A Christmas Carol

A Christmas Carol

AND OTHER CHRISTMAS CLASSICS

CHARLES DICKENS

FALL RIVER PRESS

New York

FALL RIVER PRESS

New York

An Imprint of Sterling Publishing
387 Park Avenue South
New York, NY 10016

This 2012 compilation published by Fall River Press.

ISBN: 978-1-4351-4269-5

Manufactured in the United States of America

1 3 5 7 9 10 8 6 4 2

Contents

Introduction

Charles Dickens is sometimes described as the man who invented Christmas. While this is something of an exaggeration, no writer did more to promote the virtues that we associate with the Christmas season—charity, generosity, benevolence, kindness—than Dickens did. In 1843, at the age of thirty-one, Dickens—then, the most popular living writer in England, and one of the most popular around the world—wrote his "Ghostly little book" (as he referred to it in his Preface), *A Christmas Carol.* It proved immensely popular, and was to become one of Dickens's best-known stories and one of the best-loved works of nineteenth century fiction. Nearly every year thereafter, until his death in 1870, Dickens published at least one story for the Christmas season, with the intent to (as he wrote later) "awaken some loving and forbearing thoughts, never out of season in a Christian land."

The circumstances that gave rise to the writing of the *Carol* are well known. In 1843, while immersed in the writing of monthly installments of his novel *Martin Chuzzlewit,* Dickens was distressed to read the Second Report of the Children's Employment Commission, which brimmed with first-person accounts of the wretched conditions under which children as young as age six were working. The report surely struck Dickens to the heart. At the age of twelve, with his family in debtors' prison, he had been forced to leave school and take employment at a blacking warehouse, where for ten hours each day he pasted labels on pots of boot polish. Though he had to endure it for only a few months, the experience stayed with Dickens for the rest of his life. Aspects of it crop up in his novels *Oliver Twist* and *Little Dorritt,* and it no doubt engendered the sympathy for the underprivileged and the working class that threads through much of his fiction.

In October of that year, after participating in several philanthropic events that reaffirmed the findings of the report, Dickens considered writing an appeal on behalf of impoverished children for the *Edinburgh Review.* Instead, he decided to do what he did best, producing a work of fiction that reached a much wider audience than his essay would have. *A Christmas Carol* was published by Chapman and Hall on December 17, and the reviews of it were overwhelmingly positive. The model for the *Carol* had been "The Story of the Goblins Who Stole a Sexton," Dickens's tale of curmudgeonly gravedigger Gabriel Grub who, one Christmas Eve, is confronted in the graveyard where he chooses to spend the holiday by a horde of goblins who upbraid him for being so miserable and remind him of his duties to his fellow-men. Dickens wrote this as a story within a story, told around the Christmas table in *The Pickwick Papers,* where it serves as the twenty-ninth chapter. For the *Carol,* he appropriated the story's basic structure and elaborated on its theme, incarnating the forces of neglect and indifference that he saw in society in miser Ebenezer Scrooge, who is visited by four spirits—the ghost of his dead business partner and the spirits of Christmas Past, Present, and Future—who remind him of the genial man he once was, and the dismal consequences of his behavior if he does not reacquaint himself with his humanity.

Dickens's timing couldn't have been more propitious. Although Christmas had long been celebrated as one of the most important Christian holidays, the secular trappings that we associate with it—the Christmas tree, the singing of carols, the sending of cards—were just starting to become fixtures in Victorian culture. The success of the *Carol* insured that it would become a seasonal institution as readily as the other festive filigree. Indeed, when Dickens switched publishers the following year, his new publisher stipulated that he write a follow-up to the *Carol.* Dickens would respond with another four such stories over the next five years: novellas of twenty-five thousand to thirty-thousand words, published as stand-alone books and grouped in his bibliography, today, as the Christmas Books.

The second Christmas Book, *The Chimes,* was published in 1844. It employs the supernatural in a manner similar to the *Carol,* but is set on New Year's Eve rather than Christmas Eve. Though less well-known than its predecessor, it provoked reviews in some conservative publications that accused Dickens of trying to incite class warfare. *The Cricket on the Hearth*—published in 1845 and the best seller of the all the Christmas Books—dispenses with the holiday season altogether, and for the most part the political polemics that distinguished the first two Christmas Books. In its celebration of home , hearth, and domesticity, it shows the direction in which Dickens was taking his Christmas stories: from tales set during the holiday season to tales that would provide spiritual uplift and reassurance. The only Christmas Book to feature no supernatural element, *The Battle of Life,* is a period tale set a century earlier than the other books, and the most self-consciously melodramatic of the quintet. Dickens had struggled to complete the story at the same time that he was writing serial installments of *Dombey and Son,* and he was still at work on that novel in the summer of 1847 when he conceived the idea for the final Christmas Book, *The Haunted Man.* Unable to tackle it to his satisfaction, Dickens put off completing the tale until the following year. With its Christmas setting and its overt supernaturalism, it is the Christmas Book that is closest in spirit to the *Carol,* although its theme is forgiveness rather than redemption.

Reviews of the Christmas Books were increasingly mixed with each new title, and negative reviews predominated for *The Haunted Man.* It proved the last of the Christmas Books, though not for that reason. In 1850, in the midst of writing the novel that many consider his masterpiece—*David Copperfield*—Dickens launched a new magazine, *Household Words,* for which he served as editor. The purpose of the magazine, as he wrote in the first issue, was "to bring to innumerable homes, from the stirring world around us, the knowledge of many social wonders, good and evil, that are not calculated to render any of us less ardently persevering in ourselves, less faithful in the progress of mankind, less thankful for the privilege of living in this summer-dawn of time." Dickens's plans for *Household Words* included special issues during the Christmas season in which he and his fellow contributors would promote the same ideas and themes that he had tackled in the Christmas Books. The earliest of these Christmas stories feature Christmas themes and settings. As with the Christmas Books, in succeeding Christmas issues stories were concerned less with the Yuletide than with providing entertainment appropriate for the holiday season. Because all fiction and non-fiction in the magazine, except for novels, was published anonymously, many readers would not have known the some of the longer stories were round-robin compositions for which Dickens and other authors drafted individual parts or chapters. Dickens's best-known collaborator was the popular novelist, Wilkie Collins.

Following a dispute with his magazine's publisher, Dickens discontinued publication of *Household Words* in 1859 to launch another weekly in the same spirit, *All the Year Round.* This magazine also published special Christmas issues and collaborative multi-author works. Dickens would serialize his novel *A Tale of Two Cities* in it, as well as Collins's popular thrillers *The Woman in White* and *The Moonstone.* Particularly noteworthy contributions to the magazine include the multi-contributor tale "Dr. Marigold," for which Dickens and Collins each wrote two chapters, and Dickens's solo story "Mugby Junction." Dickens's second chapter for "Dr. Marigold" is often excerpted as the stand-alone ghost story, "The Trial for Murder," as is the fourth chapter of "Mugby Junction," under the title "The Haunted Signalman." *All the Year Round* published for another twenty-five years after Dickens's death in 1870.

Had Charles Dickens never written a Christmas story other than *A Christmas Carol,* his name and literary legacy would still be inextricably bound up with the holiday season. The stories collected in this volume are a testament to his virtuosity as a writer who could find new angles from which to approach the Christmas story, and inspire readers to think of Christmas, as he wrote in *A Christmas Carol,* "as a good time; a kind, forgiving, charitable, pleasant time; the only time I know of, in the long calendar of the year, when men and women seem by one consent to open their shut-up hearts freely."

The Christmas Books

Author's Preface

The narrow space within which it was necessary to confine these Christmas Stories, when they were originally published, rendered their construction a matter of some difficulty, and almost necessitated what is peculiar in their machinery. I never attempted great elaboration of detail in the working out of character within such limits, believing that it could not succeed. My purpose was, in a whimsical kind of masque which the good-humour of the season justified, to awaken some loving and forbearing thoughts, never out of season in a Christian land.

A Christmas Carol

Stave I

Marley's Ghost

Marley was dead: to begin with. There is no doubt whatever about that. The register of his burial was signed by the clergyman, the clerk, the undertaker, and the chief mourner. Scrooge signed it: and Scrooge's name was good upon 'Change, for anything he chose to put his hand to. Old Marley was as dead as a door-nail.

Mind! I don't mean to say that I know, of my own knowledge, what there is particularly dead about a door-nail. I might have been inclined, myself, to regard a coffin-nail as the deadest piece of ironmongery in the trade. But the wisdom of our ancestors is in the simile; and my unhallowed hands shall not disturb it, or the Country's done for. You will therefore permit me to repeat, emphatically, that Marley was as dead as a door-nail.

Scrooge knew he was dead? Of course he did. How could it be otherwise? Scrooge and he were partners for I don't know how many years. Scrooge was his sole executor, his sole administrator, his sole assign, his sole residuary legatee, his sole friend, and sole mourner. And even Scrooge was not so dreadfully cut up by the sad event, but that he was an excellent man of business on the very day of the funeral, and solemnised it with an undoubted bargain.

The mention of Marley's funeral brings me back to the point I started from. There is no doubt that Marley was dead. This must be distinctly understood, or nothing wonderful can come of the story I am going to relate. If we were not perfectly convinced that Hamlet's Father died before the play began, there would be nothing more remarkable in his taking a stroll at night, in an easterly wind, upon his own ramparts, than there would be in any other middle-aged gentleman rashly turning out after dark in a breezy spot—say Saint Paul's Churchyard for instance—literally to astonish his son's weak mind.

Scrooge never painted out Old Marley's name. There it stood, years afterwards, above the warehouse door: Scrooge and Marley. The firm was known as Scrooge and Marley. Sometimes people new to the business called Scrooge Scrooge, and sometimes Marley, but he answered to both names. It was all the same to him.

Oh! but he was a tight-fisted hand at the grind-stone, Scrooge! a squeezing, wrenching, grasping, scraping, clutching, covetous, old sinner! Hard and sharp as flint, from which no steel had ever struck out generous fire; secret, and self-contained, and solitary as an oyster. The cold within him froze his old features, nipped his pointed nose, shrivelled his cheek, stiffened his gait; made his eyes red, his thin lips blue; and spoke out shrewdly in his grating voice. A frosty rime was on his head, and on his eyebrows, and his wiry chin. He carried his own low temperature always about with him; he iced his office in the dog-days, and didn't thaw it one degree at Christmas.

External heat and cold had little influence on Scrooge. No warmth could warm, no wintry weather chill him. No wind that blew was bitterer than he, no falling snow was more intent upon its purpose, no pelting rain less open to entreaty. Foul weather didn't know where to have him. The heaviest rain, and snow, and hail, and sleet, could boast of the advantage over him in only one respect. They often "came down" handsomely, and Scrooge never did.

Nobody ever stopped him in the street to say, with gladsome looks, "My dear Scrooge, how are you? When will you come to see me?" No beggars implored him to bestow a trifle, no children asked him what it was o'clock, no man or woman ever once in all his life inquired the way to such and such a place, of Scrooge. Even the blind men's dogs appeared to know him; and when they saw him coming on, would tug their owners into doorways and up courts; and then would wag their tails as though they said, "no eye at all is better than an evil eye, dark master!"

But what did Scrooge care! It was the very thing he liked. To edge his way along the crowded paths of life, warning all human sympathy to keep its distance, was what the knowing ones call "nuts" to Scrooge.

Once upon a time—of all the good days in the year, on Christmas Eve—old Scrooge sat busy in his counting-house. It was cold, bleak, biting weather: foggy withal: and he could hear the people in the court outside, go wheezing up and down, beating their hands upon their breasts, and stamping their feet upon the pavement stones to warm them. The city clocks had only just gone three, but it was quite dark already—it had not been light all day—and candles were flaring in the windows of the neighbouring offices, like ruddy smears upon the palpable brown air. The fog came pouring in at every chink and keyhole, and was so dense without, that although the court was of the narrowest, the houses opposite were mere phantoms. To see the dingy cloud come drooping down, obscuring everything, one might have thought that Nature lived hard by, and was brewing on a large scale.

The door of Scrooge's counting-house was open that he might keep his eye upon his clerk, who in a dismal little cell beyond, a sort of tank, was copying letters. Scrooge had a very small fire, but the clerk's fire was so very much smaller that it looked like one coal. But he couldn't replenish it, for Scrooge kept the coal-box in his own room; and so surely as the clerk came in with the shovel, the master predicted that it would be necessary for them to part. Wherefore the clerk put on his white comforter, and tried to warm himself at the candle; in which effort, not being a man of a strong imagination, he failed.

"A merry Christmas, uncle! God save you!" cried a cheerful voice. It was the voice of Scrooge's nephew, who came upon him so quickly that this was the first intimation he had of his approach.

"Bah!" said Scrooge, "Humbug!"

He had so heated himself with rapid walking in the fog and frost, this nephew of Scrooge's, that he was all in a glow; his face was ruddy and handsome; his eyes sparkled, and his breath smoked again.

"Christmas a humbug, uncle!" said Scrooge's nephew. "You don't mean that, I am sure?"

"I do," said Scrooge. "Merry Christmas! What right have you to be merry? What reason have you to be merry? You're poor enough."

"Come, then," returned the nephew gaily. "What right have you to be dismal? What reason have you to be morose? You're rich enough."

Scrooge having no better answer ready on the spur of the moment, said, "Bah!" again; and followed it up with "Humbug."

"Don't be cross, uncle!" said the nephew.

"What else can I be," returned the uncle, "when I live in such a world of fools as this? Merry Christmas! Out upon merry Christmas! What's Christmas time to you but a time for paying bills without money; a time for finding yourself a year older, but not an hour richer; a time for balancing your books and having every item in 'em through a round dozen of months presented dead against you? If I could work my will," said Scrooge indignantly, "every idiot who goes about with 'Merry Christmas' on his lips, should be boiled with his own pudding, and buried with a stake of holly through his heart. He should!"

"Uncle!" pleaded the nephew.

"Nephew!" returned the uncle sternly, "keep Christmas in your own way, and let me keep it in mine."

"Keep it!" repeated Scrooge's nephew. "But you don't keep it."

"Let me leave it alone, then," said Scrooge. "Much good may it do you! Much good it has ever done you!"

"There are many things from which I might have derived good, by which I have not profited, I dare say," returned the nephew. "Christmas among the rest. But I am sure I have always thought of Christmas time, when it has come round—apart from the veneration due to its sacred name and origin, if anything belonging to it can be apart from that—as a good time; a kind, forgiving, charitable, pleasant time; the only time I know of, in the long calendar of the year, when men and women seem by one consent to open their shut-up hearts freely, and to think of people below them as if they really were fellow-passengers to the grave, and not another race of creatures bound on other journeys. And therefore, uncle, though it has never put a scrap of gold or silver in my pocket, I believe that it *has* done me good, and *will* do me good; and I say, God bless it!"

The clerk in the tank involuntarily applauded. Becoming immediately sensible of the impropriety, he poked the fire, and extinguished the last frail spark for ever.

"Let me hear another sound from *you*," said Scrooge, "and you'll keep your Christmas by losing your situation! You're quite a powerful speaker, sir," he added, turning to his nephew. "I wonder you don't go into Parliament."

"Don't be angry, uncle. Come! Dine with us to-morrow."

Scrooge said that he would see him—yes, indeed he did. He went the whole length of the expression, and said that he would see him in that extremity first.

"But why?" cried Scrooge's nephew. "Why?"

"Why did you get married?" said Scrooge.

"Because I fell in love."

"Because you fell in love!" growled Scrooge, as if that were the only one thing in the world more ridiculous than a merry Christmas. "Good afternoon!"

"Nay, uncle, but you never came to see me before that happened. Why give it as a reason for not coming now?"

"Good afternoon," said Scrooge.

"I want nothing from you; I ask nothing of you; why cannot we be friends?"

"Good afternoon," said Scrooge.

"I am sorry, with all my heart, to find you so resolute. We have never had any quarrel, to which I have been a party. But I have made the trial in homage to Christmas, and I'll keep my Christmas humour to the last. So A Merry Christmas, uncle!"

"Good afternoon!" said Scrooge.

"And A Happy New Year!"

"Good afternoon!" said Scrooge.

His nephew left the room without an angry word, notwithstanding. He stopped at the outer door to bestow the greetings of the season on the clerk, who, cold as he was, was warmer than Scrooge; for he returned them cordially.

"There's another fellow," muttered Scrooge; who overheard him: "my clerk, with fifteen shillings a week, and a wife and family, talking about a merry Christmas. I'll retire to Bedlam."

This lunatic, in letting Scrooge's nephew out, had let two other people in. They were portly gentlemen, pleasant to behold, and now stood, with their hats off, in Scrooge's office. They had books and papers in their hands, and bowed to him.

"Scrooge and Marley's, I believe," said one of the gentlemen, referring to his list. "Have I the pleasure of addressing Mr. Scrooge, or Mr. Marley?"

"Mr. Marley has been dead these seven years," Scrooge replied. "He died seven years ago, this very night."

"We have no doubt his liberality is well represented by his surviving partner," said the gentleman, presenting his credentials.

It certainly was; for they had been two kindred spirits. At the ominous word "liberality," Scrooge frowned, and shook his head, and handed the credentials back.

"At this festive season of the year, Mr. Scrooge," said the gentleman, taking up a pen, "it is more than usually desirable that we should make some slight provision for the Poor and destitute, who suffer greatly at the present time. Many thousands are in want of common necessaries; hundreds of thousands are in want of common comforts, sir."

"Are there no prisons?" asked Scrooge.

"Plenty of prisons," said the gentleman, laying down the pen again.

"And the Union workhouses?" demanded Scrooge. "Are they still in operation?"

"They are. Still," returned the gentleman, "I wish I could say they were not."

"The Treadmill and the Poor Law are in full vigour, then?" said Scrooge.

"Both very busy, sir."

"Oh! I was afraid, from what you said at first, that something had occurred to stop them in their useful course," said Scrooge. "I'm very glad to hear it."

"Under the impression that they scarcely furnish Christian cheer of mind or body to the multitude," returned the gentleman, "a few of us are endeavouring to raise a fund to buy the Poor some meat and drink, and means of warmth. We choose this time, because it is a time, of all others, when Want is keenly felt, and Abundance rejoices. What shall I put you down for?"

"Nothing!" Scrooge replied.

"You wish to be anonymous?"

"I wish to be left alone," said Scrooge. "Since you ask me what I wish, gentlemen, that is my answer. I don't make merry myself at Christmas and I can't afford to make idle people merry. I help to support the establishments I have mentioned—they cost enough; and those who are badly off must go there."

"Many can't go there; and many would rather die."

"If they would rather die," said Scrooge, "they had better do it, and decrease the surplus population. Besides—excuse me—I don't know that."

"But you might know it," observed the gentleman.

"It's not my business," Scrooge returned. "It's enough for a man to understand his own business, and not to interfere with other people's. Mine occupies me constantly. Good afternoon, gentlemen!"

Seeing clearly that it would be useless to pursue their point, the gentlemen withdrew. Scrooge resumed his labours with an improved opinion of himself, and in a more facetious temper than was usual with him.

Meanwhile the fog and darkness thickened so, that people ran about with flaring links, proffering their services to go before horses in carriages, and conduct them on their way. The ancient tower of a church, whose gruff old bell was always peeping slily down at Scrooge out of a Gothic window in the wall, became invisible, and struck the hours and quarters in the clouds, with tremulous vibrations afterwards as if its teeth were chattering in its frozen head up there. The cold became intense. In the main street, at the corner of the court, some labourers were repairing the gas-pipes, and had lighted a great fire in a brazier, round which a party of ragged men and boys were gathered: warming their hands and winking their eyes before the blaze in rapture. The water-plug being left in solitude, its overflowings sullenly congealed, and turned to misanthropic ice. The brightness of the shops where holly sprigs and berries crackled in the lamp heat of the windows, made pale faces ruddy as they passed. Poulterers' and grocers' trades became a splendid joke: a glorious pageant, with which it was next to impossible to believe that such dull principles as bargain and sale had anything to do. The Lord Mayor, in the stronghold of the mighty Mansion House, gave orders to his fifty cooks and butlers to keep Christmas as a Lord Mayor's household should; and even the little tailor, whom he had fined five shillings on the previous Monday for being drunk and bloodthirsty in the streets, stirred up to-morrow's pudding in his garret, while his lean wife and the baby sallied out to buy the beef.

Foggier yet, and colder. Piercing, searching, biting cold. If the good Saint Dunstan had but nipped the Evil Spirit's nose with a touch of such weather as that, instead of using his familiar weapons, then indeed he would have roared to lusty purpose. The owner of one scant young nose, gnawed and mumbled by the hungry cold as bones are gnawed by dogs, stooped down at Scrooge's keyhole to regale him with a Christmas carol: but at the first sound of

"God bless you, merry gentleman!
May nothing you dismay!"

Scrooge seized the ruler with such energy of action, that the singer fled in terror, leaving the keyhole to the fog and even more congenial frost.

At length the hour of shutting up the counting-house arrived. With an ill-will Scrooge dismounted from his stool, and tacitly admitted the fact to the expectant clerk in the Tank, who instantly snuffed his candle out, and put on his hat.

"You'll want all day to-morrow, I suppose?" said Scrooge.

"If quite convenient, sir."

"It's not convenient," said Scrooge, "and it's not fair. If I was to stop half-a-crown for it, you'd think yourself ill used, I'll be bound?"

The clerk smiled faintly.

"And yet," said Scrooge, "you don't think *me* ill used, when I pay a day's wages for no work."

The clerk observed that it was only once a year.

"A poor excuse for picking a man's pocket every twenty-fifth of December!" said Scrooge, buttoning his great-coat to the chin. "But I suppose you must have the whole day. Be here all the earlier next morning."

The clerk promised that he would; and Scrooge walked out with a growl. The office was closed in a twinkling, and the clerk, with the long ends of his white comforter dangling below his waist (for he boasted no great-coat), went down a slide on Cornhill, at the end of a lane of boys, twenty times, in honour of its being Christmas Eve, and then ran home to Camden Town as hard as he could pelt, to play at blindman's-buff.

Scrooge took his melancholy dinner in his usual melancholy tavern; and having read all the newspapers, and beguiled the rest of the evening with his banker's-book, went home to bed. He lived in chambers which had once belonged to his deceased partner. They were a gloomy suite of rooms, in a lowering pile of building up a yard, where it had so little business to be, that one could scarcely help fancying it must have run there when it was a young house, playing at hide-and-seek with other houses, and forgotten the way out again. It was old enough now, and dreary enough, for nobody lived in it but Scrooge, the other rooms being all let out as offices. The yard was so dark that even Scrooge, who knew its every stone, was fain to grope with his hands. The fog and frost so hung about the black old gateway of the house, that it seemed as if the Genius of the Weather sat in mournful meditation on the threshold.

Now, it is a fact, that there was nothing at all particular about the knocker on the door, except that it was very large. It is also a fact, that Scrooge had seen it, night and morning, during his whole residence in that place; also that Scrooge had as little of what is called fancy about him as any man in the city of London, even including—which is a bold word—the corporation, aldermen, and livery. Let it also be borne in mind that Scrooge had not bestowed one thought on Marley, since his last mention of his seven years' dead partner that afternoon. And then let any man explain to me, if he can, how it happened that Scrooge, having his key in the lock of the door, saw in the knocker, without its undergoing any intermediate process of change--not a knocker, but Marley's face.

Marley's face. It was not in impenetrable shadow as the other objects in the yard were, but had a dismal light about it, like a bad lobster in a dark cellar. It was not angry or ferocious, but looked at Scrooge as Marley used to look: with ghostly spectacles turned up on its ghostly forehead. The hair was curiously stirred, as if by breath or hot air; and, though the eyes were wide open, they were perfectly motionless. That, and its livid colour, made it horrible; but its horror seemed to be in spite of the face and beyond its control, rather than a part of its own expression.

As Scrooge looked fixedly at this phenomenon, it was a knocker again.

To say that he was not startled, or that his blood was not conscious of a terrible sensation to which it had been a stranger from infancy, would be untrue. But he put his hand upon the key he had relinquished, turned it sturdily, walked in, and lighted his candle.

He *did* pause, with a moment's irresolution, before he shut the door; and he *did* look cautiously behind it first, as if he half expected to be terrified with the sight of Marley's pigtail sticking out into the hall. But there was nothing on the back of the door, except the screws and nuts that held the knocker on, so he said "Pooh, pooh!" and closed it with a bang.

The sound resounded through the house like thunder. Every room above, and every cask in the wine-merchant's cellars below, appeared to have a separate peal of echoes of its own. Scrooge was not a man to be frightened by echoes. He fastened the door, and walked across the hall, and up the stairs; slowly too: trimming his candle as he went.

You may talk vaguely about driving a coach-and-six up a good old flight of stairs, or through a bad young Act of Parliament; but I mean to say you might have got a hearse up that staircase, and taken it broadwise, with the splinter-bar towards the wall and the door towards the balustrades: and done it easy. There was plenty of width for that, and room to spare; which is perhaps the reason why Scrooge thought he saw a locomotive hearse going on before him in the gloom. Half a dozen gas-lamps out of the street wouldn't have lighted the entry too well, so you may suppose that it was pretty dark with Scrooge's dip.

Up Scrooge went, not caring a button for that. Darkness is cheap, and Scrooge liked it. But before he shut his heavy door, he walked through his rooms to see that all was right. He had just enough recollection of the face to desire to do that.

Sitting-room, bed-room, lumber-room. All as they should be. Nobody under the table, nobody under the sofa; a small fire in the grate; spoon and basin ready; and the little saucepan of gruel (Scrooge had a cold in his head) upon the hob. Nobody under the bed; nobody in the closet; nobody in his dressing-gown, which was hanging up in a suspicious attitude against the wall. Lumber-room as usual. Old fire-guard, old shoes, two fish-baskets, washing-stand on three legs, and a poker.

Quite satisfied, he closed his door, and locked himself in; double-locked himself in, which was not his custom. Thus secured against surprise, he took off his cravat;

put on his dressing-gown and slippers, and his night-cap; and sat down before the fire to take his gruel.

It was a very low fire indeed; nothing on such a bitter night. He was obliged to sit close to it, and brood over it, before he could extract the least sensation of warmth from such a handful of fuel. The fireplace was an old one, built by some Dutch merchant long ago, and paved all round with quaint Dutch tiles, designed to illustrate the Scriptures. There were Cains and Abels; Pharaoh's daughters; Queens of Sheba, Angelic messengers descending through the air on clouds like feather-beds, Abrahams, Belshazzars, Apostles putting off to sea in butter-boats, hundreds of figures to attract his thoughts; and yet that face of Marley, seven years dead, came like the ancient Prophet's rod, and swallowed up the whole. If each smooth tile had been a blank at first, with power to shape some picture on its surface from the disjointed fragments of his thoughts, there would have been a copy of old Marley's head on every one.

"Humbug!" said Scrooge; and walked across the room.

After several turns, he sat down again. As he threw his head back in the chair, his glance happened to rest upon a bell, a disused bell, that hung in the room, and communicated for some purpose now forgotten with a chamber in the highest story of the building. It was with great astonishment, and with a strange, inexplicable dread, that as he looked, he saw this bell begin to swing. It swung so softly in the outset that it scarcely made a sound; but soon it rang out loudly, and so did every bell in the house.

This might have lasted half a minute, or a minute, but it seemed an hour. The bells ceased as they had begun, together. They were succeeded by a clanking noise, deep down below; as if some person were dragging a heavy chain over the casks in the wine-merchant's cellar. Scrooge then remembered to have heard that ghosts in haunted houses were described as dragging chains.

The cellar-door flew open with a booming sound, and then he heard the noise much louder, on the floors below; then coming up the stairs; then coming straight towards his door.

"It's humbug still!" said Scrooge. "I won't believe it."

His colour changed though, when, without a pause, it came on through the heavy door, and passed into the room before his eyes. Upon its coming in, the dying flame leaped up, as though it cried, "I know him; Marley's Ghost!" and fell again.

The same face: the very same. Marley in his pig-tail, usual waistcoat, tights and boots; the tassels on the latter bristling, like his pigtail, and his coat-skirts, and the hair upon his head. The chain he drew was clasped about his middle. It was long, and wound about him like a tail; and it was made (for Scrooge observed it closely) of cash-boxes, keys, padlocks, ledgers, deeds, and heavy purses wrought in steel. His body was transparent; so that Scrooge, observing him, and looking through his waistcoat, could see the two buttons on his coat behind.

Scrooge had often heard it said that Marley had no bowels, but he had never believed it until now.

No, nor did he believe it even now. Though he looked the phantom through and through, and saw it standing before him; though he felt the chilling influence of its death-cold eyes; and marked the very texture of the folded kerchief bound about its head and chin, which wrapper he had not observed before; he was still incredulous, and fought against his senses.

"How now!" said Scrooge, caustic and cold as ever. "What do you want with me?"

"Much!"—Marley's voice, no doubt about it.

"Who are you?"

"Ask me who I *was*."

"Who *were* you then?" said Scrooge, raising his voice. "You're particular, for a shade." He was going to say "*to* a shade," but substituted this, as more appropriate.

"In life I was your partner, Jacob Marley."

"Can you—can you sit down?" asked Scrooge, looking doubtfully at him.

"I can."

"Do it, then."

Scrooge asked the question, because he didn't know whether a ghost so transparent might find himself in a condition to take a chair; and felt that in the event of its being impossible, it might involve the necessity of an embarrassing explanation. But the ghost sat down on the opposite side of the fireplace, as if he were quite used to it.

"You don't believe in me," observed the Ghost.

"I don't," said Scrooge.

"What evidence would you have of my reality beyond that of your senses?"

"I don't know," said Scrooge.

"Why do you doubt your senses?"

"Because," said Scrooge, "a little thing affects them. A slight disorder of the stomach makes them cheats. You may be an undigested bit of beef, a blot of mustard, a crumb of cheese, a fragment of an underdone potato. There's more of gravy than of grave about you, whatever you are!"

Scrooge was not much in the habit of cracking jokes, nor did he feel, in his heart, by any means waggish then. The truth is, that he tried to be smart, as a means of distracting his own attention, and keeping down his terror; for the spectre's voice disturbed the very marrow in his bones.

To sit, staring at those fixed glazed eyes, in silence for a moment, would play, Scrooge felt, the very deuce with him. There was something very awful, too, in the spectre's being provided with an infernal atmosphere of its own. Scrooge could not feel it himself, but this was clearly the case; for though the Ghost sat perfectly motionless, its hair, and skirts, and tassels, were still agitated as by the hot vapour from an oven.

"You see this toothpick?" said Scrooge, returning quickly to the charge, for the reason just assigned; and wishing, though it were only for a second, to divert the vision's stony gaze from himself.

"I do," replied the Ghost.

"You are not looking at it," said Scrooge.

"But I see it," said the Ghost, "notwithstanding."

"Well!" returned Scrooge, "I have but to swallow this, and be for the rest of my days persecuted by a legion of goblins, all of my own creation. Humbug, I tell you!—humbug!"

At this the spirit raised a frightful cry, and shook its chain with such a dismal and appalling noise, that Scrooge held on tight to his chair, to save himself from falling in a swoon. But how much greater was his horror, when the phantom taking off the bandage round its head, as if it were too warm to wear indoors, its lower jaw dropped down upon its breast!

Scrooge fell upon his knees, and clasped his hands before his face.

"Mercy!" he said. "Dreadful apparition, why do you trouble me?"

"Man of the worldly mind!" replied the Ghost, "do you believe in me or not?"

"I do," said Scrooge. "I must. But why do spirits walk the earth, and why do they come to me?"

"It is required of every man," the Ghost returned, "that the spirit within him should walk abroad among his fellow-men, and travel far and wide; and if that spirit goes not forth in life, it is condemned to do so after death. It is doomed to wander through the world—oh, woe is me!—and witness what it cannot share, but might have shared on earth, and turned to happiness!"

Again the spectre raised a cry, and shook its chain and wrung its shadowy hands.

"You are fettered," said Scrooge, trembling. "Tell me why?"

"I wear the chain I forged in life," replied the Ghost. "I made it link by link, and yard by yard; I girded it on of my own free will, and of my own free will I wore it. Is its pattern strange to *you*?"

Scrooge trembled more and more.

"Or would you know," pursued the Ghost, "the weight and length of the strong coil you bear yourself? It was full as heavy and as long as this, seven Christmas Eves ago. You have laboured on it, since. It is a ponderous chain!"

Scrooge glanced about him on the floor, in the expectation of finding himself surrounded by some fifty or sixty fathoms of iron cable: but he could see nothing.

"Jacob," he said, imploringly. "Old Jacob Marley, tell me more. Speak comfort to me, Jacob!"

"I have none to give," the Ghost replied. "It comes from other regions, Ebenezer Scrooge, and is conveyed by other ministers, to other kinds of men. Nor can I tell you what I would. A very little more is all permitted to me. I cannot rest, I cannot stay, I cannot linger anywhere. My spirit never walked beyond our counting-house—mark me!—in life my spirit never roved beyond the narrow limits of our money-changing hole; and weary journeys lie before me!"

It was a habit with Scrooge, whenever he became thoughtful, to put his hands in his breeches pockets. Pondering on what the Ghost had said, he did so now, but without lifting up his eyes, or getting off his knees.

"You must have been very slow about it, Jacob," Scrooge observed, in a business-like manner, though with humility and deference.

"Slow!" the Ghost repeated.

"Seven years dead," mused Scrooge. "And travelling all the time!"

"The whole time," said the Ghost. "No rest, no peace. Incessant torture of remorse."

"You travel fast?" said Scrooge.

"On the wings of the wind," replied the Ghost.

"You might have got over a great quantity of ground in seven years," said Scrooge.

The Ghost, on hearing this, set up another cry, and clanked its chain so hideously in the dead silence of the night, that the Ward would have been justified in indicting it for a nuisance.

"But you were always a good man of business, Jacob," faltered Scrooge, who now began to apply this to himself.

"Business!" cried the Ghost, wringing its hands again. "Mankind was my business. The common welfare was my business; charity, mercy, forbearance, and benevolence, were, all, my business. The dealings of my trade were but a drop of water in the comprehensive ocean of my business!"

It held up its chain at arm's length, as if that were the cause of all its unavailing grief, and flung it heavily upon the ground again.

"At this time of the rolling year," the spectre said, "I suffer most. Why did I walk through crowds of fellow-beings with my eyes turned down, and never raise them to that blessed Star which led the Wise Men to a poor abode! Were there no poor homes to which its light would have conducted *me*!"

Scrooge was very much dismayed to hear the spectre going on at this rate, and began to quake exceedingly.

"Hear me!" cried the Ghost. "My time is nearly gone."

"I will," said Scrooge. "But don't be hard upon me! Don't be flowery, Jacob! Pray!"

"How it is that I appear before you in a shape that you can see, I may not tell. I have sat invisible beside you many and many a day."

It was not an agreeable idea. Scrooge shivered, and wiped the perspiration from his brow.

"That is no light part of my penance," pursued the Ghost. "I am here to-night to warn you, that you have yet a chance and hope of escaping my fate. A chance and hope of my procuring, Ebenezer."

"You were always a good friend to me," said Scrooge. "Thank'ee!"

"You will be haunted," resumed the Ghost, "by Three Spirits."

Scrooge's countenance fell almost as low as the Ghost's had done.

"Is that the chance and hope you mentioned, Jacob?" he demanded, in a faltering voice.

"It is."

"I—I think I'd rather not," said Scrooge.

"Without their visits," said the Ghost, "you cannot hope to shun the path I tread. Expect the first to-morrow, when the bell tolls One."

"Couldn't I take 'em all at once, and have it over, Jacob?" hinted Scrooge.

"Expect the second on the next night at the same hour. The third upon the next night when the last stroke of Twelve has ceased to vibrate. Look to see me no more; and look that, for your own sake, you remember what has passed between us!"

When it had said these words, the spectre took its wrapper from the table, and bound it round its head, as before. Scrooge knew this, by the smart sound its teeth made, when the jaws were brought together by the bandage. He ventured to raise his eyes again, and found his supernatural visitor confronting him in an erect attitude, with its chain wound over and about its arm.

The apparition walked backward from him; and at every step it took, the window raised itself a little, so that when the spectre reached it, it was wide open.

It beckoned Scrooge to approach, which he did. When they were within two paces of each other, Marley's Ghost held up its hand, warning him to come no nearer. Scrooge stopped.

Not so much in obedience, as in surprise and fear: for on the raising of the hand, he became sensible of confused noises in the air; incoherent sounds of lamentation and regret; wailings inexpressibly sorrowful and self-accusatory. The spectre, after listening for a moment, joined in the mournful dirge; and floated out upon the bleak, dark night.

Scrooge followed to the window: desperate in his curiosity. He looked out.

The air was filled with phantoms, wandering hither and thither in restless haste, and moaning as they went. Every one of them wore chains like Marley's Ghost; some few (they might be guilty governments) were linked together; none were free. Many had been personally known to Scrooge in their lives. He had been quite familiar with one old ghost, in a white waistcoat, with a monstrous iron safe attached to its ankle, who cried piteously at being unable to assist a wretched woman with an infant, whom it saw below, upon a door-step. The misery with them all was, clearly, that they sought to interfere, for good, in human matters, and had lost the power for ever.

Whether these creatures faded into mist, or mist enshrouded them, he could not tell. But they and their spirit voices faded together; and the night became as it had been when he walked home.

Scrooge closed the window, and examined the door by which the Ghost had entered. It was double-locked, as he had locked it with his own hands, and the bolts were undisturbed. He tried to say "Humbug!" but stopped at the first syllable. And being, from the emotion he had undergone, or the fatigues of the day, or his glimpse of the Invisible World, or the dull conversation of the Ghost, or the lateness of the hour, much in need of repose; went straight to bed, without undressing, and fell asleep upon the instant.

Stave II

The First of the Three Spirits

When Scrooge awoke, it was so dark, that looking out of bed, he could scarcely distinguish the transparent window from the opaque walls of his chamber. He was endeavouring to pierce the darkness with his ferret eyes, when the chimes of a neighbouring church struck the four quarters. So he listened for the hour.

To his great astonishment the heavy bell went on from six to seven, and from seven to eight, and regularly up to twelve; then stopped. Twelve! It was past two when he went to bed. The clock was wrong. An icicle must have got into the works. Twelve!

He touched the spring of his repeater, to correct this most preposterous clock. Its rapid little pulse beat twelve: and stopped.

"Why, it isn't possible," said Scrooge, "that I can have slept through a whole day and far into another night. It isn't possible that anything has happened to the sun, and this is twelve at noon!"

The idea being an alarming one, he scrambled out of bed, and groped his way to the window. He was obliged to rub the frost off with the sleeve of his dressing-gown before he could see anything; and could see very little then. All he could make out was, that it was still very foggy and extremely cold, and that there was no noise of people running to and fro, and making a great stir, as there unquestionably would have been if night had beaten off bright day, and taken possession of the world. This was a great relief, because "three days after sight of this First of Exchange pay to Mr. Ebenezer Scrooge or his order," and so forth, would have become a mere United States' security if there were no days to count by.

Scrooge went to bed again, and thought, and thought, and thought it over and over and over, and could make nothing of it. The more he thought, the more perplexed he was; and the more he endeavoured not to think, the more he thought.

Marley's Ghost bothered him exceedingly. Every time he resolved within himself, after mature inquiry, that it was all a dream, his mind flew back again, like a strong spring released, to its first position, and presented the same problem to be worked all through, "Was it a dream or not?"

Scrooge lay in this state until the chime had gone three quarters more, when he remembered, on a sudden, that the Ghost had warned him of a visitation when the bell tolled one. He resolved to lie awake until the hour was passed; and, considering that he could no more go to sleep than go to Heaven, this was perhaps the wisest resolution in his power.

The quarter was so long, that he was more than once convinced he must have sunk into a doze unconsciously, and missed the clock. At length it broke upon his listening ear.

"Ding, dong!"

"A quarter past," said Scrooge, counting.

"Ding, dong!"

"Half past!" said Scrooge.

"Ding, dong!"

"A quarter to it," said Scrooge.

"Ding, dong!"

"The hour itself," said Scrooge, triumphantly, "and nothing else!"

He spoke before the hour bell sounded, which it now did with a deep, dull, hollow, melancholy ONE. Light flashed up in the room upon the instant, and the curtains of his bed were drawn.

The curtains of his bed were drawn aside, I tell you, by a hand. Not the curtains at his feet, nor the curtains at his back, but those to which his face was addressed. The curtains of his bed were drawn aside; and Scrooge, starting up into a half-recumbent attitude, found himself face to face with the unearthly visitor who drew them: as close to it as I am now to you, and I am standing in the spirit at your elbow.

It was a strange figure—like a child: yet not so like a child as like an old man, viewed through some supernatural medium, which gave him the appearance of having receded from the view, and being diminished to a child's proportions. Its hair, which hung about its neck and down its back, was white as if with age; and yet the face had not a wrinkle in it, and the tenderest bloom was on the skin. The arms were very long and muscular; the hands the same, as if its hold were of uncommon strength. Its legs and feet, most delicately formed, were, like those upper members, bare. It wore a tunic of the purest white; and round its waist was bound a lustrous belt, the sheen of which was beautiful. It held a branch of fresh green holly in its hand; and, in singular contradiction of that wintry emblem, had its dress trimmed with summer flowers. But the strangest thing about it was, that from the crown of its head there sprung a bright clear jet of light, by which all this was visible; and which was doubtless the occasion of its using, in its duller moments, a great extinguisher for a cap, which it now held under its arm.

Even this, though, when Scrooge looked at it with increasing steadiness, was *not* its strangest quality. For as its belt sparkled and glittered now in one part and now in another, and what was light one instant, at another time was dark, so the figure itself fluctuated in its distinctness: being now a thing with one arm, now with one leg, now with twenty legs, now a pair of legs without a head, now a head without a body: of which dissolving parts, no outline would be visible in the dense gloom wherein they melted away. And in the very wonder of this, it would be itself again; distinct and clear as ever.

"Are you the Spirit, sir, whose coming was foretold to me?" asked Scrooge.

"I am!"

The voice was soft and gentle. Singularly low, as if instead of being so close beside him, it were at a distance.

"Who, and what are you?" Scrooge demanded.

"I am the Ghost of Christmas Past."

"Long Past?" inquired Scrooge: observant of its dwarfish stature.

"No. Your past."

Perhaps, Scrooge could not have told anybody why, if anybody could have asked him; but he had a special desire to see the Spirit in his cap; and begged him to be covered.

"What!" exclaimed the Ghost, "would you so soon put out, with worldly hands, the light I give? Is it not enough that you are one of those whose passions made this cap, and force me through whole trains of years to wear it low upon my brow!"

Scrooge reverently disclaimed all intention to offend or any knowledge of having wilfully "bonneted" the Spirit at any period of his life. He then made bold to inquire what business brought him there.

"Your welfare!" said the Ghost.

Scrooge expressed himself much obliged, but could not help thinking that a night of unbroken rest would have been more conducive to that end. The Spirit must have heard him thinking, for it said immediately:

"Your reclamation, then. Take heed!"

It put out its strong hand as it spoke, and clasped him gently by the arm.

"Rise! and walk with me!"

It would have been in vain for Scrooge to plead that the weather and the hour were not adapted to pedestrian purposes; that bed was warm, and the thermometer a long way below freezing; that he was clad but lightly in his slippers, dressing-gown, and nightcap; and that he had a cold upon him at that time. The grasp, though gentle as a woman's hand, was not to be resisted. He rose: but finding that the Spirit made towards the window, clasped his robe in supplication.

"I am a mortal," Scrooge remonstrated, "and liable to fall."

"Bear but a touch of my hand *there*," said the Spirit, laying it upon his heart, "and you shall be upheld in more than this!"

As the words were spoken, they passed through the wall, and stood upon an open country road, with fields on either hand. The city had entirely vanished. Not a vestige of it was to be seen. The darkness and the mist had vanished with it, for it was a clear, cold, winter day, with snow upon the ground.

"Good Heaven!" said Scrooge, clasping his hands together, as he looked about him. "I was bred in this place. I was a boy here!"

The Spirit gazed upon him mildly. Its gentle touch, though it had been light and instantaneous, appeared still present to the old man's sense of feeling. He was conscious of a thousand odours floating in the air, each one connected with a thousand thoughts, and hopes, and joys, and cares long, long, forgotten!

"Your lip is trembling," said the Ghost. "And what is that upon your cheek?"

Scrooge muttered, with an unusual catching in his voice, that it was a pimple; and begged the Ghost to lead him where he would.

"You recollect the way?" inquired the Spirit.

"Remember it!" cried Scrooge with fervour; "I could walk it blindfold."

"Strange to have forgotten it for so many years!" observed the Ghost. "Let us go on."

They walked along the road, Scrooge recognising every gate, and post, and tree; until a little market-town appeared in the distance, with its bridge, its church, and winding river. Some shaggy ponies now were seen trotting towards them with boys upon their backs, who called to other boys in country gigs and carts, driven by farmers. All these boys were in great spirits, and shouted to each other, until the broad fields were so full of merry music, that the crisp air laughed to hear it!

"These are but shadows of the things that have been," said the Ghost. "They have no consciousness of us."

The jocund travellers came on; and as they came, Scrooge knew and named them every one. Why was he rejoiced beyond all bounds to see them! Why did his cold eye glisten, and his heart leap up as they went past! Why was he filled with gladness when he heard them give each other Merry Christmas, as they parted at cross-roads and bye-ways, for their several homes! What was merry Christmas to Scrooge? Out upon merry Christmas! What good had it ever done to him?

"The school is not quite deserted," said the Ghost. "A solitary child, neglected by his friends, is left there still."

Scrooge said he knew it. And he sobbed.

They left the high-road, by a well-remembered lane, and soon approached a mansion of dull red brick, with a little weathercock-surmounted cupola, on the roof, and a bell hanging in it. It was a large house, but one of broken fortunes; for the spacious offices were little used, their walls were damp and mossy, their windows broken, and their gates decayed. Fowls clucked and strutted in the stables; and the coach-houses and sheds were over-run with grass. Nor was it more retentive of its ancient state, within; for entering the dreary hall, and glancing through the open doors of many rooms, they found them poorly furnished, cold, and vast. There was an earthy savour in the air, a chilly bareness in the place, which associated itself somehow with too much getting up by candle-light, and not too much to eat.

They went, the Ghost and Scrooge, across the hall, to a door at the back of the house. It opened before them, and disclosed a long, bare, melancholy room, made barer still by lines of plain deal forms and desks. At one of these a lonely boy was reading near a feeble fire; and Scrooge sat down upon a form, and wept to see his poor forgotten self as he used to be.

Not a latent echo in the house, not a squeak and scuffle from the mice behind the panelling, not a drip from the half-thawed water-spout in the dull yard behind, not a sigh among the leafless boughs of one despondent poplar, not the idle swinging of an empty store-house door, no, not a clicking in the fire, but fell upon the heart of Scrooge with a softening influence, and gave a freer passage to his tears.

The Spirit touched him on the arm, and pointed to his younger self, intent upon his reading. Suddenly a man, in foreign garments: wonderfully real and distinct to look at: stood outside the window, with an axe stuck in his belt, and leading by the bridle an ass laden with wood.

"Why, it's Ali Baba!" Scrooge exclaimed in ecstasy. "It's dear old honest Ali Baba! Yes, yes, I know! One Christmas time, when yonder solitary child was left here all alone, he *did* come, for the first time, just like that. Poor boy! And Valentine," said Scrooge, "and his wild brother, Orson; there they go! And what's his name, who was put down in his drawers, asleep, at the Gate of Damascus; don't you see him! And the Sultan's Groom turned upside down by the Genii; there he is upon his head! Serve him right. I'm glad of it. What business had *he* to be married to the Princess!"

To hear Scrooge expending all the earnestness of his nature on such subjects, in a most extraordinary voice between laughing and crying; and to see his heightened and excited face; would have been a surprise to his business friends in the city, indeed.

"There's the Parrot!" cried Scrooge. "Green body and yellow tail, with a thing like a lettuce growing out of the top of his head; there he is! Poor Robin Crusoe, he called him, when he came home again after sailing round the island. 'Poor Robin Crusoe, where have you been, Robin Crusoe?' The man thought he was dreaming, but he wasn't. It was the Parrot, you know. There goes Friday, running for his life to the little creek! Halloa! Hoop! Halloo!"

Then, with a rapidity of transition very foreign to his usual character, he said, in pity for his former self, "Poor boy!" and cried again.

"I wish," Scrooge muttered, putting his hand in his pocket, and looking about him, after drying his eyes with his cuff: "but it's too late now."

"What is the matter?" asked the Spirit.

"Nothing," said Scrooge. "Nothing. There was a boy singing a Christmas Carol at my door last night. I should like to have given him something: that's all."

The Ghost smiled thoughtfully, and waved its hand: saying as it did so, "Let us see another Christmas!"

Scrooge's former self grew larger at the words, and the room became a little darker and more dirty. The panels shrunk, the windows cracked; fragments of plaster fell out of the ceiling, and the naked laths were shown instead; but how all this was brought about, Scrooge knew no more than you do. He only knew that it was quite correct; that everything had happened so; that there he was, alone again, when all the other boys had gone home for the jolly holidays.

He was not reading now, but walking up and down despairingly. Scrooge looked at the Ghost, and with a mournful shaking of his head, glanced anxiously towards the door.

It opened; and a little girl, much younger than the boy, came darting in, and putting her arms about his neck, and often kissing him, addressed him as her "Dear, dear brother."

"I have come to bring you home, dear brother!" said the child, clapping her tiny hands, and bending down to laugh. "To bring you home, home, home!"

"Home, little Fan?" returned the boy.

"Yes!" said the child, brimful of glee. "Home, for good and all. Home, for ever and ever. Father is so much kinder than he used to be, that home's like Heaven! He spoke so gently to me one dear night when I was going to bed, that I was not afraid to ask him once more if you might come home; and he said Yes, you should; and sent me in a coach to bring you. And you're to be a man!" said the child, opening her eyes, "and are never to come back here; but first, we're to be together all the Christmas long, and have the merriest time in all the world."

"You are quite a woman, little Fan!" exclaimed the boy.

She clapped her hands and laughed, and tried to touch his head; but being too little, laughed again, and stood on tiptoe to embrace him. Then she began to drag him, in her childish eagerness, towards the door; and he, nothing loth to go, accompanied her.

A terrible voice in the hall cried, "Bring down Master Scrooge's box, there!" and in the hall appeared the school-master himself, who glared on Master Scrooge with a ferocious condescension, and threw him into a dreadful state of mind by shaking hands with him. He then conveyed him and his sister into the veriest old well of a shivering best-parlour that ever was seen, where the maps upon the wall, and the celestial and terrestrial globes in the windows, were waxy with cold. Here he produced a decanter of curiously light wine, and a block of curiously heavy cake, and administered instalments of those dainties to the young people: at the same time, sending out a meagre servant to offer a glass of "something" to the postboy, who answered that he thanked the gentleman, but if it was the same tap as he had tasted before, he had rather not. Master Scrooge's trunk being by this time tied on to the top of the chaise, the children bade the schoolmaster good-bye right willingly; and getting into it, drove gaily down the garden-sweep: the quick wheels dashing the hoar-frost and snow from off the dark leaves of the evergreens like spray.

"Always a delicate creature, whom a breath might have withered," said the Ghost. "But she had a large heart!"

"So she had," cried Scrooge. "You're right. I will not gainsay it, Spirit. God forbid!"

"She died a woman," said the Ghost, "and had, as I think, children."

"One child," Scrooge returned.

"True," said the Ghost. "Your nephew!"

Scrooge seemed uneasy in his mind; and answered briefly, "Yes."

Although they had but that moment left the school behind them, they were now in the busy thoroughfares of a city, where shadowy passengers passed and repassed; where shadowy carts and coaches battled for the way, and all the strife and tumult of a real city were. It was made plain enough, by the dressing of the shops, that here too it was Christmas time again; but it was evening, and the streets were lighted up.

The Ghost stopped at a certain warehouse door, and asked Scrooge if he knew it.

"Know it!" said Scrooge. "Was I apprenticed here!"

They went in. At sight of an old gentleman in a Welsh wig, sitting behind such a high desk, that if he had been two inches taller he must have knocked his head against the ceiling, Scrooge cried in great excitement:

"Why, it's old Fezziwig! Bless his heart; it's Fezziwig alive again!"

Old Fezziwig laid down his pen, and looked up at the clock, which pointed to the hour of seven. He rubbed his hands; adjusted his capacious waistcoat; laughed all over himself, from his shoes to his organ of benevolence; and called out in a comfortable, oily, rich, fat, jovial voice:

"Yo ho, there! Ebenezer! Dick!"

Scrooge's former self, now grown a young man, came briskly in, accompanied by his fellow-'prentice.

"Dick Wilkins, to be sure!" said Scrooge to the Ghost. "Bless me, yes. There he is. He was very much attached to me, was Dick. Poor Dick! Dear, dear!"

"Yo ho, my boys!" said Fezziwig. "No more work to-night. Christmas Eve, Dick. Christmas, Ebenezer! Let's have the shutters up," cried old Fezziwig, with a sharp clap of his hands, "before a man can say Jack Robinson!"

You wouldn't believe how those two fellows went at it! They charged into the street with the shutters—one, two, three—had 'em up in their places—four, five, six—barred 'em and pinned 'em—seven, eight, nine—and came back before you could have got to twelve, panting like race-horses.

"Hilli-ho!" cried old Fezziwig, skipping down from the high desk, with wonderful agility. "Clear away, my lads, and let's have lots of room here! Hilli-ho, Dick! Chirrup, Ebenezer!"

Clear away! There was nothing they wouldn't have cleared away, or couldn't have cleared away, with old Fezziwig looking on. It was done in a minute. Every movable was packed off, as if it were dismissed from public life for evermore; the floor was swept and watered, the lamps were trimmed, fuel was heaped upon the fire; and the warehouse was as snug, and warm, and dry, and bright a ball-room, as you would desire to see upon a winter's night.

In came a fiddler with a music-book, and went up to the lofty desk, and made an orchestra of it, and tuned like fifty stomach-aches. In came Mrs. Fezziwig, one vast substantial smile. In came the three Miss Fezziwigs, beaming and lovable. In came the six young followers whose hearts they broke. In came all the young men and women employed in the business. In came the housemaid, with her cousin, the baker. In came the cook, with her brother's particular friend, the milkman. In came the boy from over the way, who was suspected of not having board enough from his master; trying to hide himself behind the girl from next door but one, who was proved to have had her ears pulled by her mistress. In they all came, one after another; some shyly, some boldly, some gracefully, some awkwardly, some pushing, some pulling; in they all came, anyhow and everyhow. Away they all went, twenty couple at once; hands half round and back again the other way; down the middle and up again; round and round in various stages of affectionate grouping; old top couple always turning up in the wrong place; new top couple starting off again, as soon as they got there; all top couples at last, and not a bottom one to help them! When this result was brought about, old Fezziwig, clapping his hands to stop the dance, cried out, "Well done!" and the fiddler plunged his hot face into a pot of porter, especially provided for that purpose. But scorning rest, upon his reappearance, he instantly began again, though there were no dancers yet, as if the other fiddler had been carried home, exhausted, on a shutter, and he were a bran-new man resolved to beat him out of sight, or perish.

There were more dances, and there were forfeits, and more dances, and there was cake, and there was negus, and there was a great piece of Cold Roast, and there was a great piece of Cold Boiled, and there were mince-pies, and plenty of beer. But the great effect of the evening came after the Roast and Boiled, when the fiddler (an artful dog, mind! The sort of man who knew his business better than you or I could have told it him!) struck up "Sir Roger de Coverley." Then old Fezziwig stood out to dance with Mrs. Fezziwig. Top couple, too; with a good stiff piece of work cut out for them; three or four and twenty pair of partners; people who were not to be trifled with; people who *would* dance, and had no notion of walking.

But if they had been twice as many—ah, four times—old Fezziwig would have been a match for them, and so would Mrs. Fezziwig. As to *her*, she was worthy to be his partner in every sense of the term. If that's not high praise, tell me higher, and I'll use it. A positive light appeared to issue from Fezziwig's calves. They shone in every part of the dance like moons. You couldn't have predicted, at any given time, what would have become of them next. And when old Fezziwig and Mrs. Fezziwig had gone all through the dance; advance and retire, both hands to your partner, bow and curtsey, corkscrew, thread-the-needle, and back again to your place; Fezziwig "cut"—cut so deftly, that he appeared to wink with his legs, and came upon his feet again without a stagger.

When the clock struck eleven, this domestic ball broke up. Mr. and Mrs. Fezziwig took their stations, one on either side of the door, and shaking hands with every person individually as he or she went out, wished him or her a Merry Christmas. When everybody had retired but the two 'prentices, they did the same to them; and thus the cheerful voices died away, and the lads were left to their beds; which were under a counter in the back-shop.

During the whole of this time, Scrooge had acted like a man out of his wits. His heart and soul were in the scene, and with his former self. He corroborated everything, remembered everything, enjoyed everything, and underwent the strangest agitation. It was not until now, when the bright faces of his former self and Dick were turned from them, that he remembered the Ghost, and became conscious that it was looking full upon him, while the light upon its head burnt very clear.

"A small matter," said the Ghost, "to make these silly folks so full of gratitude."

"Small!" echoed Scrooge.

The Spirit signed to him to listen to the two apprentices, who were pouring out their hearts in praise of Fezziwig: and when he had done so, said,

"Why! Is it not? He has spent but a few pounds of your mortal money: three or four perhaps. Is that so much that he deserves this praise?"

"It isn't that," said Scrooge, heated by the remark, and speaking unconsciously like his former, not his latter, self. "It isn't that, Spirit. He has the power to render us happy or unhappy; to make our service light or burdensome; a pleasure or a toil. Say that his power lies in words and looks; in things so slight and insignificant that it is impossible to add and count 'em up: what then? The happiness he gives, is quite as great as if it cost a fortune."

He felt the Spirit's glance, and stopped.

"What is the matter?" asked the Ghost.

"Nothing particular," said Scrooge.

"Something, I think?" the Ghost insisted.

"No," said Scrooge, "No. I should like to be able to say a word or two to my clerk just now. That's all."

His former self turned down the lamps as he gave utterance to the wish; and Scrooge and the Ghost again stood side by side in the open air.

"My time grows short," observed the Spirit. "Quick!"

This was not addressed to Scrooge, or to any one whom he could see, but it produced an immediate effect. For again Scrooge saw himself. He was older now; a man in the prime of life. His face had not the harsh and rigid lines of later years; but it had begun to wear the signs of care and avarice. There was an eager, greedy, restless motion in the eye, which showed the passion that had taken root, and where the shadow of the growing tree would fall.

He was not alone, but sat by the side of a fair young girl in a mourning-dress: in whose eyes there were tears, which sparkled in the light that shone out of the Ghost of Christmas Past.

"It matters little," she said, softly. "To you, very little. Another idol has displaced me; and if it can cheer and comfort you in time to come, as I would have tried to do, I have no just cause to grieve."

"What Idol has displaced you?" he rejoined.

"A golden one."

"This is the even-handed dealing of the world!" he said. "There is nothing on which it is so hard as poverty; and there is nothing it professes to condemn with such severity as the pursuit of wealth!"

"You fear the world too much," she answered, gently. "All your other hopes have merged into the hope of being beyond the chance of its sordid reproach. I have seen your nobler aspirations fall off one by one, until the master-passion, Gain, engrosses you. Have I not?"

"What then?" he retorted. "Even if I have grown so much wiser, what then? I am not changed towards you."

She shook her head.

"Am I?"

"Our contract is an old one. It was made when we were both poor and content to be so, until, in good season, we could improve our worldly fortune by our patient industry. You *are* changed. When it was made, you were another man."

"I was a boy," he said impatiently.

"Your own feeling tells you that you were not what you are," she returned. "I am. That which promised happiness when we were one in heart, is fraught with misery now that we are two. How often and how keenly I have thought of this, I will not say. It is enough that I *have* thought of it, and can release you."

"Have I ever sought release?"

"In words. No. Never."

"In what, then?"

"In a changed nature; in an altered spirit; in another atmosphere of life; another Hope as its great end. In everything that made my love of any worth or value in your sight. If this had never been between us," said the girl, looking mildly, but with steadiness, upon him; "tell me, would you seek me out and try to win me now? Ah, no!"

He seemed to yield to the justice of this supposition, in spite of himself. But he said with a struggle, "You think not."

"I would gladly think otherwise if I could," she answered, "Heaven knows! When *I* have learned a Truth like this, I know how strong and irresistible it must be. But if you were free to-day, to-morrow, yesterday, can even I believe that you would choose a dowerless girl—you who, in your very confidence with her, weigh everything by Gain: or, choosing her, if for a moment you were false enough to your one guiding principle to do so, do I not know that your repentance and regret would surely follow? I do; and I release you. With a full heart, for the love of him you once were."

He was about to speak; but with her head turned from him, she resumed.

"You may—the memory of what is past half makes me hope you will—have pain in this. A very, very brief time, and you will dismiss the recollection of it, gladly, as an unprofitable dream, from which it happened well that you awoke. May you be happy in the life you have chosen!"

She left him; and they parted.

"Spirit!" said Scrooge, "show me no more! Conduct me home. Why do you delight to torture me?"

"One shadow more!" exclaimed the Ghost.

"No more!" cried Scrooge. "No more. I don't wish to see it. Show me no more!"

But the relentless Ghost pinioned him in both his arms, and forced him to observe what happened next.

They were in another scene and place; a room, not very large or handsome, but full of comfort. Near to the winter fire sat a beautiful young girl, so like that last that Scrooge believed it was the same, until he saw *her*, now a comely matron, sitting opposite her daughter. The noise in this room was perfectly tumultuous, for there were more children there, than Scrooge in his agitated state of mind could count; and, unlike the celebrated herd in the poem, they were not forty children conducting themselves like one, but every child was conducting itself like forty.

The consequences were uproarious beyond belief; but no one seemed to care; on the contrary, the mother and daughter laughed heartily, and enjoyed it very much; and the latter, soon beginning to mingle in the sports, got pillaged by the young brigands most ruthlessly. What would I not have given to be one of them! Though I never could have been so rude, no, no! I wouldn't for the wealth of all the world have crushed that braided hair, and torn it down; and for the precious little shoe, I wouldn't have plucked it off, God bless my soul! to save my life. As to measuring her waist in sport, as they did, bold young brood, I couldn't have done it; I should have expected my arm to have grown round it for a punishment, and never come straight again. And yet I should have dearly liked, I own, to have touched her lips; to have questioned her, that she might have opened them; to have looked upon the lashes of her downcast eyes, and never raised a blush; to have let loose waves of hair, an inch of which would be a keepsake beyond price: in short, I should have liked, I do confess, to have had the lightest licence of a child, and yet to have been man enough to know its value.

But now a knocking at the door was heard, and such a rush immediately ensued that she with laughing face and plundered dress was borne towards it the centre of a flushed and boisterous group, just in time to greet the father, who came home attended by a man laden with Christmas toys and presents. Then the shouting and the struggling, and the onslaught that was made on the defenceless porter! The scaling him with chairs for ladders to dive into his pockets, despoil him of brown-paper parcels, hold on tight by his cravat, hug him round his neck, pommel his back, and kick his legs in irrepressible affection! The shouts of wonder and delight with which the development of every package was received! The terrible announcement that the baby had been taken in the act of putting a doll's frying-pan into his mouth, and was more than suspected of having swallowed a fictitious turkey, glued on a wooden platter! The immense relief of finding this a false alarm! The joy, and gratitude, and ecstasy! They are all indescribable alike. It is enough that by degrees the children and their emotions got out of the parlour, and by one stair at a time, up to the top of the house; where they went to bed, and so subsided.

And now Scrooge looked on more attentively than ever, when the master of the house, having his daughter leaning fondly on him, sat down with her and her mother at his own fireside; and when he thought that such another creature, quite as graceful and as full of promise, might have called him father, and been a spring-time in the haggard winter of his life, his sight grew very dim indeed.

"Belle," said the husband, turning to his wife with a smile, "I saw an old friend of yours this afternoon."

"Who was it?"

"Guess!"

"How can I? Tut, don't I know?" she added in the same breath, laughing as he laughed. "Mr. Scrooge."

"Mr. Scrooge it was. I passed his office window; and as it was not shut up, and he had a candle inside, I could scarcely help seeing him. His partner lies upon the point of death, I hear; and there he sat alone. Quite alone in the world, I do believe."

"Spirit!" said Scrooge in a broken voice, "remove me from this place."

"I told you these were shadows of the things that have been," said the Ghost. "That they are what they are, do not blame me!"

"Remove me!" Scrooge exclaimed, "I cannot bear it!"

He turned upon the Ghost, and seeing that it looked upon him with a face, in which in some strange way there were fragments of all the faces it had shown him, wrestled with it.

"Leave me! Take me back. Haunt me no longer!"

In the struggle, if that can be called a struggle in which the Ghost with no visible resistance on its own part was undisturbed by any effort of its adversary, Scrooge observed that its light was burning high and bright; and dimly connecting that with its influence over him, he seized the extinguisher-cap, and by a sudden action pressed it down upon its head.

The Spirit dropped beneath it, so that the extinguisher covered its whole form; but though Scrooge pressed it down with all his force, he could not hide the light: which streamed from under it, in an unbroken flood upon the ground.

He was conscious of being exhausted, and overcome by an irresistible drowsiness; and, further, of being in his own bed-room. He gave the cap a parting squeeze, in which his hand relaxed; and had barely time to reel to bed, before he sank into a heavy sleep.

Stave III

The Second of the Three Spirits

Awakening in the middle of a prodigiously tough snore, and sitting up in bed to get his thoughts together, Scrooge had no occasion to be told that the bell was again upon the stroke of One. He felt that he was restored to consciousness in the right nick of time, for the especial purpose of holding a conference with the second messenger despatched to him through Jacob Marley's intervention. But finding that he turned uncomfortably cold when he began to wonder which of his curtains this new spectre would draw back, he put them every one aside with his own hands; and lying down again, established a sharp look-out all round the bed. For he wished to challenge the Spirit on the moment of its appearance, and did not wish to be taken by surprise, and made nervous.

Gentlemen of the free-and-easy sort, who plume themselves on being acquainted with a move or two, and being usually equal to the time-of-day, express the wide range of their capacity for adventure by observing that they are good for anything from pitch-and-toss to manslaughter; between which opposite extremes, no doubt, there lies a tolerably wide and comprehensive range of subjects. Without venturing for Scrooge quite as hardily as this, I don't mind calling on you to believe that he was ready for a good broad field of strange appearances, and that nothing between a baby and rhinoceros would have astonished him very much.

Now, being prepared for almost anything, he was not by any means prepared for nothing; and, consequently, when the Bell struck One, and no shape appeared, he was taken with a violent fit of trembling. Five minutes, ten minutes, a quarter of an hour went by, yet nothing came. All this time, he lay upon his bed, the very core and centre of a blaze of ruddy light, which streamed upon it when the clock proclaimed the hour; and which, being only light, was more alarming than a dozen ghosts, as he was powerless to make out what it meant, or would be at; and was sometimes apprehensive that he might be at that very moment an interesting case of spontaneous combustion, without having the consolation of knowing it. At last, however, he began to think—as you or I would have thought at first; for it is always the person not in the predicament who knows what ought to have been done in it, and would unquestionably have done it too—at last, I say, he began to think that the source and secret of this ghostly light might be in the adjoining room, from whence, on further tracing it, it seemed to shine. This idea taking full possession of his mind, he got up softly and shuffled in his slippers to the door.

The moment Scrooge's hand was on the lock, a strange voice called him by his name, and bade him enter. He obeyed.

It was his own room. There was no doubt about that. But it had undergone a surprising transformation. The walls and ceiling were so hung with living green, that it looked a perfect grove; from every part of which, bright gleaming berries glistened. The crisp leaves of holly, mistletoe, and ivy reflected back the light, as if so many little mirrors had been scattered there; and such a mighty blaze went roaring up the chimney, as that dull petrification of a hearth had never known in Scrooge's time, or Marley's, or for many and many a winter season gone. Heaped up on the floor, to form a kind of throne, were turkeys, geese, game, poultry, brawn, great joints of meat, sucking-pigs, long wreaths of sausages, mince-pies, plum-puddings, barrels of oysters, red-hot chestnuts, cherry-cheeked apples, juicy oranges, luscious pears, immense twelfth-cakes, and seething bowls of punch, that made the chamber dim with their delicious steam. In easy state upon this couch, there sat a jolly Giant, glorious to see; who bore a glowing torch, in shape not unlike Plenty's horn, and held it up, high up, to shed its light on Scrooge, as he came peeping round the door.

"Come in!" exclaimed the Ghost. "Come in! and know me better, man!"

Scrooge entered timidly, and hung his head before this Spirit. He was not the dogged Scrooge he had been; and though the Spirit's eyes were clear and kind, he did not like to meet them.

"I am the Ghost of Christmas Present," said the Spirit. "Look upon me!"

Scrooge reverently did so. It was clothed in one simple green robe, or mantle, bordered with white fur. This garment hung so loosely on the figure, that its capacious breast was bare, as if disdaining to be warded or concealed by any artifice. Its feet, observable beneath the ample folds of the garment, were also bare; and on its head it wore no other covering than a holly wreath, set here and there with shining icicles. Its dark brown curls were long and free; free as its genial face, its sparkling eye, its open hand, its cheery voice, its unconstrained demeanour, and its joyful air. Girded round its middle was an antique scabbard; but no sword was in it, and the ancient sheath was eaten up with rust.

"You have never seen the like of me before!" exclaimed the Spirit.

"Never," Scrooge made answer to it.

"Have never walked forth with the younger members of my family; meaning (for I am very young) my elder brothers born in these later years?" pursued the Phantom.

"I don't think I have," said Scrooge. "I am afraid I have not. Have you had many brothers, Spirit?"

"More than eighteen hundred," said the Ghost.

"A tremendous family to provide for!" muttered Scrooge.

The Ghost of Christmas Present rose.

"Spirit," said Scrooge submissively, "conduct me where you will. I went forth last night on compulsion, and I learnt a lesson which is working now. To-night, if you have aught to teach me, let me profit by it."

"Touch my robe!"

Scrooge did as he was told, and held it fast.

Holly, mistletoe, red berries, ivy, turkeys, geese, game, poultry, brawn, meat, pigs, sausages, oysters, pies, puddings, fruit, and punch, all vanished instantly. So did the room, the fire, the ruddy glow, the hour of night, and they stood in the city streets on Christmas morning, where (for the weather was severe) the people made a rough, but brisk and not unpleasant kind of music, in scraping the snow from the pavement in front of their dwellings, and from the tops of their houses, whence it was mad delight to the boys to see it come plumping down into the road below, and splitting into artificial little snow-storms.

The house fronts looked black enough, and the windows blacker, contrasting with the smooth white sheet of snow upon the roofs, and with the dirtier snow upon the ground; which last deposit had been ploughed up in deep furrows by the heavy wheels of carts and waggons; furrows that crossed and re-crossed each other hundreds of times where the great streets branched off; and made intricate channels, hard to trace in the thick yellow mud and icy water. The sky was gloomy, and the shortest streets were choked up with a dingy mist, half thawed, half frozen, whose heavier particles descended in a shower of sooty atoms, as if all the chimneys in Great Britain had, by one consent, caught fire, and were blazing away to their dear hearts' content. There was nothing very cheerful in the climate or the town, and yet was there an air of cheerfulness abroad that the clearest summer air and brightest summer sun might have endeavoured to diffuse in vain.

For the people who were shovelling away on the housetops were jovial and full of glee; calling out to one another from the parapets, and now and then exchanging a facetious snowball—better-natured missile far than many a wordy jest—laughing heartily if it went right and not less heartily if it went wrong. The poulterers' shops were still half open, and the fruiterers' were radiant in their glory. There were great, round, pot-bellied baskets of chestnuts, shaped like the waistcoats of jolly old gentlemen, lolling at the doors, and tumbling out into the street in their apoplectic opulence. There were ruddy, brown-faced, broad-girthed Spanish Onions, shining in the fatness of their growth like Spanish Friars, and winking from their shelves in wanton slyness at the girls as they went by, and glanced demurely at the hung-up mistletoe. There were pears and apples, clustered high in blooming pyramids; there were bunches of grapes, made in the shopkeepers' benevolence to dangle from conspicuous hooks, that people's mouths might water gratis as they passed; there were piles of filberts, mossy and brown, recalling, in their fragrance, ancient walks among the woods, and pleasant shufflings ankle deep through withered leaves; there were Norfolk Biffins, squat and swarthy, setting off the yellow of the oranges and lemons, and, in the great compactness of their juicy persons, urgently entreating and beseeching to be carried home in paper bags and eaten after dinner. The very gold and silver fish, set forth among these choice fruits in a bowl, though members of a dull and stagnant-blooded race, appeared to know that there was something going on; and, to a fish, went gasping round and round their little world in slow and passionless excitement.

The Grocers'! oh the Grocers'! nearly closed, with perhaps two shutters down, or one; but through those gaps such glimpses! It was not alone that the scales descending on the counter made a merry sound, or that the twine and roller parted company so briskly, or that the canisters were rattled up and down like juggling tricks, or even that the blended scents of tea and coffee were so grateful to the nose, or even that the raisins were so plentiful and rare, the almonds so extremely white, the sticks of cinnamon so long and straight, the other spices so delicious, the candied fruits so caked and spotted with molten sugar as to make the coldest lookers-on feel faint and subsequently bilious. Nor was it that the figs were moist and pulpy, or that the French plums blushed in modest tartness from their highly-decorated boxes, or that everything was good to eat and in its Christmas dress; but the customers were all so hurried and so eager in the hopeful promise of the day, that they tumbled up against each other at the door, crashing their wicker baskets wildly, and left their purchases upon the counter, and came running back to fetch them, and committed hundreds of the like mistakes, in the best humour possible; while the Grocer and his people were so frank and fresh that the polished hearts with which they fastened their aprons behind might have been their own, worn outside for general inspection, and for Christmas daws to peck at if they chose.

But soon the steeples called good people all, to church and chapel, and away they came, flocking through the streets in their best clothes, and with their gayest faces. And at the same time there emerged from scores of bye-streets, lanes, and nameless turnings, innumerable people, carrying their dinners to the bakers' shops. The sight of these poor revellers appeared to interest the Spirit very much, for he stood with Scrooge beside him in a baker's doorway, and taking off the covers as their bearers passed, sprinkled incense on their dinners from his torch. And it was a very uncommon kind of torch, for once or twice when there were angry words between some dinner-carriers who had jostled each other, he shed a few drops of water on them from it, and their good humour was restored directly. For they said, it was a shame to quarrel upon Christmas Day. And so it was! God love it, so it was!

In time the bells ceased, and the bakers were shut up; and yet there was a genial shadowing forth of all these dinners and the progress of their cooking, in the thawed blotch of wet above each baker's oven; where the pavement smoked as if its stones were cooking too.

"Is there a peculiar flavour in what you sprinkle from your torch?" asked Scrooge.

"There is. My own."

"Would it apply to any kind of dinner on this day?" asked Scrooge.

"To any kindly given. To a poor one most."

"Why to a poor one most?" asked Scrooge.

"Because it needs it most."

"Spirit," said Scrooge, after a moment's thought, "I wonder you, of all the beings in the many worlds about us, should desire to cramp these people's opportunities of innocent enjoyment."

"I!" cried the Spirit.

"You would deprive them of their means of dining every seventh day, often the only day on which they can be said to dine at all," said Scrooge. "Wouldn't you?"

"I!" cried the Spirit.

"You seek to close these places on the Seventh Day?" said Scrooge. "And it comes to the same thing."

"*I* seek!" exclaimed the Spirit.

"Forgive me if I am wrong. It has been done in your name, or at least in that of your family," said Scrooge.

"There are some upon this earth of yours," returned the Spirit, "who lay claim to know us, and who do their deeds of passion, pride, ill-will, hatred, envy, bigotry, and selfishness in our name, who are as strange to us and all our kith and kin, as if they had never lived. Remember that, and charge their doings on themselves, not us."

Scrooge promised that he would; and they went on, invisible, as they had been before, into the suburbs of the town. It was a remarkable quality of the Ghost (which Scrooge had observed at the baker's), that notwithstanding his gigantic size, he could accommodate himself to any place with ease; and that he stood beneath a low roof quite as gracefully and like a supernatural creature, as it was possible he could have done in any lofty hall.

And perhaps it was the pleasure the good Spirit had in showing off this power of his, or else it was his own kind, generous, hearty nature, and his sympathy with all poor men, that led him straight to Scrooge's clerk's; for there he went, and took Scrooge with him, holding to his robe; and on the threshold of the door the Spirit smiled, and stopped to bless Bob Cratchit's dwelling with the sprinkling of his torch. Think of that! Bob had but fifteen "Bob" a-week himself; he pocketed on Saturdays but fifteen copies of his Christian name; and yet the Ghost of Christmas Present blessed his four-roomed house!

Then up rose Mrs. Cratchit, Cratchit's wife, dressed out but poorly in a twice-turned gown, but brave in ribbons, which are cheap and make a goodly show for sixpence; and she laid the cloth, assisted by Belinda Cratchit, second of her daughters, also brave in ribbons; while Master Peter Cratchit plunged a fork into the saucepan of potatoes, and getting the corners of his monstrous shirt collar (Bob's private property, conferred upon his son and heir in honour of the day) into his mouth, rejoiced to find himself so gallantly attired, and yearned to show his linen in the fashionable Parks. And now two smaller Cratchits, boy and girl, came tearing in, screaming that outside the baker's they had smelt the goose, and known it for their own; and basking in luxurious thoughts of sage and onion, these young Cratchits danced about the table, and exalted Master Peter Cratchit to the skies, while he (not proud, although his collars nearly choked him) blew the fire, until the slow potatoes bubbling up, knocked loudly at the saucepan-lid to be let out and peeled.

"What has ever got your precious father then?" said Mrs. Cratchit. "And your brother, Tiny Tim! And Martha warn't as late last Christmas Day by half-an-hour?"

"Here's Martha, mother!" said a girl, appearing as she spoke.

"Here's Martha, mother!" cried the two young Cratchits. "Hurrah! There's *such* a goose, Martha!"

"Why, bless your heart alive, my dear, how late you are!" said Mrs. Cratchit, kissing her a dozen times, and taking off her shawl and bonnet for her with officious zeal.

"We'd a deal of work to finish up last night," replied the girl, "and had to clear away this morning, mother!"

"Well! Never mind so long as you are come," said Mrs. Cratchit. "Sit ye down before the fire, my dear, and have a warm, Lord bless ye!"

"No, no! There's father coming," cried the two young Cratchits, who were everywhere at once. "Hide, Martha, hide!"

So Martha hid herself, and in came little Bob, the father, with at least three feet of comforter exclusive of the fringe, hanging down before him; and his threadbare clothes darned up and brushed, to look seasonable; and Tiny Tim upon his shoulder. Alas for Tiny Tim, he bore a little crutch, and had his limbs supported by an iron frame!

"Why, where's our Martha?" cried Bob Cratchit, looking round.

"Not coming," said Mrs. Cratchit.

"Not coming!" said Bob, with a sudden declension in his high spirits; for he had been Tim's blood horse all the way from church, and had come home rampant. "Not coming upon Christmas Day!"

Martha didn't like to see him disappointed, if it were only in joke; so she came out prematurely from behind the closet door, and ran into his arms, while the two young Cratchits hustled Tiny Tim, and bore him off into the wash-house, that he might hear the pudding singing in the copper.

"And how did little Tim behave?" asked Mrs. Cratchit, when she had rallied Bob on his credulity, and Bob had hugged his daughter to his heart's content.

"As good as gold," said Bob, "and better. Somehow he gets thoughtful, sitting by himself so much, and thinks the strangest things you ever heard. He told me, coming home, that he hoped the people saw him in the church, because he was a cripple, and it might be pleasant to them to remember upon Christmas Day, who made lame beggars walk, and blind men see."

Bob's voice was tremulous when he told them this, and trembled more when he said that Tiny Tim was growing strong and hearty.

His active little crutch was heard upon the floor, and back came Tiny Tim before another word was spoken, escorted by his brother and sister to his stool before the fire; and while Bob, turning up his cuffs—as if, poor fellow, they were capable of being made more shabby—compounded some hot mixture in a jug with gin and lemons, and stirred it round and round and put it on the hob to simmer; Master Peter, and the two ubiquitous young Cratchits went to fetch the goose, with which they soon returned in high procession.

Such a bustle ensued that you might have thought a goose the rarest of all birds; a feathered phenomenon, to which a black swan was a matter of course—and in truth it was something very like it in that house. Mrs. Cratchit made the gravy (ready beforehand in a little saucepan) hissing hot; Master Peter mashed the potatoes with incredible vigour; Miss Belinda sweetened up the apple-sauce; Martha dusted the hot plates; Bob took Tiny Tim beside him in a tiny corner at the table; the two young Cratchits set chairs for everybody, not forgetting themselves, and mounting guard upon their posts, crammed spoons into their mouths, lest they should shriek for goose before their turn came to be helped. At last the dishes were set on, and grace was said. It was succeeded by a breathless pause, as Mrs. Cratchit, looking slowly all along the carving-knife, prepared to plunge it in the breast; but when she did, and when the long expected gush of stuffing issued forth, one murmur of delight arose all round the board, and even Tiny Tim, excited by the two young Cratchits, beat on the table with the handle of his knife, and feebly cried Hurrah!

There never was such a goose. Bob said he didn't believe there ever was such a goose cooked. Its tenderness and flavour, size and cheapness, were the themes of universal admiration. Eked out by apple-sauce and mashed potatoes, it was a sufficient dinner for the whole family; indeed, as Mrs. Cratchit said with great delight (surveying one small atom of a bone upon the dish), they hadn't ate it all at last! Yet every one had had enough, and the youngest Cratchits in particular, were steeped in sage and onion to the eyebrows! But now, the plates being changed by Miss Belinda, Mrs. Cratchit left the room alone—too nervous to bear witnesses—to take the pudding up and bring it in.

Suppose it should not be done enough! Suppose it should break in turning out! Suppose somebody should have got over the wall of the back-yard, and stolen it, while they were merry with the goose—a supposition at which the two young Cratchits became livid! All sorts of horrors were supposed.

Hallo! A great deal of steam! The pudding was out of the copper. A smell like a washing-day! That was the cloth. A smell like an eating-house and a pastrycook's next door to each other, with a laundress's next door to that! That was the pudding! In half a minute Mrs. Cratchit entered—flushed, but smiling proudly— with the pudding, like a speckled cannon-ball, so hard and firm, blazing in half of half-a-quartern of ignited brandy, and bedight with Christmas holly stuck into the top.

Oh, a wonderful pudding! Bob Cratchit said, and calmly too, that he regarded it as the greatest success achieved by Mrs. Cratchit since their marriage. Mrs. Cratchit said that now the weight was off her mind, she would confess she had had her doubts about the quantity of flour. Everybody had something to say about it, but nobody said or thought it was at all a small pudding for a large family. It would have been flat heresy to do so. Any Cratchit would have blushed to hint at such a thing.

At last the dinner was all done, the cloth was cleared, the hearth swept, and the fire made up. The compound in the jug being tasted, and considered perfect, apples and oranges were put upon the table, and a shovel-full of chestnuts on the fire. Then all the Cratchit family drew round the hearth, in what Bob Cratchit called a circle, meaning half a one; and at Bob Cratchit's elbow stood the family display of glass. Two tumblers, and a custard-cup without a handle.

These held the hot stuff from the jug, however, as well as golden goblets would have done; and Bob served it out with beaming looks, while the chestnuts on the fire sputtered and cracked noisily. Then Bob proposed:

"A Merry Christmas to us all, my dears. God bless us!"

Which all the family re-echoed.

"God bless us every one!" said Tiny Tim, the last of all.

He sat very close to his father's side upon his little stool. Bob held his withered little hand in his, as if he loved the child, and wished to keep him by his side, and dreaded that he might be taken from him.

"Spirit," said Scrooge, with an interest he had never felt before, "tell me if Tiny Tim will live."

"I see a vacant seat," replied the Ghost, "in the poor chimney-corner, and a crutch without an owner, carefully preserved. If these shadows remain unaltered by the Future, the child will die."

"No, no," said Scrooge. "Oh, no, kind Spirit! say he will be spared."

"If these shadows remain unaltered by the Future, none other of my race," returned the Ghost, "will find him here. What then? If he be like to die, he had better do it, and decrease the surplus population."

Scrooge hung his head to hear his own words quoted by the Spirit, and was overcome with penitence and grief.

"Man," said the Ghost, "if man you be in heart, not adamant, forbear that wicked cant until you have discovered What the surplus is, and Where it is. Will you decide what men shall live, what men shall die? It may be, that in the sight of Heaven, you are more worthless and less fit to live than millions like this poor man's child. Oh God! to hear the Insect on the leaf pronouncing on the too much life among his hungry brothers in the dust!"

Scrooge bent before the Ghost's rebuke, and trembling cast his eyes upon the ground. But he raised them speedily, on hearing his own name.

"Mr. Scrooge!" said Bob; "I'll give you Mr. Scrooge, the Founder of the Feast!"

"The Founder of the Feast indeed!" cried Mrs. Cratchit, reddening. "I wish I had him here. I'd give him a piece of my mind to feast upon, and I hope he'd have a good appetite for it."

"My dear," said Bob, "the children; Christmas Day."

"It should be Christmas Day, I am sure," said she, "on which one drinks the health of such an odious, stingy, hard, unfeeling man as Mr. Scrooge. You know he is, Robert! Nobody knows it better than you do, poor fellow!"

"My dear," was Bob's mild answer, "Christmas Day."

"I'll drink his health for your sake and the Day's," said Mrs. Cratchit, "not for his. Long life to him! A merry Christmas and a happy new year!—he'll be very merry and very happy, I have no doubt!"

The children drank the toast after her. It was the first of their proceedings which had no heartiness. Tiny Tim drank it last of all, but he didn't care twopence for it. Scrooge was the Ogre of the family. The mention of his name cast a dark shadow on the party, which was not dispelled for full five minutes.

After it had passed away, they were ten times merrier than before, from the mere relief of Scrooge the Baleful being done with. Bob Cratchit told them how he had a situation in his eye for Master Peter, which would bring in, if obtained, full five-and-sixpence weekly. The two young Cratchits laughed tremendously at the idea of Peter's being a man of business; and Peter himself looked thoughtfully at the fire from between his collars, as if he were deliberating what particular investments he should favour when he came into the receipt of that bewildering income. Martha, who was a poor apprentice at a milliner's, then told them what kind of work she had to do, and how many hours she worked at a stretch, and how she meant to lie abed to-morrow morning for a good long rest; to-morrow being a holiday she passed at home. Also how she had seen a countess and a lord some days before, and how the lord "was much about as tall as Peter;" at which Peter pulled up his collars so high that you couldn't have seen his head if you had been there. All this time the chestnuts and the jug went round and round; and by and bye they had a song, about a lost child travelling in the snow, from Tiny Tim; who had a plaintive little voice, and sang it very well indeed.

There was nothing of high mark in this. They were not a handsome family; they were not well dressed; their shoes were far from being water-proof; their clothes were scanty; and Peter might have known, and very likely did, the inside of a pawnbroker's. But, they were happy, grateful, pleased with one another, and contented with the time; and when they faded, and looked happier yet in the bright sprinklings of the Spirit's torch at parting, Scrooge had his eye upon them, and especially on Tiny Tim, until the last.

By this time it was getting dark, and snowing pretty heavily; and as Scrooge and the Spirit went along the streets, the brightness of the roaring fires in kitchens, parlours, and all sorts of rooms, was wonderful. Here, the flickering of the blaze showed preparations for a cosy dinner, with hot plates baking through and through before the fire, and deep red curtains, ready to be drawn to shut out cold and darkness. There all the children of the house were running out into the snow to meet their married sisters, brothers, cousins, uncles, aunts, and be the first to greet them. Here, again, were shadows on the window-blind of guests assembling; and there a group of handsome girls, all hooded and fur-booted, and all chattering at once, tripped lightly off to some near neighbour's house; where, woe upon the single man who saw them enter—artful witches, well they knew it—in a glow!

But, if you had judged from the numbers of people on their way to friendly gatherings, you might have thought that no one was at home to give them welcome when they got there, instead of every house expecting company, and piling up its fires half-chimney high. Blessings on it, how the Ghost exulted! How it bared its breadth of breast, and opened its capacious palm, and floated on, outpouring, with a generous hand, its bright and harmless mirth on everything within its reach! The very lamplighter, who ran on before, dotting the dusky street with specks of light, and who was dressed to spend the evening somewhere, laughed out loudly as the Spirit passed, though little kenned the lamplighter that he had any company but Christmas!

And now, without a word of warning from the Ghost, they stood upon a bleak and desert moor, where monstrous masses of rude stone were cast about, as though it were the burial-place of giants; and water spread itself wheresoever it listed, or would have done so, but for the frost that held it prisoner; and nothing grew but moss and furze, and coarse rank grass. Down in the west the setting sun had left a streak of fiery red, which glared upon the desolation for an instant, like a sullen eye, and frowning lower, lower, lower yet, was lost in the thick gloom of darkest night.

"What place is this?" asked Scrooge.

"A place where Miners live, who labour in the bowels of the earth," returned the Spirit. "But they know me. See!"

A light shone from the window of a hut, and swiftly they advanced towards it. Passing through the wall of mud and stone, they found a cheerful company assembled round a glowing fire. An old, old man and woman, with their children and their children's children, and another generation beyond that, all decked out gaily in their holiday attire. The old man, in a voice that seldom rose above the howling of the wind upon the barren waste, was singing them a Christmas song—it had been a very old song when he was a boy—and from time to time they all joined in the chorus. So surely as they raised their voices, the old man got quite blithe and loud; and so surely as they stopped, his vigour sank again.

The Spirit did not tarry here, but bade Scrooge hold his robe, and passing on above the moor, sped—whither? Not to sea? To sea. To Scrooge's horror, looking back, he saw the last of the land, a frightful range of rocks, behind them; and his ears were deafened by the thundering of water, as it rolled and roared, and raged among the dreadful caverns it had worn, and fiercely tried to undermine the earth.

Built upon a dismal reef of sunken rocks, some league or so from shore, on which the waters chafed and dashed, the wild year through, there stood a solitary lighthouse. Great heaps of sea-weed clung to its base, and storm-birds—born of the wind one might suppose, as sea-weed of the water—rose and fell about it, like the waves they skimmed.

But even here, two men who watched the light had made a fire, that through the loophole in the thick stone wall shed out a ray of brightness on the awful sea. Joining their horny hands over the rough table at which they sat, they wished each other Merry Christmas in their can of grog; and one of them: the elder, too, with his face all damaged and scarred with hard weather, as the figure-head of an old ship might be: struck up a sturdy song that was like a Gale in itself.

Again the Ghost sped on, above the black and heaving sea—on, on—until, being far away, as he told Scrooge, from any shore, they lighted on a ship. They stood beside the helmsman at the wheel, the look-out in the bow, the officers who had the watch; dark, ghostly figures in their several stations; but every man among them hummed a Christmas tune, or had a Christmas thought, or spoke below his breath to his companion of some bygone Christmas Day, with homeward hopes belonging to it. And every man on board, waking or sleeping, good or bad, had had a kinder word for another on that day than on any day in the year; and had shared to some extent in its festivities; and had remembered those he cared for at a distance, and had known that they delighted to remember him.

It was a great surprise to Scrooge, while listening to the moaning of the wind, and thinking what a solemn thing it was to move on through the lonely darkness over an unknown abyss, whose depths were secrets as profound as Death: it was a great surprise to Scrooge, while thus engaged, to hear a hearty laugh. It was a much greater surprise to Scrooge to recognise it as his own nephew's, and to find himself in a bright, dry, gleaming room, with the Spirit standing smiling by his side, and looking at that same nephew with approving affability!

"Ha, ha!" laughed Scrooge's nephew. "Ha, ha, ha!"

If you should happen, by any unlikely chance, to know a man more blest in a laugh than Scrooge's nephew, all I can say is, I should like to know him too. Introduce him to me, and I'll cultivate his acquaintance.

It is a fair, even-handed, noble adjustment of things, that while there is infection in disease and sorrow, there is nothing in the world so irresistibly contagious as laughter and good-humour. When Scrooge's nephew laughed in this way: holding his sides, rolling his head, and twisting his face into the most extravagant contortions: Scrooge's niece, by marriage, laughed as heartily as he. And their assembled friends being not a bit behindhand, roared out lustily.

"Ha, ha! Ha, ha, ha, ha!"

"He said that Christmas was a humbug, as I live!" cried Scrooge's nephew. "He believed it too!"

"More shame for him, Fred!" said Scrooge's niece, indignantly. Bless those women; they never do anything by halves. They are always in earnest.

She was very pretty: exceedingly pretty. With a dimpled, surprised-looking, capital face; a ripe little mouth, that seemed made to be kissed—as no doubt it was; all kinds of good little dots about her chin, that melted into one another when she laughed; and the sunniest pair of eyes you ever saw in any little creature's head. Altogether she was what you would have called provoking, you know; but satisfactory, too. Oh, perfectly satisfactory.

"He's a comical old fellow," said Scrooge's nephew, "that's the truth: and not so pleasant as he might be. However, his offences carry their own punishment, and I have nothing to say against him."

"I'm sure he is very rich, Fred," hinted Scrooge's niece. "At least you always tell *me* so."

"What of that, my dear!" said Scrooge's nephew. "His wealth is of no use to him. He don't do any good with it. He don't make himself comfortable with it. He hasn't the satisfaction of thinking—ha, ha, ha!—that he is ever going to benefit Us with it."

"I have no patience with him," observed Scrooge's niece. Scrooge's niece's sisters, and all the other ladies, expressed the same opinion.

"Oh, I have!" said Scrooge's nephew. "I am sorry for him; I couldn't be angry with him if I tried. Who suffers by his ill whims! Himself, always. Here, he takes it into his head to dislike us, and he won't come and dine with us. What's the consequence? He don't lose much of a dinner."

"Indeed, I think he loses a very good dinner," interrupted Scrooge's niece. Everybody else said the same, and they must be allowed to have been competent judges, because they had just had dinner; and, with the dessert upon the table, were clustered round the fire, by lamplight.

"Well! I'm very glad to hear it," said Scrooge's nephew, "because I haven't great faith in these young housekeepers. What do *you* say, Topper?"

Topper had clearly got his eye upon one of Scrooge's niece's sisters, for he answered that a bachelor was a wretched outcast, who had no right to express an opinion on the subject. Whereat Scrooge's niece's sister—the plump one with the lace tucker: not the one with the roses—blushed.

"Do go on, Fred," said Scrooge's niece, clapping her hands. "He never finishes what he begins to say! He is such a ridiculous fellow!"

Scrooge's nephew revelled in another laugh, and as it was impossible to keep the infection off; though the plump sister tried hard to do it with aromatic vinegar; his example was unanimously followed.

"I was only going to say," said Scrooge's nephew, "that the consequence of his taking a dislike to us, and not making merry with us, is, as I think, that he loses some pleasant moments, which could do him no harm. I am sure he loses pleasanter companions than he can find in his own thoughts, either in his mouldy old office, or his dusty chambers. I mean to give him the same chance every year, whether he likes it or not, for I pity him. He may rail at Christmas till he dies, but he can't help thinking better of it—I defy him—if he finds me going there, in good temper, year after year, and saying Uncle Scrooge, how are you? If it only puts him in the vein to leave his poor clerk fifty pounds, *that's* something; and I think I shook him yesterday."

It was their turn to laugh now at the notion of his shaking Scrooge. But being thoroughly good-natured, and not much caring what they laughed at, so that they laughed at any rate, he encouraged them in their merriment, and passed the bottle joyously.

After tea, they had some music. For they were a musical family, and knew what they were about, when they sung a Glee or Catch, I can assure you: especially Topper, who could growl away in the bass like a good one, and never swell the large veins in his forehead, or get red in the face over it. Scrooge's niece played well upon the harp; and played among other tunes a simple little air (a mere nothing: you might learn to whistle it in two minutes), which had been familiar to the child who fetched Scrooge from the boarding-school, as he had been reminded by the Ghost of Christmas Past. When this strain of music sounded, all the things that Ghost had shown him, came upon his mind; he softened more and more; and thought that if he could have listened to it often, years ago, he might have cultivated the kindnesses of life for his own happiness with his own hands, without resorting to the sexton's spade that buried Jacob Marley.

But they didn't devote the whole evening to music. After a while they played at forfeits; for it is good to be children sometimes, and never better than at Christmas, when its mighty Founder was a child himself. Stop! There was first a game at blind-man's buff. Of course there was. And I no more believe Topper was really blind than I believe he had eyes in his boots. My opinion is, that it was a done thing between him and Scrooge's nephew; and that the Ghost of Christmas Present knew it. The way he went after that plump sister in the lace tucker, was an outrage on the credulity of human nature. Knocking down the fire-irons, tumbling over the chairs, bumping against the piano, smothering himself among the curtains, wherever she went, there went he! He always knew where the plump sister was. He wouldn't catch anybody else. If you had fallen up against him (as some of them did), on purpose, he would have made a feint of endeavouring to seize you, which would have been an affront to your understanding, and would instantly have sidled off in the direction of the plump sister. She often cried out that it wasn't fair; and it really was not. But when at last, he caught her; when, in spite of all her silken rustlings, and her rapid flutterings past him, he got her into a corner whence there was no escape; then his conduct was the most execrable. For his pretending not to know her; his pretending that it was necessary to touch her head-dress, and further to assure himself of her identity by pressing a certain ring upon her finger, and a certain chain about her neck; was vile, monstrous! No doubt she told him her opinion of it, when, another blind-man being in office, they were so very confidential together, behind the curtains.

Scrooge's niece was not one of the blind-man's buff party, but was made comfortable with a large chair and a footstool, in a snug corner, where the Ghost and Scrooge were close behind her. But she joined in the forfeits, and loved her love to admiration with all the letters of the alphabet. Likewise at the game of How, When, and Where, she was very great, and to the secret joy of Scrooge's nephew, beat her sisters hollow: though they were sharp girls too, as Topper could have told you. There might have been twenty people there, young and old, but they all played, and so did Scrooge; for wholly forgetting in the interest he had in what was going on, that his voice made no sound in their ears, he sometimes came out with his guess quite loud, and very often guessed quite right, too; for the sharpest needle, best Whitechapel, warranted not to cut in the eye, was not sharper than Scrooge; blunt as he took it in his head to be.

The Ghost was greatly pleased to find him in this mood, and looked upon him with such favour, that he begged like a boy to be allowed to stay until the guests departed. But this the Spirit said could not be done.

"Here is a new game," said Scrooge. "One half hour, Spirit, only one!"

It was a Game called Yes and No, where Scrooge's nephew had to think of something, and the rest must find out what; he only answering to their questions yes or no, as the case was. The brisk fire of questioning to which he was exposed, elicited from him that he was thinking of an animal, a live animal, rather a disagreeable animal, a savage animal, an animal that growled and grunted sometimes, and talked sometimes, and lived in London, and walked about the streets, and wasn't made a show of, and wasn't led by anybody, and didn't live in a menagerie, and was never killed in a market, and was not a horse, or an ass, or a cow, or a bull, or a tiger, or a dog, or a pig, or a cat, or a bear. At every fresh question that was put to him, this nephew burst into a fresh roar of laughter; and was so inexpressibly tickled, that he was obliged to get up off the sofa and stamp. At last the plump sister, falling into a similar state, cried out:

"I have found it out! I know what it is, Fred! I know what it is!"

"What is it?" cried Fred.

"It's your Uncle Scro-o-o-o-oge!"

Which it certainly was. Admiration was the universal sentiment, though some objected that the reply to "Is it a bear?" ought to have been "Yes"; inasmuch as an answer in the negative was sufficient to have diverted their thoughts from Mr. Scrooge, supposing they had ever had any tendency that way.

"He has given us plenty of merriment, I am sure," said Fred, "and it would be ungrateful not to drink his health. Here is a glass of mulled wine ready to our hand at the moment; and I say, 'Uncle Scrooge!' "

"Well! Uncle Scrooge!" they cried.

"A Merry Christmas and a Happy New Year to the old man, whatever he is!" said Scrooge's nephew. "He wouldn't take it from me, but may he have it, nevertheless. Uncle Scrooge!"

Uncle Scrooge had imperceptibly become so gay and light of heart, that he would have pledged the unconscious company in return, and thanked them in an inaudible speech, if the Ghost had given him time. But the whole scene passed off in the breath of the last word spoken by his nephew; and he and the Spirit were again upon their travels.

Much they saw, and far they went, and many homes they visited, but always with a happy end. The Spirit stood beside sick beds, and they were cheerful; on foreign lands, and they were close at home; by struggling men, and they were patient in their greater hope; by poverty, and it was rich. In almshouse, hospital, and jail, in misery's every refuge, where vain man in his little brief authority had not made fast the door, and barred the Spirit out, he left his blessing, and taught Scrooge his precepts.

It was a long night, if it were only a night; but Scrooge had his doubts of this, because the Christmas Holidays appeared to be condensed into the space of time they passed together. It was strange, too, that while Scrooge remained unaltered in his outward form, the Ghost grew older, clearly older. Scrooge had observed this change, but never spoke of it, until they left a children's Twelfth Night party, when, looking at the Spirit as they stood together in an open place, he noticed that its hair was grey.

"Are spirits' lives so short?" asked Scrooge.

"My life upon this globe, is very brief," replied the Ghost. "It ends to-night."

"To-night!" cried Scrooge.

"To-night at midnight. Hark! The time is drawing near."

The chimes were ringing the three quarters past eleven at that moment.

"Forgive me if I am not justified in what I ask," said Scrooge, looking intently at the Spirit's robe, "but I see something strange, and not belonging to yourself, protruding from your skirts. Is it a foot or a claw?"

"It might be a claw, for the flesh there is upon it," was the Spirit's sorrowful reply. "Look here."

From the foldings of its robe, it brought two children; wretched, abject, frightful, hideous, miserable. They knelt down at its feet, and clung upon the outside of its garment.

"Oh, Man! look here. Look, look, down here!" exclaimed the Ghost.

They were a boy and girl. Yellow, meagre, ragged, scowling, wolfish; but prostrate, too, in their humility. Where graceful youth should have filled their features out, and touched them with its freshest tints, a stale and shrivelled hand, like that of age, had pinched, and twisted them, and pulled them into shreds. Where angels might have sat enthroned, devils lurked, and glared out menacing. No change, no degradation, no perversion of humanity, in any grade, through all the mysteries of wonderful creation, has monsters half so horrible and dread.

Scrooge started back, appalled. Having them shown to him in this way, he tried to say they were fine children, but the words choked themselves, rather than be parties to a lie of such enormous magnitude.

"Spirit! are they yours?" Scrooge could say no more.

"They are Man's," said the Spirit, looking down upon them. "And they cling to me, appealing from their fathers. This boy is Ignorance. This girl is Want. Beware them both, and all of their degree, but most of all beware this boy, for on his brow I see that written which is Doom, unless the writing be erased. Deny it!" cried the Spirit, stretching out its hand towards the city. "Slander those who tell it ye! Admit it for your factious purposes, and make it worse. And bide the end!"

"Have they no refuge or resource?" cried Scrooge.

"Are there no prisons?" said the Spirit, turning on him for the last time with his own words. "Are there no workhouses?"

The bell struck twelve.

Scrooge looked about him for the Ghost, and saw it not. As the last stroke ceased to vibrate, he remembered the prediction of old Jacob Marley, and lifting up his eyes, beheld a solemn Phantom, draped and hooded, coming, like a mist along the ground, towards him.

Stave IV

The Last of the Spirits

The Phantom slowly, gravely, silently, approached. When it came near him, Scrooge bent down upon his knee; for in the very air through which this Spirit moved it seemed to scatter gloom and mystery.

It was shrouded in a deep black garment, which concealed its head, its face, its form, and left nothing of it visible save one outstretched hand. But for this it would have been difficult to detach its figure from the night, and separate it from the darkness by which it was surrounded.

He felt that it was tall and stately when it came beside him, and that its mysterious presence filled him with a solemn dread. He knew no more, for the Spirit neither spoke nor moved.

"I am in the presence of the Ghost of Christmas Yet To Come?" said Scrooge.

The Spirit answered not, but pointed onward with its hand.

"You are about to show me shadows of the things that have not happened, but will happen in the time before us," Scrooge pursued. "Is that so, Spirit?"

The upper portion of the garment was contracted for an instant in its folds, as if the Spirit had inclined its head. That was the only answer he received.

Although well used to ghostly company by this time, Scrooge feared the silent shape so much that his legs trembled beneath him, and he found that he could hardly stand when he prepared to follow it. The Spirit paused a moment, as observing his condition, and giving him time to recover.

But Scrooge was all the worse for this. It thrilled him with a vague uncertain horror, to know that behind the dusky shroud, there were ghostly eyes intently fixed upon him, while he, though he stretched his own to the utmost, could see nothing but a spectral hand and one great heap of black.

"Ghost of the Future!" he exclaimed, "I fear you more than any spectre I have seen. But as I know your purpose is to do me good, and as I hope to live to be another man from what I was, I am prepared to bear you company, and do it with a thankful heart. Will you not speak to me?"

It gave him no reply. The hand was pointed straight before them.

"Lead on!" said Scrooge. "Lead on! The night is waning fast, and it is precious time to me, I know. Lead on, Spirit!"

The Phantom moved away as it had come towards him. Scrooge followed in the shadow of its dress, which bore him up, he thought, and carried him along.

They scarcely seemed to enter the city; for the city rather seemed to spring up about them, and encompass them of its own act. But there they were, in the heart of it; on 'Change, amongst the merchants; who hurried up and down, and chinked the money in their pockets, and conversed in groups, and looked at their watches, and trifled thoughtfully with their great gold seals; and so forth, as Scrooge had seen them often.

The Spirit stopped beside one little knot of business men. Observing that the hand was pointed to them, Scrooge advanced to listen to their talk.

"No," said a great fat man with a monstrous chin, "I don't know much about it, either way. I only know he's dead."

"When did he die?" inquired another.

"Last night, I believe."

"Why, what was the matter with him?" asked a third, taking a vast quantity of snuff out of a very large snuff-box. "I thought he'd never die."

"God knows," said the first, with a yawn.

"What has he done with his money?" asked a red-faced gentleman with a pendulous excrescence on the end of his nose, that shook like the gills of a turkey-cock.

"I haven't heard," said the man with the large chin, yawning again. "Left it to his company, perhaps. He hasn't left it to *me*. That's all I know."

This pleasantry was received with a general laugh.

"It's likely to be a very cheap funeral," said the same speaker; "for upon my life I don't know of anybody to go to it. Suppose we make up a party and volunteer?"

"I don't mind going if a lunch is provided," observed the gentleman with the excrescence on his nose. "But I must be fed, if I make one."

Another laugh.

"Well, I am the most disinterested among you, after all," said the first speaker, "for I never wear black gloves, and I never eat lunch. But I'll offer to go, if anybody else will. When I come to think of it, I'm not at all sure that I wasn't his most particular friend; for we used to stop and speak whenever we met. Bye, bye!"

Speakers and listeners strolled away, and mixed with other groups. Scrooge knew the men, and looked towards the Spirit for an explanation.

The Phantom glided on into a street. Its finger pointed to two persons meeting. Scrooge listened again, thinking that the explanation might lie here.

He knew these men, also, perfectly. They were men of business: very wealthy, and of great importance. He had made a point always of standing well in their esteem: in a business point of view, that is; strictly in a business point of view.

"How are you?" said one.

"How are you?" returned the other.

"Well!" said the first. "Old Scratch has got his own at last, hey?"

"So I am told," returned the second. "Cold, isn't it?"

"Seasonable for Christmas time. You're not a skater, I suppose?"

"No. No. Something else to think of. Good morning!"

Not another word. That was their meeting, their conversation, and their parting.

Scrooge was at first inclined to be surprised that the Spirit should attach importance to conversations apparently so trivial; but feeling assured that they must have some hidden purpose, he set himself to consider what it was likely to be. They could scarcely be supposed to have any bearing on the death of Jacob, his old partner, for that was Past, and this Ghost's province was the Future. Nor could he think of any one immediately connected with himself, to whom he could apply them. But nothing doubting that to whomsoever they applied they had some latent moral for his own improvement, he resolved to treasure up every word he heard, and everything he saw; and especially to observe the shadow of himself when it appeared. For he had an expectation that the conduct of his future self would give him the clue he missed, and would render the solution of these riddles easy.

He looked about in that very place for his own image; but another man stood in his accustomed corner, and though the clock pointed to his usual time of day for being there, he saw no likeness of himself among the multitudes that poured in through the Porch. It gave him little surprise, however; for he had been revolving in his mind a change of life, and thought and hoped he saw his new-born resolutions carried out in this.

Quiet and dark, beside him stood the Phantom, with its outstretched hand. When he roused himself from his thoughtful quest, he fancied from the turn of the hand, and its situation in reference to himself, that the Unseen Eyes were looking at him keenly. It made him shudder, and feel very cold.

They left the busy scene, and went into an obscure part of the town, where Scrooge had never penetrated before, although he recognised its situation, and its bad repute. The ways were foul and narrow; the shops and houses wretched; the people half-naked, drunken, slipshod, ugly. Alleys and archways, like so many cesspools, disgorged their offences of smell, and dirt, and life, upon the straggling streets; and the whole quarter reeked with crime, with filth, and misery.

Far in this den of infamous resort, there was a low-browed, beetling shop, below a pent-house roof, where iron, old rags, bottles, bones, and greasy offal, were bought. Upon the floor within, were piled up heaps of rusty keys, nails, chains, hinges, files, scales, weights, and refuse iron of all kinds. Secrets that few would like to scrutinise were bred and hidden in mountains of unseemly rags, masses of corrupted fat, and sepulchres of bones. Sitting in among the wares he dealt in, by a charcoal stove, made of old bricks, was a grey-haired rascal, nearly seventy years of age; who had screened himself from the cold air without, by a frousy curtaining of miscellaneous tatters, hung upon a line; and smoked his pipe in all the luxury of calm retirement.

Scrooge and the Phantom came into the presence of this man, just as a woman with a heavy bundle slunk into the shop. But she had scarcely entered, when another woman, similarly laden, came in too; and she was closely followed by a man in faded black, who was no less startled by the sight of them, than they had been upon the recognition of each other. After a short period of blank astonishment, in which the old man with the pipe had joined them, they all three burst into a laugh.

"Let the charwoman alone to be the first!" cried she who had entered first. "Let the laundress alone to be the second; and let the undertaker's man alone to be the third. Look here, old Joe, here's a chance! If we haven't all three met here without meaning it!"

"You couldn't have met in a better place," said old Joe, removing his pipe from his mouth. "Come into the parlour. You were made free of it long ago, you know; and the other two an't strangers. Stop till I shut the door of the shop. Ah! How it skreeks! There an't such a rusty bit of metal in the place as its own hinges, I believe; and I'm sure there's no such old bones here, as mine. Ha, ha! We're all suitable to our calling, we're well matched. Come into the parlour. Come into the parlour."

The parlour was the space behind the screen of rags. The old man raked the fire together with an old stair-rod, and having trimmed his smoky lamp (for it was night), with the stem of his pipe, put it in his mouth again.

While he did this, the woman who had already spoken threw her bundle on the floor, and sat down in a flaunting manner on a stool; crossing her elbows on her knees, and looking with a bold defiance at the other two.

"What odds then! What odds, Mrs. Dilber?" said the woman. "Every person has a right to take care of themselves. *He* always did."

"That's true, indeed!" said the laundress. "No man more so."

"Why then, don't stand staring as if you was afraid, woman; who's the wiser? We're not going to pick holes in each other's coats, I suppose?"

"No, indeed!" said Mrs. Dilber and the man together. "We should hope not."

"Very well, then!" cried the woman. "That's enough. Who's the worse for the loss of a few things like these? Not a dead man, I suppose."

"No, indeed," said Mrs. Dilber, laughing.

"If he wanted to keep 'em after he was dead, a wicked old screw," pursued the woman, "why wasn't he natural in his lifetime? If he had been, he'd have had somebody to look after him when he was struck with Death, instead of lying gasping out his last there, alone by himself."

"It's the truest word that ever was spoke," said Mrs. Dilber. "It's a judgment on him."

"I wish it was a little heavier judgment," replied the woman; "and it should have been, you may depend upon it, if I could have laid my hands on anything else. Open that bundle, old Joe, and let me know the value of it. Speak out plain. I'm not afraid to be the first, nor afraid for them to see it. We know pretty well that we were helping ourselves, before we met here, I believe. It's no sin. Open the bundle, Joe."

But the gallantry of her friends would not allow of this; and the man in faded black, mounting the breach first, produced his plunder. It was not extensive. A seal or two, a pencil-case, a pair of sleeve-buttons, and a brooch of no great value, were all. They were severally examined and appraised by old Joe, who chalked the sums he was disposed to give for each, upon the wall, and added them up into a total when he found there was nothing more to come.

"That's your account," said Joe, "and I wouldn't give another sixpence, if I was to be boiled for not doing it. Who's next?"

Mrs. Dilber was next. Sheets and towels, a little wearing apparel, two old-fashioned silver teaspoons, a pair of sugar-tongs, and a few boots. Her account was stated on the wall in the same manner.

"I always give too much to ladies. It's a weakness of mine, and that's the way I ruin myself," said old Joe. "That's your account. If you asked me for another penny, and made it an open question, I'd repent of being so liberal and knock off half-a-crown."

"And now undo *my* bundle, Joe," said the first woman.

Joe went down on his knees for the greater convenience of opening it, and having unfastened a great many knots, dragged out a large and heavy roll of some dark stuff.

"What do you call this?" said Joe. "Bed-curtains!"

"Ah!" returned the woman, laughing and leaning forward on her crossed arms. "Bed-curtains!"

"You don't mean to say you took 'em down, rings and all, with him lying there?" said Joe.

"Yes I do," replied the woman. "Why not?"

"You were born to make your fortune," said Joe, "and you'll certainly do it."

"I certainly shan't hold my hand, when I can get anything in it by reaching it out, for the sake of such a man as *he* was, I promise you, Joe," returned the woman coolly. "Don't drop that oil upon the blankets, now."

"His blankets?" asked Joe.

"Whose else's do you think?" replied the woman. "He isn't likely to take cold without 'em, I dare say."

"I hope he didn't die of anything catching? Eh?" said old Joe, stopping in his work, and looking up.

"Don't you be afraid of that," returned the woman. "I an't so fond of his company that I'd loiter about him for such things, if he did. Ah! you may look through that shirt till your eyes ache; but you won't find a hole in it, nor a threadbare place. It's the best he had, and a fine one too. They'd have wasted it, if it hadn't been for me."

"What do you call wasting of it?" asked old Joe.

"Putting it on him to be buried in, to be sure," replied the woman with a laugh. "Somebody was fool enough to do it, but I took it off again. If calico an't good enough for such a purpose, it isn't good for anything. It's quite as becoming to the body. He can't look uglier than he did in that one."

Scrooge listened to this dialogue in horror. As they sat grouped about their spoil, in the scanty light afforded by the old man's lamp, he viewed them with a detestation and disgust, which could hardly have been greater, though they had been obscene demons, marketing the corpse itself.

"Ha, ha!" laughed the same woman, when old Joe, producing a flannel bag with money in it, told out their several gains upon the ground. "This is the end of it, you see! He frightened every one away from him when he was alive, to profit us when he was dead! Ha, ha, ha!"

"Spirit!" said Scrooge, shuddering from head to foot. "I see, I see. The case of this unhappy man might be my own. My life tends that way, now. Merciful Heaven, what is this!"

He recoiled in terror, for the scene had changed, and now he almost touched a bed: a bare, uncurtained bed: on which, beneath a ragged sheet, there lay a something covered up, which, though it was dumb, announced itself in awful language.

The room was very dark, too dark to be observed with any accuracy, though Scrooge glanced round it in obedience to a secret impulse, anxious to know what kind of room it was. A pale light, rising in the outer air, fell straight upon the bed; and on it, plundered and bereft, unwatched, unwept, uncared for, was the body of this man.

Scrooge glanced towards the Phantom. Its steady hand was pointed to the head. The cover was so carelessly adjusted that the slightest raising of it, the motion of a finger upon Scrooge's part, would have disclosed the face. He thought of it, felt how easy it would be to do, and longed to do it; but had no more power to withdraw the veil than to dismiss the spectre at his side.

Oh cold, cold, rigid, dreadful Death, set up thine altar here, and dress it with such terrors as thou hast at thy command: for this is thy dominion! But of the loved, revered, and honoured head, thou canst not turn one hair to thy dread purposes, or make one feature odious. It is not that the hand is heavy and will fall down when released; it is not that the heart and pulse are still; but that the hand WAS open, generous, and true; the heart brave, warm, and tender; and the pulse a man's. Strike, Shadow, strike! And see his good deeds springing from the wound, to sow the world with life immortal!

No voice pronounced these words in Scrooge's ears, and yet he heard them when he looked upon the bed. He thought, if this man could be raised up now, what would be his foremost thoughts? Avarice, hard-dealing, griping cares? They have brought him to a rich end, truly!

He lay, in the dark empty house, with not a man, a woman, or a child, to say that he was kind to me in this or that, and for the memory of one kind word I will be kind to him. A cat was tearing at the door, and there was a sound of gnawing rats beneath the hearth-stone. What *they* wanted in the room of death, and why they were so restless and disturbed, Scrooge did not dare to think.

"Spirit!" he said, "this is a fearful place. In leaving it, I shall not leave its lesson, trust me. Let us go!"

Still the Ghost pointed with an unmoved finger to the head.

"I understand you," Scrooge returned, "and I would do it, if I could. But I have not the power, Spirit. I have not the power."

Again it seemed to look upon him.

"If there is any person in the town, who feels emotion caused by this man's death," said Scrooge quite agonised, "show that person to me, Spirit, I beseech you!"

The Phantom spread its dark robe before him for a moment, like a wing; and withdrawing it, revealed a room by daylight, where a mother and her children were.

She was expecting some one, and with anxious eagerness; for she walked up and down the room; started at every sound; looked out from the window; glanced at the clock; tried, but in vain, to work with her needle; and could hardly bear the voices of the children in their play.

At length the long-expected knock was heard. She hurried to the door, and met her husband; a man whose face was careworn and depressed, though he was young. There was a remarkable expression in it now; a kind of serious delight of which he felt ashamed, and which he struggled to repress.

He sat down to the dinner that had been hoarding for him by the fire; and when she asked him faintly what news (which was not until after a long silence), he appeared embarrassed how to answer.

"Is it good?" she said, "or bad?"—to help him.

"Bad," he answered.

"We are quite ruined?"

"No. There is hope yet, Caroline."

"If *he* relents," she said, amazed, "there is! Nothing is past hope, if such a miracle has happened."

"He is past relenting," said her husband. "He is dead."

She was a mild and patient creature if her face spoke truth; but she was thankful in her soul to hear it, and she said so, with clasped hands. She prayed forgiveness the next moment, and was sorry; but the first was the emotion of her heart.

"What the half-drunken woman whom I told you of last night, said to me, when I tried to see him and obtain a week's delay; and what I thought was a mere excuse to avoid me; turns out to have been quite true. He was not only very ill, but dying, then."

"To whom will our debt be transferred?"

"I don't know. But before that time we shall be ready with the money; and even though we were not, it would be a bad fortune indeed to find so merciless a creditor in his successor. We may sleep to-night with light hearts, Caroline!"

Yes. Soften it as they would, their hearts were lighter. The children's faces, hushed and clustered round to hear what they so little understood, were brighter; and it was a happier house for this man's death! The only emotion that the Ghost could show him, caused by the event, was one of pleasure.

"Let me see some tenderness connected with a death," said Scrooge; "or that dark chamber, Spirit, which we left just now, will be for ever present to me."

The Ghost conducted him through several streets familiar to his feet; and as they went along, Scrooge looked here and there to find himself, but nowhere was he to be seen. They entered poor Bob Cratchit's house; the dwelling he had visited before; and found the mother and the children seated round the fire.

Quiet. Very quiet. The noisy little Cratchits were as still as statues in one corner, and sat looking up at Peter, who had a book before him. The mother and her daughters were engaged in sewing. But surely they were very quiet!

"'And He took a child, and set him in the midst of them.'"

Where had Scrooge heard those words? He had not dreamed them. The boy must have read them out, as he and the Spirit crossed the threshold. Why did he not go on?

The mother laid her work upon the table, and put her hand up to her face.

"The colour hurts my eyes," she said.

The colour? Ah, poor Tiny Tim!

"They're better now again," said Cratchit's wife. "It makes them weak by candle-light; and I wouldn't show weak eyes to your father when he comes home, for the world. It must be near his time."

"Past it rather," Peter answered, shutting up his book. "But I think he has walked a little slower than he used, these few last evenings, mother."

They were very quiet again. At last she said, and in a steady, cheerful voice, that only faltered once:

"I have known him walk with—I have known him walk with Tiny Tim upon his shoulder, very fast indeed."

"And so have I," cried Peter. "Often."

"And so have I," exclaimed another. So had all.

"But he was very light to carry," she resumed, intent upon her work, "and his father loved him so, that it was no trouble: no trouble. And there is your father at the door!"

She hurried out to meet him; and little Bob in his comforter—he had need of it, poor fellow—came in. His tea was ready for him on the hob, and they all tried who should help him to it most. Then the two young Cratchits got upon his knees and laid, each child a little cheek, against his face, as if they said, "Don't mind it, father. Don't be grieved!"

Bob was very cheerful with them, and spoke pleasantly to all the family. He looked at the work upon the table, and praised the industry and speed of Mrs. Cratchit and the girls. They would be done long before Sunday, he said.

"Sunday! You went to-day, then, Robert?" said his wife.

"Yes, my dear," returned Bob. "I wish you could have gone. It would have done you good to see how green a place it is. But you'll see it often. I promised him that I would walk there on a Sunday. My little, little child!" cried Bob. "My little child!"

He broke down all at once. He couldn't help it. If he could have helped it, he and his child would have been farther apart perhaps than they were.

He left the room, and went up-stairs into the room above, which was lighted cheerfully, and hung with Christmas. There was a chair set close beside the child, and there were signs of some one having been there, lately. Poor Bob sat down in it, and when he had thought a little and composed himself, he kissed the little face. He was reconciled to what had happened, and went down again quite happy.

They drew about the fire, and talked; the girls and mother working still. Bob told them of the extraordinary kindness of Mr. Scrooge's nephew, whom he had scarcely seen but once, and who, meeting him in the street that day, and seeing that he looked a little—"just a little down you know," said Bob, inquired what had happened to distress him. "On which," said Bob, "for he is the pleasantest-spoken gentleman you ever heard, I told him. 'I am heartily sorry for it, Mr. Cratchit,' he said, 'and heartily sorry for your good wife.' By the bye, how he ever knew *that*, I don't know."

"Knew what, my dear?"

"Why, that you were a good wife," replied Bob.

"Everybody knows that!" said Peter.

"Very well observed, my boy!" cried Bob. "I hope they do. 'Heartily sorry,' he said, 'for your good wife. If I can be of service to you in any way,' he said, giving me his card, 'that's where I live. Pray come to me.' Now, it wasn't," cried Bob, "for the sake of anything he might be able to do for us, so much as for his kind way, that this was quite delightful. It really seemed as if he had known our Tiny Tim, and felt with us."

"I'm sure he's a good soul!" said Mrs. Cratchit.

"You would be surer of it, my dear," returned Bob, "if you saw and spoke to him. I shouldn't be at all surprised—mark what I say!—if he got Peter a better situation."

"Only hear that, Peter," said Mrs. Cratchit.

"And then," cried one of the girls, "Peter will be keeping company with some one, and setting up for himself."

"Get along with you!" retorted Peter, grinning.

"It's just as likely as not," said Bob, "one of these days; though there's plenty of time for that, my dear. But however and whenever we part from one another, I am sure we shall none of us forget poor Tiny Tim—shall we—or this first parting that there was among us?"

"Never, father!" cried they all.

"And I know," said Bob, "I know, my dears, that when we recollect how patient and how mild he was; although he was a little, little child; we shall not quarrel easily among ourselves, and forget poor Tiny Tim in doing it."

"No, never, father!" they all cried again.

"I am very happy," said little Bob, "I am very happy!"

Mrs. Cratchit kissed him, his daughters kissed him, the two young Cratchits kissed him, and Peter and himself shook hands. Spirit of Tiny Tim, thy childish essence was from God!

"Spectre," said Scrooge, "something informs me that our parting moment is at hand. I know it, but I know not how. Tell me what man that was whom we saw lying dead?"

The Ghost of Christmas Yet To Come conveyed him, as before—though at a different time, he thought: indeed, there seemed no order in these latter visions, save that they were in the Future—into the resorts of business men, but showed him not himself. Indeed, the Spirit did not stay for anything, but went straight on, as to the end just now desired, until besought by Scrooge to tarry for a moment.

"This court," said Scrooge, "through which we hurry now, is where my place of occupation is, and has been for a length of time. I see the house. Let me behold what I shall be, in days to come!"

The Spirit stopped; the hand was pointed elsewhere.

"The house is yonder," Scrooge exclaimed. "Why do you point away?"

The inexorable finger underwent no change.

Scrooge hastened to the window of his office, and looked in. It was an office still, but not his. The furniture was not the same, and the figure in the chair was not himself. The Phantom pointed as before.

He joined it once again, and wondering why and whither he had gone, accompanied it until they reached an iron gate. He paused to look round before entering.

A churchyard. Here, then; the wretched man whose name he had now to learn, lay underneath the ground. It was a worthy place. Walled in by houses; overrun by grass and weeds, the growth of vegetation's death, not life; choked up with too much burying; fat with repleted appetite. A worthy place!

The Spirit stood among the graves, and pointed down to One. He advanced towards it trembling. The Phantom was exactly as it had been, but he dreaded that he saw new meaning in its solemn shape.

"Before I draw nearer to that stone to which you point," said Scrooge, "answer me one question. Are these the shadows of the things that Will be, or are they shadows of things that May be, only?"

Still the Ghost pointed downward to the grave by which it stood.

"Men's courses will foreshadow certain ends, to which, if persevered in, they must lead," said Scrooge. "But if the courses be departed from, the ends will change. Say it is thus with what you show me!"

The Spirit was immovable as ever.

Scrooge crept towards it, trembling as he went; and following the finger, read upon the stone of the neglected grave his own name, Ebenezer Scrooge.

"Am *I* that man who lay upon the bed?" he cried, upon his knees.

The finger pointed from the grave to him, and back again.

"No, Spirit! Oh, no, no!"

The finger still was there.

"Spirit!" he cried, tight clutching at its robe, "hear me! I am not the man I was. I will not be the man I must have been but for this intercourse. Why show me this, if I am past all hope!"

For the first time the hand appeared to shake.

"Good Spirit," he pursued, as down upon the ground he fell before it: "Your nature intercedes for me, and pities me. Assure me that I yet may change these shadows you have shown me, by an altered life!"

The kind hand trembled.

"I will honour Christmas in my heart, and try to keep it all the year. I will live in the Past, the Present, and the Future. The Spirits of all Three shall strive within me. I will not shut out the lessons that they teach. Oh, tell me I may sponge away the writing on this stone!"

In his agony, he caught the spectral hand. It sought to free itself, but he was strong in his entreaty, and detained it. The Spirit, stronger yet, repulsed him.

Holding up his hands in a last prayer to have his fate reversed, he saw an alteration in the Phantom's hood and dress. It shrunk, collapsed, and dwindled down into a bedpost.

Stave V

The End of It

Yes! and the bedpost was his own. The bed was his own, the room was his own. Best and happiest of all, the Time before him was his own, to make amends in!

"I will live in the Past, the Present, and the Future!" Scrooge repeated, as he scrambled out of bed. "The Spirits of all Three shall strive within me. Oh Jacob Marley! Heaven, and the Christmas Time be praised for this! I say it on my knees, old Jacob; on my knees!"

He was so fluttered and so glowing with his good intentions, that his broken voice would scarcely answer to his call. He had been sobbing violently in his conflict with the Spirit, and his face was wet with tears.

"They are not torn down," cried Scrooge, folding one of his bed-curtains in his arms, "they are not torn down, rings and all. They are here—I am here—the shadows of the things that would have been, may be dispelled. They will be. I know they will!"

His hands were busy with his garments all this time; turning them inside out, putting them on upside down, tearing them, mislaying them, making them parties to every kind of extravagance.

"I don't know what to do!" cried Scrooge, laughing and crying in the same breath; and making a perfect Laocoön of himself with his stockings. "I am as light as a feather, I am as happy as an angel, I am as merry as a schoolboy. I am as giddy as a drunken man. A merry Christmas to everybody! A happy New Year to all the world. Hallo here! Whoop! Hallo!"

He had frisked into the sitting-room, and was now standing there: perfectly winded.

"There's the saucepan that the gruel was in!" cried Scrooge, starting off again, and going round the fireplace. "There's the door, by which the Ghost of Jacob Marley entered! There's the corner where the Ghost of Christmas Present, sat! There's the window where I saw the wandering Spirits! It's all right, it's all true, it all happened. Ha ha ha!"

Really, for a man who had been out of practice for so many years, it was a splendid laugh, a most illustrious laugh. The father of a long, long line of brilliant laughs!

"I don't know what day of the month it is!" said Scrooge. "I don't know how long I've been among the Spirits. I don't know anything. I'm quite a baby. Never mind. I don't care. I'd rather be a baby. Hallo! Whoop! Hallo here!"

He was checked in his transports by the churches ringing out the lustiest peals he had ever heard. Clash, clang, hammer; ding, dong, bell. Bell, dong, ding; hammer, clang, clash! Oh, glorious, glorious!

Running to the window, he opened it, and put out his head. No fog, no mist; clear, bright, jovial, stirring, cold; cold, piping for the blood to dance to; Golden sunlight; Heavenly sky; sweet fresh air; merry bells. Oh, glorious. Glorious!

"What's to-day!" cried Scrooge, calling downward to a boy in Sunday clothes, who perhaps had loitered in to look about him.

"EH?" returned the boy, with all his might of wonder.

"What's to-day, my fine fellow?" said Scrooge.

"To-day!" replied the boy. "Why, CHRISTMAS DAY."

"It's Christmas Day!" said Scrooge to himself. "I haven't missed it. The Spirits have done it all in one night. They can do anything they like. Of course they can. Of course they can. Hallo, my fine fellow!"

"Hallo!" returned the boy.

"Do you know the Poulterer's, in the next street but one, at the corner?" Scrooge inquired.

"I should hope I did," replied the lad.

"An intelligent boy!" said Scrooge. "A remarkable boy! Do you know whether they've sold the prize Turkey that was hanging up there? Not the little prize Turkey: the big one?"

"What, the one as big as me?" returned the boy.

"What a delightful boy!" said Scrooge. "It's a pleasure to talk to him. Yes, my buck!"

"It's hanging there now," replied the boy.

"Is it?" said Scrooge. "Go and buy it."

"Walk-ER!" exclaimed the boy.

"No, no," said Scrooge, "I am in earnest. Go and buy it, and tell 'em to bring it here, that I may give them the direction where to take it. Come back with the man, and I'll give you a shilling. Come back with him in less than five minutes and I'll give you half-a-crown!"

The boy was off like a shot. He must have had a steady hand at a trigger who could have got a shot off half so fast.

"I'll send it to Bob Cratchit's!" whispered Scrooge, rubbing his hands, and splitting with a laugh. "He sha'n't know who sends it. It's twice the size of Tiny Tim. Joe Miller never made such a joke as sending it to Bob's will be!"

The hand in which he wrote the address was not a steady one, but write it he did, somehow, and went down-stairs to open the street door, ready for the coming of the poulterer's man. As he stood there, waiting his arrival, the knocker caught his eye.

"I shall love it, as long as I live!" cried Scrooge, patting it with his hand. "I scarcely ever looked at it before. What an honest expression it has in its face! It's a wonderful knocker!—Here's the Turkey! Hallo! Whoop! How are you! Merry Christmas!"

It *was* a Turkey! He never could have stood upon his legs, that bird. He would have snapped 'em short off in a minute, like sticks of sealing-wax.

"Why, it's impossible to carry that to Camden Town," said Scrooge. "You must have a cab."

The chuckle with which he said this, and the chuckle with which he paid for the Turkey, and the chuckle with which he paid for the cab, and the chuckle with which he recompensed the boy, were only to be exceeded by the chuckle with which he sat down breathless in his chair again, and chuckled till he cried.

Shaving was not an easy task, for his hand continued to shake very much; and shaving requires attention, even when you don't dance while you are at it. But if he had cut the end of his nose off, he would have put a piece of sticking-plaister over it, and been quite satisfied.

He dressed himself "all in his best," and at last got out into the streets. The people were by this time pouring forth, as he had seen them with the Ghost of Christmas Present; and walking with his hands behind him, Scrooge regarded every one with a delighted smile. He looked so irresistibly pleasant, in a word, that three or four good-humoured fellows said, "Good morning, sir! A merry Christmas to you!" And Scrooge said often afterwards, that of all the blithe sounds he had ever heard, those were the blithest in his ears.

He had not gone far, when coming on towards him he beheld the portly gentleman, who had walked into his counting-house the day before, and said, "Scrooge and Marley's, I believe?" It sent a pang across his heart to think how this old gentleman would look upon him when they met; but he knew what path lay straight before him, and he took it.

"My dear sir," said Scrooge, quickening his pace, and taking the old gentleman by both his hands.

"How do you do? I hope you succeeded yesterday. It was very kind of you. A merry Christmas to you, sir!"

"Mr. Scrooge?"

"Yes," said Scrooge. "That is my name, and I fear it may not be pleasant to you. Allow me to ask your pardon. And will you have the goodness"—here Scrooge whispered in his ear.

"Lord bless me!" cried the gentleman, as if his breath were taken away. "My dear Mr. Scrooge, are you serious?"

"If you please," said Scrooge. "Not a farthing less. A great many back-payments are included in it, I assure you. Will you do me that favour?"

"My dear sir," said the other, shaking hands with him. "I don't know what to say to such munifi—"

"Don't say anything, please," retorted Scrooge. "Come and see me. Will you come and see me?"

"I will!" cried the old gentleman. And it was clear he meant to do it.

"Thank'ee," said Scrooge. "I am much obliged to you. I thank you fifty times. Bless you!"

He went to church, and walked about the streets, and watched the people hurrying to and fro, and patted children on the head, and questioned beggars, and looked down into the kitchens of houses, and up to the windows, and found that everything could yield him pleasure. He had never dreamed that any walk—that anything—could give him so much happiness. In the afternoon he turned his steps towards his nephew's house.

He passed the door a dozen times, before he had the courage to go up and knock. But he made a dash, and did it:

"Is your master at home, my dear?" said Scrooge to the girl. Nice girl! Very.

"Yes, sir."

"Where is he, my love?" said Scrooge.

"He's in the dining-room, sir, along with mistress. I'll show you up-stairs, if you please."

"Thank'ee. He knows me," said Scrooge, with his hand already on the dining-room lock. "I'll go in here, my dear."

He turned it gently, and sidled his face in, round the door. They were looking at the table (which was spread out in great array); for these young housekeepers are always nervous on such points, and like to see that everything is right.

"Fred!" said Scrooge.

Dear heart alive, how his niece by marriage started! Scrooge had forgotten, for the moment, about her sitting in the corner with the footstool, or he wouldn't have done it, on any account.

"Why bless my soul!" cried Fred, "who's that?"

"It's I. Your uncle Scrooge. I have come to dinner. Will you let me in, Fred?"

Let him in! It is a mercy he didn't shake his arm off. He was at home in five minutes. Nothing could be heartier. His niece looked just the same. So did Topper when *he* came. So did the plump sister when *she* came. So did every one when *they* came. Wonderful party, wonderful games, wonderful unanimity, won-der-ful happiness!

But he was early at the office next morning. Oh, he was early there. If he could only be there first, and catch Bob Cratchit coming late! That was the thing he had set his heart upon.

And he did it; yes, he did! The clock struck nine. No Bob. A quarter past. No Bob. He was full eighteen minutes and a half behind his time. Scrooge sat with his door wide open, that he might see him come into the Tank.

His hat was off, before he opened the door; his comforter too. He was on his stool in a jiffy; driving away with his pen, as if he were trying to overtake nine o'clock.

"Hallo!" growled Scrooge, in his accustomed voice, as near as he could feign it. "What do you mean by coming here at this time of day?"

"I am very sorry, sir," said Bob. "I *am* behind my time."

"You are?" repeated Scrooge. "Yes. I think you are. Step this way, sir, if you please."

"It's only once a year, sir," pleaded Bob, appearing from the Tank. "It shall not be repeated. I was making rather merry yesterday, sir."

"Now, I'll tell you what, my friend," said Scrooge, "I am not going to stand this sort of thing any longer. And therefore," he continued, leaping from his stool, and giving Bob such a dig in the waistcoat that he staggered back into the Tank again: "and therefore I am about to raise your salary!"

Bob trembled, and got a little nearer to the ruler. He had a momentary idea of knocking Scrooge down with it, holding him, and calling to the people in the court for help and a strait-waistcoat.

"A merry Christmas, Bob!" said Scrooge, with an earnestness that could not be mistaken, as he clapped him on the back. "A merrier Christmas, Bob, my good fellow, than I have given you, for many a year! I'll raise your salary, and endeavour to assist your struggling family, and we will discuss your affairs this very afternoon, over a Christmas bowl of smoking bishop, Bob! Make up the fires, and buy another coal-scuttle before you dot another i, Bob Cratchit!"

Scrooge was better than his word. He did it all, and infinitely more; and to Tiny Tim, who did NOT die, he was a second father. He became as good a friend, as good a master, and as good a man, as the good old city knew, or any other good old city, town, or borough, in the good old world. Some people laughed to see the alteration in him, but he let them laugh, and little heeded them; for he was wise enough to know that nothing ever happened on this globe, for good, at which some people did not have their fill of laughter in the outset; and knowing that such as these would be blind anyway, he thought it quite as well that they should wrinkle up their eyes in grins, as have the malady in less attractive forms. His own heart laughed: and that was quite enough for him.

He had no further intercourse with Spirits, but lived upon the Total Abstinence Principle, ever afterwards; and it was always said of him, that he knew how to keep Christmas well, if any man alive possessed the knowledge. May that be truly said of us, and all of us! And so, as Tiny Tim observed, God bless Us, Every One!

The Chimes

First Quarter

There are not many people—and as it is desirable that a story-teller and a story-reader should establish a mutual understanding as soon as possible, I beg it to be noticed that I confine this observation neither to young people nor to little people, but extend it to all conditions of people: little and big, young and old: yet growing up, or already growing down again—there are not, I say, many people who would care to sleep in a church. I don't mean at sermon-time in warm weather (when the thing has actually been done, once or twice), but in the night, and alone. A great multitude of persons will be violently astonished, I know, by this position, in the broad bold Day. But it applies to Night. It must be argued by night, and I will undertake to maintain it successfully on any gusty winter's night appointed for the purpose, with any one opponent chosen from the rest, who will meet me singly in an old churchyard, before an old church-door; and will previously empower me to lock him in, if needful to his satisfaction, until morning.

For the night-wind has a dismal trick of wandering round and round a building of that sort, and moaning as it goes; and of trying, with its unseen hand, the windows and the doors; and seeking out some crevices by which to enter. And when it has got in; as one not finding what it seeks, whatever that may be, it wails and howls to issue forth again: and not content with stalking through the aisles, and gliding round and round the pillars, and tempting the deep organ, soars up to the roof, and strives to rend the rafters: then flings itself despairingly upon the stones below, and passes, muttering, into the vaults. Anon, it comes up stealthily, and creeps along the walls, seeming to read, in whispers, the Inscriptions sacred to the Dead. At some of these, it breaks out shrilly, as with laughter; and at others, moans and cries as if it were lamenting. It has a ghostly sound too, lingering within the altar; where it seems to chaunt, in its wild way, of Wrong and Murder done, and false Gods worshipped, in defiance of the Tables of the Law, which look so fair and smooth, but are so flawed and broken. Ugh! Heaven preserve us, sitting snugly round the fire! It has an awful voice, that wind at Midnight, singing in a church!

But, high up in the steeple! There the foul blast roars and whistles! High up in the steeple, where it is free to come and go through many an airy arch and loophole, and to twist and twine itself about the giddy stair, and twirl the groaning weather-cock, and make the very tower shake and shiver! High up in the steeple, where the belfry is, and iron rails are ragged with rust, and sheets of lead and copper, shrivelled by the changing weather, crackle and heave beneath the unaccustomed tread; and birds stuff shabby nests into corners of old oaken joists and beams; and dust grows old and grey; and speckled spiders, indolent and fat with long security, swing idly to and fro in the vibration of the bells, and never loose their hold upon their thread-spun castles in the air, or climb up sailor-like in quick alarm, or drop upon the ground and ply a score of nimble legs to save one life! High up in the steeple of an old church, far above the light and murmur of the town and far below the flying clouds that shadow it, is the wild and dreary place at night: and high up in the steeple of an old church, dwelt the Chimes I tell of.

They were old Chimes, trust me. Centuries ago, these Bells had been baptized by bishops: so many centuries ago, that the register of their baptism was lost long, long before the memory of man, and no one knew their names. They had had their Godfathers and Godmothers, these Bells (for my own part, by the way, I would rather incur the responsibility of being Godfather to a Bell than a Boy), and had their silver mugs no doubt, besides. But Time had mowed down their sponsors, and Henry the Eighth had melted down their mugs; and they now hung, nameless and mugless, in the church-tower.

Not speechless, though. Far from it. They had clear, loud, lusty, sounding voices, had these Bells; and far and wide they might be heard upon the wind. Much too sturdy Chimes were they, to be dependent on the pleasure of the wind, moreover; for, fighting gallantly against it when it took an adverse whim, they would pour their cheerful notes into a listening ear right royally; and bent on being heard on stormy nights, by some poor mother watching a sick child, or some lone wife whose husband was at sea, they had been sometimes known to beat a blustering Nor'-Wester; aye, "all to fits," as Toby Veck said;—for though they chose to call him Trotty Veck, his name was Toby, and nobody could make it anything else either (except Tobias) without a special act of parliament; he having been as lawfully christened in his day as the Bells had been in theirs, though with not quite so much of solemnity or public rejoicing.

For my part, I confess myself of Toby Veck's belief, for I am sure he had opportunities enough of forming a correct one. And whatever Toby Veck said, I say. And I take my stand by Toby Veck, although he *did* stand all day long (and weary work it was) just outside the church-door. In fact he was a ticket-porter, Toby Veck, and waited there for jobs.

And a breezy, goose-skinned, blue-nosed, red-eyed, stony-toed, tooth-chattering place it was, to wait in, in the winter-time, as Toby Veck well knew. The wind came tearing round the corner—especially the east wind—as if it had sallied forth, express, from the confines of the earth, to have a blow at Toby. And oftentimes it seemed to come upon him sooner than it had expected, for bouncing round the corner, and passing Toby, it would suddenly wheel round again, as if it cried "Why, here he is!" Incontinently his little white apron would be caught up over his head like a naughty boy's garments, and his feeble little cane would be seen to wrestle and struggle unavailingly in his hand, and his legs would undergo tremendous agitation, and Toby himself all aslant, and facing now in this direction, now in that, would be so banged and buffeted, and to touzled, and worried, and hustled, and lifted off his feet, as to render it a state of things but one degree removed from a positive miracle, that he wasn't carried up bodily into the air as a colony of frogs or snails or other very portable creatures sometimes are, and rained down again, to the great astonishment of the natives, on some strange corner of the world where ticket-porters are unknown.

But, windy weather, in spite of its using him so roughly, was, after all, a sort of holiday for Toby. That's the fact. He didn't seem to wait so long for a sixpence in the wind, as at other times; the having to fight with that boisterous element took off his attention, and quite freshened him up, when he was getting hungry and low-spirited. A hard frost too, or a fall of snow, was an Event; and it seemed to do him good, somehow or other—it would have been hard to say in what respect though, Toby! So wind and frost and snow, and perhaps a good stiff storm of hail, were Toby Veck's red-letter days.

Wet weather was the worst; the cold, damp, clammy wet, that wrapped him up like a moist great-coat—the only kind of great-coat Toby owned, or could have added to his comfort by dispensing with. Wet days, when the rain came slowly, thickly, obstinately down; when the street's throat, like his own, was choked with mist; when smoking umbrellas passed and re-passed, spinning round and round like so many teetotums, as they knocked against each other on the crowded footway, throwing off a little whirlpool of uncomfortable sprinklings; when gutters brawled and waterspouts were full and noisy; when the wet from the projecting stones and ledges of the church fell drip, drip, drip, on Toby, making the wisp of straw on which he stood mere mud in no time; those were the days that tried him. Then, indeed, you might see Toby looking anxiously out from his shelter in an angle of the church wall—such a meagre shelter that in summer time it never cast a shadow thicker than a good-sized walking stick upon the sunny pavement—with a disconsolate and lengthened face. But coming out, a minute afterwards, to warm himself by exercise, and trotting up and down some dozen times, he would brighten even then, and go back more brightly to his niche.

They called him Trotty from his pace, which meant speed if it didn't make it. He could have walked faster perhaps; most likely; but rob him of his trot, and Toby would have taken to his bed and died. It bespattered him with mud in dirty weather;

it cost him a world of trouble; he could have walked with infinitely greater ease; but that was one reason for his clinging to it so tenaciously. A weak, small, spare old man, he was a very Hercules, this Toby, in his good intentions. He loved to earn his money. He delighted to believe—Toby was very poor, and couldn't well afford to part with a delight—that he was worth his salt. With a shilling or an eighteenpenny message or small parcel in hand, his courage always high, rose higher. As he trotted on, he would call out to fast Postmen ahead of him, to get out of the way; devoutly believing that in the natural course of things he must inevitably overtake and run them down; and he had perfect faith—not often tested—in his being able to carry anything that man could lift.

Thus, even when he came out of his nook to warm himself on a wet day, Toby trotted. Making, with his leaky shoes, a crooked line of slushy footprints in the mire; and blowing on his chilly hands and rubbing them against each other, poorly defended from the searching cold by threadbare mufflers of grey worsted, with a private apartment only for the thumb, and a common room or tap for the rest of the fingers; Toby, with his knees bent and his cane beneath his arm, still trotted. Falling out into the road to look up at the belfry when the Chimes resounded, Toby trotted still.

He made this last excursion several times a day, for they were company to him; and when he heard their voices, he had an interest in glancing at their lodging-place, and thinking how they were moved, and what hammers beat upon them. Perhaps he was the more curious about these Bells, because there were points of resemblance between themselves and him. They hung there, in all weathers, with the wind and rain driving in upon them; facing only the outsides of all those houses; never getting any nearer to the blazing fires that gleamed and shone upon the windows, or came puffing out of the chimney tops; and incapable of participation in any of the good things that were constantly being handled, through the street doors and the area railings, to prodigious cooks. Faces came and went at many windows: sometimes pretty faces, youthful faces, pleasant faces: sometimes the reverse: but Toby knew no more (though he often speculated on these trifles, standing idle in the streets) whence they came, or where they went, or whether, when the lips moved, one kind word was said of him in all the year, than did the Chimes themselves.

Toby was not a casuist—that he knew of, at least—and I don't mean to say that when he began to take to the Bells, and to knit up his first rough acquaintance with them into something of a closer and more delicate woof, he passed through these considerations one by one, or held any formal review or great field-day in his thoughts. But what I mean to say, and do say is, that as the functions of Toby's body, his digestive organs for example, did of their own cunning, and by a great many operations of which he was altogether ignorant, and the knowledge of which would have astonished him very much, arrive at a certain end; so his mental faculties, without his privity or concurrence, set all these wheels and springs in motion, with a thousand others, when they worked to bring about his liking for the Bells.

And though I had said his love, I would not have recalled the word, though it would scarcely have expressed his complicated feeling. For, being but a simple man, he invested them with a strange and solemn character. They were so mysterious, often heard and never seen; so high up, so far off, so full of such a deep strong melody, that he regarded them with a species of awe; and sometimes when he looked up at the dark arched windows in the tower, he half expected to be beckoned to by something which was not a Bell, and yet was what he had heard so often sounding in the Chimes. For all this, Toby scouted with indignation a certain flying rumour that the Chimes were haunted, as implying the possibility of their being connected with any Evil thing. In short, they were very often in his ears, and very often in his thoughts, but always in his good opinion; and he very often got such a crick in his neck by staring with his mouth wide open, at the steeple where they hung, that he was fain to take an extra trot or two, afterwards, to cure it.

The very thing he was in the act of doing one cold day, when the last drowsy sound of Twelve o'clock, just struck, was humming like a melodious monster of a Bee, and not by any means a busy bee, all through the steeple.

"Dinner-time, eh!" said Toby, trotting up and down before the church. "Ah!"

Toby's nose was very red, and his eyelids were very red, and he winked very much, and his shoulders were very near his ears, and his legs were very stiff, and altogether he was evidently a long way upon the frosty side of cool.

"Dinner-time, eh!" repeated Toby, using his right-hand muffler like an infantine boxing-glove, and punishing his chest for being cold. "Ah-h-h-h!"

He took a silent trot, after that, for a minute or two.

"There's nothing," said Toby, breaking forth afresh—but here he stopped short in his trot, and with a face of great interest and some alarm, felt his nose carefully all the way up. It was but a little way (not being much of a nose) and he had soon finished.

"I thought it was gone," said Toby, trotting off again. "It's all right, however. I am sure I couldn't blame it if it was to go. It has a precious hard service of it in the bitter weather, and precious little to look forward to; for I don't take snuff myself. It's a good deal tried, poor creetur, at the best of times; for when it *does* get hold of a pleasant whiff or so (which an't too often) it's generally from somebody else's dinner, a-coming home from the baker's."

The reflection reminded him of that other reflection, which he had left unfinished.

"There's nothing," said Toby, "more regular in its coming round than dinner-time, and nothing less regular in its coming round than dinner. That's the great difference between 'em. It's took me a long time to find it out. I wonder whether it would be worth any gentleman's while, now, to buy that observation for the Papers; or the Parliament!"

Toby was only joking, for he gravely shook his head in self-depreciation.

"Why! Lord!" said Toby. "The Papers is full of obserwations as it is; and so's the Parliament. Here's last week's paper, now"; taking a very dirty one from his pocket, and holding it from him at arm's length; "full of obserwations! Full of obserwations! I like to know the news as well as any man," said Toby, slowly; folding it a little smaller, and putting it in his pocket again: "but it almost goes against the grain with me to read a paper now. It frightens me almost. I don't know what we poor people are coming to. Lord send we may be coming to something better in the New Year nigh upon us!"

"Why, father, father!" said a pleasant voice, hard by.

But Toby, not hearing it, continued to trot backwards and forwards: musing as he went, and talking to himself.

"It seems as if we can't go right, or do right, or be righted," said Toby. "I hadn't much schooling, myself, when I was young; and I can't make out whether we have any business on the face of the earth, or not. Sometimes I think we must have—a little; and sometimes I think we must be intruding. I get so puzzled sometimes that I am not even able to make up my mind whether there is any good at all in us, or whether we are born bad. We seem to be dreadful things; we seem to give a deal of trouble; we are always being complained of and guarded against. One way or other, we fill the papers. Talk of a New Year!" said Toby, mournfully. "I can bear up as well as another man at most times; better than a good many, for I am as strong as a lion, and all men an't; but supposing it should really be that we have no right to a New Year—supposing we really *are* intruding—"

"Why, father, father!" said the pleasant voice again.

Toby heard it this time; started; stopped; and shortening his sight, which had been directed a long way off as seeking the enlightenment in the very heart of the approaching year, found himself face to face with his own child, and looking close into her eyes.

Bright eyes they were. Eyes that would bear a world of looking in, before their depth was fathomed. Dark eyes, that reflected back the eyes which searched them; not flashingly, or at the owner's will, but with a clear, calm, honest, patient radiance, claiming kindred with that light which Heaven called into being. Eyes that were beautiful and true, and beaming with Hope. With Hope so young and fresh; with Hope so buoyant, vigorous, and bright, despite the twenty years of work and poverty on which they had looked; that they became a voice to Trotty Veck, and said: "I think we have some business here—a little!"

Trotty kissed the lips belonging to the eyes, and squeezed the blooming face between his hands.

"Why, Pet," said Trotty. "What's to do? I didn't expect you to-day, Meg."

"Neither did I expect to come, father," cried the girl, nodding her head and smiling as she spoke. "But here I am! And not alone; not alone!"

"Why you don't mean to say," observed Trotty, looking curiously at a covered basket which she carried in her hand. "that you—"

"Smell it, father dear," said Meg. "Only smell it!"

Trotty was going to lift up the cover at once, in a great hurry, when she gaily interposed her hand.

"No, no, no," said Meg, with the glee of a child. "Lengthen it out a little. Let me just lift up the corner; just the lit-tle ti-ny cor-ner, you know," said Meg, suiting the action to the word with the utmost gentleness, and speaking very softly, as if she were afraid of being overheard by something inside the basket; "there. Now. What's that?"

Toby took the shortest possible sniff at the edge of the basket, and cried out in a rapture:

"Why, it's hot!"

"It's burning hot!" cried Meg. "Ha, ha, ha! It's scalding hot!"

"Ha, ha, ha!" roared Toby, with a sort of kick. "It's scalding hot!"

"But what is it, father?" said Meg. "Come. You haven't guessed what it is. And you must guess what it is. I can't think of taking it out, till you guess what it is. Don't be in such a hurry! Wait a minute! A little bit more of the cover. Now guess!"

Meg was in a perfect fright lest he should guess right too soon; shrinking away, as she held the basket towards him; curling up her pretty shoulders; stopping her ear with her hand, as if by so doing she could keep the right word out of Toby's lips; and laughing softly the whole time.

Meanwhile Toby, putting a hand on each knee, bent down his nose to the basket, and took a long inspiration at the lid; the grin upon his withered face expanding in the process, as if he were inhaling laughing gas.

"Ah! It's very nice," said Toby. "It an't—I suppose it an't Polonies?"

"No, no, no!" cried Meg, delighted. "Nothing like Polonies!"

"No," said Toby, after another sniff. "It's—it's mellower than Polonies. It's very nice. It improves every moment. It's too decided for Trotters. An't it?"

Meg was in an ecstasy. He could not have gone wider of the mark than Trotters—except Polonies.

"Liver?" said Toby, communing with himself. "No. There's a mildness about it that don't answer to liver. Pettitoes? No. It an't faint enough for pettitoes. It wants the stringiness of Cocks' heads. And I know it an't sausages. I'll tell you what it is. It's chitterlings!"

"No, it an't!" cried Meg, in a burst of delight. "No, it an't!"

"Why, what am I a-thinking of!" said Toby, suddenly recovering a position as near the perpendicular as it was possible for him to assume. "I shall forget my own name next. It's tripe!"

Tripe it was; and Meg, in high joy, protested he should say, in half a minute more, it was the best tripe ever stewed.

"And so," said Meg, busying herself exultingly with the basket. "I'll lay the cloth at once, father; for I have brought the tripe in a basin, and tied the basin up in a pocket-handkerchief; and if I like to be proud for once, and spread that for a cloth, and call it a cloth, there's no law to prevent me; is there, father?"

"Not that I know of, my dear," said Toby. "But they're always a-bringing up some new law or other."

"And according to what I was reading you in the paper the other day, father; what the Judge said, you know; we poor people are supposed to know them all. Ha ha! What a mistake! My goodness me, how clever they think us!"

"Yes, my dear," cried Trotty; "and they'd be very fond of any one of us that *did* know 'em all. He'd grow fat upon the work he'd get, that man, and be popular with the gentlefolks in his neighbourhood. Very much so!"

"He'd eat his dinner with an appetite, whoever he was, if it smelt like this," said Meg, cheerfully. "Make haste, for there's a hot potato besides, and half a pint of fresh-drawn beer in a bottle. Where will you dine, father? On the Post, or on the Steps? Dear, dear, how grand we are. Two places to choose from!"

"The steps to-day, my Pet," said Trotty. "Steps in dry weather. Post in wet. There's a greater conveniency in the steps at all times, because of the sitting down; but they're rheumatic in the damp."

"Then here," said Meg, clapping her hands, after a moment's bustle; "here it is, all ready! And beautiful it looks! Come, father. Come!"

Since his discovery of the contents of the basket, Trotty had been standing looking at her—and had been speaking too—in an abstracted manner, which showed that though she was the object of his thoughts and eyes, to the exclusion even of tripe, he neither saw nor thought about her as she was at that moment, but had before him some imaginary rough sketch or drama of her future life. Roused, now, by her cheerful summons, he shook off a melancholy shake of the head which was just coming upon him, and trotted to her side. As he was stooping to sit down, the Chimes rang.

"Amen!" said Trotty, pulling off his hat and looking up towards them.

"Amen to the Bells, father?" cried Meg.

"They broke in like a grace, my dear," said Trotty, taking his seat. "They'd say a good one, I am sure, if they could. Many's the kind thing they say to me."

"The Bells do, father?" laughed Meg, as she set the basin, and a knife and fork, before him. "Well!"

"Seem to, my Pet," said Trotty, falling to with great vigour. "And where's the difference? If I hear 'em, what does it matter whether they speak it or not? Why bless you, my dear," said Toby, pointing at the tower with his fork, and becoming more animated under the influence of dinner. "how often have I heard them bells say, "Toby Veck, Toby Veck, keep a good heart, Toby! Toby Veck, Toby Veck, keep a good heart, Toby!" A million times? More!"

"Well, I never!" cried Meg.

She had, though—over and over again. For it was Toby's constant topic.

"When things is very bad," said Trotty; "very bad indeed, I mean; almost at the worst; then it's "Toby Veck, Toby Veck, job coming soon, Toby! Toby Veck, Toby Veck, job coming soon, Toby!" That way."

"And it comes—at last, father," said Meg, with a touch of sadness in her pleasant voice.

"Always," answered the unconscious Toby. "Never fails."

While this discourse was holding, Trotty made no pause in his attack upon the savoury meat before him, but cut and ate, and cut and drank, and cut and chewed, and dodged about, from tripe to hot potato, and from hot potato back again to tripe, with an unctuous and unflagging relish. But happening now to look all round the street—in case anybody should be beckoning from any door or window, for a porter—his eyes, in coming back again, encountered Meg: sitting opposite to him, with her arms folded and only busy in watching his progress with a smile of happiness.

"Why, Lord forgive me!" said Trotty, dropping his knife and fork. "My dove! Meg! why didn't you tell me what a beast I was?"

"Father?"

"Sitting here," said Trotty, in penitent explanation. "cramming, and stuffing, and gorging myself; and you before me there, never so much as breaking your precious fast, nor wanting to, when—"

"But I have broken it, father," interposed his daughter, laughing. "all to bits. I have had my dinner."

"Nonsense," said Trotty. "Two dinners in one day! It an't possible! You might as well tell me that two New Year's Days will come together, or that I have had a gold head all my life, and never changed it."

"I have had my dinner, father, for all that," said Meg, coming nearer to him. "And if you'll go on with yours, I'll tell you how and where; and how your dinner came to be brought; and—and something else besides."

Toby still appeared incredulous; but she looked into his face with her clear eyes, and laying her hand upon his shoulder, motioned him to go on while the meat was hot. So Trotty took up his knife and fork again, and went to work. But much more slowly than before, and shaking his head, as if he were not at all pleased with himself.

"I had my dinner, father," said Meg, after a little hesitation. "with—with Richard. His dinner-time was early; and as he brought his dinner with him when he came to see me, we—we had it together, father."

Trotty took a little beer, and smacked his lips. Then he said. "Oh!"—because she waited.

"And Richard says, father—" Meg resumed. Then stopped.

"What does Richard say, Meg?" asked Toby.

"Richard says, father—" Another stoppage.

"Richard's a long time saying it," said Toby.

"He says then, father," Meg continued, lifting up her eyes at last, and speaking in a tremble, but quite plainly; "another year is nearly gone, and where is the use of waiting on from year to year, when it is so unlikely we shall ever be better off than we are now? He says we are poor now, father, and we shall be poor then, but we are young now, and years will make us old before we know it. He says that if we wait: people in our condition: until we see our way quite clearly, the way will be a narrow one indeed—the common way—the Grave, father."

A bolder man than Trotty Veck must needs have drawn upon his boldness largely, to deny it. Trotty held his peace.

"And how hard, father, to grow old, and die, and think we might have cheered and helped each other! How hard in all our lives to love each other; and to grieve, apart, to see each other working, changing, growing old and grey. Even if I got the better of it, and forgot him (which I never could), oh father dear, how hard to have a heart so full as mine is now, and live to have it slowly drained out every drop, without the recollection of one happy moment of a woman's life, to stay behind and comfort me, and make me better!"

Trotty sat quite still. Meg dried her eyes, and said more gaily: that is to say, with here a laugh, and there a sob, and here a laugh and sob together:

"So Richard says, father; as his work was yesterday made certain for some time to come, and as I love him, and have loved him full three years—ah! longer than that, if he knew it!—will I marry him on New Year's Day; the best and happiest day, he says, in the whole year, and one that is almost sure to bring good fortune with it. It's a short notice, father—isn't it?—but I haven't my fortune to be settled, or my wedding dresses to be made, like the great ladies, father, have I? And he said so much, and said it in his way; so strong and earnest, and all the time so kind and gentle; that I said I'd come and talk to you, father. And as they paid the money for that work of mine this morning (unexpectedly, I am sure!) and as you have fared very poorly for a whole week, and as I couldn't help wishing there should be something to make this day a sort of holiday to you as well as a dear and happy day to me, father, I made a little treat and brought it to surprise you."

"And see how he leaves it cooling on the step!" said another voice.

It was the voice of this same Richard, who had come upon them unobserved, and stood before the father and daughter; looking down upon them with a face as glowing as the iron on which his stout sledge-hammer daily rung. A handsome, well-made, powerful youngster he was; with eyes that sparkled like the red-hot droppings from a furnace fire; black hair that curled about his swarthy temples rarely; and a smile—a smile that bore out Meg's eulogium on his style of conversation.

"See how he leaves it cooling on the step!" said Richard. "Meg don't know what he likes. Not she!"

Trotty, all action and enthusiasm, immediately reached up his hand to Richard, and was going to address him in great hurry, when the house-door opened without any warning, and a footman very nearly put his foot into the tripe.

"Out of the vays here, will you! You must always go and be a-settin on our steps, must you! You can't go and give a turn to none of the neighbours never, can't you! *Will* you clear the road, or won't you?"

Strictly speaking, the last question was irrelevant, as they had already done it.

"What's the matter, what's the matter!" said the gentleman for whom the door was opened; coming out of the house at that kind of light-heavy pace—that peculiar compromise between a walk and a jog-trot—with which a gentleman upon the smooth down-hill of life, wearing creaking boots, a watch-chain, and clean linen, *may* come out of his house: not only without any abatement of his dignity, but with an expression of having important and wealthy engagements elsewhere. "What's the matter! What's the matter!"

"You're always a-being begged, and prayed, upon your bended knees you are," said the footman with great emphasis to Trotty Veck. "to let our door-steps be. Why don't you let 'em be? CAN'T you let 'em be?"

"There! That'll do, that'll do!" said the gentleman. "Halloa there! Porter!" beckoning with his head to Trotty Veck. "Come here. What's that? Your dinner?"

"Yes, sir," said Trotty, leaving it behind him in a corner.

"Don't leave it there," exclaimed the gentleman. "Bring it here, bring it here. So! This is your dinner, is it?"

"Yes, sir," repeated Trotty, looking with a fixed eye and a watery mouth, at the piece of tripe he had reserved for a last delicious tit-bit; which the gentleman was now turning over and over on the end of the fork.

Two other gentlemen had come out with him. One was a low-spirited gentleman of middle age, of a meagre habit, and a disconsolate face; who kept his hands continually in the pockets of his scanty pepper-and-salt trousers, very large and dog's-eared from that custom; and was not particularly well brushed or washed. The other, a full-sized, sleek, well-conditioned gentleman, in a blue coat with bright buttons, and a white cravat. This gentleman had a very red face, as if an undue proportion of the blood in his body were squeezed up into his head; which perhaps accounted for his having also the appearance of being rather cold about the heart.

He who had Toby's meat upon the fork, called to the first one by the name of Filer; and they both drew near together. Mr. Filer being exceedingly short-sighted, was obliged to go so close to the remnant of Toby's dinner before he could make out what it was, that Toby's heart leaped up into his mouth. But Mr. Filer didn't eat it.

"This is a description of animal food, Alderman," said Filer, making little punches in it with a pencil-case, "commonly known to the labouring population of this country, by the name of tripe."

The Alderman laughed, and winked; for he was a merry fellow, Alderman Cute. Oh, and a sly fellow too! A knowing fellow. Up to everything. Not to be imposed upon. Deep in the people's hearts! He knew them, Cute did. I believe you!

"But who eats tripe?" said Mr. Filer, looking round. "Tripe is without an exception the least economical, and the most wasteful article of consumption that the markets of this country can by possibility produce. The loss upon a pound of tripe has been found to be, in the boiling, seven-eights of a fifth more than the loss upon a pound of any other animal substance whatever. Tripe is more expensive, properly understood, than the hothouse pine-apple. Taking into account the number of animals slaughtered yearly within the bills of mortality alone; and forming a low estimate of the quantity of tripe which the carcases of those animals, reasonably well butchered, would yield; I find that the waste on that amount of tripe, if boiled, would victual a garrison of five hundred men for five months of thirty-one days each, and a February over. The Waste, the Waste!"

Trotty stood aghast, and his legs shook under him. He seemed to have starved a garrison of five hundred men with his own hand.

"Who eats tripe?" said Mr. Filer, warmly. "Who eats tripe?"

Trotty made a miserable bow.

"You do, do you?" said Mr. Filer. "Then I'll tell you something. You snatch your tripe, my friend, out of the mouths of widows and orphans."

"I hope not, sir," said Trotty, faintly. "I'd sooner die of want!"

"Divide the amount of tripe before-mentioned, Alderman," said Mr. Filer, "by the estimated number of existing widows and orphans, and the result will be one pennyweight of tripe to each. Not a grain is left for that man. Consequently, he's a robber."

Trotty was so shocked, that it gave him no concern to see the Alderman finish the tripe himself. It was a relief to get rid of it, anyhow.

"And what do you say?" asked the Alderman, jocosely, of the red-faced gentleman in the blue coat. "You have heard friend Filer. What do *you* say?"

"What's it possible to say?" returned the gentleman. "What *is* to be said? Who can take any interest in a fellow like this," meaning Trotty; "in such degenerate times as these? Look at him. What an object! The good old times, the grand old times, the great old times! *Those* were the times for a bold peasantry, and all that sort of thing. Those were the times for every sort of thing, in fact. There's nothing now-a-days. Ah!" sighed the red-faced gentleman. "The good old times, the good old times!"

The gentleman didn't specify what particular times he alluded to; nor did he say whether he objected to the present times, from a disinterested consciousness that they had done nothing very remarkable in producing himself.

"The good old times, the good old times," repeated the gentleman. "What times they were! They were the only times. It's of no use talking about any other times, or discussing what the people are in these times. You don't call these, times, do you? I don't. Look into Strutt's Costumes, and see what a Porter used to be, in any of the good old English reigns."

"He hadn't, in his very best circumstances, a shirt to his back, or a stocking to his foot; and there was scarcely a vegetable in all England for him to put into his mouth," said Mr. Filer. "I can prove it, by tables."

But still the red-faced gentleman extolled the good old times, the grand old times, the great old times. No matter what anybody else said, he still went turning round and round in one set form of words concerning them; as a poor squirrel turns and turns in its revolving cage; touching the mechanism, and trick of which, it has probably quite as distinct perceptions, as ever this red-faced gentleman had of his deceased Millennium.

It is possible that poor Trotty's faith in these very vague Old Times was not entirely destroyed, for he felt vague enough at that moment. One thing, however, was plain to him, in the midst of his distress; to wit, that however these gentlemen might differ in details, his misgivings of that morning, and of many other mornings, were well founded. "No, no. We can't go right or do right," thought Trotty in despair. "There is no good in us. We are born bad!"

But Trotty had a father's heart within him; which had somehow got into his breast in spite of this decree; and he could not bear that Meg, in the blush of her brief joy, should have her fortune read by these wise gentlemen. "God help her," thought poor Trotty. "She will know it soon enough."

He anxiously signed, therefore, to the young smith, to take her away. But he was so busy, talking to her softly at a little distance, that he only became conscious of this desire, simultaneously with Alderman Cute. Now, the Alderman had not yet had his say, but *he* was a philosopher, too—practical, though! Oh, very practical—and, as he had no idea of losing any portion of his audience, he cried "Stop!"

"Now, you know," said the Alderman, addressing his two friends, with a self-complacent smile upon his face which was habitual to him. "I am a plain man, and a practical man; and I go to work in a plain practical way. That's my way. There is not the least mystery or difficulty in dealing with this sort of people if you only understand 'em, and can talk to 'em in their own manner. Now, you Porter! Don't you ever tell me, or anybody else, my friend, that you haven't always enough to eat, and of the best; because I know better. I have tasted your tripe, you know, and you can't "chaff" me. You understand what "chaff" means, eh? That's the right word, isn't it? Ha, ha, ha! Lord bless you," said the Alderman, turning to his friends again. "it's the easiest thing on earth to deal with this sort of people, if you understand 'em."

Famous man for the common people, Alderman Cute! Never out of temper with them! Easy, affable, joking, knowing gentleman!

"You see, my friend," pursued the Alderman, "there's a great deal of nonsense talked about Want—'hard up,' you know; that's the phrase, isn't it? ha! ha! ha!—and I intend to Put it Down. There's a certain amount of cant in vogue about Starvation, and I mean to Put it Down. That's all! Lord bless you," said the Alderman, turning to his friends again. "you may Put Down anything among this sort of people, if you only know the way to set about it."

Trotty took Meg's hand and drew it through his arm. He didn't seem to know what he was doing though.

"Your daughter, eh?" said the Alderman, chucking her familiarly under the chin.

Always affable with the working classes, Alderman Cute! Knew what pleased them! Not a bit of pride!

"Where's her mother?" asked that worthy gentleman.

"Dead," said Toby. "Her mother got up linen; and was called to Heaven when She was born."

"Not to get up linen *there*, I suppose," remarked the Alderman pleasantly.

Toby might or might not have been able to separate his wife in Heaven from her old pursuits. But query: If Mrs. Alderman Cute had gone to Heaven, would Mr. Alderman Cute have pictured her as holding any state or station there?

"And you're making love to her, are you?" said Cute to the young smith.

"Yes," returned Richard quickly, for he was nettled by the question. "And we are going to be married on New Year's Day."

"What do you mean!" cried Filer sharply. "Married!"

"Why, yes, we're thinking of it, Master," said Richard. "We're rather in a hurry, you see, in case it should be Put Down first."

"Ah!" cried Filer, with a groan. "Put *that* down indeed, Alderman, and you'll do something. Married! Married!! The ignorance of the first principles of political economy on the part of these people; their improvidence; their wickedness; is, by Heavens! enough to—Now look at that couple, will you!"

Well? They were worth looking at. And marriage seemed as reasonable and fair a deed as they need have in contemplation.

"A man may live to be as old as Methuselah," said Mr. Filer, "and may labour all his life for the benefit of such people as those; and may heap up facts on figures, facts on figures, facts on figures, mountains high and dry; and he can no more hope to persuade 'em that they have no right or business to be married, than he can hope to persuade 'em that they have no earthly right or business to be born. And *that* we know they haven't. We reduced it to a mathematical certainty long ago!"

Alderman Cute was mightily diverted, and laid his right forefinger on the side of his nose, as much as to say to both his friends. "Observe me, will you! Keep your eye on the practical man!"—and called Meg to him.

"Come here, my girl!" said Alderman Cute.

The young blood of her lover had been mounting, wrathfully, within the last few minutes; and he was indisposed to let her come. But, setting a constraint upon himself, he came forward with a stride as Meg approached, and stood beside her. Trotty kept her hand within his arm still, but looked from face to face as wildly as a sleeper in a dream.

"Now, I'm going to give you a word or two of good advice, my girl," said the Alderman, in his nice easy way. "It's my place to give advice, you know, because I'm a Justice. You know I'm a Justice, don't you?"

Meg timidly said. "Yes." But everybody knew Alderman Cute was a Justice! O dear, so active a Justice always! Who such a mote of brightness in the public eye, as Cute!

"You are going to be married, you say," pursued the Alderman. "Very unbecoming and indelicate in one of your sex! But never mind that. After you are married, you'll quarrel with your husband and come to be a distressed wife. You may think not; but you will, because I tell you so. Now, I give you fair warning, that I have made up my mind to Put distressed wives Down. So, don't be brought before me. You'll have children—boys. Those boys will grow up bad, of course, and run wild in the streets, without shoes and stockings. Mind, my young friend! I'll convict 'em summarily, every one, for I am determined to Put boys without shoes and stockings, Down. Perhaps your husband will die young (most likely) and leave you with a baby. Then you'll be turned out of doors, and wander up and down the streets. Now, don't wander near me, my dear, for I am resolved, to Put all wandering mothers Down. All young mothers, of all sorts and kinds, it's my determination to Put Down. Don't think to plead illness as an excuse with me; or babies as an excuse with me; for all sick persons and young children (I hope you know the church-service, but I'm afraid not)

I am determined to Put Down. And if you attempt, desperately, and ungratefully, and impiously, and fraudulently attempt, to drown yourself, or hang yourself, I'll have no pity for you, for I have made up my mind to Put all suicide Down! If there is one thing," said the Alderman, with his self-satisfied smile, "on which I can be said to have made up my mind more than on another, it is to Put suicide Down. So don't try it on. That's the phrase, isn't it? Ha, ha! now we understand each other."

Toby knew not whether to be agonised or glad, to see that Meg had turned a deadly white, and dropped her lover's hand.

"And as for you, you dull dog," said the Alderman, turning with even increased cheerfulness and urbanity to the young smith, "what are you thinking of being married for? What do you want to be married for, you silly fellow? If I was a fine, young, strapping chap like you, I should be ashamed of being milksop enough to pin myself to a woman's apron-strings! Why, she'll be an old woman before you're a middle-aged man! And a pretty figure you'll cut then, with a draggle-tailed wife and a crowd of squalling children crying after you wherever you go!"

O, he knew how to banter the common people, Alderman Cute!

"There! Go along with you," said the Alderman, "and repent. Don't make such a fool of yourself as to get married on New Year's Day. You'll think very differently of it, long before next New Year's Day: a trim young fellow like you, with all the girls looking after you. There! Go along with you!"

They went along. Not arm in arm, or hand in hand, or interchanging bright glances; but, she in tears; he, gloomy and down-looking. Were these the hearts that had so lately made old Toby's leap up from its faintness? No, no. The Alderman (a blessing on his head!) had Put *them* Down.

"As you happen to be here," said the Alderman to Toby, "you shall carry a letter for me. Can you be quick? You're an old man."

Toby, who had been looking after Meg, quite stupidly, made shift to murmur out that he was very quick, and very strong.

"How old are you?" inquired the Alderman.

"I'm over sixty, sir," said Toby.

"O! This man's a great deal past the average age, you know," cried Mr. Filer breaking in as if his patience would bear some trying, but this really was carrying matters a little too far.

"I feel I'm intruding, sir," said Toby. "I—I misdoubted it this morning. Oh dear me!"

The Alderman cut him short by giving him the letter from his pocket. Toby would have got a shilling too; but Mr. Filer clearly showing that in that case he would rob a certain given number of persons of ninepence-halfpenny a-piece, he only got sixpence; and thought himself very well off to get that.

Then the Alderman gave an arm to each of his friends, and walked off in high feather; but, he immediately came hurrying back alone, as if he had forgotten something.

"Porter!" said the Alderman.

"Sir!" said Toby.

"Take care of that daughter of yours. She's much too handsome."

"Even her good looks are stolen from somebody or other, I suppose," thought Toby, looking at the sixpence in his hand, and thinking of the tripe. "She's been and robbed five hundred ladies of a bloom a-piece, I shouldn't wonder. It's very dreadful!"

"She's much too handsome, my man," repeated the Alderman. "The chances are, that she'll come to no good, I clearly see. Observe what I say. Take care of her!" With which, he hurried off again.

"Wrong every way. Wrong every way!" said Trotty, clasping his hands. "Born bad. No business here!"

The Chimes came clashing in upon him as he said the words. Full, loud, and sounding—but with no encouragement. No, not a drop.

"The tune's changed," cried the old man, as he listened. "There's not a word of all that fancy in it. Why should there be? I have no business with the New Year nor with the old one neither. Let me die!"

Still the Bells, pealing forth their changes, made the very air spin. Put 'em down, Put 'em down! Good old Times, Good old Times! Facts and Figures, Facts and Figures! Put 'em down, Put 'em down! If they said anything they said this, until the brain of Toby reeled.

He pressed his bewildered head between his hands, as if to keep it from splitting asunder. A well-timed action, as it happened; for finding the letter in one of them, and being by that means reminded of his charge, he fell, mechanically, into his usual trot, and trotted off.

The Second Quarter

THE LETTER TOBY HAD RECEIVED FROM ALDERMAN CUTE, WAS ADDRESSED to a great man in the great district of the town. The greatest district of the town. It must have been the greatest district of the town, because it was commonly called The World by its inhabitants. The letter positively seemed heavier in Toby's hand, than another letter. Not because the Alderman had sealed it with a very large coat of arms and no end of wax, but because of the weighty name on the superscription, and the ponderous amount of gold and silver with which it was associated.

"How different from us!" thought Toby, in all simplicity and earnestness, as he looked at the direction. "Divide the lively turtles in the bills of mortality, by the number of gentlefolks able to buy 'em; and whose share does he take but his own! As to snatching tripe from anybody's mouth—he'd scorn it!"

With the involuntary homage due to such an exalted character, Toby interposed a corner of his apron between the letter and his fingers.

"His children," said Trotty, and a mist rose before his eyes; "his daughters—Gentlemen may win their hearts and marry them; they may be happy wives and mothers; they may be handsome like my darling M-e-"

He couldn't finish the name. The final letter swelled in his throat, to the size of the whole alphabet.

"Never mind," thought Trotty. "I know what I mean. That's more than enough for me." And with this consolatory rumination, trotted on.

It was a hard frost, that day. The air was bracing, crisp, and clear. The wintry sun, though powerless for warmth, looked brightly down upon the ice it was too weak to melt, and set a radiant glory there. At other times, Trotty might have learned a poor man's lesson from the wintry sun; but, he was past that, now.

The Year was Old, that day. The patient Year had lived through the reproaches and misuses of its slanderers, and faithfully performed its work. Spring, summer, autumn, winter. It had laboured through the destined round, and now laid down its weary head to die. Shut out from hope, high impulse, active happiness, itself, but active messenger of many joys to others, it made appeal in its decline to have its toiling days and patient hours remembered, and to die in peace. Trotty might have read a poor man's allegory in the fading year; but he was past that, now.

And only he? Or has the like appeal been ever made, by seventy years at once upon an English labourer's head, and made in vain!

The streets were full of motion, and the shops were decked out gaily. The New Year, like an Infant Heir to the whole world, was waited for, with welcomes, presents, and rejoicings. There were books and toys for the New Year, glittering trinkets for the New Year, dresses for the New Year, schemes of fortune for the New Year; new inventions to beguile it. Its life was parcelled out in almanacks and pocket-books; the coming of its moons, and stars, and tides, was known beforehand to the moment; all the workings of its seasons in their days and nights, were calculated with as much precision as Mr. Filer could work sums in men and women.

The New Year, the New Year. Everywhere the New Year! The Old Year was already looked upon as dead; and its effects were selling cheap, like some drowned mariner's aboardship. Its patterns were Last Year's, and going at a sacrifice, before its breath was gone. Its treasures were mere dirt, beside the riches of its unborn successor!

Trotty had no portion, to his thinking, in the New Year or the Old.

"Put 'em down, Put 'em down! Facts and Figures, Facts and Figures! Good old Times, Good old Times! Put 'em down, Put 'em down!"—his trot went to that measure, and would fit itself to nothing else.

But, even that one, melancholy as it was, brought him, in due time, to the end of his journey. To the mansion of Sir Joseph Bowley, Member of Parliament.

The door was opened by a Porter. Such a Porter! Not of Toby's order. Quite another thing. His place was the ticket though; not Toby's.

This Porter underwent some hard panting before he could speak; having breathed himself by coming incautiously out of his chair, without first taking time to think about it and compose his mind. When he had found his voice—which it took him a long time to do, for it was a long way off, and hidden under a load of meat—he said in a fat whisper,

"Who's it from?"

Toby told him.

"You're to take it in, yourself," said the Porter, pointing to a room at the end of a long passage, opening from the hall. "Everything goes straight in, on this day of the year. You're not a bit too soon; for the carriage is at the door now, and they have only come to town for a couple of hours, a' purpose."

Toby wiped his feet (which were quite dry already) with great care, and took the way pointed out to him; observing as he went that it was an awfully grand house, but hushed and covered up, as if the family were in the country. Knocking at the room-door, he was told to enter from within; and doing so found himself in a spacious library, where, at a table strewn with files and papers, were a stately lady in a bonnet; and a not very stately gentleman in black who wrote from her dictation; while another, and an older, and a much statelier gentleman, whose hat and cane were on the table, walked up and down, with one hand in his breast, and looked complacently from time to time at his own picture—a full length; a very full length—hanging over the fireplace.

"What is this?" said the last-named gentleman. "Mr. Fish, will you have the goodness to attend?"

Mr. Fish begged pardon, and taking the letter from Toby, handed it, with great respect.

"From Alderman Cute, Sir Joseph."

"Is this all? Have you nothing else, Porter?" inquired Sir Joseph.

Toby replied in the negative.

"You have no bill or demand upon me—my name is Bowley, Sir Joseph Bowley—of any kind from anybody, have you?" said Sir Joseph. "If you have, present it. There is a cheque-book by the side of Mr. Fish. I allow nothing to be carried into the New Year. Every description of account is settled in this house at the close of the old one. So that if death was to—to—"

"To cut," suggested Mr. Fish.

"To sever, sir," returned Sir Joseph, with great asperity, "the cord of existence—my affairs would be found, I hope, in a state of preparation."

"My dear Sir Joseph!" said the lady, who was greatly younger than the gentleman. "How shocking!"

"My lady Bowley," returned Sir Joseph, floundering now and then, as in the great depth of his observations, "at this season of the year we should think of—of—ourselves. We should look into our—our accounts. We should feel that every return of so eventful a period in human transactions, involves a matter of deep moment between a man and his—and his banker."

Sir Joseph delivered these words as if he felt the full morality of what he was saying; and desired that even Trotty should have an opportunity of being improved by such discourse. Possibly he had this end before him in still forbearing to break the seal of the letter, and in telling Trotty to wait where he was, a minute.

"You were desiring Mr. Fish to say, my lady—" observed Sir Joseph.

"Mr. Fish has said that, I believe," returned his lady, glancing at the letter. "But, upon my word, Sir Joseph, I don't think I can let it go after all. It is so very dear."

"What is dear?" inquired Sir Joseph.

"That Charity, my love. They only allow two votes for a subscription of five pounds. Really monstrous!"

"My lady Bowley," returned Sir Joseph. "you surprise me. Is the luxury of feeling in proportion to the number of votes; or is it, to a rightly constituted mind, in proportion to the number of applicants, and the wholesome state of mind to which their canvassing reduces them? Is there no excitement of the purest kind in having two votes to dispose of among fifty people?"

"Not to me, I acknowledge," replied the lady. "It bores one. Besides, one can't oblige one's acquaintance. But you are the Poor Man's Friend, you know, Sir Joseph. You think otherwise."

"I *am* the Poor Man's Friend," observed Sir Joseph, glancing at the poor man present. "As such I may be taunted. As such I have been taunted. But I ask no other title."

"Bless him for a noble gentleman!" thought Trotty.

"I don't agree with Cute here, for instance," said Sir Joseph, holding out the letter. "I don't agree with the Filer party. I don't agree with any party. My friend the Poor Man, has no business with anything of that sort, and nothing of that sort has any business with him. My friend the Poor Man, in my district, is my business. No man or body of men has any right to interfere between my friend and me. That is the ground I take. I assume a—a paternal character towards my friend. I say, 'My good fellow, I will treat you paternally.' "

Toby listened with great gravity, and began to feel more comfortable.

"Your only business, my good fellow," pursued Sir Joseph, looking abstractedly at Toby; "your only business in life is with me. You needn't trouble yourself to think about anything. I will think for you; I know what is good for you; I am your perpetual parent. Such is the dispensation of an all-wise Providence! Now, the design of your creation is—not that you should swill, and guzzle, and associate your enjoyments, brutally, with food"—Toby thought remorsefully of the tripe—"but that you should feel the Dignity of Labour. Go forth erect into the cheerful morning air, and—and stop there. Live hard and temperately, be respectful, exercise your self-denial, bring up your family on next to nothing, pay your rent as regularly as the clock strikes, be punctual in your dealings (I set you a good example; you will find Mr. Fish, my confidential secretary, with a cash-box before him at all times); and you may trust to me to be your Friend and Father."

"Nice children, indeed, Sir Joseph!" said the lady, with a shudder. "Rheumatisms, and fevers, and crooked legs, and asthmas, and all kinds of horrors!"

"My lady," returned Sir Joseph, with solemnity, "not the less am I the Poor Man's Friend and Father. Not the less shall he receive encouragement at my hands. Every quarter-day he will be put in communication with Mr. Fish. Every New Year's Day, myself and friends will drink his health. Once every year, myself and friends will address him with the deepest feeling. Once in his life, he may even perhaps receive; in public, in the presence of the gentry; a Trifle from a Friend. And when, upheld no more by these stimulants, and the Dignity of Labour, he sinks into his comfortable grave, then, my lady"—here Sir Joseph blew his nose—"I will be a Friend and a Father—on the same terms—to his children."

Toby was greatly moved.

"O! You have a thankful family, Sir Joseph!" cried his wife.

"My lady," said Sir Joseph, quite majestically. "Ingratitude is known to be the sin of that class. I expect no other return."

"Ah! Born bad!" thought Toby. "Nothing melts us."

"What man can do, *I* do," pursued Sir Joseph. "I do my duty as the Poor Man's Friend and Father; and I endeavour to educate his mind, by inculcating on all occasions the one great moral lesson which that class requires. That is, entire Dependence on myself. They have no business whatever with—with themselves. If wicked and designing persons tell them otherwise, and they become impatient and discontented, and are guilty of insubordinate conduct and black-hearted ingratitude; which is undoubtedly the case; I am their Friend and Father still. It is so Ordained. It is in the nature of things."

With that great sentiment, he opened the Alderman's letter; and read it.

"Very polite and attentive, I am sure!" exclaimed Sir Joseph. "My lady, the Alderman is so obliging as to remind me that he has had "the distinguished honour"—he is very good—of meeting me at the house of our mutual friend Deedles, the banker; and he does me the favour to inquire whether it will be agreeable to me to have Will Fern put down."

"*Most* agreeable!" replied my Lady Bowley. "The worst man among them! He has been committing a robbery, I hope?"

"Why, no," said Sir Joseph, referring to the letter. "Not quite. Very near. Not quite. He came up to London, it seems, to look for employment (trying to better himself—that's his story), and being found at night asleep in a shed, was taken into custody, and carried next morning before the Alderman. The Alderman observes (very properly) that he is determined to put this sort of thing down; and that if it will be agreeable to me to have Will Fern put down, he will be happy to begin with him."

"Let him be made an example of, by all means," returned the lady. "Last winter, when I introduced pinking and eyelet-holing among the men and boys in the village, as a nice evening employment, and had the lines,

O let us love our occupations,
Bless the squire and his relations,
Live upon our daily rations,
And always know our proper stations,

set to music on the new system, for them to sing the while; this very Fern—I see him now—touched that hat of his, and said, 'I humbly ask your pardon, my lady, but *an't* I something different from a great girl?' I expected it, of course; who can expect anything but insolence and ingratitude from that class of people! That is not to the purpose, however. Sir Joseph! Make an example of him!"

"Hem!" coughed Sir Joseph. "Mr. Fish, if you'll have the goodness to attend—"

Mr. Fish immediately seized his pen, and wrote from Sir Joseph's dictation.

"Private. My dear Sir. I am very much indebted to you for your courtesy in the matter of the man William Fern, of whom, I regret to add, I can say nothing favourable. I have uniformly considered myself in the light of his Friend and Father, but have been repaid (a common case, I grieve to say) with ingratitude, and constant opposition to my plans. He is a turbulent and rebellious spirit. His character will not bear investigation. Nothing will persuade him to be happy when he might. Under these circumstances, it appears to me, I own, that when he comes before you again (as you informed me he promised to do to-morrow, pending your inquiries, and I think he may be so far relied upon), his committal for some short term as a Vagabond, would be a service to society, and would be a salutary example in a country where—for the sake of those who are, through good and evil report, the Friends and Fathers of the Poor, as well as with a view to that, generally speaking, misguided class themselves—examples are greatly needed. And I am," and so forth.

"It appears," remarked Sir Joseph when he had signed this letter, and Mr. Fish was sealing it. "as if this were Ordained: really. At the close of the year, I wind up my account and strike my balance, even with William Fern!"

Trotty, who had long ago relapsed, and was very low-spirited, stepped forward with a rueful face to take the letter.

"With my compliments and thanks," said Sir Joseph. "Stop!"

"Stop!" echoed Mr. Fish.

"You have heard, perhaps," said Sir Joseph, oracularly, "certain remarks into which I have been led respecting the solemn period of time at which we have arrived, and the duty imposed upon us of settling our affairs, and being prepared. You have observed that I don't shelter myself behind my superior standing in society, but that Mr. Fish—that gentleman—has a cheque-book at his elbow, and is in fact here, to enable me to turn over a perfectly new leaf, and enter on the epoch before us with a clean account. Now, my friend, can you lay your hand upon your heart, and say, that you also have made preparations for a New Year?"

"I am afraid, sir," stammered Trotty, looking meekly at him, "that I am a—a—little behind-hand with the world."

"Behind-hand with the world!" repeated Sir Joseph Bowley, in a tone of terrible distinctness.

"I am afraid, sir," faltered Trotty, "that there's a matter of ten or twelve shillings owing to Mrs. Chickenstalker."

"To Mrs. Chickenstalker!" repeated Sir Joseph, in the same tone as before.

"A shop, sir," exclaimed Toby, "in the general line. Also a—a little money on account of rent. A very little, sir. It oughtn't to be owing, I know, but we have been hard put to it, indeed!"

Sir Joseph looked at his lady, and at Mr. Fish, and at Trotty, one after another, twice all round. He then made a despondent gesture with both hands at once, as if he gave the thing up altogether.

"How a man, even among this improvident and impracticable race; an old man; a man grown grey; can look a New Year in the face, with his affairs in this condition; how he can lie down on his bed at night, and get up again in the morning, and— There!" he said, turning his back on Trotty. "Take the letter. Take the letter!"

"I heartily wish it was otherwise, sir," said Trotty, anxious to excuse himself. "We have been tried very hard."

Sir Joseph still repeating "Take the letter, take the letter!" and Mr. Fish not only saying the same thing, but giving additional force to the request by motioning the bearer to the door, he had nothing for it but to make his bow and leave the house. And in the street, poor Trotty pulled his worn old hat down on his head, to hide the grief he felt at getting no hold on the New Year, anywhere.

He didn't even lift his hat to look up at the Bell tower when he came to the old church on his return. He halted there a moment, from habit: and knew that it was growing dark, and that the steeple rose above him, indistinct and faint, in the murky air. He knew, too, that the Chimes would ring immediately; and that they sounded to his fancy, at such a time, like voices in the clouds. But he only made the more haste to deliver the Alderman's letter, and get out of the way before they began; for he dreaded to hear them tagging "Friends and Fathers, Friends and Fathers," to the burden they had rung out last.

Toby discharged himself of his commission, therefore, with all possible speed, and set off trotting homeward. But what with his pace, which was at best an awkward one in the street; and what with his hat, which didn't improve it; he trotted against somebody in less than no time, and was sent staggering out into the road.

"I beg your pardon, I'm sure!" said Trotty, pulling up his hat in great confusion, and between the hat and the torn lining, fixing his head into a kind of bee-hive. "I hope I haven't hurt you."

As to hurting anybody, Toby was not such an absolute Samson, but that he was much more likely to be hurt himself: and indeed, he had flown out into the road, like a shuttlecock. He had such an opinion of his own strength, however, that he was in real concern for the other party: and said again,

"I hope I haven't hurt you?"

The man against whom he had run; a sun-browned, sinewy, country-looking man, with grizzled hair, and a rough chin; stared at him for a moment, as if he suspected him to be in jest. But, satisfied of his good faith, he answered:

"No, friend. You have not hurt me."

"Nor the child, I hope?" said Trotty.

"Nor the child," returned the man. "I thank you kindly."

As he said so, he glanced at a little girl he carried in his arms, asleep: and shading her face with the long end of the poor handkerchief he wore about his throat, went slowly on.

The tone in which he said "I thank you kindly," penetrated Trotty's heart. He was so jaded and foot-sore, and so soiled with travel, and looked about him so forlorn and strange, that it was a comfort to him to be able to thank any one: no matter for how little. Toby stood gazing after him as he plodded wearily away, with the child's arm clinging round his neck.

At the figure in the worn shoes—now the very shade and ghost of shoes—rough leather leggings, common frock, and broad slouched hat, Trotty stood gazing, blind to the whole street. And at the child's arm, clinging round its neck.

Before he merged into the darkness the traveller stopped; and looking round, and seeing Trotty standing there yet, seemed undecided whether to return or go on. After doing first the one and then the other, he came back, and Trotty went half-way to meet him.

"You can tell me, perhaps," said the man with a faint smile, "and if you can I am sure you will, and I'd rather ask you than another—where Alderman Cute lives."

"Close at hand," replied Toby. "I'll show you his house with pleasure."

"I was to have gone to him elsewhere to-morrow," said the man, accompanying Toby. "but I'm uneasy under suspicion, and want to clear myself, and to be free to go and seek my bread—I don't know where. So, maybe he'll forgive my going to his house to-night."

"It's impossible," cried Toby with a start, "that your name's Fern!"

"Eh!" cried the other, turning on him in astonishment.

"Fern! Will Fern!" said Trotty.

"That's my name," replied the other.

"Why then," said Trotty, seizing him by the arm, and looking cautiously round, "for Heaven's sake don't go to him! Don't go to him! He'll put you down as sure as ever you were born. Here! come up this alley, and I'll tell you what I mean. Don't go to *him*."

His new acquaintance looked as if he thought him mad; but he bore him company nevertheless. When they were shrouded from observation, Trotty told him what he knew, and what character he had received, and all about it.

The subject of his history listened to it with a calmness that surprised him. He did not contradict or interrupt it, once. He nodded his head now and then—more in corroboration of an old and worn-out story, it appeared, than in refutation of it; and once or twice threw back his hat, and passed his freckled hand over a brow, where every furrow he had ploughed seemed to have set its image in little. But he did no more.

"It's true enough in the main," he said, "master. I could sift grain from husk here and there, but let it be as 'tis. What odds? I have gone against his plans; to my misfortun'. I can't help it; I should do the like to-morrow. As to character, them gentlefolks will search and search, and pry and pry, and have it as free from spot or speck in us, afore they'll help us to a dry good word! Well! I hope they don't lose good opinion as easy as we do, or their lives is strict indeed, and hardly worth the keeping. For myself, master, I never took with that hand"—holding it before him—"what wasn't my own; and never held it back from work, however hard, or poorly paid. Whoever can deny it, let him chop it off! But when work won't maintain me like a human creetur; when my living is so bad, that I am Hungry, out of doors and in; when I see a whole working life begin that way, go on that way, and end that way, without a chance or change; then I say to the gentlefolks 'Keep away from me! Let my cottage be. My doors is dark enough without your darkening of 'em more. Don't look for me to come up into the Park to help the show when there's a Birthday, or a fine Speechmaking, or what not. Act your Plays and Games without me, and be welcome to 'em, and enjoy 'em. We've nowt to do with one another. I'm best let alone!'"

Seeing that the child in his arms had opened her eyes, and was looking about her in wonder, he checked himself to say a word or two of foolish prattle in her ear, and stand her on the ground beside him. Then slowly winding one of her long tresses round and round his rough forefinger like a ring, while she hung about his dusty leg, he said to Trotty:

"I'm not a cross-grained man by natur', I believe; and easy satisfied, I'm sure. I bear no ill-will against none of 'em. I only want to live like one of the Almighty's creeturs. I can't—I don't—and so there's a pit dug between me, and them that can and do. There's others like me. You might tell 'em off by hundreds and by thousands, sooner than by ones."

Trotty knew he spoke the Truth in this, and shook his head to signify as much.

"I've got a bad name this way," said Fern; "and I'm not likely, I'm afeared, to get a better. 'T'an't lawful to be out of sorts, and I AM out of sorts, though God knows I'd sooner bear a cheerful spirit if I could. Well! I don't know as this Alderman could hurt *me* much by sending me to jail; but without a friend to speak a word for me, he might do it; and you see—!" pointing downward with his finger, at the child.

"She has a beautiful face," said Trotty.

"Why, yes!" replied the other in a low voice, as he gently turned it up with both his hands towards his own, and looked upon it steadfastly. "I've thought so, many times. I've thought so, when my hearth was very cold, and cupboard very bare. I thought so t'other night, when we were taken like two thieves. But they—they shouldn't try the little face too often, should they, Lilian? That's hardly fair upon a man!"

He sunk his voice so low, and gazed upon her with an air so stern and strange, that Toby, to divert the current of his thoughts, inquired if his wife were living.

"I never had one," he returned, shaking his head. "She's my brother's child: a orphan. Nine year old, though you'd hardly think it; but she's tired and worn out now. They'd have taken care on her, the Union—eight-and-twenty mile away from where we live—between four walls (as they took care of my old father when he couldn't work no more, though he didn't trouble 'em long); but I took her instead, and she's lived with me ever since. Her mother had a friend once, in London here. We are trying to find her, and to find work too; but it's a large place. Never mind. More room for us to walk about in, Lilly!"

Meeting the child's eyes with a smile which melted Toby more than tears, he shook him by the hand.

"I don't so much as know your name," he said, "but I've opened my heart free to you, for I'm thankful to you; with good reason. I'll take your advice, and keep clear of this—"

"Justice," suggested Toby.

"Ah!" he said. "If that's the name they give him. This Justice. And to-morrow will try whether there's better fortun' to be met with, somewheres near London. Good night. A Happy New Year!"

"Stay!" cried Trotty, catching at his hand, as he relaxed his grip. "Stay! The New Year never can be happy to me, if we part like this. The New Year never can be happy to me, if I see the child and you go wandering away, you don't know where, without a shelter for your heads. Come home with me! I'm a poor man, living in a poor place; but I can give you lodging for one night and never miss it. Come home with me! Here! I'll take her!" cried Trotty, lifting up the child. "A pretty one! I'd carry twenty times her weight, and never know I'd got it. Tell me if I go too quick for you. I'm very fast. I always was!" Trotty said this, taking about six of his trotting paces to one stride of his fatigued companion; and with his thin legs quivering again, beneath the load he bore.

"Why, she's as light," said Trotty, trotting in his speech as well as in his gait; for he couldn't bear to be thanked, and dreaded a moment's pause; "as light as a feather. Lighter than a Peacock's feather—a great deal lighter. Here we are and here we go! Round this first turning to the right, Uncle Will, and past the pump, and sharp off up the passage to the left, right opposite the public-house. Here we are and here we go! Cross over, Uncle Will, and mind the kidney pieman at the corner! Here we are and here we go! Down the Mews here, Uncle Will, and stop at the black door, with "T. Veck, Ticket Porter," wrote upon a board; and here we are and here we go, and here we are indeed, my precious. Meg, surprising you!"

With which words Trotty, in a breathless state, set the child down before his daughter in the middle of the floor. The little visitor looked once at Meg; and doubting nothing in that face, but trusting everything she saw there; ran into her arms.

"Here we are and here we go!" cried Trotty, running round the room, and choking audibly. "Here, Uncle Will, here's a fire you know! Why don't you come to the fire? Oh here we are and here we go! Meg, my precious darling, where's the kettle? Here it is and here it goes, and it'll bile in no time!"

Trotty really had picked up the kettle somewhere or other in the course of his wild career and now put it on the fire: while Meg, seating the child in a warm corner, knelt down on the ground before her, and pulled off her shoes, and dried her wet feet on a cloth. Ay, and she laughed at Trotty too—so pleasantly, so cheerfully, that Trotty could have blessed her where she kneeled; for he had seen that, when they entered, she was sitting by the fire in tears.

"Why, father!" said Meg. "You're crazy to-night, I think. I don't know what the Bells would say to that. Poor little feet. How cold they are!"

"Oh, they're warmer now!" exclaimed the child. "They're quite warm now!"

"No, no, no," said Meg. "We haven't rubbed 'em half enough. We're so busy. So busy! And when they're done, we'll brush out the damp hair; and when that's done, we'll bring some colour to the poor pale face with fresh water; and when that's done, we'll be so gay, and brisk, and happy—!"

The child, in a burst of sobbing, clasped her round the neck; caressed her fair cheek with its hand; and said. "Oh Meg! oh dear Meg!"

Toby's blessing could have done no more. Who could do more!

"Why, father!" cried Meg, after a pause.

"Here I am and here I go, my dear!" said Trotty.

"Good Gracious me!" cried Meg. "He's crazy! He's put the dear child's bonnet on the kettle, and hung the lid behind the door!"

"I didn't go for to do it, my love," said Trotty, hastily repairing this mistake. "Meg, my dear?"

Meg looked towards him and saw that he had elaborately stationed himself behind the chair of their male visitor, where with many mysterious gestures he was holding up the sixpence he had earned.

"I see, my dear," said Trotty, "as I was coming in, half an ounce of tea lying somewhere on the stairs; and I'm pretty sure there was a bit of bacon too. As I don't remember where it was exactly, I'll go myself and try to find 'em."

With this inscrutable artifice, Toby withdrew to purchase the viands he had spoken of, for ready money, at Mrs. Chickenstalker's; and presently came back, pretending he had not been able to find them, at first, in the dark.

"But here they are at last," said Trotty, setting out the tea-things, "all correct! I was pretty sure it was tea, and a rasher. So it is. Meg, my pet, if you'll just make the tea, while your unworthy father toasts the bacon, we shall be ready, immediate. It's a curious circumstance," said Trotty, proceeding in his cookery, with the assistance of the toasting-fork, "curious, but well known to my friends, that I never care, myself, for rashers, nor for tea. I like to see other people enjoy 'em," said Trotty, speaking very loud, to impress the fact upon his guest, "but to me, as food, they're disagreeable."

Yet Trotty sniffed the savour of the hissing bacon—ah!—as if he liked it; and when he poured the boiling water in the tea-pot, looked lovingly down into the depths of that snug cauldron, and suffered the fragrant steam to curl about his nose, and wreathe his head and face in a thick cloud. However, for all this, he neither ate nor drank, except at the very beginning, a mere morsel for form's sake, which he appeared to eat with infinite relish, but declared was perfectly uninteresting to him.

No. Trotty's occupation was, to see Will Fern and Lilian eat and drink; and so was Meg's. And never did spectators at a city dinner or court banquet find such high delight in seeing others feast: although it were a monarch or a pope: as those two did, in looking on that night. Meg smiled at Trotty, Trotty laughed at Meg. Meg shook her head, and made belief to clap her hands, applauding Trotty; Trotty conveyed, in dumb-show, unintelligible narratives of how and when and where he had found their visitors, to Meg; and they were happy. Very happy.

"Although," thought Trotty, sorrowfully, as he watched Meg's face; "that match is broken off, I see!"

"Now, I'll tell you what," said Trotty after tea. "The little one, she sleeps with Meg, I know."

"With good Meg!" cried the child, caressing her. "With Meg."

"That's right," said Trotty. "And I shouldn't wonder if she kiss Meg's father, won't she? *I'm* Meg's father."

Mightily delighted Trotty was, when the child went timidly towards him, and having kissed him, fell back upon Meg again.

"She's as sensible as Solomon," said Trotty. "Here we come and here we—no, we don't—I don't mean that—I—what was I saying, Meg, my precious?"

Meg looked towards their guest, who leaned upon her chair, and with his face turned from her, fondled the child's head, half hidden in her lap.

"To be sure," said Toby. "To be sure! I don't know what I'm rambling on about, to-night. My wits are wool-gathering, I think. Will Fern, you come along with me. You're tired to death, and broken down for want of rest. You come along with me." The man still played with the child's curls, still leaned upon Meg's chair, still turned away his face. He didn't speak, but in his rough coarse fingers, clenching and expanding in the fair hair of the child, there was an eloquence that said enough.

"Yes, yes," said Trotty, answering unconsciously what he saw expressed in his daughter's face. "Take her with you, Meg. Get her to bed. There! Now, Will, I'll show you where you lie. It's not much of a place: only a loft; but, having a loft, I always say, is one of the great conveniences of living in a mews; and till this coach-house and stable gets a better let, we live here cheap. There's plenty of sweet hay up there, belonging to a neighbour; and it's as clean as hands, and Meg, can make it. Cheer up! Don't give way. A new heart for a New Year, always!"

The hand released from the child's hair, had fallen, trembling, into Trotty's hand. So Trotty, talking without intermission, led him out as tenderly and easily as if he had been a child himself. Returning before Meg, he listened for an instant at the door of her little chamber; an adjoining room. The child was murmuring a simple Prayer before lying down to sleep; and when she had remembered Meg's name. "Dearly, Dearly"—so her words ran—Trotty heard her stop and ask for his.

It was some short time before the foolish little old fellow could compose himself to mend the fire, and draw his chair to the warm hearth. But, when he had done so, and had trimmed the light, he took his newspaper from his pocket, and began to read. Carelessly at first, and skimming up and down the columns; but with an earnest and a sad attention, very soon.

For this same dreaded paper re-directed Trotty's thoughts into the channel they had taken all that day, and which the day's events had so marked out and shaped. His interest in the two wanderers had set him on another course of thinking, and a happier one, for the time; but being alone again, and reading of the crimes and violences of the people, he relapsed into his former train.

In this mood, he came to an account (and it was not the first he had ever read) of a woman who had laid her desperate hands not only on her own life but on that of her young child. A crime so terrible, and so revolting to his soul, dilated with the love of Meg, that he let the journal drop, and fell back in his chair, appalled!

"Unnatural and cruel!" Toby cried. "Unnatural and cruel! None but people who were bad at heart, born bad, who had no business on the earth, could do such deeds. It's too true, all I've heard to-day; too just, too full of proof. We're Bad!"

The Chimes took up the words so suddenly—burst out so loud, and clear, and sonorous—that the Bells seemed to strike him in his chair.

And what was that, they said?

"Toby Veck, Toby Veck, waiting for you Toby! Toby Veck, Toby Veck, waiting for you Toby! Come and see us, come and see us, Drag him to us, drag him to us, Haunt and hunt him, haunt and hunt him, Break his slumbers, break his slumbers! Toby Veck Toby Veck, door open wide Toby, Toby Veck Toby Veck, door open wide Toby—" then fiercely back to their impetuous strain again, and ringing in the very bricks and plaster on the walls.

Toby listened. Fancy, fancy! His remorse for having run away from them that afternoon! No, no. Nothing of the kind. Again, again, and yet a dozen times again. "Haunt and hunt him, haunt and hunt him, Drag him to us, drag him to us!" Deafening the whole town!

"Meg," said Trotty softly: tapping at her door. "Do you hear anything?"

"I hear the Bells, father. Surely they're very loud to-night."

"Is she asleep?" said Toby, making an excuse for peeping in.

"So peacefully and happily! I can't leave her yet though, father. Look how she holds my hand!"

"Meg," whispered Trotty. "Listen to the Bells!"

She listened, with her face towards him all the time. But it underwent no change. She didn't understand them.

Trotty withdrew, resumed his seat by the fire, and once more listened by himself. He remained here a little time.

It was impossible to bear it; their energy was dreadful.

"If the tower-door is really open," said Toby, hastily laying aside his apron, but never thinking of his hat, "what's to hinder me from going up into the steeple and satisfying myself? If it's shut, I don't want any other satisfaction. That's enough."

He was pretty certain as he slipped out quietly into the street that he should find it shut and locked, for he knew the door well, and had so rarely seen it open, that he couldn't reckon above three times in all. It was a low arched portal, outside the church, in a dark nook behind a column; and had such great iron hinges, and such a monstrous lock, that there was more hinge and lock than door.

But what was his astonishment when, coming bare-headed to the church; and putting his hand into this dark nook, with a certain misgiving that it might be unexpectedly seized, and a shivering propensity to draw it back again; he found that the door, which opened outwards, actually stood ajar!

He thought, on the first surprise, of going back; or of getting a light, or a companion, but his courage aided him immediately, and he determined to ascend alone.

"What have I to fear?" said Trotty. "It's a church! Besides, the ringers may be there, and have forgotten to shut the door." So he went in, feeling his way as he went, like a blind man; for it was very dark. And very quiet, for the Chimes were silent.

The dust from the street had blown into the recess; and lying there, heaped up, made it so soft and velvet-like to the foot, that there was something startling, even in that. The narrow stair was so close to the door, too, that he stumbled at the very first; and shutting the door upon himself, by striking it with his foot, and causing it to rebound back heavily, he couldn't open it again.

This was another reason, however, for going on. Trotty groped his way, and went on. Up, up, up, and round, and round; and up, up, up; higher, higher, higher up!

It was a disagreeable staircase for that groping work; so low and narrow, that his groping hand was always touching something; and it often felt so like a man or ghostly figure standing up erect and making room for him to pass without discovery, that he would rub the smooth wall upward searching for its face, and downward searching for its feet, while a chill tingling crept all over him. Twice or thrice, a door or niche broke the monotonous surface; and then it seemed a gap as wide as the whole church; and he felt on the brink of an abyss, and going to tumble headlong down, until he found the wall again.

Still up, up, up; and round and round; and up, up, up; higher, higher, higher up!

At length, the dull and stifling atmosphere began to freshen: presently to feel quite windy: presently it blew so strong, that he could hardly keep his legs. But, he got to an arched window in the tower, breast high, and holding tight, looked down upon the house-tops, on the smoking chimneys, on the blur and blotch of lights (towards the place where Meg was wondering where he was and calling to him perhaps), all kneaded up together in a leaven of mist and darkness.

This was the belfry, where the ringers came. He had caught hold of one of the frayed ropes which hung down through apertures in the oaken roof. At first he started, thinking it was hair; then trembled at the very thought of waking the deep Bell. The Bells themselves were higher. Higher, Trotty, in his fascination, or in working out the spell upon him, groped his way. By ladders now, and toilsomely, for it was steep, and not too certain holding for the feet.

Up, up, up; and climb and clamber; up, up, up; higher, higher, higher up!

Until, ascending through the floor, and pausing with his head just raised above its beams, he came among the Bells. It was barely possible to make out their great shapes in the gloom; but there they were. Shadowy, and dark, and dumb.

A heavy sense of dread and loneliness fell instantly upon him, as he climbed into this airy nest of stone and metal. His head went round and round. He listened, and then raised a wild "Holloa!"

Holloa! was mournfully protracted by the echoes.

Giddy, confused, and out of breath, and frightened, Toby looked about him vacantly, and sunk down in a swoon.

Third Quarter

BLACK ARE THE BROODING CLOUDS AND TROUBLED THE DEEP WATERS, when the Sea of Thought, first heaving from a calm, gives up its Dead. Monsters uncouth and wild, arise in premature, imperfect resurrection; the several parts and shapes of different things are joined and mixed by chance; and when, and how, and by what wonderful degrees, each separates from each, and every sense and object of the mind resumes its usual form and lives again, no man—though every man is every day the casket of this type of the Great Mystery—can tell.

So, when and how the darkness of the night-black steeple changed to shining light; when and how the solitary tower was peopled with a myriad figures; when and how the whispered "Haunt and hunt him," breathing monotonously through his sleep or swoon, became a voice exclaiming in the waking ears of Trotty. "Break his slumbers"; when and how he ceased to have a sluggish and confused idea that such things were, companioning a host of others that were not; there are no dates or means to tell. But, awake and standing on his feet upon the boards where he had lately lain, he saw this Goblin Sight.

He saw the tower, whither his charmed footsteps had brought him, swarming with dwarf phantoms, spirits, elfin creatures of the Bells. He saw them leaping, flying, dropping, pouring from the Bells without a pause. He saw them, round him on the ground; above him, in the air; clambering from him, by the ropes below; looking down upon him, from the massive iron-girded beams; peeping in upon him, through the chinks and loopholes in the walls; spreading away and away from him in enlarging circles, as the water ripples give way to a huge stone that suddenly comes plashing in among them. He saw them, of all aspects and all shapes. He saw them ugly, handsome, crippled, exquisitely formed. He saw them young, he saw them old, he saw them kind, he saw them cruel, he saw them merry, he saw them grim; he saw them dance, and heard them sing; he saw them tear their hair, and heard them howl. He saw the air thick with them. He saw them come and go, incessantly. He saw them riding downward, soaring upward, sailing off afar, perching near at hand, all restless and all violently active. Stone, and brick, and slate, and tile, became transparent to him as to them. He saw them *in* the houses, busy at the sleepers' beds. He saw them soothing people in their dreams; he saw them beating them with knotted whips; he saw them yelling in their ears; he saw them playing softest music on their pillows; he saw them cheering some with the songs of birds and the perfume of flowers; he saw them flashing awful faces on the troubled rest of others, from enchanted mirrors which they carried in their hands.

He saw these creatures, not only among sleeping men but waking also, active in pursuits irreconcilable with one another, and possessing or assuming natures the most opposite. He saw one buckling on innumerable wings to increase his speed; another loading himself with chains and weights, to retard his. He saw some putting the hands of clocks forward, some putting the hands of clocks backward, some endeavouring to stop the clock entirely. He saw them representing, here a marriage ceremony, there a funeral; in this chamber an election, in that a ball he saw, everywhere, restless and untiring motion.

Bewildered by the host of shifting and extraordinary figures, as well as by the uproar of the Bells, which all this while were ringing, Trotty clung to a wooden pillar for support, and turned his white face here and there, in mute and stunned astonishment.

As he gazed, the Chimes stopped. Instantaneous change! The whole swarm fainted! their forms collapsed, their speed deserted them; they sought to fly, but in the act of falling died and melted into air. No fresh supply succeeded them. One straggler leaped down pretty briskly from the surface of the Great Bell, and alighted on his feet, but he was dead and gone before he could turn round. Some few of the late company who had gambolled in the tower, remained there, spinning over and over a little longer; but these became at every turn more faint, and few, and feeble, and soon went the way of the rest. The last of all was one small hunchback, who had got into an echoing corner, where he twirled and twirled, and floated by himself a long time; showing such perseverance, that at last he dwindled to a leg and even to a foot, before he finally retired; but he vanished in the end, and then the tower was silent.

Then and not before, did Trotty see in every Bell a bearded figure of the bulk and stature of the Bell—incomprehensibly, a figure and the Bell itself. Gigantic, grave, and darkly watchful of him, as he stood rooted to the ground.

Mysterious and awful figures! Resting on nothing; poised in the night air of the tower, with their draped and hooded heads merged in the dim roof; motionless and shadowy. Shadowy and dark, although he saw them by some light belonging to themselves—none else was there—each with its muffled hand upon its goblin mouth.

He could not plunge down wildly through the opening in the floor; for all power of motion had deserted him. Otherwise he would have done so—aye, would have thrown himself, headforemost, from the steeple-top, rather than have seen them watching him with eyes that would have waked and watched although the pupils had been taken out.

Again, again, the dread and terror of the lonely place, and of the wild and fearful night that reigned there, touched him like a spectral hand. His distance from all help; the long, dark, winding, ghost-beleaguered way that lay between him and the earth on which men lived; his being high, high, high, up there, where it had made him dizzy to see the birds fly in the day; cut off from all good people, who at such an hour were safe at home and sleeping in their beds; all this struck coldly through him, not as a reflection but a bodily sensation. Meantime his eyes and thoughts and fears, were fixed upon the watchful figures; which, rendered unlike any figures of this world by the deep gloom and shade enwrapping and enfolding them, as well as by their looks and forms and supernatural hovering above the floor, were nevertheless as plainly to be seen as were the stalwart oaken frames, cross-pieces, bars and beams, set up there to support the Bells. These hemmed them, in a very forest of hewn timber; from the entanglements, intricacies, and depths of which, as from among the boughs of a dead wood blighted for their phantom use, they kept their darksome and unwinking watch.

A blast of air—how cold and shrill!—came moaning through the tower. As it died away, the Great Bell, or the Goblin of the Great Bell, spoke.

"What visitor is this!" it said. The voice was low and deep, and Trotty fancied that it sounded in the other figures as well.

"I thought my name was called by the Chimes!" said Trotty, raising his hands in an attitude of supplication. "I hardly know why I am here, or how I came. I have listened to the Chimes these many years. They have cheered me often."

"And you have thanked them?" said the Bell.

"A thousand times!" cried Trotty.

"How?"

"I am a poor man," faltered Trotty, "and could only thank them in words."

"And always so?" inquired the Goblin of the Bell. "Have you never done us wrong in words?"

"No!" cried Trotty eagerly.

"Never done us foul, and false, and wicked wrong, in words?" pursued the Goblin of the Bell.

Trotty was about to answer. "Never!" But he stopped, and was confused.

"The voice of Time," said the Phantom, "cries to man, Advance! Time is for his advancement and improvement; for his greater worth, his greater happiness, his better life; his progress onward to that goal within its knowledge and its view, and set there, in the period when Time and He began. Ages of darkness, wickedness, and violence, have come and gone—millions uncountable, have suffered, lived, and died—to point the way before him. Who seeks to turn him back, or stay him on his course, arrests a mighty engine which will strike the meddler dead; and be the fiercer and the wilder, ever, for its momentary check!"

"I never did so to my knowledge, sir," said Trotty. "It was quite by accident if I did. I wouldn't go to do it, I'm sure."

"Who puts into the mouth of Time, or of its servants," said the Goblin of the Bell. "a cry of lamentation for days which have had their trial and their failure, and have left deep traces of it which the blind may see—a cry that only serves the present time, by showing men how much it needs their help when any ears can listen to regrets for such a past—who does this, does a wrong. And you have done that wrong, to us, the Chimes."

Trotty's first excess of fear was gone. But he had felt tenderly and gratefully towards the Bells, as you have seen; and when he heard himself arraigned as one who had offended them so weightily, his heart was touched with penitence and grief.

"If you knew," said Trotty, clasping his hands earnestly—"or perhaps you do know—if you know how often you have kept me company; how often you have cheered me up when I've been low; how you were quite the plaything of my little daughter Meg (almost the only one she ever had) when first her mother died, and she and me were left alone; you won't bear malice for a hasty word!"

"Who hears in us, the Chimes, one note bespeaking disregard, or stern regard, of any hope, or joy, or pain, or sorrow, of the many-sorrowed throng; who hears us make response to any creed that gauges human passions and affections, as it gauges the amount of miserable food on which humanity may pine and wither; does us wrong. That wrong you have done us!" said the Bell.

"I have!" said Trotty. "Oh forgive me!"

"Who hears us echo the dull vermin of the earth: the Putters Down of crushed and broken natures, formed to be raised up higher than such maggots of the time can crawl or can conceive," pursued the Goblin of the Bell; "who does so, does us wrong. And you have done us wrong!"

"Not meaning it," said Trotty. "In my ignorance. Not meaning it!"

"Lastly, and most of all," pursued the Bell. "Who turns his back upon the fallen and disfigured of his kind; abandons them as vile; and does not trace and track with pitying eyes the unfenced precipice by which they fell from good—grasping in their fall some tufts and shreds of that lost soil, and clinging to them still when bruised and dying in the gulf below; does wrong to Heaven and man, to time and to eternity. And you have done that wrong!"

"Spare me!" cried Trotty, falling on his knees; "for Mercy's sake!"

"Listen!" said the Shadow.

"Listen!" cried the other Shadows.

"Listen!" said a clear and childlike voice, which Trotty thought he recognised as having heard before.

The organ sounded faintly in the church below. Swelling by degrees, the melody ascended to the roof, and filled the choir and nave. Expanding more and more, it rose up, up; up, up; higher, higher, higher up; awakening agitated hearts within the burly piles of oak, the hollow bells, the iron-bound doors, the stairs of solid stone; until the tower walls were insufficient to contain it, and it soared into the sky.

No wonder that an old man's breast could not contain a sound so vast and mighty. It broke from that weak prison in a rush of tears; and Trotty put his hands before his face.

"Listen!" said the Shadow.

"Listen!" said the other Shadows.

"Listen!" said the child's voice.

A solemn strain of blended voices, rose into the tower.

It was a very low and mournful strain—a Dirge—and as he listened, Trotty heard his child among the singers.

"She is dead!" exclaimed the old man. "Meg is dead! Her Spirit calls to me. I hear it!"

"The Spirit of your child bewails the dead, and mingles with the dead—dead hopes, dead fancies, dead imaginings of youth," returned the Bell, "but she is living. Learn from her life, a living truth. Learn from the creature dearest to your heart, how bad the bad are born. See every bud and leaf plucked one by one from off the fairest stem, and know how bare and wretched it may be. Follow her! To desperation!"

Each of the shadowy figures stretched its right arm forth, and pointed downward.

"The Spirit of the Chimes is your companion," said the figure.

"Go! It stands behind you!"

Trotty turned, and saw—the child! The child Will Fern had carried in the street; the child whom Meg had watched, but now, asleep!

"I carried her myself, to-night," said Trotty. "In these arms!"

"Show him what he calls himself," said the dark figures, one and all.

The tower opened at his feet. He looked down, and beheld his own form, lying at the bottom, on the outside: crushed and motionless.

"No more a living man!" cried Trotty. "Dead!"

"Dead!" said the figures all together.

"Gracious Heaven! And the New Year—"

"Past," said the figures.

"What!" he cried, shuddering. "I missed my way, and coming on the outside of this tower in the dark, fell down—a year ago?"

"Nine years ago!" replied the figures.

As they gave the answer, they recalled their outstretched hands; and where their figures had been, there the Bells were.

And they rung; their time being come again. And once again, vast multitudes of phantoms sprung into existence; once again, were incoherently engaged, as they had been before; once again, faded on the stopping of the Chimes; and dwindled into nothing.

"What are these?" he asked his guide. "If I am not mad, what are these?"

"Spirits of the Bells. Their sound upon the air," returned the child. "They take such shapes and occupations as the hopes and thoughts of mortals, and the recollections they have stored up, give them."

"And you," said Trotty wildly. "What are you?"

"Hush, hush!" returned the child. "Look here!"

In a poor, mean room; working at the same kind of embroidery which he had often, often seen before her; Meg, his own dear daughter, was presented to his view. He made no effort to imprint his kisses on her face; he did not strive to clasp her to his loving heart; he knew that such endearments were, for him, no more. But, he held his trembling breath, and brushed away the blinding tears, that he might look upon her; that he might only see her.

Ah! Changed. Changed. The light of the clear eye, how dimmed. The bloom, how faded from the cheek. Beautiful she was, as she had ever been, but Hope, Hope, Hope, oh where was the fresh Hope that had spoken to him like a voice!

She looked up from her work, at a companion. Following her eyes, the old man started back.

In the woman grown, he recognised her at a glance. In the long silken hair, he saw the self-same curls; around the lips, the child's expression lingering still. See! In the eyes, now turned inquiringly on Meg, there shone the very look that scanned those features when he brought her home!

Then what was this, beside him!

Looking with awe into its face, he saw a something reigning there: a lofty something, undefined and indistinct, which made it hardly more than a remembrance of that child—as yonder figure might be—yet it was the same: the same: and wore the dress.

Hark. They were speaking!

"Meg," said Lilian, hesitating. "How often you raise your head from your work to look at me!"

"Are my looks so altered, that they frighten you?" asked Meg.

"Nay, dear! But you smile at that, yourself! Why not smile, when you look at me, Meg?"

"I do so. Do I not?" she answered: smiling on her.

"Now you do," said Lilian, "but not usually. When you think I'm busy, and don't see you, you look so anxious and so doubtful, that I hardly like to raise my eyes. There is little cause for smiling in this hard and toilsome life, but you were once so cheerful."

"Am I not now!" cried Meg, speaking in a tone of strange alarm, and rising to embrace her. "Do I make our weary life more weary to you, Lilian!"

"You have been the only thing that made it life," said Lilian, fervently kissing her; "sometimes the only thing that made me care to live so, Meg. Such work, such work! So many hours, so many days, so many long, long nights of hopeless, cheerless, never-ending work—not to heap up riches, not to live grandly or gaily, not to live upon enough, however coarse; but to earn bare bread; to scrape together just enough to toil upon, and want upon, and keep alive in us the consciousness of our hard fate! Oh Meg, Meg!" she raised her voice and twined her arms about her as she spoke, like one in pain. "How can the cruel world go round, and bear to look upon such lives!"

"Lilly!" said Meg, soothing her, and putting back her hair from her wet face. "Why, Lilly! You! So pretty and so young!"

"Oh Meg!" she interrupted, holding her at arm's-length, and looking in her face imploringly. "The worst of all, the worst of all! Strike me old, Meg! Wither me, and shrivel me, and free me from the dreadful thoughts that tempt me in my youth!"

Trotty turned to look upon his guide. But the Spirit of the child had taken flight. Was gone.

Neither did he himself remain in the same place; for, Sir Joseph Bowley, Friend and Father of the Poor, held a great festivity at Bowley Hall, in honour of the natal day of Lady Bowley. And as Lady Bowley had been born on New Year's Day (which the local newspapers considered an especial pointing of the finger of Providence to number One, as Lady Bowley's destined figure in Creation), it was on a New Year's Day that this festivity took place.

Bowley Hall was full of visitors. The red-faced gentleman was there, Mr. Filer was there, the great Alderman Cute was there—Alderman Cute had a sympathetic feeling with great people, and had considerably improved his acquaintance with Sir Joseph Bowley on the strength of his attentive letter: indeed had become quite a friend of the family since then—and many guests were there. Trotty's ghost was there, wandering about, poor phantom, drearily; and looking for its guide.

There was to be a great dinner in the Great Hall. At which Sir Joseph Bowley, in his celebrated character of Friend and Father of the Poor, was to make his great speech. Certain plum-puddings were to be eaten by his Friends and Children in another Hall first; and, at a given signal, Friends and Children flocking in among their Friends and Fathers, were to form a family assemblage, with not one manly eye therein unmoistened by emotion.

But, there was more than this to happen. Even more than this. Sir Joseph Bowley, Baronet and Member of Parliament, was to play a match at skittles—real skittles—with his tenants!

"Which quite reminds me," said Alderman Cute, "of the days of old King Hal, stout King Hal, bluff King Hal. Ah. Fine character!"

"Very," said Mr. Filer, dryly. "For marrying women and murdering 'em. Considerably more than the average number of wives by the bye."

"You'll marry the beautiful ladies, and not murder 'em, eh?" said Alderman Cute to the heir of Bowley, aged twelve. "Sweet boy! We shall have this little gentleman in Parliament now," said the Alderman, holding him by the shoulders, and looking as reflective as he could. "before we know where we are. We shall hear of his successes at the poll; his speeches in the House; his overtures from Governments; his brilliant achievements of all kinds; ah! we shall make our little orations about him in the Common Council, I'll be bound; before we have time to look about us!"

"Oh, the difference of shoes and stockings!" Trotty thought. But his heart yearned towards the child, for the love of those same shoeless and stockingless boys, predestined (by the Alderman) to turn out bad, who might have been the children of poor Meg.

"Richard," moaned Trotty, roaming among the company, to and fro; "where is he? I can't find Richard! Where is Richard?"

Not likely to be there, if still alive! But Trotty's grief and solitude confused him; and he still went wandering among the gallant company, looking for his guide, and saying. "Where is Richard? Show me Richard!"

He was wandering thus, when he encountered Mr. Fish, the confidential Secretary: in great agitation.

"Bless my heart and soul!" cried Mr. Fish. "Where's Alderman Cute? Has anybody seen the Alderman?"

Seen the Alderman? Oh dear! Who could ever help seeing the Alderman? He was so considerate, so affable, he bore so much in mind the natural desires of folks to see him, that if he had a fault, it was the being constantly On View. And wherever the great people were, there, to be sure, attracted by the kindred sympathy between great souls, was Cute.

Several voices cried that he was in the circle round Sir Joseph. Mr. Fish made way there; found him; and took him secretly into a window near at hand. Trotty joined them. Not of his own accord. He felt that his steps were led in that direction.

"My dear Alderman Cute," said Mr. Fish. "A little more this way. The most dreadful circumstance has occurred. I have this moment received the intelligence. I think it will be best not to acquaint Sir Joseph with it till the day is over. You understand Sir Joseph, and will give me your opinion. The most frightful and deplorable event!"

"Fish!" returned the Alderman. "Fish! My good fellow, what is the matter? Nothing revolutionary, I hope! No—no attempted interference with the magistrates?"

"Deedles, the banker," gasped the Secretary. "Deedles Brothers—who was to have been here to-day—high in office in the Goldsmiths' Company—"

"Not stopped!" exclaimed the Alderman. "It can't be!"

"Shot himself."

"Good God!"

"Put a double-barrelled pistol to his mouth, in his own counting house," said Mr. Fish. "and blew his brains out. No motive. Princely circumstances!"

"Circumstances!" exclaimed the Alderman. "A man of noble fortune. One of the most respectable of men. Suicide, Mr. Fish! By his own hand!"

"This very morning," returned Mr. Fish.

"Oh the brain, the brain!" exclaimed the pious Alderman, lifting up his hands. "Oh the nerves, the nerves; the mysteries of this machine called Man! Oh the little that unhinges it: poor creatures that we are! Perhaps a dinner, Mr. Fish. Perhaps the conduct of his son, who, I have heard, ran very wild, and was in the habit of drawing bills upon him without the least authority! A most respectable man. One of the most respectable men I ever knew! A lamentable instance, Mr. Fish. A public calamity! I shall make a point of wearing the deepest mourning. A most respectable man! But there is One above. We must submit, Mr. Fish. We must submit!"

What, Alderman! No word of Putting Down? Remember, Justice, your high moral boast and pride. Come, Alderman! Balance those scales. Throw me into this, the empty one, no dinner, and Nature's founts in some poor woman, dried by starving misery and rendered obdurate to claims for which her offspring *has* authority in holy mother Eve. Weigh me the two, you Daniel, going to judgment, when your day shall come! Weigh them, in the eyes of suffering thousands, audience (not unmindful) of the grim farce you play. Or supposing that you strayed from your five wits—it's not so far to go, but that it might be—and laid hands upon that throat of yours, warning your fellows (if you have a fellow) how they croak their comfortable wickedness to raving heads and stricken hearts. What then?

The words rose up in Trotty's breast, as if they had been spoken by some other voice within him. Alderman Cute pledged himself to Mr. Fish that he would assist him in breaking the melancholy catastrophe to Sir Joseph when the day was over. Then, before they parted, wringing Mr. Fish's hand in bitterness of soul, he said.

"The most respectable of men!" And added that he hardly knew (not even he), why such afflictions were allowed on earth.

"It's almost enough to make one think, if one didn't know better," said Alderman Cute, "that at times some motion of a capsizing nature was going on in things, which affected the general economy of the social fabric. Deedles Brothers!"

The skittle-playing came off with immense success. Sir Joseph knocked the pins about quite skilfully; Master Bowley took an innings at a shorter distance also; and everybody said that now, when a Baronet and the Son of a Baronet played at skittles, the country was coming round again, as fast as it could come.

At its proper time, the Banquet was served up. Trotty involuntarily repaired to the Hall with the rest, for he felt himself conducted thither by some stronger impulse than his own free will. The sight was gay in the extreme; the ladies were very handsome; the visitors delighted, cheerful, and good-tempered. When the lower doors were opened, and the people flocked in, in their rustic dresses, the beauty of the spectacle was at its height; but Trotty only murmured more and more. "Where is Richard? He should help and comfort her! I can't see Richard!"

There had been some speeches made; and Lady Bowley's health had been proposed; and Sir Joseph Bowley had returned thanks, and had made his great speech, showing by various pieces of evidence that he was the born Friend and Father, and so forth; and had given as a Toast, his Friends and Children, and the Dignity of Labour; when a slight disturbance at the bottom of the Hall attracted Toby's notice. After some confusion, noise, and opposition, one man broke through the rest, and stood forward by himself.

Not Richard. No. But one whom he had thought of, and had looked for, many times. In a scantier supply of light, he might have doubted the identity of that worn man, so old, and grey, and bent; but with a blaze of lamps upon his gnarled and knotted head, he knew Will Fern as soon as he stepped forth.

"What is this!" exclaimed Sir Joseph, rising. "Who gave this man admittance? This is a criminal from prison! Mr. Fish, sir, *will* you have the goodness—"

"A minute!" said Will Fern. "A minute! My Lady, you was born on this day along with a New Year. Get me a minute's leave to speak."

She made some intercession for him. Sir Joseph took his seat again, with native dignity.

The ragged visitor—for he was miserably dressed—looked round upon the company, and made his homage to them with a humble bow.

"Gentlefolks!" he said. "You've drunk the Labourer. Look at me!"

"Just come from jail," said Mr. Fish.

"Just come from jail," said Will. "And neither for the first time, nor the second, nor the third, nor yet the fourth."

Mr. Filer was heard to remark testily, that four times was over the average; and he ought to be ashamed of himself.

"Gentlefolks!" repeated Will Fern. "Look at me! You see I'm at the worst. Beyond all hurt or harm; beyond your help; for the time when your kind words or kind actions could have done me good,"—he struck his hand upon his breast, and shook his head, "is gone, with the scent of last year's beans or clover on the air. Let me say a word for these," pointing to the labouring people in the Hall; "and when you're met together, hear the real Truth spoke out for once."

"There's not a man here," said the host, "who would have him for a spokesman."

"Like enough, Sir Joseph. I believe it. Not the less true, perhaps, is what I say. Perhaps that's a proof on it. Gentlefolks, I've lived many a year in this place. You may see the cottage from the sunk fence over yonder. I've seen the ladies draw it in their books, a hundred times. It looks well in a picter, I've heerd say; but there an't weather in picters, and maybe 'tis fitter for that, than for a place to live in. Well! I lived there. How hard—how bitter hard, I lived there, I won't say. Any day in the year, and every day, you can judge for your own selves."

He spoke as he had spoken on the night when Trotty found him in the street. His voice was deeper and more husky, and had a trembling in it now and then; but he never raised it passionately, and seldom lifted it above the firm stern level of the homely facts he stated.

"'Tis harder than you think for, gentlefolks, to grow up decent, commonly decent, in such a place. That I growed up a man and not a brute, says something for me—as I was then. As I am now, there's nothing can be said for me or done for me. I'm past it."

"I am glad this man has entered," observed Sir Joseph, looking round serenely. "Don't disturb him. It appears to be Ordained. He is an example: a living example. I hope and trust, and confidently expect, that it will not be lost upon my Friends here."

"I dragged on," said Fern, after a moment's silence, "somehow. Neither me nor any other man knows how; but so heavy, that I couldn't put a cheerful face upon it, or make believe that I was anything but what I was. Now, gentlemen—you gentlemen that sits at Sessions—when you see a man with discontent writ on his face, you says to one another, "He's suspicious. I has my doubts," says you, "about Will Fern. Watch that fellow!" I don't say, gentlemen, it ain't quite nat'ral, but I say 'tis so; and from that hour, whatever Will Fern does, or lets alone—all one—it goes against him."

Alderman Cute stuck his thumbs in his waistcoat-pockets, and leaning back in his chair, and smiling, winked at a neighbouring chandelier. As much as to say, "Of course! I told you so. The common cry! Lord bless you, we are up to all this sort of thing—myself and human nature."

"Now, gentlemen," said Will Fern, holding out his hands, and flushing for an instant in his haggard face, "see how your laws are made to trap and hunt us when we're brought to this. I tries to live elsewhere. And I'm a vagabond. To jail with him! I comes back here. I goes a-nutting in your woods, and breaks—who don't?—a limber branch or two. To jail with him! One of your keepers sees me in the broad day, near my own patch of garden, with a gun. To jail with him! I has a nat'ral angry word with that man, when I'm free again. To jail with him! I cuts a stick. To jail with him! I eats a rotten apple or a turnip. To jail with him! It's twenty mile away; and coming back I begs a trifle on the road. To jail with him! At last, the constable, the keeper—anybody—finds me anywhere, a-doing anything. To jail with him, for he's a vagrant, and a jail-bird known; and jail's the only home he's got."

The Alderman nodded sagaciously, as who should say. "A very good home too!"

"Do I say this to serve MY cause!" cried Fern. "Who can give me back my liberty, who can give me back my good name, who can give me back my innocent niece? Not all the Lords and Ladies in wide England. But, gentlemen, gentlemen, dealing with other men like me, begin at the right end. Give us, in mercy, better homes when we're a-lying in our cradles; give us better food when we're a-working for our lives; give us kinder laws to bring us back when were a-going wrong; and don't set Jail, Jail, Jail, afore us, everywhere we turn. There an't a condescension you can show the Labourer then, that he won't take, as ready and as grateful as a man can be; for, he has a patient, peaceful, willing heart. But you must put his rightful spirit in him first; for, whether he's a wreck and ruin such as me, or is like one of them that stand here now, his spirit is divided from you at this time. Bring it back, gentlefolks, bring it back! Bring it back, afore the day comes when even his Bible changes in his altered mind, and the words seem to him to read, as they have sometimes read in my own eyes—in jail: 'Whither thou goest, I can Not go; where thou lodgest, I do Not lodge; thy people are Not my people; Nor thy God my God!'"

A sudden stir and agitation took place in Hall. Trotty thought at first, that several had risen to eject the man; and hence this change in its appearance. But, another moment showed him that the room and all the company had vanished from his sight, and that his daughter was again before him, seated at her work. But in a poorer, meaner garret than before; and with no Lilian by her side.

The frame at which she had worked, was put away upon a shelf and covered up. The chair in which she had sat, was turned against the wall. A history was written in these little things, and in Meg's grief-worn face. Oh! who could fail to read it!

Meg strained her eyes upon her work until it was too dark to see the threads; and when the night closed in, she lighted her feeble candle and worked on. Still her old father was invisible about her; looking down upon her; loving her—how dearly loving her!—and talking to her in a tender voice about the old times, and the Bells. Though he knew, poor Trotty, though he knew she could not hear him.

A great part of the evening had worn away, when a knock came at her door. She opened it. A man was on the threshold. A slouching, moody, drunken sloven, wasted by intemperance and vice, and with his matted hair and unshorn beard in wild disorder; but with some traces on him, too, of having been a man of good proportion and good features in his youth.

He stopped until he had her leave to enter; and she, retiring a pace of two from the open door, silently and sorrowfully looked upon him. Trotty had his wish. He saw Richard.

"May I come in, Margaret?"

"Yes! Come in. Come in!"

It was well that Trotty knew him before he spoke; for with any doubt remaining on his mind, the harsh discordant voice would have persuaded him that it was not Richard but some other man.

There were but two chairs in the room. She gave him hers, and stood at some short distance from him, waiting to hear what he had to say.

He sat, however, staring vacantly at the floor; with a lustreless and stupid smile. A spectacle of such deep degradation, of such abject hopelessness, of such a miserable downfall, that she put her hands before her face and turned away, lest he should see how much it moved her.

Roused by the rustling of her dress, or some such trifling sound, he lifted his head, and began to speak as if there had been no pause since he entered.

"Still at work, Margaret? You work late."

"I generally do."

"And early?"

"And early."

"So she said. She said you never tired; or never owned that you tired. Not all the time you lived together. Not even when you fainted, between work and fasting. But I told you that, the last time I came."

"You did," she answered. "And I implored you to tell me nothing more; and you made me a solemn promise, Richard, that you never would."

"A solemn promise," he repeated, with a drivelling laugh and vacant stare. "A solemn promise. To be sure. A solemn promise!" Awakening, as it were, after a time; in the same manner as before; he said with sudden animation:

"How can I help it, Margaret? What am I to do? She has been to me again!"

"Again!" cried Meg, clasping her hands. "O, does she think of me so often! Has she been again!"

"Twenty times again," said Richard. "Margaret, she haunts me. She comes behind me in the street, and thrusts it in my hand. I hear her foot upon the ashes when I'm at my work (ha, ha! that an't often), and before I can turn my head, her voice is in my ear, saying, "Richard, don't look round. For Heaven's love, give her this!" She brings it where I live: she sends it in letters; she taps at the window and lays it on the sill. What *can* I do? Look at it!"

He held out in his hand a little purse, and chinked the money it enclosed.

"Hide it," sad Meg. "Hide it! When she comes again, tell her, Richard, that I love her in my soul. That I never lie down to sleep, but I bless her, and pray for her. That, in my solitary work, I never cease to have her in my thoughts. That she is with me, night and day. That if I died to-morrow, I would remember her with my last breath. But, that I cannot look upon it!"

He slowly recalled his hand, and crushing the purse together, said with a kind of drowsy thoughtfulness:

"I told her so. I told her so, as plain as words could speak. I've taken this gift back and left it at her door, a dozen times since then. But when she came at last, and stood before me, face to face, what could I do?"

"You saw her!" exclaimed Meg. "You saw her! O, Lilian, my sweet girl! O, Lilian, Lilian!"

"I saw her," he went on to say, not answering, but engaged in the same slow pursuit of his own thoughts. "There she stood: trembling! "How does she look, Richard? Does she ever speak of me? Is she thinner? My old place at the table: what's in my old place? And the frame she taught me our old work on—has she burnt it, Richard!" There she was. I heard her say it."

Meg checked her sobs, and with the tears streaming from her eyes, bent over him to listen. Not to lose a breath.

With his arms resting on his knees; and stooping forward in his chair, as if what he said were written on the ground in some half legible character, which it was his occupation to decipher and connect; he went on.

"'Richard, I have fallen very low; and you may guess how much I have suffered in having this sent back, when I can bear to bring it in my hand to you. But you loved her once, even in my memory, dearly. Others stepped in between you; fears, and jealousies, and doubts, and vanities, estranged you from her; but you did love her, even in my memory!' I suppose I did," he said, interrupting himself for a moment. "I did! That's neither here nor there—'O Richard, if you ever did; if you have any memory for what is gone and lost, take it to her once more. Once more! Tell her how I laid my head upon your shoulder, where her own head might have lain, and was so humble to you, Richard. Tell her that you looked into my face, and saw the beauty which she used to praise, all gone: all gone: and in its place, a poor, wan, hollow cheek, that she would weep to see. Tell her everything, and take it back, and she will not refuse again. She will not have the heart!' "

So he sat musing, and repeating the last words, until he woke again, and rose.

"You won't take it, Margaret?"

She shook her head, and motioned an entreaty to him to leave her.

"Good night, Margaret."

"Good night!"

He turned to look upon her; struck by her sorrow, and perhaps by the pity for himself which trembled in her voice. It was a quick and rapid action; and for the moment some flash of his old bearing kindled in his form. In the next he went as he had come. Nor did this glimmer of a quenched fire seem to light him to a quicker sense of his debasement.

In any mood, in any grief, in any torture of the mind or body, Meg's work must be done. She sat down to her task, and plied it. Night, midnight. Still she worked.

She had a meagre fire, the night being very cold; and rose at intervals to mend it. The Chimes rang half-past twelve while she was thus engaged; and when they ceased she heard a gentle knocking at the door. Before she could so much as wonder who was there, at that unusual hour, it opened.

O Youth and Beauty, happy as ye should be, look at this. O Youth and Beauty, blest and blessing all within your reach, and working out the ends of your Beneficent Creator, look at this!

She saw the entering figure; screamed its name; cried "Lilian!"

It was swift, and fell upon its knees before her: clinging to her dress.

"Up, dear! Up! Lilian! My own dearest!"

"Never more, Meg; never more! Here! Here! Close to you, holding to you, feeling your dear breath upon my face!"

"Sweet Lilian! Darling Lilian! Child of my heart—no mother's love can be more tender—lay your head upon my breast!"

"Never more, Meg. Never more! When I first looked into your face, you knelt before me. On my knees before you, let me die. Let it be here!"

"You have come back. My Treasure! We will live together, work together, hope together, die together!"

"Ah! Kiss my lips, Meg; fold your arms about me; press me to your bosom; look kindly on me; but don't raise me. Let it be here. Let me see the last of your dear face upon my knees!"

O Youth and Beauty, happy as ye should be, look at this! O Youth and Beauty, working out the ends of your Beneficent Creator, look at this!

"Forgive me, Meg! So dear, so dear! Forgive me! I know you do, I see you do, but say so, Meg!"

She said so, with her lips on Lilian's cheek. And with her arms twined round—she knew it now—a broken heart.

"His blessing on you, dearest love. Kiss me once more! He suffered her to sit beside His feet, and dry them with her hair. O Meg, what Mercy and Compassion!"

As she died, the Spirit of the child returning, innocent and radiant, touched the old man with its hand, and beckoned him away.

Fourth Quarter

Some new remembrance of the ghostly figures in the Bells; some faint impression of the ringing of the Chimes; some giddy consciousness of having seen the swarm of phantoms reproduced and reproduced until the recollection of them lost itself in the confusion of their numbers; some hurried knowledge, how conveyed to him he knew not, that more years had passed; and Trotty, with the Spirit of the child attending him, stood looking on at mortal company.

Fat company, rosy-cheeked company, comfortable company. They were but two, but they were red enough for ten. They sat before a bright fire, with a small low table between them; and unless the fragrance of hot tea and muffins lingered longer in that room than in most others, the table had seen service very lately. But all the cups and saucers being clean, and in their proper places in the corner-cupboard; and the brass toasting-fork hanging in its usual nook and spreading its four idle fingers out as if it wanted to be measured for a glove; there remained no other visible tokens of the meal just finished, than such as purred and washed their whiskers in the person of the basking cat, and glistened in the gracious, not to say the greasy, faces of her patrons.

This cosy couple (married, evidently) had made a fair division of the fire between them, and sat looking at the glowing sparks that dropped into the grate; now nodding off into a doze; now waking up again when some hot fragment, larger than the rest, came rattling down, as if the fire were coming with it.

It was in no danger of sudden extinction, however; for it gleamed not only in the little room, and on the panes of window-glass in the door, and on the curtain half drawn across them, but in the little shop beyond. A little shop, quite crammed and choked with the abundance of its stock; a perfectly voracious little shop, with a maw as accommodating and full as any shark's. Cheese, butter, firewood, soap, pickles, matches, bacon, table-beer, peg-tops, sweetmeats, boys' kites, bird-seed, cold ham, birch brooms, hearth-stones, salt, vinegar, blacking, red-herrings, stationery, lard, mushroom-ketchup, staylaces, loaves of bread, shuttlecocks, eggs, and slate pencil; everything was fish that came to the net of this greedy little shop, and all articles were in its net. How many other kinds of petty merchandise were there, it would be difficult to say; but balls of packthread, ropes of onions, pounds of candles, cabbage-nets, and brushes, hung in bunches from the ceiling, like extraordinary fruit; while various odd canisters emitting aromatic smells, established the veracity of the inscription over the outer door, which informed the public that the keeper of this little shop was a licensed dealer in tea, coffee, tobacco, pepper, and snuff.

Glancing at such of these articles as were visible in the shining of the blaze, and the less cheerful radiance of two smoky lamps which burnt but dimly in the shop itself, as though its plethora sat heavy on their lungs; and glancing, then, at one of the two faces by the parlour-fire; Trotty had small difficulty in recognising in the stout old lady, Mrs. Chickenstalker: always inclined to corpulency, even in the days when he had known her as established in the general line, and having a small balance against him in her books.

The features of her companion were less easy to him. The great broad chin, with creases in it large enough to hide a finger in; the astonished eyes, that seemed to expostulate with themselves for sinking deeper and deeper into the yielding fat of the soft face; the nose afflicted with that disordered action of its functions which is generally termed The Snuffles; the short thick throat and labouring chest, with other beauties of the like description; though calculated to impress the memory, Trotty could at first allot to nobody he had ever known: and yet he had some recollection of them too. At length, in Mrs. Chickenstalker's partner in the general line, and in the crooked and eccentric line of life, he recognised the former porter of Sir Joseph Bowley; an apoplectic innocent, who had connected himself in Trotty's mind with Mrs. Chickenstalker years ago, by giving him admission to the mansion where he had confessed his obligations to that lady, and drawn on his unlucky head such grave reproach.

Trotty had little interest in a change like this, after the changes he had seen; but association is very strong sometimes; and he looked involuntarily behind the parlour-door, where the accounts of credit customers were usually kept in chalk. There was no record of his name. Some names were there, but they were strange to him, and infinitely fewer than of old; from which he argued that the porter was an advocate of ready-money transactions, and on coming into the business had looked pretty sharp after the Chickenstalker defaulters.

So desolate was Trotty, and so mournful for the youth and promise of his blighted child, that it was a sorrow to him, even to have no place in Mrs. Chickenstalker's ledger.

"What sort of a night is it, Anne?" inquired the former porter of Sir Joseph Bowley, stretching out his legs before the fire, and rubbing as much of them as his short arms could reach; with an air that added, "Here I am if it's bad, and I don't want to go out if it's good."

"Blowing and sleeting hard," returned his wife; "and threatening snow. Dark. And very cold."

"I'm glad to think we had muffins," said the former porter, in the tone of one who had set his conscience at rest. "It's a sort of night that's meant for muffins. Likewise crumpets. Also Sally Lunns."

The former porter mentioned each successive kind of eatable, as if he were musingly summing up his good actions. After which he rubbed his fat legs as before, and jerking them at the knees to get the fire upon the yet unroasted parts, laughed as if somebody had tickled him.

"You're in spirits, Tugby, my dear," observed his wife.

The firm was Tugby, late Chickenstalker.

"No," said Tugby. "No. Not particular. I'm a little elewated. The muffins came so pat!"

With that he chuckled until he was black in the face; and had so much ado to become any other colour, that his fat legs took the strangest excursions into the air. Nor were they reduced to anything like decorum until Mrs. Tugby had thumped him violently on the back, and shaken him as if he were a great bottle.

"Good gracious, goodness, lord-a-mercy bless and save the man!" cried Mrs. Tugby, in great terror. "What's he doing?"

Mr. Tugby wiped his eyes, and faintly repeated that he found himself a little elewated.

"Then don't be so again, that's a dear good soul," said Mrs. Tugby. "if you don't want to frighten me to death, with your struggling and fighting!"

Mr. Tugby said he wouldn't; but, his whole existence was a fight, in which, if any judgment might be founded on the constantly-increasing shortness of his breath, and the deepening purple of his face, he was always getting the worst of it.

"So it's blowing, and sleeting, and threatening snow; and it's dark, and very cold: is it, my dear?" said Mr. Tugby, looking at the fire, and reverting to the cream and marrow of his temporary elevation.

"Hard weather indeed," returned his wife, shaking her head.

"Aye, aye! Years," said Mr. Tugby, "are like Christians in that respect. Some of 'em die hard; some of 'em die easy. This one hasn't many days to run, and is making a fight for it. I like him all the better. There's a customer, my love!"

Attentive to the rattling door, Mrs. Tugby had already risen.

"Now then!" said that lady, passing out into the little shop. "What's wanted? Oh! I beg your pardon, sir, I'm sure. I didn't think it was you."

She made this apology to a gentleman in black, who, with his wristbands tucked up, and his hat cocked loungingly on one side, and his hands in his pockets, sat down astride on the table-beer barrel, and nodded in return.

"This is a bad business up-stairs, Mrs. Tugby," said the gentleman. "The man can't live."

"Not the back-attic can't!" cried Tugby, coming out into the shop to join the conference.

"The back-attic, Mr. Tugby," said the gentleman, "is coming down-stairs fast, and will be below the basement very soon."

Looking by turns at Tugby and his wife, he sounded the barrel with his knuckles for the depth of beer, and having found it, played a tune upon the empty part.

"The back-attic, Mr. Tugby," said the gentleman: Tugby having stood in silent consternation for some time: "is Going."

"Then," said Tugby, turning to his wife, "he must Go, you know, before he's Gone."

"I don't think you can move him," said the gentleman, shaking his head. "I wouldn't take the responsibility of saying it could be done, myself. You had better leave him where he is. He can't live long."

"It's the only subject," said Tugby, bringing the butter-scale down upon the counter with a crash, by weighing his fist on it, "that we've ever had a word upon; she and me; and look what it comes to! He's going to die here, after all. Going to die upon the premises. Going to die in our house!"

"And where should he have died, Tugby?" cried his wife.

"In the workhouse," he returned. "What are workhouses made for?"

"Not for that," said Mrs. Tugby, with great energy. "Not for that! Neither did I marry you for that. Don't think it, Tugby. I won't have it. I won't allow it. I'd be separated first, and never see your face again. When my widow's name stood over that door, as it did for many years: this house being known as Mrs. Chickenstalker's far and wide, and never known but to its honest credit and its good report: when my widow's name stood over that door, Tugby, I knew him as a handsome, steady, manly, independent youth; I knew her as the sweetest-looking, sweetest-tempered girl, eyes ever saw; I knew her father (poor old creetur, he fell down from the steeple walking in his sleep, and killed himself), for the simplest, hardest-working, childest-hearted man, that ever drew the breath of life; and when I turn them out of house and home, may angels turn me out of Heaven. As they would! And serve me right!"

Her old face, which had been a plump and dimpled one before the changes which had come to pass, seemed to shine out of her as she said these words; and when she dried her eyes, and shook her head and her handkerchief at Tugby, with an expression of firmness which it was quite clear was not to be easily resisted, Trotty said. "Bless her! Bless her!"

Then he listened, with a panting heart, for what should follow. Knowing nothing yet, but that they spoke of Meg.

If Tugby had been a little elevated in the parlour, he more than balanced that account by being not a little depressed in the shop, where he now stood staring at his wife, without attempting a reply; secretly conveying, however—either in a fit of abstraction or as a precautionary measure—all the money from the till into his own pockets, as he looked at her.

The gentleman upon the table-beer cask, who appeared to be some authorised medical attendant upon the poor, was far too well accustomed, evidently, to little differences of opinion between man and wife, to interpose any remark in this instance. He sat softly whistling, and turning little drops of beer out of the tap upon the ground, until there was a perfect calm: when he raised his head, and said to Mrs. Tugby, late Chickenstalker:

"There's something interesting about the woman, even now. How did she come to marry him?"

"Why that," said Mrs. Tugby, taking a seat near him. "is not the least cruel part of her story, sir. You see they kept company, she and Richard, many years ago. When they were a young and beautiful couple, everything was settled, and they were to have been married on a New Year's Day. But, somehow, Richard got it into his head, through what the gentlemen told him, that he might do better, and that he'd soon repent it, and that she wasn't good enough for him, and that a young man of spirit had no business to be married. And the gentlemen frightened her, and made her melancholy, and timid of his deserting her, and of her children coming to the gallows, and of its being wicked to be man and wife, and a good deal more of it. And in short, they lingered and lingered, and their trust in one another was broken, and so at last was the match. But the fault was his. She would have married him, sir, joyfully. I've seen her heart swell many times afterwards, when he passed her in a proud and careless way; and never did a woman grieve more truly for a man, than she for Richard when he first went wrong."

"Oh! he went wrong, did he?" said the gentleman, pulling out the vent-peg of the table-beer, and trying to peep down into the barrel through the hole.

"Well, sir, I don't know that he rightly understood himself, you see. I think his mind was troubled by their having broke with one another; and that but for being ashamed before the gentlemen, and perhaps for being uncertain too, how she might take it, he'd have gone through any suffering or trial to have had Meg's promise and Meg's hand again. That's my belief. He never said so; more's the pity! He took to drinking, idling, bad companions: all the fine resources that were to be so much better for him than the Home he might have had. He lost his looks, his character, his health, his strength, his friends, his work: everything!"

"He didn't lose everything, Mrs. Tugby," returned the gentleman, "because he gained a wife; and I want to know how he gained her."

"I'm coming to it, sir, in a moment. This went on for years and years; he sinking lower and lower; she enduring, poor thing, miseries enough to wear her life away. At last, he was so cast down, and cast out, that no one would employ or notice him; and doors were shut upon him, go where he would. Applying from place to place, and door to door; and coming for the hundredth time to one gentleman who had often and often tried him (he was a good workman to the very end); that gentleman, who knew his history, said, 'I believe you are incorrigible; there is only one person in the world who has a chance of reclaiming you; ask me to trust you no more, until she tries to do it.' Something like that, in his anger and vexation."

"Ah!" said the gentleman. "Well?"

"Well, sir, he went to her, and kneeled to her; said it was so; said it ever had been so; and made a prayer to her to save him."

"And she?—Don't distress yourself, Mrs. Tugby."

"She came to me that night to ask me about living here. "What he was once to me," she said, "is buried in a grave, side by side with what I was to him. But I have thought of this; and I will make the trial. In the hope of saving him; for the love of the light-hearted girl (you remember her) who was to have been married on a New Year's Day; and for the love of her Richard." And she said he had come to her from Lilian, and Lilian had trusted to him, and she never could forget that. So they were married; and when they came home here, and I saw them, I hoped that such prophecies as parted them when they were young, may not often fulfil themselves as they did in this case, or I wouldn't be the makers of them for a Mine of Gold."

The gentleman got off the cask, and stretched himself, observing:

"I suppose he used her ill, as soon as they were married?"

"I don't think he ever did that," said Mrs. Tugby, shaking her head, and wiping her eyes. "He went on better for a short time; but, his habits were too old and strong to be got rid of; he soon fell back a little; and was falling fast back, when his illness came so strong upon him. I think he has always felt for her. I am sure he has. I have seen him, in his crying fits and tremblings, try to kiss her hand; and I have heard him call her "Meg," and say it was her nineteenth birthday. There he has been lying, now, these weeks and months. Between him and her baby, she has not been able to do her old work; and by not being able to be regular, she has lost it, even if she could have done it. How they have lived, I hardly know!"

"*I* know," muttered Mr. Tugby; looking at the till, and round the shop, and at his wife; and rolling his head with immense intelligence. "Like Fighting Cocks!"

He was interrupted by a cry—a sound of lamentation—from the upper story of the house. The gentleman moved hurriedly to the door.

"My friend," he said, looking back. "you needn't discuss whether he shall be removed or not. He has spared you that trouble, I believe."

Saying so, he ran up-stairs, followed by Mrs. Tugby; while Mr. Tugby panted and grumbled after them at leisure: being rendered more than commonly short-winded by the weight of the till, in which there had been an inconvenient quantity of copper. Trotty, with the child beside him, floated up the staircase like mere air.

"Follow her! Follow her! Follow her!" He heard the ghostly voices in the Bells repeat their words as he ascended. "Learn it, from the creature dearest to your heart!"

It was over. It was over. And this was she, her father's pride and joy! This haggard, wretched woman, weeping by the bed, if it deserved that name, and pressing to her breast, and hanging down her head upon, an infant. Who can tell how spare, how sickly, and how poor an infant! Who can tell how dear!

"Thank God!" cried Trotty, holding up his folded hands. "O, God be thanked! She loves her child!"

The gentleman, not otherwise hard-hearted or indifferent to such scenes, than that he saw them every day, and knew that they were figures of no moment in the Filer sums—mere scratches in the working of these calculations—laid his hand upon the heart that beat no more, and listened for the breath, and said. "His pain is over. It's better as it is!" Mrs. Tugby tried to comfort her with kindness. Mr. Tugby tried philosophy.

"Come, come!" he said, with his hands in his pockets. "you mustn't give way, you know. That won't do. You must fight up. What would have become of me if *I* had given way when I was porter, and we had as many as six runaway carriage-doubles at our door in one night! But, I fell back upon my strength of mind, and didn't open it!"

Again Trotty heard the voices saying. "Follow her!" He turned towards his guide, and saw it rising from him, passing through the air. "Follow her!" it said. And vanished.

He hovered round her; sat down at her feet; looked up into her face for one trace of her old self; listened for one note of her old pleasant voice. He flitted round the child: so wan, so prematurely old, so dreadful in its gravity, so plaintive in its feeble, mournful, miserable wail. He almost worshipped it. He clung to it as her only safeguard; as the last unbroken link that bound her to endurance. He set his father's hope and trust on the frail baby; watched her every look upon it as she held it in her arms; and cried a thousand times. "She loves it! God be thanked, she loves it!"

He saw the woman tend her in the night; return to her when her grudging husband was asleep, and all was still; encourage her, shed tears with her, set nourishment before her. He saw the day come, and the night again; the day, the night; the time go by; the house of death relieved of death; the room left to herself and to the child; he heard it moan and cry; he saw it harass her, and tire her out, and when she slumbered in exhaustion, drag her back to consciousness, and hold her with its little hands upon the rack; but she was constant to it, gentle with it, patient with it. Patient! Was its loving mother in her inmost heart and soul, and had its Being knitted up with hers as when she carried it unborn.

All this time, she was in want: languishing away, in dire and pining want. With the baby in her arms, she wandered here and there, in quest of occupation; and with its thin face lying in her lap, and looking up in hers, did any work for any wretched sum; a day and night of labour for as many farthings as there were figures on the dial. If she had quarrelled with it; if she had neglected it; if she had looked upon it with a moment's hate; if, in the frenzy of an instant, she had struck it! No. His comfort was, She loved it always.

She told no one of her extremity, and wandered abroad in the day lest she should be questioned by her only friend: for any help she received from her hands, occasioned fresh disputes between the good woman and her husband; and it was new bitterness to be the daily cause of strife and discord, where she owed so much.

She loved it still. She loved it more and more. But a change fell on the aspect of her love. One night.

She was singing faintly to it in its sleep, and walking to and fro to hush it, when her door was softly opened, and a man looked in.

"For the last time," he said.

"William Fern!"

"For the last time."

He listened like a man pursued: and spoke in whispers.

"Margaret, my race is nearly run. I couldn't finish it, without a parting word with you. Without one grateful word."

"What have you done?" she asked: regarding him with terror.

He looked at her, but gave no answer.

After a short silence, he made a gesture with his hand, as if he set her question by; as if he brushed it aside; and said:

"It's long ago, Margaret, now: but that night is as fresh in my memory as ever 'twas. We little thought, then," he added, looking round, "that we should ever meet like this. Your child, Margaret? Let me have it in my arms. Let me hold your child."

He put his hat upon the floor, and took it. And he trembled as he took it, from head to foot.

"Is it a girl?"

"Yes."

He put his hand before its little face.

"See how weak I'm grown, Margaret, when I want the courage to look at it! Let her be, a moment. I won't hurt her. It's long ago, but—What's her name?"

"Margaret," she answered, quickly.

"I'm glad of that," he said. "I'm glad of that!" He seemed to breathe more freely; and after pausing for an instant, took away his hand, and looked upon the infant's face. But covered it again, immediately.

"Margaret!" he said; and gave her back the child. "It's Lilian's."

"Lilian's!"

"I held the same face in my arms when Lilian's mother died and left her."

"When Lilian's mother died and left her!" she repeated, wildly.

"How shrill you speak! Why do you fix your eyes upon me so? Margaret!"

She sunk down in a chair, and pressed the infant to her breast, and wept over it. Sometimes, she released it from her embrace, to look anxiously in its face: then strained it to her bosom again. At those times, when she gazed upon it, then it was that something fierce and terrible began to mingle with her love. Then it was that her old father quailed.

"Follow her!" was sounded through the house. "Learn it, from the creature dearest to your heart!"

"Margaret," said Fern, bending over her, and kissing her upon the brow: "I thank you for the last time. Good night. Good bye! Put your hand in mine, and tell me you'll forget me from this hour, and try to think the end of me was here."

"What have you done?" she asked again.

"There'll be a Fire to-night," he said, removing from her. "There'll be Fires this winter-time, to light the dark nights, East, West, North, and South. When you see the distant sky red, they'll be blazing. When you see the distant sky red, think of me no more; or, if you do, remember what a Hell was lighted up inside of me, and think you see its flames reflected in the clouds. Good night. Good bye!"

She called to him; but he was gone. She sat down stupefied, until her infant roused her to a sense of hunger, cold, and darkness. She paced the room with it the livelong night, hushing it and soothing it. She said at intervals. "Like Lilian, when her mother died and left her!" Why was her step so quick, her eye so wild, her love so fierce and terrible, whenever she repeated those words?

"But, it is Love," said Trotty. "It is Love. She'll never cease to love it. My poor Meg!"

She dressed the child next morning with unusual care—ah, vain expenditure of care upon such squalid robes!—and once more tried to find some means of life. It was the last day of the Old Year. She tried till night, and never broke her fast. She tried in vain.

She mingled with an abject crowd, who tarried in the snow, until it pleased some officer appointed to dispense the public charity (the lawful charity; not that once preached upon a Mount), to call them in, and question them, and say to this one, "go to such a place," to that one, "come next week"; to make a football of another wretch, and pass him here and there, from hand to hand, from house to house, until he wearied and lay down to die; or started up and robbed, and so became a higher sort of criminal, whose claims allowed of no delay. Here, too, she failed. She loved her child, and wished to have it lying on her breast. And that was quite enough.

It was night: a bleak, dark, cutting night: when, pressing the child close to her for warmth, she arrived outside the house she called her home. She was so faint and giddy, that she saw no one standing in the doorway until she was close upon it, and about to enter. Then, she recognised the master of the house, who had so disposed himself—with his person it was not difficult—as to fill up the whole entry.

"Oh!" he said softly. "You have come back?"

She looked at the child, and shook her head.

"Don't you think you have lived here long enough without paying any rent? Don't you think that, without any money, you've been a pretty constant customer at this shop, now?" said Mr. Tugby.

She repeated the same mute appeal.

"Suppose you try and deal somewhere else," he said. "And suppose you provide yourself with another lodging. Come! Don't you think you could manage it?"

She said in a low voice, that it was very late. To-morrow.

"Now I see what you want," said Tugby; "and what you mean. You know there are two parties in this house about you, and you delight in setting 'em by the ears. I don't want any quarrels; I'm speaking softly to avoid a quarrel; but if you don't go away, I'll speak out loud, and you shall cause words high enough to please you. But you shan't come in. That I am determined."

She put her hair back with her hand, and looked in a sudden manner at the sky, and the dark lowering distance.

"This is the last night of an Old Year, and I won't carry ill-blood and quarrellings and disturbances into a New One, to please you nor anybody else," said Tugby, who was quite a retail Friend and Father. "I wonder you an't ashamed of yourself, to carry such practices into a New Year. If you haven't any business in the world, but to be always giving way, and always making disturbances between man and wife, you'd be better out of it. Go along with you."

"Follow her! To desperation!"

Again the old man heard the voices. Looking up, he saw the figures hovering in the air, and pointing where she went, down the dark street.

"She loves it!" he exclaimed, in agonised entreaty for her. "Chimes! she loves it still!"

"Follow her!" The shadow swept upon the track she had taken, like a cloud.

He joined in the pursuit; he kept close to her; he looked into her face. He saw the same fierce and terrible expression mingling with her love, and kindling in her eyes. He heard her say. "Like Lilian! To be changed like Lilian!" and her speed redoubled.

Oh, for something to awaken her! For any sight, or sound, or scent, to call up tender recollections in a brain on fire! For any gentle image of the Past, to rise before her!

"I was her father! I was her father!" cried the old man, stretching out his hands to the dark shadows flying on above. "Have mercy on her, and on me! Where does she go? Turn her back! I was her father!"

But they only pointed to her, as she hurried on; and said. "To desperation! Learn it from the creature dearest to your heart!" A hundred voices echoed it. The air was made of breath expended in those words. He seemed to take them in, at every gasp he drew. They were everywhere, and not to be escaped. And still she hurried on; the same light in her eyes, the same words in her mouth. "Like Lilian! To be changed like Lilian!"

All at once she stopped.

"Now, turn her back!" exclaimed the old man, tearing his white hair. "My child! Meg! Turn her back! Great Father, turn her back!"

In her own scanty shawl, she wrapped the baby warm. With her fevered hands, she smoothed its limbs, composed its face, arranged its mean attire. In her wasted arms she folded it, as though she never would resign it more. And with her dry lips, kissed it in a final pang, and last long agony of Love.

Putting its tiny hand up to her neck, and holding it there, within her dress, next to her distracted heart, she set its sleeping face against her: closely, steadily, against her: and sped onward to the river.

To the rolling River, swift and dim, where Winter Night sat brooding like the last dark thoughts of many who had sought a refuge there before her. Where scattered lights upon the banks gleamed sullen, red, and dull, as torches that were burning there, to show the way to Death. Where no abode of living people cast its shadow, on the deep, impenetrable, melancholy shade.

To the River! To that portal of Eternity, her desperate footsteps tended with the swiftness of its rapid waters running to the sea. He tried to touch her as she passed him, going down to its dark level: but, the wild distempered form, the fierce and terrible love, the desperation that had left all human check or hold behind, swept by him like the wind.

He followed her. She paused a moment on the brink, before the dreadful plunge. He fell down on his knees, and in a shriek addressed the figures in the Bells now hovering above them.

"I have learnt it!" cried the old man. "From the creature dearest to my heart! Oh, save her, save her!"

He could wind his fingers in her dress; could hold it! As the words escaped his lips, he felt his sense of touch return, and knew that he detained her.

The figures looked down steadfastly upon him.

"I have learnt it!" cried the old man. "Oh, have mercy on me in this hour, if, in my love for her, so young and good, I slandered Nature in the breasts of mothers rendered desperate! Pity my presumption, wickedness, and ignorance, and save her."

He felt his hold relaxing. They were silent still.

"Have mercy on her!" he exclaimed. "as one in whom this dreadful crime has sprung from Love perverted; from the strongest, deepest Love we fallen creatures know! Think what her misery must have been, when such seed bears such fruit! Heaven meant her to be good. There is no loving mother on the earth who might not come to this, if such a life had gone before. Oh, have mercy on my child, who, even at this pass, means mercy to her own, and dies herself, and perils her immortal soul, to save it!"

She was in his arms. He held her now. His strength was like a giant's.

"I see the Spirit of the Chimes among you!" cried the old man, singling out the child, and speaking in some inspiration, which their looks conveyed to him. "I know that our inheritance is held in store for us by Time. I know there is a sea of Time to rise one day, before which all who wrong us or oppress us will be swept away like leaves. I see it, on the flow! I know that we must trust and hope, and neither doubt ourselves, nor doubt the good in one another. I have learnt it from the creature dearest to my heart. I clasp her in my arms again. Oh Spirits, merciful and good, I take your lesson to my breast along with her! Oh Spirits, merciful and good, I am grateful!"

He might have said more; but the Bells, the old familiar Bells, his own dear, constant, steady friends, the Chimes, began to ring the joy-peals for a New Year: so lustily, so merrily, so happily, so gaily, that he leapt upon his feet, and broke the spell that bound him.

"And whatever you do, father," said Meg, "don't eat tripe again, without asking some doctor whether it's likely to agree with you; for how you *have* been going on, Good gracious!"

She was working with her needle, at the little table by the fire; dressing her simple gown with ribbons for her wedding. So quietly happy, so blooming and youthful, so full of beautiful promise, that he uttered a great cry as if it were an Angel in his house; then flew to clasp her in his arms.

But, he caught his feet in the newspaper, which had fallen on the hearth; and somebody came rushing in between them.

"No!" cried the voice of this same somebody; a generous and jolly voice it was! "Not even you. Not even you. The first kiss of Meg in the New Year is mine. Mine! I have been waiting outside the house, this hour, to hear the Bells and claim it. Meg, my precious prize, a happy year! A life of happy years, my darling wife!"

And Richard smothered her with kisses.

You never in all your life saw anything like Trotty after this. I don't care where you have lived or what you have seen; you never in all your life saw anything at all approaching him! He sat down in his chair and beat his knees and cried; he sat down in his chair and beat his knees and laughed; he sat down in his chair and beat his knees and laughed and cried together; he got out of his chair and hugged Meg; he got out of his chair and hugged Richard; he got out of his chair and hugged them both at once; he kept running up to Meg, and squeezing her fresh face between his hands and kissing it, going from her backwards not to lose sight of it, and running up again like a figure in a magic lantern; and whatever he did, he was constantly sitting himself down in his chair, and never stopping in it for one single moment; being—that's the truth—beside himself with joy.

"And to-morrow's your wedding-day, my pet!" cried Trotty. "Your real, happy wedding-day!"

"To-day!" cried Richard, shaking hands with him. "To-day. The Chimes are ringing in the New Year. Hear them!"

They WERE ringing! Bless their sturdy hearts, they were ringing! Great Bells as they were; melodious, deep-mouthed, noble Bells; cast in no common metal; made by no common founder; when had they ever chimed like that, before!

"But, to-day, my pet," said Trotty. "You and Richard had some words to-day."

"Because he's such a bad fellow, father," said Meg. "An't you, Richard? Such a headstrong, violent man! He'd have made no more of speaking his mind to that great Alderman, and putting *him* down I don't know where, than he would of—"

"—Kissing Meg," suggested Richard. Doing it too!

"No. Not a bit more," said Meg. "But I wouldn't let him, father. Where would have been the use!"

"Richard my boy!" cried Trotty. "You was turned up Trumps originally; and Trumps you must be, till you die! But, you were crying by the fire to-night, my pet, when I came home! Why did you cry by the fire?"

"I was thinking of the years we've passed together, father. Only that. And thinking that you might miss me, and be lonely."

Trotty was backing off to that extraordinary chair again, when the child, who had been awakened by the noise, came running in half-dressed.

"Why, here she is!" cried Trotty, catching her up. "Here's little Lilian! Ha ha ha! Here we are and here we go! O here we are and here we go again! And here we are and here we go! and Uncle Will too!" Stopping in his trot to greet him heartily. "O, Uncle Will, the vision that I've had to-night, through lodging you! O, Uncle Will, the obligations that you've laid me under, by your coming, my good friend!"

Before Will Fern could make the least reply, a band of music burst into the room, attended by a lot of neighbours, screaming "A Happy New Year, Meg!" "A Happy Wedding!" "Many of 'em!" and other fragmentary good wishes of that sort. The Drum (who was a private friend of Trotty's) then stepped forward, and said:

"Trotty Veck, my boy! It's got about, that your daughter is going to be married to-morrow. There an't a soul that knows you that don't wish you well, or that knows her and don't wish her well. Or that knows you both, and don't wish you both all the happiness the New Year can bring. And here we are, to play it in and dance it in, accordingly."

Which was received with a general shout. The Drum was rather drunk, by-the-bye; but, never mind.

"What a happiness it is, I'm sure," said Trotty. "to be so esteemed! How kind and neighbourly you are! It's all along of my dear daughter. She deserves it!"

They were ready for a dance in half a second (Meg and Richard at the top); and the Drum was on the very brink of feathering away with all his power; when a combination of prodigious sounds was heard outside, and a good-humoured comely woman of some fifty years of age, or thereabouts, came running in, attended by a man bearing a stone pitcher of terrific size, and closely followed by the marrow-bones and cleavers, and the bells; not *the* Bells, but a portable collection on a frame.

Trotty said. "It's Mrs. Chickenstalker!" And sat down and beat his knees again.

"Married, and not tell me, Meg!" cried the good woman. "Never! I couldn't rest on the last night of the Old Year without coming to wish you joy. I couldn't have done it, Meg. Not if I had been bed-ridden. So here I am; and as it's New Year's Eve, and the Eve of your wedding too, my dear, I had a little flip made, and brought it with me."

Mrs. Chickenstalker's notion of a little flip did honour to her character. The pitcher steamed and smoked and reeked like a volcano; and the man who had carried it, was faint.

"Mrs. Tugby!" said Trotty, who had been going round and round her, in an ecstasy.—"I *should* say, Chickenstalker—Bless your heart and soul! A Happy New Year, and many of 'em! Mrs. Tugby," said Trotty when he had saluted her;—"I *should* say, Chickenstalker—This is William Fern and Lilian."

The worthy dame, to his surprise, turned very pale and very red.

"Not Lilian Fern whose mother died in Dorsetshire!" said she.

Her uncle answered 'Yes," and meeting hastily, they exchanged some hurried words together; of which the upshot was, that Mrs. Chickenstalker shook him by both hands; saluted Trotty on his cheek again of her own free will; and took the child to her capacious breast.

"Will Fern!" said Trotty, pulling on his right-hand muffler. "Not the friend you was hoping to find?"

"Ay!" returned Will, putting a hand on each of Trotty's shoulders. "And like to prove a'most as good a friend, if that can be, as one I found."

"O!" said Trotty. "Please to play up there. Will you have the goodness!"

To the music of the band, and, the bells, the marrow-bones and cleavers, all at once; and while the Chimes were yet in lusty operation out of doors; Trotty, making Meg and Richard second couple, led off Mrs. Chickenstalker down the dance, and danced it in a step unknown before or since; founded on his own peculiar trot.

Had Trotty dreamed? Or, are his joys and sorrows, and the actors in them, but a dream; himself a dream; the teller of this tale a dreamer, waking but now? If it be so, O listener, dear to him in all his visions, try to bear in mind the stern realities from which these shadows come; and in your sphere—none is too wide, and none too limited for such an end—endeavour to correct, improve, and soften them. So may the New Year be a happy one to you, happy to many more whose happiness depends on you! So may each year be happier than the last, and not the meanest of our brethren or sisterhood debarred their rightful share, in what our Great Creator formed them to enjoy.

THE CRICKET ON THE HEARTH

Chirp the First

THE KETTLE BEGAN IT! DON'T TELL ME WHAT MRS. PEERYBINGLE SAID. I know better. Mrs. Peerybingle may leave it on record to the end of time that she couldn't say which of them began it; but, I say the Kettle did. I ought to know, I hope? The Kettle began it, full five minutes by the little waxy-faced Dutch clock in the corner before the Cricket uttered a chirp.

As if the clock hadn't finished striking, and the convulsive little Haymaker at the top of it, jerking away right and left with a scythe in front of a Moorish Palace, hadn't mowed down half an acre of imaginary grass before the Cricket joined in at all!

Why, I am not naturally positive. Every one knows that. I wouldn't set my own opinion against the opinion of Mrs. Peerybingle, unless I were quite sure, on any account whatever. Nothing should induce me. But this is a question of act. And the fact is, that the Kettle began it, at least five minutes before the Cricket gave any sign of being in existence. Contradict me: and I'll say ten.

Let me narrate exactly how it happened. I should have proceeded to do so, in my very first word, but for this plain consideration—if I am to tell a story I must begin at the beginning; and how is it possible to begin at the beginning, without beginning at the Kettle?

It appeared as if there were a sort of match, or trial of skill, you must understand, between the Kettle and the Cricket. And this is what led to it, and how it came about.

Mrs. Peerybingle going out into the raw twilight, and clicking over the wet stones in a pair of pattens that worked innumerable rough impressions of the first proposition in Euclid all about the yard—Mrs. Peerybingle filled the Kettle at the water butt. Presently returning, less the pattens: and a good deal less, for they were tall and Mrs. Peerybingle was but short: she set the Kettle on the fire. In doing which she lost her temper, or mislaid it for an instant; for, the water—being uncomfortably cold, and in that slippy, slushy, sleety sort of state wherein it seems to penetrate through every kind of substance, patten rings included—had laid hold of Mrs. Peerybingle's toes, and even splashed her legs. And when we rather plume ourselves (with reason too) upon our legs, and keep ourselves particularly neat in point of stockings, we find this, for the moment, hard to bear.

Besides, the Kettle was aggravating and obstinate. It wouldn't allow itself to be adjusted on the top bar; it wouldn't hear of accommodating itself kindly to the knobs of coal: it would lean forward with a drunken air, and dribble, a very Idiot of a Kettle, on the hearth. It was quarrelsome; and hissed and spluttered morosely at the fire. To sum up all, the lid, resisting Mrs. Peerybingle's fingers, first of all turned topsy-turvy, and then, with an ingenious pertinacity deserving of a better cause, dived sideways in—down to the very bottom of the Kettle. And the hull of the *Royal George* has never made half the monstrous resistance to coming out of the water, which the lid of that Kettle employed against Mrs. Peerybingle, before she got it up again.

It looked sullen and pig-headed enough, even then; carrying its handle with an air of defiance, and cocking its spout pertly and mockingly at Mrs. Peerybingle, as if it said, "I won't boil. Nothing shall induce me!"

But Mrs. Peerybingle, with restored good humour, dusted her chubby little hands against each other, and sat down before the Kettle: laughing. Meantime, the jolly blaze uprose and fell, flashing and gleaming on the little Haymaker at the top of the Dutch clock, until one might have thought he stood stock still before the Moorish Palace, and nothing was in motion but the flame.

He was on the move, however; and had his spasms, two to the second, all right and regular. But his sufferings when the clock was going to strike, were frightful to behold; and when a Cuckoo looked out of a trap-door in the Palace, and gave note six times, it shook him, each time, like a spectral voice—or like a something wiry, plucking at his legs.

It was not until a violent commotion and a whirring noise among the weights and ropes below him had quite subsided, that this terrified Haymaker became himself again. Nor was he startled without reason; for these rattling, bony skeletons of clocks are very disconcerting in their operation, and I wonder very much how any set of men, but most of all how Dutchmen, can have had a liking to invent them. There is a popular belief that Dutchmen love broad cases and much clothing for their own lower selves; and they might know better than to leave their clocks so very lank and unprotected, surely.

Now it was, you observe, that the Kettle began to spend the evening. Now it was, that the Kettle, growing mellow and musical, began to have irrepressible gurglings in its throat, and to indulge in short vocal snorts, which it checked in the bud, as if it hadn't quite made up its mind yet, to be good company. Now it was, that after two or three such vain attempts to stifle its convivial sentiments, it threw off all moroseness, all reserve, and burst into a stream of song so cosy and hilarious, as never maudlin nightingale yet formed the least idea of.

So plain, too! Bless you, you might have understood it like a book—better than some books you and I could name, perhaps. With its warm breath gushing forth in a light cloud which merrily and gracefully ascended a few feet, then hung about the chimney-corner as its own domestic Heaven, it trolled its song with that strong energy of cheerfulness, that its iron body hummed and stirred upon the fire; and the lid itself, the recently rebellious lid—such is the influence of a bright example—performed a sort of jig, and clattered like a deaf and dumb young cymbal that had never known the use of its twin brother.

That this song of the Kettle's was a song of invitation and welcome to somebody out of doors; to somebody at that moment coming on, towards the snug small home and the crisp fire; there is no doubt whatever. Mrs. Peerybingle knew it, perfectly, as she sat musing before the hearth. It's a dark night, sang the Kettle, and the rotten leaves are lying by the way; and, above, all is mist and darkness, and, below, all is mire and clay; and there's only one relief in all the sad and murky air; and I don't know that it is one, for it's nothing but a glare, of deep and angry crimson, where the sun and wind together, set a brand upon the clouds for being guilty of such weather; and the widest open country is a long dull streak of black; and there's hoar-frost on the finger-post, and thaw upon the track; and the ice it isn't water, and the water isn't free; and you couldn't say that anything is what it ought to be; but he's coming, coming, coming!—

And here, if you like, the Cricket DID chime in! with a Chirrup, Chirrup, Chirrup of such magnitude, by way of chorus; with a voice, so astoundingly disproportionate to its size, as compared with the Kettle; (size! you couldn't See it!) that if it had then and there burst itself like an overcharged gun: if it had fallen a victim on the spot, and chirruped its little body into fifty pieces: it would have seemed a natural and inevitable consequence, for which it had expressly laboured.

The Kettle had had the last of its solo performance. It persevered with undiminished ardour; but the Cricket took first fiddle and kept it. Good Heaven, how it chirped! Its shrill, sharp, piercing voice resounded through the house, and seemed to twinkle in the outer darkness like a Star. There was an indescribable little trill and tremble in it, at its loudest, which suggested its being carried off its legs, and made to leap again, by its own intense enthusiasm. Yet they went very well together, the Cricket and the Kettle. The burden of the song was still the same; and louder, louder, louder still, they sang it in their emulation.

The fair little listener; for fair she was, and young—though something of what is called the dumpling shape; but I don't myself object to that—lighted a candle, glanced at the Haymaker on the top of the clock, who was getting in a pretty average crop of minutes; and looked out of the window, where she saw nothing, owing to the darkness, but her own face imaged in the glass. And my opinion is (and so would yours have been), that she might have looked a long way, and seen nothing half so agreeable. When she came back, and sat down in her former seat, the Cricket and the

Kettle were still keeping it up, with a perfect fury of competition. The Kettle's weak side clearly being, that he didn't know when he was beat.

There was all the excitement of a race about it. Chirp, chirp, chirp! Cricket a mile ahead. Hum, hum, hum—m—m! Kettle making play in the distance, like a great top. Chirp, chirp, chirp! Cricket round the corner. Hum, hum, hum—m—m! Kettle sticking to him in his own way; no idea of giving in. Chirp, chirp, chirp! Cricket fresher than ever. Hum, hum, hum—m—m! Kettle slow and steady. Chirp, chirp, chirp! Cricket going in to finish him. Hum, hum, hum—m—m! Kettle not to be finished. Until at last they got so jumbled together, in the hurry-skurry, helter-skelter, of the match, that whether the Kettle chirped and the Cricket hummed, or the Cricket chirped and the Kettle hummed, or they both chirped and both hummed, it would have taken a clearer head than yours or mine to have decided with anything like certainty. But of this, there is no doubt: that the Kettle and the Cricket, at one and the same moment, and by some power of amalgamation best known to themselves, sent, each, his fireside song of comfort streaming into a ray of the candle that shone out through the window; and a long way down the lane. And this light, bursting on a certain person who, on the instant, approached towards it through the gloom, expressed the whole thing to him, literally in a twinkling, and cried, "Welcome home, old fellow! Welcome home, my boy!"

This end attained, the Kettle, being dead beat, boiled over, and was taken off the fire. Mrs. Peerybingle then went running to the door, where, what with the wheels of a cart, the tramp of a horse, the voice of a man, the tearing in and out of an excited dog, and the surprising and mysterious appearance of a Baby, there was soon the very What's-his-name to pay.

Where the Baby came from, or how Mrs. Peerybingle got hold of it in that flash of time, *I* don't know. But a live Baby there was, in Mrs. Peerybingle's arms; and a pretty tolerable amount of pride she seemed to have in it, when she was drawn gently to the fire, by a sturdy figure of a man, much taller and much older than herself, who had to stoop a long way down, to kiss her. But she was worth the trouble. Six foot six, with the lumbago, might have done it.

"Oh goodness, John!" said Mrs. P. "What a state you are in with the weather!"

He was something the worse for it, undeniably. The thick mist hung in clots upon his eyelashes like candied thaw; and between the fog and fire together, there were rainbows in his very whiskers.

"Why, you see, Dot," John made answer, slowly, as he unrolled a shawl from about his throat; and warmed his hands; "it—it an't exactly summer weather. So, no wonder."

"I wish you wouldn't call me Dot, John. I don't like it," said Mrs. Peerybingle: pouting in a way that clearly showed she *did* like it, very much.

"Why what else are you?" returned John, looking down upon her with a smile, and giving her waist as light a squeeze as his huge hand and arm could give. "A dot and"—here he glanced at the Baby—"a dot and carry—I won't say it, for fear I should spoil it; but I was very near a joke. I don't know as ever I was nearer."

He was often near to something or other very clever, by his own account: this lumbering, slow, honest John; this John so heavy, but so light of spirit; so rough upon the surface, but so gentle at the core; so dull without, so quick within; so stolid, but so good! Oh Mother Nature, give thy children the true Poetry of Heart that hid itself in this poor Carrier's breast—he was but a Carrier by the way—and we can bear to have them talking Prose, and leading lives of prose; and bear to bless Thee for their company!

It was pleasant to see Dot, with her little figure, and her Baby in her arms: a very doll of a Baby: glancing with a coquettish thoughtfulness at the fire, and inclining her delicate little head just enough on one side to let it rest in an odd, half-natural, half-affected, wholly nestling and agreeable manner, on the great rugged figure of the Carrier. It was pleasant to see him, with his tender awkwardness, endeavouring to adapt his rude support to her slight need, and make his burly middle-age a leaning-staff not inappropriate to her blooming youth. It was pleasant to observe how Tilly Slowboy, waiting in the background for the Baby, took special cognizance (though in her earliest teens) of this grouping; and stood with her mouth and eyes wide open, and her head thrust forward, taking it in as if it were air. Nor was it less agreeable to observe how John the Carrier, reference being made by Dot to the aforesaid Baby, checked his hand when on the point of touching the infant, as if he thought he might crack it; and bending down, surveyed it from a safe distance, with a kind of puzzled pride, such as an amiable mastiff might be supposed to show, if he found himself, one day, the father of a young canary.

"An't he beautiful, John? Don't he look precious in his sleep?"

"Very precious," said John. "Very much so. He generally *is* asleep, an't he?"

"Lor John! Good gracious no!"

"Oh," said John, pondering. "I thought his eyes was generally shut. Halloa!"

"Goodness John, how you startle one!"

"It an't right for him to turn 'em up in that way!" said the astonished Carrier, "is it? See how he's winking with both of 'em at once! And look at his mouth! Why he's gasping like a gold and silver fish!"

"You don't deserve to be a father, you don't," said Dot, with all the dignity of an experienced matron. "But how should you know what little complaints children are troubled with, John! You wouldn't so much as know their names, you stupid fellow." And when she had turned the Baby over on her left arm, and had slapped its back as a restorative, she pinched her husband's ear, laughing.

"No," said John, pulling off his outer coat. "It's very true, Dot. I don't know much about it. I only know that I've been fighting pretty stiffly with the Wind to-night. It's been blowing north-east, straight into the cart, the whole way home."

"Poor old man, so it has!" cried Mrs. Peerybingle, instantly becoming very active. "Here! Take the precious darling, Tilly, while I make myself of some use. Bless it, I could smother it with kissing it; I could! Hie then, good dog! Hie Boxer, boy! Only let me make the tea first, John; and then I'll help you with the parcels, like a busy bee. 'How doth the little'—and all the rest of it, you know, John. Did you ever learn 'how doth the little,' when you went to school, John?"

"Not to quite know it," John returned. "I was very near it once. But I should only have spoilt it, I dare say."

"Ha ha," laughed Dot. She had the blithest little laugh you ever heard. "What a dear old darling of a dunce you are, John, to be sure!"

Not at all disputing this position, John went out to see that the boy with the lantern, which had been dancing to and fro before the door and window, like a Will of the Wisp, took due care of the horse; who was fatter than you would quite believe, if I gave you his measure, and so old that his birthday was lost in the mists of antiquity. Boxer, feeling that his attentions were due to the family in general, and must be impartially distributed, dashed in and out with bewildering inconstancy; now describing a circle of short barks round the horse, where he was being rubbed down at the stable-door; now feigning to make savage rushes at his mistress, and facetiously bringing himself to sudden stops; now eliciting a shriek from Tilly Slowboy, in the low nursing-chair near the fire, by the unexpected application of his moist nose to her countenance; now exhibiting an obtrusive interest in the Baby; now going round and round upon the hearth, and lying down as if he had established himself for the night; now getting up again, and taking that nothing of a fag-end of a tail of his, out into the weather, as if he had just remembered an appointment, and was off, at a round trot, to keep it.

"There! There's the teapot, ready on the hob!" said Dot; as briskly busy as a child at play at keeping house. "And there's the old knuckle of ham; and there's the butter; and there's the crusty loaf, and all! Here's the clothes-basket for the small parcels, John, if you've got any there—where are you, John? Don't let the dear child fall under the grate, Tilly, whatever you do!"

It may be noted of Miss Slowboy, in spite of her rejecting the caution with some vivacity, that she had a rare and surprising talent for getting this Baby into difficulties: and had several times imperilled its short life, in a quiet way peculiarly her own. She was of a spare and straight shape, this young lady, insomuch that her garments appeared to be in constant danger of sliding off those sharp pegs, her shoulders, on which they were loosely hung. Her costume was remarkable for the partial development, on all possible occasions, of some flannel vestment of a singular structure; also for affording glimpses, in the region of the back, of a corset, or pair of stays, in colour a dead-green. Being always in a state of gaping admiration at everything, and absorbed, besides, in the perpetual contemplation of her mistress's perfections and the Baby's, Miss Slowboy, in her little errors of judgment, may be said to have done equal honour to her head and to her heart; and though these did less honour to the Baby's head, which they were the occasional means of bringing into contact with deal doors, dressers, stair-rails, bed posts, and other foreign substances, still they were the honest results of Tilly Slowboy's constant astonishment at finding herself so kindly treated, and installed in such a comfortable home. For the maternal and paternal Slowboy were alike unknown to Fame, and Tilly had been bred by public charity, a Foundling; which word, though only differing from Fondling by one vowel's length, is very different in meaning, and expresses quite another thing.

To have seen little Mrs. Peerybingle come back with her husband; tugging at the clothes-basket, and making the most strenuous exertions to do nothing at all (for he carried it); would have amused you almost as much as it amused him. It may have entertained the Cricket too, for anything I know; but, certainly, it now began to chirp again, vehemently.

"Heyday!" said John, in his slow way. "It's merrier than ever, to-night, I think."

"And it's sure to bring us good fortune, John! It always has done so. To have a Cricket on the Hearth, is the luckiest thing in all the world!"

John looked at her as if he had very nearly got the thought into his head, that she was his Cricket in chief, and he quite agreed with her. But it was probably one of his narrow escapes, for he said nothing.

"The first time I heard its cheerful little note, John, was on that night when you brought me home—when you brought me to my new home here; its little mistress. Nearly a year ago. You recollect, John?"

O yes. John remembered. I should think so!

"Its chirp was such a welcome to me! It seemed so full of promise and encouragement. It seemed to say, you would be kind and gentle with me, and would not expect (I had a fear of that, John, then) to find an old head on the shoulders of your foolish little wife."

John thoughtfully patted one of the shoulders, and then the head, as though he would have said No, no; he had had no such expectation; he had been quite content to take them as they were. And really he had reason. They were very comely.

"It spoke the truth, John, when it seemed to say so; for you have ever been, I am sure, the best, the most considerate, the most affectionate of husbands to me. This has been a happy home, John; and I love the Cricket for its sake!"

"Why so do I then," said the Carrier. "So do I, Dot."

"I love it for the many times I have heard it, and the many thoughts its harmless music has given me. Sometimes, in the twilight, when I have felt a little solitary and down-hearted, John—before Baby was here to keep me company and make the house gay; when I have thought how lonely you would be if I should die; how lonely I should be if I could know that you had lost me, dear; its Chirp, Chirp, Chirp upon the hearth, has seemed to tell me of another little voice, so sweet, so very dear to me, before whose coming sound, my trouble vanished like a dream. And when I used to fear—I did fear once, John, I was very young you know—that ours might prove to be an ill-assorted marriage: I being such a child, and you more like my guardian than my husband; and that you might not, however hard you tried, be able to learn to love me, as you hoped and prayed you might; its Chirp, Chirp, Chirp has cheered me up again, and filled me with new trust and confidence. I was thinking of these things to-night, dear, when I sat expecting you; and I love the Cricket for their sake!"

"And so do I," repeated John. "But, Dot? *I* hope and pray that I might learn to love you? How you talk! I had learnt that, long before I brought you here, to be the Cricket's little mistress, Dot!"

She laid her hand, an instant, on his arm, and looked up at him with an agitated face, as if she would have told him something. Next moment she was down upon her knees before the basket, speaking in a sprightly voice, and busy with the parcels.

"There are not many of them to-night, John, but I saw some goods behind the cart, just now; and though they give more trouble, perhaps, still they pay as well; so we have no reason to grumble, have we? Besides, you have been delivering, I dare say, as you came along?"

"Oh yes," John said. "A good many."

"Why what's this round box? Heart alive, John, it's a wedding-cake!"

"Leave a woman alone to find out that," said John, admiringly. "Now a man would never have thought of it. Whereas, it's my belief that if you was to pack a wedding-cake up in a tea-chest, or a turn-up bedstead, or a pickled salmon keg, or any unlikely thing, a woman would be sure to find it out directly. Yes; I called for it at the pastry-cook's."

"And it weighs I don't know what—whole hundredweights!" cried Dot, making a great demonstration of trying to lift it. "Whose is it, John? Where is it going?"

"Read the writing on the other side," said John.

"Why, John! My Goodness, John!"

"Ah! Who'd have thought it!" John returned.

"You never mean to say," pursued Dot, sitting on the floor and shaking her head at him, "that it's Gruff and Tackleton the toymaker!"

John nodded.

Mrs. Peerybingle nodded also, fifty times at least. Not in assent—in dumb and pitying amazement; screwing up her lips the while with all their little force (they were never made for screwing up; I am clear of that), and looking the good Carrier through and through, in her abstraction. Miss Slowboy, in the mean time, who had a mechanical power of reproducing scraps of current conversation for the delectation of the Baby, with all the sense struck out of them, and all the Nouns changed into the Plural number, inquired aloud of that young creature, Was it Gruffs and Tackletons the toymakers then, and Would it call at Pastry-cooks for wedding-cakes, and Did its mothers know the boxes when its fathers brought them homes; and so on.

"And that is really to come about!" said Dot. "Why, she and I were girls at school together, John."

He might have been thinking of her, or nearly thinking of her, perhaps, as she was in that same school time. He looked upon her with a thoughtful pleasure, but he made no answer.

"And he's as old! As unlike her!—Why, how many years older than you, is Gruff and Tackleton, John?"

"How many more cups of tea shall I drink to-night at one sitting, than Gruff and Tackleton ever took in four, I wonder!" replied John, good-humouredly, as he drew a chair to the round table, and began at the cold Ham. "As to eating, I eat but little; but that little I enjoy, Dot."

Even this, his usual sentiment at meal times, one of his innocent delusions (for his appetite was always obstinate, and flatly contradicted him), awoke no smile in the face of his little wife, who stood among the parcels, pushing the cake-box slowly from her with her foot, and never once looked, though her eyes were cast down too, upon the dainty shoe she generally was so mindful of. Absorbed in thought, she stood there, heedless alike of the tea and John (although he called to her, and rapped the table with his knife to startle her), until he rose and touched her on the arm; when she looked at him for a moment, and hurried to her place behind the teaboard, laughing at her negligence. But, not as she had laughed before. The manner and the music were quite changed.

The Cricket, too, had stopped. Somehow the room was not so cheerful as it had been. Nothing like it.

"So, these are all the parcels, are they, John?" she said, breaking a long silence, which the honest Carrier had devoted to the practical illustration of one part of his favourite sentiment—certainly enjoying what he ate, if it couldn't be admitted that he ate but little. "So, these are all the parcels; are they, John?"

"That's all," said John. "Why—no—I—" laying down his knife and fork, and taking a long breath. "I declare—I've clean forgotten the old gentleman!"

"The old gentleman?"

"In the cart," said John. "He was asleep, among the straw, the last time I saw him. I've very nearly remembered him, twice, since I came in; but he went out of my head again. Holloa! Yahip there! Rouse up! That's my hearty!"

John said these latter words outside the door, whither he had hurried with the candle in his hand.

Miss Slowboy, conscious of some mysterious reference to The Old Gentleman, and connecting in her mystified imagination certain associations of a religious nature with the phrase, was so disturbed, that hastily rising from the low chair by the fire to seek protection near the skirts of her mistress, and coming into contact as she crossed the doorway with an ancient Stranger, she instinctively made a charge or butt at him with the only offensive instrument within her reach. This instrument happening to be the Baby, great commotion and alarm ensued, which the sagacity of Boxer rather tended to increase; for, that good dog, more thoughtful than its master, had, it seemed, been watching the old gentleman in his sleep, lest he should walk off with a few young poplar trees that were tied up behind the cart; and he still attended on him very closely, worrying his gaiters in fact, and making dead sets at the buttons.

"You're such an undeniable good sleeper, sir," said John, when tranquillity was restored; in the mean time the old gentleman had stood, bareheaded and motionless, in the centre of the room; "that I have half a mind to ask you where the other six are—only that would be a joke, and I know I should spoil it. Very near though," murmured the Carrier, with a chuckle; "very near!"

The Stranger, who had long white hair, good features, singularly bold and well defined for an old man, and dark, bright, penetrating eyes, looked round with a smile, and saluted the Carrier's wife by gravely inclining his head.

His garb was very quaint and odd—a long, long way behind the time. Its hue was brown, all over. In his hand he held a great brown club or walking-stick; and striking this upon the floor, it fell asunder, and became a chair. On which he sat down, quite composedly.

"There!" said the Carrier, turning to his wife. "That's the way I found him, sitting by the roadside! Upright as a milestone. And almost as deaf."

"Sitting in the open air, John!"

"In the open air," replied the Carrier, "just at dusk. "Carriage Paid," he said; and gave me eighteenpence. Then he got in. And there he is."

"He's going, John, I think!"

Not at all. He was only going to speak.

"If you please, I was to be left till called for," said the Stranger, mildly. "Don't mind me."

With that, he took a pair of spectacles from one of his large pockets, and a book from another, and leisurely began to read. Making no more of Boxer than if he had been a house lamb!

The Carrier and his wife exchanged a look of perplexity. The Stranger raised his head; and glancing from the latter to the former, said,

"Your daughter, my good friend?"

"Wife," returned John.

"Niece?" said the Stranger.

"Wife," roared John.

"Indeed?" observed the Stranger. "Surely? Very young!"

He quietly turned over, and resumed his reading. But, before he could have read two lines, he again interrupted himself to say:

"Baby, yours?"

John gave him a gigantic nod; equivalent to an answer in the affirmative, delivered through a speaking trumpet.

"Girl?"

"Bo-o-oy!" roared John.

"Also very young, eh?"

Mrs. Peerybingle instantly struck in. "Two months and three da-ays! Vaccinated just six weeks ago-o! Took very fine-ly! Considered, by the doctor, a remarkably beautiful chi-ild! Equal to the general run of children at five months o-old! Takes notice, in a way quite wonderful! May seem impossible to you, but feels his legs al-ready!"

Here the breathless little mother, who had been shrieking these short sentences into the old man's ear, until her pretty face was crimsoned, held up the Baby before him as a stubborn and triumphant fact; while Tilly Slowboy, with a melodious cry of 'Ketcher, Ketcher'—which sounded like some unknown words, adapted to a popular Sneeze—performed some cow-like gambols round that all unconscious Innocent.

"Hark! He's called for, sure enough," said John. "There's somebody at the door. Open it, Tilly."

Before she could reach it, however, it was opened from without; being a primitive sort of door, with a latch, that any one could lift if he chose—and a good many people did choose, for all kinds of neighbours liked to have a cheerful word or two with the Carrier, though he was no great talker himself. Being opened, it gave admission to a little, meagre, thoughtful, dingy-faced man, who seemed to have made himself a great-coat from the sack-cloth covering of some old box; for when he turned to shut the door, and keep the weather out, he disclosed upon the back of that garment, the inscription G & T in large black capitals. Also the word GLASS in bold characters.

"Good evening, John!" said the little man. "Good evening, Mum. Good evening, Tilly. Good evening, Unbeknown! How's Baby, Mum? Boxer's pretty well I hope?"

"All thriving, Caleb," replied Dot. "I am sure you need only look at the dear child, for one, to know that."

"And I'm sure I need only look at you for another," said Caleb.

He didn't look at her though; he had a wandering and thoughtful eye which seemed to be always projecting itself into some other time and place, no matter what he said; a description which will equally apply to his voice.

"Or at John for another," said Caleb. "Or at Tilly, as far as that goes. Or certainly at Boxer."

"Busy just now, Caleb?" asked the Carrier.

"Why, pretty well, John," he returned, with the distraught air of a man who was casting about for the Philosopher's stone, at least. "Pretty much so. There's rather a run on Noah's Arks at present. I could have wished to improve upon the Family, but I don't see how it's to be done at the price. It would be a satisfaction to one's mind, to make it clearer which was Shems and Hams, and which was Wives. Flies an't on that scale neither, as compared with elephants you know! Ah! well! Have you got anything in the parcel line for me, John?"

The Carrier put his hand into a pocket of the coat he had taken off; and brought out, carefully preserved in moss and paper, a tiny flower-pot.

"There it is!" he said, adjusting it with great care. "Not so much as a leaf damaged. Full of buds!"

Caleb's dull eye brightened, as he took it, and thanked him.

"Dear, Caleb," said the Carrier. "Very dear at this season."

"Never mind that. It would be cheap to me, whatever it cost," returned the little man. "Anything else, John?"

"A small box," replied the Carrier. "Here you are!"

"'For Caleb Plummer,'" said the little man, spelling out the direction. "'With Cash.' With Cash, John? I don't think it's for me."

"With Care," returned the Carrier, looking over his shoulder. "Where do you make out cash?"

"Oh! To be sure!" said Caleb. "It's all right. With care! Yes, yes; that's mine. It might have been with cash, indeed, if my dear Boy in the Golden South Americas had lived, John. You loved him like a son; didn't you? You needn't say you did. *I* know, of course. 'Caleb Plummer. With care.' Yes, yes, it's all right. It's a box of dolls' eyes for my daughter's work. I wish it was her own sight in a box, John."

"I wish it was, or could be!" cried the Carrier.

"Thank'ee," said the little man. "You speak very hearty. To think that she should never see the Dolls—and them a-staring at her, so bold, all day long! That's where it cuts. What's the damage, John?"

"I'll damage you," said John, "if you inquire. Dot! Very near?"

"Well! it's like you to say so," observed the little man. "It's your kind way. Let me see. I think that's all."

"I think not," said the Carrier. "Try again."

"Something for our Governor, eh?" said Caleb, after pondering a little while. "To be sure. That's what I came for; but my head's so running on them Arks and things! He hasn't been here, has he?"

"Not he," returned the Carrier. "He's too busy, courting."

"He's coming round though," said Caleb; "for he told me to keep on the near side of the road going home, and it was ten to one he'd take me up. I had better go, by the bye.—You couldn't have the goodness to let me pinch Boxer's tail, Mum, for half a moment, could you?"

"Why, Caleb! what a question!"

"Oh never mind, Mum," said the little man. "He mightn't like it perhaps. There's a small order just come in, for barking dogs; and I should wish to go as close to Natur' as I could, for sixpence. That's all. Never mind, Mum."

It happened opportunely, that Boxer, without receiving the proposed stimulus, began to bark with great zeal. But, as this implied the approach of some new visitor, Caleb, postponing his study from the life to a more convenient season, shouldered the round box, and took a hurried leave. He might have spared himself the trouble, for he met the visitor upon the threshold.

"Oh! You are here, are you? Wait a bit. I'll take you home. John Peerybingle, my service to you. More of my service to your pretty wife. Handsomer every day! Better too, if possible! And younger," mused the speaker, in a low voice; "that's the Devil of it!"

"I should be astonished at your paying compliments, Mr. Tackleton," said Dot, not with the best grace in the world; "but for your condition."

"You know all about it then?"

"I have got myself to believe it, somehow," said Dot.

"After a hard struggle, I suppose?"

"Very."

Tackleton the Toy-merchant, pretty generally known as Gruff and Tackleton—for that was the firm, though Gruff had been bought out long ago; only leaving his name, and as some said his nature, according to its Dictionary meaning, in the business—Tackleton the Toy-merchant, was a man whose vocation had been quite misunderstood by his Parents and Guardians. If they had made him a Money-Lender, or a sharp Attorney, or a Sheriff's Officer, or a Broker, he might have sown his discontented oats in his youth, and, after having had the full run of himself in ill-natured transactions, might have turned out amiable, at last, for the sake of a little freshness and novelty. But, cramped and chafing in the peaceable pursuit of toy-making, he was a domestic Ogre, who had been living on children all his life, and was their implacable enemy. He despised all toys; wouldn't have bought one for the world; delighted, in his malice, to insinuate grim expressions into the faces of brown-paper farmers who drove pigs to market, bellmen who advertised lost lawyers' consciences, movable old ladies who darned stockings or carved pies; and other like samples of his stock in trade. In appalling masks; hideous, hairy, red-eyed Jacks in Boxes; Vampire Kites; demoniacal Tumblers who wouldn't lie down, and were perpetually flying forward, to stare infants out of countenance; his soul perfectly revelled. They were his only relief, and safety-valve. He was great in such inventions. Anything suggestive of a Pony-nightmare was delicious to him. He had even lost money (and he took to that toy very kindly) by getting up Goblin slides for magic-lanterns, whereon the Powers of Darkness were depicted as a sort of supernatural shell-fish, with human faces. In intensifying the portraiture of Giants, he had sunk quite a little capital; and, though no painter himself, he could indicate, for the instruction of his artists, with a piece of chalk, a certain furtive leer for the countenances of those monsters, which was safe to destroy the peace of mind of any young gentleman between the ages of six and eleven, for the whole Christmas or Midsummer Vacation.

What he was in toys, he was (as most men are) in other things. You may easily suppose, therefore, that within the great green cape, which reached down to the calves of his legs, there was buttoned up to the chin an uncommonly pleasant fellow; and that he was about as choice a spirit, and as agreeable a companion, as ever stood in a pair of bull-headed-looking boots with mahogany-coloured tops.

Still, Tackleton, the Toy-merchant, was going to be married. In spite of all this, he was going to be married. And to a young wife too, a beautiful young wife.

He didn't look much like a bridegroom, as he stood in the Carrier's kitchen, with a twist in his dry face, and a screw in his body, and his hat jerked over the bridge of his nose, and his hands tucked down into the bottoms of his pockets, and his whole sarcastic ill-conditioned self peering out of one little corner of one little eye, like the concentrated essence of any number of ravens. But, a Bridegroom he designed to be.

"In three days' time. Next Thursday. The last day of the first month in the year. That's my wedding-day," said Tackleton.

Did I mention that he had always one eye wide open, and one eye nearly shut; and that the one eye nearly shut, was always the expressive eye? I don't think I did.

"That's my wedding-day!" said Tackleton, rattling his money.

"Why, it's our wedding-day too," exclaimed the Carrier.

"Ha ha!" laughed Tackleton. "Odd! You're just such another couple. Just!"

The indignation of Dot at this presumptuous assertion is not to be described. What next? His imagination would compass the possibility of just such another Baby, perhaps. The man was mad.

"I say! A word with you," murmured Tackleton, nudging the Carrier with his elbow, and taking him a little apart. "You'll come to the wedding? We're in the same boat, you know."

"How in the same boat?" inquired the Carrier.

"A little disparity, you know," said Tackleton, with another nudge. "Come and spend an evening with us, beforehand."

"Why?" demanded John, astonished at this pressing hospitality.

"Why?" returned the other. "That's a new way of receiving an invitation. Why, for pleasure—sociability, you know, and all that!"

"I thought you were never sociable," said John, in his plain way.

"Tchah! It's of no use to be anything but free with you, I see," said Tackleton. "Why, then, the truth is you have a—what tea-drinking people call a sort of a comfortable appearance together, you and your wife. We know better, you know, but—"

"No, we don't know better," interposed John. "What are you talking about?"

"Well! We *don't* know better, then," said Tackleton. "We'll agree that we don't. As you like; what does it matter? I was going to say, as you have that sort of appearance, your company will produce a favourable effect on Mrs. Tackleton that will be. And, though I don't think your good lady's very friendly to me, in this matter, still she can't help herself from falling into my views, for there's a compactness and cosiness of appearance about her that always tells, even in an indifferent case. You'll say you'll come?"

"We have arranged to keep our Wedding-Day (as far as that goes) at home," said John. "We have made the promise to ourselves these six months. We think, you see, that home—"

"Bah! what's home?" cried Tackleton. "Four walls and a ceiling! (why don't you kill that Cricket? *I* would! I always do. I hate their noise.) There are four walls and a ceiling at my house. Come to me!"

"You kill your Crickets, eh?" said John.

"Scrunch 'em, sir," returned the other, setting his heel heavily on the floor. "You'll say you'll come? it's as much your interest as mine, you know, that the women should persuade each other that they're quiet and contented, and couldn't be better off. I know their way. Whatever one woman says, another woman is determined to clinch, always. There's that spirit of emulation among 'em, sir, that if your wife says to my wife, 'I'm the happiest woman in the world, and mine's the best husband in the world, and I dote on him,' my wife will say the same to yours, or more, and half believe it."

"Do you mean to say she don't, then?" asked the Carrier.

"Don't!" cried Tackleton, with a short, sharp laugh. "Don't what?"

The Carrier had some faint idea of adding, "dote upon you." But, happening to meet the half-closed eye, as it twinkled upon him over the turned-up collar of the cape, which was within an ace of poking it out, he felt it such an unlikely part and parcel of anything to be doted on, that he substituted, "that she don't believe it?"

"Ah you dog! You're joking," said Tackleton.

But the Carrier, though slow to understand the full drift of his meaning, eyed him in such a serious manner, that he was obliged to be a little more explanatory.

"I have the humour," said Tackleton: holding up the fingers of his left hand, and tapping the forefinger, to imply "there I am, Tackleton to wit: I have the humour, sir, to marry a young wife, and a pretty wife": here he rapped his little finger, to express the Bride; not sparingly, but sharply; with a sense of power. "I'm able to gratify that humour and I do. It's my whim. But—now look there!"

He pointed to where Dot was sitting, thoughtfully, before the fire; leaning her dimpled chin upon her hand, and watching the bright blaze. The Carrier looked at her, and then at him, and then at her, and then at him again.

"She honours and obeys, no doubt, you know," said Tackleton; "and that, as I am not a man of sentiment, is quite enough for ME. But do you think there's anything more in it?"

"I think," observed the Carrier, "that I should chuck any man out of window, who said there wasn't."

"Exactly so," returned the other with an unusual alacrity of assent. "To be sure! Doubtless you would. Of course. I'm certain of it. Good night. Pleasant dreams!"

The Carrier was puzzled, and made uncomfortable and uncertain, in spite of himself. He couldn't help showing it, in his manner.

"Good night, my dear friend!" said Tackleton, compassionately. "I'm off. We're exactly alike, in reality, I see. You won't give us to-morrow evening? Well! Next day you go out visiting, I know. I'll meet you there, and bring my wife that is to be. It'll do her good. You're agreeable? Thank'ee. What's that!"

It was a loud cry from the Carrier's wife: a loud, sharp, sudden cry, that made the room ring, like a glass vessel. She had risen from her seat, and stood like one transfixed by terror and surprise. The Stranger had advanced towards the fire to warm himself, and stood within a short stride of her chair. But quite still.

"Dot!" cried the Carrier. "Mary! Darling! What's the matter?"

They were all about her in a moment. Caleb, who had been dozing on the cake-box, in the first imperfect recovery of his suspended presence of mind, seized Miss Slowboy by the hair of her head, but immediately apologised.

"Mary!" exclaimed the Carrier, supporting her in his arms. "Are you ill! What is it? Tell me, dear!"

She only answered by beating her hands together, and falling into a wild fit of laughter. Then, sinking from his grasp upon the ground, she covered her face with her apron, and wept bitterly. And then she laughed again, and then she cried again, and then she said how cold it was, and suffered him to lead her to the fire, where she sat down as before. The old man standing, as before, quite still.

"I'm better, John," she said. "I'm quite well now—I—"

"John!" But John was on the other side of her. Why turn her face towards the strange old gentleman, as if addressing him! Was her brain wandering?

"Only a fancy, John dear—a kind of shock—a something coming suddenly before my eyes—I don't know what it was. It's quite gone, quite gone."

"I'm glad it's gone," muttered Tackleton, turning the expressive eye all round the room. "I wonder where it's gone, and what it was. Humph! Caleb, come here! Who's that with the grey hair?"

"I don't know, sir," returned Caleb in a whisper. "Never see him before, in all my life. A beautiful figure for a nutcracker; quite a new model. With a screw-jaw opening down into his waistcoat, he'd be lovely."

"Not ugly enough," said Tackleton.

"Or for a firebox, either," observed Caleb, in deep contemplation, "what a model! Unscrew his head to put the matches in; turn him heels up'ards for the light; and what a firebox for a gentleman's mantel-shelf, just as he stands!"

"Not half ugly enough," said Tackleton. "Nothing in him at all! Come! Bring that box! All right now, I hope?"

"Oh quite gone!" said the little woman, waving him hurriedly away. "Good night!"

"Good night," said Tackleton. "Good night, John Peerybingle! Take care how you carry that box, Caleb. Let it fall, and I'll murder you! Dark as pitch, and weather worse than ever, eh? Good night!"

So, with another sharp look round the room, he went out at the door; followed by Caleb with the wedding-cake on his head.

The Carrier had been so much astounded by his little wife, and so busily engaged in soothing and tending her, that he had scarcely been conscious of the Stranger's presence, until now, when he again stood there, their only guest.

"He don't belong to them, you see," said John. "I must give him a hint to go."

"I beg your pardon, friend," said the old gentleman, advancing to him; "the more so, as I fear your wife has not been well; but the Attendant whom my infirmity," he touched his ears and shook his head, "renders almost indispensable, not having arrived, I fear there must be some mistake. The bad night which made the shelter of your comfortable cart (may I never have a worse!) so acceptable, is still as bad as ever. Would you, in your kindness, suffer me to rent a bed here?"

"Yes, yes," cried Dot. "Yes! Certainly!"

"Oh!" said the Carrier, surprised by the rapidity of this consent.

"Well! I don't object; but, still I'm not quite sure that—"

"Hush!" she interrupted. "Dear John!"

"Why, he's stone deaf," urged John.

"I know he is, but—Yes, sir, certainly. Yes! certainly! I'll make him up a bed, directly, John."

As she hurried off to do it, the flutter of her spirits, and the agitation of her manner, were so strange that the Carrier stood looking after her, quite confounded.

"Did its mothers make it up a Beds then!" cried Miss Slowboy to the Baby; "and did its hair grow brown and curly, when its caps was lifted off, and frighten it, a precious Pets, a sitting by the fires!"

With that unaccountable attraction of the mind to trifles, which is often incidental to a state of doubt and confusion, the Carrier as he walked slowly to and fro, found himself mentally repeating even these absurd words, many times. So many times that he got them by heart, and was still conning them over and over, like a lesson, when Tilly, after administering as much friction to the little bald head with her hand as she thought wholesome (according to the practice of nurses), had once more tied the Baby's cap on.

"And frighten it, a precious Pets, a sitting by the fires. What frightened Dot, I wonder!" mused the Carrier, pacing to and fro.

He scouted, from his heart, the insinuations of the Toy-merchant, and yet they filled him with a vague, indefinite uneasiness. For, Tackleton was quick and sly; and he had that painful sense, himself, of being of slow perception, that a broken hint was always worrying to him. He certainly had no intention in his mind of linking anything that Tackleton had said, with the unusual conduct of his wife, but the two subjects of reflection came into his mind together, and he could not keep them asunder.

The bed was soon made ready; and the visitor, declining all refreshment but a cup of tea, retired. Then, Dot: quite well again, she said, quite well again" arranged the great chair in the chimney-corner for her husband; filled his pipe and gave it him; and took her usual little stool beside him on the hearth.

She always *would* sit on that little stool. I think she must have had a kind of notion that it was a coaxing, wheedling little stool.

She was, out and out, the very best filler of a pipe, I should say, in the four quarters of the globe. To see her put that chubby little finger in the bowl, and then blow down the pipe to clear the tube, and, when she had done so, affect to think that there was really something in the tube, and blow a dozen times, and hold it to her eye like a telescope, with a most provoking twist in her capital little face, as she looked down it, was quite a brilliant thing. As to the tobacco, she was perfect mistress of the subject; and her lighting of the pipe, with a wisp of paper, when the Carrier had it in his mouth—going so very near his nose, and yet not scorching it—was Art: high Art, Sir.

And the Cricket and the Kettle, turning up again, acknowledged it! The bright fire, blazing up again, acknowledged it! The little Mower on the clock, in his unheeded work, acknowledged it! The Carrier, in his smoothing forehead and expanding face, acknowledged it, the readiest of all.

And as he soberly and thoughtfully puffed at his old pipe; and as the Dutch clock ticked; and as the red fire gleamed; and as the Cricket chirped; that Genius of his Hearth and Home (for such the Cricket was) came out, in fairy shape, into the room, and summoned many forms of Home about him. Dots of all ages, and all sizes, filled the chamber. Dots who were merry children, running on before him gathering flowers, in the fields; coy Dots, half shrinking from, half yielding to, the pleading of his own rough image; newly-married Dots, alighting at the door, and taking wondering possession of the household keys; motherly little Dots, attended by fictitious Slowboys, bearing babies to be christened; matronly Dots, still young and blooming, watching Dots of daughters, as they danced at rustic balls; fat Dots, encircled and beset by troops of rosy grandchildren; withered Dots, who leaned on sticks, and tottered as they crept along. Old Carriers too, appeared, with blind old Boxers lying at their feet; and newer carts with younger drivers ("Peerybingle Brothers" on the tilt); and sick old Carriers, tended by the gentlest hands; and graves of dead and gone old Carriers, green in the churchyard. And as the Cricket showed him all these things—he saw them plainly, though his eyes were fixed upon the fire—the Carrier's heart grew light and happy, and he thanked his Household Gods with all his might, and cared no more for Gruff and Tackleton than you do.

But what was that young figure of a man, which the same Fairy Cricket set so near Her stool, and which remained there, singly and alone? Why did it linger still, so near her, with its arm upon the chimney-piece, ever repeating "Married! and not to me!"

Oh Dot! Oh failing Dot! There is no place for it in all your husband's visions; why has its shadow fallen on his hearth!

Chirp the Second

Caleb Plummer and his Blind Daughter lived all alone by themselves, as the Story-books say—and my blessing, with yours to back it I hope, on the Story-books, for saying anything in this workaday world!—Caleb Plummer and his Blind Daughter lived all alone by themselves, in a little cracked nutshell of a wooden house, which was, in truth, no better than a pimple on the prominent red-brick nose of Gruff and Tackleton. The premises of Gruff and Tackleton were the great feature of the street; but you might have knocked down Caleb Plummer's dwelling with a hammer or two, and carried off the pieces in a cart.

If any one had done the dwelling-house of Caleb Plummer the honour to miss it after such an inroad, it would have been, no doubt, to commend its demolition as a vast improvement. It stuck to the premises of Gruff and Tackleton, like a barnacle to a ship's keel, or a snail to a door, or a little bunch of toadstools to the stem of a tree. But it was the germ from which the full-grown trunk of Gruff and Tackleton had sprung; and, under its crazy roof, the Gruff before last, had, in a small way, made toys for a generation of old boys and girls, who had played with them, and found them out, and broken them, and gone to sleep.

I have said that Caleb and his poor Blind Daughter lived here; but I should have said that Caleb lived here, and his poor Blind Daughter somewhere else; in an enchanted home of Caleb's furnishing, where scarcity and shabbiness were not, and trouble never entered. Caleb was no sorcerer, but in the only magic art that still remains to us: the magic of devoted, deathless love: Nature had been the mistress of his study; and from her teaching, all the wonder came.

The Blind Girl never knew that ceilings were discoloured; walls blotched, and bare of plaster here and there; high crevices unstopped, and widening every day; beams mouldering and tending downward. The Blind Girl never knew that iron was rusting, wood rotting, paper peeling off; the size, and shape, and true proportion of the dwelling, withering away. The Blind Girl never knew that ugly shapes of delf and earthenware were on the board; that sorrow and faint-heartedness were in the house; that Caleb's scanty hairs were turning greyer and more grey before her sightless face. The Blind Girl never knew they had a master, cold, exacting, and uninterested: never knew that Tackleton was Tackleton in short; but lived in the belief of an eccentric humourist who loved to have his jest with them; and while he was the Guardian Angel of their lives, disdained to hear one word of thankfulness.

And all was Caleb's doing; all the doing of her simple father! But he too had a Cricket on his Hearth; and listening sadly to its music when the motherless Blind Child was very young, that Spirit had inspired him with the thought that even her great deprivation might be almost changed into a blessing, and the girl made happy by these little means. For all the Cricket tribe are potent Spirits, even though the people who hold converse with them do not know it (which is frequently the case); and there are not in the Unseen World, Voices more gentle and more true, that may be so implicitly relied on, or that are so certain to give none but tenderest counsel; as the Voices in which the Spirits of the Fireside and the Hearth, address themselves to human kind.

Caleb and his daughter were at work together in their usual working-room, which served them for their ordinary living-room as well; and a strange place it was. There were houses in it, finished and unfinished, for Dolls of all stations in life. Suburban tenements for Dolls of moderate means; kitchens and single apartments for Dolls of the lower classes; capital town residences for Dolls of high estate. Some of these establishments were already furnished according to estimate, with a view to the convenience of Dolls of limited income; others could be fitted on the most expensive scale, at a moment's notice, from whole shelves of chairs and tables, sofas, bedsteads, and upholstery. The nobility and gentry, and public in general, for whose accommodation these tenements were designed, lay, here and there, in baskets, staring straight up at the ceiling; but in denoting their degrees in society, and confining them to their respective stations (which experience shows to be lamentably difficult in real life), the makers of these Dolls had far improved on Nature, who is often froward and perverse; for they, not resting on such arbitrary marks as satin, cotton-print, and bits of rag, had superadded striking personal differences which allowed of no mistake. Thus, the Doll-lady of distinction had wax limbs of perfect symmetry; but only she and her compeers; the next grade in the social scale being made of leather; and the next of coarse linen stuff. As to the common-people, they had just so many matches out of tinder-boxes for their arms and legs, and there they were—established in their sphere at once, beyond the possibility of getting out of it.

There were various other samples of his handicraft besides Dolls, in Caleb Plummer's room. There were Noah's Arks, in which the Birds and Beasts were an uncommonly tight fit, I assure you; though they could be crammed in, anyhow, at the roof, and rattled and shaken into the smallest compass. By a bold poetical licence, most of these Noah's Arks had knockers on the doors; inconsistent appendages, perhaps, as suggestive of morning callers and a Postman, yet a pleasant finish to the outside of the building. There were scores of melancholy little carts, which, when the wheels went round, performed most doleful music. Many small fiddles, drums, and other instruments of torture; no end of cannon, shields, swords, spears, and guns. There were little tumblers in red breeches, incessantly swarming up high obstacles of red-tape, and coming down, head first, on the other side; and there were innumerable old gentlemen of respectable, not to say venerable, appearance, insanely flying over horizontal pegs, inserted, for the purpose, in their own street doors. There were beasts of all sorts; horses, in particular, of every breed, from the spotted barrel on four pegs, with a small tippet for a mane, to the thoroughbred rocker on his highest mettle. As it would have been hard to count the dozens upon dozens of grotesque figures that were ever ready to commit all sorts of absurdities on the turning of a handle so it would have been no easy task to mention any human folly, vice, or weakness, that had not its type, immediate or remote, in Caleb Plummer's room. And not in an exaggerated form, for very little handles will move men and women to as strange performances, as any Toy was ever made to undertake.

In the midst of all these objects, Caleb and his daughter sat at work. The Blind Girl busy as a Doll's dressmaker; Caleb painting and glazing the four-pair front of a desirable family mansion.

The care imprinted in the lines of Caleb's face, and his absorbed and dreamy manner, which would have sat well on some alchemist or abstruse student, were at first sight an odd contrast to his occupation, and the trivialities about him. But, trivial things, invented and pursued for bread, become very serious matters of fact; and, apart from this consideration, I am not at all prepared to say, myself, that if Caleb had been a Lord Chamberlain, or a Member of Parliament, or a lawyer, or even a great speculator, he would have dealt in toys one whit less whimsical, while I have a very great doubt whether they would have been as harmless.

"So you were out in the rain last night, father, in your beautiful new great-coat," said Caleb's daughter.

"In my beautiful new great-coat," answered Caleb, glancing towards a clothes-line in the room, on which the sackcloth garment previously described, was carefully hung up to dry.

"How glad I am you bought it, father!"

"And of such a tailor, too," said Caleb. "Quite a fashionable tailor. It's too good for me."

The Blind Girl rested from her work, and laughed with delight. "Too good, father! What can be too good for you?"

"I'm half-ashamed to wear it though," said Caleb, watching the effect of what he said, upon her brightening face; "upon my word! When I hear the boys and people say behind me, 'Hal-loa! Here's a swell!' I don't know which way to look. And when the beggar wouldn't go away last night; and when I said I was a very common man, said 'No, your Honour! Bless your Honour, don't say that!' I was quite ashamed. I really felt as if I hadn't a right to wear it."

Happy Blind Girl! How merry she was, in her exultation!

"I see you, father," she said, clasping her hands, "as plainly, as if I had the eyes I never want when you are with me. A blue coat—"

"Bright blue," said Caleb.

"Yes, yes! Bright blue!" exclaimed the girl, turning up her radiant face; "the colour I can just remember in the blessed sky! You told me it was blue before! A bright blue coat—"

"Made loose to the figure," suggested Caleb.

"Yes! loose to the figure!" cried the Blind Girl, laughing heartily; "and in it, you, dear father, with your merry eye, your smiling face, your free step, and your dark hair—looking so young and handsome!"

"Halloa! Halloa!" said Caleb. "I shall be vain, presently!"

"I think you are, already," cried the Blind Girl, pointing at him, in her glee. "I know you, father! Ha, ha, ha! I've found you out, you see!"

How different the picture in her mind, from Caleb, as he sat observing her! She had spoken of his free step. She was right in that. For years and years, he had never once crossed that threshold at his own slow pace, but with a footfall counterfeited for her ear; and never had he, when his heart was heaviest, forgotten the light tread that was to render hers so cheerful and courageous!

Heaven knows! But I think Caleb's vague bewilderment of manner may have half originated in his having confused himself about himself and everything around him, for the love of his Blind Daughter. How could the little man be otherwise than bewildered, after labouring for so many years to destroy his own identity, and that of all the objects that had any bearing on it!

"There we are," said Caleb, falling back a pace or two to form the better judgment of his work; "as near the real thing as sixpenn'orth of halfpence is to sixpence. What a pity that the whole front of the house opens at once! If there was only a staircase in it, now, and regular doors to the rooms to go in at! But that's the worst of my calling, I'm always deluding myself, and swindling myself."

"You are speaking quite softly. You are not tired, father?"

"Tired!" echoed Caleb, with a great burst of animation, "what should tire me, Bertha? *I* was never tired. What does it mean?"

To give the greater force to his words, he checked himself in an involuntary imitation of two half-length stretching and yawning figures on the mantel-shelf, who were represented as in one eternal state of weariness from the waist upwards; and hummed a fragment of a song. It was a Bacchanalian song, something about a Sparkling Bowl; and he sang it with an assumption of a Devil-may-care voice, that made his face a thousand times more meagre and more thoughtful than ever.

"What! You're singing, are you?" said Tackleton, putting his head in at the door. "Go it! *I* can't sing."

Nobody would have suspected him of it. He hadn't what is generally termed a singing face, by any means.

"I can't afford to sing," said Tackleton. "I'm glad you can. I hope you can afford to work too. Hardly time for both, I should think?"

"If you could only see him, Bertha, how he's winking at me!" whispered Caleb. "Such a man to joke! You'd think, if you didn't know him, he was in earnest—wouldn't you now?"

The Blind Girl smiled, and nodded.

"The bird that can sing and won't sing, must be made to sing, they say," grumbled Tackleton. "What about the owl that can't sing, and oughtn't to sing, and will sing; is there anything that *he* should be made to do?"

"The extent to which he's winking at this moment!" whispered Caleb to his daughter. "Oh, my gracious!"

"Always merry and light-hearted with us!" cried the smiling Bertha.

"O, you're there, are you?" answered Tackleton. "Poor Idiot!"

He really did believe she was an Idiot; and he founded the belief, I can't say whether consciously or not, upon her being fond of him.

"Well! and being there,—how are you?" said Tackleton, in his grudging way.

"Oh! well; quite well. And as happy as even you can wish me to be. As happy as you would make the whole world, if you could!"

"Poor Idiot!" muttered Tackleton. "No gleam of reason. Not a gleam!"

The Blind Girl took his hand and kissed it; held it for a moment in her own two hands; and laid her cheek against it tenderly, before releasing it. There was such unspeakable affection and such fervent gratitude in the act, that Tackleton himself was moved to say, in a milder growl than usual:

"What's the matter now?"

"I stood it close beside my pillow when I went to sleep last night, and remembered it in my dreams. And when the day broke, and the glorious red sun—the *red* sun, father?"

"Red in the mornings and the evenings, Bertha," said poor Caleb, with a woeful glance at his employer.

"When it rose, and the bright light I almost fear to strike myself against in walking, came into the room, I turned the little tree towards it, and blessed Heaven for making things so precious, and blessed you for sending them to cheer me!"

"Bedlam broke loose!" said Tackleton under his breath. "We shall arrive at the strait-waistcoat and mufflers soon. We're getting on!"

Caleb, with his hands hooked loosely in each other, stared vacantly before him while his daughter spoke, as if he really were uncertain (I believe he was) whether Tackleton had done anything to deserve her thanks, or not. If he could have been a perfectly free agent, at that moment, required, on pain of death, to kick the Toy-merchant, or fall at his feet, according to his merits, I believe it would have been an even chance which course he would have taken. Yet, Caleb knew that with his own hands he had brought the little rose-tree home for her, so carefully, and that with his own lips he had forged the innocent deception which should help to keep her from suspecting how much, how very much, he every day, denied himself, that she might be the happier.

"Bertha!" said Tackleton, assuming, for the nonce, a little cordiality. "Come here."

"Oh! I can come straight to you! You needn't guide me!" she rejoined.

"Shall I tell you a secret, Bertha?"

"If you will!" she answered, eagerly.

How bright the darkened face! How adorned with light, the listening head!

"This is the day on which little what's-her-name, the spoilt child, Peerybingle's wife, pays her regular visit to you—makes her fantastic Pic-Nic here; an't it?" said Tackleton, with a strong expression of distaste for the whole concern.

"Yes," replied Bertha. "This is the day."

"I thought so," said Tackleton. "I should like to join the party."

"Do you hear that, father!" cried the Blind Girl in an ecstacy.

"Yes, yes, I hear it," murmured Caleb, with the fixed look of a sleep-walker; "but I don't believe it. It's one of my lies, I've no doubt."

"You see I—I want to bring the Peerybingles a little more into company with May Fielding," said Tackleton. "I am going to be married to May."

"Married!" cried the Blind Girl, starting from him.

"She's such a con-founded Idiot," muttered Tackleton, "that I was afraid she'd never comprehend me. Ah, Bertha! Married! Church, parson, clerk, beadle, glass-coach, bells, breakfast, bride-cake, favours, marrow-bones, cleavers, and all the rest of the tomfoolery. A wedding, you know; a wedding. Don't you know what a wedding is?"

"I know," replied the Blind Girl, in a gentle tone. "I understand!"

"Do you?" muttered Tackleton. "It's more than I expected. Well! On that account I want to join the party, and to bring May and her mother. I'll send in a little something or other, before the afternoon. A cold leg of mutton, or some comfortable trifle of that sort. You'll expect me?"

"Yes," she answered.

She had drooped her head, and turned away; and so stood, with her hands crossed, musing.

"I don't think you will," muttered Tackleton, looking at her; "for you seem to have forgotten all about it, already. Caleb!"

"I may venture to say I'm here, I suppose," thought Caleb. "Sir!"

"Take care she don't forget what I've been saying to her."

"*She* never forgets," returned Caleb. "It's one of the few things she an't clever in."

"Every man thinks his own geese swans," observed the Toy Merchant, with a shrug. "Poor devil!"

Having delivered himself of which remark, with infinite contempt, old Gruff and Tackleton withdrew.

Bertha remained where he had left her, lost in meditation. The gaiety had vanished from her downcast face, and it was very sad. Three or four times, she shook her head, as if bewailing some remembrance or some loss; but her sorrowful reflections found no vent in words.

It was not until Caleb had been occupied, some time, in yoking a team of horses to a waggon by the summary process of nailing the harness to the vital parts of their bodies, that she drew near to his working-stool, and sitting down beside him, said:

"Father, I am lonely in the dark. I want my eyes, my patient, willing eyes."

"Here they are," said Caleb. "Always ready. They are more yours than mine, Bertha, any hour in the four-and-twenty. What shall your eyes do for you, dear?"

"Look round the room, father."

"All right," said Caleb. "No sooner said than done, Bertha."

"Tell me about it."

"It's much the same as usual," said Caleb. "Homely, but very snug. The gay colours on the walls; the bright flowers on the plates and dishes; the shining wood, where there are beams or panels; the general cheerfulness and neatness of the building; make it very pretty."

Cheerful and neat it was wherever Bertha's hands could busy themselves. But nowhere else, were cheerfulness and neatness possible, in the old crazy shed which Caleb's fancy so transformed.

"You have your working dress on, and are not so gallant as when you wear the handsome coat?" said Bertha, touching him.

"Not quite so gallant," answered Caleb. "Pretty brisk though."

"Father," said the Blind Girl, drawing close to his side, and stealing one arm round his neck, "tell me something about May. She is very fair?"

"She is indeed," said Caleb. And she was indeed. It was quite a rare thing to Caleb, not to have to draw on his invention.

"Her hair is dark," said Bertha, pensively, "darker than mine. Her voice is sweet and musical, I know. I have often loved to hear it. Her shape—"

"There's not a Doll's in all the room to equal it," said Caleb. "And her eyes!"—

He stopped; for Bertha had drawn closer round his neck, and from the arm that clung about him, came a warning pressure which he understood too well.

He coughed a moment, hammered for a moment, and then fell back upon the song about the sparkling bowl; his infallible resource in all such difficulties.

"Our friend, father; our benefactor. I am never tired, you know, of hearing about him.—Now was I, ever?" she said, hastily.

"Of course not," answered Caleb. "And with reason."

"Ah! With how much reason!" cried the Blind Girl. With such fervency, that Caleb, though his motives were so pure, could not endure to meet her face; but dropped his eyes, as if she could have read in them his innocent deceit.

"Then, tell me again about him, dear father," said Bertha. "Many times again! His face is benevolent, kind, and tender. Honest and true, I am sure it is. The manly heart that tries to cloak all favours with a show of roughness and unwillingness, beats in its every look and glance."

"And makes it noble!" added Caleb, in his quiet desperation.

"And makes it noble!" cried the Blind Girl. "He is older than May, father."

"Ye-es," said Caleb, reluctantly. "He's a little older than May. But that don't signify."

"Oh father, yes! To be his patient companion in infirmity and age; to be his gentle nurse in sickness, and his constant friend in suffering and sorrow; to know no weariness in working for his sake; to watch him, tend him, sit beside his bed and talk to him awake, and pray for him asleep; what privileges these would be! What opportunities for proving all her truth and devotion to him! Would she do all this, dear father?

"No doubt of it," said Caleb.

"I love her, father; I can love her from my soul!" exclaimed the Blind Girl. And saying so, she laid her poor blind face on Caleb's shoulder, and so wept and wept, that he was almost sorry to have brought that tearful happiness upon her.

In the mean time, there had been a pretty sharp commotion at John Peerybingle's, for little Mrs. Peerybingle naturally couldn't think of going anywhere without the Baby; and to get the Baby under weigh, took time. Not that there was much of the Baby: speaking of it as a thing of weight and measure: but there was a vast deal to do about and about it, and it all had to be done by easy stages. For instance: when the Baby was got, by hook and by crook, to a certain point of dressing, and you might have rationally supposed that another touch or two would finish him off, and turn him out a tip-top Baby challenging the world, he was unexpectedly extinguished in a flannel cap, and hustled off to bed; where he simmered (so to speak) between two blankets for the best part of an hour. From this state of inaction he was then recalled, shining very much and roaring violently, to partake of—well? I would rather say, if you'll permit me to speak generally—of a slight repast. After which, he went to sleep again. Mrs. Peerybingle took advantage of this interval, to make herself as smart in a small way as ever you saw anybody in all your life; and, during the same short truce, Miss Slowboy insinuated herself into a spencer of a fashion so surprising and ingenious, that it had no connection with herself, or anything else in the universe, but was a shrunken, dog's-eared, independent fact, pursuing its lonely course without the least regard to anybody. By this time, the Baby, being all alive again, was invested, by the united efforts of Mrs. Peerybingle and Miss Slowboy, with a cream-coloured mantle for its body, and a sort of nankeen raised-pie for its head; and so in course of time they all three got down to the door, where the old horse had already taken more than the full value of his day's toll out of the Turnpike Trust, by tearing up the road with his impatient autographs—and whence Boxer might be dimly seen in the remote perspective, standing looking back, and tempting him to come on without orders.

As to a chair, or anything of that kind for helping Mrs. Peerybingle into the cart, you know very little of John, if you think *that* was necessary. Before you could have seen him lift her from the ground, there she was in her place, fresh and rosy, saying, "John! How can you! Think of Tilly!"

If I might be allowed to mention a young lady's legs, on any terms, I would observe of Miss Slowboy's that there was a fatality about them which rendered them singularly liable to be grazed; and that she never effected the smallest ascent or descent, without recording the circumstance upon them with a notch, as Robinson Crusoe marked the days upon his wooden calendar. But as this might be considered ungenteel, I'll think of it.

"John! You've got the Basket with the Veal and Ham-Pie and things, and the bottles of Beer?" said Dot. "If you haven't, you must turn round again, this very minute."

"You're a nice little article," returned the Carrier, "to be talking about turning round, after keeping me a full quarter of an hour behind my time."

"I am sorry for it, John," said Dot in a great bustle, "but I really could not think of going to Bertha's—I would not do it, John, on any account—without the Veal and Ham-Pie and things, and the bottles of Beer. Way!"

This monosyllable was addressed to the horse, who didn't mind it at all.

"Oh *do* way, John!" said Mrs. Peerybingle. "Please!"

"It'll be time enough to do that," returned John, "when I begin to leave things behind me. The basket's here, safe enough."

"What a hard-hearted monster you must be, John, not to have said so, at once, and save me such a turn! I declared I wouldn't go to Bertha's without the Veal and Ham-Pie and things, and the bottles of Beer, for any money. Regularly once a fortnight ever since we have been married, John, have we made our little Pic-Nic there. If anything was to go wrong with it, I should almost think we were never to be lucky again."

"It was a kind thought in the first instance," said the Carrier: "and I honour you for it, little woman."

"My dear John," replied Dot, turning very red, "don't talk about honouring me. Good Gracious!"

"By the bye—" observed the Carrier. "That old gentleman—"

Again so visibly, and instantly embarrassed.

"He's an odd fish," said the Carrier, looking straight along the road before them. "I can't make him out. I don't believe there's any harm in him."

"None at all. I'm—I'm sure there's none at all."

"Yes," said the Carrier, with his eyes attracted to her face by the great earnestness of her manner. "I am glad you feel so certain of it, because it's a confirmation to me. It's curious that he should have taken it into his head to ask leave to go on lodging with us; an't it? Things come about so strangely."

"So very strangely," she rejoined in a low voice, scarcely audible.

"However, he's a good-natured old gentleman," said John, "and pays as a gentleman, and I think his word is to be relied upon, like a gentleman's. I had quite a long talk with him this morning: he can hear me better already, he says, as he gets more used to my voice. He told me a great deal about himself, and I told him a great deal about myself, and a rare lot of questions he asked me. I gave him information about my having two beats, you know, in my business; one day to the right from our house and back again; another day to the left from our house and back again (for he's a stranger and don't know the names of places about here); and he seemed quite pleased. 'Why, then I shall be returning home to-night your way,' he says, 'when I thought you'd be coming in an exactly opposite direction. That's capital! I may trouble you for another lift perhaps, but I'll engage not to fall so sound asleep again.' He *was* sound asleep, sure-ly!—Dot! what are you thinking of?"

"Thinking of, John? I—I was listening to you."

"O! That's all right!" said the honest Carrier. "I was afraid, from the look of your face, that I had gone rambling on so long, as to set you thinking about something else. I was very near it, I'll be bound."

Dot making no reply, they jogged on, for some little time, in silence. But it was not easy to remain silent very long in John Peerybingle's cart, for everybody on the road had something to say. Though it might only be "How are you!" and indeed it was very often nothing else, still, to give that back again in the right spirit of cordiality, required, not merely a nod and a smile, but as wholesome an action of the lungs withal, as a long-winded Parliamentary speech. Sometimes, passengers on foot, or horseback, plodded on a little way beside the cart, for the express purpose of having a chat; and then there was a great deal to be said, on both sides.

Then, Boxer gave occasion to more good-natured recognitions of, and by, the Carrier, than half-a-dozen Christians could have done! Everybody knew him, all along the road—especially the fowls and pigs, who when they saw him approaching, with his body all on one side, and his ears pricked up inquisitively, and that knob of a tail making the most of itself in the air, immediately withdrew into remote back settlements, without waiting for the honour of a nearer acquaintance. He had business everywhere; going down all the turnings, looking into all the wells, bolting in and out of all the cottages, dashing into the midst of all the Dame-Schools, fluttering all the pigeons, magnifying the tails of all the cats, and trotting into the public-houses like a regular customer. Wherever he went, somebody or other might have been heard to cry, "Halloa! Here's Boxer!" and out came that somebody forthwith, accompanied by at least two or three other somebodies, to give John Peerybingle and his pretty wife, Good Day.

The packages and parcels for the errand cart, were numerous; and there were many stoppages to take them in and give them out; which were not by any means the worst parts of the journey. Some people were so full of expectation about their parcels, and other people were so full of wonder about their parcels, and other people were so full of inexhaustible directions about their parcels, and John had such a lively interest in all the parcels, that it was as good as a play. Likewise, there were articles to carry, which required to be considered and discussed, and in reference to the adjustment and disposition of which, councils had to be holden by the Carrier and the senders: at which Boxer usually assisted, in short fits of the closest attention, and long fits of tearing round and round the assembled sages and barking himself hoarse. Of all these little incidents, Dot was the amused and open-eyed spectatress from her chair in the cart; and as she sat there, looking on: a charming little portrait framed to admiration by the tilt: there was no lack of nudgings and glancings and whisperings and envyings among the younger men I promise you. And this delighted John the Carrier, beyond measure; for he was proud to have his little wife admired, knowing that she didn't mind it—that, if anything, she rather liked it perhaps.

The trip was a little foggy, to be sure, in the January weather; and was raw and cold. But who cared for such trifles? Not Dot, decidedly. Not Tilly Slowboy, for she deemed sitting in a cart, on any terms, to be the highest point of human joys; the crowning circumstance of earthly hopes. Not the Baby, I'll be sworn; for it's not in Baby nature to be warmer or more sound asleep, though its capacity is great in both respects, than that blessed young Peerybingle was, all the way.

You couldn't see very far in the fog, of course; but you could see a great deal! It's astonishing how much you may see, in a thicker fog than that, if you will only take the trouble to look for it. Why, even to sit watching for the Fairy-rings in the fields, and for the patches of hoar-frost still lingering in the shade, near hedges and by trees, was a pleasant occupation: to make no mention of the unexpected shapes in which the trees themselves came starting out of the mist, and glided into it again. The hedges were tangled and bare, and waved a multitude of blighted garlands in the wind; but there was no discouragement in this. It was agreeable to contemplate;

for it made the fireside warmer in possession, and the summer greener in expectancy. The river looked chilly; but it was in motion, and moving at a good pace; which was a great point. The canal was rather slow and torpid; that must be admitted. Never mind. It would freeze the sooner when the frost set fairly in, and then there would be skating, and sliding; and the heavy old barges, frozen up somewhere near a wharf, would smoke their rusty iron chimney pipes all day, and have a lazy time of it.

In one place, there was a great mound of weeds or stubble burning; and they watched the fire, so white in the day-time, flaring through the fog, with only here and there a dash of red in it, until, in consequence, as she observed, of the smoke "getting up her nose," Miss Slowboy choked—she could do anything of that sort, on the smallest provocation—and woke the Baby, who wouldn't go to sleep again. But, Boxer, who was in advance some quarter of a mile or so, had already passed the outposts of the town, and gained the corner of the street where Caleb and his daughter lived; and long before they had reached the door, he and the Blind Girl were on the pavement waiting to receive them.

Boxer, by the way, made certain delicate distinctions of his own, in his communication with Bertha, which persuade me fully that he knew her to be blind. He never sought to attract her attention by looking at her, as he often did with other people, but touched her, invariably. What experience he could ever have had of blind people or blind dogs, I don't know. He had never lived with a blind master; nor had Mr. Boxer the elder, nor Mrs. Boxer, nor any of his respectable family on either side, ever been visited with blindness, that I am aware of. He may have found it out for himself, perhaps, but he had got hold of it somehow; and therefore he had hold of Bertha too, by the skirt, and kept hold, until Mrs. Peerybingle and the Baby, and Miss Slowboy, and the basket, were all got safely within doors.

May Fielding was already come; and so was her mother—a little querulous chip of an old lady with a peevish face, who, in right of having preserved a waist like a bedpost, was supposed to be a most transcendent figure; and who, in consequence of having once been better off, or of labouring under an impression that she might have been, if something had happened which never did happen, and seemed to have never been particularly likely to come to pass—but it's all the same—was very genteel and patronising indeed. Gruff and Tackleton was also there, doing the agreeable, with the evident sensation of being as perfectly at home, and as unquestionably in his own element, as a fresh young salmon on the top of the Great Pyramid.

"May! My dear old friend!" cried Dot, running up to meet her. "What a happiness to see you."

Her old friend was, to the full, as hearty and as glad as she; and it really was, if you'll believe me, quite a pleasant sight to see them embrace. Tackleton was a man of taste beyond all question. May was very pretty.

You know sometimes, when you are used to a pretty face, how, when it comes into contact and comparison with another pretty face, it seems for the moment to be homely and faded, and hardly to deserve the high opinion you have had of it. Now, this was not at all the case, either with Dot or May; for May's face set off Dot's, and Dot's face set off May's, so naturally and agreeably, that, as John Peerybingle was very near saying when he came into the room, they ought to have been born sisters: which was the only improvement you could have suggested.

Tackleton had brought his leg of mutton, and, wonderful to relate, a tart besides—but we don't mind a little dissipation when our brides are in the case; we don't get married every day—and in addition to these dainties, there were the Veal and Ham-Pie, and "things," as Mrs. Peerybingle called them; which were chiefly nuts and oranges, and cakes, and such small deer. When the repast was set forth on the board, flanked by Caleb's contribution, which was a great wooden bowl of smoking potatoes (he was prohibited, by solemn compact, from producing any other viands), Tackleton led his intended mother-in-law to the post of honour. For the better gracing of this place at the high Festival, the majestic old soul had adorned herself with a cap, calculated to inspire the thoughtless with sentiments of awe. She also wore her gloves. But let us be genteel, or die!

Caleb sat next his daughter; Dot and her old schoolfellow were side by side; the good Carrier took care of the bottom of the table. Miss Slowboy was isolated, for the time being, from every article of furniture but the chair she sat on, that she might have nothing else to knock the Baby's head against.

As Tilly stared about her at the Dolls and Toys, they stared at her and at the company. The venerable old gentlemen at the street doors (who were all in full action) showed especial interest in the party: pausing occasionally before leaping, as if they were listening to the conversation, and then plunging wildly over and over, a great many times, without halting for breath,—as in a frantic state of delight with the whole proceedings.

Certainly, if these old gentlemen were inclined to have a fiendish joy in the contemplation of Tackleton's discomfiture, they had good reason to be satisfied. Tackleton couldn't get on at all; and the more cheerful his intended bride became in Dot's society, the less he liked it, though he had brought them together for that purpose. For he was a regular dog in the manger, was Tackleton; and when they laughed and he couldn't, he took it into his head, immediately, that they must be laughing at him.

"Ah, May!" said Dot. "Dear dear, what changes! To talk of those merry school-days makes one young again."

"Why, you an't particularly old, at any time; are you?" said Tackleton.

"Look at my sober, plodding husband there," returned Dot. "He adds twenty years to my age at least. Don't you, John?"

"Forty," John replied.

"How many *you*'ll add to May's, I am sure I don't know," said Dot, laughing. "But she can't be much less than a hundred years of age on her next birthday."

"Ha ha!" laughed Tackleton. Hollow as a drum, that laugh though. And he looked as if he could have twisted Dot's neck: comfortably.

"Dear dear!" said Dot. "Only to remember how we used to talk, at school, about the husbands we would choose. I don't know how young, and how handsome, and how gay, and how lively, mine was not to be! And as to May's!—Ah dear! I don't know whether to laugh or cry, when I think what silly girls we were."

May seemed to know which to do; for the colour flushed into her face, and tears stood in her eyes.

"Even the very persons themselves—real live young men—we fixed on sometimes," said Dot. "We little thought how things would come about. I never fixed on John I'm sure; I never so much as thought of him. And if I had told you, you were ever to be married to Mr. Tackleton, why you'd have slapped me. Wouldn't you, May?"

Though May didn't say yes, she certainly didn't say no, or express no, by any means.

Tackleton laughed—quite shouted, he laughed so loud. John Peerybingle laughed too, in his ordinary good-natured and contented manner; but his was a mere whisper of a laugh, to Tackleton's.

"You couldn't help yourselves, for all that. You couldn't resist us, you see," said Tackleton. "Here we are! Here we are! Where are your gay young bridegrooms now?"

"Some of them are dead," said Dot; "and some of them forgotten. Some of them, if they could stand among us at this moment, would not believe we were the same creatures; would not believe that what they saw and heard was real, and we *could* forget them so. No! they would not believe one word of it!"

"Why, Dot!" exclaimed the Carrier. "Little woman!"

She had spoken with such earnestness and fire, that she stood in need of some recalling to herself, without doubt. Her husband's check was very gentle, for he merely interfered, as he supposed, to shield old Tackleton; but it proved effectual, for she stopped, and said no more. There was an uncommon agitation, even in her silence, which the wary Tackleton, who had brought his half-shut eye to bear upon her, noted closely, and remembered to some purpose too, as you will see.

May uttered no word, good or bad, but sat quite still, with her eyes cast down, and made no sign of interest in what had passed. The good lady her mother now interposed: observing, in the first instance, that girls were girls, and byegones byegones, and that so long as young people were young and thoughtless, they would probably conduct themselves like young and thoughtless persons: with two or three other positions of a no less sound and incontrovertible character. She then remarked, in a devout spirit, that she thanked Heaven she had always found in her daughter May, a dutiful and obedient child; for which she took no credit to herself, though she had every reason to believe it was entirely owing to herself. With regard to Mr. Tackleton she said, That he was in a moral point of view an undeniable individual; and That he was in an eligible point of view a son-in-law to be desired, no one in their senses could doubt. (She was very emphatic here.) With regard to the family into which he was so soon about, after some solicitation, to be admitted, she believed Mr. Tackleton knew that, although reduced in purse, it had some pretensions to gentility; and if certain circumstances, not wholly unconnected, she would go so far as to say, with the Indigo Trade, but to which she would not more particularly refer, had happened differently, it might perhaps have been in possession of Wealth. She then remarked that she would not allude to the past, and would not mention that her daughter had for some time rejected the suit of Mr. Tackleton; and that she would not say a great many other things which she did say, at great length. Finally, she delivered it as the general result of her observation and experience, that those marriages in which there was least of what was romantically and sillily called love, were always the happiest; and that she anticipated the greatest possible amount of bliss—not rapturous bliss; but the solid, steady-going article—from the approaching nuptials. She concluded by informing the company that to-morrow was the day she had lived for, expressly; and that when it was over, she would desire nothing better than to be packed up and disposed of, in any genteel place of burial.

As these remarks were quite unanswerable: which is the happy property of all remarks that are sufficiently wide of the purpose: they changed the current of the conversation, and diverted the general attention to the Veal and Ham-Pie, the cold mutton, the potatoes, and the tart. In order that the bottled beer might not be slighted, John Peerybingle proposed To-morrow: the Wedding-Day: and called upon them to drink a bumper to it, before he proceeded on his journey.

For you ought to know that he only rested there, and gave the old horse a bait. He had to go some four of five miles farther on; and when he returned in the evening, he called for Dot, and took another rest on his way home. This was the order of the day on all the Pic-Nic occasions, had been, ever since their institution.

There were two persons present, besides the bride and bridegroom elect, who did but indifferent honour to the toast. One of these was Dot, too flushed and discomposed to adapt herself to any small occurrence of the moment; the other Bertha, who rose up hurriedly, before the rest, and left the table.

"Good bye!" said stout John Peerybingle, pulling on his dreadnought coat. "I shall be back at the old time. Good bye all!"

"Good bye, John," returned Caleb.

He seemed to say it by rote, and to wave his hand in the same unconscious manner; for he stood observing Bertha with an anxious wondering face, that never altered its expression.

"Good bye young shaver!" said the jolly Carrier, bending down to kiss the child; which Tilly Slowboy, now intent upon her knife and fork, had deposited asleep (and strange to say, without damage) in a little cot of Bertha's furnishing; "good bye! Time will come, I suppose, when *you*'ll turn out into the cold, my little friend, and leave your old father to enjoy his pipe and his rheumatics in the chimney-corner; eh? Where's Dot?"

"I'm here, John!" she said, starting.

"Come, come!" returned the Carrier, clapping his sounding hands. "Where's the pipe?"

"I quite forgot the pipe, John."

Forgot the pipe! Was such a wonder ever heard of! She! Forgot the pipe!

"I'll—I'll fill it directly. It's soon done."

But it was not so soon done, either. It lay in the usual place; the Carrier's dreadnought pocket; with the little pouch, her own work; from which she was used to fill it; but her hand shook so, that she entangled it (and yet her hand was small enough to have come out easily, I am sure), and bungled terribly. The filling of the pipe and lighting it, those little offices in which I have commended her discretion, were vilely done, from first to last. During the whole process, Tackleton stood looking on maliciously with the half-closed eye; which, whenever it met hers—or caught it, for it can hardly be said to have ever met another eye: rather being a kind of trap to snatch it up—augmented her confusion in a most remarkable degree.

"Why, what a clumsy Dot you are, this afternoon!" said John. "I could have done it better myself, I verily believe!"

With these good-natured words, he strode away; and presently was heard, in company with Boxer, and the old horse, and the cart, making lively music down the road. What time the dreamy Caleb still stood, watching his blind daughter, with the same expression on his face.

"Bertha!" said Caleb, softly. "What has happened? How changed you are, my darling, in a few hours—since this morning. *You* silent and dull all day! What is it? Tell me!"

"Oh father, father!" cried the Blind Girl, bursting into tears. "Oh my hard, hard Fate!"

Caleb drew his hand across his eyes before he answered her.

"But think how cheerful and how happy you have been, Bertha! How good, and how much loved, by many people."

"That strikes me to the heart, dear father! Always so mindful of me! Always so kind to me!"

Caleb was very much perplexed to understand her.

"To be—to be blind, Bertha, my poor dear," he faultered, "is a great affliction; but—"

"I have never felt it!" cried the Blind Girl. "I have never felt it, in its fulness. Never! I have sometimes wished that I could see you, or could see him; only once, dear father; only for one little minute; that I might know what it is I treasure up," she laid her hands upon her breast, "and hold here! That I might be sure and have it right! And sometimes (but then I was a child) I have wept in my prayers at night, to think that when your images ascended from my heart to Heaven, they might not be the true resemblance of yourselves. But I have never had these feelings long. They have passed away and left me tranquil and contented."

"And they will again," said Caleb.

"But, father! Oh my good, gentle father, bear with me, if I am wicked!" said the Blind Girl. "This is not the sorrow that so weighs me down!"

Her father could not choose but let his moist eyes overflow; she was so earnest and pathetic, but he did not understand her, yet.

"Bring her to me," said Bertha. "I cannot hold it closed and shut within myself. Bring her to me, father!"

She knew he hesitated, and said, "May. Bring May!"

May heard the mention of her name, and coming quietly towards her, touched her on the arm. The Blind Girl turned immediately, and held her by both hands.

"Look into my face, Dear heart, Sweet heart!" said Bertha. "Read it with your beautiful eyes, and tell me if the truth is written on it."

"Dear Bertha, Yes!"

The Blind Girl still, upturning the blank sightless face, down which the tears were coursing fast, addressed her in these words:

"There is not, in my soul, a wish or thought that is not for your good, bright May! There is not, in my soul, a grateful recollection stronger than the deep remembrance which is stored there, of the many many times when, in the full pride of sight and beauty, you have had consideration for Blind Bertha, even when we two were children, or when Bertha was as much a child as ever blindness can be! Every blessing on your head! Light upon your happy course! Not the less, my dear May"; and she drew towards her, in a closer grasp; "not the less, my Bird, because, to-day, the knowledge that you are to be His wife has wrung my heart almost to breaking! Father, May, Mary! oh forgive me that it is so, for the sake of all he has done to relieve the weariness of my dark life: and for the sake of the belief you have in me, when I call Heaven to witness that I could not wish him married to a wife more worthy of his Goodness!"

While speaking, she had released May Fielding's hands, and clasped her garments in an attitude of mingled supplication and love. Sinking lower and lower down, as she proceeded in her strange confession, she dropped at last at the feet of her friend, and hid her blind face in the folds of her dress.

"Great Power!" exclaimed her father, smitten at one blow with the truth, "have I deceived her from the cradle, but to break her heart at last!"

It was well for all of them that Dot, that beaming, useful, busy little Dot—for such she was, whatever faults she had, and however you may learn to hate her, in good time—it was well for all of them, I say, that she was there: or where this would have ended, it were hard to tell. But Dot, recovering her self-possession, interposed, before May could reply, or Caleb say another word.

"Come, come, dear Bertha! come away with me! Give her your arm, May. So! How composed she is, you see, already; and how good it is of her to mind us," said the cheery little woman, kissing her upon the forehead. "Come away, dear Bertha! Come! and here's her good father will come with her; won't you, Caleb? To—be—sure!"

Well, well! she was a noble little Dot in such things, and it must have been an obdurate nature that could have withstood her influence. When she had got poor Caleb and his Bertha away, that they might comfort and console each other, as she knew they only could, she presently came bouncing back,—the saying is, as fresh as any daisy; *I* say fresher—to mount guard over that bridling little piece of consequence in the cap and gloves, and prevent the dear old creature from making discoveries.

"So bring me the precious Baby, Tilly," said she, drawing a chair to the fire; "and while I have it in my lap, here's Mrs. Fielding, Tilly, will tell me all about the management of Babies, and put me right in twenty points where I'm as wrong as can be. Won't you, Mrs. Fielding?"

Not even the Welsh Giant, who, according to the popular expression, was so "slow" as to perform a fatal surgical operation upon himself, in emulation of a juggling-trick achieved by his arch-enemy at breakfast-time; not even he fell half so readily into the snare prepared for him, as the old lady did into this artful Pitfall. The fact of Tackleton having walked out; and furthermore, of two or three people having been talking together at a distance, for two minutes, leaving her to her own resources; was quite enough to have put her on her dignity, and the bewailment of that mysterious convulsion in the Indigo trade, for four-and-twenty hours. But this becoming deference to her experience, on the part of the young mother, was so irresistible, that after a short affectation of humility, she began to enlighten her with the best grace in the world; and sitting bolt upright before the wicked Dot, she did, in half an hour, deliver more infallible domestic recipes and precepts, than would (if acted on) have utterly destroyed and done up that Young Peerybingle, though he had been an Infant Samson.

To change the theme, Dot did a little needlework—she carried the contents of a whole workbox in her pocket; however she contrived it, *I* don't know—then did a little nursing; then a little more needlework; then had a little whispering chat with May, while the old lady dozed; and so in little bits of bustle, which was quite her manner always, found it a very short afternoon. Then, as it grew dark, and as it was a solemn part of this Institution of the Pic-Nic that she should perform all Bertha's household tasks, she trimmed the fire, and swept the hearth, and set the tea-board out, and drew the curtain, and lighted a candle. Then she played an air or two on a rude kind of harp, which Caleb had contrived for Bertha; and played them very well; for Nature had made her delicate little ear as choice a one for music as it would have been for jewels, if she had had any to wear. By this time it was the established hour for having tea; and Tackleton came back again, to share the meal, and spend the evening.

Caleb and Bertha had returned some time before, and Caleb had sat down to his afternoon's work. But he couldn't settle to it, poor fellow, being anxious and remorseful for his daughter. It was touching to see him sitting idle on his working-stool, regarding her so wistfully, and always saying in his face, "have I deceived her from her cradle, but to break her heart!"

When it was night, and tea was done, and Dot had nothing more to do in washing up the cups and saucers; in a word—for I must come to it, and there is no use in putting it off—when the time drew nigh for expecting the Carrier's return in every sound of distant wheels; her manner changed again; her colour came and went; and she was very restless. Not as good wives are, when listening for their husbands. No, no, no. It was another sort of restlessness from that.

Wheels heard. A horse's feet. The barking of a dog. The gradual approach of all the sounds. The scratching paw of Boxer at the door!

"Whose step is that!" cried Bertha, starting up.

"Whose step?" returned the Carrier, standing in the portal, with his brown face ruddy as a winter berry from the keen night air. "Why, mine."

"The other step," said Bertha. "The man's tread behind you!"

"She is not to be deceived," observed the Carrier, laughing. "Come along, sir. You'll be welcome, never fear!"

He spoke in a loud tone; and as he spoke, the deaf old gentleman entered.

"He's not so much a stranger, that you haven't seen him once, Caleb," said the Carrier. "You'll give him house-room till we go?"

"Oh surely John, and take it as an honour."

"He's the best company on earth, to talk secrets in," said John. "I have reasonable good lungs, but he tries 'em, I can tell you. Sit down, sir. All friends here, and glad to see you!"

When he had imparted this assurance, in a voice that amply corroborated what he had said about his lungs, he added in his natural tone, "A chair in the chimney-corner, and leave to sit quite silent and look pleasantly about him, is all he cares for. He's easily pleased."

Bertha had been listening intently. She called Caleb to her side, when he had set the chair, and asked him, in a low voice, to describe their visitor. When he had done so (truly now; with scrupulous fidelity), she moved, for the first time since he had come in; and sighed; and seemed to have no further interest concerning him.

The Carrier was in high spirits, good fellow that he was; and fonder of his little wife than ever.

"A clumsy Dot she was, this afternoon!" he said, encircling her with his rough arm, as she stood, removed from the rest; "and yet I like her somehow. See yonder, Dot!"

He pointed to the old man. She looked down. I think she trembled.

"He's—ha ha ha!—he's full of admiration for you!" said the Carrier. "Talked of nothing else, the whole way here. Why, he's a brave old boy. I like him for it!"

"I wish he had had a better subject, John," she said, with an uneasy glance about the room; at Tackleton especially.

"A better subject!" cried the jovial John. "There's no such thing. Come! off with the great-coat, off with the thick shawl, off with the heavy wrappers! and a cosy half-hour by the fire! My humble service, Mistress. A game at cribbage, you and I? That's hearty. The cards and board, Dot. And a glass of beer here, if there's any left, small wife!"

His challenge was addressed to the old lady, who accepting it with gracious readiness, they were soon engaged upon the game. At first, the Carrier looked about him sometimes, with a smile, or now and then called Dot to peep over his shoulder at his hand, and advise him on some knotty point. But his adversary being a rigid disciplinarian, and subject to an occasional weakness in respect of pegging more than she was entitled to, required such vigilance on his part, as left him neither eyes nor ears to spare. Thus, his whole attention gradually became absorbed upon the cards; and he thought of nothing else, until a hand upon his shoulder restored him to a consciousness of Tackleton.

"I am sorry to disturb you—but a word, directly."

"I'm going to deal," returned the Carrier. "It's a crisis."

"It is," said Tackleton. "Come here, man!"

There was that in his pale face which made the other rise immediately, and ask him, in a hurry, what the matter was.

"Hush! John Peerybingle," said Tackleton. "I am sorry for this. I am indeed. I have been afraid of it. I have suspected it from the first."

"What is it?" asked the Carrier, with a frightened aspect.

"Hush! I'll show you, if you'll come with me."

The Carrier accompanied him, without another word. They went across a yard, where the stars were shining, and by a little side-door, into Tackleton's own counting-house, where there was a glass window, commanding the ware-room, which was closed for the night. There was no light in the counting-house itself, but there were lamps in the long narrow ware-room; and consequently the window was bright.

"A moment!" said Tackleton. "Can you bear to look through that window, do you think?"

"Why not?" returned the Carrier.

"A moment more," said Tackleton. "Don't commit any violence. It's of no use. It's dangerous too. You're a strong-made man; and you might do murder before you know it."

The Carrier looked him in the face, and recoiled a step as if he had been struck. In one stride he was at the window, and he saw—

Oh Shadow on the Hearth! Oh truthful Cricket! Oh perfidious Wife!

He saw her, with the old man; old no longer, but erect and gallant: bearing in his hand the false white hair that had won his way into their desolate and miserable home. He saw her listening to him, as he bent his head to whisper in her ear; and suffering him to clasp her round the waist, as they moved slowly down the dim wooden gallery towards the door by which they had entered it. He saw them stop, and saw her turn—to have the face, the face he loved so, so presented to his view!—and saw her, with her own hands, adjust the Lie upon his head, laughing, as she did it, at his unsuspicious nature!

He clenched his strong right hand at first, as if it would have beaten down a lion. But opening it immediately again, he spread it out before the eyes of Tackleton (for he was tender of her, even then), and so, as they passed out, fell down upon a desk, and was as weak as any infant.

He was wrapped up to the chin, and busy with his horse and parcels, when she came into the room, prepared for going home.

"Now John, dear! Good night May! Good night, Bertha!"

Could she kiss them? Could she be blithe and cheerful in her parting? Could she venture to reveal her face to them without a blush? Yes. Tackleton observed her closely, and she did all this.

Tilly was hushing the Baby, and she crossed and re-crossed Tackleton, a dozen times, repeating drowsily:

"Did the knowledge that it was to be its wifes, then, wring its hearts almost to breaking; and did its fathers deceive it from its cradles but to break its hearts at last!"

"Now, Tilly, give me the Baby! Good night, Mr. Tackleton. Where's John, for Goodness' sake?"

"He's going to walk beside the horse's head," said Tackleton; who helped her to her seat.

"My dear John. Walk? To-night?"

The muffled figure of her husband made a hasty sign in the affirmative; and the false Stranger and the little nurse being in their places, the old horse moved off. Boxer, the unconscious Boxer, running on before, running back, running round and round the cart, and barking as triumphantly and merrily as ever.

When Tackleton had gone off likewise, escorting May and her mother home, poor Caleb sat down by the fire beside his daughter; anxious and remorseful at the core; and still saying in his wistful contemplation of her, "have I deceived her from her cradle, but to break her heart at last!"

The toys that had been set in motion for the Baby, had all stopped, and run down, long ago. In the faint light and silence, the imperturbably calm dolls; the agitated rocking-horses with distended eyes and nostrils; the old gentlemen at the street-doors, standing half doubled up upon their failing knees and ankles; the wry-faced nut-crackers; the very Beasts upon their way into the Ark, in twos, like a Boarding School out walking; might have been imagined to be stricken motionless with fantastic wonder, at Dot being false, or Tackleton beloved, under any combination of circumstances.

Chirp the Third

THE DUTCH CLOCK IN THE CORNER STRUCK TEN, WHEN THE CARRIER SAT down by his fireside. So troubled and grief-worn, that he seemed to scare the Cuckoo, who, having cut his ten melodious announcements as short as possible, plunged back into the Moorish Palace again, and clapped his little door behind him, as if the unwonted spectacle were too much for his feelings.

If the little Haymaker had been armed with the sharpest of scythes, and had cut at every stroke into the Carrier's heart, he never could have gashed and wounded it, as Dot had done.

It was a heart so full of love for her; so bound up and held together by innumerable threads of winning remembrance, spun from the daily working of her many qualities of endearment; it was a heart in which she had enshrined herself so gently and so closely; a heart so single and so earnest in its Truth: so strong in right, so weak in wrong; that it could cherish neither passion nor revenge at first, and had only room to hold the broken image of its Idol.

But slowly, slowly; as the Carrier sat brooding on his hearth, now cold and dark; other and fiercer thoughts began to rise within him, as an angry wind comes rising in the night. The Stranger was beneath his outraged roof. Three steps would take him to his chamber door. One blow would beat it in. "You might do Murder before you know it," Tackleton had said. How could it be murder, if he gave the villain time to grapple with him hand to hand! He was the younger man.

It was an ill-timed thought, bad for the dark mood of his mind. It was an angry thought, goading him to some avenging act, that should change the cheerful house into a haunted place which lonely travellers would dread to pass by night; and where the timid would see shadows struggling in the ruined windows when the moon was dim, and hear wild noises in the stormy weather.

He was the younger man! Yes, yes; some lover who had won the heart that *he* had never touched. Some lover of her early choice: of whom she had thought and dreamed: for whom she had pined and pined: when he had fancied her so happy by his side. Oh agony to think of it!

She had been above-stairs with the Baby, getting it to bed. As he sat brooding on the hearth, she came close beside him, without his knowledge—in the turning of the rack of his great misery, he lost all other sounds—and put her little stool at his feet. He only knew it, when he felt her hand upon his own, and saw her looking up into his face.

With wonder? No. It was his first impression, and he was fain to look at her again, to set it right. No, not with wonder. With an eager and inquiring look; but not with wonder. At first it was alarmed and serious; then, it changed into a strange, wild, dreadful smile of recognition of his thoughts; then, there was nothing but her clasped hands on her brow, and her bent head, and falling hair.

Though the power of Omnipotence had been his to wield at that moment, he had too much of its Diviner property of Mercy in his breast, to have turned one feather's weight of it against her. But he could not bear to see her crouching down upon the little seat where he had often looked on her, with love and pride, so innocent and gay; and, when she rose and left him, sobbing as she went, he felt it a relief to have the vacant place beside him rather than her so long cherished presence. This in itself was anguish keener than all: reminding him how desolate he was become, and how the great bond of his life was rent asunder.

The more he felt this, and the more he knew he could have better borne to see her lying prematurely dead before him with their little child upon her breast, the higher and the stronger rose his wrath against his enemy. He looked about him for a weapon.

There was a Gun, hanging on the wall. He took it down, and moved a pace or two towards the door of the perfidious Stranger's room. He knew the Gun was loaded. Some shadowy idea that it was just to shoot this man like a Wild Beast, seized him, and dilated in his mind until it grew into a monstrous demon in complete possession of him, casting out all milder thoughts and setting up its undivided empire.

That phrase is wrong. Not casting out his milder thoughts, but artfully transforming them. Changing them into scourges to drive him on. Turning water into blood, love into hate, gentleness into blind ferocity. Her image, sorrowing, humbled, but still pleading to his tenderness and mercy with resistless power, never left his mind; but, staying there, it urged him to the door; raised the weapon to his shoulder; fitted and nerved his finger to the trigger; and cried "Kill him! In his Bed!"

He reversed the Gun to beat the stock upon the door; he already held it lifted in the air; some indistinct design was in his thoughts of calling out to him to fly, for God's sake, by the window—

When, suddenly, the struggling fire illumined the whole chimney with a glow of light; and the Cricket on the Hearth began to Chirp!

No sound he could have heard; no human voice, not even hers; could so have moved and softened him. The artless words in which she had told him of her love for this same Cricket, were once more freshly spoken; her trembling, earnest manner at the moment, was again before him; her pleasant voice—oh what a voice it was, for making household music at the fireside of an honest man!—thrilled through and through his better nature, and awoke it into life and action.

He recoiled from the door, like a man walking in his sleep, awakened from a frightful dream; and put the Gun aside. Clasping his hands before his face, he then sat down again beside the fire, and found relief in tears.

The Cricket on the Hearth came out into the room, and stood in Fairy shape before him.

"'I love it,'" said the Fairy Voice, repeating what he well remembered, "'for the many times I have heard it, and the many thoughts its harmless music has given me.'"

"She said so!" cried the Carrier. "True!"

"'This has been a happy home, John; and I love the Cricket for its sake!'"

"It has been, Heaven knows," returned the Carrier. "She made it happy, always,—until now."

"So gracefully sweet-tempered; so domestic, joyful, busy, and light-hearted!" said the Voice.

"Otherwise I never could have loved her as I did," returned the Carrier.

The Voice, correcting him, said "do."

The Carrier repeated "as I did." But not firmly. His faltering tongue resisted his control, and would speak in its own way, for itself and him.

The Figure, in an attitude of invocation, raised its hand and said:

"Upon your own hearth—"

"The hearth she has blighted," interposed the Carrier.

"The hearth she has—how often!—blessed and brightened," said the Cricket; "the hearth which, but for her, were only a few stones and bricks and rusty bars, but which has been, through her, the Altar of your Home; on which you have nightly sacrificed some petty passion, selfishness, or care, and offered up the homage of a tranquil mind, a trusting nature, and an overflowing heart; so that the smoke from this poor chimney has gone upward with a better fragrance than the richest incense that is burnt before the richest shrines in all the gaudy Temples of this World!—Upon your own hearth; in its quiet sanctuary; surrounded by its gentle influences and associations; hear her! Hear me! Hear everything that speaks the language of your hearth and home!"

"And pleads for her?" inquired the Carrier.

"All things that speak the language of your hearth and home, *must* plead for her!" returned the Cricket. "For they speak the truth."

And while the Carrier, with his head upon his hands, continued to sit meditating in his chair, the Presence stood beside him, suggesting his reflections by its power, and presenting them before him, as in a Glass or Picture. It was not a solitary Presence. From the hearthstone, from the chimney, from the clock, the pipe, the kettle, and the cradle; from the floor, the walls, the ceiling, and the stairs; from the cart without, and the cupboard within, and the household implements; from every thing and every place with which she had ever been familiar, and with which she had ever entwined one recollection of herself in her unhappy husband's mind; Fairies came trooping forth. Not to stand beside him as the Cricket did, but to busy and bestir themselves. To do all honour to her image. To pull him by the skirts, and point to it when it appeared. To cluster round it, and embrace it, and strew flowers for it to tread on. To try to crown its fair head with their tiny hands. To show that they were fond of it and loved it; and that there was not one ugly, wicked or accusatory creature to claim knowledge of it—none but their playful and approving selves.

His thoughts were constant to her Image. It was always there.

She sat plying her needle, before the fire, and singing to herself. Such a blithe, thriving, steady little Dot! The fairy figures turned upon him all at once, by one consent, with one prodigious concentrated stare, and seemed to say, "Is this the light wife you are mourning for!"

There were sounds of gaiety outside, musical instruments, and noisy tongues, and laughter. A crowd of young merry-makers came pouring in, among whom were May Fielding and a score of pretty girls. Dot was the fairest of them all; as young as any of them too. They came to summon her to join their party. It was a dance. If ever little foot were made for dancing, hers was, surely. But she laughed, and shook her head, and pointed to her cookery on the fire, and her table ready spread: with an exulting defiance that rendered her more charming than she was before. And so she merrily dismissed them, nodding to her would-be partners, one by one, as they passed, but with a comical indifference, enough to make them go and drown themselves immediately if they were her admirers—and they must have been so, more or less; they couldn't help it. And yet indifference was not her character. Oh no! For presently, there came a certain Carrier to the door; and bless her what a welcome she bestowed upon him!

Again the staring figures turned upon him all at once, and seemed to say, "Is this the wife who has forsaken you!"

A shadow fell upon the mirror or the picture: call it what you will. A great shadow of the Stranger, as he first stood underneath their roof; covering its surface, and blotting out all other objects. But the nimble Fairies worked like bees to clear it off again; and Dot again was there. Still bright and beautiful.

Rocking her little Baby in its cradle; singing to it softly; and resting her head upon a shoulder which had its counterpart in the musing figure by which the Fairy Cricket stood.

The night —I mean the real night: not going by Fairy clocks—was wearing now; and in this stage of the Carrier's thoughts, the moon burst out, and shone brightly in the sky. Perhaps some calm and quiet light had risen also, in his mind; and he could think more soberly of what had happened.

Although the shadow of the Stranger fell at intervals upon the glass—always distinct, and big, and thoroughly defined—it never fell so darkly as at first. Whenever it appeared, the Fairies uttered a general cry of consternation, and plied their little arms and legs, with inconceivable activity, to rub it out. And whenever they got at Dot again, and showed her to him once more, bright and beautiful, they cheered in the most inspiring manner.

They never showed her, otherwise than beautiful and bright, for they were Household Spirits to whom Falsehood is annihilation; and being so, what Dot was there for them, but the one active, beaming, pleasant little creature who had been the light and sun of the Carrier's Home!

The Fairies were prodigiously excited when they showed her, with the Baby, gossiping among a knot of sage old matrons, and affecting to be wondrous old and matronly herself, and leaning in a staid, demure old way upon her husband's arm, attempting—she! such a bud of a little woman—to convey the idea of having abjured the vanities of the world in general, and of being the sort of person to whom it was no novelty at all to be a mother; yet in the same breath, they showed her, laughing at the Carrier for being awkward, and pulling up his shirt-collar to make him smart, and mincing merrily about that very room to teach him how to dance!

They turned, and stared immensely at him when they showed her with the Blind Girl; for though she carried cheerfulness and animation with her wheresoever she went, she bore those influences into Caleb Plummer's home, heaped up and running over. The Blind Girl's love for her, and trust in her, and gratitude to her; her own good busy way of setting Bertha's thanks aside; her dexterous little arts for filling up each moment of the visit in doing something useful to the house, and really working hard while feigning to make holiday; her bountiful provision of those standing delicacies, the Veal and Ham-Pie and the bottles of Beer; her radiant little face arriving at the door, and taking leave; the wonderful expression in her whole self, from her neat foot to the crown of her head, of being a part of the establishment—a something necessary to it, which it couldn't be without; all this the Fairies revelled in, and loved her for. And once again they looked upon him all at once, appealingly, and seemed to say, while some among them nestled in her dress and fondled her, "Is this the Wife who has betrayed your confidence!"

More than once, or twice, or thrice, in the long thoughtful night, they showed her to him sitting on her favourite seat, with her bent head, her hands clasped on her brow, her falling hair. As he had seen her last. And when they found her thus, they neither turned nor looked upon him, but gathered close round her, and comforted and kissed her, and pressed on one another to show sympathy and kindness to her, and forgot him altogether.

Thus the night passed. The moon went down; the stars grew pale; the cold day broke; the sun rose. The Carrier still sat, musing, in the chimney corner. He had sat there, with his head upon his hands, all night. All night the faithful Cricket had been Chirp, Chirp, Chirping on the Hearth. All night he had listened to its voice. All night, the household Fairies had been busy with him. All night, she had been amiable and blameless in the Glass, except when that one shadow fell upon it.

He rose up when it was broad day, and washed and dressed himself. He couldn't go about his customary cheerful avocations; he wanted spirit for them; but it mattered the less, that it was Tackleton's wedding-day, and he had arranged to make his rounds by proxy. He thought to have gone merrily to church with Dot. But such plans were at an end. It was their own wedding-day too. Ah! how little he had looked for such a close to such a year!

The Carrier had expected that Tackleton would pay him an early visit; and he was right. He had not walked to and fro before his own door, many minutes, when he saw the Toy-merchant coming in his chaise along the road. As the chaise drew nearer, he perceived that Tackleton was dressed out sprucely, for his marriage: and had decorated his horse's head with flowers and favours.

The horse looked much more like a bridegroom than Tackleton, whose half-closed eye was more disagreeably expressive than ever. But the Carrier took little heed of this. His thoughts had other occupation.

"John Peerybingle!" said Tackleton, with an air of condolence. "My good fellow, how do you find yourself this morning?"

"I have had but a poor night, Master Tackleton," returned the Carrier, shaking his head: "for I have been a good deal disturbed in my mind. But it's over now! Can you spare me half an hour or so, for some private talk?"

"I came on purpose," returned Tackleton, alighting. "Never mind the horse. He'll stand quiet enough, with the reins over this post, if you'll give him a mouthful of hay."

The Carrier having brought it from his stable, and set it before him, they turned into the house.

"You are not married before noon," he said, "I think?"

"No," answered Tackleton. "Plenty of time. Plenty of time."

When they entered the kitchen, Tilly Slowboy was rapping at the Stranger's door; which was only removed from it by a few steps. One of her very red eyes (for Tilly had been crying all night long, because her mistress cried) was at the keyhole; and she was knocking very loud; and seemed frightened.

"If you please I can't make nobody hear," said Tilly, looking round. "I hope nobody an't gone and been and died if you please!"

This philanthropic wish, Miss Slowboy emphasised with various new raps and kicks at the door; which led to no result whatever.

"Shall I go?" said Tackleton. "It's curious."

The Carrier, who had turned his face from the door, signed to him to go if he would.

So Tackleton went to Tilly Slowboy's relief; and he too kicked and knocked; and he too failed to get the least reply. But he thought of trying the handle of the door; and as it opened easily, he peeped in, looked in, went in, and soon came running out again.

"John Peerybingle," said Tackleton, in his ear. "I hope there has been nothing—nothing rash in the night?"

The Carrier turned upon him quickly.

"Because he's gone!" said Tackleton; "and the window's open. I don't see any marks—to be sure it's almost on a level with the garden: but I was afraid there might have been some—some scuffle. Eh?"

He nearly shut up the expressive eye altogether; he looked at him so hard. And he gave his eye, and his face, and his whole person, a sharp twist. As if he would have screwed the truth out of him.

"Make yourself easy," said the Carrier. "He went into that room last night, without harm in word or deed from me, and no one has entered it since. He is away of his own free will. I'd go out gladly at that door, and beg my bread from house to house, for life, if I could so change the past that he had never come. But he has come and gone. And I have done with him!"

"Oh!—Well, I think he has got off pretty easy," said Tackleton, taking a chair.

The sneer was lost upon the Carrier, who sat down too, and shaded his face with his hand, for some little time, before proceeding.

"You showed me last night," he said at length, "my wife; my wife that I love; secretly—"

"And tenderly," insinuated Tackleton.

"Conniving at that man's disguise, and giving him opportunities of meeting her alone. I think there's no sight I wouldn't have rather seen than that. I think there's no man in the world I wouldn't have rather had to show it me."

"I confess to having had my suspicions always," said Tackleton. "And that has made me objectionable here, I know."

"But as you did show it me," pursued the Carrier, not minding him; "and as you saw her, my wife, my wife that I love"—his voice, and eye, and hand, grew steadier and firmer as he repeated these words: evidently in pursuance of a steadfast purpose—"as you saw her at this disadvantage, it is right and just that you should also see with my eyes, and look into my breast, and know what my mind is, upon the subject. For it's settled," said the Carrier, regarding him attentively. "And nothing can shake it now."

Tackleton muttered a few general words of assent, about its being necessary to vindicate something or other; but he was overawed by the manner of his companion. Plain and unpolished as it was, it had a something dignified and noble in it, which nothing but the soul of generous honour dwelling in the man could have imparted.

"I am a plain, rough man," pursued the Carrier, "with very little to recommend me. I am not a clever man, as you very well know. I am not a young man. I loved my little Dot, because I had seen her grow up, from a child, in her father's house; because I knew how precious she was; because she had been my life, for years and years. There's many men I can't compare with, who never could have loved my little Dot like me, I think!"

He paused, and softly beat the ground a short time with his foot, before resuming:

"I often thought that though I wasn't good enough for her, I should make her a kind husband, and perhaps know her value better than another; and in this way I reconciled it to myself, and came to think it might be possible that we should be married. And in the end it came about, and we *were* married."

"Hah!" said Tackleton, with a significant shake of the head.

"I had studied myself; I had had experience of myself; I knew how much I loved her, and how happy I should be," pursued the Carrier. "But I had not—I feel it now—sufficiently considered her."

"To be sure," said Tackleton. "Giddiness, frivolity, fickleness, love of admiration! Not considered! All left out of sight! Hah!"

"You had best not interrupt me," said the Carrier, with some sternness, "till you understand me; and you're wide of doing so. If, yesterday, I'd have struck that man down at a blow, who dared to breathe a word against her, to-day I'd set my foot upon his face, if he was my brother!"

The Toy-merchant gazed at him in astonishment. He went on in a softer tone:

"Did I consider," said the Carrier, "that I took her; at her age, and with her beauty; from her young companions, and the many scenes of which she was the ornament; in which she was the brightest little star that ever shone, to shut her up from day to day in my dull house, and keep my tedious company? Did I consider how little suited I was to her sprightly humour, and how wearisome a plodding man like me must be, to one of her quick spirit? Did I consider that it was no merit in me, or claim in me, that I loved her, when everybody must, who knew her? Never. I took advantage of her hopeful nature and her cheerful disposition; and I married her. I wish I never had! For her sake; not for mine!"

The Toy-merchant gazed at him, without winking. Even the half-shut eye was open now.

"Heaven bless her!" said the Carrier, "for the cheerful constancy with which she tried to keep the knowledge of this from me! And Heaven help me, that, in my slow mind, I have not found it out before! Poor child! Poor Dot! *I* not to find it out, who have seen her eyes fill with tears, when such a marriage as our own was spoken of! I, who have seen the secret trembling on her lips a hundred times, and never suspected it till last night! Poor girl! That I could ever hope she would be fond of me! That I could ever believe she was!"

"She made a show of it," said Tackleton. "She made such a show of it, that to tell you the truth it was the origin of my misgivings."

And here he asserted the superiority of May Fielding, who certainly made no sort of show of being fond of *him*.

"She has tried," said the poor Carrier, with greater emotion than he had exhibited yet; "I only now begin to know how hard she has tried, to be my dutiful and zealous wife. How good she has been; how much she has done; how brave and strong a heart she has; let the happiness I have known under this roof bear witness! It will be some help and comfort to me, when I am here alone."

"Here alone?" said Tackleton. "Oh! Then you do mean to take some notice of this?"

"I mean," returned the Carrier, "to do her the greatest kindness, and make her the best reparation, in my power. I can release her from the daily pain of an unequal marriage, and the struggle to conceal it. She shall be as free as I can render her."

"Make *her* reparation!" exclaimed Tackleton, twisting and turning his great ears with his hands. "There must be something wrong here. You didn't say that, of course."

The Carrier set his grip upon the collar of the Toy-merchant, and shook him like a reed.

"Listen to me!" he said. "And take care that you hear me right. Listen to me. Do I speak plainly?"

"Very plainly indeed," answered Tackleton.

"As if I meant it?"

"Very much as if you meant it."

"I sat upon that hearth, last night, all night," exclaimed the Carrier. "On the spot where she has often sat beside me, with her sweet face looking into mine. I called up her whole life, day by day. I had her dear self, in its every passage, in review before me. And upon my soul she is innocent, if there is One to judge the innocent and guilty!"

Staunch Cricket on the Hearth! Loyal household Fairies!

"Passion and distrust have left me!" said the Carrier; "and nothing but my grief remains. In an unhappy moment some old lover, better suited to her tastes and years than I; forsaken, perhaps, for me, against her will; returned. In an unhappy moment:

taken by surprise, and wanting time to think of what she did: she made herself a party to his treachery, by concealing it. Last night she saw him, in the interview we witnessed. It was wrong. But otherwise than this she is innocent if there is Truth on earth!"

"If that is your opinion"—Tackleton began.

"So, let her go!" pursued the Carrier. "Go, with my blessing for the many happy hours she has given me, and my forgiveness for any pang she has caused me. Let her go, and have the peace of mind I wish her! She'll never hate me. She'll learn to like me better, when I'm not a drag upon her, and she wears the chain I have riveted, more lightly. This is the day on which I took her, with so little thought for her enjoyment, from her home. To-day she shall return to it, and I will trouble her no more. Her father and mother will be here to-day—we had made a little plan for keeping it together—and they shall take her home. I can trust her, there, or anywhere. She leaves me without blame, and she will live so I am sure. If I should die—I may perhaps while she is still young; I have lost some courage in a few hours—she'll find that I remembered her, and loved her to the last! This is the end of what you showed me. Now, it's over!"

"Oh no, John, not over. Do not say it's over yet! Not quite yet. I have heard your noble words. I could not steal away, pretending to be ignorant of what has affected me with such deep gratitude. Do not say it's over, 'till the clock has struck again!"

She had entered shortly after Tackleton, and had remained there. She never looked at Tackleton, but fixed her eyes upon her husband. But she kept away from him, setting as wide a space as possible between them; and though she spoke with most impassioned earnestness, she went no nearer to him even then. How different in this from her old self!

"No hand can make the clock which will strike again for me the hours that are gone," replied the Carrier, with a faint smile. "But let it be so, if you will, my dear. It will strike soon. It's of little matter what we say. I'd try to please you in a harder case than that."

"Well!" muttered Tackleton. "I must be off, for when the clock strikes again, it'll be necessary for me to be upon my way to church. Good morning, John Peerybingle. I'm sorry to be deprived of the pleasure of your company. Sorry for the loss, and the occasion of it too!"

"I have spoken plainly?" said the Carrier, accompanying him to the door.

"Oh quite!"

"And you'll remember what I have said?"

"Why, if you compel me to make the observation," said Tackleton, previously taking the precaution of getting into his chaise; "I must say that it was so very unexpected, that I'm far from being likely to forget it."

"The better for us both," returned the Carrier. "Good bye. I give you joy!"

"I wish I could give it to *you*," said Tackleton. "As I can't; thank'ee. Between ourselves (as I told you before, eh?) I don't much think I shall have the less joy in my married life, because May hasn't been too officious about me, and too demonstrative. Good bye! Take care of yourself."

The Carrier stood looking after him until he was smaller in the distance than his horse's flowers and favours near at hand; and then, with a deep sigh, went strolling like a restless, broken man, among some neighbouring elms; unwilling to return until the clock was on the eve of striking.

His little wife, being left alone, sobbed piteously; but often dried her eyes and checked herself, to say how good he was, how excellent he was! and once or twice she laughed; so heartily, triumphantly, and incoherently (still crying all the time), that Tilly was quite horrified.

"Ow if you please don't!" said Tilly. "It's enough to dead and bury the Baby, so it is if you please."

"Will you bring him sometimes, to see his father, Tilly," inquired her mistress, drying her eyes; "when I can't live here, and have gone to my old home?"

"Ow if you please don't!" cried Tilly, throwing back her head, and bursting out into a howl—she looked at the moment uncommonly like Boxer. "Ow if you please don't! Ow, what has everybody gone and been and done with everybody, making everybody else so wretched! Ow-w-w-w!"

The soft-hearted Slowboy trailed off at this juncture, into such a deplorable howl, the more tremendous from its long suppression, that she must infallibly have awakened the Baby, and frightened him into something serious (probably convulsions), if her eyes had not encountered Caleb Plummer, leading in his daughter. This spectacle restoring her to a sense of the proprieties, she stood for some few moments silent, with her mouth wide open; and then, posting off to the bed on which the Baby lay asleep, danced in a weird, Saint Vitus manner on the floor, and at the same time rummaged with her face and head among the bedclothes: apparently deriving much relief from those extraordinary operations.

"Mary!" said Bertha. "Not at the marriage!"

"I told her you would not be there, mum," whispered Caleb. "I heard as much last night. But bless you," said the little man, taking her tenderly by both hands, "*I* don't care for what they say. *I* don't believe them. There an't much of me, but that little should be torn to pieces sooner than I'd trust a word against you!"

He put his arms about her and hugged her, as a child might have hugged one of his own dolls.

"Bertha couldn't stay at home this morning," said Caleb. "She was afraid, I know, to hear the Bells ring: and couldn't trust herself to be so near them on their wedding-day. So we started in good time, and came here. I have been thinking of what I have done," said Caleb, after a moment's pause; "I have been blaming myself 'till I hardly knew what to do or where to turn, for the distress of mind I have caused her; and I've come to the conclusion that I'd better, if you'll stay with me, mum, the while, tell her the truth. You'll stay with me the while?" he inquired, trembling from head to foot. "I don't know what effect it may have upon her; I don't know what she'll think of me; I don't know that she'll ever care for her poor father afterwards. But it's best for her that she should be undeceived, and I must bear the consequences as I deserve!"

"Mary," said Bertha, "where is your hand! Ah! Here it is; here it is!" pressing it to her lips, with a smile, and drawing it through her arm. "I heard them speaking softly among themselves, last night, of some blame against you. They were wrong."

The Carrier's Wife was silent. Caleb answered for her.

"They were wrong," he said.

"I knew it!" cried Bertha, proudly. "I told them so. I scorned to hear a word! Blame *her* with justice!" she pressed the hand between her own, and the soft cheek against her face. "No! I am not so Blind as that."

Her father went on one side of her, while Dot remained upon the other: holding her hand.

"I know you all," said Bertha, "better than you think. But none so well as her. Not even you, father. There is nothing half so real and so true about me, as she is. If I could be restored to sight this instant, and not a word were spoken, I could choose her from a crowd! My Sister!"

"Bertha, my dear!" said Caleb, "I have something on my mind I want to tell you, while we three are alone. Hear me kindly! I have a confession to make to you, my darling."

"A confession, father?"

"I have wandered from the truth and lost myself, my child," said Caleb, with a pitiable expression in his bewildered face. "I have wandered from the truth, intending to be kind to you; and have been cruel."

She turned her wonder-stricken face towards him, and repeated "Cruel!"

"He accuses himself too strongly, Bertha," said Dot. "You'll say so, presently. You'll be the first to tell him so."

"He cruel to me!" cried Bertha, with a smile of incredulity.

"Not meaning it, my child," said Caleb. "But I have been; though I never suspected it, 'till yesterday. My dear blind daughter, hear me and forgive me! The world you live in, heart of mine, doesn't exist as I have represented it. The eyes you have trusted in, have been false to you."

She turned her wonder-stricken face towards him still; but drew back, and clung closer to her friend.

"Your road in life was rough, my poor one," said Caleb, "and I meant to smooth it for you. I have altered objects, changed the characters of people, invented many things that never have been, to make you happier. I have had concealments from you, put deceptions on you, God forgive me! and surrounded you with fancies."

"But living people are not fancies!" she said hurriedly, and turning very pale, and still retiring from him. "You can't change them."

"I have done so, Bertha," pleaded Caleb. "There is one person that you know, my Dove—"

"Oh father! why do you say, I know?" she answered, in a term of keen reproach. "What and whom do *I* know! I who have no leader! I so miserably blind."

In the anguish of her heart, she stretched out her hands, as if she were groping her way; then spread them, in a manner most forlorn and sad, upon her face.

"The marriage that takes place to-day," said Caleb, "is with a stern, sordid, grinding man. A hard master to you and me, my dear, for many years. Ugly in his looks, and in his nature. Cold and callous always. Unlike what I have painted him to you in everything, my child. In everything."

"Oh why," cried the Blind Girl, tortured, as it seemed, almost beyond endurance, "why did you ever do this! Why did you ever fill my heart so full, and then come in like Death, and tear away the objects of my love! Oh Heaven, how blind I am! How helpless and alone!"

Her afflicted father hung his head, and offered no reply but in his penitence and sorrow.

She had been but a short time in this passion of regret, when the Cricket on the Hearth, unheard by all but her, began to chirp. Not merrily, but in a low, faint, sorrowing way. It was so mournful that her tears began to flow; and when the Presence which had been beside the Carrier all night, appeared behind her, pointing to her father, they fell down like rain.

She heard the Cricket-voice more plainly soon; and was conscious, through her blindness, of the Presence hovering about her father.

"Mary," said the Blind Girl, "tell me what my home is. What it truly is."

"It is a poor place, Bertha; very poor and bare indeed. The house will scarcely keep out wind and rain another winter. It is as roughly shielded from the weather, Bertha," Dot continued in a low, clear voice, "as your poor father in his sack cloth coat."

The Blind Girl, greatly agitated, rose, and led the Carrier's little wife aside.

"Those presents that I took such care of; that came almost at my wish, and were so dearly welcome to me," she said, trembling; "where did they come from? Did you send them?"

"No."

"Who then?"

Dot saw she knew, already, and was silent. The Blind Girl spread her hands before her face again. But in quite another manner now.

"Dear Mary, a moment. One moment? More this way. Speak softly to me. You are true, I know. You'd not deceive me now; would you?"

"No, Bertha, indeed!"

"No, I am sure you would not. You have too much pity for me. Mary, look across the room to where we were just now—to where my father is—my father, so compassionate and loving to me—and tell me what you see."

"I see," said Dot, who understood her well, "an old man sitting in a chair, and leaning sorrowfully on the back, with his face resting on his hand. As if his child should comfort him, Bertha."

"Yes, yes. She will. Go on."

"He is an old man, worn with care and work. He is a spare, dejected, thoughtful, grey-haired man. I see him now, despondent and bowed down, and striving against nothing. But, Bertha, I have seen him many times before, and striving hard in many ways for one great sacred object. And I honour his grey head, and bless him!"

The Blind Girl broke away from her; and throwing herself upon her knees before him, took the grey head to her breast.

"It is my sight restored. It is my sight!" she cried. "I have been blind, and now my eyes are open. I never knew him! To think I might have died, and never truly seen the father who has been so loving to me!"

There were no words for Caleb's emotion.

"There is not a gallant figure on this earth," exclaimed the Blind Girl, holding him in her embrace, "that I would love so dearly, and would cherish so devotedly, as this! The greyer, and more worn, the dearer, father! Never let them say I am blind again. There's not a furrow in his face, there's not a hair upon his head, that shall be forgotten in my prayers and thanks to Heaven!"

Caleb managed to articulate "My Bertha!"

"And in my Blindness, I believed him," said the girl, caressing him with tears of exquisite affection, "to be so different! And having him beside me, day by day, so mindful of me—always, never dreamed of this!"

"The fresh smart father in the blue coat, Bertha," said poor Caleb. "He's gone!"

"Nothing is gone," she answered. "Dearest father, no! Everything is here—in you. The father that I loved so well; the father that I never loved enough, and never knew; the benefactor whom I first began to reverence and love, because he had such sympathy for me; All are here in you. Nothing is dead to me. The soul of all that was most dear to me is here—here, with the worn face, and the grey head. And I am NOT blind, father, any longer!"

Dot's whole attention had been concentrated, during this discourse, upon the father and daughter; but looking, now, towards the little Haymaker in the Moorish meadow, she saw that the clock was within a few minutes of striking, and fell, immediately, into a nervous and excited state.

"Father," said Bertha, hesitating. "Mary."

"Yes, my dear," returned Caleb. "Here she is."

"There is no change in *her*. You never told me anything of *her* that was not true?"

"I should have done it, my dear, I am afraid," returned Caleb, "if I could have made her better than she was. But I must have changed her for the worse, if I had changed her at all. Nothing could improve her, Bertha."

Confident as the Blind Girl had been when she asked the question, her delight and pride in the reply and her renewed embrace of Dot, were charming to behold.

"More changes than you think for, may happen though, my dear," said Dot. "Changes for the better, I mean; changes for great joy to some of us. You mustn't let them startle you too much, if any such should ever happen, and affect you? Are those wheels upon the road? You've a quick ear, Bertha. Are they wheels?"

"Yes. Coming very fast."

"I—I—I know you have a quick ear," said Dot, placing her hand upon her heart, and evidently talking on, as fast as she could to hide its palpitating state, "because I have noticed it often, and because you were so quick to find out that strange step last night. Though why you should have said, as I very well recollect you did say, Bertha, 'whose step is that!' and why you should have taken any greater observation of it than of any other step, I don't know. Though as I said just now, there are great changes in the world: great changes: and we can't do better than prepare ourselves to be surprised at hardly anything."

Caleb wondered what this meant; perceiving that she spoke to him, no less than to his daughter. He saw her, with astonishment, so fluttered and distressed that she could scarcely breathe; and holding to a chair, to save herself from falling.

"They are wheels indeed!" she panted. "Coming nearer! Nearer! Very close! And now you hear them stopping at the garden-gate! And now you hear a step outside the door—the same step, Bertha, is it not!—and now!"—

She uttered a wild cry of uncontrollable delight; and running up to Caleb put her hands upon his eyes, as a young man rushed into the room, and flinging away his hat into the air, came sweeping down upon them.

"Is it over?" cried Dot.

"Yes!"

"Happily over?"

"Yes!"

"Do you recollect the voice, dear Caleb? Did you ever hear the like of it before?" cried Dot.

"If my boy in the Golden South Americas was alive"—said Caleb, trembling.

"He is alive!" shrieked Dot, removing her hands from his eyes, and clapping them in ecstasy; "look at him! See where he stands before you, healthy and strong! Your own dear son! Your own dear living, loving brother, Bertha!"

All honour to the little creature for her transports! All honour to her tears and laughter, when the three were locked in one another's arms! All honour to the heartiness with which she met the sunburnt Sailor-fellow, with his dark streaming hair, half-way, and never turned her rosy little mouth aside, but suffered him to kiss it, freely, and to press her to his bounding heart!

And honour to the Cuckoo too—why not!—for bursting out of the trap-door in the Moorish Palace like a house-breaker, and hiccoughing twelve times on the assembled company, as if he had got drunk for joy!

The Carrier, entering, started back: and well he might, to find himself in such good company.

"Look, John!" said Caleb, exultingly, "look here! My own boy from the Golden South Americas! My own son! Him that you fitted out, and sent away yourself! Him that you were always such a friend to!"

The Carrier advanced to seize him by the hand; but, recoiling, as some feature in his face awakened a remembrance of the Deaf Man in the Cart, said:

"Edward! Was it you?"

"Now tell him all!" cried Dot. "Tell him all, Edward; and don't spare me, for nothing shall make me spare myself in his eyes, ever again."

"I was the man," said Edward.

"And could you steal, disguised, into the house of your old friend?" rejoined the Carrier. "There was a frank boy once—how many years is it, Caleb, since we heard that he was dead, and had it proved, we thought?—who never would have done that."

"There was a generous friend of mine, once; more a father to me than a friend"; said Edward, "who never would have judged me, or any other man, unheard. You were he. So I am certain you will hear me now."

The Carrier, with a troubled glance at Dot, who still kept far away from him, replied, "Well! that's but fair. I will."

"You must know that when I left here, a boy," said Edward, "I was in love, and my love was returned. She was a very young girl, who perhaps (you may tell me) didn't know her own mind. But I knew mine; and I had a passion for her."

"You had!" exclaimed the Carrier. "You!"

"Indeed I had," returned the other. "And she returned it. I have ever since believed she did; and now I am sure she did."

"Heaven help me!" said the Carrier. "This is worse than all."

"Constant to her," said Edward, "and returning, full of hope, after many hardships and perils, to redeem my part of our old contract, I heard, twenty miles away, that she was false to me; that she had forgotten me; and had bestowed herself upon another and a richer man. I had no mind to reproach her; but I wished to see her, and to prove beyond dispute that this was true. I hoped she might have been forced into it, against her own desire and recollection. It would be small comfort, but it would be some, I thought: and on I came. That I might have the truth, the real truth; observing freely for myself, and judging for myself, without obstruction on the one hand, or presenting my own influence (if I had any) before her, on the other; I dressed myself unlike myself—you know how; and waited on the road—you know where. You had no suspicion of me; neither had—had she," pointing to Dot, "until I whispered in her ear at that fireside, and she so nearly betrayed me."

"But when she knew that Edward was alive, and had come back," sobbed Dot, now speaking for herself, as she had burned to do, all through this narrative; "and when she knew his purpose, she advised him by all means to keep his secret close; for his old friend John Peerybingle was much too open in his nature, and too clumsy in all artifice—being a clumsy man in general," said Dot, half laughing and half crying—"to keep it for him. And when she—that's me, John," sobbed the little woman—"told him all, and how his sweetheart had believed him to be dead; and how she had at last been over-persuaded by her mother into a marriage which the silly, dear old thing called advantageous; and when she—that's me again, John—told him they were not yet married (though close upon it), and that it would be nothing but a sacrifice if it went on, for there was no love on her side; and when he went nearly mad with joy to hear it; then she—that's me again—said she would go between them, as she had often done before in old times, John, and would sound his sweetheart and be sure that what she—me again, John—said and thought was right. And it WAS right, John! And they were brought together, John! And they were married, John, an hour ago! And here's the Bride! And Gruff and Tackleton may die a bachelor! And I'm a happy little woman, May, God bless you!"

She was an irresistible little woman, if that be anything to the purpose; and never so completely irresistible as in her present transports. There never were congratulations so endearing and delicious, as those she lavished on herself and on the Bride.

Amid the tumult of emotions in his breast, the honest Carrier had stood, confounded. Flying, now, towards her, Dot stretched out her hand to stop him, and retreated as before.

"No, John, no! Hear all! Don't love me any more, John, 'till you've heard every word I have to say. It was wrong to have a secret from you, John. I'm very sorry. I didn't think it any harm, till I came and sat down by you on the little stool last night;

but when I knew by what was written in your face, that you had seen me walking in the gallery with Edward; and when I knew what you thought; I felt how giddy and how wrong it was. But oh, dear John, how could you, could you, think so!"

Little woman, how she sobbed again! John Peerybingle would have caught her in his arms. But no; she wouldn't let him.

"Don't love me yet, please John! Not for a long time yet! When I was sad about this intended marriage, dear, it was because I remembered May and Edward such young lovers; and knew that her heart was far away from Tackleton. You believe that, now. Don't you, John?"

John was going to make another rush at this appeal; but she stopped him again.

"No; keep there, please, John! When I laugh at you, as I sometimes do, John; and call you clumsy and a dear old goose, and names of that sort, it's because I love you, John, so well, and take such pleasure in your ways; and wouldn't see you altered in the least respect to have you made a King to-morrow."

"Hooroar!" said Caleb with unusual vigour. "My opinion!"

"And when I speak of people being middle-aged, and steady, John, and pretend that we are a humdrum couple, going on in a jog-trot sort of way, it's only because I'm such a silly little thing, John, that I like, sometimes, to act a kind of Play with Baby, and all that: and make believe."

She saw that he was coming; and stopped him again. But she was very nearly too late.

"No, don't love me for another minute or two, if you please, John! What I want most to tell you, I have kept to the last. My dear, good, generous John, when we were talking the other night about the Cricket, I had it on my lips to say, that at first I did not love you quite so dearly as I do now; that when I first came home here, I was half afraid I mightn't learn to love you every bit as well as I hoped and prayed I might—being so very young, John! But, dear John, every day and hour I loved you more and more. And if I could have loved you better than I do, the noble words I heard you say this morning, would have made me. But I can't. All the affection that I had (it was a great deal, John) I gave you, as you well deserve, long, long ago, and I have no more left to give. Now, my dear husband, take me to your heart again! That's my home, John; and never, never think of sending me to any other!"

You never will derive so much delight from seeing a glorious little woman in the arms of a third party, as you would have felt if you had seen Dot run into the Carrier's embrace. It was the most complete, unmitigated, soul-fraught little piece of earnestness that ever you beheld in all your days.

You may be sure the Carrier was in a state of perfect rapture; and you may be sure Dot was likewise; and you may be sure they all were, inclusive of Miss Slowboy, who wept copiously for joy, and, wishing to include her young charge in the general interchange of congratulations, handed round the Baby to everybody in succession, as if it were something to drink.

But, now, the sound of wheels was heard again outside the door; and somebody exclaimed that Gruff and Tackleton was coming back. Speedily that worthy gentleman appeared, looking warm and flustered.

"Why, what the Devil's this, John Peerybingle!" said Tackleton. "There's some mistake. I appointed Mrs. Tackleton to meet me at the church; and I'll swear I passed her on the road, on her way here. Oh! here she is! I beg your pardon, Sir; I haven't the pleasure of knowing you; but if you can do me the favour to spare this young lady, she has rather a particular engagement this morning."

"But I can't spare her," returned Edward. "I couldn't think of it."

"What do you mean, you vagabond?" said Tackleton.

"I mean, that as I can make allowance for your being vexed," returned the other, with a smile, "I am as deaf to harsh discourse this morning, as I was to all discourse last night."

The look that Tackleton bestowed upon him, and the start he gave!

"I am sorry, sir," said Edward, holding out May's left hand, and especially the third finger; "that the young lady can't accompany you to church; but as she has been there once, this morning, perhaps you'll excuse her."

Tackleton looked hard at the third finger, and took a little piece of silver-paper, apparently containing a ring, from his waistcoat-pocket.

"Miss Slowboy," said Tackleton. "Will you have the kindness to throw that in the fire? Thank'ee."

"It was a previous engagement, quite an old engagement, that prevented my wife from keeping her appointment with you, I assure you," said Edward.

"Mr. Tackleton will do me the justice to acknowledge that I revealed it to him faithfully; and that I told him, many times, I never could forget it," said May, blushing.

"Oh certainly!" said Tackleton. "Oh to be sure. Oh it's all right. It's quite correct. Mrs. Edward Plummer, I infer?"

"That's the name," returned the bridegroom.

"Ah, I shouldn't have known you, sir," said Tackleton, scrutinising his face narrowly, and making a low bow. "I give you joy Sir!"

"Thank'ee."

"Mrs. Peerybingle," said Tackleton, turning suddenly to where she stood with her husband; "I am sorry. You haven't done me a very great kindness, but, upon my life I am sorry. You are better than I thought you. John Peerybingle, I am sorry. You understand me; that's enough. It's quite correct, ladies and gentlemen all, and perfectly satisfactory. Good morning!"

With these words he carried it off, and carried himself off too: merely stopping at the door, to take the flowers and favours from his horse's head, and to kick that animal once, in the ribs, as a means of informing him that there was a screw loose in his arrangements.

Of course it became a serious duty now, to make such a day of it, as should mark these events for a high Feast and Festival in the Peerybingle Calendar for evermore. Accordingly, Dot went to work to produce such an entertainment, as should reflect undying honour on the house and on every one concerned; and in a very short space of time, she was up to her dimpled elbows in flour, and whitening the Carrier's coat, every time he came near her, by stopping him to give him a kiss. That good fellow washed the greens, and peeled the turnips, and broke the plates, and upset iron pots full of cold water on the fire, and made himself useful in all sorts of ways: while a couple of professional assistants, hastily called in from somewhere in the neighbourhood, as on a point of life or death, ran against each other in all the doorways and round all the corners; and everybody tumbled over Tilly Slowboy and the Baby, everywhere. Tilly never came out in such force before. Her ubiquity was the theme of general admiration. She was a stumbling-block in the passage at five-and-twenty minutes past two; a man-trap in the kitchen at half-past two precisely; and a pitfall in the garret at five-and-twenty minutes to three. The Baby's head was, as it were, a test and touchstone for every description of matter, animal, vegetable, and mineral. Nothing was in use that day that didn't come, at some time or other, into close acquaintance with it.

Then, there was a great Expedition set on foot to go and find out Mrs. Fielding; and to be dismally penitent to that excellent gentlewoman; and to bring her back, by force, if needful, to be happy and forgiving. And when the Expedition first discovered her, she would listen to no terms at all, but said, an unspeakable number of times, that ever she should have lived to see the day! and couldn't be got to say anything else, except, "Now carry me to the grave": which seemed absurd, on account of her not being dead, or anything at all like it. After a time, she lapsed into a state of dreadful calmness, and observed, that when that unfortunate train of circumstances had occurred in the Indigo Trade, she had foreseen that she would be exposed, during her whole life, to every species of insult and contumely; and that she was glad to find it was the case; and begged they wouldn't trouble themselves about her,—for what was she? oh, dear! a nobody!—but would forget that such a being lived, and would take their course in life without her. From this bitterly sarcastic mood, she passed into an angry one, in which she gave vent to the remarkable expression that the worm would turn if trodden on; and, after that, she yielded to a soft regret, and said, if they had only given her their confidence, what might she not have had it in her power to suggest! Taking advantage of this crisis in her feelings, the Expedition embraced her; and she very soon had her gloves on, and was on her way to John Peerybingle's in a state of unimpeachable gentility; with a paper parcel at her side containing a cap of state, almost as tall, and quite as stiff, as a Mitre.

Then, there were Dot's father and mother to come, in another little chaise; and they were behind their time; and fears were entertained; and there was much looking out for them down the road; and Mrs. Fielding always would look in the wrong and morally impossible direction; and being apprised thereof, hoped she might take the liberty of looking where she pleased. At last they came: a chubby little couple, jogging along in a snug and comfortable little way that quite belonged to the Dot family; and Dot and her mother, side by side, were wonderful to see. They were so like each other.

Then, Dot's mother had to renew her acquaintance with May's mother; and May's mother always stood on her gentility; and Dot's mother never stood on anything but her active little feet. And old Dot: so to call Dot's father; I forgot it wasn't his right name, but never mind: took liberties, and shook hands at first sight, and seemed to think a cap but so much starch and muslin, and didn't defer himself at all to the Indigo Trade, but said there was no help for it now; and, in Mrs. Fielding's summing up, was a good-natured kind of man—but coarse, my dear.

I wouldn't have missed Dot, doing the honours in her wedding-gown: my benison on her bright face! for any money. No! nor the good Carrier, so jovial and so ruddy, at the bottom of the table. Nor the brown, fresh sailor-fellow, and his handsome wife. Nor any one among them. To have missed the dinner would have been to miss as jolly and as stout a meal as man need eat; and to have missed the overflowing cups in which they drank The Wedding-Day, would have been the greatest miss of all.

After dinner, Caleb sang the song about the Sparkling Bowl! As I'm a living man, hoping to keep so, for a year or two: he sang it through.

And, by-the-by, a most unlooked-for incident occurred, just as he finished the last verse.

There was a tap at the door; and a man came staggering in, without saying with your leave, or by your leave, with something heavy on his head. Setting this down in the middle of the table, symmetrically in the centre of the nuts and apples, he said:

"Mr. Tackleton's compliments, and as he hasn't got no use for the cake himself, p'raps you'll eat it."

And with those words, he walked off.

There was some surprise among the company, as you may imagine. Mrs. Fielding, being a lady of infinite discernment, suggested that the cake was poisoned; and related a narrative of a cake, which, within her knowledge, had turned a seminary for young ladies, blue. But she was overruled by acclamation; and the cake was cut by May, with much ceremony and rejoicing.

I don't think any one had tasted it, when there came another tap at the door; and the same man appeared again, having under his arm a vast brown-paper parcel.

"Mr. Tackleton's compliments, and he's sent a few toys for the Babby. They ain't ugly."

After the delivery of which expressions, he retired again.

The whole party would have experienced great difficulty in finding words for their astonishment, even if they had had ample time to seek them. But they had none at all; for the messenger had scarcely shut the door behind him, when there came another tap, and Tackleton himself walked in.

"Mrs. Peerybingle!" said the Toy-merchant, hat in hand. "I'm sorry. I'm more sorry than I was this morning. I have had time to think of it. John Peerybingle! I'm sour by disposition; but I can't help being sweetened, more or less, by coming face to face with such a man as you. Caleb! This unconscious little nurse gave me a broken hint last night, of which I have found the thread. I blush to think how easily I might have bound you and your daughter to me; and what a miserable idiot I was, when I took her for one! Friends, one and all, my house is very lonely to-night. I have not so much as a Cricket on my Hearth. I have scared them all away. Be gracious to me; let me join this happy party!"

He was at home in five minutes. You never saw such a fellow. What *had* he been doing with himself all his life, never to have known, before, his great capacity of being jovial! Or what had the Fairies been doing with him, to have effected such a change!

"John! you won't send me home this evening; will you?" whispered Dot.

He had been very near it though!

There wanted but one living creature to make the party complete; and, in the twinkling of an eye, there he was, very thirsty with hard running, and engaged in hopeless endeavours to squeeze his head into a narrow pitcher. He had gone with the cart to its journey's-end, very much disgusted with the absence of his master, and stupendously rebellious to the Deputy. After lingering about the stable for some little time, vainly attempting to incite the old horse to the mutinous act of returning on his own account, he had walked into the tap-room and laid himself down before the fire. But suddenly yielding to the conviction that the Deputy was a humbug, and must be abandoned, he had got up again, turned tail, and come home.

There was a dance in the evening. With which general mention of that recreation, I should have left it alone, if I had not some reason to suppose that it was quite an original dance, and one of a most uncommon figure. It was formed in an odd way; in this way. Edward, that Sailor-fellow—a good free dashing sort of a fellow he was—had been telling them various marvels concerning parrots, and mines, and Mexicans, and gold dust, when all at once he took it in his head to jump up from his seat and propose a dance; for Bertha's harp was there, and she had such a hand upon it as you seldom hear. Dot (sly little piece of affectation when she chose) said her dancing days were over; *I* think because the Carrier was smoking his pipe, and she liked sitting by him, best. Mrs. Fielding had no choice, of course, but to say her dancing days were over, after that; and everybody said the same, except May; May was ready.

So, May and Edward get up, amid great applause, to dance alone; and Bertha plays her liveliest tune.

Well! if you'll believe me, they have not been dancing five minutes, when suddenly the Carrier flings his pipe away, takes Dot round the waist, dashes out into the room, and starts off with her, toe and heel, quite wonderfully. Tackleton no sooner sees this, than he skims across to Mrs. Fielding, takes her round the waist, and follows suit. Old Dot no sooner sees this, than up he is, all alive, whisks off Mrs. Dot in the middle of the dance, and is the foremost there. Caleb no sooner sees this, than he clutches Tilly Slowboy by both hands and goes off at score; Miss Slowboy, firm in the belief that diving hotly in among the other couples, and effecting any number of concussions with them, is your only principle of footing it.

Hark! how the Cricket joins the music with its Chirp, Chirp, Chirp; and how the kettle hums!

* * *

But what is this! Even as I listen to them, blithely, and turn towards Dot, for one last glimpse of a little figure very pleasant to me, she and the rest have vanished into air, and I am left alone. A Cricket sings upon the Hearth; a broken child's-toy lies upon the ground; and nothing else remains.

The Battle of Life

Part the First

Once upon a time, it matters little when, and in stalwart England, it matters little where, a fierce battle was fought. It was fought upon a long summer day when the waving grass was green. Many a wild flower formed by the Almighty Hand to be a perfumed goblet for the dew, felt its enamelled cup filled high with blood that day, and shrinking dropped. Many an insect deriving its delicate colour from harmless leaves and herbs, was stained anew that day by dying men, and marked its frightened way with an unnatural track. The painted butterfly took blood into the air upon the edges of its wings. The stream ran red. The trodden ground became a quagmire, whence, from sullen pools collected in the prints of human feet and horses' hoofs, the one prevailing hue still lowered and glimmered at the sun.

Heaven keep us from a knowledge of the sights the moon beheld upon that field, when, coming up above the black line of distant rising-ground, softened and blurred at the edge by trees, she rose into the sky and looked upon the plain, strewn with upturned faces that had once at mothers' breasts sought mothers' eyes, or slumbered happily. Heaven keep us from a knowledge of the secrets whispered afterwards upon the tainted wind that blew across the scene of that day's work and that night's death and suffering! Many a lonely moon was bright upon the battle-ground, and many a star kept mournful watch upon it, and many a wind from every quarter of the earth blew over it, before the traces of the fight were worn away.

They lurked and lingered for a long time, but survived in little things; for, Nature, far above the evil passions of men, soon recovered Her serenity, and smiled upon the guilty battle-ground as she had done before, when it was innocent. The larks sang high above it; the swallows skimmed and dipped and flitted to and fro; the shadows of the flying clouds pursued each other swiftly, over grass and corn and turnip-field and wood, and over roof and church-spire in the nestling town among the trees, away into the bright distance on the borders of the sky and earth, where the red sunsets faded. Crops were sown, and grew up, and were gathered in; the stream that had been crimsoned, turned a watermill; men whistled at the plough; gleaners and haymakers were seen in quiet groups at work; sheep and oxen pastured; boys whooped and called, in fields, to scare away the birds; smoke rose from cottage chimneys; sabbath bells rang peacefully; old people lived and died; the timid creatures of the field, the simple flowers of the bush and garden, grew and withered in their destined terms: and all upon the fierce and bloody battle-ground, where thousands upon thousands had been killed in the great fight.

But, there were deep green patches in the growing corn at first, that people looked at awfully. Year after year they re-appeared; and it was known that underneath those fertile spots, heaps of men and horses lay buried, indiscriminately, enriching the ground. The husbandmen who ploughed those places, shrunk from the great worms abounding there; and the sheaves they yielded, were, for many a long year, called the Battle Sheaves, and set apart; and no one ever knew a Battle Sheaf to be among the last load at a Harvest Home. For a long time, every furrow that was turned, revealed some fragments of the fight. For a long time, there were wounded trees upon the battle-ground; and scraps of hacked and broken fence and wall, where deadly struggles had been made; and trampled parts where not a leaf or blade would grow. For a long time, no village girl would dress her hair or bosom with the sweetest flower from that field of death: and after many a year had come and gone, the berries growing there, were still believed to leave too deep a stain upon the hand that plucked them.

The Seasons in their course, however, though they passed as lightly as the summer clouds themselves, obliterated, in the lapse of time, even these remains of the old conflict; and wore away such legendary traces of it as the neighbouring people carried in their minds, until they dwindled into old wives' tales, dimly remembered round the winter fire, and waning every year. Where the wild flowers and berries had so long remained upon the stem untouched, gardens arose, and houses were built, and children played at battles on the turf. The wounded trees had long ago made Christmas logs, and blazed and roared away. The deep green patches were no greener now than the memory of those who lay in dust below. The ploughshare still turned up from time to time some rusty bits of metal, but it was hard to say what use they had ever served, and those who found them wondered and disputed. An old dinted corselet, and a helmet, had been hanging in the church so long, that the same weak half-blind old man who tried in vain to make them out above the white-washed arch, had marvelled at them as a baby. If the host slain upon the field, could have been for a moment reanimated in the forms in which they fell, each upon the spot that was the bed of his untimely death, gashed and ghastly soldiers would have stared in, hundreds deep, at household door and window; and would have risen on the hearths of quiet homes; and would have been the garnered store of barns and granaries; and would have started up between the cradled infant and its nurse; and would have floated with the stream, and whirled round on the mill, and crowded the orchard, and burdened the meadow, and piled the rickyard high with dying men. So altered was the battle-ground, where thousands upon thousands had been killed in the great fight.

Nowhere more altered, perhaps, about a hundred years ago, than in one little orchard attached to an old stone house with a honeysuckle porch; where, on a bright autumn morning, there were sounds of music and laughter, and where two girls danced merrily together on the grass, while some half-dozen peasant women standing on ladders, gathering the apples from the trees, stopped in their work to look down, and share their enjoyment. It was a pleasant, lively, natural scene; a beautiful day, a retired spot; and the two girls, quite unconstrained and careless, danced in the freedom and gaiety of their hearts.

If there were no such thing as display in the world, my private opinion is, and I hope you agree with me, that we might get on a great deal better than we do, and might be infinitely more agreeable company than we are. It was charming to see how these girls danced. They had no spectators but the apple-pickers on the ladders. They were very glad to please them, but they danced to please themselves (or at least you would have supposed so); and you could no more help admiring, than they could help dancing. How they did dance!

Not like opera-dancers. Not at all. And not like Madame Anybody's finished pupils. Not the least. It was not quadrille dancing, nor minuet dancing, nor even country-dance dancing. It was neither in the old style, nor the new style, nor the French style, nor the English style; though it may have been, by accident, a trifle in the Spanish style, which is a free and joyous one, I am told, deriving a delightful air of off-hand inspiration, from the chirping little castanets. As they danced among the orchard trees, and down the groves of stems and back again, and twirled each other lightly round and round, the influence of their airy motion seemed to spread and spread, in the sun-lighted scene, like an expanding circle in the water. Their streaming hair and fluttering skirts, the elastic grass beneath their feet, the boughs that rustled in the morning air—the flashing leaves, the speckled shadows on the soft green ground—the balmy wind that swept along the landscape, glad to turn the distant windmill, cheerily—everything between the two girls, and the man and team at plough upon the ridge of land, where they showed against the sky as if they were the last things in the world—seemed dancing too.

At last, the younger of the dancing sisters, out of breath, and laughing gaily, threw herself upon a bench to rest. The other leaned against a tree hard by. The music, a wandering harp and fiddle, left off with a flourish, as if it boasted of its freshness; though the truth is, it had gone at such a pace, and worked itself to such a pitch of competition with the dancing, that it never could have held on, half a minute longer. The apple-pickers on the ladders raised a hum and murmur of applause, and then, in keeping with the sound, bestirred themselves to work again like bees.

The more actively, perhaps, because an elderly gentleman, who was no other than Doctor Jeddler himself—it was Doctor Jeddler's house and orchard, you should know, and these were Doctor Jeddler's daughters—came bustling out to see what was the matter, and who the deuce played music on his property, before breakfast. For he was a great philosopher, Doctor Jeddler, and not very musical.

"Music and dancing *to-day!*" said the Doctor, stopping short, and speaking to himself. "I thought they dreaded to-day. But it's a world of contradictions. Why, Grace, why, Marion!" he added, aloud, "is the world more mad than usual this morning?"

"Make some allowance for it, father, if it be," replied his younger daughter, Marion, going close to him, and looking into his face, "for it's somebody's birth-day."

"Somebody's birth-day, Puss!" replied the Doctor. "Don't you know it's always somebody's birth-day? Did you never hear how many new performers enter on this—ha! ha! ha!—it's impossible to speak gravely of it—on this preposterous and ridiculous business called Life, every minute?"

"No, father!"

"No, not you, of course; you're a woman—almost," said the Doctor. "By-the-by," and he looked into the pretty face, still close to his, "I suppose it's *your* birth-day."

"No! Do you really, father?" cried his pet daughter, pursing up her red lips to be kissed.

"There! Take my love with it," said the Doctor, imprinting his upon them; "and many happy returns of the—the idea!—of the day. The notion of wishing happy returns in such a farce as this," said the Doctor to himself, "is good! Ha! ha! ha!"

Doctor Jeddler was, as I have said, a great philosopher, and the heart and mystery of his philosophy was, to look upon the world as a gigantic practical joke; as something too absurd to be considered seriously, by any rational man. His system of belief had been, in the beginning, part and parcel of the battle-ground on which he lived, as you shall presently understand.

"Well! But how did you get the music?" asked the Doctor. "Poultry-stealers, of course! Where did the minstrels come from?"

"Alfred sent the music," said his daughter Grace, adjusting a few simple flowers in her sister's hair, with which, in her admiration of that youthful beauty, she had herself adorned it half-an-hour before, and which the dancing had disarranged.

"Oh! Alfred sent the music, did he?" returned the Doctor.

"Yes. He met it coming out of the town as he was entering early. The men are travelling on foot, and rested there last night; and as it was Marion's birth-day, and he thought it would please her, he sent them on, with a pencilled note to me, saying that if I thought so too, they had come to serenade her."

"Ay, ay," said the Doctor, carelessly, "he always takes your opinion."

"And my opinion being favourable," said Grace, good-humouredly; and pausing for a moment to admire the pretty head she decorated, with her own thrown back; "and Marion being in high spirits, and beginning to dance, I joined her. And so we danced to Alfred's music till we were out of breath. And we thought the music all the gayer for being sent by Alfred. Didn't we, dear Marion?"

"Oh, I don't know, Grace. How you tease me about Alfred."

"Tease you by mentioning your lover?" said her sister.

"I am sure I don't much care to have him mentioned," said the wilful beauty, stripping the petals from some flowers she held, and scattering them on the ground. "I am almost tired of hearing of him; and as to his being my lover—"

"Hush! Don't speak lightly of a true heart, which is all your own, Marion," cried her sister, "even in jest. There is not a truer heart than Alfred's in the world!"

"No-no," said Marion, raising her eyebrows with a pleasant air of careless consideration, "perhaps not. But I don't know that there's any great merit in that. I—I don't want him to be so very true. I never asked him. If he expects that I—But, dear Grace, why need we talk of him at all, just now!"

It was agreeable to see the graceful figures of the blooming sisters, twined together, lingering among the trees, conversing thus, with earnestness opposed to lightness, yet, with love responding tenderly to love. And it was very curious indeed to see the younger sister's eyes suffused with tears, and something fervently and deeply felt, breaking through the wilfulness of what she said, and striving with it painfully.

The difference between them, in respect of age, could not exceed four years at most; but Grace, as often happens in such cases, when no mother watches over both (the Doctor's wife was dead), seemed, in her gentle care of her young sister, and in the steadiness of her devotion to her, older than she was; and more removed, in course of nature, from all competition with her, or participation, otherwise than through her sympathy and true affection, in her wayward fancies, than their ages seemed to warrant. Great character of mother, that, even in this shadow and faint reflection of it, purifies the heart, and raises the exalted nature nearer to the angels!

The Doctor's reflections, as he looked after them, and heard the purport of their discourse, were limited at first to certain merry meditations on the folly of all loves and likings, and the idle imposition practised on themselves by young people, who believed for a moment, that there could be anything serious in such bubbles, and were always undeceived—always!

But, the home-adorning, self-denying qualities of Grace, and her sweet temper, so gentle and retiring, yet including so much constancy and bravery of spirit, seemed all expressed to him in the contrast between her quiet household figure and that of his younger and more beautiful child; and he was sorry for her sake—sorry for them both—that life should be such a very ridiculous business as it was.

The Doctor never dreamed of inquiring whether his children, or either of them, helped in any way to make the scheme a serious one. But then he was a Philosopher.

A kind and generous man by nature, he had stumbled, by chance, over that common Philosopher's stone (much more easily discovered than the object of the alchemist's researches), which sometimes trips up kind and generous men, and has the fatal property of turning gold to dross and every precious thing to poor account.

"Britain!" cried the Doctor. "Britain! Holloa!"

A small man, with an uncommonly sour and discontented face, emerged from the house, and returned to this call the unceremonious acknowledgment of "Now then!"

"Where's the breakfast table?" said the Doctor.

"In the house," returned Britain.

"Are you going to spread it out here, as you were told last night?" said the Doctor. "Don't you know that there are gentlemen coming? That there's business to be done this morning, before the coach comes by? That this is a very particular occasion?"

"I couldn't do anything, Dr. Jeddler, till the women had done getting in the apples, could I?" said Britain, his voice rising with his reasoning, so that it was very loud at last.

"Well, have they done now?" replied the Doctor, looking at his watch, and clapping his hands. "Come! make haste! where's Clemency?"

"Here am I, Mister," said a voice from one of the ladders, which a pair of clumsy feet descended briskly. "It's all done now. Clear away, gals. Everything shall be ready for you in half a minute, Mister."

With that she began to bustle about most vigorously; presenting, as she did so, an appearance sufficiently peculiar to justify a word of introduction.

She was about thirty years old, and had a sufficiently plump and cheerful face, though it was twisted up into an odd expression of tightness that made it comical. But, the extraordinary homeliness of her gait and manner, would have superseded any face in the world. To say that she had two left legs, and somebody else's arms, and that all four limbs seemed to be out of joint, and to start from perfectly wrong places when they were set in motion, is to offer the mildest outline of the reality. To say that she was perfectly content and satisfied with these arrangements, and regarded them as being no business of hers, and that she took her arms and legs as they came, and allowed them to dispose of themselves just as it happened, is to render faint justice to her equanimity. Her dress was a prodigious pair of self-willed shoes, that never wanted to go where her feet went; blue stockings; a printed gown of many colours, and the most hideous pattern procurable for money; and a white apron. She always wore short sleeves, and always had, by some accident, grazed elbows, in which she took so lively an interest, that she was continually trying to turn them round and get impossible views of them. In general, a little cap placed somewhere on her head; though it was rarely to be met with in the place usually occupied in other subjects, by that article of dress; but, from head to foot she was scrupulously clean, and maintained a kind of dislocated tidiness. Indeed her laudable anxiety to be tidy and compact in her own conscience as well as in the public eye, gave rise to one of her most startling evolutions, which was to grasp herself sometimes by a sort of wooden handle (part of her clothing, and familiarly called a busk), and wrestle as it were with her garments, until they fell into a symmetrical arrangement.

Such, in outward form and garb, was Clemency Newcome; who was supposed to have unconsciously originated a corruption of her own Christian name, from Clementina (but nobody knew, for the deaf old mother, a very phenomenon of age, whom she had supported almost from a child, was dead, and she had no other relation); who now busied herself in preparing the table, and who stood, at intervals, with her bare red arms crossed, rubbing her grazed elbows with opposite hands, and staring at it very composedly, until she suddenly remembered something else she wanted, and jogged off to fetch it.

"Here are them two lawyers a-coming, Mister!" said Clemency, in a tone of no very great good-will.

"Ah!" cried the Doctor, advancing to the gate to meet them. "Good morning, good morning! Grace, my dear! Marion! Here are Messrs. Snitchey and Craggs. Where's Alfred!"

"He'll be back directly, father, no doubt," said Grace. "He had so much to do this morning in his preparations for departure, that he was up and out by daybreak. Good morning, gentlemen."

"Ladies!" said Mr. Snitchey, "for Self and Craggs," who bowed, "good morning! Miss," to Marion, "I kiss your hand." Which he did. "And I wish you"—which he might or might not, for he didn't look, at first sight, like a gentleman troubled with many warm outpourings of soul, in behalf of other people, "a hundred happy returns of this auspicious day."

"Ha ha ha!" laughed the Doctor thoughtfully, with his hands in his pockets. "The great farce in a hundred acts!"

"You wouldn't, I am sure," said Mr. Snitchey, standing a small professional blue bag against one leg of the table, "cut the great farce short for this actress, at all events, Doctor Jeddler."

"No," returned the Doctor. "God forbid! May she live to laugh at it, as long as she *can* laugh, and then say, with the French wit, 'The farce is ended; draw the curtain.'"

"The French wit," said Mr. Snitchey, peeping sharply into his blue bag, "was wrong, Doctor Jeddler, and your philosophy is altogether wrong, depend upon it, as I have often told you. Nothing serious in life! What do you call law?"

"A joke," replied the Doctor.

"Did you ever go to law?" asked Mr. Snitchey, looking out of the blue bag.

"Never," returned the Doctor.

"If you ever do," said Mr. Snitchey, "perhaps you'll alter that opinion."

Craggs, who seemed to be represented by Snitchey, and to be conscious of little or no separate existence or personal individuality, offered a remark of his own in this place. It involved the only idea of which he did not stand seized and possessed in equal moieties with Snitchey; but he had some partners in it among the wise men of the world.

"It's made a great deal too easy," said Mr. Craggs.

"Law is?" asked the Doctor.

"Yes," said Mr. Craggs, "everything is. Everything appears to me to be made too easy, now-a-days. It's the vice of these times. If the world is a joke (I am not prepared to say it isn't), it ought to be made a very difficult joke to crack. It ought to be as hard a struggle, sir, as possible. That's the intention. But, it's being made far too easy. We are oiling the gates of life. They ought to be rusty. We shall have them beginning to turn, soon, with a smooth sound. Whereas they ought to grate upon their hinges, sir."

Mr. Craggs seemed positively to grate upon his own hinges, as he delivered this opinion; to which he communicated immense effect—being a cold, hard, dry, man, dressed in grey and white, like a flint; with small twinkles in his eyes, as if something struck sparks out of them. The three natural kingdoms, indeed, had each a fanciful representative among this brotherhood of disputants; for Snitchey was like a magpie or raven (only not so sleek), and the Doctor had a streaked face like a winter-pippin, with here and there a dimple to express the peckings of the birds, and a very little bit of pigtail behind that stood for the stalk.

As the active figure of a handsome young man, dressed for a journey, and followed by a porter bearing several packages and baskets, entered the orchard at a brisk pace, and with an air of gaiety and hope that accorded well with the morning, these three drew together, like the brothers of the sister Fates, or like the Graces most effectually disguised, or like the three weird prophets on the heath, and greeted him.

"Happy returns, Alf!" said the Doctor, lightly.

"A hundred happy returns of this auspicious day, Mr. Heathfield!" said Snitchey, bowing low.

"Returns!" Craggs murmured in a deep voice, all alone.

"Why, what a battery!" exclaimed Alfred, stopping short, "and one—two—three—all foreboders of no good, in the great sea before me. I am glad you are not the first I have met this morning: I should have taken it for a bad omen. But Grace was the first—sweet, pleasant Grace—so I defy you all!"

"If you please, Mister, *I* was the first you know," said Clemency Newcome. "She was walking out here, before sunrise, you remember. I was in the house."

"That's true! Clemency was the first," said Alfred. "So I defy you with Clemency."

"Ha, ha, ha,—for Self and Craggs," said Snitchey. "What a defiance!"

"Not so bad a one as it appears, may be," said Alfred, shaking hands heartily with the Doctor, and also with Snitchey and Craggs, and then looking round. "Where are the—Good Heavens!"

With a start, productive for the moment of a closer partnership between Jonathan Snitchey and Thomas Craggs than the subsisting articles of agreement in that wise contemplated, he hastily betook himself to where the sisters stood together, and—however, I needn't more particularly explain his manner of saluting Marion first, and Grace afterwards, than by hinting that Mr. Craggs may possibly have considered it "too easy."

Perhaps to change the subject, Dr. Jeddler made a hasty move towards the breakfast, and they all sat down at table. Grace presided; but so discreetly stationed herself, as to cut off her sister and Alfred from the rest of the company. Snitchey and Craggs sat at opposite corners, with the blue bag between them for safety; the Doctor took his usual position, opposite to Grace. Clemency hovered galvanically about the table, as waitress; and the melancholy Britain, at another and a smaller board, acted as Grand Carver of a round of beef and a ham.

"Meat?" said Britain, approaching Mr. Snitchey, with the carving knife and fork in his hands, and throwing the question at him like a missile.

"Certainly," returned the lawyer.

"Do *you* want any?" to Craggs.

"Lean and well done," replied that gentleman.

Having executed these orders, and moderately supplied the Doctor (he seemed to know that nobody else wanted anything to eat), he lingered as near the Firm as he decently could, watching with an austere eye their disposition of the viands, and but once relaxing the severe expression of his face. This was on the occasion of Mr. Craggs, whose teeth were not of the best, partially choking, when he cried out with great animation, "I thought he was gone!"

"Now, Alfred," said the Doctor, "for a word or two of business, while we are yet at breakfast."

"While we are yet at breakfast," said Snitchey and Craggs, who seemed to have no present idea of leaving off.

Although Alfred had not been breakfasting, and seemed to have quite enough business on his hands as it was, he respectfully answered:

"If you please, Sir."

"If anything could be serious," the Doctor began, "in such a—"

"Farce as this, Sir," hinted Alfred.

"In such a farce as this," observed the Doctor, "it might be this recurrence, on the eve of separation, of a double birth-day, which is connected with many associations pleasant to us four, and with the recollection of a long and amicable intercourse. That's not to the purpose."

"Ah! yes, yes, Dr. Jeddler," said the young man. "It is to the purpose. Much to the purpose, as my heart bears witness this morning; and as yours does too, I know, if you would let it speak. I leave your house to-day; I cease to be your ward to-day; we part with tender relations stretching far behind us, that never can be exactly renewed, and with others dawning—yet before us," he looked down at Marion beside him, "fraught with such considerations as I must not trust myself to speak of now. Come, come!" he added, rallying his spirits and the Doctor at once, "there's a serious grain in this large foolish dust-heap, Doctor. Let us allow to-day, that there is One."

"To-day!" cried the Doctor. "Hear him! Ha, ha, ha! Of all days in the foolish year. Why, on this day, the great battle was fought on this ground. On this ground where we now sit, where I saw my two girls dance this morning, where the fruit has just been gathered for our eating from these trees, the roots of which are struck in Men, not earth,—so many lives were lost, that within my recollection, generations afterwards, a churchyard full of bones, and dust of bones, and chips of cloven skulls, has been dug up from underneath our feet here. Yet not a hundred people in that battle knew for what they fought, or why; not a hundred of the inconsiderate rejoicers in the victory, why they rejoiced. Not half a hundred people were the better for the gain or loss. Not half-a-dozen men agree to this hour on the cause or merits; and nobody, in short, ever knew anything distinct about it, but the mourners of the slain. Serious, too!" said the Doctor, laughing. "Such a system!"

"But, all this seems to me," said Alfred, "to be very serious."

"Serious!" cried the Doctor. "If you allowed such things to be serious, you must go mad, or die, or climb up to the top of a mountain, and turn hermit."

"Besides—so long ago," said Alfred.

"Long ago!" returned the Doctor. "Do you know what the world has been doing, ever since? Do you know what else it has been doing? I don't!"

"It has gone to law a little," observed Mr. Snitchey, stirring his tea.

"Although the way out has been always made too easy," said his partner.

"And you'll excuse my saying, Doctor," pursued Mr. Snitchey, "having been already put a thousand times in possession of my opinion, in the course of our discussions, that, in its having gone to law, and in its legal system altogether, I do observe a serious side—now, really, a something tangible, and with a purpose and intention in it—"

Clemency Newcome made an angular tumble against the table, occasioning a sounding clatter among the cups and saucers.

"Heyday! what's the matter there?" exclaimed the Doctor.

"It's this evil-inclined blue bag," said Clemency, "always tripping up somebody!"

"With a purpose and intention in it, I was saying," resumed Snitchey, "that commands respect. Life a farce, Dr. Jeddler? With law in it?"

The Doctor laughed, and looked at Alfred.

"Granted, if you please, that war is foolish," said Snitchey. "There we agree. For example. Here's a smiling country," pointing it out with his fork, "once overrun by soldiers—trespassers every man of 'em—and laid waste by fire and sword. He, he, he! The idea of any man exposing himself, voluntarily, to fire and sword! Stupid, wasteful, positively ridiculous; you laugh at your fellow-creatures, you know, when you think of it! But take this smiling country as it stands. Think of the laws appertaining to real property; to the bequest and devise of real property; to the mortgage and redemption of real property; to leasehold, freehold, and copyhold estate; think," said Mr. Snitchey, with such great emotion that he actually smacked his lips, "of the complicated laws relating to title and proof of title, with all the contradictory precedents and numerous acts of parliament connected with them; think of the infinite number of ingenious and interminable chancery suits, to which this pleasant prospect may give rise; and acknowledge, Dr. Jeddler, that there is a green spot in the scheme about us! I believe," said Mr. Snitchey, looking at his partner, "that I speak for Self and Craggs?"

Mr. Craggs having signified assent, Mr. Snitchey, somewhat freshened by his recent eloquence, observed that he would take a little more beef and another cup of tea.

"I don't stand up for life in general," he added, rubbing his hands and chuckling, "it's full of folly; full of something worse. Professions of trust, and confidence, and unselfishness, and all that! Bah, bah, bah! We see what they're worth. But, you mustn't laugh at life; you've got a game to play; a very serious game indeed! Everybody's playing against you, you know, and you're playing against them. Oh! it's a very interesting thing. There are deep moves upon the board. You must only laugh, Dr. Jeddler, when you win—and then not much. He, he, he! And then not much," repeated Snitchey, rolling his head and winking his eye, as if he would have added, "you may do this instead!"

"Well, Alfred!" cried the Doctor, "what do you say now?"

"I say, sir," replied Alfred, "that the greatest favour you could do me, and yourself too, I am inclined to think, would be to try sometimes to forget this battle-field and others like it in that broader battle-field of Life, on which the sun looks every day."

"Really, I'm afraid that wouldn't soften his opinions, Mr. Alfred," said Snitchey. "The combatants are very eager and very bitter in that same battle of Life. There's a great deal of cutting and slashing, and firing into people's heads from behind. There is terrible treading down, and trampling on. It is rather a bad business."

"I believe, Mr. Snitchey," said Alfred, "there are quiet victories and struggles, great sacrifices of self, and noble acts of heroism, in it—even in many of its apparent lightnesses and contradictions—not the less difficult to achieve, because they have no earthly chronicle or audience—done every day in nooks and corners, and in little households, and in men's and women's hearts—any one of which might reconcile the sternest man to such a world, and fill him with belief and hope in it, though two-fourths of its people were at war, and another fourth at law; and that's a bold word."

Both the sisters listened keenly.

"Well, well!" said the Doctor, "I am too old to be converted, even by my friend Snitchey here, or my good spinster sister, Martha Jeddler; who had what she calls her domestic trials ages ago, and has led a sympathising life with all sorts of people ever since; and who is so much of your opinion (only she's less reasonable and more obstinate, being a woman), that we can't agree, and seldom meet. I was born upon this battle-field. I began, as a boy, to have my thoughts directed to the real history of a battle-field. Sixty years have gone over my head, and I have never seen the Christian world, including Heaven knows how many loving mothers and good enough girls like mine here, anything but mad for a battle-field. The same contradictions prevail in everything. One must either laugh or cry at such stupendous inconsistencies; and I prefer to laugh."

Britain, who had been paying the profoundest and most melancholy attention to each speaker in his turn, seemed suddenly to decide in favour of the same preference, if a deep sepulchral sound that escaped him might be construed into a demonstration of risibility. His face, however, was so perfectly unaffected by it, both before and afterwards, that although one or two of the breakfast party looked round as being startled by a mysterious noise, nobody connected the offender with it.

Except his partner in attendance, Clemency Newcome; who rousing him with one of those favourite joints, her elbows, inquired, in a reproachful whisper, what he laughed at.

"Not you!" said Britain.

"Who then?"

"Humanity," said Britain. "That's the joke!"

"What between master and them lawyers, he's getting more and more addle-headed every day!" cried Clemency, giving him a lunge with the other elbow, as a mental stimulant. "Do you know where you are? Do you want to get warning?"

"I don't know anything," said Britain, with a leaden eye and an immovable visage. "I don't care for anything. I don't make out anything. I don't believe anything. And I don't want anything."

Although this forlorn summary of his general condition may have been overcharged in an access of despondency, Benjamin Britain—sometimes called Little Britain, to distinguish him from Great; as we might say Young England, to express Old England with a decided difference—had defined his real state more accurately than might be supposed. For, serving as a sort of man Miles to the Doctor's Friar Bacon, and listening day after day to innumerable orations addressed by the Doctor to various people, all tending to show that his very existence was at best a mistake and an absurdity, this unfortunate servitor had fallen, by degrees, into such an abyss of confused and contradictory suggestions from within and without, that Truth at the bottom of her well, was on the level surface as compared with Britain in the depths of his mystification. The only point he clearly comprehended, was, that the new element usually brought into these discussions by Snitchey and Craggs, never served to make them clearer, and always seemed to give the Doctor a species of advantage and confirmation. Therefore, he looked upon the Firm as one of the proximate causes of his state of mind, and held them in abhorrence accordingly.

"But, this is not our business, Alfred," said the Doctor. "Ceasing to be my ward (as you have said) to-day; and leaving us full to the brim of such learning as the Grammar School down here was able to give you, and your studies in London could add to that, and such practical knowledge as a dull old country Doctor like myself could graft upon both; you are away, now, into the world. The first term of probation appointed by your poor father, being over, away you go now, your own master, to fulfil his second desire: and long before your three years' tour among the foreign schools of medicine is finished, you'll have forgotten us. Lord, you'll forget us easily in six months!"

"If I do—But you know better; why should I speak to you!" said Alfred, laughing.

"I don't know anything of the sort," returned the Doctor. "What do you say, Marion?"

Marion, trifling with her teacup, seemed to say—but she didn't say it—that he was welcome to forget, if he could. Grace pressed the blooming face against her cheek, and smiled.

"I haven't been, I hope, a very unjust steward in the execution of my trust," pursued the Doctor; "but I am to be, at any rate, formally discharged, and released, and what not this morning; and here are our good friends Snitchey and Craggs, with a bagful of papers, and accounts, and documents, for the transfer of the balance of the trust fund to you (I wish it was a more difficult one to dispose of, Alfred, but you must get to be a great man and make it so), and other drolleries of that sort, which are to be signed, sealed, and delivered."

"And duly witnessed as by law required," said Snitchey, pushing away his plate, and taking out the papers, which his partner proceeded to spread upon the table; "and Self and Craggs having been co-trustees with you, Doctor, in so far as the fund was concerned, we shall want your two servants to attest the signatures—can you read, Mrs. Newcome?"

"I an't married, Mister," said Clemency.

"Oh! I beg your pardon. I should think not," chuckled Snitchey, casting his eyes over her extraordinary figure. "You *can* read?"

"A little," answered Clemency.

"The marriage service, night and morning, eh?" observed the lawyer, jocosely.

"No," said Clemency. "Too hard. I only reads a thimble."

"Read a thimble!" echoed Snitchey. "What are you talking about, young woman?"

Clemency nodded. "And a nutmeg-grater."

"Why, this is a lunatic! a subject for the Lord High Chancellor!" said Snitchey, staring at her.

"If possessed of any property," stipulated Craggs.

Grace, however, interposing, explained that each of the articles in question bore an engraved motto, and so formed the pocket library of Clemency Newcome, who was not much given to the study of books.

"Oh, that's it, is it, Miss Grace!" said Snitchey.

"Yes, yes. Ha, ha, ha! I thought our friend was an idiot. She looks uncommonly like it," he muttered, with a supercilious glance. "And what does the thimble say, Mrs. Newcome?"

"I an't married, Mister," observed Clemency.

"Well, Newcome. Will that do?" said the lawyer. "What does the thimble say, Newcome?"

How Clemency, before replying to this question, held one pocket open, and looked down into its yawning depths for the thimble which wasn't there,—and how she then held an opposite pocket open, and seeming to descry it, like a pearl of great price, at the bottom, cleared away such intervening obstacles as a handkerchief, an end of wax candle, a flushed apple, an orange, a lucky penny, a cramp bone, a padlock, a pair of scissors in a sheath more expressively describable as promising young shears, a handful or so of loose beads, several balls of cotton, a needle-case, a cabinet collection of curl-papers, and a biscuit, all of which articles she entrusted individually and separately to Britain to hold,—is of no consequence. Nor how, in her determination to grasp this pocket by the throat and keep it prisoner (for it had a tendency to swing, and twist itself round the nearest corner), she assumed and calmly maintained, an attitude apparently inconsistent with the human anatomy and the laws of gravity. It is enough that at last she triumphantly produced the thimble on her finger, and rattled the nutmeg-grater: the literature of both those trinkets being obviously in course of wearing out and wasting away, through excessive friction.

"That's the thimble, is it, young woman?" said Mr. Snitchey, diverting himself at her expense. "And what does the thimble say?"

"It says," replied Clemency, reading slowly round as if it were a tower, "For-get and For-give."

Snitchey and Craggs laughed heartily. "So new!" said Snitchey. "So easy!" said Craggs. "Such a knowledge of human nature in it!" said Snitchey. "So applicable to the affairs of life!" said Craggs.

"And the nutmeg-grater?" inquired the head of the Firm.

"The grater says," returned Clemency, "Do as you—wold—be—done by."

"Do, or you'll be done brown, you mean," said Mr. Snitchey.

"I don't understand," retorted Clemency, shaking her head vaguely. "I an't no lawyer."

"I am afraid that if she was, Doctor," said Mr. Snitchey, turning to him suddenly, as if to anticipate any effect that might otherwise be consequent on this retort, "she'd find it to be the golden rule of half her clients. They are serious enough in that—whimsical as your world is—and lay the blame on us afterwards. We, in our profession, are little else than mirrors after all, Mr. Alfred; but, we are generally consulted by angry and quarrelsome people who are not in their best looks, and it's rather hard to quarrel with us if we reflect unpleasant aspects. I think," said Mr. Snitchey, "that I speak for Self and Craggs?"

"Decidedly," said Craggs.

"And so, if Mr. Britain will oblige us with a mouthful of ink," said Mr. Snitchey, returning to the papers, "we'll sign, seal, and deliver as soon as possible, or the coach will be coming past before we know where we are."

If one might judge from his appearance, there was every probability of the coach coming past before Mr. Britain knew where *he* was; for he stood in a state of abstraction, mentally balancing the Doctor against the lawyers, and the lawyers against the Doctor, and their clients against both, and engaged in feeble attempts to make the thimble and nutmeg-grater (a new idea to him) square with anybody's system of philosophy; and, in short, bewildering himself as much as ever his great namesake has done with theories and schools. But Clemency, who was his good Genius—though he had the meanest possible opinion of her understanding, by reason of her seldom troubling herself with abstract speculations, and being always at hand to do the right thing at the right time—having produced the ink in a twinkling, tendered him the further service of recalling him to himself by the application of her elbows; with which gentle flappers she so jogged his memory, in a more literal construction of that phrase than usual, that he soon became quite fresh and brisk.

How he laboured under an apprehension not uncommon to persons in his degree, to whom the use of pen and ink is an event, that he couldn't append his name to a document, not of his own writing, without committing himself in some shadowy manner, or somehow signing away vague and enormous sums of money; and how he approached the deeds under protest, and by dint of the Doctor's coercion, and insisted on pausing to look at them before writing (the cramped hand, to say nothing of the phraseology, being so much Chinese to him), and also on turning them round to see whether there was anything fraudulent underneath; and how, having signed his name, he became desolate as one who had parted with his property and rights; I want the time to tell. Also, how the blue bag containing his signature, afterwards had a mysterious interest for him, and he couldn't leave it; also, how Clemency Newcome, in an ecstasy of laughter at the idea of her own importance and dignity, brooded over the whole table with her two elbows, like a spread eagle, and reposed her head upon her left arm as a preliminary to the formation of certain cabalistic characters, which required a deal of ink, and imaginary counterparts whereof she executed at the same time with her tongue. Also, how, having once tasted ink, she became thirsty in that regard, as tame tigers are said to be after tasting another sort of fluid, and wanted to sign everything, and put her name in all kinds of places. In brief, the Doctor was discharged of his trust and all its responsibilities; and Alfred, taking it on himself, was fairly started on the journey of life.

"Britain!" said the Doctor. "Run to the gate, and watch for the coach. Time flies, Alfred!"

"Yes, sir, yes," returned the young man, hurriedly. "Dear Grace! a moment! Marion—so young and beautiful, so winning and so much admired, dear to my heart as nothing else in life is—remember! I leave Marion to you!"

"She has always been a sacred charge to me, Alfred. She is doubly so, now. I will be faithful to my trust, believe me."

"I do believe it, Grace. I know it well. Who could look upon your face, and hear your voice, and not know it! Ah, Grace! If I had your well-governed heart, and tranquil mind, how bravely I would leave this place to-day!"

"Would you?" she answered with a quiet smile.

"And yet, Grace—Sister, seems the natural word."

"Use it!" she said quickly. "I am glad to hear it. Call me nothing else."

"And yet, sister, then," said Alfred, "Marion and I had better have your true and steadfast qualities serving us here, and making us both happier and better. I wouldn't carry them away, to sustain myself, if I could!"

"Coach upon the hill-top!" exclaimed Britain.

"Time flies, Alfred," said the Doctor.

Marion had stood apart, with her eyes fixed upon the ground; but, this warning being given, her young lover brought her tenderly to where her sister stood, and gave her into her embrace.

"I have been telling Grace, dear Marion," he said, "that you are her charge; my precious trust at parting. And when I come back and reclaim you, dearest, and the bright prospect of our married life lies stretched before us, it shall be one of our chief pleasures to consult how we can make Grace happy; how we can anticipate her wishes; how we can show our gratitude and love to her; how we can return her something of the debt she will have heaped upon us."

The younger sister had one hand in his; the other rested on her sister's neck. She looked into that sister's eyes, so calm, serene, and cheerful, with a gaze in which affection, admiration, sorrow, wonder, almost veneration, were blended. She looked into that sister's face, as if it were the face of some bright angel. Calm, serene, and cheerful, the face looked back on her and on her lover.

"And when the time comes, as it must one day," said Alfred,—"I wonder it has never come yet, but Grace knows best, for Grace is always right,—when *she* will want a friend to open her whole heart to, and to be to her something of what she has been to us,—then, Marion, how faithful we will prove, and what delight to us to know that she, our dear good sister, loves and is loved again, as we would have her!"

Still the younger sister looked into her eyes, and turned not—even towards him. And still those honest eyes looked back, so calm, serene, and cheerful, on herself and on her lover.

"And when all that is past, and we are old, and living (as we must!) together—close together; talking often of old times," said Alfred—"these shall be our favourite times among them—this day most of all; and, telling each other what we thought and felt, and hoped and feared at parting; and how we couldn't bear to say good bye—"

"Coach coming through the wood!" cried Britain.

"Yes! I am ready—and how we met again, so happily in spite of all; we'll make this day the happiest in all the year, and keep it as a treble birth-day. Shall we, dear?"

"Yes!" interposed the elder sister, eagerly, and with a radiant smile. "Yes! Alfred, don't linger. There's no time. Say good bye to Marion. And Heaven be with you!"

He pressed the younger sister to his heart. Released from his embrace, she again clung to her sister; and her eyes, with the same blended look, again sought those so calm, serene, and cheerful.

"Farewell, my boy!" said the Doctor. "To talk about any serious correspondence or serious affections, and engagements and so forth, in such a—ha ha ha!—you know what I mean—why that, of course, would be sheer nonsense. All I can say is, that if you and Marion should continue in the same foolish minds, I shall not object to have you for a son-in-law one of these days."

"Over the bridge!" cried Britain.

"Let it come!" said Alfred, wringing the Doctor's hand stoutly. "Think of me sometimes, my old friend and guardian, as seriously as you can! Adieu, Mr. Snitchey! Farewell, Mr. Craggs!"

"Coming down the road!" cried Britain.

"A kiss of Clemency Newcome for long acquaintance' sake! Shake hands, Britain! Marion, dearest heart, good bye! Sister Grace! remember!"

The quiet household figure, and the face so beautiful in its serenity, were turned towards him in reply; but Marion's look and attitude remained unchanged.

The coach was at the gate. There was a bustle with the luggage. The coach drove away. Marion never moved.

"He waves his hat to you, my love," said Grace. "Your chosen husband, darling. Look!"

The younger sister raised her head, and, for a moment, turned it. Then, turning back again, and fully meeting, for the first time, those calm eyes, fell sobbing on her neck.

"Oh, Grace. God bless you! But I cannot bear to see it, Grace! It breaks my heart."

Part the Second

SNITCHEY AND CRAGGS HAD A SNUG LITTLE OFFICE ON THE OLD BATTLE Ground, where they drove a snug little business, and fought a great many small pitched battles for a great many contending parties. Though it could hardly be said of these conflicts that they were running fights—for in truth they generally proceeded at a snail's pace—the part the Firm had in them came so far within the general denomination, that now they took a shot at this Plaintiff, and now aimed a chop at that Defendant, now made a heavy charge at an estate in Chancery, and now had some light skirmishing among an irregular body of small debtors, just as the occasion served, and the enemy happened to present himself. The Gazette was an important and profitable feature in some of their fields, as in fields of greater renown; and in most of the Actions wherein they showed their generalship, it was afterwards observed by the combatants that they had had great difficulty in making each other out, or in knowing with any degree of distinctness what they were about, in consequence of the vast amount of smoke by which they were surrounded.

The offices of Messrs. Snitchey and Craggs stood convenient with an open door, down two smooth steps, in the market-place: so that any angry farmer inclining towards hot water, might tumble into it at once. Their special council-chamber and hall of conference was an old back-room up-stairs, with a low dark ceiling, which seemed to be knitting its brows gloomily in the consideration of tangled points of law. It was furnished with some high-backed leathern chairs, garnished with great goggle-eyed brass nails, of which, every here and there, two or three had fallen out; or had been picked out, perhaps, by the wandering thumbs and forefingers of bewildered clients. There was a framed print of a great judge in it, every curl in whose dreadful wig had made a man's hair stand on end. Bales of papers filled the dusty closets, shelves, and tables; and round the wainscot there were tiers of boxes, padlocked and fireproof, with people's names painted outside, which anxious visitors felt themselves, by a cruel enchantment, obliged to spell backwards and forwards, and to make anagrams of, while they sat, seeming to listen to Snitchey and Craggs, without comprehending one word of what they said.

Snitchey and Craggs had each, in private life as in professional existence, a partner of his own. Snitchey and Craggs were the best friends in the world, and had a real confidence in one another; but Mrs. Snitchey, by a dispensation not uncommon in the affairs of life, was on principle suspicious of Mr. Craggs; and Mrs. Craggs was on principle suspicious of Mr. Snitchey. "Your Snitcheys indeed," the latter lady would observe, sometimes, to Mr. Craggs; using that imaginative plural as if in disparagement of an objectionable pair of pantaloons, or other articles not possessed of a singular number; "I don't see what you want with your Snitcheys, for my part. You trust a great deal too much to your Snitcheys, *I* think, and I hope you may never find my words come true." While Mrs. Snitchey would observe to Mr. Snitchey, of Craggs, "that if ever he was led away by man he was led away by that man, and that if ever she read a double purpose in a mortal eye, she read that purpose in Craggs's eye." Notwithstanding this, however, they were all very good friends in general: and Mrs. Snitchey and Mrs. Craggs maintained a close bond of alliance against "the office," which they both considered the Blue chamber, and common enemy, full of dangerous (because unknown) machinations.

In this office, nevertheless, Snitchey and Craggs made honey for their several hives. Here, sometimes, they would linger, of a fine evening, at the window of their council-chamber overlooking the old battle-ground, and wonder (but that was generally at assize time, when much business had made them sentimental) at the folly of mankind, who couldn't always be at peace with one another and go to law comfortably. Here, days, and weeks, and months, and years, passed over them: their calendar, the gradually diminishing number of brass nails in the leathern chairs, and the increasing bulk of papers on the tables. Here, nearly three years' flight had thinned the one and swelled the other, since the breakfast in the orchard; when they sat together in consultation at night.

Not alone; but, with a man of about thirty, or that time of life, negligently dressed, and somewhat haggard in the face, but well-made, well-attired, and well-looking, who sat in the arm-chair of state, with one hand in his breast, and the other in his dishevelled hair, pondering moodily. Messrs. Snitchey and Craggs sat opposite each other at a neighbouring desk. One of the fire-proof boxes, unpadlocked and opened, was upon it; a part of its contents lay strewn upon the table, and the rest was then in course of passing through the hands of Mr. Snitchey; who brought it to the candle, document by document; looked at every paper singly, as he produced it; shook his head, and handed it to Mr. Craggs, who looked it over also, shook his head, and laid it down. Sometimes they would stop, and shaking their heads in concert, look towards the abstracted client; and the name on the box being Michael Warden, Esquire, we may conclude from these premises that the name and the box were both his, and that the affairs of Michael Warden, Esquire, were in a bad way.

"That's all," said Mr. Snitchey, turning up the last paper. "Really there's no other resource. No other resource."

"All lost, spent, wasted, pawned, borrowed, and sold, eh?" said the client, looking up.

"All," returned Mr. Snitchey.

"Nothing else to be done, you say?"

"Nothing at all."

The client bit his nails, and pondered again.

"And I am not even personally safe in England? You hold to that, do you?"

"In no part of the United Kingdom of Great Britain and Ireland," replied Mr. Snitchey.

"A mere prodigal son with no father to go back to, no swine to keep, and no husks to share with them? Eh?" pursued the client, rocking one leg over the other, and searching the ground with his eyes.

Mr. Snitchey coughed, as if to deprecate the being supposed to participate in any figurative illustration of a legal position. Mr. Craggs, as if to express that it was a partnership view of the subject, also coughed.

"Ruined at thirty!" said the client. "Humph!"

"Not ruined, Mr. Warden," returned Snitchey. "Not so bad as that. You have done a good deal towards it, I must say, but you are not ruined. A little nursing—"

"A little Devil," said the client.

"Mr. Craggs," said Snitchey, "will you oblige me with a pinch of snuff? Thank you, Sir."

As the imperturbable lawyer applied it to his nose with great apparent relish and a perfect absorption of his attention in the proceeding, the client gradually broke into a smile, and, looking up, said:

"You talk of nursing. How long nursing?"

"How long nursing?" repeated Snitchey, dusting the snuff from his fingers, and making a slow calculation in his mind. "For your involved estate, sir? In good hands? S. and C.'s, say? Six or seven years."

"To starve for six or seven years!" said the client with a fretful laugh, and an impatient change of his position.

"To starve for six or seven years, Mr. Warden," said Snitchey, "would be very uncommon indeed. You might get another estate by showing yourself, the while. But, we don't think you could do it—speaking for Self and Craggs—and consequently don't advise it."

"What *do* you advise?"

"Nursing, I say," repeated Snitchey. "Some few years of nursing by Self and Craggs would bring it round. But to enable us to make terms, and hold terms, and you to keep terms, you must go away; you must live abroad. As to starvation, we could ensure you some hundreds a-year to starve upon, even in the beginning—I dare say, Mr. Warden."

"Hundreds," said the client. "And I have spent thousands!"

"That," retorted Mr. Snitchey, putting the papers slowly back into the cast-iron box, "there is no doubt about. No doubt a—bout," he repeated to himself, as he thoughtfully pursued his occupation.

The lawyer very likely knew *his* man; at any rate his dry, shrewd, whimsical manner, had a favourable influence on the client's moody state, and disposed him to be more free and unreserved. Or, perhaps the client knew *his* man, and had elicited such encouragement as he had received, to render some purpose he was about to disclose the more defensible in appearance. Gradually raising his head, he sat looking at his immovable adviser with a smile, which presently broke into a laugh.

"After all," he said, "my iron-headed friend—"

Mr. Snitchey pointed out his partner. "Self and—excuse me—Craggs."

"I beg Mr. Craggs's pardon," said the client. "After all, my iron-headed friends," he leaned forward in his chair, and dropped his voice a little, "you don't know half my ruin yet."

Mr. Snitchey stopped and stared at him. Mr. Craggs also stared.

"I am not only deep in debt," said the client, "but I am deep in—"

"Not in love!" cried Snitchey.

"Yes!" said the client, falling back in his chair, and surveying the Firm with his hands in his pockets. "Deep in love."

"And not with an heiress, sir?" said Snitchey.

"Not with an heiress."

"Nor a rich lady?"

"Nor a rich lady that I know of—except in beauty and merit."

"A single lady, I trust?" said Mr. Snitchey, with great expression.

"Certainly."

"It's not one of Dr. Jeddler's daughters?" said Snitchey, suddenly squaring his elbows on his knees, and advancing his face at least a yard.

"Yes!" returned the client.

"Not his younger daughter?" said Snitchey.

"Yes!" returned the client.

"Mr. Craggs," said Snitchey, much relieved, "will you oblige me with another pinch of snuff? Thank you! I am happy to say it don't signify, Mr. Warden; she's engaged, Sir, she's bespoke. My partner can corroborate me. We know the fact."

"We know the fact," repeated Craggs.

"Why, so do I perhaps," returned the client quietly. "What of that! Are you men of the world, and did you never hear of a woman changing her mind?"

"There certainly have been actions for breach," said Mr. Snitchey, "brought against both spinsters and widows, but, in the majority of cases—"

"Cases!" interposed the client, impatiently. "Don't talk to me of cases. The general precedent is in a much larger volume than any of your law books. Besides, do you think I have lived six weeks in the Doctor's house for nothing?"

"I think, Sir," observed Mr. Snitchey, gravely addressing himself to his partner, "that of all the scrapes Mr. Warden's horses have brought him into at one time and another—and they have been pretty numerous, and pretty expensive, as none know better than himself, and you, and I—the worst scrape may turn out to be, if he talks in this way, this having ever been left by one of them at the Doctor's garden wall, with three broken ribs, a snapped collar-bone, and the Lord knows how many bruises. We didn't think so much of it, at the time when we knew he was going on well under the Doctor's hands and roof; but it looks bad now, sir. Bad? It looks very bad. Doctor Jeddler too—our client, Mr. Craggs."

"Mr. Alfred Heathfield too—a sort of client, Mr. Snitchey," said Craggs.

"Mr. Michael Warden too, a kind of client," said the careless visitor, "and no bad one either: having played the fool for ten or twelve years. However, Mr. Michael Warden has sown his wild oats now—there's their crop, in that box; and he means to repent and be wise. And in proof of it, Mr. Michael Warden means, if he can, to marry Marion, the Doctor's lovely daughter, and to carry her away with him."

"Really, Mr. Craggs," Snitchey began.

"Really, Mr. Snitchey, and Mr. Craggs, partners both," said the client, interrupting him; "you know your duty to your clients, and you know well enough, I am sure, that it is no part of it to interfere in a mere love affair, which I am obliged to confide to you. I am not going to carry the young lady off, without her own consent. There's nothing illegal in it. I never was Mr. Heathfield's bosom friend. I violate no confidence of his. I love where he loves, and I mean to win where he would win, if I can."

"He can't, Mr. Craggs," said Snitchey, evidently anxious and discomfited. "He can't do it, sir. She dotes on Mr. Alfred."

"Does she?" returned the client.

"Mr. Craggs, she dotes on him, sir," persisted Snitchey.

"I didn't live six weeks, some few months ago, in the Doctor's house for nothing; and I doubted that soon," observed the client. "She would have doted on him, if her sister could have brought it about; but I watched them. Marion avoided his name, avoided the subject: shrunk from the least allusion to it, with evident distress."

"Why should she, Mr. Craggs, you know? Why should she, Sir?" inquired Snitchey.

"I don't know why she should, though there are many likely reasons," said the client, smiling at the attention and perplexity expressed in Mr. Snitchey's shining eye, and at his cautious way of carrying on the conversation, and making himself informed upon the subject; "but I know she does. She was very young when she made the engagement—if it may be called one, I am not even sure of that—and has repented of it, perhaps. Perhaps—it seems a foppish thing to say, but upon my soul I don't mean it in that light—she may have fallen in love with me, as I have fallen in love with her."

"He, he! Mr. Alfred, her old playfellow too, you remember, Mr. Craggs," said Snitchey, with a disconcerted laugh; "knew her almost from a baby!"

"Which makes it the more probable that she may be tired of his idea," calmly pursued the client, "and not indisposed to exchange it for the newer one of another lover, who presents himself (or is presented by his horse) under romantic circumstances; has the not unfavourable reputation—with a country girl—of having lived thoughtlessly and gaily, without doing much harm to anybody; and who, for his youth and figure, and so forth—this may seem foppish again, but upon my soul I don't mean it in that light—might perhaps pass muster in a crowd with Mr. Alfred himself."

There was no gainsaying the last clause, certainly; and Mr. Snitchey, glancing at him, thought so. There was something naturally graceful and pleasant in the very carelessness of his air. It seemed to suggest, of his comely face and well-knit figure, that they might be greatly better if he chose: and that, once roused and made earnest (but he never had been earnest yet), he could be full of fire and purpose. "A dangerous sort of libertine," thought the shrewd lawyer, "to seem to catch the spark he wants, from a young lady's eyes."

"Now, observe, Snitchey," he continued, rising and taking him by the button, "and Craggs," taking him by the button also, and placing one partner on either side of him, so that neither might evade him. "I don't ask you for any advice. You are right to keep quite aloof from all parties in such a matter, which is not one in which grave men like you could interfere, on any side. I am briefly going to review in half-a-dozen words, my position and intention, and then I shall leave it to you to do the best for me, in money matters, that you can: seeing that, if I run away with the Doctor's beautiful daughter (as I hope to do, and to become another man under her bright influence), it will be, for the moment, more chargeable than running away alone. But I shall soon make all that up in an altered life."

"I think it will be better not to hear this, Mr. Craggs?" said Snitchey, looking at him across the client.

"*I* think not," said Craggs.—Both listened attentively.

"Well! You needn't hear it," replied their client. "I'll mention it, however. I don't mean to ask the Doctor's consent, because he wouldn't give it me. But I mean to do the Doctor no wrong or harm, because (besides there being nothing serious in such trifles, as he says) I hope to rescue his child, my Marion, from what I see—I *know*—she dreads, and contemplates with misery: that is, the return of this old lover. If anything in the world is true, it is true that she dreads his return. Nobody is injured so far. I am so harried and worried here just now, that I lead the life of a flying-fish. I skulk about in the dark, I am shut out of my own house, and warned off my own grounds: but that house, and those grounds, and many an acre besides, will come back to me one day, as you know and say; and Marion will probably be richer—on your showing, who are never sanguine—ten years hence as my wife, than as the wife of Alfred Heathfield, whose return she dreads (remember that), and in whom or in any man, my passion is not surpassed. Who is injured yet? It is a fair case throughout. My right is as good as his, if she decide in my favour; and I will try my right by her alone. You will like to know no more after this, and I will tell you no more. Now you know my purpose, and wants. When must I leave here?"

"In a week," said Snitchey. "Mr. Craggs?—"

"In something less, I should say," responded Craggs.

"In a month," said the client, after attentively watching the two faces. "This day month. To-day is Thursday. Succeed or fail, on this day month I go."

"It's too long a delay," said Snitchey; "much too long. But let it be so. I thought he'd have stipulated for three," he murmured to himself. "Are you going? Good night, Sir!"

"Good night!" returned the client, shaking hands with the Firm. "You'll live to see me making a good use of riches yet. Henceforth the star of my destiny is, Marion!"

"Take care of the stairs, Sir," replied Snitchey; "for she don't shine there. Good night!"

"Good night!"

So they both stood at the stair-head with a pair of office-candles, watching him down. When he had gone away, they stood looking at each other.

"What do you think of all this, Mr. Craggs?" said Snitchey.

Mr. Craggs shook his head.

"It was our opinion, on the day when that release was executed, that there was something curious in the parting of that pair, I recollect," said Snitchey.

"It was," said Mr. Craggs.

"Perhaps he deceives himself altogether," pursued Mr. Snitchey, locking up the fire-proof box, and putting it away; "or, if he don't, a little bit of fickleness and perfidy is not a miracle, Mr. Craggs. And yet I thought that pretty face was very true. I thought," said Mr. Snitchey, putting on his great-coat (for the weather was very cold), drawing on his gloves, and snuffing out one candle, "that I had even seen her character becoming stronger and more resolved of late. More like her sister's."

"Mrs. Craggs was of the same opinion," returned Craggs.

"I'd really give a trifle to-night," observed Mr. Snitchey, who was a good-natured man, "if I could believe that Mr. Warden was reckoning without his host; but, light-headed, capricious, and unballasted as he is, he knows something of the world and its people (he ought to, for he has bought what he does know, dear enough); and I can't quite think that. We had better not interfere: we can do nothing, Mr. Craggs, but keep quiet."

"Nothing," returned Craggs.

"Our friend the Doctor makes light of such things," said Mr. Snitchey, shaking his head. "I hope he mayn't stand in need of his philosophy. Our friend Alfred talks of the battle of life," he shook his head again, "I hope he mayn't be cut down early in the day. Have you got your hat, Mr. Craggs? I am going to put the other candle out."

Mr. Craggs replying in the affirmative, Mr. Snitchey suited the action to the word, and they groped their way out of the council-chamber, now dark as the subject, or the law in general.

My story passes to a quiet little study, where, on that same night, the sisters and the hale old Doctor sat by a cheerful fireside. Grace was working at her needle. Marion read aloud from a book before her. The Doctor, in his dressing-gown and slippers, with his feet spread out upon the warm rug, leaned back in his easy-chair, and listened to the book, and looked upon his daughters.

They were very beautiful to look upon. Two better faces for a fireside, never made a fireside bright and sacred. Something of the difference between them had been softened down in three years' time; and enthroned upon the clear brow of the younger sister, looking through her eyes, and thrilling in her voice, was the same earnest nature that her own motherless youth had ripened in the elder sister long ago. But she still appeared at once the lovelier and weaker of the two; still seemed to rest her head upon her sister's breast, and put her trust in her, and look into her eyes for counsel and reliance. Those loving eyes, so calm, serene, and cheerful, as of old.

"'And being in her own home,'" read Marion, from the book; "'her home made exquisitely dear by these remembrances, she now began to know that the great trial of her heart must soon come on, and could not be delayed. Oh Home, our comforter and friend when others fall away, to part with whom, at any step between the cradle and the grave'"—

"Marion, my love!" said Grace.

"Why, Puss!" exclaimed her father, "what's the matter?"

She put her hand upon the hand her sister stretched towards her, and read on; her voice still faltering and trembling, though she made an effort to command it when thus interrupted.

"'To part with whom, at any step between the cradle and the grave, is always sorrowful. O Home, so true to us, so often slighted in return, be lenient to them that turn away from thee, and do not haunt their erring footsteps too reproachfully! Let no kind looks, no well-remembered smiles, be seen upon thy phantom face. Let no ray of affection, welcome, gentleness, forbearance, cordiality, shine from thy white head. Let no old loving word, or tone, rise up in judgment against thy deserter; but if thou canst look harshly and severely, do, in mercy to the Penitent!'"

"Dear Marion, read no more to-night," said Grace—for she was weeping.

"I cannot," she replied, and closed the book. "The words seem all on fire!"

The Doctor was amused at this; and laughed as he patted her on the head.

"What! overcome by a story-book!" said Doctor Jeddler. "Print and paper! Well, well, it's all one. It's as rational to make a serious matter of print and paper as of anything else. But dry your eyes, love, dry your eyes. I dare say the heroine has got home again long ago, and made it up all round—and if she hasn't, a real home is only four walls; and a fictitious one, mere rags and ink. What's the matter now?"

"It's only me, Mister," said Clemency, putting in her head at the door.

"And what's the matter with *you*?" said the Doctor.

"Oh, bless you, nothing an't the matter with me," returned Clemency—and truly too, to judge from her well-soaped face, in which there gleamed as usual the very soul of good-humour, which, ungainly as she was, made her quite engaging. Abrasions on the elbows are not generally understood, it is true, to range within that class of personal charms called beauty-spots. But it is better, going through the world, to have the arms chafed in that narrow passage, than the temper: and Clemency's was sound and whole as any beauty's in the land.

"Nothing an't the matter with me," said Clemency, entering, "but—come a little closer, Mister."

The Doctor, in some astonishment, complied with this invitation.

"You said I wasn't to give you one before them, you know," said Clemency.

A novice in the family might have supposed, from her extraordinary ogling as she said it, as well as from a singular rapture or ecstasy which pervaded her elbows, as if she were embracing herself, that "one," in its most favourable interpretation, meant a chaste salute. Indeed the Doctor himself seemed alarmed, for the moment; but quickly regained his composure, as Clemency, having had recourse to both her pockets—beginning with the right one, going away to the wrong one, and afterwards coming back to the right one again—produced a letter from the Post-office.

"Britain was riding by on a errand," she chuckled, handing it to the Doctor, "and see the mail come in, and waited for it. There's A. H. in the corner. Mr. Alfred's on his journey home, I bet. We shall have a wedding in the house—there was two spoons in my saucer this morning. Oh Luck, how slow he opens it!"

All this she delivered, by way of soliloquy, gradually rising higher and higher on tiptoe, in her impatience to hear the news, and making a corkscrew of her apron, and a bottle of her mouth. At last, arriving at a climax of suspense, and seeing the Doctor still engaged in the perusal of the letter, she came down flat upon the soles of her feet again, and cast her apron, as a veil, over her head, in a mute despair, and inability to bear it any longer.

"Here! Girls!" cried the Doctor. "I can't help it: I never could keep a secret in my life. There are not many secrets, indeed, worth being kept in such a—well! never mind that. Alfred's coming home, my dears, directly."

"Directly!" exclaimed Marion.

"What! The story-book is soon forgotten!" said the Doctor, pinching her cheek. "I thought the news would dry those tears. Yes. "Let it be a surprise," he says, here. But I can't let it be a surprise. He must have a welcome."

"Directly!" repeated Marion.

"Why, perhaps not what your impatience calls 'directly,'" returned the doctor; "but pretty soon too. Let us see. Let us see. To-day is Thursday, is it not? Then he promises to be here, this day month."

"This day month!" repeated Marion, softly.

"A gay day and a holiday for us," said the cheerful voice of her sister Grace, kissing her in congratulation. "Long looked forward to, dearest, and come at last."

She answered with a smile; a mournful smile, but full of sisterly affection. As she looked in her sister's face, and listened to the quiet music of her voice, picturing the happiness of this return, her own face glowed with hope and joy.

And with a something else; a something shining more and more through all the rest of its expression; for which I have no name. It was not exultation, triumph, proud enthusiasm. They are not so calmly shown. It was not love and gratitude alone, though love and gratitude were part of it. It emanated from no sordid thought, for sordid thoughts do not light up the brow, and hover on the lips, and move the spirit like a fluttered light, until the sympathetic figure trembles.

Dr. Jeddler, in spite of his system of philosophy—which he was continually contradicting and denying in practice, but more famous philosophers have done that—could not help having as much interest in the return of his old ward and pupil as if it had been a serious event. So he sat himself down in his easy-chair again, stretched out his slippered feet once more upon the rug, read the letter over and over a great many times, and talked it over more times still.

"Ah! The day was," said the Doctor, looking at the fire, "when you and he, Grace, used to trot about arm-in-arm, in his holiday time, like a couple of walking dolls. You remember?"

"I remember," she answered, with her pleasant laugh, and plying her needle busily.

"This day month, indeed!" mused the Doctor. "That hardly seems a twelvemonth ago. And where was my little Marion then!"

"Never far from her sister," said Marion, cheerily, "however little. Grace was everything to me, even when she was a young child herself."

"True, Puss, true," returned the Doctor. "She was a staid little woman, was Grace, and a wise housekeeper, and a busy, quiet, pleasant body; bearing with our humours and anticipating our wishes, and always ready to forget her own, even in those times. I never knew you positive or obstinate, Grace, my darling, even then, on any subject but one."

"I am afraid I have changed sadly for the worse, since," laughed Grace, still busy at her work. "What was that one, father?"

"Alfred, of course," said the Doctor. "Nothing would serve you but you must be called Alfred's wife; so we called you Alfred's wife; and you liked it better, I believe (odd as it seems now), than being called a Duchess, if we could have made you one."

"Indeed?" said Grace, placidly.

"Why, don't you remember?" inquired the Doctor.

"I think I remember something of it," she returned, "but not much. It's so long ago." And as she sat at work, she hummed the burden of an old song, which the Doctor liked.

"Alfred will find a real wife soon," she said, breaking off; "and that will be a happy time indeed for all of us. My three years' trust is nearly at an end, Marion. It has been a very easy one. I shall tell Alfred, when I give you back to him, that you have loved him dearly all the time, and that he has never once needed my good services. May I tell him so, love?"

"Tell him, dear Grace," replied Marion, "that there never was a trust so generously, nobly, steadfastly discharged; and that I have loved *you*, all the time, dearer and dearer every day; and O! how dearly now!"

"Nay," said her cheerful sister, returning her embrace, "I can scarcely tell him that; we will leave my deserts to Alfred's imagination. It will be liberal enough, dear Marion; like your own."

With that, she resumed the work she had for a moment laid down, when her sister spoke so fervently: and with it the old song the Doctor liked to hear. And the Doctor, still reposing in his easy-chair, with his slippered feet stretched out before him on the rug, listened to the tune, and beat time on his knee with Alfred's letter, and looked at his two daughters, and thought that among the many trifles of the trifling world, these trifles were agreeable enough.

Clemency Newcome, in the meantime, having accomplished her mission and lingered in the room until she had made herself a party to the news, descended to the kitchen, where her coadjutor, Mr. Britain, was regaling after supper, surrounded by such a plentiful collection of bright pot-lids, well-scoured saucepans, burnished dinner-covers, gleaming kettles, and other tokens of her industrious habits, arranged upon the walls and shelves, that he sat as in the centre of a hall of mirrors. The majority did not give forth very flattering portraits of him, certainly; nor were they by any means unanimous in their reflections; as some made him very long-faced, others very broad-faced, some tolerably well-looking, others vastly ill-looking, according to their several manners of reflecting: which were as various, in respect of one fact, as those of so many kinds of men. But they all agreed that in the midst of them sat, quite at his ease, an individual with a pipe in his mouth, and a jug of beer at his elbow, who nodded condescendingly to Clemency, when she stationed herself at the same table.

"Well, Clemmy," said Britain, "how are you by this time, and what's the news?"

Clemency told him the news, which he received very graciously. A gracious change had come over Benjamin from head to foot. He was much broader, much redder, much more cheerful, and much jollier in all respects. It seemed as if his face had been tied up in a knot before, and was now untwisted and smoothed out.

"There'll be another job for Snitchey and Craggs, I suppose," he observed, puffing slowly at his pipe. "More witnessing for you and me, perhaps, Clemmy!"

"Lor!" replied his fair companion, with her favourite twist of her favourite joints. "I wish it was me, Britain!"

"Wish what was you?"

"A going to be married," said Clemency.

Benjamin took his pipe out of his mouth and laughed heartily. "Yes! you're a likely subject for that!" he said. "Poor Clem!" Clemency for her part laughed as heartily as he, and seemed as much amused by the idea. "Yes," she assented, "I'm a likely subject for that; an't I?"

"*You'll* never be married, you know," said Mr. Britain, resuming his pipe.

"Don't you think I ever shall though?" said Clemency, in perfect good faith.

Mr. Britain shook his head. "Not a chance of it!"

"Only think!" said Clemency. "Well!—I suppose you mean to, Britain, one of these days; don't you?"

A question so abrupt, upon a subject so momentous, required consideration. After blowing out a great cloud of smoke, and looking at it with his head now on this side and now on that, as if it were actually the question, and he were surveying it in various aspects, Mr. Britain replied that he wasn't altogether clear about it, but—ye-es—he thought he might come to that at last.

"I wish her joy, whoever she may be!" cried Clemency.

"Oh she'll have that," said Benjamin, "safe enough."

"But she wouldn't have led quite such a joyful life as she will lead, and wouldn't have had quite such a sociable sort of husband as she will have," said Clemency, spreading herself half over the table, and staring retrospectively at the candle, "if it hadn't been for—not that I went to do it, for it was accidental, I am sure—if it hadn't been for me; now would she, Britain?"

"Certainly not," returned Mr. Britain, by this time in that high state of appreciation of his pipe, when a man can open his mouth but a very little way for speaking purposes; and sitting luxuriously immovable in his chair, can afford to turn only his eyes towards a companion, and that very passively and gravely. "Oh! I'm greatly beholden to you, you know, Clem."

"Lor, how nice that is to think of!" said Clemency.

At the same time, bringing her thoughts as well as her sight to bear upon the candle-grease, and becoming abruptly reminiscent of its healing qualities as a balsam, she anointed her left elbow with a plentiful application of that remedy.

"You see I've made a good many investigations of one sort and another in my time," pursued Mr. Britain, with the profundity of a sage, "having been always of an inquiring turn of mind; and I've read a good many books about the general Rights of things and Wrongs of things, for I went into the literary line myself, when I began life."

"Did you though!" cried the admiring Clemency.

"Yes," said Mr. Britain: "I was hid for the best part of two years behind a bookstall, ready to fly out if anybody pocketed a volume; and after that, I was light porter to a stay and mantua maker, in which capacity I was employed to carry about, in oilskin baskets, nothing but deceptions—which soured my spirits and disturbed my confidence in human nature; and after that, I heard a world of discussions in this house, which soured my spirits fresh; and my opinion after all is, that, as a safe and comfortable sweetener of the same, and as a pleasant guide through life, there's nothing like a nutmeg-grater."

Clemency was about to offer a suggestion, but he stopped her by anticipating it.

"Com-bined," he added gravely, "with a thimble."

"Do as you wold, you know, and cetrer, eh!" observed Clemency, folding her arms comfortably in her delight at this avowal, and patting her elbows. "Such a short cut, an't it?"

"I'm not sure," said Mr. Britain, "that it's what would be considered good philosophy. I've my doubts about that; but it wears well, and saves a quantity of snarling, which the genuine article don't always."

"See how you used to go on once, yourself, you know!" said Clemency.

"Ah!" said Mr. Britain. "But the most extraordinary thing, Clemmy, is that I should live to be brought round, through you. That's the strange part of it. Through you! Why, I suppose you haven't so much as half an idea in your head."

Clemency, without taking the least offence, shook it, and laughed and hugged herself, and said, "No, she didn't suppose she had."

"I'm pretty sure of it," said Mr. Britain.

"Oh! I dare say you're right," said Clemency. "I don't pretend to none. I don't want any."

Benjamin took his pipe from his lips, and laughed till the tears ran down his face. "What a natural you are, Clemmy!" he said, shaking his head, with an infinite relish of the joke, and wiping his eyes. Clemency, without the smallest inclination to dispute it, did the like, and laughed as heartily as he.

"I can't help liking you," said Mr. Britain; "you're a regular good creature in your way, so shake hands, Clem. Whatever happens, I'll always take notice of you, and be a friend to you."

"Will you?" returned Clemency. "Well! that's very good of you."

"Yes, yes," said Mr. Britain, giving her his pipe to knock the ashes out of it; "I'll stand by you. Hark! That's a curious noise!"

"Noise!" repeated Clemency.

"A footstep outside. Somebody dropping from the wall, it sounded like," said Britain. "Are they all abed up-stairs?"

"Yes, all abed by this time," she replied.

"Didn't you hear anything?"

"No."

They both listened, but heard nothing.

"I tell you what," said Benjamin, taking down a lantern. "I'll have a look round, before I go to bed myself, for satisfaction's sake. Undo the door while I light this, Clemmy."

Clemency complied briskly; but observed as she did so, that he would only have his walk for his pains, that it was all his fancy, and so forth. Mr. Britain said "very likely"; but sallied out, nevertheless, armed with the poker, and casting the light of the lantern far and near in all directions.

"It's as quiet as a churchyard," said Clemency, looking after him; "and almost as ghostly too!"

Glancing back into the kitchen, she cried fearfully, as a light figure stole into her view, "What's that!"

"Hush!" said Marion in an agitated whisper. "You have always loved me, have you not?"

"Loved you, child! You may be sure I have."

"I am sure. And I may trust you, may I not? There is no one else just now, in whom I *can* trust."

"Yes," said Clemency, with all her heart.

"There is some one out there," pointing to the door, "whom I must see, and speak with, to-night. Michael Warden, for God's sake retire! Not now!"

Clemency started with surprise and trouble as, following the direction of the speaker's eyes, she saw a dark figure standing in the doorway.

"In another moment you may be discovered," said Marion. "Not now! Wait, if you can, in some concealment. I will come presently."

He waved his hand to her, and was gone. "Don't go to bed. Wait here for me!" said Marion, hurriedly. "I have been seeking to speak to you for an hour past. Oh, be true to me!"

Eagerly seizing her bewildered hand, and pressing it with both her own to her breast—an action more expressive, in its passion of entreaty, than the most eloquent appeal in words,—Marion withdrew; as the light of the returning lantern flashed into the room.

"All still and peaceable. Nobody there. Fancy, I suppose," said Mr. Britain, as he locked and barred the door. "One of the effects of having a lively imagination. Halloa! Why, what's the matter?"

Clemency, who could not conceal the effects of her surprise and concern, was sitting in a chair: pale, and trembling from head to foot.

"Matter!" she repeated, chafing her hands and elbows, nervously, and looking anywhere but at him. "That's good in you, Britain, that is! After going and frightening one out of one's life with noises and lanterns, and I don't know what all. Matter! Oh, yes!"

"If you're frightened out of your life by a lantern, Clemmy," said Mr. Britain, composedly blowing it out and hanging it up again, "that apparition's very soon got rid of. But you're as bold as brass in general," he said, stopping to observe her; "and were, after the noise and the lantern too. What have you taken into your head? Not an idea, eh?"

But, as Clemency bade him good night very much after her usual fashion, and began to bustle about with a show of going to bed herself immediately, Little Britain, after giving utterance to the original remark that it was impossible to account for a woman's whims, bade her good night in return, and taking up his candle strolled drowsily away to bed.

When all was quiet, Marion returned.

"Open the door," she said; "and stand there close beside me, while I speak to him, outside."

Timid as her manner was, it still evinced a resolute and settled purpose, such as Clemency could not resist. She softly unbarred the door: but before turning the key, looked round on the young creature waiting to issue forth when she should open it.

The face was not averted or cast down, but looking full upon her, in its pride of youth and beauty. Some simple sense of the slightness of the barrier that interposed itself between the happy home and honoured love of the fair girl, and what might be the desolation of that home, and shipwreck of its dearest treasure, smote so keenly on the tender heart of Clemency, and so filled it to overflowing with sorrow and compassion, that, bursting into tears, she threw her arms round Marion's neck.

"It's little that I know, my dear," cried Clemency, "very little; but I know that this should not be. Think of what you do!"

"I have thought of it many times," said Marion, gently.

"Once more," urged Clemency. "Till to-morrow." Marion shook her head.

"For Mr. Alfred's sake," said Clemency, with homely earnestness. "Him that you used to love so dearly, once!"

She hid her face, upon the instant, in her hands, repeating "Once!" as if it rent her heart.

"Let me go out," said Clemency, soothing her. "I'll tell him what you like. Don't cross the door-step to-night. I'm sure no good will come of it. Oh, it was an unhappy day when Mr. Warden was ever brought here! Think of your good father, darling: of your sister."

"I have," said Marion, hastily raising her head. "You don't know what I do. I *must* speak to him. You are the best and truest friend in all the world for what you have said to me, but I must take this step. Will you go with me, Clemency," she kissed her on her friendly face, "or shall I go alone?"

Sorrowing and wondering, Clemency turned the key, and opened the door. Into the dark and doubtful night that lay beyond the threshold, Marion passed quickly, holding by her hand.

In the dark night he joined her, and they spoke together earnestly and long; and the hand that held so fast by Clemeney's, now trembled, now turned deadly cold, now clasped and closed on hers, in the strong feeling of the speech it emphasised unconsciously. When they returned, he followed to the door, and pausing there a moment, seized the other hand, and pressed it to his lips. Then, stealthily withdrew.

The door was barred and locked again, and once again she stood beneath her father's roof. Not bowed down by the secret that she brought there, though so young; but, with that same expression on her face for which I had no name before, and shining through her tears.

Again she thanked and thanked her humble friend, and trusted to her, as she said, with confidence, implicitly. Her chamber safely reached, she fell upon her knees; and with her secret weighing on her heart, could pray!

Could rise up from her prayers, so tranquil and serene, and bending over her fond sister in her slumber, look upon her face and smile: though sadly: murmuring as she kissed her forehead, how that Grace had been a mother to her, ever, and she loved her as a child!

Could draw the passive arm about her neck when lying down to rest—it seemed to cling there, of its own will, protectingly and tenderly even in sleep—and breathe upon the parted lips, God bless her!

Could sink into a peaceful sleep, herself; but for one dream, in which she cried out, in her innocent and touching voice, that she was quite alone, and they had all forgotten her.

A month soon passes, even at its tardiest pace. The month appointed to elapse between that night and the return, was quick of foot, and went by like a vapour.

The day arrived. A raging winter day, that shook the old house, sometimes, as if it shivered in the blast. A day to make home doubly home. To give the chimney-corner new delights. To shed a ruddier glow upon the faces gathered round the hearth, and draw each fireside group into a closer and more social league, against the roaring elements without. Such a wild winter day as best prepares the way for shut-out night; for curtained rooms, and cheerful looks; for music, laughter, dancing, light, and jovial entertainment!

All these the Doctor had in store to welcome Alfred back. They knew that he could not arrive till night; and they would make the night air ring, he said, as he approached. All his old friends should congregate about him. He should not miss a face that he had known and liked. No! They should every one be there!

So, guests were bidden, and musicians were engaged, and tables spread, and floors prepared for active feet, and bountiful provision made, of every hospitable kind. Because it was the Christmas season, and his eyes were all unused to English holly and its sturdy green, the dancing-room was garlanded and hung with it; and the red berries gleamed an English welcome to him, peeping from among the leaves.

It was a busy day for all of them: a busier day for none of them than Grace, who noiselessly presided everywhere, and was the cheerful mind of all the preparations. Many a time that day (as well as many a time within the fleeting month preceding it), did Clemency glance anxiously, and almost fearfully, at Marion. She saw her paler, perhaps, than usual; but there was a sweet composure on her face that made it lovelier than ever.

At night when she was dressed, and wore upon her head a wreath that Grace had proudly twined about it—its mimic flowers were Alfred's favourites, as Grace remembered when she chose them—that old expression, pensive, almost sorrowful, and yet so spiritual, high, and stirring, sat again upon her brow, enhanced a hundred-fold.

"The next wreath I adjust on this fair head, will be a marriage wreath," said Grace; "or I am no true prophet, dear."

Her sister smiled, and held her in her arms.

"A moment, Grace. Don't leave me yet. Are you sure that I want nothing more?"

Her care was not for that. It was her sister's face she thought of, and her eyes were fixed upon it, tenderly.

"My art," said Grace, "can go no farther, dear girl; nor your beauty. I never saw you look so beautiful as now."

"I never was so happy," she returned.

"Ay, but there is a greater happiness in store. In such another home, as cheerful and as bright as this looks now," said Grace, "Alfred and his young wife will soon be living."

She smiled again. "It is a happy home, Grace, in your fancy. I can see it in your eyes. I know it WILL be happy, dear. How glad I am to know it."

"Well," cried the Doctor, bustling in. "Here we are, all ready for Alfred, eh? He can't be here until pretty late—an hour or so before midnight—so there'll be plenty of time for making merry before he comes. He'll not find us with the ice unbroken. Pile up the fire here, Britain! Let it shine upon the holly till it winks again. It's a world of nonsense, Puss; true lovers and all the rest of it—all nonsense; but we'll be nonsensical with the rest of 'em, and give our true lover a mad welcome. Upon my word!" said the old Doctor, looking at his daughters proudly, "I'm not clear to-night, among other absurdities, but that I'm the father of two handsome girls."

"All that one of them has ever done, or may do—may do, dearest father—to cause you pain or grief, forgive her," said Marion, "forgive her now, when her heart is full. Say that you forgive her. That you will forgive her. That she shall always share your love, and—," and the rest was not said, for her face was hidden on the old man's shoulder.

"Tut, tut, tut," said the Doctor gently. "Forgive! What have I to forgive? Heyday, if our true lovers come back to flurry us like this, we must hold 'em at a distance; we must send expresses out to stop 'em short upon the road, and bring 'em on a mile or two a day, until we're properly prepared to meet 'em. Kiss me, Puss. Forgive! Why, what a silly child you are! If you had vexed and crossed me fifty times a day, instead of not at all, I'd forgive you everything, but such a supplication. Kiss me again, Puss. There! Prospective and retrospective—a clear score between us. Pile up the fire here! Would you freeze the people on this bleak December night! Let us be light, and warm, and merry, or I'll not forgive some of you!"

So gaily the old Doctor carried it! And the fire was piled up, and the lights were bright, and company arrived, and a murmuring of lively tongues began, and already there was a pleasant air of cheerful excitement stirring through all the house.

More and more company came flocking in. Bright eyes sparkled upon Marion; smiling lips gave her joy of his return; sage mothers fanned themselves, and hoped she mightn't be too youthful and inconstant for the quiet round of home; impetuous fathers fell into disgrace for too much exaltation of her beauty; daughters envied her; sons envied him; innumerable pairs of lovers profited by the occasion; all were interested, animated, and expectant.

Mr. and Mrs. Craggs came arm in arm, but Mrs. Snitchey came alone. "Why, what's become of *him?*" inquired the Doctor.

The feather of a Bird of Paradise in Mrs. Snitchey's turban, trembled as if the Bird of Paradise were alive again, when she said that doubtless Mr. Craggs knew. *SHE* was never told.

"That nasty office," said Mrs. Craggs.

"I wish it was burnt down," said Mrs. Snitchey.

"He's—he's—there's a little matter of business that keeps my partner rather late," said Mr. Craggs, looking uneasily about him.

"Oh—h! Business. Don't tell me!" said Mrs. Snitchey.

"*We* know what business means," said Mrs. Craggs.

But their not knowing what it meant, was perhaps the reason why Mrs. Snitchey's Bird of Paradise feather quivered so portentously, and why all the pendant bits on Mrs. Craggs's ear-rings shook like little bells.

"I wonder *you* could come away, Mr. Craggs," said his wife.

"Mr. Craggs is fortunate, I'm sure!" said Mrs. Snitchey.

"That office so engrosses 'em," said Mrs. Craggs.

"A person with an office has no business to be married at all," said Mrs. Snitchey.

Then, Mrs. Snitchey said, within herself, that that look of hers had pierced to Craggs's soul, and he knew it; and Mrs. Craggs observed to Craggs, that "his Snitcheys" were deceiving him behind his back, and he would find it out when it was too late.

Still, Mr. Craggs, without much heeding these remarks, looked uneasily about until his eye rested on Grace, to whom he immediately presented himself.

"Good evening, ma'am," said Craggs. "You look charmingly. Your—Miss—your sister, Miss Marion, is she—"

"Oh, she's quite well, Mr. Craggs."

"Yes—I—is she here?" asked Craggs.

"Here! Don't you see her yonder? Going to dance?" said Grace.

Mr. Craggs put on his spectacles to see the better; looked at her through them, for some time; coughed; and put them, with an air of satisfaction, in their sheath again, and in his pocket.

Now the music struck up, and the dance commenced. The bright fire crackled and sparkled, rose and fell, as though it joined the dance itself, in right good fellowship. Sometimes, it roared as if it would make music too. Sometimes, it flashed and beamed as if it were the eye of the old room: it winked too, sometimes, like a knowing patriarch, upon the youthful whisperers in corners. Sometimes, it sported with the holly-boughs; and, shining on the leaves by fits and starts, made them look as if they were in the cold winter night again, and fluttering in the wind. Sometimes its genial humour grew obstreperous, and passed all bounds; and then it cast into the room, among the twinkling feet, with a loud burst, a shower of harmless little sparks, and in its exultation leaped and bounded, like a mad thing, up the broad old chimney.

Another dance was near its close, when Mr. Snitchey touched his partner, who was looking on, upon the arm.

Mr. Craggs started, as if his familiar had been a spectre.

"Is he gone?" he asked.

"Hush! He has been with me," said Snitchey, "for three hours and more. He went over everything. He looked into all our arrangements for him, and was very particular indeed. He—Humph!"

The dance was finished. Marion passed close before him, as he spoke. She did not observe him, or his partner; but looked over her shoulder towards her sister in the distance, as she slowly made her way into the crowd, and passed out of their view.

"You see! All safe and well," said Mr. Craggs. "He didn't recur to that subject, I suppose?"

"Not a word."

"And is he really gone? Is he safe away?"

"He keeps to his word. He drops down the river with the tide in that shell of a boat of his, and so goes out to sea on this dark night!—a dare-devil he is—before the wind. There's no such lonely road anywhere else. That's one thing. The tide flows, he says, an hour before midnight—about this time. I'm glad it's over." Mr. Snitchey wiped his forehead, which looked hot and anxious.

"What do you think," said Mr. Craggs, "about—"

"Hush!" replied his cautious partner, looking straight before him. "I understand you. Don't mention names, and don't let us, seem to be talking secrets. I don't know what to think; and to tell you the truth, I don't care now. It's a great relief. His self-love deceived him, I suppose. Perhaps the young lady coquetted a little. The evidence would seem to point that way. Alfred not arrived?"

"Not yet," said Mr. Craggs. "Expected every minute."

"Good." Mr. Snitchey wiped his forehead again. "It's a great relief. I haven't been so nervous since we've been in partnership. I intend to spend the evening now, Mr. Craggs."

Mrs. Craggs and Mrs. Snitchey joined them as he announced this intention. The Bird of Paradise was in a state of extreme vibration, and the little bells were ringing quite audibly.

"It has been the theme of general comment, Mr. Snitchey," said Mrs. Snitchey. "I hope the office is satisfied."

"Satisfied with what, my dear?" asked Mr. Snitchey.

"With the exposure of a defenceless woman to ridicule and remark," returned his wife. "That is quite in the way of the office, *that* is."

"I really, myself," said Mrs. Craggs, "have been so long accustomed to connect the office with everything opposed to domesticity, that I am glad to know it as the avowed enemy of my peace. There is something honest in that, at all events."

"My dear," urged Mr. Craggs, "your good opinion is invaluable, but *I* never avowed that the office was the enemy of your peace."

"No," said Mrs. Craggs, ringing a perfect peal upon the little bells. "Not you, indeed. You wouldn't be worthy of the office, if you had the candour to."

"As to my having been away to-night, my dear," said Mr. Snitchey, giving her his arm, "the deprivation has been mine, I'm sure; but, as Mr. Craggs knows—"

Mrs. Snitchey cut this reference very short by hitching her husband to a distance, and asking him to look at that man. To do her the favour to look at him!

"At which man, my dear?" said Mr. Snitchey.

"Your chosen companion; *I*'m no companion to you, Mr. Snitchey."

"Yes, yes, you are, my dear," he interposed.

"No, no, I'm not," said Mrs. Snitchey with a majestic smile. "I know my station. Will you look at your chosen companion, Mr. Snitchey; at your referee, at the keeper of your secrets, at the man you trust; at your other self, in short?"

The habitual association of Self with Craggs, occasioned Mr. Snitchey to look in that direction.

"If you can look that man in the eye this night," said Mrs. Snitchey, "and not know that you are deluded, practised upon, made the victim of his arts, and bent down prostrate to his will by some unaccountable fascination which it is impossible to explain and against which no warning of mine is of the least avail, all I can say is—I pity you!"

At the very same moment Mrs. Craggs was oracular on the cross subject. Was it possible, she said, that Craggs could so blind himself to his Snitcheys, as not to feel his true position? Did he mean to say that he had seen his Snitcheys come into that room, and didn't plainly see that there was reservation, cunning, treachery, in the man? Would he tell her that his very action, when he wiped his forehead and looked so stealthily about him, didn't show that there was something weighing on the conscience of his precious Snitcheys (if he had a conscience), that wouldn't bear the light? Did anybody but his Snitcheys come to festive entertainments like a burglar?—which, by the way, was hardly a clear illustration of the case, as he had walked in very mildly at the door. And would he still assert to her at noon-day (it being nearly midnight), that his Snitcheys were to be justified through thick and thin, against all facts, and reason, and experience?

Neither Snitchey nor Craggs openly attempted to stem the current which had thus set in, but, both were content to be carried gently along it, until its force abated; which happened at about the same time as a general movement for a country dance; when Mr. Snitchey proposed himself as a partner to Mrs. Craggs, and Mr. Craggs gallantly offered himself to Mrs. Snitchey; and after some such slight evasions as "why don't you ask somebody else?" and "you'll be glad, I know, if I decline," and "I wonder you can dance out of the office" (but this jocosely now), each lady graciously accepted, and took her place.

It was an old custom among them, indeed, to do so, and to pair off, in like manner, at dinners and suppers; for they were excellent friends, and on a footing of easy familiarity. Perhaps the false Craggs and the wicked Snitchey were a recognised fiction with the two wives, as Doe and Roe, incessantly running up and down bailiwicks, were with the two husbands: or, perhaps the ladies had instituted, and taken upon themselves, these two shares in the business, rather than be left out of it altogether. But, certain it is, that each wife went as gravely and steadily to work in her vocation as her husband did in his, and would have considered it almost impossible for the Firm to maintain a successful and respectable existence, without her laudable exertions.

But now the Bird of Paradise was seen to flutter down the middle; and the little bells began to bounce and jingle in poussette; and the Doctor's rosy face spun round and round, like an expressive pegtop highly varnished; and breathless Mr. Craggs began to doubt already, whether country dancing had been made "too easy," like the rest of life; and Mr. Snitchey, with his nimble cuts and capers, footed it for Self and Craggs, and half-a-dozen more.

Now, too, the fire took fresh courage, favoured by the lively wind the dance awakened, and burnt clear and high. It was the Genius of the room, and present everywhere. It shone in people's eyes, it sparkled in the jewels on the snowy necks of girls, it twinkled at their ears as if it whispered to them slyly, it flashed about their waists, it flickered on the ground and made it rosy for their feet, it bloomed upon the ceiling that its glow might set off their bright faces, and it kindled up a general illumination in Mrs. Craggs's little belfry.

Now, too, the lively air that fanned it, grew less gentle as the music quickened and the dance proceeded with new spirit; and a breeze arose that made the leaves and berries dance upon the wall, as they had often done upon the trees; and the breeze rustled in the room as if an invisible company of fairies, treading in the footsteps of the good substantial revellers, were whirling after them. Now, too, no feature of the Doctor's face could be distinguished as he spun and spun; and now there seemed a dozen Birds of Paradise in fitful flight; and now there were a thousand little bells at work; and now a fleet of flying skirts was ruffled by a little tempest, when the music gave in, and the dance was over.

Hot and breathless as the Doctor was, it only made him the more impatient for Alfred's coming.

"Anything been seen, Britain? Anything been heard?"

"Too dark to see far, Sir. Too much noise inside the house to hear."

"That's right! The gayer welcome for him. How goes the time?"

"Just twelve, Sir. He can't be long, Sir."

"Stir up the fire, and throw another log upon it," said the Doctor. "Let him see his welcome blazing out upon the night—good boy!—as he comes along!"

He saw it—Yes! From the chaise he caught the light, as he turned the corner by the old church. He knew the room from which it shone. He saw the wintry branches of the old trees between the light and him. He knew that one of those trees rustled musically in the summer time at the window of Marion's chamber.

The tears were in his eyes. His heart throbbed so violently that he could hardly bear his happiness. How often he had thought of this time—pictured it under all circumstances—feared that it might never come—yearned, and wearied for it—far away!

Again the light! Distinct and ruddy; kindled, he knew, to give him welcome, and to speed him home. He beckoned with his hand, and waved his hat, and cheered out, loud, as if the light were they, and they could see and hear him, as he dashed towards them through the mud and mire, triumphantly.

"Stop!" He knew the Doctor, and understood what he had done. He would not let it be a surprise to them. But he could make it one, yet, by going forward on foot. If the orchard-gate were open, he could enter there; if not, the wall was easily climbed, as he knew of old; and he would be among them in an instant.

He dismounted from the chaise, and telling the driver—even that was not easy in his agitation—to remain behind for a few minutes, and then to follow slowly, ran on with exceeding swiftness, tried the gate, scaled the wall, jumped down on the other side, and stood panting in the old orchard.

There was a frosty rime upon the trees, which, in the faint light of the clouded moon, hung upon the smaller branches like dead garlands. Withered leaves crackled and snapped beneath his feet, as he crept softly on towards the house. The desolation of a winter night sat brooding on the earth, and in the sky. But, the red light came cheerily towards him from the windows; figures passed and repassed there; and the hum and murmur of voices greeted his ear sweetly.

Listening for hers: attempting, as he crept on, to detach it from the rest, and half believing that he heard it: he had nearly reached the door, when it was abruptly opened, and a figure coming out encountered his. It instantly recoiled with a half-suppressed cry.

"Clemency," he said, "don't you know me?"

"Don't come in!" she answered, pushing him back. "Go away. Don't ask me why. Don't come in."

"What is the matter?" he exclaimed.

"I don't know. I—I am afraid to think. Go back. Hark!"

There was a sudden tumult in the house. She put her hands upon her ears. A wild scream, such as no hands could shut out, was heard; and Grace—distraction in her looks and manner—rushed out at the door.

"Grace!" He caught her in his arms. "What is it! Is she dead!"

She disengaged herself, as if to recognise his face, and fell down at his feet.

A crowd of figures came about them from the house. Among them was her father, with a paper in his hand.

"What is it!" cried Alfred, grasping his hair with his hands, and looking in an agony from face to face, as he bent upon his knee beside the insensible girl. "Will no one look at me? Will no one speak to me? Does no one know me? Is there no voice among you all, to tell me what it is!"

There was a murmur among them. "She is gone."

"Gone!" he echoed.

"Fled, my dear Alfred!" said the Doctor, in a broken voice, and with his hands before his face. "Gone from her home and us. To-night! She writes that she has made her innocent and blameless choice—entreats that we will forgive her—prays that we will not forget her—and is gone."

"With whom? Where?"

He started up, as if to follow in pursuit, but, when they gave way to let him pass, looked wildly round upon them, staggered back, and sunk down in his former attitude, clasping one of Grace's cold hands in his own.

There was a hurried running to and fro, confusion, noise, disorder, and no purpose. Some proceeded to disperse themselves about the roads, and some took horse, and some got lights, and some conversed together, urging that there was no trace or track to follow. Some approached him kindly, with the view of offering consolation; some admonished him that Grace must be removed into the house, and that he prevented it. He never heard them, and he never moved.

The snow fell fast and thick. He looked up for a moment in the air, and thought that those white ashes strewn upon his hopes and misery, were suited to them well. He looked round on the whitening ground, and thought how Marion's footprints would be hushed and covered up, as soon as made, and even that remembrance of her blotted out. But he never felt the weather and he never stirred.

Part the Third

The world had grown six years older since that night of the return. It was a warm autumn afternoon, and there had been heavy rain. The sun burst suddenly from among the clouds; and the old battle-ground, sparkling brilliantly and cheerfully at sight of it in one green place, flashed a responsive welcome there, which spread along the country side as if a joyful beacon had been lighted up, and answered from a thousand stations.

How beautiful the landscape kindling in the light, and that luxuriant influence passing on like a celestial presence, brightening everything! The wood, a sombre mass before, revealed its varied tints of yellow, green, brown, red: its different forms of trees, with raindrops glittering on their leaves and twinkling as they fell. The verdant meadowland, bright and glowing, seemed as if it had been blind, a minute since, and now had found a sense of sight where-with to look up at the shining sky. Corn-fields, hedge-rows, fences, homesteads, and clustered roofs, the steeple of the church, the stream, the water-mill, all sprang out of the gloomy darkness smiling. Birds sang sweetly, flowers raised their drooping heads, fresh scents arose from the invigorated ground; the blue expanse above extended and diffused itself; already the sun's slanting rays pierced mortally the sullen bank of cloud that lingered in its flight; and a rainbow, spirit of all the colours that adorned the earth and sky, spanned the whole arch with its triumphant glory.

At such a time, one little roadside Inn, snugly sheltered behind a great elm-tree with a rare seat for idlers encircling its capacious bole, addressed a cheerful front towards the traveller, as a house of entertainment ought, and tempted him with many mute but significant assurances of a comfortable welcome. The ruddy sign-board perched up in the tree, with its golden letters winking in the sun, ogled the passer-by, from among the green leaves, like a jolly face, and promised good cheer. The horse-trough, full of clear fresh water, and the ground below it sprinkled with droppings of fragrant hay, made every horse that passed, prick up his ears. The crimson curtains in the lower rooms, and the pure white hangings in the little bed-chambers above, beckoned, Come in! with every breath of air. Upon the bright green shutters, there were golden legends about beer and ale, and neat wines, and good beds; and an affecting picture of a brown jug frothing over at the top. Upon the window-sills were flowering plants in bright red pots, which made a lively show against the white front of the house; and in the darkness of the doorway there were streaks of light, which glanced off from the surfaces of bottles and tankards.

On the door-step, appeared a proper figure of a landlord, too; for, though he was a short man, he was round and broad, and stood with his hands in his pockets, and his legs just wide enough apart to express a mind at rest upon the subject of the cellar, and an easy confidence—too calm and virtuous to become a swagger—in the general resources of the Inn. The superabundant moisture, trickling from everything after the late rain, set him off well. Nothing near him was thirsty. Certain top-heavy dahlias, looking over the palings of his neat well-ordered garden, had swilled as much as they could carry—perhaps a trifle more—and may have been the worse for liquor; but the sweet-briar, roses, wall-flowers, the plants at the windows, and the leaves on the old tree, were in the beaming state of moderate company that had taken no more than was wholesome for them, and had served to develop their best qualities. Sprinkling dewy drops about them on the ground, they seemed profuse of innocent and sparkling mirth, that did good where it lighted, softening neglected corners which the steady rain could seldom reach, and hurting nothing.

This village Inn had assumed, on being established, an uncommon sign. It was called The Nutmeg-Grater. And underneath that household word, was inscribed, up in the tree, on the same flaming board, and in the like golden characters, By Benjamin Britain.

At a second glance, and on a more minute examination of his face, you might have known that it was no other than Benjamin Britain himself who stood in the doorway—reasonably changed by time, but for the better; a very comfortable host indeed.

"Mrs. B.," said Mr. Britain, looking down the road, "is rather late. It's tea-time."

As there was no Mrs. Britain coming, he strolled leisurely out into the road and looked up at the house, very much to his satisfaction. "It's just the sort of house," said Benjamin, "I should wish to stop at, if I didn't keep it."

Then, he strolled towards the garden-paling, and took a look at the dahlias. They looked over at him, with a helpless drowsy hanging of their heads: which bobbed again, as the heavy drops of wet dripped off them.

"You must be looked after," said Benjamin. "Memorandum, not to forget to tell her so. She's a long time coming!"

Mr. Britain's better half seemed to be by so very much his better half, that his own moiety of himself was utterly cast away and helpless without her.

"She hadn't much to do, I think," said Ben. "There were a few little matters of business after market, but not many. Oh! here we are at last!"

A chaise-cart, driven by a boy, came clattering along the road: and seated in it, in a chair, with a large well-saturated umbrella spread out to dry behind her, was the plump figure of a matronly woman, with her bare arms folded across a basket which she carried on her knee, several other baskets and parcels lying crowded around her, and a certain bright good nature in her face and contented awkwardness in her manner, as she jogged to and fro with the motion of her carriage, which smacked of old times, even in the distance. Upon her nearer approach, this relish of bygone days was not diminished; and when the cart stopped at the Nutmeg-Grater door, a pair of shoes, alighting from it, slipped nimbly through Mr. Britain's open arms, and came down with a substantial weight upon the pathway, which shoes could hardly have belonged to any one but Clemency Newcome.

In fact they did belong to her, and she stood in them, and a rosy comfortable-looking soul she was: with as much soap on her glossy face as in times of yore, but with whole elbows now, that had grown quite dimpled in her improved condition.

"You're late, Clemmy!" said Mr. Britain.

"Why, you see, Ben, I've had a deal to do!" she replied, looking busily after the safe removal into the house of all the packages and baskets: "eight, nine, ten—where's eleven? Oh! my basket's eleven! It's all right. Put the horse up, Harry, and if he coughs again give him a warm mash to-night. Eight, nine, ten. Why, where's eleven? Oh! forgot, it's all right. How's the children, Ben?"

"Hearty, Clemmy, hearty."

"Bless their precious faces!" said Mrs. Britain, unbonneting her own round countenance (for she and her husband were by this time in the bar), and smoothing her hair with her open hands. "Give us a kiss, old man!"

Mr. Britain promptly complied.

"I think," said Mrs. Britain, applying herself to her pockets and drawing forth an immense bulk of thin books and crumpled papers: a very kennel of dogs'-ears: "I've done everything. Bills all settled—turnips sold—brewer's account looked into and paid—'bacco pipes ordered—seventeen pound four, paid into the Bank—Doctor Heathfield's charge for little Clem—you'll guess what that is—Doctor Heathfield won't take nothing again, Ben."

"I thought he wouldn't," returned Ben.

"No. He says whatever family you was to have, Ben, he'd never put you to the cost of a halfpenny. Not if you was to have twenty."

Mr. Britain's face assumed a serious expression, and he looked hard at the wall.

"An't it kind of him?" said Clemency.

"Very," returned Mr. Britain. "It's the sort of kindness that I wouldn't presume upon, on any account."

"No," retorted Clemency. "Of course not. Then there's the pony—he fetched eight pound two; and that an't bad, is it?"

"It's very good," said Ben.

"I'm glad you're pleased!" exclaimed his wife. "I thought you would be; and I think that's all, and so no more at present from yours and cetrer, C. Britain. Ha, ha, ha!

There! Take all the papers, and lock 'em up. Oh! Wait a minute. Here's a printed bill to stick on the wall. Wet from the printer's. How nice it smells!"

"What's this?" said Ben, looking over the document.

"I don't know," replied his wife. "I haven't read a word of it."

" 'To be sold by Auction,' " read the host of the Nutmeg-Grater, " 'unless previously disposed of by private contract.' "

"They always put that," said Clemency.

"Yes, but they don't always put this," he returned. "Look here, 'Mansion,' &c.—'offices,' &c., 'shrubberies,' &c., 'ring fence,' &c. 'Messrs. Snitchey and Craggs,' &c., 'ornamental portion of the unencumbered freehold property of Michael Warden, Esquire, intending to continue to reside abroad!' "

"Intending to continue to reside abroad!" repeated Clemency.

"Here it is," said Britain. "Look!"

"And it was only this very day that I heard it whispered at the old house, that better and plainer news had been half promised of her, soon!" said Clemency, shaking her head sorrowfully, and patting her elbows as if the recollection of old times unconsciously awakened her old habits. "Dear, dear, dear! There'll be heavy hearts, Ben, yonder."

Mr. Britain heaved a sigh, and shook his head, and said he couldn't make it out: he had left off trying long ago. With that remark, he applied himself to putting up the bill just inside the bar window. Clemency, after meditating in silence for a few moments, roused herself, cleared her thoughtful brow, and bustled off to look after the children.

Though the host of the Nutmeg-Grater had a lively regard for his good-wife, it was of the old patronising kind, and she amused him mightily. Nothing would have astonished him so much, as to have known for certain from any third party, that it was she who managed the whole house, and made him, by her plain straightforward thrift, good-humour, honesty, and industry, a thriving man. So easy it is, in any degree of life (as the world very often finds it), to take those cheerful natures that never assert their merit, at their own modest valuation; and to conceive a flippant liking of people for their outward oddities and eccentricities, whose innate worth, if we would look so far, might make us blush in the comparison!

It was comfortable to Mr. Britain, to think of his own condescension in having married Clemency. She was a perpetual testimony to him of the goodness of his heart, and the kindness of his disposition; and he felt that her being an excellent wife was an illustration of the old precept that virtue is its own reward.

He had finished wafering up the bill, and had locked the vouchers for her day's proceedings in the cupboard—chuckling all the time, over her capacity for business—when, returning with the news that the two Master Britains were playing in the coach-house under the superintendence of one Betsey, and that little Clem was sleeping "like a picture," she sat down to tea, which had awaited her arrival, on a little table. It was a very neat little bar, with the usual display of bottles and glasses; a sedate clock, right to the minute (it was half-past five); everything in its place, and everything furbished and polished up to the very utmost.

"It's the first time I've sat down quietly to-day, I declare," said Mrs. Britain, taking a long breath, as if she had sat down for the night; but getting up again immediately to hand her husband his tea, and cut him his bread-and-butter; "how that bill does set me thinking of old times!"

"Ah!" said Mr. Britain, handling his saucer like an oyster, and disposing of its contents on the same principle.

"That same Mr. Michael Warden," said Clemency, shaking her head at the notice of sale, "lost me my old place."

"And got you your husband," said Mr. Britain.

"Well! So he did," retorted Clemency, "and many thanks to him."

"Man's the creature of habit," said Mr. Britain, surveying her, over his saucer. "I had somehow got used to you, Clem; and I found I shouldn't be able to get on without you. So we went and got made man and wife. Ha! ha! We! Who'd have thought it!"

"Who indeed!" cried Clemency. "It was very good of you, Ben."

"No, no, no," replied Mr. Britain, with an air of self-denial. "Nothing worth mentioning."

"Oh yes it was, Ben," said his wife, with great simplicity; "I'm sure I think so, and am very much obliged to you. Ah!" looking again at the bill; "when she was known to be gone, and out of reach, dear girl, I couldn't help telling—for her sake quite as much as theirs—what I knew, could I?"

"You told it, anyhow," observed her husband.

"And Dr. Jeddler," pursued Clemency, putting down her tea-cup, and looking thoughtfully at the bill, "in his grief and passion turned me out of house and home! I never have been so glad of anything in all my life, as that I didn't say an angry word to him, and hadn't any angry feeling towards him, even then; for he repented that truly, afterwards. How often he has sat in this room, and told me over and over again he was sorry for it!—the last time, only yesterday, when you were out. How often he has sat in this room, and talked to me, hour after hour, about one thing and another, in which he made believe to be interested!—but only for the sake of the days that are gone by, and because he knows she used to like me, Ben!"

"Why, how did you ever come to catch a glimpse of that, Clem?" asked her husband: astonished that she should have a distinct perception of a truth which had only dimly suggested itself to his inquiring mind.

"I don't know, I'm sure," said Clemency, blowing her tea, to cool it. "Bless you, I couldn't tell you, if you was to offer me a reward of a hundred pound."

He might have pursued this metaphysical subject but for her catching a glimpse of a substantial fact behind him, in the shape of a gentleman attired in mourning, and cloaked and booted like a rider on horseback, who stood at the bar-door. He seemed attentive to their conversation, and not at all impatient to interrupt it.

Clemency hastily rose at this sight. Mr. Britain also rose and saluted the guest. "Will you please to walk up-stairs, Sir? There's a very nice room up-stairs, Sir."

"Thank you," said the stranger, looking earnestly at Mr. Britain's wife. "May I come in here?"

"Oh, surely, if you like, Sir," returned Clemency, admitting him. "What would you please to want, sir?"

The bill had caught his eye, and he was reading it.

"Excellent property that, Sir," observed Mr. Britain.

He made no answer; but, turning round, when he had finished reading, looked at Clemency with the same observant curiosity as before. "You were asking me,"—he said, still looking at her,—

"What you would please to take, sir," answered Clemency, stealing a glance at him in return.

"If you will let me have a draught of ale," he said, moving to a table by the window, "and will let me have it here, without being any interruption to your meal, I shall be much obliged to you."

He sat down as he spoke, without any further parley, and looked out at the prospect. He was an easy, well-knit figure of a man in the prime of life. His face, much browned by the sun, was shaded by a quantity of dark hair; and he wore a moustache. His beer being set before him, he filled out a glass, and drank, good-humouredly, to the house; adding, as he put the tumbler down again:

"It's a new house, is it not?"

"Not particularly new, Sir," replied Mr. Britain.

"Between five and six years old," said Clemency; speaking very distinctly.

"I think I heard you mention Dr. Jeddler's name, as I came in," inquired the stranger. "That bill reminds me of him; for I happen to know something of that story, by hearsay, and through certain connexions of mine.—Is the old man living?"

"Yes, he's living, Sir," said Clemency.

"Much changed?"

"Since when, Sir?" returned Clemency, with remarkable emphasis and expression.

"Since his daughter—went away."

"Yes! he's greatly changed since then," said Clemency. "He's grey and old, and hasn't the same way with him at all; but, I think he's happy now. He has taken on with his sister since then, and goes to see her very often. That did him good, directly. At first, he was sadly broken down; and it was enough to make one's heart bleed, to see him wandering about, railing at the world; but a great change for the better came over him after a year or two, and then he began to like to talk about his lost daughter, and to praise her, ay and the world too! and was never tired of saying, with the tears in his poor eyes, how beautiful and good she was. He had forgiven her then. That was about the same time as Miss Grace's marriage. Britain, you remember?"

Mr. Britain remembered very well.

"The sister *is* married then," returned the stranger. He paused for some time before he asked, "To whom?"

Clemency narrowly escaped oversetting the tea-board, in her emotion at this question.

"Did *you* never hear?" she said.

"I should like to hear," he replied, as he filled his glass again, and raised it to his lips.

"Ah! It would be a long story, if it was properly told," said Clemency, resting her chin on the palm of her left hand, and supporting that elbow on her right hand, as she shook her head, and looked back through the intervening years, as if she were looking at a fire. "It would be a long story, I am sure."

"But told as a short one," suggested the stranger.

Told as a short one," repeated Clemency in the same thoughtful tone, and without any apparent reference to him, or consciousness of having auditors, "what would there be to tell? That they grieved together, and remembered her together, like a person dead; that they were so tender of her, never would reproach her, called her back to one another as she used to be, and found excuses for her! Every one knows that. I'm sure *I* do. No one better," added Clemency, wiping her eyes with her hand.

"And so," suggested the stranger.

"And so," said Clemency, taking him up mechanically, and without any change in her attitude or manner, "they at last were married. They were married on her birth-day—it comes round again to-morrow—very quiet, very humble like, but very happy. Mr. Alfred said, one night when they were walking in the orchard, 'Grace, shall our wedding-day be Marion's birth-day?' And it was."

"And they have lived happily together?" said the stranger.

"Ay," said Clemency. "No two people ever more so. They have had no sorrow but this."

She raised her head as with a sudden attention to the circumstances under which she was recalling these events, and looked quickly at the stranger. Seeing that his face was turned toward the window, and that he seemed intent upon the prospect, she made some eager signs to her husband, and pointed to the bill, and moved her mouth as if she were repeating with great energy, one word or phrase to him over and over again. As she uttered no sound, and as her dumb motions like most of her gestures were of a very extraordinary kind, this unintelligible conduct reduced Mr. Britain to the confines of despair. He stared at the table, at the stranger, at the spoons, at his wife—followed her pantomime with looks of deep amazement and perplexity—asked in the same language, was it property in danger, was it he in danger, was it she—answered her signals with other signals expressive of the deepest distress and confusion—followed the motions of her lips—guessed half aloud "milk and water," "monthly warning," "mice and walnuts"—and couldn't approach her meaning.

Clemency gave it up at last, as a hopeless attempt; and moving her chair by very slow degrees a little nearer to the stranger, sat with her eyes apparently cast down but glancing sharply at him now and then, waiting until he should ask some other question. She had not to wait long; for he said, presently,

"And what is the after history of the young lady who went away? They know it, I suppose?"

Clemency shook her head. "I've heard," she said, "that Doctor Jeddler is thought to know more of it than he tells. Miss Grace has had letters from her sister, saying that she was well and happy, and made much happier by her being married to Mr. Alfred: and has written letters back. But there's a mystery about her life and fortunes, altogether, which nothing has cleared up to this hour, and which—"

She faltered here, and stopped.

"And which"—repeated the stranger.

"Which only one other person, I believe, could explain," said Clemency, drawing her breath quickly.

"Who may that be?" asked the stranger.

"Mr. Michael Warden!" answered Clemency, almost in a shriek: at once conveying to her husband what she would have had him understand before, and letting Michael Warden know that he was recognised.

"You remember me, Sir?" said Clemency, trembling with emotion; "I saw just now you did! You remember me, that night in the garden. I was with her!"

"Yes. You were," he said.

"Yes, sir," returned Clemency. "Yes, to be sure. This is my husband, if you please. Ben, my dear Ben, run to Miss Grace—run to Mr. Alfred—run somewhere, Ben! Bring somebody here, directly!"

"Stay!" said Michael Warden, quietly interposing himself between the door and Britain. "What would you do?"

"Let them know that you are here, sir," answered Clemency, clapping her hands in sheer agitation. "Let them know that they may hear of her, from your own lips; let them know that she is not quite lost to them, but that she will come home again yet, to bless her father and her loving sister—even her old servant, even me," she struck herself upon the breast with both hands, "with a sight of her sweet face. Run, Ben, run!" And still she pressed him on towards the door, and still Mr. Warden stood before it, with his hand stretched out, not angrily, but sorrowfully.

"Or perhaps," said Clemency, running past her husband, and catching in her emotion at Mr. Warden's cloak, "perhaps she's here now; perhaps she's close by. I think from your manner she is. Let me see her, sir, if you please. I waited on her when she was a little child. I saw her grow to be the pride of all this place. I knew her when she was Mr. Alfred's promised wife. I tried to warn her when you tempted her away. I know what her old home was when she was like the soul of it, and how it changed when she was gone and lost. Let me speak to her, if you please!"

He gazed at her with compassion, not unmixed with wonder: but, he made no gesture of assent.

"I don't think she *can* know," pursued Clemency, "how truly they forgive her; how they love her; what joy it would be to them, to see her once more. She may be timorous of going home. Perhaps if she sees me, it may give her new heart. Only tell me truly, Mr. Warden, is she with you?"

"She is not," he answered, shaking his head.

This answer, and his manner, and his black dress, and his coming back so quietly, and his announced intention of continuing to live abroad, explained it all. Marion was dead.

He didn't contradict her; yes, she was dead! Clemency sat down, hid her face upon the table, and cried.

At that moment, a grey-headed old gentleman came running in: quite out of breath, and panting so much that his voice was scarcely to be recognised as the voice of Mr. Snitchey.

"Good Heaven, Mr. Warden!" said the lawyer, taking him aside, "what wind has blown—" He was so blown himself, that he couldn't get on any further until after a pause, when he added, feebly, "you here?"

"An ill-wind, I am afraid," he answered. "If you could have heard what has just passed—how I have been besought and entreated to perform impossibilities—what confusion and affliction I carry with me!"

"I can guess it all. But why did you ever come here, my good sir?" retorted Snitchey.

"Come! How should I know who kept the house? When I sent my servant on to you, I strolled in here because the place was new to me; and I had a natural curiosity in everything new and old, in these old scenes; and it was outside the town. I wanted to communicate with you, first, before appearing there. I wanted to know what people would say to me. I see by your manner that you can tell me. If it were not for your confounded caution, I should have been possessed of everything long ago."

"Our caution!" returned the lawyer, "speaking for Self and Craggs—deceased," here Mr. Snitchey, glancing at his hat-band, shook his head, "how can you reasonably blame us, Mr. Warden? It was understood between us that the subject was never to be renewed, and that it wasn't a subject on which grave and sober men like us (I made a note of your observations at the time) could interfere. Our caution too! When Mr. Craggs, sir, went down to his respected grave in the full belief—"

"I had given a solemn promise of silence until I should return, whenever that might be," interrupted Mr. Warden; "and I have kept it."

"Well, sir, and I repeat it," returned Mr. Snitchey, "we were bound to silence too. We were bound to silence in our duty towards ourselves, and in our duty towards a variety of clients, you among them, who were as close as wax. It was not our place to make inquiries of you on such a delicate subject. I had my suspicions, sir; but, it is not six months since I have known the truth, and been assured that you lost her."

"By whom?" inquired his client.

"By Doctor Jeddler himself, Sir, who at last reposed that confidence in me voluntarily. He, and only he, has known the whole truth, years and years."

"And you know it?" said his client.

"I do, Sir!" replied Snitchey; "and I have also reason to know that it will be broken to her sister to-morrow evening. They have given her that promise. In the meantime, perhaps you'll give me the honour of your company at my house; being unexpected at your own. But, not to run the chance of any more such difficulties as you have had here, in case you should be recognised—though you're a good deal changed; I think I might have passed you myself, Mr. Warden—we had better dine here, and walk on in the evening. It's a very good place to dine at, Mr. Warden: your own property, by-the-bye. Self and Craggs (deceased) took a chop here sometimes, and had it very comfortably served. Mr. Craggs, sir," said Snitchey, shutting his eyes tight for an instant, and opening them again, "was struck off the roll of life too soon."

"Heaven forgive me for not condoling with you," returned Michael Warden, passing his hand across his forehead, "but I'm like a man in a dream at present. I seem to want my wits. Mr. Craggs—yes—I am very sorry we have lost Mr. Craggs." But he looked at Clemency as he said it, and seemed to sympathise with Ben, consoling her.

"Mr. Craggs, Sir," observed Snitchey, "didn't find life, I regret to say, as easy to have and to hold as his theory made it out, or he would have been among us now. It's a great loss to me. He was my right arm, my right leg, my right ear, my right eye, was Mr. Craggs. I am paralytic without him. He bequeathed his share of the business to Mrs. Craggs, her executors, administrators, and assigns. His name remains in the Firm to this hour. I try, in a childish sort of a way, to make believe, sometimes, he's alive. You may observe that I speak for Self and Craggs—deceased, Sir—deceased," said the tender-hearted attorney, waving his pocket-handkerchief.

Michael Warden, who had still been observant of Clemency, turned to Mr. Snitchey when he ceased to speak, and whispered in his ear.

"Ah, poor thing!" said Snitchey, shaking his head. "Yes. She was always very faithful to Marion. She was always very fond of her. Pretty Marion! Poor Marion! Cheer up, Mistress—you *are* married now, you know, Clemency."

Clemency only sighed, and shook her head.

"Well, well! Wait till to-morrow," said the lawyer, kindly.

"To-morrow can't bring back the dead to life, Mister," said Clemency, sobbing.

"No. It can't do that, or it would bring back Mr. Craggs, deceased," returned the lawyer. "But it may bring some soothing circumstances; it may bring some comfort. Wait till to-morrow!"

So Clemency, shaking his proffered hand, said she would; and Britain, who had been terribly cast down at sight of his despondent wife (which was like the business hanging its head), said that was right; and Mr. Snitchey and Michael Warden went up-stairs; and there they were soon engaged in a conversation so cautiously conducted, that no murmur of it was audible above the clatter of plates and dishes, the hissing of the frying-pan, the bubbling of saucepans, the low monotonous waltzing of the jack—with a dreadful click every now and then as if it had met with some mortal accident to its head, in a fit of giddiness—and all the other preparations in the kitchen for their dinner.

To-morrow was a bright and peaceful day; and nowhere were the autumn tints more beautifully seen, than from the quiet orchard of the Doctor's house. The snows of many winter nights had melted from that ground, the withered leaves of many summer times had rustled there, since she had fled. The honey-suckle porch was green again, the trees cast bountiful and changing shadows on the grass, the landscape was as tranquil and serene as it had ever been; but where was she!

Not there. Not there. She would have been a stranger sight in her old home now, even than that home had been at first, without her. But, a lady sat in the familiar place, from whose heart she had never passed away; in whose true memory she lived, unchanging, youthful, radiant with all promise and all hope; in whose affection—and it was a mother's now, there was a cherished little daughter playing by her side—she had no rival, no successor; upon whose gentle lips her name was trembling then.

The spirit of the lost girl looked out of those eyes. Those eyes of Grace, her sister, sitting with her husband in the orchard, on their wedding-day, and his and Marion's birth-day.

He had not become a great man; he had not grown rich; he had not forgotten the scenes and friends of his youth; he had not fulfilled any one of the Doctor's old predictions. But, in his useful, patient, unknown visiting of poor men's homes; and in his watching of sick beds; and in his daily knowledge of the gentleness and goodness flowering the bye-paths of this world, not to be trodden down beneath the heavy foot of poverty, but springing up, elastic, in its track, and making its way beautiful; he had better learned and proved, in each succeeding year, the truth of his old faith. The manner of his life, though quiet and remote, had shown him how often men still entertained angels, unawares, as in the olden time; and how the most unlikely forms—even some that were mean and ugly to the view, and poorly clad—became irradiated by the couch of sorrow, want, and pain, and changed to ministering spirits with a glory round their heads.

He lived to better purpose on the altered battle-ground, perhaps, than if he had contended restlessly in more ambitious lists; and he was happy with his wife, dear Grace.

And Marion. Had *he* forgotten her?

"The time has flown, dear Grace," he said, "since then"; they had been talking of that night; "and yet it seems a long long while ago. We count by changes and events within us. Not by years."

"Yet we have years to count by, too, since Marion was with us," returned Grace. "Six times, dear husband, counting to-night as one, we have sat here on her birth-day, and spoken together of that happy return, so eagerly expected and so long deferred. Ah when will it be! When will it be!"

Her husband attentively observed her, as the tears collected in her eyes; and drawing nearer, said:

"But, Marion told you, in that farewell letter which she left for you upon your table, love, and which you read so often, that years must pass away before it *could* be. Did she not?"

She took a letter from her breast, and kissed it, and said "Yes."

"That through these intervening years, however happy she might be, she would look forward to the time when you would meet again, and all would be made clear; and that she prayed you, trustfully and hopefully to do the same. The letter runs so, does it not, my dear?"

"Yes, Alfred."

"And every other letter she has written since?"

"Except the last—some months ago—in which she spoke of you, and what you then knew, and what I was to learn to-night."

He looked towards the sun, then fast declining, and said that the appointed time was sunset.

"Alfred!" said Grace, laying her hand upon his shoulder earnestly, "there is something in this letter—this old letter, which you say I read so often—that I have never told you. But to-night, dear husband, with that sunset drawing near, and all our life seeming to sof ten and become hushed with the departing day, I cannot keep it secret."

"What is it, love?"

"When Marion went away, she wrote me, here, that you had once left her a sacred trust to me, and that now she left you, Alfred, such a trust in my hands: praying and beseeching me, as I loved her, and as I loved you, not to reject the affection she believed (she knew, she said) you would transfer to me when the new wound was healed, but to encourage and return it."

"—And make me a proud, and happy man again, Grace. Did she say so?"

"She meant, to make myself so blest and honoured in your love," was his wife's answer, as he held her in his arms.

"Hear me, my dear!" he said.—"No. Hear me so!"—and as he spoke, he gently laid the head she had raised, again upon his shoulder. "I know why I have never heard this passage in the letter until now. I know why no trace of it ever showed itself in any word or look of yours at that time. I know why Grace, although so true a friend to me, was hard to win to be my wife. And knowing it, my own! I know the priceless value of the heart I gird within my arms, and thank God for the rich possession!"

She wept, but not for sorrow, as he pressed her to his heart. After a brief space, he looked down at the child, who was sitting at their feet playing with a little basket of flowers, and bade her look how golden and how red the sun was.

"Alfred," said Grace, raising her head quickly at these words. "The sun is going down. You have not forgotten what I am to know before it sets."

"You are to know the truth of Marion's history, my love," he answered.

"All the truth," she said, imploringly. "Nothing veiled from me, any more. That was the promise. Was it not?"

"It was," he answered.

"Before the sun went down on Marion's birth-day. And you see it, Alfred? It is sinking fast."

He put his arm about her waist, and, looking steadily into her eyes, rejoined:

"That truth is not reserved so long for me to tell, dear Grace. It is to come from other lips."

"From other lips!" she faintly echoed.

"Yes. I know your constant heart, I know how brave you are, I know that to you a word of preparation is enough. You have said, truly, that the time is come. It is. Tell me that you have present fortitude to bear a trial—a surprise—a shock: and the messenger is waiting at the gate."

"What messenger?" she said. "And what intelligence does he bring?"

"I am pledged," he answered her, preserving his steady look, "to say no more. Do you think you understand me?"

"I am afraid to think," she said.

There was that emotion in his face, despite its steady gaze, which frightened her. Again she hid her own face on his shoulder, trembling, and entreated him to pause—a moment.

"Courage, my wife! When you have firmness to receive the messenger, the messenger is waiting at the gate. The sun is setting on Marion's birth-day. Courage, courage, Grace!"

She raised her head, and, looking at him, told him she was ready. As she stood, and looked upon him going away, her face was so like Marion's as it had been in her later days at home, that it was wonderful to see. He took the child with him. She called her back—she bore the lost girl's name—and pressed her to her bosom. The little creature, being released again, sped after him, and Grace was left alone.

She knew not what she dreaded, or what hoped; but remained there, motionless, looking at the porch by which they had disappeared.

Ah! what was that, emerging from its shadow; standing on its threshold! That figure, with its white garments rustling in the evening air; its head laid down upon her father's breast, and pressed against it to his loving heart! O God! was it a vision that came bursting from the old man's arms, and with a cry, and with a waving of its hands, and with a wild precipitation of itself upon her in its boundless love, sank down in her embrace!

"Oh, Marion, Marion! Oh, my sister! Oh, my heart's dear love! Oh, joy and happiness unutterable, so to meet again!"

It was no dream, no phantom conjured up by hope and fear, but Marion, sweet Marion! So beautiful, so happy, so unalloyed by care and trial, so elevated and exalted in her loveliness, that as the setting sun shone brightly on her upturned face, she might have been a spirit visiting the earth upon some healing mission.

Clinging to her sister, who had dropped upon a seat and bent down over her: and smiling through her tears and kneeling, close before her, with both arms twining round her, and never turning for an instant from her face: and with the glory of the setting sun upon her brow, and with the soft tranquillity of evening gathering around them: Marion at length broke silence; her voice, so calm, low, clear, and pleasant, well-tuned to the time.

"When this was my dear home, Grace, as it will be now again—"

"Stay, my sweet love! A moment! O Marion, to hear you speak again."

She could not bear the voice she loved so well, at first.

"When this was my dear home, Grace, as it will be now again, I loved him from my soul. I loved him most devotedly. I would have died for him, though I was so young. I never slighted his affection in my secret breast for one brief instant. It was far beyond all price to me. Although it is so long ago, and past, and gone, and everything is wholly changed, I could not bear to think that you, who love so well, should think I did not truly love him once. I never loved him better, Grace, than when he left this very scene upon this very day. I never loved him better, dear one, than I did that night when *I* left here."

Her sister, bending over her, could look into her face, and hold her fast.

"But he had gained, unconsciously," said Marion, with a gentle smile, "another heart, before I knew that I had one to give him. That heart—yours, my sister!—was so yielded up, in all its other tenderness, to me; was so devoted, and so noble; that it plucked its love away, and kept its secret from all eyes but mine—Ah! what other eyes were quickened by such tenderness and gratitude!—and was content to sacrifice itself to me. But, I knew something of its depths. I knew the struggle it had made. I knew its high, inestimable worth to him, and his appreciation of it, let him love me as he would. I knew the debt I owed it. I had its great example every day before me. What you had done for me, I knew that I could do, Grace, if I would, for you. I never laid my head down on my pillow, but I prayed with tears to do it. I never laid my head down on my pillow, but I thought of Alfred's own words on the day of his departure, and how truly he had said (for I knew that, knowing you) that there were victories gained every day, in struggling hearts, to which these fields of battle were nothing. Thinking more and more upon the great endurance cheerfully sustained, and never known or cared for, that there must be, every day and hour, in that great strife of which he spoke, my trial seemed to grow light and easy: and He who knows our hearts, my dearest, at this moment, and who knows there is no drop of bitterness or grief—of anything but unmixed happiness—in mine, enabled me to make the resolution that I never would be Alfred's wife. That he should be my brother, and your husband, if the course I took could bring that happy end to pass; but that I never would (Grace, I then loved him dearly, dearly!) be his wife!"

"O Marion! O Marion!"

"I had tried to seem indifferent to him"; and she pressed her sister's face against her own; "but that was hard, and you were always his true advocate. I had tried to tell you of my resolution, but you would never hear me; you would never understand me. The time was drawing near for his return. I felt that I must act, before the daily intercourse between us was renewed. I knew that one great pang, undergone at that time, would save a lengthened agony to all of us. I knew that if I went away then, that end must follow which *has* followed, and which has made us both so happy, Grace! I wrote to good Aunt Martha, for a refuge in her house: I did not then tell her all, but something of my story, and she freely promised it. While I was contesting that step with myself, and with my love of you, and home, Mr. Warden, brought here by an accident, became, for some time, our companion."

"I have sometimes feared of late years, that this might have been," exclaimed her sister; and her countenance was ashy-pale. "You never loved him—and you married him in your self-sacrifice to me!"

"He was then," said Marion, drawing her sister closer to her, "on the eve of going secretly away for a long time. He wrote to me, after leaving here; told me what his condition and prospects really were; and offered me his hand. He told me he had seen I was not happy in the prospect of Alfred's return. I believe he thought my heart had no part in that contract; perhaps thought I might have loved him once, and did not then; perhaps thought that when I tried to seem indifferent, I tried to hide indifference—I cannot tell. But I wished that you should feel me wholly lost to Alfred—hopeless to him—dead. Do you understand me, love?"

Her sister looked into her face, attentively. She seemed in doubt.

"I saw Mr. Warden, and confided in his honour; charged him with my secret, on the eve of his and my departure. He kept it. Do you understand me, dear?"

Grace looked confusedly upon her. She scarcely seemed to hear.

"My love, my sister!" said Marion, "recall your thoughts a moment; listen to me. Do not look so strangely on me. There are countries, dearest, where those who would abjure a misplaced passion, or would strive, against some cherished feeling of their hearts and conquer it, retire into a hopeless solitude, and close the world against themselves and worldly loves and hopes for ever. When women do so, they assume that name which is so dear to you and me, and call each other Sisters. But, there may be sisters, Grace, who, in the broad world out of doors, and underneath its free sky, and in its crowded places, and among its busy life, and trying to assist and cheer it and to do some good,—learn the same lesson; and who, with hearts still fresh and young, and open to all happiness and means of happiness, can say the battle is long past, the victory long won. And such a one am I! You understand me now?"

Still she looked fixedly upon her, and made no reply.

"Oh Grace, dear Grace," said Marion, clinging yet more tenderly and fondly to that breast from which she had been so long exiled, "if you were not a happy wife and mother—if I had no little namesake here—if Alfred, my kind brother, were not your own fond husband—from whence could I derive the ecstasy I feel to-night!

But, as I left here, so I have returned. My heart has known no other love, my hand has never been bestowed apart from it. I am still your maiden sister, unmarried, unbetrothed: your own loving old Marion, in whose affection you exist alone and have no partner, Grace!"

She understood her now. Her face relaxed: sobs came to her relief; and falling on her neck, she wept and wept, and fondled her as if she were a child again.

When they were more composed, they found that the Doctor, and his sister good Aunt Martha, were standing near at hand, with Alfred.

"This is a weary day for me," said good Aunt Martha, smiling through her tears, as she embraced her nieces; "for I lose my dear companion in making you all happy; and what can you give me, in return for my Marion?"

"A converted brother," said the Doctor.

"That's something, to be sure," retorted Aunt Martha, "in such a farce as—"

"No, pray don't," said the Doctor penitently.

"Well, I won't," replied Aunt Martha. "But, I consider myself ill used. I don't know what's to become of me without my Marion, after we have lived together half-a-dozen years."

"You must come and live here, I suppose," replied the Doctor. "We shan't quarrel now, Martha."

"Or you must get married, Aunt," said Alfred.

"Indeed," returned the old lady, "I think it might be a good speculation if I were to set my cap at Michael Warden, who, I hear, is come home much the better for his absence in all respects. But as I knew him when he was a boy, and I was not a very young woman then, perhaps he mightn't respond. So I'll make up my mind to go and live with Marion, when she marries, and until then (it will not be very long, I dare say) to live alone. What do *you* say, Brother?"

"I've a great mind to say it's a ridiculous world altogether, and there's nothing serious in it," observed the poor old Doctor.

"You might take twenty affidavits of it if you chose, Anthony," said his sister; "but nobody would believe you with such eyes as those."

"It's a world full of hearts," said the Doctor, hugging his youngest daughter, and bending across her to hug Grace—for he couldn't separate the sisters; "and a serious world, with all its folly—even with mine, which was enough to have swamped the whole globe; and it is a world on which the sun never rises, but it looks upon a thousand bloodless battles that are some set-off against the miseries and wickedness of Battle-Fields; and it is a world we need be careful how we libel, Heaven forgive us, for it is a world of sacred mysteries, and its Creator only knows what lies beneath the surface of His lightest image!"

* * *

You would not be the better pleased with my rude pen, if it dissected and laid open to your view the transports of this family, long severed and now reunited. Therefore, I will not follow the poor Doctor through his humbled recollection of the sorrow he had had, when Marion was lost to him; nor, will I tell how serious he had found that world to be, in which some love, deep-anchored, is the portion of all human creatures; nor, how such a trifle as the absence of one little unit in the great absurd account, had stricken him to the ground. Nor how, in compassion for his distress, his sister had, long ago, revealed the truth to him by slow degrees, and brought him to the knowledge of the heart of his self-banished daughter, and to that daughter's side.

Nor, how Alfred Heathfield had been told the truth, too, in the course of that then current year; and Marion had seen him, and had promised him, as her brother, that on her birth-day, in the evening, Grace should know it from her lips at last.

"I beg your pardon, Doctor," said Mr. Snitchey, looking into the orchard, "but have I liberty to come in?"

Without waiting for permission, he came straight to Marion, and kissed her hand, quite joyfully.

"If Mr. Craggs had been alive, my dear Miss Marion," said Mr. Snitchey, "he would have had great interest in this occasion. It might have suggested to him, Mr. Alfred, that our life is not too easy perhaps: that, taken altogether, it will bear any little smoothing we can give it; but Mr. Craggs was a man who could endure to be convinced, sir. He was always open to conviction. If he were open to conviction, now, I—this is weakness. Mrs. Snitchey, my dear,"—at his summons that lady appeared from behind the door, "you are among old friends."

Mrs. Snitchey having delivered her congratulations, took her husband aside.

"One moment, Mr. Snitchey," said that lady. "It is not in my nature to rake up the ashes of the departed."

"No, my dear," returned her husband.

"Mr. Craggs is—"

"Yes, my dear, he is deceased," said Snitchey.

"But I ask you if you recollect," pursued his wife, "that evening of the ball? I only ask you that. If you do; and if your memory has not entirely failed you, Mr. Snitchey; and if you are not absolutely in your dotage; I ask you to connect this time with that—to remember how I begged and prayed you, on my knees—"

"Upon your knees, my dear?" said Mr. Snitchey.

"Yes," said Mrs. Snitchey, confidently, "and you know it—to beware of that man—to observe his eye—and now to tell me whether I was right, and whether at that moment he knew secrets which he didn't choose to tell."

"Mrs. Snitchey," returned her husband, in her ear, "Madam. Did you ever observe anything in *my* eye?"

"No," said Mrs. Snitchey, sharply. "Don't flatter yourself."

"Because, Madam, that night," he continued, twitching her by the sleeve, "it happens that we both knew secrets which we didn't choose to tell, and both knew just the same professionally. And so the less you say about such things the better, Mrs. Snitchey; and take this as a warning to have wiser and more charitable eyes another time. Miss Marion, I brought a friend of yours along with me. Here! Mistress!"

Poor Clemency, with her apron to her eyes, came slowly in, escorted by her husband; the latter doleful with the presentiment, that if she abandoned herself to grief, the Nutmeg-Grater was done for.

"Now, Mistress," said the lawyer, checking Marion as she ran towards her, and interposing himself between them, "what's the matter with *you?*"

"The matter!" cried poor Clemency.—When, looking up in wonder, and in indignant remonstrance, and in the added emotion of a great roar from Mr. Britain, and seeing that sweet face so well remembered close before her, she stared, sobbed, laughed, cried, screamed, embraced her, held her fast, released her, fell on Mr. Snitchey and embraced him (much to Mrs. Snitchey's indignation), fell on the Doctor and embraced him, fell on Mr. Britain and embraced him, and concluded by embracing herself, throwing her apron over her head, and going into hysterics behind it.

A stranger had come into the orchard after Mr. Snitchey, and had remained apart, near the gate, without being observed by any of the group; for they had little spare attention to bestow, and that had been monopolised by the ecstasies of Clemency. He did not appear to wish to be observed, but stood alone, with downcast eyes; and there was an air of dejection about him (though he was a gentleman of a gallant appearance) which the general happiness rendered more remarkable.

None but the quick eyes of Aunt Martha, however, remarked him at all; but, almost as soon as she espied him, she was in conversation with him. Presently, going to where Marion stood with Grace and her little namesake, she whispered something in Marion's ear, at which she started, and appeared surprised; but soon recovering from her confusion, she timidly approached the stranger, in Aunt Martha's company, and engaged in conversation with him too.

"Mr. Britain," said the lawyer, putting his hand in his pocket, and bringing out a legal-looking document, while this was going on, "I congratulate you. You are now the whole and sole proprietor of that freehold tenement, at present occupied and held by yourself as a licensed tavern, or house of public entertainment, and commonly called or known by the sign of the Nutmeg-Grater. Your wife lost one house, through my client Mr. Michael Warden; and now gains another. I shall have the pleasure of canvassing you for the county, one of these fine mornings."

"Would it make any difference in the vote if the sign was altered, sir?" asked Britain.

"Not in the least," replied the lawyer.

"Then," said Mr. Britain, handing him back the conveyance, "just clap in the words, 'and Thimble,' will you be so good; and I'll have the two mottoes painted up in the parlour instead of my wife's portrait."

"And let me," said a voice behind them; it was the stranger's—Michael Warden's; "let me claim the benefit of those inscriptions. Mr. Heathfield and Dr. Jeddler, I might have deeply wronged you both. That I did not, is no virtue of my own. I will not say that I am six years wiser than I was, or better. But I have known, at any rate, that term of self-reproach. I can urge no reason why you should deal gently with me. I abused the hospitality of this house; and learnt by my own demerits, with a shame I never have forgotten, yet with some profit too, I would fain hope, from one," he glanced at Marion, "to whom I made my humble supplication for forgiveness, when I knew her merit and my deep unworthiness. In a few days I shall quit this place for ever. I entreat your pardon. Do as you would be done by! Forget and Forgive!"

TIME—from whom I had the latter portion of this story, and with whom I have the pleasure of a personal acquaintance of some five-and-thirty years' duration—informed me, leaning easily upon his scythe, that Michael Warden never went away again, and never sold his house, but opened it afresh, maintained a golden means of hospitality, and had a wife, the pride and honour of that country-side, whose name was Marion. But, as I have observed that Time confuses facts occasionally, I hardly know what weight to give to his authority.

The Haunted Man

Chapter I

The Gift Bestowed

EVERYBODY SAID SO.

Far be it from me to assert that what everybody says must be true. Everybody is, often, as likely to be wrong as right. In the general experience, everybody has been wrong so often, and it has taken, in most instances, such a weary while to find out how wrong, that the authority is proved to be fallible. Everybody may sometimes be right; "but *that's* no rule," as the ghost of Giles Scroggins says in the ballad.

The dread word, GHOST, recalls me.

Everybody said he looked like a haunted man. The extent of my present claim for everybody is, that they were so far right. He did.

Who could have seen his hollow cheek; his sunken brilliant eye; his black-attired figure, indefinably grim, although well-knit and well-proportioned; his grizzled hair hanging, like tangled sea-weed, about his face,—as if he had been, through his whole life, a lonely mark for the chafing and beating of the great deep of humanity,—but might have said he looked like a haunted man?

Who could have observed his manner, taciturn, thoughtful, gloomy, shadowed by habitual reserve, retiring always and jocund never, with a distraught air of reverting to a bygone place and time, or of listening to some old echoes in his mind, but might have said it was the manner of a haunted man?

Who could have heard his voice, slow-speaking, deep, and grave, with a natural fulness and melody in it which he seemed to set himself against and stop, but might have said it was the voice of a haunted man?

Who that had seen him in his inner chamber, part library and part laboratory,—for he was, as the world knew, far and wide, a learned man in chemistry, and a teacher on whose lips and hands a crowd of aspiring ears and eyes hung daily,—who that had seen him there, upon a winter night, alone, surrounded by his drugs and instruments and books; the shadow of his shaded lamp a monstrous beetle on the wall, motionless among a crowd of spectral shapes raised there by the flickering of the fire upon the quaint objects around him; some of these phantoms (the reflection of glass vessels that held liquids), trembling at heart like things that knew his power to uncombine them, and to give back their component parts to fire and vapour;—who that had seen him then, his work done, and he pondering in his chair before the rusted grate and red flame, moving his thin mouth as if in speech, but silent as the dead, would not have said that the man seemed haunted and the chamber too?

Who might not, by a very easy flight of fancy, have believed that everything about him took this haunted tone, and that he lived on haunted ground?

His dwelling was so solitary and vault-like,—an old, retired part of an ancient endowment for students, once a brave edifice, planted in an open place, but now the obsolete whim of forgotten architects; smoke-age-and-weather-darkened, squeezed on every side by the overgrowing of the great city, and choked, like an old well, with stones and bricks; its small quadrangles, lying down in very pits formed by the streets and buildings, which, in course of time, had been constructed above its heavy chimney stalks; its old trees, insulted by the neighbouring smoke, which deigned to droop so low when it was very feeble and the weather very moody; its grass-plots, struggling with the mildewed earth to be grass, or to win any show of compromise; its silent pavements, unaccustomed to the tread of feet, and even to the observation of eyes, except when a stray face looked down from the upper world, wondering what nook it was; its sun-dial in a little bricked-up corner, where no sun had straggled for a hundred years, but where, in compensation for the sun's neglect, the snow would lie for weeks when it lay nowhere else, and the black east wind would spin like a huge humming-top, when in all other places it was silent and still.

His dwelling, at its heart and core—within doors—at his fireside—was so lowering and old, so crazy, yet so strong, with its worn-eaten beams of wood in the ceiling, and its sturdy floor shelving downward to the great oak chimney-piece; so environed and hemmed in by the pressure of the town yet so remote in fashion, age, and custom; so quiet, yet so thundering with echoes when a distant voice was raised or a door was shut,—echoes, not confined to the many low passages and empty rooms, but rumbling and grumbling till they were stifled in the heavy air of the forgotten Crypt where the Norman arches were half-buried in the earth.

You should have seen him in his dwelling about twilight, in the dead winter time.

When the wind was blowing, shrill and shrewd, with the going down of the blurred sun. When it was just so dark, as that the forms of things were indistinct and big—but not wholly lost. When sitters by the fire began to see wild faces and figures, mountains and abysses, ambuscades and armies, in the coals. When people in the streets bent down their heads and ran before the weather. When those who were obliged to meet it, were stopped at angry corners, stung by wandering snow-flakes alighting on the lashes of their eyes,—which fell too sparingly, and were blown away too quickly, to leave a trace upon the frozen ground. When windows of private houses closed up tight and warm. When lighted gas began to burst forth in the busy and the quiet streets, fast blackening otherwise. When stray pedestrians, shivering along the latter, looked down at the glowing fires in kitchens, and sharpened their sharp appetites by sniffing up the fragrance of whole miles of dinners.

When travellers by land were bitter cold, and looked wearily on gloomy landscapes, rustling and shuddering in the blast. When mariners at sea, outlying upon icy yards, were tossed and swung above the howling ocean dreadfully. When lighthouses, on rocks and headlands, showed solitary and watchful; and benighted sea-birds breasted on against their ponderous lanterns, and fell dead. When little readers of story-books, by the firelight, trembled to think of Cassim Baba cut into quarters, hanging in the Robbers' Cave, or had some small misgivings that the fierce little old woman with the crutch, who used to start out of the box in the merchant Abudah's bedroom, might, one of these nights, be found upon the stairs, in the long, cold, dusky journey up to bed.

When, in rustic places, the last glimmering of daylight died away from the ends of avenues; and the trees, arching overhead, were sullen and black. When, in parks and woods, the high wet fern and sodden moss, and beds of fallen leaves, and trunks of trees, were lost to view, in masses of impenetrable shade. When mists arose from dyke, and fen, and river. When lights in old halls and in cottage windows, were a cheerful sight. When the mill stopped, the wheelwright and the blacksmith shut their workshops, the turnpike-gate closed, the plough and harrow were left lonely in the fields, the labourer and team went home, and the striking of the church clock had a deeper sound than at noon, and the churchyard wicket would be swung no more that night.

When twilight everywhere released the shadows, prisoned up all day, that now closed in and gathered like mustering swarms of ghosts. When they stood lowering, in corners of rooms, and frowned out from behind half-opened doors. When they had full possession of unoccupied apartments. When they danced upon the floors, and walls, and ceilings of inhabited chambers, while the fire was low, and withdrew like ebbing waters when it sprang into a blaze. When they fantastically mocked the shapes of household objects, making the nurse an ogress, the rocking-horse a monster, the wondering child half-scared and half-amused, a stranger to itself,—the very tongs upon the hearth, a straddling giant with his arms a-kimbo, evidently smelling the blood of Englishmen, and wanting to grind people's bones to make his bread.

When these shadows brought into the minds of older people, other thoughts, and showed them different images. When they stole from their retreats, in the likenesses of forms and faces from the past, from the grave, from the deep, deep gulf, where the things that might have been, and never were, are always wandering.

When he sat, as already mentioned, gazing at the fire. When, as it rose and fell, the shadows went and came. When he took no heed of them, with his bodily eyes; but, let them come or let them go, looked fixedly at the fire. You should have seen him then.

When the sounds that had arisen with the shadows, and come out of their lurking-places at the twilight summons, seemed to make a deeper stillness all about him. When the wind was rumbling in the chimney, and sometimes crooning, sometimes howling, in the house. When the old trees outside were so shaken and beaten, that one querulous old rook, unable to sleep, protested now and then, in a feeble, dozy, high-up "Caw!" When, at intervals, the window trembled, the rusty vane upon the turret-top complained, the clock beneath it recorded that another quarter of an hour was gone, or the fire collapsed and fell in with a rattle.

—When a knock came at his door, in short, as he was sitting so, and roused him.

"Who's that?" said he. "Come in!"

Surely there had been no figure leaning on the back of his chair; no face looking over it. It is certain that no gliding footstep touched the floor, as he lifted up his head, with a start, and spoke. And yet there was no mirror in the room on whose surface his own form could have cast its shadow for a moment; and Something had passed darkly and gone!

"I'm humbly fearful, sir," said a fresh-coloured busy man, holding the door open with his foot for the admission of himself and a wooden tray he carried, and letting it go again by very gentle and careful degrees, when he and the tray had got in, lest it should close noisily, "that it's a good bit past the time to-night. But Mrs. William has been taken off her legs so often—"

"By the wind? Ay! I have heard it rising."

"—By the wind, sir—that it's a mercy she got home at all. Oh dear, yes. Yes. It was by the wind, Mr. Redlaw. By the wind."

He had, by this time, put down the tray for dinner, and was employed in lighting the lamp, and spreading a cloth on the table. From this employment he desisted in a hurry, to stir and feed the fire, and then resumed it; the lamp he had lighted, and the blaze that rose under his hand, so quickly changing the appearance of the room, that it seemed as if the mere coming in of his fresh red face and active manner had made the pleasant alteration.

"Mrs. William is of course subject at any time, sir, to be taken off her balance by the elements. She is not formed superior to *that*."

"No," returned Mr. Redlaw good-naturedly, though abruptly.

"No, sir. Mrs. William may be taken off her balance by Earth; as, for example, last Sunday week, when sloppy and greasy, and she going out to tea with her newest sister-in-law, and having a pride in herself, and wishing to appear perfectly spotless though pedestrian. Mrs. William may be taken off her balance by Air; as being once over-persuaded by a friend to try a swing at Peckham Fair, which acted on her constitution instantly like a steam-boat. Mrs. William may be taken off her balance by Fire; as on a false alarm of engines at her mother's, when she went two miles in her nightcap. Mrs. William may be taken off her balance by Water; as at Battersea, when rowed into the piers by her young nephew, Charley Swidger junior, aged twelve, which had no idea of boats whatever. But these are elements. Mrs. William must be taken out of elements for the strength of *her* character to come into play."

As he stopped for a reply, the reply was "Yes," in the same tone as before.

"Yes, sir. Oh dear, yes!" said Mr. Swidger, still proceeding with his preparations, and checking them off as he made them. "That's where it is, sir. That's what I always say myself, sir. Such a many of us Swidgers!—Pepper. Why there's my father, sir, superannuated keeper and custodian of this Institution, eighty-seven year old. He's a Swidger!—Spoon."

"True, William," was the patient and abstracted answer, when he stopped again.

"Yes, sir," said Mr. Swidger. "That's what I always say, sir. You may call him the trunk of the tree!—Bread. Then you come to his successor, my unworthy self—Salt—and Mrs. William, Swidgers both.—Knife and fork. Then you come to all my brothers and their families, Swidgers, man and woman, boy and girl. Why, what with cousins, uncles, aunts, and relationships of this, that, and t'other degree, and what-not degree, and marriages, and lyings-in, the Swidgers—Tumblers—might take hold of hands, and make a ring round England!"

Receiving no reply at all here, from the thoughtful man whom he addressed, Mr. William approached him nearer, and made a feint of accidentally knocking the table with a decanter, to rouse him. The moment he succeeded, he went on, as if in great alacrity of acquiescence.

"Yes, sir! That's just what I say myself, sir. Mrs. William and me have often said so. 'There's Swidgers enough,' we say, 'without *our* voluntary contributions,'—Butter. In fact, sir, my father is a family in himself—Castors—to take care of; and it happens all for the best that we have no child of our own, though it's made Mrs. William rather quiet-like, too. Quite ready for the fowl and mashed potatoes, sir? Mrs. William said she'd dish in ten minutes when I left the Lodge."

"I am quite ready," said the other, waking as from a dream, and walking slowly to and fro.

"Mrs. William has been at it again, sir!" said the keeper, as he stood warming a plate at the fire, and pleasantly shading his face with it. Mr. Redlaw stopped in his walking, and an expression of interest appeared in him.

"What I always say myself, sir. She *will* do it! There's a motherly feeling in Mrs. William's breast that must and will have went."

"What has she done?"

"Why, sir, not satisfied with being a sort of mother to all the young gentlemen that come up from a variety of parts, to attend your courses of lectures at this ancient foundation—its surprising how stone-chaney catches the heat this frosty weather, to be sure!" Here he turned the plate, and cooled his fingers.

"Well?" said Mr. Redlaw.

"That's just what I say myself, sir," returned Mr. William, speaking over his shoulder, as if in ready and delighted assent. "That's exactly where it is, sir! There ain't one of our students but appears to regard Mrs. William in that light. Every day, right through the course, they puts their heads into the Lodge, one after another, and have all got something to tell her, or something to ask her. 'Swidge' is the appellation by which they speak of Mrs. William in general, among themselves, I'm told; but that's what I say, sir. Better be called ever so far out of your name, if it's done in real liking, than have it made ever so much of, and not cared about! What's a name for? To know a person by. If Mrs. William is known by something better than her name—I allude to Mrs. William's qualities and disposition—never mind her name, though it *is* Swidger, by rights. Let 'em call her Swidge, Widge, Bridge—Lord! London Bridge, Blackfriars, Chelsea, Putney, Waterloo, or Hammersmith Suspension—if they like!"

The close of this triumphant oration brought him and the plate to the table, upon which he half laid and half dropped it, with a lively sense of its being thoroughly heated, just as the subject of his praises entered the room, bearing another tray and a lantern, and followed by a venerable old man with long grey hair.

Mrs. William, like Mr. William, was a simple, innocent-looking person, in whose smooth cheeks the cheerful red of her husband's official waistcoat was very pleasantly repeated. But whereas Mr. William's light hair stood on end all over his head, and seemed to draw his eyes up with it in an excess of bustling readiness for anything, the dark brown hair of Mrs. William was carefully smoothed down, and waved away under a trim tidy cap, in the most exact and quiet manner imaginable. Whereas Mr. William's very trousers hitched themselves up at the ankles, as if it were not in their iron-grey nature to rest without looking about them, Mrs. William's neatly-flowered skirts—red and white, like her own pretty face—were as composed and orderly, as if the very wind that blew so hard out of doors could not disturb one of their folds. Whereas his coat had something of a fly-away and half-off appearance about the collar and breast, her little bodice was so placid and neat, that there should have been protection for her, in it, had she needed any, with the roughest people. Who could have had the heart to make so calm a bosom swell with grief, or throb with fear, or flutter with a thought of shame! To whom would its repose and peace have not appealed against disturbance, like the innocent slumber of a child!

"Punctual, of course, Milly," said her husband, relieving her of the tray, "or it wouldn't be you. Here's Mrs. William, sir!—He looks lonelier than ever to-night," whispering to his wife, as he was taking the tray, "and ghostlier altogether."

Without any show of hurry or noise, or any show of herself even, she was so calm and quiet, Milly set the dishes she had brought upon the table,—Mr. William, after much clattering and running about, having only gained possession of a butter-boat of gravy, which he stood ready to serve.

"What is that the old man has in his arms?" asked Mr. Redlaw, as he sat down to his solitary meal.

"Holly, sir," replied the quiet voice of Milly.

"That's what I say myself, sir," interposed Mr. William, striking in with the butter-boat. "Berries is so seasonable to the time of year!—Brown gravy!"

"Another Christmas come, another year gone!" murmured the Chemist, with a gloomy sigh. "More figures in the lengthening sum of recollection that we work and work at to our torment, till Death idly jumbles all together, and rubs all out. So, Philip!" breaking off, and raising his voice, as he addressed the old man standing apart, with his glistening burden in his arms, from which the quiet Mrs. William took small branches, which she noiselessly trimmed with her scissors, and decorated the room with, while her aged father-in-law looked on much interested in the ceremony.

"My duty to you, sir," returned the old man. "Should have spoke before, sir, but know your ways, Mr. Redlaw—proud to say—and wait till spoke to! Merry Christmas, sir, and happy New Year, and many of 'em. Have had a pretty many of 'em myself—ha, ha!—and may take the liberty of wishing 'em. I'm eighty-seven!"

"Have you had so many that were merry and happy?" asked the other.

"Ay, sir, ever so many," returned the old man.

"Is his memory impaired with age? It is to be expected now," said Mr. Redlaw, turning to the son, and speaking lower.

"Not a morsel of it, sir," replied Mr. William. "That's exactly what I say myself, sir. There never was such a memory as my father's. He's the most wonderful man in the world. He don't know what forgetting means. It's the very observation I'm always making to Mrs. William, sir, if you'll believe me!"

Mr. Swidger, in his polite desire to seem to acquiesce at all events, delivered this as if there were no iota of contradiction in it, and it were all said in unbounded and unqualified assent.

The Chemist pushed his plate away, and, rising from the table, walked across the room to where the old man stood looking at a little sprig of holly in his hand.

"It recalls the time when many of those years were old and new, then?" he said, observing him attentively, and touching him on the shoulder. "Does it?"

"Oh many, many!" said Philip, half awaking from his reverie. "I'm eighty-seven!"

"Merry and happy, was it?" asked the Chemist in a low voice. "Merry and happy, old man?"

"May-be as high as that, no higher," said the old man, holding out his hand a little way above the level of his knee, and looking retrospectively at his questioner, "when I first remember 'em! Cold, sunshiny day it was, out a-walking, when some one—it was my mother as sure as you stand there, though I don't know what her blessed face was like, for she took ill and died that Christmas-time—told me they were food for birds. The pretty little fellow thought—that's me, you understand—that birds' eyes were so bright, perhaps, because the berries that they lived on in the winter were so bright. I recollect that. And I'm eighty-seven!"

"Merry and happy!" mused the other, bending his dark eyes upon the stooping figure, with a smile of compassion. "Merry and happy—and remember well!"

"Ay, ay, ay!" resumed the old man, catching the last words. "I remember 'em well in my school time, year after year, and all the merry-making that used to come along with them. I was a strong chap then, Mr. Redlaw; and, if you'll believe me, hadn't my match at foot-ball within ten mile. Where's my son, William? Hadn't my match at football, William, within ten mile!"

"That's what I always say, father!" returned the son promptly, and with great respect. "You ARE a Swidger, if ever there was one of the family!"

"Dear!" said the old man, shaking his head as he again looked at the holly. "His mother—my son William's my youngest son—and I, have sat among 'em all, boys and girls, little children and babies, many a year, when the berries like these were not shining half so bright all round us, as their bright faces. Many of 'em are gone; she's gone; and my son George (our eldest, who was her pride more than all the rest!) is fallen very low: but I can see them, when I look here, alive and healthy, as they used to be in those days; and I can see him, thank God, in his innocence. It's a blessed thing to me, at eighty-seven."

The keen look that had been fixed upon him with so much earnestness, had gradually sought the ground.

"When my circumstances got to be not so good as formerly, through not being honestly dealt by, and I first come here to be custodian," said the old man, "—which was upwards of fifty years ago—where's my son William? More than half a century ago, William!"

"That's what I say, father," replied the son, as promptly and dutifully as before, "that's exactly where it is. Two times ought's an ought, and twice five ten, and there's a hundred of 'em."

"It was quite a pleasure to know that one of our founders—or more correctly speaking," said the old man, with a great glory in his subject and his knowledge of it, "one of the learned gentlemen that helped endow us in Queen Elizabeth's time, for we were founded afore her day—left in his will, among the other bequests he made us, so much to buy holly, for garnishing the walls and windows, come Christmas. There was something homely and friendly in it. Being but strange here, then, and coming at Christmas-time, we took a liking for his very picter that hangs in what used to be, anciently, afore our ten poor gentlemen commuted for an annual stipend in money, our great Dinner Hall.—A sedate gentleman in a peaked beard, with a ruff round his neck, and a scroll below him, in old English letters, 'Lord! keep my memory green!' You know all about him, Mr. Redlaw?"

"I know the portrait hangs there, Philip."

"Yes, sure, it's the second on the right, above the panelling. I was going to say—he has helped to keep *my* memory green, I thank him; for going round the building every year, as I'm a doing now, and freshening up the bare rooms with these branches and berries, freshens up my bare old brain. One year brings back another, and that year another, and those others numbers! At last, it seems to me as if the birth-time of our Lord was the birth-time of all I have ever had affection for, or mourned for, or delighted in,—and they're a pretty many, for I'm eighty-seven!"

"Merry and happy," murmured Redlaw to himself.

The room began to darken strangely.

"So you see, sir," pursued old Philip, whose hale wintry cheek had warmed into a ruddier glow, and whose blue eyes had brightened while he spoke, "I have plenty to keep, when I keep this present season. Now, where's my quiet Mouse? Chattering's the sin of my time of life, and there's half the building to do yet, if the cold don't freeze us first, or the wind don't blow us away, or the darkness don't swallow us up."

The quiet Mouse had brought her calm face to his side, and silently taken his arm, before he finished speaking.

"Come away, my dear," said the old man. "Mr. Redlaw won't settle to his dinner, otherwise, till it's cold as the winter. I hope you'll excuse me rambling on, sir, and I wish you good night, and, once again, a merry—"

"Stay!" said Mr. Redlaw, resuming his place at the table, more, it would have seemed from his manner, to reassure the old keeper, than in any remembrance of his own appetite. "Spare me another moment, Philip. William, you were going to tell me something to your excellent wife's honour. It will not be disagreeable to her to hear you praise her. What was it?"

"Why, that's where it is, you see, sir," returned Mr. William Swidger, looking towards his wife in considerable embarrassment. "Mrs. William's got her eye upon me."

"But you're not afraid of Mrs. William's eye?"

"Why, no, sir," returned Mr. Swidger, "that's what I say myself. It wasn't made to be afraid of. It wouldn't have been made so mild, if that was the intention. But I wouldn't like to—Milly!—him, you know. Down in the Buildings."

Mr. William, standing behind the table, and rummaging disconcertedly among the objects upon it, directed persuasive glances at Mrs. William, and secret jerks of his head and thumb at Mr. Redlaw, as alluring her towards him.

"Him, you know, my love," said Mr. William. "Down in the Buildings. Tell, my dear! You're the works of Shakespeare in comparison with myself. Down in the Buildings, you know, my love.—Student."

"Student?" repeated Mr. Redlaw, raising his head.

"That's what I say, sir!" cried Mr. William, in the utmost animation of assent. "If it wasn't the poor student down in the Buildings, why should you wish to hear it from Mrs. William's lips? Mrs. William, my dear—Buildings."

"I didn't know," said Milly, with a quiet frankness, free from any haste or confusion, "that William had said anything about it, or I wouldn't have come. I asked him not to. It's a sick young gentleman, sir—and very poor, I am afraid—who is too ill to go home this holiday-time, and lives, unknown to any one, in but a common kind of lodging for a gentleman, down in Jerusalem Buildings. That's all, sir."

"Why have I never heard of him?" said the Chemist, rising hurriedly. "Why has he not made his situation known to me? Sick!—give me my hat and cloak. Poor!—what house?—what number?"

"Oh, you mustn't go there, sir," said Milly, leaving her father-in-law, and calmly confronting him with her collected little face and folded hands.

"Not go there?"

"Oh dear, no!" said Milly, shaking her head as at a most manifest and self-evident impossibility. "It couldn't be thought of!"

"What do you mean? Why not?"

"Why, you see, sir," said Mr. William Swidger, persuasively and confidentially, "that's what I say. Depend upon it, the young gentleman would never have made his situation known to one of his own sex. Mrs. Williams has got into his confidence, but that's quite different. They all confide in Mrs. William; they all trust *her*. A man, sir, couldn't have got a whisper out of him; but woman, sir, and Mrs. William combined—!"

"There is good sense and delicacy in what you say, William," returned Mr. Redlaw, observant of the gentle and composed face at his shoulder. And laying his finger on his lip, he secretly put his purse into her hand.

"Oh dear no, sir!" cried Milly, giving it back again. "Worse and worse! Couldn't be dreamed of!"

Such a staid matter-of-fact housewife she was, and so unruffled by the momentary haste of this rejection, that, an instant afterwards, she was tidily picking up a few leaves which had strayed from between her scissors and her apron, when she had arranged the holly.

Finding, when she rose from her stooping posture, that Mr. Redlaw was still regarding her with doubt and astonishment, she quietly repeated—looking about, the while, for any other fragments that might have escaped her observation:

"Oh dear no, sir! He said that of all the world he would not be known to you, or receive help from you—though he is a student in your class. I have made no terms of secrecy with you, but I trust to your honour completely."

Why did he say so?"

"Indeed I can't tell, sir," said Milly, after thinking a little, "because I am not at all clever, you know; and I wanted to be useful to him in making things neat and comfortable about him, and employed myself that way. But I know he is poor, and lonely, and I think he is somehow neglected too.—How dark it is!"

The room had darkened more and more. There was a very heavy gloom and shadow gathering behind the Chemist's chair.

"What more about him?" he asked.

"He is engaged to be married when he can afford it," said Milly, "and is studying, I think, to qualify himself to earn a living. I have seen, a long time, that he has studied hard and denied himself much.—How very dark it is!"

"It's turned colder, too," said the old man, rubbing his hands. "There's a chill and dismal feeling in the room. Where's my son William? William, my boy, turn the lamp, and rouse the fire!"

Milly's voice resumed, like quiet music very softly played:

"He muttered in his broken sleep yesterday afternoon, after talking to me" (this was to herself) "about some one dead, and some great wrong done that could never be forgotten; but whether to him or to another person, I don't know. Not *by* him, I am sure."

"And, in short, Mrs. William, you see—which she wouldn't say herself, Mr. Redlaw, if she was to stop here till the new year after this next one—" said Mr. William, coming up to him to speak in his ear, "has done him worlds of good! Bless you, worlds of good! All at home just the same as ever—my father made as snug and comfortable—not a crumb of litter to be found in the house, if you were to offer fifty pound ready money for it—Mrs. William apparently never out of the way—yet Mrs. William backwards and forwards, backwards and forwards, up and down, up and down, a mother to him!"

The room turned darker and colder, and the gloom and shadow gathering behind the chair was heavier.

"Not content with this, sir, Mrs. William goes and finds, this very night, when she was coming home (why it's not above a couple of hours ago), a creature more like a young wild beast than a young child, shivering upon a door-step. What does Mrs. William do, but brings it home to dry it, and feed it, and keep it till our old Bounty of food and flannel is given away, on Christmas morning! If it ever felt a fire before, it's as much as ever it did; for it's sitting in the old Lodge chimney, staring at ours as if its ravenous eyes would never shut again. It's sitting there, at least," said Mr. William, correcting himself, on reflection, "unless it's bolted!"

"Heaven keep her happy!" said the Chemist aloud, "and you too, Philip! and you, William! I must consider what to do in this. I may desire to see this student, I'll not detain you any longer now. Good-night!"

"I thank'ee, sir, I thank'ee!" said the old man, "for Mouse, and for my son William, and for myself. Where's my son William? William, you take the lantern and go on first, through them long dark passages, as you did last year and the year afore. Ha, ha! *I* remember—though I'm eighty-seven! 'Lord, keep my memory green!' It's a very good prayer, Mr. Redlaw, that of the learned gentleman in the peaked beard, with a ruff round his neck—hangs up, second on the right above the panelling, in what used to be, afore our ten poor gentlemen commuted, our great Dinner Hall. 'Lord, keep my memory green!' It's very good and pious, sir. Amen! Amen!"

As they passed out and shut the heavy door, which, however carefully withheld, fired a long train of thundering reverberations when it shut at last, the room turned darker.

As he fell a-musing in his chair alone, the healthy holly withered on the wall, and dropped—dead branches.

As the gloom and shadow thickened behind him, in that place where it had been gathering so darkly, it took, by slow degrees,—or out of it there came, by some unreal, unsubstantial process—not to be traced by any human sense,—an awful likeness of himself!

Ghastly and cold, colourless in its leaden face and hands, but with his features, and his bright eyes, and his grizzled hair, and dressed in the gloomy shadow of his dress, it came into his terrible appearance of existence, motionless, without a sound. As *he* leaned his arm upon the elbow of his chair, ruminating before the fire, *it* leaned upon the chair-back, close above him, with its appalling copy of his face looking where his face looked, and bearing the expression his face bore.

This, then, was the Something that had passed and gone already. This was the dread companion of the haunted man!

It took, for some moments, no more apparent heed of him, than he of it. The Christmas Waits were playing somewhere in the distance, and, through his thoughtfulness, he seemed to listen to the music. It seemed to listen too.

At length he spoke; without moving or lifting up his face.

"Here again!" he said.

"Here again!" replied the Phantom.

"I see you in the fire," said the haunted man; "I hear you in music, in the wind, in the dead stillness of the night."

The Phantom moved its head, assenting.

"Why do you come, to haunt me thus?"

"I come as I am called," replied the Ghost.

"No. Unbidden," exclaimed the Chemist.

"Unbidden be it," said the Spectre. "It is enough. I am here."

Hitherto the light of the fire had shone on the two faces—if the dread lineaments behind the chair might be called a face—both addressed towards it, as at first, and neither looking at the other. But, now, the haunted man turned, suddenly, and stared upon the Ghost. The Ghost, as sudden in its motion, passed to before the chair, and stared on him.

The living man, and the animated image of himself dead, might so have looked, the one upon the other. An awful survey, in a lonely and remote part of an empty old pile of building, on a winter night, with the loud wind going by upon its journey of mystery—whence or whither, no man knowing since the world began—and the stars, in unimaginable millions, glittering through it, from eternal space, where the world's bulk is as a grain, and its hoary age is infancy.

"Look upon me!" said the Spectre. "I am he, neglected in my youth, and miserably poor, who strove and suffered, and still strove and suffered, until I hewed out knowledge from the mine where it was buried, and made rugged steps thereof, for my worn feet to rest and rise on."

"I *am* that man," returned the Chemist.

"No mother's self-denying love," pursued the Phantom, "no father's counsel, aided *me*. A stranger came into my father's place when I was but a child, and I was easily an alien from my mother's heart. My parents, at the best, were of that sort whose care soon ends, and whose duty is soon done; who cast their offspring loose, early, as birds do theirs; and, if they do well, claim the merit; and, if ill, the pity."

It paused, and seemed to tempt and goad him with its look, and with the manner of its speech, and with its smile.

"I am he," pursued the Phantom, "who, in this struggle upward, found a friend. I made him—won him—bound him to me! We worked together, side by side. All the love and confidence that in my earlier youth had had no outlet, and found no expression, I bestowed on him."

"Not all," said Redlaw, hoarsely.

"No, not all," returned the Phantom. "I had a sister."

The haunted man, with his head resting on his hands, replied "I had!" The Phantom, with an evil smile, drew closer to the chair, and resting its chin upon its folded hands, its folded hands upon the back, and looking down into his face with searching eyes, that seemed instinct with fire, went on:

"Such glimpses of the light of home as I had ever known, had streamed from her. How young she was, how fair, how loving! I took her to the first poor roof that I was master of, and made it rich. She came into the darkness of my life, and made it bright.—She is before me!"

"I saw her, in the fire, but now. I hear her in music, in the wind, in the dead stillness of the night," returned the haunted man.

"*Did* he love her?" said the Phantom, echoing his contemplative tone. "I think he did, once. I am sure he did. Better had she loved him less—less secretly, less dearly, from the shallower depths of a more divided heart!"

"Let me forget it!" said the Chemist, with an angry motion of his hand. "Let me blot it from my memory!"

The Spectre, without stirring, and with its unwinking, cruel eyes still fixed upon his face, went on:

"A dream, like hers, stole upon my own life."

"It did," said Redlaw.

"A love, as like hers," pursued the Phantom, "as my inferior nature might cherish, arose in my own heart. I was too poor to bind its object to my fortune then, by any thread of promise or entreaty. I loved her far too well, to seek to do it. But, more than ever I had striven in my life, I strove to climb! Only an inch gained, brought me something nearer to the height. I toiled up! In the late pauses of my labour at that time—my sister (sweet companion!) still sharing with me the expiring embers and the cooling hearth,—when day was breaking, what pictures of the future did I see!"

"I saw them, in the fire, but now," he murmured. "They come back to me in music, in the wind, in the dead stillness of the night, in the revolving years."

"—Pictures of my own domestic life, in after-time, with her who was the inspiration of my toil. Pictures of my sister, made the wife of my dear friend, on equal terms—for he had some inheritance, we none—pictures of our sobered age and mellowed happiness, and of the golden links, extending back so far, that should bind us, and our children, in a radiant garland," said the Phantom.

"Pictures," said the haunted man, "that were delusions. Why is it my doom to remember them too well!"

"Delusions," echoed the Phantom in its changeless voice, and glaring on him with its changeless eyes. "For my friend (in whose breast my confidence was locked as in my own), passing between me and the centre of the system of my hopes and struggles, won her to himself, and shattered my frail universe. My sister, doubly dear, doubly devoted, doubly cheerful in my home, lived on to see me famous, and my old ambition so rewarded when its spring was broken, and then—"

"Then died," he interposed. "Died, gentle as ever; happy; and with no concern but for her brother. Peace!"

The Phantom watched him silently.

"Remembered!" said the haunted man, after a pause. "Yes. So well remembered, that even now, when years have passed, and nothing is more idle or more visionary to me than the boyish love so long outlived, I think of it with sympathy, as if it were a younger brother's or a son's. Sometimes I even wonder when her heart first inclined to him, and how it had been affected towards me.—Not lightly, once, I think.—But that is nothing. Early unhappiness, a wound from a hand I loved and trusted, and a loss that nothing can replace, outlive such fancies."

"Thus," said the Phantom, "I bear within me a Sorrow and a Wrong. Thus I prey upon myself. Thus, memory is my curse; and, if I could forget my sorrow and my wrong, I would!"

"Mocker!" said the Chemist, leaping up, and making, with a wrathful hand, at the throat of his other self. "Why have I always that taunt in my ears?"

"Forbear!" exclaimed the Spectre in an awful voice. "Lay a hand on me, and die!"

He stopped midway, as if its words had paralysed him, and stood looking on it. It had glided from him; it had its arm raised high in warning; and a smile passed over its unearthly features, as it reared its dark figure in triumph.

"If I could forget my sorrow and wrong, I would," the Ghost repeated. "If I could forget my sorrow and my wrong, I would!"

"Evil spirit of myself," returned the haunted man, in a low, trembling tone, "my life is darkened by that incessant whisper."

"It is an echo," said the Phantom.

"If it be an echo of my thoughts—as now, indeed, I know it is," rejoined the haunted man, "why should I, therefore, be tormented? It is not a selfish thought. I suffer it to range beyond myself. All men and women have their sorrows,—most of them their wrongs; ingratitude, and sordid jealousy, and interest, besetting all degrees of life. Who would not forget their sorrows and their wrongs?"

"Who would not, truly, and be happier and better for it?" said the Phantom.

"These revolutions of years, which we commemorate," proceeded Redlaw, "what do *they* recall! Are there any minds in which they do not re-awaken some sorrow, or some trouble? What is the remembrance of the old man who was here to-night? A tissue of sorrow and trouble."

"But common natures," said the Phantom, with its evil smile upon its glassy face, "unenlightened minds and ordinary spirits, do not feel or reason on these things like men of higher cultivation and profounder thought."

"Tempter," answered Redlaw, "whose hollow look and voice I dread more than words can express, and from whom some dim foreshadowing of greater fear is stealing over me while I speak, I hear again an echo of my own mind."

"Receive it as a proof that I am powerful," returned the Ghost. "Hear what I offer! Forget the sorrow, wrong, and trouble you have known!"

"Forget them!" he repeated.

"I have the power to cancel their remembrance—to leave but very faint, confused traces of them, that will die out soon," returned the Spectre. "Say! Is it done?"

"Stay!" cried the haunted man, arresting by a terrified gesture the uplifted hand. "I tremble with distrust and doubt of you; and the dim fear you cast upon me deepens into a nameless horror I can hardly bear.—I would not deprive myself of any kindly recollection, or any sympathy that is good for me, or others. What shall I lose, if I assent to this? What else will pass from my remembrance?"

"No knowledge; no result of study; nothing but the intertwisted chain of feelings and associations, each in its turn dependent on, and nourished by, the banished recollections. Those will go."

"Are they so many?" said the haunted man, reflecting in alarm.

"They have been wont to show themselves in the fire, in music, in the wind, in the dead stillness of the night, in the revolving years," returned the Phantom scornfully.

The Phantom held its peace.

But, having stood before him, silent, for a little while, it moved towards the fire; then stopped.

"Decide!" it said, "before the opportunity is lost!"

"A moment! I call Heaven to witness," said the agitated man, "that I have never been a hater of any kind,—never morose, indifferent, or hard, to anything around me. If, living here alone, I have made too much of all that was and might have been, and too little of what is, the evil, I believe, has fallen on me, and not on others. But, if there were poison in my body, should I not, possessed of antidotes and knowledge how to use them, use them? If there be poison in my mind, and through this fearful shadow I can cast it out, shall I not cast it out?"

"Say," said the Spectre, "is it done?"

"A moment longer!" he answered hurriedly. "*I would forget it if I could*! Have *I* thought that, alone, or has it been the thought of thousands upon thousands, generation after generation? All human memory is fraught with sorrow and trouble. My memory is as the memory of other men, but other men have not this choice. Yes, I close the bargain. Yes! I WILL forget my sorrow, wrong, and trouble!"

"Say," said the Spectre, "is it done?"

"It is!"

"It is. And take this with you, man whom I here renounce! The gift that I have given, you shall give again, go where you will. Without recovering yourself the power that you have yielded up, you shall henceforth destroy its like in all whom you approach. Your wisdom has discovered that the memory of sorrow, wrong, and trouble is the lot of all mankind, and that mankind would be the happier, in its other memories, without it. Go! Be its benefactor! Freed from such remembrance, from this hour, carry involuntarily the blessing of such freedom with you. Its diffusion is inseparable and inalienable from you. Go! Be happy in the good you have won, and in the good you do!"

The Phantom, which had held its bloodless hand above him while it spoke, as if in some unholy invocation, or some ban; and which had gradually advanced its eyes so close to his, that he could see how they did not participate in the terrible smile upon its face, but were a fixed, unalterable, steady horror melted before him and was gone.

As he stood rooted to the spot, possessed by fear and wonder, and imagining he heard repeated in melancholy echoes, dying away fainter and fainter, the words, "Destroy its like in all whom you approach!" a shrill cry reached his ears. It came, not from the passages beyond the door, but from another part of the old building, and sounded like the cry of some one in the dark who had lost the way.

He looked confusedly upon his hands and limbs, as if to be assured of his identity, and then shouted in reply, loudly and wildly; for there was a strangeness and terror upon him, as if he too were lost.

The cry responding, and being nearer, he caught up the lamp, and raised a heavy curtain in the wall, by which he was accustomed to pass into and out of the theatre where he lectured,—which adjoined his room. Associated with youth and animation, and a high amphitheatre of faces which his entrance charmed to interest in a moment, it was a ghostly place when all this life was faded out of it, and stared upon him like an emblem of Death.

"Halloa!" he cried. "Halloa! This way! Come to the light!" When, as he held the curtain with one hand, and with the other raised the lamp and tried to pierce the gloom that filled the place, something rushed past him into the room like a wild-cat, and crouched down in a corner.

"What is it?" he said, hastily.

He might have asked "What is it?" even had he seen it well, as presently he did when he stood looking at it gathered up in its corner.

A bundle of tatters, held together by a hand, in size and form almost an infant's, but, in its greedy, desperate little clutch, a bad old man's. A face rounded and smoothed by some half-dozen years, but pinched and twisted by the experiences of a life. Bright eyes, but not youthful. Naked feet, beautiful in their childish delicacy,—ugly in the blood and dirt that cracked upon them. A baby savage, a young monster, a child who had never been a child, a creature who might live to take the outward form of man, but who, within, would live and perish a mere beast.

Used, already, to be worried and hunted like a beast, the boy crouched down as he was looked at, and looked back again, and interposed his arm to ward off the expected blow.

"I'll bite," he said, "if you hit me!"

The time had been, and not many minutes since, when such a sight as this would have wrung the Chemist's heart. He looked upon it now, coldly; but with a heavy effort to remember something—he did not know what—he asked the boy what he did there, and whence he came.

"Where's the woman?" he replied. "I want to find the woman."

"Who?"

"The woman. Her that brought me here, and set me by the large fire. She was so long gone, that I went to look for her, and lost myself. I don't want you. I want the woman."

He made a spring, so suddenly, to get away, that the dull sound of his naked feet upon the floor was near the curtain, when Redlaw caught him by his rags.

"Come! you let me go!" muttered the boy, struggling, and clenching his teeth. "I've done nothing to you. Let me go, will you, to the woman!"

"That is not the way. There is a nearer one," said Redlaw, detaining him, in the same blank effort to remember some association that ought, of right, to bear upon this monstrous object. "What is your name?"

"Got none."

"Where do you live?

"Live! What's that?"

The boy shook his hair from his eyes to look at him for a moment, and then, twisting round his legs and wrestling with him, broke again into his repetition of "You let me go, will you? I want to find the woman."

The Chemist led him to the door. "This way," he said, looking at him still confusedly, but with repugnance and avoidance, growing out of his coldness. "I'll take you to her."

The sharp eyes in the child's head, wandering round the room, lighted on the table where the remnants of the dinner were.

"Give me some of that!" he said, covetously.

"Has she not fed you?"

"I shall be hungry again to-morrow, sha'n't I? Ain't I hungry every day?"

Finding himself released, he bounded at the table like some small animal of prey, and hugging to his breast bread and meat, and his own rags, all together, said:

"There! Now take me to the woman!"

As the Chemist, with a new-born dislike to touch him, sternly motioned him to follow, and was going out of the door, he trembled and stopped.

"The gift that I have given, you shall give again, go where you will!"

The Phantom's words were blowing in the wind, and the wind blew chill upon him.

"I'll not go there, to-night," he murmured faintly.

"I'll go nowhere to-night. Boy! straight down this long-arched passage, and past the great dark door into the yard,—you see the fire shining on the window there."

"The woman's fire?" inquired the boy.

He nodded, and the naked feet had sprung away. He came back with his lamp, locked his door hastily, and sat down in his chair, covering his face like one who was frightened at himself.

For now he was, indeed, alone. Alone, alone.

Chapter II

The Gift Diffused

A SMALL MAN SAT IN A SMALL PARLOUR, PARTITIONED OFF FROM A SMALL shop by a small screen, pasted all over with small scraps of newspapers. In company with the small man, was almost any amount of small children you may please to name—at least it seemed so; they made, in that very limited sphere of action, such an imposing effect, in point of numbers.

Of these small fry, two had, by some strong machinery, been got into bed in a corner, where they might have reposed snugly enough in the sleep of innocence, but for a constitutional propensity to keep awake, and also to scuffle in and out of bed. The immediate occasion of these predatory dashes at the waking world, was the construction of an oyster-shell wall in a corner, by two other youths of tender age; on which fortification the two in bed made harassing descents (like those accursed Picts and Scots who beleaguer the early historical studies of most young Britons), and then withdrew to their own territory.

In addition to the stir attendant on these inroads, and the retorts of the invaded, who pursued hotly, and made lunges at the bed-clothes under which the marauders took refuge, another little boy, in another little bed, contributed his mite of confusion to the family stock, by casting his boots upon the waters; in other words, by launching these and several small objects, inoffensive in themselves, though of a hard substance considered as missiles, at the disturbers of his repose,—who were not slow to return these compliments.

Besides which, another little boy—the biggest there, but still little—was tottering to and fro, bent on one side, and considerably affected in his knees by the weight of a large baby, which he was supposed by a fiction that obtains sometimes in sanguine families, to be hushing to sleep. But oh! the inexhaustible regions of contemplation and watchfulness into which this baby's eyes were then only beginning to compose themselves to stare, over his unconscious shoulder!

It was a very Moloch of a baby, on whose insatiate altar the whole existence of this particular young brother was offered up a daily sacrifice. Its personality may be said to have consisted in its never being quiet, in any one place, for five consecutive minutes, and never going to sleep when required. "Tetterby's baby" was as well known in the neighbourhood as the postman or the pot-boy. It roved from door-step to door-step, in the arms of little Johnny Tetterby, and lagged heavily at the rear of troops of juveniles who followed the Tumblers or the Monkey, and came up, all on one side, a little too late for everything that was attractive, from Monday morning until Saturday night. Wherever childhood congregated to play, there was little Moloch making Johnny fag and toil. Wherever Johnny desired to stay, little Moloch became fractious, and would not remain. Whenever Johnny wanted to go out, Moloch was asleep, and must be watched. Whenever Johnny wanted to stay at home, Moloch was awake, and must be taken out. Yet Johnny was verily persuaded that it was a faultless baby, without its peer in the realm of England; and was quite content to catch meek glimpses of things in general from behind its skirts, or over its limp flapping bonnet, and to go staggering about with it like a very little porter with a very large parcel, which was not directed to anybody, and could never be delivered anywhere.

The small man who sat in the small parlour, making fruitless attempts to read his newspaper peaceably in the midst of this disturbance, was the father of the family, and the chief of the firm described in the inscription over the little shop front, by the name and title of A. TETTERBY AND CO., NEWSMEN. Indeed, strictly speaking, he was the only personage answering to that designation, as Co. was a mere poetical abstraction, altogether baseless and impersonal.

Tetterby's was the corner shop in Jerusalem Buildings. There was a good show of literature in the window, chiefly consisting of picture-newspapers out of date, and serial pirates, and footpads. Walking-sticks, likewise, and marbles, were included in the stock in trade. It had once extended into the light confectionery line; but it would seem that those elegancies of life were not in demand about Jerusalem Buildings, for nothing connected with that branch of commerce remained in the window, except a sort of small glass lantern containing a languishing mass of bull's-eyes, which had melted in the summer and congealed in the winter until all hope of ever getting them out, or of eating them without eating the lantern too, was gone for ever. Tetterby's had tried its hand at several things. It had once made a feeble little dart at the toy business; for, in another lantern, there was a heap of minute wax dolls, all sticking together upside down, in the direst confusion, with their feet on one another's heads, and a precipitate of broken arms and legs at the bottom. It had made a move in the millinery direction, which a few dry, wiry bonnet-shapes remained in a corner of the window to attest. It had fancied that a living might lie hidden in the tobacco trade, and had stuck up a representation of a native of each of the three integral portions of the British Empire, in the act of consuming that fragrant weed; with a poetic legend attached, importing that united in one cause they sat and joked, one chewed tobacco, one took snuff, one smoked: but nothing seemed to have come of it,—except flies. Time had been when it had put a forlorn trust in imitative jewellery, for in one pane of glass there was a card of cheap seals, and another of pencil-cases, and a mysterious black amulet of inscrutable intention, labelled ninepence. But, to that hour,

Jerusalem Buildings had bought none of them. In short, Tetterby's had tried so hard to get a livelihood out of Jerusalem Buildings in one way or other, and appeared to have done so indifferently in all, that the best position in the firm was too evidently Co.'s; Co., as a bodiless creation, being untroubled with the vulgar inconveniences of hunger and thirst, being chargeable neither to the poor's-rates nor the assessed taxes, and having no young family to provide for.

Tetterby himself, however, in his little parlour, as already mentioned, having the presence of a young family impressed upon his mind in a manner too clamorous to be disregarded, or to comport with the quiet perusal of a newspaper, laid down his paper, wheeled, in his distraction, a few times round the parlour, like an undecided carrier-pigeon, made an ineffectual rush at one or two flying little figures in bed-gowns that skimmed past him, and then, bearing suddenly down upon the only unoffending member of the family, boxed the ears of little Moloch's nurse.

"You bad boy!" said Mr. Tetterby, "haven't you any feeling for your poor father after the fatigues and anxieties of a hard winter's day, since five o'clock in the morning, but must you wither his rest, and corrode his latest intelligence, with *your* wicious tricks? Isn't it enough, sir, that your brother 'Dolphus is toiling and moiling in the fog and cold, and you rolling in the lap of luxury with a—with a baby, and everything you can wish for," said Mr. Tetterby, heaping this up as a great climax of blessings, "but must you make a wilderness of home, and maniacs of your parents? Must you, Johnny? Hey?" At each interrogation, Mr. Tetterby made a feint of boxing his ears again, but thought better of it, and held his hand.

"Oh, father!" whimpered Johnny, "when I wasn't doing anything, I'm sure, but taking such care of Sally, and getting her to sleep. Oh, father!"

"I wish my little woman would come home!" said Mr. Tetterby, relenting and repenting, "I only wish my little woman would come home! I ain't fit to deal with 'em. They make my head go round, and get the better of me. Oh, Johnny! Isn't it enough that your dear mother has provided you with that sweet sister?" indicating Moloch; "isn't it enough that you were seven boys before without a ray of gal, and that your dear mother went through what she *did* go through, on purpose that you might all of you have a little sister, but must you so behave yourself as to make my head swim?"

Softening more and more, as his own tender feelings and those of his injured son were worked on, Mr. Tetterby concluded by embracing him, and immediately breaking away to catch one of the real delinquents. A reasonably good start occurring, he succeeded, after a short but smart run, and some rather severe cross-country work under and over the bedsteads, and in and out among the intricacies of the chairs, in capturing this infant, whom he condignly punished, and bore to bed. This example had a powerful, and apparently, mesmeric influence on him of the boots, who instantly fell into a deep sleep, though he had been, but a moment before, broad awake, and in the highest possible feather. Nor was it lost upon the two young architects, who retired to bed, in an adjoining closet, with great privacy and speed. The comrade of the Intercepted One also shrinking into his nest with similar discretion, Mr. Tetterby, when he paused for breath, found himself unexpectedly in a scene of peace.

"My little woman herself," said Mr. Tetterby, wiping his flushed face, "could hardly have done it better! I only wish my little woman had had it to do, I do indeed!"

Mr. Tetterby sought upon his screen for a passage appropriate to be impressed upon his children's minds on the occasion, and read the following.

"'It is an undoubted fact that all remarkable men have had remarkable mothers, and have respected them in after life as their best friends.' Think of your own remarkable mother, my boys," said Mr. Tetterby, "and know her value while she is still among you!"

He sat down again in his chair by the fire, and composed himself, cross-legged, over his newspaper.

"Let anybody, I don't care who it is, get out of bed again," said Tetterby, as a general proclamation, delivered in a very soft-hearted manner, "and astonishment will be the portion of that respected contemporary!"—which expression Mr. Tetterby selected from his screen. "Johnny, my child, take care of your only sister, Sally; for she's the brightest gem that ever sparkled on your early brow."

Johnny sat down on a little stool, and devotedly crushed himself beneath the weight of Moloch.

"Ah, what a gift that baby is to you, Johnny!" said his father, "and how thankful you ought to be! 'It is not generally known, Johnny,'" he was now referring to the screen again, "'but it is a fact ascertained, by accurate calculations, that the following immense percentage of babies never attain to two years old; that is to say—'"

"Oh, don't, father, please!" cried Johnny. "I can't bear it, when I think of Sally."

Mr. Tetterby desisting, Johnny, with a profound sense of his trust, wiped his eyes, and hushed his sister.

"Your brother 'Dolphus," said his father, poking the fire, "is late to-night, Johnny, and will come home like a lump of ice. What's got your precious mother?"

"Here's mother, and 'Dolphus too, father!" exclaimed Johnny, "I think."

"You're right!" returned his father, listening. "Yes, that's the footstep of my little woman."

The process of induction, by which Mr. Tetterby had come to the conclusion that his wife was a little woman, was his own secret. She would have made two editions of himself, very easily. Considered as an individual, she was rather remarkable for being robust and portly; but considered with reference to her husband, her dimensions became magnificent. Nor did they assume a less imposing proportion, when studied with reference to the size of her seven sons, who were but diminutive. In the case of Sally, however, Mrs. Tetterby had asserted herself, at last; as nobody knew better than the victim Johnny, who weighed and measured that exacting idol every hour in the day.

Mrs. Tetterby, who had been marketing, and carried a basket, threw back her bonnet and shawl, and sitting down, fatigued, commanded Johnny to bring his sweet charge to her straightway, for a kiss. Johnny having complied, and gone back to his stool, and again crushed himself, Master Adolphus Tetterby, who had by this time unwound his torso out of a prismatic comforter, apparently interminable, requested the same favour. Johnny having again complied, and again gone back to his stool, and again crushed himself, Mr. Tetterby, struck by a sudden thought, preferred the same claim on his own parental part. The satisfaction of this third desire completely exhausted the sacrifice, who had hardly breath enough left to get back to his stool, crush himself again, and pant at his relations.

"Whatever you do, Johnny," said Mrs. Tetterby, shaking her head, "take care of her, or never look your mother in the face again."

"Nor your brother," said Adolphus.

"Nor your father, Johnny," added Mr. Tetterby.

Johnny, much affected by this conditional renunciation of him, looked down at Moloch's eyes to see that they were all right, so far, and skilfully patted her back (which was uppermost), and rocked her with his foot.

"Are you wet, 'Dolphus, my boy?" said his father. "Come and take my chair, and dry yourself."

"No, father, thank'ee," said Adolphus, smoothing himself down with his hands. "I an't very wet, I don't think. Does my face shine much, father?"

"Well, it *does* look waxy, my boy," returned Mr. Tetterby.

"It's the weather, father," said Adolphus, polishing his cheeks on the worn sleeve of his jacket. "What with rain, and sleet, and wind, and snow, and fog, my face gets quite brought out into a rash sometimes. And shines, it does—oh, don't it, though!"

Master Adolphus was also in the newspaper line of life, being employed, by a more thriving firm than his father and Co., to vend newspapers at a railway station, where his chubby little person, like a shabbily-disguised Cupid, and his shrill little voice (he was not much more than ten years old), were as well known as the hoarse panting of the locomotives, running in and out. His juvenility might have been at some loss for a harmless outlet, in this early application to traffic, but for a fortunate discovery he made of a means of entertaining himself, and of dividing the long day into stages of interest, without neglecting business. This ingenious invention, remarkable, like many great discoveries, for its simplicity, consisted in varying the first vowel in the word "paper," and substituting, in its stead, at different periods of the day, all the other vowels in grammatical succession. Thus, before daylight in the winter time, he went to and fro, in his little oilskin cap and cape, and his big comforter, piercing the heavy air with his cry of "Morn-ing Pa-per!" which, about an hour before noon, changed to "Morn-ing Pepper!" which, at about two, changed to "Morn-ing Pip-per!" which in a couple of hours changed to "Morn-ing Pop-per!" and so declined with the sun into "Eve-ning Pup-per!" to the great relief and comfort of this young gentleman's spirits.

Mrs. Tetterby, his lady-mother, who had been sitting with her bonnet and shawl thrown back, as aforesaid, thoughtfully turning her wedding-ring round and round upon her finger, now rose, and divesting herself of her out-of-door attire, began to lay the cloth for supper.

"Ah, dear me, dear me, dear me!" said Mrs. Tetterby. "That's the way the world goes!"

"Which is the way the world goes, my dear?" asked Mr. Tetterby, looking round.

"Oh, nothing!" said Mrs. Tetterby.

Mr. Tetterby elevated his eyebrows, folded his newspaper afresh, and carried his eyes up it, and down it, and across it, but was wandering in his attention, and not reading it.

Mrs. Tetterby, at the same time, laid the cloth, but rather as if she were punishing the table than preparing the family supper; hitting it unnecessarily hard with the knives and forks, slapping it with the plates, dinting it with the salt-cellar, and coming heavily down upon it with the loaf.

"Ah, dear me, dear me, dear me!" said Mrs. Tetterby. "That's the way the world goes!"

"My duck," returned her husband, looking round again, "you said that before. Which is the way the world goes?"

"Oh, nothing!" said Mrs. Tetterby.

"Sophia!" remonstrated her husband, "you said *that* before, too."

"Well, I'll say it again if you like," returned Mrs. Tetterby. "Oh nothing—there! And again if you like, oh nothing—there! And again if you like, oh nothing—now then!"

Mr. Tetterby brought his eye to bear upon the partner of his bosom, and said, in mild astonishment:

"My little woman, what has put you out?"

"I'm sure *I* don't know," she retorted. "Don't ask me. Who said I was put out at all? *I* never did."

Mr. Tetterby gave up the perusal of his newspaper as a bad job, and, taking a slow walk across the room, with his hands behind him, and his shoulders raised—his gait according perfectly with the resignation of his manner—addressed himself to his two eldest offspring.

"Your supper will be ready in a minute, 'Dolphus," said Mr. Tetterby. "Your mother has been out in the wet, to the cook's shop, to buy it. It was very good of your mother so to do. *You* shall get some supper too, very soon, Johnny. Your mother's pleased with you, my man, for being so attentive to your precious sister."

Mrs. Tetterby, without any remark, but with a decided subsidence of her animosity towards the table, finished her preparations, and took, from her ample basket, a substantial slab of hot pease pudding wrapped in paper, and a basin covered with a saucer, which, on being uncovered, sent forth an odour so agreeable, that the three pair of eyes in the two beds opened wide and fixed themselves upon the banquet. Mr. Tetterby, without regarding this tacit invitation to be seated, stood repeating slowly, "Yes, yes, your supper will be ready in a minute, 'Dolphus—your mother went out in the wet, to the cook's shop, to buy it. It was very good of your mother so to do"—until Mrs. Tetterby, who had been exhibiting sundry tokens of contrition behind him, caught him round the neck, and wept.

"Oh, 'Dolphus!" said Mrs. Tetterby, "how could I go and behave so?"

This reconciliation affected Adolphus the younger and Johnny to that degree, that they both, as with one accord, raised a dismal cry, which had the effect of immediately shutting up the round eyes in the beds, and utterly routing the two remaining little Tetterbys, just then stealing in from the adjoining closet to see what was going on in the eating way.

"I am sure, 'Dolphus," sobbed Mrs. Tetterby, "coming home, I had no more idea than a child unborn—"

Mr. Tetterby seemed to dislike this figure of speech, and observed, "Say than the baby, my dear."

"—Had no more idea than the baby," said Mrs. Tetterby.—"Johnny, don't look at me, but look at her, or she'll fall out of your lap and be killed, and then you'll die in agonies of a broken heart, and serve you right.—No more idea I hadn't than that darling, of being cross when I came home; but somehow, 'Dolphus—" Mrs. Tetterby paused, and again turned her wedding-ring round and round upon her finger.

"I see!" said Mr. Tetterby. "I understand! My little woman was put out. Hard times, and hard weather, and hard work, make it trying now and then. I see, bless your soul! No wonder! Dolf, my man," continued Mr. Tetterby, exploring the basin with a fork, "here's your mother been and bought, at the cook's shop, besides pease pudding, a whole knuckle of a lovely roast leg of pork, with lots of crackling left upon it, and with seasoning gravy and mustard quite unlimited. Hand in your plate, my boy, and begin while it's simmering."

Master Adolphus, needing no second summons, received his portion with eyes rendered moist by appetite, and withdrawing to his particular stool, fell upon his supper tooth and nail. Johnny was not forgotten, but received his rations on bread, lest he should, in a flush of gravy, trickle any on the baby. He was required, for similar reasons, to keep his pudding, when not on active service, in his pocket.

There might have been more pork on the knucklebone,—which knucklebone the carver at the cook's shop had assuredly not forgotten in carving for previous customers—but there was no stint of seasoning, and that is an accessory dreamily suggesting pork, and pleasantly cheating the sense of taste. The pease pudding, too, the gravy and mustard, like the Eastern rose in respect of the nightingale, if they were not absolutely pork, had lived near it; so, upon the whole, there was the flavour of a middle-sized pig. It was irresistible to the Tetterbys in bed, who, though professing to slumber peacefully, crawled out when unseen by their parents, and silently appealed to their brothers for any gastronomic token of fraternal affection. They, not hard of heart, presenting scraps in return, it resulted that a party of light skirmishers in night-gowns were careering about the parlour all through supper, which harassed Mr. Tetterby exceedingly, and once or twice imposed upon him the necessity of a charge, before which these guerilla troops retired in all directions and in great confusion.

Mrs. Tetterby did not enjoy her supper. There seemed to be something on Mrs. Tetterby's mind. At one time she laughed without reason, and at another time she cried without reason, and at last she laughed and cried together in a manner so very unreasonable that her husband was confounded.

"My little woman," said Mr. Tetterby, "if the world goes that way, it appears to go the wrong way, and to choke you."

"Give me a drop of water," said Mrs. Tetterby, struggling with herself, "and don't speak to me for the present, or take any notice of me. Don't do it!"

Mr. Tetterby having administered the water, turned suddenly on the unlucky Johnny (who was full of sympathy), and demanded why he was wallowing there, in gluttony and idleness, instead of coming forward with the baby, that the sight of her might revive his mother. Johnny immediately approached, borne down by its weight; but Mrs. Tetterby holding out her hand to signify that she was not in a condition to bear that trying appeal to her feelings, he was interdicted from advancing another inch, on pain of perpetual hatred from all his dearest connections; and accordingly retired to his stool again, and crushed himself as before.

After a pause, Mrs. Tetterby said she was better now, and began to laugh.

"My little woman," said her husband, dubiously, "are you quite sure you're better? Or are you, Sophia, about to break out in a fresh direction?"

"No, 'Dolphus, no," replied his wife. "I'm quite myself." With that, settling her hair, and pressing the palms of her hands upon her eyes, she laughed again.

"What a wicked fool I was, to think so for a moment!" said Mrs. Tetterby. "Come nearer, 'Dolphus, and let me ease my mind, and tell you what I mean. Let me tell you all about it."

Mr. Tetterby bringing his chair closer, Mrs. Tetterby laughed again, gave him a hug, and wiped her eyes.

"You know, 'Dolphus, my dear," said Mrs. Tetterby, "that when I was single, I might have given myself away in several directions. At one time, four after me at once; two of them were sons of Mars."

"We're all sons of Ma's, my dear," said Mr. Tetterby, "jointly with Pa's."

"I don't mean that," replied his wife, "I mean soldiers—serjeants."

"Oh!" said Mr. Tetterby.

"Well, 'Dolphus, I'm sure I never think of such things now, to regret them; and I'm sure I've got as good a husband, and would do as much to prove that I was fond of him, as—"

"As any little woman in the world," said Mr. Tetterby. "Very good. *Very* good."

If Mr. Tetterby had been ten feet high, he could not have expressed a gentler consideration for Mrs. Tetterby's fairy-like stature; and if Mrs. Tetterby had been two feet high, she could not have felt it more appropriately her due.

"But you see, 'Dolphus," said Mrs. Tetterby, "this being Christmas-time, when all people who can, make holiday, and when all people who have got money, like to spend some, I did, somehow, get a little out of sorts when I was in the streets just now. There were so many things to be sold—such delicious things to eat, such fine things to look at, such delightful things to have—and there was so much calculating and calculating necessary, before I durst lay out a sixpence for the commonest thing; and the basket was so large, and wanted so much in it; and my stock of money was so small, and would go such a little way;—you hate me, don't you, 'Dolphus?"

"Not quite," said Mr. Tetterby, "as yet."

"Well! I'll tell you the whole truth," pursued his wife, penitently, "and then perhaps you will. I felt all this, so much, when I was trudging about in the cold, and when I saw a lot of other calculating faces and large baskets trudging about, too, that I began to think whether I mightn't have done better, and been happier, if—I—hadn't—" the wedding-ring went round again, and Mrs. Tetterby shook her downcast head as she turned it.

"I see," said her husband quietly; "if you hadn't married at all, or if you had married somebody else?"

"Yes," sobbed Mrs. Tetterby. "That's really what I thought. Do you hate me now, 'Dolphus?"

"Why no," said Mr. Tetterby. "I don't find that I do, as yet."

Mrs. Tetterby gave him a thankful kiss, and went on.

"I begin to hope you won't, now, 'Dolphus, though I'm afraid I haven't told you the worst. I can't think what came over me. I don't know whether I was ill, or mad, or what I was, but I couldn't call up anything that seemed to bind us to each other, or to reconcile me to my fortune. All the pleasures and enjoyments we had ever had—*they* seemed so poor and insignificant, I hated them. I could have trodden on them. And I could think of nothing else, except our being poor, and the number of mouths there were at home."

"Well, well, my dear," said Mr. Tetterby, shaking her hand encouragingly, "that's truth, after all. We *are* poor, and there *are* a number of mouths at home here."

"Ah! but, Dolf, Dolf!" cried his wife, laying her hands upon his neck, "my good, kind, patient fellow, when I had been at home a very little while—how different! Oh, Dolf, dear, how different it was! I felt as if there was a rush of recollection on me, all at once, that softened my hard heart, and filled it up till it was bursting. All our struggles for a livelihood, all our cares and wants since we have been married, all the times of sickness, all the hours of watching, we have ever had, by one another, or by the children, seemed to speak to me, and say that they had made us one, and that I never might have been, or could have been, or would have been, any other than the wife and mother I am. Then, the cheap enjoyments that I could have trodden on so cruelly, got to be so precious to me—oh, so priceless, and dear!—that I couldn't bear to think how much I had wronged them; and I said, and say again a hundred times, how could I ever behave so, 'Dolphus, how could I ever have the heart to do it!"

The good woman, quite carried away by her honest tenderness and remorse, was weeping with all her heart, when she started up with a scream, and ran behind her husband. Her cry was so terrified, that the children started from their sleep and from their beds, and clung about her. Nor did her gaze belie her voice, as she pointed to a pale man in a black cloak who had come into the room.

"Look at that man! Look there! What does he want?"

"My dear," returned her husband, "I'll ask him if you'll let me go. What's the matter! How you shake!"

"I saw him in the street, when I was out just now. He looked at me, and stood near me. I am afraid of him."

"Afraid of him! Why?"

"I don't know why—I—stop! husband!" for he was going towards the stranger.

She had one hand pressed upon her forehead, and one upon her breast; and there was a peculiar fluttering all over her, and a hurried unsteady motion of her eyes, as if she had lost something.

"Are you ill, my dear?"

"What is it that is going from me again?" she muttered, in a low voice. "What *is* this that is going away?"

Then she abruptly answered: "Ill? No, I am quite well," and stood looking vacantly at the floor.

Her husband, who had not been altogether free from the infection of her fear at first, and whom the present strangeness of her manner did not tend to reassure, addressed himself to the pale visitor in the black cloak, who stood still, and whose eyes were bent upon the ground.

"What may be your pleasure, sir," he asked, "with us?"

"I fear that my coming in unperceived," returned the visitor, "has alarmed you; but you were talking and did not hear me."

"My little woman says—perhaps you heard her say it," returned Mr. Tetterby, "that it's not the first time you have alarmed her to-night."

"I am sorry for it. I remember to have observed her, for a few moments only, in the street. I had no intention of frightening her."

As he raised his eyes in speaking, she raised hers. It was extraordinary to see what dread she had of him, and with what dread he observed it—and yet how narrowly and closely.

"My name," he said, "is Redlaw. I come from the old college hard by. A young gentleman who is a student there, lodges in your house, does he not?"

"Mr. Denham?" said Tetterby.

"Yes."

It was a natural action, and so slight as to be hardly noticeable; but the little man, before speaking again, passed his hand across his forehead, and looked quickly round the room, as though he were sensible of some change in its atmosphere. The Chemist, instantly transferring to him the look of dread he had directed towards the wife, stepped back, and his face turned paler.

"The gentleman's room," said Tetterby, "is upstairs, sir. There's a more convenient private entrance; but as you have come in here, it will save your going out into the cold, if you'll take this little staircase," showing one communicating directly with the parlour, "and go up to him that way, if you wish to see him."

"Yes, I wish to see him," said the Chemist. "Can you spare a light?"

The watchfulness of his haggard look, and the inexplicable distrust that darkened it, seemed to trouble Mr. Tetterby. He paused; and looking fixedly at him in return, stood for a minute or so, like a man stupefied, or fascinated.

At length he said, "I'll light you, sir, if you'll follow me."

"No," replied the Chemist, "I don't wish to be attended, or announced to him. He does not expect me. I would rather go alone. Please to give me the light, if you can spare it, and I'll find the way."

In the quickness of his expression of this desire, and in taking the candle from the newsman, he touched him on the breast. Withdrawing his hand hastily, almost as though he had wounded him by accident (for he did not know in what part of himself his new power resided, or how it was communicated, or how the manner of its reception varied in different persons), he turned and ascended the stair.

But when he reached the top, he stopped and looked down. The wife was standing in the same place, twisting her ring round and round upon her finger. The husband, with his head bent forward on his breast, was musing heavily and sullenly. The children, still clustering about the mother, gazed timidly after the visitor, and nestled together when they saw him looking down.

"Come!" said the father, roughly. "There's enough of this. Get to bed here!"

"The place is inconvenient and small enough," the mother added, "without you. Get to bed!"

The whole brood, scared and sad, crept away; little Johnny and the baby lagging last. The mother, glancing contemptuously round the sordid room, and tossing from her the fragments of their meal, stopped on the threshold of her task of clearing the table, and sat down, pondering idly and dejectedly. The father betook himself to the chimney-corner, and impatiently raking the small fire together, bent over it as if he would monopolise it all. They did not interchange a word.

The Chemist, paler than before, stole upward like a thief; looking back upon the change below, and dreading equally to go on or return.

"What have I done!" he said, confusedly. "What am I going to do!"

"To be the benefactor of mankind," he thought he heard a voice reply.

He looked round, but there was nothing there; and a passage now shutting out the little parlour from his view, he went on, directing his eyes before him at the way he went.

"It is only since last night," he muttered gloomily, "that I have remained shut up, and yet all things are strange to me. I am strange to myself. I am here, as in a dream. What interest have I in this place, or in any place that I can bring to my remembrance? My mind is going blind!"

There was a door before him, and he knocked at it. Being invited, by a voice within, to enter, he complied.

"Is that my kind nurse?" said the voice. "But I need not ask her. There is no one else to come here."

It spoke cheerfully, though in a languid tone, and attracted his attention to a young man lying on a couch, drawn before the chimney-piece, with the back towards the door. A meagre scanty stove, pinched and hollowed like a sick man's cheeks, and bricked into the centre of a hearth that it could scarcely warm, contained the fire, to which his face was turned. Being so near the windy house-top, it wasted quickly, and with a busy sound, and the burning ashes dropped down fast.

"They chink when they shoot out here," said the student, smiling, "so, according to the gossips, they are not coffins, but purses. I shall be well and rich yet, some day, if it please God, and shall live perhaps to love a daughter Milly, in remembrance of the kindest nature and the gentlest heart in the world."

He put up his hand as if expecting her to take it, but, being weakened, he lay still, with his face resting on his other hand, and did not turn round.

The Chemist glanced about the room;—at the student's books and papers, piled upon a table in a corner, where they, and his extinguished reading-lamp, now prohibited and put away, told of the attentive hours that had gone before this illness, and perhaps caused it;—at such signs of his old health and freedom, as the out-of-door attire that hung idle on the wall;—at those remembrances of other and less solitary scenes, the little miniatures upon the chimney-piece, and the drawing of home;—at that token of his emulation, perhaps, in some sort, of his personal attachment too, the framed engraving of himself, the looker-on. The time had been, only yesterday, when not one of these objects, in its remotest association of interest with the living figure before him, would have been lost on Redlaw. Now, they were but objects; or, if any gleam of such connexion shot upon him, it perplexed, and not enlightened him, as he stood looking round with a dull wonder.

The student, recalling the thin hand which had remained so long untouched, raised himself on the couch, and turned his head.

"Mr. Redlaw!" he exclaimed, and started up.

Redlaw put out his arm.

"Don't come nearer to me. I will sit here. Remain you, where you are!"

He sat down on a chair near the door, and having glanced at the young man standing leaning with his hand upon the couch, spoke with his eyes averted towards the ground.

"I heard, by an accident, by what accident is no matter, that one of my class was ill and solitary. I received no other description of him, than that he lived in this street. Beginning my inquiries at the first house in it, I have found him."

"I have been ill, sir," returned the student, not merely with a modest hesitation, but with a kind of awe of him, "but am greatly better. An attack of fever—of the brain, I believe—has weakened me, but I am much better. I cannot say I have been solitary, in my illness, or I should forget the ministering hand that has been near me."

"You are speaking of the keeper's wife," said Redlaw.

"Yes." The student bent his head, as if he rendered her some silent homage.

The Chemist, in whom there was a cold, monotonous apathy, which rendered him more like a marble image on the tomb of the man who had started from his dinner yesterday at the first mention of this student's case, than the breathing man himself, glanced again at the student leaning with his hand upon the couch, and looked upon the ground, and in the air, as if for light for his blinded mind.

"I remembered your name," he said, "when it was mentioned to me down stairs, just now; and I recollect your face. We have held but very little personal communication together?"

"Very little."

"You have retired and withdrawn from me, more than any of the rest, I think?"

The student signified assent.

"And why?" said the Chemist; not with the least expression of interest, but with a moody, wayward kind of curiosity. "Why? How comes it that you have sought to keep especially from me, the knowledge of your remaining here, at this season, when all the rest have dispersed, and of your being ill? I want to know why this is?"

The young man, who had heard him with increasing agitation, raised his downcast eyes to his face, and clasping his hands together, cried with sudden earnestness and with trembling lips:

"Mr. Redlaw! You have discovered me. You know my secret!"

"Secret?" said the Chemist, harshly. "*I* know?"

"Yes! Your manner, so different from the interest and sympathy which endear you to so many hearts, your altered voice, the constraint there is in everything you say, and in your looks," replied the student, "warn me that you know me. That you would conceal it, even now, is but a proof to me (God knows I need none!) of your natural kindness and of the bar there is between us."

A vacant and contemptuous laugh, was all his answer.

"But, Mr. Redlaw," said the student, "as a just man, and a good man, think how innocent I am, except in name and descent, of participation in any wrong inflicted on you or in any sorrow you have borne."

"Sorrow!" said Redlaw, laughing. "Wrong! What are those to me?"

"For Heaven's sake," entreated the shrinking student, "do not let the mere interchange of a few words with me change you like this, sir! Let me pass again from your knowledge and notice. Let me occupy my old reserved and distant place among those whom you instruct. Know me only by the name I have assumed, and not by that of Longford—"

"Longford!" exclaimed the other.

He clasped his head with both his hands, and for a moment turned upon the young man his own intelligent and thoughtful face. But the light passed from it, like the sunbeam of an instant, and it clouded as before.

"The name my mother bears, sir," faltered the young man, "the name she took, when she might, perhaps, have taken one more honoured. Mr. Redlaw," hesitating,

"I believe I know that history. Where my information halts, my guesses at what is wanting may supply something not remote from the truth. I am the child of a marriage that has not proved itself a well-assorted or a happy one. From infancy, I have heard you spoken of with honour and respect—with something that was almost reverence. I have heard of such devotion, of such fortitude and tenderness, of such rising up against the obstacles which press men down, that my fancy, since I learnt my little lesson from my mother, has shed a lustre on your name. At last, a poor student myself, from whom could I learn but you?"

Redlaw, unmoved, unchanged, and looking at him with a staring frown, answered by no word or sign.

"I cannot say," pursued the other, "I should try in vain to say, how much it has impressed me, and affected me, to find the gracious traces of the past, in that certain power of winning gratitude and confidence which is associated among us students (among the humblest of us, most) with Mr. Redlaw's generous name. Our ages and positions are so different, sir, and I am so accustomed to regard you from a distance, that I wonder at my own presumption when I touch, however lightly, on that theme. But to one who—I may say, who felt no common interest in my mother once—it may be something to hear, now that all is past, with what indescribable feelings of affection I have, in my obscurity, regarded him; with what pain and reluctance I have kept aloof from his encouragement, when a word of it would have made me rich; yet how I have felt it fit that I should hold my course, content to know him, and to be unknown. Mr. Redlaw," said the student, faintly, "what I would have said, I have said ill, for my strength is strange to me as yet; but for anything unworthy in this fraud of mine, forgive me, and for all the rest forget me!"

The staring frown remained on Redlaw's face, and yielded to no other expression until the student, with these words, advanced towards him, as if to touch his hand, when he drew back and cried to him:

"Don't come nearer to me!"

The young man stopped, shocked by the eagerness of his recoil, and by the sternness of his repulsion; and he passed his hand, thoughtfully, across his forehead.

"The past is past," said the Chemist. "It dies like the brutes. Who talks to me of its traces in my life? He raves or lies! What have I to do with your distempered dreams? If you want money, here it is. I came to offer it; and that is all I came for. There can be nothing else that brings me here," he muttered, holding his head again, with both his hands. "There *can* be nothing else, and yet—"

He had tossed his purse upon the table. As he fell into this dim cogitation with himself, the student took it up, and held it out to him.

"Take it back, sir," he said proudly, though not angrily. "I wish you could take from me, with it, the remembrance of your words and offer."

"You do?" he retorted, with a wild light in his eyes. "You do?"

"I do!"

The Chemist went close to him, for the first time, and took the purse, and turned him by the arm, and looked him in the face.

"There is sorrow and trouble in sickness, is there not?" he demanded, with a laugh.

The wondering student answered, "Yes."

"In its unrest, in its anxiety, in its suspense, in all its train of physical and mental miseries?" said the Chemist, with a wild unearthly exultation. "All best forgotten, are they not?"

The student did not answer, but again passed his hand, confusedly, across his forehead. Redlaw still held him by the sleeve, when Milly's voice was heard outside.

"I can see very well now," she said, "thank you, Dolf. Don't cry, dear. Father and mother will be comfortable again, to-morrow, and home will be comfortable too. A gentleman with him, is there!"

Redlaw released his hold, as he listened.

"I have feared, from the first moment," he murmured to himself, "to meet her. There is a steady quality of goodness in her, that I dread to influence. I may be the murderer of what is tenderest and best within her bosom."

She was knocking at the door.

"Shall I dismiss it as an idle foreboding, or still avoid her?" he muttered, looking uneasily around.

She was knocking at the door again.

"Of all the visitors who could come here," he said, in a hoarse alarmed voice, turning to his companion, "this is the one I should desire most to avoid. Hide me!"

The student opened a frail door in the wall, communicating where the garret-roof began to slope towards the floor, with a small inner room. Redlaw passed in hastily, and shut it after him.

The student then resumed his place upon the couch, and called to her to enter.

"Dear Mr. Edmund," said Milly, looking round, "they told me there was a gentleman here."

"There is no one here but I."

"There has been some one?"

"Yes, yes, there has been some one."

She put her little basket on the table, and went up to the back of the couch, as if to take the extended hand—but it was not there. A little surprised, in her quiet way, she leaned over to look at his face, and gently touched him on the brow.

"Are you quite as well to-night? Your head is not so cool as in the afternoon."

"Tut!" said the student, petulantly, "very little ails me."

A little more surprise, but no reproach, was expressed in her face, as she withdrew to the other side of the table, and took a small packet of needlework from her basket. But she laid it down again, on second thoughts, and going noiselessly about the room, set everything exactly in its place, and in the neatest order; even to the cushions on the couch, which she touched with so light a hand, that he hardly seemed to know it, as he lay looking at the fire. When all this was done, and she had swept the hearth, she sat down, in her modest little bonnet, to her work, and was quietly busy on it directly.

"It's the new muslin curtain for the window, Mr. Edmund," said Milly, stitching away as she talked. "It will look very clean and nice, though it costs very little, and will save your eyes, too, from the light. My William says the room should not be too light just now, when you are recovering so well, or the glare might make you giddy."

He said nothing; but there was something so fretful and impatient in his change of position, that her quick fingers stopped, and she looked at him anxiously.

"The pillows are not comfortable," she said, laying down her work and rising. "I will soon put them right."

"They are very well," he answered. "Leave them alone, pray. You make so much of everything."

He raised his head to say this, and looked at her so thanklessly, that, after he had thrown himself down again, she stood timidly pausing. However, she resumed her seat, and her needle, without having directed even a murmuring look towards him, and was soon as busy as before.

"I have been thinking, Mr. Edmund, that *you* have been often thinking of late, when I have been sitting by, how true the saying is, that adversity is a good teacher. Health will be more precious to you, after this illness, than it has ever been. And years hence, when this time of year comes round, and you remember the days when you lay here sick, alone, that the knowledge of your illness might not afflict those who are dearest to you, your home will be doubly dear and doubly blest. Now, isn't that a good, true thing?"

She was too intent upon her work, and too earnest in what she said, and too composed and quiet altogether, to be on the watch for any look he might direct towards her in reply; so the shaft of his ungrateful glance fell harmless, and did not wound her.

"Ah!" said Milly, with her pretty head inclining thoughtfully on one side, as she looked down, following her busy fingers with her eyes. "Even on me—and I am very different from you, Mr. Edmund, for I have no learning, and don't know how to think properly—this view of such things has made a great impression, since you have been lying ill. When I have seen you so touched by the kindness and attention of the poor people down-stairs, I have felt that you thought even that experience some repayment for the loss of health, and I have read in your face, as plain as if it was a book, that but for some trouble and sorrow we should never know half the good there is about us."

His getting up from the couch, interrupted her, or she was going on to say more.

"We needn't magnify the merit, Mrs. William," he rejoined slightingly. "The people down-stairs will be paid in good time I dare say, for any little extra service they may have rendered me; and perhaps they anticipate no less. I am much obliged to you, too."

Her fingers stopped, and she looked at him.

"I can't be made to feel the more obliged by your exaggerating the case," he said. "I am sensible that you have been interested in me, and I say I am much obliged to you. What more would you have?"

Her work fell on her lap, as she still looked at him walking to and fro with an intolerant air, and stopping now and then.

"I say again, I am much obliged to you. Why weaken my sense of what is your due in obligation, by preferring enormous claims upon me? Trouble, sorrow, affliction, adversity! One might suppose I had been dying a score of deaths here!"

"Do you believe, Mr. Edmund," she asked, rising and going nearer to him, "that I spoke of the poor people of the house, with any reference to myself? To me?" laying her hand upon her bosom with a simple and innocent smile of astonishment.

"Oh! I think nothing about it, my good creature," he returned. "I have had an indisposition, which your solicitude—observe! I say solicitude—makes a great deal more of, than it merits; and it's over, and we can't perpetuate it."

He coldly took a book, and sat down at the table.

She watched him for a little while, until her smile was quite gone, and then, returning to where her basket was, said gently:

"Mr. Edmund, would you rather be alone?"

"There is no reason why I should detain you here," he replied.

"Except—" said Milly, hesitating, and showing her work.

"Oh! the curtain," he answered, with a supercilious laugh. "That's not worth staying for."

She made up the little packet again, and put it in her basket. Then, standing before him with such an air of patient entreaty that he could not choose but look at her, she said:

"If you should want me, I will come back willingly. When you did want me, I was quite happy to come; there was no merit in it. I think you must be afraid, that, now you are getting well, I may be troublesome to you; but I should not have been, indeed. I should have come no longer than your weakness and confinement lasted. You owe me nothing; but it is right that you should deal as justly by me as if I was a lady—even the very lady that you love; and if you suspect me of meanly making much of the little I have tried to do to comfort your sick room, you do yourself more wrong than ever you can do me. That is why I am sorry. That is why I am very sorry."

If she had been as passionate as she was quiet, as indignant as she was calm, as angry in her look as she was gentle, as loud of tone as she was low and clear, she might have left no sense of her departure in the room, compared with that which fell upon the lonely student when she went away.

He was gazing drearily upon the place where she had been, when Redlaw came out of his concealment, and came to the door.

"When sickness lays its hand on you again," he said, looking fiercely back at him, "—may it be soon!—Die here! Rot here!"

"What have you done?" returned the other, catching at his cloak. "What change have you wrought in me? What curse have you brought upon me? Give me back myself!"

"Give me back *my*self!" exclaimed Redlaw like a madman. "I am infected! I am infectious! I am charged with poison for my own mind, and the minds of all mankind. Where I felt interest, compassion, sympathy, I am turning into stone. Selfishness and ingratitude spring up in my blighting footsteps. I am only so much less base than the wretches whom I make so, that in the moment of their transformation I can hate them."

As he spoke—the young man still holding to his cloak—he cast him off, and struck him: then, wildly hurried out into the night air where the wind was blowing, the snow falling, the cloud-drift sweeping on, the moon dimly shining; and where, blowing in the wind, falling with the snow, drifting with the clouds, shining in the moonlight, and heavily looming in the darkness, were the Phantom's words, "The gift that I have given, you shall give again, go where you will!"

Whither he went, he neither knew nor cared, so that he avoided company. The change he felt within him made the busy streets a desert, and himself a desert, and the multitude around him, in their manifold endurances and ways of life, a mighty waste of sand, which the winds tossed into unintelligible heaps and made a ruinous confusion of. Those traces in his breast which the Phantom had told him would "die out soon," were not, as yet, so far upon their way to death, but that he understood enough of what he was, and what he made of others, to desire to be alone.

This put it in his mind—he suddenly bethought himself, as he was going along, of the boy who had rushed into his room. And then he recollected, that of those with whom he had communicated since the Phantom's disappearance, that boy alone had shown no sign of being changed.

Monstrous and odious as the wild thing was to him, he determined to seek it out, and prove if this were really so; and also to seek it with another intention, which came into his thoughts at the same time.

So, resolving with some difficulty where he was, he directed his steps back to the old college, and to that part of it where the general porch was, and where, alone, the pavement was worn by the tread of the students' feet.

The keeper's house stood just within the iron gates, forming a part of the chief quadrangle. There was a little cloister outside, and from that sheltered place he knew he could look in at the window of their ordinary room, and see who was within. The iron gates were shut, but his hand was familiar with the fastening, and drawing it back by thrusting in his wrist between the bars, he passed through softly, shut it again, and crept up to the window, crumbling the thin crust of snow with his feet.

The fire, to which he had directed the boy last night, shining brightly through the glass, made an illuminated place upon the ground. Instinctively avoiding this, and going round it, he looked in at the window. At first, he thought that there was no one there, and that the blaze was reddening only the old beams in the ceiling and the dark walls; but peering in more narrowly, he saw the object of his search coiled asleep before it on the floor. He passed quickly to the door, opened it, and went in.

The creature lay in such a fiery heat, that, as the Chemist stooped to rouse him, it scorched his head. So soon as he was touched, the boy, not half awake, clutching his rags together with the instinct of flight upon him, half rolled and half ran into a distant corner of the room, where, heaped upon the ground, he struck his foot out to defend himself.

"Get up!" said the Chemist. "You have not forgotten me?"

"You let me alone!" returned the boy. "This is the woman's house—not yours."

The Chemist's steady eye controlled him somewhat, or inspired him with enough submission to be raised upon his feet, and looked at.

"Who washed them, and put those bandages where they were bruised and cracked?" asked the Chemist, pointing to their altered state.

"The woman did."

"And is it she who has made you cleaner in the face, too?"

"Yes, the woman."

Redlaw asked these questions to attract his eyes towards himself, and with the same intent now held him by the chin, and threw his wild hair back, though he loathed to touch him. The boy watched his eyes keenly, as if he thought it needful to his own defence, not knowing what he might do next; and Redlaw could see well that no change came over him.

"Where are they?" he inquired.

"The woman's out."

"I know she is. Where is the old man with the white hair, and his son?"

"The woman's husband, d'ye mean?" inquired the boy.

"Aye. Where are those two?"

"Out. Something's the matter, somewhere. They were fetched out in a hurry, and told me to stop here."

"Come with me," said the Chemist, "and I'll give you money."

"Come where? and how much will you give?"

"I'll give you more shillings than you ever saw, and bring you back soon. Do you know your way to where you came from?"

"You let me go," returned the boy, suddenly twisting out of his grasp. "I'm not a going to take you there. Let me be, or I'll heave some fire at you!"

He was down before it, and ready, with his savage little hand, to pluck the burning coals out.

What the Chemist had felt, in observing the effect of his charmed influence stealing over those with whom he came in contact, was not nearly equal to the cold vague terror with which he saw this baby-monster put it at defiance. It chilled his blood to look on the immovable impenetrable thing, in the likeness of a child, with its sharp malignant face turned up to his, and its almost infant hand, ready at the bars.

"Listen, boy!" he said. "You shall take me where you please, so that you take me where the people are very miserable or very wicked. I want to do them good, and not to harm them. You shall have money, as I have told you, and I will bring you back. Get up! Come quickly!" He made a hasty step towards the door, afraid of her returning.

"Will you let me walk by myself, and never hold me, nor yet touch me?" said the boy, slowly withdrawing the hand with which he threatened, and beginning to get up.

"I will!"

"And let me go, before, behind, or anyways I like?"

"I will!"

"Give me some money first then, and go."

The Chemist laid a few shillings, one by one, in his extended hand. To count them was beyond the boy's knowledge, but he said "one," every time, and avariciously looked at each as it was given, and at the donor. He had nowhere to put them, out of his hand, but in his mouth; and he put them there.

Redlaw then wrote with his pencil on a leaf of his pocket-book, that the boy was with him; and laying it on the table, signed to him to follow. Keeping his rags together, as usual, the boy complied, and went out with his bare head and naked feet into the winter night.

Preferring not to depart by the iron gate by which he had entered, where they were in danger of meeting her whom he so anxiously avoided, the Chemist led the way, through some of those passages among which the boy had lost himself, and by that portion of the building where he lived, to a small door of which he had the key. When they got into the street, he stopped to ask his guide—who instantly retreated from him—if he knew where they were.

The savage thing looked here and there, and at length, nodding his head, pointed in the direction he designed to take. Redlaw going on at once, he followed, something less suspiciously; shifting his money from his mouth into his hand, and back again into his mouth, and stealthily rubbing it bright upon his shreds of clothes, as he went along.

Three times, in their progress, they were side by side. Three times they stopped, being side by side. Three times the Chemist glanced down at his face, and shuddered as it forced upon him one reflection.

The first occasion was when they were crossing an old churchyard, and Redlaw stopped among the graves, utterly at a loss how to connect them with any tender, softening, or consolatory thought.

The second was, when the breaking forth of the moon induced him to look up at the Heavens, where he saw her in her glory, surrounded by a host of stars he still knew by the names and histories which human science has appended to them; but where he saw nothing else he had been wont to see, felt nothing he had been wont to feel, in looking up there, on a bright night.

The third was when he stopped to listen to a plaintive strain of music, but could only hear a tune, made manifest to him by the dry mechanism of the instruments and his own ears, with no address to any mystery within him, without a whisper in it of the past, or of the future, powerless upon him as the sound of last year's running water, or the rushing of last year's wind.

At each of these three times, he saw with horror that, in spite of the vast intellectual distance between them, and their being unlike each other in all physical respects, the expression on the boy's face was the expression on his own.

They journeyed on for some time—now through such crowded places, that he often looked over his shoulder thinking he had lost his guide, but generally finding him within his shadow on his other side; now by ways so quiet, that he could have counted his short, quick, naked footsteps coming on behind—until they arrived at a ruinous collection of houses, and the boy touched him and stopped.

"In there!" he said, pointing out one house where there were shattered lights in the windows, and a dim lantern in the doorway, with "Lodgings for Travellers" painted on it.

Redlaw looked about him; from the houses to the waste piece of ground on which the houses stood, or rather did not altogether tumble down, unfenced, undrained, unlighted, and bordered by a sluggish ditch; from that, to the sloping line of arches, part of some neighbouring viaduct or bridge with which it was surrounded, and which lessened gradually towards them, until the last but one was a mere kennel for a dog, the last a plundered little heap of bricks; from that, to the child, close to him, cowering and trembling with the cold, and limping on one little foot, while he coiled the other round his leg to warm it, yet staring at all these things with that frightful likeness of expression so apparent in his face, that Redlaw started from him.

"In there!" said the boy, pointing out the house again. "I'll wait."

"Will they let me in?" asked Redlaw.

"Say you're a doctor," he answered with a nod. "There's plenty ill here."

Looking back on his way to the house-door, Redlaw saw him trail himself upon the dust and crawl within the shelter of the smallest arch, as if he were a rat. He had no pity for the thing, but he was afraid of it; and when it looked out of its den at him, he hurried to the house as a retreat.

"Sorrow, wrong, and trouble," said the Chemist, with a painful effort at some more distinct remembrance, "at least haunt this place darkly. He can do no harm, who brings forgetfulness of such things here!"

With these words, he pushed the yielding door, and went in.

There was a woman sitting on the stairs, either asleep or forlorn, whose head was bent down on her hands and knees. As it was not easy to pass without treading on her, and as she was perfectly regardless of his near approach, he stopped, and touched her on the shoulder. Looking up, she showed him quite a young face, but one whose bloom and promise were all swept away, as if the haggard winter should unnaturally kill the spring.

With little or no show of concern on his account, she moved nearer to the wall to leave him a wider passage.

"What are you?" said Redlaw, pausing, with his hand upon the broken stair-rail.

"What do you think I am?" she answered, showing him her face again.

He looked upon the ruined Temple of God, so lately made, so soon disfigured; and something, which was not compassion—for the springs in which a true compassion for such miseries has its rise, were dried up in his breast—but which was nearer to it, for the moment, than any feeling that had lately struggled into the darkening, but not yet wholly darkened, night of his mind—mingled a touch of softness with his next words.

"I am come here to give relief, if I can," he said. "Are you thinking of any wrong?"

She frowned at him, and then laughed; and then her laugh prolonged itself into a shivering sigh, as she dropped her head again, and hid her fingers in her hair.

"Are you thinking of a wrong?" he asked once more.

"I am thinking of my life," she said, with a momentary look at him.

He had a perception that she was one of many, and that he saw the type of thousands, when he saw her, drooping at his feet.

"What are your parents?" he demanded.

"I had a good home once. My father was a gardener, far away, in the country."

"Is he dead?"

"He's dead to me. All such things are dead to me. You a gentleman, and not know that!" She raised her eyes again, and laughed at him.

"Girl!" said Redlaw, sternly, "before this death, of all such things, was brought about, was there no wrong done to you? In spite of all that you can do, does no remembrance of wrong cleave to you? Are there not times upon times when it is misery to you?"

So little of what was womanly was left in her appearance, that now, when she burst into tears, he stood amazed. But he was more amazed, and much disquieted, to note that in her awakened recollection of this wrong, the first trace of her old humanity and frozen tenderness appeared to show itself.

He drew a little off, and in doing so, observed that her arms were black, her face cut, and her bosom bruised.

"What brutal hand has hurt you so?" he asked.

"My own. I did it myself!" she answered quickly.

"It is impossible."

"I'll swear I did! He didn't touch me. I did it to myself in a passion, and threw myself down here. He wasn't near me. He never laid a hand upon me!"

In the white determination of her face, confronting him with this untruth, he saw enough of the last perversion and distortion of good surviving in that miserable breast, to be stricken with remorse that he had ever come near her.

"Sorrow, wrong, and trouble!" he muttered, turning his fearful gaze away. "All that connects her with the state from which she has fallen, has those roots! In the name of God, let me go by!"

Afraid to look at her again, afraid to touch her, afraid to think of having sundered the last thread by which she held upon the mercy of Heaven, he gathered his cloak about him, and glided swiftly up the stairs.

Opposite to him, on the landing, was a door, which stood partly open, and which, as he ascended, a man with a candle in his hand, came forward from within to shut. But this man, on seeing him, drew back, with much emotion in his manner, and, as if by a sudden impulse, mentioned his name aloud.

In the surprise of such a recognition there, he stopped, endeavouring to recollect the wan and startled face. He had no time to consider it, for, to his yet greater amazement, old Philip came out of the room, and took him by the hand.

"Mr. Redlaw," said the old man, "this is like you, this is like you, sir! you have heard of it, and have come after us to render any help you can. Ah, too late, too late!"

Redlaw, with a bewildered look, submitted to be led into the room. A man lay there, on a truckle-bed, and William Swidger stood at the bedside.

"Too late!" murmured the old man, looking wistfully into the Chemist's face; and the tears stole down his cheeks.

"That's what I say, father," interposed his son in a low voice. "That's where it is, exactly. To keep as quiet as ever we can while he's a-dozing, is the only thing to do. You're right, father!"

Redlaw paused at the bedside, and looked down on the figure that was stretched upon the mattress. It was that of a man, who should have been in the vigour of his life, but on whom it was not likely the sun would ever shine again. The vices of his forty or fifty years' career had so branded him, that, in comparison with their effects upon his face, the heavy hand of time upon the old man's face who watched him had been merciful and beautifying.

"Who is this?" asked the Chemist, looking round.

"My son George, Mr. Redlaw," said the old man, wringing his hands. "My eldest son, George, who was more his mother's pride than all the rest!"

Redlaw's eyes wandered from the old man's grey head, as he laid it down upon the bed, to the person who had recognised him, and who had kept aloof, in the remotest corner of the room. He seemed to be about his own age; and although he knew no such hopeless decay and broken man as he appeared to be, there was something in the turn of his figure, as he stood with his back towards him, and now went out at the door, that made him pass his hand uneasily across his brow.

"William," he said in a gloomy whisper, "who is that man?"

"Why you see, sir," returned Mr. William, "that's what I say, myself. Why should a man ever go and gamble, and the like of that, and let himself down inch by inch till he can't let himself down any lower!"

"Has *he* done so?" asked Redlaw, glancing after him with the same uneasy action as before.

"Just exactly that, sir," returned William Swidger, "as I'm told. He knows a little about medicine, sir, it seems; and having been wayfaring towards London with my unhappy brother that you see here," Mr. William passed his coat-sleeve across his eyes, "and being lodging up-stairs for the night—what I say, you see, is that strange companions come together here sometimes—he looked in to attend upon him, and came for us at his request. What a mournful spectacle, sir! But that's where it is. It's enough to kill my father!"

Redlaw looked up, at these words, and, recalling where he was and with whom, and the spell he carried with him—which his surprise had obscured—retired a little, hurriedly, debating with himself whether to shun the house that moment, or remain.

Yielding to a certain sullen doggedness, which it seemed to be a part of his condition to struggle with, he argued for remaining.

"Was it only yesterday," he said, "when I observed the memory of this old man to be a tissue of sorrow and trouble, and shall I be afraid, to-night, to shake it? Are such remembrances as I can drive away, so precious to this dying man that I need fear for *him*? No! I'll stay here."

But he stayed in fear and trembling none the less for these words; and, shrouded in his black cloak with his face turned from them, stood away from the bedside, listening to what they said, as if he felt himself a demon in the place.

"Father!" murmured the sick man, rallying a little from stupor.

"My boy! My son George!" said old Philip.

"You spoke, just now, of my being mother's favourite, long ago. It's a dreadful thing to think now, of long ago!"

"No, no, no!" returned the old man. "Think of it. Don't say it's dreadful. It's not dreadful to me, my son."

"It cuts you to the heart, father." For the old man's tears were falling on him.

"Yes, yes," said Philip, "so it does; but it does me good. It's a heavy sorrow to think of that time, but it does me good, George. Oh, think of it too, think of it too, and your heart will be softened more and more! Where's my son William? William, my boy, your mother loved him dearly to the last, and with her latest breath said, 'Tell him I forgave him, blessed him, and prayed for him.' Those were her words to me. I have never forgotten them, and I'm eighty-seven!"

"Father!" said the man upon the bed, "I am dying, I know. I am so far gone, that I can hardly speak, even of what my mind most runs on. Is there any hope for me beyond this bed?"

"There is hope," returned the old man, "for all who are softened and penitent. There is hope for all such. Oh!" he exclaimed, clasping his hands and looking up, "I was thankful, only yesterday, that I could remember this unhappy son when he was an innocent child. But what a comfort it is, now, to think that even God himself has that remembrance of him!"

Redlaw spread his hands upon his face, and shrank, like a murderer.

"Ah!" feebly moaned the man upon the bed. "The waste since then, the waste of life since then!"

"But he was a child once," said the old man. "He played with children. Before he lay down on his bed at night, and fell into his guiltless rest, he said his prayers at his poor mother's knee. I have seen him do it, many a time; and seen her lay his head upon her breast, and kiss him. Sorrowful as it was to her and me, to think of this, when he went so wrong, and when our hopes and plans for him were all broken, this gave him still a hold upon us, that nothing else could have given. Oh, Father, so much better than the fathers upon earth! Oh, Father, so much more afflicted by the errors of thy children! take this wanderer back! Not as he is, but as he was then, let him cry to thee, as he has so often seemed to cry to us!"

As the old man lifted up his trembling hands, the son, for whom he made the supplication, laid his sinking head against him for support and comfort, as if he were indeed the child of whom he spoke.

When did man ever tremble, as Redlaw trembled, in the silence that ensued! He knew it must come upon them, knew that it was coming fast.

"My time is very short, my breath is shorter," said the sick man, supporting himself on one arm, and with the other groping in the air, "and I remember there is something on my mind concerning the man who was here just now, Father and William—wait!—is there really anything in black, out there?"

"Yes, yes, it is real," said his aged father.

"Is it a man?"

"What I say myself, George," interposed his brother, bending kindly over him. "It's Mr. Redlaw."

"I thought I had dreamed of him. Ask him to come here."

The Chemist, whiter than the dying man, appeared before him. Obedient to the motion of his hand, he sat upon the bed.

"It has been so ripped up, to-night, sir," said the sick man, laying his hand upon his heart, with a look in which the mute, imploring agony of his condition was concentrated, "by the sight of my poor old father, and the thought of all the trouble I have been the cause of, and all the wrong and sorrow lying at my door, that—"

Was it the extremity to which he had come, or was it the dawning of another change, that made him stop?

"—that what I *can* do right, with my mind running on so much, so fast, I'll try to do. There was another man here. Did you see him?"

Redlaw could not reply by any word; for when he saw that fatal sign he knew so well now, of the wandering hand upon the forehead, his voice died at his lips. But he made some indication of assent.

"He is penniless, hungry, and destitute. He is completely beaten down, and has no resource at all. Look after him! Lose no time! I know he has it in his mind to kill himself."

It was working. It was on his face. His face was changing, hardening, deepening in all its shades, and losing all its sorrow.

"Don't you remember? Don't you know him?" he pursued.

He shut his face out for a moment, with the hand that again wandered over his forehead, and then it lowered on Redlaw, reckless, ruffianly, and callous.

"Why, d—n you!" he said, scowling round, "what have you been doing to me here! I have lived bold, and I mean to die bold. To the Devil with you!"

And so lay down upon his bed, and put his arms up, over his head and ears, as resolute from that time to keep out all access, and to die in his indifference.

If Redlaw had been struck by lightning, it could not have struck him from the bedside with a more tremendous shock. But the old man, who had left the bed while his son was speaking to him, now returning, avoided it quickly likewise, and with abhorrence.

"Where's my boy William?" said the old man hurriedly. "William, come away from here. We'll go home."

"Home, father!" returned William. "Are you going to leave your own son?"

"Where's my own son?" replied the old man.

"Where? why, there!"

"That's no son of mine," said Philip, trembling with resentment. "No such wretch as that, has any claim on me. My children are pleasant to look at, and they wait upon me, and get my meat and drink ready, and are useful to me. I've a right to it! I'm eighty-seven!"

"You're old enough to be no older," muttered William, looking at him grudgingly, with his hands in his pockets. "I don't know what good you are, myself. We could have a deal more pleasure without you."

"*My* son, Mr. Redlaw!" said the old man. "*My* son, too! The boy talking to me of *my* son! Why, what has he ever done to give me any pleasure, I should like to know?"

"I don't know what you have ever done to give *me* any pleasure," said William, sulkily.

"Let me think," said the old man. "For how many Christmas times running, have I sat in my warm place, and never had to come out in the cold night air; and have made good cheer, without being disturbed by any such uncomfortable, wretched sight as him there? Is it twenty, William?"

"Nigher forty, it seems," he muttered. "Why, when I look at my father, sir, and come to think of it," addressing Redlaw, with an impatience and irritation that were quite new, "I'm whipped if I can see anything in him but a calendar of ever so many years of eating and drinking, and making himself comfortable, over and over again."

"I—I'm eighty-seven," said the old man, rambling on, childishly and weakly, "and I don't know as I ever was much put out by anything. I'm not going to begin now, because of what he calls my son. He's not my son. I've had a power of pleasant times. I recollect once—no I don't—no, it's broken off. It was something about a game of cricket and a friend of mine, but it's somehow broken off. I wonder who he was—I suppose I liked him? And I wonder what became of him—I suppose he died? But I don't know. And I don't care, neither; I don't care a bit."

In his drowsy chuckling, and the shaking of his head, he put his hands into his waistcoat pockets. In one of them he found a bit of holly (left there, probably last night), which he now took out, and looked at.

"Berries, eh?" said the old man. "Ah! It's a pity they're not good to eat. I recollect, when I was a little chap about as high as that, and out a walking with—let me see—who was I out a walking with?—no, I don't remember how that was. I don't remember as I ever walked with any one particular, or cared for any one, or any one for me. Berries, eh? There's good cheer when there's berries. Well; I ought to have my share of it, and to be waited on, and kept warm and comfortable; for I'm eighty-seven, and a poor old man. I'm eigh-ty-seven. Eigh-ty-seven!"

The drivelling, pitiable manner in which, as he repeated this, he nibbled at the leaves, and spat the morsels out; the cold, uninterested eye with which his youngest son (so changed) regarded him; the determined apathy with which his eldest son lay hardened in his sin; impressed themselves no more on Redlaw's observation,—for he broke his way from the spot to which his feet seemed to have been fixed, and ran out of the house.

His guide came crawling forth from his place of refuge, and was ready for him before he reached the arches.

"Back to the woman's?" he inquired.

"Back, quickly!" answered Redlaw. "Stop nowhere on the way!"

For a short distance the boy went on before; but their return was more like a flight than a walk, and it was as much as his bare feet could do, to keep pace with the Chemist's rapid strides. Shrinking from all who passed, shrouded in his cloak, and keeping it drawn closely about him, as though there were mortal contagion in any fluttering touch of his garments, he made no pause until they reached the door by which they had come out. He unlocked it with his key, went in, accompanied by the boy, and hastened through the dark passages to his own chamber.

The boy watched him as he made the door fast, and withdrew behind the table, when he looked round.

"Come!" he said. "Don't you touch me! You've not brought me here to take my money away."

Redlaw threw some more upon the ground. He flung his body on it immediately, as if to hide it from him, lest the sight of it should tempt him to reclaim it; and not until he saw him seated by his lamp, with his face hidden in his hands, began furtively to pick it up. When he had done so, he crept near the fire, and, sitting down in a great chair before it, took from his breast some broken scraps of food, and fell to munching, and to staring at the blaze, and now and then to glancing at his shillings, which he kept clenched up in a bunch, in one hand.

"And this," said Redlaw, gazing on him with increased repugnance and fear, "is the only one companion I have left on earth!"

How long it was before he was aroused from his contemplation of this creature, whom he dreaded so—whether half an hour, or half the night—he knew not. But the stillness of the room was broken by the boy (whom he had seen listening) starting up, and running towards the door.

"Here's the woman coming!" he exclaimed.

The Chemist stopped him on his way, at the moment when she knocked.

"Let me go to her, will you?" said the boy.

"Not now," returned the Chemist. "Stay here. Nobody must pass in or out of the room now. Who's that?"

"It's I, sir," cried Milly. "Pray, sir, let me in!"

"No! not for the world!" he said.

"Mr. Redlaw, Mr. Redlaw, pray, sir, let me in."

"What is the matter?" he said, holding the boy.

"The miserable man you saw, is worse, and nothing I can say will wake him from his terrible infatuation. William's father has turned childish in a moment. William himself is changed. The shock has been too sudden for him; I cannot understand him; he is not like himself. Oh, Mr. Redlaw, pray advise me, help me!"

"No! No! No!" he answered.

"Mr. Redlaw! Dear sir! George has been muttering, in his doze, about the man you saw there, who, he fears, will kill himself."

"Better he should do it, than come near me!"

"He says, in his wandering, that you know him; that he was your friend once, long ago; that he is the ruined father of a student here—my mind misgives me, of the young gentleman who has been ill. What is to be done? How is he to be followed? How is he to be saved? Mr. Redlaw, pray, oh, pray, advise me! Help me!"

All this time he held the boy, who was half-mad to pass him, and let her in.

"Phantoms! Punishers of impious thoughts!" cried Redlaw, gazing round in anguish, "Look upon me! From the darkness of my mind, let the glimmering of contrition that I know is there, shine up and show my misery! In the material world, as I have long taught, nothing can be spared; no step or atom in the wondrous structure could be lost, without a blank being made in the great universe. I know, now, that it is the same with good and evil, happiness and sorrow, in the memories of men. Pity me! Relieve me!"

There was no response, but her "Help me, help me, let me in!" and the boy's struggling to get to her.

"Shadow of myself! Spirit of my darker hours!" cried Redlaw, in distraction, "Come back, and haunt me day and night, but take this gift away! Or, if it must still rest with me, deprive me of the dreadful power of giving it to others. Undo what I have done. Leave me benighted, but restore the day to those whom I have cursed. As I have spared this woman from the first, and as I never will go forth again, but will die here, with no hand to tend me, save this creature's who is proof against me,—hear me!"

The only reply still was, the boy struggling to get to her, while he held him back; and the cry, increasing in its energy, "Help! let me in. He was your friend once, how shall he be followed, how shall he be saved? They are all changed, there is no one else to help me, pray, pray, let me in!"

Chapter III

The Gift Reversed

NIGHT WAS STILL HEAVY IN THE SKY. ON OPEN PLAINS, FROM HILL-TOPS, and from the decks of solitary ships at sea, a distant low-lying line, that promised by-and-by to change to light, was visible in the dim horizon; but its promise was remote and doubtful, and the moon was striving with the night-clouds busily.

The shadows upon Redlaw's mind succeeded thick and fast to one another, and obscured its light as the night-clouds hovered between the moon and earth, and kept the latter veiled in darkness. Fitful and uncertain as the shadows which the night-clouds cast, were their concealments from him, and imperfect revelations to him; and, like the night-clouds still, if the clear light broke forth for a moment, it was only that they might sweep over it, and make the darkness deeper than before.

Without, there was a profound and solemn hush upon the ancient pile of building, and its buttresses and angles made dark shapes of mystery upon the ground, which now seemed to retire into the smooth white snow and now seemed to come out of it, as the moon's path was more or less beset. Within, the Chemist's room was indistinct and murky, by the light of the expiring lamp; a ghostly silence had succeeded to the knocking and the voice outside; nothing was audible but, now and then, a low sound among the whitened ashes of the fire, as of its yielding up its last breath. Before it on the ground the boy lay fast asleep. In his chair, the Chemist sat, as he had sat there since the calling at his door had ceased—like a man turned to stone.

At such a time, the Christmas music he had heard before, began to play. He listened to it at first, as he had listened in the churchyard; but presently—it playing still, and being borne towards him on the night air, in a low, sweet, melancholy strain—he rose, and stood stretching his hands about him, as if there were some friend approaching within his reach, on whom his desolate touch might rest, yet do no harm. As he did this, his face became less fixed and wondering; a gentle trembling came upon him; and at last his eyes filled with tears, and he put his hands before them, and bowed down his head.

His memory of sorrow, wrong, and trouble, had not come back to him; he knew that it was not restored; he had no passing belief or hope that it was. But some dumb stir within him made him capable, again, of being moved by what was hidden, afar off, in the music. If it were only that it told him sorrowfully the value of what he had lost, he thanked Heaven for it with a fervent gratitude.

As the last chord died upon his ear, he raised his head to listen to its lingering vibration. Beyond the boy, so that his sleeping figure lay at its feet, the Phantom stood, immovable and silent, with its eyes upon him.

Ghastly it was, as it had ever been, but not so cruel and relentless in its aspect—or he thought or hoped so, as he looked upon it trembling. It was not alone, but in its shadowy hand it held another hand.

And whose was that? Was the form that stood beside it indeed Milly's, or but her shade and picture? The quiet head was bent a little, as her manner was, and her eyes were looking down, as if in pity, on the sleeping child. A radiant light fell on her face, but did not touch the Phantom; for, though close beside her, it was dark and colourless as ever.

"Spectre!" said the Chemist, newly troubled as he looked, "I have not been stubborn or presumptuous in respect of her. Oh, do not bring her here. Spare me that!"

"This is but a shadow," said the Phantom; "when the morning shines seek out the reality whose image I present before you."

"Is it my inexorable doom to do so?" cried the Chemist.

"It is," replied the Phantom.

"To destroy her peace, her goodness; to make her what I am myself, and what I have made of others!"

"I have said 'seek her out,'" returned the Phantom. "I have said no more."

"Oh, tell me," exclaimed Redlaw, catching at the hope which he fancied might lie hidden in the words. "Can I undo what I have done?"

"No," returned the Phantom.

"I do not ask for restoration to myself," said Redlaw. "What I abandoned, I abandoned of my own free will, and have justly lost. But for those to whom I have transferred the fatal gift; who never sought it; who unknowingly received a curse of which they had no warning, and which they had no power to shun; can I do nothing?"

"Nothing," said the Phantom.

"If I cannot, can any one?"

The Phantom, standing like a statue, kept its gaze upon him for a while; then turned its head suddenly, and looked upon the shadow at its side.

"Ah! Can she?" cried Redlaw, still looking upon the shade.

The Phantom released the hand it had retained till now, and softly raised its own with a gesture of dismissal. Upon that, her shadow, still preserving the same attitude, began to move or melt away.

"Stay," cried Redlaw with an earnestness to which he could not give enough expression. "For a moment! As an act of mercy! I know that some change fell upon me, when those sounds were in the air just now. Tell me, have I lost the power of harming her? May I go near her without dread? Oh, let her give me any sign of hope!"

The Phantom looked upon the shade as he did—not at him—and gave no answer.

"At least, say this—has she, henceforth, the consciousness of any power to set right what I have done?"

"She has not," the Phantom answered.

"Has she the power bestowed on her without the consciousness?"

The Phantom answered: "Seek her out." And her shadow slowly vanished.

They were face to face again, and looking on each other, as intently and awfully as at the time of the bestowal of the gift, across the boy who still lay on the ground between them, at the Phantom's feet.

"Terrible instructor," said the Chemist, sinking on his knee before it, in an attitude of supplication, "by whom I was renounced, but by whom I am revisited (in which, and in whose milder aspect, I would fain believe I have a gleam of hope), I will obey without inquiry, praying that the cry I have sent up in the anguish of my soul has been, or will be, heard, in behalf of those whom I have injured beyond human reparation. But there is one thing—"

"You speak to me of what is lying here," the Phantom interposed, and pointed with its finger to the boy.

"I do," returned the Chemist. "You know what I would ask. Why has this child alone been proof against my influence, and why, why, have I detected in its thoughts a terrible companionship with mine?"

"This," said the Phantom, pointing to the boy, "is the last, completest illustration of a human creature, utterly bereft of such remembrances as you have yielded up. No softening memory of sorrow, wrong, or trouble enters here, because this wretched mortal from his birth has been abandoned to a worse condition than the beasts, and has, within his knowledge, no one contrast, no humanising touch, to make a grain of such a memory spring up in his hardened breast. All within this desolate creature is barren wilderness. All within the man bereft of what you have resigned, is the same barren wilderness. Woe to such a man! Woe, tenfold, to the nation that shall count its monsters such as this, lying here, by hundreds and by thousands!"

Redlaw shrank, appalled, from what he heard

"There is not," said the Phantom, "one of these—not one—but sows a harvest that mankind MUST REAP. From every seed of evil in this boy, a field of ruin is grown that shall be gathered in, and garnered up, and sown again in many places in the world, until regions are overspread with wickedness enough to raise the waters of another Deluge. Open and unpunished murder in a city's streets would be less guilty in its daily toleration, than one such spectacle as this."

It seemed to look down upon the boy in his sleep. Redlaw, too, looked down upon him with a new emotion.

"There is not a father," said the Phantom, "by whose side in his daily or his nightly walk, these creatures pass; there is not a mother among all the ranks of loving mothers in this land; there is no one risen from the state of childhood, but shall be responsible in his or her degree for this enormity. There is not a country throughout the earth on which it would not bring a curse. There is no religion upon earth that it would not deny; there is no people upon earth it would not put to shame."

The Chemist clasped his hands, and looked, with trembling fear and pity, from the sleeping boy to the Phantom, standing above him with his finger pointing down.

"Behold, I say," pursued the Spectre, "the perfect type of what it was your choice to be. Your influence is powerless here, because from this child's bosom you can banish nothing. His thoughts have been in 'terrible companionship' with yours, because you have gone down to his unnatural level. He is the growth of man's indifference; you are the growth of man's presumption. The beneficent design of Heaven is, in each case, overthrown, and from the two poles of the immaterial world you come together."

The Chemist stooped upon the ground beside the boy, and, with the same kind of compassion for him that he now felt for himself, covered him as he slept, and no longer shrank from him with abhorrence or indifference.

Soon, now, the distant line on the horizon brightened, the darkness faded, the sun rose red and glorious, and the chimney stacks and gables of the ancient building gleamed in the clear air, which turned the smoke and vapour of the city into a cloud of gold. The very sun-dial in his shady corner, where the wind was used to spin with such unwindy constancy, shook off the finer particles of snow that had accumulated on his dull old face in the night, and looked out at the little white wreaths eddying round and round him. Doubtless some blind groping of the morning made its way down into the forgotten crypt so cold and earthy, where the Norman arches were half buried in the ground, and stirred the dull sap in the lazy vegetation hanging to the walls, and quickened the slow principle of life within the little world of wonderful and delicate creation which existed there, with some faint knowledge that the sun was up.

The Tetterbys were up, and doing. Mr. Tetterby took down the shutters of the shop, and, strip by strip, revealed the treasures of the window to the eyes, so proof against their seductions, of Jerusalem Buildings. Adolphus had been out so long already, that he was halfway on to "Morning Pep-per." Five small Tetterbys, whose ten round eyes were much inflamed by soap and friction, were in the tortures of a cool wash in the back kitchen; Mrs. Tetterby presiding. Johnny, who was pushed and hustled through his toilet with great rapidity when Moloch chanced to be in an exacting frame of mind (which was always the case), staggered up and down with his charge before the shop door, under greater difficulties than usual; the weight of Moloch being much increased by a complication of defences against the cold, composed of knitted worsted-work, and forming a complete suit of chain-armour, with a head-piece and blue gaiters.

It was a peculiarity of this baby to be always cutting teeth. Whether they never came, or whether they came and went away again, is not in evidence; but it had certainly cut enough, on the showing of Mrs. Tetterby, to make a handsome dental provision for the sign of the Bull and Mouth. All sorts of objects were impressed for the rubbing of its gums, notwithstanding that it always carried, dangling at its waist (which was immediately under its chin), a bone ring, large enough to have represented the rosary of a young nun. Knife-handles, umbrella-tops, the heads of walking-sticks selected from the stock, the fingers of the family in general, but especially of Johnny, nutmeg-graters, crusts, the handles of doors, and the cool knobs on the tops of pokers, were among the commonest instruments indiscriminately applied for this baby's relief. The amount of electricity that must have been rubbed out of it in a week, is not to be calculated. Still Mrs. Tetterby always said "it was coming through, and then the child would be herself"; and still it never did come through, and the child continued to be somebody else.

The tempers of the little Tetterbys had sadly changed with a few hours. Mr. and Mrs. Tetterby themselves were not more altered than their offspring. Usually they were an unselfish, good-natured, yielding little race, sharing short commons when it happened (which was pretty often) contentedly and even generously, and taking a great deal of enjoyment out of a very little meat. But they were fighting now, not only for the soap and water, but even for the breakfast which was yet in perspective. The hand of every little Tetterby was against the other little Tetterbys; and even Johnny's hand—the patient, much-enduring, and devoted Johnny—rose against the baby! Yes, Mrs. Tetterby, going to the door by mere accident, saw him viciously pick out a weak place in the suit of armour where a slap would tell, and slap that blessed child.

Mrs. Tetterby had him into the parlour by the collar, in that same flash of time, and repaid him the assault with usury thereto.

"You brute, you murdering little boy," said Mrs. Tetterby. "Had you the heart to do it?"

"Why don't her teeth come through, then," retorted Johnny, in a loud rebellious voice, "instead of bothering me? How would you like it yourself?"

"Like it, sir!" said Mrs. Tetterby, relieving him of his dishonoured load.

"Yes, like it," said Johnny. "How would you? Not at all. If you was me, you'd go for a soldier. I will, too. There an't no babies in the army."

Mr. Tetterby, who had arrived upon the scene of action, rubbed his chin thoughtfully, instead of correcting the rebel, and seemed rather struck by this view of a military life.

"I wish I was in the army myself, if the child's in the right," said Mrs. Tetterby, looking at her husband, "for I have no peace of my life here. I'm a slave—a Virginia slave"; some indistinct association with their weak descent on the tobacco trade perhaps suggested this aggravated expression to Mrs. Tetterby. "I never have a holiday, or any pleasure at all, from year's end to year's end! Why, Lord bless and save the child," said Mrs. Tetterby, shaking the baby with an irritability hardly suited to so pious an aspiration, "what's the matter with her now?"

Not being able to discover, and not rendering the subject much clearer by shaking it, Mrs. Tetterby put the baby away in a cradle, and, folding her arms, sat rocking it angrily with her foot.

"How you stand there, 'Dolphus," said Mrs. Tetterby to her husband. "Why don't you do something?"

"Because I don't care about doing anything," Mr. Tetterby replied.

"I am sure *I* don't," said Mrs. Tetterby.

"I'll take my oath *I* don't," said Mr. Tetterby.

A diversion arose here among Johnny and his five younger brothers, who, in preparing the family breakfast table, had fallen to skirmishing for the temporary possession of the loaf, and were buffeting one another with great heartiness; the smallest boy of all, with precocious discretion, hovering outside the knot of combatants, and harassing their legs. Into the midst of this fray, Mr. and Mrs. Tetterby both precipitated themselves with great ardour, as if such ground were the only ground on which they could now agree; and having, with no visible remains of their late soft-heartedness, laid about them without any lenity, and done much execution, resumed their former relative positions.

"You had better read your paper than do nothing at all," said Mrs. Tetterby.

"What's there to read in a paper?" returned Mr. Tetterby, with excessive discontent.

"What?" said Mrs. Tetterby. "Police!"

"It's nothing to me," said Tetterby. "What do I care what people do, or are done to?"

"Suicides," suggested Mrs. Tetterby.

"No business of mine," replied her husband.

"Births, deaths, and marriages, are those nothing to you?" said Mrs. Tetterby.

"If the births were all over for good, and all to-day; and the deaths were all to begin to come off to-morrow; I don't see why it should interest me, till I thought it was a coming to my turn," grumbled Tetterby. "As to marriages, I've done it myself. I know quite enough about *them*."

To judge from the dissatisfied expression of her face and manner, Mrs. Tetterby appeared to entertain the same opinions as her husband; but she opposed him, nevertheless, for the gratification of quarrelling with him.

"Oh, you're a consistent man," said Mrs. Tetterby, "an't you? You, with the screen of your own making there, made of nothing else but bits of newspapers, which you sit and read to the children by the half-hour together!"

"Say used to, if you please," returned her husband. "You won't find me doing so any more. I'm wiser now."

"Bah! wiser, indeed!" said Mrs. Tetterby. "Are you better?"

The question sounded some discordant note in Mr. Tetterby's breast. He ruminated dejectedly, and passed his hand across and across his forehead.

"Better!" murmured Mr. Tetterby. "I don't know as any of us are better, or happier either. Better, is it?"

He turned to the screen, and traced about it with his finger, until he found a certain paragraph of which he was in quest.

"This used to be one of the family favourites, I recollect," said Tetterby, in a forlorn and stupid way, "and used to draw tears from the children, and make 'em good, if there was any little bickering or discontent among 'em, next to the story of the robin redbreasts in the wood. 'Melancholy case of destitution. Yesterday a small man, with a baby in his arms, and surrounded by half-a-dozen ragged little ones, of various ages between ten and two, the whole of whom were evidently in a famishing condition, appeared before the worthy magistrate, and made the following recital':—Ha! I don't understand it, I'm sure," said Tetterby; "I don't see what it has got to do with us."

"How old and shabby he looks," said Mrs. Tetterby, watching him. "I never saw such a change in a man. Ah! dear me, dear me, dear me, it was a sacrifice!"

"What was a sacrifice?" her husband sourly inquired.

Mrs. Tetterby shook her head; and without replying in words, raised a complete sea-storm about the baby, by her violent agitation of the cradle.

"If you mean your marriage was a sacrifice, my good woman—" said her husband.

"I *do* mean it" said his wife.

"Why, then I mean to say," pursued Mr. Tetterby, as sulkily and surlily as she, "that there are two sides to that affair; and that *I* was the sacrifice; and that I wish the sacrifice hadn't been accepted."

"I wish it hadn't, Tetterby, with all my heart and soul I do assure you," said his wife. "You can't wish it more than I do, Tetterby."

"I don't know what I saw in her," muttered the newsman, "I'm sure:—certainly, if I saw anything, it's not there now. I was thinking so, last night, after supper, by the fire. She's fat, she's ageing, she won't bear comparison with most other women."

"He's common-looking, he has no air with him, he's small, he's beginning to stoop and he's getting bald," muttered Mrs. Tetterby.

"I must have been half out of my mind when I did it," muttered Mr. Tetterby.

"My senses must have forsook me. That's the only way in which I can explain it to myself," said Mrs. Tetterby with elaboration.

In this mood they sat down to breakfast. The little Tetterbys were not habituated to regard that meal in the light of a sedentary occupation, but discussed it as a dance or trot; rather resembling a savage ceremony, in the occasionally shrill whoops, and brandishings of bread and butter, with which it was accompanied, as well as in the intricate filings off into the street and back again, and the hoppings up and down the doorsteps, which were incidental to the performance. In the present instance, the contentions between these Tetterby children for the milk-and-water jug, common to all, which stood upon the table, presented so lamentable an instance of angry passions risen very high indeed, that it was an outrage on the memory of Doctor Watts. It was not until Mr. Tetterby had driven the whole herd out at the front door, that a moment's peace was secured; and even that was broken by the discovery that Johnny had surreptitiously come back, and was at that instant choking in the jug like a ventriloquist, in his indecent and rapacious haste.

"These children will be the death of me at last!" said Mrs. Tetterby, after banishing the culprit. "And the sooner the better, I think."

"Poor people," said Mr. Tetterby, "ought not to have children at all. They give *us* no pleasure."

He was at that moment taking up the cup which Mrs. Tetterby had rudely pushed towards him, and Mrs. Tetterby was lifting her own cup to her lips, when they both stopped, as if they were transfixed.

"Here! Mother! Father!" cried Johnny, running into the room. "Here's Mrs. William coming down the street!"

And if ever, since the world began, a young boy took a baby from a cradle with the care of an old nurse, and hushed and soothed it tenderly, and tottered away with it cheerfully, Johnny was that boy, and Moloch was that baby, as they went out together!

Mr. Tetterby put down his cup; Mrs. Tetterby put down her cup. Mr. Tetterby rubbed his forehead; Mrs. Tetterby rubbed hers. Mr. Tetterby's face began to smooth and brighten; Mrs. Tetterby's began to smooth and brighten.

"Why, Lord forgive me," said Mr. Tetterby to himself, "what evil tempers have I been giving way to? What has been the matter here!"

"How could I ever treat him ill again, after all I said and felt last night!" sobbed Mrs. Tetterby, with her apron to her eyes.

"Am I a brute," said Mr. Tetterby, "or is there any good in me at all? Sophia! My little woman!"

"'Dolphus dear," returned his wife.

"I—I've been in a state of mind," said Mr. Tetterby, "that I can't abear to think of, Sophy."

"Oh! It's nothing to what I've been in, Dolf," cried his wife in a great burst of grief.

"My Sophia," said Mr. Tetterby, "don't take on. I never shall forgive myself. I must have nearly broke your heart, I know."

"No, Dolf, no. It was me! Me!" cried Mrs. Tetterby.

"My little woman," said her husband, "don't. You make me reproach myself dreadful, when you show such a noble spirit. Sophia, my dear, you don't know what I thought. I showed it bad enough, no doubt; but what I thought, my little woman!—"

"Oh, dear Dolf, don't! Don't!" cried his wife.

"Sophia," said Mr. Tetterby, "I must reveal it. I couldn't rest in my conscience unless I mentioned it. My little woman—"

"Mrs. William's very nearly here!" screamed Johnny at the door.

"My little woman, I wondered how," gasped Mr. Tetterby, supporting himself by his chair, "I wondered how I had ever admired you—I forgot the precious children you have brought about me, and thought you didn't look as slim as I could wish. I—I never gave a recollection," said Mr. Tetterby, with severe self-accusation, "to the cares you've had as my wife, and along of me and mine, when you might have had hardly any with another man, who got on better and was luckier than me (anybody might have found such a man easily I am sure); and I quarrelled with you for having aged a little in the rough years you have lightened for me. Can you believe it, my little woman? I hardly can myself."

Mrs. Tetterby, in a whirlwind of laughing and crying, caught his face within her hands, and held it there.

"Oh, Dolf!" she cried. "I am so happy that you thought so; I am so grateful that you thought so! For I thought that you were common-looking, Dolf; and so you are, my dear, and may you be the commonest of all sights in my eyes, till you close them with your own good hands. I thought that you were small; and so you are, and I'll make much of you because you are, and more of you because I love my husband. I thought that you began to stoop; and so you do, and you shall lean on me, and I'll do all I can to keep you up. I thought there was no air about you; but there is, and it's the air of home, and that's the purest and the best there is, and God bless home once more, and all belonging to it, Dolf!"

"Hurrah! Here's Mrs. William!" cried Johnny.

So she was, and all the children with her; and so she came in, they kissed her, and kissed one another, and kissed the baby, and kissed their father and mother, and then ran back and flocked and danced about her, trooping on with her in triumph.

Mr. and Mrs. Tetterby were not a bit behind-hand in the warmth of their reception. They were as much attracted to her as the children were; they ran towards her, kissed her hands, pressed round her, could not receive her ardently or enthusiastically enough. She came among them like the spirit of all goodness, affection, gentle consideration, love, and domesticity.

"What! are *you* all so glad to see me, too, this bright Christmas morning?" said Milly, clapping her hands in a pleasant wonder. "Oh dear, how delightful this is!"

More shouting from the children, more kissing, more trooping round her, more happiness, more love, more joy, more honour, on all sides, than she could bear.

"Oh dear!" said Milly, "what delicious tears you make me shed. How can I ever have deserved this! What have I done to be so loved?"

"Who can help it?" cried Mr. Tetterby.

"Who can help it?" cried Mrs. Tetterby.

"Who can help it?" echoed the children, in a joyful chorus. And they danced and trooped about her again, and clung to her, and laid their rosy faces against her dress, and kissed and fondled it, and could not fondle it, or her, enough.

"I never was so moved," said Milly, drying her eyes, "as I have been this morning. I must tell you, as soon as I can speak.—Mr. Redlaw came to me at sunrise, and with a tenderness in his manner, more as if I had been his darling daughter than myself, implored me to go with him to where William's brother George is lying ill. We went together, and all the way along he was so kind, and so subdued, and seemed to put such trust and hope in me, that I could not help trying with pleasure. When we got to the house, we met a woman at the door (somebody had bruised and hurt her, I am afraid), who caught me by the hand, and blessed me as I passed."

"She was right," said Mr. Tetterby. Mrs. Tetterby said she was right. All the children cried out that she was right.

"Ah, but there's more than that," said Milly. "When we got up-stairs, into the room, the sick man who had lain for hours in a state from which no effort could rouse him, rose up in his bed, and, bursting into tears, stretched out his arms to me, and said that he had led a mis-spent life, but that he was truly repentant now, in his sorrow for the past, which was all as plain to him as a great prospect, from which a dense black cloud had cleared away, and that he entreated me to ask his poor old father for his pardon and his blessing, and to say a prayer beside his bed. And when

I did so, Mr. Redlaw joined in it so fervently, and then so thanked and thanked me, and thanked Heaven, that my heart quite overflowed, and I could have done nothing but sob and cry, if the sick man had not begged me to sit down by him,—which made me quiet of course. As I sat there, he held my hand in his until he sank in a doze; and even then, when I withdrew my hand to leave him to come here (which Mr. Redlaw was very earnest indeed in wishing me to do), his hand felt for mine, so that some one else was obliged to take my place and make believe to give him my hand back. Oh dear, oh dear," said Milly, sobbing. "How thankful and how happy I should feel, and do feel, for all this!"

While she was speaking, Redlaw had come in, and, after pausing for a moment to observe the group of which she was the centre, had silently ascended the stairs. Upon those stairs he now appeared again; remaining there, while the young student passed him, and came running down.

"Kind nurse, gentlest, best of creatures," he said, falling on his knee to her, and catching at her hand, "forgive my cruel ingratitude!"

"Oh dear, oh dear!" cried Milly innocently, "here's another of them! Oh dear, here's somebody else who likes me. What shall I ever do!"

The guileless, simple way in which she said it, and in which she put her hands before her eyes and wept for very happiness, was as touching as it was delightful.

"I was not myself," he said. "I don't know what it was—it was some consequence of my disorder perhaps—I was mad. But I am so no longer. Almost as I speak, I am restored. I heard the children crying out your name, and the shade passed from me at the very sound of it. Oh don't weep! Dear Milly, if you could read my heart, and only knew with what affection and what grateful homage it is glowing, you would not let me see you weep. It is such deep reproach."

"No, no," said Milly, "it's not that. It's not indeed. It's joy. It's wonder that you should think it necessary to ask me to forgive so little, and yet it's pleasure that you do."

"And will you come again? and will you finish the little curtain?"

"No," said Milly, drying her eyes, and shaking her head. "You won't care for *my* needlework now."

"Is it forgiving me, to say that?"

She beckoned him aside, and whispered in his ear.

"There is news from your home, Mr. Edmund."

"News? How?"

"Either your not writing when you were very ill, or the change in your handwriting when you began to be better, created some suspicion of the truth; however that is—but you're sure you'll not be the worse for any news, if it's not bad news?"

"Sure."

"Then there's some one come!" said Milly.

"My mother?" asked the student, glancing round involuntarily towards Redlaw, who had come down from the stairs.

"Hush! No," said Milly.

"It can be no one else."

"Indeed?" said Milly, "are you sure?"

"It is not—" Before he could say more, she put her hand upon his mouth.

"Yes it is!" said Milly. "The young lady (she is very like the miniature, Mr. Edmund, but she is prettier) was too unhappy to rest without satisfying her doubts, and came up, last night, with a little servant-maid. As you always dated your letters from the college, she came there; and before I saw Mr. Redlaw this morning, I saw her. *She* likes me too!" said Milly. "Oh dear, that's another!"

"This morning! Where is she now?"

"Why, she is now," said Milly, advancing her lips to his ear, "in my little parlour in the Lodge, and waiting to see you."

He pressed her hand, and was darting off, but she detained him.

"Mr. Redlaw is much altered, and has told me this morning that his memory is impaired. Be very considerate to him, Mr. Edmund; he needs that from us all."

The young man assured her, by a look, that her caution was not ill-bestowed; and as he passed the Chemist on his way out, bent respectfully and with an obvious interest before him.

Redlaw returned the salutation courteously and even humbly, and looked after him as he passed on. He dropped his head upon his hand too, as trying to reawaken something he had lost. But it was gone.

The abiding change that had come upon him since the influence of the music, and the Phantom's reappearance, was, that now he truly felt how much he had lost, and could compassionate his own condition, and contrast it, clearly, with the natural state of those who were around him. In this, an interest in those who were around him was revived, and a meek, submissive sense of his calamity was bred, resembling that which sometimes obtains in age, when its mental powers are weakened, without insensibility or sullenness being added to the list of its infirmities.

He was conscious that, as he redeemed, through Milly, more and more of the evil he had done, and as he was more and more with her, this change ripened itself within him. Therefore, and because of the attachment she inspired him with (but without other hope), he felt that he was quite dependent on her, and that she was his staff in his affliction.

So, when she asked him whether they should go home now, to where the old man and her husband were, and he readily replied "yes"—being anxious in that regard—he put his arm through hers, and walked beside her; not as if he were the wise and learned man to whom the wonders of nature were an open book, and hers were the uninstructed mind, but as if their two positions were reversed, and he knew nothing, and she all.

He saw the children throng about her, and caress her, as he and she went away together thus, out of the house; he heard the ringing of their laughter, and their merry voices; he saw their bright faces, clustering around him like flowers; he witnessed the renewed contentment and affection of their parents; he breathed the simple air of their poor home, restored to its tranquillity; he thought of the unwholesome blight he had shed upon it, and might, but for her, have been diffusing then; and perhaps it is no wonder that he walked submissively beside her, and drew her gentle bosom nearer to his own.

When they arrived at the Lodge, the old man was sitting in his chair in the chimney-corner, with his eyes fixed on the ground, and his son was leaning against the opposite side of the fire-place, looking at him. As she came in at the door, both started, and turned round towards her, and a radiant change came upon their faces.

"Oh dear, dear, dear, they are all pleased to see me like the rest!" cried Milly, clapping her hands in an ecstasy, and stopping short. "Here are two more!"

Pleased to see her! Pleasure was no word for it. She ran into her husband's arms, thrown wide open to receive her, and he would have been glad to have her there, with her head lying on his shoulder, through the short winter's day. But the old man couldn't spare her. He had arms for her too, and he locked her in them.

"Why, where has my quiet Mouse been all this time?" said the old man. "She has been a long while away. I find that it's impossible for me to get on without Mouse. I—where's my son William?—I fancy I have been dreaming, William."

"That's what I say myself, father," returned his son. "*I* have been in an ugly sort of dream, I think.—How are you, father? Are you pretty well?"

"Strong and brave, my boy," returned the old man.

It was quite a sight to see Mr. William shaking hands with his father, and patting him on the back, and rubbing him gently down with his hand, as if he could not possibly do enough to show an interest in him.

"What a wonderful man you are, father!—How are you, father? Are you really pretty hearty, though?" said William, shaking hands with him again, and patting him again, and rubbing him gently down again.

"I never was fresher or stouter in my life, my boy."

"What a wonderful man you are, father! But that's exactly where it is," said Mr. William, with enthusiasm. "When I think of all that my father's gone through, and all the chances and changes, and sorrows and troubles, that have happened to him in the course of his long life, and under which his head has grown grey, and years upon years have gathered on it, I feel as if we couldn't do enough to honour the old gentleman, and make his old age easy.—How are you, father? Are you really pretty well, though?"

Mr. William might never have left off repeating this inquiry, and shaking hands with him again, and patting him again, and rubbing him down again, if the old man had not espied the Chemist, whom until now he had not seen.

"I ask your pardon, Mr. Redlaw," said Philip, "but didn't know you were here, sir, or should have made less free. It reminds me, Mr. Redlaw, seeing you here on a Christmas morning, of the time when you was a student yourself, and worked so hard that you were backwards and forwards in our Library even at Christmas-time. Ha! ha! I'm old enough to remember that; and I remember it right well, I do, though I am eight-seven. It was after you left here that my poor wife died. You remember my poor wife, Mr. Redlaw?"

The Chemist answered yes.

"Yes," said the old man. "She was a dear creetur.—I recollect you come here one Christmas morning with a young lady—I ask your pardon, Mr. Redlaw, but I think it was a sister you was very much attached to?"

The Chemist looked at him, and shook his head. "I had a sister," he said vacantly. He knew no more.

"One Christmas morning," pursued the old man, "that you come here with her—and it began to snow, and my wife invited the lady to walk in, and sit by the fire that is always a burning on Christmas Day in what used to be, before our ten poor gentlemen commuted, our great Dinner Hall. I was there; and I recollect, as I was stirring up the blaze for the young lady to warm her pretty feet by, she read the scroll out loud, that is underneath that picter, 'Lord, keep my memory green!' She and my poor wife fell a-talking about it; and it's a strange thing to think of, now, that they both said (both being so unlike to die) that it was a good prayer, and that it was one they would put up very earnestly, if they were called away young, with reference to those who were dearest to them. 'My brother,' says the young lady—'My husband,' says my poor wife.—'Lord, keep his memory of me, green, and do not let me be forgotten!'"

Tears more painful, and more bitter than he had ever shed in all his life, coursed down Redlaw's face. Philip, fully occupied in recalling his story, had not observed him until now, nor Milly's anxiety that he should not proceed.

"Philip!" said Redlaw, laying his hand upon his arm, "I am a stricken man, on whom the hand of Providence has fallen heavily, although deservedly. You speak to me, my friend, of what I cannot follow; my memory is gone."

"Merciful Power!" cried the old man.

"I have lost my memory of sorrow, wrong, and trouble," said the Chemist, "and with that I have lost all man would remember!"

To see old Philip's pity for him, to see him wheel his own great chair for him to rest in, and look down upon him with a solemn sense of his bereavement, was to know, in some degree, how precious to old age such recollections are.

The boy came running in, and ran to Milly.

"Here's the man," he said, "in the other room. I don't want *him*."

"What man does he mean?" asked Mr. William.

"Hush!" said Milly.

Obedient to a sign from her, he and his old father softly withdrew. As they went out, unnoticed, Redlaw beckoned to the boy to come to him.

"I like the woman best," he answered, holding to her skirts.

"You are right," said Redlaw, with a faint smile. "But you needn't fear to come to me. I am gentler than I was. Of all the world, to you, poor child!"

The boy still held back at first, but yielding little by little to her urging, he consented to approach, and even to sit down at his feet. As Redlaw laid his hand upon the shoulder of the child, looking on him with compassion and a fellow-feeling, he put out his other hand to Milly. She stooped down on that side of him, so that she could look into his face, and after silence, said:

"Mr. Redlaw, may I speak to you?"

"Yes," he answered, fixing his eyes upon her. "Your voice and music are the same to me."

"May I ask you something?"

"What you will."

"Do you remember what I said, when I knocked at your door last night? About one who was your friend once, and who stood on the verge of destruction?"

"Yes. I remember," he said, with some hesitation.

"Do you understand it?"

He smoothed the boy's hair—looking at her fixedly the while, and shook his head.

"This person," said Milly, in her clear, soft voice, which her mild eyes, looking at him, made clearer and softer, "I found soon afterwards. I went back to the house, and, with Heaven's help, traced him. I was not too soon. A very little and I should have been too late."

He took his hand from the boy, and laying it on the back of that hand of hers, whose timid and yet earnest touch addressed him no less appealingly than her voice and eyes, looked more intently on her.

"He *is* the father of Mr. Edmund, the young gentleman we saw just now. His real name is Longford.—You recollect the name?"

"I recollect the name."

"And the man?"

"No, not the man. Did he ever wrong me?"

"Yes."

"Ah! Then it's hopeless—hopeless."

He shook his head, and softly beat upon the hand he held, as though mutely asking her commiseration.

"I did not go to Mr. Edmund last night," said Milly,—"You will listen to me just the same as if you did remember all?"

"To every syllable you say."

"Both, because I did not know, then, that this really was his father, and because I was fearful of the effect of such intelligence upon him, after his illness, if it should be. Since I have known who this person is, I have not gone either; but that is for another reason. He has long been separated from his wife and son—has been a stranger to his home almost from this son's infancy, I learn from him—and has abandoned and deserted what he should have held most dear. In all that time he has been falling from the state of a gentleman, more and more, until—" she rose up, hastily, and going out for a moment, returned, accompanied by the wreck that Redlaw had beheld last night.

"Do you know me?" asked the Chemist.

"I should be glad," returned the other, "and that is an unwonted word for me to use, if I could answer no."

The Chemist looked at the man, standing in self-abasement and degradation before him, and would have looked longer, in an ineffectual struggle for enlightenment, but that Milly resumed her late position by his side, and attracted his attentive gaze to her own face.

"See how low he is sunk, how lost he is!" she whispered, stretching out her arm towards him, without looking from the Chemist's face. "If you could remember all that is connected with him, do you not think it would move your pity to reflect that one you ever loved (do not let us mind how long ago, or in what belief that he has forfeited), should come to this?"

"I hope it would," he answered. "I believe it would."

His eyes wandered to the figure standing near the door, but came back speedily to her, on whom he gazed intently, as if he strove to learn some lesson from every tone of her voice, and every beam of her eyes.

"I have no learning, and you have much," said Milly; "I am not used to think, and you are always thinking. May I tell you why it seems to me a good thing for us, to remember wrong that has been done us?"

"Yes."

"That we may forgive it."

"Pardon me, great Heaven!" said Redlaw, lifting up his eyes, "for having thrown away thine own high attribute!"

"And if," said Milly, "if your memory should one day be restored, as we will hope and pray it may be, would it not be a blessing to you to recall at once a wrong and its forgiveness?"

He looked at the figure by the door, and fastened his attentive eyes on her again; a ray of clearer light appeared to him to shine into his mind, from her bright face.

"He cannot go to his abandoned home. He does not seek to go there. He knows that he could only carry shame and trouble to those he has so cruelly neglected; and that the best reparation he can make them now, is to avoid them. A very little money carefully bestowed, would remove him to some distant place, where he might live and do no wrong, and make such atonement as is left within his power for the wrong he has done. To the unfortunate lady who is his wife, and to his son, this would be the best and kindest boon that their best friend could give them—one too that they need never know of; and to him, shattered in reputation, mind, and body, it might be salvation."

He took her head between her hands, and kissed it, and said: "It shall be done. I trust to you to do it for me, now and secretly; and to tell him that I would forgive him, if I were so happy as to know for what."

As she rose, and turned her beaming face towards the fallen man, implying that her mediation had been successful, he advanced a step, and without raising his eyes, addressed himself to Redlaw.

"You are so generous," he said, "—you ever were—that you will try to banish your rising sense of retribution in the spectacle that is before you. I do not try to banish it from myself, Redlaw. If you can, believe me."

The Chemist entreated Milly, by a gesture, to come nearer to him; and, as he listened looked in her face, as if to find in it the clue to what he heard.

"I am too decayed a wretch to make professions; I recollect my own career too well, to array any such before you. But from the day on which I made my first step downward, in dealing falsely by you, I have gone down with a certain, steady, doomed progression. That, I say."

Redlaw, keeping her close at his side, turned his face towards the speaker, and there was sorrow in it. Something like mournful recognition too.

"I might have been another man, my life might have been another life, if I had avoided that first fatal step. I don't know that it would have been. I claim nothing for the possibility. Your sister is at rest, and better than she could have been with me, if I had continued even what you thought me: even what I once supposed myself to be."

Redlaw made a hasty motion with his hand, as if he would have put that subject on one side.

"I speak," the other went on, "like a man taken from the grave. I should have made my own grave, last night, had it not been for this blessed hand."

"Oh dear, he likes me too!" sobbed Milly, under her breath. "That's another!"

"I could not have put myself in your way, last night, even for bread. But, to-day, my recollection of what has been is so strongly stirred, and is presented to me, I don't know how, so vividly, that I have dared to come at her suggestion, and to take your bounty, and to thank you for it, and to beg you, Redlaw, in your dying hour, to be as merciful to me in your thoughts, as you are in your deeds."

He turned towards the door, and stopped a moment on his way forth.

"I hope my son may interest you, for his mother's sake. I hope he may deserve to do so. Unless my life should be preserved a long time, and I should know that I have not misused your aid, I shall never look upon him more."

Going out, he raised his eyes to Redlaw for the first time. Redlaw, whose steadfast gaze was fixed upon him, dreamily held out his hand. He returned and touched it—little more—with both his own—and bending down his head, went slowly out.

In the few moments that elapsed, while Milly silently took him to the gate, the Chemist dropped into his chair, and covered his face with his hands. Seeing him thus, when she came back, accompanied by her husband and his father (who were both greatly concerned for him), she avoided disturbing him, or permitting him to be disturbed; and kneeled down near the chair to put some warm clothing on the boy.

"That's exactly where it is. That's what I always say, father!" exclaimed her admiring husband. "There's a motherly feeling in Mrs. William's breast that must and will have went!"

"Ay, ay," said the old man; "you're right. My son William's right!"

"It happens all for the best, Milly dear, no doubt," said Mr. William, tenderly, "that we have no children of our own; and yet I sometimes wish you had one to love and cherish. Our little dead child that you built such hopes upon, and that never breathed the breath of life—it has made you quiet-like, Milly."

"I am very happy in the recollection of it, William dear," she answered. "I think of it every day."

"I was afraid you thought of it a good deal."

"Don't say, afraid; it is a comfort to me; it speaks to me in so many ways. The innocent thing that never lived on earth, is like an angel to me, William."

"You are like an angel to father and me," said Mr. William, softly. "I know that."

"When I think of all those hopes I built upon it, and the many times I sat and pictured to myself the little smiling face upon my bosom that never lay there, and the sweet eyes turned up to mine that never opened to the light," said Milly, "I can feel a greater tenderness, I think, for all the disappointed hopes in which there is no harm. When I see a beautiful child in its fond mother's arms, I love it all the better, thinking that my child might have been like that, and might have made my heart as proud and happy."

Redlaw raised his head, and looked towards her.

"All through life, it seems by me," she continued, "to tell me something. For poor neglected children, my little child pleads as if it were alive, and had a voice I knew, with which to speak to me. When I hear of youth in suffering or shame, I think that my child might have come to that, perhaps, and that God took it from me in His mercy. Even in age and grey hair, such as father's is at present: saying that it too might have lived to be old, long and long after you and I were gone, and to have needed the respect and love of younger people."

Her quiet voice was quieter than ever, as she took her husband's arm, and laid her head against it.

"Children love me so, that sometimes I half fancy—it's a silly fancy, William—they have some way I don't know of, of feeling for my little child, and me, and understanding why their love is precious to me. If I have been quiet since, I have been more happy, William, in a hundred ways. Not least happy, dear, in this—that even when my little child was born and dead but a few days, and I was weak and sorrowful, and could not help grieving a little, the thought arose, that if I tried to lead a good life, I should meet in Heaven a bright creature, who would call me, Mother!"

Redlaw fell upon his knees, with a loud cry.

"O Thou," he said, "who through the teaching of pure love, hast graciously restored me to the memory which was the memory of Christ upon the cross, and of all the good who perished in His cause, receive my thanks, and bless her!"

Then, he folded her to his heart; and Milly, sobbing more than ever, cried, as she laughed, "He is come back to himself! He likes me very much indeed, too! Oh dear, dear, dear me, here's another!"

Then, the student entered, leading by the hand a lovely girl, who was afraid to come. And Redlaw so changed towards him, seeing in him and his youthful choice, the softened shadow of that chastening passage in his own life, to which, as to a shady tree, the dove so long imprisoned in his solitary ark might fly for rest and company, fell upon his neck, entreating them to be his children.

Then, as Christmas is a time in which, of all times in the year, the memory of every remediable sorrow, wrong, and trouble in the world around us, should be active with us, not less than our own experiences, for all good, he laid his hand upon the boy, and, silently calling Him to witness who laid His hand on children in old time, rebuking, in the majesty of His prophetic knowledge, those who kept them from Him, vowed to protect him, teach him, and reclaim him.

Then, he gave his right hand cheerily to Philip, and said that they would that day hold a Christmas dinner in what used to be, before the ten poor gentlemen commuted, their great Dinner Hall; and that they would bid to it as many of that Swidger family, who, his son had told him, were so numerous that they might join hands and make a ring round England, as could be brought together on so short a notice.

And it was that day done. There were so many Swidgers there, grown up and children, that an attempt to state them in round numbers might engender doubts, in the distrustful, of the veracity of this history. Therefore the attempt shall not be made. But there they were, by dozens and scores—and there was good news and good hope there, ready for them, of George, who had been visited again by his father and brother, and by Milly, and again left in a quiet sleep. There, present at the dinner, too, were the Tetterbys, including young Adolphus, who arrived in his prismatic comforter, in good time for the beef. Johnny and the baby were too late, of course, and came in all on one side, the one exhausted, the other in a supposed state of double-tooth; but that was customary, and not alarming.

It was sad to see the child who had no name or lineage, watching the other children as they played, not knowing how to talk with them, or sport with them, and more strange to the ways of childhood than a rough dog. It was sad, though in a different way, to see what an instinctive knowledge the youngest children there had of his being different from all the rest, and how they made timid approaches to him with soft words, and touches, and with little presents, that he might not be unhappy. But he kept by Milly, and began to love her—that was another, as she said!—and, as they all liked her dearly, they were glad of that, and when they saw him peeping at them from behind her chair, they were pleased that he was so close to it.

All this, the Chemist, sitting with the student and his bride that was to be, Philip, and the rest, saw.

Some people have said since, that he only thought what has been herein set down; others, that he read it in the fire, one winter night about the twilight time; others, that the Ghost was but the representation of his gloomy thoughts, and Milly the embodiment of his better wisdom. *I* say nothing.

—Except this. That as they were assembled in the old Hall, by no other light than that of a great fire (having dined early), the shadows once more stole out of their hiding-places, and danced about the room, showing the children marvellous shapes and faces on the walls, and gradually changing what was real and familiar there, to what was wild and magical. But that there was one thing in the Hall, to which the eyes of Redlaw, and of Milly and her husband, and of the old man, and of the student, and his bride that was to be, were often turned, which the shadows did not obscure or change. Deepened in its gravity by the firelight, and gazing from the darkness of the panelled wall like life, the sedate face in the portrait, with the beard and ruff, looked down at them from under its verdant wreath of holly, as they looked up at it; and, clear and plain below, as if a voice had uttered them, were the words, "Lord keep my Memory green."

Other Christmas Stories

The Story of the Goblins Who Stole a Sexton

In an old abbey town, down in this part of the country, a long, long while ago—so long, that the story must be a true one, because our great-grandfathers implicitly believed it—there officiated as sexton and grave-digger in the churchyard, one Gabriel Grub. It by no means follows that because a man is a sexton, and constantly surrounded by the emblems of mortality, therefore he should be a morose and melancholy man; your undertakers are the merriest fellows in the world; and I once had the honour of being on intimate terms with a mute, who in private life, and off duty, was as comical and jocose a little fellow as ever chirped out a devil-may-care song, without a hitch in his memory, or drained off a good stiff glass without stopping for breath. But notwithstanding these precedents to the contrary, Gabriel Grub was an ill-conditioned, cross-grained, surly fellow—a morose and lonely man, who consorted with nobody but himself, and an old wicker bottle which fitted into his large deep waistcoat pocket—and who eyed each merry face, as it passed him by, with such a deep scowl of malice and ill-humour, as it was difficult to meet without feeling something the worse for.

A little before twilight, one Christmas Eve, Gabriel shouldered his spade, lighted his lantern, and betook himself towards the old churchyard; for he had got a grave to finish by next morning, and, feeling very low, he thought it might raise his spirits, perhaps, if he went on with his work at once. As he went his way, up the ancient street, he saw the cheerful light of the blazing fires gleam through the old casements, and heard the loud laugh and the cheerful shouts of those who were assembled around them; he marked the bustling preparations for next day's cheer, and smelled the numerous savoury odours consequent thereupon, as they steamed up from the kitchen windows in clouds. All this was gall and wormwood to the heart of Gabriel Grub; and when groups of children bounded out of the houses, tripped across the road, and were met, before they could knock at the opposite door, by half a dozen curly-headed little rascals who crowded round them as they flocked upstairs to spend the evening in their Christmas games, Gabriel smiled grimly, and clutched the handle of his spade with a firmer grasp, as he thought of measles, scarlet fever, thrush, whooping-cough, and a good many other sources of consolation besides.

In this happy frame of mind, Gabriel strode along, returning a short, sullen growl to the good-humoured greetings of such of his neighbours as now and then passed him, until he turned into the dark lane which led to the churchyard. Now, Gabriel had been looking forward to reaching the dark lane, because it was, generally speaking, a nice, gloomy, mournful place, into which the townspeople did not much care to go, except in broad daylight, and when the sun was shining; consequently, he was not a little indignant to hear a young urchin roaring out some jolly song about a merry Christmas, in this very sanctuary which had been called Coffin Lane ever since the days of the old abbey, and the time of the shaven-headed monks. As Gabriel walked on, and the voice drew nearer, he found it proceeded from a small boy, who was hurrying along, to join one of the little parties in the old street, and who, partly to keep himself company, and partly to prepare himself for the occasion, was shouting out the song at the highest pitch of his lungs. So Gabriel waited until the boy came up, and then dodged him into a corner, and rapped him over the head with his lantern five or six times, just to teach him to modulate his voice. And as the boy hurried away with his hand to his head, singing quite a different sort of tune, Gabriel Grub chuckled very heartily to himself, and entered the churchyard, locking the gate behind him.

He took off his coat, set down his lantern, and getting into the unfinished grave, worked at it for an hour or so with right good-will. But the earth was hardened with the frost, and it was no very easy matter to break it up, and shovel it out; and although there was a moon, it was a very young one, and shed little light upon the grave, which was in the shadow of the church. At any other time, these obstacles would have made Gabriel Grub very moody and miserable, but he was so well pleased with having stopped the small boy's singing, that he took little heed of the scanty progress he had made, and looked down into the grave, when he had finished work for the night, with grim satisfaction, murmuring as he gathered up his things—

Brave lodgings for one, brave lodgings for one,
A few feet of cold earth, when life is done;
A stone at the head, a stone at the feet,
A rich, juicy meal for the worms to eat;
Rank grass overhead, and damp clay around,
Brave lodgings for one, these, in holy ground!

"Ho! ho!" laughed Gabriel Grub, as he sat himself down on a flat tombstone which was a favourite resting-place of his, and drew forth his wicker bottle. "A coffin at Christmas! A Christmas box! Ho! ho! ho!"

'"Ho! ho! ho!" repeated a voice which sounded close behind him.

Gabriel paused, in some alarm, in the act of raising the wicker bottle to his lips, and looked round. The bottom of the oldest grave about him was not more still and quiet than the churchyard in the pale moonlight. The cold hoar frost glistened on the tombstones, and sparkled like rows of gems, among the stone carvings of the old church. The snow lay hard and crisp upon the ground; and spread over the thickly-strewn mounds of earth, so white and smooth a cover that it seemed as if corpses lay there, hidden only by their winding sheets. Not the faintest rustle broke the profound tranquillity of the solemn scene. Sound itself appeared to be frozen up, all was so cold and still.

"It was the echoes," said Gabriel Grub, raising the bottle to his lips again.

"It was *not*," said a deep voice.

Gabriel started up, and stood rooted to the spot with astonishment and terror; for his eyes rested on a form that made his blood run cold.

Seated on an upright tombstone, close to him, was a strange, unearthly figure, whom Gabriel felt at once, was no being of this world. His long, fantastic legs which might have reached the ground, were cocked up, and crossed after a quaint, fantastic fashion; his sinewy arms were bare; and his hands rested on his knees. On his short, round body, he wore a close covering, ornamented with small slashes; a short cloak dangled at his back; the collar was cut into curious peaks, which served the goblin in lieu of ruff or neckerchief; and his shoes curled up at his toes into long points. On his head, he wore a broad-brimmed sugar-loaf hat, garnished with a single feather. The hat was covered with the white frost; and the goblin looked as if he had sat on the same tombstone very comfortably, for two or three hundred years. He was sitting perfectly still; his tongue was put out, as if in derision; and he was grinning at Gabriel Grub with such a grin as only a goblin could call up.

"It was *not* the echoes," said the goblin.

Gabriel Grub was paralysed, and could make no reply.

"What do you do here on Christmas Eve?" said the goblin sternly.

"I came to dig a grave, Sir," stammered Gabriel Grub.

"What man wanders among graves and churchyards on such a night as this?" cried the goblin.

"Gabriel Grub! Gabriel Grub!" screamed a wild chorus of voices that seemed to fill the churchyard. Gabriel looked fearfully round—nothing was to be seen.

"What have you got in that bottle?" said the goblin.

"Hollands, sir," replied the sexton, trembling more than ever; for he had bought it of the smugglers, and he thought that perhaps his questioner might be in the excise department of the goblins.

"Who drinks Hollands alone, and in a churchyard, on such a night as this?" said the goblin.

"Gabriel Grub! Gabriel Grub!" exclaimed the wild voices again.

The goblin leered maliciously at the terrified sexton, and then raising his voice, exclaimed—

"And who, then, is our fair and lawful prize?"

To this inquiry the invisible chorus replied, in a strain that sounded like the voices of many choristers singing to the mighty swell of the old church organ—a strain that seemed borne to the sexton's ears upon a wild wind, and to die away as it passed onward; but the burden of the reply was still the same, "Gabriel Grub! Gabriel Grub!"

The goblin grinned a broader grin than before, as he said, "Well, Gabriel, what do you say to this?"

The sexton gasped for breath. "What do you think of this, Gabriel?" said the goblin, kicking up his feet in the air on either side of the tombstone, and looking at the turned-up points with as much complacency as if he had been contemplating the most fashionable pair of Wellingtons in all Bond Street.

"It's—it's—very curious, Sir," replied the sexton, half dead with fright; "very curious, and very pretty, but I think I'll go back and finish my work, Sir, if you please."

"Work!" said the goblin, "what work?"

"The grave, Sir; making the grave," stammered the sexton.

"Oh, the grave, eh?" said the goblin; "who makes graves at a time when all other men are merry, and takes a pleasure in it?"

Again the mysterious voices replied, "Gabriel Grub! Gabriel Grub!"

"I am afraid my friends want you, Gabriel," said the goblin, thrusting his tongue farther into his cheek than ever—and a most astonishing tongue it was—"I'm afraid my friends want you, Gabriel," said the goblin.

"Under favour, Sir," replied the horror-stricken sexton, "I don't think they can, Sir; they don't know me, Sir; I don't think the gentlemen have ever seen me, Sir."

"Oh, yes, they have," replied the goblin; "we know the man with the sulky face and grim scowl, that came down the street to-night, throwing his evil looks at the children, and grasping his burying-spade the tighter. We know the man who struck the boy in the envious malice of his heart, because the boy could be merry, and he could not. We know him, we know him."

Here, the goblin gave a loud, shrill laugh, which the echoes returned twentyfold; and throwing his legs up in the air, stood upon his head, or rather upon the very point of his sugar-loaf hat, on the narrow edge of the tombstone, whence he threw a Somerset with extraordinary agility, right to the sexton's feet, at which he planted himself in the attitude in which tailors generally sit upon the shop-board.

"I—I—am afraid I must leave you, Sir," said the sexton, making an effort to move.

"Leave us!" said the goblin, "Gabriel Grub going to leave us. Ho! ho! ho!"

As the goblin laughed, the sexton observed, for one instant, a brilliant illumination within the windows of the church, as if the whole building were lighted up; it disappeared, the organ pealed forth a lively air, and whole troops of goblins, the very counterpart of the first one, poured into the churchyard, and began playing at leap-frog with the tombstones, never stopping for an instant to take breath, but "overing" the highest among them, one after the other, with the most marvellous dexterity. The first goblin was a most astonishing leaper, and none of the others could come near him; even in the extremity of his terror the sexton could not help observing, that while his friends were content to leap over the common-sized gravestones, the first one took the family vaults, iron railings and all, with as much ease as if they had been so many street-posts.

At last the game reached to a most exciting pitch; the organ played quicker and quicker, and the goblins leaped faster and faster, coiling themselves up, rolling head over heels upon the ground, and bounding over the tombstones like footballs. The sexton's brain whirled round with the rapidity of the motion he beheld, and his legs reeled beneath him, as the spirits flew before his eyes; when the goblin king, suddenly darting towards him, laid his hand upon his collar, and sank with him through the earth.

When Gabriel Grub had had time to fetch his breath, which the rapidity of his descent had for the moment taken away, he found himself in what appeared to be a large cavern, surrounded on all sides by crowds of goblins, ugly and grim; in the centre of the room, on an elevated seat, was stationed his friend of the churchyard; and close behind him stood Gabriel Grub himself, without power of motion.

"Cold to-night," said the king of the goblins, "very cold. A glass of something warm here!"

At this command, half a dozen officious goblins, with a perpetual smile upon their faces, whom Gabriel Grub imagined to be courtiers, on that account, hastily disappeared, and presently returned with a goblet of liquid fire, which they presented to the king.

"Ah!" cried the goblin, whose cheeks and throat were transparent, as he tossed down the flame, "this warms one, indeed! Bring a bumper of the same, for Mr. Grub."

It was in vain for the unfortunate sexton to protest that he was not in the habit of taking anything warm at night; one of the goblins held him while another poured the blazing liquid down his throat; the whole assembly screeched with laughter, as he coughed and choked, and wiped away the tears which gushed plentifully from his eyes, after swallowing the burning draught.

"And now," said the king, fantastically poking the taper corner of his sugar-loaf hat into the sexton's eye, and thereby occasioning him the most exquisite pain; "and now, show the man of misery and gloom, a few of the pictures from our own great storehouse!"

As the goblin said this, a thick cloud which obscured the remoter end of the cavern rolled gradually away, and disclosed, apparently at a great distance, a small and scantily furnished, but neat and clean apartment. A crowd of little children were gathered round a bright fire, clinging to their mother's gown, and gambolling around her chair. The mother occasionally rose, and drew aside the window-curtain, as if to look for some expected object; a frugal meal was ready spread upon the table; and an elbow chair was placed near the fire. A knock was heard at the door; the mother opened it, and the children crowded round her, and clapped their hands for joy, as their father entered. He was wet and weary, and shook the snow from his garments, as the children crowded round him, and seizing his cloak, hat, stick, and gloves, with busy zeal, ran with them from the room. Then, as he sat down to his meal before the fire, the children climbed about his knee, and the mother sat by his side, and all seemed happiness and comfort.

But a change came upon the view, almost imperceptibly. The scene was altered to a small bedroom, where the fairest and youngest child lay dying; the roses had fled from his cheek, and the light from his eye; and even as the sexton looked upon him with an interest he had never felt or known before, he died. His young brothers and sisters crowded round his little bed, and seized his tiny hand, so cold and heavy; but they shrank back from its touch, and looked with awe on his infant face; for calm and tranquil as it was, and sleeping in rest and peace as the beautiful child seemed to be, they saw that he was dead, and they knew that he was an angel looking down upon, and blessing them, from a bright and happy Heaven.

Again the light cloud passed across the picture, and again the subject changed. The father and mother were old and helpless now, and the number of those about them was diminished more than half; but content and cheerfulness sat on every face, and beamed in every eye, as they crowded round the fireside, and told and listened to old stories of earlier and bygone days. Slowly and peacefully, the father sank into the grave, and, soon after, the sharer of all his cares and troubles followed him to a place of rest. The few who yet survived them, kneeled by their tomb, and watered the green turf which covered it with their tears; then rose, and turned away, sadly and mournfully, but not with bitter cries, or despairing lamentations, for they knew that they should one day meet again; and once more they mixed with the busy world, and their content and cheerfulness were restored. The cloud settled upon the picture, and concealed it from the sexton's view.

"What do you think of *that*?" said the goblin, turning his large face towards Gabriel Grub.

Gabriel murmured out something about its being very pretty, and looked somewhat ashamed, as the goblin bent his fiery eyes upon him.

"You miserable man!" said the goblin, in a tone of excessive contempt. "You!" He appeared disposed to add more, but indignation choked his utterance, so he lifted up one of his very pliable legs, and, flourishing it above his head a little, to insure his aim, administered a good sound kick to Gabriel Grub; immediately after which, all the goblins in waiting crowded round the wretched sexton, and kicked him without mercy, according to the established and invariable custom of courtiers upon earth, who kick whom royalty kicks, and hug whom royalty hugs.

"Show him some more!" said the king of the goblins.

At these words, the cloud was dispelled, and a rich and beautiful landscape was disclosed to view—there is just such another, to this day, within half a mile of the old abbey town. The sun shone from out the clear blue sky, the water sparkled beneath his rays, and the trees looked greener, and the flowers more gay, beneath its cheering influence. The water rippled on with a pleasant sound, the trees rustled in the light wind that murmured among their leaves, the birds sang upon the boughs, and the lark carolled on high her welcome to the morning. Yes, it was morning; the bright, balmy morning of summer; the minutest leaf, the smallest blade of grass, was instinct with life. The ant crept forth to her daily toil, the butterfly fluttered and basked in the warm rays of the sun; myriads of insects spread their transparent wings, and revelled in their brief but happy existence. Man walked forth, elated with the scene; and all was brightness and splendour.

"*You* a miserable man!" said the king of the goblins, in a more contemptuous tone than before. And again the king of the goblins gave his leg a flourish; again it descended on the shoulders of the sexton; and again the attendant goblins imitated the example of their chief.

Many a time the cloud went and came, and many a lesson it taught to Gabriel Grub, who, although his shoulders smarted with pain from the frequent applications of the goblins' feet thereunto, looked on with an interest that nothing could diminish. He saw that men who worked hard, and earned their scanty bread with lives of labour, were cheerful and happy; and that to the most ignorant, the sweet face of Nature was a never-failing source of cheerfulness and joy. He saw those who had been delicately nurtured, and tenderly brought up, cheerful under privations, and superior to suffering, that would have crushed many of a rougher grain, because they bore within their own bosoms the materials of happiness, contentment, and peace. He saw that women, the tenderest and most fragile of all God's creatures, were the oftenest superior to sorrow, adversity, and distress; and he saw that it was because they bore, in their own hearts, an inexhaustible well-spring of affection and devotion. Above all, he saw that men like himself, who snarled at the mirth and cheerfulness of others, were the foulest weeds on the fair surface of the earth; and setting all the good of the world against the evil, he came to the conclusion that it was a very decent and respectable sort of world after all. No sooner had he formed it, than the cloud which had closed over the last picture, seemed to settle on his senses, and lull him to repose. One by one, the goblins faded from his sight; and, as the last one disappeared, he sank to sleep.

The day had broken when Gabriel Grub awoke, and found himself lying at full length on the flat gravestone in the churchyard, with the wicker bottle lying empty by his side, and his coat, spade, and lantern, all well whitened by the last night's frost, scattered on the ground. The stone on which he had first seen the goblin seated, stood bolt upright before him, and the grave at which he had worked, the night before, was not far off. At first, he began to doubt the reality of his adventures, but the acute pain in his shoulders when he attempted to rise, assured him that the kicking of the goblins was certainly not ideal. He was staggered again, by observing no traces of footsteps in the snow on which the goblins had played at leap-frog with the gravestones, but he speedily accounted for this circumstance when he remembered that, being spirits, they would leave no visible impression behind them. So, Gabriel Grub got on his feet as well as he could, for the pain in his back; and, brushing the frost off his coat, put it on, and turned his face towards the town.

But he was an altered man, and he could not bear the thought of returning to a place where his repentance would be scoffed at, and his reformation disbelieved. He hesitated for a few moments; and then turned away to wander where he might, and seek his bread elsewhere.

The lantern, the spade, and the wicker bottle were found, that day, in the churchyard. There were a great many speculations about the sexton's fate, at first, but it was speedily determined that he had been carried away by the goblins; and there were not wanting some very credible witnesses who had distinctly seen him whisked through the air on the back of a chestnut horse blind of one eye, with the hind-quarters of a lion, and the tail of a bear. At length all this was devoutly believed; and the new sexton used to exhibit to the curious, for a trifling emolument, a good-sized piece of the church weathercock which had been accidentally kicked off by the aforesaid horse in his aerial flight, and picked up by himself in the churchyard, a year or two afterwards.

Unfortunately, these stories were somewhat disturbed by the unlooked-for reappearance of Gabriel Grub himself, some ten years afterwards, a ragged, contented, rheumatic old man. He told his story to the clergyman, and also to the mayor; and in course of time it began to be received as a matter of history, in which form it has continued down to this very day. The believers in the weathercock tale, having misplaced their confidence once, were not easily prevailed upon to part with it again, so they looked as wise as they could, shrugged their shoulders, touched their foreheads, and murmured something about Gabriel Grub having drunk all the Hollands, and then fallen asleep on the flat tombstone; and they affected to explain what he supposed he had witnessed in the goblin's cavern, by saying that he had seen the world, and grown wiser. But this opinion, which was by no means a popular one at any time, gradually died off; and be the matter how it may, as Gabriel Grub was afflicted with rheumatism to the end of his days, this story has at least one moral, if it teach no better one—and that is, that if a man turn sulky and drink by himself at Christmas time, he may make up his mind to be not a bit the better for it: let the spirits be never so good, or let them be even as many degrees beyond proof, as those which Gabriel Grub saw in the goblin's cavern.

A Christmas Tree

I have been looking on, this evening, at a merry company of children assembled round that pretty German toy, a Christmas Tree. The tree was planted in the middle of a great round table, and towered high above their heads. It was brilliantly lighted by a multitude of little tapers; and everywhere sparkled and glittered with bright objects. There were rosy-cheeked dolls, hiding behind the green leaves; and there were real watches (with movable hands, at least, and an endless capacity of being wound up) dangling from innumerable twigs; there were French-polished tables, chairs, bedsteads, wardrobes, eight-day clocks, and various other articles of domestic furniture (wonderfully made, in tin, at Wolverhampton), perched among the boughs, as if in preparation for some fairy housekeeping; there were jolly, broad-faced little men, much more agreeable in appearance than many real men—and no wonder, for their heads took off, and showed them to be full of sugar-plums; there were fiddles and drums; there were tambourines, books, work-boxes, paint-boxes, sweetmeat-boxes, peep-show boxes, and all kinds of boxes; there were trinkets for the elder girls, far brighter than any grown-up gold and jewels; there were baskets and pincushions in all devices; there were guns, swords, and banners; there were witches standing in enchanted rings of pasteboard, to tell fortunes; there were teetotums, humming-tops, needle-cases, pen-wipers, smelling-bottles, conversation-cards, bouquet-holders; real fruit, made artificially dazzling with gold leaf; imitation apples, pears, and walnuts, crammed with surprises; in short, as a pretty child, before me, delightedly whispered to another pretty child, her bosom friend, "There was everything, and more." This motley collection of odd objects, clustering on the tree like magic fruit, and flashing back the bright looks directed towards it from every side—some of the diamond-eyes admiring it were hardly on a level with the table, and a few were languishing in timid wonder on the bosoms of pretty mothers, aunts, and nurses—made a lively realisation of the fancies of childhood; and set me thinking how all the trees that grow and all the things that come into existence on the earth, have their wild adornments at that well-remembered time.

Being now at home again, and alone, the only person in the house awake, my thoughts are drawn back, by a fascination which I do not care to resist, to my own childhood. I begin to consider, what do we all remember best upon the branches of the Christmas Tree of our own young Christmas days, by which we climbed to real life.

Straight, in the middle of the room, cramped in the freedom of its growth by no encircling walls or soon-reached ceiling, a shadowy tree arises; and, looking up into the dreamy brightness of its top—for I observe in this tree the singular property that it appears to grow downward towards the earth—I look into my youngest Christmas recollections!

All toys at first, I find. Up yonder, among the green holly and red berries, is the Tumbler with his hands in his pockets, who wouldn't lie down, but whenever he was put upon the floor, persisted in rolling his fat body about, until he rolled himself still, and brought those lobster eyes of his to bear upon me—when I affected to laugh very much, but in my heart of hearts was extremely doubtful of him. Close beside him is that infernal snuff-box, out of which there sprang a demoniacal Counsellor in a black gown, with an obnoxious head of hair, and a red cloth mouth, wide open, who was not to be endured on any terms, but could not be put away either; for he used suddenly, in a highly magnified state, to fly out of Mammoth Snuff-boxes in dreams, when least expected. Nor is the frog with cobbler's wax on his tail, far off; for there was no knowing where he wouldn't jump; and when he flew over the candle, and came upon one's hand with that spotted back—red on a green ground—he was horrible. The cardboard lady in a blue-silk skirt, who was stood up against the candlestick to dance, and whom I see on the same branch, was milder, and was beautiful; but I can't say as much for the larger cardboard man, who used to be hung against the wall and pulled by a string; there was a sinister expression in that nose of his; and when he got his legs round his neck (which he very often did), he was ghastly, and not a creature to be alone with.

When did that dreadful Mask first look at me? Who put it on, and why was I so frightened that the sight of it is an era in my life? It is not a hideous visage in itself; it is even meant to be droll, why then were its stolid features so intolerable? Surely not because it hid the wearer's face. An apron would have done as much; and though I should have preferred even the apron away, it would not have been absolutely insupportable, like the mask. Was it the immovability of the mask? The doll's face was immovable, but I was not afraid of *her*. Perhaps that fixed and set change coming over a real face, infused into my quickened heart some remote suggestion and dread of the universal change that is to come on every face, and make it still? Nothing reconciled me to it. No drummers, from whom proceeded a melancholy chirping on the turning of a handle; no regiment of soldiers, with a mute band, taken out of a box, and fitted, one by one, upon a stiff and lazy little set of lazy-tongs; no old woman, made of wires and a brown-paper composition, cutting up a pie for two small children; could give me a permanent comfort, for a long time. Nor was it any satisfaction to be shown the Mask, and see that it was made of paper, or to have it locked up and be assured that no one wore it. The mere recollection of that fixed face, the mere knowledge of its existence anywhere, was sufficient to awake me in the night all perspiration and horror, with, "O I know it's coming! O the mask!"

I never wondered what the dear old donkey with the panniers—there he is! was made of, then! His hide was real to the touch, I recollect. And the great black horse with the round red spots all over him—the horse that I could even get upon—I never wondered what had brought him to that strange condition, or thought that such a horse was not commonly seen at Newmarket. The four horses of no colour, next to him, that went into the waggon of cheeses, and could be taken out and stabled under the piano, appear to have bits of fur-tippet for their tails, and other bits for their manes, and to stand on pegs instead of legs, but it was not so when they were brought home for a Christmas present. They were all right, then; neither was their harness unceremoniously nailed into their chests, as appears to be the case now. The tinkling works of the music-cart, I *did* find out, to be made of quill toothpicks and wire; and I always thought that little tumbler in his shirt sleeves, perpetually swarming up one side of a wooden frame, and coming down, head foremost, on the other, rather a weak-minded person—though good-natured; but the Jacob's Ladder, next him, made of little squares of red wood, that went flapping and clattering over one another, each developing a different picture, and the whole enlivened by small bells, was a mighty marvel and a great delight.

Ah! The Doll's house!—of which I was not proprietor, but where I visited. I don't admire the Houses of Parliament half so much as that stone-fronted mansion with real glass windows, and door-steps, and a real balcony—greener than I ever see now, except at watering places; and even they afford but a poor imitation. And though it *did* open all at once, the entire house-front (which was a blow, I admit, as cancelling the fiction of a staircase), it was but to shut it up again, and I could believe. Even open, there were three distinct rooms in it: a sitting-room and bed-room, elegantly furnished, and best of all, a kitchen, with uncommonly soft fire-irons, a plentiful assortment of diminutive utensils—oh, the warming-pan!—and a tin man-cook in profile, who was always going to fry two fish. What Barmecide justice have I done to the noble feasts wherein the set of wooden platters figured, each with its own peculiar delicacy, as a ham or turkey, glued tight on to it, and garnished with something green, which I recollect as moss! Could all the Temperance Societies of these later days, united, give me such a tea-drinking as I have had through the means of yonder little set of blue crockery, which really would hold liquid (it ran out of the small wooden cask, I recollect, and tasted of matches), and which made tea, nectar. And if the two legs of the ineffectual little sugar-tongs did tumble over one another, and want purpose, like Punch's hands, what does it matter? And if I did once shriek out, as a poisoned child, and strike the fashionable company with consternation, by reason of having drunk a little teaspoon, inadvertently dissolved in too hot tea, I was never the worse for it, except by a powder!

Upon the next branches of the tree, lower down, hard by the green roller and miniature gardening-tools, how thick the books begin to hang. Thin books, in themselves, at first, but many of them, and with deliciously smooth covers of bright red or green. What fat black letters to begin with! "A was an archer, and shot at a frog." Of course he was. He was an apple-pie also, and there he is! He was a good many things in his time, was A, and so were most of his friends, except X, who had so little versatility, that I never knew him to get beyond Xerxes or Xantippe—like Y, who was always confined to a Yacht or a Yew Tree; and Z condemned for ever to be a Zebra or a Zany. But, now, the very tree itself changes, and becomes a bean-stalk—the marvellous bean-stalk up which Jack climbed to the Giant's house! And now, those dreadfully interesting, double-headed giants, with their clubs over their shoulders, begin to stride along the boughs in a perfect throng, dragging knights and ladies home for dinner by the hair of their heads. And Jack—how noble, with his sword of sharpness, and his shoes of swiftness! Again those old meditations come upon me as I gaze up at him; and I debate within myself whether there was more than one Jack (which I am loth to believe possible), or only one genuine original admirable Jack, who achieved all the recorded exploits.

Good for Christmas-time is the ruddy colour of the cloak, in which—the tree making a forest of itself for her to trip through, with her basket—Little Red Riding-Hood comes to me one Christmas Eve to give me information of the cruelty and treachery of that dissembling Wolf who ate her grandmother, without making any impression on his appetite, and then ate her, after making that ferocious joke about his teeth. She was my first love. I felt that if I could have married Little Red Riding-Hood, I should have known perfect bliss. But, it was not to be; and there was nothing for it but to look out the Wolf in the Noah's Ark there, and put him late in the procession on the table, as a monster who was to be degraded. O the wonderful Noah's Ark! It was not found seaworthy when put in a washing-tub, and the animals were crammed in at the roof, and needed to have their legs well shaken down before they could be got in, even there—and then, ten to one but they began to tumble out at the door, which was but imperfectly fastened with a wire latch—but what was *that* against it! Consider the noble fly, a size or two smaller than the elephant: the lady-bird, the butterfly—all triumphs of art! Consider the goose, whose feet were so small, and whose balance was so indifferent, that he usually tumbled forward, and knocked down all the animal creation. Consider Noah and his family, like idiotic tobacco-stoppers; and how the leopard stuck to warm little fingers; and how the tails of the larger animals used gradually to resolve themselves into frayed bits of string!

Hush! Again a forest, and somebody up in a tree—not Robin Hood, not Valentine, not the Yellow Dwarf (I have passed him and all Mother Bunch's wonders, without mention), but an Eastern King with a glittering scimitar and turban. By Allah! two Eastern Kings, for I see another, looking over his shoulder! Down upon the grass, at the tree's foot, lies the full length of a coal-black Giant, stretched asleep, with his head in a lady's lap; and near them is a glass box, fastened with four locks of shining steel, in which he keeps the lady prisoner when he is awake. I see the four keys at his girdle now. The lady makes signs to the two kings in the tree, who softly descend. It is the setting-in of the bright Arabian Nights.

Oh, now all common things become uncommon and enchanted to me. All lamps are wonderful; all rings are talismans. Common flower-pots are full of treasure, with a little earth scattered on the top; trees are for Ali Baba to hide in; beefsteaks are to throw down into the Valley of Diamonds, that the precious stones may stick to them, and be carried by the eagles to their nests, whence the traders, with loud cries, will scare them. Tarts are made, according to the recipe of the Vizier's son of Bussorah, who turned pastrycook after he was set down in his drawers at the gate of Damascus; cobblers are all Mustaphas, and in the habit of sewing up people cut into four pieces, to whom they are taken blind-fold.

Any iron ring let into stone is the entrance to a cave which only waits for the magician, and the little fire, and the necromancy, that will make the earth shake. All the dates imported come from the same tree as that unlucky date, with whose shell the merchant knocked out the eye of the genie's invisible son. All olives are of the stock of that fresh fruit, concerning which the Commander of the Faithful overheard the boy conduct the fictitious trial of the fraudulent olive merchant; all apples are akin to the apple purchased (with two others) from the Sultan's gardener for three sequins, and which the tall black slave stole from the child. All dogs are associated with the dog, really a transformed man, who jumped upon the baker's counter, and put his paw on the piece of bad money. All rice recalls the rice which the awful lady, who was a ghoule, could only peck by grains, because of her nightly feasts in the burial-place. My very rocking-horse,—there he is, with his nostrils turned completely inside-out, indicative of Blood!—should have a peg in his neck, by virtue thereof to fly away with me, as the wooden horse did with the Prince of Persia, in the sight of all his father's Court.

Yes, on every object that I recognise among those upper branches of my Christmas Tree, I see this fairy light! When I wake in bed, at daybreak, on the cold dark winter mornings, the white snow dimly beheld, outside, through the frost on the window-pane, I hear Dinarzade. "Sister, sister, if you are yet awake, I pray you finish the history of the Young King of the Black Islands." Scheherazade replies, "If my lord the Sultan will suffer me to live another day, sister, I will not only finish that, but tell you a more wonderful story yet." Then, the gracious Sultan goes out, giving no orders for the execution, and we all three breathe again.

At this height of my tree I begin to see, cowering among the leaves—it may be born of turkey, or of pudding, or mince pie, or of these many fancies, jumbled with Robinson Crusoe on his desert island, Philip Quarll among the monkeys, Sandford and Merton with Mr. Barlow, Mother Bunch, and the Mask—or it may be the result of indigestion, assisted by imagination and over-doctoring—a prodigious nightmare. It is so exceedingly indistinct, that I don't know why it's frightful—but I know it is. I can only make out that it is an immense array of shapeless things, which appear to be planted on a vast exaggeration of the lazy-tongs that used to bear the toy soldiers, and to be slowly coming close to my eyes, and receding to an immeasurable distance. When it comes closest, it is worse. In connection with it I descry remembrances of winter nights incredibly long; of being sent early to bed, as a punishment for some small offence, and waking in two hours, with a sensation of having been asleep two nights; of the laden hopelessness of morning ever dawning; and the oppression of a weight of remorse.

And now, I see a wonderful row of little lights rise smoothly out of the ground, before a vast green curtain. Now, a bell rings—a magic bell, which still sounds in my ears unlike all other bells—and music plays, amidst a buzz of voices, and a fragrant smell of orange-peel and oil. Anon, the magic bell commands the music to cease, and the great green curtain rolls itself up majestically, and The Play begins! The devoted dog of Montargis avenges the death of his master, foully murdered in the Forest of Bondy; and a humorous Peasant with a red nose and a very little hat, whom I take from this hour forth to my bosom as a friend (I think he was a Waiter or an Hostler at a village Inn, but many years have passed since he and I have met), remarks that the sassigassity of that dog is indeed surprising; and evermore this jocular conceit will live in my remembrance fresh and unfading, overtopping all possible jokes, unto the end of time. Or now, I learn with bitter tears how poor Jane Shore, dressed all in white, and with her brown hair hanging down, went starving through the streets; or how George Barnwell killed the worthiest uncle that ever man had, and was afterwards so sorry for it that he ought to have been let off. Comes swift to comfort me, the Pantomime—stupendous Phenomenon!—when clowns are shot from loaded mortars into the great chandelier, bright constellation that it is; when Harlequins, covered all over with scales of pure gold, twist and sparkle, like amazing fish; when Pantaloon (whom I deem it no irreverence to compare in my own mind to my grandfather) puts red-hot pokers in his pocket, and cries "Here's somebody coming!" or taxes the Clown with petty larceny, by saying, "Now, I sawed you do it!" when Everything is capable, with the greatest ease, of being changed into Anything; and "Nothing is, but thinking makes it so." Now, too, I perceive my first experience of the dreary sensation—often to return in after-life—of being unable, next day, to get back to the dull, settled world; of wanting to live for ever in the bright atmosphere I have quitted; of doting on the little Fairy, with the wand like a celestial Barber's Pole, and pining for a Fairy immortality along with her. Ah, she comes back, in many shapes, as my eye wanders down the branches of my Christmas Tree, and goes as often, and has never yet stayed by me!

Out of this delight springs the toy-theatre,—there it is, with its familiar proscenium, and ladies in feathers, in the boxes!—and all its attendant occupation with paste and glue, and gum, and water colours, in the getting-up of The Miller and his Men, and Elizabeth, or the Exile of Siberia. In spite of a few besetting accidents and failures (particularly an unreasonable disposition in the respectable Kelmar, and some others, to become faint in the legs, and double up, at exciting points of the drama), a teeming world of fancies so suggestive and all-embracing, that, far below it on my Christmas Tree, I see dark, dirty, real Theatres in the day-time, adorned with these associations as with the freshest garlands of the rarest flowers, and charming me yet.

But hark! The Waits are playing, and they break my childish sleep! What images do I associate with the Christmas music as I see them set forth on the Christmas Tree? Known before all the others, keeping far apart from all the others, they gather round my little bed. An angel, speaking to a group of shepherds in a field; some travellers, with eyes uplifted, following a star; a baby in a manger; a child in a spacious temple, talking with grave men; a solemn figure, with a mild and beautiful face, raising a dead girl by the hand; again, near a city gate, calling back the son of a widow, on his bier, to life; a crowd of people looking through the opened roof of a chamber where he sits, and letting down a sick person on a bed, with ropes; the same, in a tempest, walking on the water to a ship; again, on a sea-shore, teaching a great multitude; again, with a child upon his knee, and other children round; again, restoring sight to the blind, speech to the dumb, hearing to the deaf, health to the sick, strength to the lame, knowledge to the ignorant; again, dying upon a Cross, watched by armed soldiers, a thick darkness coming on, the earth beginning to shake, and only one voice heard, "Forgive them, for they know not what they do."

Still, on the lower and maturer branches of the Tree, Christmas associations cluster thick. School-books shut up; Ovid and Virgil silenced; the Rule of Three, with its cool impertinent inquiries, long disposed of; Terence and Plautus acted no more, in an arena of huddled desks and forms, all chipped, and notched, and inked; cricket-bats, stumps, and balls, left higher up, with the smell of trodden grass and the softened noise of shouts in the evening air; the tree is still fresh, still gay. If I no more come home at Christmas-time, there will be boys and girls (thank Heaven!) while the World lasts; and they do! Yonder they dance and play upon the branches of my Tree, God bless them, merrily, and my heart dances and plays too!

And I *do* come home at Christmas. We all do, or we all should. We all come home, or ought to come home, for a short holiday—the longer, the better—from the great boarding-school, where we are for ever working at our arithmetical slates, to take, and give a rest. As to going a visiting, where can we not go, if we will; where have we not been, when we would; starting our fancy from our Christmas Tree!

Away into the winter prospect. There are many such upon the tree! On, by low-lying, misty grounds, through fens and fogs, up long hills, winding dark as caverns between thick plantations, almost shutting out the sparkling stars; so, out on broad heights, until we stop at last, with sudden silence, at an avenue. The gate-bell has a deep, half-awful sound in the frosty air; the gate swings open on its hinges; and, as we drive up to a great house, the glancing lights grow larger in the windows, and the opposing rows of trees seem to fall solemnly back on either side, to give us place. At intervals, all day, a frightened hare has shot across this whitened turf; or the distant clatter of a herd of deer trampling the hard frost, has, for the minute, crushed the silence too. Their watchful eyes beneath the fern may be shining now, if we could see them, like the icy dewdrops on the leaves; but they are still, and all is still. And so, the lights growing larger, and the trees falling back before us, and closing up again behind us, as if to forbid retreat, we come to the house.

There is probably a smell of roasted chestnuts and other good comfortable things all the time, for we are telling Winter Stories—Ghost Stories, or more shame for us—round the Christmas fire; and we have never stirred, except to draw a little nearer to it. But, no matter for that. We came to the house, and it is an old house, full of great chimneys where wood is burnt on ancient dogs upon the hearth, and grim portraits (some of them with grim legends, too) lower distrustfully from the oaken panels of the walls. We are a middle-aged nobleman, and we make a generous supper with our host and hostess and their guests—it being Christmas-time, and the old house full of company—and then we go to bed. Our room is a very old room. It is hung with tapestry. We don't like the portrait of a cavalier in green, over the fire-place. There are great black beams in the ceiling, and there is a great black bedstead, supported at the foot by two great black figures, who seem to have come off a couple of tombs in the old baronial church in the park, for our particular accommodation. But, we are not a superstitious nobleman, and we don't mind. Well! we dismiss our servant, lock the door, and sit before the fire in our dressing-gown, musing about a great many things. At length we go to bed. Well! we can't sleep. We toss and tumble, and can't sleep. The embers on the hearth burn fitfully and make the room look ghostly. We can't help peeping out over the counterpane, at the two black figures and the cavalier—that wicked-looking cavalier—in green. In the flickering light they seem to advance and retire: which, though we are not by any means a superstitious nobleman, is not agreeable. Well! we get nervous—more and more nervous. We say

"This is very foolish, but we can't stand this; we'll pretend to be ill, and knock up somebody." Well! we are just going to do it, when the locked door opens, and there comes in a young woman, deadly pale, and with long fair hair, who glides to the fire, and sits down in the chair we have left there, wringing her hands. Then, we notice that her clothes are wet. Our tongue cleaves to the roof of our mouth, and we can't speak; but, we observe her accurately. Her clothes are wet; her long hair is dabbled with moist mud; she is dressed in the fashion of two hundred years ago; and she has at her girdle a bunch of rusty keys. Well! there she sits, and we can't even faint, we are in such a state about it. Presently she gets up, and tries all the locks in the room with the rusty keys, which won't fit one of them; then, she fixes her eyes on the portrait of the cavalier in green, and says, in a low, terrible voice, "The stags know it!" After that, she wrings her hands again, passes the bedside, and goes out at the door. We hurry on our dressing-gown, seize our pistols (we always travel with pistols), and are following, when we find the door locked. We turn the key, look out into the dark gallery; no one there. We wander away, and try to find our servant. Can't be done. We pace the gallery till daybreak; then return to our deserted room, fall asleep, and are awakened by our servant (nothing ever haunts *him*) and the shining sun. Well! we make a wretched breakfast, and all the company say we look queer. After breakfast, we go over the house with our host, and then we take him to the portrait of the cavalier in green, and then it all comes out. He was false to a young housekeeper once attached to that family, and famous for her beauty, who drowned herself in a pond, and whose body was discovered, after a long time, because the stags refused to drink of the water. Since which, it has been whispered that she traverses the house at midnight (but goes especially to that room where the cavalier in green was wont to sleep), trying the old locks with the rusty keys. Well! we tell our host of what we have seen, and a shade comes over his features, and he begs it may be hushed up; and so it is. But, it's all true; and we said so, before we died (we are dead now) to many responsible people.

There is no end to the old houses, with resounding galleries, and dismal state-bedchambers, and haunted wings shut up for many years, through which we may ramble, with an agreeable creeping up our back, and encounter any number of ghosts, but (it is worthy of remark perhaps) reducible to a very few general types and classes; for, ghosts have little originality, and "walk" in a beaten track. Thus, it comes to pass, that a certain room in a certain old hall, where a certain bad lord, baronet, knight, or gentleman, shot himself, has certain planks in the floor from which the blood *will not* be taken out. You may scrape and scrape, as the present owner has done, or plane and plane, as his father did, or scrub and scrub, as his grandfather did, or burn and burn with strong acids, as his great-grandfather did, but, there the blood will still be—no redder and no paler—no more and no less—always just the same. Thus, in such another house there is a haunted door, that never will keep open; or another door that never will keep shut, or a haunted sound of a spinning-wheel, or a hammer, or a footstep, or a cry, or a sigh, or a horse's tramp, or the rattling of a chain. Or else, there is a turret-clock, which, at the midnight hour, strikes thirteen when the head of the family is going to die; or a shadowy, immovable black carriage which at such a time is always seen by somebody, waiting near the great gates in the stable-yard. Or thus, it came to pass how Lady Mary went to pay a visit at a large wild house in the Scottish Highlands, and, being fatigued with her long journey, retired to bed early, and innocently said, next morning, at the breakfast-table, "How odd, to have so late a party last night, in this remote place, and not to tell me of it, before I went to bed!" Then, every one asked Lady Mary what she meant? Then, Lady Mary replied, "Why, all night long, the carriages were driving round and round the terrace, underneath my window!" Then, the owner of the house turned pale, and so did his Lady, and Charles Macdoodle of Macdoodle signed to Lady Mary to say no more, and every one was silent. After breakfast, Charles Macdoodle told Lady Mary that it was a tradition in the family that those rumbling carriages on the terrace betokened death. And so it proved, for, two months afterwards, the Lady of the mansion died. And Lady Mary, who was a Maid of Honour at Court, often told this story to the old Queen Charlotte; by this token that the old King always said, "Eh, eh? What, what? Ghosts, ghosts? No such thing, no such thing!" And never left off saying so, until he went to bed.

Or, a friend of somebody's whom most of us know, when he was a young man at college, had a particular friend, with whom he made the compact that, if it were possible for the Spirit to return to this earth after its separation from the body, he of the twain who first died, should reappear to the other. In course of time, this compact was forgotten by our friend; the two young men having progressed in life, and taken diverging paths that were wide asunder. But, one night, many years afterwards, our friend being in the North of England, and staying for the night in an inn, on the Yorkshire Moors, happened to look out of bed; and there, in the moonlight, leaning on a bureau near the window, steadfastly regarding him, saw his old college friend! The appearance being solemnly addressed, replied, in a kind of whisper, but very audibly, "Do not come near me. I am dead. I am here to redeem my promise. I come from another world, but may not disclose its secrets!" Then, the whole form becoming paler, melted, as it were, into the moonlight, and faded away.

Or, there was the daughter of the first occupier of the picturesque Elizabethan house, so famous in our neighbourhood. You have heard about her? No! Why, *she* went out one summer evening at twilight, when she was a beautiful girl, just seventeen years of age, to gather flowers in the garden; and presently came running, terrified, into the hall to her father, saying, "Oh, dear father, I have met myself!" He took her in his arms, and told her it was fancy, but she said, "Oh no! I met myself in the broad walk, and I was pale and gathering withered flowers, and I turned my head, and held them up!" And, that night, she died; and a picture of her story was begun, though never finished, and they say it is somewhere in the house to this day, with its face to the wall.

Or, the uncle of my brother's wife was riding home on horseback, one mellow evening at sunset, when, in a green lane close to his own house, he saw a man standing before him, in the very centre of a narrow way. "Why does that man in the cloak stand there!" he thought. "Does he want me to ride over him?" But the figure never moved. He felt a strange sensation at seeing it so still, but slackened his trot and rode forward. When he was so close to it, as almost to touch it with his stirrup, his horse shied, and the figure glided up the bank, in a curious, unearthly manner—backward, and without seeming to use its feet—and was gone. The uncle of my brother's wife, exclaiming, "Good Heaven! It's my cousin Harry, from Bombay!" put spurs to his horse, which was suddenly in a profuse sweat, and, wondering at such strange behaviour, dashed round to the front of his house. There, he saw the same figure, just passing in at the long French window of the drawing-room, opening on the ground. He threw his bridle to a servant, and hastened in after it. His sister was sitting there, alone. "Alice, where's my cousin Harry?" "Your cousin Harry, John?" "Yes. From Bombay. I met him in the lane just now, and saw him enter here, this instant." Not a creature had been seen by any one; and in that hour and minute, as it afterwards appeared, this cousin died in India.

Or, it was a certain sensible old maiden lady, who died at ninety-nine, and retained her faculties to the last, who really did see the Orphan Boy; a story which has often been incorrectly told, but, of which the real truth is this—because it is, in fact, a story belonging to our family—and she was a connexion of our family. When she was about forty years of age, and still an uncommonly fine woman (her lover died young, which was the reason why she never married, though she had many offers), she went to stay at a place in Kent, which her brother, an Indian-Merchant, had newly bought. There was a story that this place had once been held in trust by the guardian of a young boy; who was himself the next heir, and who killed the young boy by harsh and cruel treatment. She knew nothing of that. It has been said that there was a Cage in her bedroom in which the guardian used to put the boy. There was no such thing. There was only a closet. She went to bed, made no alarm whatever in the night, and in the morning said composedly to her maid when she came in, "Who is the pretty forlorn-looking child who has been peeping out of that closet all night?" The maid replied by giving a loud scream, and instantly decamping. She was surprised; but she was a woman of remarkable strength of mind, and she dressed herself and went downstairs, and closeted herself with her brother. "Now,

Walter," she said, "I have been disturbed all night by a pretty, forlorn-looking boy, who has been constantly peeping out of that closet in my room, which I can't open. This is some trick." "I am afraid not, Charlotte," said he, "for it is the legend of the house. It is the Orphan Boy. What did he do?" "He opened the door softly," said she, "and peeped out. Sometimes, he came a step or two into the room. Then, I called to him, to encourage him, and he shrunk, and shuddered, and crept in again, and shut the door." "The closet has no communication, Charlotte," said her brother, "with any other part of the house, and it's nailed up." This was undeniably true, and it took two carpenters a whole forenoon to get it open, for examination. Then, she was satisfied that she had seen the Orphan Boy. But, the wild and terrible part of the story is, that he was also seen by three of her brother's sons, in succession, who all died young. On the occasion of each child being taken ill, he came home in a heat, twelve hours before, and said, Oh, mama, he had been playing under a particular oak-tree, in a certain meadow, with a strange boy—a pretty, forlorn-looking boy, who was very timid, and made signs! From fatal experience, the parents came to know that this was the Orphan Boy, and that the course of that child whom he chose for his little playmate was surely run.

Legion is the name of the German castles, where we sit up alone to wait for the Spectre—where we are shown into a room, made comparatively cheerful for our reception—where we glance round at the shadows, thrown on the blank walls by the crackling fire—where we feel very lonely when the village innkeeper and his pretty daughter have retired, after laying down a fresh store of wood upon the hearth, and setting forth on the small table such supper-cheer as a cold roast capon, bread, grapes, and a flask of old Rhine wine—where the reverberating doors close on their retreat, one after another, like so many peals of sullen thunder—and where, about the small hours of the night, we come into the knowledge of divers supernatural mysteries. Legion is the name of the haunted German students, in whose society we draw yet nearer to the fire, while the schoolboy in the corner opens his eyes wide and round, and flies off the footstool he has chosen for his seat, when the door accidentally blows open. Vast is the crop of such fruit, shining on our Christmas Tree; in blossom, almost at the very top; ripening all down the boughs!

Among the later toys and fancies hanging there—as idle often and less pure—be the images once associated with the sweet old Waits, the softened music in the night, ever unalterable! Encircled by the social thoughts of Christmas-time, still let the benignant figure of my childhood stand unchanged! In every cheerful image and suggestion that the season brings, may the bright star that rested above the poor roof, be the star of all the Christian World! A moment's pause, O vanishing tree, of which the lower boughs are dark to me as yet, and let me look once more! I know there are blank spaces on thy branches, where eyes that I have loved have shone and smiled;

from which they are departed. But, far above, I see the raiser of the dead girl, and the Widow's Son; and God is good! If Age be hiding for me in the unseen portion of thy downward growth, O may I, with a grey head, turn a child's heart to that figure yet, and a child's trustfulness and confidence!

Now, the tree is decorated with bright merriment, and song, and dance, and cheerfulness. And they are welcome. Innocent and welcome be they ever held, beneath the branches of the Christmas Tree, which cast no gloomy shadow! But, as it sinks into the ground, I hear a whisper going through the leaves. "This, in commemoration of the law of love and kindness, mercy and compassion. This, in remembrance of Me!"

What Christmas Is as We Grow Older

Time was, with most of us, when Christmas Day encircling all our limited world like a magic ring, left nothing out for us to miss or seek; bound together all our home enjoyments, affections, and hopes; grouped everything and every one around the Christmas fire; and made the little picture shining in our bright young eyes, complete.

Time came, perhaps, all too soon, when our thoughts over-leaped that narrow boundary; when there was some one (very dear, we thought then, very beautiful, and absolutely perfect) wanting to the fulness of our happiness; when we were wanting too (or we thought so, which did just as well) at the Christmas hearth by which that some one sat; and when we intertwined with every wreath and garland of our life that some one's name.

That was the time for the bright visionary Christmases which have long arisen from us to show faintly, after summer rain, in the palest edges of the rainbow! That was the time for the beatified enjoyment of the things that were to be, and never were, and yet the things that were so real in our resolute hope that it would be hard to say, now, what realities achieved since, have been stronger!

What! Did that Christmas never really come when we and the priceless pearl who was our young choice were received, after the happiest of totally impossible marriages, by the two united families previously at daggers—drawn on our account? When brothers and sisters-in-law who had always been rather cool to us before our relationship was effected, perfectly doted on us, and when fathers and mothers overwhelmed us with unlimited incomes? Was that Christmas dinner never really eaten, after which we arose, and generously and eloquently rendered honour to our late rival, present in the company, then and there exchanging friendship and forgiveness, and founding an attachment, not to be surpassed in Greek or Roman story, which subsisted until death? Has that same rival long ceased to care for that same priceless pearl, and married for money, and become usurious? Above all, do we really know, now, that we should probably have been miserable if we had won and worn the pearl, and that we are better without her?

That Christmas when we had recently achieved so much fame; when we had been carried in triumph somewhere, for doing something great and good; when we had won an honoured and ennobled name, and arrived and were received at home in a shower of tears of joy; is it possible that *that* Christmas has not come yet?

And is our life here, at the best, so constituted that, pausing as we advance at such a noticeable mile-stone in the track as this great birthday, we look back on the things that never were, as naturally and full as gravely as on the things that have been and are gone, or have been and still are? If it be so, and so it seems to be, must we come to the conclusion that life is little better than a dream, and little worth the loves and strivings that we crowd into it?

No! Far be such miscalled philosophy from us, dear Reader, on Christmas Day! Nearer and closer to our hearts be the Christmas spirit, which is the spirit of active usefulness, perseverance, cheerful discharge of duty, kindness and forbearance! It is in the last virtues especially, that we are, or should be, strengthened by the unaccomplished visions of our youth; for, who shall say that they are not our teachers to deal gently even with the impalpable nothings of the earth!

Therefore, as we grow older, let us be more thankful that the circle of our Christmas associations and of the lessons that they bring, expands! Let us welcome every one of them, and summon them to take their places by the Christmas hearth.

Welcome, old aspirations, glittering creatures of an ardent fancy, to your shelter underneath the holly! We know you, and have not outlived you yet. Welcome, old projects and old loves, however fleeting, to your nooks among the steadier lights that burn around us. Welcome, all that was ever real to our hearts; and for the earnestness that made you real, thanks to Heaven! Do we build no Christmas castles in the clouds now? Let our thoughts, fluttering like butterflies among these flowers of children, bear witness! Before this boy, there stretches out a Future, brighter than we ever looked on in our old romantic time, but bright with honour and with truth. Around this little head on which the sunny curls lie heaped, the graces sport, as prettily, as airily, as when there was no scythe within the reach of Time to shear away the curls of our first-love. Upon another girl's face near it—placider but smiling bright—a quiet and contented little face, we see Home fairly written. Shining from the word, as rays shine from a star, we see how, when our graves are old, other hopes than ours are young, other hearts than ours are moved; how other ways are smoothed; how other happiness blooms, ripens, and decays—no, not decays, for other homes and other bands of children, not yet in being nor for ages yet to be, arise, and bloom and ripen to the end of all!

Welcome, everything! Welcome, alike what has been, and what never was, and what we hope may be, to your shelter underneath the holly, to your places round the Christmas fire, where what is sits open-hearted! In yonder shadow, do we see obtruding furtively upon the blaze, an enemy's face? By Christmas Day we do forgive him! If the injury he has done us may admit of such companionship, let him come here and take his place. If otherwise, unhappily, let him go hence, assured that we will never injure nor accuse him.

On this day we shut out Nothing!

"Pause," says a low voice. "Nothing? Think!"

"On Christmas Day, we will shut out from our fireside, Nothing."

"Not the shadow of a vast City where the withered leaves are lying deep?" the voice replies. "Not the shadow that darkens the whole globe? Not the shadow of the City of the Dead?"

Not even that. Of all days in the year, we will turn our faces towards that City upon Christmas Day, and from its silent hosts bring those we loved, among us. City of the Dead, in the blessed name wherein we are gathered together at this time, and in the Presence that is here among us according to the promise, we will receive, and not dismiss, thy people who are dear to us!

Yes. We can look upon these children angels that alight, so solemnly, so beautifully among the living children by the fire, and can bear to think how they departed from us. Entertaining angels unawares, as the Patriarchs did, the playful children are unconscious of their guests; but we can see them—can see a radiant arm around one favourite neck, as if there were a tempting of that child away. Among the celestial figures there is one, a poor misshapen boy on earth, of a glorious beauty now, of whom his dying mother said it grieved her much to leave him here, alone, for so many years as it was likely would elapse before he came to her—being such a little child. But he went quickly, and was laid upon her breast, and in her hand she leads him.

There was a gallant boy, who fell, far away, upon a burning sand beneath a burning sun, and said, "Tell them at home, with my last love, how much I could have wished to kiss them once, but that I died contented and had done my duty!" Or there was another, over whom they read the words, "Therefore we commit his body to the deep," and so consigned him to the lonely ocean and sailed on. Or there was another, who lay down to his rest in the dark shadow of great forests, and, on earth, awoke no more. O shall they not, from sand and sea and forest, be brought home at such a time?

There was a dear girl—almost a woman—never to be one—who made a mourning Christmas in a house of joy, and went her trackless way to the silent City. Do we recollect her, worn out, faintly whispering what could not be heard, and falling into that last sleep for weariness? O look upon her now! O look upon her beauty, her serenity, her changeless youth, her happiness! The daughter of Jairus was recalled to life, to die; but she, more blest, has heard the same voice, saying unto her, "Arise for ever!"

We had a friend who was our friend from early days, with whom we often pictured the changes that were to come upon our lives, and merrily imagined how we would speak, and walk, and think, and talk, when we came to be old. His destined habitation in the City of the Dead received him in his prime. Shall he be shut out from our Christmas remembrance? Would his love have so excluded us? Lost friend, lost child, lost parent, sister, brother, husband, wife, we will not so discard you! You shall hold your cherished places in our Christmas hearts, and by our Christmas fires; and in the season of immortal hope, and on the birthday of immortal mercy, we will shut out Nothing!

The winter sun goes down over town and village; on the sea it makes a rosy path, as if the Sacred tread were fresh upon the water. A few more moments, and it sinks, and night comes on, and lights begin to sparkle in the prospect. On the hill-side beyond the shapelessly-diffused town, and in the quiet keeping of the trees that gird the village-steeple, remembrances are cut in stone, planted in common flowers, growing in grass, entwined with lowly brambles around many a mound of earth. In town and village, there are doors and windows closed against the weather, there are flaming logs heaped high, there are joyful faces, there is healthy music of voices. Be all ungentleness and harm excluded from the temples of the Household Gods, but be those remembrances admitted with tender encouragement! They are of the time and all its comforting and peaceful reassurances; and of the history that reunited even upon earth the living and the dead; and of the broad beneficence and goodness that too many men have tried to tear to narrow shreds.

The Poor Relation's Story

He was very reluctant to take precedence of so many respected members of the family, by beginning the round of stories they were to relate as they sat in a goodly circle by the Christmas fire; and he modestly suggested that it would be more correct if "John our esteemed host" (whose health he begged to drink) would have the kindness to begin. For as to himself, he said, he was so little used to lead the way that really—But as they all cried out here, that he must begin, and agreed with one voice that he might, could, would, and should begin, he left off rubbing his hands, and took his legs out from under his armchair, and did begin.

I have no doubt (said the poor relation) that I shall surprise the assembled members of our family, and particularly John our esteemed host to whom we are so much indebted for the great hospitality with which he has this day entertained us, by the confession I am going to make. But, if you do me the honour to be surprised at anything that falls from a person so unimportant in the family as I am, I can only say that I shall be scrupulously accurate in all I relate.

I am not what I am supposed to be. I am quite another thing. Perhaps before I go further, I had better glance at what I *am* supposed to be.

It is supposed, unless I mistake—the assembled members of our family will correct me if I do, which is very likely (here the poor relation looked mildly about him for contradiction); that I am nobody's enemy but my own. That I never met with any particular success in anything. That I failed in business because I was unbusiness-like and credulous—in not being prepared for the interested designs of my partner. That I failed in love, because I was ridiculously trustful—in thinking it impossible that Christiana could deceive me. That I failed in my expectations from my uncle Chill, on account of not being as sharp as he could have wished in worldly matters. That, through life, I have been rather put upon and disappointed in a general way. That I am at present a bachelor of between fifty-nine and sixty years of age, living on a limited income in the form of a quarterly allowance, to which I see that John our esteemed host wishes me to make no further allusion.

The supposition as to my present pursuits and habits is to the following effect.

I live in a lodging in the Clapham Road—a very clean back room, in a very respectable house—where I am expected not to be at home in the day-time, unless poorly; and which I usually leave in the morning at nine o'clock, on pretence of going to business. I take my breakfast—my roll and butter, and my half-pint of coffee—at the old-established coffee-shop near Westminster Bridge; and then I go into the City—I don't know why—and sit in Garraway's Coffee House, and on 'Change, and walk about, and look into a few offices and counting-houses where some of my relations or acquaintance are so good as to tolerate me, and where I stand by the fire if the weather happens to be cold. I get through the day in this way until five o'clock, and then I dine: at a cost, on the average, of one and threepence. Having still a little money to spend on my evening's entertainment, I look into the old-established coffee-shop as I go home, and take my cup of tea, and perhaps my bit of toast. So, as the large hand of the clock makes its way round to the morning hour again, I make my way round to the Clapham Road again, and go to bed when I get to my lodging—fire being expensive, and being objected to by the family on account of its giving trouble and making a dirt.

Sometimes, one of my relations or acquaintances is so obliging as to ask me to dinner. Those are holiday occasions, and then I generally walk in the Park. I am a solitary man, and seldom walk with anybody. Not that I am avoided because I am shabby; for I am not at all shabby, having always a very good suit of black on (or rather Oxford mixture, which has the appearance of black and wears much better); but I have got into a habit of speaking low, and being rather silent, and my spirits are not high, and I am sensible that I am not an attractive companion.

The only exception to this general rule is the child of my first cousin, Little Frank. I have a particular affection for that child, and he takes very kindly to me. He is a diffident boy by nature; and in a crowd he is soon run over, as I may say, and forgotten. He and I, however, get on exceedingly well. I have a fancy that the poor child will in time succeed to my peculiar position in the family. We talk but little; still, we understand each other. We walk about, hand in hand; and without much speaking he knows what I mean, and I know what he means. When he was very little indeed, I used to take him to the windows of the toy-shops, and show him the toys inside. It is surprising how soon he found out that I would have made him a great many presents if I had been in circumstances to do it.

Little Frank and I go and look at the outside of the Monument—he is very fond of the Monument—and at the Bridges, and at all the sights that are free. On two of my birthdays, we have dined on à-la-mode beef, and gone at half-price to the play, and been deeply interested. I was once walking with him in Lombard Street, which we often visit on account of my having mentioned to him that there are great riches there—he is very fond of Lombard Street—when a gentleman said to me as he passed by, "Sir, your little son has dropped his glove." I assure you, if you will excuse my remarking on so trivial a circumstance, this accidental mention of the child as mine, quite touched my heart and brought the foolish tears into my eyes.

When Little Frank is sent to school in the country, I shall be very much at a loss what to do with myself, but I have the intention of walking down there once a month and seeing him on a half holiday. I am told he will then be at play upon the Heath; and if my visits should be objected to, as unsettling the child, I can see him from a distance without his seeing me, and walk back again. His mother comes of a highly genteel family, and rather disapproves, I am aware, of our being too much together. I know that I am not calculated to improve his retiring disposition; but I think he would miss me beyond the feeling of the moment if we were wholly separated.

When I die in the Clapham Road, I shall not leave much more in this world than I shall take out of it; but, I happen to have a miniature of a bright-faced boy, with a curling head, and an open shirt-frill waving down his bosom (my mother had it taken for me, but I can't believe that it was ever like), which will be worth nothing to sell, and which I shall beg may he given to Frank. I have written my dear boy a little letter with it, in which I have told him that I felt very sorry to part from him, though bound to confess that I knew no reason why I should remain here. I have given him some short advice, the best in my power, to take warning of the consequences of being nobody's enemy but his own; and I have endeavoured to comfort him for what I fear he will consider a bereavement, by pointing out to him, that I was only a superfluous something to every one but him; and that having by some means failed to find a place in this great assembly, I am better out of it.

Such (said the poor relation, clearing his throat and beginning to speak a little louder) is the general impression about me. Now, it is a remarkable circumstance which forms the aim and purpose of my story, that this is all wrong. This is not my life, and these are not my habits. I do not even live in the Clapham Road. Comparatively speaking, I am very seldom there. I reside, mostly, in a—I am almost ashamed to say the word, it sounds so full of pretension—in a Castle. I do not mean that it is an old baronial habitation, but still it is a building always known to every one by the name of a Castle. In it, I preserve the particulars of my history; they run thus:

It was when I first took John Spatter (who had been my clerk) into partnership, and when I was still a young man of not more than five-and-twenty, residing in the house of my uncle Chill, from whom I had considerable expectations, that I ventured to propose to Christiana. I had loved Christiana a long time. She was very beautiful, and very winning in all respects. I rather mistrusted her widowed mother, who I feared was of a plotting and mercenary turn of mind; but, I thought as well of her as I could, for Christiana's sake. I never had loved any one but Christiana, and she had been all the world, and O far more than all the world, to me, from our childhood!

Christiana accepted me with her mother's consent, and I was rendered very happy indeed. My life at my uncle Chill's was of a spare dull kind, and my garret chamber was as dull, and bare, and cold, as an upper prison room in some stern northern fortress. But, having Christiana's love, I wanted nothing upon earth. I would not have changed my lot with any human being.

Avarice was, unhappily, my uncle Chill's master-vice. Though he was rich, he pinched, and scraped, and clutched, and lived miserably. As Christiana had no fortune, I was for some time a little fearful of confessing our engagement to him; but, at length I wrote him a letter, saying how it all truly was. I put it into his hand one night, on going to bed.

As I came downstairs next morning, shivering in the cold December air; colder in my uncle's unwarmed house than in the street, where the winter sun did sometimes shine, and which was at all events enlivened by cheerful faces and voices passing along; I carried a heavy heart towards the long, low breakfast-room in which my uncle sat. It was a large room with a small fire, and there was a great bay window in it which the rain had marked in the night as if with the tears of houseless people. It stared upon a raw yard, with a cracked stone pavement, and some rusted iron railings half uprooted, whence an ugly out-building that had once been a dissecting-room (in the time of the great surgeon who had mortgaged the house to my uncle), stared at it.

We rose so early always, that at that time of the year we breakfasted by candle-light. When I went into the room, my uncle was so contracted by the cold, and so huddled together in his chair behind the one dim candle, that I did not see him until I was close to the table.

As I held out my hand to him, he caught up his stick (being infirm, he always walked about the house with a stick), and made a blow at me, and said, "You fool!"

"Uncle," I returned, "I didn't expect you to be so angry as this." Nor had I expected it, though he was a hard and angry old man.

"You didn't expect!" said he; "when did you ever expect? When did you ever calculate, or look forward, you contemptible dog?"

"These are hard words, uncle!"

"Hard words? Feathers, to pelt such an idiot as you with," said he. "Here! Betsy Snap! Look at him!"

Betsy Snap was a withered, hard-favoured, yellow old woman—our only domestic—always employed, at this time of the morning, in rubbing my uncle's legs. As my uncle adjured her to look at me, he put his lean grip on the crown of her head, she kneeling beside him, and turned her face towards me. An involuntary thought connecting them both with the Dissecting Room, as it must often have been in the surgeon's time, passed across my mind in the midst of my anxiety.

"Look at the snivelling milksop!" said my uncle. "Look at the baby! This is the gentleman who, people say, is nobody's enemy but his own. This is the gentleman who can't say no. This is the gentleman who was making such large profits in his business that he must needs take a partner, t'other day. This is the gentleman who is going to marry a wife without a penny, and who falls into the hands of Jezebels who are speculating on my death!"

I knew, now, how great my uncle's rage was; for nothing short of his being almost beside himself would have induced him to utter that concluding word, which he held in such repugnance that it was never spoken or hinted at before him on any account.

"On my death," he repeated, as if he were defying me by defying his own abhorrence of the word. "On my death—death—Death! But I'll spoil the speculation. Eat your last under this roof, you feeble wretch, and may it choke you!"

You may suppose that I had not much appetite for the breakfast to which I was bidden in these terms; but, I took my accustomed seat. I saw that I was repudiated henceforth by my uncle; still I could bear that very well, possessing Christiana's heart.

He emptied his basin of bread and milk as usual, only that he took it on his knees with his chair turned away from the table where I sat. When he had done, he carefully snuffed out the candle; and the cold, slate-coloured, miserable day looked in upon us.

"Now, Mr. Michael," said he, "before we part, I should like to have a word with these ladies in your presence."

"As you will, Sir," I returned; "but you deceive yourself, and wrong us, cruelly, if you suppose that there is any feeling at stake in this contract but pure, disinterested, faithful love."

To this, he only replied, "You lie!" and not one other word.

We went, through half-thawed snow and half-frozen rain, to the house where Christiana and her mother lived. My uncle knew them very well. They were sitting at their breakfast, and were surprised to see us at that hour.

"Your servant, ma'am," said my uncle to the mother. "You divine the purpose of my visit, I dare say, ma'am. I understand there is a world of pure, disinterested, faithful love cooped up here. I am happy to bring it all it wants, to make it complete. I bring you your son-in-law, ma'am—and you, your husband, miss. The gentleman is a perfect stranger to me, but I wish him joy of his wise bargain."

He snarled at me as he went out, and I never saw him again.

It is altogether a mistake (continued the poor relation) to suppose that my dear Christiana, over-persuaded and influenced by her mother, married a rich man, the dirt from whose carriage wheels is often, in these changed times, thrown upon me as she rides by. No, no. She married me.

The way we came to be married rather sooner than we intended, was this. I took a frugal lodging and was saving and planning for her sake, when, one day, she spoke to me with great earnestness, and said:

"My dear Michael, I have given you my heart. I have said that I loved you, and I have pledged myself to be your wife. I am as much yours through all changes of good and evil as if we had been married on the day when such words passed between us. I know you well, and know that if we should be separated and our union broken off, your whole life would be shadowed, and all that might, even now, be stronger in your character for the conflict with the world would then be weakened to the shadow of what it is!"

"God help me, Christiana!" said I. "You speak the truth."

"Michael!" said she, putting her hand in mine, in all maidenly devotion, "let us keep apart no longer. It is but for me to say that I can live contented upon such means as you have, and I well know you are happy. I say so from my heart. Strive no more alone; let us strive together. My dear Michael, it is not right that I should keep secret from you what you do not suspect, but what distresses my whole life. My mother: without considering that what you have lost, you have lost for me, and on the assurance of my faith: sets her heart on riches, and urges another suit upon me, to my misery. I cannot bear this, for to bear it is to be untrue to you. I would rather share your struggles than look on. I want no better home than you can give me. I know that you will aspire and labour with a higher courage if I am wholly yours, and let it be so when you will!"

I was blest indeed, that day, and a new world opened to me. We were married in a very little while, and I took my wife to our happy home. That was the beginning of the residence I have spoken of; the Castle we have ever since inhabited together, dates from that time. All our children have been born in it. Our first child—now married—was a little girl, whom we called Christiana. Her son is so like Little Frank, that I hardly know which is which.

The current impression as to my partner's dealings with me is also quite erroneous. He did not begin to treat me coldly, as a poor simpleton, when my uncle and I so fatally quarrelled; nor did he afterwards gradually possess himself of our business and edge me out. On the contrary, he behaved to me with the utmost good faith and honour.

Matters between us took this turn:—On the day of my separation from my uncle, and even before the arrival at our counting-house of my trunks (which he sent after me, *not* carriage paid), I went down to our room of business, on our little wharf, overlooking the river; and there I told John Spatter what had happened. John did not say, in reply, that rich old relatives were palpable facts, and that love and sentiment were moonshine and fiction. He addressed me thus:

"Michael," said John, "we were at school together, and I generally had the knack of getting on better than you, and making a higher reputation."

"You had, John," I returned.

"Although" said John, "I borrowed your books and lost them; borrowed your pocket-money, and never repaid it; got you to buy my damaged knives at a higher price than I had given for them new; and to own to the windows that I had broken."

"All not worth mentioning, John Spatter," said I, "but certainly true."

"When you were first established in this infant business, which promises to thrive so well," pursued John, "I came to you, in my search for almost any employment, and you made me your clerk."

"Still not worth mentioning, my dear John Spatter," said I; "still, equally true."

"And finding that I had a good head for business, and that I was really useful *to* the business, you did not like to retain me in that capacity, and thought it an act of justice soon to make me your partner."

"Still less worth mentioning than any of those other little circumstances you have recalled, John Spatter," said I; "for I was, and am, sensible of your merits and my deficiencies."

"Now, my good friend," said John, drawing my arm through his, as he had had a habit of doing at school; while two vessels outside the windows of our counting-house—which were shaped like the stern windows of a ship—went lightly down the river with the tide, as John and I might then be sailing away in company, and in trust and confidence, on our voyage of life; "let there, under these friendly circumstances, be a right understanding between us. You are too easy, Michael. You are nobody's enemy but your own. If I were to give you that damaging character among our connexion, with a shrug, and a shake of the head, and a sigh; and if I were further to abuse the trust you place in me—"

"But you never will abuse it at all, John," I observed.

"Never!" said he; "but I am putting a case—I say, and if I were further to abuse that trust by keeping this piece of our common affairs in the dark, and this other piece in the light, and again this other piece in the twilight, and so on, I should strengthen my strength, and weaken your weakness, day by day, until at last I found myself on the high road to fortune, and you left behind on some bare common, a hopeless number of miles out of the way."

"Exactly so," said I.

"To prevent this, Michael," said John Spatter, "or the remotest chance of this, there must be perfect openness between us. Nothing must be concealed, and we must have but one interest."

"My dear John Spatter," I assured him, "that is precisely what I mean."

"And when you are too easy," pursued John, his face glowing with friendship, "you must allow me to prevent that imperfection in your nature from being taken advantage of, by any one; you must not expect me to humour it—"

"My dear John Spatter," I interrupted, "I *don't* expect you to humour it. I want to correct it."

"And I, too," said John.

"Exactly so!" cried I. "We both have the same end in view; and, honourably seeking it, and fully trusting one another, and having but one interest, ours will be a prosperous and happy partnership."

"I am sure of it!" returned John Spatter. And we shook hands most affectionately.

I took John home to my Castle, and we had a very happy day. Our partnership throve well. My friend and partner supplied what I wanted, as I had foreseen that he would, and by improving both the business and myself, amply acknowledged any little rise in life to which I had helped him.

I am not (said the poor relation, looking at the fire as he slowly rubbed his hands) very rich, for I never cared to be that; but I have enough, and am above all moderate wants and anxieties. My Castle is not a splendid place, but it is very comfortable, and it has a warm and cheerful air, and is quite a picture of Home.

Our eldest girl, who is very like her mother, married John Spatter's eldest son. Our two families are closely united in other ties of attachment. It is very pleasant of an evening, when we are all assembled together—which frequently happens—and when John and I talk over old times, and the one interest there has always been between us.

I really do not know, in my Castle, what loneliness is. Some of our children or grandchildren are always about it, and the young voices of my descendants are delightful—O, how delightful!—to me to hear. My dearest and most devoted wife, ever faithful, ever loving, ever helpful and sustaining and consoling, is the priceless blessing of my house; from whom all its other blessings spring. We are rather a musical family, and when Christiana sees me, at any time, a little weary or depressed, she steals to the piano and sings a gentle air she used to sing when we were first betrothed. So weak a man am I, that I cannot bear to hear it from any other source. They played it once, at the Theatre, when I was there with Little Frank; and the child said wondering, "Cousin Michael, whose hot tears are these that have fallen on my hand?"

Such is my Castle, and such are the real particulars of my life therein preserved. I often take Little Frank home there. He is very welcome to my grandchildren, and they play together. At this time of the year—the Christmas and New Year time—I am seldom out of my Castle. For, the associations of the season seem to hold me there, and the precepts of the season seem to teach me that it is well to be there.

* * *

"And the Castle is—" observed a grave, kind voice among the company.

"Yes. My Castle," said the poor relation, shaking his head as he still looked at the fire, "is in the Air. John our esteemed host suggests its situation accurately. My Castle is in the Air! I have done. Will you be so good as to pass the story!"

THE CHILD'S STORY

ONCE UPON A TIME, A GOOD MANY YEARS AGO, THERE WAS A TRAVELLER, and he set out upon a journey. It was a magic journey, and was to seem very long when he began it, and very short when he got half way through.

He travelled along a rather dark path for some little time, without meeting anything, until at last he came to a beautiful child. So he said to the child, "What do you do here?" And the child said, "I am always at play. Come and play with me!"

So, he played with that child, the whole day long, and they were very merry. The sky was so blue, the sun was so bright, the water was so sparkling, the leaves were so green, the flowers were so lovely, and they heard such singing-birds and saw so many butteries, that everything was beautiful. This was in fine weather. When it rained, they loved to watch the falling drops, and to smell the fresh scents. When it blew, it was delightful to listen to the wind, and fancy what it said, as it came rushing from its home—where was that, they wondered!—whistling and howling, driving the clouds before it, bending the trees, rumbling in the chimneys, shaking the house, and making the sea roar in fury. But, when it snowed, that was best of all; for, they liked nothing so well as to look up at the white flakes falling fast and thick, like down from the breasts of millions of white birds; and to see how smooth and deep the drift was; and to listen to the hush upon the paths and roads.

They had plenty of the finest toys in the world, and the most astonishing picture-books: all about scimitars and slippers and turbans, and dwarfs and giants and genii and fairies, and blue-beards and bean-stalks and riches and caverns and forests and Valentines and Orsons: and all new and all true.

But, one day, of a sudden, the traveller lost the child. He called to him over and over again, but got no answer. So, he went upon his road, and went on for a little while without meeting anything, until at last he came to a handsome boy. So, he said to the boy, "What do you do here?" And the boy said, "I am always learning. Come and learn with me."

So he learned with that boy about Jupiter and Juno, and the Greeks and the Romans, and I don't know what, and learned more than I could tell—or he either, for he soon forgot a great deal of it. But, they were not always learning; they had the merriest games that ever were played. They rowed upon the river in summer, and skated on the ice in winter; they were active afoot, and active on horseback; at cricket, and all games at ball; at prisoner's base, hare and hounds, follow my leader, and more sports than I can think of; nobody could beat them. They had holidays too, and Twelfth cakes, and parties where they danced till midnight, and real Theatres where they saw palaces of real gold and silver rise out of the real earth, and saw all the wonders of the world at once. As to friends, they had such dear friends and so many of them, that I want the time to reckon them up. They were all young, like the handsome boy, and were never to be strange to one another all their lives through.

Still, one day, in the midst of all these pleasures, the traveller lost the boy as he had lost the child, and, after calling to him in vain, went on upon his journey. So he went on for a little while without seeing anything, until at last he came to a young man. So, he said to the young man, "What do you do here?" And the young man said, "I am always in love. Come and love with me."

So, he went away with that young man, and presently they came to one of the prettiest girls that ever was seen—just like Fanny in the corner there—and she had eyes like Fanny, and hair like Fanny, and dimples like Fanny's, and she laughed and coloured just as Fanny does while I am talking about her. So, the young man fell in love directly—just as Somebody I won't mention, the first time he came here, did with Fanny. Well! he was teased sometimes—just as Somebody used to be by Fanny; and they quarrelled sometimes—just as Somebody and Fanny used to quarrel; and they made it up, and sat in the dark, and wrote letters every day, and never were happy asunder, and were always looking out for one another and pretending not to, and were engaged at Christmas-time, and sat close to one another by the fire, and were going to be married very soon—all exactly like Somebody I won't mention, and Fanny!

But, the traveller lost them one day, as he had lost the rest of his friends, and, after calling to them to come back, which they never did, went on upon his journey. So, he went on for a little while without seeing anything, until at last he came to a middle-aged gentleman. So, he said to the gentleman, "What are you doing here?" And his answer was, "I am always busy. Come and be busy with me!"

So, he began to be very busy with that gentleman, and they went on through the wood together. The whole journey was through a wood, only it had been open and green at first, like a wood in spring; and now began to be thick and dark, like a wood in summer; some of the little trees that had come out earliest, were even turning brown. The gentleman was not alone, but had a lady of about the same age with him, who was his Wife; and they had children, who were with them too. So, they all went on together through the wood, cutting down the trees, and making a path through the branches and the fallen leaves, and carrying burdens, and working hard.

Sometimes, they came to a long green avenue that opened into deeper woods. Then they would hear a very little, distant voice crying, "Father, father, I am another child! Stop for me!" And presently they would see a very little figure, growing larger as it came along, running to join them. When it came up, they all crowded round it, and kissed and welcomed it; and then they all went on together.

Sometimes, they came to several avenues at once, and then they all stood still, and one of the children said, "Father, I am going to sea," and another said, "Father, I am going to India," and another, "Father, I am going to seek my fortune where I can," and another, "Father, I am going to Heaven!" So, with many tears at parting, they went, solitary, down those avenues, each child upon its way; and the child who went to Heaven, rose into the golden air and vanished.

Whenever these partings happened, the traveller looked at the gentleman, and saw him glance up at the sky above the trees, where the day was beginning to decline, and the sunset to come on. He saw, too, that his hair was turning grey. But, they never could rest long, for they had their journey to perform, and it was necessary for them to be always busy.

At last, there had been so many partings that there were no children left, and only the traveller, the gentleman, and the lady, went upon their way in company. And now the wood was yellow; and now brown; and the leaves, even of the forest trees, began to fall.

So, they came to an avenue that was darker than the rest, and were pressing forward on their journey without looking down it when the lady stopped.

"My husband," said the lady. "I am called."

They listened, and they heard a voice a long way down the avenue, say, "Mother, mother!"

It was the voice of the first child who had said, "I am going to Heaven!" and the father said, "I pray not yet. The sunset is very near. I pray not yet!"

But, the voice cried, "Mother, mother!" without minding him, though his hair was now quite white, and tears were on his face.

Then, the mother, who was already drawn into the shade of the dark avenue and moving away with her arms still round his neck, kissed him, and said, "My dearest, I am summoned, and I go!" And she was gone. And the traveller and he were left alone together.

And they went on and on together, until they came to very near the end of the wood: so near, that they could see the sunset shining red before them through the trees.

Yet, once more, while he broke his way among the branches, the traveller lost his friend. He called and called, but there was no reply, and when he passed out of the wood, and saw the peaceful sun going down upon a wide purple prospect, he came to an old man sitting on a fallen tree. So, he said to the old man, "What do you do here?" And the old man said with a calm smile, "I am always remembering. Come and remember with me!"

So the traveller sat down by the side of that old man, face to face with the serene sunset; and all his friends came softly back and stood around him. The beautiful child, the handsome boy, the young man in love, the father, mother, and children: every one of them was there, and he had lost nothing. So, he loved them all, and was kind and forbearing with them all, and was always pleased to watch them all, and they all honoured and loved him. And I think the traveller must be yourself, dear Grandfather, because this what you do to us, and what we do to you.

The Schoolboy's Story

Being rather young at present—I am getting on in years, but still I am rather young—I have no particular adventures of my own to fall back upon. It wouldn't much interest anybody here, I suppose, to know what a screw the Reverend is, or what a griffin *she* is, or how they do stick it into parents—particularly hair-cutting, and medical attendance. One of our fellows was charged in his half's account twelve and sixpence for two pills—tolerably profitable at six and threepence a-piece, I should think—and he never took them either, but put them up the sleeve of his jacket.

As to the beef, it's shameful. It's *not* beef. Regular beef isn't veins. You can chew regular beef. Besides which, there's gravy to regular beef, and you never see a drop to ours. Another of our fellows went home ill, and heard the family doctor tell his father that he couldn't account for his complaint unless it was the beer. Of course it was the beer, and well it might be!

However, beef and Old Cheeseman are two different things. So is beer. It was Old Cheeseman I meant to tell about; not the manner in which our fellows get their constitutions destroyed for the sake of profit.

Why, look at the pie-crust alone. There's no flakiness in it. It's solid—like damp lead. Then our fellows get nightmares, and are bolstered for calling out and waking other fellows. Who can wonder!

Old Cheeseman one night walked in his sleep, put his hat on over his night-cap, got hold of a fishing-rod and a cricket-bat, and went down into the parlour, where they naturally thought from his appearance he was a Ghost. Why, he never would have done that if his meals had been wholesome. When we all begin to walk in our sleeps, I suppose they'll be sorry for it.

Old Cheeseman wasn't second Latin Master then; he was a fellow himself. He was first brought there, very small, in a post-chaise, by a woman who was always taking snuff and shaking him—and that was the most he remembered about it. He never went home for the holidays. His accounts (he never learnt any extras) were sent to a Bank, and the Bank paid them; and he had a brown suit twice a-year, and went into boots at twelve. They were always too big for him, too.

In the Midsummer holidays, some of our fellows who lived within walking distance, used to come back and climb the trees outside the playground wall, on purpose to look at Old Cheeseman reading there by himself. He was always as mild as the tea—and *that's* pretty mild, I should hope!—so when they whistled to him, he looked up and nodded; and when they said, "Halloa, Old Cheeseman, what have you had for dinner?" he said, "Boiled mutton"; and when they said, "An't it solitary, Old Cheeseman?" he said, "It is a little dull sometimes": and then they said, "Well good-bye, Old Cheeseman!" and climbed down again. Of course it was imposing on Old Cheeseman to give him nothing but boiled mutton through a whole Vacation, but that was just like the system. When they didn't give him boiled mutton, they gave him rice pudding, pretending it was a treat. And saved the butcher.

So Old Cheeseman went on. The holidays brought him into other trouble besides the loneliness; because when the fellows began to come back, not wanting to, he was always glad to see them; which was aggravating when they were not at all glad to see him, and so he got his head knocked against walls, and that was the way his nose bled. But he was a favourite in general. Once a subscription was raised for him; and, to keep up his spirits, he was presented before the holidays with two white mice, a rabbit, a pigeon, and a beautiful puppy. Old Cheeseman cried about it—especially soon afterwards, when they all ate one another.

Of course Old Cheeseman used to be called by the names of all sorts of cheeses—Double Glo'sterman, Family Cheshireman, Dutchman, North Wiltshireman, and all that. But he never minded it. And I don't mean to say he was old in point of years—because he wasn't—only he was called from the first, Old Cheeseman.

At last, Old Cheeseman was made second Latin Master. He was brought in one morning at the beginning of a new half, and presented to the school in that capacity as "Mr. Cheeseman." Then our fellows all agreed that Old Cheeseman was a spy, and a deserter, who had gone over to the enemy's camp, and sold himself for gold. It was no excuse for him that he had sold himself for very little gold—two pound ten a quarter and his washing, as was reported. It was decided by a Parliament which sat about it, that Old Cheeseman's mercenary motives could alone be taken into account, and that he had "coined our blood for drachmas." The Parliament took the expression out of the quarrel scene between Brutus and Cassius.

When it was settled in this strong way that Old Cheeseman was a tremendous traitor, who had wormed himself into our fellows' secrets on purpose to get himself into favour by giving up everything he knew, all courageous fellows were invited to come forward and enrol themselves in a Society for making a set against him. The President of the Society was First boy, named Bob Tarter. His father was in the West Indies, and he owned, himself, that his father was worth millions. He had great power among our fellows, and he wrote a parody, beginning—

"Who made believe to be so meek
That we could hardly hear him speak,
Yet turned out an Informing Sneak?
Old Cheeseman."

—and on in that way through more than a dozen verses, which he used to go and sing, every morning, close by the new master's desk. He trained one of the low boys, too, a rosy-cheeked little Brass who didn't care what he did, to go up to him with his Latin Grammar one morning, and say it so: *Nominativus pronominum*—Old Cheeseman, *raro exprimitur*—was never suspected, *nisi distinctionis*—of being an informer, *aut emphasis gratiâ*—until he proved one. *Ut*—for instance, *Vos damnastis*—when he sold the boys. *Quasi*—as though, *dicat*—he should say, *Præterea nemo*—I'm a Judas! All this produced a great effect on Old Cheeseman. He had never had much hair; but what he had, began to get thinner and thinner every day. He grew paler and more worn; and sometimes of an evening he was seen sitting at his desk with a precious long snuff to his candle, and his hands before his face, crying. But no member of the Society could pity him, even if he felt inclined, because the President said it was Old Cheeseman's conscience.

So Old Cheeseman went on, and didn't he lead a miserable life! Of course the Reverend turned up his nose at him, and of course *she* did—because both of them always do that at all the masters—but he suffered from the fellows most, and he suffered from them constantly. He never told about it, that the Society could find out; but he got no credit for that, because the President said it was Old Cheeseman's cowardice.

He had only one friend in the world, and that one was almost as powerless as he was, for it was only Jane. Jane was a sort of wardrobe woman to our fellows, and took care of the boxes. She had come at first, I believe, as a kind of apprentice—some of our fellows say from a Charity, but I don't know—and after her time was out, had stopped at so much a year. So little a year, perhaps I ought to say, for it is far more likely. However, she had put some pounds in the Savings' Bank, and she was a very nice young woman. She was not quite pretty; but she had a very frank, honest, bright face, and all our fellows were fond of her. She was uncommonly neat and cheerful, and uncommonly comfortable and kind. And if anything was the matter with a fellow's mother, he always went and showed the letter to Jane.

Jane was Old Cheeseman's friend. The more the Society went against him, the more Jane stood by him. She used to give him a good-humoured look out of her still-room window, sometimes, that seemed to set him up for the day. She used to pass out of the orchard and the kitchen garden (always kept locked, I believe you!) through the playground, when she might have gone the other way, only to give a turn of her head, as much as to say "Keep up your spirits!" to Old Cheeseman. His slip of a room was so fresh and orderly that it was well known who looked after it while he was at his desk; and when our fellows saw a smoking hot dumpling on his plate at dinner, they knew with indignation who had sent it up.

Under these circumstances, the Society resolved, after a quantity of meeting and debating, that Jane should be requested to cut Old Cheeseman dead; and that if she refused, she must be sent to Coventry herself. So a deputation, headed by the President, was appointed to wait on Jane, and inform her of the vote the Society had been under the painful necessity of passing. She was very much respected for all her good qualities, and there was a story about her having once waylaid the Reverend in his own study, and got a fellow off from severe punishment, of her own kind comfortable heart. So the deputation didn't much like the job. However, they went up, and the President told Jane all about it. Upon which Jane turned very red, burst into tears, informed the President and the deputation, in a way not at all like her usual way, that they were a parcel of malicious young savages, and turned the whole respected body out of the room. Consequently it was entered in the Society's book (kept in astronomical cypher for fear of detection), that all communication with Jane was interdicted: and the President addressed the members on this convincing instance of Old Cheeseman's undermining.

But Jane was as true to Old Cheeseman as Old Cheeseman was false to our fellows—in their opinion, at all events—and steadily continued to be his only friend. It was a great exasperation to the Society, because Jane was as much a loss to them as she was a gain to him; and being more inveterate against him than ever, they treated him worse than ever. At last, one morning, his desk stood empty, his room was peeped into, and found to be vacant, and a whisper went about among the pale faces of our fellows that Old Cheeseman, unable to bear it any longer, had got up early and drowned himself.

The mysterious looks of the other masters after breakfast, and the evident fact that old Cheeseman was not expected, confirmed the Society in this opinion. Some began to discuss whether the President was liable to hanging or only transportation for life, and the President's face showed a great anxiety to know which. However, he said that a jury of his country should find him game; and that in his address he should put it to them to lay their hands upon their hearts and say whether they as Britons approved of informers, and how they thought they would like it themselves. Some of the Society considered that he had better run away until he found a forest where he might change clothes with a wood-cutter, and stain his face with blackberries; but the majority believed that if he stood his ground, his father—belonging as he did to the West Indies, and being worth millions—could buy him off.

All our fellows' hearts beat fast when the Reverend came in, and made a sort of a Roman, or a Field-Marshal, of himself with the ruler; as he always did before delivering an address. But their fears were nothing to their astonishment when he came out with the story that Old Cheeseman, "so long our respected friend and fellow-pilgrim in the pleasant plains of knowledge," he called him—O yes! I dare say! Much of that!—was the orphan child of a disinherited young lady who had married against her father's wish, and whose young husband had died, and who had died of sorrow herself, and whose unfortunate baby (Old Cheeseman) had been brought up at the cost of a grandfather who would never consent to see it, baby, boy, or man: which grandfather was now dead, and serve him right—that's my putting in—and which grandfather's large property, there being no will, was now, and all of a sudden and for ever, Old Cheeseman's! Our so long respected friend and fellow-pilgrim in the pleasant plains of knowledge, the Reverend wound up a lot of bothering quotations by saying, would "come among us once more" that day fortnight, when he desired to take leave of us himself, in a more particular manner. With these words, he stared severely round at our fellows, and went solemnly out.

There was precious consternation among the members of the Society, now. Lots of them wanted to resign, and lots more began to try to make out that they had never belonged to it. However, the President stuck up, and said that they must stand or fall together, and that if a breach was made it should be over his body—which was meant to encourage the Society: but it didn't. The President further said, he would consider the position in which they stood, and would give them his best opinion and advice in a few days. This was eagerly looked for, as he knew a good deal of the world on account of his father's being in the West Indies.

After days and days of hard thinking, and drawing armies all over his slate, the President called our fellows together, and made the matter clear. He said it was plain that when Old Cheeseman came on the appointed day, his first revenge would be to impeach the Society, and have it flogged all round. After witnessing with joy the torture of his enemies, and gloating over the cries which agony would extort from them, the probability was that he would invite the Reverend, on pretence of conversation, into a private room—say the parlour into which Parents were shown, where the two great globes were which were never used—and would there reproach him with the various frauds and oppressions he had endured at his hands. At the close of his observations he would make a signal to a Prizefighter concealed in the passage, who would then appear and pitch into the Reverend, till he was left insensible. Old Cheeseman would then make Jane a present of from five to ten pounds, and would leave the establishment in fiendish triumph.

The President explained that against the parlour part, or the Jane part, of these arrangements he had nothing to say; but, on the part of the Society, he counselled deadly resistance. With this view he recommended that all available desks should be filled with stones, and that the first word of the complaint should be the signal to every fellow to let fly at Old Cheeseman. The bold advice put the Society in better spirits, and was unanimously taken. A post about Old Cheeseman's size was put up in the playground, and all our fellows practised at it till it was dinted all over.

When the day came, and Places were called, every fellow sat down in a tremble. There had been much discussing and disputing as to how Old Cheeseman would come; but it was the general opinion that he would appear in a sort of triumphal car drawn by four horses, with two livery servants in front, and the Prizefighter in disguise up behind. So, all our fellows sat listening for the sound of wheels. But no wheels were heard, for Old Cheeseman walked after all, and came into the school without any preparation. Pretty much as he used to be, only dressed in black.

"Gentlemen," said the Reverend, presenting him, "our so long respected friend and fellow-pilgrim in the pleasant plains of knowledge, is desirous to offer a word or two. Attention, gentlemen, one and all!"

Every fellow stole his hand into his desk and looked at the President. The President was all ready, and taking aim at old Cheeseman with his eyes.

What did Old Cheeseman then, but walk up to his old desk, look round him with a queer smile as if there was a tear in his eye, and begin in a quavering, mild voice, "My dear companions and old friends!"

Every fellow's hand came out of his desk, and the President suddenly began to cry.

"My dear companions and old friends," said Old Cheeseman, "you have heard of my good fortune. I have passed so many years under this roof—my entire life so far, I may say—that I hope you have been glad to hear of it for my sake. I could never enjoy it without exchanging congratulations with you. If we have ever misunderstood one another at all, pray, my dear boys, let us forgive and forget. I have a great tenderness for you, and I am sure you return it. I want in the fulness of a grateful heart to shake hands with you every one. I have come back to do it, if you please, my dear boys."

Since the President had begun to cry, several other fellows had broken out here and there: but now, when Old Cheeseman began with him as first boy, laid his left hand affectionately on his shoulder and gave him his right; and when the President said "Indeed, I don't deserve it, sir; upon my honour I don't;" there was sobbing and crying all over the school. Every other fellow said he didn't deserve it, much in the same way; but Old Cheeseman, not minding that a bit, went cheerfully round to every boy, and wound up with every master—finishing off the Reverend last.

Then a snivelling little chap in a corner, who was always under some punishment or other, set up a shrill cry of "Success to Old Cheeseman! Hooray!" The Reverend glared upon him, and said, "*Mr.* Cheeseman, Sir." But, Old Cheeseman protesting that he liked his old name a great deal better than his new one, all our fellows took up the cry; and, for I don't know how many minutes, there was such a thundering of feet and hands, and such a roaring of Old Cheeseman, as never was heard.

After that, there was a spread in the dining-room of the most magnificent kind. Fowls, tongues, preserves, fruits, confectionaries, jellies, neguses, barley-sugar temples, trifles, crackers—eat all you can and pocket what you like—all at Old Cheeseman's expense. After that, speeches, whole holiday, double and treble sets of all manners of things for all manners of games, donkeys, pony-chaises and drive yourself, dinner for all the masters at the Seven Bells (twenty pounds a-head our fellows estimated it at), an annual holiday and feast fixed for that day every year, and another on Old Cheeseman's birthday—Reverend bound down before the fellows to allow it, so that he could never back out—all at Old Cheeseman's expense.

And didn't our fellows go down in a body and cheer outside the Seven Bells? O no!

But there's something else besides. Don't look at the next story-teller, for there's more yet. Next day, it was resolved that the Society should make it up with Jane, and then be dissolved. What do you think of Jane being gone, though? "What? Gone for ever?" said our fellows, with long faces. "Yes, to be sure," was all the answer they could get. None of the people about the house would say anything more. At length, the first boy took upon himself to ask the Reverend whether our old friend Jane was really gone? The Reverend (he has got a daughter at home—turn-up nose, and red) replied severely, "Yes, sir, Miss Pitt is gone." The idea of calling Jane, Miss Pitt! Some said she had been sent away in disgrace for taking money from Old Cheeseman; others said she had gone into Old Cheeseman's service at a rise of ten pounds a year. All that our fellows knew, was, she was gone.

It was two or three months afterwards, when, one afternoon, an open carriage stopped at the cricket field, just outside bounds, with a lady and gentleman in it, who looked at the game a long time and stood up to see it played. Nobody thought much about them, until the same little snivelling chap came in, against all rules, from the post where he was Scout, and said, "It's Jane!" Both Elevens forgot the game directly, and ran crowding round the carriage. It *was* Jane! In such a bonnet! And if you'll believe me, Jane was married to Old Cheeseman.

It soon became quite a regular thing when our fellows were hard at it in the playground, to see a carriage at the low part of the wall where it joins the high part, and a lady and gentleman standing up in it, looking over. The gentleman was always Old Cheeseman, and the lady was always Jane.

The first time I ever saw them, I saw them in that way. There had been a good many changes among our fellows then, and it had turned out that Bob Tarter's father wasn't worth Millions! He wasn't worth anything. Bob had gone for a soldier, and

Old Cheeseman had purchased his discharge. But that's not the carriage. The carriage stopped, and all our fellows stopped as soon as it was seen.

"So you have never sent me to Coventry after all!" said the lady, laughing, as our fellows swarmed up the wall to shake hands with her. "Are you never going to do it?"

"Never! never! never!" on all sides.

I didn't understand what she meant then, but of course I do now. I was very much pleased with her face though, and with her good way, and I couldn't help looking at her—and at him too—with all our fellows clustering so joyfully about them.

They soon took notice of me as a new boy, so I thought I might as well swarm up the wall myself, and shake hands with them as the rest did. I was quite as glad to see them as the rest were, and was quite as familiar with them in a moment.

"Only a fortnight now," said Old Cheeseman, "to the holidays. Who stops? Anybody?"

A good many fingers pointed at me, and a good many voices cried "He does!" For it was the year when you were all away; and rather low I was about it, I can tell you.

"Oh!" said Old Cheeseman. "But it's solitary here in the holiday time. He had better come to us."

So I went to their delightful house, and was as happy as I could possibly be. They understand how to conduct themselves towards boys, *they* do. When they take a boy to the play, for instance, they *do* take him. They don't go in after it's begun, or come out before it's over. They know how to bring a boy up, too. Look at their own! Though he is very little as yet, what a capital boy he is! Why, my next favourite to Mrs. Cheeseman and Old Cheeseman, is young Cheeseman.

So, now I have told you all I know about Old Cheeseman. And it's not much after all, I am afraid. Is it?

Nobody's Story

HE LIVED ON THE BANK OF A MIGHTY RIVER, BROAD AND DEEP, WHICH was always silently rolling on to a vast undiscovered ocean. It had rolled on, ever since the world began. It had changed its course sometimes, and turned into new channels, leaving its old ways dry and barren; but it had ever been upon the flow, and ever was to flow until Time should be no more. Against its strong, unfathomable stream, nothing made head. No living creature, no flower, no leaf, no particle of animate or inanimate existence, ever strayed back from the undiscovered ocean. The tide of the river set resistlessly towards it; and the tide never stopped, any more than the earth stops in its circling round the sun.

He lived in a busy place, and he worked very hard to live. He had no hope of ever being rich enough to live a month without hard work, but he was quite content, GOD knows, to labour with a cheerful will. He was one of an immense family, all of whose sons and daughters gained their daily bread by daily work, prolonged from their rising up betimes until their lying down at night. Beyond this destiny he had no prospect, and he sought none.

There was over-much drumming, trumpeting, and speech-making, in the neighbourhood where he dwelt; but he had nothing to do with that. Such clash and uproar came from the Bigwig family, at the unaccountable proceedings of which race, he marvelled much. They set up the strangest statues, in iron, marble, bronze, and brass, before his door; and darkened his house with the legs and tails of uncouth images of horses. He wondered what it all meant, smiled in a rough good-humoured way he had, and kept at his hard work.

The Bigwig family (composed of all the stateliest people thereabouts, and all the noisiest) had undertaken to save him the trouble of thinking for himself, and to manage him and his affairs. "Why truly," said he, "I have little time upon my hands; and if you will be so good as to take care of me, in return for the money I pay over"—for the Bigwig family were not above his money—"I shall be relieved and much obliged, considering that you know best." Hence the drumming, trumpeting, and speech-making, and the ugly images of horses which he was expected to fall down and worship.

"I don't understand all this," said he, rubbing his furrowed brow confusedly. "But it *has* a meaning, maybe, if I could find it out."

"It means," returned the Bigwig family, suspecting something of what he said, "honour and glory in the highest, to the highest merit."

"Oh!" said he. And he was glad to hear that.

But, when he looked among the images in iron, marble, bronze, and brass, he failed to find a rather meritorious countryman of his, once the son of a Warwickshire wool-dealer, or any single countryman whomsoever of that kind. He could find none of the men whose knowledge had rescued him and his children from terrific and disfiguring disease, whose boldness had raised his forefathers from the condition of serfs, whose wise fancy had opened a new and high existence to the humblest, whose skill had filled the working man's world with accumulated wonders. Whereas, he did find others whom he knew no good of, and even others whom he knew much ill of.

"Humph!" said he. "I don't quite understand it."

So, he went home, and sat down by his fireside to get it out of his mind.

Now, his fireside was a bare one, all hemmed in by blackened streets; but it was a precious place to him. The hands of his wife were hardened with toil, and she was old before her time; but she was dear to him. His children, stunted in their growth, bore traces of unwholesome nurture; but they had beauty in his sight. Above all other things, it was an earnest desire of this man's soul that his children should be taught. "If I am sometimes misled," said he, "for want of knowledge, at least let them know better, and avoid my mistakes. If it is hard to me to reap the harvest of pleasure and instruction that is stored in books, let it be easier to them."

But, the Bigwig family broke out into violent family quarrels concerning what it was lawful to teach to this man's children. Some of the family insisted on such a thing being primary and indispensable above all other things; and others of the family insisted on such another thing being primary and indispensable above all other things; and the Bigwig family, rent into factions, wrote pamphlets, held convocations, delivered charges, orations, and all varieties of discourses; impounded one another in courts Lay and courts Ecclesiastical; threw dirt, exchanged pummelings, and fell together by the ears in unintelligible animosity. Meanwhile, this man, in his short evening snatches at his fireside, saw the demon Ignorance arise there, and take his children to itself. He saw his daughter perverted into a heavy, slatternly drudge; he saw his son go moping down the ways of low sensuality, to brutality and crime; he saw the dawning light of intelligence in the eyes of his babies so changing into cunning and suspicion, that he could have rather wished them idiots.

"I don't understand this any the better," said he; "but I think it cannot be right. Nay, by the clouded Heaven above me, I protest against this as my wrong!"

Becoming peaceable again (for his passion was usually short-lived, and his nature kind), he looked about him on his Sundays and holidays, and he saw how much monotony and weariness there was, and thence how drunkenness arose with all its train of ruin. Then he appealed to the Bigwig family, and said, "We are a labouring people, and I have a glimmering suspicion in me that labouring people of whatever condition were made—by a higher intelligence than yours, as I poorly understand it—to be in need of mental refreshment and recreation. See what we fall into, when we rest without it. Come! Amuse me harmlessly, show me something, give me an escape!"

But, here the Bigwig family fell into a state of uproar absolutely deafening. When some few voices were faintly heard, proposing to show him the wonders of the world, the greatness of creation, the mighty changes of time, the workings of nature and the beauties of art—to show him these things, that is to say, at any period of his life when he could look upon them—there arose among the Bigwigs such roaring and raving, such pulpiting and petitioning, such maundering and memorialising, such name-calling and dirt-throwing, such a shrill wind of parliamentary questioning and feeble replying—where "I dare not" waited on "I would"—that the poor fellow stood aghast, staring wildly around.

"Have I provoked all this," said he, with his hands to his affrighted ears, "by what was meant to be an innocent request, plainly arising out of my familiar experience, and the common knowledge of all men who choose to open their eyes? I don't understand, and I am not understood. What is to come of such a state of things?"

He was bending over his work, often asking himself the question, when the news began to spread that a pestilence had appeared among the labourers, and was slaying them by thousands. Going forth to look about him, he soon found this to be true. The dying and the dead were mingled in the close and tainted houses among which his life was passed. New poison was distilled into the always murky, always sickening air. The robust and the weak, old age and infancy, the father and the mother, all were stricken down alike.

What means of flight had he? He remained there, where he was, and saw those who were dearest to him die. A kind preacher came to him, and would have said some prayers to soften his heart in his gloom, but he replied:

"O what avails it, missionary, to come to me, a man condemned to residence in this foetid place, where every sense bestowed upon me for my delight becomes a torment, and where every minute of my numbered days is new mire added to the heap under which I lie oppressed! But, give me my first glimpse of Heaven, through a little of its light and air; give me pure water; help me to be clean; lighten this heavy atmosphere and heavy life, in which our spirits sink, and we become the indifferent and callous creatures you too often see us; gently and kindly take the bodies of those who die among us, out of the small room where we grow to be so familiar with the awful change that even its sanctity is lost to us; and, Teacher, then I will hear—none know better than you, how willingly—of Him whose thoughts were so much with the poor, and who had compassion for all human sorrow!"

He was at work again, solitary and sad, when his Master came and stood near to him dressed in black. He, also, had suffered heavily. His young wife, his beautiful and good young wife, was dead; so, too, his only child.

"Master, 'tis hard to bear—I know it—but be comforted. I would give you comfort, if I could."

The Master thanked him from his heart, but, said he, "O you labouring men! The calamity began among you. If you had but lived more healthily and decently, I should not be the widowed and bereft mourner that I am this day."

"Master," returned the other, shaking his head, "I have begun to understand a little that most calamities will come from us, as this one did, and that none will stop at our poor doors, until we are united with that great squabbling family yonder, to do the things that are right. We cannot live healthily and decently, unless they who undertook to manage us provide the means. We cannot be instructed unless they will teach us; we cannot be rationally amused, unless they will amuse us; we cannot but have some false gods of our own, while they set up so many of theirs in all the public places. The evil consequences of imperfect instruction, the evil consequences of pernicious neglect, the evil consequences of unnatural restraint and the denial of humanising enjoyments, will all come from us, and none of them will stop with us. They will spread far and wide. They always do; they always have done—just like the pestilence. I understand so much, I think, at last."

But the Master said again, "O you labouring men! How seldom do we ever hear of you, except in connection with some trouble!"

"Master," he replied, "I am Nobody, and little likely to be heard of (nor yet much wanted to be heard of, perhaps), except when there is some trouble. But it never begins with me, and it never can end with me. As sure as Death, it comes down to me, and it goes up from me."

There was so much reason in what he said, that the Bigwig family, getting wind of it, and being horribly frightened by the late desolation, resolved to unite with him to do the things that were right—at all events, so far as the said things were associated with the direct prevention, humanly speaking, of another pestilence. But, as their fear wore off, which it soon began to do, they resumed their falling out among themselves, and did nothing. Consequently the scourge appeared again—low down as before—and spread avengingly upward as before, and carried off vast numbers of the brawlers. But not a man among them ever admitted, if in the least degree he ever perceived, that he had anything to do with it.

So Nobody lived and died in the old, old, old way; and this, in the main, is the whole of Nobody's story.

Had he no name, you ask? Perhaps it was Legion. It matters little what his name was. Let us call him Legion.

If you were ever in the Belgian villages near the field of Waterloo, you will have seen, in some quiet little church, a monument erected by faithful companions in arms to the memory of Colonel A, Major B, Captains C, D and E, Lieutenants F and G, Ensigns H, I and J, seven non-commissioned officers, and one hundred and thirty rank and file, who fell in the discharge of their duty on the memorable day. The story of Nobody is the story of the rank and file of the earth. They bear their share of the battle; they have their part in the victory; they fall; they leave no name but in the mass. The march of the proudest of us, leads to the dusty way by which they go. O! Let us think of them this year at the Christmas fire, and not forget them when it is burnt out.

The Seven Poor Travellers

IN THREE CHAPTERS

Chapter I

In the Old City of Rochester

Strictly speaking, there were only six Poor Travellers; but, being a Traveller myself, though an idle one, and being withal as poor as I hope to be, I brought the number up to seven. This word of explanation is due at once, for what says the inscription over the quaint old door?

Richard Watts, Esq.
by his Will, dated 22 Aug. 1579,
founded this Charity
for Six poor Travellers,
who not being Rogues, or Proctors,
May receive gratis for one Night,
Lodging, Entertainment,
and Fourpence each.

It was in the ancient little city of Rochester in Kent, of all the good days in the year upon a Christmas-eve, that I stood reading this inscription over the quaint old door in question. I had been wandering about the neighbouring Cathedral, and had seen the tomb of Richard Watts, with the effigy of worthy Master Richard starting out of it like a ship's figure-head; and I had felt that I could do no less, as I gave the Verger his fee, than inquire the way to Watts's Charity. The way being very short and very plain, I had come prosperously to the inscription and the quaint old door.

"Now," said I to myself, as I looked at the knocker, "I know I am not a Proctor; I wonder whether I am a Rogue!"

Upon the whole, though Conscience reproduced two or three pretty faces which might have had smaller attraction for a moral Goliath than they had had for me, who am but a Tom Thumb in that way, I came to the conclusion that I was not a Rogue. So, beginning to regard the establishment as in some sort my property, bequeathed to me and divers co-legatees, share and share alike, by the Worshipful Master Richard Watts, I stepped backward into the road to survey my inheritance.

I found it to be a clean white house, of a staid and venerable air, with the quaint old door already three times mentioned (an arched door), choice little long low lattice-windows, and a roof of three gables. The silent High street of Rochester is full of gables, with old beams and timbers carved into strange faces. It is oddly garnished with a queer old clock that projects over the pavement out of a grave red-brick building, as if Time carried on business there, and hung out his sign. Sooth to say, he did an active stroke of work in Rochester, in the old days of the Romans, and the Saxons, and the Normans; and down to the times of King John, when the rugged castle—I will not undertake to say how many hundreds of years old then—was abandoned to the centuries of weather which have so defaced the dark apertures in its walls, that the ruin looks as if the rooks and daws had pecked its eyes out.

I was very well pleased, both with my property and its situation. While I was yet surveying it with growing content, I espied, at one of the upper lattices which stood open, a decent body, of a wholesome matronly appearance, whose eyes I caught inquiringly addressed to mine. They said so plainly, "Do you wish to see the house?" that I answered aloud, "Yes, if you please." And within a minute the old door opened, and I bent my head, and went down two steps into the entry.

"This," said the matronly presence, ushering me into a low room on the right, "is where the Travellers sit by the fire, and cook what bits of suppers they buy with their fourpences."

"O! Then they have no Entertainment?" said I. For the inscription over the outer door was still running in my head, and I was mentally repeating, in a kind of tune, "Lodging, entertainment, and fourpence each."

"They have a fire provided for 'em," returned the matron—a mighty civil person, not, as I could make out, overpaid; "and these cooking utensils. And this what's painted on a board is the rules for their behaviour. They have their fourpences when they get their tickets from the steward over the way,—for I don't admit 'em myself, they must get their tickets first,—and sometimes one buys a rasher of bacon, and another a herring, and another a pound of potatoes, or what not. Sometimes two or three of 'em will club their fourpences together, and make a supper that way. But not much of anything is to be got for fourpence, at present, when provisions is so dear."

"True indeed," I remarked. I had been looking about the room, admiring its snug fireside at the upper end, its glimpse of the street through the low mullioned window, and its beams overhead. "It is very comfortable," said I.

"Ill-conwenient," observed the matronly presence.

I liked to hear her say so; for it showed a commendable anxiety to execute in no niggardly spirit the intentions of Master Richard Watts. But the room was really so well adapted to its purpose that I protested, quite enthusiastically, against her disparagement.

"Nay, ma'am," said I, "I am sure it is warm in winter and cool in summer. It has a look of homely welcome and soothing rest. It has a remarkably cosey fireside, the very blink of which, gleaming out into the street upon a winter night, is enough to warm all Rochester's heart. And as to the convenience of the six Poor Travellers—"

"I don't mean them," returned the presence. "I speak of its being an ill-conwenience to myself and my daughter, having no other room to sit in of a night."

This was true enough, but there was another quaint room of corresponding dimensions on the opposite side of the entry: so I stepped across to it, through the open doors of both rooms, and asked what this chamber was for.

"This," returned the presence, "is the Board Room. Where the gentlemen meet when they come here."

Let me see. I had counted from the street six upper windows besides these on the ground-story. Making a perplexed calculation in my mind, I rejoined, "Then the six Poor Travellers sleep upstairs?"

My new friend shook her head. "They sleep," she answered, "in two little outer galleries at the back, where their beds has always been, ever since the Charity was founded. It being so very ill-conwenient to me as things is at present, the gentlemen are going to take off a bit of the back yard, and make a slip of a room for 'em there, to sit in before they go to bed."

"And then the six Poor Travellers," said I, "will be entirely out of the house?"

"Entirely out of the house," assented the presence, comfortably smoothing her hands. "Which is considered much better for all parties, and much more conwenient."

I had been a little startled, in the Cathedral, by the emphasis with which the effigy of Master Richard Watts was bursting out of his tomb; but I began to think, now, that it might be expected to come across the High Street some stormy night, and make a disturbance here.

Howbeit, I kept my thoughts to myself, and accompanied the presence to the little galleries at the back. I found them on a tiny scale, like the galleries in old inn-yards; and they were very clean. While I was looking at them, the matron gave me to understand that the prescribed number of Poor Travellers were forthcoming every night from year's end to year's end; and that the beds were always occupied. My questions upon this, and her replies, brought us back to the Board Room so essential to the dignity of "the gentlemen," where she showed me the printed accounts of the Charity hanging up by the window. From them I gathered that the greater part of the property bequeathed by the Worshipful Master Richard Watts for the maintenance of this foundation was, at the period of his death, mere marsh-land; but that, in course of time, it had been reclaimed and built upon, and was very considerably increased in value. I found, too, that about a thirtieth part of the annual revenue was now expended on the purposes commemorated in the inscription over the door; the rest being handsomely laid out in Chancery, law expenses, collectorship, receivership, poundage, and other appendages of management, highly complimentary to the importance of the six Poor Travellers. In short, I made the not entirely new discovery that it may be said of an establishment like this, in dear old England, as of the fat oyster in the American story, that it takes a good many men to swallow it whole.

"And pray, ma'am," said I, sensible that the blankness of my face began to brighten as the thought occurred to me, "could one see these Travellers?"

"Well!" she returned dubiously, "no!"

"Not to-night, for instance!" said I.

"Well!" she returned more positively, "no. Nobody ever asked to see them, and nobody ever did see them."

As I am not easily balked in a design when I am set upon it, I urged to the good lady that this was Christmas-eve; that Christmas comes but once a year,—which is unhappily too true, for when it begins to stay with us the whole year round we shall make this earth a very different place; that I was possessed by the desire to treat the Travellers to a supper and a temperate glass of hot Wassail; that the voice of Fame had been heard in that land, declaring my ability to make hot Wassail; that if I were permitted to hold the feast, I should be found conformable to reason, sobriety, and good hours; in a word, that I could be merry and wise myself, and had been even known at a pinch to keep others so, although I was decorated with no badge or medal, and was not a Brother, Orator, Apostle, Saint, or Prophet of any denomination whatever. In the end I prevailed, to my great joy. It was settled that at nine o'clock that night a Turkey and a piece of Roast Beef should smoke upon the board; and that I, faint and unworthy minister for once of Master Richard Watts, should preside as the Christmas-supper host of the six Poor Travellers.

I went back to my inn to give the necessary directions for the Turkey and Roast Beef, and, during the remainder of the day, could settle to nothing for thinking of the Poor Travellers. When the wind blew hard against the windows,—it was a cold day, with dark gusts of sleet alternating with periods of wild brightness, as if the year were dying fitfully,—I pictured them advancing towards their resting-place along various cold roads, and felt delighted to think how little they foresaw the supper that awaited them. I painted their portraits in my mind, and indulged in little heightening touches. I made them footsore; I made them weary; I made them carry packs and bundles; I made them stop by finger-posts and milestones, leaning on their bent sticks, and looking wistfully at what was written there; I made them lose their way; and filled their five wits with apprehensions of lying out all night, and being frozen to death. I took up my hat, and went out, climbed to the top of the Old Castle, and looked over the windy hills that slope down to the Medway, almost believing that I could descry some of my Travellers in the distance. After it fell dark, and the Cathedral bell was heard in the invisible steeple—quite a bower of frosty rime when I had last seen it—striking five, six, seven, I became so full of my Travellers that I could eat no dinner, and felt constrained to watch them still in the red coals of my fire. They were all arrived by this time, I thought, had got their tickets, and were gone in.—There my pleasure was dashed by the reflection that probably some Travellers had come too late and were shut out.

After the Cathedral bell had struck eight, I could smell a delicious savour of Turkey and Roast Beef rising to the window of my adjoining bedroom, which looked down into the inn-yard just where the lights of the kitchen reddened a massive fragment of the Castle Wall. It was high time to make the Wassail now; therefore I had up the materials (which, together with their proportions and combinations, I must decline to impart, as the only secret of my own I was ever known to keep), and made a glorious jorum. Not in a bowl; for a bowl anywhere but on a shelf is a low superstition, fraught with cooling and slopping; but in a brown earthenware pitcher, tenderly suffocated, when full, with a coarse cloth. It being now upon the stroke of nine, I set out for Watts's Charity, carrying my brown beauty in my arms. I would trust Ben, the waiter, with untold gold; but there are strings in the human heart which must never be sounded by another, and drinks that I make myself are those strings in mine.

The Travellers were all assembled, the cloth was laid, and Ben had brought a great billet of wood, and had laid it artfully on the top of the fire, so that a touch or two of the poker after supper should make a roaring blaze. Having deposited my brown beauty in a red nook of the hearth, inside the fender, where she soon began to sing like an ethereal cricket, diffusing at the same time odours as of ripe vineyards, spice forests, and orange groves,—I say, having stationed my beauty in a place of security and improvement, I introduced myself to my guests by shaking hands all round, and giving them a hearty welcome.

I found the party to be thus composed. Firstly, myself. Secondly, a very decent man indeed, with his right arm in a sling, who had a certain clean agreeable smell of wood about him, from which I judged him to have something to do with shipbuilding. Thirdly, a little sailor-boy, a mere child, with a profusion of rich dark brown hair, and deep womanly-looking eyes. Fourthly, a shabby-genteel personage in a threadbare black suit, and apparently in very bad circumstances, with a dry suspicious look; the absent buttons on his waistcoat eked out with red tape; and a bundle of extraordinarily tattered papers sticking out of an inner breast-pocket. Fifthly, a foreigner by birth, but an Englishman in speech, who carried his pipe in the band of his hat, and lost no time in telling me, in an easy, simple, engaging way, that he was a watchmaker from Geneva, and travelled all about the Continent, mostly on foot, working as a journeyman, and seeing new countries,—possibly (I thought) also smuggling a watch or so, now and then. Sixthly, a little widow, who had been very pretty and was still very young, but whose beauty had been wrecked in some great misfortune, and whose manner was remarkably timid, scared, and solitary. Seventhly and lastly, a Traveller of a kind familiar to my boyhood, but now almost obsolete,—a Book-Pedler, who had a quantity of Pamphlets and Numbers with him, and who presently boasted that he could repeat more verses in an evening than he could sell in a twelvemonth.

All these I have mentioned in the order in which they sat at table. I presided, and the matronly presence faced me. We were not long in taking our places, for the supper had arrived with me, in the following procession:

Myself with the pitcher.
Ben with Beer.
Inattentive Boy with hot plates. Inattentive Boy with hot plates.
THE TURKEY.
Female carrying sauces to be heated on the spot.
THE BEEF.
Man with Tray on his head, containing Vegetables and Sundries.
Volunteer Hostler from Hotel, grinning,
And rendering no assistance.

As we passed along the High Street, comet-like, we left a long tail of fragrance behind us which caused the public to stop, sniffing in wonder. We had previously left at the corner of the inn-yard a wall-eyed young man connected with the Fly department, and well accustomed to the sound of a railway whistle which Ben always carries in his pocket, whose instructions were, so soon as he should hear the whistle blown, to dash into the kitchen, seize the hot plum-pudding and mince-pies, and speed with them to Watts's Charity, where they would be received (he was further instructed) by the sauce-female, who would be provided with brandy in a blue state of combustion.

All these arrangements were executed in the most exact and punctual manner. I never saw a finer turkey, finer beef, or greater prodigality of sauce and gravy;—and my Travellers did wonderful justice to everything set before them. It made my heart rejoice to observe how their wind and frost hardened faces softened in the clatter of plates and knives and forks, and mellowed in the fire and supper heat. While their hats and caps and wrappers, hanging up, a few small bundles on the ground in a corner, and in another corner three or four old walking-sticks, worn down at the end to mere fringe, linked this smug interior with the bleak outside in a golden chain.

When supper was done, and my brown beauty had been elevated on the table, there was a general requisition to me to "take the corner"; which suggested to me comfortably enough how much my friends here made of a fire,—for when had *I* ever thought so highly of the corner, since the days when I connected it with Jack

Horner? However, as I declined, Ben, whose touch on all convivial instruments is perfect, drew the table apart, and instructing my Travellers to open right and left on either side of me, and form round the fire, closed up the centre with myself and my chair, and preserved the order we had kept at table. He had already, in a tranquil manner, boxed the ears of the inattentive boys until they had been by imperceptible degrees boxed out of the room; and he now rapidly skirmished the sauce-female into the High Street, disappeared, and softly closed the door.

This was the time for bringing the poker to bear on the billet of wood. I tapped it three times, like an enchanted talisman, and a brilliant host of merry-makers burst out of it, and sported off by the chimney,—rushing up the middle in a fiery country dance, and never coming down again. Meanwhile, by their sparkling light, which threw our lamp into the shade, I filled the glasses, and gave my Travellers, Christmas!—Christmas-eve, my friends, when the shepherds, who were Poor Travellers, too, in their way, heard the Angels sing, "On earth, peace. Good-will towards men!"

I don't know who was the first among us to think that we ought to take hands as we sat, in deference to the toast, or whether any one of us anticipated the others, but at any rate we all did it. We then drank to the memory of the good Master Richard Watts. And I wish his Ghost may never have had worse usage under that roof than it had from us.

It was the witching time for Story-telling. "Our whole life, Travellers," said I, "is a story more or less intelligible,—generally less; but we shall read it by a clearer light when it is ended. I, for one, am so divided this night between fact and fiction, that I scarce know which is which. Shall I beguile the time by telling you a story as we sit here?"

They all answered, yes. I had little to tell them, but I was bound by my own proposal. Therefore, after looking for awhile at the spiral column of smoke wreathing up from my brown beauty, through which I could have almost sworn I saw the effigy of Master Richard Watts less startled than usual, I fired away.

Chapter II

The Story of Richard Doubledick

In the year one thousand seven hundred and ninety-nine, a relative of mine came limping down, on foot, to this town of Chatham. I call it this town, because if anybody present knows to a nicety where Rochester ends and Chatham begins, it is more than I do. He was a poor traveller, with not a farthing in his pocket. He sat by the fire in this very room, and he slept one night in a bed that will be occupied to-night by some one here.

My relative came down to Chatham to enlist in a cavalry regiment, if a cavalry regiment would have him; if not, to take King George's shilling from any corporal or sergeant who would put a bunch of ribbons in his hat. His object was to get shot; but he thought he might as well ride to death as be at the trouble of walking.

My relative's Christian name was Richard, but he was better known as Dick. He dropped his own surname on the road down, and took up that of Doubledick. He was passed as Richard Doubledick; age, twenty-two; height, five foot ten; native place, Exmouth, which he had never been near in his life. There was no cavalry in Chatham when he limped over the bridge here with half a shoe to his dusty feet, so he enlisted into a regiment of the line, and was glad to get drunk and forget all about it.

You are to know that this relative of mine had gone wrong, and run wild. His heart was in the right place, but it was sealed up. He had been betrothed to a good and beautiful girl, whom he had loved better than she—or perhaps even he—believed; but in an evil hour he had given her cause to say to him solemnly, "Richard, I will never marry another man. I will live single for your sake, but Mary Marshall's lips"—her name was Mary Marshall—"never address another word to you on earth. Go, Richard! Heaven forgive you!" This finished him. This brought him down to Chatham. This made him Private Richard Doubledick, with a determination to be shot.

There was not a more dissipated and reckless soldier in Chatham barracks, in the year one thousand seven hundred and ninety-nine, than Private Richard Doubledick. He associated with the dregs of every regiment; he was as seldom sober as he could be, and was constantly under punishment. It became clear to the whole barracks that Private Richard Doubledick would very soon be flogged.

Now the Captain of Richard Doubledick's company was a young gentleman not above five years his senior, whose eyes had an expression in them which affected Private Richard Doubledick in a very remarkable way. They were bright, handsome, dark eyes,—what are called laughing eyes generally, and, when serious, rather steady than severe,—but they were the only eyes now left in his narrowed world that Private Richard Doubledick could not stand. Unabashed by evil report and punishment, defiant of everything else and everybody else, he had but to know that those eyes looked at him for a moment, and he felt ashamed. He could not so much as salute Captain Taunton in the street like any other officer. He was reproached and confused,—troubled by the mere possibility of the captain's looking at him. In his worst moments, he would rather turn back, and go any distance out of his way, than encounter those two handsome, dark, bright eyes.

One day, when Private Richard Doubledick came out of the Black hole, where he had been passing the last eight-and-forty hours, and in which retreat he spent a good deal of his time, he was ordered to betake himself to Captain Taunton's quarters. In the stale and squalid state of a man just out of the Black hole, he had less fancy than ever for being seen by the captain; but he was not so mad yet as to disobey orders, and consequently went up to the terrace overlooking the parade-ground, where the officers' quarters were; twisting and breaking in his hands, as he went along, a bit of the straw that had formed the decorative furniture of the Black hole.

"Come in!" cried the Captain, when he had knocked with his knuckles at the door. Private Richard Doubledick pulled off his cap, took a stride forward, and felt very conscious that he stood in the light of the dark, bright eyes.

There was a silent pause. Private Richard Doubledick had put the straw in his mouth, and was gradually doubling it up into his windpipe and choking himself.

"Doubledick," said the Captain, "do you know where you are going to?"

"To the Devil, Sir?" faltered Doubledick.

"Yes," returned the Captain. "And very fast."

Private Richard Doubledick turned the straw of the Black hole in his month, and made a miserable salute of acquiescence.

"Doubledick," said the Captain, "since I entered his Majesty's service, a boy of seventeen, I have been pained to see many men of promise going that road; but I have never been so pained to see a man make the shameful journey as I have been, ever since you joined the regiment, to see you."

Private Richard Doubledick began to find a film stealing over the floor at which he looked; also to find the legs of the Captain's breakfast-table turning crooked, as if he saw them through water.

"I am only a common soldier, sir," said he. "It signifies very little what such a poor brute comes to."

"You are a man," returned the Captain, with grave indignation, "of education and superior advantages; and if you say that, meaning what you say, you have sunk lower than I had believed. How low that must be, I leave you to consider, knowing what I know of your disgrace, and seeing what I see."

"I hope to get shot soon, Sir," said Private Richard Doubledick; "and then the regiment and the world together will be rid of me."

The legs of the table were becoming very crooked. Doubledick, looking up to steady his vision, met the eyes that had so strong an influence over him. He put his hand before his own eyes, and the breast of his disgrace-jacket swelled as if it would fly asunder.

"I would rather," said the young Captain, "see this in you, Doubledick, than I would see five thousand guineas counted out upon this table for a gift to my good mother. Have you a mother?"

"I am thankful to say she is dead, Sir."

"If your praises," returned the Captain, "were sounded from mouth to mouth through the whole regiment, through the whole army, through the whole country, you would wish she had lived to say, with pride and joy, 'He is my son!'"

"Spare me, Sir," said Doubledick. "She would never have heard any good of me. She would never have had any pride and joy in owning herself my mother. Love and compassion she might have had, and would have always had, I know but not—Spare me, Sir! I am a broken wretch, quite at your mercy!" And he turned his face to the wall, and stretched out his imploring hand.

"My friend—" began the Captain.

"God bless you, Sir!" sobbed Private Richard Doubledick.

"You are at the crisis of your fate. Hold your course unchanged a little longer, and you know what must happen. *I* know even better than you can imagine, that, after that has happened, you are lost. No man who could shed those tears could bear those marks."

"I fully believe it, Sir," in a low, shivering voice said Private Richard Doubledick.

"But a man in any station can do his duty," said the young Captain, "and, in doing it, can earn his own respect, even if his case should be so very unfortunate and so very rare that he can earn no other man's. A common soldier, poor brute though you called him just now, has this advantage in the stormy times we live in, that he always does his duty before a host of sympathising witnesses. Do you doubt that he may so do it as to be extolled through a whole regiment, through a whole army, through a whole country? Turn while you may yet retrieve the past, and try."

"I will! I ask for only one witness, sir," cried Richard, with a bursting heart.

"I understand you. I will be a watchful and a faithful one."

I have heard from Private Richard Doubledick's own lips, that he dropped down upon his knee, kissed that officer's hand, arose, and went out of the light of the dark, bright eyes, an altered man.

In that year, one thousand seven hundred and ninety-nine, the French were in Egypt, in Italy, in Germany, where not? Napoleon Bonaparte had likewise begun to stir against us in India, and most men could read the signs of the great troubles that were coming on. In the very next year, when we formed an alliance with Austria against him, Captain Taunton's regiment was on service in India. And there was not a finer non-commissioned officer in it,—no, nor in the whole line—than Corporal Richard Doubledick.

In eighteen hundred and one, the Indian army were on the coast of Egypt. Next year was the year of the proclamation of the short peace, and they were recalled. It had then become well known to thousands of men, that wherever Captain Taunton, with the dark, bright eyes, led, there, close to him, ever at his side, firm as a rock, true as the sun, and brave as Mars, would be certain to be found, while life beat in their hearts, that famous soldier, Sergeant Richard Doubledick.

Eighteen hundred and five, besides being the great year of Trafalgar, was a year of hard fighting in India. That year saw such wonders done by a Sergeant-Major, who cut his way single-handed through a solid mass of men, recovered the colours of his regiment, which had been seized from the hand of a poor boy shot through the heart, and rescued his wounded Captain, who was down, and in a very jungle of horses' hoofs and sabres,—saw such wonders done, I say, by this brave Sergeant-Major, that he was specially made the bearer of the colours he had won; and Ensign Richard Doubledick had risen from the ranks.

Sorely cut up in every battle, but always reinforced by the bravest of men,—for the fame of following the old colours, shot through and through, which Ensign Richard Doubledick had saved, inspired all breasts,—this regiment fought its way through the Peninsular war, up to the investment of Badajos in eighteen hundred and twelve. Again and again it had been cheered through the British ranks until the tears had sprung into men's eyes at the mere hearing of the mighty British voice, so exultant in their valour; and there was not a drummer-boy but knew the legend, that wherever the two friends, Major Taunton, with the dark, bright eyes, and Ensign Richard Doubledick, who was devoted to him, were seen to go, there the boldest spirits in the English army became wild to follow.

One day, at Badajos,—not in the great storming, but in repelling a hot sally of the besieged upon our men at work in the trenches, who had given way,—the two officers found themselves hurrying forward, face to face, against a party of French infantry, who made a stand. There was an officer at their head, encouraging his men,—a courageous, handsome, gallant officer of five-and-thirty, whom Doubledick saw hurriedly, almost momentarily, but saw well. He particularly noticed this officer waving his sword, and rallying his men with an eager and excited cry, when they fired in obedience to his gesture, and Major Taunton dropped.

It was over in ten minutes more, and Doubledick returned to the spot where he had laid the best friend man ever had on a coat spread upon the wet clay. Major Taunton's uniform was opened at the breast, and on his shirt were three little spots of blood.

"Dear Doubledick," said he, "I am dying."

"For the love of Heaven, no!" exclaimed the other, kneeling down beside him, and passing his arm round his neck to raise his head. "Taunton! My preserver, my guardian angel, my witness! Dearest, truest, kindest of human beings! Taunton! For God's sake!"

The bright, dark eyes—so very, very dark now, in the pale face—smiled upon him; and the hand he had kissed thirteen years ago laid itself fondly on his breast.

"Write to my mother. You will see Home again. Tell her how we became friends. It will comfort her, as it comforts me."

He spoke no more, but faintly signed for a moment towards his hair as it fluttered in the wind. The Ensign understood him. He smiled again when he saw that, and, gently turning his face over on the supporting arm as if for rest, died, with his hand upon the breast in which he had revived a soul.

No dry eye looked on Ensign Richard Doubledick that melancholy day. He buried his friend on the field, and became a lone, bereaved man. Beyond his duty he appeared to have but two remaining cares in life,—one, to preserve the little packet of hair he was to give to Taunton's mother; the other, to encounter that French officer who had rallied the men under whose fire Taunton fell. A new legend now began to circulate among our troops; and it was, that when he and the French officer came face to face once more, there would be weeping in France.

The war went on—and through it went the exact picture of the French officer on the one side, and the bodily reality upon the other—until the Battle of Toulouse was fought. In the returns sent home appeared these words: "Severely wounded, but not dangerously, Lieutenant Richard Doubledick."

At Midsummer-time, in the year eighteen hundred and fourteen, Lieutenant Richard Doubledick, now a browned soldier, seven-and-thirty years of age, came home to England invalided. He brought the hair with him, near his heart. Many a French officer had he seen since that day; many a dreadful night, in searching with men and lanterns for his wounded, had he relieved French officers lying disabled; but the mental picture and the reality had never come together.

Though he was weak and suffered pain, he lost not an hour in getting down to Frome in Somersetshire, where Taunton's mother lived. In the sweet, compassionate words that naturally present themselves to the mind to-night, "he was the only son of his mother, and she was a widow."

It was a Sunday evening, and the lady sat at her quiet garden-window, reading the Bible; reading to herself, in a trembling voice, that very passage in it, as I have heard him tell. He heard the words: "Young man, I say unto thee, arise!"

He had to pass the window; and the bright, dark eyes of his debased time seemed to look at him. Her heart told her who he was; she came to the door quickly, and fell upon his neck.

"He saved me from ruin, made me a human creature, won me from infamy and shame. O, God for ever bless him! As He will, He will!"

"He will!" the lady answered. "I know he is in Heaven!" Then she piteously cried, "But O, my darling boy, my darling boy!"

Never from the hour when Private Richard Doubledick enlisted at Chatham had the Private, Corporal, Sergeant, Sergeant-Major, Ensign, or Lieutenant breathed his right name, or the name of Mary Marshall, or a word of the story of his life, into any ear except his reclaimer's. That previous scene in his existence was closed. He had firmly resolved that his expiation should be to live unknown; to disturb no more the peace that had long grown over his old offences; to let it be revealed, when he was dead, that he had striven and suffered, and had never forgotten; and then, if they could forgive him and believe him—well, it would be time enough—time enough!

But that night, remembering the words he had cherished for two years, "Tell her how we became friends. It will comfort her, as it comforts me," he related everything. It gradually seemed to him as if in his maturity he had recovered a mother; it gradually seemed to her as if in her bereavement she had found a son. During his stay in England, the quiet garden into which he had slowly and painfully crept, a stranger, became the boundary of his home; when he was able to rejoin his regiment in the spring, he left the garden, thinking was this indeed the first time he had ever turned his face towards the old colours with a woman's blessing!

He followed them—so ragged, so scarred and pierced now, that they would scarcely hold together—to Quatre Bras and Ligny. He stood beside them, in an awful stillness of many men, shadowy through the mist and drizzle of a wet June forenoon, on the field of Waterloo. And down to that hour the picture in his mind of the French officer had never been compared with the reality.

The famous regiment was in action early in the battle, and received its first check in many an eventful year, when he was seen to fall. But it swept on to avenge him, and left behind it no such creature in the world of consciousness as Lieutenant Richard Doubledick.

Through pits of mire, and pools of rain; along deep ditches, once roads, that were pounded and ploughed to pieces by artillery, heavy waggons, tramp of men and horses, and the struggle of every wheeled thing that could carry wounded soldiers; jolted among the dying and the dead, so disfigured by blood and mud as to be hardly recognisable for humanity; undisturbed by the moaning of men and the shrieking of horses, which, newly taken from the peaceful pursuits of life, could not endure the sight of the stragglers lying by the wayside, never to resume their toilsome journey; dead, as to any sentient life that was in it, and yet alive,—the form that had been Lieutenant Richard Doubledick, with whose praises England rang, was conveyed to Brussels. There it was tenderly laid down in hospital; and there it lay, week after week, through the long bright summer days, until the harvest, spared by war, had ripened and was gathered in.

Over and over again the sun rose and set upon the crowded city; over and over again the moonlight nights were quiet on the plains of Waterloo: and all that time was a blank to what had been Lieutenant Richard Doubledick. Rejoicing troops marched into Brussels, and marched out; brothers and fathers, sisters, mothers, and wives, came thronging thither, drew their lots of joy or agony, and departed; so many times a day the bells rang; so many times the shadows of the great buildings changed; so many lights sprang up at dusk; so many feet passed here and there upon the pavements; so many hours of sleep and cooler air of night succeeded: indifferent to all, a marble face lay on a bed, like the face of a recumbent statue on the tomb of Lieutenant Richard Doubledick.

Slowly labouring, at last, through a long heavy dream of confused time and place, presenting faint glimpses of army surgeons whom he knew, and of faces that had been familiar to his youth,—dearest and kindest among them, Mary Marshall's, with a solicitude upon it more like reality than anything he could discern,—Lieutenant Richard Doubledick came back to life. To the beautiful life of a calm autumn evening sunset, to the peaceful life of a fresh quiet room with a large window standing open; a balcony beyond, in which were moving leaves and sweet-smelling flowers; beyond, again, the clear sky, with the sun full in his sight, pouring its golden radiance on his bed.

It was so tranquil and so lovely that he thought he had passed into another world. And he said in a faint voice, "Taunton, are you near me?"

A face bent over him. Not his, his mother's.

"I came to nurse you. We have nursed you many weeks. You were moved here long ago. Do you remember nothing?"

"Nothing."

The lady kissed his cheek, and held his hand, soothing him.

"Where is the regiment? What has happened? Let me call you mother. What has happened, mother?"

"A great victory, dear. The war is over, and the regiment was the bravest in the field."

His eyes kindled, his lips trembled, he sobbed, and the tears ran down his face. He was very weak, too weak to move his hand.

"Was it dark just now?" he asked presently.

"No."

"It was only dark to me? Something passed away, like a black shadow. But as it went, and the sun—O the blessed sun, how beautiful it is!—touched my face, I thought I saw a light white cloud pass out at the door. Was there nothing that went out?"

She shook her head, and in a little while he fell asleep, she still holding his hand, and soothing him.

From that time, he recovered. Slowly, for he had been desperately wounded in the head, and had been shot in the body, but making some little advance every day. When he had gained sufficient strength to converse as he lay in bed, he soon began to remark that Mrs. Taunton always brought him back to his own history. Then he recalled his preserver's dying words, and thought, "It comforts her."

One day he awoke out of a sleep, refreshed, and asked her to read to him. But the curtain of the bed, softening the light, which she always drew back when he awoke, that she might see him from her table at the bedside where she sat at work, was held undrawn; and a woman's voice spoke, which was not hers.

"Can you bear to see a stranger?" it said softly. "Will you like to see a stranger?"

"Stranger!" he repeated. The voice awoke old memories, before the days of Private Richard Doubledick.

"A stranger now, but not a stranger once," it said in tones that thrilled him. "Richard, dear Richard, lost through so many years, my name—"

He cried out her name, "Mary," and she held him in her arms, and his head lay on her bosom.

"I am not breaking a rash vow, Richard. These are not Mary Marshall's lips that speak. I have another name."

She was married.

"I have another name, Richard. Did you ever hear it?"

"Never!"

He looked into her face, so pensively beautiful, and wondered at the smile upon it through her tears.

"Think again, Richard. Are you sure you never heard my altered name?"

"Never!"

"Don't move your head to look at me, dear Richard. Let it lie here, while I tell my story. I loved a generous, noble man; loved him with my whole heart; loved him for years and years; loved him faithfully, devotedly; loved him without hope of return; loved him, knowing nothing of his highest qualities—not even knowing that he was alive. He was a brave soldier. He was honoured and beloved by thousands of thousands, when the mother of his dear friend found me, and showed me that in all his triumphs he had never forgotten me. He was wounded in a great battle. He was brought, dying, here, into Brussels. I came to watch and tend him, as I would have joyfully gone, with such a purpose, to the dreariest ends of the earth. When he knew no one else, he knew me. When he suffered most, he bore his sufferings barely murmuring, content to rest his head where your rests now. When he lay at the point of death, he married me, that he might call me Wife before he died. And the name, my dear love, that I took on that forgotten night—"

"I know it now!" he sobbed. "The shadowy remembrance strengthens. It is come back. I thank Heaven that my mind is quite restored! My Mary, kiss me; lull this weary head to rest, or I shall die of gratitude. His parting words were fulfilled. I see Home again!"

Well! They were happy. It was a long recovery, but they were happy through it all. The snow had melted on the ground, and the birds were singing in the leafless thickets of the early spring, when those three were first able to ride out together, and when people flocked about the open carriage to cheer and congratulate Captain Richard Doubledick.

But even then it became necessary for the Captain, instead of returning to England, to complete his recovery in the climate of Southern France. They found a spot upon the Rhône, within a ride of the old town of Avignon, and within view of its broken bridge, which was all they could desire; they lived there, together, six months; then returned to England. Mrs. Taunton, growing old after three years—though not so old as that her bright, dark eyes were dimmed—and remembering that her strength had been benefited by the change resolved to go back for a year to those parts. So she went with a faithful servant, who had often carried her son in his arms; and she was to be rejoined and escorted home, at the year's end, by Captain Richard Doubledick.

She wrote regularly to her children (as she called them now), and they to her. She went to the neighbourhood of Aix; and there, in their own château near the farmer's house she rented, she grew into intimacy with a family belonging to that part of France. The intimacy began in her often meeting among the vineyards a pretty child, a girl with a most compassionate heart, who was never tired of listening to the solitary English lady's stories of her poor son and the cruel wars. The family were as gentle as the child, and at length she came to know them so well that she accepted their invitation to pass the last month of her residence abroad under their roof. All this intelligence she wrote home, piecemeal as it came about, from time to time; and at last enclosed a polite note, from the head of the château, soliciting, on the occasion of his approaching mission to that neighbourhood, the honour of the company of cet homme si justement célèbre, Monsieur le Capitaine Richard Doubledick.

Captain Doubledick, now a hardy, handsome man in the full vigour of life, broader across the chest and shoulders than he had ever been before, dispatched a courteous reply, and followed it in person. Travelling through all that extent of country after three years of Peace, he blessed the better days on which the world had fallen. The corn was golden, not drenched in unnatural red; was bound in sheaves for food, not trodden underfoot by men in mortal fight. The smoke rose up from peaceful hearths, not blazing ruins. The carts were laden with the fair fruits of the earth, not with wounds and death. To him who had so often seen the terrible reverse, these things were beautiful indeed; and they brought him in a softened spirit to the old château near Aix upon a deep blue evening.

It was a large château of the genuine old ghostly kind, with round towers, and extinguishers, and a high leaden roof, and more windows than Aladdin's Palace. The lattice blinds were all thrown open after the heat of the day, and there were glimpses of rambling walls and corridors within. Then there were immense out-buildings fallen into partial decay, masses of dark trees, terrace-gardens, balustrades; tanks of water, too weak to play and too dirty to work; statues, weeds, and thickets of iron railing that seemed to have overgrown themselves like the shrubberies, and to have branched out in all manner of wild shapes. The entrance doors stood open, as doors often do in that country when the heat of the day is past; and the Captain saw no bell or knocker, and walked in.

He walked into a lofty stone hall, refreshingly cool and gloomy after the glare of a Southern day's travel. Extending along the four sides of this hall was a gallery, leading to suites of rooms; and it was lighted from the top. Still no bell was to be seen.

"Faith," said the Captain halting, ashamed of the clanking of his boots, "this is a ghostly beginning!"

He started back, and felt his face turn white. In the gallery, looking down at him, stood the French officer—the officer whose picture he had carried in his mind so long and so far. Compared with the original, at last—in every lineament how like it was!

He moved, and disappeared, and Captain Richard Doubledick heard his steps coming quickly down own into the hall. He entered through an archway. There was a bright, sudden look upon his face, much such a look as it had worn in that fatal moment.

Monsieur le Capitaine Richard Doubledick? Enchanted to receive him! A thousand apologies! The servants were all out in the air. There was a little fête among them in the garden. In effect, it was the fête day of my daughter, the little cherished and protected of Madame Taunton.

He was so gracious and so frank that Monsieur le Capitaine Richard Doubledick could not withhold his hand. "It is the hand of a brave Englishman," said the French officer, retaining it while he spoke. "I could respect a brave Englishman, even as my foe, how much more as my friend! I also am a soldier."

"He has not remembered me, as I have remembered him; he did not take such note of my face, that day, as I took of his," thought Captain Richard Doubledick. "How shall I tell him?"

The French officer conducted his guest into a garden and presented him to his wife, an engaging and beautiful woman, sitting with Mrs. Taunton in a whimsical old-fashioned pavilion. His daughter, her fair young face beaming with joy, came running to embrace him; and there was a boy-baby to tumble down among the orange trees on the broad steps, in making for his father's legs. A multitude of children visitors were dancing to sprightly music; and all the servants and peasants about the château were dancing too. It was a scene of innocent happiness that might have been invented for the climax of the scenes of peace which had soothed the Captain's journey.

He looked on, greatly troubled in his mind, until a resounding bell rang, and the French officer begged to show him his rooms. They went upstairs into the gallery from which the officer had looked down; and Monsieur le Capitaine Richard Doubledick was cordially welcomed to a grand outer chamber, and a smaller one within, all clocks and draperies, and hearths, and brazen dogs, and tiles, and cool devices, and elegance, and vastness.

"You were at Waterloo," said the French officer.

"I was," said Captain Richard Doubledick. "And at Badajos."

Left alone with the sound of his own stern voice in his ears, he sat down to consider, What shall I do, and how shall I tell him? At that time, unhappily, many deplorable duels had been fought between English and French officers, arising out of the recent war; and these duels, and how to avoid this officer's hospitality, were the uppermost thought in Captain Richard Doubledick's mind.

He was thinking, and letting the time run out in which he should have dressed for dinner, when Mrs. Taunton spoke to him outside the door, asking if he could give her the letter he had brought from Mary. "His mother, above all," the Captain thought. "How shall I tell *her*?"

"You will form a friendship with your host, I hope," said Mrs. Taunton, whom he hurriedly admitted, "that will last for life. He is so true-hearted and so generous, Richard, that you can hardly fail to esteem one another. If He had been spared," she kissed (not without tears) the locket in which she wore his hair, "he would have appreciated him with his own magnanimity, and would have been truly happy that the evil days were past which made such a man his enemy."

She left the room; and the Captain walked, first to one window, whence he could see the dancing in the garden, then to another window, whence he could see the smiling prospect and the peaceful vineyards.

"Spirit of my departed friend," said he, "is it through thee these better thoughts are rising in my mind? Is it thou who hast shown me, all the way I have been drawn to meet this man, the blessings of the altered time? Is it thou who hast sent thy stricken mother to me, to stay my angry hand? Is it from thee the whisper comes, that this man did his duty as thou didst,—and as I did, through thy guidance, which has wholly saved me here on earth,—and that he did no more?"

He sat down, with his head buried in his hands, and, when he rose up, made the second strong resolution of his life,—that neither to the French officer, nor to the mother of his departed friend, nor to any soul, while either of the two was living, would he breathe what only he knew. And when he touched that French officer's glass with his own, that day at dinner, he secretly forgave him in the name of the Divine Forgiver of injuries.

* * *

Here I ended my story as the first Poor Traveller. But, if I had told it now, I could have added that the time has since come when the son of Major Richard Doubledick, and the son of that French officer, friends as their fathers were before them, fought side by side in one cause, with their respective nations, like long-divided brothers whom the better times have brought together, fast united.

Chapter III

The Road

My story being finished, and the Wassail too, we broke up as the Cathedral bell struck Twelve. I did not take leave of my travellers that night; for it had come into my head to reappear, in conjunction with some hot coffee, at seven in the morning.

As I passed along the High-street, I heard the Waits at a distance, and struck off to find them. They were playing near one of the old gates of the City, at the corner of a wonderfully quaint row of red-brick tenements, which the clarionet obligingly informed me were inhabited by the Minor-Canons. They had odd little porches over the doors, like sounding-boards over old pulpits; and I thought I should like to see one of the Minor-Canons come out upon his top stop, and favour us with a little Christmas discourse about the poor scholars of Rochester; taking for his text the words of his Master relative to the devouring of Widows' houses.

The clarionet was so communicative, and my inclinations were (as they generally are) of so vagabond a tendency, that I accompanied the Waits across an open green called the Vines, and assisted—in the French sense—at the performance of two waltzes, two polkas, and three Irish melodies, before I thought of my inn any more. However, I returned to it then, and found a fiddle in the kitchen, and Ben, the wall-eyed young man, and two chambermaids, circling round the great deal table with the utmost animation.

I had a very bad night. It cannot have been owing to the turkey or the beef,—and the Wassail is out of the question,—but in every endeavour that I made to get to sleep I failed most dismally. I was never asleep; and in whatsoever unreasonable direction my mind rambled, the effigy of Master Richard Watts perpetually embarrassed it.

In a word, I only got out of the Worshipful Master Richard Watts's way by getting out of bed in the dark at six o'clock, and tumbling, as my custom is, into all the cold water that could be accumulated for the purpose. The outer air was dull and cold enough in the street, when I came down there; and the one candle in our supper-room at Watts's Charity looked as pale in the burning as if it had had a bad night too.

But my Travellers had all slept soundly, and they took to the hot coffee, and the piles of bread-and-butter, which Ben had arranged like deals in a timber-yard, as kindly as I could desire.

While it was yet scarcely daylight, we all came out into the street together, and there shook hands. The widow took the little sailor towards Chatham, where he was to find a steamboat for Sheerness; the lawyer, with an extremely knowing look, went his own way, without committing himself by announcing his intentions; two more struck off by the cathedral and old castle for Maidstone; and the book-pedler accompanied me over the bridge. As for me, I was going to walk by Cobham Woods, as far upon my way to London as I fancied.

When I came to the stile and footpath by which I was to diverge from the main road, I bade farewell to my last remaining Poor Traveller, and pursued my way alone. And now the mists began to rise in the most beautiful manner, and the sun to shine; and as I went on through the bracing air, seeing the hoarfrost sparkle everywhere, I felt as if all Nature shared in the joy of the great Birthday.

Going through the woods, the softness of my tread upon the mossy ground and among the brown leaves enhanced the Christmas sacredness by which I felt surrounded. As the whitened stems environed me, I thought how the Founder of the time had never raised his benignant hand, save to bless and heal, except in the case of one unconscious tree. By Cobham Hall, I came to the village, and the churchyard where the dead had been quietly buried, "in the sure and certain hope" which Christmas time inspired. What children could I see at play, and not be loving of, recalling who had loved them! No garden that I passed was out of unison with the day, for I remembered that the tomb was in a garden, and that "she, supposing him to be the gardener," had said, "Sir, if thou have borne him hence, tell me where thou hast laid him, and I will take him away." In time, the distant river with the ships came full in view, and with it pictures of the poor fishermen, mending their nets, who arose and followed him,—of the teaching of the people from a ship pushed off a little way from shore, by reason of the multitude,—of a majestic figure walking on the water, in the loneliness of night. My very shadow on the ground was eloquent of Christmas; for did not the people lay their sick where the more shadows of the men who had heard and seen him might fall as they passed along?

Thus Christmas begirt me, far and near, until I had come to Blackheath, and had walked down the long vista of gnarled old trees in Greenwich Park, and was being steam-rattled through the mists now closing in once more, towards the lights of London. Brightly they shone, but not so brightly as my own fire, and the brighter faces around it, when we came together to celebrate the day. And there I told of worthy Master Richard Watts, and of my supper with the Six Poor Travellers who were neither Rogues nor Proctors, and from that hour to this I have never seen one of them again.

The Holly-Tree

THREE BRANCHES

First Branch

MYSELF

I HAVE KEPT ONE SECRET IN THE COURSE OF MY LIFE. I AM A BASHFUL MAN. Nobody would suppose it, nobody ever does suppose it, nobody ever did suppose it, but I am naturally a bashful man. This is the secret which I have never breathed until now.

I might greatly move the reader by some account of the innumerable places I have not been to, the innumerable people I have not called upon or received, the innumerable social evasions I have been guilty of, solely because I am by original constitution and character a bashful man. But I will leave the reader unmoved, and proceed with the object before me.

That object is to give a plain account of my travels and discoveries in the Holly-Tree Inn; in which place of good entertainment for man and beast I was once snowed up.

It happened in the memorable year when I parted for ever from Angela Leath, whom I was shortly to have married, on making the discovery that she preferred my bosom friend. From our school-days I had freely admitted Edwin, in my own mind, to be far superior to myself; and, though I was grievously wounded at heart, I felt the preference to be natural, and tried to forgive them both. It was under these circumstances that I resolved to go to America—on my way to the Devil.

Communicating my discovery neither to Angela nor to Edwin, but resolving to write each of them an affecting letter conveying my blessing and forgiveness, which the steam-tender for shore should carry to the post when I myself should be bound for the New World, far beyond recall,—I say, locking up my grief in my own breast, and consoling myself as I could with the prospect of being generous, I quietly left all I held dear, and started on the desolate journey I have mentioned.

The dead winter-time was in full dreariness when I left my chambers for ever, at five o'clock in the morning. I had shaved by candle-light, of course, and was miserably cold, and experienced that general all-pervading sensation of getting up to be hanged which I have usually found inseparable from untimely rising under such circumstances.

How well I remember the forlorn aspect of Fleet-street when I came out of the Temple! The street-lamps flickering in the gusty north-east wind, as if the very gas were contorted with cold; the white-topped houses; the bleak, star-lighted sky; the market people and other early stragglers, trotting to circulate their almost frozen blood; the hospitable light and warmth of the few coffee-shops and public-houses that were open for such customers; the hard, dry, frosty rime with which the air was charged (the wind had already beaten it into every crevice), and which lashed my face like a steel whip.

It wanted nine days to the end of the month, and end of the year. The Post-office packet for the United States was to depart from Liverpool, weather permitting, on the first of the ensuing month, and I had the intervening time on my hands. I had taken this into consideration, and had resolved to make a visit to a certain spot (which I need not name) on the farther borders of Yorkshire. It was endeared to me by my having first seen Angela at a farmhouse in that place, and my melancholy was gratified by the idea of taking a wintry leave of it before my expatriation. I ought to explain, that, to avoid being sought out before my resolution should have been rendered irrevocable by being carried into full effect, I had written to Angela overnight, in my usual manner, lamenting that urgent business, of which she should know all particulars by-and-by—took me unexpectedly away from her for a week or ten days.

There was no Northern Railway at that time, and in its place there were stage-coaches; which I occasionally find myself, in common with some other people, affecting to lament now, but which everybody dreaded as a very serious penance then. I had secured the box-seat on the fastest of these, and my business in Fleet-street was to get into a cab with my portmanteau, so to make the best of my way to the Peacock at Islington, where I was to join this coach. But when one of our Temple watchmen, who carried my portmanteau into Fleet Street for me, told me about the huge blocks of ice that had for some days past been floating in the river, having closed up in the night, and made a walk from the Temple Gardens over to the Surrey shore, I began to ask myself the question, whether the box-seat would not be likely to put a sudden and a frosty end to my unhappiness. I was heart-broken, it is true, and yet I was not quite so far gone as to wish to be frozen to death.

When I got up to the Peacock,—where I found everybody drinking hot purl, in self-preservation,—I asked if there were an inside seat to spare. I then discovered that, inside or out, I was the only passenger. This gave me a still livelier idea of the great inclemency of the weather, since that coach always loaded particularly well. However, I took a little purl (which I found uncommonly good), and got into the coach. When I was seated, they built me up with straw to the waist, and, conscious of making a rather ridiculous appearance, I began my journey.

It was still dark when we left the Peacock. For a little while, pale, uncertain ghosts of houses and trees appeared and vanished, and then it was hard, black, frozen day. People were lighting their fires; smoke was mounting straight up high into the rarified air; and we were rattling for Highgate Archway over the hardest ground I have ever heard the ring of iron shoes on. As we got into the country, everything seemed to have grown old and gray. The roads, the trees, thatched roofs of cottages and homesteads, the ricks in farmers' yards. Out-door work was abandoned, horse-troughs at roadside inns were frozen hard, no stragglers lounged about, doors were close shut, little turnpike houses had blazing fires inside, and children (even turnpike people have children, and seem to like them) rubbed the frost from the little panes of glass with their chubby arms, that their bright eyes might catch a glimpse of the solitary coach going by. I don't know when the snow begin to set in; but I know that we were changing horses somewhere when I heard the guard remark, "That the old lady up in the sky was picking her geese pretty hard to-day." Then, indeed, I found the white down falling fast and thick.

The lonely day wore on, and I dozed it out, as a lonely traveller does. I was warm and valiant after eating and drinking,—particularly after dinner; cold and depressed at all other times. I was always bewildered as to time and place, and always more or less out of my senses. The coach and horses seemed to execute in chorus Auld Lang Syne, without a moment's intermission. They kept the time and tune with the greatest regularity, and rose into the swell at the beginning of the Refrain, with a precision that worried me to death. While we changed horses, the guard and coachman went stumping up and down the road, printing off their shoes in the snow, and poured so much liquid consolation into themselves without being any the worse for it, that I began to confound them, as it darkened again, with two great white casks standing on end. Our horses tumbled down in solitary places, and we got them up,—which was the pleasantest variety *I* had, for it warmed me. And it snowed and snowed, and still it snowed, and never left off snowing. All night long we went on in this manner. Thus we came round the clock, upon the Great North Road, to the performance of Auld Lang Syne by day again. And it snowed and snowed, and still it snowed, and never left off snowing.

I forget now where we were at noon on the second day, and where we ought to have been; but I know that we were scores of miles behindhand, and that our case was growing worse every hour. The drift was becoming prodigiously deep; landmarks were getting snowed out; the road and the fields were all one; instead of having fences and hedge-rows to guide us, we went crunching on over an unbroken surface of ghastly white that might sink beneath us at any moment and drop us down a whole hillside. Still the coachman and guard—who kept together on the box, always in council, and looking well about them—made out the track with astonishing sagacity.

When we came in sight of a town, it looked, to my fancy, like a large drawing on a slate, with abundance of slate-pencil expended on the churches and houses where the snow lay thickest. When we came within a town, and found the church clocks all stopped, the dial-faces choked with snow, and the inn-signs blotted out, it seemed as if the whole place were overgrown with white moss. As to the coach, it was a mere snowball; similarly, the men and boys who ran along beside us to the town's end, turning our clogged wheels and encouraging our horses, were men and boys of snow; and the bleak wild solitude to which they at last dismissed us was a snowy Sahara. One would have thought this enough: notwithstanding which, I pledge my word that it snowed and snowed, and still it snowed, and never left off snowing.

We performed Auld Lang Syne the whole day; seeing nothing, out of towns and villages, but the track of stoats, hares, and foxes, and sometimes of birds. At nine o'clock at night, on a Yorkshire moor, a cheerful burst from our horn, and a welcome sound of talking, with a glimmering and moving about of lanterns, roused me from my drowsy state. I found that we were going to change.

They helped me out, and I said to a waiter, whose bare head became as white as King Lear's in a single minute, "What Inn is this?"

"The Holly-Tree, Sir," said he.

"Upon my word, I believe," said I, apologetically, to the guard and coachman, "that I must stop here."

Now the landlord, and the landlady, and the ostler, and the post-boy, and all the stable authorities, had already asked the coachman, to the wide-eyed interest of all the rest of the establishment, if he meant to go on. The coachman had already replied, "Yes, he'd take her through it,"—meaning by Her the coach,—"if so be as George would stand by him." George was the guard, and he had already sworn that he would stand by him. So the helpers were already getting the horses out.

My declaring myself beaten, after this parley, was not an announcement without preparation. Indeed, but for the way to the announcement being smoothed by the parley, I more than doubt whether, as an innately bashful man, I should have had the confidence to make it. As it was, it received the approval even of the guard and coachman. Therefore, with many confirmations of my inclining, and many remarks from one bystander to another, that the gentleman could go for'ard by the mail to-morrow, whereas to-night he would only be froze, and where was the good of a gentleman being froze—ah, let alone buried alive (which latter clause was added by a humorous helper as a joke at my expense, and was extremely well received), I saw my portmanteau got out stiff, like a frozen body; did the handsome thing by the guard and coachman; wished them good-night and a prosperous journey; and, a little ashamed of myself, after all, for leaving them to fight it out alone, followed the landlord, landlady, and waiter of the Holly-Tree upstairs.

I thought I had never seen such a large room as that into which they showed me. It had five windows, with dark red curtains that would have absorbed the light of a general illumination; and there were complications of drapery at the top of the curtains, that went wandering about the wall in a most extraordinary manner. I asked for a smaller room, and they told me there was no smaller room.

They could screen me in, however, the landlord said. They brought a great old japanned screen, with natives (Japanese, I suppose) engaged in a variety of idiotic pursuits all over it; and left me roasting whole before an immense fire.

My bedroom was some quarter of a mile off, up a great staircase at the end of a long gallery; and nobody knows what a misery this is to a bashful man who would rather not meet people on the stairs. It was the grimmest room I have ever had the nightmare in; and all the furniture, from the four posts of the bed to the two old silver candlesticks, was tall, high-shouldered, and spindle-waisted. Below, in my sitting-room, if I looked round my screen, the wind rushed at me like a mad bull; if I stuck to my arm-chair, the fire scorched me to the colour of a new brick. The chimneypiece was very high, and there was a bad glass—what I may call a wavy glass—above it, which, when I stood up, just showed me my anterior phrenological developments,—and these never look well, in any subject, cut short off at the eyebrow. If I stood with my back to the fire, a gloomy vault of darkness above and beyond the screen insisted on being looked at; and, in its dim remoteness, the drapery of the ten curtains of the five windows went twisting and creeping about, like a nest of gigantic worms.

I suppose that what I observe in myself must be observed by some other men of similar character in *themselves*; therefore I am emboldened to mention, that, when I travel, I never arrive at a place but I immediately want to go away from it. Before I had finished my supper of broiled fowl and mulled port, I had impressed upon the waiter in detail my arrangements for departure in the morning. Breakfast and bill at eight. Fly at nine. Two horses, or, if needful, even four.

Tired though I was, the night appeared about a week long. In cases of nightmare, I thought of Angela, and felt more depressed than ever by the reflection that I was on the shortest road to Gretna Green. What had *I* to do with Gretna Green? I was not going *that* way to the Devil, but by the American route, I remarked in my bitterness.

In the morning I found that it was snowing still, that it had snowed all night, and that I was snowed up. Nothing could get out of that spot on the moor, or could come at it, until the road had been cut out by labourers from the market-town. When they might cut their way to the Holly-Tree nobody could tell me.

It was now Christmas-eve. I should have had a dismal Christmas-time of it anywhere, and consequently that did not so much matter; still, being snowed up was like dying of frost, a thing I had not bargained for. I felt very lonely. Yet I could no more have proposed to the landlord and landlady to admit me to their society (though I should have liked it—very much) than I could have asked them to present me with a piece of plate. Here my great secret, the real bashfulness of my character, is to be observed. Like most bashful men, I judge of other people as if they were bashful too. Besides being far too shamefaced to make the proposal myself, I really had a delicate misgiving that it would be in the last degree disconcerting to them.

Trying to settle down, therefore, in my solitude, I first of all asked what books there were in the house. The waiter brought me a *Book of Roads*, two or three old Newspapers, a little Song-Book, terminating in a collection of Toasts and Sentiments, a little Jest-Book, an odd volume of *Peregrine Pickle*, and the *Sentimental Journey*. I knew every word of the two last already, but I read them through again, then tried to hum all the songs (Auld Lang Syne was among them); went entirely through the jokes,—in which I found a fund of melancholy adapted to my state of mind; proposed all the toasts, enunciated all the sentiments, and mastered the papers. The latter had nothing in them but stock advertisements, a meeting about a county rate, and a highway robbery. As I am a greedy reader, I could not make this supply hold out until night; it was exhausted by tea-time. Being then entirely cast upon my own resources, I got through an hour in considering what to do next. Ultimately, it came into my head (from which I was anxious by any means to exclude Angela and Edwin), that I would endeavour to recall my experience of Inns, and would try how long it lasted me. I stirred the fire, moved my chair a little to one side of the screen,—not daring to go far, for I knew the wind was waiting to make a rush at me, I could hear it growling,—and began.

My first impressions of an Inn dated from the Nursery; consequently I went back to the Nursery for a starting-point, and found myself at the knee of a sallow woman with a fishy eye, an aquiline nose, and a green gown, whose specially was a dismal narrative of a landlord by the roadside, whose visitors unaccountably disappeared for many years, until it was discovered that the pursuit of his life had been to convert them into pies. For the better devotion of himself to this branch of industry, he had constructed a secret door behind the head of the bed; and when the visitor (oppressed with pie) had fallen asleep, this wicked landlord would look softly in with a lamp in one hand and a knife in the other, would cut his throat, and would make him into pies; for which purpose he had coppers, underneath a trap-door, always boiling; and rolled out his pastry in the dead of the night. Yet even he was not insensible to the stings of conscience, for he never went to sleep without being heard to mutter, "Too much pepper!" which was eventually the cause of his being brought to justice. I had no sooner disposed of this criminal than there started up another of the same period, whose profession was originally house-breaking; in the pursuit of which art he had had his right ear chopped off one night, as he was burglariously getting in at a window, by a brave and lovely servant-maid (whom the aquiline-nosed woman, though not at all answering the description, always mysteriously implied to be herself). After several years, this brave and lovely servant-maid was married to the landlord of a country Inn; which landlord had this remarkable characteristic, that he always wore a silk nightcap, and never would on any consideration take it off. At last, one night, when he was fast asleep, the brave and lovely woman lifted up his silk nightcap on the right side, and found that he had no ear there; upon which she sagaciously perceived that he was the clipped housebreaker, who had married her with the intention of putting her to death. She immediately heated the poker and terminated his career, for which she was taken to King George upon his throne, and received the compliments of royalty on her great discretion and valour. This same narrator, who had a Ghoulish pleasure, I have long been persuaded, in terrifying me to the utmost confines of my reason, had another authentic anecdote within her own experience, founded, I now believe, upon *Raymond and Agnes, or the Bleeding Nun*. She said it happened to her brother-in-law, who was immensely rich,—which my father was not; and immensely tall,—which my father was not. It was always a point with this Ghoul to present my clearest relations and friends to my youthful mind under circumstances of disparaging contrast. The brother-in-law was riding once through a forest on a magnificent horse (we had no magnificent horse at our house), attended by a favourite and valuable Newfoundland dog (we had no dog), when he found himself benighted, and came to an Inn. A dark woman opened the door, and he asked her if he could have a bed there. She answered yes, and put his horse in the stable, and took him into a room where there were two dark men. While he was at supper, a parrot in the room began to talk, saying, "Blood, blood! Wipe up the blood!" Upon which one of the dark men wrung the parrot's neck, and said he was fond of roasted parrots, and he meant to have this one for breakfast in the morning. After eating and drinking heartily, the immensely rich, tall brother-in-law went up to bed; but he was rather vexed, because they had shut his dog in the stable, saying that they never allowed dogs in the house. He sat very quiet for more than an hour, thinking and thinking, when, just as his candle was burning out, he heard a scratch at the door. He opened the door, and there was the Newfoundland dog! The dog came softly in, smelt about him, went straight to some straw in the corner which the dark men had said covered apples, tore the straw away, and disclosed two sheets steeped in blood. Just at that moment the candle went out, and the brother-in-law, looking through a chink in the door, saw the two dark men stealing upstairs; one armed with a dagger that long (about five feet); the other carrying a chopper, a sack, and a spade. Having no remembrance of the close of this adventure, I suppose my faculties to have been always so frozen with terror at this stage of it, that the power of listening stagnated within me for some quarter of an hour.

These barbarous stories carried me, sitting there on the Holly-Tree hearth, to the Roadside Inn, renowned in my time in a sixpenny book with a folding plate, representing in a central compartment of oval form the portrait of Jonathan Bradford, and in four corner compartments four incidents of the tragedy with which the name is associated,—coloured with a hand at once so free and economical, that the bloom of Jonathan's complexion passed without any pause into the breeches of the ostler, and, smearing itself off into the next division, became rum in a bottle. Then I remembered how the landlord was found at the murdered traveller's bedside, with his own knife at his feet, and blood upon his hand; how he was hanged for the murder, notwithstanding his protestation that he had indeed come there to kill the traveller for his saddle-bags, but had been stricken motionless on finding him already slain; and how the ostler, years afterwards, owned the deed. By this time I had made myself quite uncomfortable. I stirred the fire, and stood with my back to it as long as I could bear the heat, looking up at the darkness beyond the screen, and at the wormy curtains creeping in and creeping out, like the worms in the ballad of Alonzo the Brave and the Fair Imogene.

There was an Inn in the cathedral town where I went to school, which had pleasanter recollections about it than any of these. I took it next. It was the Inn where friends used to put up, and where we used to go to see parents, and to have salmon and fowls, and be tipped. It had an ecclesiastical sign,—the Mitre,—and a bar that seemed to be the next best thing to a bishopric, it was so snug. I loved the landlord's youngest daughter to distraction,—but let that pass. It was in this Inn that I was cried over by my rosy little sister, because I had acquired a black eye in a fight. And though she had been, that Holly-Tree night, for many a long year where all tears are dried, the Mitre softened me yet.

"To be continued to-morrow," said I, when I took my candle to go to bed. But my bed took it upon itself to continue the train of thought that night. It carried me away, like the enchanted carpet, to a distant place (though still in England), and there, alighting from a stage-coach at another Inn in the snow, as I had actually done some years before, I repeated in my sleep a curious experience I had really had there. More than a year before I made the journey in the course of which I put up at that Inn, I had lost a very near and dear friend by death. Every night since, at home or away from home, I had dreamed of that friend; sometimes as still living; sometimes as returning from the world of shadows to comfort me; always as being beautiful, placid, and happy, never in association with any approach to fear or distress. It was at a lonely Inn in a wide moorland place, that I halted to pass the night. When I had looked from my bedroom window over the waste of snow on which the moon was shining, I sat down by my fire to write a letter. I had always, until that hour, kept it within my own breast that I dreamed every night of the dear lost one. But in the letter that I wrote I recorded the circumstance, and added that I felt much interested in proving whether the subject of my dream would still be faithful to me, travel-tired, and in that remote place. No. I lost the beloved figure of my vision in parting with the secret. My sleep has never looked upon it since, in sixteen years, but once. I was in Italy, and awoke (or seemed to awake), the well-remembered voice distinctly in my ears, conversing with it. I entreated it, as it rose above my bed and soared up to the vaulted roof of the old room, to answer me a question I had asked touching the Future Life. My hands were still outstretched towards it as it vanished, when I heard a bell ringing by the garden wall, and a voice in the deep stillness of the night calling on all good Christians to pray for the souls of the dead; it being All Souls' Eve.

To return to the Holly-Tree. When I awoke next day, it was freezing hard, and the lowering sky threatened more snow. My breakfast cleared away, I drew my chair into its former place, and, with the fire getting so much the better of the landscape that I sat in twilight, resumed my Inn remembrances.

That was a good Inn down in Wiltshire where I put up once, in the days of the hard Wiltshire ale, and before all beer was bitterness. It was on the skirts of Salisbury Plain, and the midnight wind that rattled my lattice window came moaning at me from Stonehenge. There was a hanger-on at that establishment (a supernaturally preserved Druid I believe him to have been, and to be still), with long white hair, and a flinty blue eye always looking afar off; who claimed to have been a shepherd, and who seemed to be ever watching for the reappearance, on the verge of the horizon, of some ghostly flock of sheep that had been mutton for many ages. He was a man with a weird belief in him that no one could count the stones of Stonehenge twice, and make the same number of them; likewise, that any one who counted them three times nine times, and then stood in the centre and said, "I dare!" would behold a tremendous apparition, and be stricken dead. He pretended to have seen a bustard (I suspect him to have been familiar with the dodo), in manner following: He was out upon the plain at the close of a late autumn day, when he dimly discerned, going on before him at a curious fitfully bounding pace, what he at first supposed to be a gig-umbrella that had been blown from some conveyance, but what he presently believed to be a lean dwarf man upon a little pony. Having followed this object for some distance without gaining on it, and having called to it many times without receiving any answer, he pursued it for miles and miles, when, at length coming up with it, he discovered it to be the last bustard in Great Britain, degenerated into a wingless state, and running along the ground. Resolved to capture him or perish in the attempt, he closed with the bustard; but the bustard, who had formed a counter-resolution that he should do neither, threw him, stunned him, and was last seen making off due west. This weird main, at that stage of metempsychosis, may have been a sleep-walker or an enthusiast or a robber; but I awoke one night to find him in the dark at my bedside, repeating the Athanasian Creed in a terrific voice. I paid my bill next day, and retired from the county with all possible precipitation.

That was not a commonplace story which worked itself out at a little Inn in Switzerland, while I was staying there. It was a very homely place, in a village of one narrow zigzag street, among mountains, and you went in at the main door through the cow-house, and among the mules and the dogs and the fowls, before ascending a great bare staircase to the rooms; which were all of unpainted wood, without plastering or papering,—like rough packing-cases. Outside there was nothing but the straggling street, a little toy church with a copper-coloured steeple, a pine forest, a torrent, mists, and mountain-sides. A young man belonging to this Inn had disappeared eight weeks before (it was winter-time), and was supposed to have had some undiscovered love affair, and to have gone for a soldier. He had got up in the night, and dropped into the village street from the loft in which he slept with another man; and he had done it so quietly, that his companion and fellow-labourer had heard no movement when he was awakened in the morning, and they said, "Louis, where is Henri?" They looked for him high and low, in vain, and gave him up. Now, outside this Inn, there stood, as there stood outside every dwelling in the village, a stack of firewood; but the stack belonging to the Inn was higher than any of the rest, because the Inn was the richest house, and burnt the most fuel. It began to be noticed, while they were looking high and low, that a Bantam cock, part of the live stock of the Inn, put himself wonderfully out of his way to get to the top of this wood-stack; and that he would stay there for hours and hours, crowing, until he appeared in danger of splitting himself. Five weeks went on,—six weeks,—and still this terrible Bantam, neglecting his domestic affairs, was always on the top of the wood-stack, crowing the very eyes out of his head. By this time it was perceived that Louis had become inspired with a violent animosity towards the terrible Bantam, and one morning he was seen by a woman, who sat nursing her goître at a little window in a gleam of sun, to catch up a rough billet of wood, with a great oath, hurl it at the terrible Bantam crowing on the wood-stack, and bring him down dead. Hereupon the woman, with a sudden light in her mind, stole round to the back of the wood-stack, and, being a good climber, as all those women are, climbed up, and soon was seen upon the summit, screaming, looking down the hollow within, and crying, "Seize Louis, the murderer! Ring the church bell! Here is the body!" I saw the murderer that day, and I saw him as I sat by my fire at the Holly-Tree Inn, and I see him now, lying shackled with cords on the stable litter, among the mild eyes and the smoking breath of the cows, waiting to be taken away by the police, and stared at by the fearful village. A heavy animal,—the dullest animal in the stables,—with a stupid head, and a lumpish face devoid of any trace of insensibility, who had been, within the knowledge of the murdered youth, an embezzler of certain small moneys belonging to his master, and who had taken this hopeful mode of putting a possible accuser out of his way. All of which he confessed next day, like a sulky wretch who couldn't be troubled any more, now that they had got hold of him, and meant to make an end of him. I saw him once again, on the day of my departure from the Inn. In that Canton the headsman still does his office with a sword; and I came upon this murderer sitting bound, to a chair, with his eyes bandaged, on a scaffold in a little market-place. In that instant, a great sword (loaded with quicksilver in the thick part of the blade) swept round him like a gust of wind or fire, and there was no such creature in the world. My wonder was, not that he was so suddenly dispatched, but that any head was left unreaped, within a radius of fifty yards of that tremendous sickle.

That was a good Inn, too, with the kind, cheerful landlady and the honest landlord, where I lived in the shadow of Mont Blanc, and where one of the apartments has a zoological papering on the walls, not so accurately joined but that the elephant occasionally rejoices in a tiger's hind legs and tail, while the lion puts on a trunk and tusks, and the bear, moulting as it were, appears as to portions of himself like a leopard. I made several American friends at that Inn, who all called Mont Blanc Mount Blank,—except one good-humoured gentleman, of a very sociable nature, who became on such intimate terms with it that he spoke of it familiarly as "Blank"; observing, at breakfast, "Blank looks pretty tall this morning;" or considerably doubting in the courtyard in the evening, whether there warn't some go-ahead naters in our country, sir, that would make out the top of Blank in a couple of hours from first start—now!

Once I passed a fortnight at an Inn in the North of England, where I was haunted by the ghost of a tremendous pie. It was a Yorkshire pie, like a fort,—an abandoned fort with nothing in it; but the waiter had a fixed idea that it was a point of ceremony at every meal to put the pie on the table. After some days I tried to hint, in several delicate ways, that I considered the pie done with; as, for example, by emptying fag-ends of glasses of wine into it; putting cheese-plates and spoons into it, as into a basket; putting wine-bottles into it, as into a cooler; but always in vain, the pie being invariably cleaned out again and brought up as before. At last, beginning to be doubtful whether I was not the victim of a spectral illusion, and whether my health and spirits might not sink under the horrors of an imaginary pie, I cut a triangle out of it, fully as large as the musical instrument of that name in a powerful orchestra. Human provision could not have foreseen the result—but the waiter mended the pie. With some effectual species of cement, he adroitly fitted the triangle in again, and I paid my reckoning and fled.

The Holly-Tree was getting rather dismal. I made an overland expedition beyond the screen, and penetrated as far as the fourth window. Here I was driven back by stress of weather. Arrived at my winter-quarters once more, I made up the fire, and took another Inn.

It was in the remotest part of Cornwall. A great annual Miners' Feast was being holden at the Inn, when I and my travelling companions presented ourselves at night among the wild crowd that were dancing before it by torchlight. We had had a break-down in the dark, on a stony morass some miles away; and I had the honour of leading one of the unharnessed post-horses. If any lady or gentleman, on perusal of the present lines, will take any very tall post-horse with his traces hanging about his legs, and will conduct him by the bearing-rein into the heart of a country dance of a hundred and fifty couples, that lady or gentleman will then, and only then, form an adequate idea of the extent to which that post-horse will tread on his conductor's toes. Over and above which, the post-horse, finding three hundred people whirling about him, will probably rear, and also lash out with his hind legs, in a manner incompatible with dignity or self-respect on his conductor's part. With such little drawbacks on my usually impressive aspect, I appeared at this Cornish Inn, to the unutterable wonder of the Cornish Miners. It was full, and twenty times full, and nobody could be received but the post-horse,—though to get rid of that noble animal was something. While my fellow-travellers and I were discussing how to pass the night and so much of the next day as must intervene before the jovial blacksmith and the jovial wheelwright would be in a condition to go out on the morass and mend the coach, an honest man stepped forth from the crowd and proposed his unlet floor of two rooms, with supper of eggs and bacon, ale and punch. We joyfully accompanied him home to the strangest of clean houses, where we were well entertained to the satisfaction of all parties. But the novel feature of the entertainment was, that our host was a chair-maker, and that the chairs assigned to us were mere frames, altogether without bottoms of any sort; so that we passed the evening on perches. Nor was this the absurdest consequence; for when we unbent at supper, and any one of us gave way to laughter, he forgot the peculiarity of his position, and instantly disappeared. I myself, doubled up into an attitude from which self-extrication was impossible, was taken out of my frame, like a clown in a comic pantomime who has tumbled into a tub, five times by the taper's light during the eggs and bacon.

The Holly-Tree was fast reviving within me a sense of loneliness. I began to feel conscious that my subject would never carry on until I was dug out. I might be a week here,—weeks!

There was a story with a singular idea in it, connected with an Inn I once passed a night at in a picturesque old town on the Welsh border. In a large double-bedded room of this Inn there had been a suicide committed by poison, in one bed, while a tired traveller slept unconscious in the other. After that time, the suicide bed was never used, but the other constantly was; the disused bedstead remaining in the room empty, though as to all other respects in its old state. The story ran, that whosoever slept in this room, though never so entire a stranger, from never so far off, was invariably observed to come down in the morning with an impression that he smelt Laudanum, and that his mind always turned upon the subject of suicide; to which, whatever kind of man he might be, he was certain to make some reference if he conversed with any one. This went on for years, until it at length induced the landlord to take the disused bedstead down, and bodily burn it,—bed, hangings, and all. The strange influence (this was the story) now changed to a fainter one, but never changed afterwards. The occupant of that room, with occasional but very rare exceptions, would come down in the morning, trying to recall a forgotten dream he had had in the night. The landlord, on his mentioning his perplexity, would suggest various commonplace subjects, not one of which, as he very well knew, was the true subject. But the moment the landlord suggested "Poison," the traveller started, and cried, "Yes!" He never failed to accept that suggestion, and he never recalled any more of the dream.

This reminiscence brought the Welsh Inns in general before me; with the women in their round hats, and the harpers with their white beards (venerable, but humbugs, I am afraid), playing outside the door while I took my dinner. The transition was natural to the Highland Inns, with the oatmeal bannocks, the honey, the venison steaks, the trout from the loch, the whisky, and perhaps (having the materials so temptingly at hand) the Athol brose. Once was I coming south from the Scottish Highlands in hot haste, hoping to change quickly at the station at the bottom of a certain wild historical glen, when these eyes did with mortification see the landlord come out with a telescope and sweep the whole prospect for the horses; which horses were away picking up their own living, and did not heave in sight under four hours. Having thought of the loch-trout, I was taken by quick association to the Anglers' Inns of England (I have assisted at innumerable feats of angling by lying in the bottom of the boat, whole summer days, doing nothing with the greatest perseverance; which I have generally found to be as effectual towards the taking of fish as the finest tackle and the utmost science), and to the pleasant white, clean, flower-pot-decorated bedrooms of those inns, overlooking the river, and the ferry, and the green ait, and the church-spire, and the country bridge; and to the pearless Emma with the bright eyes and the pretty smile, who waited, bless her! with a natural grace that would have converted Blue-Beard. Casting my eyes upon my Holly-Tree fire, I next discerned among the glowing coals the pictures of a score or more of those wonderful English posting-inns which we are all so sorry to have lost, which were so large and so comfortable, and which were such monuments of British submission to rapacity and extortion. He who would see these houses pining away, let him walk from Basingstoke, or even Windsor, to London, by way of Hounslow, and moralise on their perishing remains; the stables crumbling to dust; unsettled labourers and wanderers bivouacking in the outhouses;

grass growing in the yards; the rooms, where erst so many hundred beds of down were made up, let off to Irish lodgers at eighteenpence a week; a little ill-looking beer-shop shrinking in the tap of former days, burning coach-house gates for firewood, having one of its two windows bunged up, as if it had received punishment in a fight with the Railroad; a low, bandy-legged, brick-making bulldog standing in the doorway. What could I next see in my fire so naturally as the new railway-house of these times near the dismal country station; with nothing particular on draught but cold air and damp, nothing worth mentioning in the larder but new mortar, and no business doing beyond a conceited affectation of luggage in the hall? Then I came to the Inns of Paris, with the pretty apartment of four pieces up one hundred and seventy-five waxed stairs, the privilege of ringing the bell all day long without influencing anybody's mind or body but your own, and the not-too-much-for-dinner, considering the price. Next to the provincial Inns of France, with the great church-tower rising above the courtyard, the horse-bells jingling merrily up and down the street beyond, and the clocks of all descriptions in all the rooms, which are never right, unless taken at the precise minute when, by getting exactly twelve hours too fast or too slow, they unintentionally become so. Away I went, next, to the lesser roadside Inns of Italy; where all the dirty clothes in the house (not in wear) are always lying in your anteroom; where the mosquitoes make a raisin pudding of your face in summer, and the cold bites it blue in winter; where you get what you can, and forget what you can't: where I should again like to be boiling my tea in a pocket-handkerchief dumpling, for want of a teapot. So to the old palace Inns and old monastery Inns, in towns and cities of the same bright country; with their massive quadrangular staircases, whence you may look from among clustering pillars high into the blue vault of heaven; with their stately banqueting-rooms, and vast refectories; with their labyrinths of ghostly bedchambers, and their glimpses into gorgeous streets that have no appearance of reality or possibility. So to the close little Inns of the Malaria districts, with their pale attendants, and their peculiar smell of never letting in the air. So to the immense fantastic Inns of Venice, with the cry of the gondolier below, as he skims the corner; the grip of the watery odours on one particular little bit of the bridge of your nose (which is never released while you stay there); and the great bell of St. Mark's Cathedral tolling midnight. Next I put up for a minute at the restless Inns upon the Rhine, where your going to bed, no matter at what hour, appears to be the tocsin for everybody else's getting up; and where, in the table-d'hôte room at the end of the long table (with several Towers of Babel on it at the other end, all made of white plates), one knot of stoutish men, entirely dressed in jewels and dirt, and having nothing else upon them, *will* remain all night, clinking glasses, and singing about the river that flows, and the grape that grows, and Rhine wine that beguiles, and Rhine woman that smiles and hi drink drink my friend and ho drink drink my brother, and all the rest of it. I departed thence, as a matter of course, to other German Inns, where all the eatables are soddened down to the same flavour, and where the mind is disturbed by the apparition of hot puddings, and boiled cherries, sweet and slab, at awfully unexpected periods of the repast. After a draught of sparkling beer from a foaming glass jug, and a glance of recognition through the windows of the student beer-houses at Heidelberg and elsewhere, I put out to sea for the Inns of America, with their four hundred beds apiece, and their eight or nine hundred ladies and gentlemen at dinner every day. Again I stood in the bar-rooms thereof, taking my evening cobbler, julep, sling, or cocktail. Again I listened to my friend the General,—whom I had known for five minutes, in the course of which period he had made me intimate for life with two Majors, who again had made me intimate for life with three Colonels, who again had made me brother to twenty-two civilians,—again, I say, I listened to my friend the General, leisurely expounding the resources of the establishment, as to gentlemen's morning-room, Sir; ladies' morning-room, Sir; gentlemen's evening-room, Sir; ladies' evening-room, Sir; ladies' and gentlemen's evening reuniting-room, Sir; music-room, Sir; reading-room, Sir; over four hundred sleeping-rooms, Sir; and the entire planned and finited within twelve calendar months from the first clearing off of the old encumbrances on the plot, at a cost of five hundred thousand dollars, Sir. Again I found, as to my individual way of thinking, that the greater, the more gorgeous, and the more dollarous the establishment was, the less desirable it was. Nevertheless, again I drank my cobbler, julep, sling, or cocktail, in all good-will, to my friend the General, and my friends the Majors, Colonels, and civilians all; full well knowing that, whatever little motes my beamy eyes may have descried in theirs, they belong to a kind, generous, large-hearted, and great people.

I had been going on lately at a quick pace to keep my solitude out of my mind; but here I broke down for good, and gave up the subject. What was I to do? What was to become of me? Into what extremity was I submissively to sink? Supposing that, like Baron Trenck, I looked out for a mouse or spider, and found one, and beguiled my imprisonment by training it? Even that might be dangerous with a view to the future. I might be so far gone when the road did come to be cut through the snow, that, on my way forth, I might burst into tears, and beseech, like the prisoner who was released in his old age from the Bastille, to be taken back again to the five windows, the ten curtains, and the sinuous drapery.

A desperate idea came into my head. Under any other circumstances I should have rejected it; but, in the strait at which I was, I held it fast. Could I so far overcome the inherent bashfulness which withheld me from the landlord's table and the company I might find there, as to call up the Boots, and ask him to take a chair,—and something in a liquid form,—and talk to me? I could, I would, I did.

Second Branch

THE BOOTS

WHERE HAD HE BEEN IN HIS TIME? HE REPEATED, WHEN I ASKED HIM THE question. Lord, he had been everywhere! And what had he been? Bless you, he had been everything you could mention a'most!

Seen a good deal? Why, of course he had. I should say so, he could assure me, if I only knew about a twentieth part of what had come in his way. Why, it would be easier for him, he expected, to tell what he hadn't seen than what he had. Ah! A deal, it would.

What was the curiousest thing he had seen? Well! He didn't know. He couldn't momently name what was the curiousest thing he had seen,—unless it was a Unicorn, and he see *him* once at a Fair. But supposing a young gentleman not eight year old was to run away with a fine young woman of seven, might I think *that* a queer start? Certainly. Then that was a start as he himself had had his blessed eyes on, and he had cleaned the shoes they run away in—and they was so little that he couldn't get his hand into 'em.

Master Harry Walmers' father, you see, he lived at the Elmses, down away by Shooter's Hill there, six or seven miles from Lunnon. He was a gentleman of spirit, and good-looking, and held his head up when he walked, and had what you may call Fire about him. He wrote poetry, and he rode, and he ran, and he cricketed, and he danced, and he acted, and he done it all equally beautiful. He was uncommon proud of Master Harry as was his only child; but he didn't spoil him neither. He was a gentleman that had a will of his own and a eye of his own, and that would be minded. Consequently, though he made quite a companion of the fine bright boy, and was delighted to see him so fond of reading his fairy books, and was never tired of hearing him say my name is Norval, or hearing him sing his songs about Young May Moons is beaming love, and When he as adores thee has left but the name, and that; still he kept the command over the child, and the child *was* a child, and it's to be wished more of 'em was!

How did Boots happen to know all this? Why, through being under-gardener. Of course he couldn't be under-gardener, and be always about, in the summer-time, near the windows on the lawn, a mowing, and sweeping, and weeding, and pruning, and this and that, without getting acquainted with the ways of the family. Even supposing Master Harry hadn't come to him one morning early, and said, "Cobbs, how should you spell Norah, if you was asked?" and then began cutting it in print all over the fence.

He couldn't say he had taken particular notice of children before that; but really it was pretty to see them two mites a going about the place together, deep in love.

And the courage of the boy! Bless your soul, he'd have throwed off his little hat, and tucked up his little sleeves, and gone in at a Lion, he would, if they had happened to meet one, and she had been frightened of him. One day he stops, along with her, where Boots was hoeing weeds in the gravel, and says, speaking up, "Cobbs," he says, "I like *you*." "Do you, Sir? I'm proud to hear it." "Yes, I do, Cobbs. Why do I like you, do you think, Cobbs?" "Don't know, Master Harry, I am sure." "Because Norah likes you, Cobbs." "Indeed, Sir? That's very gratifying." "Gratifying, Cobbs? It's better than millions of the brightest diamonds to be liked by Norah." "Certainly, Sir." "You're going away, ain't you, Cobbs?" "Yes, Sir." "Would you like another situation, Cobbs?" "Well, Sir, I shouldn't object, if it was a good 'un." "Then, Cobbs," says he, "you shall be our Head Gardener when we are married." And he tucks her, in her little sky-blue mantle, under his arm, and walks away.

Boots could assure me that it was better than a picter, and equal to a play, to see them babies, with their long, bright, curling hair, their sparkling eyes, and their beautiful light tread, a rambling about the garden, deep in love. Boots was of opinion that the birds believed they was birds, and kept up with 'em, singing to please 'em. Sometimes they would creep under the Tulip-tree, and would sit there with their arms round one another's necks, and their soft cheeks touching, a reading about the Prince and the Dragon, and the good and bad enchanters, and the king's fair daughter. Sometimes he would hear them planning about having a house in a forest, keeping bees and a cow, and living entirely on milk and honey. Once he came upon them by the pond, and heard Master Harry say, "Adorable Norah, kiss me, and say you love me to distraction, or I'll jump in head-foremost." And Boots made no question he would have done it if she hadn't complied. On the whole, Boots said it had a tendency to make him feel as if he was in love himself—only he didn't exactly know who with.

"Cobbs," said Master Harry, one evening, when Cobbs was watering the flowers, "I am going on a visit, this present Midsummer, to my grandmamma's at York."

"Are you indeed, Sir? I hope you'll have a pleasant time. I am going into Yorkshire, myself, when I leave here."

"Are you going to your grandmamma's, Cobbs?"

"No, Sir. I haven't got such a thing."

"Not as a grandmamma, Cobbs?"

"No, Sir."

The boy looked on at the watering of the flowers for a little while, and then said, "I shall be very glad indeed to go, Cobbs,—Norah's going."

"You'll be all right then, Sir," says Cobbs, "with your beautiful sweetheart by your side."

"Cobbs," returned the boy, flushing, "I never let anybody joke about it, when I can prevent them."

"It wasn't a joke, Sir," says Cobbs, with humility,—"wasn't so meant."

"I am glad of that, Cobbs, because I like you, you know, and you're going to live with us.—Cobbs!"

"Sir."

"What do you think my grandmamma gives me when I go down there?"

"I couldn't so much as make a guess, Sir."

"A Bank of England five-pound note, Cobbs."

"Whew!" says Cobbs, "that's a spanking sum of money, Master Harry."

"A person could do a good deal with such a sum of money as that,—couldn't a person, Cobbs?"

"I believe you, Sir!"

"Cobbs," said the boy, "I'll tell you a secret. At Norah's house, they have been joking her about me, and pretending to laugh at our being engaged,—pretending to make game of it, Cobbs!"

"Such, Sir," says Cobbs, "is the depravity of human natur."

The boy, looking exactly like his father, stood for a few minutes with his glowing face towards the sunset, and then departed with, "Good-night, Cobbs. I'm going in."

If I was to ask Boots how it happened that he was a-going to leave that place just at that present time, well, he couldn't rightly answer me. He did suppose he might have stayed there till now if he had been anyways inclined. But, you see, he was younger then, and he wanted change. That's what he wanted,—change. Mr. Walmers, he said to him when he gave him notice of his intentions to leave, "Cobbs," he says, "have you anythink to complain of? I make the inquiry because if I find that any of my people really has anythink to complain of, I wish to make it right if I can." "No, Sir," says Cobbs; "thanking you, Sir, I find myself as well sitiwated here as I could hope to be anywheres. The truth is, Sir, that I'm a-going to seek my fortun'." "O, indeed, Cobbs!" he says; "I hope you may find it." And Boots could assure me—which he did, touching his hair with his bootjack, as a salute in the way of his present calling—that he hadn't found it yet.

Well, Sir! Boots left the Elmses when his time was up, and Master Harry, he went down to the old lady's at York, which old lady would have given that child the teeth out of her head (if she had had any), she was so wrapped up in him. What does that Infant do,—for Infant you may call him and be within the mark,—but cut away from that old lady's with his Norah, on a expedition to go to Gretna Green and be married!

Sir, Boots was at this identical Holly-Tree Inn (having left it several times since to better himself, but always come back through one thing or another), when, one summer afternoon, the coach drives up, and out of the coach gets them two children. The Guard says to our Governor, "I don't quite make out these little passengers, but the young gentleman's words was, that they was to be brought here." The young gentleman gets out; hands his lady out; gives the Guard something for himself; says to our Governor, "We're to stop here to-night, please. Sitting-room and two bedrooms will be required. Chops and cherry-pudding for two!" and tucks her, in her sky-blue mantle, under his arm, and walks into the house much bolder than Brass.

Boots leaves me to judge what the amazement of that establishment was, when these two tiny creatures all alone by themselves was marched into the Angel,—much more so, when he, who had seen them without their seeing him, give the Governor his views of the expedition they was upon. "Cobbs," says the Governor, "if this is so, I must set off myself to York, and quiet their friends' minds. In which case you must keep your eye upon 'em, and humour 'em, till I come back. But before I take these measures, Cobbs, I should wish you to find from themselves whether your opinion is correct." "Sir, to you," says Cobbs, "that shall be done directly."

So Boots goes upstairs to the Angel, and there he finds Master Harry on a e-normous sofa,—immense at any time, but looking like the Great Bed of Ware, compared with him,—a drying the eyes of Miss Norah with his pocket-hankecher. Their little legs was entirely off the ground, of course, and it really is not possible for Boots to express to me how small them children looked.

"It's Cobbs! It's Cobbs!" cries Master Harry, and comes running to him, and catching hold of his hand. Miss Norah comes running to him on t'other side and catching hold of his t'other hand, and they both jump for joy.

"I see you a getting out, Sir," says Cobbs. "I thought it was you. I thought I couldn't be mistaken in your height and figure. What's the object of your journey, sir?—Matrimonial?"

"We are going to be married, Cobbs, at Gretna Green," returned the boy. "We have run away on purpose. Norah has been in rather low spirits, Cobbs; but she'll be happy, now we have found you to be our friend."

"Thank you, Sir, and thank *you*, Miss," says Cobbs, "for your good opinion. *Did* you bring any luggage with you, Sir?"

If I will believe Boots when he gives me his word and honour upon it, the lady had got a parasol, a smelling-bottle, a round and a half of cold buttered toast, eight peppermint drops, and a hair-brush,—seemingly a doll's. The gentleman had got about half a dozen yards of string, a knife, three or four sheets of writing-paper folded up surprising small, a orange, and a Chaney mug with his name upon it.

"What may be the exact natur of your plans, Sir?" says Cobbs.

"To go on," replied the boy,—which the courage of that boy was something wonderful!—"in the morning, and be married to-morrow."

"Just so, Sir," says Cobbs. "Would it meet your views, Sir, if I was to accompany you?"

When Cobbs said this, they both jumped for joy again, and cried out, "Oh, yes, yes, Cobbs! Yes!"

"Well, Sir," says Cobbs. "If you will excuse my having the freedom to give an opinion, what I should recommend would be this. I'm acquainted with a pony, Sir, which, put in a pheayton that I could borrow, would take you and Mrs. Harry Walmers, Junior, (myself driving, if you approved,) to the end of your journey in a very short space of time. I am not altogether sure, Sir, that this pony will be at liberty to-morrow, but even if you had to wait over to-morrow for him, it might be worth your while. As to the small account here, Sir, in case you was to find yourself running at all short, that don't signify; because I'm a part proprietor of this inn, and it could stand over."

Boots assures me that when they clapped their hands, and jumped for joy again, and called him "Good Cobbs!" and "Dear Cobbs!" and bent across him to kiss one another in the delight of their confiding hearts, he felt himself the meanest rascal for deceiving 'em that ever was born.

"Is there anything you want just at present, Sir?" says Cobbs, mortally ashamed of himself.

"We should like some cakes after dinner," answered Master Harry, folding his arms, putting out one leg, and looking straight at him, "and two apples,—and jam. With dinner we should like to have toast-and-water. But Norah has always been accustomed to half a glass of currant wine at dessert. And so have I."

"It shall be ordered at the bar, Sir," says Cobbs; and away he went.

Boots has the feeling as fresh upon him at this minute of speaking as he had then, that he would far rather have had it out in half-a-dozen rounds with the Governor than have combined with him; and that he wished with all his heart there was any impossible place where those two babies could make an impossible marriage, and live impossibly happy ever afterwards. However, as it couldn't be, he went into the Governor's plans, and the Governor set off for York in half an hour.

The way in which the women of that house—without exception—every one of 'em—married *and* single—took to that boy when they heard the story, Boots considers surprising. It was as much as he could do to keep 'em from dashing into the room and kissing him. They climbed up all sorts of places, at the risk of their lives, to look at him through a pane of glass. They was seven deep at the keyhole. They was out of their minds about him and his bold spirit.

In the evening, Boots went into the room to see how the runaway couple was getting on. The gentleman was on the window-seat, supporting the lady in his arms. She had tears upon her face, and was lying, very tired and half asleep, with her head upon his shoulder.

"Mrs. Harry Walmers, Junior, fatigued, Sir?" says Cobbs.

"Yes, she is tired, Cobbs; but she is not used to be away from home, and she has been in low spirits again. Cobbs, do you think you could bring a biffin, please?"

"I ask your pardon, Sir," says Cobbs. "What was it you—?"

"I think a Norfolk biffin would rouse her, Cobbs. She is very fond of them."

Boots withdrew in search of the required restorative, and when he brought it in, the gentleman handed it to the lady, and fed her with a spoon, and took a little himself; the lady being heavy with sleep, and rather cross. "What should you think, Sir," says Cobbs, "of a chamber candlestick?" The gentleman approved; the chambermaid went first, up the great staircase; the lady, in her sky-blue mantle, followed, gallantly escorted by the gentleman; the gentleman embraced her at her door, and retired to his own apartment, where Boots softly locked him up.

Boots couldn't but feel with increased acuteness what a base deceiver he was, when they consulted him at breakfast (they had ordered sweet milk-and-water, and toast and currant jelly, overnight) about the pony. It really was as much as he could do, he don't mind confessing to me, to look them two young things in the face, and think what a wicked old father of lies he had grown up to be. Howsomever, he went on a lying like a Trojan about the pony. He told 'em that it did so unfortunately happen that the pony was half clipped, you see, and that he couldn't be taken out in that state, for fear it should strike to his inside. But that he'd be finished clipping in the course of the day, and that to-morrow morning at eight o'clock the pheayton would be ready. Boots's view of the whole case, looking back on it in my room, is, that Mrs. Harry Walmers, Junior, was beginning to give in. She hadn't had her hair curled when she went to bed, and she didn't seem quite up to brushing it herself, and its getting in her eyes put her out. But nothing put out Master Harry. He sat behind his breakfast-cup, a tearing away at the jelly, as if he had been his own father.

After breakfast, Boots is inclined to consider that they drawed soldiers,—at least, he knows that many such was found in the fire-place, all on horseback. In the course of the morning, Master Harry rang the bell,—it was surprising how that there boy did carry on,—and said, in a sprightly way, "Cobbs, is there any good walks in this neighbourhood?"

"Yes, Sir," says Cobbs. "There's Love-lane."

"Get out with you, Cobbs!"—that was that there boy's expression,—"you're joking."

"Begging your pardon, Sir," says Cobbs, "there really is Love-lane. And a pleasant walk it is, and proud shall I be to show it to yourself and Mrs. Harry Walmers, Junior."

"Norah, dear," said Master Harry, "this is curious. We really ought to see Love-lane. Put on your bonnet, my sweetest darling, and we will go there with Cobbs."

Boots leaves me to judge what a Beast he felt himself to be, when that young pair told him, as they all three jogged along together, that they had made up their minds to give him two thousand guineas a year as head-gardener, on accounts of his being so true a friend to 'em. Boots could have wished at the moment that the earth would have opened and swallowed him up, he felt so mean, with their beaming eyes a looking at him, and believing him. Well, Sir, he turned the conversation as well as he could, and he took 'em down Love-lane to the water-meadows, and there Master Harry would have drowned himself in half a moment more, a getting out a water-lily for her,—but nothing daunted that boy. Well, Sir, they was tired out. All being so new and strange to 'em, they was tired as tired could be. And they laid down on a bank of daisies, like the children in the wood, leastways meadows, and fell asleep.

Boots don't know—perhaps I do,—but never mind, it don't signify either way—why it made a man fit to make a fool of himself to see them two pretty babies a lying there in the clear still sunny day, not dreaming half so hard when they was asleep as they done when they was awake. But, Lord! when you come to think of yourself, you know, and what a game you have been up to ever since you was in your own cradle, and what a poor sort of a chap you are, and how it's always either Yesterday with you, or else To-morrow, and never To-day, that's where it is!

Well, Sir, they woke up at last, and then one thing was getting pretty clear to Boots, namely, that Mrs. Harry Walmerses, Junior's, temper was on the move. When Master Harry took her round the waist, she said he "teased her so"; and when he says, "Norah, my young May Moon, your Harry tease you?" she tells him, "Yes; and I want to go home!"

A biled fowl, and baked bread-and-butter pudding, brought Mrs. Walmers up a little; but Boots could have wished, he must privately own to me, to have seen her more sensible of the woice of love, and less abandoning of herself to currants. However, Master Harry, he kept up, and his noble heart was as fond as ever. Mrs. Walmers turned very sleepy about dusk, and began to cry. Therefore, Mrs. Walmers went off to bed as per yesterday; and Master Harry ditto repeated.

About eleven or twelve at night comes back the Governor in a chaise, along with Mr. Walmers and a elderly lady. Mr. Walmers looks amused and very serious, both at once, and says to our missis, "We are much indebted to you, ma'am, for your kind care of our little children, which we can never sufficiently acknowledge. Pray, ma'am, where is my boy?" Our missis says, "Cobbs has the dear child in charge, Sir. Cobbs, show Forty!" Then he says to Cobbs, "Ah, Cobbs, I am glad to see *you*! I understood you was here!" And Cobbs says, "Yes, Sir. Your most obedient, Sir."

I may be surprised to hear Boots say it, perhaps; but Boots assures me that his heart beat like a hammer, going upstairs. "I beg your pardon, Sir," says he, while unlocking the door; "I hope you are not angry with Master Harry. For Master Harry is a fine boy, Sir, and will do you credit and honour." And Boots signifies to me, that, if the fine boy's father had contradicted him in the daring state of mind in which he then was, he thinks he should have "fetched him a crack," and taken the consequences.

But Mr. Walmers only says, "No, Cobbs. No, my good fellow. Thank you!" And, the door being opened, goes in.

Boots goes in too, holding the light, and he sees Mr. Walmers go up to the bedside, bend gently down, and kiss the little sleeping face. Then he stands looking at it for a minute, looking wonderfully like it (they do say he ran away with Mrs. Walmers); and then he gently shakes the little shoulder.

"Harry, my dear boy! Harry!"

Master Harry starts up and looks at him. Looks at Cobbs too. Such is the honour of that mite, that he looks at Cobbs, to see whether he has brought him into trouble.

"I am not angry, my child. I only want you to dress yourself and come home."

"Yes, pa."

Master Harry dresses himself quickly. His breast begins to swell when he has nearly finished, and it swells more and more as he stands, at last, a looking at his father: his father standing a looking at him, the quiet image of him.

"Please may I"—the spirit of that little creatur, and the way he kept his rising tears down!—"please, dear pa—may I—kiss Norah before I go?"

"You may, my child."

So he takes Master Harry in his hand, and Boots leads the way with the candle, and they come to that other bedroom, where the elderly lady is seated by the bed, and poor little Mrs. Harry Walmers, Junior, is fast asleep. There the father lifts the child up to the pillow, and he lays his little face down for an instant by the little warm face of poor unconscious little Mrs. Harry Walmers, Junior, and gently draws it to him,—a sight so touching to the chambermaids who are peeping through the door, that one of them calls out, "It's a shame to part 'em!" But this chambermaid was always, as Boots informs me, a soft-hearted one. Not that there was any harm in that girl. Far from it.

Finally, Boots says, that's all about it. Mr. Walmers drove away in the chaise, having hold of Master Harry's hand. The elderly lady and Mrs. Harry Walmers, Junior, that was never to be (she married a Captain long afterwards, and died in India), went off next day. In conclusion, Boots put it to me whether I hold with him in two opinions: firstly, that there are not many couples on their way to be married who are half as innocent of guile as those two children; secondly, that it would be a jolly good thing for a great many couples on their way to be married, if they could only be stopped in time, and brought back separately.

Third Branch

THE BILL

I HAD BEEN SNOWED UP A WHOLE WEEK. THE TIME HAD HUNG SO LIGHTLY ON MY hands, that I should have been in great doubt of the fact but for a piece of documentary evidence that lay upon my table.

The road had been dug out of the snow on the previous day, and the document in question was my bill. It testified emphatically to my having eaten and drunk, and warmed myself, and slept among the sheltering branches of the Holly-Tree, seven days and nights.

I had yesterday allowed the road twenty-four hours to improve itself, finding that I required that additional margin of time for the completion of my task. I had ordered my bill to be upon the table, and a chaise to be at the door, "at eight o'clock to-morrow evening." It was eight o'clock to-morrow evening when I buckled up my travelling writing-desk in its leather case, paid my bill, and got on my warm coats and wrappers. Of course, no time now remained for my travelling on to add a frozen tear to the icicles which were doubtless hanging plentifully about the farmhouse where I had first seen Angela. What I had to do was to get across to Liverpool by the shortest open road, there to meet my heavy baggage and embark. It was quite enough to do, and I had not an hour too much time to do it in.

I had taken leave of all my Holly-Tree friends—almost, for the time being, of my bashfulness too—and was standing for half a minute at the Inn door watching the ostler as he took another turn at the cord which tied my portmanteau on the chaise, when I saw lamps coming down towards the Holly-Tree. The road was so padded with snow that no wheels were audible; but all of us who were standing at the Inn door saw lamps coming on, and at a lively rate too, between the walls of snow that had been heaped up on either side of the track. The chambermaid instantly divined how the case stood, and called to the ostler, "Tom, this is a Gretna job!" The ostler, knowing that her sex instinctively scented a marriage, or anything in that direction, rushed up the yard bawling, "Next four out!" and in a moment the whole establishment was thrown into commotion.

I had a melancholy interest in seeing the happy man who loved and was beloved; and therefore, instead of driving off at once, I remained at the Inn door when the fugitives drove up. A bright-eyed fellow, muffled in a mantle, jumped out so briskly that he almost overthrew me. He turned to apologise, and, by heaven, it was Edwin!

"Charley!" said he, recoiling. "Gracious powers, what do you do here?"

"Edwin," said I, recoiling, "gracious powers, what do *you* do here?" I struck my forehead as I said it, and an insupportable blaze of light seemed to shoot before my eyes.

He hurried me into the little parlour (always kept with a slow fire in it and no poker), where posting company waited while their horses were putting to, and, shutting the door, said:

"Charley, forgive me!"

"Edwin!" I returned. "Was this well? When I loved her so dearly! When I had garnered up my heart so long!" I could say no more.

He was shocked when he saw how moved I was, and made the cruel observation, that he had not thought I should have taken it so much to heart.

I looked at him. I reproached him no more. But I looked at him.

"My dear, dear Charley," said he, "don't think ill of me, I beseech you! I know you have a right to my utmost confidence, and, believe me, you have ever had it until now. I abhor secrecy. Its meanness is intolerable to me. But I and my dear girl have observed it for your sake."

He and his dear girl! It steeled me.

"You have observed it for my sake, Sir?" said I, wondering how his frank face could face it out so.

"Yes!—and Angela's," said he.

I found the room reeling round in an uncertain way, like a labouring, humming-top. "Explain yourself," said I, holding on by one hand to an armchair.

"Dear old darling Charley!" returned Edwin, in his cordial manner, "consider! When you were going on so happily with Angela, why should I compromise you with the old gentleman by making you a party to our engagement, and (after he had declined my proposals) to our secret intention? Surely it was better that you should be able honourably to say, 'He never took counsel with me, never told me, never breathed a word of it.' If Angela suspected it, and showed me all the favour and support she could—God bless her for a precious creature and a priceless wife!—I couldn't help that. Neither I nor Emmeline ever told her, any more than we told you. And for the same good reason, Charley; trust me, for the same good reason, and no other upon earth!"

Emmeline was Angela's cousin. Lived with her. Had been brought up with her. Was her father's ward. Had property.

"Emmeline is in the chaise, my dear Edwin!" said I, embracing him with the greatest affection.

"My good fellow!" said he, "do you suppose I should be going to Gretna Green without her?"

I ran out with Edwin, I opened the chaise door, I took Emmeline in my arms, I folded her to my heart. She was wrapped in soft white fur, like the snowy landscape: but was warm, and young, and lovely. I put their leaders to with my own hands, I gave the boys a five-pound note apiece, I cheered them as they drove away, I drove the other way myself as hard as I could pelt.

I never went to Liverpool, I never went to America, I went straight back to London, and I married Angela. I have never until this time, even to her, disclosed the secret of my character, and the mistrust and the mistaken journey into which it led me. When she, and they, and our eight children and their seven—I mean Edwin and Emmeline's, whose oldest girl is old enough now to wear white for herself, and to look very like her mother in it—come to read these pages, as of course they will, I shall hardly fail to be found out at last. Never mind! I can bear it. I began at the Holly-Tree, by idle accident, to associate the Christmas-time of year with human interest, and with some inquiry into, and some care for, the lives of those by whom I find myself surrounded. I hope that I am none the worse for it, and that no one near me or afar off is the worse for it. And I say, May the green Holly-Tree flourish, striking its roots deep into our English ground, and having its germinating qualities carried by the birds of Heaven all over the world!

Going into Society

At one period of its reverses, the House fell into the occupation of a Showman. He was found registered as its occupier, on the parish books of the time when he rented the House, and there was therefore no need of any clue to his name. But, he himself was less easy to be found; for, he had led a wandering life, and settled people had lost sight of him, and people who plumed themselves on being respectable were shy of admitting that they had ever known anything of him. At last, among the marsh lands near the river's level, that lie about Deptford and the neighbouring market-gardens, a Grizzled Personage in velveteen, with a face so cut up by varieties of weather that he looked as if he had been tattooed, was found smoking a pipe at the door of a wooden house on wheels. The wooden house was laid up in ordinary for the winter, near the mouth of a muddy creek; and everything near it, the foggy river, the misty marshes, and the steaming market-gardens, smoked in company with the grizzled man. In the midst of this smoking party, the funnel-chimney of the wooden house on wheels was not remiss, but took its pipe with the rest in a companionable manner.

On being asked if it were he who had once rented the House to Let, Grizzled Velveteen looked surprised, and said yes. Then his name was Magsman? That was it, Toby Magsman—which lawfully christened Robert; but called in the line, from a infant, Toby. There was nothing agin Toby Magsman, he believed? If there was suspicion of such—mention it!

There was no suspicion of such, he might rest assured. But, some inquiries were making about that House, and would he object to say why he left it?

Not at all; why should he? He left it, along of a Dwarf.

Along of a Dwarf?

Mr. Magsman repeated, deliberately and emphatically, Along of a Dwarf.

Might it be compatible with Mr. Magsman's inclination and convenience to enter, as a favour, into a few particulars?

Mr. Magsman entered into the following particulars.

It was a long time ago, to begin with;—afore lotteries and a deal more was done away with. Mr. Magsman was looking about for a good pitch, and he see that house, and he says to himself, "I'll have you, if you're to be had. If money'll get you, I'll have you."

The neighbours cut up rough, and made complaints; but Mr. Magsman don't know what they *would* have had. It was a lovely thing. First of all, there was the canvas, representin the picter of the Giant, in Spanish trunks and a ruff, who was himself half the heighth of the house, and was run up with a line and pulley to a pole on the roof, so that his Ed was coeval with the parapet. Then, there was the canvass, representin the picter of the Albina lady, showing her white air to the Army and Navy in correct uniform. Then, there was the canvas, representin the picter of the Wild Indian a scalpin a member of some foreign nation. Then, there was the canvas, representin the picter of a child of a British Planter, seized by two Boa Constrictors—not that *we* never had no child, nor no Constrictors neither. Similarly, there was the canvas, representin the picter of the Wild Ass of the Prairies—not that *we* never had no wild asses, nor wouldn't have had 'em at a gift. Last, there was the canvas, representin the picter of the Dwarf, and like him too (considerin), with George the Fourth in such a state of astonishment at him as His Majesty couldn't with his utmost politeness and stoutness express. The front of the House was so covered with canvasses, that there wasn't a spark of daylight ever visible on that side. "MAGSMAN'S AMUSEMENTS," fifteen foot long by two foot high, ran over the front door and parlour winders. The passage was a Arbour of green baize and gardenstuff. A barrel-organ performed there unceasing. And as to respectability,—if threepence ain't respectable, what is?

But, the Dwarf is the principal article at present, and he was worth the money. He was wrote up as MAJOR TPSCHOFFKI, OF THE IMPERIAL BULGRADERIAN BRIGADE. Nobody couldn't pronounce the name, and it never was intended anybody should. The public always turned it, as a regular rule, into Chopski. In the line he was called Chops; partly on that account, and partly because his real name, if he ever had any real name (which was very dubious), was Stakes.

He was a uncommon small man, he really was. Certainly not so small as he was made out to be, but where *is* your Dwarf as is? He was a most uncommon small man, with a most uncommon large Ed; and what he had inside that Ed, nobody ever knowed but himself: even supposin himself to have ever took stock of it, which it would have been a stiff job for even him to do.

The kindest little man as never growed! Spirited, but not proud. When he travelled with the Spotted Baby—though he knowed himself to be a nat'ral Dwarf, and knowed the Baby's spots to be put upon him artificial, he nursed that Baby like a mother. You never heerd him give a ill-name to a Giant. He *did* allow himself to break out into strong language respectin the Fat Lady from Norfolk; but that was an affair of the 'art; and when a man's 'art has been trifled with by a lady, and the preference giv to a Indian, he ain't master of his actions.

He was always in love, of course; every human nat'ral phenomenon is. And he was always in love with a large woman; I never knowed the Dwarf as could be got to love a small one. Which helps to keep 'em the Curiosities they are.

One sing'ler idea he had in that Ed of his, which must have meant something, or it wouldn't have been there. It was always his opinion that he was entitled to property. He never would put his name to anything. He had been taught to write, by the young man without arms, who got his living with his toes (quite a writing master *he* was, and taught scores in the line), but Chops would have starved to death, afore he'd have gained a bit of bread by putting his hand to a paper. This is the more curious to bear in mind, because *he* had no property, nor hope of property, except his house and a sarser. When I say his house, I mean the box, painted and got up outside like a reg'lar six-roomer, that he used to creep into, with a diamond ring (or quite as good to look at) on his forefinger, and ring a little bell out of what the Public believed to be the Drawing-room winder. And when I say a sarser, I mean a Chaney sarser in which he made a collection for himself at the end of every Entertainment. His cue for that, he took from me; "Ladies and gentlemen, the little man will now walk three times round the Cairawan, and retire behind the curtain." When he said anything important, in private life, he mostly wound it up with this form of words, and they was generally the last thing he said to me at night afore he went to bed.

He had what I consider a fine mind—a poetic mind. His ideas respectin his property never come upon him so strong as when he sat upon a barrel-organ and had the handle turned. Arter the wibration had run through him a little time, he would screech out, "Toby, I feel my property coming—grind away! I'm counting my guineas by thousands, Toby—grind away! Toby, I shall be a man of fortun! I feel the Mint a jingling in me, Toby, and I'm swelling out into the Bank of England!" Such is the influence of music on a poetic mind. Not that he was partial to any other music but a barrel-organ; on the contrary, hated it.

He had a kind of a everlasting grudge agin the Public: which is a thing you may notice in many phenomenons that get their living out of it. What riled him most in the nater of his occupation was, that it kep him out of Society. He was continiwally saying, "Toby, my ambition is, to go into Society. The curse of my position towards the Public is, that it keeps me hout of Society. This don't signify to a low beast of a Indian; he an't formed for Society. This don't signify to a Spotted Baby; *he* an't formed for Society.—I am."

Nobody never could make out what Chops done with his money. He had a good salary, down on the drum every Saturday as the day came round, besides having the run of his teeth—and he was a Woodpecker to eat—but all Dwarfs are. The sarser was a little income, bringing him in so many halfpence that he'd carry 'em for a week together, tied up in a pocket-handkercher. And yet he never had money. And it couldn't be the Fat Lady from Norfolk, as was once supposed; because it stands to reason that when you have a animosity towards a Indian, which makes you grind your teeth at him to his face, and which can hardly hold you from Goosing him audible when he's going through his War-Dance—it stands to reason you wouldn't under them circumstances deprive yourself, to support that Indian in the lap of luxury.

Most unexpected, the mystery come out one day at Egham Races. The Public was shy of bein pulled in, and Chops was ringin his little bell out of his drawing-room winder, and was snarlin to me over his shoulder as he kneeled down with his legs out at the back-door—for he couldn't be shoved into his house without kneeling down, and the premises wouldn't accommodate his legs—was snarlin, "Here's a precious Public for you; why the Devil don't they tumble up?" when a man in the crowd holds up a carrier-pigeon, and cries out, "If there's any person here as has got a ticket, the Lottery's just drawed, and the number as has come up for the great prize is three, seven, forty-two! Three, seven, forty-two!" I was givin the man to the Furies myself, for calling off the Public's attention—for the Public will turn away, at any time, to look at anything in preference to the thing showed 'em; and if you doubt it, get 'em together for any indiwidual purpose on the face of the earth, and send only two people in late, and see if the whole company an't far more interested in takin particular notice of them two than of you—I say, I wasn't best pleased with the man for callin out, and wasn't blessin him in my own mind, when I see Chops's little bell fly out of winder at a old lady, and he gets up and kicks his box over, exposin the whole secret, and he catches hold of the calves of my legs and he says to me, "Carry me into the wan, Toby, and throw a pail of water over me or I'm a dead man, for I've come into my property!"

Twelve thousand odd hundred pound, was Chops's winnins. He had bought a half-ticket for the twenty-five thousand prize, and it had come up. The first use he made of his property, was, to offer to fight the Wild Indian for five hundred pound a side, him with a poisoned darnin-needle and the Indian with a club; but the Indian being in want of backers to that amount, it went no further.

Arter he had been mad for a week—in a state of mind, in short, in which, if I had let him sit on the organ for only two minutes, I believe he would have bust—but we kep the organ from him—Mr. Chops come round, and behaved liberal and beautiful to all. He then sent for a young man he knowed, as had a wery genteel appearance and was a Bonnet at a gaming-booth (most respectable brought up, father havin been imminent in the livery stable line but unfort'nate in a commercial crisis, through paintin a old gray, ginger-bay, and sellin him with a Pedigree), and Mr. Chops said to this Bonnet, who said his name was Normandy, which it wasn't:

"Normandy, I'm a goin into Society. Will you go with me?"

Says Normandy: "Do I understand you, Mr. Chops, to hintimate that the 'ole of the expenses of that move will be borne by yourself?"

"Correct," says Mr. Chops. "And you shall have a Princely allowance too."

The Bonnet lifted Mr. Chops upon a chair, to shake hands with him, and replied in poetry, with his eyes seemingly full of tears:

"My boat is on the shore,
And my bark is on the sea,
And I do not ask for more,
But I'll Go:—along with thee."

They went into Society, in a chay and four grays with silk jackets. They took lodgings in Pall Mall, London, and they blazed away.

In consequence of a note that was brought to Bartlemy Fair in the autumn of next year by a servant, most wonderful got up in milk-white cords and tops, I cleaned myself and went to Pall Mall, one evening appinted. The gentlemen was at their wine arter dinner, and Mr. Chops's eyes was more fixed in that Ed of his than I thought good for him. There was three of 'em (in company, I mean), and I knowed the third well. When last met, he had on a white Roman shirt, and a bishop's mitre covered with leopard-skin, and played the clarionet all wrong, in a band at a Wild Beast Show.

This gent took on not to know me, and Mr. Chops said: "Gentlemen, this is a old friend of former days": and Normandy looked at me through a eye-glass, and said, "Magsman, glad to see you!"—which I'll take my oath he wasn't. Mr. Chops, to git him convenient to the table, had his chair on a throne (much of the form of George the Fourth's in the canvas), but he hardly appeared to me to be King there in any other pint of view, for his two gentlemen ordered about like Emperors. They was all dressed like May-Day—gorgeous!—And as to Wine, they swam in all sorts.

I made the round of the bottles, first separate (to say I had done it), and then mixed 'em all together (to say I had done it), and then tried two of 'em as half-and-half, and then t'other two. Altogether, I passed a pleasin evenin, but with a tendency to feel muddled, until I considered it good manners to get up and say, "Mr. Chops, the best of friends must part, I thank you for the wariety of foreign drains you have stood so 'ansome, I looks towards you in red wine, and I takes my leave." Mr. Chops replied, "If you'll just hitch me out of this over your right arm, Magsman, and carry me down-stairs, I'll see you out." I said I couldn't think of such a thing, but he would have it, so I lifted him off his throne. He smelt strong of Maideary, and I couldn't help thinking as I carried him down that it was like carrying a large bottle full of wine, with a rayther ugly stopper, a good deal out of proportion.

When I set him on the door-mat in the hall, he kep me close to him by holding on to my coat-collar, and he whispers:

"I ain't 'appy, Magsman."

"What's on your mind, Mr. Chops?"

"They don't use me well. They an't grateful to me. They puts me on the mantel-piece when I won't have in more Champagne-wine, and they locks me in the side-board when I won't give up my property."

"Get rid of 'em, Mr. Chops."

"I can't. We're in Society together, and what would Society say?"

"Come out of Society!" says I.

"I can't. You don't know what you're talking about. When you have once gone into Society, you mustn't come out of it."

"Then if you'll excuse the freedom, Mr. Chops," were my remark, shaking my head grave, "I think it's a pity you ever went in."

Mr. Chops shook that deep Ed of his, to a surprisin extent, and slapped it half a dozen times with his hand, and with more Wice than I thought were in him. Then, he says, "You're a good fellow, but you don't understand. Good night, go along. Magsman, the little man will now walk three times round the Cairawan, and retire behind the curtain." The last I see of him on that occasion was his tryin, on the extremest werge of insensibility, to climb up the stairs, one by one, with his hands and knees. They'd have been much too steep for him, if he had been sober; but he wouldn't be helped.

It warn't long after that, that I read in the newspaper of Mr. Chops's being presented at court. It was printed, "It will be recollected"—and I've noticed in my life, that it is sure to be printed that it *will* be recollected, whenever it won't—"that Mr. Chops is the individual of small stature, whose brilliant success in the last State Lottery attracted so much attention." Well, I says to myself, Such is Life! He has been and done it in earnest at last. He has astonished George the Fourth!

(On account of which, I had that canvas new-painted, him with a bag of money in his hand, a presentin it to George the Fourth, and a lady in Ostrich Feathers fallin in love with him in a bag-wig, sword, and buckles correct.)

I took the House as is the subject of present inquiries—though not the honour of bein acquainted—and I run Magsman's Amusements in it thirteen months—sometimes one thing, sometimes another, sometimes nothin particular, but always all the canvasses outside. One night, when we had played the last company out, which was a shy company, through its raining Heavens hard, I was takin a pipe in the one pair back along with the young man with the toes, which I had taken on for a month (though he never drawed—except on paper), and I heard a kickin at the street door. "Halloa!" I says to the young man, "what's up?" He rubs his eyebrows with his toes, and he says, "I can't imagine, Mr. Magsman"—which he never could imagine nothin, and was monotonous company.

The noise not leavin off, I laid down my pipe, and I took up a candle, and I went down and opened the door. I looked out into the street; but nothin could I see, and nothin was I aware of, until I turned round quick, because some creetur run between my legs into the passage. There was Mr. Chops!

"Magsman," he says, "take me, on the old terms, and you've got me; if it's done, say done!"

I was all of a maze, but I said, "Done, Sir."

"Done to your done, and double done!" says he. "Have you got a bit of supper in the house?"

Bearin in mind them sparklin warieties of foreign drains as we'd guzzled away at in Pall Mall, I was ashamed to offer him cold sassages and gin-and-water; but he took 'em both and took 'em free; havin a chair for his table, and sittin down at it on a stool, like hold times. I, all of a maze all the while.

It was arter he had made a clean sweep of the sassages (beef, and to the best of my calculations two pound and a quarter), that the wisdom as was in that little man began to come out of him like prespiration.

"Magsman," he says, "look upon me! You see afore you, One as has both gone into Society and come out."

"O! You *are* out of it, Mr. Chops? How did you get out, Sir?"

"Sold out!" says he. You never saw the like of the wisdom as his Ed expressed, when he made use of them two words.

"My friend Magsman, I'll impart to you a discovery I've made. It's wallable; it's cost twelve thousand five hundred pound; it may do you good in life—The secret of this matter is, that it ain't so much that a person goes into Society, as that Society goes into a person."

Not exactly keepin up with his meanin, I shook my head, put on a deep look, and said, "You're right there, Mr. Chops."

"Magsman," he says, twitchin me by the leg, "Society has gone into me, to the tune of every penny of my property."

I felt that I went pale, and though nat'rally a bold speaker, I couldn't hardly say, "Where's Normandy?"

"Bolted. With the plate," said Mr. Chops.

"And t'other one?" meaning him as formerly wore the bishop's mitre.

"Bolted. With the jewels," said Mr. Chops.

I sat down and looked at him, and he stood up and looked at me.

"Magsman," he says, and he seemed to myself to get wiser as he got hoarser; "Society, taken in the lump, is all dwarfs. At the court of St. James's, they was all a doing my old business—all a goin three times round the Cairawan, in the hold court-suits and properties. Elsewheres, they was most of 'em ringin their little bells out of make-believes. Everywheres, the sarser was a goin round. Magsman, the sarser is the uniwersal Institution!"

I perceived, you understand, that he was soured by his misfortunes, and I felt for Mr. Chops.

"As to Fat Ladies," he says, giving his head a tremendious one agin the wall, "there's lots of *them* in Society, and worse than the original. *Hers* was a outrage upon Taste—simply a outrage upon Taste—awakenin contempt—carryin its own punishment in the form of a Indian." Here he giv himself another tremendious one. "But *theirs*, Magsman, *theirs* is mercenary outrages. Lay in Cashmeer shawls, buy bracelets, strew 'em and a lot of 'andsome fans and things about your rooms, let it be known that you give away like water to all as come to admire, and the Fat Ladies that don't exhibit for so much down upon the drum, will come from all the pints of the compass to flock about you, whatever you are. They'll drill holes in your 'art, Magsman, like a Cullender. And when you've no more left to give, they'll laugh at you to your face, and leave you to have your bones picked dry by Wulturs, like the dead Wild Ass of the Prairies that you deserve to be!" Here he giv himself the most tremendious one of all, and dropped.

I thought he was gone. His Ed was so heavy, and he knocked it so hard, and he fell so stoney, and the sassagerial disturbance in him must have been so immense, that I thought he was gone. But, he soon come round with care, and he sat up on the floor, and he said to me, with wisdom comin out of his eyes, if ever it come:

"Magsman! The most material difference between the two states of existence through which your unhappy friend has passed"; he reached out his poor little hand, and his tears dropped down on the moustachio which it was a credit to him to have done his best to grow, but it is not in mortals to command success,—"the difference this. When I was out of Society, I was paid light for being seen. When I went into Society, I paid heavy for being seen. I prefer the former, even if I wasn't forced upon it. Give me out through the trumpet, in the hold way, to-morrow."

Arter that, he slid into the line again as easy as if he had been iled all over. But the organ was kep from him, and no allusions was ever made, when a company was in, to his property. He got wiser every day; his views of Society and the Public was luminous, bewilderin, awful; and his Ed got bigger and bigger as his Wisdom expanded it.

He took well, and pulled 'em in most excellent for nine weeks. At the expiration of that period, when his Ed was a sight, he expressed one evenin, the last Company havin been turned out, and the door shut, a wish to have a little music.

"Mr. Chops," I said (I never dropped the "Mr." with him; the world might do it, but not me); "Mr. Chops, are you sure as you are in a state of mind and body to sit upon the organ?"

His answer was this: "Toby, when next met with on the tramp, I forgive her and the Indian. And I am."

It was with fear and trembling that I began to turn the handle; but he sat like a lamb. I will be my belief to my dying day, that I see his Ed expand as he sat; you may therefore judge how great his thoughts was. He sat out all the changes, and then he come off.

"Toby," he says, with a quiet smile, "the little man will now walk three times round the Cairawan, and retire behind the curtain."

When we called him in the morning, we found him gone into a much better Society than mine or Pall Mall's. I giv Mr. Chops as comfortable a funeral as lay in my power, followed myself as Chief, and had the George the Fourth canvas carried first, in the form of a banner. But, the House was so dismal arterwards, that I giv it up, and took to the Wan again.

"I don't triumph," said Jarber, folding up the second manuscript, and looking hard at Trottle. "I don't triumph over this worthy creature. I merely ask him if he is satisfied now?"

"How can he be anything else?" I said, answering for Trottle, who sat obstinately silent. "This time, Jarber, you have not only read us a delightfully amusing story, but you have also answered the question about the House. Of course it stands empty now. Who would think of taking it after it had been turned into a caravan?" I looked at Trottle, as I said those last words, and Jarber waved his hand indulgently in the same direction.

"Let this excellent person speak," said Jarber. "You were about to say, my good man—?"

"I only wished to ask, Sir," said Trottle doggedly, "if you could kindly oblige me with a date or two in connection with that last story?"

"A date!" repeated Jarber. "What does the man want with dates!"

"I should be glad to know, with great respect," persisted Trottle, "if the person named Magsman was the last tenant who lived in the House. It's my opinion—if I may be excused for giving it—that he most decidedly was not."

With those words, Trottle made a low bow, and quietly left the room.

There is no denying that Jarber, when we were left together, looked sadly discomposed. He had evidently forgotten to inquire about dates; and, in spite of his magnificent talk about his series of discoveries, it was quite as plain that the two stories he had just read, had really and truly exhausted his present stock. I thought myself bound, in common gratitude, to help him out of his embarrassment by a timely suggestion. So I proposed that he should come to tea again, on the next Monday evening, the thirteenth, and should make such inquiries in the meantime, as might enable him to dispose triumphantly of Trottle's objection.

He gallantly kissed my hand, made a neat little speech of acknowledgment, and took his leave. For the rest of the week I would not encourage Trottle by allowing him to refer to the House at all. I suspected he was making his own inquiries about dates, but I put no questions to him.

On Monday evening, the thirteenth, that dear unfortunate Jarber came, punctual to the appointed time. He looked so terribly harassed, that he was really quite a spectacle of feebleness and fatigue. I saw, at a glance, that the question of dates had gone against him, that Mr. Magsman had not been the last tenant of the House, and that the reason of its emptiness was still to seek.

"What I have gone through," said Jarber, "words are not eloquent enough to tell. O Sophonisba, I have begun another series of discoveries! Accept the last two as stories laid on your shrine; and wait to blame me for leaving your curiosity unappeased, until you have heard Number Three."

Number Three looked like a very short manuscript, and I said as much. Jarber explained to me that we were to have some poetry this time. In the course of his investigations he had stepped into the Circulating Library, to seek for information on the one important subject. All the Library-people knew about the House was, that a female relative of the last tenant, as they believed, had, just after that tenant left, sent a little manuscript poem to them which she described as referring to events that had actually passed in the House; and which she wanted the proprietor of the Library to publish. She had written no address on her letter; and the proprietor had kept the manuscript ready to be given back to her (the publishing of poems not being in his line) when she might call for it. She had never called for it; and the poem had been lent to Jarber, at his express request, to read to me.

Before he began, I rang the bell for Trottle; being determined to have him present at the new reading, as a wholesome check on his obstinacy. To my surprise Peggy answered the bell, and told me, that Trottle had stepped out without saying where. I instantly felt the strongest possible conviction that he was at his old tricks: and that his stepping out in the evening, without leave, meant—Philandering.

Controlling myself on my visitor's account, I dismissed Peggy, stifled my indignation, and prepared, as politely as might be, to listen to Jarber.

Mrs. Lirriper's Lodgings

IN TWO CHAPTERS

Chapter I

How Mrs. Lirriper Carried On The Business

Whoever would begin to be worried with letting Lodgings that wasn't a lone woman with a living to get is a thing inconceivable to me, my dear; excuse the familiarity, but it comes natural to me in my own little room, when wishing to open my mind to those that I can trust, and I should be truly thankful if they were all mankind, but such is not so, for have but a Furnished bill in the window and your watch on the mantelpiece, and farewell to it if you turn your back for but a second, however gentlemanly the manners; nor is being of your own sex any safeguard, as I have reason, in the form of sugar-tongs to know, for that lady (and a fine woman she was) got me to run for a glass of water, on the plea of going to be confined, which certainly turned out true, but it was in the Station-house.

Number Eighty-one Norfolk Street, Strand—situated midway between the City and St. James's, and within five minutes' walk of the principal places of public amusement—is my address. I have rented this house many years, as the parish rate-books will testify; and I could wish my landlord was as alive to the fact as I am myself; but no, bless you, not a half a pound of paint to save his life, nor so much, my dear, as a tile upon the roof, though on your bended knees.

My dear, you never have found Number Eighty-one Norfolk Street Strand advertised in Bradshaw's *Railway Guide*, and with the blessing of Heaven you never will or shall so find it. Some there are who do not think it lowering themselves to make their names that cheap, and even going the lengths of a portrait of the house not like it with a blot in every window and a coach and four at the door, but what will suit Wozenham's lower down on the other side of the way will not suit me, Miss Wozenham having her opinions and me having mine, though when it comes to systematic underbidding capable of being proved on oath in a court of justice and taking the form of "If Mrs. Lirriper names eighteen shillings a week, I name fifteen and six," it then comes to a settlement between yourself and your conscience, supposing for the sake of argument your name to be Wozenham, which I am well aware it is not or my opinion of you would be greatly lowered, and as to airy bedrooms and a night-porter in constant attendance the less said the better, the bedrooms being stuffy and the porter stuff.

It is forty years ago since me and my poor Lirriper got married at St. Clement's Danes, where I now have a sitting in a very pleasant pew with genteel company and my own hassock, and being partial to evening service not too crowded. My poor Lirriper was a handsome figure of a man, with a beaming eye and a voice as mellow as a musical instrument made of honey and steel, but he had ever been a free liver being in the commercial travelling line and travelling what he called a limekiln road—"a dry road, Emma my dear," my poor Lirriper says to me, "where I have to lay the dust with one drink or another all day long and half the night, and it wears me Emma"—and this led to his running through a good deal and might have run through the turnpike too when that dreadful horse that never would stand still for a single instant set off, but for its being night and the gate shut and consequently took his wheel, my poor Lirriper and the gig smashed to atoms and never spoke afterwards. He was a handsome figure of a man, and a man with a jovial heart and a sweet temper; but if they had come up then they never could have given you the mellowness of his voice, and indeed I consider photographs wanting in mellowness as a general rule and making you look like a new-ploughed field.

My poor Lirriper being behindhand with the world and being buried at Hatfield church in Hertfordshire, not that it was his native place but that he had a liking for the Salisbury Arms where we went upon our wedding-day and passed as happy a fortnight as ever happy was, I went round to the creditors and I says "Gentlemen I am acquainted with the fact that I am not answerable for my late husband's debts but I wish to pay them for I am his lawful wife and his good name is dear to me. I am going into the Lodgings gentlemen as a business and if I prosper every farthing that my late husband owed shall be paid for the sake of the love I bore him, by this right hand." It took a long time to do but it was done, and the silver cream-jug which is between ourselves and the bed and the mattress in my room upstairs (or it would have found legs so sure as ever the Furnished bill was up) being presented by the gentlemen engraved "To Mrs. Lirriper a mark of grateful respect for her honourable conduct" gave me a turn which was too much for my feelings, till Mr. Betley which at that time had the parlours and loved his joke says "Cheer up Mrs. Lirriper, you should feel as if it was only your christening and they were your godfathers and godmothers which did promise for you." And it brought me round, and I don't mind confessing to you my dear that I then put a sandwich and a drop of sherry in a little basket and went down to Hatfield churchyard outside the coach and kissed my hand and laid it with a kind of proud and swelling love on my husband's grave, though bless you it had taken me so long to clear his name that my wedding-ring was worn quite fine and smooth when I laid it on the green waving grass.

I am an old woman now and my good looks are gone but that's me my dear over the plate-warmer and considered like in the times when you used to pay two guineas on ivory and took your chance pretty much how you came out, which made you very careful how you left it about afterwards because people were turned so red and uncomfortable by mostly guessing it was somebody else quite different, and there was once a certain person that had put his money in a hop business that came in one morning to pay his rent and his respects being the second floor that would have taken it down from its hook and put it in his breast-pocket—you understand my dear—for the L, he says of the original—only there was no mellowness in *his* voice and I wouldn't let him, but his opinion of it you may gather from his saying to it "Speak to me Emma!" which was far from a rational observation no doubt but still a tribute to its being a likeness, and I think myself it *was* like me when I was young and wore that sort of stays.

But it was about the Lodgings that I was intending to hold forth and certainly I ought to know something of the business having been in it so long, for it was early in the second year of my married life that I lost my poor Lirriper and I set up at Islington directly afterwards and afterwards came here, being two houses and eight-and-thirty years and some losses and a deal of experience.

Girls are your first trial after fixtures and they try you even worse than what I call the Wandering Christians, though why *they* should roam the earth looking for bills and then coming in and viewing the apartments and stickling about terms and never at all wanting them or dreaming of taking them being already provided, is a mystery I should be thankful to have explained if by any miracle it could be. It's wonderful they live so long and thrive so on it but I suppose the exercise makes it healthy, knocking so much and going from house to house and up and downstairs all day, and then their pretending to be so particular and punctual is a most astonishing thing, looking at their watches and saying "Could you give me the refusal of the rooms till twenty minutes past eleven the day after to-morrow in the forenoon, and supposing it to be considered essential by my friend from the country could there be a small iron bedstead put in the little room upon the stairs?" Why when I was new to it my dear I used to consider before I promised and to make my mind anxious with calculations and to get quite wearied out with disappointments, but now I says "Certainly by all means" well knowing it's a Wandering Christian and I shall hear no more about it, indeed by this time I know most of the Wandering Christians by sight as well as they know me, it being the habit of each individual revolving round London in that capacity to come back about twice a year, and it's very remarkable that it runs in families and the children grow up to it, but even were it otherwise I should no sooner hear of the friend from the country which is a certain sign than I should nod and say to myself You're a Wandering Christian, though whether they are (as I *have* heard) persons of small property with a taste for regular employment and frequent change of scene I cannot undertake to tell you.

Girls as I was beginning to remark are one of your first and your lasting troubles, being like your teeth which begin with convulsions and never cease tormenting you from the time you cut them till they cut you, and then you don't want to part with them which seems hard but we must all succumb or buy artificial, and even where you get a will nine times out of ten you'll get a dirty face with it and naturally lodgers do not like good society to be shown in with a smear of black across the nose or a smudgy eyebrow. Where they pick the black up is a mystery I cannot solve, as in the case of the willingest girl that ever came into a house half-starved poor thing, a girl so willing that I called her Willing Sophy down upon her knees scrubbing early and late and ever cheerful but always smiling with a black face. And I says to Sophy, "Now Sophy my good girl have a regular day for your stoves and keep the width of the Airy between yourself and the blacking and do not brush your hair with the bottoms of the saucepans and do not meddle with the snuffs of the candles and it stands to reason that it can no longer be" yet there it was and always on her nose, which turning up and being broad at the end seemed to boast of it and caused warning from a steady gentleman and excellent lodger with breakfast by the week but a little irritable and use of a sitting-room when required, his words being "Mrs. Lirriper I have arrived at the point of admitting that the Black is a man and a brother, but only in a natural form and when it can't be got off." Well consequently I put poor Sophy on to other work and forbid her answering the door or answering a bell on any account but she was so unfortunately willing that nothing would stop her flying up the kitchen-stairs whenever a bell was heard to tingle. I put it to her "O Sophy Sophy for goodness' goodness' sake where does it come from?" To which that poor unlucky willing mortal—bursting out crying to see me so vexed replied "I took a deal of black into me ma'am when I was a small child being much neglected and I think it must be, that it works out," so it continuing to work out of that poor thing and not having another fault to find with her I says "Sophy what do you seriously think of my helping you away to New South Wales where it might not be noticed?" Nor did I ever repent the money which was well spent, for she married the ship's cook on the voyage (himself a Mulotter) and did well and lived happy, and so far as ever I heard it was *not* noticed in a new state of society to her dying day.

In what way Miss Wozenham lower down on the other side of the way reconciled it to her feelings as a lady (which she is not) to entice Mary Anne Perkinsop from my service is best known to herself, I do not know and I do not wish to know how opinions are formed at Wozenham's on any point. But Mary Anne Perkinsop although I behaved handsomely to her and she behaved unhandsomely to me was worth her weight in gold as overawing lodgers without driving them away, for lodgers would be far more sparing of their bells with Mary Anne than I ever knew them to be with Maid or Mistress, which is a great triumph especially when accompanied with a cast in the eye and a bag of bones, but it was the steadiness of her way with them through her father's having failed in Pork. It was Mary Anne's looking so respectable in her person and being so strict in her spirits that conquered the tea-and-sugarest gentleman (for he weighed them both in a pair of scales every morning) that I have ever had to deal with and no lamb grew meeker, still it afterwards came round to me that Miss Wozenham happening to pass and seeing Mary Anne take in the milk of a milkman that made free in a rosy-faced way (I think no worse of him) with every girl in the street but was quite frozen up like the statue at Charing-cross by her, saw Mary Anne's value in the lodging business and went as high as one pound per quarter more, consequently Mary Anne with not a word betwixt us says "If you will provide yourself Mrs. Lirriper in a month from this day I have already done the same," which hurt me and I said so, and she then hurt me more by insinuating that her father having failed in Pork had laid her open to it.

My dear I do assure you it's a harassing thing to know what kind of girls to give the preference to, for if they are lively they get bell'd off their legs and if they are sluggish you suffer from it yourself in complaints and if they are sparkling-eyed they get made love to, and if they are smart in their persons they try on your Lodgers' bonnets and if they are musical I defy you to keep them away from bands and organs, and allowing for any difference you like in their heads their heads will be always out of window just the same. And then what the gentlemen like in girls the ladies don't, which is fruitful hot water for all parties, and then there's temper though such a temper as Caroline Maxey's I hope not often. A good-looking black-eyed girl was Caroline and a comely-made girl to your cost when she did break out and laid about her, as took place first and last through a new-married couple come to see London in the first floor and the lady very high and it *was* supposed not liking the good looks of Caroline having none of her own to spare, but anyhow she did try Caroline though that was no excuse. So one afternoon Caroline comes down into the kitchen flushed and flashing, and she says to me "Mrs. Lirriper that woman in the first has aggravated me past bearing," I says "Caroline keep your temper," Caroline says with a curdling laugh "Keep my temper? You're right Mrs. Lirriper, so I will. Capital D her!" bursts out Caroline (you might have struck me into the centre of the earth with a feather when she said it) "I'll give her a touch of the temper that *I* keep!" Caroline downs with her hair my dear, screeches and rushes upstairs, I following as fast as my trembling legs could bear me, but before I got into the room the dinner-cloth and pink-and-white service all dragged off upon the floor with a crash and the new-married couple on their backs in the firegrate, him with the shovel and tongs and a dish of cucumber across him and a mercy it was summer-time. "Caroline"

I says "be calm," but she catches off my cap and tears it in her teeth as she passes me, then pounces on the new-married lady makes her a bundle of ribbons takes her by the two ears and knocks the back of her head upon the carpet Murder screaming all the time Policemen running down the street and Wozenham's windows (judge of my feelings when I came to know it) thrown up and Miss Wozenham calling out from the balcony with crocodile's tears "It's Mrs. Lirriper been overcharging somebody to madness—she'll be murdered—I always thought so—Pleeseman save her!" My dear four of them and Caroline behind the chiffoniere attacking with the poker and when disarmed prize-fighting with her double fists, and down and up and up and down and dreadful! But I couldn't bear to see the poor young creature roughly handled and her hair torn when they got the better of her, and I says "Gentlemen Policemen pray remember that her sex is the sex of your mothers and sisters and your sweethearts, and God bless them and you!" And there she was sitting down on the ground handcuffed, taking breath against the skirting-board and them cool with their coats in strips, and all she says was "Mrs. Lirriper I'm sorry as ever I touched *you*, for you're a kind motherly old thing," and it made me think that I had often wished I had been a mother indeed and how would my heart have felt if I had been the mother of that girl! Well you know it turned out at the Police-office that she had done it before, and she had her clothes away and was sent to prison, and when she was to come out I trotted off to the gate in the evening with just a morsel of jelly in that little basket of mine to give her a mite of strength to face the world again, and there I met with a very decent mother waiting for her son through bad company and a stubborn one he was with his half-boots not laced. So out came Caroline and I says "Caroline come along with me and sit down under the wall where it's retired and eat a little trifle that I have brought with me to do you good," and she throws her arms round my neck and says sobbing "O why were you never a mother when there are such mothers as there are?" she says, and in half a minute more she begins to laugh and says "Did I really tear your cap to shreds?" and when I told her "You certainly did so Caroline" she laughed again and said while she patted my face "Then why do you wear such queer old caps you dear old thing? if you hadn't worn such queer old caps I don't think I should have done it even then." Fancy the girl! Nothing could get out of her what she was going to do except O she would do well enough, and we parted she being very thankful and kissing my hands, and I nevermore saw or heard of that girl, except that I shall always believe that a very genteel cap which was brought anonymous to me one Saturday night in an oilskin basket by a most impertinent young sparrow of a monkey whistling with dirty shoes on the clean steps and playing the harp on the Airy railings with a hoop-stick came from Caroline.

What you lay yourself open to my dear in the way of being the object of uncharitable suspicions when you go into the Lodging business I have not the words to tell you, but never was I so dishonourable as to have two keys nor would I willingly think it even of Miss Wozenham lower down on the other side of the way sincerely hoping that it may not be, though doubtless at the same time money cannot come from nowhere and it is not reason to suppose that Bradshaws put it in for love be it blotty as it may. It *is* a hardship hurting to the feelings that Lodgers open their minds so wide to the idea that you are trying to get the better of them and shut their minds so close to the idea that they are trying to get the better of you, but as Major Jackman says to me "I know the ways of this circular world Mrs. Lirriper, and that's one of 'em all round it" and many is the little ruffle in my mind that the Major has smoothed, for he is a clever man who has seen much. Dear dear, thirteen years have passed though it seems but yesterday since I was sitting with my glasses on at the open front parlour window one evening in August (the parlours being then vacant) reading yesterday's paper my eyes for print being poor though still I am thankful to say a long sight at a distance, when I hear a gentleman come posting across the road and up the street in a dreadful rage talking to himself in a fury and d'ing and c'ing somebody. "By George!" says he out loud and clutching his walking-stick, "I'll go to Mrs. Lirriper's. Which is Mrs. Lirriper's?" Then looking round and seeing me he flourishes his hat right off his head as if I had been the queen and he says, "Excuse the intrusion madam, but pray madam can you tell me at what number in this street there resides a well-known and much-respected lady by the name of Lirriper?" A little flustered though I must say gratified I took off my glasses and courtesied and said "Sir, Mrs. Lirriper is your humble servant." "Astonishing!" says he. "A million pardons! Madam, may I ask you to have the kindness to direct one of your domestics to open the door to a gentleman in search of apartments, by the name of Jackman?" I had never heard the name but a politer gentleman I never hope to see, for says he, "Madam I am shocked at your opening the door yourself to no worthier a fellow than Jemmy Jackman. After you madam. I never precede a lady." Then he comes into the parlours and he sniffs, and he says "Hah! These are parlours! Not musty cupboards" he says "but parlours, and no smell of coal-sacks." Now my dear it having been remarked by some inimical to the whole neighbourhood that it always smells of coal-sacks which might prove a drawback to Lodgers if encouraged, I says to the Major gently though firmly that I think he is referring to Arundel or Surrey or Howard but not Norfolk. "Madam" says he "I refer to Wozenham's lower down over the way—Madam you can form no notion what Wozenham's is—Madam it is a vast coal-sack, and Miss Wozenham has the principles and manners of a female heaver—Madam from the manner in which I have heard her mention you I know she has no appreciation of a lady, and from the manner in which she has conducted herself towards me I know she has no appreciation of a gentleman—madam my name is Jackman—should you require any other reference than what I have already said, I name the Bank of England—perhaps you know it!" Such was the beginning of the Major's occupying the parlours and from that hour to this the same and a most obliging Lodger and punctual in all respects except one irregular which I need not particularly specify, but made up for by his being a protection and at all times ready to fill in the papers of the Assessed Taxes and Juries and that, and once collared a young man with the drawing-room clock under his coat, and once on the parapets with his own hands and blankets put out the kitchen chimney and afterwards attending the summons made a most eloquent speech against the Parish before the magistrates and saved the engine, and ever quite the gentleman though passionate. And certainly Miss Wozenham's detaining the trunks and umbrella was not in a liberal spirit though it may have been according to her rights in law or an act *I* would myself have stooped to, the Major being so much the gentleman that though he is far from tall he seems almost so when he has his shirt-frill out and his frock-coat on and his hat with the curly brims, and in what service he was I cannot truly tell you my dear whether Militia or Foreign, for I never heard him even name himself as Major but always simple "Jemmy Jackman" and once soon after he came when I felt it my duty to let him know that Miss Wozenham had put it about that he was no Major and I took the liberty of adding "which you are Sir" his words were "Madam at any rate I am not a Minor, and sufficient for the day is the evil thereof" which cannot be denied to be the sacred truth, nor yet his military ways of having his boots with only the dirt brushed off taken to him in the front parlour every morning on a clean plate and varnishing them himself with a little sponge and a saucer and a whistle in a whisper so sure as ever his breakfast is ended, and so neat his ways that it never soils his linen which is scrupulous though more in quality than quantity, neither that nor his mustachios which to the best of my belief are done at the same time and which are as black and shining as his boots, his head of hair being a lovely white.

It was the third year nearly up of the Major's being in the parlours that early one morning in the month of February when Parliament was coming on and you may therefore suppose a number of impostors were about ready to take hold of anything they could get, a gentleman and a lady from the country came in to view the Second, and I well remember that I had been looking out of window and had watched them and the heavy sleet driving down the street together looking for bills. I did not quite take to the face of the gentleman though he was good-looking too but the lady was a very pretty young thing and delicate, and it seemed too rough for her to be out at all though she had only come from the Adelphi Hotel which would not have been much above a quarter of a mile if the weather had been less severe. Now it did so happen my dear that I had been forced to put five shillings weekly additional on the second in consequence of a loss from running away full dressed as if going out to a dinner-party, which was very artful and had made me rather suspicious taking it along with Parliament, so when the gentleman proposed three months certain and the money in advance and leave then reserved to renew on the same terms for six months more, I says I was not quite certain but that I might have engaged myself to another party but would step down-stairs and look into it if they would take a seat. They took a seat and I went down to the handle of the Major's door that I had already began to consult finding it a great blessing, and I knew by his whistling in a whisper that he was varnishing his boots which was generally considered private, however he kindly calls out "If it's you, madam, come in," and I went in and told him.

"Well, madam," says the Major rubbing his nose—as I did fear at the moment with the black sponge but it was only his knuckle, he being always neat and dexterous with his fingers—"well, madam, I suppose you would be glad of the money?"

I was delicate of saying "Yes" too out, for a little extra colour rose into the Major's cheeks and there was irregularity which I will not particularly specify in a quarter which I will not name.

"I am of opinion, madam," says the Major, "that when money is ready for you—when it is ready for you, Mrs. Lirriper—you ought to take it. What is there against it, madam, in this case upstairs?"

"I really cannot say there is anything against it, sir, still I thought I would consult you."

"You said a newly-married couple, I think, madam?" says the Major.

I says "Ye-es. Evidently. And indeed the young lady mentioned to me in a casual way that she had not been married many months."

The Major rubbed his nose again and stirred the varnish round and round in its little saucer with his piece of sponge and took to his whistling in a whisper for a few moments. Then he says "You would call it a Good Let, madam?"

"O certainly a Good Let Sir."

"Say they renew for the additional six months. Would it put you about very much madam if—if the worst was to come to the worst?" said the Major.

"Well I hardly know," I says to the Major. "It depends upon circumstances. Would *you* object Sir for instance?"

"I?" says the Major. "Object? Jemmy Jackman? Mrs. Lirriper close with the proposal."

So I went upstairs and accepted, and they came in next day which was Saturday and the Major was so good as to draw up a Memorandum of an agreement in a beautiful round hand and expressions that sounded to me equally legal and military, and Mr. Edson signed it on the Monday morning and the Major called upon Mr. Edson on the Tuesday and Mr. Edson called upon the Major on the Wednesday and the Second and the parlours were as friendly as could be wished.

The three months paid for had run out and we had got without any fresh overtures as to payment into May my dear, when there came an obligation upon Mr. Edson to go a business expedition right across the Isle of Man, which fell quite unexpected upon that pretty little thing and is not a place that according to my views is particularly in the way to anywhere at any time but that may be a matter of opinion. So short a notice was it that he was to go next day, and dreadfully she cried poor pretty, and I am sure I cried too when I saw her on the cold pavement in the sharp east wind—it being a very backward spring that year—taking a last leave of him with her pretty bright hair blowing this way and that and her arms clinging round his neck and him saying "There there there. Now let me go Peggy." And by that time it was plain that what the Major had been so accommodating as to say he would not object to happening in the house, would happen in it, and I told her as much when he was gone while I comforted her with my arm up the staircase, for I says "You will soon have others to keep up for my pretty and you must think of that."

His letter never came when it ought to have come and what she went through morning after morning when the postman brought none for her the very postman himself compassionated when she ran down to the door, and yet we cannot wonder at its being calculated to blunt the feelings to have all the trouble of other people's letters and none of the pleasure and doing it oftener in the mud and mizzle than not and at a rate of wages more resembling Little Britain than Great. But at last one morning when she was too poorly to come running downstairs he says to me with a pleased look in his face that made me next to love the man in his uniform coat though he was dripping wet "I have taken you first in the street this morning Mrs. Lirriper, for here's the one for Mrs. Edson." I went up to her bedroom with it as fast as ever I could go, and she sat up in bed when she saw it and kissed it and tore it open and then a blank stare came upon her. "It's very short!" she says lifting her large eyes to my face. "O Mrs. Lirriper it's very short!" I says "My dear Mrs. Edson no doubt that's because your husband hadn't time to write more just at that time." "No doubt, no doubt," says she, and puts her two hands on her face and turns round in her bed.

I shut her softly in and I crept downstairs and I tapped at the Major's door, and when the Major having his thin slices of bacon in his own Dutch oven saw me he came out of his chair and put me down on the sofa. "Hush!" says he, "I see something's the matter. Don't speak—take time." I says "O Major I'm afraid there's cruel work upstairs." "Yes yes," says he "I had begun to be afraid of it—take time." And then in opposition to his own words he rages out frightfully, and says "I shall never forgive myself Madam, that I, Jemmy Jackman, didn't see it all that morning—didn't go straight upstairs when my boot-sponge was in my hand—didn't force it down his throat—and choke him dead with it on the spot!"

The Major and me agreed when we came to ourselves that just at present we could do no more than take on to suspect nothing and use our best endeavours to keep that poor young creature quiet, and what I ever should have done without the Major when it got about among the organ-men that quiet was our object is unknown, for he made lion and tiger war upon them to that degree that without seeing it I could not have believed it was in any gentleman to have such a power of bursting out with fire-irons walking-sticks water-jugs coals potatoes off his table the very hat off his head, and at the same time so furious in foreign languages that they would stand with their handles half-turned fixed like the Sleeping Ugly—for I cannot say Beauty.

Ever to see the postman come near the house now gave me such I fear that it was a reprieve when he went by, but in about another ten days or a fortnight he says again, "Here's one for Mrs. Edson.—Is she pretty well?" "She is pretty well postman, but not well enough to rise so early as she used" which was so far gospel-truth.

I carried the letter in to the Major at his breakfast and I says tottering "Major I have not the courage to take it up to her."

"It's an ill-looking villain of a letter," says the Major.

"I have not the courage Major" I says again in a tremble "to take it up to her."

After seeming lost in consideration for some moments the Major says, raising his head as if something new and useful had occurred to his mind "Mrs. Lirriper, I shall never forgive myself that I, Jemmy Jackman, didn't go straight up-stairs that morning when my boot-sponge was in my hand—and force it down his throat—and choke him dead with it."

"Major" I says a little hasty "you didn't do it which is a blessing, for it would have done no good and I think your sponge was better employed on your own honourable boots."

So we got to be rational, and planned that I should tap at her bedroom door and lay the letter on the mat outside and wait on the upper landing for what might happen, and never was gunpowder cannon-balls or shells or rockets more dreaded than that dreadful letter was by me as I took it to the second floor.

A terrible loud scream sounded through the house the minute after she had opened it, and I found her on the floor lying as if her life was gone. My dear I never looked at the face of the letter which was lying open by her, for there was no occasion.

Everything I needed to bring her round the Major brought up with his own hands, besides running out to the chemist's for what was not in the house and likewise having the fiercest of all his many skirmishes with a musical instrument representing a ball-room I do not know in what particular country and company waltzing in and out at folding-doors with rolling eyes. When after a long time I saw her coming to, I slipped on the landing till I heard her cry, and then I went in and says cheerily "Mrs. Edson you're not well my dear and it's not to be wondered at," as if I had not been in before. Whether she believed or disbelieved I cannot say and it would signify nothing if I could, but I stayed by her for hours and then she God ever blesses me! and says she will try to rest for her head is bad.

"Major," I whispers, looking in at the parlours, "I beg and pray of you don't go out."

The Major whispers, "Madam, trust me I will do no such a thing. How is she?"

I says "Major the good Lord above us only knows what burns and rages in her poor mind. I left her sitting at her window. I am going to sit at mine."

It came on afternoon and it came on evening. Norfolk is a delightful street to lodge in—provided you don't go lower down—but of a summer evening when the dust and waste paper lie in it and stray children play in it and a kind of a gritty calm and bake settles on it and a peal of church-bells is practising in the neighbourhood it is a trifle dull, and never have I seen it since at such a time and never shall I see it evermore at such a time without seeing the dull June evening when that forlorn young creature sat at her open corner window on the Second and me at my open corner window (the other corner) on the Third. Something merciful, something wiser and better far than my own self, had moved me while it was yet light to sit in my bonnet and shawl, and as the shadows fell and the tide rose I could sometimes—when I put out my head and looked at her window below—see that she leaned out a little looking down the street. It was just settling dark when I saw *her* in the street.

So fearful of losing sight of her that it almost stops my breath while I tell it, I went downstairs faster than I ever moved in all my life and only tapped with my hand at the Major's door in passing it and slipping out. She was gone already. I made the same speed down the street and when I came to the corner of Howard-street I saw that she had turned it and was there plain before me going towards the west. O with what a thankful heart I saw her going along!

She was quite unacquainted with London and had very seldom been out for more than an airing in our own street where she knew two or three little children belonging to neighbours and had sometimes stood among them at the street looking at the water. She must be going at hazard I knew, still she kept the bye-streets quite correctly as long as they would serve her, and then turned up into the Strand. But at every corner I could see her head turned one way, and that way was always the river way.

It may have been only the darkness and quiet of the Adelphi that caused her to strike into it but she struck into it much as readily as if she had set out to go there, which perhaps was the case. She went straight down to the Terrace and along it and looked over the iron rail, and I often woke afterwards in my own bed with the horror of seeing her do it. The desertion of the wharf below and the flowing of the high water there seemed to settle her purpose. She looked about as if to make out the way down, and she struck out the right way or the wrong way—I don't know which, for I don't know the place before or since—and I followed her the way she went.

It was noticeable that all this time she never once looked back. But there was now a great change in the manner of her going, and instead of going at a steady quick walk with her arms folded before her,—among the dark dismal arches she went in a wild way with her arms opened wide, as if they were wings and she was flying to her death.

We were on the wharf and she stopped. I stopped. I saw her hands at her bonnet-strings, and I rushed between her and the brink and took her round the waist with both my arms. She might have drowned me, I felt then, but she could never have got quit of me.

Down to that moment my mind had been all in a maze and not half an idea had I had in it what I should say to her, but the instant I touched her it came to me like magic and I had my natural voice and my senses and even almost my breath.

"Mrs. Edson!" I says "My dear! Take care. How ever did you lose your way and stumble on a dangerous place like this? Why you must have come here by the most perplexing streets in all London. No wonder you are lost, I'm sure. And this place too! Why I thought nobody ever got here, except me to order my coals and the Major in the parlours to smoke his cigar!"—for I saw that blessed man close by, pretending to it.

"Hah—Hah—Hum!" coughs the Major.

"And good gracious me" I says, "why here he is!"

"Halloa! who goes there?" says the Major in a military manner.

"Well!" I says, "if this don't beat everything! Don't you know us Major Jackman?"

"Halloa!" says the Major. "Who calls on Jemmy Jackman?" (and more out of breath he was, and did it less like life than I should have expected.)

"Why here's Mrs. Edson Major" I says, "strolling out to cool her poor head which has been very bad, has missed her way and got lost, and Goodness knows where she might have got to but for me coming here to drop an order into my coal merchant's letter-box and you coming here to smoke your cigar!—And you really are not well enough my dear" I says to her "to be half so far from home without me. And your arm will be very acceptable I am sure Major" I says to him "and I know she may lean upon it as heavy as she likes." And now we had both got her—thanks be Above!—one on each side.

She was all in a cold shiver and she so continued till I laid her on her own bed, and up to the early morning she held me by the hand and moaned and moaned "O wicked, wicked, wicked!" But when at last I made believe to droop my head and be overpowered with a dead sleep, I heard that poor young creature give such touching and such humble thanks for being preserved from taking her own life in her madness that I thought I should have cried my eyes out on the counterpane and I knew she was safe.

Being well enough to do and able to afford it, me and the Major laid our little plans next day while she was asleep worn out, and so I says to her as soon as I could do it nicely: "Mrs. Edson my dear, when Mr. Edson paid me the rent for these farther six months—"

She gave a start and I felt her large eyes look at me, but I went on with it and with my needlework.

"—I can't say that I am quite sure I dated the receipt right. Could you let me look at it?"

She laid her frozen cold hand upon mine and she looked through me when I was forced to look up from my needlework, but I had taken the precaution of having on my spectacles.

"I have no receipt" says she.

"Ah! Then he has got it" I says in a careless way. "It's of no great consequence. A receipt's a receipt."

From that time she always had hold of my hand when I could spare it which was generally only when I read to her, for of course she and me had our bits of needlework to plod at and neither of us was very handy at those little things, though I am still rather proud of my share in them too considering. And though she took to all I read to her, I used to fancy that next to what was taught upon the Mount she took most of all to His gentle compassion for us poor women and to His young life and to how His mother was proud of Him and treasured His sayings in her heart. She had a grateful look in her eyes that never never never will be out of mine until they are closed in my last sleep, and when I chanced to look at her without thinking of it I would always meet that look, and she would often offer me her trembling lip to kiss, much more like a little affectionate half broken-hearted child than ever I can imagine any grown person.

One time the trembling of this poor lip was so strong and her tears ran down so fast that I thought she was going to tell me all her woe, so I takes her two hands in mine and I says:

"No my dear not now, you had best not try to do it now. Wait for better times when you have got over this and are strong, and then you shall tell me whatever you will. Shall it be agreed?"

With our hands still joined she nodded her head many times, and she lifted my hands and put them to her lips and to her bosom.

"Only one word now my dear" I says. "Is there any one?"

She looked inquiringly "Any one?"

"That I can go to?"

She shook her head.

"No one that I can bring?"

She shook her head.

"No one is wanted by *me* my dear. Now that may be considered past and gone."

Not much more than a week afterwards—for this was far on in the time of our being so together—I was bending over at her bedside with my ear down to her lips, by turns listening for her breath and looking for a sign of life in her face. At last it came in a solemn way—not in a flash but like a kind of pale faint light brought very slow to the face.

She said something to me that had no sound in it, but I saw she asked me:

"Is this death?"

And I says:

"Poor dear poor dear, I think it is."

Knowing somehow that she wanted me to move her weak right hand, I took it and laid it on her breast and then folded her other hand upon it, and she prayed a good good prayer and I joined in it poor me though there were no words spoke. Then I brought the baby in its wrappers from where it lay, and I says:

"My dear this is sent to a childless old woman. This is for me to take care of."

The trembling lip was put up towards my face for the last time, and I dearly kissed it.

"Yes my dear," I says. "Please God! Me and the Major."

I don't know how to tell it right, but I saw her soul brighten and leap up, and get free and fly away in the grateful look.

So this is the why and wherefore of its coming to pass my dear that we called him Jemmy, being after the Major his own godfather with Lirriper for a surname being after myself, and never was a dear child such a brightening thing in a Lodgings or such a playmate to his grandmother as Jemmy to this house and me, and always good and minding what he was told (upon the whole) and soothing for the temper and making everything pleasanter except when he grew old enough to drop his cap down Wozenham's Airy and they wouldn't hand it up to him, and being worked into a state I put on my best bonnet and gloves and parasol with the child in my hand and I says "Miss Wozenham I little thought ever to have entered *your* house but unless my grandson's cap is instantly restored, the laws of this country regulating the property of the Subject shall at length decide betwixt yourself and me, cost what it may." With a sneer upon her face which did strike me I must say as being expressive of two keys but it may have been a mistake and if there is any doubt let Miss Wozenham have the full benefit of it as is but right, she rang the bell and she says "Jane, is there a street-child's old cap down our Airy?" I says "Miss Wozenham before your house-maid answers that question you must allow me to inform you to your face that my grandson is *not* a street-child and is *not* in the habit of wearing old caps. In fact" I says "Miss Wozenham I am far from sure that my grandson's cap may not be newer than your own" which was perfectly savage in me, her lace being the commonest machine-make washed and torn besides, but I had been put into a state to begin with fomented by impertinence. Miss Wozenham says red in the face "Jane you heard my question, is there any child's cap down our Airy?" "Yes ma'am" says Jane, "I think I did see some such rubbish a-lying there." "Then" says Miss Wozenham "let these visitors out, and then throw up that worthless article out of my premises." But here the child who had been staring at Miss Wozenham with all his eyes and more, frowns down his little eyebrows purses up his little mouth puts his chubby legs far apart turns his little dimpled fists round and round slowly over one another like a little coffee-mill, and says to her "Oo impdent to mi Gran, me tut oor hi!" "O!" says Miss Wozenham looking down scornfully at the Mite "this is not a street-child is it not! Really!" I bursts out laughing and I says "Miss Wozenham if this ain't a pretty sight to you I don't envy your feelings and I wish you good-day. Jemmy come along with Gran." And I was still in the best of humours though his cap came flying up into the street as if it had been just turned on out of the water-plug, and I went home laughing all the way, all owing to that dear boy.

The miles and miles that me and the Major have travelled with Jemmy in the dusk between the lights are not to be calculated, Jemmy driving on the coach-box which is the Major's brass-bound writing desk on the table, me inside in the easy-chair and the Major Guard up behind with a brown-paper horn doing it really wonderful. I do assure you my dear that sometimes when I have taken a few winks in my place inside the coach and have come half awake by the flashing light of the fire and have heard that precious pet driving and the Major blowing up behind to have the change of horses ready when we got to the Inn, I have half believed we were on the old North Road that my poor Lirriper knew so well. Then to see that child and the Major both wrapped up getting down to warm their feet and going stamping about and having glasses of ale out of the paper match-boxes on the chimney-piece is to see the Major enjoying it fully as much as the child I am very sure, and it's equal to any play when Coachee opens the coach-door to look in at me inside and say "Wery 'past that 'tage.—'Prightened old lady?"

But what my inexpressible feelings were when we lost that child can only be compared to the Major's which were not a shade better, through his straying out at five years old and eleven o'clock in the forenoon and never heard of by word or sign or deed till half-past nine at night, when the Major had gone to the Editor of the *Times* newspaper to put in an advertisement, which came out next day four-and-twenty hours after he was found, and which I mean always carefully to keep in my lavender drawer as the first printed account of him. The more the day got on, the more I got distracted and the Major too and both of us made worse by the composed ways of the police though very civil and obliging and what I must call their obstinacy in not entertaining the idea that he was stolen. "We mostly find mum" says the sergeant who came round to comfort me, which he didn't at all and he had been one of the private constables in Caroline's time to which he referred in his opening words when he said "Don't give way to uneasiness in your mind mum, it'll all come as right as my nose did when I got the same barked by that young woman in your second floor"—says this sergeant "we mostly find mum as people ain't over-anxious to have what I may call second-hand children. *You'll* get him back mum." "O but my dear good Sir" I says clasping my hands and wringing them and clasping them again "he is such an uncommon child!" "Yes mum" says the sergeant, "we mostly find that too mum. The question is what his clothes were worth." "His clothes" I says "were not worth much Sir for he had only got his playing-dress on, but the dear child!—" "All right mum" says the sergeant. "*You'll* get him back mum. And even if he'd had his best clothes on, it wouldn't come to worse than his being found wrapped up in a cabbage-leaf, a shivering in a lane." His words pierced my heart like daggers and daggers, and me and the Major ran in and out like wild things all day long till the Major returning from his interview with the Editor of the *Times* at night rushes into my little room hysterical and squeezes my hand and wipes his eyes and says "Joy joy—officer in plain clothes came up on the steps as I was letting myself in—compose your feelings—Jemmy's found." Consequently I fainted away and when I came to, embraced the legs of the officer in plain clothes who seemed to be taking a kind of a quiet inventory in his mind of the property in my little room with brown whiskers, and I says "Blessings on you Sir where is the Darling!" and he says "In Kennington Station House." I was dropping at his feet Stone at the image of that Innocence in cells with murderers when he adds "He followed the Monkey." I says deeming it slang language "O Sir explain for a loving grandmother what Monkey!" He says "Him in the spangled cap with the strap under the chin, as won't keep on—him as sweeps the crossings on a round table and don't want to draw his sabre more than he can help." Then I understood it all and most thankfully thanked him, and me and the Major and him drove over to Kennington and there we found our boy lying quite comfortable before a blazing fire having sweetly played himself to sleep upon a small accordion nothing like so big as a flat-iron which they had been so kind as to lend him for the purpose and which it appeared had been stopped upon a very young person.

My dear the system upon which the Major commenced and as I may say perfected Jemmy's learning when he was so small that if the dear was on the other side of the table you had to look under it instead of over it to see him with his mother's own bright hair in beautiful curls, is a thing that ought to be known to the Throne and Lords and Commons and then might obtain some promotion for the Major which he well deserves and would be none the worse for (speaking between friends) L. S. D.-ically. When the Major first undertook his learning he says to me:

"I'm going madam," he says "to make our child a Calculating Boy.

"Major," I says, "you terrify me and may do the pet a permanent injury you would never forgive yourself."

"Madam," says the Major, "next to my regret that when I had my boot-sponge in my hand, I didn't choke that scoundrel with it—on the spot—"

"There! For Gracious' sake," I interrupts, "let his conscience find him without sponges."

"—I say next to that regret, madam," says the Major "would be the regret with which my breast," which he tapped, "would be surcharged if this fine mind was not early cultivated. But mark me madam," says the Major holding up his forefinger "cultivated on a principle that will make it a delight."

"Major" I says "I will be candid with you and tell you openly that if ever I find the dear child fall off in his appetite I shall know it is his calculations and shall put a stop to them at two minutes' notice. Or if I find them mounting to his head" I says, "or striking anyways cold to his stomach or leading to anything approaching flabbiness in his legs, the result will be the same, but Major you are a clever man and have seen much and you love the child and are his own godfather, and if you feel a confidence in trying try."

"Spoken madam" says the Major "like Emma Lirriper. All I have to ask, madam, is that you will leave my godson and myself to make a week or two's preparations for surprising you, and that you will give me leave to have up and down any small articles not actually in use that I may require from the kitchen."

"From the kitchen Major?" I says half feeling as if he had a mind to cook the child.

"From the kitchen" says the Major, and smiles and swells, and at the same time looks taller.

So I passed my word and the Major and the dear boy were shut up together for half an hour at a time through a certain while, and never could I hear anything going on betwixt them but talking and laughing and Jemmy clapping his hands and screaming out numbers, so I says to myself "it has not harmed him yet" nor could I on examining the dear find any signs of it anywhere about him which was likewise a great relief. At last one day Jemmy brings me a card in joke in the Major's neat writing "The Messrs. Jemmy Jackman" for we had given him the Major's other name too "request the honour of Mrs. Lirriper's company at the Jackman Institution in the front parlour this evening at five, military time, to witness a few slight feats of elementary arithmetic." And if you'll believe me there in the front parlour at five punctual to the moment was the Major behind the Pembroke table with both leaves up and a lot of things from the kitchen tidily set out on old newspapers spread atop of it, and there was the Mite stood upon a chair with his rosy cheeks flushing and his eyes sparkling clusters of diamonds.

"Now Gran" says he, "oo tit down and don't oo touch ler people"—for he saw with every one of those diamonds of his that I was going to give him a squeeze.

"Very well Sir" I says "I am obedient in this good company I am sure." And I sits down in the easy-chair that was put for me, shaking my sides.

But picture my admiration when the Major going on almost as quick as if he was conjuring sets out all the articles he names, and says "Three saucepans, an Italian iron, a hand-bell, a toasting-fork, a nutmeg-grater, four potlids, a spice-box, two egg-cups, and a chopping-board—how many?" and when that Mite instantly cries "Tifteen, tut down tive and carry ler 'toppin-board" and then claps his hands draws up his legs and dances on his chair.

My dear with the same astonishing ease and correctness him and the Major added up the tables chairs and sofy, the picters fenders and fire-irons their own selves me and the cat and the eyes in Miss Wozenham's head, and whenever the sum was done Young Roses and Diamonds claps his hands and draws up his legs and dances on his chair.

The pride of the Major! ("*Here's* a mind ma'am!" he says to me behind his hand.)

Then he says aloud, "We now come to the next elementary rule,—which is called—"

"Umtraction!" cries Jemmy.

"Right," says the Major. "We have here a toasting-fork, a potato in its natural state, two potlids, one egg-cup, a wooden spoon, and two skewers, from which it is necessary for commercial purposes to subtract a sprat-gridiron, a small pickle-jar, two lemons, one pepper-castor, a blackbeetle-trap, and a knob of the dresser-drawer—what remains?"

"Toatin-fork!" cries Jemmy.

"In numbers how many?" says the Major.

"One!" cries Jemmy.

("*Here's* a boy, ma'am!" says the Major to me behind his hand.) Then the Major goes on:

"We now approach the next elementary rule,—which is entitled—"

"Tickleication" cries Jemmy.

"Correct" says the Major.

But my dear to relate to you in detail the way in which they multiplied fourteen sticks of firewood by two bits of ginger and a larding-needle, or divided pretty well everything else there was on the table by the heater of the Italian iron and a chamber candlestick, and got a lemon over, would make my head spin round and round and round as it did at the time. So I says "if you'll excuse my addressing the chair Professor Jackman I think the period of the lecture has now arrived when it becomes necessary that I should take a good hug of this young scholar." Upon which Jemmy calls out from his station on the chair, "Gran oo open oor arms and me'll make a 'pring into 'em." So I opened my arms to him as I had opened my sorrowful heart when his poor young mother lay a dying, and he had his jump and we had a good long hug together and the Major prouder than any peacock says to me behind his hand, "You need not let him know it madam" (which I certainly need not for the Major was quite audible) "but he *is* a boy!"

In this way Jemmy grew and grew and went to day-school and continued under the Major too, and in summer we were as happy as the days were long, and in winter we were as happy as the days were short and there seemed to rest a Blessing on the Lodgings for they as good as Let themselves and would have done it if there had been twice the accommodation, when sore and hard against my will I one day says to the Major:

"Major you know what I am going to break to you. Our boy must go to boarding-school."

It was a sad sight to see the Major's countenance drop, and I pitied the good soul with all my heart.

"Yes Major" I says, "though he is as popular with the Lodgers as you are yourself and though he is to you and me what only you and me know, still it is in the course of things and Life is made of partings and we must part with our Pet."

Bold as I spoke, I saw two Majors and half-a-dozen fireplaces, and when the poor Major put one of his neat bright-varnished boots upon the fender and his elbow on his knee and his head upon his hand and rocked himself a little to and fro, I was dreadfully cut up.

"But" says I clearing my throat "you have so well prepared him Major—he has had such a Tutor in you—that he will have none of the first drudgery to go through. And he is so clever besides that he'll soon make his way to the front rank."

"He is a boy" says the Major—having sniffed—"that has not his like on the face of the earth."

"True as you say Major, and it is not for us merely for our own sakes to do anything to keep him back from being a credit and an ornament wherever he goes and perhaps even rising to be a great man, is it Major? He will have all my little savings when my work is done (being all the world to me) and we must try to make him a wise man and a good man, mustn't we Major?"

"Madam" says the Major rising "Jemmy Jackman is becoming an older file than I was aware of, and you put him to shame. You are thoroughly right madam. You are simply and undeniably right.—And if you'll excuse me, I'll take a walk."

So the Major being gone out and Jemmy being at home, I got the child into my little room here and I stood him by my chair and I took his mother's own curls in my hand and I spoke to him loving and serious. And when I had reminded the darling how that he was now in his tenth year and when I had said to him about his getting on in life pretty much what I had said to the Major I broke to him how that we must have this same parting, and there I was forced to stop for there I saw of a sudden the well-remembered lip with its tremble, and it so brought back that time! But with the spirit that was in him he controlled it soon and he says gravely nodding through his tears, "I understand Gran—I know it *must* be, Gran—go on Gran, don't be afraid of *me*." And when I had said all that ever I could think of, he turned his bright steady face to mine and he says just a little broken here and there "You shall see Gran that I can be a man and that I can do anything that is grateful and loving to you—and if I don't grow up to be what you would like to have me—I hope it will be—because I shall die." And with that he sat down by me and I went on to tell him of the school of which I had excellent recommendations and where it was and how many scholars and what games they played as I had heard and what length of holidays, to all of which he listened bright and clear. And so it came that at last he says "And now dear Gran let me kneel down here where I have been used to say my prayers and let me fold my face for just a minute in your gown and let me cry, for you have been more than father—more than mother—more than brothers sisters friends—to me!" And so he did cry and I too and we were both much the better for it.

From that time forth he was true to his word and ever blithe and ready, and even when me and the Major took him down into Lincolnshire he was far the gayest of the party though for sure and certain he might easily have been that, but he really was and put life into us only when it came to the last Good-bye, he says with a wistful look, "You wouldn't have me not really sorry would you Gran?" and when I says "No dear, Lord forbid!" he says "I am glad of that!" and ran in out of sight.

But now that the child was gone out of the Lodgings the Major fell into a regularly moping state. It was taken notice of by all the Lodgers that the Major moped. He hadn't even the same air of being rather tall than he used to have, and if he varnished his boots with a single gleam of interest it was as much as he did.

One evening the Major came into my little room to take a cup of tea and a morsel of buttered toast and to read Jemmy's newest letter which had arrived that afternoon (by the very same postman more than middle-aged upon the Beat now), and the letter raising him up a little I says to the Major:

"Major you mustn't get into a moping way."

The Major shook his head. "Jemmy Jackman madam," he says with a deep sigh, "is an older file than I thought him."

"Moping is not the way to grow younger Major."

"My dear madam," says the Major, "is there *any* way of growing younger?"

Feeling that the Major was getting rather the best of that point I made a diversion to another.

"Thirteen years! Thir-teen years! Many Lodgers have come and gone, in the thirteen years that you have lived in the parlours Major."

"Hah!" says the Major warming. "Many madam, many."

"And I should say you have been familiar with them all?"

"As a rule (with its exceptions like all rules) my dear madam" says the Major, "they have honoured me with their acquaintance, and not unfrequently with their confidence."

Watching the Major as he drooped his white head and stroked his black mustachios and moped again, a thought which I think must have been going about looking for an owner somewhere dropped into my old noddle if you will excuse the expression.

"The walls of my Lodgings" I says in a casual way—for my dear it is of no use going straight at a man who mopes—"might have something to tell if they could tell it."

The Major neither moved nor said anything but I saw he was attending with his shoulders my dear—attending with his shoulders to what I said. In fact I saw that his shoulders were struck by it.

"The dear boy was always fond of story-books" I went on, like as if I was talking to myself. "I am sure this house—his own home—might write a story or two for his reading one day or another."

The Major's shoulders gave a dip and a curve and his head came up in his shirt-collar. The Major's head came up in his shirt-collar as I hadn't seen it come up since Jemmy went to school.

"It is unquestionable that in intervals of cribbage and a friendly rubber, my dear madam," says the Major, "and also over what used to be called in my young times—in the salad days of Jemmy Jackman—the social glass, I have exchanged many a reminiscence with your Lodgers."

My remark was—I confess I made it with the deepest and artfullest of intentions—"I wish our dear boy had heard them!"

"Are you serious madam?" asked the Major starting and turning full round.

"Why not Major?"

"Madam" says the Major, turning up one of his cuffs, "they shall be written for him."

"Ah! Now you speak" I says giving my hands a pleased clap. "Now you are in a way out of moping Major!"

"Between this and my holidays—I mean the dear boy's" says the Major turning up his other cuff, "a good deal may be done towards it."

"Major you are a clever man and you have seen much and not a doubt of it."

"I'll begin," says the Major looking as tall as ever he did, "to-morrow."

My dear the Major was another man in three days and he was himself again in a week and he wrote and wrote and wrote with his pen scratching like rats behind the wainscot, and whether he had many grounds to go upon or whether he did at all romance I cannot tell you, but what he has written is in the left-hand glass closet of the little bookcase close behind you.

Chapter II

How the Parlours Added a Few Words

I have the honour of presenting myself by the name of Jackman. I esteem it a proud privilege to go down to posterity through the instrumentality of the most remarkable boy that ever lived,—by the name of Jemmy Jackman Lirriper,—and of my most worthy and most highly respected friend, Mrs. Emma Lirriper, of Eighty-one, Norfolk Street, Strand, in the County of Middlesex, in the United Kingdom of Great Britain and Ireland.

It is not for me to express the rapture with which we received that dear and eminently remarkable boy, on the occurrence of his first Christmas holidays. Suffice it to observe that when he came flying into the house with two splendid prizes (Arithmetic, and Exemplary Conduct), Mrs. Lirriper and myself embraced with emotion, and instantly took him to the Play, where we were all three admirably entertained.

Nor is it to render homage to the virtues of the best of her good and honoured sex—whom, in deference to her unassuming worth, I will only here designate by the initials E. L.—that I add this record to the bundle of papers with which our, in a most distinguished degree, remarkable boy has expressed himself delighted, before reconsigning the same to the left-hand glass closet of Mrs. Lirriper's little bookcase.

Neither is it to obtrude the name of the old original superannuated obscure Jemmy Jackman, once (to his degradation) of Wozenham's, long (to his elevation) of Lirriper's. If I could be consciously guilty of that piece of bad taste, it would indeed be a work of supererogation, now that the name is borne by Jemmy Jackman Lirriper.

No, I take up my humble pen to register a little record of our strikingly remarkable boy, which my poor capacity regards as presenting a pleasant little picture of the dear boy's mind. The picture may be interesting to himself when he is a man.

Our first reunited Christmas-day was the most delightful one we have ever passed together. Jemmy was never silent for five minutes, except in church-time. He talked as we sat by the fire, he talked when we were out walking, he talked as we sat by the fire again, he talked incessantly at dinner, though he made a dinner almost as remarkable as himself. It was the spring of happiness in his fresh young heart flowing and flowing, and it fertilised (if I may be allowed so bold a figure) my much-esteemed friend, and J. J. the present writer.

There were only we three. We dined in my esteemed friend's little room, and our entertainment was perfect. But everything in the establishment is, in neatness, order, and comfort, always perfect. After dinner our boy slipped away to his old stool at my esteemed friend's knee, and there, with his hot chestnuts and his glass of brown sherry (really, a most excellent wine!) on a chair for a table, his face outshone the apples in the dish.

We talked of these jottings of mine, which Jemmy had read through and through by that time; and so it came about that my esteemed friend remarked, as she sat smoothing Jemmy's curls:

"And as you belong to the house too, Jemmy,—and so much more than the Lodgers, having been born in it,—why, your story ought to be added to the rest, I think, one of these days."

Jemmy's eyes sparkled at this, and he said, "So *I* think, Gran."

Then he sat looking at the fire, and then he began to laugh in a sort of confidence with the fire, and then he said, folding his arms across my esteemed friend's lap, and raising his bright face to hers: "Would you like to hear a boy's story, Gran?"

"Of all things," replied my esteemed friend.

"Would you, godfather?"

"Of all things," I too replied.

"Well, then," said Jemmy, "I'll tell you one."

Here our indisputably remarkable boy gave himself a hug, and laughed again, musically, at the idea of his coming out in that new line. Then he once more took the fire into the same sort of confidence as before, and began:

"Once upon a time, When pigs drank wine, And monkeys chewed tobaccer, 'Twas neither in your time nor mine, But that's no macker—"

"Bless the child!" cried my esteemed friend, "what's amiss with his brain?"

"It's poetry, Gran," returned Jemmy, shouting with laughter. "We always begin stories that way at school."

"Gave me quite a turn, Major," said my esteemed friend, fanning herself with a plate. "Thought he was light-headed!"

"In those remarkable times, Gran and godfather, there was once a boy,—not me, you know."

"No, no," says my respected friend, "not you. Not him, Major, you understand?"

"No, no," says I.

"And he went to school in Rutlandshire—"

"Why not Lincolnshire?" says my respected friend.

"Why not, you dear old Gran? Because *I* go to school in Lincolnshire, don't I?"

"Ah, to be sure!" says my respected friend. "And it's not Jemmy, you understand, Major?"

"No, no," says I.

"Well!" our boy proceeded, hugging himself comfortably, and laughing merrily (again in confidence with the fire), before he again looked up in Mrs. Lirriper's face, "and so he was tremendously in love with his schoolmaster's daughter, and she was the most beautiful creature that ever was seen, and she had brown eyes, and she had brown hair all curling beautifully, and she had a delicious voice, and she was delicious altogether, and her name was Seraphina."

"What's the name of *your* schoolmaster's daughter, Jemmy?" asks my respected friend.

"Polly!" replied Jemmy, pointing his forefinger at her. "There now! Caught you! Ha, ha, ha!"

When he and my respected friend had had a laugh and a hug together, our admittedly remarkable boy resumed with a great relish:

"Well! And so he loved her. And so he thought about her, and dreamed about her, and made her presents of oranges and nuts, and would have made her presents of pearls and diamonds if he could have afforded it out of his pocket-money, but he couldn't. And so her father—O, he WAS a Tartar! Keeping the boys up to the mark, holding examinations once a month, lecturing upon all sorts of subjects at all sorts of times, and knowing everything in the world out of book. And so this boy—"

"Had he any name?" asks my respected friend.

"No, he hadn't, Gran. Ha, ha! There now! Caught you again!"

After this, they had another laugh and another hug, and then our boy went on.

"Well! And so this boy, he had a friend about as old as himself at the same school, and his name (for He *had* a name, as it happened) was—let me remember—was Bobbo."

"Not Bob," says my respected friend.

"Of course not," says Jemmy. "What made you think it was, Gran? Well! And so this friend was the cleverest and bravest and best-looking and most generous of all the friends that ever were, and so he was in love with Seraphina's sister, and so Seraphina's sister was in love with him, and so they all grew up."

"Bless us!" says my respected friend. "They were very sudden about it."

"So they all grew up," our boy repeated, laughing heartily, "and Bobbo and this boy went away together on horseback to seek their fortunes, and they partly got their horses by favour, and partly in a bargain; that is to say, they had saved up between them seven and fourpence, and the two horses, being Arabs, were worth more, only the man said he would take that, to favour them. Well! And so they made their fortunes and came prancing back to the school, with their pockets full of gold, enough to last for ever. And so they rang at the parents' and visitors' bell (not the back gate), and when the bell was answered they proclaimed 'The same as if it was scarlet fever! Every boy goes home for an indefinite period!' And then there was great hurrahing, and then they kissed Seraphina and her sister,—each his own love, and not the other's on any account,—and then they ordered the Tartar into instant confinement."

"Poor man!" said my respected friend.

"Into instant confinement, Gran," repeated Jemmy, trying to look severe and roaring with laughter; "and he was to have nothing to eat but the boys' dinners, and was to drink half a cask of their beer every day. And so then the preparations were made for the two weddings, and there were hampers, and potted things, and sweet things, and nuts, and postage-stamps, and all manner of things. And so they were so jolly, that they let the Tartar out, and he was jolly too."

"I am glad they let him out," says my respected friend, "because he had only done his duty."

"O, but hadn't he overdone it, though!" cried Jemmy. "Well! And so then this boy mounted his horse, with his bride in his arms, and cantered away, and cantered on and on till he came to a certain place where he had a certain Gran and a certain godfather,—not you two, you know."

"No, no," we both said.

"And there he was received with great rejoicings, and he filled the cupboard and the bookcase with gold, and he showered it out on his Gran and his godfather because they were the two kindest and dearest people that ever lived in this world. And so while they were sitting up to their knees in gold, a knocking was heard at the street door, and who should it be but Bobbo, also on horseback with his bride in his arms, and what had he come to say but that he would take (at double rent) all the Lodgings for ever, that were not wanted by this a boy and this Gran and this godfather, and that they would all live together, and all be happy! And so they were, and so it never ended!"

"And was there no quarrelling?" asked my respected friend, as Jemmy sat upon her lap and hugged her.

"No! Nobody ever quarrelled."

"And did the money never melt away?"

"No! Nobody could ever spend it all."

"And did none of them ever grow older?"

"No! Nobody ever grew older after that."

"And did none of them ever die?"

"O, no, no, no, Gran!" exclaimed our dear boy, laying his cheek upon her breast, and drawing her closer to him. "Nobody ever died."

"Ah, Major, Major!" says my respected friend, smiling benignly upon me, "this beats our stories. Let us end with the Boy's story, Major, for the Boy's story is the best that is ever told!"

In submission to which request on the part of the best of women, I have here noted it down as faithfully as my best abilities, coupled with my best intentions, would admit, subscribing it with my name,

J. JACKMAN

The parlours.
Mrs. Lirriper's Lodgings.

Mrs. Lirriper's Legacy

IN TWO CHAPTERS

Chapter I

Mrs. Lirriper Relates How She Went On, and Went Over

Ah! It's pleasant to drop into my own easy-chair my dear though a little palpitating what with trotting upstairs and what with trotting down, and why kitchen stairs should all be corner stairs is for the builders to justify though I do not think they fully understand their trade and never did, else why the sameness and why not more conveniences and fewer draughts and likewise making a practice of laying the plaster on too thick I am well convinced which holds the damp, and as to chimney-pots putting them on by guess-work like hats at a party and no more knowing what their effect will be upon the smoke bless you than I do if so much, except that it will mostly be either to send it down your throat in a straight form or give it a twist before it goes there. And what I says speaking as I find of those new metal chimneys all manner of shapes (there's a row of 'em at Miss Wozenham's lodging-house lower down on the other side of the way) is that they only work your smoke into artificial patterns for you before you swallow it and that I'd quite as soon swallow mine plain, the flavour being the same, not to mention the conceit of putting up signs on the top of your house to show the forms in which you take your smoke into your inside.

Being here before your eyes my dear in my own easy-chair in my own quiet room in my own Lodging-House Number Eighty-one Norfolk Street Strand London situated midway between the City and St. James's—if anything is where it used to be with these hotels calling themselves Limited but called unlimited by Major Jackman rising up everywhere and rising up into flagstaffs where they can't go any higher, but my mind of those monsters is give me a landlord's or landlady's wholesome face when I come off a journey and not a brass plate with an electrified number clicking out of it which it's not in nature can be glad to see me and to which I don't want to be hoisted like molasses at the Docks and left there telegraphing for help with the most ingenious instruments but quite in vain—being here my dear I have no call to mention that I am still in the Lodgings as a business hoping to die in the same and if agreeable to the clergy partly read over at Saint Clement's Danes and concluded in Hatfield churchyard when lying once again by my poor Lirriper ashes to ashes and dust to dust.

Neither should I tell you any news my dear in telling you that the Major is still a fixture in the Parlours quite as much so as the roof of the house, and that Jemmy is of boys the best and brightest and has ever had kept from him the cruel story of his poor pretty young mother Mrs. Edson being deserted in the second floor and dying in my arms, fully believing that I am his born Gran and him an orphan, though what with engineering since he took a taste for it and him and the Major making Locomotives out of parasols broken iron pots and cotton-reels and them absolutely a getting off the line and falling over the table and injuring the passengers almost equal to the originals it really is quite wonderful. And when I says to the Major, "Major can't you by *any* means give us a communication with the guard?" the Major says quite huffy, "No madam it's not to be done," and when I says "Why not?" the Major says, "That is between us who are in the Railway Interest madam and our friend the Right Honourable Vice-President of the Board of Trade" and if you'll believe me my dear the Major wrote to Jemmy at school to consult him on the answer I should have before I could get even that amount of unsatisfactoriness out of the man, the reason being that when we first began with the little model and the working signals beautiful and perfect (being in general as wrong as the real) and when I says laughing "What appointment am I to hold in this undertaking gentlemen?" Jemmy hugs me round the neck and tells me dancing, "You shall be the Public Gran" and consequently they put upon me just as much as ever they like and I sit a growling in my easy-chair.

My dear whether it is that a grown man as clever as the Major cannot give half his heart and mind to anything—even a plaything—but must get into right down earnest with it, whether it is so or whether it is not so I do not undertake to say, but Jemmy is far out-done by the serious and believing ways of the Major in the management of the United Grand Junction Lirriper and Jackman Great Norfolk Parlour Line, "For" says my Jemmy with the sparkling eyes when it was christened, "we must have a whole mouthful of name Gran or our dear old Public" and there the young rogue kissed me, "won't stump up." So the Public took the shares—ten at ninepence, and immediately when that was spent twelve Preference at one and sixpence—and they were all signed by Jemmy and countersigned by the Major, and between ourselves much better worth the money than some shares I have paid for in my time. In the same holidays the line was made and worked and opened and ran excursions and had collisions and burst its boilers and all sorts of accidents and offences all most regular correct and pretty. The sense of responsibility entertained by the Major as a military style of station-master my dear starting the down train behind time and ringing one of those little bells that you buy with the little coal-scuttles off the tray round the man's neck in the street did him honour, but noticing the Major of a night when he is writing out his monthly report to Jemmy at school of the state of the Rolling Stock and the Permanent Way and all the rest of it (the whole kept upon the Major's sideboard and dusted with his own hands every morning before varnishing his boots) I notice him as full of thought and care as full can be and frowning in a fearful manner, but indeed the Major does nothing by halves as witness his great delight in going out surveying with Jemmy when he has Jemmy to go with, carrying a chain and a measuring-tape and driving I don't know what improvements right through Westminster Abbey and fully believed in the streets to be knocking everything upside down by Act of Parliament. As please Heaven will come to pass when Jemmy takes to that as a profession!

Mentioning my poor Lirriper brings into my head his own youngest brother the Doctor though Doctor of what I am sure it would be hard to say unless Liquor, for neither Physic nor Music nor yet Law does Joshua Lirriper know a morsel of except continually being summoned to the County Court and having orders made upon him which he runs away from, and once was taken in the passage of this very house with an umbrella up and the Major's hat on, giving his name with the door-mat round him as Sir Johnson Jones, K.C.B. in spectacles residing at the Horse Guards. On which occasion he had got into the house not a minute before, through the girl letting him on the mat when he sent in a piece of paper twisted more like one of those spills for lighting candles than a note, offering me the choice between thirty shillings in hand and his brains on the premises marked immediate and waiting for an answer. My dear it gave me such a dreadful turn to think of the brains of my poor dear Lirriper's own flesh and blood flying about the new oilcloth however unworthy to be so assisted, that I went out of my room here to ask him what he would take once for all not to do it for life when I found him in the custody of two gentlemen that I should have judged to be in the feather-bed trade if they had not announced the law, so fluffy were their personal appearance. "Bring your chains, Sir," says Joshua to the littlest of the two in the biggest hat, "rivet on my fetters!" Imagine my feelings when I pictered him clanking up Norfolk Street in irons and Miss Wozenham looking out of window! "Gentlemen," I says all of a tremble and ready to drop "please to bring him into Major Jackman's apartments." So they brought him into the Parlours, and when the Major spies his own curly-brimmed hat on him which Joshua Lirriper had whipped off its peg in the passage for a military disguise he goes into such a tearing passion that he tips it off his head with his hand and kicks it up to the ceiling with his foot where it grazed long afterwards. "Major" I says "be cool and advise me what to do with Joshua my dead and gone Lirriper's own youngest brother." "Madam" says the Major "my advice is that you board and lodge him in a Powder Mill, with a handsome gratuity to the proprietor when exploded." "Major" I says "as a Christian you cannot mean your words." "Madam" says the Major "by the Lord I do!" and indeed the Major besides being with all his merits a very passionate man for his size had a bad opinion of Joshua on account of former troubles even unattended by liberties taken with his apparel. When Joshua Lirriper hears this conversation betwixt us he turns upon the littlest one with the biggest hat and says "Come Sir! Remove me to my vile dungeon. Where is my mouldy straw?" My dear at the picter of him rising in my mind dressed almost entirely in padlocks like Baron Trenck in Jemmy's book I was so overcome that I burst into tears and I says to the Major, "Major take my keys and settle with these gentlemen or I shall never know a happy minute more," which was done several times both before and since, but still I must remember that Joshua Lirriper has his good feelings and shows them in being always so troubled in his mind when he cannot wear mourning for his brother. Many a long year have I left off my widow's mourning not being wishful to intrude, but the tender point in Joshua that I cannot help a little yielding to is when he writes "One single sovereign would enable me to wear a decent suit of mourning for my much-loved brother. I vowed at the time of his lamented death that I would ever wear sables in memory of him but Alas how short-sighted is man, How keep that vow when penniless!" It says a good deal for the strength of his feelings that he couldn't have been seven year old when my poor Lirriper died and to have kept to it ever since is highly creditable. But we know there's good in all of us,—if we only knew where it was in some of us,—and though it was far from delicate in Joshua to work upon the dear child's feelings when first sent to school and write down into Lincolnshire for his pocket-money by return of post and got it, still he is my poor Lirriper's own youngest brother and mightn't have meant not paying his bill at the Salisbury Arms when his affection took him down to stay a fortnight at Hatfield churchyard and might have meant to keep sober but for bad company. Consequently if the Major *had* played on him with the garden-engine which he got privately into his room without my knowing of it, I think that much as I should have regretted it there would have been words betwixt the Major and me. Therefore my dear though he played on Mr. Buffle by mistake being hot in his head, and though it might have been misrepresented down at Wozenham's into not being ready for Mr. Buffle in other respects he being the Assessed Taxes, still I do not so much regret it as perhaps I ought. And whether Joshua Lirriper will yet do well in life I cannot say, but I did hear of his coming, out at a Private Theatre in the character of a Bandit without receiving any offers afterwards from the regular managers.

Mentioning Mr. Buffle gives an instance of there being good in persons where good is not expected, for it cannot be denied that Mr. Buffle's manners when engaged in his business were not agreeable. To collect is one thing, and to look about as if suspicious of the goods being gradually removing in the dead of the night by a back door is another, over taxing you have no control but suspecting is voluntary. Allowances too must ever be made for a gentleman of the Major's warmth not relishing being spoke to with a pen in the mouth, and while I do not know that it is more irritable to my own feelings to have a low-crowned hat with a broad brim kept on in doors than any other hat still I can appreciate the Major's, besides which without bearing malice or vengeance the Major is a man that scores up arrears as his habit always was with Joshua Lirriper. So at last my dear the Major lay in wait for Mr. Buffle, and it worrited me a good deal. Mr. Buffle gives his rap of two sharp knocks one day and the Major bounces to the door. "Collector has called for two quarters' Assessed Taxes" says Mr. Buffle. "They are ready for him" says the Major and brings him in here. But on the way Mr. Buffle looks about him in his usual suspicious manner and the Major fires and asks him "Do you see a Ghost Sir?" "No Sir" says Mr. Buffle. "Because I have before noticed you" says the Major "apparently looking for a spectre very hard beneath the roof of my respected friend. When you find that supernatural agent, be so good as point him out Sir." Mr. Buffle stares at the Major and then nods at me. "Mrs. Lirriper Sir" says the Major going off into a perfect steam and introducing me with his hand. "Pleasure of knowing her" says Mr. Buffle. "A—hum!—Jemmy Jackman Sir!" says the Major introducing himself. "Honour of knowing you by sight" says Mr. Buffle. "Jemmy Jackman Sir" says the Major wagging his head sideways in a sort of obstinate fury "presents to you his esteemed friend that lady Mrs. Emma Lirriper of Eighty-one Norfolk Street Strand London in the County of Middlesex in the United Kingdom of Great Britain and Ireland. Upon which occasion Sir," says the Major, "Jemmy Jackman takes your hat off." Mr. Buffle looks at his hat where the Major drops it on the floor, and he picks it up and puts it on again. "Sir" says the Major very red and looking him full in the face "there are two quarters of the Gallantry Taxes due and the Collector has called." Upon which if you can believe my words my dear the Major drops Mr. Buffle's hat off again. "This—" Mr. Buffle begins very angry with his pen in his mouth, when the Major steaming more and more says "Take your bit out Sir! Or by the whole infernal system of Taxation of this country and every individual figure in the National Debt, I'll get upon your back and ride you like a horse!" which it's my belief he would have done and even actually jerking his neat little legs ready for a spring as it was. "This," says Mr. Buffle without his pen "is an assault and I'll have the law of you." "Sir" replies the Major "if you are a man of honour, your Collector of whatever may be due on the Honourable Assessment by applying to Major Jackman at the Parlours Mrs. Lirriper's Lodgings, may obtain what he wants in full at any moment."

When the Major glared at Mr. Buffle with those meaning words my dear I literally gasped for a teaspoonful of salvolatile in a wine-glass of water, and I says "Pray let it go no farther gentlemen I beg and beseech of you!" But the Major could be got to do nothing else but snort long after Mr. Buffle was gone, and the effect it had upon my whole mass of blood when on the next day of Mr. Buffle's rounds the Major spruced himself up and went humming a tune up and down the street with one eye almost obliterated by his hat there are not expressions in Johnson's Dictionary to state. But I safely put the street door on the jar and got behind the Major's blinds with my shawl on and my mind made up the moment I saw danger to rush out screeching till my voice failed me and catch the Major round the neck till my strength went and have all parties bound. I had not been behind the blinds a quarter of an hour when I saw Mr. Buffle approaching with his Collecting-books in his hand. The Major likewise saw him approaching and hummed louder and himself approached. They met before the Airy railings. The Major takes off his hat at arm's length and says "Mr. Buffle I believe?" Mr. Buffle takes off *his* hat at arm's length and says "That is my name Sir." Says the Major "Have you any commands for me, Mr. Buffle?" Says Mr. Buffle "Not any Sir." Then my dear both of 'em bowed very low and haughty and parted, and whenever Mr. Buffle made his rounds in future him and the Major always met and bowed before the Airy railings, putting me much in mind of Hamlet and the other gentleman in mourning before killing one another, though I could have wished the other gentleman had done it fairer and even if less polite no poison.

Mr. Buffle's family were not liked in this neighbourhood, for when you are a householder my dear you'll find it does not come by nature to like the Assessed, and it was considered besides that a one-horse pheayton ought not to have elevated Mrs. Buffle to that height especially when purloined from the Taxes which I myself did consider uncharitable. But they were *not* liked and there was that domestic unhappiness in the family in consequence of their both being very hard with Miss Buffle and one another on account of Miss Buffle's favouring Mr. Buffle's articled young gentleman, that it *was* whispered that Miss Buffle would go either into a consumption or a convent she being so very thin and off her appetite and two close-shaved gentlemen with white bands round their necks peeping round the corner whenever she went out in waistcoats resembling black pinafores. So things stood towards Mr. Buffle when one night I was woke by a frightful noise and a smell of burning, and going to my bedroom window saw the whole street in a glow. Fortunately we had two sets empty just then and before I could hurry on some clothes I heard the Major hammering at the attics' doors and calling out "Dress yourselves!—Fire! Don't be frightened!—Fire! Collect your presence of mind!—Fire! All right—Fire!" most tremenjously. As I opened my bedroom door the Major came tumbling in over himself and me, and caught me in his arms. "Major" I says breathless "where is it?" "I don't know dearest madam" says the Major—"Fire! Jemmy Jackman will defend you to the last drop of his blood—Fire! If the dear boy was at home what a treat this would be for him—Fire!" and altogether very collected and bold except that he couldn't say a single sentence without shaking me to the very centre with roaring Fire. We ran down to the drawing-room and put our heads out of window, and the Major calls to an unfeeling young monkey, scampering by be joyful and ready to split "Where is it?—Fire!" The monkey answers without stopping "O here's a lark! Old Buffle's been setting his house alight to prevent its being found out that he boned the Taxes. Hurrah! Fire!" And then the sparks came flying up and the smoke came pouring down and the crackling of flames and spatting of water and banging of engines and hacking of axes and breaking of glass and knocking at doors and the shouting and crying and hurrying and the heat and altogether gave me a dreadful palpitation. "Don't be frightened dearest madam," says the Major, "—Fire! There's nothing to be alarmed at—Fire! Don't open the street door till I come back—Fire! I'll go and see if I can be of any service—Fire! You're quite composed and comfortable ain't you?—Fire, Fire, Fire!" It was in vain for me to hold the man and tell him he'd be galloped to death by the engines—pumped to death by his over-exertions—wet-feeted to death by the slop and mess—flattened to death when the roofs fell in—his spirit was up and he went scampering off after the young monkey with all the breath he had and none to spare, and me and the girls huddled together at the parlour windows looking at the dreadful flames above the houses over the way, Mr. Buffle's being round the corner. Presently what should we see but some people running down the street straight to our door, and then the Major directing operations in the busiest way, and then some more people and then—carried in a chair similar to Guy Fawkes—Mr. Buffle in a blanket!

My dear the Major has Mr. Buffle brought up our steps and whisked into the parlour and carted out on the sofy, and then he and all the rest of them without so much as a word burst away again full speed leaving the impression of a vision except for Mr. Buffle awful in his blanket with his eyes a rolling. In a twinkling they all burst back again with Mrs. Buffle in another blanket, which whisked in and carted out on the sofy they all burst off again and all burst back again with Miss Buffle in another blanket, which again whisked in and carted out they all burst off again and all burst back again with Mr. Buffle's articled young gentleman in another blanket—him a holding round the necks of two men carrying him by the legs, similar to the picter of the disgraceful creetur who has lost the fight (but where the chair I do not know) and his hair having the appearance of newly played upon. When all four of a row, the Major rubs his hands and whispers me with what little hoarseness he can get together, "If our dear remarkable boy was only at home what a delightful treat this would be for him!"

My dear we made them some hot tea and toast and some hot brandy-and-water with a little comfortable nutmeg in it, and at first they were scared and low in their spirits but being fully insured got sociable. And the first use Mr. Buffle made of his tongue was to call the Major his Preserver and his best of friends and to say "My for ever dearest sir let me make you known to Mrs. Buffle" which also addressed him as her Preserver and her best of friends and was fully as cordial as the blanket would admit of. Also Miss Buffle. The articled young gentleman's head was a little light and he sat a moaning "Robina is reduced to cinders, Robina is reduced to cinders!" Which went more to the heart on account of his having got wrapped in his blanket as if he was looking out of a violinceller case, until Mr. Buffle says "Robina speak to him!" Miss Buffle says "Dear George!" and but for the Major's pouring down brandy-and-water on the instant which caused a catching in his throat owing to the nutmeg and a violent fit of coughing it might have proved too much for his strength. When the articled young gentleman got the better of it Mr. Buffle leaned up against Mrs. Buffle being two bundles, a little while in confidence, and then says with tears in his eyes which the Major noticing wiped, "We have not been an united family, let us after this danger become so, take her George." The young gentleman could not put his arm out far to do it, but his spoken expressions were very beautiful though of a wandering class. And I do not know that I ever had a much pleasanter meal than the breakfast we took together after we had all dozed, when Miss Buffle made tea very sweetly in quite the Roman style as depicted formerly at Covent Garden Theatre and when the whole family was most agreeable, as they have ever proved since that night when the Major stood at the foot of the Fire-Escape and claimed them as they came down—the young gentleman head-foremost, which accounts. And though I do not say that we should be less liable to think ill of one another if strictly limited to blankets, still I do say that we might most of us come to a better understanding if we kept one another less at a distance.

Why there's Wozenham's lower down on the other side of the street. I had a feeling of much soreness several years respecting what I must still ever call Miss Wozenham's systematic underbidding and the likeness of the house in Bradshaw having far too many windows and a most umbrageous and outrageous Oak which never yet was seen in Norfolk Street nor yet a carriage and four at Wozenham's door, which it would have been far more to Bradshaw's credit to have drawn a cab. This frame of mind continued bitter down to the very afternoon in January last when one of my girls, Sally Rairyganoo which I still suspect of Irish extraction though family represented Cambridge, else why abscond with a bricklayer of the Limerick persuasion and be married in pattens not waiting till his black eye was decently got round with all the company fourteen in number and one horse fighting outside on the roof of the vehicle,—I repeat my dear my ill-regulated state of mind towards Miss Wozenham continued down to the very afternoon of January last past when Sally Rairyganoo came banging (I can use no milder expression) into my room with a jump which may be Cambridge and may not, and said "Hurroo Missis! Miss Wozenham's sold up!" My dear when I had it thrown in my face and conscience that the girl Sally had reason to think I could be glad of the ruin of a fellow-creeter, I burst into tears and dropped back in my chair and I says "I am ashamed of myself!"

Well! I tried to settle to my tea but I could not do it what with thinking of Miss Wozenham and her distresses. It was a wretched night and I went up to a front window and looked over at Wozenham's and as well as I could make it out down the street in the fog it was the dismallest of the dismal and not a light to be seen. So at last I save to myself "This will not do," and I puts on my oldest bonnet and shawl not wishing Miss Wozenham to be reminded of my best at such a time, and lo and behold you I goes over to Wozenham's and knocks. "Miss Wozenham at home?" I says turning my head when I heard the door go. And then I saw it was Miss Wozenham herself who had opened it and sadly worn she was poor thing and her eyes all swelled and swelled with crying. "Miss Wozenham" I says "it is several years since there was a little unpleasantness betwixt us on the subject of my grandson's cap being down your Airy. I have overlooked it and I hope you have done the same." "Yes Mrs. Lirriper" she says in a surprise, "I have." "Then my dear" I says "I should be glad to come in and speak a word to you." Upon my calling her my dear Miss Wozenham breaks out a crying most pitiful, and a not unfeeling elderly person that might have been better shaved in a nightcap with a hat over it offering a polite apology for the mumps having worked themselves into his constitution, and also for sending home to his wife on the bellows which was in his hand as a writing-desk, looks out of the back parlour and says "The lady wants a word of comfort" and goes in again. So I was able to say quite natural "Wants a word of comfort does she Sir? Then please the pigs she shall have it!" And Miss Wozenham and me we go into the front room with a wretched light that seemed to have been crying too and was sputtering out, and I says "Now my dear, tell me all," and she wrings her hands and says "O Mrs. Lirriper that man is in possession here, and I have not a friend in the world who is able to help me with a shilling."

It doesn't signify a bit what a talkative old body like me said to Miss Wozenham when she said that, and so I'll tell you instead my dear that I'd have given thirty shillings to have taken her over to tea, only I durstn't on account of the Major. Not you see but what I knew I could draw the Major out like thread and wind him round my finger on most subjects and perhaps even on that if I was to set myself to it, but him and me had so often belied Miss Wozenham to one another that I was shamefaced, and I knew she had offended his pride and never mine, and likewise I felt timid that that Rairyganoo girl might make things awkward. So I says "My dear if you could give me a cup of tea to clear my muddle of a head I should better understand your affairs." And we had the tea and the affairs too and after all it was but forty pound, and—There! she's as industrious and straight a creeter as ever lived and has paid back half of it already, and where's the use of saying more, particularly when it ain't the point? For the point is that when she was a kissing my hands and holding them in hers and kissing them again and blessing blessing blessing, I cheered up at last and

I says "Why what a waddling old goose I have been my dear to take you for something so very different!" "Ah but I too" says she "how have *I* mistaken *you!*" "Come for goodness' sake tell me" I says "what you thought of me?" "O" says she "I thought you had no feeling for such a hard hand-to-mouth life as mine, and were rolling in affluence." I says shaking my sides (and very glad to do it for I had been a choking quite long enough) "Only look at my figure my dear and give me your opinion whether if I was in affluence I should be likely to roll in it?" That did it! We got as merry as grigs (whatever *they* are, if you happen to know my dear—*I* don't) and I went home to my blessed home as happy and as thankful as could be. But before I make an end of it, think even of my having misunderstood the Major! Yes! For next forenoon the Major came into my little room with his brushed hat in his hand and he begins "My dearest madam—" and then put his face in his hat as if he had just come into church. As I sat all in a maze he came out of his hat and began again. "My esteemed and beloved friend—" and then went into his hat again. "Major," I cries out frightened "has anything happened to our darling boy?" "No, no, no" says the Major "but Miss Wozenham has been here this morning to make her excuses to me, and by the Lord I can't get over what she told me." "Hoity toity, Major," I says "you don't know yet that I was afraid of you last night and didn't think half as well of you as I ought! So come out of church Major and forgive me like a dear old friend and I'll never do so any more." And I leave you to judge my dear whether I ever did or will. And how affecting to think of Miss Wozenham out of her small income and her losses doing so much for her poor old father, and keeping a brother that had had the misfortune to soften his brain against the hard mathematics as neat as a new pin in the three back represented to lodgers as a lumber-room and consuming a whole shoulder of mutton whenever provided!

And now my dear I really am a going to tell you about my Legacy if you're inclined to favour me with your attention, and I did fully intend to have come straight to it only one thing does so bring up another. It was the month of June and the day before Midsummer Day when my girl Winifred Madgers—she was what is termed a Plymouth Sister, and the Plymouth Brother that made away with her was quite right, for a tidier young woman for a wife never came into a house and afterwards called with the beautifullest Plymouth Twins—it was the day before Midsummer Day when Winifred Madgers comes and says to me "A gentleman from the Consul's wishes particular to speak to Mrs. Lirriper." If you'll believe me my dear the Consols at the bank where I have a little matter for Jemmy got into my head, and I says "Good gracious I hope he ain't had any dreadful fall!" Says Winifred "He don't look as if he had ma'am." And I says "Show him in."

The gentleman came in dark and with his hair cropped what I should consider too close, and he says very polite "Madame Lirrwiper!" I says, "Yes Sir. Take a chair." "I come," says he "frrwom the Frrwench Consul's." So I saw at once that it wasn't the Bank of England. "We have rrweceived," says the gentleman turning his r's very curious and skilful, "frrwom the Mairrwie at Sens, a communication which I will have the honour to rrwead. Madame Lirrwiper understands Frrwench?" "O dear no Sir!" says I. "Madame Lirriper don't understand anything of the sort." "It matters not," says the gentleman, "I will trrwanslate."

With that my dear the gentleman after reading something about a Department and a Marie (which Lord forgive me I supposed till the Major came home was Mary, and never was I more puzzled than to think how that young woman came to have so much to do with it) translated a lot with the most obliging pains, and it came to this:—That in the town of Sens in France an unknown Englishman lay a dying. That he was speechless and without motion. That in his lodging there was a gold watch and a purse containing such and such money and a trunk containing such and such clothes, but no passport and no papers, except that on his table was a pack of cards and that he had written in pencil on the back of the ace of hearts: "To the authorities. When I am dead, pray send what is left, as a last Legacy, to Mrs. Lirriper Eighty-one Norfolk Street Strand London." When the gentleman had explained all this, which seemed to be drawn up much more methodical than I should have given the French credit for, not at that time knowing the nation, he put the document into my hand. And much the wiser I was for that you may be sure, except that it had the look of being made out upon grocery paper and was stamped all over with eagles.

"Does Madame Lirrwiper" says the gentleman "believe she rrwecognises her unfortunate compatrrwiot?"

You may imagine the flurry it put me into my dear to be talked to about my compatriots.

I says "Excuse me. Would you have the kindness sir to make your language as simple as you can?"

"This Englishman unhappy, at the point of death. This compatrrwiot afflicted," says the gentleman.

"Thank you, Sir" I says "I understand you now. No sir I have not the least idea who this can be."

"Has Madame Lirrwiper no son, no nephew, no godson, no frrwiend, no acquaintance of any kind in Frrwance?"

"To my certain knowledge" says I "no relation or friend, and to the best of my belief no acquaintance."

"Pardon me. You take Locataires?" says the gentleman.

My dear fully believing he was offering me something with his obliging foreign manners,—snuff for anything I knew,—I gave a little bend of my head and I says if you'll credit it, "No I thank you. I have not contracted the habit."

The gentleman looks perplexed and says "Lodgers!"

"Oh!" says I laughing. "Bless the man! Why yes to be sure!"

"May it not be a former lodger?" says the gentleman. "Some lodger that you pardoned some rrwent? You have pardoned lodgers some rrwent?"

"Hem! It has happened Sir" says I, "but I assure you I can call to mind no gentleman of that description that this is at all likely to be."

In short my dear, we could make nothing of it, and the gentleman noted down what I said and went away. But he left me the paper of which he had two with him, and when the Major came in I says to the Major as I put it in his hand "Major here's Old Moore's Almanac with the hieroglyphic complete, for your opinion."

It took the Major a little longer to read than I should have thought, judging from the copious flow with which he seemed to be gifted when attacking the organ-men, but at last he got through it, and stood a gazing at me in amazement.

"Major" I says "you're paralysed."

"Madam" says the Major, "Jemmy Jackman is doubled up."

Now it did so happen that the Major had been out to get a little information about railroads and steamboats, as our boy was coming home for his Midsummer holidays next day and we were going to take him somewhere for a treat and a change. So while the Major stood a gazing it came into my head to say to him "Major I wish you'd go and look at some of your books and maps, and see whereabouts this same town of Sens is in France."

The Major he roused himself and he went into the Parlours and he poked about a little, and he came back to me and he says, "Sens my dearest madam is seventy-odd miles south of Paris."

With what I may truly call a desperate effort "Major," I says "we'll go there with our blessed boy."

If ever the Major was beside himself it was at the thoughts of that journey. All day long he was like the wild man of the woods after meeting with an advertisement in the papers telling him something to his advantage, and early next morning hours before Jemmy could possibly come home he was outside in the street ready to call out to him that we was all a going to France. Young Rosycheeks you may believe was as wild as the Major, and they did carry on to that degree that I says "If you two children ain't more orderly I'll pack you both off to bed." And then they fell to cleaning up the Major's telescope to see France with, and went out and bought a leather bag with a snap to hang round Jemmy, and him to carry the money like a little Fortunatus with his purse.

If I hadn't passed my word and raised their hopes, I doubt if I could have gone through with the undertaking but it was too late to go back now. So on the second day after Midsummer Day we went off by the morning mail. And when we came to the sea which I had never seen but once in my life and that when my poor Lirriper was courting me, the freshness of it and the deepness and the airiness and to think that it had been rolling ever since and that it was always a rolling and so few of us minding, made me feel quite serious. But I felt happy too and so did Jemmy and the Major and not much motion on the whole, though me with a swimming in the head and a sinking but able to take notice that the foreign insides appear to be constructed hollower than the English, leading to much more tremenjous noises when bad sailors.

But my dear the blueness and the lightness and the coloured look of everything and the very sentry-boxes striped and the shining rattling drums and the little soldiers with their waists and tidy gaiters, when we got across to the Continent—it made me feel as if I don't know what—as if the atmosphere had been lifted off me. And as to lunch why bless you if I kept a man-cook and two kitchen-maids I couldn't got it done for twice the money, and no injured young woman a glaring at you and grudging you and acknowledging your patronage by wishing that your food might choke you, but so civil and so hot and attentive and every way comfortable except Jemmy pouring wine down his throat by tumblers-full and me expecting to see him drop under the table.

And the way in which Jemmy spoke his French was a real charm. It was often wanted of him, for whenever anybody spoke a syllable to me I says "Non-comprenny, you're very kind, but it's no use—Now Jemmy!" and then Jemmy he fires away at 'em lovely, the only thing wanting in Jemmy's French being as it appeared to me that he hardly ever understood a word of what they said to him which made it scarcely of the use it might have been though in other respects a perfect Native, and regarding the Major's fluency I should have been of the opinion judging French by English that there might have been a greater choice of words in the language though still I must admit that if I hadn't known him when he asked a military gentleman in a gray cloak what o'clock it was I should have took him for a Frenchman born.

Before going on to look after my Legacy we were to make one regular day in Paris, and I leave you to judge my dear what a day *that* was with Jemmy and the Major and the telescope and me and the prowling young man at the inn door (but very civil too) that went along with us to show the sights. All along the railway to Paris Jemmy and the Major had been frightening me to death by stooping down on the platforms at stations to inspect the engines underneath their mechanical stomachs, and by creeping in and out I don't know where all, to find improvements for the United Grand Junction Parlour, but when we got out into the brilliant streets on a bright morning they gave up all their London improvements as a bad job and gave their minds to Paris. Says the prowling young man to me "Will I speak Inglis No?" So I says "If you can young man I shall take it as a favour," but after half-an-hour of it when I fully believed the man had gone mad and me too I says "Be so good as fall back on your French Sir," knowing that then I shouldn't have the agonies of trying to understand him, which was a happy release. Not that I lost much more than the rest either, for I generally noticed that when he had described something very long indeed and I says to Jemmy "What does he say Jemmy?" Jemmy says looking with vengeance in his eye "He is so jolly indistinct!" and that when he had described it longer all over again and I says to Jemmy "Well Jemmy what's it all about?" Jemmy says "He says the building was repaired in seventeen hundred and four, Gran."

Wherever that prowling young man formed his prowling habits I cannot be expected to know, but the way in which he went round the corner while we had our breakfasts and was there again when we swallowed the last crumb was most marvellous, and just the same at dinner and at night, prowling equally at the theatre and the inn gateway and the shop doors when we bought a trifle or two and everywhere else but troubled with a tendency to spit. And of Paris I can tell you no more my dear than that it's town and country both in one, and carved stone and long streets of high houses and gardens and fountains and statues and trees and gold, and immensely big soldiers and immensely little soldiers and the pleasantest nurses with the whitest caps a playing at skipping-rope with the bunchiest babies in the flattest caps, and clean table-cloths spread everywhere for dinner and people sitting out of doors smoking and sipping all day long and little plays being acted in the open air for little people and every shop a complete and elegant room, and everybody seeming to play at everything in this world. And as to the sparkling lights my dear after dark, glittering high up and low down and on before and on behind and all round, and the crowd of theatres and the crowd of people and the crowd of all sorts, it's pure enchantment. And pretty well the only thing that grated on me was that whether you pay your fare at the railway or whether you change your money at a money-dealer's or whether you take your ticket at the theatre, the lady or gentleman is caged up (I suppose by government) behind the strongest iron bars having more of a Zoological appearance than a free country.

Well to be sure when I did after all get my precious bones to bed that night, and my Young Rogue came in to kiss me and asks "What do you think of this lovely lovely Paris, Gran?" I says "Jemmy I feel as if it was beautiful fireworks being let off in my head." And very cool and refreshing the pleasant country was next day when we went on to look after my Legacy, and rested me much and did me a deal of good.

So at length and at last my dear we come to Sens, a pretty little town with a great two-towered cathedral and the rooks flying in and out of the loopholes and another tower atop of one of the towers like a sort of a stone pulpit. In which pulpit with the birds skimming below him if you'll believe me, I saw a speck while I was resting at the inn before dinner which they made signs to me was Jemmy and which really was. I had been a fancying as I sat in the balcony of the hotel that an Angel might light there and call down to the people to be good, but I little thought what Jemmy all unknown to himself was a calling down from that high place to some one in the town.

The pleasantest-situated inn my dear! Right under the two towers, with their shadows a changing upon it all day like a kind of a sundial, and country people driving in and out of the courtyard in carts and hooded cabriolets and such like, and a market outside in front of the cathedral, and all so quaint and like a picter. The Major and me agreed that whatever came of my Legacy this was the place to stay in for our holiday, and we also agreed that our dear boy had best not be checked in his joy that night by the sight of the Englishman if he was still alive, but that we would go together and alone. For you are to understand that the Major not feeling himself quite equal in his wind to the height to which Jemmy had climbed, had come back to me and left him with the Guide.

So after dinner when Jemmy had set off to see the river, the Major went down to the Mairie, and presently came back with a military character in a sword and spurs and a cocked hat and a yellow shoulder-belt and long tags about him that he must have found inconvenient. And the Major says "The Englishman still lies in the same state dearest madam. This gentleman will conduct us to his lodging." Upon which the military character pulled off his cocked hat to me, and I took notice that he had shaved his forehead in imitation of Napoleon Bonaparte but not like.

We wont out at the courtyard gate and past the great doors of the cathedral and down a narrow High-street where the people were sitting chatting at their shop doors and the children were at play. The military character went in front and he stopped at a pork-shop with a little statue of a pig sitting up, in the window, and a private door that a donkey was looking out of.

When the donkey saw the military character he came slipping out on the pavement to turn round and then clattered along the passage into a back yard. So the coast being clear, the Major and me were conducted up the common stair and into the front room on the second, a bare room with a red tiled floor and the outside lattice blinds pulled close to darken it. As the military character opened the blinds I saw the tower where I had seen Jemmy, darkening as the sun got low, and I turned to the bed by the wall and saw the Englishman.

It was some kind of brain fever he had had, and his hair was all gone, and some wetted folded linen lay upon his head. I looked at him very attentive as he lay there all wasted away with his eyes closed, and I says to the Major—

"I never saw this face before."

The Major looked at him very attentive too, and he says:

"*I* never saw this face before."

When the Major explained our words to the military character, that gentleman shrugged his shoulders and showed the Major the card on which it was written about the Legacy for me. It had been written with a weak and trembling hand in bed, and I knew no more of the writing than of the face. Neither did the Major.

Though lying there alone, the poor creetur was as well taken care of as could be hoped, and would have been quite unconscious of any one's sitting by him then. I got the Major to say that we were not going away at present and that I would come back to-morrow and watch a bit by the bedside. But I got him to add—and I shook my head hard to make it stronger—"We agree that we never saw this face before."

Our boy was greatly surprised when we told him sitting out in the balcony in the starlight, and he ran over some of those stories of former Lodgers, of the Major's putting down, and asked wasn't it possible that it might be this lodger or that lodger. It was not possible, and we went to bed.

In the morning just at breakfast-time the military character came jingling round, and said that the doctor thought from the signs he saw there might be some rally before the end. So I says to the Major and Jemmy, "You two boys go and enjoy yourselves, and I'll take my Prayer Book and go sit by the bed." So I went, and I sat there some hours, reading a prayer for him poor soul now and then, and it was quite on in the day when he moved his hand.

He had been so still, that the moment he moved I knew of it, and I pulled off my spectacles and laid down my book and rose and looked at him. From moving one hand he began to move both, and then his action was the action of a person groping in the dark. Long after his eyes had opened, there was a film over them and he still felt for his way out into light. But by slow degrees his sight cleared and his hands stopped. He saw the ceiling, he saw the wall, he saw me. As his sight cleared, mine cleared too, and when at last we looked in one another's faces, I started back, and I cries passionately:

"O you wicked wicked man! Your sin has found you out!"

For I knew him, the moment life looked out of his eyes, to be Mr. Edson, Jemmy's father who had so cruelly deserted Jemmy's young unmarried mother who had died in my arms, poor tender creetur, and left Jemmy to me.

"You cruel wicked man! You bad black traitor!"

With the little strength he had, he made an attempt to turn over on his wretched face to hide it. His arm dropped out of the bed and his head with it, and there he lay before me crushed in body and in mind. Surely the miserablest sight under the summer sun!

"O blessed Heaven," I says a crying, "teach me what to say to this broken mortal! I am a poor sinful creetur, and the Judgment is not mine."

As I lifted my eyes up to the clear bright sky, I saw the high tower where Jemmy had stood above the birds, seeing that very window; and the last look of that poor pretty young mother when her soul brightened and got free, seemed to shine down from it.

"O man, man, man!" I says, and I went on my knees beside the bed; "if your heart is rent asunder and you are truly penitent for what you did, Our Saviour will have mercy on you yet!"

As I leaned my face against the bed, his feeble hand could just move itself enough to touch me. I hope the touch was penitent. It tried to hold my dress and keep hold, but the fingers were too weak to close.

I lifted him back upon the pillows and I says to him:

"Can you hear me?"

He looked yes.

"Do you know me?"

He looked yes, even yet more plainly.

"I am not here alone. The Major is with me. You recollect the Major?"

Yes. That is to say he made out yes, in the same way as before.

"And even the Major and I are not alone. My grandson—his godson—is with us. Do you hear? My grandson."

The fingers made another trial to catch my sleeve, but could only creep near it and fall.

"Do you know who my grandson is?"

Yes.

"I pitied and loved his lonely mother. When his mother lay a dying I said to her, 'My dear, this baby is sent to a childless old woman.' He has been my pride and joy ever since. I love him as dearly as if he had drunk from my breast. Do you ask to see my grandson before you die?"

Yes.

"Show me, when I leave off speaking, if you correctly understand what I say. He has been kept unacquainted with the story of his birth. He has no knowledge of it. No suspicion of it. If I bring him here to the side of this bed, he will suppose you to be a perfect stranger. It is more than I can do to keep from him the knowledge that there is such wrong and misery in the world; but that it was ever so near him in his innocent cradle I have kept from him, and I do keep from him, and I ever will keep from him, for his mother's sake, and for his own."

He showed me that he distinctly understood, and the tears fell from his eyes.

"Now rest, and you shall see him."

So I got him a little wine and some brandy, and I put things straight about his bed. But I began to be troubled in my mind lest Jemmy and the Major might be too long of coming back. What with this occupation for my thoughts and hands, I didn't hear a foot upon the stairs, and was startled when I saw the Major stopped short in the middle of the room by the eyes of the man upon the bed, and knowing him then, as I had known him a little while ago.

There was anger in the Major's face, and there was horror and repugnance and I don't know what. So I went up to him and I led him to the bedside, and when I clasped my hands and lifted of them up, the Major did the like.

"O Lord" I says "Thou knowest what we two saw together of the sufferings and sorrows of that young creetur now with Thee. If this dying man is truly penitent, we two together humbly pray Thee to have mercy on him!"

The Major says "Amen!" and then after a little stop I whispers him, "Dear old friend fetch our beloved boy." And the Major, so clever as to have got to understand it all without being told a word, went away and brought him.

Never never never shall I forget the fair bright face of our boy when he stood at the foot of the bed, looking at his unknown father. And O so like his dear young mother then!

"Jemmy" I says, "I have found out all about this poor gentleman who is so ill, and he did lodge in the old house once. And as he wants to see all belonging to it, now that he is passing away, I sent for you."

"Ah poor man!" says Jemmy stepping forward and touching one of his hands with great gentleness. "My heart melts for him. Poor, poor man!"

The eyes that were so soon to close for ever turned to me, and I was not that strong in the pride of my strength that I could resist them.

"My darling boy, there is a reason in the secret history of this fellow-creetur lying as the best and worst of us must all lie one day, which I think would ease his spirit in his last hour if you would lay your cheek against his forehead and say, 'May God forgive you!'"

"O Gran," says Jemmy with a full heart, "I am not worthy!" But he leaned down and did it. Then the faltering fingers made out to catch hold of my sleeve at last, and I believe he was a-trying to kiss me when he died.

There my dear! There you have the story of my Legacy in full, and it's worth ten times the trouble I have spent upon it if you are pleased to like it.

You might suppose that it set us against the little French town of Sens, but no we didn't find that. I found myself that I never looked up at the high tower atop of the other tower, but the days came back again when that fair young creetur with her pretty bright hair trusted in me like a mother, and the recollection made the place so peaceful to me as I can't express. And every soul about the hotel down to the pigeons in the courtyard made friends with Jemmy and the Major, and went lumbering away with them on all sorts of expeditions in all sorts of vehicles drawn by rampagious cart-horses,—with heads and without,—mud for paint and ropes for harness,—and every new friend dressed in blue like a butcher, and every new horse standing on his hind legs wanting to devour and consume every other horse, and every man that had a whip to crack crack-crack-crack-crack-cracking it as if it was a schoolboy with his first. As to the Major my dear that man lived the greater part of his time with a little tumbler in one hand and a bottle of small wine in the other, and whenever he saw anybody else with a little tumbler, no matter who it was,—the military character with the tags, or the inn-servants at their supper in the courtyard, or townspeople a chatting on a bench, or country people a starting home after market,—down rushes the Major to clink his glass against their glasses and cry,—Hola! Vive Somebody! or Vive Something! as if he was beside himself. And though I could not quite approve of the Major's doing it, still the ways of the world are the ways of the world varying according to the different parts of it, and dancing at all in the open Square with a lady that kept a barber's shop my opinion is that the Major was right to dance his best and to lead off with a power that I did not think was in him, though I was a little uneasy at the Barricading sound of the cries that were set up by the other dancers and the rest of the company, until when I says "What are they ever calling out Jemmy?" Jemmy says, "They're calling out Gran, Bravo the Military English! Bravo the Military English!" which was very gratifying to my feelings as a Briton and became the name the Major was known by.

But every evening at a regular time we all three sat out in the balcony of the hotel at the end of the courtyard, looking up at the golden and rosy light as it changed on the great towers, and looking at the shadows of the towers as they changed on all about us ourselves included, and what do you think we did there? My dear, if Jemmy hadn't brought some other of those stories of the Major's taking down from the telling of former lodgers at Eighty-one Norfolk Street, and if he didn't bring 'em out with this speech:

"Here you are Gran! Here you are godfather! More of 'em! I'll read. And though you wrote 'em for me, godfather, I know you won't disapprove of my making 'em over to Gran; will you?"

"No, my dear boy," says the Major. "Everything we have is hers, and we are hers."

"Hers ever affectionately and devotedly J. Jackman, and J. Jackman Lirriper," cries the Young Rogue giving me a close hug. "Very well then godfather. Look here. As Gran is in the Legacy way just now, I shall make these stories a part of Gran's Legacy. I'll leave 'em to her. What do you say godfather?"

"Hip hip Hurrah!" says the Major.

"Very well then," cries Jemmy all in a bustle. "Vive the Military English! Vive the Lady Lirriper! Vive the Jemmy Jackman Ditto! Vive the Legacy! Now, you look out, Gran. And you look out, godfather. *I*'ll read! And I'll tell you what I'll do besides. On the last night of our holiday here when we are all packed and going away, I'll top up with something of my own."

"Mind you do Sir" says I.

Chapter II

Mrs. Lirriper Relates How Jemmy Topped Up

Well my dear and so the evening readings of those jottings of the Major's brought us round at last to the evening when we were all packed and going away next day, and I do assure you that by that time though it was deliciously comfortable to look forward to the dear old house in Norfolk-street again, I had formed quite a high opinion of the French nation and had noticed them to be much more homely and domestic in their families and far more simple and amiable in their lives than I had ever been led to expect, and it did strike me between ourselves that in one particular they might be imitated to advantage by another nation which I will not mention, and that is in the courage with which they take their little enjoyments on little means and with little things and don't let solemn big-wigs stare them out of countenance or speechify them dull, of which said solemn big-wigs I have ever had the one opinion that I wish they were all made comfortable separately in coppers with the lids on and never let out any more.

"Now young man," I says to Jemmy when we brought our chairs into the balcony that last evening, "you please to remember who was to 'top up.'"

"All right Gran" says Jemmy. "I am the illustrious personage."

But he looked so serious after he had made me that light answer, that the Major raised his eyebrows at me and I raised mine at the Major.

"Gran and godfather," says Jemmy, "you can hardly think how much my mind has run on Mr. Edson's death."

It gave me a little check. "Ah! it was a sad scene my love" I says, "and sad remembrances come back stronger than merry. But this" I says after a little silence, to rouse myself and the Major and Jemmy all together, "is not topping up. Tell us your story my dear."

"I will" says Jemmy.

"What is the date Sir?" says I. "Once upon a time when pigs drank wine?"

"No Gran," says Jemmy, still serious; "once upon a time when the French drank wine."

Again I glanced at the Major, and the Major glanced at me.

"In short, Gran and godfather," says Jemmy, looking up, "the date is this time, and I'm going to tell you Mr. Edson's story."

The flutter that it threw me into. The change of colour on the part of the Major!

"That is to say, you understand," our bright-eyed boy says, "I am going to give you my version of it. I shall not ask whether it's right or not, firstly because you said you knew very little about it, Gran, and secondly because what little you did know was a secret."

I folded my hands in my lap and I never took my eyes off Jemmy as he went running on.

"The unfortunate gentleman" Jemmy commences, "who is the subject of our present narrative was the son of Somebody, and was born Somewhere, and chose a profession Somehow. It is not with those parts of his career that we have to deal; but with his early attachment to a young and beautiful lady."

I thought I should have dropped. I durstn't look at the Major; but I know what his state was, without looking at him.

"The father of our ill-starred hero" says Jemmy, copying as it seemed to me the style of some of his story-books, "was a worldly man who entertained ambitious views for his only son and who firmly set his face against the contemplated alliance with a virtuous but penniless orphan. Indeed he went so far as roundly to assure our hero that unless he weaned his thoughts from the object of his devoted affection, he would disinherit him. At the same time, he proposed as a suitable match the daughter of a neighbouring gentleman of a good estate, who was neither ill-favoured nor unamiable, and whose eligibility in a pecuniary point of view could not be disputed. But young Mr. Edson, true to the first and only love that had inflamed his breast, rejected all considerations of self-advancement, and, deprecating his father's anger in a respectful letter, ran away with her."

My dear I had begun to take a turn for the better, but when it come to running away I began to take another turn for the worse.

"The lovers" says Jemmy "fled to London and were united at the altar of Saint Clement's Danes. And it is at this period of their simple but touching story that we find them inmates of the dwelling of a highly-respected and beloved lady of the name of Gran, residing within a hundred miles of Norfolk-street."

I felt that we were almost safe now, I felt that the dear boy had no suspicion of the bitter truth, and I looked at the Major for the first time and drew a long breath. The Major gave me a nod.

"Our hero's father" Jemmy goes on "proving implacable and carrying his threat into unrelenting execution, the struggles of the young couple in London were severe, and would have been far more so, but for their good angel's having conducted them to the abode of Mrs. Gran; who, divining their poverty (in spite of their endeavours to conceal it from her), by a thousand delicate arts smoothed their rough way, and alleviated the sharpness of their first distress."

Here Jemmy took one of my hands in one of his, and began a marking the turns of his story by making me give a beat from time to time upon his other hand.

"After a while, they left the house of Mrs. Gran, and pursued their fortunes through a variety of successes and failures elsewhere. But in all reverses, whether for good or evil, the words of Mr. Edson to the fair young partner of his life were, 'Unchanging Love and Truth will carry us through all!'"

My hand trembled in the dear boy's, those words were so wofully unlike the fact.

"Unchanging Love and Truth" says Jemmy over again, as if he had a proud kind of a noble pleasure in it, "will carry us through all! Those were his words. And so they fought their way, poor but gallant and happy, until Mrs. Edson gave birth to a child."

"A daughter," I says.

"No," says Jemmy, "a son. And the father was so proud of it that he could hardly bear it out of his sight. But a dark cloud overspread the scene. Mrs. Edson sickened, drooped, and died."

"Ah! Sickened, drooped, and died!" I says.

"And so Mr. Edson's only comfort, only hope on earth, and only stimulus to action, was his darling boy. As the child grew older, he grew so like his mother that he was her living picture. It used to make him wonder why his father cried when he kissed him. But unhappily he was like his mother in constitution as well as in face, and lo, died too before he had grown out of childhood. Then Mr. Edson, who had good abilities, in his forlornness and despair, threw them all to the winds. He became apathetic, reckless, lost. Little by little he sank down, down, down, down, until at last he almost lived (I think) by gaming. And so sickness overtook him in the town of Sens in France, and he lay down to die. But now that he laid him down when all was done, and looked back upon the green Past beyond the time when he had covered it with ashes, he thought gratefully of the good Mrs. Gran long lost sight of, who had been so kind to him and his young wife in the early days of their marriage, and he left the little that he had as a last Legacy to her. And she, being brought to see him, at first no more knew him than she would know from seeing the ruin of a Greek or Roman Temple, what it used to be before it fell; but at length she remembered him. And then he told her, with tears, of his regret for the misspent part of his life, and besought her to think as mildly of it as she could, because it was the poor fallen Angel of his unchanging Love and Constancy after all. And because she had her grandson with her, and he fancied that his own boy, if he had lived, might have grown to be something like him, he asked her to let him touch his forehead with his cheek and say certain parting words."

Jemmy's voice sank low when it got to that, and tears filled my eyes, and filled the Major's.

"You little Conjurer" I says, "how did you ever make it all out? Go in and write it every word down, for it's a wonder."

Which Jemmy did, and I have repeated it to you my dear from his writing.

Then the Major took my hand and kissed it, and said, "Dearest madam all has prospered with us."

"Ah Major" I says drying my eyes, "we needn't have been afraid. We might have known it. Treachery don't come natural to beaming youth; but trust and pity, love and constancy,—they do, thank God!"

Doctor Marigold

IN THREE CHAPTERS

Chapter I

To Be Taken Immediately

I AM A CHEAP JACK, AND MY OWN FATHER'S NAME WAS WILLUM MARIGOLD. It was in his lifetime supposed by some that his name was William, but my own father always consistently said, No, it was Willum. On which point I content myself with looking at the argument this way: If a man is not allowed to know his own name in a free country, how much is he allowed to know in a land of slavery? As to looking at the argument through the medium of the Register, Willum Marigold come into the world before Registers come up much,—and went out of it too. They wouldn't have been greatly in his line neither, if they had chanced to come up before him.

I was born on the Queen's highway, but it was the King's at that time. A doctor was fetched to my own mother by my own father, when it took place on a common; and in consequence of his being a very kind gentleman, and accepting no fee but a tea-tray, I was named Doctor, out of gratitude and compliment to him. There you have me. Doctor Marigold.

I am at present a middle-aged man of a broadish build, in cords, leggings, and a sleeved waistcoat the strings of which is always gone behind. Repair them how you will, they go like fiddle-strings. You have been to the theatre, and you have seen one of the wiolin-players screw up his wiolin, after listening to it as if it had been whispering the secret to him that it feared it was out of order, and then you have heard it snap. That's as exactly similar to my waistcoat as a waistcoat and a wiolin can be like one another.

I am partial to a white hat, and I like a shawl round my neck wore loose and easy. Sitting down is my favourite posture. If I have a taste in point of personal jewelry, it is mother-of-pearl buttons. There you have me again, as large as life.

The doctor having accepted a tea-tray, you'll guess that my father was a Cheap Jack before me. You are right. He was. It was a pretty tray. It represented a large lady going along a serpentining up-hill gravel-walk, to attend a little church. Two swans had likewise come astray with the same intentions. When I call her a large lady, I don't mean in point of breadth, for there she fell below my views, but she more than made it up in heighth; her heighth and slimness was—in short THE heighth of both.

I often saw that tray, after I was the innocently smiling cause (or more likely screeching one) of the doctor's standing it up on a table against the wall in his consulting-room. Whenever my own father and mother were in that part of the country, I used to put my head (I have heard my own mother say it was flaxen curls at that time, though you wouldn't know an old hearth-broom from it now till you come to the handle, and found it wasn't me) in at the doctor's door, and the doctor was always glad to see me, and said, "Aha, my brother practitioner! Come in, little M.D. How are your inclinations as to sixpence?"

You can't go on for ever, you'll find, nor yet could my father nor yet my mother. If you don't go off as a whole when you are about due, you're liable to go off in part, and two to one your head's the part. Gradually my father went off his, and my mother went off hers. It was in a harmless way, but it put out the family where I boarded them. The old couple, though retired, got to be wholly and solely devoted to the Cheap Jack business, and were always selling the family off. Whenever the cloth was laid for dinner, my father began rattling the plates and dishes, as we do in our line when we put up crockery for a bid, only he had lost the trick of it, and mostly let 'em drop and broke 'em. As the old lady had been used to sit in the cart, and hand the articles out one by one to the old gentleman on the footboard to sell, just in the same way she handed him every item of the family's property, and they disposed of it in their own imaginations from morning to night. At last the old gentleman, lying bedridden in the same room with the old lady, cries out in the old patter, fluent, after having been silent for two days and nights: "Now here, my jolly companions every one,—which the Nightingale club in a village was held, At the sign of the Cabbage and Shears, Where the singers no doubt would have greatly excelled, But for want of taste, voices and ears,—now, here, my jolly companions, every one, is a working model of a used-up old Cheap Jack, without a tooth in his head, and with a pain in every bone: so like life that it would be just as good if it wasn't better, just as bad if it wasn't worse, and just as new if it wasn't worn out. Bid for the working model of the old Cheap Jack, who has drunk more gunpowder-tea with the ladies in his time than would blow the lid off a washerwoman's copper, and carry it as many thousands of miles higher than the moon as naught nix naught, divided by the national debt, carry nothing to the poor-rates, three under, and two over. Now, my hearts of oak and men of straw, what do you say for the lot? Two shillings, a shilling, tenpence, eightpence, sixpence, fourpence. Twopence? Who said twopence? The gentleman in the scarecrow's hat? I am ashamed of the gentleman in the scarecrow's hat. I really am ashamed of him for his want of public spirit. Now I'll tell you what I'll do with you. Come! I'll throw you in a working model of a old woman that was married to the old Cheap Jack so long ago that upon my word and honour it took place in Noah's Ark, before the Unicorn could get in to forbid the banns by blowing a tune upon his horn. There now! Come! What do you say for both? I'll tell you what I'll do with you. I don't bear you malice for being so backward. Here! If you make me a bid that'll only reflect a little credit on your town, I'll throw you in a warming-pan for nothing, and lend you a toasting-fork for life. Now come; what do you say after that splendid offer? Say two pound, say thirty shillings, say a pound, say ten shillings, say five, say two and six? You don't say even two and six? You say two and three? No. You shan't have the lot for two and three. I'd sooner give it to you, if you was good-looking enough. Here! Missis! Chuck the old man and woman into the cart, put the horse to, and drive 'em away and bury 'em!" Such were the last words of Willum Marigold, my own father, and they were carried out, by him and by his wife, my own mother, on one and the same day, as I ought to know, having followed as mourner.

My father had been a lovely one in his time at the Cheap Jack work, as his dying observations went to prove. But I top him. I don't say it because it's myself, but because it has been universally acknowledged by all that has had the means of comparison. I have worked at it. I have measured myself against other public speakers,—Members of Parliament, Platforms, Pulpits, Counsel learned in the law,—and where I have found 'em good, I have took a bit of imagination from 'em, and where I have found 'em bad, I have let 'em alone. Now I'll tell you what. I mean to go down into my grave declaring that of all the callings ill used in Great Britain, the Cheap Jack calling is the worst used. Why ain't we a profession? Why ain't we endowed with privileges? Why are we forced to take out a hawker's license, when no such thing is expected of the political hawkers? Where's the difference betwixt us? Except that we are Cheap Jacks and they are Dear Jacks, *I* don't see any difference but what's in our favour.

For look here! Say it's election time. I am on the footboard of my cart in the market-place, on a Saturday night. I put up a general miscellaneous lot. I say: "Now here, my free and independent woters, I'm a going to give you such a chance as you never had in all your born days, nor yet the days preceding. Now I'll show you what I am a going to do with you. Here's a pair of razors that'll shave you closer than the Board of Guardians; here's a flat-iron worth its weight in gold; here's a frying-pan artificially flavoured with essence of beefsteaks to that degree that you've only got for the rest of your lives to fry bread and dripping in it and there you are replete with animal food; here's a genuine chronometer watch in such a solid silver case that you may knock at the door with it when you come home late from a social meeting, and rouse your wife and family, and save up your knocker for the postman; and here's half-a-dozen dinner plates that you may play the cymbals with to charm baby when it's fractious. Stop! I'll throw in another article, and I'll give you that, and it's a rolling-pin; and if the baby can only get it well into its mouth when its teeth is coming and rub the gums once with it, they'll come through double, in a fit of laughter equal to being tickled. Stop again! I'll throw you in another article, because I don't like the looks of you, for you haven't the appearance of buyers unless I lose by you, and because I'd rather lose than not take money to-night, and that's a looking-glass in which you may see how ugly you look when you don't bid. What do you say now? Come! Do you say a pound? Not you, for you haven't got it. Do you say ten shillings? Not you, for you owe more to the tallyman. Well then, I'll tell you what I'll do with you. I'll heap 'em all on the footboard of the cart,—there they are! razors, flat watch, dinner plates, rolling-pin, and away for four shillings, and I'll give you sixpence for your trouble!" This is me, the Cheap Jack. But on the Monday morning, in the same market-place, comes the Dear Jack on the hustings—*his* cart—and, what does *he* say? "Now my free and independent woters, I am a going to give you such a chance" (he begins just like me) "as you never had in all your born days, and that's the chance of sending Myself to Parliament. Now I'll tell you what I am a going to do for you. Here's the interests of this magnificent town promoted above all the rest of the civilised and uncivilised earth. Here's your railways carried, and your neighbours' railways jockeyed. Here's all your sons in the Post-office. Here's Britannia smiling on you. Here's the eyes of Europe on you. Here's uniwersal prosperity for you, repletion of animal food, golden cornfields, gladsome homesteads, and rounds of applause from your own hearts, all in one lot, and that's myself. Will you take me as I stand? You won't? Well, then, I'll tell you what I'll do with you. Come now! I'll throw you in anything you ask for. There! Church-rates, abolition of church-rates, more malt tax, no malt tax, uniwersal education to the highest mark, or uniwersal ignorance to the lowest, total abolition of flogging in the army or a dozen for every private once a month all round, Wrongs of Men or Rights of Women—only say which it shall be, take 'em or leave 'em, and I'm of your opinion altogether, and the lot's your own on your own terms. There! You won't take it yet! Well, then, I'll tell you what I'll do with you. Come! You *are* such free and independent woters, and I *am* so proud of you,—you *are* such a noble and enlightened constituency, and I *am* so ambitious of the honour and dignity of being your member, which is by far the highest level to which the wings of the human mind can soar,—that I'll tell you what I'll do with you. I'll throw you in all the public-houses in your magnificent town for nothing. Will that content you? It won't? You won't take the lot yet? Well, then, before I put the horse in and drive away, and make the offer to the next most magnificent town that can be discovered, I'll tell you what I'll do. Take the lot, and I'll drop two thousand pound in the streets of your magnificent town for them to pick up that can. Not enough? Now look here. This is the very furthest that I'm a going to. I'll make it two thousand five hundred. And still you won't? Here, missis! Put the horse—no, stop half a moment, I shouldn't like to turn my back upon you neither for a trifle, I'll make it two thousand seven hundred and fifty pound. There! Take the lot on your own terms, and I'll count out two thousand seven hundred and fifty pound on the footboard of the cart, to be dropped in the streets of your magnificent town for them to pick up that can. What do you say? Come now! You won't do better, and you may do worse. You take it? Hooray! Sold again, and got the seat!"

These Dear Jacks soap the people shameful, but we Cheap Jacks don't. We tell 'em the truth about themselves to their faces, and scorn to court 'em. As to wenturesomeness in the way of puffing up the lots, the Dear Jacks beat us hollow. It is considered in the Cheap Jack calling, that better patter can be made out of a gun than any article we put up from the cart, except a pair of spectacles. I often hold forth about a gun for a quarter of an hour, and feel as if I need never leave off. But when I tell 'em what the gun can do, and what the gun has brought down, I never go half so far as the Dear Jacks do when they make speeches in praise of *their* guns—their great guns that set 'em on to do it. Besides, I'm in business for myself: I ain't sent down into the market-place to order, as they are. Besides, again, my guns don't know what I say in their laudation, and their guns do, and the whole concern of 'em have reason to be sick and ashamed all round. These are some of my arguments for declaring that the Cheap Jack calling is treated ill in Great Britain, and for turning warm when I think of the other Jacks in question setting themselves up to pretend to look down upon it.

I courted my wife from the footboard of the cart. I did indeed. She was a Suffolk young woman, and it was in Ipswich market-place right opposite the corn-chandler's shop. I had noticed her up at a window last Saturday that was, appreciating highly. I had took to her, and I had said to myself, "If not already disposed of, I'll have that lot." Next Saturday that come, I pitched the cart on the same pitch, and I was in very high feather indeed, keeping 'em laughing the whole of the time, and getting off the goods briskly. At last I took out of my waistcoat-pocket a small lot wrapped in soft paper, and I put it this way (looking up at the window where she was). "Now here, my blooming English maidens, is an article, the last article of the present evening's sale, which I offer to only you, the lovely Suffolk Dumplings biling over with beauty, and I won't take a bid of a thousand pounds for from any man alive. Now what is it? Why, I'll tell you what it is. It's made of fine gold, and it's not broke, though there's a hole in the middle of it, and it's stronger than any fetter that ever was forged, though it's smaller than any finger in my set of ten. Why ten? Because, when my parents made over my property to me, I tell you true, there was twelve sheets, twelve towels, twelve table-cloths, twelve knives, twelve forks, twelve tablespoons, and twelve teaspoons, but my set of fingers was two short of a dozen, and could never since be matched. Now what else is it? Come, I'll tell you. It's a hoop of solid gold, wrapped in a silver curl-paper, that I myself took off the shining locks of the ever beautiful old lady in Threadneedle-street, London city; I wouldn't tell you so if I hadn't the paper to show, or you mightn't believe it even of me. Now what else is it? It's a man-trap and a handcuff, the parish stocks and a leg-lock, all in gold and all in one. Now what else is it? It's a wedding-ring. Now I'll tell you what I'm a going to do with it. I'm not a going to offer this lot for money; but I mean to give it to the next of you beauties that laughs, and I'll pay her a visit to-morrow morning at exactly half after nine o'clock as the chimes go, and I'll take her out for a walk to put up the banns." *She* laughed, and got the ring handed up to her. When I called in the morning, she says, "O dear! It's never you, and you never mean it?" "It's ever me," says I, "and I am ever yours, and I ever mean it." So we got married, after being put up three times—which, by the bye, is quite in the Cheap Jack way again, and shows once more how the Cheap Jack customs pervade society.

She wasn't a bad wife, but she had a temper. If she could have parted with that one article at a sacrifice, I wouldn't have swopped her away in exchange for any other woman in England. Not that I ever did swop her away, for we lived together till she died, and that was thirteen year. Now, my lords and ladies and gentlefolks all, I'll let you into a secret, though you won't believe it. Thirteen year of temper in a Palace would try the worst of you, but thirteen year of temper in a Cart would try the best of you. You are kept so very close to it in a cart, you see. There's thousands of couples among you getting on like sweet ile upon a whetstone in houses five and six pairs of stairs high, that would go to the Divorce Court in a cart. Whether the jolting makes it worse, I don't undertake to decide; but in a cart it does come home to you, and stick to you. Wiolence in a cart is *so* wiolent, and aggrawation in a cart is *so* aggrawating.

We might have had such a pleasant life! A roomy cart, with the large goods hung outside, and the bed slung underneath it when on the road, an iron pot and a kettle, a fireplace for the cold weather, a chimney for the smoke, a hanging-shelf and a cupboard, a dog and a horse. What more do you want? You draw off upon a bit of turf in a green lane or by the roadside, you hobble your old horse and turn him grazing, you light your fire upon the ashes of the last visitors, you cook your stew, and you wouldn't call the Emperor of France your father. But have a temper in the cart, flinging language and the hardest goods in stock at you, and where are you then? Put a name to your feelings.

My dog knew as well when she was on the turn as I did. Before she broke out, he would give a howl, and bolt. How he knew it, was a mystery to me; but the sure and certain knowledge of it would wake him up out of his soundest sleep, and he would give a howl, and bolt. At such times I wished I was him.

The worst of it was, we had a daughter born to us, and I love children with all my heart. When she was in her furies she beat the child. This got to be so shocking, as the child got to be four or five year old, that I have many a time gone on with my whip over my shoulder, at the old horse's head, sobbing and crying worse than ever little Sophy did. For how could I prevent it? Such a thing is not to be tried with such a temper—in a cart—without coming to a fight. It's in the natural size and formation of a cart to bring it to a fight. And then the poor child got worse terrified than before, as well as worse hurt generally, and her mother made complaints to the next people we lighted on, and the word went round, "Here's a wretch of a Cheap Jack been a beating his wife."

Little Sophy was such a brave child! She grew to be quite devoted to her poor father, though he could do so little to help her. She had a wonderful quantity of shining dark hair, all curling natural about her. It is quite astonishing to me now, that I didn't go tearing mad when I used to see her run from her mother before the cart, and her mother catch her by this hair, and pull her down by it, and beat her.

Such a brave child I said she was! Ah! with reason.

"Don't you mind next time, father dear," she would whisper to me, with her little face still flushed, and her bright eyes still wet; "if I don't cry out, you may know I am not much hurt. And even if I do cry out, it will only be to get mother to let go and leave off." What I have seen the little spirit bear—for me—without crying out!

Yet in other respects her mother took great care of her. Her clothes were always clean and neat, and her mother was never tired of working at 'em. Such is the inconsistency in things. Our being down in the marsh country in unhealthy weather, I consider the cause of Sophy's taking bad low fever; but however she took it, once she got it she turned away from her mother for evermore, and nothing would persuade her to be touched by her mother's hand. She would shiver and say, "No, no, no," when it was offered at, and would hide her face on my shoulder, and hold me tighter round the neck.

The Cheap Jack business had been worse than ever I had known it, what with one thing and what with another (and not least with railroads, which will cut it all to pieces, I expect, at last), and I was run dry of money. For which reason, one night at that period of little Sophy's being so bad, either we must have come to a dead-lock for victuals and drink, or I must have pitched the cart as I did.

I couldn't get the dear child to lie down or leave go of me, and indeed I hadn't the heart to try, so I stepped out on the footboard with her holding round my neck. They all set up a laugh when they see us, and one chuckle-headed Joskin (that I hated for it) made the bidding, "Tuppence for her!"

"Now, you country boobies," says I, feeling as if my heart was a heavy weight at the end of a broken sashline, "I give you notice that I am a going to charm the money out of your pockets, and to give you so much more than your money's worth that you'll only persuade yourselves to draw your Saturday night's wages ever again arterwards by the hopes of meeting me to lay 'em out with, which you never will, and why not? Because I've made my fortunes by selling my goods on a large scale for seventy-five per cent. less than I give for 'em, and I am consequently to be elevated to the House of Peers next week, by the title of the Duke of Cheap and Markis Jackaloorul. Now let's know what you want to-night, and you shall have it. But first of all, shall I tell you why I have got this little girl round my neck? You don't want to know? Then you shall. She belongs to the Fairies. She's a fortune-teller. She can tell me all about you in a whisper, and can put me up to whether you're going to buy a lot or leave it. Now do you want a saw? No, she says you don't, because you're too clumsy to use one. Else here's a saw which would be a lifelong blessing to a handy man, at four shillings, at three and six, at three, at two and six, at two, at eighteen-pence. But none of you shall have it at any price, on account of your well-known awkwardness, which would make it manslaughter. The same objection applies to this set of three planes which I won't let you have neither, so don't bid for 'em. Now I am a going to ask her what you do want." (Then I whispered, "Your head burns so, that I am afraid it hurts you bad, my pet," and she answered, without opening her heavy eyes, "Just a little, father.") "O! This little fortune-teller says it's a memorandum-book you want. Then why didn't you mention it? Here it is. Look at it. Two hundred superfine hot-pressed wire-wove pages—if you don't believe me, count 'em—ready ruled for your expenses, an everlastingly pointed pencil to put 'em down with, a double-bladed penknife to scratch 'em out with, a book of printed tables to calculate your income with, and a camp-stool to sit down upon while you give your mind to it! Stop! And an umbrella to keep the moon off when you give your mind to it on a pitch-dark night. Now I won't ask you how much for the lot, but how little? How little are you thinking of? Don't be ashamed to mention it, because my fortune-teller knows already." (Then making believe to whisper, I kissed her, and she kissed me.) "Why, she says you are thinking of as little as three and threepence! I couldn't have believed it, even of you, unless she told me. Three and threepence! And a set of printed tables in the lot that'll calculate your income up to forty thousand a year! With an income of forty thousand a year, you grudge three and sixpence. Well then, I'll tell you my opinion. I so despise the threepence, that I'd sooner take three shillings. There. For three shillings, three shillings, three shillings! Gone. Hand 'em over to the lucky man."

As there had been no bid at all, everybody looked about and grinned at everybody, while I touched little Sophy's face and asked her if she felt faint, or giddy. "Not very, father. It will soon be over." Then turning from the pretty patient eyes, which were opened now, and seeing nothing but grins across my lighted grease-pot, I went on again in my Cheap Jack style. "Where's the butcher?" (My sorrowful eye had just caught sight of a fat young butcher on the outside of the crowd.) "She says the good luck is the butcher's. Where is he?" Everybody handed on the blushing butcher to the front, and there was a roar, and the butcher felt himself obliged to put his hand in his pocket, and take the lot. The party so picked out, in general, does feel obliged to take the lot—good four times out of six. Then we had another lot, the counterpart of that one, and sold it sixpence cheaper, which is always wery much enjoyed. Then we had the spectacles. It ain't a special profitable lot, but I put 'em on, and I see what the Chancellor of the Exchequer is going to take off the taxes, and I see what the sweetheart of the young woman in the shawl is doing at home, and I see what the Bishops has got for dinner, and a deal more that seldom fails to fetch 'em 'up in their spirits; and the better their spirits, the better their bids. Then we had the ladies' lot—the teapot, tea-caddy, glass sugar-basin, half-a-dozen spoons, and caudle-cup—and all the time I was making similar excuses to give a look or two and say a word or two to my poor child. It was while the second ladies' lot was holding 'em enchained that I felt her lift herself a little on my shoulder, to look across the dark street. "What troubles you, darling?" "Nothing troubles me, father. I am not at all troubled. But don't I see a pretty churchyard over there?" "Yes, my dear." "Kiss me twice, dear father, and lay me down to rest upon that churchyard grass so soft and green." I staggered back into the cart with her head dropped on my shoulder, and I says to her mother, "Quick. Shut the door! Don't let those laughing people see!" "What's the matter?" she cries. "O woman, woman," I tells her, "you'll never catch my little Sophy by her hair again, for she has flown away from you!"

Maybe those were harder words than I meant 'em; but from that time forth my wife took to brooding, and would sit in the cart or walk beside it, hours at a stretch, with her arms crossed, and her eyes looking on the ground. When her furies took her (which was rather seldomer than before) they took her in a new way, and she banged herself about to that extent that I was forced to hold her. She got none the better for a little drink now and then, and through some years I used to wonder, as I plodded along at the old horse's head, whether there was many carts upon the road that held so much dreariness as mine, for all my being looked up to as the King of the Cheap Jacks. So sad our lives went on till one summer evening, when, as we were coming into Exeter, out of the farther West of England, we saw a woman beating a child in a cruel manner, who screamed, "Don't beat me! O mother, mother, mother!" Then my wife stopped her ears, and ran away like a wild thing, and next day she was found in the river.

Me and my dog were all the company left in the cart now; and the dog learned to give a short bark when they wouldn't bid, and to give another and a nod of his head when I asked him, "Who said half a crown? Are you the gentleman, sir, that offered half a crown?" He attained to an immense height of popularity, and I shall always believe taught himself entirely out of his own head to growl at any person in the crowd that bid as low as sixpence. But he got to be well on in years, and one night when I was conwulsing York with the spectacles, he took a conwulsion on his own account upon the very footboard by me, and it finished him.

Being naturally of a tender turn, I had dreadful lonely feelings on me arter this. I conquered 'em at selling times, having a reputation to keep (not to mention keeping myself), but they got me down in private, and rolled upon me. That's often the way with us public characters. See us on the footboard, and you'd give pretty well anything you possess to be us. See us off the footboard, and you'd add a trifle to be off your bargain. It was under those circumstances that I come acquainted with a giant. I might have been too high to fall into conversation with him, had it not been for my lonely feelings. For the general rule is, going round the country, to draw the line at dressing up. When a man can't trust his getting a living to his undisguised abilities, you consider him below your sort. And this giant when on view figured as a Roman.

He was a languid young man, which I attribute to the distance betwixt his extremities. He had a little head and less in it, he had weak eyes and weak knees, and altogether you couldn't look at him without feeling that there was greatly too much of him both for his joints and his mind. But he was an amiable though timid young man (his mother let him out, and spent the money), and we come acquainted when he was walking to ease the horse betwixt two fairs. He was called Rinaldo di Velasco, his name being Pickleson.

This giant, otherwise Pickleson, mentioned to me under the seal of confidence that, beyond his being a burden to himself, his life was made a burden to him by the cruelty of his master towards a step-daughter who was deaf and dumb. Her mother was dead, and she had no living soul to take her part, and was used most hard. She travelled with his master's caravan only because there was nowhere to leave her, and this giant, otherwise Pickleson, did go so far as to believe that his master often tried to lose her. He was such a very languid young man, that I don't know how long it didn't take him to get this story out, but it passed through his defective circulation to his top extremity in course of time.

When I heard this account from the giant, otherwise Pickleson, and likewise that the poor girl had beautiful long dark hair, and was often pulled down by it and beaten, I couldn't see the giant through what stood in my eyes. Having wiped 'em, I give him sixpence (for he was kept as short as he was long), and he laid it out in two three-penn'orths of gin-and-water, which so brisked him up, that he sang the Favourite Comic of Shivery Shakey, ain't it cold?—a popular effect which his master had tried every other means to get out of him as a Roman wholly in vain.

His master's name was Mim, a wery hoarse man, and I knew him to speak to. I went to that Fair as a mere civilian, leaving the cart outside the town, and I looked about the back of the Vans while the performing was going on, and at last, sitting dozing against a muddy cart-wheel, I come upon the poor girl who was deaf and dumb. At the first look I might almost have judged that she had escaped from the Wild Beast Show; but at the second I thought better of her, and thought that if she was more cared for and more kindly used she would be like my child. She was just the same age that my own daughter would have been, if her pretty head had not fell down upon my shoulder that unfortunate night.

To cut it short, I spoke confidential to Mim while he was beating the gong outside betwixt two lots of Pickleson's publics, and I put it to him, "She lies heavy on your own hands; what'll you take for her?" Mim was a most ferocious swearer. Suppressing that part of his reply which was much the longest part, his reply was, "A pair of braces." "Now I'll tell you," says I, "what I'm a going to do with you. I'm a going to fetch you half-a-dozen pair of the primest braces in the cart, and then to take her away with me." Says Mim (again ferocious), "I'll believe it when I've got the goods, and no sooner." I made all the haste I could, lest he should think twice of it, and the bargain was completed, which Pickleson he was thereby so relieved in his mind that he come out at his little back door, longways like a serpent, and give us Shivery Shakey in a whisper among the wheels at parting.

It was happy days for both of us when Sophy and me began to travel in the cart. I at once give her the name of Sophy, to put her ever towards me in the attitude of my own daughter. We soon made out to begin to understand one another, through the goodness of the Heavens, when she knowed that I meant true and kind by her. In a very little time she was wonderful fond of me. You have no idea what it is to have anybody wonderful fond of you, unless you have been got down and rolled upon by the lonely feelings that I have mentioned as having once got the better of me.

You'd have laughed—or the rewerse—it's according to your disposition—if you could have seen me trying to teach Sophy. At first I was helped—you'd never guess by what—milestones. I got some large alphabets in a box, all the letters separate on bits of bone, and saying we was going to Windsor, I give her those letters in that order, and then at every milestone I showed her those same letters in that same order again, and pointed towards the abode of royalty. Another time I give her CART, and then chalked the same upon the cart. Another time I give her DOCTOR MARIGOLD, and hung a corresponding inscription outside my waistcoat. People that met us might stare a bit and laugh, but what did *I* care, if she caught the idea? She caught it after long patience and trouble, and then we did begin to get on swimmingly, I believe you! At first she was a little given to consider me the cart, and the cart the abode of royalty, but that soon wore off.

We had our signs, too, and they was hundreds in number. Sometimes she would sit looking at me and considering hard how to communicate with me about something fresh,—how to ask me what she wanted explained,—and then she was (or I thought she was; what does it signify?) so like my child with those years added to her, that I half-believed it was herself, trying to tell me where she had been to up in the skies, and what she had seen since that unhappy night when she flied away. She had a pretty face, and now that there was no one to drag at her bright dark hair, and it was all in order, there was a something touching in her looks that made the cart most peaceful and most quiet, though not at all melancholy. [N.B. In the Cheap Jack patter, we generally sound it lemonjolly, and it gets a laugh.]

The way she learnt to understand any look of mine was truly surprising. When I sold of a night, she would sit in the cart unseen by them outside, and would give a eager look into my eyes when I looked in, and would hand me straight the precise article or articles I wanted. And then she would clap her hands, and laugh for joy. And as for me, seeing her so bright, and remembering what she was when I first lighted on her, starved and beaten and ragged, leaning asleep against the muddy cart-wheel, it give me such heart that I gained a greater heighth of reputation than ever, and I put Pickleson down (by the name of Mim's Travelling Giant otherwise Pickleson) for a fypunnote in my will.

This happiness went on in the cart till she was sixteen year old. By which time I began to feel not satisfied that I had done my whole duty by her, and to consider that she ought to have better teaching than I could give her. It drew a many tears on both sides when I commenced explaining my views to her; but what's right is right, and you can't neither by tears nor laughter do away with its character.

So I took her hand in mine, and I went with her one day to the Deaf and Dumb Establishment in London, and when the gentleman come to speak to us, I says to him: "Now I'll tell you what I'll do with you, Sir. I am nothing but a Cheap Jack, but of late years I have laid by for a rainy day notwithstanding. This is my only daughter (adopted), and you can't produce a deafer nor a dumber. Teach her the most that can be taught her in the shortest separation that can be named,—state the figure for it,—and I am game to put the money down. I won't bate you a single farthing, Sir, but I'll put down the money here and now, and I'll thankfully throw you in a pound to take it. There!" The gentleman smiled, and then, "Well, well," says he, "I must first know what she has learned already. How do you communicate with her?" Then I showed him, and she wrote in printed writing many names of things and so forth; and we held some sprightly conversation, Sophy and me, about a little story in a book which the gentleman showed her, and which she was able to read. "This is most extraordinary," says the gentleman; "is it possible that you have been her only teacher?" "I have been her only teacher, Sir," I says, "besides herself." "Then," says the gentleman, and more acceptable words was never spoke to me, "you're a clever fellow, and a good fellow." This he makes known to Sophy, who kisses his hands, claps her own, and laughs and cries upon it.

We saw the gentleman four times in all, and when he took down my name and asked how in the world it ever chanced to be Doctor, it come out that he was own nephew by the sister's side, if you'll believe me, to the very Doctor that I was called after. This made our footing still easier, and he says to me:

"Now, Marigold, tell me what more do you want your adopted daughter to know?"

"I want her, Sir, to be cut off from the world as little as can be, considering her deprivations, and therefore to be able to read whatever is wrote with perfect ease and pleasure."

"My good fellow," urges the gentleman, opening his eyes wide, "why *I* can't do that myself!"

I took his joke, and gave him a laugh (knowing by experience how flat you fall without it), and I mended my words accordingly.

"What do you mean to do with her afterwards?" asks the gentleman, with a sort of a doubtful eye. "To take her about the country?"

"In the cart, Sir, but only in the cart. She will live a private life, you understand, in the cart. I should never think of bringing her infirmities before the public. I wouldn't make a show of her for any money."

The gentleman nodded, and seemed to approve.

"Well," says he, "can you part with her for two years?"

"To do her that good,—yes, Sir."

"There's another question," says the gentleman, looking towards her,—"can she part with you for two years?"

I don't know that it was a harder matter of itself (for the other was hard enough to me), but it was harder to get over. However, she was pacified to it at last, and the separation betwixt us was settled. How it cut up both of us when it took place, and when I left her at the door in the dark of an evening, I don't tell. But I know this; remembering that night, I shall never pass that same establishment without a heart-ache and a swelling in the throat; and I couldn't put you up the best of lots in sight of it with my usual spirit,—no, not even the gun, nor the pair of spectacles,—for five hundred pound reward from the Secretary of State for the Home Department, and throw in the honour of putting my legs under his mahogany arterwards.

Still, the loneliness that followed in the cart was not the old loneliness, because there was a term put to it, however long to look forward to; and because I could think, when I was anyways down, that she belonged to me and I belonged to her. Always planning for her coming back, I bought in a few months' time another cart, and what do you think I planned to do with it? I'll tell you. I planned to fit it up with shelves and books for her reading, and to have a seat in it where I could sit and see her read, and think that I had been her first teacher. Not hurrying over the job, I had the fittings knocked together in contriving ways under my own inspection, and here was her bed in a berth with curtains, and there was her reading-table, and here was her writing-desk, and elsewhere was her books in rows upon rows, picters and no picters, bindings and no bindings, gilt-edged and plain, just as I could pick 'em up for her in lots up and down the country, North and South and West and East, Winds liked best and winds liked least, Here and there and gone astray, Over the hills and far away. And when I had got together pretty well as many books as the cart would neatly hold, a new scheme come into my head, which, as it turned out, kept my time and attention a good deal employed, and helped me over the two years' stile.

Without being of an awaricious temper, I like to be the owner of things. I shouldn't wish, for instance, to go partners with yourself in the Cheap Jack cart. It's not that I mistrust you, but that I'd rather know it was mine. Similarly, very likely you'd rather know it was yours. Well! A kind of a jealousy began to creep into my mind when I reflected that all those books would have been read by other people long before they was read by her. It seemed to take away from her being the owner of 'em like. In this way, the question got into my head: Couldn't I have a book new-made express for her, which she should be the first to read?

It pleased me, that thought did; and as I never was a man to let a thought sleep (you must wake up all the whole family of thoughts you've got and burn their night-caps, or you won't do in the Cheap Jack line), I set to work at it. Considering that I was in the habit of changing so much about the country, and that I should have to find out a literary character here to make a deal with, and another literary character there to make a deal with, as opportunities presented, I hit on the plan that this same book should be a general miscellaneous lot,—like the razors, flat-iron, chronometer watch, dinner plates, rolling-pin, and looking-glass,—and shouldn't be offered as a single indiwidual article, like the spectacles or the gun. When I had come to that conclusion, I come to another, which shall likewise be yours.

Often had I regretted that she never had heard me on the footboard, and that she never could hear me. It ain't that *I* am vain, but that *you* don't like to put your own light under a bushel. What's the worth of your reputation, if you can't convey the reason for it to the person you most wish to value it? Now I'll put it to you. Is it worth sixpence, fippence, fourpence, threepence, twopence, a penny, a halfpenny, a farthing? No, it ain't. Not worth a farthing. Very well, then. My conclusion was that I would begin her book with some account of myself. So that, through reading a specimen or two of me on the footboard, she might form an idea of my merits there. I was aware that I couldn't do myself justice. A man can't write his eye (at least *I* don't know how to), nor yet can a man write his voice, nor the rate of his talk, nor the quickness of his action, nor his general spicy way. But he can write his turns of speech, when he is a public speaker,—and indeed I have heard that he very often does, before he speaks 'em.

Well! Having formed that resolution, then come the question of a name. How did I hammer that hot iron into shape? This way. The most difficult explanation I had ever had with her was, how I come to be called Doctor, and yet was no Doctor.

After all, I felt that I had failed of getting it correctly into her mind, with my utmost pains. But trusting to her improvement in the two years, I thought that I might trust to her understanding it when she should come to read it as put down by my own hand. Then I thought I would try a joke with her and watch how it took, by which of itself I might fully judge of her understanding it. We had first discovered the mistake we had dropped into, through her having asked me to prescribe for her when she had supposed me to be a Doctor in a medical point of view; so thinks I, "Now, if I give this book the name of my Prescriptions, and if she catches the idea that my only Prescriptions are for her amusement and interest,—to make her laugh in a pleasant way, or to make her cry in a pleasant way,—it will be a delightful proof to both of us that we have got over our difficulty." It fell out to absolute perfection. For when she saw the book, as I had it got up,—the printed and pressed book,—lying on her desk in her cart, and saw the title, Doctor Marigold's Prescriptions, she looked at me for a moment with astonishment, then fluttered the leaves, then broke out a laughing in the charmingest way, then felt her pulse and shook her head, then turned the pages pretending to read them most attentive, then kissed the book to me, and put it to her bosom with both her hands. I never was better pleased in all my life!

But let me not anticipate. (I take that expression out of a lot of romances I bought for her. I never opened a single one of 'em—and I have opened many—but I found the romancer saying "let me not anticipate." Which being so, I wonder why he did anticipate, or who asked him to it.) Let me not, I say, anticipate. This same book took up all my spare time. It was no play to get the other articles together in the general miscellaneous lot, but when it come to my own article! There! I couldn't have believed the blotting, nor yet the buckling to at it, nor the patience over it. Which again is like the footboard. The public have no idea.

At last it was done, and the two years' time was gone after all the other time before it, and where it's all gone to, who knows? The new cart was finished,—yellow outside, relieved with wermilion and brass fittings,—the old horse was put in it, a new 'un and a boy being laid on for the Cheap Jack cart,—and I cleaned myself up to go and fetch her. Bright cold weather it was, cart-chimneys smoking, carts pitched private on a piece of waste ground over at Wandsworth, where you may see 'em from the Sou'western Railway when not upon the road. (Look out of the right-hand window going down.)

"Marigold," says the gentleman, giving his hand hearty, "I am very glad to see you."

"Yet I have my doubts, Sir," says I, "if you can be half as glad to see me as I am to see you."

"The time has appeared so long,—has it, Marigold?"

"I won't say that, Sir, considering its real length; but—"

"What a start, my good fellow!"

Ah! I should think it was! Grown such a woman, so pretty, so intelligent, so expressive! I knew then that she must be really like my child, or I could never have known her, standing quiet by the door.

"You are affected," says the gentleman in a kindly manner.

"I feel, Sir," says I, "that I am but a rough chap in a sleeved waistcoat."

"I feel," says the gentleman, "that it was you who raised her from misery and degradation, and brought her into communication with her kind. But why do we converse alone together, when we can converse so well with her? Address her in your own way."

"I am such a rough chap in a sleeved waistcoat, Sir," says I, "and she is such a graceful woman, and she stands so quiet at the door!"

"Try if she moves at the old sign," says the gentleman.

They had got it up together o' purpose to please me! For when I give her the old sign, she rushed to my feet, and dropped upon her knees, holding up her hands to me with pouring tears of love and joy; and when I took her hands and lifted her, she clasped me round the neck, and lay there; and I don't know what a fool I didn't make of myself, until we all three settled down into talking without sound, as if there was a something soft and pleasant spread over the whole world for us.

[A portion is here omitted from the text, having reference to the sketches contributed by other writers; but the reader will be pleased to have what follows retained in a note:

"Now I'll tell you what I am a-going to do with you. I am a-going to offer you the general miscellaneous lot, her own book, never read by anybody else but me, added to and completed by me after her first reading of it, eight-and-forty printed pages, six-and-ninety columns, Whiting's own work, Beaufort House to wit, thrown off by the steam-ingine, best of paper, beautiful green wrapper, folded like clean linen come home from the clear-starcher's, and so exquisitely stitched that, regarded as a piece of needlework alone, it's better than the sampler of a seamstress undergoing a Competitive examination for Starvation before the Civil Service Commissioners—and I offer the lot for what? For eight pound? Not so much. For six pound? Less. For four pound. Why, I hardly expect you to believe me, but that's the sum. Four pound! The stitching alone cost half as much again. Here's forty-eight original pages, ninety-six original columns, for four pound. You want more for the money? Take it. Three whole pages of advertisements of thrilling interest thrown in for nothing. Read 'em and believe 'em. More? My best of wishes for your merry Christmases and your happy New Years, your long lives and your true prosperities. Worth twenty pound good if they are delivered as I send them. Remember! Here's a final prescription added, "To be taken for life," which will tell you how the cart broke down, and where the journey ended. You think Four Pound too much? And still you think so? Come! I'll tell you what then. Say Four Pence, and keep the secret."]

Chapter II

To Be Taken With a Grain of Salt

I HAVE ALWAYS NOTICED A PREVALENT WANT OF COURAGE, EVEN AMONG PERSONS of superior intelligence and culture, as to imparting their own psychological experiences when those have been of a strange sort. Almost all men are afraid that what they could relate in such wise would find no parallel or response in a listener's internal life, and might be suspected or laughed at. A truthful traveller, who should have seen some extraordinary creature in the likeness of a sea-serpent, would have no fear of mentioning it; but the same traveller, having had some singular presentiment, impulse, vagary of thought, vision (so called), dream, or other remarkable mental impression, would hesitate considerably before he would own to it. To this reticence I attribute much of the obscurity in which such subjects are involved. We do not habitually communicate our experiences of these subjective things as we do our experiences of objective creation. The consequence is, that the general stock of experience in this regard appears exceptional, and really is so, in respect of being miserably imperfect.

In what I am going to relate, I have no intention of setting up, opposing, or supporting, any theory whatever. I know the history of the Bookseller of Berlin, I have studied the case of the wife of a late Astronomer Royal as related by Sir David Brewster, and I have followed the minutest details of a much more remarkable case of Spectral Illusion occurring within my private circle of friends. It may be necessary to state as to this last, that the sufferer (a lady) was in no degree, however distant, related to me. A mistaken assumption on that head might suggest an explanation of a part of my own case,—but only a part,—which would be wholly without foundation. It cannot be referred to my inheritance of any developed peculiarity, nor had I ever before any at all similar experience, nor have I ever had any at all similar experience since.

It does not signify how many years ago, or how few, a certain murder was committed in England, which attracted great attention. We hear more than enough of murderers as they rise in succession to their atrocious eminence, and I would bury the memory of this particular brute, if I could, as his body was buried, in Newgate Jail. I purposely abstain from giving any direct clue to the criminal's individuality.

When the murder was first discovered, no suspicion fell—or I ought rather to say, for I cannot be too precise in my facts, it was nowhere publicly hinted that any suspicion fell—on the man who was afterwards brought to trial. As no reference was at that time made to him in the newspapers, it is obviously impossible that any description of him can at that time have been given in the newspapers. It is essential that this fact be remembered.

Unfolding at breakfast my morning paper, containing the account of that first discovery, I found it to be deeply interesting, and I read it with close attention. I read it twice, if not three times. The discovery had been made in a bedroom, and, when I laid down the paper, I was aware of a flash—rush—flow—I do not know what to call it,—no word I can find is satisfactorily descriptive,—in which I seemed to see that bedroom passing through my room, like a picture impossibly painted on a running river. Though almost instantaneous in its passing, it was perfectly clear; so clear that I distinctly, and with a sense of relief, observed the absence of the dead body from the bed.

It was in no romantic place that I had this curious sensation, but in chambers in Piccadilly, very near to the corner of St. James's-street. It was entirely new to me. I was in my easy-chair at the moment, and the sensation was accompanied with a peculiar shiver which started the chair from its position. (But it is to be noted that the chair ran easily on castors.) I went to one of the windows (there are two in the room, and the room is on the second floor) to refresh my eyes with the moving objects down in Piccadilly. It was a bright autumn morning, and the street was sparkling and cheerful. The wind was high. As I looked out, it brought down from the Park a quantity of fallen leaves, which a gust took, and whirled into a spiral pillar. As the pillar fell and the leaves dispersed, I saw two men on the opposite side of the way, going from West to East. They were one behind the other. The foremost man often looked back over his shoulder. The second man followed him, at a distance of some thirty paces, with his right hand menacingly raised. First, the singularity and steadiness of this threatening gesture in so public a thoroughfare attracted my attention; and next, the more remarkable circumstance that nobody heeded it. Both men threaded their way among the other passengers with a smoothness hardly consistent even with the action of walking on a pavement; and no single creature, that I could see, gave them place, touched them, or looked after them. In passing before my windows, they both stared up at me. I saw their two faces very distinctly, and I knew that I could recognise them anywhere. Not that I had consciously noticed anything very remarkable in either face, except that the man who went first had an unusually lowering appearance, and that the face of the man who followed him was of the colour of impure wax.

I am a bachelor, and my valet and his wife constitute my whole establishment. My occupation is in a certain Branch Bank, and I wish that my duties as head of a Department were as light as they are popularly supposed to be. They kept me in town that autumn, when I stood in need of change. I was not ill, but I was not well. My reader is to make the most that can be reasonably made of my feeling jaded, having a depressing sense upon me of a monotonous life, and being "slightly dyspeptic." I am assured by my renowned doctor that my real state of health at that time justifies no stronger description, and I quote his own from his written answer to my request for it.

As the circumstances of the murder, gradually unravelling, took stronger and stronger possession of the public mind, I kept them away from mine by knowing as little about them as was possible in the midst of the universal excitement. But I knew that a verdict of Wilful Murder had been found against the suspected murderer, and that he had been committed to Newgate for trial. I also knew that his trial had been postponed over one Sessions of the Central Criminal Court, on the ground of general prejudice and want of time for the preparation of the defence. I may further have known, but I believe I did not, when, or about when, the Sessions to which his trial stood postponed would come on.

My sitting-room, bedroom, and dressing-room, are all on one floor. With the last there is no communication but through the bedroom. True, there is a door in it, once communicating with the staircase; but a part of the fitting of my bath has been—and had then been for some years—fixed across it. At the same period, and as a part of the same arrangement,—the door had been nailed up and canvased over.

I was standing in my bedroom late one night, giving some directions to my servant before he went to bed. My face was towards the only available door of communication with the dressing-room, and it was closed. My servant's back was towards that door. While I was speaking to him, I saw it open, and a man look in, who very earnestly and mysteriously beckoned to me. That man was the man who had gone second of the two along Piccadilly, and whose face was of the colour of impure wax.

The figure, having beckoned, drew back, and closed the door. With no longer pause than was made by my crossing the bedroom, I opened the dressing-room door, and looked in. I had a lighted candle already in my hand. I felt no inward expectation of seeing the figure in the dressing-room, and I did not see it there.

Conscious that my servant stood amazed, I turned round to him, and said: "Derrick, could you believe that in my cool senses I fancied I saw a—" As I there laid my hand upon his breast, with a sudden start he trembled violently, and said, "O Lord, yes, Sir! A dead man beckoning!"

Now I do not believe that this John Derrick, my trusty and attached servant for more than twenty years, had any impression whatever of having seen any such figure, until I touched him. The change in him was so startling, when I touched him, that I fully believe he derived his impression in some occult manner from me at that instant.

I bade John Derrick bring some brandy, and I gave him a dram, and was glad to take one myself. Of what had preceded that night's phenomenon, I told him not a single word. Reflecting on it, I was absolutely certain that I had never seen that face before, except on the one occasion in Piccadilly. Comparing its expression when beckoning at the door with its expression when it had stared up at me as I stood at my window, I came to the conclusion that on the first occasion it had sought to fasten itself upon my memory, and that on the second occasion it had made sure of being immediately remembered.

I was not very comfortable that night, though I felt a certainty, difficult to explain, that the figure would not return. At daylight I fell into a heavy sleep, from which I was awakened by John Derrick's coming to my bedside with a paper in his hand.

This paper, it appeared, had been the subject of an altercation at the door between its bearer and my servant. It was a summons to me to serve upon a Jury at the forthcoming Sessions of the Central Criminal Court at the Old Bailey. I had never before been summoned on such a Jury, as John Derrick well knew. He believed—I am not certain at this hour whether with reason or otherwise—that that class of Jurors were customarily chosen on a lower qualification than mine, and he had at first refused to accept the summons. The man who served it had taken the matter very coolly. He had said that my attendance or non-attendance was nothing to him; there the summons was; and I should deal with it at my own peril, and not at his.

For a day or two I was undecided whether to respond to this call, or take no notice of it. I was not conscious of the slightest mysterious bias, influence, or attraction, one way or other. Of that I am as strictly sure as of every other statement that I make here. Ultimately I decided, as a break in the monotony of my life, that I would go.

The appointed morning was a raw morning in the month of November. There was a dense brown fog in Piccadilly, and it became positively black and in the last degree oppressive East of Temple Bar. I found the passages and staircases of the Court-House flaringly lighted with gas, and the Court itself similarly illuminated. I *think* that, until I was conducted by officers into the Old Court and saw its crowded state, I did not know that the Murderer was to be tried that day. I *think* that, until I was so helped into the Old Court with considerable difficulty, I did not know into which of the two Courts sitting my summons would take me. But this must not be received as a positive assertion, for I am not completely satisfied in my mind on either point.

I took my seat in the place appropriated to Jurors in waiting, and I looked about the Court as well as I could through the cloud of fog and breath that was heavy in it. I noticed the black vapour hanging like a murky curtain outside the great windows, and I noticed the stifled sound of wheels on the straw or tan that was littered in the street; also, the hum of the people gathered there, which a shrill whistle, or a louder song or hail than the rest, occasionally pierced. Soon afterwards the Judges, two in number, entered, and took their seats. The buzz in the Court was awfully hushed. The direction was given to put the Murderer to the bar. He appeared there. And in that same instant I recognised in him the first of the two men who had gone down Piccadilly.

If my name had been called then, I doubt if I could have answered to it audibly. But it was called about sixth or eighth in the panel, and I was by that time able to say, "Here!" Now, observe. As I stepped into the box, the prisoner, who had been looking on attentively, but with no sign of concern, became violently agitated, and beckoned to his attorney. The prisoner's wish to challenge me was so manifest, that it occasioned a pause, during which the attorney, with his hand upon the dock, whispered with his client, and shook his head. I afterwards had it from that gentleman, that the prisoner's first affrighted words to him were, "*At all hazards, challenge that man!*" But that, as he would give no reason for it, and admitted that he had not even known my name until he heard it called and I appeared, it was not done.

Both on the ground already explained, that I wish to avoid reviving the unwholesome memory of that Murderer, and also because a detailed account of his long trial is by no means indispensable to my narrative, I shall confine myself closely to such incidents in the ten days and nights during which we, the Jury, were kept together, as directly bear on my own curious personal experience. It is in that, and not in the Murderer, that I seek to interest my reader. It is to that, and not to a page of the Newgate Calendar, that I beg attention.

I was chosen Foreman of the Jury. On the second morning of the trial, after evidence had been taken for two hours (I heard the church clocks strike), happening to cast my eyes over my brother jurymen, I found an inexplicable difficulty in counting them. I counted them several times, yet always with the same difficulty. In short, I made them one too many.

I touched the brother jurymen whose place was next me, and I whispered to him, "Oblige me by counting us." He looked surprised by the request, but turned his head and counted. "Why," says he, suddenly, "we are Thirt—; but no, it's not possible. No. We are twelve."

According to my counting that day, we were always right in detail, but in the gross we were always one too many. There was no appearance—no figure—to account for it; but I had now an inward foreshadowing of the figure that was surely coming.

The Jury were housed at the London Tavern. We all slept in one large room on separate tables, and we were constantly in the charge and under the eye of the officer sworn to hold us in safe-keeping. I see no reason for suppressing the real name of that officer. He was intelligent, highly polite, and obliging, and (I was glad to hear) much respected in the City. He had an agreeable presence, good eyes, enviable black whiskers, and a fine sonorous voice. His name was Mr. Harker.

When we turned into our twelve beds at night, Mr. Harker's bed was drawn across the door. On the night of the second day, not being disposed to lie down, and seeing Mr. Harker sitting on his bed, I went and sat beside him, and offered him a pinch of snuff. As Mr. Harker's hand touched mine in taking it from my box, a peculiar shiver crossed him, and he said, "Who is this?"

Following Mr. Harker's eyes, and looking along the room, I saw again the figure I expected,—the second of the two men who had gone down Piccadilly. I rose, and advanced a few steps; then stopped, and looked round at Mr. Harker. He was quite unconcerned, laughed, and said in a pleasant way, "I thought for a moment we had a thirteenth juryman, without a bed. But I see it is the moonlight."

Making no revelation to Mr. Harker, but inviting him to take a walk with me to the end of the room, I watched what the figure did. It stood for a few moments by the bedside of each of my eleven brother jurymen, close to the pillow. It always went to the right-hand side of the bed, and always passed out crossing the foot of the next bed. It seemed, from the action of the head, merely to look down pensively at each recumbent figure. It took no notice of me, or of my bed, which was that nearest to Mr. Harker's. It seemed to go out where the moonlight came in, through a high window, as by an aërial flight of stairs.

Next morning at breakfast, it appeared that everybody present had dreamed of the murdered man last night, except myself and Mr. Harker.

I now felt as convinced that the second man who had gone down Piccadilly was the murdered man (so to speak), as if it had been borne into my comprehension by his immediate testimony. But even this took place, and in a manner for which I was not at all prepared.

On the fifth day of the trial, when the case for the prosecution was drawing to a close, a miniature of the murdered man, missing from his bedroom upon the discovery of the deed, and afterwards found in a hiding-place where the Murderer had been seen digging, was put in evidence. Having been identified by the witness under examination, it was handed up to the Bench, and thence handed down to be inspected by the Jury. As an officer in a black gown was making his way with it across to me, the figure of the second man who had gone down Piccadilly impetuously started from the crowd, caught the miniature from the officer, and gave it to me with his own hands, at the same time saying, in a low and hollow tone,—before I saw the miniature, which was in a locket,—"*I was younger then, and my face was not then drained of blood.*" It also came between me and the brother juryman to whom I would have given the miniature, and between him and the brother juryman to whom he would have given it, and so passed it on through the whole of our number, and back into my possession. Not one of them, however, detected this.

At table, and generally when we were shut up together in Mr. Harker's custody, we had from the first naturally discussed the day's proceedings a good deal. On that fifth day, the case for the prosecution being closed, and we having that side of the question in a completed shape before us, our discussion was more animated and serious. Among our number was a vestryman,—the densest idiot I have ever seen at large,—who met the plainest evidence with the most preposterous objections, and who was sided with by two flabby parochial parasites; all the three impanelled from a district so delivered over to Fever that they ought to have been upon their own trial for five hundred Murders. When these mischievous blockheads were at their loudest, which was towards midnight, while some of us were already preparing for bed, I again saw the murdered man. He stood grimly behind them, beckoning to me. On my going towards them, and striking into the conversation, he immediately retired. This was the beginning of a separate series of appearances, confined to that long room in which we were confined. Whenever a knot of my brother jurymen laid their heads together, I saw the head of the murdered man among theirs. Whenever their comparison of notes was going against him, he would solemnly and irresistibly beckon to me.

It will be borne in mind that down to the production of the miniature, on the fifth day of the trial, I had never seen the Appearance in Court. Three changes occurred now that we entered on the case for the defence. Two of them I will mention together, first. The figure was now in Court continually, and it never there addressed itself to me, but always to the person who was speaking at the time. For instance: the throat of the murdered man had been cut straight across. In the opening speech for the defence, it was suggested that the deceased might have cut his own throat. At that very moment, the figure, with its throat in the dreadful condition referred to (this it had concealed before), stood at the speaker's elbow, motioning across and across its windpipe, now with the right hand, now with the left, vigorously suggesting to the speaker himself the impossibility of such a wound having been self-inflicted by either hand. For another instance: a witness to character, a woman, deposed to the prisoner's being the most amiable of mankind. The figure at that instant stood on the floor before her, looking her full in the face, and pointing out the prisoner's evil countenance with an extended arm and an outstretched finger.

The third change now to be added impressed me strongly as the most marked and striking of all. I do not theorise upon it; I accurately state it, and there leave it. Although the Appearance was not itself perceived by those whom it addressed, its coming close to such persons was invariably attended by some trepidation or disturbance on their part. It seemed to me as if it were prevented, by laws to which I was not amenable, from fully revealing itself to others, and yet as if it could invisibly, dumbly, and darkly overshadow their minds. When the leading counsel for the defence suggested that hypothesis of suicide, and the figure stood at the learned gentleman's elbow, frightfully sawing at its severed throat, it is undeniable that the counsel faltered in his speech, lost for a few seconds the thread of his ingenious discourse, wiped his forehead with his handkerchief, and turned extremely pale. When the witness to character was confronted by the Appearance, her eyes most certainly did follow the direction of its pointed finger, and rest in great hesitation and trouble upon the prisoner's face. Two additional illustrations will suffice. On the eighth day of the trial, after the pause which was every day made early in the afternoon for a few minutes' rest and refreshment, I came back into Court with the rest of the Jury some little time before the return of the Judges. Standing up in the box and looking about me, I thought the figure was not there, until, chancing to raise my eyes to the gallery, I saw it bending forward, and leaning over a very decent woman, as if to assure itself whether the Judges had resumed their seats or not. Immediately afterwards that woman screamed, fainted, and was carried out. So with the venerable, sagacious, and patient Judge who conducted the trial. When the case was over, and he settled himself and his papers to sum up, the murdered man, entering by the Judges' door, advanced to his Lordship's desk, and looked eagerly over his shoulder at the pages of his notes which he was turning. A change came over his Lordship's face; his hand stopped; the peculiar shiver, that I knew so well, passed over him; he faltered, "Excuse me, gentlemen, for a few moments. I am somewhat oppressed by the vitiated air"; and did not recover until he had drunk a glass of water.

Through all the monotony of six of those interminable ten days,—the same Judges and others on the bench, the same Murderer in the dock, the same lawyers at the table, the same tones of question and answer rising to the roof of the court, the same scratching of the Judge's pen, the same ushers going in and out, the same lights kindled at the same hour when there had been any natural light of day, the same foggy curtain outside the great windows when it was foggy, the same rain pattering and dripping when it was rainy, the same footmarks of turnkeys and prisoner day after day on the same sawdust, the same keys locking and unlocking the same heavy doors,—through all the wearisome monotony which made me feel as if I had been Foreman of the Jury for a vast period of time, and Piccadilly had flourished coevally with Babylon, the murdered man never lost one trace of his distinctness in my eyes, nor was he at any moment less distinct than anybody else. I must not omit, as a matter of fact, that I never once saw the Appearance which I call by the name of the murdered man look at the Murderer. Again and again I wondered, "Why does he not?" But he never did.

Nor did he look at me, after the production of the miniature, until the last closing minutes of the trial arrived. We retired to consider, at seven minutes before ten at night. The idiotic vestryman and his two parochial parasites gave us so much trouble that we twice returned into Court to beg to have certain extracts from the Judge's notes re-read. Nine of us had not the smallest doubt about those passages, neither, I believe, had any one in the Court; the dunder-headed triumvirate, having no idea but obstruction, disputed them for that very reason. At length we prevailed, and finally the Jury returned into Court at ten minutes past twelve.

The murdered man at that time stood directly opposite the Jury-box, on the other side of the Court. As I took my place, his eyes rested on me with great attention; he seemed satisfied, and slowly shook a great gray veil, which he carried on his arm for the first time, over his head and whole form. As I gave in our verdict, "Guilty," the veil collapsed, all was gone, and his place was empty.

The Murderer, being asked by the Judge, according to usage, whether he had anything to say before sentence of Death should be passed upon him, indistinctly muttered something which was described in the leading newspapers of the following day as "a few rambling, incoherent, and half-audible words, in which he was understood to complain that he had not had a fair trial, because the Foreman of the Jury was prepossessed against him." The remarkable declaration that he really made was this: "*My Lord, I knew I was a doomed man, when the Foreman of my Jury came into the box. My Lord, I knew he would never let me off, because, before I was taken, he somehow got to my bedside in the night, woke me, and put a rope round my neck.*"

Chapter III

To Be Taken for Life

So every item of my plan was crowned with success. Our reunited life was more than all that we had looked forward to. Content and joy went with us as the wheels of the two carts went round, and the same stopped with us when the two carts stopped. I was as pleased and as proud as a Pug-Dog with his muzzle black-leaded for a evening party, and his tail extra curled by machinery.

But I had left something out of my calculations. Now, what had I left out? To help you to guess I'll say, a figure. Come. Make a guess and guess right. Nought? No. Nine? No. Eight? No. Seven? No. Six? No. Five? No. Four? No. Three? No. Two? No. One? No. Now I'll tell you what I'll do with you. I'll say it's another sort of figure altogether. There. Why then, says you, it's a mortal figure. No, nor yet a mortal figure. By such means you got yourself penned into a corner, and you can't help guessing a *im*mortal figure. That's about it. Why didn't you say so sooner?

Yes. It was a immortal figure that I had altogether left out of my calculations. Neither man's, nor woman's, but a child's. Girl's or boy's? Boy's. "I, says the sparrow with my bow and arrow." Now you have got it.

We were down at Lancaster, and I had done two nights more than fair average business (though I cannot in honour recommend them as a quick audience) in the open square there, near the end of the street where Mr. Sly's King's Arms and Royal Hotel stands. Mim's travelling giant, otherwise Pickleson, happened at the self-same time to be trying it on in the town. The genteel lay was adopted with him. No hint of a van. Green baize alcove leading up to Pickleson in a Auction Room. Printed poster, "Free list suspended, with the exception of that proud boast of an enlightened country, a free press. Schools admitted by private arrangement. Nothing to raise a blush in the cheek of youth or shock the most fastidious." Mim swearing most horrible and terrific, in a pink calico pay-place, at the slackness of the public. Serious handbill in the shops, importing that it was all but impossible to come to a right understanding of the history of David without seeing Pickleson.

I went to the Auction Room in question, and I found it entirely empty of everything but echoes and mouldiness, with the single exception of Pickleson on a piece of red drugget. This suited my purpose, as I wanted a private and confidential word with him, which was: "Pickleson. Owing much happiness to you, I put you in my will for a fypunnote; but, to save trouble, here's fourpunten down, which may equally suit your views, and let us so conclude the transaction." Pickleson, who up to that remark had had the dejected appearance of a long Roman rushlight that couldn't anyhow get lighted, brightened up at his top extremity, and made his acknowledgments in a way which (for him) was parliamentary eloquence. He likewise did add, that, having ceased to draw as a Roman, Mim had made proposals for his going in as a conwerted Indian Giant worked upon by The Dairyman's Daughter. This, Pickleson, having no acquaintance with the tract named after that young woman, and not being willing to couple gag with his serious views, had declined to do, thereby leading to words and the total stoppage of the unfortunate young man's beer. All of which, during the whole of the interview, was confirmed by the ferocious growling of Mim down below in the pay-place, which shook the giant like a leaf.

But what was to the present point in the remarks of the travelling giant, otherwise Pickleson, was this: "Doctor Marigold,"—I give his words without a hope of conweying their feebleness,—"who is the strange young man that hangs about your carts?"—"The strange young *man*?" I gives him back, thinking that he meant her, and his languid circulation had dropped a syllable. "Doctor," he returns, with a pathos calculated to draw a tear from even a manly eye, "I am weak, but not so weak yet as that I don't know my words. I repeat them, Doctor. The strange young man." It then appeared that Pickleson, being forced to stretch his legs (not that they wanted it) only at times when he couldn't be seen for nothing, to wit in the dead of the night and towards daybreak, had twice seen hanging about my carts, in that same town of Lancaster where I had been only two nights, this same unknown young man.

It put me rather out of sorts. What it meant as to particulars I no more foreboded then than you forebode now, but it put me rather out of sorts. Howsoever, I made light of it to Pickleson, and I took leave of Pickleson, advising him to spend his legacy in getting up his stamina, and to continue to stand by his religion. Towards morning I kept a look out for the strange young man, and—what was more—I saw the strange young man. He was well dressed and well looking. He loitered very nigh my carts, watching them like as if he was taking care of them, and soon after daybreak turned and went away. I sent a hail after him, but he never started or looked round, or took the smallest notice.

We left Lancaster within an hour or two, on our way towards Carlisle. Next morning, at daybreak, I looked out again for the strange young man. I did not see him. But next morning I looked out again, and there he was once more. I sent another hail after him, but as before he gave not the slightest sign of being anyways disturbed. This put a thought into my head. Acting on it I watched him in different manners and at different times not necessary to enter into, till I found that this strange young man was deaf and dumb.

The discovery turned me over, because I knew that a part of that establishment where she had been was allotted to young men (some of them well off), and I thought to myself, "If she favours him, where am I? and where is all that I have worked and planned for?" Hoping—I must confess to the selfishness—that she might *not* favour him, I set myself to find out. At last I was by accident present at a meeting between them in the open air, looking on leaning behind a fir-tree without their knowing of it. It was a moving meeting for all the three parties concerned. I knew every syllable that passed between them as well as they did. I listened with my eyes, which had come to be as quick and true with deaf and dumb conversation as my ears with the talk of people that can speak. He was a-going out to China as clerk in a merchant's house, which his father had been before him. He was in circumstances to keep a wife, and he wanted her to marry him and go along with him. She persisted, no. He asked if she didn't love him. Yes, she loved him dearly, dearly; but she could never disappoint her beloved, good, noble, generous, and I-don't-know-what-all father (meaning me, the Cheap Jack in the sleeved waistcoat) and she would stay with him, Heaven bless him! though it was to break her heart. Then she cried most bitterly, and that made up my mind.

While my mind had been in an unsettled state about her favouring this young man, I had felt that unreasonable towards Pickleson, that it was well for him he had got his legacy down. For I often thought, "If it hadn't been for this same weak-minded giant, I might never have come to trouble my head and wex my soul about the young man." But, once that I knew she loved him,—once that I had seen her weep for him,—it was a different thing. I made it right in my mind with Pickleson on the spot, and I shook myself together to do what was right by all.

She had left the young man by that time (for it took a few minutes to get me thoroughly well shook together), and the young man was leaning against another of the fir-trees,—of which there was a cluster,—with his face upon his arm. I touched him on the back. Looking up and seeing me, he says, in our deaf-and-dumb talk, "Do not be angry."

"I am not angry, good boy. I am your friend. Come with me."

I left him at the foot of the steps of the Library Cart, and I went up alone. She was drying her eyes.

"You have been crying, my dear."

"Yes, father."

"Why?"

"A headache."

"Not a heartache?"

"I said a headache, father."

"Doctor Marigold must prescribe for that headache."

She took up the book of my Prescriptions, and held it up with a forced smile; but seeing me keep still and look earnest, she softly laid it down again, and her eyes were very attentive.

"The Prescription is not there, Sophy."

"Where is it?"

"Here, my dear."

I brought her young husband in, and I put her hand in his, and my only farther words to both of them were these: "Doctor Marigold's last Prescription. To be taken for life." After which I bolted.

When the wedding come off, I mounted a coat (blue, and bright buttons), for the first and last time in all my days, and I give Sophy away with my own hand. There were only us three and the gentleman who had had charge of her for those two years. I give the wedding dinner of four in the Library Cart. Pigeon-pie, a leg of pickled pork, a pair of fowls, and suitable garden stuff. The best of drinks. I give them a speech, and the gentleman give us a speech, and all our jokes told, and the whole went off like a sky-rocket. In the course of the entertainment I explained to Sophy that I should keep the Library Cart as my living-cart when not upon the road, and that I should keep all her books for her just as they stood, till she come back to claim them. So she went to China with her young husband, and it was a parting sorrowful and heavy, and I got the boy I had another service; and so as of old, when my child and wife were gone, I went plodding along alone, with my whip over my shoulder, at the old horse's head.

Sophy wrote me many letters, and I wrote her many letters. About the end of the first year she sent me one in an unsteady hand: "Dearest father, not a week ago I had a darling little daughter, but I am so well that they let me write these words to you. Dearest and best father, I hope my child may not be deaf and dumb, but I do not yet know." When I wrote back, I hinted the question; but as Sophy never answered that question, I felt it to be a sad one, and I never repeated it. For a long time our letters were regular, but then they got irregular, through Sophy's husband being moved to another station, and through my being always on the move. But we were in one another's thoughts, I was equally sure, letters or no letters.

Five years, odd months, had gone since Sophy went away. I was still the King of the Cheap Jacks, and at a greater height of popularity than ever. I had had a first-rate autumn of it, and on the twenty-third of December, one thousand eight hundred and sixty-four, I found myself at Uxbridge, Middlesex, clean sold out. So I jogged up to London with the old horse, light and easy, to have my Christmas-eve and Christmas-day alone by the fire in the Library Cart, and then to buy a regular new stock of goods all round, to sell 'em again and get the money.

I am a neat hand at cookery, and I'll tell you what I knocked up for my Christmas-eve dinner in the Library Cart. I knocked up a beefsteak-pudding for one, with two kidneys, a dozen oysters, and a couple of mushrooms thrown in. It's a pudding to put a man in good humour with everything, except the two bottom buttons of his waistcoat. Having relished that pudding and cleared away, I turned the lamp low, and sat down by the light of the fire, watching it as it shone upon the backs of Sophy's books.

Sophy's books so brought Sophy's self, that I saw her touching face quite plainly, before I dropped off dozing by the fire. This may be a reason why Sophy, with her deaf-and-dumb child in her arms, seemed to stand silent by me all through my nap. I was on the road, off the road, in all sorts of places, North and South and West and East, Winds liked best and winds liked least, Here and there and gone astray, Over the hills and far away, and still she stood silent by me, with her silent child in her arms. Even when I woke with a start, she seemed to vanish, as if she had stood by me in that very place only a single instant before.

I had started at a real sound, and the sound was on the steps of the cart. It was the light hurried tread of a child, coming clambering up. That tread of a child had once been so familiar to me, that for half a moment I believed I was a-going to see a little ghost.

But the touch of a real child was laid upon the outer handle of the door, and the handle turned, and the door opened a little way, and a real child peeped in. A bright little comely girl with large dark eyes.

Looking full at me, the tiny creature took off her mite of a straw hat, and a quantity of dark curls fell about her face. Then she opened her lips, and said in a pretty voice,

"Grandfather!"

"Ah, my God!" I cries out. "She can speak!"

"Yes, dear grandfather. And I am to ask you whether there was ever any one that I remind you of?"

In a moment Sophy was round my neck, as well as the child, and her husband was a-wringing my hand with his face hid, and we all had to shake ourselves together before we could get over it. And when we did begin to get over it, and I saw the pretty child a-talking, pleased and quick and eager and busy, to her mother, in the signs that I had first taught her mother, the happy and yet pitying tears fell rolling down my face.

Mugby Junction

IN FOUR CHAPTERS

Chapter I

Barbox Brothers

I

"Guard! What place is this?"

"Mugby Junction, Sir."

"A windy place!"

"Yes, it mostly is, Sir."

"And looks comfortless indeed!"

"Yes, it generally does, Sir."

"Is it a rainy night still?"

"Pours, Sir."

"Open the door. I'll get out."

"You'll have, Sir," said the guard, glistening with drops of wet, and looking at the tearful face of his watch by the light of his lantern as the traveller descended, "three minutes here."

"More, I think.—For I am not going on."

"Thought you had a through ticket, Sir?"

"So I have, but I shall sacrifice the rest of it. I want my luggage."

"Please to come to the van and point it out, Sir. Be good enough to look very sharp, Sir. Not a moment to spare."

The guard hurried to the luggage van, and the traveller hurried after him. The guard got into it, and the traveller looked into it.

"Those two large black portmanteaus in the corner where your light shines. Those are mine."

"Name upon 'em, Sir?"

"Barbox Brothers."

"Stand clear, Sir, if you please. One. Two. Right!" Lamp waved. Signal lights ahead already changing. Shriek from engine. Train gone.

"Mugby Junction!" said the traveller, pulling up the woollen muffler round his throat with both hands. "At past three o'clock of a tempestuous morning! So!"

He spoke to himself. There was no one else to speak to. Perhaps, though there had been any one else to speak to, he would have preferred to speak to himself. Speaking to himself he spoke to a man within five years of fifty either way, who had turned grey too soon, like a neglected fire; a man of pondering habit, brooding carriage of the head, and suppressed internal voice; a man with many indications on him of having been much alone.

He stood unnoticed on the dreary platform, except by the rain and by the wind. Those two vigilant assailants made a rush at him. "Very well," said he, yielding. "It signifies nothing to me to what quarter I turn my face."

Thus, at Mugby Junction, at past three o'clock of a tempestuous morning, the traveller went where the weather drove him.

Not but what he could make a stand when he was so minded, for, coming to the end of the roofed shelter (it is of considerable extent at Mugby Junction), and looking out upon the dark night, with a yet darker spirit-wing of storm beating its wild way through it, he faced about, and held his own as ruggedly in the difficult direction as he had held it in the easier one. Thus, with a steady step, the traveller went up and down, up and down, up and down, seeking nothing and finding it.

A place replete with shadowy shapes, this Mugby Junction in the black hours of the four-and-twenty. Mysterious goods trains, covered with palls and gliding on like vast weird funerals, conveying themselves guiltily away from the presence of the few lighted lamps, as if their freight had come to a secret and unlawful end. Half-miles of coal pursuing in a Detective manner, following when they lead, stopping when they stop, backing when they back. Red-hot embers showering out upon the ground, down this dark avenue, and down the other, as if torturing fires were being raked clear; concurrently, shrieks and groans and grinds invading the ear, as if the tortured were at the height of their suffering. Iron-barred cages full of cattle jangling by midway, the drooping beasts with horns entangled, eyes frozen with terror, and mouths too: at least they have long icicles (or what seem so) hanging from their lips. Unknown languages in the air, conspiring in red, green, and white characters. An earthquake, accompanied with thunder and lightning, going up express to London. Now, all quiet, all rusty, wind and rain in possession, lamps extinguished, Mugby Junction dead and indistinct, with its robe drawn over its head, like Cæsar.

Now, too, as the belated traveller plodded up and down, a shadowy train went by him in the gloom which was no other than the train of a life. From whatsoever intangible deep cutting or dark tunnel it emerged, here it came, unsummoned and unannounced, stealing upon him, and passing away into obscurity. Here mournfully went by a child who had never had a childhood or known a parent, inseparable from a youth with a bitter sense of his namelessness, coupled to a man the enforced business of whose best years had been distasteful and oppressive, linked to an ungrateful friend, dragging after him a woman once beloved. Attendant, with many a clank and wrench, were lumbering cares, dark meditations, huge dim disappointments, monotonous years, a long jarring line of the discords of a solitary and unhappy existence.

"—Yours, Sir?"

The traveller recalled his eyes from the waste into which they had been staring, and fell back a step or so under the abruptness, and perhaps the chance appropriateness, of the question.

"Oh! My thoughts were not here for the moment. Yes. Yes. Those two portmanteaus are mine. Are you a Porter?"

"On Porter's wages, Sir. But I am Lamps."

The traveller looked a little confused.

"Who did you say you are?"

"Lamps, Sir," showing an oily cloth in his hand, as farther explanation.

"Surely, surely. Is there any hotel or tavern here?"

"Not exactly here, Sir. There is a Refreshment Room here, but—" Lamps, with a mighty serious look, gave his head a warning roll that plainly added—"but it's a blessed circumstance for you that it's not open."

"You couldn't recommend it, I see, if it was available?"

"Ask your pardon, Sir. If it was—?"

"Open?"

"It ain't my place, as a paid servant of the company, to give my opinion on any of the company's toepics,"—he pronounced it more like toothpicks,—"beyond lampile and cottons," returned Lamps in a confidential tone; "but, speaking as a man, I wouldn't recommend my father (if he was to come to life again) to go and try how he'd be treated at the Refreshment Room. Not speaking as a man, no, I would *not*."

The traveller nodded conviction. "I suppose I can put up in the town? There is a town here?" For the traveller (though a stay-at-home compared with most travellers) had been, like many others, carried on the steam winds and the iron tides through that Junction before, without having ever, as one might say, gone ashore there.

"Oh yes, there's a town, Sir! Anyways, there's town enough to put up in. But," following the glance of the other at his luggage, "this is a very dead time of the night with us, Sir. The deadest time. I might a'most call it our deadest and buriedest time."

"No porters about?"

"Well, Sir, you see," returned Lamps, confidential again, "they in general goes off with the gas. That's how it is. And they seem to have overlooked you, through your walking to the furder end of the platform. But, in about twelve minutes or so, she may be up."

"Who may be up?"

"The three forty-two, Sir. She goes off in a sidin' till the Up X passes, and then she"—here an air of hopeful vagueness pervaded Lamps—"does all as lays in her power."

"I doubt if I comprehend the arrangement."

"I doubt if anybody do, Sir. She's a Parliamentary, Sir. And, you see, a Parliamentary, or a Skirmishun—"

"Do you mean an Excursion?"

"That's it, Sir.—A Parliamentary or a Skirmishun, she mostly *doos* go off into a sidin'. But, when she *can* get a chance, she's whistled out of it, and she's whistled up into doin' all as,"—Lamps again wore the air of a highly sanguine man who hoped for the best,—"all as lays in her power."

He then explained that the porters on duty, being required to be in attendance on the Parliamentary matron in question, would doubtless turn up with the gas. In the meantime, if the gentleman would not very much object to the smell of lamp-oil, and would accept the warmth of his little room—The gentleman, being by this time very cold, instantly closed with the proposal.

A greasy little cabin it was, suggestive, to the sense of smell, of a cabin in a Whaler. But there was a bright fire burning in its rusty grate, and on the floor there stood a wooden stand of newly trimmed and lighted lamps, ready for carriage service. They made a bright show, and their light, and the warmth, accounted for the popularity of the room, as borne witness to by many impressions of velveteen trousers on a form by the fire, and many rounded smears and smudges of stooping velveteen shoulders on the adjacent wall. Various untidy shelves accommodated a quantity of lamps and oil-cans, and also a fragrant collection of what looked like the pocket-handkerchiefs of the whole lamp family.

As Barbox Brothers (so to call the traveller on the warranty of his luggage) took his seat upon the form, and warmed his now ungloved hands at the fire, he glanced aside at a little deal desk, much blotched with ink, which his elbow touched. Upon it were some scraps of coarse paper, and a superannuated steel pen in very reduced and gritty circumstances.

From glancing at the scraps of paper, he turned involuntarily to his host, and said, with some roughness:

"Why, you are never a poet, man?"

Lamps had certainly not the conventional appearance of one, as he stood modestly rubbing his squab nose with a handkerchief so exceedingly oily, that he might have been in the act of mistaking himself for one of his charges. He was a spare man of about the Barbox Brothers time of life, with his features whimsically drawn upward as if they were attracted by the roots of his hair. He had a peculiarly shining transparent complexion, probably occasioned by constant oleaginous application;

and his attractive hair, being cut short, and being grizzled, and standing straight up on end as if it in its turn were attracted by some invisible magnet above it, the top of his head was not very unlike a lamp-wick.

"But, to be sure, it's no business of mine," said Barbox Brothers. "That was an impertinent observation on my part. Be what you like."

"Some people, Sir," remarked Lamps in a tone of apology, "are sometimes what they don't like."

"Nobody knows that better than I do," sighed the other. "I have been what I don't like, all my life."

"When I first took, Sir," resumed Lamps, "to composing little Comic-Songs-like—"

Barbox Brothers eyed him with great disfavour.

"—To composing little Comic-Songs-like—and what was more hard—to singing 'em afterwards," said Lamps, "it went against the grain at that time, it did indeed."

Something that was not all oil here shining in Lamps's eye, Barbox Brothers withdrew his own a little disconcerted, looked at the fire, and put a foot on the top bar. "Why did you do it, then?" he asked after a short pause; abruptly enough, but in a softer tone. "If you didn't want to do it, why did you do it? Where did you sing them? Public-house?"

To which Mr. Lamps returned the curious reply: "Bedside."

At this moment, while the traveller looked at him for elucidation, Mugby Junction started suddenly, trembled violently, and opened its gas eyes. "She's got up!" Lamps announced, excited. "What lays in her power is sometimes more, and sometimes less; but it's laid in her power to get up to-night, by George!"

The legend "Barbox Brothers," in large white letters on two black surfaces, was very soon afterwards trundling on a truck through a silent street, and, when the owner of the legend had shivered on the pavement half an hour, what time the porter's knocks at the Inn Door knocked up the whole town first, and the Inn last, he groped his way into the close air of a shut-up house, and so groped between the sheets of a shut-up bed that seemed to have been expressly refrigerated for him when last made.

II

"You remember me, Young Jackson?"

"What do I remember if not you? You are my first remembrance. It was you who told me that was my name. It was you who told me that on every twentieth of December my life had a penitential anniversary in it called a birthday. I suppose the last communication was truer than the first!"

"What am I like, Young Jackson?"

"You are like a blight all through the year to me. You hard-lined, thin-lipped, repressive, changeless woman with a wax mask on. You are like the Devil to me; most of all when you teach me religious things, for you make me abhor them."

"You remember me, Mr. Young Jackson?" In another voice from another quarter.

"Most gratefully, Sir. You were the ray of hope and prospering ambition in my life. When I attended your course, I believed that I should come to be a great healer, and I felt almost happy—even though I was still the one boarder in the house with that horrible mask, and ate and drank in silence and constraint with the mask before me, every day. As I had done every, every, every day, through my school-time and from my earliest recollection."

"What am I like, Mr. Young Jackson?"

"You are like a Superior Being to me. You are like Nature beginning to reveal herself to me. I hear you again, as one of the hushed crowd of young men kindling under the power of your presence and knowledge, and you bring into my eyes the only exultant tears that ever stood in them."

"You remember Me, Mr. Young Jackson?" In a grating voice from quite another quarter.

"Too well. You made your ghostly appearance in my life one day, and announced that its course was to be suddenly and wholly changed. You showed me which was my wearisome seat in the Galley of Barbox Brothers. (When *they* were, if they ever were, is unknown to me; there was nothing of them but the name when I bent to the oar.) You told me what I was to do, and what to be paid; you told me afterwards, at intervals of years, when I was to sign for the Firm, when I became a partner, when I became the Firm. I know no more of it, or of myself."

"What am I like, Mr. Young Jackson?"

"You are like my father, I sometimes think. You are hard enough and cold enough so to have brought up an acknowledged son. I see your scanty figure, your close brown suit, and your tight brown wig; but you, too, wear a wax mask to your death. You never by a chance remove it—it never by a chance falls off—and I know no more of you."

Throughout this dialogue, the traveller spoke to himself at his window in the morning, as he had spoken to himself at the Junction overnight. And as he had then looked in the darkness, a man who had turned grey too soon, like a neglected fire: so he now looked in the sun-light, an ashier grey, like a fire which the brightness of the sun put out.

The firm of Barbox Brothers had been some offshoot or irregular branch of the Public Notary and bill-broking tree. It had gained for itself a griping reputation before the days of Young Jackson, and the reputation had stuck to it and to him.

As he had imperceptibly come into possession of the dim den up in the corner of a court off Lombard Street, on whose grimy windows the inscription Barbox Brothers had for many long years daily interposed itself between him and the sky, so he had insensibly found himself a personage held in chronic distrust, whom it was essential to screw tight to every transaction in which he engaged, whose word was never to be taken without his attested bond, whom all dealers with openly set up guards and wards against. This character had come upon him through no act of his own. It was as if the original Barbox had stretched himself down upon the office floor, and had thither caused to be conveyed Young Jackson in his sleep, and had there effected a metempsychosis and exchange of persons with him. The discovery—aided in its turn by the deceit of the only woman he had ever loved, and the deceit of the only friend he had ever made: who eloped from him to be married together—the discovery, so followed up, completed what his earliest rearing had begun. He shrank, abashed, within the form of Barbox, and lifted up his head and heart no more.

But he did at last effect one great release in his condition. He broke the oar he had plied so long, and he scuttled and sank the galley. He prevented the gradual retirement of an old conventional business from him, by taking the initiative and retiring from it. With enough to live on (though, after all, with not too much), he obliterated the firm of Barbox Brothers from the pages of the Post-Office Directory and the face of the earth, leaving nothing of it but its name on two portmanteaus.

"For one must have some name in going about, for people to pick up," he explained to Mugby High Street, through the Inn window, "and that name at least was real once. Whereas, Young Jackson!—Not to mention its being a sadly satirical misnomer for Old Jackson."

He took up his hat and walked out, just in time to see, passing along on the opposite side of the way, a velveteen man, carrying his day's dinner in a small bundle that might have been larger without suspicion of gluttony, and pelting away towards the Junction at a great pace.

"There's Lamps!" said Barbox Brothers. "And by-the-bye—"

Ridiculous, surely, that a man so serious, so self-contained, and not yet three days emancipated from a routine of drudgery, should stand rubbing his chin in the street, in a brown study about Comic Songs.

"Bedside?" said Barbox Brothers testily. "Sings them at the bedside? Why at the bedside, unless he goes to bed drunk? Does, I shouldn't wonder. But it's no business of mine. Let me see. Mugby Junction, Mugby Junction. Where shall I go next? As it came into my head last night when I woke from an uneasy sleep in the carriage and found myself here, I can go anywhere from here. Where shall I go? I'll go and look at the Junction by daylight. There's no hurry, and I may like the look of one Line better than another."

But there were so many Lines. Gazing down upon them from a bridge at the Junction, it was as if the concentrating Companies formed a great Industrial Exhibition of the works of extraordinary ground spiders that spun iron. And then so many of the Lines went such wonderful ways, so crossing and curving among one another, that the eye lost them. And then some of them appeared to start with the fixed intention of going five hundred miles, and all of a sudden gave it up at an insignificant barrier, or turned off into a workshop. And then others, like intoxicated men, went a little way very straight, and surprisingly slued round and came back again. And then others were so chock-full of trucks of coal, others were so blocked with trucks of casks, others were so gorged with trucks of ballast, others were so set apart for wheeled objects like immense iron cotton-reels: while others were so bright and clear, and others were so delivered over to rust and ashes and idle wheelbarrows out of work, with their legs in the air (looking much like their masters on strike), that there was no beginning, middle, or end to the bewilderment.

Barbox Brothers stood puzzled on the bridge, passing his right hand across the lines on his forehead, which multiplied while he looked down, as if the railway Lines were getting themselves photographed on that sensitive plate. Then was heard a distant ringing of bells and blowing of whistles. Then, puppet-looking heads of men popped out of boxes in perspective, and popped in again. Then, prodigious wooden razors, set up on end, began shaving the atmosphere. Then, several locomotive engines in several directions began to scream and be agitated. Then, along one avenue a train came in. Then, along another two trains appeared that didn't come in, but stopped without. Then, bits of trains broke off. Then, a struggling horse became involved with them. Then, the locomotives shared the bits of trains, and ran away with the whole.

"I have not made my next move much clearer by this. No hurry. No need to make up my mind to-day, or to-morrow, nor yet the day after. I'll take a walk."

It fell out somehow (perhaps he meant it should) that the walk tended to the platform at which he had alighted, and to Lamps's room. But Lamps was not in his room. A pair of velveteen shoulders were adapting themselves to one of the impressions on the wall by Lamps's fireplace, but otherwise the room was void. In passing back to get out of the station again, he learnt the cause of this vacancy, by catching sight of Lamps on the opposite line of railway, skipping along the top of a train, from carriage to carriage, and catching lighted namesakes thrown up to him by a coadjutor.

"He is busy. He has not much time for composing or singing Comic Songs this morning, I take it."

The direction he pursued now was into the country, keeping very near to the side of one great Line of railway, and within easy view of others. "I have half a mind,"' he said, glancing around, "to settle the question from this point, by saying,

'I'll take this set of rails, or that, or t'other, and stick to it.' They separate themselves from the confusion, out here, and go their ways."

Ascending a gentle hill of some extent, he came to a few cottages. There, looking about him as a very reserved man might who had never looked about him in his life before, he saw some six or eight young children come merrily trooping and whooping from one of the cottages, and disperse. But not until they had all turned at the little garden-gate, and kissed their hands to a face at the upper window: a low window enough, although the upper, for the cottage had but a story of one room above the ground.

Now, that the children should do this was nothing; but that they should do this to a face lying on the sill of the open window, turned towards them in a horizontal position, and apparently only a face, was something noticeable. He looked up at the window again. Could only see a very fragile, though a very bright face, lying on one cheek on the window-sill. The delicate smiling face of a girl or woman. Framed in long bright brown hair, round which was tied a light blue band or fillet, passing under the chin.

He walked on, turned back, passed the window again, shyly glanced up again. No change. He struck off by a winding branch-road at the top of the hill—which he must otherwise have descended—kept the cottages in view, worked his way round at a distance so as to come out once more into the main road, and be obliged to pass the cottages again. The face still lay on the window-sill, but not so much inclined towards him. And now there were a pair of delicate hands too. They had the action of performing on some musical instrument, and yet it produced no sound that reached his ears.

"Mugby Junction must be the maddest place in England," said Barbox Brothers, pursuing his way down the hill. "The first thing I find here is a Railway Porter who composes comic songs to sing at his bedside. The second thing I find here is a face, and a pair of hands playing a musical instrument that *don't* play!"

The day was a fine bright day in the early beginning of November, the air was clear and inspiriting, and the landscape was rich in beautiful colours. The prevailing colours in the court off Lombard Street, London city, had been few and sombre. Sometimes, when the weather elsewhere was very bright indeed, the dwellers in those tents enjoyed a pepper-and-salt-coloured day or two, but their atmosphere's usual wear was slate or snuff coloured.

He relished his walk so well that he repeated it next day. He was a little earlier at the cottage than on the day before, and he could hear the children upstairs singing to a regular measure, and clapping out the time with their hands.

"Still, there is no sound of any musical instrument," he said, listening at the corner, "and yet I saw the performing hands again as I came by. What are the children singing? Why, good Lord, they can never be singing the multiplication table?"

They were, though, and with infinite enjoyment. The mysterious face had a voice attached to it, which occasionally led or set the children right. Its musical cheerfulness was delightful. The measure at length stopped, and was succeeded by a murmuring of young voices, and then by a short song which he made out to be about the current month of the year, and about what work it yielded to the labourers in the fields and farmyards. Then there was a stir of little feet, and the children came trooping and whooping out, as on the previous day. And again, as on the previous day, they all turned at the garden-gate, and kissed their hands—evidently to the face on the window-sill, though Barbox Brothers from his retired post of disadvantage at the corner could not see it.

But, as the children dispersed, he cut off one small straggler—a brown-faced boy with flaxen hair—and said to him:

"Come here, little one. Tell me, whose house is that?"

The child, with one swarthy arm held up across his eyes, half in shyness, and half ready for defence, said from behind the inside of his elbow:

"Phœbe's."

"And who," said Barbox Brothers, quite as much embarrassed by his part in the dialogue as the child could possibly be by his, "is Phœbe?"

To which the child made answer: "Why, Phœbe, of course."

The small but sharp observer had eyed his questioner closely, and had taken his moral measure. He lowered his guard, and rather assumed a tone with him: as having discovered him to be an unaccustomed person in the art of polite conversation.

"Phœbe," said the child, "can't be anybobby else but Phœbe. Can she?"

"No, I suppose not."

"Well," returned the child, "then why did you ask me?"

Deeming it prudent to shift his ground, Barbox Brothers took up a new position.

"What do you do there? Up there in that room where the open window is. What do you do there?"

"Cool," said the child.

"Eh?"

"Co-o-ol," the child repeated in a louder voice, lengthening out the word with a fixed look and great emphasis, as much as to say: "What's the use of your having grown up, if you're such a donkey as not to understand me?"

"Ah! School, school," said Barbox Brothers. "Yes, yes, yes. And Phœbe teaches you?"

The child nodded.

"Good boy."

"Tound it out, have you?" said the child.

"Yes, I have found it out. What would you do with twopence, if I gave it you?"

"Pend it."

The knock-down promptitude of this reply leaving him not a leg to stand upon, Barbox Brothers produced the twopence with great lameness, and withdrew in a state of humiliation.

But, seeing the face on the window-sill as he passed the cottage, he acknowledged its presence there with a gesture, which was not a nod, not a bow, not a removal of his hat from his head, but was a diffident compromise between or struggle with all three. The eyes in the face seemed amused, or cheered, or both, and the lips modestly said: "Good day to you, Sir."

"I find I must stick for a time to Mugby Junction," said Barbox Brothers with much gravity, after once more stopping on his return road to look at the Lines where they went their several ways so quietly. "I can't make up my mind yet which iron road to take. In fact, I must get a little accustomed to the Junction before I can decide."

So, he announced at the Inn that he was "going to stay on for the present," and improved his acquaintance with the Junction that night, and again next morning, and again next night and morning: going down to the station, mingling with the people there, looking about him down all the avenues of railway, and beginning to take an interest in the incomings and outgoings of the trains. At first, he often put his head into Lamps's little room, but he never found Lamps there. A pair or two of velveteen shoulders he usually found there, stooping over the fire, sometimes in connection with a clasped knife and a piece of bread and meat; but the answer to his inquiry, "Where's Lamps?" was, either that he was "t'other side the line," or, that it was his off-time, or (in the latter case) his own personal introduction to another Lamps who was not his Lamps. However, he was not so desperately set upon seeing Lamps now, but he bore the disappointment. Nor did he so wholly devote himself to his severe application to the study of Mugby Junction as to neglect exercise. On the contrary, he took a walk every day, and always the same walk. But the weather turned cold and wet again, and the window was never open.

III

At length, after a lapse of some days, there came another streak of fine bright hardy autumn weather. It was a Saturday. The window was open, and the children were gone. Not surprising, this, for he had patiently watched and waited at the corner until they *were* gone.

"Good day," he said to the face; absolutely getting his hat clear off his head this time.

"Good day to you, Sir."

"I am glad you have a fine sky again to look at."

"Thank you, Sir. It is kind of you."

"You are an invalid, I fear?"

"No, Sir. I have very good health."

"But are you not always lying down?"

"Oh yes, I am always lying down, because I cannot sit up! But I am not an invalid."

The laughing eyes seemed highly to enjoy his great mistake.

"Would you mind taking the trouble to come in, Sir? There is a beautiful view from this window. And you would see that I am not at all ill—being so good as to care."

It was said to help him, as he stood irresolute, but evidently desiring to enter, with his diffident hand on the latch of the garden-gate. It did help him, and he went in.

The room upstairs was a very clean white room with a low roof. Its only inmate lay on a couch that brought her face to a level with the window. The couch was white too; and her simple dress or wrapper being light blue, like the band around her hair, she had an ethereal look, and a fanciful appearance of lying among clouds. He felt that she instinctively perceived him to be by habit a downcast taciturn man; it was another help to him to have established that understanding so easily, and got it over.

There was an awkward constraint upon him, nevertheless, as he touched her hand, and took a chair at the side of her couch.

"I see now," he began, not at all fluently, "how you occupy your hand. Only seeing you from the path outside, I thought you were playing upon something."

She was engaged in very nimbly and dexterously making lace. A lace-pillow lay upon her breast; and the quick movements and changes of her hands upon it, as she worked, had given them the action he had misinterpreted.

"That is curious," she answered with a bright smile. "For I often fancy, myself, that I play tunes while I am at work."

"Have you any musical knowledge?"

She shook her head.

"I think I could pick out tunes, if I had any instrument, which could be made as handy to me as my lace-pillow. But I dare say I deceive myself. At all events, I shall never know."

"You have a musical voice. Excuse me; I have heard you sing."

"With the children?" she answered, slightly colouring. "Oh yes. I sing with the dear children, if it can be called singing."

Barbox Brothers glanced at the two small forms in the room, and hazarded the speculation that she was fond of children, and that she was learned in new systems of teaching them?

"Very fond of them," she said, shaking her head again; "but I know nothing of teaching, beyond the interest I have in it, and the pleasure it gives me when they learn. Perhaps your overhearing my little scholars sing some of their lessons has led you so far astray as to think me a grand teacher? Ah! I thought so! No, I have only read and been told about that system. It seemed so pretty and pleasant, and to treat them so like the merry Robins they are, that I took up with it in my little way. You don't need to be told what a very little way mine is, Sir," she added with a glance at the small forms and round the room.

All this time her hands were busy at her lace-pillow. As they still continued so, and as there was a kind of substitute for conversation in the click and play of its pegs, Barbox Brothers took the opportunity of observing her. He guessed her to be thirty. The charm of her transparent face and large bright brown eyes was, not that they were passively resigned, but that they were actively and thoroughly cheerful. Even her busy hands, which of their own thinness alone might have besought compassion, plied their task with a gay courage that made mere compassion an unjustifiable assumption of superiority, and an impertinence.

He saw her eyes in the act of rising towards his, and he directed his towards the prospect, saying: "Beautiful, indeed!"

"Most beautiful, Sir. I have sometimes had a fancy that I would like to sit up, for once, only to try how it looks to an erect head. But what a foolish fancy that would be to encourage! It cannot look more lovely to any one than it does to me."

Her eyes were turned to it, as she spoke, with most delighted admiration and enjoyment. There was not a trace in it of any sense of deprivation.

"And those threads of railway, with their puffs of smoke and steam changing places so fast, make it so lively for me," she went on. "I think of the number of people who can go where they wish, on their business, or their pleasure; I remember that the puffs make signs to me that they are actually going while I look; and that enlivens the prospect with abundance of company, if I want company. There is the great Junction, too. I don't see it under the foot of the hill, but I can very often hear it, and I always know it is there. It seems to join me, in a way, to I don't know how many places and things that *I* shall never see."

With an abashed kind of idea that it might have already joined himself to something he had never seen, he said constrainedly: "Just so."

"And so you see, Sir," pursued Phœbe, "I am not the invalid you thought me, and I am very well off indeed."

"You have a happy disposition," said Barbox Brothers: perhaps with a slight excusatory touch for his own disposition.

"Ah! But you should know my father," she replied. "His is the happy disposition!—Don't mind, Sir!" For his reserve took the alarm at a step upon the stairs, and he distrusted that he would be set down for a troublesome intruder. "This is my father coming."

The door opened, and the father paused there.

"Why, Lamps!" exclaimed Barbox Brothers, starting from his chair. "How do you DO, Lamps?"

To which Lamps responded: "The gentleman for Nowhere! How do you DO, Sir?"

And they shook hands, to the greatest admiration and surprise of Lamp's daughter.

"I have looked you up half-a-dozen times since that night," said Barbox Brothers, "but have never found you."

"So I've heerd on, Sir, so I've heerd on," returned Lamps. "It's your being noticed so often down at the Junction, without taking any train, that has begun to get you the name among us of the gentleman for Nowhere. No offence in my having called you by it when took by surprise, I hope, Sir?"

"None at all. It's as good a name for me as any other you could call me by. But may I ask you a question in the corner here?"

Lamps suffered himself to be led aside from his daughter's couch by one of the buttons of his velveteen jacket.

"Is this the bedside where you sing your songs?"

Lamps nodded.

The gentleman for Nowhere clapped him on the shoulder, and they faced about again.

"Upon my word, my dear," said Lamps then to his daughter, looking from her to her visitor, "it is such an amaze to me, to find you brought acquainted with this gentleman, that I must (if this gentleman will excuse me) take a rounder."

Mr. Lamps demonstrated in action what this meant, by pulling out his oily handkerchief rolled up in the form of a ball, and giving himself an elaborate smear, from behind the right ear, up the cheek, across the forehead, and down the other cheek to behind his left ear. After this operation he shone exceedingly.

"It's according to my custom when particular warmed up by any agitation, Sir," he offered by way of apology. "And really, I am throwed into that state of amaze by finding you brought acquainted with Phœbe, that I—that I think I will, if you'll excuse me, take another rounder." Which he did, seeming to be greatly restored by it.

They were now both standing by the side of her couch, and she was working at her lace-pillow. "Your daughter tells me," said Barbox Brothers, still in a half-reluctant shamefaced way, "that she never sits up."

"No, Sir, nor never has done. You see, her mother (who died when she was a year and two months old) was subject to very bad fits, and as she had never mentioned to me that she *was* subject to fits, they couldn't be guarded against. Consequently, she dropped the baby when took, and this happened."

"It was very wrong of her," said Barbox Brothers with a knitted brow, "to marry you, making a secret of her infirmity."

"Well, Sir!" pleaded Lamps in behalf of the long-deceased. "You see, Phœbe and me, we have talked that over too. And Lord bless us! Such a number on us has our infirmities, what with fits, and what with misfits, of one sort and another, that if we confessed to 'em all before we got married, most of us might never get married."

"Might not that be for the better?"

"Not in this case, Sir," said Phœbe, giving her hand to her father.

"No, not in this case, Sir," said her father, patting it between his own.

"You correct me," returned Barbox Brothers with a blush; "and I must look so like a Brute, that at all events it would be superfluous in me to confess to *that* infirmity. I wish you would tell me a little more about yourselves. I hardly knew how to ask it of you, for I am conscious that I have a bad stiff manner, a dull discouraging way with me, but I wish you would."

"With all our hearts, Sir," returned Lamps gaily for both. "And first of all, that you may know my name—"

"Stay!" interposed the visitor with a slight flush. "What signifies your name? Lamps is name enough for me. I like it. It is bright and expressive. What do I want more?"

"Why, to be sure, Sir," returned Lamps. "I have in general no other name down at the Junction; but I thought, on account of your being here as a first-class single, in a private character, that you might—"

The visitor waved the thought away with his hand, and Lamps acknowledged the mark of confidence by taking another rounder.

"You are hard-worked, I take for granted?" said Barbox Brothers, when the subject of the rounder came out of it much dirtier than be went into it.

Lamps was beginning, "Not particular so"—when his daughter took him up.

"Oh yes, Sir, he is very hard-worked. Fourteen, fifteen, eighteen hours a day. Sometimes twenty-four hours at a time."

"And you," said Barbox Brothers, "what with your school, Phœbe, and what with your lace-making—"

"But my school is a pleasure to me," she interrupted, opening her brown eyes wider, as if surprised to find him so obtuse. "I began it when I was but a child, because it brought me and other children into company, don't you see? *That* was not work. I carry it on still, because it keeps children about me. *That* is not work. I do it as love, not as work. Then my lace-pillow"; her busy hands had stopped, as if her argument required all her cheerful earnestness, but now went on again at the name; "it goes with my thoughts when I think, and it goes with my tunes when I hum any, and *that's* not work. Why, you yourself thought it was music, you know, Sir. And so it is to me."

"Everything is!" cried Lamps radiantly. "Everything is music to her, Sir."

"My father is, at any rate," said Phœbe, exultingly pointing her thin forefinger at him. "There is more music in my father than there is in a brass band."

"I say! My dear! It's very fillyillially done, you know; but you are flattering your father," he protested, sparkling.

"No, I am not, Sir, I assure you. No, I am not. If you could hear my father sing, you would know I am not. But you never will hear him sing, because he never sings to any one but me. However tired he is, he always sings to me when he comes home. When I lay here long ago, quite a poor little broken doll, he used to sing to me. More than that, he used to make songs, bringing in whatever little jokes we had between us. More than that, he often does so to this day. Oh! I'll tell of you, father, as the gentleman has asked about you. He is a poet, Sir."

"I shouldn't wish the gentleman, my dear," observed Lamps, for the moment turning grave, "to carry away that opinion of your father, because it might look as if I was given to asking the stars in a molloncolly manner what they was up to. Which I wouldn't at once waste the time, and take the liberty, my dear."

"My father," resumed Phœbe, amending her text, "is always on the bright side, and the good side. You told me, just now, I had a happy disposition. How can I help it?"

"Well; but, my dear," returned Lamps argumentatively, "how can I help it? Put it to yourself, Sir. Look at her. Always as you see her now. Always working—and after all, Sir, for but a very few shillings a week—always contented, always lively, always interested in others, of all sorts. I said, this moment, she was always as you see her now. So she is, with a difference that comes to much the same. For, when it is my Sunday off and the morning bells have done ringing, I hear the prayers and thanks read in the touchingest way, and I have the hymns sung to me—so soft, Sir, that you couldn't hear 'em out of this room—in notes that seem to me, I am sure, to come from Heaven and go back to it."

It might have been merely through the association of these words with their sacredly quiet time, or it might have been through the larger association of the words with the Redeemer's presence beside the bedridden; but here her dexterous fingers came to a stop on the lace-pillow, and clasped themselves around his neck as he bent down. There was great natural sensibility in both father and daughter, the visitor could easily see; but each made it, for the other's sake, retiring, not demonstrative; and perfect cheerfulness, intuitive or acquired, was either the first or second nature of both. In a very few moments Lamps was taking another rounder with his comical features beaming, while Phœbe's laughing eyes (just a glistening speck or so upon their lashes) were again directed by turns to him, and to her work, and to Barbox Brothers.

"When my father, Sir," she said brightly, "tells you about my being interested in other people, even though they know nothing about me—which, by the bye, I told you myself—you ought to know how that comes about. That's my father's doing."

"No, it isn't!" he protested.

"Don't you believe him, Sir; yes, it is. He tells me of everything he sees down at his work. You would be surprised what a quantity he gets together for me every day. He looks into the carriages, and tells me how the ladies are dressed—so that I know all the fashions! He looks into the carriages, and tells me what pairs of lovers he sees, and what new-married couples on their wedding trip—so that I know all about that! He collects chance newspapers and books—so that I have plenty to read! He tells me about the sick people who are travelling to try to get better—so that I know all about them! In short, as I began by saying, he tells me everything he sees and makes out down at his work, and you can't think what a quantity he does see and make out."

"As to collecting newspapers and books, my dear," said Lamps, "it's clear I can have no merit in that, because they're not my perquisites. You see, sir, it's this way: A Guard, he'll say to me, 'Hallo, here you are, Lamps. I've saved this paper for your daughter. How is she a-going on?' A Head Porter, he'll say to me, 'Here! Catch hold, Lamps. Here's a couple of wollumes for your daughter. Is she pretty much where she were?' And that's what makes it double welcome, you see. If she had a thousand pound in a box, they wouldn't trouble themselves about her; but being what she is—that is, you understand," Lamps added, somewhat hurriedly, "not having a thousand pound in a box—they take thought for her. And as concerning the young pairs, married and unmarried, it's only natural I should bring home what little I can about *them*, seeing that there's not a Couple of either sort in the neighbourhood that don't come of their own accord to confide in Phœbe."

She raised her eyes triumphantly to Barbox Brothers as she said:

"Indeed, Sir, that is true. If I could have got up and gone to church, I don't know how often I should have been a bridesmaid. But, if I could have done that, some girls in love might have been jealous of me, and, as it is, no girl is jealous of me. And my pillow would not have been half as ready to put the piece of cake under, as I always find it," she added, turning her face on it with a light sigh, and a smile at her father.

The arrival of a little girl, the biggest of the scholars, now led to an understanding on the part of Barbox Brothers, that she was the domestic of the cottage, and had come to take active measures in it, attended by a pail that might have extinguished her, and a broom three times her height. He therefore rose to take his leave, and took it; saying that, if Phœbe had no objection, he would come again.

He had muttered that he would come "in the course of his walks." The course of his walks must have been highly favourable to his return, for he returned after an interval of a single day.

"You thought you would never see me any more, I suppose?" he said to Phœbe as he touched her hand, and sat down by her couch.

"Why should I think so?" was her surprised rejoinder.

"I took it for granted you would mistrust me."

"For granted, Sir? Have you been so much mistrusted?"

"I think I am justified in answering yes. But I may have mistrusted, too, on my part. No matter just now. We were speaking of the Junction last time. I have passed hours there since the day before yesterday."

"Are you now the gentleman for Somewhere?" she asked with a smile.

"Certainly for Somewhere; but I don't yet know Where. You would never guess what I am travelling from. Shall I tell you? I am travelling from my birthday."

Her hands stopped in her work, and she looked at him with incredulous astonishment.

"Yes," said Barbox Brothers, not quite easy in his chair, "from my birthday. I am, to myself, an unintelligible book with the earlier chapters all torn out, and thrown away. My childhood had no grace of childhood, my youth had no charm of youth, and what can be expected from such a lost beginning?" His eyes meeting hers as they were addressed intently to him, something seemed to stir within his breast, whispering: "Was this bed a place for the graces of childhood and the charms of youth to take to kindly? Oh, shame, shame!"

"It is a disease with me," said Barbox Brothers, checking himself, and making as though he had a difficulty in swallowing something, "to go wrong about that. I don't know how I came to speak of that. I hope it is because of an old misplaced confidence in one of your sex involving an old bitter treachery. I don't know. I am all wrong together."

Her hands quietly and slowly resumed their work. Glancing at her, he saw that her eyes were thoughtfully following them.

"I am travelling from my birthday," he resumed, "because it has always been a dreary day to me. My first free birthday coming round some five or six weeks hence, I am travelling to put its predecessors far behind me, and to try to crush the day—or, at all events, put it out of my sight—by heaping new objects on it."

As he paused, she looked at him; but only shook her head as being quite at a loss.

"This is unintelligible to your happy disposition," he pursued, abiding by his former phrase as if there were some lingering virtue of self-defence in it. "I knew it would be, and am glad it is. However, on this travel of mine (in which I mean to pass the rest of my days, having abandoned all thought of a fixed home), I stopped, as you have heard from your father, at the Junction here. The extent of its ramifications quite confused me as to whither I should go, *from* here. I have not yet settled, being still perplexed among so many roads. What do you think I mean to do? How many of the branching roads can you see from your window?"

Looking out, full of interest, she answered, "Seven."

"Seven," said Barbox Brothers, watching her with a grave smile. "Well! I propose to myself at once to reduce the gross number to those very seven, and gradually to fine them down to one—the most promising for me—and to take that."

"But how will you know, Sir, which *is* the most promising?" she asked, with her brightened eyes roving over the view.

"Ah!" said Barbox Brothers with another grave smile, and considerably improving in his ease of speech. "To be sure. In this way. Where your father can pick up so much every day for a good purpose, I may once and again pick up a little for an indifferent purpose. The gentleman for Nowhere must become still better known at the Junction. He shall continue to explore it, until he attaches something that he has seen, heard, or found out, at the head of each of the seven roads, to the road itself. And so his choice of a road shall be determined by his choice among his discoveries."

Her hands still busy, she again glanced at the prospect, as if it comprehended something that had not been in it before, and laughed as if it yielded her new pleasure.

"But I must not forget," said Barbox Brothers, "(having got so far) to ask a favour. I want your help in this expedient of mine. I want to bring you what I pick up at the heads of the seven roads that you lie here looking out at, and to compare notes with you about it. May I? They say two heads are better than one. I should say myself that probably depends upon the heads concerned. But I am quite sure, though we are so newly acquainted, that your head and your father's have found out better things, Phœbe, than ever mine of itself discovered."

She gave him her sympathetic right hand, in perfect rapture with his proposal, and eagerly and gratefully thanked him.

"That's well!" said Barbox Brothers. "Again I must not forget (having got so far) to ask a favour. Will you shut your eyes?"

Laughing playfully at the strange nature of the request, she did so.

"Keep them shut," said Barbox Brothers, going softly to the door, and coming back. "You are on your honour, mind, not to open you eyes until I tell you that you may?"

"Yes! On my honour."

"Good. May I take your lace-pillow from you for a minute?"

Still laughing and wondering, she removed her hands from it, and he put it aside.

"Tell me. Did you see the puffs of smoke and steam made by the morning fast-train yesterday on road number seven from here?"

"Behind the elm-trees and the spire?"

"That's the road," said Barbox Brothers, directing his eyes towards it.

"Yes. I watched them melt away."

"Anything unusual in what they expressed?"

"No!" she answered merrily.

"Not complimentary to me, for I was in that train. I went—don't open your eyes—to fetch you this, from the great ingenious town. It is not half so large as your lace-pillow, and lies easily and lightly in its place. These little keys are like the keys of a miniature piano, and you supply the air required with your left hand. May you pick out delightful music from it, my dear! For the present—you can open your eyes now—good-bye!"

In his embarrassed way, he closed the door upon himself, and only saw, in doing so, that she ecstatically took the present to her bosom and caressed it. The glimpse gladdened his heart, and yet saddened it; for so might she, if her youth had flourished in its natural course, having taken to her breast that day the slumbering music of her own child's voice.

Chapter II

Barbox Brothers and Co.

WITH GOOD-WILL AND EARNEST PURPOSE, THE GENTLEMAN FOR NOWHERE began, on the very next day, his researches at the heads of the seven roads. The results of his researches, as he and Phœbe afterwards set them down in fair writing, hold their due places in this veracious chronicle. But they occupied a much longer time in the getting together than they ever will in the perusal. And this is probably the case with most reading matter, except when it is of that highly beneficial kind (for Posterity) which is "thrown off in a few moments of leisure" by the superior poetic geniuses who scorn to take prose pains.

It must be admitted, however, that Barbox by no means hurried himself. His heart being in his work of good-nature, he revelled in it. There was the joy, too (it was a true joy to him), of sometimes sitting by, listening to Phœbe as she picked out more and more discourse from her musical instrument, and as her natural taste and ear refined daily upon her first discoveries. Besides being a pleasure, this was an occupation, and in the course of weeks it consumed hours. It resulted that his dreaded birthday was close upon him before he had troubled himself any more about it.

The matter was made more pressing by the unforeseen circumstance that the councils held (at which Mr. Lamps, beaming most brilliantly, on a few rare occasions assisted) respecting the road to be selected were, after all, in nowise assisted by his investigations. For, he had connected this interest with this road, or that interest with the other, but could deduce no reason from it for giving any road the preference. Consequently, when the last council was holden, that part of the business stood, in the end, exactly where it had stood in the beginning.

"But, Sir," remarked Phœbe, "we have only six roads after all. Is the seventh road dumb?"

"The seventh road? Oh!" said Barbox Brothers, rubbing his chin. "That is the road I took, you know, when I went to get your little present. That is *its* story. Phœbe."

"Would you mind taking that road again, Sir?" she asked with hesitation.

"Not in the least; it is a great high-road after all."

"I should like you to take it," returned Phœbe with a persuasive smile, "for the love of that little present which must ever be so dear to me. I should like you to take it, because that road can never be again like any other road to me. I should like you to take it, in remembrance of your having done me so much good: of your having made me so much happier! If you leave me by the road you travelled when you went to do me this great kindness," sounding a faint chord as she spoke, "I shall feel, lying here watching at my window, as if it must conduct you to a prosperous end, and bring you back some day."

"It shall be done, my dear; it shall be done."

So at last the gentleman for Nowhere took a ticket for Somewhere, and his destination was the great ingenious town.

He had loitered so long about the Junction that it was the eighteenth of December when he left it. "High time," he reflected, as he seated himself in the train, "that I started in earnest! Only one clear day remains between me and the day I am running away from. I'll push onward for the hill-country to-morrow. I'll go to Wales."

It was with some pains that he placed before himself the undeniable advantages to be gained in the way of novel occupation for his senses from misty mountains, swollen streams, rain, cold, a wild seashore, and rugged roads. And yet he scarcely made them out as distinctly as he could have wished. Whether the poor girl, in spite of her new resource, her music, would have any feeling of loneliness upon her now—just at first—that she had not had before; whether she saw those very puffs of steam and smoke that he saw, as he sat in the train thinking of her; whether her face would have any pensive shadow on it as they died out of the distant view from her window; whether, in telling him he had done her so much good, she had not unconsciously corrected his old moody bemoaning of his station in life, by setting him thinking that a man might be a great healer, if he would, and yet not be a great doctor; these and other similar meditations got between him and his Welsh picture.

There was within him, too, that dull sense of vacuity which follows separation from an object of interest, and cessation of a pleasant pursuit; and this sense, being quite new to him, made him restless. Further, in losing Mugby Junction, he had found himself again; and he was not the more enamoured of himself for having lately passed his time in better company.

But surely here, not far ahead, must be the great ingenious town. This crashing and clashing that the train was undergoing, and this coupling on to it of a multitude of new echoes, could mean nothing less than approach to the great station. It did mean nothing less. After some stormy flashes of town lightning, in the way of swift revelations of red brick blocks of houses, high red brick chimney-shafts, vistas of red brick railway arches, tongues of fire, blocks of smoke, valleys of canal, and hills if coal, there came the thundering in at the journey's end.

Having seen his portmanteaus safely housed in the hotel he chose, and having appointed his dinner hour, Barbox Brothers went out for a walk in the busy streets. And now it began to be suspected by him that Mugby Junction was a Junction of many branches, invisible as well as visible, and had joined him to an endless number of by-ways. For, whereas he would, but a little while ago, have walked these streets blindly brooding, he now had eyes and thoughts for a new external world. How the many toiling people lived, and loved, and died; how wonderful it was to consider the various trainings of eye and hand, the nice distinctions of sight and touch, that separated them into classes of workers, and even into classes of workers at subdivisions of one complete whole which combined their many intelligences and forces, though of itself but some cheap object of use or ornament in common life; how good it was to know that such assembling in a multitude on their part, and such contribution of their several dexterities towards a civilising end, did not deteriorate them as it was the fashion of the supercilious Mayflies of humanity to pretend, but engendered among them a self-respect, and yet a modest desire to be much wiser than they were (the first evinced in their well-balanced bearing and manner of speech when he stopped to ask a question; the second, in the announcements of their popular studies and amusements on the public walls); these considerations, and a host of such, made his walk a memorable one. "I too am but a little part of a great whole," he began to think; "and to be serviceable to myself and others, or to be happy, I must cast my interest into, and draw it out of, the common stock."

Although he had arrived at his journey's end for the day by noon, he had since insensibly walked about the town so far and so long that the lamp-lighters were now at their work in the streets, and the shops were sparkling up brilliantly. Thus reminded to turn towards his quarters, he was in the act of doing so, when a very little hand crept into his, and a very little voice said:

"Oh! if you please, I am lost!"

He looked down, and saw a very little fair-haired girl.

"Yes," she said, confirming her words with a serious nod. "I am indeed. I am lost!"

Greatly perplexed, he stopped, looked about him for help, descried none, and said, bending low.

"Where do you live, my child?"

"I don't know where I live," she returned. "I am lost."

"What is your name?"

"Polly."

"What is your other name?"

The reply was prompt, but unintelligible.

Imitating the sound as he caught it, he hazarded the guess, "Trivits."

"Oh no!" said the child, shaking her head. "Nothing like that."

"Say it again, little one."

An unpromising business. For this time it had quite a different sound.

He made the venture, "Paddens?"

"Oh no!" said the child. "Nothing like that."

"Once more. Let us try it again, dear."

A most hopeless business. This time it swelled into four syllables. "It can't be Tappitarver?" said Barbox Brothers, rubbing his head with his hat in discomfiture.

"No! It ain't," thc child quietly assented.

On her trying this unfortunate name once more, with extraordinary efforts at distinctness, it swelled into eight syllables at least.

"Ah! I think," said Barbox Brothers with a desperate air of resignation, "that we had better give it up."

"But I am lost," said the child, nestling her little hand more closely in his, "and you'll take care of me, won't you?"

If ever a man were disconcerted by division between compassion on the one hand, and the very imbecility of irresolution on the other, here the man was. "Lost!" he repeated, looking down at the child. "I am sure *I* am. What is to be done?"

"Where do you live?" asked the child, looking up at him wistfully.

"Over there," he answered, pointing vaguely in the direction of his hotel.

"Hadn't we better go there?" said the child.

"Really," he replied, "I don't know but what we had."

So they set off, hand-in-hand. He, through comparison of himself against his little companion, with a clumsy feeling on him as if he had just developed into a foolish giant. She, clearly elevated in her own tiny opinion by having got him so neatly out of his embarrassment.

"We are going to have dinner when we get there, I suppose?" said Polly.

"Well," he rejoined, "I—Yes, I suppose we are."

"Do you like your dinner?" asked the child.

"Why, on the whole," said Barbox Brothers, "yes, I think I do."

"I do mine," said Polly. "Have you any brothers and sisters?"

"No. Have you?"

"Mine are dead."

"Oh!" said Barbox Brothers. With that absurd sense of unwieldiness of mind and body weighing him down, he would have not known how to pursue the conversation beyond this curt rejoinder, but that the child was always ready for him.

"What," she asked, turning her soft hand coaxingly in his, "are you going to do to amuse me after dinner?"

"Upon my soul, Polly," exclaimed Barbox Brothers, very much at a loss, "I have not the slightest idea!"

"Then I tell you what," said Polly. "Have you got any cards at your house?"

"Plenty," said Barbox Brothers in a boastful vein.

"Very well. Then I'll build houses, and you shall look at me. You mustn't blow, you know."

"Oh no," said Barbox Brothers. "No, no, no. No blowing. Blowing's not fair."

He flattered himself that he had said this pretty well for an idiotic monster; but the child, instantly perceiving the awkwardness of his attempt to adapt himself to her level, utterly destroyed his hopeful opinion of himself by saying compassionately: "What a funny man you are!"

Feeling, after this melancholy failure, as if he every minute grew bigger and heavier in person, and weaker in mind, Barbox gave himself up for a bad job. No giant ever submitted more meekly to be led in triumph by all-conquering Jack than he to be bound in slavery to Polly.

"Do you know any stories?" she asked him.

He was reduced to the humiliating confession: "No."

"What a dunce you must be, mustn't you?" said Polly.

He was reduced to the humiliating confession: "Yes."

"Would you like me to teach you a story? But you must remember it, you know, and be able to tell it right to somebody else afterwards."

He professed that it would afford him the highest mental gratification to be taught a story, and that he would humbly endeavour to retain it in his mind. Whereupon Polly, giving her hand a new little turn in his, expressive of settling down for enjoyment, commenced a long romance, of which every relishing clause began with the words: "So this," or, "And so this." As, "So this boy"; or, "So this fairy"; or, "And so this pie was four yards round, and two yards and a quarter deep." The interest of the romance was derived from the intervention of this fairy to punish this boy for having a greedy appetite. To achieve which purpose, this fairy made this pie, and this boy ate and ate and ate, and his cheeks swelled and swelled and swelled. There were many tributary circumstances, but the forcible interest culminated in the total consumption of this pie, and the bursting of this boy. Truly he was a fine sight, Barbox Brothers, with serious attentive face, and ear bent down, much jostled on the pavements of the busy town, but afraid of losing a single incident of the epic, lest he should be examined in it by-and-by, and found deficient.

Thus they arrived at the hotel. And there he had to say at the bar, and said awkwardly enough: "I have found a little girl!"

The whole establishment turned out to look at the little girl. Nobody knew her; nobody could make out her name, as she set it forth—except one chambermaid, who said it was Constantinople—which it wasn't.

"I will dine with my young friend in a private room," said Barbox Brothers to the hotel authorities, "and perhaps you will be so good as to let the police know that the pretty baby is here. I suppose she is sure to be inquired for soon, if she has not been already. Come along, Polly."

Perfectly at ease and peace, Polly came along, but, finding the stairs rather stiff work, was carried up by Barbox Brothers. The dinner was a most transcendant success, and the Barbox sheepishness, under Polly's directions how to mince her meat for her, and how to diffuse gravy over the plate with a liberal and equal hand, was another fine sight.

"And now," said Polly, "while we are at dinner, you be good, and tell me that story I taught you."

With the tremors of a Civil Service examination upon him, and very uncertain indeed, not only as to the epoch at which the pie appeared in history, but also as to the measurements of that indispensable fact, Barbox Brothers made a shaky beginning, but under encouragement did very fairly. There was a want of breadth observable in his rendering of the cheeks, as well as the appetite, of the boy; and there was a certain tameness in his fairy, referable to an under-current of desire to account for her. Still, as the first lumbering performance of a good-humoured monster, it passed muster.

"I told you to be good," said Polly, "and you are good, ain't you?"

"I hope so," replied Barbox Brothers.

Such was his deference that Polly, elevated on a platform of sofa cushions in a chair at his right hand, encouraged him with a pat or two on the face from the greasy bowl of her spoon, and even with a gracious kiss. In getting on her feet upon her chair, however, to give him this last reward, she toppled forward among the dishes, and caused him to exclaim, as he effected her rescue: "Gracious Angels! Whew! I thought we were in the fire, Polly!"

"What a coward you are, ain't you?" said Polly when replaced.

"Yes, I am rather nervous," he replied. "Whew! Don't, Polly! Don't flourish your spoon, or you'll go over sideways. Don't tilt up your legs when you laugh, Polly, or you'll go over backwards. Whew! Polly, Polly, Polly," said Barbox Brothers, nearly succumbing to despair, "we are environed with dangers!"

Indeed, he could descry no security from the pitfalls that were yawning for Polly, but in proposing to her, after dinner, to sit upon a low stool. "I will, if you will," said Polly. So, as peace of mind should go before all, he begged the waiter to wheel aside the table, bring a pack of cards, a couple of footstools, and a screen, and close in Polly and himself before the fire, as it were in a snug room within the room. Then, finest sight of all, was Barbox Brothers on his footstool, with a pint decanter on the rug, contemplating Polly as she built successfully, and growing blue in the face with holding his breath, lest he should blow the house down.

"How you stare, don't you?" said Polly in a houseless pause.

Detected in the ignoble fact, he felt obliged to admit, apologetically: "I am afraid I was looking rather hard at you, Polly."

"Why do you stare?" asked Polly.

"I cannot," he murmured to himself, "recall why.—I don't know, Polly."

"You must be a simpleton to do things and not know why, mustn't you?" said Polly.

In spite of which reproof, he looked at the child again intently, as she bent her head over her card structure, her rich curls shading her face. "It is impossible," he thought, "that I can ever have seen this pretty baby before. Can I have dreamed of her? In some sorrowful dream?"

He could make nothing of it. So he went into the building trade as a journeyman under Polly, and they built three stories high, four stories high; even five.

"I say! Who do you think is coming?" asked Polly, rubbing her eyes after tea.

He guessed: "The waiter?"

"No," said Polly, "the dustman. I am getting sleepy."

A new embarrassment for Barbox Brothers!

"I don't think I am going to be fetched to-night," said Polly. "What do you think?"

He thought not, either. After another quarter of an hour, the dustman not merely impending, but actually arriving, recourse was had to the Constantinopolitan chambermaid: who cheerily undertook that the child should sleep in a comfortable and wholesome room, which she herself would share.

"And I know you will be careful, won't you," said Barbox Brothers, as a new fear dawned upon him, "that she don't fall out of bed?"

Polly found this so highly entertaining that she was under the necessity of clutching him round the neck with both arms as he sat on his footstool picking up the cards, and rocking him to and fro, with her dimpled chin on his shoulder.

"Oh, what a coward you are, ain't you?" said Polly. "Do *you* fall out of bed?"

"N—not generally, Polly."

"No more do I."

With that, Polly gave him a reassuring hug or two to keep him going, and then giving that confiding mite of a hand of hers to be swallowed up in the hand of the Constantinopolitan chambermaid, trotted off, chattering, without a vestige of anxiety.

He looked after her, had the screen removed and the table and chairs replaced, and still looked after her. He paced the room for half an hour. "A most engaging little creature, but it's not that. A most winning little voice, but it's not that. That has much to do with it, but there is something more. How can it be that I seem to know this child? What was it she imperfectly recalled to me when I felt her touch in the street, and, looking down at her, saw her looking up at me?"

"Mr. Jackson!"

With a start he turned towards the sound of the subdued voice, and saw his answer standing at the door.

"Oh, Mr. Jackson, do not be severe with me! Speak a word of encouragement to me, I beseech you."

"You are Polly's mother."

"Yes."

Yes. Polly herself might come to this, one day. As you see what the rose was in its faded leaves; as you see what the summer growth of the woods was in their wintry branches; so Polly might be traced, one day, in a careworn woman like this, with her hair turned grey. Before him were the ashes of a dead fire that had once burned bright. This was the woman he had loved. This was the woman he had lost. Such had been the constancy of his imagination to her, so had Time spared her under its withholding, that now, seeing how roughly the inexorable hand had struck her, his soul was filled with pity and amazement.

He led her to a chair, and stood leaning on a corner of the chimney-piece, with his head resting on his hand, and his face half averted.

"Did you see me in the street, and show me to your child?" he asked.

"Yes."

"Is the little creature, then, a party to deceit?"

"I hope there is no deceit. I said to her, 'We have lost our way, and I must try to find mine by myself. Go to that gentleman, and tell him you are lost. You shall be fetched by-and-by.' Perhaps you have not thought how very young she is?"

"She is very self-reliant."

"Perhaps because she is so young."

He asked, after a short pause, "Why did you do this?"

"Oh, Mr. Jackson, do you ask me? In the hope that you might see something in my innocent child to soften your heart towards me. Not only towards me, but towards my husband."

He suddenly turned about, and walked to the opposite end of the room. He came back again with a slower step, and resumed his former attitude, saying:

"I thought you had emigrated to America?"

"We did. But life went ill with us there, and we came back."

"Do you live in this town?"

"Yes. I am a daily teacher of music here. My husband is a bookkeeper."

"Are you—forgive my asking—poor?"

"We earn enough for our wants. That is not our distress. My husband is very, very ill of a lingering disorder. He will never recover—"

"You check yourself. If it is for want of the encouraging word you spoke of, take it from me. I cannot forget the old time, Beatrice."

"God bless you!" she replied with a burst of tears, and gave him her trembling hand.

"Compose yourself. I cannot be composed if you are not, for to see you weep distresses me beyond expression. Speak freely to me. Trust me."

She shaded her face with her veil, and after a little while spoke calmly. Her voice had the ring of Polly's.

"It is not that my husband's mind is at all impaired by his bodily suffering, for I assure you that is not the case. But in his weakness, and in his knowledge that he is incurably ill, he cannot overcome the ascendancy of one idea. It preys upon him, embitters every moment of his painful life, and will shorten it."

She stopping, he said again: "Speak freely to me. Trust me."

"We have had five children before this darling, and they all lie in their little graves. He believes that they have withered away under a curse, and that it will blight this child like the rest."

"Under what curse?"

"Both I and he have it on our conscience that we tried you very heavily, and I do not know but that, if I were as ill as he, I might suffer in my mind as he does. This is the constant burden:—'I believe, Beatrice, I was the only friend that Mr. Jackson ever cared to make, though I was so much his junior. The more influence he acquired in the business, the higher he advanced me, and I was alone in his private confidence. I came between him and you, and I took you from him. We were both secret, and the blow fell when he was wholly unprepared. The anguish it caused a man so compressed must have been terrible; the wrath it awakened inappeasable. So, a curse came to be invoked on our poor, pretty little flowers, and they fall.'"

"And you, Beatrice," he asked, when she had ceased to speak, and there had been a silence afterwards, "how say you?"

"Until within these few weeks I was afraid of you, and I believed that you would never, never forgive."

"Until within these few weeks," he repeated. "Have you changed your opinion of me within these few weeks?"

"Yes."

"For what reason?"

"I was getting some pieces of music in a shop in this town, when, to my terror, you came in. As I veiled my face and stood in the dark end of the shop, I heard you explain that you wanted a musical instrument for a bedridden girl. Your voice and manner were so softened, you showed such interest in its selection, you took it away yourself with so much tenderness of care and pleasure, that I knew you were a man with a most gentle heart. Oh, Mr. Jackson, Mr. Jackson, if you could have felt the refreshing rain of tears that followed for me!"

Was Phœbe playing at that moment on her distant couch? He seemed to hear her.

"I inquired in the shop where you lived, but could get no information. As I had heard you say that you were going back by the next train (but you did not say where), I resolved to visit the station at about that time of day, as often as I could, between my lessons, on the chance of seeing you again. I have been there very often, but saw you no more until to-day. You were meditating as you walked the street, but the calm expression of your face emboldened me to send my child to you. And when I saw you bend your head to speak tenderly to her, I prayed to God to forgive me for having ever brought a sorrow on it. I now pray to you to forgive me, and to forgive my husband. I was very young, he was young too, and, in the ignorant hardihood of such a time of life, we don't know what we do to those who have undergone more discipline. You generous man! You good man! So to raise me up and make nothing of my crime against you!"—for he would not see her on her knees, and soothed her as a kind father might have soothed an erring daughter—"thank you, bless you, thank you!"

When he next spoke, it was after having drawn aside the window curtain and looked out awhile. Then he only said:

"Is Polly asleep?"

"Yes. As I came in, I met her going away upstairs, and put her to bed myself."

"Leave her with me for to-morrow, Beatrice, and write me your address on this leaf of my pocket-book. In the evening I will bring her home to you—and to her father."

"Hallo!" cried Polly, putting her saucy sunny face in at the door next morning when breakfast was ready: "I thought I was fetched last night?"

"So you were, Polly, but I asked leave to keep you here for the day, and to take you home in the evening."

"Upon my word!" said Polly. "You are very cool, ain't you?"

However, Polly seemed to think it a good idea, and added:

"I suppose I must give you a kiss, though you *are* cool."

The kiss given and taken, they sat down to breakfast in a highly conversational tone.

"Of course, you are going to amuse me?" said Polly.

"Oh, of course!" said Barbox Brothers.

In the pleasurable height of her anticipations, Polly found it indispensable to put down her piece of toast, cross one of her little fat knees over the other, and bring her little fat right hand down into her left hand with a business-like slap. After this gathering of herself together, Polly, by that time a mere heap of dimples, asked in a wheedling manner:

"What are we going to do, you dear old thing?"

"Why, I was thinking," said Barbox Brothers, "—but are you fond of horses, Polly?"

"Ponies, I am," said Polly, "especially when their tails are long. But horses—n-no—too big, you know."

"Well," pursued Barbox Brothers, in a spirit of grave mysterious confidence adapted to the importance of the consultation, "I did see yesterday, Polly, on the walls, pictures of two long-tailed ponies, speckled all over—"

"No, no, NO!" cried Polly, in an ecstatic desire to linger on the charming details. "Not speckled all over!"

"Speckled all over. Which ponies jump through hoops—"

"No, no, NO!" cried Polly as before. "They never jump through hoops!"

"Yes, they do. Oh, I assure you they do! And eat pie in pinafores—"

"Ponies eating pie in pinafores!" said Polly. "What a story-teller you are, ain't you?"

"Upon my honour.—And fire off guns."

(Polly hardly seemed to see the force of the ponies resorting to fire-arms.)

"And I was thinking," pursued the exemplary Barbox, "that if you and I were to go to the Circus where these ponies are, it would do our constitutions good."

"Does that mean amuse us?" inquired Polly. "What long words you do use, don't you?"

Apologetic for having wandered out of his depth, he replied:

"That means amuse us. That is exactly what it means. There are many other wonders besides the ponies, and we shall see them all. Ladies and gentlemen in spangled dresses, and elephants and lions and tigers."

Polly became observant of the teapot, with a curled-up nose indicating some uneasiness of mind.

"They never get out, of course," she remarked as a mere truism.

"The elephants and lions and tigers? Oh, dear no!"

"Oh, dear no!" said Polly. "And of course nobody's afraid of the ponies shooting anybody."

"Not the least in the world."

"No, no, not the least in the world," said Polly.

"I was also thinking," proceeded Barbox, "that if we were to look in at the toy-shop, to choose a doll—"

"Not dressed!" cried Polly with a clap of her hands. "No, no, NO, not dressed!"

"Full-dressed. Together with a house, and all things necessary for house-keeping—"

Polly gave a little scream, and seemed in danger of falling into a swoon of bliss.

"What a darling you are!" she languidly exclaimed, leaning back in her chair. "Come and be hugged, or I must come and hug you."

This resplendent programme was carried into execution with the utmost rigour of the law. It being essential to make the purchase of the doll its first feature—or that lady would have lost the ponies—the toy-shop expedition took precedence. Polly in the magic warehouse, with a doll as large as herself under each arm, and a neat assortment of some twenty more on view upon the counter, did indeed present a spectacle of indecision not quite compatible with unalloyed happiness, but the light cloud passed. The lovely specimen oftenest chosen, oftenest rejected, and finally abided by, was of Circassian descent, possessing as much boldness of beauty as was reconcilable with extreme feebleness of mouth, and combining a sky-blue silk pelisse with rose-coloured satin trousers, and a black velvet hat: which this fair stranger to our northern shores would seem to have founded on the portraits of the late Duchess of Kent. The name this distinguished foreigner brought with her from beneath the glowing skies of a sunny clime was (on Polly's authority) Miss Melluka, and the costly nature of her outfit as a housekeeper, from the Barbox coffers, may be inferred from the two facts that her silver tea-spoons were as large as her kitchen poker, and that the proportions of her watch exceeded those of her frying-pan. Miss Melluka was graciously pleased to express her entire approbation of the Circus, and so was Polly; for the ponies were speckled, and brought down nobody when they fired, and the savagery of the wild beasts appeared to be mere smoke—which article, in fact, they did produce in large quantities from their insides. The Barbox absorption in the general subject throughout the realisation of these delights was again a sight to see, nor was it less worthy to behold at dinner, when he drank to Miss Melluka, tied stiff in a chair opposite to Polly (the fair Circassian possessing an unbendable spine), and even induced the waiter to assist in carrying out with due decorum the prevailing glorious idea. To wind up, there came the agreeable fever of getting Miss Melluka and all her wardrobe and rich possessions into a fly with Polly, to be taken home. But, by that time, Polly had become unable to look upon such accumulated joys with waking eyes, and had withdrawn her consciousness into the wonderful Paradise of a child's sleep. "Sleep, Polly, sleep," said Barbox Brothers, as her head dropped on his shoulder; "you shall not fall out of this bed easily, at any rate!"

What rustling piece of paper he took from his pocket, and carefully folded into the bosom of Polly's frock, shall not be mentioned. He said nothing about it, and nothing shall be said about it. They drove to a modest suburb of the great ingenious town, and stopped at the fore-court of a small house. "Do not wake the child," said Barbox Brothers softly to the driver; "I will carry her in as she is."

Greeting the light at the opened door which was held by Polly's mother, Polly's bearer passed on with mother and child in to a ground-floor room. There, stretched on a sofa, lay a sick man, sorely wasted, who covered his eyes with his emaciated hand.

"Tresham," said Barbox in a kindly voice, "I have brought you back your Polly, fast asleep. Give me your hand, and tell me you are better."

The sick man reached forth his right hand, and bowed his head over the hand into which it was taken, and kissed it. "Thank you, thank you! I may say that I am well and happy."

"That's brave," said Barbox. "Tresham, I have a fancy—Can you make room for me beside you here?"

He sat down on the sofa as he said the words, cherishing the plump peachey cheek that lay uppermost on his shoulder.

"I have a fancy, Tresham (I am getting quite an old fellow now, you know, and old fellows may take fancies into their heads sometimes), to give up Polly, having found her, to no one but you. Will you take her from me?"

As the father held out his arms for the child, each of the two men looked steadily at the other.

"She is very dear to you, Tresham?"

"Unutterably dear."

"God bless her! It is not much, Polly," he continued, turning his eyes upon her peaceful face as he apostrophized her, "it is not much, Polly, for a blind and sinful man to invoke a blessing on something so far better than himself as a little child is; but it would be much—much upon his cruel head, and much upon his guilty soul—if he could be so wicked as to invoke a curse. He had better have a millstone round his neck, and be cast into the deepest sea. Live and thrive, my pretty baby!" Here he kissed her. "Live and prosper, and become in time the mother of other little children, like the Angels who behold The Father's face!"

He kissed her again, gave her up gently to both her parents, and went out.

But he went not to Wales. No, he never went to Wales. He went straightway for another stroll about the town, and he looked in upon the people at their work, and at their play, here, there, every-there, and where not. For he was Barbox Brothers and Co. now, and had taken thousands of partners into the solitary firm.

He had at length got back to his hotel room, and was standing before his fire refreshing himself with a glass of hot drink which he had stood upon the chimney-piece, when he heard the town clocks striking, and, referring to his watch, found the evening to have so slipped away, that they were striking twelve. As he put up his watch again, his eyes met those of his reflection in the chimney-glass.

"Why, it's your birthday already," he said, smiling. "You are looking very well. I wish you many happy returns of the day."

He had never before bestowed that wish upon himself. "By Jupiter!" he discovered, "it alters the whole case of running away from one's birthday! It's a thing to explain to Phoebe. Besides, here is quite a long story to tell her, that has sprung out of the road with no story. I'll go back, instead of going on. I'll go back by my friend Lamps's Up X presently."

He went back to Mugby Junction, and, in point of fact, he established himself at Mugby Junction. It was the convenient place to live in, for brightening Phoebe's life. It was the convenient place to live in, for having her taught music by Beatrice. It was the convenient place to live in, for occasionally borrowing Polly. It was the convenient place to live in, for being joined at will to all sorts of agreeable places and persons. So, he became settled there, and, his house standing in an elevated situation, it is noteworthy of him in conclusion, as Polly herself might (not irreverently) have put it:

"There was an Old Barbox who lived on a hill,
And if he ain't gone, he lives there still."

HERE FOLLOWS THE SUBSTANCE OF WHAT WAS SEEN, HEARD, OR OTHERWISE PICKED UP, BY THE GENTLEMAN FOR NOWHERE, IN HIS CAREFUL STUDY OF THE JUNCTION.

Chapter III

Main Line: The Boy at Mugby

I AM THE BOY AT MUGBY. THAT'S ABOUT WHAT *I* AM.

You don't know what I mean? What a pity! But I think you do. I think you must. Look here. I am the boy at what is called The Refreshment Room at Mugby Junction, and what's proudest boast is, that it never yet refreshed a mortal being.

Up in a corner of the Down Refreshment Room at Mugby Junction, in the height of twenty-seven cross draughts (I've often counted 'em while they brush the First-Class hair twenty-seven ways), behind the bottles, among the glasses, bounded on the nor'west by the beer, stood pretty far to the right of a metallic object that's at times the tea-urn and at times the soup-tureen, according to the nature of the last twang imparted to its contents which are the same groundwork, fended off from the traveller by a barrier of stale sponge-cakes erected atop of the counter, and lastly exposed sideways to the glare of Our Missis's eye—you ask a Boy so sitiwated, next time you stop in a hurry at Mugby, for anything to drink; you take particular notice that he'll try to seem not to hear you, that he'll appear in a absent manner to survey the Line through a transparent medium composed of your head and body, and that he won't serve you as long as you can possibly bear it. That's me.

What a lark it is! We are the Model Establishment, we are, at Mugby. Other Refreshment Rooms send their imperfect young ladies up to be finished off by our Missis. For some of the young ladies, when they're new to the business, come into it mild! Ah! Our Missis, she soon takes that out of 'em. Why, I originally come into the business meek myself. But Our Missis, she soon took that out of *me*.

What a delightful lark it is! I look upon us Refreshmenters as ockipying the only proudly independent footing on the Line. There's Papers, for instance,—my honourable friend, if he will allow me to call him so,—him as belongs to Smith's bookstall. Why, he no more dares to be up to our Refreshmenting games than he dares to jump a top of a locomotive with her steam at full pressure, and cut away upon her alone, driving himself, at limited-mail speed. Papers, he'd get his head punched at every compartment, first, second, and third, the whole length of a train, if he was to ventur to imitate my demeanour. It's the same with the porters, the same with the guards, the same with the ticket clerks, the same the whole way up to the secretary, traffic-manager, or very chairman. There ain't a one among 'em on the nobly independent footing we are. Did you ever catch one of them, when you wanted anything of him, making a system of surveying the Line through a transparent medium composed of your head and body? I should hope not.

You should see our Bandolining Room at Mugby Junction. It's led to by the door behind the counter, which you'll notice usually stands ajar, and it's the room where Our Missis and our young ladies Bandolines their hair. You should see 'em at it, betwixt trains, Bandolining away, as if they was anointing themselves for the combat. When you're telegraphed, you should see their noses all a-going up with scorn, as if it was a part of the working of the same Cooke and Wheatstone electrical machinery. You should hear Our Missis give the word, "Here comes the Beast to be Fed!" and then you should see 'em indignantly skipping across the Line, from the Up to the Down, or Wicer Warsaw, and begin to pitch the stale pastry into the plates, and chuck the sawdust sangwiches under the glass covers, and get out the—ha, ha, ha!—the sherry,—O my eye, my eye!—for your Refreshment.

It's only in the Isle of the Brave and Land of the Free (by which, of course, I mean to say Britannia) that Refreshmenting is so effective, so 'olesome, so constitutional a check upon the public. There was a Foreigner, which having politely, with his hat off, beseeched our young ladies and Our Missis for "a leetel gloss host prarndee," and having had the Line surveyed through him by all and no other acknowledgment, was a-proceeding at last to help himself, as seems to be the custom in his own country, when Our Missis, with her hair almost a-coming un-Bandolined with rage, and her eyes omitting sparks, flew at him, cotched the decanter out of his hand, and said, "Put it down! I won't allow that!" The foreigner turned pale, stepped back with his arms stretched out in front of him, his hands clasped, and his shoulders riz, and exclaimed: "Ah! Is it possible, this! That these disdaincous females and this ferocious old woman are placed here by the administration, not only to empoison the voyagers, but to affront them! Great Heaven! How arrives it? The English people. Or is he then a slave? Or idiot?" Another time, a merry, wideawake American gent had tried the sawdust and spit it out, and had tried the Sherry and spit that out, and had tried in vain to sustain exhausted natur upon Butter-Scotch, and had been rather extra Bandolined and Line-surveyed through, when, as the bell was ringing and he paid Our Missis, he says, very loud and good-tempered: "I tell Yew what 'tis, ma'arm. I la'af. Theer! I la'af. I Dew. I oughter ha' seen most things, for I hail from the Onlimited side of the Atlantic Ocean, and I haive travelled right slick over the Limited, head on through Jeerusalemm and the East, and likeways France and Italy, Europe Old World, and am now upon the track to the Chief Europian Village; but such an Institution as Yew, and Yewer young ladies, and Yewer fixin's solid and liquid, afore the glorious Tarnal I never did see yet! And if I hain't found the eighth wonder of monarchical Creation, in finding Yew and Yewer young ladies, and Yewer fixin's solid and liquid, all as aforesaid, established in a country where the people air not absolute Loo-naticks, I am Extra Double Darned with a Nip and Frizzle to the innermostest grit! Wheerfur—Theer!—I la'af! I Dew, ma'arm. I la'af!" And so he went, stamping and shaking his sides, along the platform all the way to his own compartment.

I think it was her standing up agin the Foreigner as giv' Our Missis the idea of going over to France, and droring a comparison betwixt Refreshmenting as followed among the frog-eaters, and Refreshmenting as triumphant in the Isle of the Brave and Land of the Free (by which, of course, I mean to say agin, Britannia). Our young ladies, Miss Whiff, Miss Piff, and Mrs. Sniff, was unanimous opposed to her going; for, as they says to Our Missis one and all, it is well beknown to the hends of the herth as no other nation except Britain has a idea of anythink, but above all of business. Why then should you tire yourself to prove what is already proved? Our Missis, however (being a teazer at all pints) stood out grim obstinate, and got a return pass by Southeastern Tidal, to go right through, if such should be her dispositions, to Marseilles.

Sniff is husband to Mrs. Sniff, and is a regular insignificant cove. He looks arter the sawdust department in a back room, and is sometimes, when we are very hard put to it, let behind the counter with a corkscrew; but never when it can be helped, his demeanour towards the public being disgusting servile. How Mrs. Sniff ever come so far to lower herself as to marry him, I don't know; but I suppose *he* does, and I should think he wished he didn't, for he leads a awful life. Mrs. Sniff couldn't be much harder with him if he was public. Similarly, Miss Whiff and Miss Piff, taking the tone of Mrs. Sniff, they shoulder Sniff about when he *is* let in with a corkscrew, and they whisk things out of his hands when in his servility he is a-going to let the public have 'em, and they snap him up when in the crawling baseness of his spirit he is a-going to answer a public question, and they drore more tears into his eyes than ever the mustard does which he all day long lays on to the sawdust. (But it ain't strong.) Once, when Sniff had the repulsiveness to reach across to get the milk-pot to hand over for a baby, I see Our Missis in her rage catch him by both his shoulders, and spin him out into the Bandolining Room.

But Mrs. Sniff,—how different! She's the one! She's the one as you'll notice to be always looking another way from you, when you look at her. She's the one with the small waist buckled in tight in front, and with the lace cuffs at her wrists, which she puts on the edge of the counter before her, and stands a smoothing while the public foams. This smoothing the cuffs and looking another way while the public foams is the last accomplishment taught to the young ladies as come to Mugby to be finished by Our Missis; and it's always taught by Mrs. Sniff.

When Our Missis went away upon her journey, Mrs. Sniff was left in charge. She did hold the public in check most beautiful! In all my time, I never see half so many cups of tea given without milk to people as wanted it with, nor half so many cups of tea with milk given to people as wanted it without. When foaming ensued, Mrs. Sniff would say: "Then you'd better settle it among yourselves, and change with one another." It was a most highly delicious lark. I enjoyed the Refreshmenting business more than ever, and was so glad I had took to it when young.

Our Missis returned. It got circulated among the young ladies, and it as it might be penetrated to me through the crevices of the Bandolining Room, that she had Orrors to reveal, if revelations so contemptible could be dignified with the name. Agitation become awakened. Excitement was up in the stirrups. Expectation stood a-tiptoe. At length it was put forth that on our slacked evening in the week, and at our slackest time of that evening betwixt trains, Our Missis would give her views of foreign Refreshmenting, in the Bandolining Room.

It was arranged tasteful for the purpose. The Bandolining table and glass was hid in a corner, a arm-chair was elevated on a packing-case for Our Missis's ockypation, a table and a tumbler of water (no sherry in it, thankee) was placed beside it. Two of the pupils, the season being autumn, and hollyhocks and dahlias being in, ornamented the wall with three devices in those flowers. On one might be read, "MAY ALBION NEVER LEARN"; on another "KEEP THE PUBLIC DOWN"; on another, "OUR REFRESHMENTING CHARTER." The whole had a beautiful appearance, with which the beauty of the sentiments corresponded.

On Our Missis's brow was wrote Severity, as she ascended the fatal platform. (Not that that was anythink new.) Miss Whiff and Miss Piff sat at her feet. Three chairs from the Waiting Room might have been perceived by a average eye, in front of her, on which the pupils was accommodated. Behind them a very close observer might have discerned a Boy. Myself.

"Where," said Our Missis, glancing gloomily around, "is Sniff?"

"I thought it better," answered Mrs. Sniff, "that he should not be let to come in. He is such an Ass."

"No doubt," assented Our Missis. "But for that reason is it not desirable to improve his mind?"

"Oh, nothing will ever improve *him*," said Mrs. Sniff.

"However," pursued Our Missis, "call him in, Ezekiel."

I called him in. The appearance of the low-minded cove was hailed with disapprobation from all sides, on account of his having brought his corkscrew with him. He pleaded "the force of habit."

"The force!" said Mrs. Sniff. "Don't let us have you talking about force, for Gracious' sake. There! Do stand still where you are, with your back against the wall."

He is a smiling piece of vacancy, and he smiled in the mean way in which he will even smile at the public if he gets a chance (language can say no meaner of him), and he stood upright near the door with the back of his head agin the wall, as if he was a waiting for somebody to come and measure his heighth for the Army.

"I should not enter, ladies," says Our Missis, "on the revolting disclosures I am about to make, if it was not in the hope that they will cause you to be yet more implacable in the exercise of the power you wield in a constitutional country, and yet more devoted to the constitutional motto which I see before me,"—it was behind her, but the words sounded better so,—"'May Albion never learn!'"

Here the pupils as had made the motto admired it, and cried, "Hear! Hear! Hear!" Sniff, showing an inclination to join in chorus, got himself frowned down by every brow.

"The baseness of the French," pursued Our Missis, "as displayed in the fawning nature of their Refreshmenting, equals, if not surpasses, anythink as was ever heard of the baseness of the celebrated Bonaparte."

Miss Whiff, Miss Piff, and me, we drored a heavy breath, equal to saying, "We thought as much!" Miss Whiff and Miss Piff seeming to object to my droring mine along with theirs, I drored another to aggravate 'em.

"Shall I be believed," says Our Missis, with flashing eyes, "when I tell you that no sooner had I set my foot upon that treacherous shore—"

Here Sniff, either bursting out mad, or thinking aloud, says, in a low voice: "Feet. Plural, you know."

The cowering that come upon him when he was spurned by all eyes, added to his being beneath contempt, was sufficient punishment for a cove so grovelling. In the midst of a silence rendered more impressive by the turned-up female noses with which it was pervaded, Our Missis went on:

"Shall I be believed when I tell you, that no sooner had I landed," this word with a killing look at Sniff, "on that treacherous shore, than I was ushered into a Refreshment Room where there were—I do not exaggerate—actually eatable things to eat?"

A groan burst from the ladies. I not only did myself the honour of jining, but also of lengthening it out.

"Where there were," Our Missis added, "not only eatable things to eat, but also drinkable things to drink?"

A murmur, swelling almost into a scream, ariz. Miss Piff, trembling with indignation, called out, "Name!"

"I *will* name," said Our Missis. "There was roast fowls, hot and cold; there was smoking roast veal surrounded with browned potatoes; there was hot soup with (again I ask shall I be credited?) nothing bitter in it, and no flour to choke off the consumer; there was a variety of cold dishes set off with jelly; there was salad; there was—mark me! *fresh* pastry, and that of a light construction; there was a luscious show of fruit; there was bottles and decanters of sound small wine, of every size, and adapted to every pocket; the same odious statement will apply to brandy; and these were set out upon the counter so that all could help themselves."

Our Missis's lips so quivered, that Mrs. Sniff, though scarcely less convulsed than she were, got up and held the tumbler to them.

"This," proceeds Our Missis, "was my first unconstitutional experience. Well would it have been if it had been my last and worst. But no. As I proceeded farther into that enslaved and ignorant land, its aspect became more hideous. I need not explain to this assembly the ingredients and formation of the British Refreshment sangwich?"

Universal laughter,—except from Sniff, who, as sangwich-cutter, shook his head in a state of the utmost dejection as he stood with it agin the wall.

"Well!" said Our Missis, with dilated nostrils. "Take a fresh, crisp, long, crusty penny loaf made of the whitest and best flour. Cut it longwise through the middle. Insert a fair and nicely fitting slice of ham. Tie a smart piece of ribbon round the middle of the whole to bind it together. Add at one end a neat wrapper of clean white paper by which to hold it. And the universal French Refreshment sangwich busts on your disgusted vision."

A cry of "Shame!" from all—except Sniff, which rubbed his stomach with a soothing hand.

"I need not," said Our Missis, "explain to this assembly the usual formation and fitting of the British Refreshment Room?"

No, no, and laughter. Sniff agin shaking his head in low spirits agin the wall.

"Well," said Our Missis, "what would you say to a general decoration of everythink, to hangings (sometimes elegant), to easy velvet furniture, to abundance of little tables, to abundance of little seats, to brisk bright waiters, to great convenience, to a pervading cleanliness and tastefulness positively addressing the public, and making the Beast thinking itself worth the pains?"

Contemptuous fury on the part of all the ladies. Mrs. Sniff looking as if she wanted somebody to hold her, and everbody else looking as if they'd rayther not.

"Three times," said Our Missis, working herself into a truly terrimenjious state,—"three times did I see these shameful things, only between the coast and Paris, and not counting either: at Hazebroucke, at Arras, at Amiens. But worse remains. Tell me, what would you call a person who should propose in England that there should be kept, say at our own model Mugby Junction, pretty baskets, each holding an assorted cold lunch and dessert for one, each at a certain fixed price, and each within a passenger's power to take away, to empty in the carriage at perfect leisure, and to return at another station fifty or a hundred miles farther on?"

There was disagreement what such a person should be called. Whether revolutionise, atheist, Bright (*I* said him), or Un-English. Miss Piff screeched her shrill opinion last, in the words: "A malignant maniac!"

"I adopt," says Our Missis, "the brand set upon such a person by the righteous indignation of my friend Miss Piff. A malignant maniac. Know, then, that that malignant maniac has sprung from the congenial soil of France, and that his malignant madness was in unchecked action on this same part of my journey."

I noticed that Sniff was a-rubbing his hands, and that Mrs. Sniff had got her eye upon him. But I did not take more particular notice, owing to the excited state in which the young ladies was, and to feeling myself called upon to keep it up with a howl.

"On my experience south of Paris," said Our Missis, in a deep tone, "I will not expatiate. Too loathsome were the task! But fancy this. Fancy a guard coming round, with the train at full speed, to inquire how many for dinner. Fancy his telegraphing forward the number of dinners. Fancy every one expected, and the table elegantly laid for the complete party. Fancy a charming dinner, in a charming room, and the head-cook, concerned for the honour of every dish, superintending in his clean white jacket and cap. Fancy the Beast travelling six hundred miles on end, very fast, and with great punctuality, yet being taught to expect all this to be done for it!"

A spirited chorus of "The Beast!"

I noticed that Sniff was agin a-rubbing his stomach with a soothing hand, and that he had drored up one leg. But agin I didn't take particular notice, looking on myself as called upon to stimulate public feeling. It being a lark besides.

"Putting everything together," said Our Missis, "French Refreshmenting comes to this, and oh, it comes to a nice total! First: eatable things to eat, and drinkable things to drink."

A groan from the young ladies, kep' up by me.

"Second: convenience, and even elegance."

Another groan from the young ladies, kep' up by me.

"Third: moderate charges."

This time a groan from me, kep' up by the young ladies.

"Fourth:—and here," says Our Missis, "I claim your angriest sympathy,—attention, common civility, nay, even politeness!"

Me and the young ladies regularly raging mad all together.

"And I cannot in conclusion," says Our Missis, with her spitefullest sneer, "give you a completer pictur of that despicable nation (after what I have related), than assuring you that they wouldn't bear our constitutional ways and noble independence at Mugby Junction, for a single month, and that they would turn us to the right-about and put another system in our places, as soon as look at us; perhaps sooner, for I do not believe they have the good taste to care to look at us twice."

The swelling tumult was arrested in its rise. Sniff, bore away by his servile disposition, had drored up his leg with a higher and a higher relish, and was now discovered to be waving his corkscrew over his head. It was at this moment that Mrs. Sniff, who had kep' her eye upon him like the fabled obelisk, descended on her victim. Our Missis followed them both out, and cries was heard in the sawdust department.

You come into the Down Refreshment Room, at the Junction, making believe you don't know me, and I'll pint you out with my right thumb over my shoulder which is Our Missis, and which is Miss Whiff, and which is Miss Piff, and which is Mrs. Sniff. But you won't get a chance to see Sniff, because he disappeared that night. Whether he perished, tore to pieces, I cannot say; but his corkscrew alone remains, to bear witness to the servility of his disposition.

Chapter IV

No. 1 Branch Line: The Signal-Man

"Halloa! Below there!"

When he heard a voice thus calling to him, he was standing at the door of his box, with a flag in his hand, furled round its short pole. One would have thought, considering the nature of the ground, that he could not have doubted from what quarter the voice came; but instead of looking up to where I stood on the top of the steep cutting nearly over his head, he turned himself about, and looked down the Line. There was something remarkable in his manner of doing so, though I could not have said for my life what. But I know it was remarkable enough to attract my notice, even though his figure was foreshortened and shadowed, down in the deep trench, and mine was high above him, so steeped in the glow of an angry sunset, that I had shaded my eyes with my hand before I saw him at all.

"Halloa! Below!"

From looking down the Line, he turned himself about again, and, raising his eyes, saw my figure high above him.

"Is there any path by which I can come down and speak to you?"

He looked up at me without replying, and I looked down at him without pressing him too soon with a repetition of my idle question. Just then there came a vague vibration in the earth and air, quickly changing into a violent pulsation, and an oncoming rush that caused me to start back, as though it had force to draw me down. When such vapour as rose to my height from this rapid train had passed me, and was skimming away over the landscape, I looked down again, and saw him refurling the flag he had shown while the train went by.

I repeated my inquiry. After a pause, during which he seemed to regard me with fixed attention, he motioned with his rolled-up flag towards a point on my level, some two or three hundred yards distant. I called down to him, "All right!" and made for that point. There, by dint of looking closely about me, I found a rough zigzag descending path notched out, which I followed.

The cutting was extremely deep, and unusually precipitate. It was made through a clammy stone, that became oozier and wetter as I went down. For these reasons, I found the way long enough to give me time to recall a singular air of reluctance or compulsion with which he had pointed out the path.

When I came down low enough upon the zigzag descent to see him again, I saw that he was standing between the rails on the way by which the train had lately passed, in an attitude as if he were waiting for me to appear. He had his left hand at his chin, and that left elbow rested on his right hand, crossed over his breast. His attitude was one of such expectation and watchfulness that I stopped a moment, wondering at it.

I resumed my downward way, and stepping out upon the level of the railroad, and drawing nearer to him, saw that he was a dark, sallow man, with a dark beard and rather heavy eyebrows. His post was in as solitary and dismal a place as ever I saw. On either side, a dripping-wet wall of jagged stone, excluding all view but a strip of sky; the perspective one way only a crooked prolongation of this great dungeon; the shorter perspective in the other direction terminating in a gloomy red light, and the gloomier entrance to a black tunnel, in whose massive architecture there was a barbarous, depressing, and forbidding air. So little sunlight ever found its way to this spot, that it had an earthy, deadly smell; and so much cold wind rushed through it, that it struck chill to me, as if I had left the natural world.

Before he stirred, I was near enough to him to have touched him. Not even then removing his eyes from mine, he stepped back one step, and lifted his hand.

This was a lonesome post to occupy (I said), and it had riveted my attention when I looked down from up yonder. A visitor was a rarity, I should suppose; not an unwelcome rarity, I hoped? In me, he merely saw a man who had been shut up within narrow limits all his life, and who, being at last set free, had a newly-awakened interest in these great works. To such purpose I spoke to him; but I am far from sure of the terms I used; for, besides that I am not happy in opening any conversation, there was something in the man that daunted me.

He directed a most curious look towards the red light near the tunnel's mouth, and looked all about it, as if something were missing from it, and then looked at me.

That light was part of his charge? Was it not?

He answered in a low voice,—"Don't you know it is?"

The monstrous thought came into my mind, as I perused the fixed eyes and the saturnine face, that this was a spirit, not a man. I have speculated since, whether there may have been infection in his mind.

In my turn, I stepped back. But in making the action, I detected in his eyes some latent fear of me. This put the monstrous thought to flight.

"You look at me," I said, forcing a smile, "as if you had a dread of me."

"I was doubtful," he returned, "whether I had seen you before."

"Where?"

He pointed to the red light he had looked at.

"There?" I said.

Intently watchful of me, he replied (but without sound), "Yes."

"My good fellow, what should I do there? However, be that as it may, I never was there, you may swear."

"I think I may," he rejoined. "Yes; I am sure I may."

His manner cleared, like my own. He replied to my remarks with readiness, and in well-chosen words. Had he much to do there? Yes; that was to say, he had enough responsibility to bear; but exactness and watchfulness were what was required of him, and of actual work—manual labour—he had next to none. To change that signal, to trim those lights, and to turn this iron handle now and then, was all he had to do under that head. Regarding those many long and lonely hours of which I seemed to make so much, he could only say that the routine of his life had shaped itself into that form, and he had grown used to it. He had taught himself a language down here,—if only to know it by sight, and to have formed his own crude ideas of its pronunciation, could be called learning it. He had also worked at fractions and decimals, and tried a little algebra; but he was, and had been as a boy, a poor hand at figures. Was it necessary for him when on duty always to remain in that channel of damp air, and could he never rise into the sunshine from between those high stone walls? Why, that depended upon times and circumstances. Under some conditions there would be less upon the Line than under others, and the same held good as to certain hours of the day and night. In bright weather, he did choose occasions for getting a little above these lower shadows; but, being at all times liable to be called by his electric bell, and at such times listening for it with redoubled anxiety, the relief was less than I would suppose.

He took me into his box, where there was a fire, a desk for an official book in which he had to make certain entries, a telegraphic instrument with its dial, face, and needles, and the little bell of which he had spoken. On my trusting that he would excuse the remark that he had been well educated, and (I hoped I might say without offence) perhaps educated above that station, he observed that instances of slight incongruity in such wise would rarely be found wanting among large bodies of men; that he had heard it was so in workhouses, in the police force, even in that last desperate resource, the army; and that he knew it was so, more or less, in any great railway staff. He had been, when young (if I could believe it, sitting in that hut,—he scarcely could), a student of natural philosophy, and had attended lectures; but he had run wild, misused his opportunities, gone down, and never risen again. He had no complaint to offer about that. He had made his bed, and he lay upon it. It was far too late to make another.

All that I have here condensed he said in a quiet manner, with his grave, dark regards divided between me and the fire. He threw in the word, "Sir," from time to time, and especially when he referred to his youth,—as though to request me to understand that he claimed to be nothing but what I found him. He was several times interrupted by the little bell, and had to read off messages, and send replies. Once he had to stand without the door, and display a flag as a train passed, and make some verbal communication to the driver. In the discharge of his duties, I observed him to be remarkably exact and vigilant, breaking off his discourse at a syllable, and remaining silent until what he had to do was done.

In a word, I should have set this man down as one of the safest of men to be employed in that capacity, but for the circumstance that while he was speaking to me he twice broke off with a fallen colour, turned his face towards the little bell when it did NOT ring, opened the door of the hut (which was kept shut to exclude the unhealthy damp), and looked out towards the red light near the mouth of the tunnel. On both of those occasions, he came back to the fire with the inexplicable air upon him which I had remarked, without being able to define, when we were so far asunder.

Said I, when I rose to leave him, "You almost make me think that I have met with a contented man."

(I am afraid I must acknowledge that I said it to lead him on.)

"I believe I used to be so," he rejoined, in the low voice in which he had first spoken; "but I am troubled, Sir, I am troubled."

He would have recalled the words if he could. He had said them, however, and I took them up quickly.

"With what? What is your trouble?"

"It is very difficult to impart, Sir. It is very, very difficult to speak of. If ever you make me another visit, I will try to tell you."

"But I expressly intend to make you another visit. Say, when shall it be?"

"I go off early in the morning, and I shall be on again at ten to-morrow night, Sir."

"I will come at eleven."

He thanked me, and went out at the door with me. "I'll show my white light, Sir," he said, in his peculiar low voice, "till you have found the way up. When you have found it, don't call out! And when you are at the top, don't call out!"

His manner seemed to make the place strike colder to me, but I said no more than, "Very well."

"And when you come down to-morrow night, don't call out! Let me ask you a parting question. What made you cry, 'Halloa! Below there!' to-night?"

"Heaven knows," said I. "I cried something to that effect—"

"Not to that effect, Sir. Those were the very words. I know them well."

"Admit those were the very words. I said them, no doubt, because I saw you below."

"For no other reason?"

"What other reason could I possibly have?"

"You had no feeling that they were conveyed to you in any supernatural way?"

"No."

He wished me good-night, and held up his light. I walked by the side of the down Line of rails (with a very disagreeable sensation of a train coming behind me) until I found the path. It was easier to mount than to descend, and I got back to my inn without any adventure.

Punctual to my appointment, I placed my foot on the first notch of the zigzag next night, as the distant clocks were striking eleven. He was waiting for me at the bottom, with his white light on. "I have not called out," I said, when we came close together; "may I speak now?" "By all means, Sir." "Good night, then, and here's my hand." "Good night, Sir, and here's mine." With that we walked side by side to his box, entered it, closed the door, and sat down by the fire.

"I have made up my mind, Sir," he began, bending forward as soon as we were seated, and speaking in a tone but a little above a whisper, "that you shall not have to ask me twice what troubles me. I took you for some one else yesterday evening. That troubles me."

"That mistake?"

"No. That some one else."

"Who is it?"

"I don't know."

"Like me?"

"I don't know. I never saw the face. The left arm is across the face, and the right arm is waved,—violently waved. This way."

I followed his action with my eyes, and it was the action of an arm gesticulating, with the utmost passion and vehemence, "For God's sake, clear the way!"

"One moonlight night," said the man, "I was sitting here, when I heard a voice cry, 'Halloa! Below there!' I started up, looked from that door, and saw this Some one else standing by the red light near the tunnel, waving as I just now showed you. The voice seemed hoarse with shouting, and it cried, 'Look out! Look out!' And then again, 'Halloa! Below there! Look out!' I caught up my lamp, turned it on red, and ran towards the figure, calling, 'What's wrong? What has happened? Where?' It stood just outside the blackness of the tunnel. I advanced so close upon it that I wondered at its keeping the sleeve across its eyes. I ran right up at it, and had my hand stretched out to pull the sleeve away, when it was gone."

"Into the tunnel?" said I.

"No. I ran on into the tunnel, five hundred yards. I stopped, and held my lamp above my head, and saw the figures of the measured distance, and saw the wet stains stealing down the walls and trickling through the arch. I ran out again faster than I had run in (for I had a mortal abhorrence of the place upon me), and I looked all round the red light with my own red light, and I went up the iron ladder to the gallery atop of it, and I came down again, and ran back here. I telegraphed both ways, 'An alarm has been given. Is anything wrong?' The answer came back, both ways, 'All well.'"

Resisting the slow touch of a frozen finger tracing out my spine, I showed him how that this figure must be a deception of his sense of sight; and how that figures, originating in disease of the delicate nerves that minister to the functions of the eye, were known to have often troubled patients, some of whom had become conscious of the nature of their affliction, and had even proved it by experiments upon themselves. "As to an imaginary cry," said I, "do but listen for a moment to the wind in this unnatural valley while we speak so low, and to the wild harp it makes of the telegraph wires."

That was all very well, he returned, after we had sat listening for a while, and he ought to know something of the wind and the wires,—he who so often passed long winter nights there, alone and watching. But he would beg to remark that he had not finished.

I asked his pardon, and he slowly added these words, touching my arm,—

"Within six hours after the Appearance, the memorable accident on this Line happened, and within ten hours the dead and wounded were brought along through the tunnel over the spot where the figure had stood."

A disagreeable shudder crept over me, but I did my best against it. It was not to be denied, I rejoined, that this was a remarkable coincidence, calculated deeply to impress his mind. But it was unquestionable that remarkable coincidences did continually occur, and they must be taken into account in dealing with such a subject. Though to be sure I must admit, I added (for I thought I saw that he was going to bring the objection to bear upon me), men of common sense did not allow much for coincidences in making the ordinary calculations of life.

He again begged to remark that he had not finished.

I again begged his pardon for being betrayed into interruptions.

"This," he said, again laying his hand upon my arm, and glancing over his shoulder with hollow eyes, "was just a year ago. Six or seven months passed, and I had recovered from the surprise and shock, when one morning, as the day was breaking, I, standing at the door, looked towards the red light, and saw the spectre again." He stopped, with a fixed look at me.

"Did it cry out?"

"No. It was silent."

"Did it wave its arm?"

"No. It leaned against the shaft of the light, with both hands before the face. Like this."

Once more I followed his action with my eyes. It was an action of mourning. I have seen such an attitude in stone figures on tombs.

"Did you go up to it?"

"I came in and sat down, partly to collect my thoughts, partly because it had turned me faint. When I went to the door again, daylight was above me, and the ghost was gone."

"But nothing followed? Nothing came of this?"

He touched me on the arm with his forefinger twice or thrice giving a ghastly nod each time:—

"That very day, as a train came out of the tunnel, I noticed, at a carriage window on my side, what looked like a confusion of hands and heads, and something waved. I saw it just in time to signal the driver, Stop! He shut off, and put his brake on, but the train drifted past here a hundred and fifty yards or more. I ran after it, and, as I went along, heard terrible screams and cries. A beautiful young lady had died instantaneously in one of the compartments, and was brought in here, and laid down on this floor between us."

Involuntarily I pushed my chair back, as I looked from the boards at which he pointed to himself.

"True, Sir. True. Precisely as it happened, so I tell it you."

I could think of nothing to say, to any purpose, and my mouth was very dry. The wind and the wires took up the story with a long lamenting wail.

He resumed. "Now, Sir, mark this, and judge how my mind is troubled. The spectre came back a week ago. Ever since, it has been there, now and again, by fits and starts."

"At the light?"

"At the Danger-light."

"What does it seem to do?"

He repeated, if possible with increased passion and vehemence, that former gesticulation of, "For God's sake, clear the way!"

Then he went on. "I have no peace or rest for it. It calls to me, for many minutes together, in an agonised manner, 'Below there! Look out! Look out!' It stands waving to me. It rings my little bell—"

I caught at that. "Did it ring your bell yesterday evening when I was here, and you went to the door?"

"Twice."

"Why, see," said I, "how your imagination misleads you. My eyes were on the bell, and my ears were open to the bell, and if I am a living man, it did NOT ring at those times. No, nor at any other time, except when it was rung in the natural course of physical things by the station communicating with you."

He shook his head. "I have never made a mistake as to that yet, Sir. I have never confused the spectre's ring with the man's. The ghost's ring is a strange vibration in the bell that it derives from nothing else, and I have not asserted that the bell stirs to the eye. I don't wonder that you failed to hear it. But *I* heard it."

"And did the spectre seem to be there, when you looked out?"

"It WAS there."

"Both times?"

He repeated firmly: "Both times."

"Will you come to the door with me, and look for it now?"

He bit his under lip as though he were somewhat unwilling, but arose. I opened the door, and stood on the step, while he stood in the doorway. There was the Danger-light. There was the dismal mouth of the tunnel. There were the high, wet stone walls of the cutting. There were the stars above them.

"Do you see it?" I asked him, taking particular note of his face. His eyes were prominent and strained, but not very much more so, perhaps, than my own had been when I had directed them earnestly towards the same spot.

"No," he answered. "It is not there."

"Agreed," said I.

We went in again, shut the door, and resumed our seats. I was thinking how best to improve this advantage, if it might be called one, when he took up the conversation in such a matter-of-course way, so assuming that there could be no serious question of fact between us, that I felt myself placed in the weakest of positions.

"By this time you will fully understand, Sir," he said, "that what troubles me so dreadfully is the question, What does the spectre mean?"

I was not sure, I told him, that I did fully understand.

"What is its warning against?" he said, ruminating, with his eyes on the fire, and only by times turning them on me. "What is the danger? Where is the danger? There is danger overhanging somewhere on the Line. Some dreadful calamity will happen. It is not to be doubted this third time, after what has gone before. But surely this is a cruel haunting of *me*. What can *I* do?"

He pulled out his handkerchief, and wiped the drops from his heated forehead.

"If I telegraph Danger, on either side of me, or on both, I can give no reason for it," he went on, wiping the palms of his hands. "I should get into trouble, and do no good. They would think I was mad. This is the way it would work,—Message:

'Danger! Take care!' Answer: 'What Danger? Where?' Message: 'Don't know. But, for God's sake, take care!' They would displace me. What else could they do?"

His pain of mind was most pitiable to see. It was the mental torture of a conscientious man, oppressed beyond endurance by an unintelligible responsibility involving life.

"When it first stood under the Danger-light," he went on, putting his dark hair back from his head, and drawing his hands outward across and across his temples in an extremity of feverish distress, "why not tell me where that accident was to happen,—if it must happen? Why not tell me how it could be averted,—if it could have been averted? When on its second coming it hid its face, why not tell me, instead, 'She is going to die. Let them keep her at home?' If it came, on those two occasions, only to show me that its warnings were true, and so to prepare me for the third, why not warn me plainly now? And I, Lord help me! A mere poor signal-man on this solitary station! Why not go to somebody with credit to be believed, and power to act?"

When I saw him in this state, I saw that for the poor man's sake, as well as for the public safety, what I had to do for the time was to compose his mind. Therefore, setting aside all question of reality or unreality between us, I represented to him that whoever thoroughly discharged his duty must do well, and that at least it was his comfort that he understood his duty, though he did not understand these confounding Appearances. In this effort I succeeded far better than in the attempt to reason him out of his conviction. He became calm; the occupations incidental to his post as the night advanced began to make larger demands on his attention: and I left him at two in the morning. I had offered to stay through the night, but he would not hear of it.

That I more than once looked back at the red light as I ascended the pathway, that I did not like the red light, and that I should have slept but poorly if my bed had been under it, I see no reason to conceal. Nor did I like the two sequences of the accident and the dead girl. I see no reason to conceal that either.

But what ran most in my thoughts was the consideration how ought I to act, having become the recipient of this disclosure? I had proved the man to be intelligent, vigilant, painstaking, and exact; but how long might he remain so, in his state of mind? Though in a subordinate position, still he held a most important trust, and would I (for instance) like to stake my own life on the chances of his continuing to execute it with precision?

Unable to overcome a feeling that there would be something treacherous in my communicating what he had told me to his superiors in the Company, without first being plain with himself and proposing a middle course to him, I ultimately resolved to offer to accompany him (otherwise keeping his secret for the present) to the wisest medical practitioner we could hear of in those parts, and to take his opinion. A change in his time of duty would come round next night, he had apprised me, and he would be off an hour or two after sunrise, and on again soon after sunset. I had appointed to return accordingly.

Next evening was a lovely evening, and I walked out early to enjoy it. The sun was not yet quite down when I traversed the field-path near the top of the deep cutting. I would extend my walk for an hour, I said to myself, half an hour on and half an hour back, and it would then be time to go to my signal-man's box.

Before pursuing my stroll, I stepped to the brink, and mechanically looked down, from the point from which I had first seen him. I cannot describe the thrill that seized upon me, when, close at the mouth of the tunnel, I saw the appearance of a man, with his left sleeve across his eyes, passionately waving his right arm.

The nameless horror that oppressed me passed in a moment, for in a moment I saw that this appearance of a man was a man indeed, and that there was a little group of other men, standing at a short distance, to whom he seemed to be rehearsing the gesture he made. The Danger-light was not yet lighted. Against its shaft, a little low hut, entirely new to me, had been made of some wooden supports and tarpaulin. It looked no bigger than a bed.

With an irresistible sense that something was wrong,—with a flashing self-reproachful fear that fatal mischief had come of my leaving the man there, and causing no one to be sent to overlook or correct what he did,—I descended the notched path with all the speed I could make.

"What is the matter?" I asked the men.

"Signal-man killed this morning, Sir."

"Not the man belonging to that box?"

"Yes, Sir."

"Not the man I know?"

"You will recognise him, Sir, if you knew him," said the man who spoke for the others, solemnly uncovering his own head, and raising an end of the tarpaulin, "for his face is quite composed."

"O, how did this happen, how did this happen?" I asked, turning from one to another as the hut closed in again.

"He was cut down by an engine, Sir. No man in England knew his work better. But somehow he was not clear of the outer rail. It was just at broad day. He had struck the light, and had the lamp in his hand. As the engine came out of the tunnel, his back was towards her, and she cut him down. That man drove her, and was showing how it happened. Show the gentleman, Tom."

The man, who wore a rough dark dress, stepped back to his former place at the mouth of the tunnel.

"Coming round the curve in the tunnel, Sir," he said, "I saw him at the end, like as if I saw him down a perspective-glass. There was no time to check speed, and

I knew him to be very careful. As he didn't seem to take heed of the whistle, I shut it off when we were running down upon him, and called to him as loud as I could call."

"What did you say?"

"I said, 'Below there! Look out! Look out! For God's sake, clear the way!' "

I started.

"Ah! it was a dreadful time, Sir. I never left off calling to him. I put this arm before my eyes not to see, and I waved this arm to the last; but it was no use."

Without prolonging the narrative to dwell on any one of its curious circumstances more than on any other, I may, in closing it, point out the coincidence that the warning of the Engine-Driver included, not only the words which the unfortunate Signalman had repeated to me as haunting him, but also the words which I myself—not he—had attached, and that only in my own mind, to the gesticulation he had imitated.

The Wreck of the *Golden Mary*

(Written with Wilkie Collins)

The Wreck

I was apprenticed to the Sea when I was twelve years old, and I have encountered a great deal of rough weather, both literal and metaphorical. It has always been my opinion since I first possessed such a thing as an opinion, that the man who knows only one subject is next tiresome to the man who knows no subject. Therefore, in the course of my life I have taught myself whatever I could, and although I am not an educated man, I am able, I am thankful to say, to have an intelligent interest in most things.

A person might suppose, from reading the above, that I am in the habit of holding forth about number one. That is not the case. Just as if I was to come into a room among strangers, and must either be introduced or introduce myself, so I have taken the liberty of passing these few remarks, simply and plainly that it may be known who and what I am. I will add no more of the sort than that my name is William George Ravender, that I was born at Penrith half a year after my own father was drowned, and that I am on the second day of this present blessed Christmas week of one thousand eight hundred and fifty-six, fifty-six years of age.

When the rumour first went flying up and down that there was gold in California—which, as most people know, was before it was discovered in the British colony of Australia—I was in the West Indies, trading among the Islands. Being in command and likewise part-owner of a smart schooner, I had my work cut out for me, and I was doing it. Consequently, gold in California was no business of mine.

But, by the time when I came home to England again, the thing was as clear as your hand held up before you at noonday. There was Californian gold in the museums and in the goldsmiths' shops, and the very first time I went upon 'Change, I met a friend of mine (a seafaring man like myself), with a Californian nugget hanging to his watch-chain. I handled it. It was as like a peeled walnut with bits unevenly broken off here and there, and then electrotyped all over, as ever I saw anything in my life.

I am a single man (she was too good for this world and for me, and she died six weeks before our marriage-day), so when I am ashore, I live in my house at Poplar. My house at Poplar is taken care of and kept ship-shape by an old lady who was my mother's maid before I was born. She is as handsome and as upright as any old lady in the world. She is as fond of me as if she had ever had an only son, and I was he. Well do I know wherever I sail that she never lays down her head at night without having said, "Merciful Lord! bless and preserve William George Ravender, and send him safe home, through Christ our Saviour!" I have thought of it in many a dangerous moment, when it has done me no harm, I am sure.

In my house at Poplar, along with this old lady, I lived quiet for best part of a year: having had a long spell of it among the Islands, and having (which was very uncommon in me) taken the fever rather badly. At last, being strong and hearty, and having read every book I could lay hold of, right out, I was walking down Leadenhall Street in the City of London, thinking of turning-to again, when I met what I call Smithick and Watersby of Liverpool. I chanced to lift up my eyes from looking in at a ship's chronometer in a window, and I saw him bearing down upon me, head on.

It is, personally, neither Smithick, nor Watersby, that I here mention, nor was I ever acquainted with any man of either of those names, nor do I think that there has been any one of either of those names in that Liverpool House for years back. But, it is in reality the House itself that I refer to; and a wiser merchant or a truer gentleman never stepped.

"My dear Captain Ravender," says he. "Of all the men on earth, I wanted to see you most. I was on my way to you."

"Well!" says I. "That looks as if you *were* to see me, don't it?" With that I put my arm in his, and we walked on towards the Royal Exchange, and when we got there, walked up and down at the back of it where the Clock-Tower is. We walked an hour and more, for he had much to say to me. He had a scheme for chartering a new ship of their own to take out cargo to the diggers and emigrants in California, and to buy and bring back gold. Into the particulars of that scheme I will not enter, and I have no right to enter. All I say of it is, that it was a very original one, a very fine one, a very sound one, and a very lucrative one beyond doubt.

He imparted it to me as freely as if I had been a part of himself. After doing so, he made me the handsomest sharing offer that ever was made to me, boy or man—or I believe to any other captain in the Merchant Navy—and he took this round turn to finish with:

"Ravender, you are well aware that the lawlessness of that coast and country at present, is as special as the circumstances in which it is placed. Crews of vessels outward-bound, desert as soon as they make the land; crews of vessels homeward-bound, ship at enormous wages, with the express intention of murdering the captain and seizing the gold freight; no man can trust another, and the devil seems let loose. Now," says he, "you know my opinion of you, and you know I am only expressing it, and with no singularity, when I tell you that you are almost the only man on whose integrity, discretion, and energy—" &c., &c. For, I don't want to repeat what he said, though I was and am sensible of it.

Notwithstanding my being, as I have mentioned, quite ready for a voyage, still I had some doubts of this voyage. Of course I knew, without being told, that there were peculiar difficulties and dangers in it, a long way over and above those which attend all voyages. It must not be supposed that I was afraid to face them; but, in my opinion a man has no manly motive or sustainment in his own breast for facing dangers, unless he has well considered what they are, and is able quietly to say to himself, "None of these perils can now take me by surprise; I shall know what to do for the best in any of them; all the rest lies in the higher and greater hands to which I humbly commit myself." On this principle I have so attentively considered (regarding it as my duty) all the hazards I have ever been able to think of, in the ordinary way of storm, shipwreck, and fire at sea, that I hope I should be prepared to do, in any of those cases, whatever could be done, to save the lives intrusted to my charge.

As I was thoughtful, my good friend proposed that he should leave me to walk there as long as I liked, and that I should dine with him by-and-by at his club in Pall Mall. I accepted the invitation and I walked up and down there, quarter-deck fashion, a matter of a couple of hours; now and then looking up at the weathercock as I might have looked up aloft; and now and then taking a look into Cornhill, as I might have taken a look over the side.

All dinner-time, and all after dinner-time, we talked it over again. I gave him my views of his plan, and he very much approved of the same. I told him I had nearly decided, but not quite. "Well, well," says he, "come down to Liverpool to-morrow with me, and see the *Golden Mary*." I liked the name (her name was Mary, and she was golden, if golden stands for good), so I began to feel that it was almost done when I said I would go to Liverpool. On the next morning but one we were on board the *Golden Mary*. I might have known, from his asking me to come down and see her, what she was. I declare her to have been the completest and most exquisite Beauty that ever I set my eyes upon.

We had inspected every timber in her, and had come back to the gangway to go ashore from the dock-basin, when I put out my hand to my friend. "Touch upon it," says I, "and touch heartily. I take command of this ship, and I am hers and yours, if I can get John Steadiman for my chief mate."

John Steadiman had sailed with me four voyages. The first voyage John was third mate out to China, and came home second. The other three voyages he was my first officer. At this time of chartering the *Golden Mary*, he was aged thirty-two. A brisk, bright, blue-eyed fellow, a very neat figure and rather under the middle size, never out of the way and never in it, a face that pleased everybody and that all children took to, a habit of going about singing as cheerily as a blackbird, and a perfect sailor.

We were in one of those Liverpool hackney-coaches in less than a minute, and we cruised about in her upwards of three hours, looking for John. John had come home from Van Diemen's Land barely a month before, and I had heard of him as taking a frisk in Liverpool. We asked after him, among many other places, at the two boarding-houses he was fondest of, and we found he had had a week's spell at each of them; but, he had gone here and gone there, and had set off "to lay out on the main-to'-gallant-yard of the highest Welsh mountain" (so he had told the people of the house), and where he might be then, or when he might come back, nobody could tell us. But it was surprising, to be sure, to see how every face brightened the moment there was mention made of the name of Mr. Steadiman.

We were taken aback at meeting with no better luck, and we had wore ship and put her head for my friends, when as we were jogging through the streets, I clap my eyes on John himself coming out of a toyshop! He was carrying a little boy, and conducting two uncommon pretty women to their coach, and he told me afterwards that he had never in his life seen one of the three before, but that he was so taken with them on looking in at the toyshop while they were buying the child a cranky Noah's Ark, very much down by the head, that he had gone in and asked the ladies' permission to treat him to a tolerably correct Cutter there was in the window, in order that such a handsome boy might not grow up with a lubberly idea of naval architecture.

We stood off and on until the ladies' coachman began to give way, and then we hailed John. On his coming aboard of us, I told him, very gravely, what I had said to my friend. It struck him, as he said himself, amidships. He was quite shaken by it. "Captain Ravender," were John Steadiman's words, "such an opinion from you is true commendation, and I'll sail round the world with you for twenty years if you hoist the signal, and stand by you for ever!" And now indeed I felt that it was done, and that the *Golden Mary* was afloat.

Grass never grew yet under the feet of Smithick and Watersby. The riggers were out of that ship in a fortnight's time, and we had begun taking in cargo. John was always aboard, seeing everything stowed with his own eyes; and whenever I went aboard myself early or late, whether he was below in the hold, or on deck at the hatchway, or overhauling his cabin, nailing up pictures in it of the Blush Roses of England, the Blue Belles of Scotland, and the female Shamrock of Ireland: of a certainty I heard John singing like a blackbird.

We had room for twenty passengers. Our sailing advertisement was no sooner out, than we might have taken these twenty times over. In entering our men, I and John (both together) picked them, and we entered none but good hands—as good as were to be found in that port. And so, in a good ship of the best build, well owned, well arranged, well officered, well manned, well found in all respects, we parted with our pilot at a quarter past four o'clock in the afternoon of the seventh of March, one thousand eight hundred and fifty-one, and stood with a fair wind out to sea.

It may be easily believed that up to that time I had had no leisure to be intimate with my passengers. The most of them were then in their berths sea-sick; however, in going among them, telling them what was good for them, persuading them not to be there, but to come up on deck and feel the breeze, and in rousing them with a joke, or a comfortable word, I made acquaintance with them, perhaps, in a more friendly and confidential way from the first, than I might have done at the cabin table.

Of my passengers, I need only particularise, just at present, a bright-eyed blooming young wife who was going out to join her husband in California, taking with her their only child, a little girl of three years old, whom he had never seen; a sedate young woman in black, some five years older (about thirty as I should say), who was going out to join a brother; and an old gentleman, a good deal like a hawk if his eyes had been better and not so red, who was always talking, morning, noon, and night, about the gold discovery. But, whether he was making the voyage, thinking his old arms could dig for gold, or whether his speculation was to buy it, or to barter for it, or to cheat for it, or to snatch it anyhow from other people, was his secret. He kept his secret.

These three and the child were the soonest well. The child was a most engaging child, to be sure, and very fond of me: though I am bound to admit that John Steadiman and I were borne on her pretty little books in reverse order, and that he was captain there, and I was mate. It was beautiful to watch her with John, and it was beautiful to watch John with her. Few would have thought it possible, to see John playing at bo-peep round the mast, that he was the man who had caught up an iron bar and struck a Malay and a Maltese dead, as they were gliding with their knives down the cabin stair aboard the barque *Old England*, when the captain lay ill in his cot, off Saugar Point. But he was; and give him his back against a bulwark, he would have done the same by half a dozen of them. The name of the young mother was Mrs. Atherfield, the name of the young lady in black was Miss Coleshaw, and the name of the old gentleman was Mr. Rarx.

As the child had a quantity of shining fair hair, clustering in curls all about her face, and as her name was Lucy, Steadiman gave her the name of the *Golden Lucy*. So, we had the *Golden Lucy* and the *Golden Mary*; and John kept up the idea to that extent as he and the child went playing about the decks, that I believe she used to think the ship was alive somehow—a sister or companion, going to the same place as herself. She liked to be by the wheel, and in fine weather, I have often stood by the man whose trick it was at the wheel, only to hear her, sitting near my feet, talking to the ship. Never had a child such a doll before, I suppose; but she made a doll of the *Golden Mary*, and used to dress her up by tying ribbons and little bits of finery to the belaying-pins; and nobody ever moved them, unless it was to save them from being blown away.

Of course I took charge of the two young women, and I called them "my dear," and they never minded, knowing that whatever I said was said in a fatherly and protecting spirit. I gave them their places on each side of me at dinner, Mrs. Atherfield on my right and Miss Coleshaw on my left; and I directed the unmarried lady to serve out the breakfast, and the married lady to serve out the tea. Likewise I said to my black steward in their presence, "Tom Snow, these two ladies are equally the mistresses of this house, and do you obey their orders equally"; at which Tom laughed, and they all laughed.

Old Mr. Rarx was not a pleasant man to look at, nor yet to talk to, or to be with, for no one could help seeing that he was a sordid and selfish character, and that he had warped further and further out of the straight with time. Not but what he was on his best behaviour with us, as everybody was; for we had no bickering among us, for'ard or aft. I only mean to say, he was not the man one would have chosen for a messmate. If choice there had been, one might even have gone a few points out of one's course, to say, "No! Not him!" But, there was one curious inconsistency in Mr. Rarx. That was, that he took an astonishing interest in the child. He looked, and I may add, he was, one of the last of men to care at all for a child, or to care much for any human creature. Still, he went so far as to be habitually uneasy, if the child was long on deck, out of his sight. He was always afraid of her falling overboard, or falling down a hatchway, or of a block or what not coming down upon her from the rigging in the working of the ship, or of her getting some hurt or other. He used to look at her and touch her, as if she was something precious to him. He was always solicitous about her not injuring her health, and constantly entreated her mother to be careful of it. This was so much the more curious, because the child did not like him, but used to shrink away from him, and would not even put out her hand to him without coaxing from others. I believe that every soul on board frequently noticed this, and not one of us understood it. However, it was such a plain fact, that John Steadiman said more than once when old Mr. Rarx was not within earshot, that if the *Golden Mary* felt a tenderness for the dear old gentleman she carried in her lap, she must be bitterly jealous of the *Golden Lucy*.

Before I go any further with this narrative, I will state that our ship was a barque of three hundred tons, carrying a crew of eighteen men, a second mate in addition to John, a carpenter, an armourer or smith, and two apprentices (one a Scotch boy, poor little fellow). We had three boats; the Long-boat, capable of carrying twenty-five men; the Cutter, capable of carrying fifteen; and the Surf-boat, capable of carrying ten. I put down the capacity of these boats according to the numbers they were really meant to hold.

We had tastes of bad weather and head-winds, of course; but, on the whole we had as fine a run as any reasonable man could expect, for sixty days. I then began to enter two remarks in the ship's Log and in my Journal; first, that there was an unusual and amazing quantity of ice; second, that the nights were most wonderfully dark, in spite of the ice.

For five days and a half, it seemed quite useless and hopeless to alter the ship's course so as to stand out of the way of this ice. I made what southing I could; but, all that time, we were beset by it. Mrs. Atherfield after standing by me on deck once, looking for some time in an awed manner at the great bergs that surrounded us, said in a whisper, "O! Captain Ravender, it looks as if the whole solid earth had changed into ice, and broken up!" I said to her, laughing, "I don't wonder that it does, to your inexperienced eyes, my dear." But I had never seen a twentieth part of the quantity, and, in reality, I was pretty much of her opinion.

However, at two P.M. on the afternoon of the sixth day, that is to say, when we were sixty-six days out, John Steadiman who had gone aloft, sang out from the top, that the sea was clear ahead. Before four P.M. a strong breeze springing up right astern, we were in open water at sunset. The breeze then freshening into half a gale of wind, and the *Golden Mary* being a very fast sailer, we went before the wind merrily, all night.

I had thought it impossible that it could be darker than it had been, until the sun, moon, and stars should fall out of the Heavens, and Time should be destroyed; but, it had been next to light, in comparison with what it was now. The darkness was so profound, that looking into it was painful and oppressive—like looking, without a ray of light, into a dense black bandage put as close before the eyes as it could be, without touching them. I doubled the look-out, and John and I stood in the bow side-by-side, never leaving it all night. Yet I should no more have known that he was near me when he was silent, without putting out my arm and touching him, than I should if he had turned in and been fast asleep below. We were not so much looking out, all of us, as listening to the utmost, both with our eyes and ears.

Next day, I found that the mercury in the barometer, which had risen steadily since we cleared the ice, remained steady. I had had very good observations, with now and then the interruption of a day or so, since our departure. I got the sun at noon, and found that we were in Lat. 58 ° S., Long. 60 ° W., off New South Shetland; in the neighbourhood of Cape Horn. We were sixty-seven days out, that day. The ship's reckoning was accurately worked and made up. The ship did her duty admirably, all on board were well, and all hands were as smart, efficient, and contented, as it was possible to be.

When the night came on again as dark as before, it was the eighth night I had been on deck. Nor had I taken more than a very little sleep in the day-time, my station being always near the helm, and often at it, while we were among the ice. Few but those who have tried it can imagine the difficulty and pain of only keeping the eyes open—physically open—under such circumstances, in such darkness. They get struck by the darkness, and blinded by the darkness. They make patterns in it, and they flash in it, as if they had gone out of your head to look at you. On the turn of midnight, John Steadiman, who was alert and fresh (for I had always made him turn in by day), said to me, "Captain Ravender, I entreat of you to go below. I am sure you can hardly stand, and your voice is getting weak, sir. Go below, and take a little rest. I'll call you if a block chafes." I said to John in answer, "Well, well, John! Let us wait till the turn of one o'clock, before we talk about that." I had just had one of the ship's lanterns held up, that I might see how the night went by my watch, and it was then twenty minutes after twelve.

At five minutes before one, John sang out to the boy to bring the lantern again, and when I told him once more what the time was, entreated and prayed of me to go below. "Captain Ravender," says he, "all's well; we can't afford to have you laid up for a single hour; and I respectfully and earnestly beg of you to go below." The end of it was, that I agreed to do so, on the understanding that if I failed to come up of my own accord within three hours, I was to be punctually called. Having settled that, I left John in charge. But I called him to me once afterwards, to ask him a question. I had been to look at the barometer, and had seen the mercury still perfectly steady, and had come up the companion again to take a last look about me—if I can use such a word in reference to such darkness—when I thought that the waves, as the *Golden Mary* parted them and shook them off, had a hollow sound in them; something that I fancied was a rather unusual reverberation. I was standing by the quarter-deck rail on the starboard side, when I called John aft to me, and bade him listen. He did so with the greatest attention. Turning to me he then said, "Rely upon it, Captain Ravender, you have been without rest too long, and the novelty is only in the state of your sense of hearing." I thought so too by that time, and I think so now, though I can never know for absolute certain in this world, whether it was or not.

When I left John Steadiman in charge, the ship was still going at a great rate through the water. The wind still blew right astern. Though she was making great way, she was under shortened sail, and had no more than she could easily carry. All was snug, and nothing complained. There was a pretty sea running, but not a very high sea neither, nor at all a confused one.

I turned in, as we seamen say, all standing. The meaning of that is, I did not pull my clothes off—no, not even so much as my coat: though I did my shoes, for my feet were badly swelled with the deck. There was a little swing-lamp alight in my cabin. I thought, as I looked at it before shutting my eyes, that I was so tired of darkness, and troubled by darkness, that I could have gone to sleep best in the midst of a million of flaming gas-lights. That was the last thought I had before I went off, except the prevailing thought that I should not be able to get to sleep at all.

I dreamed that I was back at Penrith again, and was trying to get round the church, which had altered its shape very much since I last saw it, and was cloven all down the middle of the steeple in a most singular manner. Why I wanted to get round the church I don't know; but I was as anxious to do it as if my life depended on it. Indeed, I believe it did in the dream. For all that, I could not get round the church. I was still trying, when I came against it with a violent shock, and was flung out of my cot against the ship's side. Shrieks and a terrific outcry struck me far harder than the bruising timbers, and amidst sounds of grinding and crashing, and a heavy rushing and breaking of water—sounds I understood too well—I made my way on deck. It was not an easy thing to do, for the ship heeled over frightfully, and was beating in a furious manner.

I could not see the men as I went forward, but I could hear that they were hauling in sail, in disorder. I had my trumpet in my hand, and, after directing and encouraging them in this till it was done, I hailed first John Steadiman, and then my second mate, Mr. William Rames. Both answered clearly and steadily. Now, I had practised them and all my crew, as I have ever made it a custom to practise all who sail with me, to take certain stations and wait my orders, in case of any unexpected crisis. When my voice was heard hailing, and their voices were heard answering, I was aware, through all the noises of the ship and sea, and all the crying of the passengers below, that there was a pause. "Are you ready, Rames?"—"Ay, ay, Sir!"—"Then light up, for God's sake!" In a moment he and another were burning blue-lights, and the ship and all on board seemed to be enclosed in a mist of light, under a great black dome.

The light shone up so high that I could see the huge Iceberg upon which we had struck, cloven at the top and down the middle, exactly like Penrith Church in my dream. At the same moment I could see the watch last relieved, crowding up and down on deck; I could see Mrs. Atherfield and Miss Coleshaw thrown about on the top of the companion as they struggled to bring the child up from below; I could see that the masts were going with the shock and the beating of the ship; I could see the frightful breach stove in on the starboard side, half the length of the vessel, and the sheathing and timbers spirting up; I could see that the Cutter was disabled, in a wreck of broken fragments; and I could see every eye turned upon me. It is my belief that if there had been ten thousand eyes there, I should have seen them all, with their different looks. And all this in a moment. But you must consider what a moment.

I saw the men, as they looked at me, fall towards their appointed stations, like good men and true. If she had not righted, they could have done very little there or anywhere but die—not that it is little for a man to die at his post—I mean they could have done nothing to save the passengers and themselves. Happily, however, the violence of the shock with which we had so determinedly borne down direct on that fatal Iceberg, as if it had been our destination instead of our destruction, had so smashed and pounded the ship that she got off in this same instant and righted. I did not want the carpenter to tell me she was filling and going down; I could see and hear that. I gave Rames the word to lower the Long-boat and the Surf-boat, and I myself told off the men for each duty. Not one hung back, or came before the other. I now whispered to John Steadiman, "John, I stand at the gangway here, to see every soul on board safe over the side. You shall have the next post of honour, and shall be the last but one to leave the ship. Bring up the passengers, and range them behind me; and put what provision and water you can got at, in the boats. Cast your eye for'ard, John, and you'll see you have not a moment to lose."

My noble fellows got the boats over the side as orderly as I ever saw boats lowered with any sea running, and, when they were launched, two or three of the nearest men in them as they held on, rising and falling with the swell, called out, looking up at me, "Captain Ravender, if anything goes wrong with us, and you are saved, remember we stood by you!"—"We'll all stand by one another ashore, yet, please God, my lads!" says I. "Hold on bravely, and be tender with the women."

The women were an example to us. They trembled very much, but they were quiet and perfectly collected. "Kiss me, Captain Ravender," says Mrs. Atherfield, "and God in heaven bless you, you good man!" "My dear," says I, "those words are better for me than a lifeboat." I held her child in my arms till she was in the boat, and then kissed the child and handed her safe down. I now said to the people in her, "You have got your freight, my lads, all but me, and I am not coming yet awhile. Pull away from the ship, and keep off!"

That was the Long-boat. Old Mr. Rarx was one of her complement, and he was the only passenger who had greatly misbehaved since the ship struck. Others had been a little wild, which was not to be wondered at, and not very blamable; but, he had made a lamentation and uproar which it was dangerous for the people to hear, as there is always contagion in weakness and selfishness. His incessant cry had been that he must not be separated from the child, that he couldn't see the child, and that he and the child must go together. He had even tried to wrest the child out of my arms, that he might keep her in his. "Mr. Rarx," said I to him when it came to that, "I have a loaded pistol in my pocket; and if you don't stand out of the gangway, and keep perfectly quiet, I shall shoot you through the heart, if you have got one." Says he, "You won't do murder, Captain Ravender!" "No, Sir," says I, "I won't murder forty-four people to humour you, but I'll shoot you to save them." After that he was quiet, and stood shivering a little way off, until I named him to go over the side.

The Long-boat being cast off, the Surf-boat was soon filled. There only remained aboard the *Golden Mary*, John Mullion the man who had kept on burning the blue-lights (and who had lighted every new one at every old one before it went out, as quietly as if he had been at an illumination); John Steadiman; and myself. I hurried those two into the Surf-boat, called to them to keep off, and waited with a grateful and relieved heart for the Long-boat to come and take me in, if she could. I looked at my watch, and it showed me, by the blue-light, ten minutes past two. They lost no time. As soon as she was near enough, I swung myself into her, and called to the men, "With a will, lads! She's reeling!" We were not an inch too far out of the inner vortex of her going down, when, by the blue-light which John Mullion still burnt in the bow of the Surf-boat, we saw her lurch, and plunge to the bottom head-foremost. The child cried, weeping wildly, "O the dear *Golden Mary*! O look at her! Save her! Save the poor *Golden Mary*!" And then the light burnt out, and the black dome seemed to come down upon us.

I suppose if we had all stood a-top of a mountain, and seen the whole remainder of the world sink away from under us, we could hardly have felt more shocked and solitary than we did when we knew we were alone on the wide ocean, and that the beautiful ship in which most of us had been securely asleep within half an hour was gone for ever. There was an awful silence in our boat, and such a kind of palsy on the rowers and the man at the rudder, that I felt they were scarcely keeping her before the sea. I spoke out then, and said, "Let every one here thank the Lord for our preservation!" All the voices answered (even the child's), "We thank the Lord!" I then said the Lord's Prayer, and all hands said it after me with a solemn murmuring. Then I gave the word "Cheerily, O men, Cheerily!" and I felt that they were handling the boat again as a boat ought to be handled.

The Surf-boat now burnt another blue-light to show us where they were, and we made for her, and laid ourselves as nearly alongside of her as we dared. I had always kept my boats with a coil or two of good stout stuff in each of them, so both boats had a rope at hand. We made a shift, with much labour and trouble, to got near enough to one another to divide the blue-lights (they were no use after that night, for the sea-water soon got at them), and to get a tow-rope out between us. All night long we kept together, sometimes obliged to cast off the rope, and sometimes getting it out again, and all of us wearying for the morning—which appeared so long in coming that old Mr. Rarx screamed out, in spite of his fears of me, "The world is drawing to an end, and the sun will never rise any more!"

When the day broke, I found that we were all huddled together in a miserable manner. We were deep in the water; being, as I found on mustering, thirty-one in number, or at least six too many. In the Surf-boat they were fourteen in number, being at least four too many. The first thing I did, was to get myself passed to the rudder—which I took from that time—and to get Mrs. Atherfield, her child, and Miss Coleshaw, passed on to sit next me. As to old Mr. Rarx, I put him in the bow, as far from us as I could. And I put some of the best men near us in order that if I should drop there might be a skilful hand ready to take the helm.

The sea moderating as the sun came up, though the sky was cloudy and wild, we spoke the other boat, to know what stores they had, and to overhaul what we had. I had a compass in my pocket, a small telescope, a double-barrelled pistol, a knife, and a fire-box and matches. Most of my men had knives, and some had a little tobacco: some, a pipe as well. We had a mug among us, and an iron spoon. As to provisions, there were in my boat two bags of biscuit, one piece of raw beef, one piece of raw pork, a bag of coffee, roasted but not ground (thrown in, I imagine, by mistake, for something else), two small casks of water, and about half-a-gallon of rum in a keg. The Surf-boat, having rather more rum than we, and fewer to drink it, gave us, as I estimated, another quart into our keg. In return, we gave them three double handfuls of coffee, tied up in a piece of a handkerchief; they reported that they had aboard besides, a bag of biscuit, a piece of beef, a small cask of water, a small box of lemons, and a Dutch cheese. It took a long time to make these exchanges, and they were not made without risk to both parties; the sea running quite high enough to make our approaching near to one another very hazardous. In the bundle with the coffee, I conveyed to John Steadiman (who had a ship's compass with him), a paper written in pencil, and torn from my pocket-book, containing the course I meant to steer, in the hope of making land, or being picked up by some vessel—I say in the hope, though I had little hope of either deliverance. I then sang out to him, so as all might hear, that if we two boats could live or die together, we would; but, that if we should be parted by the weather, and join company no more, they should have our prayers and blessings, and we asked for theirs. We then gave them three cheers, which they returned, and I saw the men's heads droop in both boats as they fell to their oars again.

These arrangements had occupied the general attention advantageously for all, though (as I expressed in the last sentence) they ended in a sorrowful feeling. I now said a few words to my fellow-voyagers on the subject of the small stock of food on which our lives depended if they were preserved from the great deep, and on the rigid necessity of our eking it out in the most frugal manner. One and all replied that whatever allowance I thought best to lay down should be strictly kept to. We made a pair of scales out of a thin scrap of iron-plating and some twine, and I got together for weights such of the heaviest buttons among us as I calculated made up some fraction over two ounces. This was the allowance of solid food served out once a-day to each, from that time to the end; with the addition of a coffee-berry, or sometimes half a one, when the weather was very fair, for breakfast. We had nothing else whatever, but half a pint of water each per day, and sometimes, when we were coldest and weakest, a teaspoonful of rum each, served out as a dram. I know how learnedly it can be shown that rum is poison, but I also know that in this case, as in all similar cases I have ever read of—which are numerous—no words can express the comfort and support derived from it. Nor have I the least doubt that it saved the lives of far more than half our number. Having mentioned half a pint of water as our daily allowance, I ought to observe that sometimes we had less, and sometimes we had more; for much rain fell, and we caught it in a canvas stretched for the purpose.

Thus, at that tempestuous time of the year, and in that tempestuous part of the world, we shipwrecked people rose and fell with the waves. It is not my intention to relate (if I can avoid it) such circumstances appertaining to our doleful condition as have been better told in many other narratives of the kind than I can be expected to tell them. I will only note, in so many passing words, that day after day and night after night, we received the sea upon our backs to prevent it from swamping the boat; that one party was always kept baling, and that every hat and cap among us soon got worn out, though patched up fifty times, as the only vessels we had for that service; that another party lay down in the bottom of the boat, while a third rowed; and that we were soon all in boils and blisters and rags.

The other boat was a source of such anxious interest to all of us that I used to wonder whether, if we were saved, the time could ever come when the survivors in this boat of ours could be at all indifferent to the fortunes of the survivors in that. We got out a tow-rope whenever the weather permitted, but that did not often happen, and how we two parties kept within the same horizon, as we did, He, who mercifully permitted it to be so for our consolation, only knows. I never shall forget the looks with which, when the morning light came, we used to gaze about us over the stormy waters, for the other boat. We once parted company for seventy-two hours, and we believed them to have gone down, as they did us. The joy on both sides when we came within view of one another again, had something in a manner Divine in it; each was so forgetful of individual suffering, in tears of delight and sympathy for the people in the other boat.

I have been wanting to get round to the individual or personal part of my subject, as I call it, and the foregoing incident puts me in the right way. The patience and good disposition aboard of us, was wonderful. I was not surprised by it in the women; for all men born of women know what great qualities they will show when men will fail; but, I own I was a little surprised by it in some of the men. Among one-and-thirty people assembled at the best of times, there will usually, I should say, be two or three uncertain tempers. I knew that I had more than one rough temper with me among my own people, for I had chosen those for the Long-boat that I might have them under my eye. But, they softened under their misery, and were as considerate of the ladies, and as compassionate of the child, as the best among us, or among men—they could not have been more so. I heard scarcely any complaining. The party lying down would moan a good deal in their sleep, and I would often notice a man—not always the same man, it is to be understood, but nearly all of them at one time or other—sitting moaning at his oar, or in his place, as he looked mistily over the sea. When it happened to be long before I could catch his eye, he would go on moaning all the time in the dismallest manner; but, when our looks met, he would brighten and leave off. I almost always got the impression that he did not know what sound he had been making, but that he thought he had been humming a tune.

Our sufferings from cold and wet were far greater than our sufferings from hunger. We managed to keep the child warm; but, I doubt if any one else among us ever was warm for five minutes together; and the shivering, and the chattering of teeth, were sad to hear. The child cried a little at first for her lost playfellow, the *Golden Mary*; but hardly ever whimpered afterwards; and when the state of the weather made it possible, she used now and then to be held up in the arms of some of us, to look over the sea for John Steadiman's boat. I see the golden hair and the innocent face now, between me and the driving clouds, like an angel going to fly away.

It had happened on the second day, towards night, that Mrs. Atherfield, in getting Little Lucy to sleep, sang her a song. She had a soft, melodious voice, and, when she had finished it, our people up and begged for another. She sang them another, and after it had fallen dark ended with the Evening Hymn. From that time, whenever anything could be heard above the sea and wind, and while she had any voice left, nothing would serve the people but that she should sing at sunset. She always did, and always ended with the Evening Hymn. We mostly took up the last line, and shed tears when it was done, but not miserably. We had a prayer night and morning, also, when the weather allowed of it.

Twelve nights and eleven days we had been driving in the boat, when old Mr. Rarx began to be delirious, and to cry out to me to throw the gold overboard or it would sink us, and we should all be lost. For days past the child had been declining, and that was the great cause of his wildness. He had been over and over again shrieking out to me to give her all the remaining meat, to give her all the remaining rum, to save her at any cost, or we should all be ruined. At this time, she lay in her mother's arms at my feet. One of her little hands was almost always creeping about her mother's neck or chin. I had watched the wasting of the little hand, and I knew it was nearly over.

The old man's cries were so discordant with the mother's love and submission, that I called out to him in an angry voice, unless he held his peace on the instant, I would order him to be knocked on the head and thrown overboard. He was mute then, until the child died, very peacefully, an hour afterwards: which was known to all in the boat by the mother's breaking out into lamentations for the first time since the wreck—for, she had great fortitude and constancy, though she was a little gentle woman. Old Mr. Rarx then became quite ungovernable, tearing what rags he had on him, raging in imprecations, and calling to me that if I had thrown the gold overboard (always the gold with him!) I might have saved the child. "And now," says he, in a terrible voice, "we shall founder, and all go to the Devil, for our sins will sink us, when we have no innocent child to bear us up!" We so discovered with amazement, that this old wretch had only cared for the life of the pretty little creature dear to all of us, because of the influence he superstitiously hoped she might have in preserving him! Altogether it was too much for the smith or armourer, who was sitting next the old man, to bear. He took him by the throat and rolled him under the thwarts, where he lay still enough for hours afterwards.

All that thirteenth night, Miss Coleshaw, lying across my knees as I kept the helm, comforted and supported the poor mother. Her child, covered with a pea-jacket of mine, lay in her lap. It troubled me all night to think that there was no Prayer-Book among us, and that I could remember but very few of the exact words of the burial service. When I stood up at broad day, all knew what was going to be done, and I noticed that my poor fellows made the motion of uncovering their heads, though their heads had been stark bare to the sky and sea for many a weary hour. There was a long heavy swell on, but otherwise it was a fair morning, and there were broad fields of sunlight on the waves in the east. I said no more than this: "I am the Resurrection and the Life, saith the Lord. He raised the daughter of Jairus the ruler, and said she was not dead but slept. He raised the widow's son. He arose Himself, and was seen of many. He loved little children, saying, Suffer them to come unto Me and rebuke them not, for of such is the kingdom of heaven. In His name, my friends, and committed to His merciful goodness!" With those words I laid my rough face softly on the placid little forehead, and buried the *Golden Lucy* in the grave of the *Golden Mary*.

Having had it on my mind to relate the end of this dear little child, I have omitted something from its exact place, which I will supply here. It will come quite as well here as anywhere else.

Foreseeing that if the boat lived through the stormy weather, the time must come, and soon come, when we should have absolutely no morsel to eat, I had one momentous point often in my thoughts. Although I had, years before that, fully satisfied myself that the instances in which human beings in the last distress have fed upon each other, are exceedingly few, and have very seldom indeed (if ever) occurred when the people in distress, however dreadful their extremity, have been accustomed to moderate forbearance and restraint; I say, though I had long before quite satisfied my mind on this topic, I felt doubtful whether there might not have been in former cases some harm and danger from keeping it out of sight and pretending not to think of it. I felt doubtful whether some minds, growing weak with fasting and exposure and having such a terrific idea to dwell upon in secret, might not magnify it until it got to have an awful attraction about it. This was not a new thought of mine, for it had grown out of my reading. However, it came over me stronger than it had ever done before—as it had reason for doing—in the boat, and on the fourth day I decided that I would bring out into the light that unformed fear which must have been more or less darkly in every brain among us. Therefore, as a means of beguiling the time and inspiring hope, I gave them the best summary in my power of Bligh's voyage of more than three thousand miles, in an open boat, after the Mutiny of the *Bounty*, and of the wonderful preservation of that boat's crew. They listened throughout with great interest, and I concluded by telling them, that, in my opinion, the happiest circumstance in the whole narrative was, that Bligh, who was no delicate man either, had solemnly placed it on record therein that he was sure and certain that under no conceivable circumstances whatever would that emaciated party, who had gone through all the pains of famine, have preyed on one another. I cannot describe the visible relief which this spread through the boat, and how the tears stood in every eye. From that time I was as well convinced as Bligh himself that there was no danger, and that this phantom, at any rate, did not haunt us.

Now, it was a part of Bligh's experience that when the people in his boat were most cast down, nothing did them so much good as hearing a story told by one of their number. When I mentioned that, I saw that it struck the general attention as much as it did my own, for I had not thought of it until I came to it in my summary. This was on the day after Mrs. Atherfield first sang to us. I proposed that, whenever the weather would permit, we should have a story two hours after dinner (I always issued the allowance I have mentioned at one o'clock, and called it by that name), as well as our song at sunset. The proposal was received with a cheerful satisfaction that warmed my heart within me; and I do not say too much when I say that those two periods in the four-and-twenty hours were expected with positive pleasure, and were really enjoyed by all hands. Spectres as we soon were in our bodily wasting, our imaginations did not perish like the gross flesh upon our bones. Music and Adventure, two of the great gifts of Providence to mankind, could charm us long after that was lost.

The wind was almost always against us after the second day; and for many days together we could not nearly hold our own. We had all varieties of bad weather. We had rain, hail, snow, wind, mist, thunder and lightning. Still the boats lived through the heavy seas, and still we perishing people rose and fell with the great waves.

Sixteen nights and fifteen days, twenty nights and nineteen days, twenty-four nights and twenty-three days. So the time went on. Disheartening as I knew that our progress, or want of progress, must be, I never deceived them as to my calculations of it. In the first place, I felt that we were all too near eternity for deceit; in the second place, I knew that if I failed, or died, the man who followed me must have a knowledge of the true state of things to begin upon. When I told them at noon, what I reckoned we had made or lost, they generally received what I said in a tranquil and resigned manner, and always gratefully towards me. It was not unusual at any time of the day for some one to burst out weeping loudly without any new cause; and, when the burst was over, to calm down a little better than before. I had seen exactly the same thing in a house of mourning.

During the whole of this time, old Mr. Rarx had had his fits of calling out to me to throw the gold (always the gold!) overboard, and of heaping violent reproaches upon me for not having saved the child; but now, the food being all gone, and I having nothing left to serve out but a bit of coffee-berry now and then, he began to be too weak to do this, and consequently fell silent. Mrs. Atherfield and Miss Coleshaw generally lay, each with an arm across one of my knees, and her head upon it. They never complained at all. Up to the time of her child's death, Mrs. Atherfield had bound up her own beautiful hair every day; and I took particular notice that this was always before she sang her song at night, when everyone looked at her. But she never did it after the loss of her darling; and it would have been now all tangled with dirt and wet, but that Miss Coleshaw was careful of it long after she was herself, and would sometimes smooth it down with her weak thin hands.

We were past mustering a story now; but one day, at about this period, I reverted to the superstition of old Mr. Rarx, concerning the *Golden Lucy*, and told them that nothing vanished from the eye of God, though much might pass away from the eyes of men. "We were all of us," says I, "children once; and our baby feet have strolled in green woods ashore; and our baby hands have gathered flowers in gardens, where the birds were singing. The children that we were, are not lost to the great knowledge of our Creator. Those innocent creatures will appear with us before Him, and plead for us. What we were in the best time of our generous youth will arise and go with us too. The purest part of our lives will not desert us at the pass to which all of us here present are gliding. What we were then, will be as much in existence before Him, as what we are now." They were no less comforted by this consideration, than I was myself; and Miss Coleshaw, drawing my ear nearer to her lips, said, "Captain Ravender, I was on my way to marry a disgraced and broken man, whom I dearly loved when he was honourable and good. Your words seem to have come out of my own poor heart." She pressed my hand upon it, smiling.

Twenty-seven nights and twenty-six days. We were in no want of rain-water, but we had nothing else. And yet, even now, I never turned my eyes upon a waking face but it tried to brighten before mine. O, what a thing it is, in a time of danger and in the presence of death, the shining of a face upon a face! I have heard it broached that orders should be given in great new ships by electric telegraph. I admire machinery as much is any man, and am as thankful to it as any man can be for what it does for us. But it will never be a substitute for the face of a man, with his soul in it, encouraging another man to be brave and true. Never try it for that. It will break down like a straw.

I now began to remark certain changes in myself which I did not like. They caused me much disquiet. I often saw the *Golden Lucy* in the air above the boat. I often saw her I have spoken of before, sitting beside me. I saw the *Golden Mary* go down, as she really had gone down, twenty times in a day. And yet the sea was mostly, to my thinking, not sea neither, but moving country and extraordinary mountainous regions, the like of which have never been beheld. I felt it time to leave my last words regarding John Steadiman, in case any lips should last out to repeat them to any living ears. I said that John had told me (as he had on deck) that he had sung out "Breakers ahead!" the instant they were audible, and had tried to wear ship, but she struck before it could be done. (His cry, I dare say, had made my dream.) I said that the circumstances were altogether without warning, and out of any course that could have been guarded against; that the same loss would have happened if I had been in charge; and that John was not to blame, but from first to last had done his duty nobly, like the man he was. I tried to write it down in my pocket-book, but could make no words, though I knew what the words were that I wanted to make. When it had come to that, her hands—though she was dead so long—laid me down gently in the bottom of the boat, and she and the *Golden Lucy* swung me to sleep.

All that follows, was written by John Steadiman, Chief Mate:

On the twenty-sixth day after the foundering of the *Golden Mary* at sea, I, John Steadiman, was sitting in my place in the stern-sheets of the Surf-boat, with just sense enough left in me to steer—that is to say, with my eyes strained, wide-awake, over the bows of the boat, and my brains fast asleep and dreaming—when I was roused upon a sudden by our second mate, Mr. William Rames.

"Let me take a spell in your place," says he. "And look you out for the Long-boat astern. The last time she rose on the crest of a wave, I thought I made out a signal flying aboard her."

We shifted our places, clumsily and slowly enough, for we were both of us weak and dazed with wet, cold, and hunger. I waited some time, watching the heavy rollers astern, before the Long-boat rose a-top of one of them at the same time with us. At last, she was heaved up for a moment well in view, and there, sure enough, was the signal flying aboard of her—a strip of rag of some sort, rigged to an oar, and hoisted in her bows.

"What does it mean?" says Rames to me in a quavering, trembling sort of voice. "Do they signal a sail in sight?"

"Hush, for God's sake!" says I, clapping my hand over his mouth. "Don't let the people hear you. They'll all go mad together if we mislead them about that signal. Wait a bit, till I have another look at it."

I held on by him, for he had set me all of a tremble with his notion of a sail in sight, and watched for the Long-boat again. Up she rose on the top of another roller. I made out the signal clearly, that second time, and saw that it was rigged half-mast high.

"Rames," says I, "it's a signal of distress. Pass the word forward to keep her before the sea, and no more. We must get the Long-boat within hailing distance of us, as soon as possible."

I dropped down into my old place at the tiller without another word—for the thought went through me like a knife that something had happened to Captain Ravender. I should consider myself unworthy to write another line of this statement, if I had not made up my mind to speak the truth, the whole truth, and nothing but the truth—and I must, therefore, confess plainly that now, for the first time, my heart sank within me. This weakness on my part was produced in some degree, as I take it, by the exhausting effects of previous anxiety and grief.

Our provisions—if I may give that name to what we had left—were reduced to the rind of one lemon and about a couple of handsfull of coffee-berries. Besides these great distresses, caused by the death, the danger, and the suffering among my crew and passengers, I had had a little distress of my own to shake me still more, in the death of the child whom I had got to be very fond of on the voyage out—so fond that I was secretly a little jealous of her being taken in the Long-boat instead of mine when the ship foundered. It used to be a great comfort to me, and I think to those with me also, after we had seen the last of the *Golden Mary*, to see the *Golden Lucy*, held up by the men in the Long-boat, when the weather allowed it, as the best and brightest sight they had to show. She looked, at the distance we saw her from, almost like a little white bird in the air. To miss her for the first time, when the weather lulled a little again, and we all looked out for our white bird and looked in vain, was a sore disappointment. To see the men's heads bowed down and the captain's hand pointing into the sea when we hailed the Long-boat, a few days after, gave me as heavy a shock and as sharp a pang of heartache to bear as ever I remember suffering in all my life. I only mention these things to show that if I did give way a little at first, under the dread that our captain was lost to us, it was not without having been a good deal shaken beforehand by more trials of one sort or another than often fall to one man's share.

I had got over the choking in my throat with the help of a drop of water, and had steadied my mind again so as to be prepared against the worst, when I heard the hail (Lord help the poor fellows, how weak it sounded!)—

"Surf-boat, ahoy!"

I looked up, and there were our companions in misfortune tossing abreast of us; not so near that we could make out the features of any of them, but near enough, with some exertion for people in our condition, to make their voices heard in the intervals when the wind was weakest.

I answered the hail, and waited a bit, and heard nothing, and then sung out the captain's name. The voice that replied did not sound like his; the words that reached us were:

"Chief-mate wanted on board!"

Every man of my crew knew what that meant as well as I did. As second officer in command, there could be but one reason for wanting me on board the Long-boat. A groan went all round us, and my men looked darkly in each other's faces, and whispered under their breaths:

"The captain is dead!"

I commanded them to be silent, and not to make too sure of bad news, at such a pass as things had now come to with us. Then, hailing the Long-boat, I signified that I was ready to go on board when the weather would let me—stopped a bit to draw a good long breath—and then called out as loud as I could the dreadful question:

"Is the captain dead?"

The black figures of three or four men in the after-part of the Long-boat all stooped down together as my voice reached them. They were lost to view for about a minute; then appeared again—one man among them was held up on his feet by the rest, and he hailed back the blessed words (a very faint hope went a very long way with people in our desperate situation): "Not yet!"

The relief felt by me, and by all with me, when we knew that our captain, though unfitted for duty, was not lost to us, it is not in words—at least, not in such words as a man like me can command—to express. I did my best to cheer the men by telling them what a good sign it was that we were not as badly off yet as we had feared; and then communicated what instructions I had to give, to William Rames, who was to be left in command in my place when I took charge of the Long-boat. After that, there was nothing to be done, but to wait for the chance of the wind dropping at sunset, and the sea going down afterwards, so as to enable our weak crews to lay the two boats alongside of each other, without undue risk—or, to put it plainer, without saddling ourselves with the necessity for any extraordinary exertion of strength or skill. Both the one and the other had now been starved out of us for days and days together.

At sunset the wind suddenly dropped, but the sea, which had been running high for so long a time past, took hours after that before it showed any signs of getting to rest. The moon was shining, the sky was wonderfully clear, and it could not have been, according to my calculations, far off midnight, when the long, slow, regular swell of the calming ocean fairly set in, and I took the responsibility of lessening the distance between the Long-boat and ourselves.

It was, I dare say, a delusion of mine; but I thought I had never seen the moon shine so white and ghastly anywhere, either on sea or on land, as she shone that night while we were approaching our companions in misery. When there was not much more than a boat's length between us, and the white light streamed cold and clear over all our faces, both crews rested on their oars with one great shudder, and stared over the gunwale of either boat, panic-stricken at the first sight of each other.

"Any lives lost among you?" I asked, in the midst of that frightful silence.

The men in the Long-bout huddled together like sheep at the sound of my voice.

"None yet, but the child, thanks be to God!" answered one among them.

And at the sound of his voice, all my men shrank together like the men in the Long-boat. I was afraid to let the horror produced by our first meeting at close quarters after the dreadful changes that wet, cold, and famine had produced, last one moment longer than could be helped; so, without giving time for any more questions and answers, I commanded the men to lay the two boats close alongside of each other. When I rose up and committed the tiller to the hands of Rames, all my poor follows raised their white faces imploringly to mine. "Don't leave us, Sir," they said, "don't leave us." "I leave you," says I, "under the command and the guidance of Mr. William Rames, as good a sailor as I am, and as trusty and kind a man as ever stepped. Do your duty by him, as you have done it by me; and remember to the last, that while there is life there is hope. God bless and help you all!" With those words I collected what strength I had left, and caught at two arms that were held out to me, and so got from the stern-sheets of one boat into the stern-sheets of the other.

"Mind where you step, Sir," whispered one of the men who had helped me into the Long-boat. I looked down as he spoke. Three figures were huddled up below me, with the moonshine falling on them in ragged streaks through the gaps between the men standing or sitting above them. The first face I made out was the face of Miss Coleshaw; her eyes were wide open and fixed on me. She seemed still to keep her senses, and, by the alternate parting and closing of her lips, to be trying to speak, but I could not hear that she uttered a single word. On her shoulder rested the head of Mrs. Atherfield. The mother of our poor little *Golden Lucy* must, I think, have been dreaming of the child she had lost; for there was a faint smile just ruffling the white stillness of her face, when I first saw it turned upward, with peaceful closed eyes towards the heavens. From her, I looked down a little, and there, with his head on her lap, and with one of her hands resting tenderly on his cheek—there lay the Captain, to whose help and guidance, up to this miserable time, we had never looked in vain,—there, worn out at last in our service, and for our sakes, lay the best and bravest man of all our company. I stole my hand in gently through his clothes and laid it on his heart, and felt a little feeble warmth over it, though my cold dulled touch could not detect even the faintest beating. The two men in the stern-sheets with me, noticing what I was doing—knowing I loved him like a brother—and seeing, I suppose, more distress in my face than I myself was conscious of its showing, lost command over themselves altogether, and burst into a piteous moaning, sobbing lamentation over him. One of the two drew aside a jacket from his feet, and showed me that they were bare, except where a wet, ragged strip of stocking still clung to one of them. When the ship struck the Iceberg, he had run on deck leaving his shoes in his cabin. All through the voyage in the boat his feet had been unprotected; and not a soul had discovered it until he dropped! As long as he could keep his eyes open, the very look of them had cheered the men, and comforted and upheld the women. Not one living creature in the boat, with any sense about him, but had felt the good influence of that brave man in one way or another. Not one but had heard him, over and over again, give the credit to others which was due only to himself; praising this man for patience, and thanking that man for help, when the patience and the help had really and truly, as to the best part of both, come only from him. All this, and much more, I heard pouring confusedly from the men's lips while they crouched down, sobbing and crying over their commander, and wrapping the jacket as warmly and tenderly as they could over is cold feet. It went to my heart to check them; but I knew that if this lamenting spirit spread any further, all chance of keeping alight any last sparks of hope and resolution among the boat's company would be lost for ever. Accordingly I sent them to their places, spoke a few encouraging words to the men forward, promising to serve out, when the morning came, as much as I dared, of any eatable thing left in the lockers; called to Rames, in my old boat, to keep as near us as he safely could; drew the garments and coverings of the two poor suffering women more closely about them; and, with a secret prayer to be directed for the best in bearing the awful responsibility now laid on my shoulders, took my Captain's vacant place at the helm of the Long-boat.

This, as well as I can tell it, is the full and true account of how I came to be placed in charge of the lost passengers and crew of the *Golden Mary*, on the morning of the twenty-seventh day after the ship struck the Iceberg, and foundered at sea.

No Thoroughfare

(Written with Wilkie Collins)

The Overture

Day of the month and year, November the thirtieth, one thousand eight hundred and thirty-five. London Time by the great clock of Saint Paul's, ten at night. All the lesser London churches strain their metallic throats. Some, flippantly begin before the heavy bell of the great cathedral; some, tardily begin three, four, half a dozen, strokes behind it; all are in sufficiently near accord, to leave a resonance in the air, as if the winged father who devours his children, had made a sounding sweep with his gigantic scythe in flying over the city.

What is this clock lower than most of the rest, and nearer to the ear, that lags so far behind to-night as to strike into the vibration alone? This is the clock of the Hospital for Foundling Children. Time was, when the Foundlings were received without question in a cradle at the gate. Time is, when inquiries are made respecting them, and they are taken as by favour from the mothers who relinquish all natural knowledge of them and claim to them for evermore.

The moon is at the full, and the night is fair with light clouds. The day has been otherwise than fair, for slush and mud, thickened with the droppings of heavy fog, lie black in the streets. The veiled lady who flutters up and down near the postern-gate of the Hospital for Foundling Children has need to be well shod to-night.

She flutters to and fro, avoiding the stand of hackney-coaches, and often pausing in the shadow of the western end of the great quadrangle wall, with her face turned towards the gate. As above her there is the purity of the moonlit sky, and below her there are the defilements of the pavement, so may she, haply, be divided in her mind between two vistas of reflection or experience. As her footprints crossing and recrossing one another have made a labyrinth in the mire, so may her track in life have involved itself in an intricate and unravellable tangle.

The postern-gate of the Hospital for Foundling Children opens, and a young woman comes out. The lady stands aside, observes closely, sees that the gate is quietly closed again from within, and follows the young woman.

Two or three streets have been traversed in silence before she, following close behind the object of her attention, stretches out her hand and touches her. Then the young woman stops and looks round, startled.

"You touched me last night, and, when I turned my head, you would not speak. Why do you follow me like a silent ghost?"

"It was not," returned the lady, in a low voice, "that I would not speak, but that I could not when I tried."

"What do you want of me? I have never done you any harm?"

"Never."

"Do I know you?"

"No."

"Then what can you want of me?"

"Here are two guineas in this paper. Take my poor little present, and I will tell you."

Into the young woman's face, which is honest and comely, comes a flush as she replies: "There is neither grown person nor child in all the large establishment that belong to, who hasn't a good word for Sally. I am Sally. Could I be so well thought of, if I was to be bought?"

"I do not mean to buy you; I mean only to reward you very slightly."

Sally firmly, but not ungently, closes and puts back the offering hand. "If there is anything I can do for you, ma'am, that I will not do for its own sake, you are much mistaken in me if you think that I will do it for money. What is it you want?"

"You are one of the nurses or attendants at the Hospital; I saw you leave to-night and last night."

"Yes, I am. I am Sally."

"There is a pleasant patience in your face which makes me believe that very young children would take readily to you."

"God bless 'em! So they do."

The lady lifts her veil, and shows a face no older than the nurse's. A face far more refined and capable than hers, but wild and worn with sorrow.

"I am the miserable mother of a baby lately received under your care. I have a prayer to make to you."

Instinctively respecting the confidence which has drawn aside the veil, Sally—whose ways are all ways of simplicity and spontaneity—replaces it, and begins to cry.

"You will listen to my prayer?" the lady urges. "You will not be deaf to the agonised entreaty of such a broken suppliant as I am?"

"O dear, dear, dear!" cries Sally. "What shall I say, or can say! Don't talk of prayers. Prayers are to be put up to the Good Father of All, and not to nurses and such. And there! I am only to hold my place for half a year longer, till another young woman can be trained up to it. I am going to be married. I shouldn't have been out last night, and I shouldn't have been out to-night, but that my Dick (he is the young man I am going to be married to) lies ill, and I help his mother and sister to watch him. Don't take on so, don't take on so!"

"O good Sally, dear Sally," moans the lady, catching at her dress entreatingly. "As you are hopeful, and I am hopeless; as a fair way in life is before you, which can never, never, be before me; as you can aspire to become a respected wife, and as you can aspire to become a proud mother, as you are a living loving woman, and must die; for GOD's sake hear my distracted petition!"

"Deary, deary, deary ME!" cries Sally, her desperation culminating in the pronoun, "what am I ever to do? And there! See how you turn my own words back upon me. I tell you I am going to be married, on purpose to make it clearer to you that I am going to leave, and therefore couldn't help you if I would, Poor Thing, and you make it seem to my own self as if I was cruel in going to be married and not helping you. It ain't kind. Now, is it kind, Poor Thing?"

"Sally! Hear me, my dear. My entreaty is for no help in the future. It applies to what is past. It is only to be told in two words."

"There! This is worse and worse," cries Sally, "supposing that I understand what two words you mean."

"You do understand. What are the names they have given my poor baby? I ask no more than that. I have read of the customs of the place. He has been christened in the chapel, and registered by some surname in the book. He was received last Monday evening. What have they called him?"

Down upon her knees in the foul mud of the bye-way into which they have strayed—an empty street without a thoroughfare giving on the dark gardens of the Hospital—the lady would drop in her passionate entreaty, but that Sally prevents her.

"Don't! Don't! You make me feel as if I was setting myself up to be good. Let me look in your pretty face again. Put your two hands in mine. Now, promise. You will never ask me anything more than the two words?"

"Never! Never!"

"You will never put them to a bad use, if I say them?"

"Never! Never!"

"Walter Wilding."

The lady lays her face upon the nurse's breast, draws her close in her embrace with both arms, murmurs a blessing and the words, "Kiss him for me!" and is gone.

Day of the month and year, the first Sunday in October, one thousand eight hundred and forty-seven. London Time by the great clock of Saint Paul's, half-past one in the afternoon. The clock of the Hospital for Foundling Children is well up with the Cathedral to-day. Service in the chapel is over, and the Foundling children are at dinner.

There are numerous lookers-on at the dinner, as the custom is. There are two or three governors, whole families from the congregation, smaller groups of both sexes, individual stragglers of various degrees. The bright autumnal sun strikes freshly into the wards; and the heavy-framed windows through which it shines, and the panelled walls on which it strikes, are such windows and such walls as pervade Hogarth's pictures. The girls' refectory (including that of the younger children) is the principal attraction. Neat attendants silently glide about the orderly and silent tables; the lookers-on move or stop as the fancy takes them; comments in whispers on face such a number from such a window are not unfrequent; many of the faces are of a character to fix attention. Some of the visitors from the outside public are accustomed visitors. They have established a speaking acquaintance with the occupants of particular seats at the tables, and halt at those points to bend down and say a word or two. It is no disparagement to their kindness that those points are generally points where personal attractions are. The monotony of the long spacious rooms and the double lines of faces is agreeably relieved by these incidents, although so slight.

A veiled lady, who has no companion, goes among the company. It would seem that curiosity and opportunity have never brought her there before. She has the air of being a little troubled by the sight, and, as she goes the length of the tables, it is with a hesitating step and an uneasy manner. At length she comes to the refectory of the boys. They are so much less popular than the girls that it is bare of visitors when she looks in at the doorway.

But just within the doorway, chances to stand, inspecting, an elderly female attendant: some order of matron or housekeeper. To whom the lady addresses natural questions: As, how many boys? At what age are they usually put out in life? Do they often take a fancy to the sea? So, lower and lower in tone until the lady puts the question: "Which is Walter Wilding?"

Attendant's head shaken. Against the rules.

"You know which is Walter Wilding?"

So keenly does the attendant feel the closeness with which the lady's eyes examine her face, that she keeps her own eyes fast upon the floor, lest by wandering in the right direction they should betray her.

"I know which is Walter Wilding, but it is not my place, ma'am, to tell names to visitors."

"But you can show me without telling me."

The lady's hand moves quietly to the attendant's hand. Pause and silence.

"I am going to pass round the tables," says the lady's interlocutor, without seeming to address her. "Follow me with your eyes. The boy that I stop at and speak to, will not matter to you. But the boy that I touch, will be Walter Wilding. Say nothing more to me, and move a little away."

Quickly acting on the hint, the lady passes on into the room, and looks about her. After a few moments, the attendant, in a staid official way, walks down outside the line of tables commencing on her left hand. She goes the whole length of the line, turns, and comes back on the inside. Very slightly glancing in the lady's direction, she stops, bends forward, and speaks. The boy whom she addresses, lifts his head and replies. Good humouredly and easily, as she listens to what he says, she lays her hand upon the shoulder of the next boy on his right. That the action may be well noted, she keeps her hand on the shoulder while speaking in return, and pats it twice or thrice before moving away. She completes her tour of the tables, touching no one else, and passes out by a door at the opposite end of the long room.

Dinner is done, and the lady, too, walks down outside the line of tables commencing on her left hand, goes the whole length of the line, turns, and comes back on the inside. Other people have strolled in, fortunately for her, and stand sprinkled about. She lifts her veil, and, stopping at the touched boy, asks how old he is?

"I am twelve, ma'am," he answers, with his bright eyes fixed on hers.

"Are you well and happy?"

"Yes, ma'am."

"May you take these sweetmeats from my hand?"

"If you please to give them to me."

In stooping low for the purpose, the lady touches the boy's face with her forehead and with her hair. Then, lowering her veil again, she passes on, and passes out without looking back.

Act I

The Curtain Rises

In a court-yard in the City of London, which was No Thoroughfare either for vehicles or foot-passengers; a court-yard diverging from a steep, a slippery, and a winding street connecting Tower Street with the Middlesex shore of the Thames; stood the place of business of Wilding & Co., Wine Merchants. Probably as a jocose acknowledgment of the obstructive character of this main approach, the point nearest to its base at which one could take the river (if so inodorously minded) bore the appellation Break-Neck-Stairs. The court-yard itself had likewise been descriptively entitled in old time, Cripple Corner.

Years before the year one thousand eight hundred and sixty-one, people had left off taking boat at Break-Neck-Stairs, and watermen had ceased to ply there. The slimy little causeway had dropped into the river by a slow process of suicide, and two or three stumps of piles and a rusty iron mooring-ring were all that remained of the departed Break-Neck glories. Sometimes, indeed, a laden coal barge would bump itself into the place, and certain laborious heavers, seemingly mud-engendered, would arise, deliver the cargo in the neighbourhood, shove off, and vanish; but at most times the only commerce of Break-Neck-Stairs arose out of the conveyance of casks and bottles, both full and empty, both to and from the cellars of Wilding & Co., Wine Merchants. Even that commerce was but occasional, and through three-fourths of its rising tides the dirty indecorous drab of a river would come solitarily oozing and lapping at the rusty ring, as if it had heard of the Doge and the Adriatic, and wanted to be married to the great conserver of its filthiness, the Right Honourable the Lord Mayor.

Some two hundred and fifty yards on the right, up the opposite hill (approaching it from the low ground of Break-Neck-Stairs) was Cripple Corner. There was a pump in Cripple Corner, there was a tree in Cripple Corner. All Cripple Corner belonged to Wilding and Co., Wine Merchants. Their cellars burrowed under it, their mansion towered over it. It really had been a mansion in the days when merchants inhabited the City, and had a ceremonious shelter to the doorway without visible support, like the sounding-board over an old pulpit. It had also a number of long narrow strips of window, so disposed in its grave brick front as to render it symmetrically ugly. It had also, on its roof, a cupola with a bell in it.

"When a man at five-and-twenty can put his hat on, and can say 'this hat covers the owner of this property and of the business which is transacted on this property,' I consider, Mr. Bintrey, that, without being boastful, he may be allowed to be deeply thankful. I don't know how it may appear to you, but so it appears to me."

Thus Mr. Walter Wilding to his man of law, in his own counting-house; taking his hat down from its peg to suit the action to the word, and hanging it up again when he had done so, not to overstep the modesty of nature.

An innocent, open-speaking, unused-looking man, Mr. Walter Wilding, with a remarkably pink and white complexion, and a figure much too bulky for so young a man, though of a good stature. With crispy curling brown hair, and amiable bright blue eyes. An extremely communicative man: a man with whom loquacity was the irrestrainable outpouring of contentment and gratitude. Mr. Bintrey, on the other hand, a cautious man, with twinkling beads of eyes in a large overhanging bald head, who inwardly but intensely enjoyed the comicality of openness of speech, or hand, or heart.

"Yes," said Mr. Bintrey. "Yes. Ha, ha!"

A decanter, two wine-glasses, and a plate of biscuits, stood on the desk.

"You like this forty-five year old port-wine?" said Mr. Wilding.

"Like it?" repeated Mr. Bintrey. "Rather, Sir!"

"It's from the best corner of our best forty-five year old bin," said Mr. Wilding.

"Thank you, Sir," said Mr. Bintrey. "It's most excellent."

He laughed again, as he held up his glass and ogled it, at the highly ludicrous idea of giving away such wine.

"And now," said Wilding, with a childish enjoyment in the discussion of affairs, "I think we have got everything straight, Mr. Bintrey."

"Everything straight," said Bintrey.

"A partner secured—"

"Partner secured," said Bintrey.

"A housekeeper advertised for—"

"Housekeeper advertised for," said Bintrey, "'apply personally at Cripple Corner, Great Tower Street, from ten to twelve'—to-morrow, by-the-bye."

"My late dear mother's affairs wound up—"

"Wound up," said Bintrey.

"And all charges paid."

"And all charges paid," said Bintrey, with a chuckle: probably occasioned by the droll circumstance that they had been paid without a haggle.

"The mention of my late dear mother," Mr. Wilding continued, his eyes filling with tears and his pocket-handkerchief drying them, "unmans me still, Mr. Bintrey. You know how I loved her; you (her lawyer) know how she loved me. The utmost love of mother and child was cherished between us, and we never experienced one moment's division or unhappiness from the time when she took me under her care. Thirteen years in all! Thirteen years under my late dear mother's care, Mr. Bintrey, and eight of them her confidentially acknowledged son! You know the story, Mr. Bintrey, who but you, Sir!" Mr. Wilding sobbed and dried his eyes, without attempt at concealment, during these remarks.

Mr. Bintrey enjoyed his comical port, and said, after rolling it in his mouth: "I know the story."

"My late dear mother, Mr. Bintrey," pursued the wine-merchant, "had been deeply deceived, and had cruelly suffered. But on that subject my late dear mother's lips were for ever sealed. By whom deceived, or under what circumstances, Heaven only knows. My late dear mother never betrayed her betrayer."

"She had made up her mind," said Mr. Bintrey, again turning his wine on his palate, "and she could hold her peace." An amused twinkle in his eyes pretty plainly added—"A devilish deal better than *you* ever will!"

"'Honour,'" said Mr. Wilding, sobbing as he quoted from the Commandments, "'thy father and thy mother, that thy days may be long in the land.' When I was in the Foundling, Mr. Bintrey, I was at such a loss how to do it, that I apprehended my days would be short in the land. But I afterwards came to honour my mother deeply, profoundly. And I honour and revere her memory. For seven happy years, Mr. Bintrey," pursued Wilding, still with the same innocent catching in his breath, and the same unabashed tears, "did my excellent mother article me to my predecessors in this business, Pebbleson Nephew. Her affectionate forethought likewise apprenticed me to the Vintners' Company, and made me in time a free Vintner, and—and—everything else that the best of mothers could desire. When I came of age, she bestowed her inherited share in this business upon me; it was her money that afterwards bought out Pebbleson Nephew, and painted in Wilding and Co.; it was she who left me everything she possessed, but the mourning ring you wear. And yet, Mr. Bintrey," with a fresh burst of honest affection, "she is no more. It is little over half a year since she came into the Corner to read on that door-post with her own eyes, Wilding and Co., Wine Merchants. And yet she is no more!"

"Sad. But the common lot, Mr. Wilding," observed Bintrey. "At some time or other we must all be no more." He placed the forty-five-year-old port wine in the universal condition, with a relishing sigh.

"So now, Mr. Bintrey," pursued Wilding, putting away his pocket-handkerchief, and smoothing his eyelids with his fingers, "now that I can no longer show my love and honour for the dear parent to whom my heart was mysteriously turned by Nature when she first spoke to me, a strange lady, I sitting at our Sunday dinner-table in the Foundling, I can at least show that I am not ashamed of having been a Foundling, and that I, who never knew a father of my own, wish to be a father to all in my employment. Therefore," continued Wilding, becoming enthusiastic in his loquacity, "therefore, I want a thoroughly good housekeeper to undertake this dwelling-house of Wilding and Co., Wine Merchants, Cripple Corner, so that I may restore in it some of the old relations betwixt employer and employed! So that I may live in it on the spot where my money is made! So that I may daily sit at the head of the table at which the people in my employment eat together, and may eat of the same roast and boiled, and drink of the same beer! So that the people in my employment may lodge under the same roof with me! So that we may one and all—I beg your pardon, Mr. Bintrey, but that old singing in my head has suddenly come on, and I shall feel obliged if you will lead me to the pump."

Alarmed by the excessive pinkness of his client, Mr. Bintrey lost not a moment in leading him forth into the court-yard. It was easily done; for the counting-house in which they talked together opened on to it, at one side of the dwelling-house. There the attorney pumped with a will, obedient to a sign from the client, and the client laved his head and face with both hands, and took a hearty drink. After these remedies, he declared himself much better.

"Don't let your good feelings excite you," said Bintrey, as they returned to the counting-house, and Mr. Wilding dried himself on a jack-towel behind an inner door.

"No, no. I won't," he returned, looking out of the towel. "I won't. I have not been confused, have I?"

"Not at all. Perfectly clear."

"Where did I leave off, Mr. Bintrey?"

"Well, you left off—but I wouldn't excite myself, if I was you, by taking it up again just yet."

"I'll take care. I'll take care. The singing in my head came on at where, Mr. Bintrey?"

"At roast, and boiled, and beer," answered the lawyer,—"prompting lodging under the same roof—and one and all—"

"Ah! And one and all singing in the head together—"

"Do you know, I really *would not* let my good feelings excite me, if I was you," hinted the lawyer again, anxiously. "Try some more pump."

"No occasion, no occasion. All right, Mr. Bintrey. And one and all forming a kind of family! You see, Mr. Bintrey, I was not used in my childhood to that sort of individual existence which most individuals have led, more or less, in their childhood. After that time I became absorbed in my late dear mother. Having lost her, I find that I am more fit for being one of a body than one by myself one. To be that, and at the same time to do my duty to those dependent on me, and attach them to me, has a patriarchal and pleasant air about it. I don't know how it may appear to you, Mr Bintrey, but so it appears to me."

"It is not I who am all-important in the case, but you," returned Bintrey. "Consequently, how it may appear to me is of very small importance."

"It appears to me," said Mr. Wilding, in a glow, "hopeful, useful, delightful!"

"Do you know," hinted the lawyer again, "I really would not ex—"

"I am not going to. Then there's Handel."

"There's who?" asked Bintrey.

"Handel, Mozart, Haydn, Kent, Purcell, Doctor Arne, Greene, Mendelssohn. I know the choruses to those anthems by heart. Foundling Chapel Collection. Why shouldn't we learn them together?"

"Who learn them together?" asked the lawyer, rather shortly.

"Employer and employed."

"Ay, ay," returned Bintrey, mollified; as if he had half expected the answer to be, Lawyer and client. "That's another thing."

"Not another thing, Mr. Bintrey! The same thing. A part of the bond among us. We will form a Choir in some quiet church near the Corner here, and, having sung together of a Sunday with a relish, we will come home and take an early dinner together with a relish. The object that I have at heart now is, to get this system well in action without delay, so that my new partner may find it founded when he enters on his partnership."

"All good be with it!" exclaimed Bintrey, rising. "May it prosper! Is Joey Ladle to take a share in Handel, Mozart, Haydn, Kent, Purcell, Doctor Arne, Greene, and Mendelssohn?"

"I hope so."

"I wish them all well out of it," returned Bintrey, with much heartiness. "Goodbye, Sir."

They shook hands and parted. Then (first knocking with his knuckles for leave) entered to Mr. Wilding from a door of communication between his private counting-house and that in which his clerks sat, the Head Cellarman of the cellars of Wilding and Co., Wine Merchants, and erst Head Cellarman of the cellars of Pebbleson Nephew. The Joey Ladle in question. A slow and ponderous man, of the drayman order of human architecture, dressed in a corrugated suit and bibbed apron, apparently a composite of door-mat and rhinoceros-hide.

"Respecting this same boarding and lodging, Young Master Wilding," said he.

"Yes, Joey?"

"Speaking for myself, Young Master Wilding—and I never did speak and I never do speak for no one else—*I* don't want no boarding nor yet no lodging. But if you wish to board me and to lodge me, take me. I can peck as well as most men. Where I peck ain't so high a object with me as What I peck. Nor even so high a object with me as How Much I peck. Is all to live in the house, Young Master Wilding? The two other cellarmen, the three porters, the two 'prentices, and the odd men?"

"Yes. I hope we shall all be an united family, Joey."

"Ah!" said Joey. "I hope they may be."

"They? Rather say we, Joey."

Joey Ladle shook his held. "Don't look to me to make we on it, Young Master Wilding, not at my time of life and under the circumstances which has formed my disposition. I have said to Pebbleson Nephew many a time, when they have said to me, 'Put a livelier face upon it, Joey'—I have said to them, 'Gentlemen, it is all wery well for you that has been accustomed to take your wine into your systems by the conwivial channel of your throttles, to put a lively face upon it; but,' I says, 'I have been accustomed to take *my* wine in at the pores of the skin, and, took that way, it acts different. It acts depressing. It's one thing, gentlemen,' I says to Pebbleson Nephew, 'to charge your glasses in a dining-room with a Hip Hurrah and a Jolly Companions Every One, and it's another thing to be charged yourself, through the pores, in a low dark cellar and a mouldy atmosphere. It makes all the difference betwixt bubbles and wapours,' I tells Pebbleson Nephew. And so it do. I've been a cellarman my life through, with my mind fully given to the business. What's the consequence? I'm as muddled a man as lives—you won't find a muddleder man than me—nor yet you won't find my equal in molloncolly. Sing of Filling the bumper fair, Every drop you sprinkle, O'er the brow of care, Smooths away a wrinkle? Yes. P'r'aps so. But try filling yourself through the pores, underground, when you don't want to it!"

"I am sorry to hear this, Joey. I had even thought that you might join a singing-class in the house."

"Me, Sir? No, no, Young Master Wilding, you won't catch Joey Ladle muddling the Armony. A pecking-machine, Sir, is all that I am capable of proving myself, out of my cellars; but that you're welcome to, if you think it is worth your while to keep such a thing on your premises."

"I do, Joey."

"Say no more, Sir. The Business's word is my law. And you're a going to take Young Master George Vendale partner into the old Business?"

"I am, Joey."

"More changes, you see! But don't change the name of the Firm again. Don't do it, Young Master Wilding. It was bad luck enough to make it Yourself and Co. Better by far have left it Pebbleson Nephew that good luck always stuck to. You should never change luck when it's good, Sir."

"At all events, I have no intention of changing the name of the House again, Joey."

"Glad to hear it, and wish you good-day, Young Master Wilding. But you had better by half," muttered Joey Ladle inaudibly, as he closed the door and shook his head, "have let the name alone from the first. You had better by half have followed the luck instead of crossing it."

ENTER THE HOUSEKEEPER

The wine-merchant sat in his dining-room next morning, to receive the personal applicants for the vacant post in his establishment. It was an old-fashioned wainscoted room; the panels ornamented with festoons of flowers carved in wood; with an oaken floor, a well-worn Turkey carpet, and dark mahogany furniture, all of which had seen service and polish under Pebbleson Nephew. The great sideboard had assisted at many business-dinners given by Pebbleson Nephew to their connexion, on the principle of throwing sprats overboard to catch whales; and Pebbleson Nephew's comprehensive three-sided plate-warmer, made to fit the whole front of the large fireplace, kept watch beneath it over a sarcophagus-shaped cellaret that had in its time held many a dozen of Pebbleson Nephew's wine. But the little rubicund old bachelor with a pigtail, whose portrait was over the sideboard (and who could easily be identified as decidedly Pebbleson and decidedly not Nephew), had retired into another sarcophagus, and the plate-warmer had grown as cold as he. So, the golden and black griffins that supported the candelabra, with black balls in their mouths at the end of gilded chains, looked as if in their old age they had lost all heart for playing at ball, and were dolefully exhibiting their chains in the Missionary line of inquiry, whether they had not earned emancipation by this time, and were not griffins and brothers.

Such a Columbus of a morning was the summer morning, that it discovered Cripple Corner. The light and warmth pierced in at the open windows, and irradiated the picture of a lady hanging over the chimneypiece, the only other decoration of the walls.

"My mother at five-and-twenty," said Mr. Wilding to himself, as his eyes enthusiastically followed the light to the portrait's face, "I hang up here, in order that visitors may admire my mother in the bloom of her youth and beauty. My mother at fifty I hang in the seclusion of my own chamber, as a remembrance sacred to me. O! It's you, Jarvis!"

These latter words he addressed to a clerk who had tapped at the door, and now looked in.

"Yes, Sir. I merely wished to mention that it's gone ten, sir, and that there are several females in the Counting-house."

"Dear me!" said the wine-merchant, deepening in the pink of his complexion and whitening in the white, "are there several? So many as several? I had better begin before there are more. I'll see them one by one, Jarvis, in the order of their arrival."

Hastily entrenching himself in his easy-chair at the table behind a great inkstand, having first placed a chair on the other side of the table opposite his own seat, Mr. Wilding entered on his task with considerable trepidation.

He ran the gauntlet that must be run on any such occasion. There were the usual species of profoundly unsympathetic women, and the usual species of much too sympathetic women. There were buccaneering widows who came to seize him, and who griped umbrellas under their arms, as if each umbrella were he, and each griper had got him. There were towering maiden ladies who had seen better days, and who came armed with clerical testimonials to their theology, as if he were Saint Peter with his keys. There were gentle maiden ladies who came to marry him. There were professional housekeepers, like non-commissioned officers, who put him through his domestic exercise, instead of submitting themselves to catechism. There were languid invalids, to whom salary was not so much an object as the comforts of a private hospital. There were sensitive creatures who burst into tears on being addressed, and had to be restored with glasses of cold water. There were some respondents who came two together, a highly promising one and a wholly unpromising one: of whom the promising one answered all questions charmingly, until it would at last appear that she was not a candidate at all, but only the friend of the unpromising one, who had glowered in absolute silence and apparent injury.

At last, when the good wine-merchant's simple heart was failing him, there entered an applicant quite different from all the rest. A woman, perhaps fifty, but looking younger, with a face remarkable for placid cheerfulness, and a manner no less remarkable for its quiet expression of equability of temper. Nothing in her dress could have been changed to her advantage. Nothing in the noiseless self-possession of her manner could have been changed to her advantage. Nothing could have been in better unison with both, than her voice when she answered the question: "What name shall I have the pleasure of noting down?" with the words, "My name is Sarah Goldstraw. Mrs. Goldstraw. My husband has been dead many years, and we had no family."

Half-a-dozen questions had scarcely extracted as much to the purpose from any one else. The voice dwelt so agreeably on Mr. Wilding's ear as he made his note, that he was rather long about it. When he looked up again, Mrs. Goldstraw's glance had naturally gone round the room, and now returned to him from the chimneypiece. Its expression was one of frank readiness to be questioned, and to answer straight.

"You will excuse my asking you a few questions?" said the modest wine-merchant.

"O, surely, Sir. Or I should have no business here."

"Have you filled the station of housekeeper before?"

"Only once. I have lived with the same widow lady for twelve years. Ever since I lost my husband. She was an invalid, and is lately dead: which is the occasion of my now wearing black."

"I do not doubt that she has left you the best credentials?" said Mr. Wilding.

"I hope I may say, the very best. I thought it would save trouble, Sir, if I wrote down the name and address of her representatives, and brought it with me." Laying a card on the table.

"You singularly remind me, Mrs. Goldstraw," said Wilding, taking the card beside him, "of a manner and tone of voice that I was once acquainted with. Not of an individual—I feel sure of that, though I cannot recall what it is I have in my mind—but of a general bearing. I ought to add, it was a kind and pleasant one."

She smiled, as she rejoined: "At least, I am very glad of that, Sir."

"Yes," said the wine-merchant, thoughtfully repeating his last phrase, with a momentary glance at his future housekeeper, "it was a kind and pleasant one. But that is the most I can make of it. Memory is sometimes like a half-forgotten dream. I don't know how it may appear to you, Mrs. Goldstraw, but so it appears to me."

Probably it appeared to Mrs. Goldstraw in a similar light, for she quietly assented to the proposition. Mr. Wilding then offered to put himself at once in communication with the gentlemen named upon the card: a firm of proctors in Doctors' Commons. To this, Mrs. Goldstraw thankfully assented. Doctors' Commons not being far off,

Mr. Wilding suggested the feasibility of Mrs. Goldstraw's looking in again, say in three hours' time. Mrs. Goldstraw readily undertook to do so. In fine, the result of Mr. Wilding's inquiries being eminently satisfactory, Mrs. Goldstraw was that afternoon engaged (on her own perfectly fair terms) to come to-morrow and set up her rest as housekeeper in Cripple Corner.

THE HOUSEKEEPER SPEAKS

On the next day Mrs. Goldstraw arrived, to enter on her domestic duties.

Having settled herself in her own room, without troubling the servants, and without wasting time, the new housekeeper announced herself as waiting to be favoured with any instructions which her master might wish to give her. The wine-merchant received Mrs. Goldstraw in the dining-room, in which he had seen her on the previous day; and, the usual preliminary civilities having passed on either side, the two sat down to take counsel together on the affairs of the house.

"About the meals, Sir?" said Mrs. Goldstraw. "Have I a large, or a small, number to provide for?"

"If I can carry out a certain old-fashioned plan of mine," replied Mr. Wilding, "you will have a large number to provide for. I am a lonely single man, Mrs. Goldstraw; and I hope to live with all the persons in my employment as if they were members of my family. Until that time comes, you will only have me, and the new partner whom I expect immediately, to provide for. What my partner's habits may be, I cannot yet say. But I may describe myself as a man of regular hours, with an invariable appetite that you may depend upon to an ounce."

"About breakfast, Sir?" asked Mrs. Goldstraw. "Is there anything particular—?"

She hesitated, and left the sentence unfinished. Her eyes turned slowly away from her master, and looked towards the chimneypiece. If she had been a less excellent and experienced housekeeper, Mr. Wilding might have fancied that her attention was beginning to wander at the very outset of the interview.

"Eight o'clock is my breakfast-hour," he resumed. "It is one of my virtues to be never tired of broiled bacon, and it is one of my vices to be habitually suspicious of the freshness of eggs." Mrs. Goldstraw looked back at him, still a little divided between her master's chimneypiece and her master. "I take tea," Mr. Wilding went on; "and I am perhaps rather nervous and fidgety about drinking it, within a certain time after it is made. If my tea stands too long—"

He hesitated, on his side, and left the sentence unfinished. If he had not been engaged in discussing a subject of such paramount interest to himself as his breakfast, Mrs. Goldstraw might have fancied that his attention was beginning to wander at the very outset of the interview.

"If your tea stands too long, Sir—?" said the housekeeper, politely taking up her master's lost thread.

"If my tea stands too long," repeated the wine-merchant mechanically, his mind getting farther and farther away from his breakfast, and his eyes fixing themselves more and more inquiringly on his housekeeper's face. "If my tea—Dear, dear me, Mrs. Goldstraw! what *is* the manner and tone of voice that you remind me of? It strikes me even more strongly to-day, than it did when I saw you yesterday. What can it be?"

"What can it be?" repeated Mrs. Goldstraw.

She said the words, evidently thinking while she spoke them of something else. The wine-merchant, still looking at her inquiringly, observed that her eyes wandered towards the chimneypiece once more. They fixed on the portrait of his mother, which hung there, and looked at it with that slight contraction of the brow which accompanies a scarcely conscious effort of memory. Mr. Wilding remarked:

"My late dear mother, when she was five-and-twenty."

Mrs. Goldstraw thanked him with a movement of the head for being at the pains to explain the picture, and said, with a cleared brow, that it was the portrait of a very beautiful lady.

Mr. Wilding, falling back into his former perplexity, tried once more to recover that lost recollection, associated so closely, and yet so undiscoverably, with his new housekeeper's voice and manner.

"Excuse my asking you a question which has nothing to do with me or my breakfast," he said. "May I inquire if you have ever occupied any other situation than the situation of housekeeper?"

"O yes, Sir. I began life as one of the nurses at the Foundling."

"Why, that's it!" cried the wine-merchant, pushing back his chair. "By heaven! Their manner is the manner you remind me of!"

In an astonished look at him, Mrs. Goldstraw changed colour, checked herself, turned her eyes upon the ground, and sat still and silent.

"What is the matter?" asked Mr. Wilding.

"Do I understand that you were in the Foundling, Sir?"

"Certainly. I am not ashamed to own it."

"Under the name you now bear?"

"Under the name of Walter Wilding."

"And the lady—?" Mrs. Goldstraw stopped short with a look at the portrait which was now unmistakably a look of alarm.

"You mean my mother," interrupted Mr. Wilding.

"Your—mother," repeated the housekeeper, a little constrainedly, "removed you from the Foundling? At what age, Sir?"

"At between eleven and twelve years old. It's quite a romantic adventure, Mrs. Goldstraw."

He told the story of the lady having spoken to him, while he sat at dinner with the other boys in the Foundling, and of all that had followed in his innocently communicative way. "My poor mother could never have discovered me," he added, "if she had not met with one of the matrons who pitied her. The matron consented to touch the boy whose name was 'Walter Wilding' as she went round the dinner-tables—and so my mother discovered me again, after having parted from me as an infant at the Foundling doors."

At those words Mrs. Goldstraw's hand, resting on the table, dropped helplessly into her lap. She sat, looking at her new master, with a face that had turned deadly pale, and with eyes that expressed an unutterable dismay.

"What does this mean?" asked the wine-merchant. "Stop!" he cried. "Is there something else in the past time which I ought to associate with you? I remember my mother telling me of another person at the Foundling, to whose kindness she owed a debt of gratitude. When she first parted with me, as an infant, one of the nurses informed her of the name that had been given to me in the institution. You were that nurse?"

"God forgive me, Sir—I was that nurse!"

"God forgive you?"

"We had better get back, Sir (if I may make so bold as to say so), to my duties in the house," said Mrs. Goldstraw. "Your breakfast-hour is eight. Do you lunch, or dine, in the middle of the day?"

The excessive pinkness which Mr. Bintrey had noticed in his client's face began to appear there once more. Mr. Wilding put his hand to his head, and mastered some momentary confusion in that quarter, before he spoke again.

"Mrs. Goldstraw," he said, "you are concealing something from me!"

The housekeeper obstinately repeated, "Please to favour me, Sir, by saying whether you lunch, or dine, in the middle of the day?"

"I don't know what I do in the middle of the day. I can't enter into my household affairs, Mrs. Goldstraw, till I know why you regret an act of kindness to my mother, which she always spoke of gratefully to the end of her life. You are not doing me a service by your silence. You are agitating me, you are alarming me, you are bringing on the singing in my head."

His hand went up to his head again, and the pink in his face deepened by a shade or two.

"It's hard, Sir, on just entering your service," said the housekeeper, "to say what may cost me the loss of your good will. Please to remember, end how it may, that I only speak because you have insisted on my speaking, and because I see that

I am alarming you by my silence. When I told the poor lady, whose portrait you have got there, the name by which her infant was christened in the Foundling, I allowed myself to forget my duty, and dreadful consequences, I am afraid, have followed from it. I'll tell you the truth, as plainly as I can. A few months from the time when I had informed the lady of her baby's name, there came to our institution in the country another lady (a stranger), whose object was to adopt one of our children. She brought the needful permission with her, and after looking at a great many of the children, without being able to make up her mind, she took a sudden fancy to one of the babies—a boy—under my care. Try, pray try, to compose yourself, Sir! It's no use disguising it any longer. The child the stranger took away was the child of that lady whose portrait hangs there!"

Mr. Wilding started to his feet. "Impossible!" he cried out, vehemently. "What are you talking about? What absurd story are you telling me now? There's her portrait! Haven't I told you so already? The portrait of my mother!"

"When that unhappy lady removed you from the Foundling, in after years," said Mrs. Goldstraw, gently, "she was the victim, and you were the victim, Sir, of a dreadful mistake."

He dropped back into his chair. "The room goes round with me," he said. "My head! my head!" The housekeeper rose in alarm, and opened the windows. Before she could get to the door to call for help, a sudden burst of tears relieved the oppression which had at first almost appeared to threaten his life. He signed entreatingly to Mrs. Goldstraw not to leave him. She waited until the paroxysm of weeping had worn itself out. He raised his head as he recovered himself, and looked at her with the angry unreasoning suspicion of a weak man.

"Mistake?" he said, wildly repeating her last word. "How do I know you are not mistaken yourself?"

"There is no hope that I am mistaken, Sir. I will tell you why, when you are better fit to hear it."

"Now! now!"

The tone in which he spoke warned Mrs. Goldstraw that it would be cruel kindness to let him comfort himself a moment longer with the vain hope that she might be wrong. A few words more would end it, and those few words she determined to speak.

"I have told you," she said, "that the child of the lady whose portrait hangs there, was adopted in its infancy, and taken away by a stranger. I am as certain of what I say as that I am now sitting here, obliged to distress you, Sir, sorely against my will. Please to carry your mind on, now, to about three months after that time. I was then at the Foundling, in London, waiting to take some children to our institution in the country. There was a question that day about naming an infant—a boy—who had just been received. We generally named them out of the Directory. On this occasion, one of the gentlemen who managed the Hospital happened to be looking over the Register. He noticed that the name of the baby who had been adopted ('Walter Wilding') was scratched out—for the reason, of course, that the child had been removed for good from our care. 'Here's a name to let,' he said. 'Give it to the new foundling who has been received to-day.' The name was given, and the child was christened. You, Sir, were that child."

The wine-merchant's head dropped on his breast. "I was that child!" he said to himself, trying helplessly to fix the idea in his mind. "I was that child!"

"Not very long after you had been received into the Institution, Sir," pursued Mrs. Goldstraw, "I left my situation there, to be married. If you will remember that, and if you can give your mind to it, you will see for yourself how the mistake happened. Between eleven and twelve years passed before the lady, whom you have believed to be your mother, returned to the Foundling, to find her son, and to remove him to her own home. The lady only knew that her infant had been called 'Walter Wilding.' The matron who took pity on her, could but point out the only 'Walter Wilding' known in the Institution. I, who might have set the matter right, was far away from the Foundling and all that belonged to it. There was nothing—there was really nothing that could prevent this terrible mistake from taking place. I feel for you—I do indeed, Sir! You must think—and with reason—that it was in an evil hour that I came here (innocently enough, I'm sure), to apply for your housekeeper's place. I feel as if I was to blame—I feel as if I ought to have had more self-command. If I had only been able to keep my face from showing you what that portrait and what your own words put into my mind, you need never, to your dying day, have known what you know now."

Mr. Wilding looked up suddenly. The inbred honesty of the man rose in protest against the housekeeper's last words. His mind seemed to steady itself, for the moment, under the shock that had fallen on it.

"Do you mean to say that you would have concealed this from me if you could?" he exclaimed.

"I hope I should always tell the truth, Sir, if I was asked," said Mrs. Goldstraw. "And I know it is better for *me* that I should not have a secret of this sort weighing on my mind. But is it better for *you*? What use can it serve now—?"

"What use? Why, good Lord! if your story is true—"

"Should I have told it, Sir, as I am now situated, if it had not been true?"

"I beg your pardon," said the wine-merchant. "You must make allowance for me. This dreadful discovery is something I can't realise even yet. We loved each other so dearly—I felt so fondly that I was her son. She died, Mrs. Goldstraw, in my arms—she died blessing me as only a mother *could* have blessed me. And now, after all these years, to be told she was *not* my mother! O me, O me! I don't know what I am saying!" he cried, as the impulse of self-control under which he had spoken a moment since, flickered, and died out. "It was not this dreadful grief—it was something else that I had it in my mind to speak of. Yes, yes. You surprised me—you wounded me just now. You talked as if you would have hidden this from me, if you could. Don't talk in that way again. It would have been a crime to have hidden it. You mean well, I know. I don't want to distress you—you are a kind-hearted woman. But you don't remember what my position is. She left me all that I possess, in the firm persuasion that I was her son. I am not her son. I have taken the place, I have innocently got the inheritance of another man. He must be found! How do I know he is not at this moment in misery, without bread to eat? He must be found! My only hope of bearing up against the shock that has fallen on me, is the hope of doing something which *she* would have approved. You must know more, Mrs. Goldstraw, than you have told me yet. Who was the stranger who adopted the child? You must have heard the lady's name?"

"I never heard it, Sir. I have never seen her, or heard of her, since."

"Did she say nothing when she took the child away? Search your memory. She must have said something."

"Only one thing, Sir, that I can remember. It was a miserably bad season, that year; and many of the children were suffering from it. When she took the baby away, the lady said to me, laughing, 'Don't be alarmed about his health. He will be brought up in a better climate than this—I am going to take him to Switzerland.'"

"To Switzerland? What part of Switzerland?"

"She didn't say, Sir."

"Only that faint clue!" said Mr. Wilding. "And a quarter of a century has passed since the child was taken away! What am I to do?"

"I hope you won't take offence at my freedom, Sir," said Mrs. Goldstraw; "but why should you distress yourself about what is to be done? He may not be alive now, for anything you know. And, if he is alive, it's not likely he can be in any distress. The, lady who adopted him was a bred and born lady—it was easy to see that. And she must have satisfied them at the Foundling that she could provide for the child, or they would never have let her take him away. If I was in your place, Sir—please to excuse my saying so—I should comfort myself with remembering that I had loved that poor lady whose portrait you have got there—truly loved her as my mother, and that she had truly loved me as her son. All she gave to you, she gave for the sake of that love. It never altered while she lived; and it won't alter, I'm sure, as long as *you* live. How can you have a better right, Sir, to keep what you have got than that?"

Mr. Wilding's immovable honesty saw the fallacy in his housekeeper's point of view at a glance.

"You don't understand me," he said. "It's *because* I loved her that I feel it a duty—a sacred duty—to do justice to her son. If he is a living man, I must find him: for my own sake, as well as for his. I shall break down under this dreadful trial, unless I employ myself—actively, instantly employ myself—in doing what my conscience tells me ought to be done. I must speak to my lawyer; I must set my lawyer at work before I sleep to-night." He approached a tube in the wall of the room, and called down through it to the office below. "Leave me for a little, Mrs. Goldstraw," he resumed; "I shall be more composed, I shall be better able to speak to you later in the day. We shall get on well—I hope we shall get on well together—in spite of what has happened. It isn't your fault; I know it isn't your fault. There! there! shake hands; and—and do the best you can in the house—I can't talk about it now."

The door opened as Mrs. Goldstraw advanced towards it; and Mr. Jarvis appeared.

"Send for Mr. Bintrey," said the wine-merchant. "Say I want to see him directly."

The clerk unconsciously suspended the execution of the order, by announcing "Mr. Vendale," and showing in the new partner in the firm of Wilding and Co.

"Pray excuse me for one moment, George Vendale," said Wilding. "I have a word to say to Jarvis. Send for Mr. Bintrey," he repeated—"send at once."

Mr. Jarvis laid a letter on the table before he left the room.

"From our correspondents at Neuchâtel, I think, Sir. The letter has got the Swiss postmark."

NEW CHARACTERS ON THE SCENE

The words, "The Swiss Postmark," following so soon upon the housekeeper's reference to Switzerland, wrought Mr. Wilding's agitation to such a remarkable height, that his new partner could not decently make a pretence of letting it pass unnoticed.

"Wilding," he asked hurriedly, and yet stopping short and glancing around as if for some visible cause of his state of mind: "what is the matter?"

"My good George Vendale," returned the wine-merchant, giving his hand with an appealing look, rather as if he wanted help to get over some obstacle, than as if he gave it in welcome or salutation: "my good George Vendale, so much is the matter, that I shall never be myself again. It is impossible that I can ever be myself again. For, in fact, I am not myself."

The new partner, a brown-cheeked handsome fellow, of about his own age, with a quick determined eye and an impulsive manner, retorted with natural astonishment: "Not yourself?"

"Not what I supposed myself to be," said Wilding.

"What, in the name of wonder, *did* you suppose yourself to be that you are not?" was the rejoinder, delivered with a cheerful frankness, inviting confidence from a more reticent man. "I may ask without impertinence, now that we are partners."

"There again!" cried Wilding, leaning back in his chair, with a lost look at the other. "Partners! I had no right to come into this business. It was never meant for me. My mother never meant it should be mine. I mean, his mother meant it should be his—if I mean anything—or if I am anybody."

"Come, come," urged his partner, after a moment's pause, and taking possession of him with that calm confidence which inspires a strong nature when it honestly desires to aid a weak one. "Whatever has gone wrong, has gone wrong through no fault of yours, I am very sure. I was not in this counting-house with you, under the old *régime*, for three years, to doubt you, Wilding. We were not younger men than we are, together, for that. Let me begin our partnership by being a serviceable partner, and setting right whatever is wrong. Has that letter anything to do with it?"

"Hah!" said Wilding, with his hand to his temple. "There again! My head! I was forgetting the coincidence. The Swiss postmark."

"At a second glance I see that the letter is unopened, so it is not very likely to have much to do with the matter," said Vendale, with comforting composure. "Is it for you, or for us?"

"For us," said Wilding.

"Suppose I open it and read it aloud, to get it out of our way?"

"Thank you, thank you."

"The letter is only from our champagne-making friends, the house at Neuchâtel. 'Dear Sir. We are in receipt of yours of the 28th ult., informing us that you have taken your Mr. Vendale into partnership, whereon we beg you to receive the assurance of our felicitations. Permit us to embrace the occasion of specially commanding to you M. Jules Obenreizer.' Impossible!"

Wilding looked up in quick apprehension, and cried, "Eh?"

"Impossible sort of name," returned his partner, slightly—"Obenreizer. '—Of specially commanding to you M. Jules Obenreizer, of Soho Square, London (north side), henceforth fully accredited as our agent, and who has already had the honour of making the acquaintance of your Mr. Vendale, in his (said M. Obenreizer's) native country, Switzerland.' To be sure! pooh pooh, what have I been thinking of! I remember now; 'when travelling with his niece.'"

"With his—?" Vendale had so slurred the last word, that Wilding had not heard it.

"When travelling with his Niece. Obenreizer's Niece," said Vendale, in a somewhat superfluously lucid manner. "Niece of Obenreizer. (I met them in my first Swiss tour, travelled a little with them, and lost them for two years; met them again, my

Swiss tour before last, and have lost them ever since.) Obenreizer. Niece of Obenreizer. To be sure! Possible sort of name, after all! 'M. Obenreizer is in possession of our absolute confidence, and we do not doubt you will esteem his merits.' Duly signed by the House, 'Defresnier et Cie.' Very well. I undertake to see M. Obenreizer presently, and clear him out of the way. That clears the Swiss postmark out of the way. So now, my dear Wilding, tell me what I can clear out of *your* way, and I'll find a way to clear it."

More than ready and grateful to be thus taken charge of, the honest wine-merchant wrung his partner's hand, and, beginning his tale by pathetically declaring himself an Impostor, told it.

"It was on this matter, no doubt, that you were sending for Bintrey when I came in?" said his partner, after reflecting.

"It was."

"He has experience and a shrewd head; I shall be anxious to know his opinion. It is bold and hazardous in me to give you mine before I know his, but I am not good at holding back. Plainly, then, I do not see these circumstances as you see them. I do not see your position as you see it. As to your being an Impostor, my dear Wilding, that is simply absurd, because no man can be that without being a consenting party to an imposition. Clearly you never were so. As to your enrichment by the lady who believed you to be her son, and whom you were forced to believe, on her showing, to be your mother, consider whether that did not arise out of the personal relations between you. You gradually became much attached to her; she gradually became much attached to you. It was on you, personally you, as I see the case, that she conferred these worldly advantages; it was from her, personally her, that you took them."

"She supposed me," objected Wilding, shaking his head, "to have a natural claim upon her, which I had not."

"I must admit that," replied his partner, "to be true. But if she had made the discovery that you have made, six months before she died, do you think it would have cancelled the years you were together, and the tenderness that each of you had conceived for the other, each on increasing knowledge of the other?"

"What I think," said Wilding, simply but stoutly holding to the bare fact, "can no more change the truth than it can bring down the sky. The truth is that I stand possessed of what was meant for another man."

"He may be dead," said Vendale.

"He may be alive," said Wilding. "And if he is alive, have I not—innocently, I grant you innocently—robbed him of enough? Have I not robbed him of all the happy time that I enjoyed in his stead? Have I not robbed him of the exquisite delight that filled my soul when that dear lady," stretching his hand towards the picture, "told me she was my mother? Have I not robbed him of all the care she lavished on me? Have I not even robbed him of all the devotion and duty that I so proudly gave to her? Therefore it is that I ask myself, George Vendale, and I ask you, where is he? What has become of him?"

"Who can tell?"

"I must try to find out who can tell. I must institute inquiries. I must never desist from prosecuting inquiries. I will live upon the interest of my share—I ought to say his share—in this business, and will lay up the rest for him. When I find him, I may perhaps throw myself upon his generosity; but I will yield up all to him. I will, I swear. As I loved and honoured her," said Wilding, reverently kissing his hand towards the picture, and then covering his eyes with it. "As I loved and honoured her, and have a world of reasons to be grateful to her!" And so broke down again.

His partner rose from the chair he had occupied, and stood beside him with a hand softly laid upon his shoulder. "Walter, I knew you before to-day to be an upright man, with a pure conscience and a fine heart. It is very fortunate for me that I have the privilege to travel on in life so near to so trustworthy a man. I am thankful for it. Use me as your right hand, and rely upon me to the death. Don't think the worse of me if I protest to you that my uppermost feeling at present is a confused, you may call it an unreasonable, one. I feel far more pity for the lady and for you, because you did not stand in your supposed relations, than I can feel for the unknown man (if he ever became a man), because he was unconsciously displaced. You have done well in sending for Mr. Bintrey. What I think will be a part of his advice, I know is the whole of mine. Do not move a step in this serious matter precipitately. The secret must be kept among us with great strictness, for to part with it lightly would be to invite fraudulent claims, to encourage a host of knaves, to let loose a flood of perjury and plotting. I have no more to say now, Walter, than to remind you that you sold me a share in your business, expressly to save yourself from more work than your present health is fit for, and that I bought it expressly to do work, and mean to do it."

With these words, and a parting grip of his partner's shoulder that gave them the best emphasis they could have had, George Vendale betook himself presently to the counting-house, and presently afterwards to the address of M. Jules Obenreizer.

As he turned into Soho-square, and directed his steps towards its north side, a deepened colour shot across his sun-browned face, which Wilding, if he had been a better observer, or had been less occupied with his own trouble, might have noticed when his partner read aloud a certain passage in their Swiss correspondent's letter, which he had not read so distinctly as the rest.

A curious colony of mountaineers has long been enclosed within that small flat London district of Soho. Swiss watchmakers, Swiss silver-chasers, Swiss jewellers, Swiss importers of Swiss musical boxes and Swiss toys of various kinds, draw close together there. Swiss professors of music, painting, and languages; Swiss artificers in steady work; Swiss couriers, and other Swiss servants chronically out of place; industrious Swiss laundresses and clear-starchers; mysteriously existing Swiss of both sexes; Swiss creditable and Swiss discreditable; Swiss to be trusted by all means, and Swiss to be trusted by no means; these diverse Swiss particles are attracted to a centre in the district of Soho. Shabby Swiss eating-houses, coffee-houses, and lodging-houses, Swiss drinks and dishes, Swiss service for Sundays, and Swiss schools for week-days, are all to be found there. Even the native-born English taverns drive a sort of broken-English trade; announcing in their windows Swiss whets and drams, and sheltering in their bars Swiss skirmishes of love and animosity on most nights in the year.

When the new partner in Wilding and Co. rang the bell of a door bearing the blunt inscription OBENREIZER on a brass plate—the inner door of a substantial house, whose ground story was devoted to the sale of Swiss clocks—he passed at once into domestic Switzerland. A white-tiled stove for winter-time filled the fireplace of the room into which he was shown, the room's bare floor was laid together in a neat pattern of several ordinary woods, the room had a prevalent air of surface bareness and much scrubbing; and the little square of flowery carpet by the sofa, and the velvet chimney-board with its capacious clock and vases of artificial flowers, contended with that tone, as if, in bringing out the whole effect, a Parisian had adapted a dairy to domestic purposes.

Mimic water was dropping off a mill-wheel under the clock. The visitor had not stood before it, following it with his eyes, a minute, when M. Obenreizer, at his elbow, startled him by saying, in very good English, very slightly clipped: "How do you do? So glad!"

"I beg your pardon. I didn't hear you come in."

"Not at all! Sit, please."

Releasing his visitor's two arms, which he had lightly pinioned at the elbows by way of embrace, M. Obenreizer also sat, remarking, with a smile: "You are well? So glad!" and touching his elbows again.

"I don't know," said Vendale, after exchange of salutations, "whether you may yet have heard of me from your House at Neuchâtel?"

"Ah, yes!"

"In connexion with Wilding and Co.?"

"Ah, surely!"

"Is it not odd that I should come to you, in London here, as one of the Firm of Wilding and Co., to pay the Firm's respects?"

"Not at all! What did I always observe when we were on the mountains? We call them vast; but the world is so little. So little is the world, that one cannot keep away from persons. There are so few persons in the world, that they continually cross and re-cross. So very little is the world, that one cannot get rid of a person. Not," touching his elbows again, with an ingratiatory smile, "that one would desire to get rid of you."

"I hope not, M. Obenreizer."

"Please call me, in your country, Mr. I call myself so, for I love your country. If I *could* be English! But I am born. And you? Though descended from so fine a family, you have had the condescension to come into trade? Stop though. Wines? Is it trade in England or profession? Not fine art?"

"Mr. Obenreizer," returned Vendale, somewhat out of countenance, "I was but a silly young fellow, just of age, when I first had the pleasure of travelling with you, and when you and I and Mademoiselle your niece—who is well?"

"Thank you. Who is well."

"—Shared some slight glacier dangers together. If, with a boy's vanity, I rather vaunted my family, I hope I did so as a kind of introduction of myself. It was very weak, and in very bad taste; but perhaps you know our English proverb, 'Live and Learn.'"

"You make too much of it," returned the Swiss. "And what the devil! After all, yours *was* a fine family."

George Vendale's laugh betrayed a little vexation as he rejoined: "Well! I was strongly attached to my parents, and when we first travelled together, Mr. Obenreizer, I was in the first flush of coming into what my father and mother left me. So I hope it may have been, after all, more youthful openness of speech and heart than boastfulness."

"All openness of speech and heart! No boastfulness!" cried Obenreizer. "You tax yourself too heavily. You tax yourself, my faith! as if you was your Government taxing you! Besides, it commenced with me. I remember, that evening in the boat upon the lake, floating among the reflections of the mountains and valleys, the crags and pine woods, which were my earliest remembrance, I drew a word-picture of my sordid childhood. Of our poor hut, by the waterfall which my mother showed to travellers; of the cow-shed where I slept with the cow; of my idiot half-brother always sitting at the door, or limping down the Pass to beg; of my half-sister always spinning, and resting her enormous goître on a great stone; of my being a famished naked little wretch of two or three years, when they were men and women with hard hands to beat me, I, the only child of my father's second marriage—if it even was a marriage. What more natural than for you to compare notes with me, and say, 'We are as one by age; at that same time I sat upon my mother's lap in my father's carriage, rolling through the rich English streets, all luxury surrounding me, all squalid poverty kept far from me. Such is *my* earliest remembrance as opposed to yours!'"

Mr. Obenreizer was a black-haired young man of a dark complexion, through whose swarthy skin no red glow ever shone. When colour would have come into another cheek, a hardly discernible beat would come into his, as if the machinery for bringing up the ardent blood were there, but the machinery were dry. He was robustly made, well proportioned, and had handsome features. Many would have perceived that some surface change in him would have set them more at their ease with him, without being able to define what change. If his lips could have been made much thicker, and his neck much thinner, they would have found their want supplied.

But the great Obenreizer peculiarity was, that a certain nameless film would come over his eyes—apparently by the action of his own will—which would impenetrably veil, not only from those tellers of tales, but from his face at large, every expression save one of attention. It by no means followed that his attention should be wholly given to the person with whom he spoke, or even wholly bestowed on present sounds and objects. Rather, it was a comprehensive watchfulness of everything he had in his own mind, and everything that he knew to be, or suspected to be, in the minds of other men.

At this stage of the conversation, Mr. Obenreizer's film came over him.

"The object of my present visit," said Vendale, "is, I need hardly say, to assure you of the friendliness of Wilding and Co., and of the goodness of your credit with us, and of our desire to be of service to you. We hope shortly to offer you our hospitality. Things are not quite in train with us yet, for my partner, Mr. Wilding, is reorganising the domestic part of our establishment, and is interrupted by some private affairs. You don't know Mr. Wilding, I believe?"

Mr. Obenreizer did not.

"You must come together soon. He will be glad to have made your acquaintance, and I think I may predict that you will be glad to have made his. You have not been long established in London, I suppose, Mr. Obenreizer?"

"It is only now that I have undertaken this agency."

"Mademoiselle your niece—is—not married?"

"Not married."

George Vendale glanced about him, as if for any tokens of her.

"She has been in London?"

"She *is* in London."

"When, and where, might I have the honour of recalling myself to her remembrance?"

Mr. Obenreizer, discarding his film and touching his visitor's elbows as before, said lightly: "Come upstairs."

Fluttered enough by the suddenness with which the interview he had sought was coming upon him after all, George Vendale followed upstairs. In a room over the chamber he had just quitted—a room also Swiss-appointed—a young lady sat near one of three windows, working at an embroidery-frame; and an older lady sat with her face turned close to another white-tiled stove (though it was summer, and the stove was not lighted), cleaning gloves. The young lady wore an unusual quantity of fair bright hair, very prettily braided about a rather rounder white forehead than the average English type, and so her face might have been a shade—or say a light—rounder than the average English face, and her figure slightly rounder than the figure of the average English girl at nineteen. A remarkable indication of freedom and grace of limb, in her quiet attitude, and a wonderful purity and freshness of colour in her dimpled face and bright gray eyes, seemed fraught with mountain air. Switzerland too, though the general fashion of her dress was English, peeped out of the fanciful bodice she wore, and lurked in the curious clocked red stocking, and in its little silver-buckled shoe. As to the elder lady, sitting with her feet apart upon the lower brass ledge of the stove, supporting a lap-full of gloves while she cleaned one stretched on her left hand, she was a true Swiss impersonation of another kind; from the breadth of her cushion-like back, and the ponderosity of her respectable legs (if the word be admissible), to the black velvet band tied tightly round her throat for the repression of a rising tendency to goître; or, higher still, to her great copper-coloured gold ear-rings; or, higher still, to her head-dress of black gauze stretched on wire.

"Miss Marguerite," said Obenreizer to the young lady, "do you recollect this gentleman?"

"I think," she answered, rising from her seat, surprised and a little confused: "it is Mr. Vendale?"

"I think it is," said Obenreizer, dryly. "Permit me, Mr. Vendale. Madame Dor."

The elder lady by the stove, with the glove stretched on her left hand, like a glover's sign, half got up, half looked over her broad shoulder, and wholly plumped down again and rubbed away.

"Madame Dor," said Obenreizer, smiling, "is so kind as to keep me free from stain or tear. Madame Dor humours my weakness for being always neat, and devotes her time to removing every one of my specks and spots."

Madame Dor, with the stretched glove in the air, and her eyes closely scrutinizing its palm, discovered a tough spot in Mr. Obenreizer at that instant, and rubbed hard at him. George Vendale took his seat by the embroidery-frame (having first taken the fair right hand that his entrance had checked), and glanced at the gold cross that dipped into the bodice, with something of the devotion of a pilgrim who had reached his shrine at last. Obenreizer stood in the middle of the room with his thumbs in his waistcoat-pockets, and became filmy.

"He was saying downstairs, Miss Obenreizer," observed Vendale, "that the world is so small a place, that people cannot escape one another. I have found it much too large for me since I saw you last."

"Have you travelled so far, then?" she inquired.

"Not so far, for I have only gone back to Switzerland each year; but I could have wished—and indeed I have wished very often—that the little world did not afford such opportunities for long escapes as it does. If it had been less, I might have found my follow-travellers sooner, you know."

The pretty Marguerite coloured, and very slightly glanced in the direction of Madame Dor.

"You find us at length, Mr. Vendale. Perhaps you may lose us again."

"I trust not. The curious coincidence that has enabled me to find you, encourages me to hope not."

"What is that coincidence, Sir, if you please?" A dainty little native touch in this turn of speech, and in its tone, made it perfectly captivating, thought George Vendale, when again he noticed an instantaneous glance towards Madame Dor. A caution seemed to be conveyed in it, rapid flash though it was; so he quietly took heed of Madame Dor from that time forth.

"It is that I happen to have become a partner in a House of business in London, to which Mr. Obenreizer happens this very day to be expressly recommended: and that, too, by another house of business in Switzerland, in which (as it turns out) we both have a commercial interest. He has not told you?"

"Ah!" cried Obenreizer, striking in, filmless. "No. I had not told Miss Marguerite. The world is so small and so monotonous that a surprise is worth having in such a little jog-trot place. It is as he tells you, Miss Marguerite. He, of so fine a family, and so proudly bred, has condescended to trade. To trade! Like us poor peasants who have risen from ditches!"

A cloud crept over the fair brow, and she cast down her eyes.

"Why, it is good for trade!" pursued Obenreizer, enthusiastically. "It ennobles trade! It is the misfortune of trade, it is its vulgarity, that any low people—for example, we poor peasants—may take to it and climb by it. See you, my dear Vendale!" He spoke with great energy. "The father of Miss Marguerite, my eldest half-brother, more than two times your age or mine, if living now, wandered without shoes, almost without rags, from that wretched Pass—wandered—wandered—got to be fed with the mules and dogs at an Inn in the main valley far away—got to be Boy there—got to be Ostler—got to be Waiter—got to be Cook—got to be Landlord. As Landlord, he took me (could he take the idiot beggar his brother, or the spinning monstrosity his sister?) to put as pupil to the famous watchmaker, his neighbour and friend. His wife dies when Miss Marguerite is born. What is his will, and what are his words to me, when he dies, she being between girl and woman? 'All for Marguerite, except so much by the year for you. You are young, but I make her your ward, for you were of the obscurest and the poorest peasantry, and so was I, and so was her mother; we were abject peasants all, and you will remember it.' The thing is equally true of most of my countrymen, now in trade in this your London quarter of Soho. Peasants once; low-born drudging Swiss Peasants. Then how good and great for trade": here, from having been warm, he became playfully jubilant, and touched the young wine-merchant's elbows again with his light embrace: "to be exalted by gentlemen."

"I do not think so," said Marguerite, with a flushed cheek, and a look away from the visitor, that was almost defiant. "I think it is as much exalted by us peasants."

"Fie, fie, Miss Marguerite," said Obenreizer. "You speak in proud England."

"I speak in proud earnest," she answered, quietly resuming her work, "and I am not English, but a Swiss peasant's daughter."

There was a dismissal of the subject in her words, which Vendale could not contend against. He only said in an earnest manner, "I most heartily agree with you, Miss Obenreizer, and I have already said so, as Mr. Obenreizer will bear witness," which he by no means did, "in this house."

Now, Vendale's eyes were quick eyes, and sharply watching Madame Dor by times, noted something in the broad back view of that lady. There was considerable pantomimic expression in her glove-cleaning. It had been very softly done when he spoke with Marguerite, or it had altogether stopped, like the action of a listener. When Obenreizer's peasant-speech came to an end, she rubbed most vigorously, as if applauding it. And once or twice, as the glove (which she always held before her a little above her face) turned in the air, or as this finger went down, or that went up, he even fancied that it made some telegraphic communication to Obenreizer: whose back was certainly never turned upon it, though he did not seem at all to heed it.

Vendale observed too, that in Marguerite's dismissal of the subject twice forced upon him to his misrepresentation, there was an indignant treatment of her guardian which she tried to cheek: as though she would have flamed out against him, but for the influence of fear. He also observed—though this was not much—that he never advanced within the distance of her at which he first placed himself: as though there were limits fixed between them. Neither had he ever spoken of her without the prefix "Miss," though whenever he uttered it, it was with the faintest trace of an air of mockery. And now it occurred to Vendale for the first time that something curious in the man, which he had never before been able to define, was definable as a certain subtle essence of mockery that eluded touch or analysis. He felt convinced that Marguerite was in some sort a prisoner as to her freewill—though she held her own against those two combined, by the force of her character, which was nevertheless inadequate to her release. To feel convinced of this, was not to feel less disposed to love her than he had always been. In a word, he was desperately in love with her, and thoroughly determined to pursue the opportunity which had opened at last.

For the present, he merely touched upon the pleasure that Wilding and Co. would soon have in entreating Miss Obenreizer to honour their establishment with her presence—a curious old place, though a bachelor house withal—and so did not protract his visit beyond such a visit's ordinary length. Going downstairs, conducted by his host, he found the Obenreizer counting-house at the back of the entrance-hall, and several shabby men in outlandish garments hanging about, whom Obenreizer put aside that he might pass, with a few words in *patois*.

"Countrymen," he explained, as he attended Vendale to the door. "Poor compatriots. Grateful and attached, like dogs! Good-bye. To meet again. So glad!"

Two more light touches on his elbows dismissed him into the street.

Sweet Marguerite at her frame, and Madame Dor's broad back at her telegraph, floated before him to Cripple Corner. On his arrival there, Wilding was closeted with Bintrey. The cellar doors happening to be open, Vendale lighted a candle in a cleft stick, and went down for a cellarous stroll. Graceful Marguerite floated before him faithfully, but Madame Dor's broad back remained outside.

The vaults were very spacious, and very old. There had been a stone crypt down there, when bygones were not bygones; some said, part of a monkish refectory; some said, of a chapel; some said, of a Pagan temple. It was all one now. Let who would make what he liked of a crumbled pillar and a broken arch or so. Old Time had made what *he* liked of it, and was quite indifferent to contradiction.

The close air, the musty smell, and the thunderous rumbling in the streets above, as being, out of the routine of ordinary life, went well enough with the picture of pretty Marguerite holding her own against those two. So Vendale went on until, at a turning in the vaults, he saw a light like the light he carried.

"O! You are here, are you, Joey?"

"Oughtn't it rather to go, 'O! *You're* here, are you, Master George?' For it's my business to be here. But it ain't yourn."

"Don't grumble, Joey."

"O! *I* don't grumble," returned the Cellarman. "If anything grumbles, it's what I've took in through the pores; it ain't me. Have a care as something in you don't begin a grumbling, Master George. Stop here long enough for the wapours to work, and they'll be at it."

His present occupation consisted of poking his head into the bins, making measurements and mental calculations, and entering them in a rhinoceros-hide-looking note-book, like a piece of himself.

"They'll be at it," he resumed, laying the wooden rod that he measured with across two casks, entering his last calculation, and straightening his back, "trust 'em! And so you've regularly come into the business, Master George?"

"Regularly. I hope you don't object, Joey?"

"*I* don't, bless you. But Wapours objects that you're too young. You're both on you too young."

"We shall got over that objection day by day, Joey."

"Ay, Master George; but I shall day by day get over the objection that I'm too old, and so I shan't be capable of seeing much improvement in you."

The retort so tickled Joey Ladle that he grunted forth a laugh and delivered it again, grunting forth another laugh after the second edition of "improvement in you."

"But what's no laughing matter, Master George," he resumed, straightening his back once more, "is, that young Master Wilding has gone and changed the luck. Mark my words. He has changed the luck, and he'll find it out. *I* ain't been down here all my life for nothing! *I* know by what I notices down here, when it's a-going to rain, when it's a-going to hold up, when it's a-going to blow, when it's a-going to be calm. *I* know, by what I notices down here, when the luck's changed, quite as well."

"Has this growth on the roof anything to do with your divination?" asked Vendale, holding his light towards a gloomy ragged growth of dark fungus, pendent from the arches with a very disagreeable and repellent effect. "We are famous for this growth in this vault, aren't we?"

"We are Master George," replied Joey Ladle, moving a step or two away, "and if you'll be advised by me, you'll let it alone."

Taking up the rod just now laid across the two casks, and faintly moving the languid fungus with it, Vendale asked, "Ay, indeed? Why so?"

"Why, not so much because it rises from the casks of wine, and may leave you to judge what sort of stuff a Cellarman takes into himself when he walks in the same all the days of his life, nor yet so much because at a stage of its growth it's maggots, and you'll fetch 'em down upon you," returned Joey Ladle, still keeping away, "as for another reason, Master George."

"What other reason?"

"(I wouldn't keep on touchin' it, if I was you, Sir.) I'll tell you if you'll come out of the place. First, take a look at its colour, Master George."

"I am doing so."

"Done, Sir. Now, come out of the place."

He moved away with his light, and Vendale followed with his. When Vendale came up with him, and they were going back together, Vendale, eyeing him as they walked through the arches, said: "Well, Joey? The colour."

"Is it like clotted blood, Master George?"

"Like enough, perhaps."

"More than enough, I think," muttered Joey Ladle, shaking his head solemnly.

"Well, say it is like; say it is exactly like. What then?"

"Master George, they do say—"

"Who?"

"How should I know who?" rejoined the Cellarman, apparently much exasperated by the unreasonable nature of the question. "Them! Them as says pretty well everything, you know. How should I know who They are, if you don't?"

"True. Go on."

"They do say that the man that gets by any accident a piece of that dark growth right upon his breast, will, for sure and certain, die by murder."

As Vendale laughingly stopped to meet the Cellarman's eyes, which he had fastened on his light while dreamily saying those words, he suddenly became conscious of being struck upon his own breast by a heavy hand. Instantly following with his eyes the action of the hand that struck him—which was his companion's—he saw that it had beaten off his breast a web or clot of the fungus even then floating to the ground.

For a moment he turned upon the Cellarman almost as scared a look as the Cellarman turned upon him. But in another moment they had reached the daylight at the foot of the cellar-steps, and before he cheerfully sprang up them, he blew out his candle and the superstition together.

EXIT WILDING

On the morning of the next day, Wilding went out alone, after leaving a message with his clerk. "If Mr. Vendale should ask for me," he said, "or if Mr. Bintrey should call, tell them I am gone to the Foundling." All that his partner had said to him, all that his lawyer, following on the same side, could urge, had left him persisting unshaken in his own point of view. To find the lost man, whose place he had usurped, was now the paramount interest of his life, and to inquire at the Foundling was plainly to take the first step in the direction of discovery. To the Foundling, accordingly, the wine-merchant now went.

The once familiar aspect of the building was altered to him, as the look of the portrait over the chimneypiece was altered to him. His one dearest association with the place which had sheltered his childhood had been broken away from it for ever. A strange reluctance possessed him, when he stated his business at the door. His heart ached as he sat alone in the waiting-room while the Treasurer of the Institution was being sent for to see him. When the interview began, it was only by a painful effort that he could compose himself sufficiently to mention the nature of his errand.

The Treasurer listened with a face which promised all needful attention, and promised nothing more.

"We are obliged to be cautious," he said, when it came to his turn to speak, "about all inquiries which are made by strangers."

"You can hardly consider me a stranger," answered Wilding, simply. "I was one of your poor lost children here, in the bygone time."

The Treasurer politely rejoined that this circumstance inspired him with a special interest in his visitor. But he pressed, nevertheless, for that visitor's motive in making his inquiry. Without further preface, Wilding told him his motive, suppressing nothing. The Treasurer rose, and led the way into the room in which the registers of the institution were kept. "All the information which our books can give is heartily at your service," he said. "After the time that has elapsed, I am afraid it is the only information we have to offer you."

The books were consulted, and the entry was found expressed as follows:

"3d March, 1836. Adopted, and removed from the Foundling Hospital, a male infant, named Walter Wilding. Name and condition of the person adopting the child—Mrs. Jane Ann Miller, widow. Address—Lime-Tree Lodge, Groombridge Wells. References—the Reverend John Harker, Groombridge Wells; and Messrs. Giles, Jeremie, and Giles, bankers, Lombard-street."

"Is that all?" asked the wine-merchant. "Had you no after-communication with Mrs. Miller?"

"None—or some reference to it must have appeared in this book."

"May I take a copy of the entry?"

"Certainly! You are a little agitated. Let me make a copy for you."

"My only chance, I suppose," said Wilding, looking sadly at the copy, "is to inquire at Mrs. Miller's residence, and to try if her references can help me?"

"That is the only chance I see at present," answered the Treasurer. "I heartily wish I could have been of some further assistance to you."

With those farewell words to comfort him, Wilding set forth on the journey of investigation which began from the Foundling doors. The first stage to make for, was plainly the house of business of the bankers in Lombard-street. Two of the partners in the firm were inaccessible to chance-visitors when he asked for them. The third, after raising certain inevitable difficulties, consented to let a clerk examine the ledger marked with the initial letter "M." The account of Mrs. Miller, widow, of Groombridge Wells, was found. Two long lines, in faded ink, were drawn across it; and at the bottom of the page there appeared this note: "Account closed, September 30th, 1837."

So the first stage of the journey was reached—and so it ended in No Thoroughfare! After sending a note to Cripple Corner to inform his partner that his absence might be prolonged for some hours, Wilding took his place in the train, and started for the second stage on the journey—Mrs. Miller's residence at Groombridge Wells.

Mothers and children travelled with him; mothers and children met each other at the station; mothers and children were in the shops when he entered them to inquire for Lime-Tree Lodge. Everywhere, the nearest and dearest of human relations showed itself happily in the happy light of day. Everywhere, he was reminded of the treasured delusion from which he had been awakened so cruelly—of the lost memory which had passed from him like a reflection from a glass.

Inquiring here, inquiring there, he could hear of no such place as Lime-Tree Lodge. Passing a house-agent's office, he went in wearily, and put the question for the last time. The house-agent pointed across the street to a dreary mansion of many windows, which might have been a manufactory, but which was an hotel. "That's where Lime-Tree Lodge stood, Sir," said the man, "ten years ago."

The second stage reached, and No Thoroughfare again!

But one chance was left. The clerical reference, Mr. Harker, still remained to be found. Customers coming in at the moment to occupy the house-agent's attention, Wilding went down the street, and entering a bookseller's shop, asked if he could be informed of the Reverend John Harker's present address.

The bookseller looked unaffectedly shocked and astonished, and made no answer.

Wilding repeated his question.

The bookseller took up from his counter a prim little volume in a binding of sober gray. He handed it to his visitor, open at the title-page. Wilding read:

"The martyrdom of the Reverend John Harker in New Zealand. Related by a former member of his flock."

Wilding put the book down on the counter. "I beg your pardon," he said thinking a little, perhaps, of his own present martyrdom while he spoke. The silent bookseller acknowledged the apology by a bow. Wilding went out.

Third and last stage, and No Thoroughfare for the third and last time.

There was nothing more to be done; there was absolutely no choice but to go back to London, defeated at all points. From time to time on the return journey, the wine-merchant looked at his copy of the entry in the Foundling Register. There is one among the many forms of despair—perhaps the most pitiable of all—which persists in disguising itself as Hope. Wilding checked himself in the act of throwing the useless morsel of paper out of the carriage window. "It may lead to something yet," he thought. "While I live, I won't part with it. When I die, my executors shall find it sealed up with my will."

Now, the mention of his will set the good wine-merchant on a new track of thought, without diverting his mind from its engrossing subject. He must make his will immediately.

The application of the phrase No Thoroughfare to the case had originated with Mr. Bintrey. In their first long conference following the discovery, that sagacious personage had a hundred times repeated, with an obstructive shake of the head, "No Thoroughfare, Sir, No Thoroughfare. My belief is that there is no way out of this at this time of day, and my advice is, make yourself comfortable where you are."

In the course of the protracted consultation, a magnum of the forty-five year old port-wine had been produced for the wetting of Mr. Bintrey's legal whistle; but the more clearly he saw his way through the wine, the more emphatically he did not see his way through the case; repeating as often as he set his glass down empty. "Mr. Wilding, No Thoroughfare. Rest and be thankful."

It is certain that the honest wine-merchant's anxiety to make a will originated in profound conscientiousness; though it is possible (and quite consistent with his rectitude) that he may unconsciously have derived some feeling of relief from the prospect of delegating his own difficulty to two other men who were to come after him. Be that as it may, he pursued his new track of thought with great ardour, and lost no time in begging George Vendale and Mr. Bintrey to meet him in Cripple Corner and share his confidence.

"Being all three assembled with closed doors," said Mr. Bintrey, addressing the new partner on the occasion, "I wish to observe, before our friend (and my client) entrusts us with his further views, that I have endorsed what I understand from him to have been your advice, Mr. Vendale, and what would be the advice of every sensible man. I have told him that he positively must keep his secret. I have spoken with Mrs. Goldstraw, both in his presence and in his absence; and if anybody is to be trusted (which is a very large IF), I think she is to be trusted to that extent. I have pointed out to our friend (and my client), that to set on foot random inquiries would not only be to raise the Devil, in the likeness of all the swindlers in the kingdom, but would also be to waste the estate. Now, you see, Mr. Vendale, our friend (and my client), does not desire to waste the estate, but, on the contrary, desires to husband it for what he considers—but I can't say I do—the rightful owner, if such rightful owner should ever be found. I am very much mistaken if he ever will be, but never mind that. Mr. Wilding and I are, at least, agreed that the estate is not to be wasted. Now, I have yielded to Mr. Wilding's desire to keep an advertisement at intervals flowing through the newspapers, cautiously inviting any person who may know anything about that adopted infant, taken from the Foundling Hospital, to come to my office; and I have pledged myself that such advertisement shall regularly appear. I have gathered from our friend (and my client) that I meet you here to-day to take his instructions, not to give him advice. I am prepared to receive his instructions, and to respect his wishes; but you will please observe that this does not imply my approval of either as a matter of professional opinion."

Thus Mr. Bintrey; talking quite is much *at* Wilding as *to* Vendale. And yet, in spite of his care for his client, he was so amused by his client's Quixotic conduct, as to eye him from time to time with twinkling eyes, in the light of a highly comical curiosity.

"Nothing," observed Wilding, "can be clearer. I only wish my head were as clear as yours, Mr. Bintrey."

"If you feel that singing in it coming on," hinted the lawyer, with an alarmed glance, "put it off.—I mean the interview."

"Not at all, I thank you," said Wilding. "What was I going to—"

"Don't excite yourself, Mr. Wilding," urged the lawyer.

"No; I *wasn't* going to," said the wine-merchant. "Mr. Bintrey and George Vendale, would you have any hesitation or objection to become my joint trustees and executors, or can you at once consent?"

"*I* consent," replied George Vendale, readily.

"*I* consent," said Bintrey, not so readily.

"Thank you both. Mr. Bintrey, my instructions for my last will and testament are short and plain. Perhaps you will now have the goodness to take them down. I leave the whole of my real and personal estate, without any exception or reservation whatsoever, to you two, my joint trustees and executors, in trust to pay over the whole to the true Walter Wilding, if he shall be found and identified within two years after the day of my death. Failing that, in trust to you two to pay over the whole as a benefaction and legacy to the Foundling Hospital."

"Those are all your instructions, are they, Mr. Wilding?" demanded Bintrey, after a blank silence, during which nobody had looked at anybody.

"The whole."

"And as to those instructions, you have absolutely made up your mind, Mr. Wilding?"

"Absolutely, decidedly, finally."

"It only remains," said the lawyer, with one shrug of his shoulders, "to get them into technical and binding form, and to execute and attest. Now, does that press? Is there any hurry about it? You are not going to die yet, Sir."

"Mr. Bintrey," answered Wilding, gravely, "when I am going to die is within other knowledge than yours or mine. I shall be glad to have this matter off my mind, if you please."

"We are lawyer and client again," rejoined Bintrey, who, for the nonce, had become almost sympathetic. "If this day week—here, at the same hour—will suit Mr. Vendale and yourself, I will enter in my Diary that I attend you accordingly."

The appointment was made, and in due sequence, kept. The will was formally signed, sealed, delivered, and witnessed, and was carried off by Mr. Bintrey for safe storage among the papers of his clients, ranged in their respective iron boxes, with their respective owners' names outside, on iron tiers in his consulting-room, as if that legal sanctuary were a condensed Family Vault of Clients.

With more heart than he had lately had for former subjects of interest, Wilding then set about completing his patriarchal establishment, being much assisted not only by Mrs. Goldstraw but by Vendale too: who, perhaps, had in his mind the giving of an Obenreizer dinner as soon as possible. Anyhow, the establishment being reported in sound working order, the Obenreizers, Guardian and Ward, were asked to dinner, and Madame Dor was included in the invitation. If Vendale had been over head and ears in love before—a phrase not to be taken as implying the faintest doubt about it—this dinner plunged him down in love ten thousand fathoms deep. Yet, for the life of him, he could not get one word alone with charming Marguerite. So surely as a blessed moment seemed to come, Obenreizer, in his filmy state, would stand at Vendale's elbow, or the broad back of Madame Dor would appear before his eyes. That speechless matron was never seen in a front view, from the moment of her arrival to that of her departure—except at dinner. And from the instant of her retirement to the drawing-room, after a hearty participation in that meal, she turned her face to the wall again.

Yet, through four or five delightful though distracting hours, Marguerite was to be seen, Marguerite was to be heard, Marguerite was to be occasionally touched. When they made the round of the old dark cellars, Vendale led her by the hand; when she sang to him in the lighted room at night, Vendale, standing by her, held her relinquished gloves, and would have bartered against them every drop of the forty-five year old, though it had been forty-five times forty-five years old, and its nett price forty-five times forty-five pounds per dozen. And still, when she was gone, and a great gap of an extinguisher was clapped on Cripple Corner, he tormented himself by wondering, Did she think that he admired her! Did she think that he adored her! Did she suspect that she had won him, heart and soul! Did she care to think at all about it! And so, Did she and Didn't she, up and down the gamut, and above the line and below the line, dear, dear! Poor restless heart of humanity! To think that the men who were mummies thousands of years ago, did the same, and ever found the secret how to be quiet after it!

"What do you think, George," Wilding asked him next day, "of Mr. Obenreizer? (I won't ask you what you think of Miss Obenreizer.)"

"I don't know," said Vendale, "and I never did know, what to think of him."

"He is well informed and clever," said Wilding.

"Certainly clever."

"A good musician." (He had played very well, and sung very well, overnight.)

"Unquestionably a good musician."

"And talks well."

"Yes," said George Vendale, ruminating, "and talks well. Do you know, Wilding, it oddly occurs to me, as I think about him, that he doesn't keep silence well!"

"How do you mean? He is not obtrusively talkative."

"No, and I don't mean that. But when he is silent, you can hardly help vaguely, though perhaps most unjustly, mistrusting him. Take people whom you know and like. Take any one you know and like."

"Soon done, my good fellow," said Wilding. "I take you."

"I didn't bargain for that, or foresee it," returned Vendale, laughing. "However, take me. Reflect for a moment. Is your approving knowledge of my interesting face mainly founded (however various the momentary expressions it may include) on my face when I am silent?"

"I think it is," said Wilding.

"I think so too. Now, you see, when Obenreizer speaks—in other words, when he is allowed to explain himself away—he comes out right enough; but when he has not the opportunity of explaining himself away, he comes out rather wrong. Therefore it is, that I say he does not keep silence well. And passing hastily in review such faces as I know, and don't trust, I am inclined to think, now I give my mind to it, that none of them keep silence well."

This proposition in Physiognomy being new to Wilding, he was at first slow to admit it, until asking himself the question whether Mrs. Goldstraw kept silence well, and remembering that her face in repose decidedly invited trustfulness, he was as glad as men usually are to believe what they desire to believe.

But, as he was very slow to regain his spirits or his health, his partner, as another means of setting him up—and perhaps also with contingent Obenreizer views—reminded him of those musical schemes of his in connection with his family, and how a singing-class was to be formed in the house, and a Choir in a neighbouring church. The class was established speedily, and, two or three of the people having already some musical knowledge, and singing tolerably, the Choir soon followed. The latter was led, and chiefly taught, by Wilding himself: who had hopes of converting his dependents into so many Foundlings, in respect of their capacity to sing sacred choruses.

Now, the Obenreizers being skilled musicians, it was easily brought to pass that they should be asked to join these musical unions. Guardian and Ward consenting, or Guardian consenting for both, it was necessarily brought to pass that Vendale's life became a life of absolute thraldom and enchantment. For, in the mouldy Christopher-Wren church on Sundays, with its dearly beloved brethren assembled and met together, five-and-twenty strong, was not that Her voice that shot like light into the darkest places, thrilling the walls and pillars as though they were pieces of his heart! What time, too, Madame Dor in a corner of the high pew, turning her back upon everybody and everything, could not fail to be Ritualistically right at some moment of the service; like the man whom the doctors recommended to get drunk once a month, and who, that he might not overlook it, got drunk every day.

But, even those seraphic Sundays were surpassed by the Wednesday concerts established for the patriarchal family. At those concerts she would sit down to the piano and sing them, in her own tongue, songs of her own land, songs calling from the mountain-tops to Vendale, "Rise above the grovelling level country; come far away from the crowd; pursue me as I mount higher; higher, higher, melting into the azure distance; rise to my supremest height of all, and love me here!" Then would the pretty bodice, the clocked stocking, and the silver-buckled shoe be, like the broad forehead and the bright eyes, fraught with the spring of a very chamois, until the strain was over.

Not even over Vendale himself did these songs of hers cast a more potent spell than over Joey Ladle in his different way. Steadily refusing to muddle the harmony by taking any share in it, and evincing the supremest contempt for scales and such-like rudiments of music—which, indeed, seldom captivate mere listeners—Joey did at first give up the whole business for a bad job, and the whole of the performers for a set of howling Dervishes. But, descrying traces of unmuddled harmony in a part-song one day, he gave his two under cellarmen faint hopes of getting on towards something in course of time. An anthem of Handel's led to further encouragement from him: though he objected that that great musician must have been down in some of them foreign cellars pretty much, for to go and say the same thing so many times over; which, took it in how you might, he considered a certain sign of your having took it in somehow. On a third occasion, the public appearance of Mr. Jarvis with a flute, and of an odd man with a violin, and the performance of a duet by the two, did so astonish him that, solely of his own impulse and motion, he became inspired with the words, "Ann Koar!" repeatedly pronouncing them as if calling in a familiar manner for some lady who had distinguished herself in the orchestra. But this was his final testimony to the merits of his mates, for, the instrumental duet being performed at the first Wednesday concert, and being presently followed by the voice of Marguerite Obenreizer, he sat with his mouth wide open, entranced, until she had finished; when, rising in his place with much solemnity, and prefacing what he was about to say with a bow that specially included Mr. Wilding in it, he delivered himself of the gratifying sentiment: "Arter that, ye may all on ye get to bed!" And ever afterwards declined to render homage in any other words to the musical powers of the family.

Thus began a separate personal acquaintance between Marguerite Obenreizer and Joey Ladle. She laughed so heartily at his compliment, and yet was so abashed by it, that Joey made bold to say to her, after the concert was over, he hoped he wasn't so muddled in his head as to have took a liberty? She made him a gracious reply, and Joey ducked in return.

"You'll change the luck time about, Miss," said Joey, ducking again. "It's such as you in the place that can bring round the luck of the place."

"Can I? Round the luck?" she answered, in her pretty English, and with a pretty wonder. "I fear I do not understand. I am so stupid."

"Young Master Wilding, Miss," Joey explained confidentially, though not much to her enlightenment, "changed the luck, afore he took in young Master George. So I say, and so they'll find. Lord! Only come into the place and sing over the luck a few times, Miss, and it won't be able to help itself!"

With this, and with a whole brood of ducks, Joey backed out of the presence. But Joey being a privileged person, and even an involuntary conquest being pleasant to youth and beauty, Marguerite merrily looked out for him next time.

"Where is my Mr. Joey, please?" she asked Vendale.

So Joey was produced, and shaken hands with, and that became an Institution.

Another Institution arose in this wise. Joey was a little hard of hearing. He himself said it was "Wapours," and perhaps it might have been; but whatever the cause of the effect, there the effect was, upon him. On this first occasion he had been seen to sidle along the wall, with his left hand to his left ear, until he had sidled himself into a seat pretty near the singer, in which place and position he had remained, until addressing to his friends the amateurs the compliment before mentioned. It was observed on the following Wednesday that Joey's action as a Pecking Machine was impaired at dinner, and it was rumoured about the table that this was explainable by his high-strung expectations of Miss Obenreizer's singing, and his fears of not getting a place where he could hear every note and syllable. The rumour reaching Wilding's ears, he in his good nature called Joey to the front at night before Marguerite began. Thus the Institution came into being that on succeeding nights, Marguerite, running her hands over the keys before singing, always said to Vendale, "Where is my Mr. Joey, please?" and that Vendale always brought him forth, and stationed him near by. That he should then, when all eyes were upon him, express in his face the utmost contempt for the exertions of his friends and confidence in Marguerite alone, whom he would stand contemplating, not unlike the rhinocerous out of the spelling-book, tamed and on his hind legs, was a part of the Institution. Also that when he remained after the singing in his most ecstatic state, some bold spirit from the back should say, "What do you think of it, Joey?" and he should be goaded to reply, as having that instant conceived the retort, "Arter that ye may all on ye get to bed!" These were other parts of the Institution.

But, the simple pleasures and small jests of Cripple Corner were not destined to have a long life. Underlying them from the first was a serious matter, which every member of the patriarchal family knew of, but which, by tacit agreement, all forbore to speak of. Mr. Wilding's health was in a bad way.

He might have overcome the shock he had sustained in the one great affection of his life, or he might have overcome his consciousness of being in the enjoyment of another man's property; but the two together were too much for him. A man haunted by twin ghosts, he became deeply depressed. The inseparable spectres sat at the board with him, ate from his platter, drank from his cup, and stood by his bedside at night. When he recalled his supposed mother's love, he felt as though he had stolen it. When he rallied a little under the respect and attachment of his dependants, he felt as though he were even fraudulent in making them happy, for that should have been the unknown man's duty and gratification.

Gradually, under the pressure of his brooding mind, his body stooped, his step lost its elasticity, his eyes were seldom lifted from the ground. He knew he could not help the deplorable mistake that had been made, but he knew he could not mend it; for the days and weeks went by, and no one claimed his name or his possessions. And now there began to creep over him a cloudy consciousness of often-recurring confusion in his head. He would unaccountably lose, sometimes whole hours, sometimes a whole day and night. Once, his remembrance stopped as he sat at the head of the dinner-table, and was blank until daybreak. Another time, it stopped as he was beating time to their singing, and went on again when he and his partner were walking in the court-yard by the light of the moon, half the night later. He asked Vendale (always full of consideration, work, and help) how this was? Vendale only replied, "You have not been quite well; that's all." He looked for explanation into the faces of his people. But they would put it off with "Glad to see you looking so much better, Sir;" or "Hope you're doing nicely now, Sir;" in which was no information at all.

At length, when the partnership was but five months old, Walter Wilding took to his bed, and his housekeeper became his nurse.

"Lying here, perhaps you will not mind my calling you Sally, Mrs. Goldstraw?" said the poor wine-merchant.

"It sounds more natural to me, Sir, than any other name, and I like it better."

"Thank you, Sally. I think, Sally, I must of late have been subject to fits. Is that so, Sally? Don't mind telling me now."

"It has happened, Sir."

"Ah! That is the explanation!" he quietly remarked. "Mr. Obenreizer, Sally, talks of the world being so small that it is not strange how often the same people come together, and come together at various places, and in various stages of life. But it does seem strange, Sally, that I should, as I may say, come round to the Foundling to die."

He extended his hand to her, and she gently took it.

"You are not going to die, dear Mr. Wilding."

"So Mr. Bintrey said, but I think he was wrong. The old child-feeling is coming back upon me, Sally. The old hush and rest, as I used to fall asleep."

After an interval he said, in a placid voice, "Please kiss me, Nurse," and, it was evident, believed himself to be lying in the old Dormitory.

As she had been used to bend over the fatherless and motherless children, Sally bent over the fatherless and motherless man, and put her lips to his forehead, murmuring:

"God bless you!"

"God bless you!" he replied, in the same tone.

After another interval, he opened his eyes in his own character, and said: "Don't move me, Sally, because of what I am going to say; I lie quite easily. I think my time is come, I don't know how it may appear to you, Sally, but—"

Insensibility fell upon him for a few minutes; he emerged from it once more.

"—I don't know how it may appear to you, Sally, but so it appears to me."

When he had thus conscientiously finished his favourite sentence, his time came, and he died.

Act II

Vendale Makes Love

The summer and the autumn passed. Christmas and the New Year were at hand.

As executors honestly bent on performing their duty towards the dead, Vendale and Bintrey had held more than one anxious consultation on the subject of Wilding's will. The lawyer had declared, from the first, that it was simply impossible to take any useful action in the matter at all. The only obvious inquiries to make, in relation to the lost man, had been made already by Wilding himself; with this result, that time and death together had not left a trace of him discoverable. To advertise for the claimant to the property, it would be necessary to mention particulars—a course of proceeding which would invite half the impostors in England to present themselves in the character of the true Walter Wilding. "If we find a chance of tracing the lost man, we will take it. If we don't, let us meet for another consultation on the first anniversary of Wilding's death." So Bintrey advised. And so, with the most earnest desire to fulfil his dead friend's wishes, Vendale was fain to let the matter rest for the present.

Turning from his interest in the past to his interest in the future, Vendale still found himself confronting a doubtful prospect. Months on months had passed since his first visit to Soho Square—and through all that time, the one language in which he had told Marguerite that he loved her was the language of the eyes, assisted, at convenient opportunities, by the language of the hand.

What was the obstacle in his way? The one immovable obstacle which had been in his way from the first. No matter how fairly the opportunities looked, Vendale's efforts to speak with Marguerite alone ended invariably in one and the same result. Under the most accidental circumstances, in the most innocent manner possible, Obenreizer was always in the way.

With the last days of the old year came an unexpected chance of spending an evening with Marguerite, which Vendale resolved should be a chance of speaking privately to her as well. A cordial note from Obenreizer invited him, on New Year's Day, to a little family dinner in Soho-square. "We shall be only four," the note said. "We shall be only two," Vendale determined, "before the evening is out!"

New Year's Day, among the English, is associated with the giving and receiving of dinners, and with nothing more. New Year's Day, among the foreigners, is the grand opportunity of the year for the giving and receiving of presents. It is occasionally possible to acclimatise a foreign custom. In this instance Vendale felt no hesitation about making the attempt. His one difficulty was to decide what his New Year's gift to Marguerite should be. The defensive pride of the peasant's daughter—morbidly sensitive to the inequality between her social position and his—would be secretly roused against him if he ventured on a rich offering. A gift, which a poor man's purse might purchase, was the one gift that could be trusted to find its way to her heart, for the giver's sake. Stoutly resisting temptation, in the form of diamonds and rubies, Vendale bought a brooch of the filagree-work of Genoa—the simplest and most unpretending ornament that he could find in the jeweller's shop.

He slipped his gift into Marguerite's hand as she held it out to welcome him on the day of the dinner.

"This is your first New Year's Day in England," he said. "Will you let me help to make it like a New Year's Day at home?"

She thanked him, a little constrainedly, as she looked at the jeweller's box, uncertain what it might contain. Opening the box, and discovering the studiously simple form under which Vendale's little keepsake offered itself to her, she penetrated his motive on the spot. Her face turned on him brightly, with a look which said, "I own you have pleased and flattered me." Never had she been so charming, in Vendale's eyes, as she was at that moment. Her winter dress—a petticoat of dark silk, with a bodice of black velvet rising to her neck, and enclosing it softly in a little circle of swansdown—heightened, by all the force of contrast, the dazzling fairness of her hair and her complexion. It was only when she turned aside from him to the glass, and, taking out the brooch that she wore, put his New Year's gift in its place, that Vendale's attention wandered far enough away from her to discover the presence of other persons in the room. He now became conscious that the hands of Obenreizer were affectionately in possession of his elbows. He now heard the voice of Obenreizer thanking him for his attention to Marguerite, with the faintest possible ring of mockery in its tone. ("Such a simple present, dear Sir! and showing such nice tact!") He now discovered, for the first time, that there was one other guest, and but one, besides himself, whom Obenreizer presented as a compatriot and friend. The friend's face was mouldy, and the friend's figure was fat. His age was suggestive of the autumnal period of human life. In the course of the evening he developed two extraordinary capacities. One was a capacity for silence; the other was a capacity for emptying bottles.

Madame Dor was not in the room. Neither was there any visible place reserved for her when they sat down to table. Obenreizer explained that it was "the good Dor's simple habit to dine always in the middle of the day. She would make her excuses later in the evening." Vendale wondered whether the good Dor had, on this occasion, varied her domestic employment from cleaning Obenreizer's gloves to cooking Obenreizer's dinner. This at least was certain—the dishes served were, one and all, as achievements in cookery, high above the reach of the rude elementary art of England. The dinner was unobtrusively perfect. As for the wine, the eyes of the speechless friend rolled over it, as in solemn ecstasy. Sometimes he said "Good!" when a bottle came in full; and sometimes he said "Ah!" when a bottle went out empty—and there his contributions to the gaiety of the evening ended.

Silence is occasionally infectious. Oppressed by private anxieties of their own, Marguerite and Vendale appeared to feel the influence of the speechless friend. The whole responsibility of keeping the talk going rested on Obenreizer's shoulders, and manfully did Obenreizer sustain it. He opened his heart in the character of an enlightened foreigner, and sang the praises of England. When other topics ran dry, he returned to this inexhaustible source, and always set the stream running again as copiously as ever. Obenreizer would have given an arm, an eye, or a leg to have been born an Englishman. Out of England there was no such institution as a home, no such thing as a fireside, no such object as a beautiful woman. His dear Miss Marguerite would excuse him, if he accounted for *her* attractions on the theory that English blood must have mixed at some former time with their obscure and unknown ancestry. Survey this English nation, and behold a tall, clean, plump, and solid people! Look at their cities! What magnificence in their public buildings! What admirable order and propriety in their streets! Admire their laws, combining the eternal principle of justice with the other eternal principle of pounds, shillings, and pence; and applying the product to all civil injuries, from an injury to a man's honour, to an injury to a man's nose! You have ruined my daughter—pounds, shillings, and pence! You have knocked me down with a blow in my face—pounds, shillings, and pence! Where was the material prosperity of such a country as *that* to stop? Obenreizer, projecting himself into the future, failed to see the end of it. Obenreizer's enthusiasm entreated permission to exhale itself, English fashion, in a toast. Here is our modest little dinner over, here is our frugal dessert on the table, and here is the admirer of England conforming to national customs, and making a speech! A toast to your white cliffs of Albion, Mr. Vendale! to your national virtues, your charming climate, and your fascinating women! to your Hearths, to your Homes, to your Habeas Corpus, and to all your other institutions! In one word—to England! Heep-heep-heep! hooray!

Obenreizer's voice had barely chanted the last note of the English cheer, the speechless friend had barely drained the last drop out of his glass, when the festive proceedings were interrupted by a modest tap at the door. A woman-servant came in, and approached her master with a little note in her hand. Obenreizer opened the note with a frown; and, after reading it with an expression of genuine annoyance, passed it on to his compatriot and friend. Vendale's spirits rose as he watched these proceedings. Had he found an ally in the annoying little note? Was the long-looked-for chance actually coming at last?

"I am afraid there is no help for it?" said Obenreizer, addressing his fellow-countryman. "I am afraid we must go."

The speechless friend handed back the letter, shrugged his heavy shoulders, and poured himself out a last glass of wine. His fat fingers lingered fondly round the neck of the bottle. They pressed it with a little amatory squeeze at parting. His globular eyes looked dimly, as through an intervening haze, at Vendale and Marguerite. His heavy articulation laboured, and brought forth a whole sentence at a birth. "I think," he said, "I should have liked a little more wine." His breath failed him after that effort; he gasped, and walked to the door.

Obenreizer addressed himself to Vendale with an appearance of the deepest distress.

"I am so shocked, so confused, so distressed," he began. "A misfortune has happened to one of my compatriots. He is alone, he is ignorant of your language—I and my good friend, here, have no choice but to go and help him. What can I say in my excuse? How can I describe my affliction at depriving myself in this way of the honour of your company?"

He paused, evidently expecting to see Vendale take up his hat and retire. Discerning his opportunity at last, Vendale determined to do nothing of the kind. He met Obenreizer dexterously, with Obenreizer's own weapons.

"Pray don't distress yourself," he said. "I'll wait here with the greatest pleasure till you come back."

Marguerite blushed deeply, and turned away to her embroidery-frame in a corner by the window. The film showed itself in Obenreizer's eyes, and the smile came something sourly to Obenreizer's lips. To have told Vendale that there was no reasonable prospect of his coming back in good time, would have been to risk offending a man whose favourable opinion was of solid commercial importance to him. Accepting his defeat with the best possible grace, he declared himself to be equally honoured and delighted by Vendale's proposal. "So frank, so friendly, so English!" He bustled about, apparently looking for something he wanted, disappeared for a moment through the folding-doors communicating with the next room, came back with his hat and coat, and protesting that he would return at the earliest possible moment, embraced Vendale's elbows, and vanished from the scene in company with the speechless friend.

Vendale turned to the corner by the window, in which Marguerite had placed herself with her work. There, as if she had dropped from the ceiling, or come up through the floor— there, in the old attitude, with her face to the stove—sat an Obstacle that had not been foreseen, in the person of Madame Dor! She half got up, half looked over her broad shoulder at Vendale, and plumped down again. Was she at work? Yes. Cleaning Obenreizer's gloves, as before? No; darning Obenreizer's stockings.

The case was now desperate. Two serious considerations presented themselves to Vendale. Was it possible to put Madame Dor into the stove? The stove wouldn't hold her. Was it possible to treat Madame Dor, not as a living woman, but as an article of furniture? Could the mind be brought to contemplate this respectable matron purely in the light of a chest of drawers, with a black gauze held-dress accidentally left on the top of it? Yes, the mind could be brought to do that. With a comparatively trifling effort, Vendale's mind did it. As he took his place on the old-fashioned window-seat, close by Marguerite and her embroidery, a slight movement appeared in the chest of drawers, but no remark issued from it. Let it be remembered that solid furniture is not easy to move, and that it has this advantage in consequence—there is no fear of upsetting it.

Unusually silent and unusually constrained—with the bright colour fast fading from her face, with a feverish energy possessing her fingers—the pretty Marguerite bent over her embroidery, and worked as if her life depended on it. Hardly less agitated himself, Vendale felt the importance of leading her very gently to the avowal which he was eager to make—to the other sweeter avowal still, which he was longing to hear. A woman's love is never to be taken by storm; it yields insensibly to a system of gradual approach. It ventures by the roundabout way, and listens to the low voice. Vendale led her memory back to their past meetings when they were travelling together in Switzerland. They revived the impressions, they recalled the events, of the happy bygone time. Little by little, Marguerite's constraint vanished. She smiled, she was interested, she looked at Vendale, she grew idle with her needle, she made false stitches in her work. Their voices sank lower and lower; their faces bent nearer and nearer to each other as they spoke. And Madame Dor? Madame Dor behaved like an angel. She never looked round; she never said a word; she went on with Obenreizer's stockings. Pulling each stocking up tight over her left arm, and holding that arm aloft from time to time, to catch the light on her work, there were moments—delicate and indescribable moments—when Madame Dor appeared to be sitting upside down, and contemplating one of her own respectable legs, elevated in the air. As the minutes wore on, these elevations followed each other at longer and longer intervals. Now and again, the black gauze head-dress nodded, dropped forward, recovered itself. A little heap of stockings slid softly from Madame Dor's lap, and remained unnoticed on the floor. A prodigious ball of worsted followed the stockings, and rolled lazily under the table. The black gauze head-dress nodded, dropped forward, recovered itself, nodded again, dropped forward again, and recovered itself no more. A composite sound, partly as of the purring of an immense cat, partly as of the planing of a soft board, rose over the hushed voices of the lovers, and hummed at regular intervals through the room. Nature and Madame Dor had combined together in Vendale's interests. The best of women was asleep.

Marguerite rose to stop—not the snoring—let us say, the audible repose of Madame Dor. Vendale laid his hand on her arm, and pressed her back gently into her chair.

"Don't disturb her," he whispered. "I have been waiting to tell you a secret. Let me tell it now."

Marguerite resumed her seat. She tried to resume her needle. It was useless; her eyes failed her; her hand failed her; she could find nothing.

"We have been talking," said Vendale, "of the happy time when we first met, and first travelled together. I have a confession to make. I have been concealing something. When we spoke of my first visit to Switzerland, I told you of all the impressions I had brought back with me to England—except one. Can you guess what that one is?"

Her eyes looked stedfastly at the embroidery, and her face turned a little away from him. Signs of disturbance began to appear in her neat velvet bodice, round the region of the brooch. She made no reply. Vendale pressed the question without mercy.

"Can you guess what the one Swiss impression is which I have not told you yet?"

Her face turned back towards him, and a faint smile trembled on her lips.

"An impression of the mountains, perhaps?" she said slyly.

"No; a much more precious impression than that."

"Of the lakes?"

"No. The lakes have not grown dearer and dearer in remembrance to me every day. The lakes are not associated with my happiness in the present, and my hopes in the future. Marguerite! all that makes life worth having hangs, for me, on a word from your lips. Marguerite! I love you!"

Her head drooped as he took her hand. He drew her to him, and looked at her. The tears escaped from her downcast eyes, and fell slowly over her cheeks.

"O, Mr. Vendale," she said sadly, "it would have been kinder to have kept your secret. Have you forgotten the distance between us? It can never, never be!"

"There can be but one distance between us, Marguerite—a distance of your making. My love, my darling, there is no higher rank in goodness, there is no higher rank in beauty, than yours! Come! whisper the one little word which tells me you will be my wife!"

She sighed bitterly. "Think of your family," she murmured; "and think of mine!"

Vendale drew her a little nearer to him.

"If you dwell on such an obstacle as that," he said, "I shall think but one thought—I shall think I have offended you."

She started, and looked up. "O, no!" she exclaimed innocently. The instant the words passed her lips, she saw the construction that might be placed on them. Her confession had escaped her in spite of herself. A lovely flush of colour overspread her face. She made a momentary effort to disengage herself from her lover's embrace. She looked up at him entreatingly. She tried to speak. The words died on her lips in the kiss that Vendale pressed on them. "Let me go, Mr. Vendale!" she said faintly.

"Call me George."

She laid her head on his bosom. All her heart went out to him at last. "George!" she whispered.

"Say you love me!"

Her arms twined themselves gently round his neck. Her lips, timidly touching his cheek, murmured the delicious words—"I love you!"

In the moment of silence that followed, the sound of the opening and closing of the house-door came clear to them through the wintry stillness of the street.

Marguerite started to her feet.

"Let me go!" she said. "He has come back!"

She hurried from the room, and touched Madame Dor's shoulder in passing. Madame Dor woke up with a loud snort, looked first over one shoulder and then over the other, peered down into her lap, and discovered neither stockings, worsted, nor darning-needle in it. At the same moment, footsteps became audible ascending the stairs. "Mon Dieu!" said Madame Dor, addressing herself to the stove, and trembling violently. Vendale picked up the stockings and the ball, and huddled them all back in a heap over her shoulder. "Mon Dieu!" said Madame Dor, for the second time, as the avalanche of worsted poured into her capacious lap.

The door opened, and Obenreizer came in. His first glance round the room showed him that Marguerite was absent.

"What!" he exclaimed, "my niece is away? My niece is not here to entertain you in my absence? This is unpardonable. I shall bring her back instantly."

Vendale stopped him.

"I beg you will not disturb Miss Obenreizer," he said. "You have returned, I see, without your friend?"

"My friend remains, and consoles our afflicted compatriot. A heart-rending scene, Mr. Vendale! The household gods at the pawnbroker's—the family immersed in tears. We all embraced in silence. My admirable friend alone possessed his composure. He sent out, on the spot, for a bottle of wine."

"Can I say a word to you in private, Mr. Obenreizer?"

"Assuredly." He turned to Madame Dor. "My good creature, you are sinking for want of repose. Mr. Vendale will excuse you."

Madame Dor rose, and set forth sideways on her journey from the stove to bed. She dropped a stocking. Vendale picked it up for her, and opened one of the folding-doors. She advanced a step, and dropped three more stockings. Vendale stooping to recover them as before, Obenreizer interfered with profuse apologies, and with a warning look at Madame Dor. Madame Dor acknowledged the look by dropping the whole of the stockings in a heap, and then shuffling away panic-stricken from the scene of disaster. Obenreizer swept up the complete collection fiercely in both hands. "Go!" he cried, giving his prodigious handful a preparatory swing in the air. Madame Dor said, "Mon Dieu," and vanished into the next room, pursued by a shower of stockings.

"What must you think, Mr. Vendale," said Obenreizer, closing the door, "of this deplorable intrusion of domestic details? For myself, I blush at it. We are beginning the New Year as badly as possible; everything has gone wrong to-night. Be seated, pray—and say, what may I offer you? Shall we pay our best respects to another of your noble English institutions? It is my study to be, what you call, jolly. I propose a grog."

Vendale declined the grog with all needful respect for that noble institution.

"I wish to speak to you on a subject in which I am deeply interested," he said. "You must have observed, Mr. Obenreizer, that I have, from the first, felt no ordinary admiration for your charming niece?"

"You are very good. In my niece's name, I thank you."

"Perhaps you may have noticed, latterly, that my admiration for Miss Obenreizer has grown into a tenderer and deeper feeling—?"

"Shall we say friendship, Mr. Vendale?"

"Say love—and we shall be nearer to the truth."

Obenreizer started out of his chair. The faintly discernible beat, which was his nearest approach to a change of colour, showed itself suddenly in his cheeks.

"You are Miss Obenreizer's guardian," pursued Vendale. "I ask you to confer upon me the greatest of all favours—I ask you to give me her hand in marriage."

Obenreizer dropped back into his chair. "Mr. Vendale," he said, "you petrify me."

"I will wait," rejoined Vendale, "until you have recovered yourself."

"One word before I recover myself. You have said nothing about this to my niece?"

"I have opened my whole heart to your niece. And I have reason to hope—"

"What!" interposed Obenreizer. "You have made a proposal to my niece, without first asking for my authority to pay your addresses to her?" He struck his hand on the table, and lost his hold over himself for the first time in Vendale's experience of him. "Sir!" he exclaimed, indignantly, "what sort of conduct is this? As a man of honour, speaking to a man of honour, how can you justify it?"

"I can only justify it as one of our English institutions," said Vendale quietly. "You admire our English institutions. I can't honestly tell you, Mr. Obenreizer, that I regret what I have done. I can only assure you that I have not acted in the matter with any intentional disrespect towards yourself. This said, may I ask you to tell me plainly what objection you see to favouring my suit?"

"I see this immense objection," answered Obenreizer, "that my niece and you are not on a social equality together. My niece is the daughter of a poor peasant; and you are the son of a gentleman. You do us an honour," he added, lowering himself again gradually to his customary polite level, "which deserves, and has, our most grateful acknowledgments. But the inequality is too glaring; the sacrifice is too great. You English are a proud people, Mr. Vendale. I have observed enough of this country to see that such a marriage as you propose would be a scandal here. Not a hand would be held out to your peasant-wife; and all your best friends would desert you."

"One moment," said Vendale, interposing on his side. "I may claim, without any great arrogance, to know more of my country people in general, and of my own friends in particular, than you do. In the estimation of everybody whose opinion is worth having, my wife herself would be the one sufficient justification of my marriage. If I did not feel certain—observe, I say certain—that I am offering her a position which she can accept without so much as the shadow of a humiliation—I would never (cost me what it might) have asked her to be my wife. Is there any other obstacle that you see? Have you any personal objection to me?"

Obenreizer spread out both his hands in courteous protest. "Personal objection!" he exclaimed. "Dear Sir, the bare question is painful to me."

"We are both men of business," pursued Vendale, "and you naturally expect me to satisfy you that I have the means of supporting a wife. I can explain my pecuniary position in two words. I inherit from my parents a fortune of twenty thousand pounds. In half of that sum I have only a life-interest, to which, if I die, leaving a widow, my widow succeeds. If I die, leaving children, the money itself is divided among them, as they come of age. The other half of my fortune is at my own disposal, and is invested in the wine-business. I see my way to greatly improving that business. As it stands at present, I cannot state my return from my capital embarked at more than twelve hundred a year. Add the yearly value of my life-interest—and the total reaches a present annual income of fifteen hundred pounds. I have the fairest prospect of soon making it more. In the meantime, do you object to me on pecuniary grounds?"

Driven back to his last entrenchment, Obenreizer rose, and took a turn backwards and forwards in the room. For the moment, he was plainly at a loss what to say or do next.

"Before I answer that last question," he said, after a little close consideration with himself, "I beg leave to revert for a moment to Miss Marguerite. You said something just now which seemed to imply that she returns the sentiment with which you are pleased to regard her?"

"I have the inestimable happiness," said Vendale, "of knowing that she loves me."

Obenreizer stood silent for a moment, with the film over his eyes, and the faintly perceptible beat becoming visible again in his cheeks.

"If you will excuse me for a few minutes," he said, with ceremonious politeness, "I should like to have the opportunity of speaking to my niece." With those words, he bowed, and quitted the room.

Left by himself, Vendale's thoughts (as a necessary result of the interview, thus far) turned instinctively to the consideration of Obenreizer's motives. He had put obstacles in the way of the courtship; he was now putting obstacles in the way of the marriage—a marriage offering advantages which even his ingenuity could not dispute. On the face of it, his conduct was incomprehensible. What did it mean?

Seeking, under the surface, for the answer to that question—and remembering that Obenreizer was a man of about his own age; also, that Marguerite was, strictly speaking, his half-niece only—Vendale asked himself, with a lover's ready jealousy, whether he had a rival to fear, as well as a guardian to conciliate. The thought just crossed his mind, and no more. The sense of Marguerite's kiss still lingering on his cheek reminded him gently that even the jealousy of a moment was now a treason to *her*.

On reflection, it seemed most likely that a personal motive of another kind might suggest the true explanation of Obenreizer's conduct. Marguerite's grace and beauty were precious ornaments in that little household. They gave it a special social attraction and a special social importance. They armed Obenreizer with a certain influence in reserve, which he could always depend upon to make his house attractive, and which he might always bring more or less to bear on the forwarding of his own private ends. Was he the sort of man to resign such advantages as were here implied, without obtaining the fullest possible compensation for the loss? A connection by marriage with Vendale offered him solid advantages, beyond all doubt. But there were hundreds of men in London with far greater power and far wider influence than Vendale possessed. Was it possible that this man's ambition secretly looked higher than the highest prospects that could be offered to him by the alliance now proposed for his niece? As the question passed through Vendale's mind, the man himself reappeared—to answer it, or not to answer it, as the event might prove.

A marked change was visible in Obenreizer when he resumed his place. His manner was less assured, and there were plain traces about his mouth of recent agitation which had not been successfully composed. Had he said something, referring either to Vendale or to himself, which had raised Marguerite's spirit, and which had placed him, for the first time, face to face with a resolute assertion of his niece's will? It might or might not be. This only was certain—he looked like a man who had met with a repulse.

"I have spoken to my niece," he began. "I find, Mr. Vendale, that even your influence has not entirely blinded her to the social objections to your proposal."

"May I ask," returned Vendale, "if that is the only result of your interview with Miss Obenreizer?"

A momentary flash leapt out through the Obenreizer film.

"You are master of the situation," he answered, in a tone of sardonic submission. "If you insist on my admitting it, I do admit it in those words. My niece's will and mine used to be one, Mr. Vendale. You have come between us, and her will is now yours. In my country, we know when we are beaten, and we submit with our best grace. I submit, with my best grace, on certain conditions. Let us revert to the statement of your pecuniary position. I have an objection to you, my dear Sir—a most amazing, a most audacious objection, from a man in my position to a man in yours."

"What is it?"

"You have honoured me by making a proposal for my niece's hand. For the present (with best thanks and respects), I beg to decline it."

"Why?"

"Because you are not rich enough."

The objection, as the speaker had foreseen, took Vendale completely by surprise. For the moment he was speechless.

"Your income is fifteen hundred a year," pursued Obenreizer. "In my miserable country I should fall on my knees before your income, and say, 'What a princely fortune!' In wealthy England, I sit as I am, and say, 'A modest independence, dear Sir; nothing more. Enough, perhaps, for a wife in your own rank of life who has no social prejudices to conquer. Not more than half enough for a wife who is a meanly born foreigner, and who has all your social prejudices against her.' Sir! if my niece is ever to marry you, she will have what you call uphill work of it in taking her place at starting. Yes, yes; this is not your view, but it remains, immovably remains, my view for all that. For my niece's sake, I claim that this uphill work shall be made as smooth as possible. Whatever material advantages she can have to help her, ought, in common justice, to be hers. Now, tell me, Mr. Vendale, on your fifteen hundred a year can your wife have a house in a fashionable quarter, a footman to open her door, a butler to wait at her table, and a carriage and horses to drive about in? I see the answer in your face—your face says, No. Very good. Tell me one more thing, and I have done. Take the mass of your educated, accomplished, and lovely country-women, is it, or is it not, the fact that a lady who has a house in a fashionable quarter, a footman to open her door, a butler to wait at her table, and a carriage and horses to drive about in, is a lady who has gained four steps, in female estimation, at starting? Yes? or No?"

"Come to the point," said Vendale. "You view this question as a question of terms. What are your terms?"

"The lowest terms, dear Sir, on which you can provide your wife with those four steps at starting. Double your present income—the most rigid economy cannot do it in England on less. You said just now that you expected greatly to increase the value of your business. To work—and increase it! I am a good devil after all! On the day when you satisfy me, by plain proofs, that your income has risen to three thousand a year, ask me for my niece's hand, and it is yours."

"May I inquire if you have mentioned this arrangement to Miss Obenreizer?"

"Certainly. She has a last little morsel of regard still left for me, Mr. Vendale, which is not yours yet; and she accepts my terms. In other words, she submits to be guided by her guardian's regard for her welfare, and by her guardian's superior knowledge of the world." He threw himself back in his chair, in firm reliance on his position, and in full possession of his excellent temper.

Any open assertion of his own interests, in the situation in which Vendale was now placed, seemed to be (for the present at least) hopeless. He found himself literally left with no ground to stand on. Whether Obenreizer's objections were the genuine product of Obenreizer's own view of the case, or whether he was simply delaying the marriage in the hope of ultimately breaking it off altogether—in either of these events, any present resistance on Vendale's part would be equally useless. There was no help for it but to yield, making the best terms that he could on his own side.

"I protest against the conditions you impose on me," he began.

"Naturally," said Obenreizer; "I dare say I should protest, myself, in your place."

"Say, however," pursued Vendale, "that I accept your terms. In that case, I must be permitted to make two stipulations on my part. In the first place, I shall expect to be allowed to see your niece."

"Aha! to see my niece? and to make her in as great a hurry to be married as you are yourself? Suppose I say, No? you would see her perhaps without my permission?"

"Decidedly!"

"How delightfully frank! How exquisitely English! You shall see her, Mr. Vendale, on certain days, which we will appoint together. What next?"

"Your objection to my income," proceeded Vendale, "has taken me completely by surprise. I wish to be assured against any repetition of that surprise. Your present views of my qualification for marriage require me to have an income of three thousand a year. Can I be certain, in the future, as your experience of England enlarges, that your estimate will rise no higher?"

"In plain English," said Obenreizer, "you doubt my word?"

"Do you purpose to take *my* word for it when I inform you that I have doubled my income?" asked Vendale. "If my memory does not deceive me, you stipulated, a minute since, for plain proofs?"

"Well played, Mr. Vendale! You combine the foreign quickness with the English solidity. Accept my best congratulations. Accept, also, my written guarantee."

He rose; seated himself at a writing-desk at a side-table, wrote a few lines, and presented them to Vendale with a low bow. The engagement was perfectly explicit, and was signed and dated with scrupulous care.

"Are you satisfied with your guarantee?"

"I am satisfied."

"Charmed to hear it, I am sure. We have had our little skirmish—we have really been wonderfully clever on both sides. For the present our affairs are settled. I bear no malice. You bear no malice. Come, Mr. Vendale, a good English shake hands."

Vendale gave his hand, a little bewildered by Obenreizer's sudden transitions from one humour to another.

"When may I expect to see Miss Obenreizer again?" he asked, as he rose to go.

"Honour me with a visit to-morrow," said Obenreizer, "and we will settle it then. Do have a grog before you go! No? Well! well! we will reserve the grog till you have your three thousand a year, and are ready to be married. Aha! When will that be?"

"I made an estimate, some months since, of the capacities of my business," said Vendale. "If that estimate is correct, I shall double my present income—"

"And be married!" added Obenreizer.

"And be married," repeated Vendale, "within a year from this time. Good Night."

VENDALE MAKES MISCHIEF

When Vendale entered his office the next morning, the dull commercial routine at Cripple Corner met him with a new face. Marguerite had an interest in it now! The whole machinery which Wilding's death had set in motion, to realise the value of the business—the balancing of ledgers, the estimating of debts, the taking of stock, and the rest of it—was now transformed into machinery which indicated the chances for and against a speedy marriage. After looking over results, as presented by his accountant, and checking additions and subtractions, as rendered by the clerks,

Vendale turned his attention to the stock-taking department next, and sent a message to the cellars, desiring to see the report.

The Cellarman's appearance, the moment he put his head in at the door of his master's private room, suggested that something very extraordinary must have happened that morning. There was an approach to alacrity in Joey Ladle's movements! There was something which actually simulated cheerfulness in Joey Ladle's face!

"What's the matter?" asked Vendale. "Anything wrong?"

"I should wish to mention one thing," answered Joey. "Young Mr. Vendale, I have never set myself up for a prophet."

"Who ever said you did?"

"No prophet, as far as I've heard I tell of that profession," proceeded Joey, "ever lived principally underground. No prophet, whatever else he might take in at the pores, ever took in wine from morning to night, for a number of years together. When I said to young Master Wilding, respecting his changing the name of the firm, that one of these days he might find he'd changed the luck of the firm—did I put myself forward as a prophet? No, I didn't. Has what I said to him come true? Yes, it has. In the time of Pebbleson Nephew, Young Mr. Vendale, no such thing was ever known as a mistake made in a consignment delivered at these doors. There's a mistake been made now. Please to remark that it happened before Miss Margaret came here. For which reason it don't go against what I've said respecting Miss Margaret singing round the luck. Read that, sir," concluded Joey, pointing attention to a special passage in the report, with a forefinger which appeared to be in process of taking in through the pores nothing more remarkable than dirt. "It's foreign to my nature to crow over the house I serve, but I feel it a kind of solemn duty to ask you to read that."

Vendale read as follows:—"Note, respecting the Swiss champagne. An irregularity has been discovered in the last consignment received from the firm of Defresnier and Co." Vendale stopped, and referred to a memorandum-book by his side. "That was in Mr. Wilding's time," he said. "The vintage was a particularly good one, and he took the whole of it. The Swiss champagne has done very well, hasn't it?"

"I don't say it's done badly," answered the Cellarman. "It may have got sick in our customers' bins, or it may have bust in our customers' hands. But I don't say it's done badly with us."

Vendale resumed the reading of the note: "We find the number of the cases to be quite correct by the books. But six of them, which present a slight difference from the rest in the brand, have been opened, and have been found to contain a red wine instead of champagne. The similarity in the brands, we suppose, caused a mistake to be made in sending the consignment from Neuchâtel. The error has not been found to extend beyond six cases."

"Is that all!" exclaimed Vendale, tossing the note away from him.

Joey Ladle's eye followed the flying morsel of paper drearily.

"I'm glad to see you take it easy, Sir," he said. "Whatever happens, it will be always a comfort to you to remember that you took it easy at first. Sometimes one mistake leads to another. A man drops a bit of orange-peel on the pavement by mistake, and another man treads on it by mistake, and there's a job at the hospital, and a party crippled for life. I'm glad you take it easy, Sir. In Pebbleson Nephew's time we shouldn't have taken it easy till we had seen the end of it. Without desiring to crow over the house, young Mr. Vendale, I wish you well through it. No offence, Sir," said the Cellarman, opening the door to go out, and looking in again ominously before he shut it. "I'm muddled and molloncolly, I grant you. But I'm an old servant of Pebbleson Nephew, and I wish you well through them six cases of red wine."

Left by himself, Vendale laughed, and took up his pen. "I may as well send a line to Defresnier and Company," he thought, "before I forget it." He wrote at once in these terms:

> "Dear Sirs. We are taking stock, and a trifling mistake has been discovered in the last consignment of champagne sent by your house to ours. Six of the cases contain red wine—which we hereby return to you. The matter can easily be set right, either by your sending us six cases of the champagne, if they can be produced, or, if not, by your crediting us with the value of six cases on the amount last paid (five hundred pounds) by our firm to yours. Your faithful servants,
>
> "Wilding and Co."

This letter despatched to the post, the subject dropped at once out of Vendale's mind. He had other and far more interesting matters to think of. Later in the day he paid the visit to Obenreizer which had been agreed on between them. Certain evenings in the week were set apart which he was privileged to spend with Marguerite—always, however, in the presence of a third person. On this stipulation Obenreizer politely but positively insisted. The one concession he made was to give Vendale his choice of who the third person should be. Confiding in past experience, his choice fell unhesitatingly upon the excellent woman who mended Obenreizer's stockings. On hearing of the responsibility entrusted to her, Madame Dor's intellectual nature burst suddenly into a new stage of development. She waited till Obenreizer's eye was off her—and then she looked at Vendale, and dimly winked.

The time passed—the happy evenings with Marguerite came and went. It was the tenth morning since Vendale had written to the Swiss firm, when the answer appeared, on his desk, with the other letters of the day:

"DEAR SIRS. We beg to offer our excuses for the little mistake which has happened. At the same time, we regret to add that the statement of our error, with which you have favoured us, has led to a very unexpected discovery. The affair is a most serious one for you and for us. The particulars are as follows:

"Having no more champagne of the vintage last sent to you, we made arrangements to credit your firm to the value of six cases, as suggested by yourself. On taking this step, certain forms observed in our mode of doing business necessitated a reference to our bankers' book, as well as to our ledger. The result is a moral certainty that no such remittance as you mention can have reached our house, and a literal certainty that no such remittance has been paid to our account at the bank.

"It is needless, at this stage of the proceedings, to trouble you with details. The money has unquestionably been stolen in the course of its transit from you to us. Certain peculiarities which we observe, relating to the manner in which the fraud has been perpetrated, lead us to conclude that the thief may have calculated on being able to pay the missing sum to our bankers, before an inevitable discovery followed the annual striking of our balance. This would not have happened, in the usual course, for another three months. During that period, but for your letter, we might have remained perfectly unconscious of the robbery that has been committed.

"We mention this last circumstance, as it may help to show you that we have to do, in this case, with no ordinary thief. Thus far we have not even a suspicion of who that thief is. But we believe you will assist us in making some advance towards discovery, by examining the receipt (forged, of course) which has no doubt purported to come to you from our house. Be pleased to look and see whether it is a receipt entirely in manuscript, or whether it is a numbered and printed form which merely requires the filling in of the amount. The settlement of this apparently trivial question is, we assure you, a matter of vital importance. Anxiously awaiting your reply, we remain, with high esteem and consideration,

"Defresnier & Cie."

Vendale had the letter on his desk, and waited a moment to steady his mind under the shock that had fallen on it. At the time of all others when it was most important to him to increase the value of his business, that business was threatened with a loss of five hundred pounds. He thought of Marguerite, as he took the key from his pocket and opened the iron chamber in the wall in which the books and papers of the firm were kept.

He was still in the chamber, searching for the forged receipt, when he was startled by a voice speaking close behind him.

"A thousand pardons," said the voice; "I am afraid I disturb you."

He turned, and found himself face to face with Marguerite's guardian.

"I have called," pursued Obenreizer, "to know if I can be of any use. Business of my own takes me away for some days to Manchester and Liverpool. Can I combine any business of yours with it? I am entirely at your disposal, in the character of commercial traveller for the firm of Wilding and Co."

"Excuse me for one moment," said Vendale; "I will speak to you directly." He turned round again, and continued his search among the papers. "You come at a time when friendly offers are more than usually precious to me," he resumed. "I have had very bad news this morning from Neuchâtel."

"Bad news!" exclaimed Obenreizer. "From Defresnier and Company?"

"Yes. A remittance we sent to them has been stolen. I am threatened with a loss of five hundred pounds. What's that?"

Turning sharply, and looking into the room for the second time, Vendale discovered his envelope case overthrown on the floor, and Obenreizer on his knees picking up the contents.

"All my awkwardness," said Obenreizer. "This dreadful news of yours startled me; I stepped back—" He became too deeply interested in collecting the scattered envelopes to finish the sentence.

"Don't trouble yourself," said Vendale. "The clerk will pick the things up."

"This dreadful news!" repeated Obenreizer, persisting in collecting the envelopes. "This dreadful news!"

"If you will read the letter," said Vendale, "you will find I have exaggerated nothing. There it is, open on my desk."

He resumed his search, and in a moment more discovered the forged receipt. It was on the numbered and printed form, described by the Swiss firm. Vendale made a memorandum of the number and the date. Having replaced the receipt and locked up the iron chamber, he had leisure to notice Obenreizer, reading the letter in the recess of a window at the far end of the room.

"Come to the fire," said Vendale. "You look perished with the cold out there. I will ring for some more coals."

Obenreizer rose, and came slowly back to the desk. "Marguerite will be as sorry to hear of this as I am," he said, kindly. "What do you mean to do?"

"I am in the hands of Defresnier and Company," answered Vendale. "In my total ignorance of the circumstances, I can only do what they recommend. The receipt which I have just found, turns out to be the numbered and printed form. They seem to attach some special importance to its discovery. You have had experience, when you were in the Swiss house, of their way of doing business. Can you guess what object they have in view?"

Obenreizer offered a suggestion.

"Suppose I examine the receipt?" he said.

"Are you ill?" asked Vendale, startled by the change in his face, which now showed itself plainly for the first time. "Pray go to the fire. You seem to be shivering—I hope you are not going to be ill?"

"Not I!" said Obenreizer. "Perhaps I have caught cold. Your English climate might have spared an admirer of your English institutions. Let me look at the receipt."

Vendale opened the iron chamber. Obenreizer took a chair, and drew it close to the fire. He held both hands over the flames. "Let me look at the receipt," he repeated, eagerly, as Vendale reappeared with the paper in his hand. At the same moment a porter entered the room with a fresh supply of coals. Vendale told him to make a good fire. The man obeyed the order with a disastrous alacrity. As he stepped forward and raised the scuttle, his foot caught in a fold of the rug, and he discharged his entire cargo of coals into the grate. The result was an instant smothering of the flame, and the production of a stream of yellow smoke, without a visible morsel of fire to account for it.

"Imbecile!" whispered Obenreizer to himself, with a look at the man which the man remembered for many a long day afterwards.

"Will you come into the clerks' room?" asked Vendale. "They have a stove there."

"No, no. No matter."

Vendale handed him the receipt. Obenreizer's interest in examining it appeared to have been quenched as suddenly and as effectually as the fire itself. He just glanced over the document, and said, "No; I don't understand it! I am sorry to be of no use."

"I will write to Neuchâtel by to-night's post," said Vendale, putting away the receipt for the second time. "We must wait, and see what comes of it."

"By to-night's post," repeated Obenreizer. "Let me see. You will get the answer in eight or nine days' time. I shall be back before that. If I can be of any service, as commercial traveller, perhaps you will let me know between this and then. You will send me written instructions? My best thanks. I shall be most anxious for your answer from Neuchâtel. Who knows? It may be a mistake, my dear friend, after all. Courage! courage! courage!" He had entered the room with no appearance of being pressed for time. He now snatched up his hat, and took his leave with the air of a man who had not another moment to lose.

Left by himself, Vendale took a turn thoughtfully in the room.

His previous impression of Obenreizer was shaken by what he had heard and seen at the interview which had just taken place. He was disposed, for the first time, to doubt whether, in this case, he had not been a little hasty and hard in his judgment on another man. Obenreizer's surprise and regret, on hearing the news from Neuchâtel, bore the plainest marks of being honestly felt—not politely assumed for the occasion. With troubles of his own to encounter, suffering, to all appearance, from the first insidious attack of a serious illness, he had looked and spoken like a man who really deplored the disaster that had fallen on his friend. Hitherto Vendale had tried vainly to alter his first opinion of Marguerite's guardian, for Marguerite's sake. All the generous instincts in his nature now combined together and shook the evidence which had seemed unanswerable up to this time. "Who knows?" he thought. "I may have read that man's face wrongly, after all."

The time passed—the happy evenings with Marguerite came and went. It was again the tenth morning since Vendale had written to the Swiss firm; and again the answer appeared on his desk with the other letters of the day:

> "Dear Sir. My senior partner, M. Defresnier, has been called away, by urgent business, to Milan. In his absence (and with his full concurrence and authority), I now write to you again on the subject of the missing five hundred pounds.
>
> "Your discovery that the forged receipt is executed upon one of our numbered and printed forms has caused inexpressible surprise and distress to my partner and to myself. At the time when your remittance was stolen, but three keys were in existence opening the strong-box in which our receipt-forms are invariably kept. My partner had one key; I had the other. The third was in the possession of a gentleman who, at that period, occupied a position of trust in our house. We should as soon have thought of suspecting one of ourselves as of suspecting this person. Suspicion now points at him, nevertheless. I cannot prevail on myself to inform you who the person is, so long as there is the shadow of a chance that he may come innocently out of the inquiry which must now be instituted. Forgive my silence; the motive of it is good.
>
> "The form our investigation must now take is simple enough. The handwriting of your receipt must be compared, by competent persons whom we have at our disposal, with certain specimens of handwriting in our possession. I cannot send you the specimens for business reasons, which, when you hear them, you are sure to approve. I must beg you to send me the receipt to Neuchâtel—and, in making this request, I must accompany it by a word of necessary warning.
>
> "If the person, at whom suspicion now points, really proves to be the person who has committed this forger and theft, I have reason to fear that circumstances may have already put him on his guard. The only evidence

against him is the evidence in your hands, and he will move heaven and earth to obtain and destroy it. I strongly urge you not to trust the receipt to the post. Send it to me, without loss of time, by a private hand, and choose nobody for your messenger but a person long established in your own employment, accustomed to travelling, capable of speaking French; a man of courage, a man of honesty, and, above all things, a man who can be trusted to let no stranger scrape acquaintance with him on the route. Tell no one—absolutely no one—but your messenger of the turn this matter has now taken. The safe transit of the receipt may depend on your interpreting *literally* the advice which I give you at the end of this letter.

"I have only to add that every possible saving of time is now of the last importance. More than one of our receipt-forms is missing—and it is impossible to say what new frauds may not be committed if we fail to lay our hands on the thief.

"Your faithful servant,
"ROLLAND,
"(Signing for Defresnier and Cie.)"

Who was the suspected man? In Vendale's position, it seemed useless to inquire.

Who was to be sent to Neuchâtel with the receipt? Men of courage and men of honesty were to be had at Cripple Corner for the asking. But where was the man who was accustomed to foreign travelling, who could speak the French language, and who could be really relied on to let no stranger scrape acquaintance with him on his route? There was but one man at hand who combined all those requisites in his own person, and that man was Vendale himself.

It was a sacrifice to leave his business; it was a greater sacrifice to leave Marguerite. But a matter of five hundred pounds was involved in the pending inquiry; and a literal interpretation of M. Rolland's advice was insisted on in terms which there was no trifling with. The more Vendale thought of it, the more plainly the necessity faced him, and said, "Go!"

As he locked up the letter with the receipt, the association of ideas reminded him of Obenreizer. A guess at the identity of the suspected man looked more possible now. Obenreizer might know.

The thought had barely passed through his mind, when the door opened, and Obenreizer entered the room.

"They told me at Soho-square you were expected back last night," said Vendale, greeting him. "Have you done well in the country? Are you better?"

A thousand thanks. Obenreizer had done admirably well; Obenreizer was infinitely better. And now, what news? Any letter from Neuchâtel?

"A very strange letter," answered Vendale. "The matter has taken a new turn, and the letter insists—without excepting anybody—on my keeping our next proceedings a profound secret."

"Without excepting anybody?" repeated Obenreizer. As he said the words, he walked away again, thoughtfully, to the window at the other end of the room, looked out for a moment, and suddenly came back to Vendale. "Surely they must have forgotten?" he resumed, "or they would have excepted *me*?"

"It is Monsieur Rolland who writes," said Vendale. "And, as you say, he must certainly have forgotten. That view of the matter quite escaped me. I was just wishing I had you to consult, when you came into the room. And here I am tried by a formal prohibition, which cannot possibly have been intended to include you. How very annoying!"

Obenreizer's filmy eyes fixed on Vendale attentively.

"Perhaps it is more than annoying!" he said. "I came this morning not only to hear the news, but to offer myself as messenger, negotiator—what you will. Would you believe it? I have letters which oblige me to go to Switzerland immediately. Messages, documents, anything—I could have taken them all to Defresnier and Rolland for you."

"You are the very man I wanted," returned Vendale. "I had decided, most unwillingly, on going to Neuchâtel myself, not five minutes since, because I could find no one here capable of taking my place. Let me look at the letter again."

He opened the strong room to get at the letter. Obenreizer, after first glancing round him to make sure that they were alone, followed a step or two and waited, measuring Vendale with his eye. Vendale was the tallest man, and unmistakably the strongest man also of the two. Obenreizer turned away, and warmed himself at the fire.

Meanwhile, Vendale read the last paragraph in the letter for the third time. There was the plain warning—there was the closing sentence, which insisted on a literal interpretation of it. The hand, which was leading Vendale in the dark, led him on that condition only. A large sum was at stake: a terrible suspicion remained to be verified. If he acted on his own responsibility, and if anything happened to defeat the object in view, who would be blamed? As a man of business, Vendale had but one course to follow. He locked the letter up again.

"It is most annoying," he said to Obenreizer—"it is a piece of forgetfulness on Monsieur Rolland's part which puts me to serious inconvenience, and places me in an absurdly false position towards you. What am I to do? I am acting in a very serious matter, and acting entirely in the dark. I have no choice but to be guided, not by the spirit, but by the letter of my instructions. You understand me, I am sure? You know, if I had not been fettered in this way, how gladly I should have accepted your services?"

"Say no more!" returned Obenreizer. "In your place I should have done the same. My good friend, I take no offence. I thank you for your compliment. We shall be travelling companions, at any rate," added Obenreizer. "You go, as I go, at once?"

"At once. I must speak to Marguerite first, of course!"

"Surely! surely! Speak to her this evening. Come, and pick me up on the way to the station. We go together by the mail train to-night?"

"By the mail train to-night."

It was later than Vendale had anticipated when he drove up to the house in Soho-square. Business difficulties, occasioned by his sudden departure, had presented themselves by dozens. A cruelly large share of the time which he had hoped to devote to Marguerite had been claimed by duties at his office which it was impossible to neglect.

To his surprise and delight, she was alone in the drawing-room when he entered it.

"We have only a few minutes, George," she said. "But Madame Dor has been good to me—and we can have those few minutes alone." She threw her arms round his neck, and whispered eagerly, "Have you done anything to offend Mr. Obenreizer?"

"I!" exclaimed Vendale, in amazement.

"Hush!" she said, "I want to whisper it. You know the little photograph I have got of you. This afternoon it happened to be on the chimneypiece. He took it up and looked at it—and I saw his face in the glass. I know you have offended him! He is merciless; he is revengeful; he is as secret as the grave. Don't go with him, George—don't go with him!"

"My own love," returned Vendale, "you are letting your fancy frighten you! Obenreizer and I were never better friends than we are at this moment."

Before a word more could be said, the sudden movement of some ponderous body shook the floor of the next room. The shock was followed by the appearance of Madame Dor. "Obenreizer" exclaimed this excellent person in a whisper, and plumped down instantly in her regular place by the stove.

Obenreizer came in with a courier's big strapped over his shoulder. "Are you ready?" he asked, addressing Vendale. "Can I take anything for you? You have no travelling-bag. I have got one. Here is the compartment for papers, open at your service."

"Thank you," said Vendale. "I have only one paper of importance with me; and that paper I am bound to take charge of myself. Here it is," he added, touching the breast-pocket of his coat, "and here it must remain till we get to Neuchâtel."

As he said those words, Marguerite's hand caught his, and pressed it significantly. She was looking towards Obenreizer. Before Vendale could look, in his turn, Obenreizer had wheeled round, and was taking leave of Madame Dor.

"Adieu, my charming niece!" he said, turning to Marguerite next. "En route, my friend, for Neuchâtel!" He tapped Vendale lightly over the breast-pocket of his coat and led the way to the door.

Vendale's last look was for Marguerite. Marguerite's last words to him were, "Don't go!"

Act III

In the Valley

It was about the middle of the month of February when Vendale and Obenreizer set forth on their expedition. The winter being a hard one, the time was bad for travellers. So bad was it that these two travellers, coming to Strasbourg, found its great inns almost empty. And even the few people they did encounter in that city, who had started from England or from Paris on business journeys towards the interior of Switzerland, were turning back.

Many of the railroads in Switzerland that tourists pass easily enough now, were almost or quite impracticable then. Some were not begun; more were not completed. On such as were open, there were still large gaps of old road where communication in the winter season was often stopped; on others, there were weak points where the new work was not safe, either under conditions of severe frost, or of rapid thaw. The running of trains on this last class was not to be counted on in the worst time of the year, was contingent upon weather, or was wholly abandoned through the months considered the most dangerous.

At Strasbourg there were more travellers' stories afloat, respecting the difficulties of the way further on, than there were travellers to relate them. Many of these tales were as wild as usual; but the more modestly marvellous did derive some colour from the circumstance that people were indisputably turning back. However, as the road to Basle was open, Vendale's resolution to push on was in no wise disturbed. Obenreizer's resolution was necessarily Vendale's, seeing that he stood at bay thus desperately: He must be ruined, or must destroy the evidence that Vendale carried about him, even if he destroyed Vendale with it.

The state of mind of each of these two fellow-travellers towards the other was this. Obenreizer, encircled by impending ruin through Vendale's quickness of action, and seeing the circle narrowed every hour by Vendale's energy, hated him with the animosity of a fierce cunning lower animal. He had always had instinctive movements in his breast against him; perhaps, because of that old sore of gentleman and peasant; perhaps, because of the openness of his nature, perhaps, because of his better looks; perhaps, because of his success with Marguerite; perhaps, on all those grounds, the two last not the least. And now he saw in him, besides, the hunter who was tracking him down. Vendale, on the other hand, always contending generously against his first vague mistrust, now felt bound to contend against it more than ever: reminding himself, "He is Marguerite's guardian. We are on perfectly friendly terms; he is my companion of his own proposal, and can have no interested motive in sharing this undesirable journey." To which pleas in behalf of Obenreizer, chance added one consideration more, when they came to Basle after a journey of more than twice the average duration.

They had had a late dinner, and were alone in an inn room there, overhanging the Rhine: at that place rapid and deep, swollen and loud. Vendale lounged upon a couch, and Obenreizer walked to and fro: now, stopping at the window, looking at the crooked reflection of the town lights in the dark water (and peradventure thinking, "If I could fling him into it!"); now, resuming his walk with his eyes upon the floor.

"Where shall I rob him, if I can? Where shall I murder him, if I must?" So, as he paced the room, ran the river, ran the river, ran the river.

The burden seemed to him, at last, to be growing so plain, that he stopped; thinking it as well to suggest another burden to his companion.

"The Rhine sounds to-night," he said with a smile, "like the old waterfall at home. That waterfall which my mother showed to travellers (I told you of it once). The sound of it changed with the weather, as does the sound of all falling waters and flowing waters. When I was pupil of the watchmaker, I remembered it as sometimes saying to me for whole days, 'Who are you, my little wretch? Who are you, my little wretch?' I remembered it as saying, other times, when its sound was hollow, and storm was coming up the Pass: 'Boom, boom, boom. Beat him, beat him, beat him.' Like my mother enraged—if she was my mother."

"If she was?" said Vendale, gradually changing his attitude to a sitting one. "If she was? Why do you say 'if'?"

"What do I know?" replied the other negligently, throwing up his hands and letting them fall as they would. "What would you have? I am so obscurely born, that how can I say? I was very young, and all the rest of the family were men and women, and my so-called parents were old. Anything is possible of a case like that."

"Did you ever doubt—"

"I told you once, I doubt the marriage of those two," he replied, throwing up his hands again, as if he were throwing the unprofitable subject away. "But here I am in Creation. *I* come of no fine family. What does it matter?"

"At least you are Swiss," said Vendale, after following him with his eyes to and fro.

"How do I know?" he retorted abruptly, and stopping to look back over his shoulder. "I say to you, at least you are English. How do you know?"

"By what I have been told from infancy."

"Ah! I know of myself that way."

"And," added Vendale, pursuing the thought that he could not drive back, "by my earliest recollections."

"I also. I know of myself that way—if that way satisfies."

"Does it not satisfy you?"

"It must. There is nothing like 'it must' in this little world. It must. Two short words those, but stronger than long proof or reasoning."

"You and poor Wilding were born in the same year. You were nearly of an age," said Vendale, again thoughtfully looking after him as he resumed his pacing up and down.

"Yes. Very nearly."

Could Obenreizer be the missing man? In the unknown associations of things, was there a subtler meaning than he himself thought, in that theory so often on his lips about the smallness of the world? Had the Swiss letter presenting him followed so close on Mrs. Goldstraw's revelation concerning the infant who had been taken away to Switzerland, because he was that infant grown a man? In a world where so many depths lie unsounded, it might be. The chances, or the laws—call them either—that had wrought out the revival of Vendale's own acquaintance with Obenreizer, and had ripened it into intimacy, and had brought them here together this present winter night, were hardly less curious; while read by such a light, they were seen to cohere towards the furtherance of a continuous and an intelligible purpose.

Vendale's awakened thoughts ran high while his eyes musingly followed Obenreizer pacing up and down the room, the river ever running to the tune: "Where shall I rob him, if I can? Where shall I murder him, if I must?" The secret of his dead friend was in no hazard from Vendale's lips; but just as his friend had died of its weight, so did he in his lighter succession feel the burden of the trust, and the obligation to follow any clue, however obscure. He rapidly asked himself, would he like this man to be the real Wilding? No. Argue down his mistrust as he might, he was unwilling to put such a substitute in the place of his late guileless, outspoken childlike partner. He rapidly asked himself, would he like this man to be rich? No. He had more power than enough over Marguerite as it was, and wealth might invest him with more. Would he like this man to be Marguerite's Guardian, and yet proved to stand in no degree of relationship towards her, however disconnected and distant? No. But these were not considerations to come between him and fidelity to the dead. Let him see to it that they passed him with no other notice than the knowledge that they *had* passed him, and left him bent on the discharge of a solemn duty. And he did see to it, so soon that he followed his companion with ungrudging eyes, while he still paced the room; that companion, whom he supposed to be moodily reflecting on his own birth, and not on another man's—least of all what man's—violent Death.

The road in advance from Basle to Neuchâtel was better than had been represented. The latest weather had done it good. Drivers, both of horses and mules, had come in that evening after dark, and had reported nothing more difficult to be overcome than trials of patience, harness, wheels, axles, and whipcord. A bargain was soon struck for a carriage and horses, to take them on in the morning, and to start before daylight.

"Do you lock your door at night when travelling?" asked Obenreizer, standing warming his hands by the wood fire in Vendale's chamber, before going to his own.

"Not I. I sleep too soundly."

"You are so sound a sleeper?" he retorted, with an admiring look. "What a blessing!"

"Anything but a blessing to the rest of the house," rejoined Vendale, "if I had to be knocked up in the morning from the outside of my bedroom door."

"I, too," said Obenreizer, "leave open my room. But let me advise you, as a Swiss who knows: always, when you travel in my country, put your papers—and, of course, your money—under your pillow. Always the same place."

"You are not complimentary to your countrymen," laughed Vendale.

"My countrymen," said Obenreizer, with that light touch of his friend's elbows by way of Good Night and benediction, "I suppose are like the majority of men. And the majority of men will take what they can get. Adieu! At four in the morning."

"Adieu! At four."

Left to himself, Vendale raked the logs together, sprinkled over them the white wood-ashes lying on the hearth, and sat down to compose his thoughts. But they still ran high on their latest theme, and the running of the river tended to agitate rather than to quiet them. As he sat thinking, what little disposition he had had to sleep departed. He felt it hopeless to lie down yet, and sat dressed by the fire. Marguerite, Wilding, Obenreizer, the business he was then upon, and a thousand hopes and doubts that had nothing to do with it, occupied his mind at once. Everything seemed to have power over him but slumber. The departed disposition to sleep kept far away.

He had sat for a long time thinking, on the hearth, when his candle burned down and its light went out. It was of little moment; there was light enough in the fire. He changed his attitude, and, leaning his arm on the chair-back, and his chin upon that hand, sat thinking still.

But he sat between the fire and the bed, and, as the fire flickered in the play of air from the fast-flowing river, his enlarged shadow fluttered on the white wall by the bedside. His attitude gave it an air, half of mourning and half of bending over the bed imploring. His eyes were observant of it, when he became troubled by the disagreeable fancy that it was like Wilding's shadow, and not his own.

A slight change of place would cause it to disappear. He made the change, and the apparition of his disturbed fancy vanished. He now sat in the shade of a little nook beside the fire, and the door of the room was before him.

It had a long cumbrous iron latch. He saw the latch slowly and softly rise. The door opened a very little, and came to again, as though only the air had moved it. But he saw that the latch was out of the hasp.

The door opened again very slowly, until it opened wide enough to admit some one. It afterwards remained still for a while, as though cautiously held open on the other side. The figure of a man then entered, with its face turned towards the bed, and stood quiet just within the door. Until it said, in a low half-whisper, at the same time taking one stop forward: "Vendale!"

"What now?" he answered, springing from his seat; "who is it?"

It was Obenreizer, and he uttered a cry of surprise as Vendale came upon him from that unexpected direction. "Not in bed?" he said, catching him by both shoulders with an instinctive tendency to a struggle. "Then something *is* wrong!"

"What do you mean?" said Vendale, releasing himself.

"First tell me; you are not ill?"

"Ill? No."

"I have had a bad dream about you. How is it that I see you up and dressed?"

"My good fellow, I may as well ask you how it is that I see *you* up and undressed?"

"I have told you why. I have had a bad dream about you. I tried to rest after it, but it was impossible. I could not make up my mind to stay where I was without knowing you were safe; and yet I could not make up my mind to come in here. I have been minutes hesitating at the door. It is so easy to laugh at a dream that you have not dreamed. Where is your candle?"

"Burnt out."

"I have a whole one in my room. Shall I fetch it?"

"Do so."

His room was very near, and he was absent for but a few seconds. Coming back with the candle in his hand, he kneeled down on the hearth and lighted it. As he blew with his breath a charred billet into flame for the purpose, Vendale, looking down at him, saw that his lips were white and not easy of control.

"Yes!" said Obenreizer, setting the lighted candle on the table, "it was a bad dream. Only look at me!"

His feet were bare; his red-flannel shirt was thrown back at the throat, and its sleeves were rolled above the elbows; his only other garment, a pair of under pantaloons or drawers, reaching to the ankles, fitted him close and tight. A certain lithe and savage appearance was on his figure, and his eyes were very bright.

"If there had been a wrestle with a robber, as I dreamed," said Obenreizer, "you see, I was stripped for it."

"And armed too," said Vendale, glancing at his girdle.

"A traveller's dagger, that I always carry on the road," he answered carelessly, half drawing it from its sheath with his left hand, and putting it back again. "Do you carry no such thing?"

"Nothing of the kind."

"No pistols?" said Obenreizer, glancing at the table, and from it to the untouched pillow.

"Nothing of the sort."

"You Englishmen are so confident! You wish to sleep?"

"I have wished to sleep this long time, but I can't do it."

"I neither, after the bad dream. My fire has gone the way of your candle. May I come and sit by yours? Two o'clock! It will so soon be four, that it is not worth the trouble to go to bed again."

"I shall not take the trouble to go to bed at all, now," said Vendale; "sit here and keep me company, and welcome."

Going back to his room to arrange his dress, Obenreizer soon returned in a loose cloak and slippers, and they sat down on opposite sides of the hearth. In the interval Vendale had replenished the fire from the wood-basket in his room, and Obenreizer had put upon the table a flask and cup from his.

"Common cabaret brandy, I am afraid," he said, pouring out; "bought upon the road, and not like yours from Cripple Corner. But yours is exhausted; so much the worse. A cold night, a cold time of night, a cold country, and a cold house. This may be better than nothing; try it."

Vendale took the cup, and did so.

"How do you find it?"

"It has a coarse after-flavour," said Vendale, giving back the cup with a slight shudder, "and I don't like it."

"You are right," said Obenreizer, tasting, and smacking his lips; "it *has* a coarse after-flavour, and *I* don't like it. Booh! It burns, though!" He had flung what remained in the cup upon the fire.

Each of them leaned an elbow on the table, reclined his head upon his hand, and sat looking at the flaring logs. Obenreizer remained watchful and still; but Vendale, after certain nervous twitches and starts, in one of which he rose to his feet and looked wildly about him, fell into the strangest confusion of dreams. He carried his papers in a leather case or pocket-book, in an inner breast-pocket of his buttoned travelling-coat; and whatever he dreamed of, in the lethargy that got possession of him, something importunate in those papers called him out of that dream, though he could not wake from it. He was berated on the steppes of Russia (some shadowy person gave that name to the place) with Marguerite; and yet the sensation of a hand at his breast, softly feeling the outline of the packet-book as he lay asleep before the fire, was present to him. He was ship-wrecked in an open boat at sea, and having lost his clothes, had no other covering than an old sail; and yet a creeping hand, tracing outside all the other pockets of the dress he actually wore, for papers, and finding none answer its touch, warned him to rouse himself. He was in the ancient vault at Cripple Corner, to which was transferred the very bed substantial and present in that very room at Basle; and Wilding (not dead, as he had supposed, and yet he did not wonder much) shook him, and whispered, "Look at that man! Don't you see he has risen, and is turning the pillow? Why should he turn the pillow, if not to seek those papers that are in your breast? Awake!" And yet he slept, and wandered off into other dreams.

Watchful and still, with his elbow on the table, and his head upon that hand, his companion at length said: "Vendale! We are called. Past Four!" Then, opening his eyes, he saw, turned sideways on him, the filmy face of Obenreizer.

"You have been in a heavy sleep," he said. "The fatigue of constant travelling and the cold!"

"I am broad awake now," cried Vendale, springing up, but with an unsteady footing. "Haven't you slept at all?"

"I may have dozed, but I seem to have been patiently looking at the fire. Whether or no, we must wash, and breakfast, and turn out. Past four, Vendale; past four!"

It was said in a tone to rouse him, for already he was half asleep again. In his preparation for the day, too, and at his breakfast, he was often virtually asleep while in mechanical action. It was not until the cold dark day was closing in, that he had any distincter impressions of the ride than jingling bells, bitter weather, slipping horses, frowning hill-sides, bleak woods, and a stoppage at some wayside house of entertainment, where they had passed through a cow-house to reach the travellers' room above. He had been conscious of little more, except of Obenreizer sitting thoughtful at his side all day, and eyeing him much.

But when he shook off his stupor, Obenreizer was not at his side. The carriage was stopping to bait at another wayside house; and a line of long narrow carts, laden with casks of wine, and drawn by horses with a quantity of blue collar and head-gear, were baiting too. These came from the direction in which the travellers were going, and Obenreizer (not thoughtful now, but cheerful and alert) was talking with the foremost driver. As Vendale stretched his limbs, circulated his blood, and cleared off the lees of his lethargy, with a sharp run to and fro in the bracing air, the line of carts moved on: the drivers all saluting Obenreizer as they passed him.

"Who are those?" asked Vendale.

"They are our carriers—Defresnier and Company's," replied Obenreizer. "Those are our casks of wine." He was singing to himself, and lighting a cigar.

"I have been drearily dull company to-day," said Vendale. "I don't know what has been the matter with me."

"You had no sleep last night; and a kind of brain-congestion frequently comes, at first, of such cold," said Obenreizer. "I have seen it often. After all, we shall have our journey for nothing, it seems."

"How for nothing?"

"The House is at Milan. You know, we are a Wine House at Neuchâtel, and a Silk House at Milan? Well, Silk happening to press of a sudden, more than Wine, Defresnier was summoned to Milan. Rolland, the other partner, has been taken ill since his departure, and the doctors will allow him to see no one. A letter awaits you at Neuchâtel to tell you so. I have it from our chief carrier whom you saw me talking with. He was surprised to see me, and said he had that word for you if he met you. What do you do? Go back?"

"Go on," said Vendale.

"On?"

"On? Yes. Across the Alps, and down to Milan."

Obenreizer stopped in his smoking to look at Vendale, and then smoked heavily, looked up the road, looked down the road, looked down at the stones in the road at his feet.

"I have a very serious matter in charge," said Vendale; "more of these missing forms may be turned to as bad account, or worse: I am urged to lose no time in helping the House to take the thief; and nothing shall turn me back."

"No?" cried Obenreizer, taking out his cigar to smile, and giving his hand to his fellow-traveller. "Then nothing shall turn *me* back. Ho, driver! Dispatch. Quick there! Let us push on!"

They travelled through the night. There had been snow, and there was a partial thaw, and they mostly travelled at a foot-pace, and always with many stoppages to breathe the splashed and floundering horses. After an hour's broad daylight, they drew rein at the inn-door at Neuchâtel, having been some eight-and-twenty hours in conquering some eighty English miles.

When they had hurriedly refreshed and changed, they went together to the house of business of Defresnier and Company. There they found the letter which the wine-carrier had described, enclosing the tests and comparisons of handwriting essential to the discovery of the Forger. Vendale's determination to press forward, without resting, being already taken, the only question to delay them was by what Pass could they cross the Alps? Respecting the state of the two Passes of the St. Gotthard and the Simplon, the guides and mule-drivers differed greatly; and both passes were still far enough off, to prevent the travellers from having the benefit of any recent experience of either. Besides which, they well knew that a fall of snow might altogether change the described conditions in a single hour, even if they were correctly stated. But, on the whole, the Simplon appearing to be the hopefuller route, Vendale decided to take it. Obenreizer bore little or no part in the discussion, and scarcely spoke.

To Geneva, to Lausanne, along the level margin of the lake to Vevay, so into the winding valley between the spurs of the mountains, and into the valley of the Rhone. The sound of the carriage-wheels, as they rattled on, through the day, through the night, became as the wheels of a great clock, recording the hours. No change of weather varied the journey, after it had hardened into a sullen frost. In a sombre-yellow sky, they saw the Alpine ranges; and they saw enough of snow on nearer and much lower hill-tops and hill-sides, to sully, by contrast, the purity of lake, torrent, and waterfall, and make the villages look discoloured and dirty. But no snow fell, nor was there any snow-drift on the road. The stalking along the valley of more or less of white mist, changing on their hair and dress into icicles, was the only variety between them and the gloomy sky. And still by day, and still by night, the wheels. And still they rolled, in the hearing of one of them, to the burden, altered from the burden of the Rhine: "The time is gone for robbing him alive, and I must murder him."

They came, at length, to the poor little town of Brieg, at the foot of the Simplon. They came there after dark, but yet could see how dwarfed men's works and men became with the immense mountains towering over them. Here they must lie for the night; and here was warmth of fire, and lamp, and dinner, and wine, and after-conference resounding, with guides and drivers. No human creature had come across the Pass for four days. The snow above the snow-line was too soft for wheeled carriage, and not hard enough for sledge. There was snow in the sky. There had been snow in the sky for days past, and the marvel was that it had not fallen, and the certainty was that it must fall. No vehicle could cross. The journey might be tried on mules, or it might be tried on foot; but the best guides must be paid danger-price in either case, and that, too, whether they succeeded in taking the two travellers across, or turned for safety and brought them back.

In this discussion, Obenreizer bore no part whatever. He sat silently smoking by the fire until the room was cleared and Vendale referred to him.

"Bah! I am weary of these poor devils and their trade," he said, in reply. "Always the same story. It is the story of their trade to-day, as it was the story of their trade when I was a ragged boy. What do you and I want? We want a knapsack each, and a mountain-staff each. We want no guide; we should guide him; he would not guide us. We leave our portmanteaus here, and we cross together. We have been on the mountains together before now, and I am mountain-born, and I know this Pass—Pass!—rather High Road!—by heart. We will leave these poor devils, in pity, to trade with others; but they must not delay us to make a pretence of earning money. Which is all they mean."

Vendale, glad to be quit of the dispute, and to cut the knot: active, adventurous, bent on getting forward, and therefore very susceptible to the last hint: readily assented. Within two hours, they had purchased what they wanted for the expedition, had packed their knapsacks, and lay down to sleep.

At break of day, they found half the town collected in the narrow street to see them depart. The people talked together in groups; the guides and drivers whispered apart, and looked up at the sky; no one wished them a good journey.

As they began the ascent, a gleam of run shone from the otherwise unaltered sky, and for a moment turned the tin spires of the town to silver.

"A good omen!" said Vendale (though it died out while he spoke). "Perhaps our example will open the Pass on this side."

"No; we shall not be followed," returned Obenreizer, looking up at the sky and back at the valley. "We shall be alone up yonder."

ON THE MOUNTAIN

The road was fair enough for stout walkers, and the air grew lighter and easier to breathe as the two ascended. But the settled gloom remained as it had remained for days back. Nature seemed to have come to a pause. The sense of hearing, no less than the sense of sight, was troubled by having to wait so long for the change, whatever it might be, that impended. The silence was as palpable and heavy as the lowering clouds—or rather cloud, for there seemed to be but one in all the sky, and that one covering the whole of it.

Although the light was thus dismally shrouded, the prospect was not obscured. Down in the valley of the Rhone behind them, the stream could be traced through all its many windings, oppressively sombre and solemn in its one leaden hue, a colourless waste. Far and high above them, glaciers and suspended avalanches overhung the spots where they must pass, by-and-by; deep and dark below them on their right, were awful precipice and roaring torrent; tremendous mountains arose in every vista. The gigantic landscape, uncheered by a touch of changing light or a solitary ray of sun, was yet terribly distinct in its ferocity. The hearts of two lonely men might shrink a little, if they had to win their way for miles and hours among a legion of silent and motionless men—mere men like themselves—all looking at them with fixed and frowning front. But how much more, when the legion is of Nature's mightiest works, and the frown may turn to fury in an instant!

As they ascended, the road became gradually more rugged and difficult. But the spirits of Vendale rose as they mounted higher, leaving so much more of the road behind them conquered. Obenreizer spoke little, and held on with a determined purpose. Both, in respect of agility and endurance, were well qualified for the expedition. Whatever the born mountaineer read in the weather-tokens that was illegible to the other, he kept to himself.

"Shall we get across to-day?" asked Vendale.

"No," replied the other. "You see how much deeper the snow lies here than it lay half a league lower. The higher we mount the deeper the snow will lie. Walking is half wading even now. And the days are so short! If we get as high as the fifth Refuge, and lie to-night at the Hospice, we shall do well."

"Is there no danger of the weather rising in the night," asked Vendale, anxiously, "and snowing us up?"

"There is danger enough about us," said Obenreizer, with a cautious glance onward and upward, "to render silence our best policy. You have heard of the Bridge of the Ganther?"

"I have crossed it once."

"In the summer?"

"Yes; in the travelling season."

"Yes; but it is another thing at this season"; with a sneer, as though he were out of temper. "This is not a time of year, or a state of things, on an Alpine Pass, that you gentlemen holiday-travellers know much about."

"You are my Guide," said Vendale, good humouredly. "I trust to you."

"I am your Guide," said Obenreizer, "and I will guide you to your journey's end. There is the Bridge before us."

They had made a turn into a desolate and dismal ravine, where the snow lay deep below them, deep above them, deep on every side. While speaking, Obenreizer stood pointing at the Bridge, and observing Vendale's face, with a very singular expression on his own.

"If I, as Guide, had sent you over there, in advance, and encouraged you to give a shout or two, you might have brought down upon yourself tons and tons and tons of snow, that would not only have struck you dead, but buried you deep, at a blow."

"No doubt," said Vendale.

"No doubt. But that is not what I have to do, as Guide. So pass silently. Or, going as we go, our indiscretion might else crush and bury *me*. Let us get on!"

There was a great accumulation of snow on the Bridge; and such enormous accumulations of snow overhung them from protecting masses of rock, that they might have been making their way through a stormy sky of white clouds. Using his staff skilfully, sounding as he went, and looking upward, with bent shoulders, as it were to resist the mere idea of a fall from above, Obenreizer softly led. Vendale closely followed. They were yet in the midst of their dangerous way, when there came a mighty rush, followed by a sound as of thunder. Obenreizer clapped his hand on Vendale's mouth and pointed to the track behind them. Its aspect had been wholly changed in a moment. An avalanche had swept over it, and plunged into the torrent at the bottom of the gulf below.

Their appearance at the solitary Inn not far beyond this terrible Bridge, elicited many expressions of astonishment from the people shut up in the house. "We stay but to rest," said Obenreizer, shaking the snow from his dress at the fire. "This gentleman has very pressing occasion to get across; tell them, Vendale."

"Assuredly, I have very pressing occasion. I must cross."

"You hear, all of you. My friend has very pressing occasion to get across, and we want no advice and no help. I am as good a guide, my fellow-countrymen, as any of you. Now, give us to eat and drink."

In exactly the same way, and in nearly the same words, when it was coming on dark and they had struggled through the greatly increased difficulties of the road, and had at last reached their destination for the night, Obenreizer said to the astonished people of the Hospice, gathering about them at the fire, while they were yet in the act of getting their wet shoes off, and shaking the snow from their clothes:

"It is well to understand one another, friends all. This gentleman—"

"—Has," said Vendale, readily taking him up with a smile, "very pressing occasion to get across. Must cross."

"You hear?—has very pressing occasion to get across, must cross. We want no advice and no help. I am mountain-born, and act as Guide. Do not worry us by talking about it, but let us have supper, and wine, and bed."

All through the intense cold of the night, the same awful stillness. Again at sunrise, no sunny tinge to gild or redden the snow. The same interminable waste of deathly white; the same immovable air; the same monotonous gloom in the sky.

"Travellers!" a friendly voice called to them from the door, after they were afoot, knapsack on back and staff in hand, as yesterday; "recollect! There are five places of shelter, near together, on the dangerous road before you; and there is the wooden cross, and there is the next Hospice. Do not stray from the track. If the *Tourmente* comes on, take shelter instantly!"

"The trade of these poor devils!" said Obenreizer to his friend, with a contemptuous backward wave of his hand towards the voice. "How they stick to their trade! You Englishmen say we Swiss are mercenary. Truly, it does look like it."

They had divided between the two knapsacks such refreshments as they had been able to obtain that morning, and as they deemed it prudent to take. Obenreizer carried the wine as his share of the burden; Vendale, the bread and meat and cheese, and the flask of brandy.

They had for some time laboured upward and onward through the snow—which was now above their knees in the track, and of unknown depth elsewhere—and they were still labouring upward and onward through the most frightful part of that tremendous desolation, when snow begin to fall. At first, but a few flakes descended slowly and steadily. After a little while the fall grew much denser, and suddenly it began without apparent cause to whirl itself into spiral shapes. Instantly ensuing upon this last change, an icy blast came roaring at them, and every sound and force imprisoned until now was let loose.

One of the dismal galleries through which the road is carried at that perilous point, a cave eked out by arches of great strength, was near at hand. They struggled into it, and the storm raged wildly. The noise of the wind, the noise of the water, the thundering down of displaced masses of rock and snow, the awful voices with which not only that gorge but every gorge in the whole monstrous range seemed to be suddenly endowed, the darkness as of night, the violent revolving of the snow which beat and broke it into spray and blinded them, the madness of everything around insatiate for destruction, the rapid substitution of furious violence for unnatural calm, and hosts of appalling sounds for silence: these were things, on the edge of a deep abyss, to chill the blood, though the fierce wind, made actually solid by ice and snow, had failed to chill it.

Obenreizer, walking to and fro in the gallery without ceasing, signed to Vendale to help him unbuckle his knapsack. They could see each other, but could not have heard each other speak. Vendale complying, Obenreizer produced his bottle of wine, and poured some out, motioning Vendale to take that for warmth's sake, and not brandy. Vendale again complying, Obenreizer seemed to drink after him, and the two walked backwards and forwards side by side; both well knowing that to rest or sleep would be to die.

The snow came driving heavily into the gallery by the upper end at which they would pass out of it, if they ever passed out; for greater dangers lay on the road behind them than before. The snow soon began to choke the arch. An hour more, and it lay so high as to block out half the returning daylight. But it froze hard now, as it fell, and could be clambered through or over. The violence of the mountain storm was gradually yielding to steady snowfall. The wind still raged at intervals, but not incessantly; and when it paused, the snow fell in heavy flakes.

They might have been two hours in their frightful prison, when Obenreizer, now crunching into the mound, now creeping over it with his head bowed down and his body touching the top of the arch, made his way out. Vendale followed close upon him, but followed without clear motive or calculation. For the lethargy of Basle was creeping over him again, and mastering his senses.

How far he had followed out of the gallery, or with what obstacles he had since contended, he knew not. He became roused to the knowledge that Obenreizer had set upon him, and that they were struggling desperately in the snow. He became roused to the remembrance of what his assailant carried in a girdle. He felt for it, drew it, struck at him, struggled again, struck at him again, cast him off, and stood face to face with him.

"I promised to guide you to your journey's end," said Obenreizer, "and I have kept my promise. The journey of your life ends here. Nothing can prolong it. You are sleeping as you stand."

"You are a villain. What have you done to me?"

"You are a fool. I have drugged you. You are doubly a fool, for I drugged you once before upon the journey, to try you. You are trebly a fool, for I am the thief and forger, and in a few moments I shall take those proofs against the thief and forger from your insensible body."

The entrapped man tried to throw off the lethargy, but its fatal hold upon him was so sure that, even while he heard those words, he stupidly wondered which of them had been wounded, and whose blood it was that he saw sprinkled on the snow.

"What have I done to you," he asked, heavily and thickly, "that you should be—so base—a murderer?"

"Done to me? You would have destroyed me, but that you have come to your journey's end. Your cursed activity interposed between me, and the time I had counted on in which I might have replaced the money. Done to me? You have come in my way—not once, not twice, but again and again and again. Did I try to shake you off in the beginning, or no? You were not to be shaken off. Therefore you die here."

Vendale tried to think coherently, tried to speak coherently, tried to pick up the iron-shod staff he had let fall; failing to touch it, tried to stagger on without its aid. All in vain, all in vain! He stumbled, and fell heavily forward on the brink of the deep chasm.

Stupefied, dozing, unable to stand upon his feet, a veil before his eyes, his sense of hearing deadened, he made such a vigorous rally that, supporting himself on his hands, he saw his enemy standing calmly over him, and heard him speak. "You call me murderer," said Obenreizer, with a grim laugh. "The name matters very little. But at least I have set my life against yours, for I am surrounded by dangers, and may never make my way out of this place. The *Tourmente* is rising again. The snow is on the whirl. I must have the papers now. Every moment has my life in it."

"Stop!" cried Vendale, in a terrible voice, staggering up with a last flash of fire breaking out of him, and clutching the thievish hands at his breast, in both of his.

"Stop! Stand away from me! God bless my Marguerite! Happily she will never know how I died. Stand off from me, and let me look at your murderous face. Let it remind me—of something—left to say."

The sight of him fighting so hard for his senses, and the doubt whether he might not for the instant be possessed by the strength of a dozen men, kept his opponent still. Wildly glaring at him, Vendale faltered out the broken words:

"It shall not be—the trust—of the dead—betrayed by me—reputed parents—misinherited fortune—see to it!"

As his head dropped on his breast, and he stumbled on the brink of the chasm as before, the thievish hands went once more, quick and busy, to his breast. He made a convulsive attempt to cry "No!" desperately rolled himself over into the gulf; and sank away from his enemy's touch, like a phantom in a dreadful dream.

The mountain storm raged again, and passed again. The awful mountain-voices died away, the moon rose, and the soft and silent snow fell.

Two men and two large dogs came out at the door of the Hospice. The men looked carefully around them, and up at the sky. The dogs rolled in the snow, and took it into their mouths, and cast it up with their paws.

One of the men said to the other: "We may venture now. We may find them in one of the five Refuges." Each fastened on his back a basket; each took in his hand a strong spiked pole; each girded under his arms a looped end of a stout rope, so that they were tied together.

Suddenly the dogs desisted from their gambols in the snow, stood looking down the ascent, put their noses up, put their noses down, became greatly excited, and broke into a deep loud bay together.

The two men looked in the faces of the two dogs. The two dogs looked, with at least equal intelligence, in the faces of the two men.

"Au secours, then! Help! To the rescue!" cried the two men. The two dogs, with a glad, deep, generous bark, bounded away.

"Two more mad ones!" said the men, stricken motionless, and looking away in the moonlight. "Is it possible in such weather! And one of them a woman!"

Each of the dogs had the corner of a woman's dress in its mouth, and drew her along. She fondled their heads as she came up, and she came up through the snow with an accustomed tread. Not so the large man with her, who was spent and winded.

"Dear guides, dear friends of travellers! I am of your country. We seek two gentlemen crossing the Pass, who should have reached the Hospice this evening."

"They have reached it, Ma'amselle."

"Thank Heaven! O thank Heaven!"

"But, unhappily, they have gone on again. We are setting forth to seek them even now. We had to wait until the *Tourmente* passed. It has been fearful up here."

"Dear guides, dear friends of travellers! Let me go with you. Let me go with you for the love of GOD! One of those gentlemen is to be my husband. I love him, O, so dearly. O so dearly! You see I am not faint, you see I am not tired. I am born a peasant girl. I will show you that I know well how to fasten myself to your ropes. I will do it with my own hands. I will swear to be brave and good. But let me go with you, let me go with you! If any mischance should have befallen him, my love would find him, when nothing else could. On my knees, dear friends of travellers! By the love your dear mothers had for your fathers!"

The good rough fellows were moved. "After all," they murmured to one another, "she speaks but the truth. She knows the ways of the mountains. See how marvellously she has come here. But as to Monsieur there, Ma'amselle?"

"Dear Mr. Joey," said Marguerite, addressing him in his own tongue, "you will remain at the house, and wait for me; will you not?"

"If I know'd which o' you two recommended it," growled Joey Ladle, eyeing the two men with great indignation, "I'd fight you for sixpence, and give you half-a-crown towards your expenses. No, Miss. I'll stick by you as long as there's any sticking left in me, and I'll die for you when I can't do better."

The state of the moon rendering it highly important that no time should be lost, and the dogs showing signs of great uneasiness, the two men quickly took their resolution. The rope that yoked them together was exchanged for a longer one; the party were secured, Marguerite second, and the Cellarman last; and they set out for the Refuges. The actual distance of those places was nothing: the whole five, and the next Hospice to boot, being within two miles; but the ghastly way was whitened out and sheeted over.

They made no miss in reaching the Gallery where the two had taken shelter. The second storm of wind and snow had so wildly swept over it since, that their tracks were gone. But the dogs went to and fro with their noses down, and were confident. The party stopping, however, at the further arch, where the second storm had been especially furious, and where the drift was deep, the dogs became troubled, and went about and about, in quest of a lost purpose.

The great abyss being known to lie on the right, they wandered too much to the left, and had to regain the way with infinite labour through a deep field of snow. The leader of the line had stopped it, and was taking note of the landmarks, when one of the dogs fell to tearing up the snow a little before them. Advancing and stooping to look at it, thinking that some one might be overwhelmed there, they saw that it was stained, and that the stain was red.

The other dog was now seen to look over the brink of the gulf, with his fore legs straightened out, lest he should fall into it, and to tremble in every limb. Then the dog who had found the stained snow joined him, and then they ran to and fro, distressed and whining. Finally, they both stopped on the brink together, and setting up their heads, howled dolefully.

"There is some one lying below," said Marguerite.

"I think so," said the foremost man. "Stand well inward, the two last, and let us look over."

The last man kindled two torches from his basket, and handed them forward. The leader taking one, and Marguerite the other, they looked down; now shading the torches, now moving them to the right or left, now raising them, now depressing them, as moonlight far below contended with black shadows. A piercing cry from Marguerite broke a long silence.

"My God! On a projecting point, where a wall of ice stretches forward over the torrent, I see a human form!"

"Where, Ma'amselle, where?"

"See, there! On the shelf of ice below the dogs!"

The leader, with a sickened aspect, drew inward, and they were all silent. But they were not all inactive, for Marguerite, with swift and skilful fingers, had detached both herself and him from the rope in a few seconds.

"Show me the baskets. These two are the only ropes?"

"The only ropes here, Ma'amselle; but at the Hospice—"

"If he is alive—I know it is my lover—he will be dead before you can return. Dear Guides! Blessed friends of travellers! Look at me. Watch my hands. If they falter or go wrong, make me your prisoner by force. If they are steady and go right, help me to save him!"

She girded herself with a cord under the breast and arms, she formed it into a kind of jacket, she drew it into knots, she laid its end side by side with the end of the other cord, she twisted and twined the two together, she knotted them together, she set her foot upon the knots, she strained them, she held them for the two men to strain at.

"She is inspired," they said to one another.

"By the Almighty's mercy!" she exclaimed. "You both know that I am by far the lightest here. Give me the brandy and the wine, and lower me down to him. Then go for assistance and a stronger rope. You see that when it is lowered to me—look at this about me now—I can make it fast and safe to his body. Alive or dead, I will bring him up, or die with him. I love him passionately. Can I say more?"

They turned to her companion, but he was lying senseless on the snow.

"Lower me down to him," she said, taking two little kegs they had brought, and hanging them about her, "or I will dash myself to pieces! I am a peasant, and I know no giddiness or fear; and this is nothing to me, and I passionately love him. Lower me down!"

"Ma'amselle, Ma'amselle, he must be dying or dead."

"Dying or dead, my husband's head shall lie upon my breast, or I will dash myself to pieces."

They yielded, overborne. With such precautions as their skill and the circumstances admitted, they let her slip from the summit, guiding herself down the precipitous icy wall with her hand, and they lowered down, and lowered down, and lowered down, until the cry came up: "Enough!"

"Is it really he, and is he dead?" they called down, looking over.

The cry came up: "He is insensible; but his heart beats. It beats against mine."

"How does he lie?"

The cry came up: "Upon a ledge of ice. It has thawed beneath him, and it will thaw beneath me. Hasten. If we die, I am content."

One of the two men hurried off with the dogs at such topmost speed as he could make; the other set up the lighted torches in the snow, and applied himself to recovering the Englishman. Much snow-chafing and some brandy got him on his legs, but delirious and quite unconscious where he was.

The watch remained upon the brink, and his cry went down continually: "Courage! They will soon be here. How goes it?" And the cry came up: "His heart still beats against mine. I warm him in my arms. I have cast off the rope, for the ice melts under us, and the rope would separate me from him; but I am not afraid."

The moon went down behind the mountain tops, and all the abyss lay in darkness. The cry went down: "How goes it?" The cry came up: "We are sinking lower, but his heart still beats against mine."

At length the eager barking of the dogs, and a flare of light upon the snow, proclaimed that help was coming on. Twenty or thirty men, lamps, torches, litters, ropes, blankets, wood to kindle a great fire, restoratives and stimulants, came in fast. The dogs ran from one man to another, and from this thing to that, and ran to the edge of the abyss, dumbly entreating Speed, speed, speed!

The cry went down: "Thanks to God, all is ready. How goes it?"

The cry came up: "We are sinking still, and we are deadly cold. His heart no longer beats against mine. Let no one come down, to add to our weight. Lower the rope only."

The fire was kindled high, a great glare of torches lighted the sides of the precipice, lamps were lowered, a strong rope was lowered. She could be seen passing it round him, and making it secure.

The cry came up into a deathly silence: "Raise! Softly!" They could see her diminished figure shrink, as he was swung into the air.

They gave no shout when some of them laid him on a litter, and others lowered another strong rope. The cry again came up into a deathly silence: "Raise! Softly!" But when they caught her at the brink, then they shouted, then they wept, then they gave thanks to Heaven, then they kissed her feet, then they kissed her dress, then the dogs caressed her, licked her icy hands, and with their honest faces warmed her frozen bosom!

She broke from them all, and sank over him on his litter, with both her loving hands upon the heart that stood still.

Act IV

The Clock-Lock

The pleasant scene was Neuchâtel; the pleasant month was April; the pleasant place was a notary's office; the pleasant person in it was the notary: a rosy, hearty, handsome old man, chief notary of Neuchâtel, known far and wide in the canton as Maître Voigt. Professionally and personally, the notary was a popular citizen. His innumerable kindnesses and his innumerable oddities had for years made him one of the recognised public characters of the pleasant Swiss town. His long brown frock-coat and his black skull-cap, were among the institutions of the place: and he carried a snuff-box which, in point of size, was popularly believed to be without a parallel in Europe.

There was another person in the notary's office, not so pleasant as the notary. This was Obenreizer.

An oddly pastoral kind of office it was, and one that would never have answered in England. It stood in a neat back yard, fenced off from a pretty flower-garden. Goats browsed in the doorway, and a cow was within half-a-dozen feet of keeping company with the clerk. Maître Voigt's room was a bright and varnished little room, with panelled walls, like a toy-chamber. According to the seasons of the year, roses, sunflowers, hollyhocks, peeped in at the windows. Maître Voigt's bees hummed through the office all the summer, in at this window and out at that, taking it frequently in their day's work, as if honey were to be made from Maître Voigt's sweet disposition. A large musical box on the chimney-piece often trilled away at the Overture to Fra Diavolo, or a Selection from William Tell, with a chirruping liveliness that had to be stopped by force on the entrance of a client, and irrepressibly broke out again the moment his back was turned.

"Courage, courage, my good fellow!" said Maître Voigt, patting Obenreizer on the knee, in a fatherly and comforting way. "You will begin a new life to-morrow morning in my office here."

Obenreizer—dressed in mourning, and subdued in manner—lifted his hand, with a white handkerchief in it, to the region of his heart. "The gratitude is here," he said. "But the words to express it are not here."

"Ta-ta-ta! Don't talk to me about gratitude!" said Maître Voigt. "I hate to see a man oppressed. I see you oppressed, and I hold out my hand to you by instinct. Besides, I am not too old yet, to remember my young days. Your father sent me my first client. (It was on a question of half an acre of vineyard that seldom bore any grapes.) Do I owe nothing to your father's son? I owe him a debt of friendly obligation, and I pay it to you. That's rather neatly expressed, I think," added Maître Voigt, in high good humour with himself. "Permit me to reward my own merit with a pinch of snuff!"

Obenreizer dropped his eyes to the ground, as though he were not even worthy to see the notary take snuff.

"Do me one last favour, Sir," he said, when he raised his eyes. "Do not act on impulse. Thus far, you have only a general knowledge of my position. Hear the case for and against me, in its details, before you take me into your office. Let my claim on your benevolence be recognised by your sound reason as well as by your excellent heart. In *that* case, I may hold up my head against the bitterest of my enemies, and build myself a new reputation on the ruins of the character I have lost."

"As you will," said Maître Voigt. "You speak well, my son. You will be a fine lawyer one of these days."

"The details are not many," pursued Obenreizer. "My troubles begin with the accidental death of my late travelling companion, my lost dear friend Mr. Vendale."

"Mr. Vendale," repeated the notary. "Just so. I have heard and read of the name, several times within these two months. The name of the unfortunate English gentleman who was killed on the Simplon. When you got that scar upon your cheek and neck."

"—From my own knife," said Obenreizer, touching what must have been an ugly gash at the time of its infliction.

"From your own knife," assented the notary, "and in trying to save him. Good, good, good. That was very good. Vendale. Yes. I have several times, lately, thought it droll that I should once have had a client of that name."

"But the world, Sir," returned Obenreizer, "is *so* small!" Nevertheless he made a mental note that the notary had once had a client of that name.

"As I was saying, Sir, the death of that dear travelling comrade begins my troubles. What follows? I save myself. I go down to Milan. I am received with coldness by Defresnier and Company. Shortly afterwards, I am discharged by Defresnier and Company. Why? They give no reason why. I ask, do they assail my honour? No answer. I ask, what is the imputation against me? No answer. I ask, where are their proofs against me? No answer. I ask, what am I to think? The reply is, 'M. Obenreizer is free to think what he will. What M. Obenreizer thinks, is of no importance to Defresnier and Company.' And that is all."

"Perfectly. That is all," asserted the notary, taking a large pinch of snuff.

"But is that enough, Sir?"

"That is not enough," said Maître Voigt. "The House of Defresnier are my fellow townsmen—much respected, much esteemed—but the House of Defresnier must not silently destroy a man's character. You can rebut assertion. But how can you rebut silence?"

"Your sense of justice, my dear patron," answered Obenreizer, "states in a word the cruelty of the case. Does it stop there? No. For, what follows upon that?"

"True, my poor boy," said the notary, with a comforting nod or two; "your ward rebels upon that."

"Rebels is too soft a word," retorted Obenreizer. "My ward revolts from me with horror. My ward defies me. My ward withdraws herself from my authority, and takes shelter (Madame Dor with her) in the house of that English lawyer, Mr. Bintrey, who replies to your summons to her to submit herself to my authority, that she will not do so."

"—And who afterwards writes," said the notary, moving his large snuff-box to look among the papers underneath it for the letter, "that he is coming to confer with me."

"Indeed?" replied Obenreizer, rather checked. "Well, Sir. Have I no legal rights?"

"Assuredly, my poor boy," returned the notary. "All but felons have their legal rights."

"And who calls me felon?" said Obenreizer, fiercely.

"No one. Be calm under your wrongs. If the House of Defresnier would call you felon, indeed, we should know how to deal with them."

While saying these words, he had handed Bintrey's very short letter to Obenreizer, who now read it and gave it back.

"In saying," observed Obenreizer, with recovered composure, "that he is coming to confer with you, this English lawyer means that he is coming to deny my authority over my ward."

"You think so?"

"I am sure of it. I know him. He is obstinate and contentious. You will tell me, my dear Sir, whether my authority is unassailable, until my ward is of age?"

"Absolutely unassailable."

"I will enforce it. I will make her submit herself to it. For," said Obenreizer, changing his angry tone to one of grateful submission, "I owe it to you, Sir; to you, who have so confidingly taken an injured man under your protection, and into your employment."

"Make your mind easy," said Maître Voigt. "No more of this now, and no thanks! Be here to-morrow morning, before the other clerk comes—between seven and eight. You will find me in this room; and I will myself initiate you in your work. Go away! go away! I have letters to write. I won't hear a word more."

Dismissed with this generous abruptness, and satisfied with the favourable impression he had left on the old man's mind, Obenreizer was at leisure to revert to the mental note he had made that Maître Voigt once had a client whose name was Vendale.

"I ought to know England well enough by this time"; so his meditations ran, as he sat on a bench in the yard; "and it is not a name I ever encountered there, except—" he looked involuntarily over his shoulder—"as *his* name. Is the world so small that I cannot get away from him, even now when he is dead? He confessed at the last that he had betrayed the trust of the dead, and misinherited a fortune. And I was to see to it. And I was to stand off, that my face might remind him of it. Why *my* face, unless it concerned *me*? I am sure of his words, for they have been in my ears ever since. Can there be anything bearing on them, in the keeping of this old idiot? Anything to repair my fortunes, and blacken his memory? He dwelt upon my earliest remembrances, that night at Basle. Why, unless he had a purpose in it?"

Maître Voigt's two largest he-goats were butting at him to butt him out of the place, as if for that disrespectful mention of their master. So he got up and left the place. But he walked alone for a long time on the border of the lake, with his head drooped in deep thought.

Between seven and eight next morning, he presented himself again at the office. He found the notary ready for him, at work on some papers which had come in on the previous evening. In a few clear words, Maître Voigt explained the routine of the office, and the duties Obenreizer would be expected to perform. It still wanted five minutes to eight, when the preliminary instructions were declared to be complete.

"I will show you over the house and the offices," said Maître Voigt, "but I must put away these papers first. They come from the municipal authorities, and they must be taken special care of."

Obenreizer saw his chance, here, of finding out the repository in which his employer's private papers were kept.

"Can't I save you the trouble, Sir?" he asked. "Can't I put those documents away under your directions?"

Maître Voigt laughed softly to himself; closed the portfolio in which the papers had been sent to him; handed it to Obenreizer.

"Suppose you try," he said. "All my papers of importance are kept yonder."

He pointed to a heavy oaken door, thickly studded with nails, at the lower end of the room. Approaching the door, with the portfolio, Obenreizer discovered, to his astonishment, that there were no means whatever of opening it from the outside. There was no handle, no bolt, no key, and (climax of passive obstruction!) no keyhole.

"There is a second door to this room?" said Obenreizer, appealing to the notary.

"No," said Maître Voigt. "Guess again."

"There is a window?"

"Nothing of the sort. The window has been bricked up. The only way in, is the way by that door. Do you give it up?" cried Maître Voigt, in high triumph. "Listen, my good fellow, and tell me if you hear nothing inside?"

Obenreizer listened for a moment, and started back from the door.

"I know!" he exclaimed. "I heard of this when I was apprenticed here at the watchmaker's. Perrin Brothers have finished their famous clock-lock at last—and you have got it?"

"Bravo!" said Maître Voigt. "The clock-lock it is! There, my son! There you have one more of what the good people of this town call, 'Daddy Voigt's follies.' With all my heart! Let those laugh who win. No thief can steal *my* keys. No burglar can pick *my* lock. No power on earth, short of a battering-ram or a barrel of gunpowder, can move that door, till my little sentinel inside—my worthy friend who goes 'Tick, Tick,' as I tell him—says, 'Open!' The big door obeys the little Tick, Tick, and the little Tick, Tick, obeys *me*. That!" cried Daddy Voigt, snapping his fingers, "for all the thieves in Christendom!"

"May I see it in action?" asked Obenreizer. "Pardon my curiosity, dear Sir! You know that I was once a tolerable worker in the clock trade."

"Certainly you shall see it in action," said Maître Voigt. "What is the time now? One minute to eight. Watch, and in one minute you will see the door open of itself."

In one minute, smoothly and slowly and silently, as if invisible hands had set it free, the heavy door opened inward, and disclosed a dark chamber beyond. On three sides, shelves filled the walls, from floor to ceiling. Arranged on the shelves, were rows upon rows of boxes made in the pretty inlaid woodwork of Switzerland, and bearing inscribed on their fronts (for the most part in fanciful coloured letters) the names of the notary's clients.

Maître Voigt lighted a taper, and led the way into the room.

"You shall see the clock," he said proudly. "I possess the greatest curiosity in Europe. It is only a privileged few whose eyes can look at it. I give the privilege to your good father's son—you shall be one of the favoured few who enter the room with me. See! here it is, on the right-hand wall at the side of the door."

"An ordinary clock," exclaimed Obenreizer. "No! Not an ordinary clock. It has only one hand."

"Aha!" said Maître Voigt. "Not an ordinary clock, my friend. No, no. That one hand goes round the dial. As I put it, so it regulates the hour at which the door shall open. See! The hand points to eight. At eight the door opened, as you saw for yourself."

"Does it open more than once in the four-and-twenty hours?" asked Obenreizer.

"More than once?" repeated the notary, with great scorn. "You don't know my good friend, Tick-Tick! He will open the door as often as I ask him. All he wants is his directions, and he gets them here. Look below the dial. Here is a half-circle of steel let into the wall, and here is a hand (called the regulator) that travels round it, just as *my* hand chooses. Notice, if you please, that there are figures to guide me on the half-circle of steel. Figure I. means: Open once in the four-and-twenty hours. Figure II. means: Open twice; and so on to the end. I set the regulator every morning, after I have read my letters, and when I know what my day's work is to be. Would you like to see me set it now? What is to-day? Wednesday. Good! This is the day of our rifle-club; there is little business to do; I grant a half-holiday. No work here to-day, after three o'clock. Let us first put away this portfolio of municipal papers. There! No need to trouble Tick-Tick to open the door until eight to-morrow. Good! I leave the dial-hand at eight; I put back the regulator to I.; I close the door; and closed the door remains, past all opening by anybody, till to-morrow morning at eight."

Obenreizer's quickness instantly saw the means by which he might make the clock-lock betray its master's confidence, and place its master's papers at his disposal.

"Stop, Sir!" he cried, at the moment when the notary was closing the door. "Don't I see something moving among the boxes—on the floor there?"

(Maître Voigt turned his back for a moment to look. In that moment, Obenreizer's ready hand put the regulator on, from the figure "I." to the figure "II." Unless the notary looked again at the half-circle of steel, the door would open at eight that evening, as well as at eight next morning, and nobody but Obenreizer would know it.)

"There is nothing!" said Maître Voigt. "Your troubles have shaken your nerves, my son. Some shadow thrown by my taper; or some poor little beetle, who lives among the old lawyer's secrets, running away from the light. Hark! I hear your fellow-clerk in the office. To work! to work! and build to-day the first step that leads to your new fortunes!"

He good-humouredly pushed Obenreizer out before him; extinguished the taper, with a last fond glance at his clock which passed harmlessly over the regulator beneath; and closed the oaken door.

At three, the office was shut up. The notary and everybody in the notary's employment, with one exception, went to see the rifle-shooting. Obenreizer had pleaded that he was not in spirits for a public festival. Nobody knew what had become of him. It was believed that he had slipped away for a solitary walk.

The house and offices had been closed but a few minutes, when the door of a shining wardrobe in the notary's shining room opened, and Obenreizer stopped out. He walked to a window, unclosed the shutters, satisfied himself that he could escape unseen by way of the garden, turned back into the room, and took his place in the notary's easy chair. He was locked up in the house, and there were five hours to wait before eight o'clock came.

He wore his way through the five hours: sometimes reading the books and newspapers that lay on the table: sometimes thinking: sometimes walking to and fro. Sunset came on. He closed the window-shutters before he kindled a light. The candle lighted, and the time drawing nearer and nearer, he sat, watch in hand, with his eyes on the oaken door.

At eight, smoothly and softly and silently the door opened.

One after another, he read the names on the outer rows of boxes. No such name as Vendale! He removed the outer row, and looked at the row behind. These were older boxes, and shabbier boxes. The four first that he examined, were inscribed with French and German names. The fifth bore a name which was almost illegible. He brought it out into the room, and examined it closely. There, covered thickly with time-stains and dust, was the name: "Vendale."

The key hung to the box by a string. He unlocked the box, took out four loose papers that were in it, spread them open on the table, and began to read them. He had not so occupied a minute, when his face fell from its expression of eagerness and avidity, to one of haggard astonishment and disappointment. But, after a little consideration, he copied the papers. He then replaced the papers, replaced the box, closed the door, extinguished the candle, and stole away.

As his murderous and thievish footfall passed out of the garden, the steps of the notary and some one accompanying him stopped at the front door of the house. The lamps were lighted in the little street, and the notary had his door-key in his hand.

"Pray do not pass my house, Mr. Bintrey," he said. "Do me the honour to come in. It is one of our town half-holidays—our Tir—but my people will be back directly. It is droll that you should ask your way to the Hotel of me. Let us eat and drink before you go there."

"Thank you; not to-night," said Bintrey. "Shall I come to you at ten to-morrow?"

"I shall be enchanted, Sir, to take so early an opportunity of redressing the wrongs of my injured client," returned the good notary.

"Yes," retorted Bintrey; "your injured client is all very well—but—a word in your ear."

He whispered to the notary and walked off. When the notary's housekeeper came home, she found him standing at his door motionless, with the key still in his hand, and the door unopened.

OBENREIZER'S VICTORY

The scene shifts again—to the foot of the Simplon, on the Swiss side.

In one of the dreary rooms of the dreary little inn at Brieg, Mr. Bintrey and Maître Voigt sat together at a professional council of two. Mr. Bintrey was searching in his dispatch-box. Maître Voigt was looking towards a closed door, painted brown to imitate mahogany, and communicating with an inner room.

"Isn't it time he was here?" asked the notary, shifting his position, and glancing at a second door at the other end of the room, painted yellow to imitate deal.

"He *is* here," answered Bintrey, after listening for a moment.

The yellow door was opened by a waiter, and Obenreizer walked in.

After greeting Maître Voigt with a cordiality which appeared to cause the notary no little embarrassment, Obenreizer bowed with grave and distant politeness to Bintrey. "For what reason have I been brought from Neuchâtel to the foot of the mountain?" he inquired, taking the seat which the English lawyer had indicated to him.

"You shall be quite satisfied on that head before our interview is over," returned Bintrey. "For the present, permit me to suggest proceeding at once to business. There has been a correspondence, Mr. Obenreizer, between you and your niece. I am here to represent your niece."

"In other words, you, a lawyer, are here to represent an infraction of the law."

"Admirably put!" said Bintrey. "If all the people I have to deal with were only like you, what an easy profession mine would be! I am here to represent an infraction of the law—that is your point of view. I am here to make a compromise between you and your niece—that is my point of view."

"There must be two parties to a compromise," rejoined Obenreizer. "I decline, in this case, to be one of them. The law gives me authority to control my niece's actions, until she comes of age. She is not yet of age; and I claim my authority."

At this point Maître attempted to speak. Bintrey silenced him with a compassionate indulgence of tone and manner, as if he was silencing a favourite child.

"No, my worthy friend, not a word. Don't excite yourself unnecessarily; leave it to me." He turned, and addressed himself again to Obenreizer. "I can think of nothing comparable to you, Mr. Obenreizer, but granite—and even that wears out in course of time. In the interests of peace and quietness—for the sake of your own dignity—relax a little. If you will only delegate your authority to another person whom I know of, that person may be trusted never to lose sight of your niece, night or day!"

"You are wasting your time and mine," returned Obenreizer. "If my niece is not rendered up to my authority within one week from this day, I invoke the law. If you resist the law, I take her by force."

He rose to his feet as he said the last word. Maître Voigt looked round again towards the brown door which led into the inner room.

"Have some pity on the poor girl," pleaded Bintrey. "Remember how lately she lost her lover by a dreadful death! Will nothing move you?"

"Nothing."

Bintrey, in his turn, rose to his feet, and looked at Maître Voigt. Maître Voigt's hand, resting on the table, began to tremble. Maître Voigt's eyes remained fixed, as if by irresistible fascination, on the brown door. Obenreizer, suspiciously observing him, looked that way too.

"There is somebody listening in there!" he exclaimed, with a sharp backward glance at Bintrey.

"There are two people listening," answered Bintrey.

"Who are they?"

"You shall see."

With this answer, he raised his voice and spoke the next words—the two common words which are on everybody's lips, at every hour of the day: "Come in!"

The brown door opened. Supported on Marguerite's arm—his sun-burnt colour gone, his right arm bandaged and clung over his breast—Vendale stood before the murderer, a man risen from the dead.

In the moment of silence that followed, the singing of a caged bird in the courtyard outside was the one sound stirring in the room. Maître Voigt touched Bintrey, and pointed to Obenreizer. "Look at him!" said the notary, in a whisper.

The shock had paralysed every movement in the villain's body, but the movement of the blood. His face was like the face of a corpse. The one vestige of colour left in it was a livid purple streak which marked the course of the scar where his victim had wounded him on the cheek and neck. Speechless, breathless, motionless alike in eye and limb, it seemed as if, at the sight of Vendale, the death to which he had doomed Vendale had struck him where he stood.

"Somebody ought to speak to him," said Maître Voigt. "Shall I?"

Even at that moment Bintrey persisted in silencing the notary, and in keeping the lead in the proceedings to himself. Checking Maître Voigt by a gesture, he dismissed Marguerite and Vendale in these words:—"The object of your appearance here is answered," he said. "If you will withdraw for the present, it may help Mr. Obenreizer to recover himself."

It did help him. As the two passed through the door and closed it behind them, he drew a deep breath of relief. He looked round him for the chair from which he had risen, and dropped into it.

"Give him time!" pleaded Maître Voigt.

"No," said Bintrey. "I don't know what use he may make of it if I do." He turned once more to Obenreizer, and went on. "I owe it to myself," he said—"I don't admit, mind, that I owe it to you—to account for my appearance in these proceedings, and to state what has been done under my advice, and on my sole responsibility. Can you listen to me?"

"I can listen to you."

"Recall the time when you started for Switzerland with Mr. Vendale," Bintrey begin. "You had not left England four-and-twenty hours before your niece committed an act of imprudence which not even your penetration could foresee. She followed her promised husband on his journey, without asking anybody's advice or permission, and without any better companion to protect her than a Cellarman in Mr. Vendale's employment."

"Why did she follow me on the journey? and how came the Cellarman to be the person who accompanied her?"

"She followed you on the journey," answered Bintrey, "because she suspected there had been some serious collision between you and Mr. Vendale, which had been kept secret from her; and because she rightly believed you to be capable of serving your interests, or of satisfying your enmity, at the price of a crime. As for the Cellarman, he was one, among the other people in Mr. Vendale's establishment, to whom she had applied (the moment your back was turned) to know if anything had happened between their master and you. The Cellarman alone had something to tell her. A senseless superstition, and a common accident which had happened to his master, in his master's cellar, had connected Mr. Vendale in this man's mind with the idea of danger by murder. Your niece surprised him into a confession, which aggravated tenfold the terrors that possessed her. Aroused to a sense of the mischief he had done, the man, of his own accord, made the one atonement in his power. 'If my master is in danger, miss,' he said, 'it's my duty to follow him, too; and it's more than my duty to take care of *you*.' The two set forth together—and, for once, a superstition has had its use. It decided your niece on taking the journey; and it led the way to saving a man's life. Do you understand me, so far?"

"I understand you, so far."

"My first knowledge of the crime that you had committed," pursued Bintrey, "came to me in the form of a letter from your niece. All you need know is that her love and her courage recovered the body of your victim, and aided the after-efforts which brought him back to life. While he lay helpless at Brieg, under her care, she wrote to me to come out to him. Before starting, I informed Madame Dor that I knew Miss Obenreizer to be safe, and knew where she was. Madame Dor informed me, in return, that a letter had come for your niece, which she knew to be in your handwriting. I took possession of it, and arranged for the forwarding of any other letters which might follow. Arrived at Brieg, I found Mr. Vendale out of danger, and at once devoted myself to hastening the day of reckoning with you. Defresnier and Company turned you off on suspicion; acting on information privately supplied by me. Having stripped you of your false character, the next thing to do was to strip you of your authority over your niece. To reach this end, I not only had no scruple in digging the pitfall under your feet in the dark—I felt a certain professional pleasure in fighting you with your own weapons. By my advice the truth has been carefully concealed from you up to this day. By my advice the trap into which you have walked was set for you (you know why, now, as well as I do) in this place. There was but one certain way of shaking the devilish self-control which has hitherto made you a formidable man. That way has been tried, and (look at me as you may) that way has succeeded. The last thing that remains to be done," concluded Bintrey, producing two little slips of manuscript from his dispatch-box, "is to set your niece free. You have attempted murder, and you have committed forgery and theft. We have the evidence ready against you in both cases. If you are convicted as a felon, you know as well as I do what becomes of your authority over your niece. Personally, I should have preferred taking that way out of it. But considerations are pressed on me which I am not able to resist, and this interview must end, as I have told you already, in a compromise. Sign those lines, resigning all authority over Miss Obenreizer, and pledging yourself never to be seen in England or in Switzerland again; and I will sign an indemnity which secures you against further proceedings on our part."

Obenreizer took the pen in silence, and signed his niece's release. On receiving the indemnity in return, he rose, but made no movement to leave the room. He stood looking at Maître Voigt with a strange smile gathering at his lips, and a strange light flashing in his filmy eyes.

"What are you waiting for?" asked Bintrey.

Obenreizer pointed to the brown door. "Call them back," he answered. "I have something to say in their presence before I go."

"Say it in my presence," retorted Bintrey. "I decline to call them back."

Obenreizer turned to Maître Voigt. "Do you remember telling me that you once had an English client named Vendale?" he asked.

"Well," answered the notary. "And what of that?"

"Maître Voigt, your clock-lock has betrayed you."

"What do you mean?"

"I have read the letters and certificates in your client's box. I have taken copies of them. I have got the copies here. Is there, or is there not, a reason for calling them back?"

For a moment the notary looked to and fro, between Obenreizer and Bintrey, in helpless astonishment. Recovering himself, he drew his brother-lawyer aside, and hurriedly spoke a few words close at his ear. The face of Bintrey—after first faithfully reflecting the astonishment on the face of Maître Voigt—suddenly altered its expression. He sprang, with the activity of a young man, to the door of the inner room, entered it, remained inside for a minute, and returned followed by Marguerite and Vendale. "Now, Mr. Obenreizer," said Bintrey, "the last move in the game is yours. Play it."

"Before I resign my position as that young lady's guardian," said Obenreizer, "I have a secret to reveal in which she is interested. In making my disclosure, I am not claiming her attention for a narrative which she, or any other person present, is expected to take on trust. I am possessed of written proofs, copies of originals, the authenticity of which Maître Voigt himself can attest. Bear that in mind, and permit me to refer you, at starting, to a date long past—the month of February, in the year one thousand eight hundred and thirty-six."

"Mark the date, Mr. Vendale," said Bintrey.

"My first proof," said Obenreizer, taking a paper from his pocket-book. "Copy of a letter, written by an English lady (married) to her sister, a widow. The name of the person writing the letter I shall keep suppressed until I have done. The name of the person to whom the letter is written I am willing to reveal. It is addressed to 'Mrs. Jane Anne Miller, of Groombridge-wells, England.'"

Vendale started, and opened his lips to speak. Bintrey instantly stopped him, as he had stopped Maître Voigt. "No," said the pertinacious lawyer. "Leave it to me."

Obenreizer went on:

"It is needless to trouble you with the first half of the letter," he said. "I can give the substance of it in two words. The writer's position at the time is this. She has been long living in Switzerland with her husband—obliged to live there for the sake of her husband's health. They are about to move to a new residence on the Lake of Neuchâtel in a week, and they will be ready to receive Mrs. Miller as visitor in a fortnight from that time. This said, the writer next enters into an important domestic detail. She has been childless for years—she and her husband have now no hope of children; they are lonely; they want an interest in life; they have decided on adopting a child. Here the important part of the letter begins; and here, therefore, I read it to you word for word."

He folded back the first page of the letter and read as follows:

"* * * Will you help us, my dear sister, to realise our new project? As English people, we wish to adopt an English child. This may be done, I believe, at the Foundling: my husband's lawyers in London will tell you how. I leave the choice to you, with only these conditions attached to it—that the child is to be an infant under a year old, and is to be a boy. Will you pardon the trouble I am giving you, for my sake; and will you bring our adopted child to us, with your own children, when you come to Neuchâtel?

"I must add a word as to my husband's wishes in this matter. He is resolved to spare the child whom we make our own any future mortification and loss of self-respect which might be caused by a discovery of his true origin. He will bear my husband's name, and he will be brought up in the belief that he is really our son. His inheritance of what we have to leave will be secured to him—not only according to the laws of England in such cases, but according to the laws of Switzerland also; for we have lived so long in this country, that there is a doubt whether we may not be considered as I domiciled, in Switzerland. The one precaution left to take is to prevent any after-discovery at the Foundling. Now, our name is a very uncommon one; and if we appear on the Register of the Institution as the persons adopting the child, there is just a chance that something might result from it. Your name, my dear, is the name of thousands of other people; and if you will consent to appear on the Register, there need be no fear of any discoveries in that quarter. We are moving, by the doctor's orders, to a part of Switzerland in which our circumstances are quite unknown; and you, as I understand, are about to engage a new nurse for the journey when you come to see us. Under these circumstances, the child may appear as my child, brought back to me under my sister's care. The only servant we take with us from our old home is my own maid, who can be safely trusted. As for the lawyers in England and in Switzerland, it is their profession to keep secrets—and we may feel quite easy in that direction. So there you have our harmless little conspiracy! Write by return of post, my love, and tell me you will join it." * * *

"Do you still conceal the name of the writer of that letter?" asked Vendale.

"I keep the name of the writer till the last," answered Obenreizer, "and I proceed to my second proof—a mere slip of paper this time, as you see. Memorandum given to the Swiss lawyer, who drew the documents referred to in the letter I have just read, expressed as follows:—'Adopted from the Foundling Hospital of England, 3d March, 1836, a male infant, called, in the Institution, Walter Wilding. Person appearing on the register, as adopting the child, Mrs. Jane Anne Miller, widow, acting in this matter for her married sister, domiciled in Switzerland.' Patience!" resumed Obenreizer, as Vendale, breaking loose from Bintrey, started to his feet. "I shall not keep the name concealed much longer. Two more little slips of paper, and I have done. Third proof! Certificate of Doctor Ganz, still living in practice at Neuchâtel, dated July, 1838. The doctor certifies (you shall read it for yourselves directly), first, that he attended the adopted child in its infant maladies; second, that, three months before the date of the certificate, the gentleman adopting the child as his son died; third, that on the date of the certificate, his widow and her maid, taking the adopted child with them, left Neuchâtel on their return to England. One more link now added to this, and my chain of evidence is complete. The maid remained with her mistress till her mistress's death, only a few years since. The maid can swear to the identity of the adopted infant, from his childhood to his youth—from his youth to his manhood, as he is now. There is her address in England—and there, Mr. Vendale, is the fourth, and final proof!"

"Why do you address yourself to *me*?" said Vendale, as Obenreizer threw the written address on the table.

Obenreizer turned on him, in a sudden frenzy of triumph.

"*Because you are the man!* If my niece marries you, she marries a bastard, brought up by public charity. If my niece marries you, she marries an impostor, without name or lineage, disguised in the character of a gentleman of rank and family."

"Bravo!" cried Bintrey. "Admirably put, Mr. Obenreizer! It only wants one word more to complete it. She marries—thanks entirely to your exertions—a man who inherits a handsome fortune, and a man whose origin will make him prouder than ever of his peasant-wife. George Vendale, as brother-executors, let us congratulate each other! Our dear dead friend's last wish on earth is accomplished. We have found the lost Walter Wilding. As Mr. Obenreizer said just now—you are the man!"

The words passed by Vendale unheeded. For the moment he was conscious of but one sensation; he heard but one voice. Marguerite's hand was clasping his. Marguerite's voice was whispering to him: "I never loved you, George, as I love you now!"

THE CURTAIN FALLS

May-day. There is merry-making in Cripple Corner, the chimneys smoke, the patriarchal dining-hall is hung with garlands, and Mrs. Goldstraw, the respected housekeeper, is very busy. For, on this bright morning the young master of Cripple Corner is married to its young mistress, far away: to wit, in the little town of Brieg, in Switzerland, lying at the foot of the Simplon Pass where she saved his life.

The bells ring gaily in the little town of Brieg, and flags are stretched across the street, and rifle shots are heard, and sounding music from brass instruments. Streamer-decorated casks of wine have been rolled out under a gay awning in the public way before the Inn, and there will be free feasting and revelry. What with bells and banners, draperies hanging from windows, explosion of gunpowder, and reverberation of brass music, the little town of Brieg is all in a flutter, like the hearts of its simple people.

It was a stormy night last night, and the mountains are covered with snow. But the sun is bright to-day, the sweet air is fresh, the tin spires of the little town of Brieg are burnished silver, and the Alps are ranges of far-off white cloud in a deep blue sky.

The primitive people of the little town of Brieg have built a greenwood arch across the street, under which the newly married pair shall pass in triumph from the church. It is inscribed, on that side, "Honour and Love to Marguerite Vendale!" for the people are proud of her to enthusiasm. This greeting of the bride under her new name is affectionately meant as a surprise, and therefore the arrangement has been made that she, unconscious why, shall be taken to the church by a tortuous back way. A scheme not difficult to carry into execution in the crooked little town of Brieg.

So, all things are in readiness, and they are to go and come on foot. Assembled in the Inn's best chamber, festively adorned, are the bride and bridegroom, the Neuchâtel notary, the London lawyer, Madame Dor, and a certain large mysterious Englishman, popularly known as Monsieur Zhoé-Ladelle. And behold Madame Dor, arrayed in a spotless pair of gloves of her own, with no hand in the air, but both hands clasped round the neck of the bride; to embrace whom Madame Dor has turned her broad back on the company, consistent to the last.

"Forgive me, my beautiful," pleads Madame Dor, "for that I ever was his she-cat!"

"She-cat, Madame Dor?"

"Engaged to sit watching my so charming mouse," are the explanatory words of Madame Dor, delivered with a penitential sob.

"Why, you were our best friend! George, dearest, tell Madame Dor. Was she not our best friend?"

"Undoubtedly, darling. What should we have done without her?"

"You are both so generous," cries Madame Dor, accepting consolation, and immediately relapsing. "But I commenced as a she-cat."

"Ah! But like the cat in the fairy-story, good Madame Dor," says Vendale, saluting her cheek, "you were a true woman. And, being a true woman, the sympathy of your heart was with true love."

"I don't wish to deprive Madame Dor of her share in the embraces that are going on," Mr. Bintrey puts in, watch in hand, "and I don't presume to offer any objection to your having got yourselves mixed together, in the corner there, like the three Graces. I merely remark that I think it's time we were moving. What are *your* sentiments on that subject, Mr. Ladle?"

"Clear, Sir," replies Joey, with a gracious grin. "I'm clearer altogether, sir, for having lived so many weeks upon the surface. I never was half so long upon the surface afore, and it's done me a power of good. At Cripple Corner, I was too much below it. Atop of the Simpleton, I was a deal too high above it. I've found the medium here, Sir. And if ever I take it in convivial, in all the rest of my days, I mean to do it this day, to the toast of 'Bless 'em both.'"

"I, too!" says Bintrey. "And now, Monsieur Voigt, let you and me be two men of Marseilles, and allons, marchons, arm-in-arm!"

They go down to the door, where others are waiting for them, and they go quietly to the church, and the happy marriage takes place. While the ceremony is yet in progress, the notary is called out. When it is finished, he has returned, is standing behind Vendale, and touches him on the shoulder.

"Go to the side door, one moment, Monsieur Vendale. Alone. Leave Madame to me."

At the side door of the church, are the same two men from the Hospice. They are snow-stained and travel-worn. They wish him joy, and then each lays his broad hand upon Vendale's breast, and one says in a low voice, while the other steadfastly regards him:

"It is here, Monsieur. Your litter. The very same."

"My litter is here? Why?"

"Hush! For the sake of Madame. Your companion of that day—"

"What of him?"

The man looks at his comrade, and his comrade takes him up. Each keeps his hand laid earnestly on Vendale's breast.

"He had been living at the first Refuge, Monsieur, for some days. The weather was now good, now bad."

"Yes?"

"He arrived at our Hospice the day before yesterday, and, having refreshed himself with sleep on the floor before the fire, wrapped in his cloak, was resolute to go on, before dark, to the next Hospice. He had a great fear of that part of the way, and thought it would be worse to-morrow."

"Yes?"

"He went on alone. He had passed the gallery when an avalanche—like that which fell behind you near the Bridge of the Ganther—"

"Killed him?"

"We dug him out, suffocated and broken all to pieces! But, Monsieur, as to Madame. We have brought him here on the litter, to be buried. We must ascend the street outside. Madame must not see. It would be an accursed thing to bring the litter through the arch across the street, until Madame has passed through. As you descend, we who accompany the litter will set it down on the stones of the street the second to the right, and will stand before it. But do not let Madame turn her head towards the street the second to the right. There is no time to lose. Madame will be alarmed by your absence. Adieu!"

Vendale returns to his bride, and draws her hand through his unmaimed arm. A pretty procession awaits them at the main door of the church. They take their station in it, and descend the street amidst the ringing of the bells, the firing of the guns, the waving of the flags, the playing of the music, the shouts, the smiles, and tears, of the excited town. Heads are uncovered as she passes, hands are kissed to her, all the people bless her. "Heaven's benediction on the dear girl! See where she goes in her youth and beauty; she who so nobly saved his life!"

Near the corner of the street the second to the right, he speaks to her, and calls her attention to the windows on the opposite side. The corner well passed, he says: "Do not look round, my darling, for a reason that I have," and turns his head. Then, looking back along the street, he sees the litter and its bearers passing up alone under the arch, as he and she and their marriage train go down towards the shining valley.

The Lazy Tour of Two Idle Apprentices

(Written with Wilkie Collins)

Chapter I

IN THE AUTUMN MONTH OF SEPTEMBER, EIGHTEEN HUNDRED AND FIFTY-SEVEN, wherein these presents bear date, two idle apprentices, exhausted by the long, hot summer, and the long, hot work it had brought with it, ran away from their employer. They were bound to a highly meritorious lady (named Literature), of fair credit and repute, though, it must be acknowledged, not quite so highly esteemed in the City as she might be. This is the more remarkable, as there is nothing against the respectable lady in that quarter, but quite the contrary; her family having rendered eminent service to many famous citizens of London. It may be sufficient to name Sir William Walworth, Lord Mayor under King Richard II., at the time of Wat Tyler's insurrection, and Sir Richard Whittington: which latter distinguished man and magistrate was doubtless indebted to the lady's family for the gift of his celebrated cat. There is also strong reason to suppose that they rang the Highgate bells for him with their own hands.

The misguided young men who thus shirked their duty to the mistress from whom they had received many favours, were actuated by the low idea of making a perfectly idle trip, in any direction. They had no intention of going anywhere in particular; they wanted to see nothing, they wanted to know nothing, they wanted to learn nothing, they wanted to do nothing. They wanted only to be idle. They took to themselves (after HOGARTH), the names of Mr. Thomas Idle and Mr. Francis Goodchild; but there was not a moral pin to choose between them, and they were both idle in the last degree.

Between Francis and Thomas, however, there was this difference of character: Goodchild was laboriously idle, and would take upon himself any amount of pains and labour to assure himself that he was idle; in short, had no better idea of idleness than that it was useless industry. Thomas Idle, on the other hand, was an idler of the unmixed Irish or Neapolitan type; a passive idler, a born-and-bred idler, a consistent idler, who practised what he would have preached if he had not been too idle to preach; a one entire and perfect chrysolite of idleness.

The two idle apprentices found themselves, within a few hours of their escape, walking down into the North of England, that is to say, Thomas was lying in a meadow, looking at the railway trains as they passed over a distant viaduct—which was *his* idea of walking down into the North; while Francis was walking a mile due South against time—which was *his* idea of walking down into the North. In the meantime the day waned, and the milestones remained unconquered.

"Tom," said Goodchild, "the sun is getting low. Up, and let us go forward!"

"Nay," quoth Thomas Idle, "I have not done with Annie Laurie yet." And he proceeded with that idle but popular ballad, to the effect that for the bonnie young person of that name he would 'lay him doon and dee'—equivalent, in prose, to lay him down and die.

"What an ass that fellow was!" cried Goodchild, with the bitter emphasis of contempt.

"Which fellow?" asked Thomas Idle.

"The fellow in your song. Lay him doon and dee! Finely he'd show off before the girl by doing *that*. A sniveller! Why couldn't he get up, and punch somebody's head!"

"Whose?" asked Thomas Idle.

"Anybody's. Everybody's would be better than nobody's! If I fell into that state of mind about a girl, do you think I'd lay me doon and dee? No, Sir," proceeded Goodchild, with a disparaging assumption of the Scottish accent, "I'd get me oop and peetch into somebody. Wouldn't you?"

"I wouldn't have anything to do with her," yawned Thomas Idle. "Why should I take the trouble?"

"It's no trouble, Tom, to fall in love," said Goodchild, shaking his head.

"It's trouble enough to fall out of it, once you're in it," retorted Tom. "So I keep out of it altogether. It would be better for you, if you did the same."

Mr. Goodchild, who is always in love with somebody, and not unfrequently with several objects at once, made no reply. He heaved a sigh of the kind which is termed by the lower orders "a bellowser," and then, heaving Mr. Idle on his feet (who was not half so heavy as the sigh), urged him northward.

These two had sent their personal baggage on by train: only retaining each a knapsack. Idle now applied himself to constantly regretting the train, to tracking it through the intricacies of Bradshaw's Guide, and finding out where it is now—and where now—and where now—and to asking what was the use of walking, when you could ride at such a pace as that. Was it to see the country? If that was the object, look at it out of the carriage windows. There was a great deal more of it to be seen there than here. Besides, who wanted to see the country? Nobody. And again, whoever did walk? Nobody. Fellows set off to walk, but they never did it. They came back and said they did, but they didn't. Then why should he walk? He wouldn't walk. He swore it by this milestone!

It was the fifth from London, so far had they penetrated into the North. Submitting to the powerful chain of argument, Goodchild proposed a return to the Metropolis, and a falling back upon Euston Square Terminus. Thomas assented with alacrity, and so they walked down into the North by the next morning's express, and carried their knapsacks in the luggage-van.

It was like all other expresses, as every express is and must be. It bore through the harvest country a smell like a large washing-day, and a sharp issue of steam as from a huge brazen tea-urn. The greatest power in nature and art combined, it yet glided over dangerous heights in the sight of people looking up from fields and roads, as smoothly and unreally as a light miniature plaything. Now, the engine shrieked in hysterics of such intensity, that it seemed desirable that the men who had her in charge should hold her feet, slap her hands, and bring her to; now, burrowed into tunnels with a stubborn and undemonstrative energy so confusing that the train seemed to be flying back into leagues of darkness. Here, were station after station, swallowed up by the express without stopping; here, stations where it fired itself in like a volley of cannon-balls, swooped away four country-people with nosegays, and three men of business with portmanteaus, and fired itself off again, bang, bang, bang! At long intervals were uncomfortable refreshment-rooms, made more uncomfortable by the scorn of Beauty towards Beast, the public (but to whom she never relented, as Beauty did in the story, towards the other Beast), and where sensitive stomachs were fed, with a contemptuous sharpness occasioning indigestion. Here, again, were stations with nothing going but a bell, and wonderful wooden razors set aloft on great posts, shaving the air. In these fields, the horses, sheep, and cattle were well used to the thundering meteor, and didn't mind; in those, they were all set scampering together, and a herd of pigs scoured after them. The pastoral country darkened, became coaly, became smoky, became infernal, got better, got worse, improved again, grew rugged, turned romantic; was a wood, a stream, a chain of hills, a gorge, a moor, a cathedral town, a fortified place, a waste. Now, miserable black dwellings, a black canal, and sick black towers of chimneys; now, a trim garden, where the flowers were bright and fair; now, a wilderness of hideous altars all a-blaze; now, the water meadows with their fairy rings; now, the mangy patch of unlet building ground outside the stagnant town, with the larger ring where the Circus was last week. The temperature changed, the dialect changed, the people changed, faces got sharper, manner got shorter, eyes got shrewder and harder; yet all so quickly, that the spruce guard in the London uniform and silver lace, had not yet rumpled his shirt-collar, delivered half the dispatches in his shiny little pouch, or read his newspaper.

Carlisle! Idle and Goodchild had got to Carlisle. It looked congenially and delightfully idle. Something in the way of public amusement had happened last month, and something else was going to happen before Christmas; and, in the meantime there was a lecture on India for those who liked it—which Idle and Goodchild did not. Likewise, by those who liked them, there were impressions to be bought of all the vapid prints, going and gone, and of nearly all the vapid books. For those who wanted to put anything in missionary boxes, here were the boxes. For those who wanted the Reverend Mr. Podgers (artist's proofs, thirty shillings), here was Mr. Podgers to any amount. Not less gracious and abundant, Mr. Codgers also of the vineyard, but opposed to Mr. Podgers, brotherly tooth and nail. Here, were guide-books to the neighbouring antiquities, and eke the Lake country, in several dry and husky sorts; here, many physically and morally impossible heads of both sexes, for young ladies to copy, in the exercise of the art of drawing; here, further, a large impression of MR. SPURGEON, solid as to the flesh, not to say even something gross. The working young men of Carlisle were drawn up, with their hands in their pockets, across the pavements, four and six abreast, and appeared (much to the satisfaction of Mr. Idle) to have nothing else to do. The working and growing young women of Carlisle, from the age of twelve upwards, promenaded the streets in the cool of the evening, and rallied the said young men. Sometimes the young men rallied the young women, as in the case of a group gathered round an accordion-player, from among whom a young man advanced behind a young woman for whom he appeared to have a tenderness, and hinted to her that he was there and playful, by giving her (he wore clogs) a kick.

On market morning, Carlisle woke up amazingly, and became (to the two Idle Apprentices) disagreeably and reproachfully busy. There were its cattle market, its sheep market, and its pig market down by the river, with raw-boned and shock-headed Rob Roys hiding their Lowland dresses beneath heavy plaids, prowling in and out among the animals, and flavouring the air with fumes of whiskey. There was its corn market down the main street, with hum of chaffering over open sacks. There was its general market in the street too, with heather brooms on which the purple flower still flourished, and heather baskets primitive and fresh to behold. With women trying on clogs and caps at open stalls, and "Bible stalls" adjoining. With "Doctor Mantle's Dispensary for the cure of all Human Maladies and no charge for advice," and with Doctor Mantle's "Laboratory of Medical, Chemical, and Botanical Science"—both healing institutions established on one pair of trestles, one board, and one sun-blind. With the renowned phrenologist from London, begging to be favoured (at sixpence each) with the company of clients of both sexes, to whom, on examination of their heads, he would make revelations "enabling him or her to know themselves." Through all these bargains and blessings, the recruiting-sergeant watchfully elbowed his way, a thread of War in the peaceful skein. Likewise on the walls were printed hints that the Oxford Blues might not be indisposed to hear of a few fine active young men; and that whereas the standard of that distinguished corps is full six feet, "growing lads of five feet eleven" need not absolutely despair of being accepted.

Scenting the morning air more pleasantly than the buried majesty of Denmark did, Messrs. Idle and Goodchild rode away from Carlisle at eight o'clock one forenoon, bound for the village of Hesket, Newmarket, some fourteen miles distant. Goodchild (who had already begun to doubt whether he was idle: as his way always is when he has nothing to do) had read of a certain black old Cumberland hill or mountain, called Carrock, or Carrock Fell; and had arrived at the conclusion that it would be the culminating triumph of Idleness to ascend the same. Thomas Idle, dwelling on the pains inseparable from that achievement, had expressed the strongest doubts of the expediency, and even of the sanity, of the enterprise; but Goodchild had carried his point, and they rode away.

Up hill and down hill, and twisting to the right, and twisting to the left, and with old Skiddaw (who has vaunted himself a great deal more than his merits deserve; but that is rather the way of the Lake country), dodging the apprentices in a picturesque and pleasant manner. Good, weather-proof, warm, pleasant houses, well white-limed, scantily dotting the road. Clean children coming out to look, carrying other clean children as big as themselves. Harvest still lying out and much rained upon; here and there, harvest still unreaped. Well-cultivated gardens attached to the cottages, with plenty of produce forced out of their hard soil. Lonely nooks, and wild; but people can be born, and married, and buried in such nooks, and can live and love, and be loved, there as elsewhere, thank God! (Mr. Goodchild's remark.) By-and-by, the village. Black, coarse-stoned, rough-windowed houses; some with outer staircases, like Swiss houses; a sinuous and stony gutter winding up hill and round the corner, by way of street. All the children running out directly. Women pausing in washing, to peep from doorways and very little windows. Such were the observations of Messrs. Idle and Goodchild, as their conveyance stopped at the village shoemaker's. Old Carrock gloomed down upon it all in a very ill-tempered state; and rain was beginning.

The village shoemaker declined to have anything to do with Carrock. No visitors went up Carrock. No visitors came there at all. Aa' the world ganged awa' yon. The driver appealed to the Innkeeper. The Innkeeper had two men working in the fields, and one of them should be called in, to go up Carrock as guide. Messrs. Idle and Goodchild, highly approving, entered the Innkeeper's house, to drink whiskey and eat oatcake.

The Innkeeper was not idle enough—was not idle at all, which was a great fault in him—but was a fine specimen of a north-country man, or any kind of man.

He had a ruddy cheek, a bright eye, a well-knit frame, an immense hand, a cheery, outspeaking voice, and a straight, bright, broad look. He had a drawing-room, too, upstairs, which was worth a visit to the Cumberland Fells. (This was Mr. Francis Goodchild's opinion, in which Mr. Thomas Idle did not concur.)

The ceiling of this drawing-room was so crossed and recrossed by beams of unequal lengths, radiating from a centre, in a corner, that it looked like a broken star-fish. The room was comfortably and solidly furnished with good mahogany and horsehair. It had a snug fireside, and a couple of well-curtained windows, looking out upon the wild country behind the house. What it most developed was, an unexpected taste for little ornaments and nick-nacks, of which it contained a most surprising number. They were not very various, consisting in great part of waxen babies with their limbs more or less mutilated, appealing on one leg to the parental affections from under little cupping glasses; but, Uncle Tom was there, in crockery, receiving theological instructions from Miss Eva, who grew out of his side like a wen, in an exceedingly rough state of profile propagandism. Engravings of Mr. Hunt's country boy, before and after his pie, were on the wall, divided by a highly-coloured nautical piece, the subject of which had all her colours (and more) flying, and was making great way through a sea of a regular pattern, like a lady's collar. A benevolent, elderly gentleman of the last century, with a powdered head, kept guard, in oil and varnish, over a most perplexing piece of furniture on a table; in appearance between a driving seat and an angular knife-box, but, when opened, a musical instrument of tinkling wires, exactly like David's harp packed for travelling. Everything became a nick-nack in this curious room. The copper tea-kettle, burnished up to the highest point of glory, took his station on a stand of his own at the greatest possible distance from the fireplace, and said: "By your leave, not a kettle, but a bijou." The Staffordshire-ware butter-dish with the cover on, got upon a little round occasional table in a window, with a worked top, and announced itself to the two chairs accidentally placed there, as an aid to polite conversation, a graceful trifle in china to be chatted over by callers, as they airily trifled away the visiting moments of a butterfly existence, in that rugged old village on the Cumberland Fells. The very footstool could not keep the floor, but got upon a sofa, and there-from proclaimed itself, in high relief of white and liver-coloured wool, a favourite spaniel coiled up for repose. Though, truly, in spite of its bright glass eyes, the spaniel was the least successful assumption in the collection: being perfectly flat, and dismally suggestive of a recent mistake in sitting down on the part of some corpulent member of the family.

There were books, too, in this room; books on the table, books on the chimney-piece, books in an open press in the corner. Fielding was there, and Smollett was there, and Steele and Addison were there, in dispersed volumes; and there were tales of those who go down to the sea in ships, for windy nights; and there was really a choice of good books for rainy days or fine. It was so very pleasant to see these things in such a lonesome by-place—so very agreeable to find these evidences of a taste, however homely, that went beyond the beautiful cleanliness and trimness of the house—so fanciful to imagine what a wonder a room must be to the little children born in the gloomy village—what grand impressions of it those of them who became wanderers over the earth would carry away; and how, at distant ends of the world, some old voyagers would die, cherishing the belief that the finest apartment known to men was once in the Hesket-Newmarket Inn, in rare old Cumberland—it was such a charmingly lazy pursuit to entertain these rambling thoughts over the choice oatcake and the genial whiskey, that Mr. Idle and Mr. Goodchild never asked themselves how it came to pass that the men in the fields were never heard of more, how the stalwart landlord replaced them without explanation, how his dog-cart came to be waiting at the door, and how everything was arranged without the least arrangement for climbing to old Carrock's shoulders, and standing on his head.

Without a word of inquiry, therefore, the Two Idle Apprentices drifted out resignedly into a fine, soft, close, drowsy, penetrating rain; got into the landlord's light dog-cart, and rattled off through the village for the foot of Carrock. The journey at the outset was not remarkable. The Cumberland road went up and down like all other roads; the Cumberland curs burst out from backs of cottages and barked like other curs, and the Cumberland peasantry stared after the dog-cart amazedly, as long as it was in sight, like the rest of their race. The approach to the foot of the mountain resembled the approaches to the feet of most other mountains all over the world. The cultivation gradually ceased, the trees grew gradually rare, the road became gradually rougher, and the sides of the mountain looked gradually more and more lofty, and more and more difficult to get up. The dog-cart was left at a lonely farmhouse. The landlord borrowed a large umbrella, and, assuming in an instant the character of the most cheerful and adventurous of guides, led the way to the ascent. Mr. Goodchild looked eagerly at the top of the mountain, and, feeling apparently that he was now going to be very lazy indeed, shone all over wonderfully to the eye, under the influence of the contentment within and the moisture without. Only in the bosom of Mr. Thomas Idle did Despondency now hold her gloomy state. He kept it a secret; but he would have given a very handsome sum, when the ascent began, to have been back again at the inn. The sides of Carrock looked fearfully steep, and the top of Carrock was hidden in mist. The rain was falling faster and faster. The knees of Mr. Idle—always weak on walking excursions—shivered and shook with fear and damp. The wet was already penetrating through the young man's outer coat to a brand-new shooting-jacket, for which he had reluctantly paid the large sum of two guineas on leaving town; he had no stimulating refreshment about him but a small packet of clammy gingerbread nuts; he had nobody to give him an arm, nobody to push him gently behind, nobody to pull him up tenderly in front, nobody to speak to who really felt the difficulties of the ascent, the dampness of the rain, the denseness of the mist, and the unutterable folly of climbing, undriven, up any steep place in the world, when there is level ground within reach to walk on instead. Was it for this that Thomas had left London? London, where there are nice short walks in level public gardens, with benches of repose set up at convenient distances for weary travellers—London, where rugged stone is humanely pounded into little lumps for the road, and intelligently shaped into smooth slabs for the pavement! No! it was not for the laborious ascent of the crags of Carrock that Idle had left his native city, and travelled to Cumberland. Never did he feel more disastrously convinced that he had committed a very grave error in judgment than when he found himself standing in the rain at the bottom of a steep mountain, and knew that the responsibility rested on his weak shoulders of actually getting to the top of it.

The honest landlord went first, the beaming Goodchild followed, the mournful Idle brought up the rear. From time to time, the two foremost members of the expedition changed places in the order of march; but the rearguard never altered his position. Up the mountain or down the mountain, in the water or out of it, over the rocks, through the bogs, skirting the heather, Mr. Thomas Idle was always the last, and was always the man who had to be looked after and waited for. At first the ascent was delusively easy, the sides of the mountain sloped gradually, and the material of which they were composed was a soft spongy turf, very tender and pleasant to walk upon. After a hundred yards or so, however, the verdant scene and the easy slope disappeared, and the rocks began. Not noble, massive rocks, standing upright, keeping a certain regularity in their positions, and possessing, now and then, flat tops to sit upon, but little irritating, comfortless rocks, littered about anyhow, by Nature; treacherous, disheartening rocks of all sorts of small shapes and small sizes, bruisers of tender toes and trippers-up of wavering feet. When these impediments were passed, heather and slough followed. Here the steepness of the ascent was slightly mitigated; and here the exploring party of three turned round to look at the view below them. The scene of the moorland and the fields was like a feeble water-colour drawing half sponged out. The mist was darkening, the rain was thickening, the trees were dotted about like spots of faint shadow, the division-lines which mapped out the fields were all getting blurred together, and the lonely farm-house where the dog-cart had been left, loomed spectral in the grey light like the last human dwelling at the end of the habitable world. Was this a sight worth climbing to see? Surely—surely not!

Up again—for the top of Carrock is not reached yet. The landlord, just as good-tempered and obliging as he was at the bottom of the mountain. Mr. Goodchild brighter in the eyes and rosier in the face than ever; full of cheerful remarks and apt quotations; and walking with a springiness of step wonderful to behold. Mr. Idle, farther and farther in the rear, with the water squeaking in the toes of his boots, with his two-guinea shooting-jacket clinging damply to his aching sides, with his overcoat so full of rain, and standing out so pyramidically stiff, in consequence, from his shoulders downwards, that he felt as if he was walking in a gigantic extinguisher—the despairing spirit within him representing but too aptly the candle that had just been put out. Up and up and up again, till a ridge is reached and the outer edge of the mist on the summit of Carrock is darkly and drizzingly near. Is this the top? No, nothing like the top. It is an aggravating peculiarity of all mountains, that, although they have only one top when they are seen (as they ought always to be seen) from below, they turn out to have a perfect eruption of false tops whenever the traveller is sufficiently ill-advised to go out of his way for the purpose of ascending them. Carrock is but a trumpery little mountain of fifteen hundred feet, and it presumes to have false tops, and even precipices, as if it were Mont Blanc. No matter; Goodchild enjoys it, and will go on; and Idle, who is afraid of being left behind by himself, must follow. On entering the edge of the mist, the landlord stops, and says he hopes that it will not get any thicker. It is twenty years since he last ascended Carrock, and it is barely possible, if the mist increases, that the party may be lost on the mountain. Goodchild hears this dreadful intimation, and is not in the least impressed by it. He marches for the top that is never to be found, as if he was the Wandering Jew, bound to go on for ever, in defiance of everything. The landlord faithfully accompanies him. The two, to the dim eye of Idle, far below, look in the exaggerative mist, like a pair of friendly giants, mounting the steps of some invisible castle together. Up and up, and then down a little, and then up, and then along a strip of level ground, and then up again. The wind, a wind unknown in the happy valley, blows keen and strong; the rain-mist gets impenetrable; a dreary little cairn of stones appears. The landlord adds one to the heap, first walking all round the cairn as if he were about to perform an incantation, then dropping the stone on to the top of the heap with the gesture of a magician adding an ingredient to a cauldron in full bubble. Goodchild sits down by the cairn as if it was his study-table at home; Idle, drenched and panting, stands up with his back to the wind, ascertains distinctly that this is the top at last, looks round with all the little curiosity that is left in him, and gets, in return, a magnificent view of—Nothing!

The effect of this sublime spectacle on the minds of the exploring party is a little injured by the nature of the direct conclusion to which the sight of it points—the said conclusion being that the mountain mist has actually gathered round them, as the landlord feared it would. It now becomes imperatively necessary to settle the exact situation of the farm-house in the valley at which the dog-cart has been left, before the travellers attempt to descend. While the landlord is endeavouring to make this discovery in his own way, Mr. Goodchild plunges his hand under his wet coat, draws out a little red morocco-case, opens it, and displays to the view of his companions a neat pocket-compass. The north is found, the point at which the farm-house is situated is settled, and the descent begins. After a little downward walking, Idle (behind as usual) sees his fellow-travellers turn aside sharply—tries to follow them—loses them in the mist—is shouted after, waited for, recovered—and then finds that a halt has been ordered, partly on his account, partly for the purpose of again consulting the compass.

The point in debate is settled as before between Goodchild and the landlord, and the expedition moves on, not down the mountain, but marching straight forward round the slope of it. The difficulty of following this new route is acutely felt by Thomas Idle. He finds the hardship of walking at all greatly increased by the fatigue of moving his feet straight forward along the side of a slope, when their natural tendency, at every step, is to turn off at a right angle, and go straight down the declivity. Let the reader imagine himself to be walking along the roof of a barn, instead of up or down it, and he will have an exact idea of the pedestrian difficulty in which the travellers had now involved themselves. In ten minutes more Idle was lost in the distance again, was shouted for, waited for, recovered as before; found Goodchild repeating his observation of the compass, and remonstrated warmly against the sideway route that his companions persisted in following. It appeared to the uninstructed mind of Thomas that when three men want to get to the bottom of a mountain, their business is to walk down it; and he put this view of the case, not only with emphasis, but even with some irritability. He was answered from the scientific eminence of the compass on which his companions were mounted, that there was a frightful chasm somewhere near the foot of Carrock, called The Black Arches, into which the travellers were sure to march in the mist, if they risked continuing the descent from the place where they had now halted. Idle received this answer with the silent respect which was due to the commanders of the expedition, and followed along the roof of the barn, or rather the side of the mountain, reflecting upon the assurance which he received on starting again, that the object of the party was only to gain "a certain point," and, this haven attained, to continue the descent afterwards until the foot of Carrock was reached. Though quite unexceptionable as an abstract form of expression, the phrase "a certain point" has the disadvantage of sounding rather vaguely when it is pronounced on unknown ground, under a canopy of mist much thicker than a London fog. Nevertheless, after the compass, this phrase was all the clue the party had to hold by, and Idle clung to the extreme end of it as hopefully as he could.

More sideway walking, thicker and thicker mist, all sorts of points reached except the "certain point"; third loss of Idle, third shouts for him, third recovery of him, third consultation of compass. Mr. Goodchild draws it tenderly from his pocket, and prepares to adjust it on a stone. Something falls on the turf—it is the glass.

Something else drops immediately after—it is the needle. The compass is broken, and the exploring party is lost!

It is the practice of the English portion of the human race to receive all great disasters in dead silence. Mr. Goodchild restored the useless compass to his pocket without saying a word, Mr. Idle looked at the landlord, and the landlord looked at Mr. Idle. There was nothing for it now but to go on blindfold, and trust to the chapter of chances. Accordingly, the lost travellers moved forward, still walking round the slope of the mountain, still desperately resolved to avoid the Black Arches, and to succeed in reaching the "certain point."

A quarter of an hour brought them to the brink of a ravine, at the bottom of which there flowed a muddy little stream. Here another halt was called, and another consultation took place. The landlord, still clinging pertinaciously to the idea of reaching the "point," voted for crossing the ravine, and going on round the slope of the mountain. Mr. Goodchild, to the great relief of his fellow-traveller, took another view of the case, and backed Mr. Idle's proposal to descend Carrock at once, at any hazard—the rather as the running stream was a sure guide to follow from the mountain to the valley. Accordingly, the party descended to the rugged and stony banks of the stream; and here again Thomas lost ground sadly, and fell far behind his travelling companions. Not much more than six weeks had elapsed since he had sprained one of his ankles, and he began to feel this same ankle getting rather weak when he found himself among the stones that were strewn about the running water. Goodchild and the landlord were getting farther and farther ahead of him. He saw them cross the stream and disappear round a projection on its banks. He heard them shout the moment after as a signal that they had halted and were waiting for him. Answering the shout, he mended his pace, crossed the stream where they had crossed it, and was within one step of the opposite bank, when his foot slipped on a wet stone, his weak ankle gave a twist outwards, a hot, rending, tearing pain ran through it at the same moment, and down fell the idlest of the Two Idle Apprentices, crippled in an instant.

The situation was now, in plain terms, one of absolute danger. There lay Mr. Idle writhing with pain, there was the mist as thick as ever, there was the landlord as completely lost as the strangers whom he was conducting, and there was the compass broken in Goodchild's pocket. To leave the wretched Thomas on unknown ground was plainly impossible; and to get him to walk with a badly sprained ankle seemed equally out of the question. However, Goodchild (brought back by his cry for help) bandaged the ankle with a pocket-handkerchief, and assisted by the landlord, raised the crippled Apprentice to his legs, offered him a shoulder to lean on, and exhorted him for the sake of the whole party to try if he could walk. Thomas, assisted by the shoulder on one side, and a stick on the other, did try, with what pain and difficulty those only can imagine who have sprained an ankle and have had to tread on it afterwards. At a pace adapted to the feeble hobbling of a newly-lamed man, the lost party moved on, perfectly ignorant whether they were on the right side of the mountain or the wrong, and equally uncertain how long Idle would be able to contend with the pain in his ankle, before he gave in altogether and fell down again, unable to stir another step.

Slowly and more slowly, as the clog of crippled Thomas weighed heavily and more heavily on the march of the expedition, the lost travellers followed the windings of the stream, till they came to a faintly-marked cart-track, branching off nearly at right angles, to the left. After a little consultation it was resolved to follow this dim vestige of a road in the hope that it might lead to some farm or cottage, at which Idle could be left in safety. It was now getting on towards the afternoon, and it was fast becoming more than doubtful whether the party, delayed in their progress as they now were, might not be overtaken by the darkness before the right route was found, and be condemned to pass the night on the mountain, without bit or drop to comfort them, in their wet clothes.

The cart-track grew fainter and fainter, until it was washed out altogether by another little stream, dark, turbulent, and rapid. The landlord suggested, judging by the colour of the water, that it must be flowing from one of the lead mines in the neighbourhood of Carrock; and the travellers accordingly kept by the stream for a little while, in the hope of possibly wandering towards help in that way. After walking forward about two hundred yards, they came upon a mine indeed, but a mine, exhausted and abandoned; a dismal, ruinous place, with nothing but the wreck of its works and buildings left to speak for it. Here, there were a few sheep feeding. The landlord looked at them earnestly, thought he recognised the marks on them—then thought he did not—finally gave up the sheep in despair—and walked on just as ignorant of the whereabouts of the party as ever.

The march in the dark, literally as well as metaphorically in the dark, had now been continued for three-quarters of an hour from the time when the crippled Apprentice had met with his accident. Mr. Idle, with all the will to conquer the pain in his ankle, and to hobble on, found the power rapidly failing him, and felt that another ten minutes at most would find him at the end of his last physical resources. He had just made up his mind on this point, and was about to communicate the dismal result of his reflections to his companions, when the mist suddenly brightened, and begun to lift straight ahead. In another minute, the landlord, who was in advance, proclaimed that he saw a tree. Before long, other trees appeared—then a cottage—then a house beyond the cottage, and a familiar line of road rising behind it. Last of all, Carrock itself loomed darkly into view, far away to the right hand. The party had not only got down the mountain without knowing how, but had wandered away from it in the mist, without knowing why—away, far down on the very moor by which they had approached the base of Carrock that morning.

The happy lifting of the mist, and the still happier discovery that the travellers had groped their way, though by a very roundabout direction, to within a mile or so of the part of the valley in which the farm-house was situated, restored Mr. Idle's sinking spirits and reanimated his failing strength. While the landlord ran off to get the dog-cart, Thomas was assisted by Goodchild to the cottage which had been the first building seen when the darkness brightened, and was propped up against the garden wall, like an artist's lay figure waiting to be forwarded, until the dog-cart should arrive from the farm-house below. In due time—and a very long time it seemed to Mr. Idle—the rattle of wheels was heard, and the crippled Apprentice was lifted into the seat. As the dog-cart was driven back to the inn, the landlord related an anecdote which he had just heard at the farm-house, of an unhappy man who had been lost, like his two guests and himself, on Carrock; who had passed the night there alone; who had been found the next morning, "scared and starved"; and who never went out afterwards, except on his way to the grave. Mr. Idle heard this sad story, and derived at least one useful impression from it. Bad as the pain in his ankle was, he contrived to bear it patiently, for he felt grateful that a worse accident had not befallen him in the wilds of Carrock.

Chapter II

THE DOG-CART, WITH MR. THOMAS IDLE AND HIS ANKLE ON THE HANGING SEAT behind, Mr. Francis Goodchild and the Innkeeper in front, and the rain in spouts and splashes everywhere, made the best of its way back to the little inn; the broken moor country looking like miles upon miles of Pre-Adamite sop, or the ruins of some enormous jorum of antediluvian toast-and-water. The trees dripped; the eaves of the scattered cottages dripped; the barren stone walls dividing the land, dripped; the yelping dogs dripped; carts and waggons under ill-roofed penthouses, dripped; melancholy cocks and hens perching on their shafts, or seeking shelter underneath them, dripped; Mr. Goodchild dripped; Thomas Idle dripped; the Innkeeper dripped; the mare dripped; the vast curtains of mist and cloud passed before the shadowy forms of the hills, streamed water as they were drawn across the landscape. Down such steep pitches that the mare seemed to be trotting on her head, and up such steep pitches that she seemed to have a supplementary leg in her tail, the dog-cart jolted and tilted back to the village. It was too wet for the women to look out, it was too wet even for the children to look out; all the doors and windows were closed, and the only sign of life or motion was in the rain-punctured puddles.

Whiskey and oil to Thomas Idle's ankle, and whiskey without oil to Francis Goodchild's stomach, produced an agreeable change in the systems of both; soothing Mr. Idle's pain, which was sharp before, and sweetening Mr. Goodchild's temper, which was sweet before. Portmanteaus being then opened and clothes changed, Mr. Goodchild, through having no change of outer garments but broadcloth and velvet, suddenly became a magnificent portent in the Innkeeper's house, a shining frontispiece to the fashions for the month, and a frightful anomaly in the Cumberland village.

Greatly ashamed of his splendid appearance, the conscious Goodchild quenched it as much as possible, in the shadow of Thomas Idle's ankle, and in a corner of the little covered carriage that started with them for Wigton—a most desirable carriage for any country, except for its having a flat roof and no sides; which caused the plumps of rain accumulating on the roof to play vigorous games of bagatelle into the interior all the way, and to score immensely. It was comfortable to see how the people coming back in open carts from Wigton market made no more of the rain than if it were sunshine; how the Wigton policeman taking a country walk of half-a-dozen miles (apparently for pleasure), in resplendent uniform, accepted saturation as his normal state; how clerks and schoolmasters in black, loitered along the road without umbrellas, getting varnished at every step; how the Cumberland girls, coming out to look after the Cumberland cows, shook the rain from their eyelashes and laughed it away; and how the rain continued to fall upon all, as it only does fall in hill countries.

Wigton market was over, and its bare booths were smoking with rain all down the street. Mr. Thomas Idle, melodramatically carried to the inn's first floor, and laid upon three chairs (he should have had the sofa, if there had been one), Mr. Goodchild went to the window to take an observation of Wigton, and report what he saw to his disabled companion.

"Brother Francis, brother Francis," cried Thomas Idle, "What do you see from the turret?"

"I see," said Brother Francis, "what I hope and believe to be one of the most dismal places ever seen by eyes. I see the houses with their roofs of dull black, their stained fronts, and their dark-rimmed windows, looking as if they were all in mourning. As every little puff of wind comes down the street, I see a perfect train of rain let off along the wooden stalls in the market-place and exploded against me. I see a very big gas lamp in the centre which I know, by a secret instinct, will not be lighted to-night. I see a pump, with a trivet underneath its spout whereon to stand the vessels that are brought to be filled with water. I see a man come to pump, and he pumps very hard, but no water follows, and he strolls empty away."

"Brother Francis, brother Francis," cried Thomas Idle, "what more do you see from the turret, besides the man and the pump, and the trivet and the houses all in mourning and the rain?"

"I see," said Brother Francis, "one, two, three, four, five, linen-drapers' shops in front of me. I see a linen-draper's shop next door to the right—and there are five more linen-drapers' shops down the corner to the left. Eleven homicidal linen-drapers' shops within a short stone's throw, each with its hands at the throats of all the rest! Over the small first-floor of one of these linen-drapers' shops appears the wonderful inscription, BANK."

"Brother Francis, brother Francis," cried Thomas Idle, "what more do you see from the turret, besides the eleven homicidal linen-drapers' shops, and the wonderful inscription, "Bank,"—on the small first-floor, and the man and the pump and the trivet and the houses all in mourning and the rain?"

"I see," said Brother Francis, "the depository for Christian Knowledge, and through the dark vapour I think I again make out Mr. Spurgeon looming heavily. Her Majesty the Queen, God bless her, printed in colours, I am sure I see. I see the *Illustrated London News* of several years ago, and I see a sweetmeat shop—which the proprietor calls a "Salt Warehouse"—with one small female child in a cotton bonnet looking in on tip-toe, oblivious of rain. And I see a watchmaker's with only three great pale watches of a dull metal hanging in his window, each in a separate pane."

"Brother Francis, brother Francis," cried Thomas Idle, "what more do you see of Wigton, besides these objects, and the man and the pump and the trivet and the houses all in mourning and the rain?"

"I see nothing more," said Brother Francis, "and there is nothing more to see, except the curlpaper bill of the theatre, which was opened and shut last week (the manager's family played all the parts), and the short, square, chinky omnibus that goes to the railway, and leads too rattling a life over the stones to hold together long. O yes! Now, I see two men with their hands in their pockets and their backs towards me."

"Brother Francis, brother Francis," cried Thomas Idle, "what do you make out from the turret, of the expression of the two men with their hands in their pockets and their backs towards you?"

"They are mysterious men," said Brother Francis, "with inscrutable backs. They keep their backs towards me with persistency. If one turns an inch in any direction, the other turns an inch in the same direction, and no more. They turn very stiffly, on a very little pivot, in the middle of the market-place. Their appearance is partly of a mining, partly of a ploughing, partly of a stable, character. They are looking at nothing—very hard. Their backs are slouched, and their legs are curved with much standing about. Their pockets are loose and dog's-eared, on account of their hands being always in them. They stand to be rained upon, without any movement of impatience or dissatisfaction, and they keep so close together that an elbow of each jostles an elbow of the other, but they never speak. They spit at times, but speak not. I see it growing darker and darker, and still I see them, sole visible population of the place, standing to be rained upon with their backs towards me, and looking at nothing very hard."

"Brother Francis, brother Francis," cried Thomas Idle, "before you draw down the blind of the turret and come in to have your head scorched by the hot gas, see if you can, and impart to me, something of the expression of those two amazing men."

"The murky shadows," said Francis Goodchild, "are gathering fast; and the wings of evening, and the wings of coal, are folding over Wigton. Still, they look at nothing very hard, with their backs towards me. Ah! Now, they turn, and I see—"

"Brother Francis, brother Francis," cried Thomas Idle, "tell me quickly what you see of the two men of Wigton!"

"I see," said Francis Goodchild, "that they have no expression at all. And now the town goes to sleep, undazzled by the large unlighted lamp in the market-place; and let no man wake it."

At the close of the next day's journey, Mr. Thomas Idle's ankle became much swollen and inflamed. There are reasons which will presently explain themselves for not publicly indicating the exact direction in which that journey lay, or the place in which it ended. It was a long day's shaking of Thomas Idle over the rough roads, and a long day's getting out and going on before the horses, and fagging up hills, and scouring down hills, on the part of Mr. Goodchild, who in the fatigues of such labours congratulated himself on attaining a high point of idleness. It was at a little town, still in Cumberland, that they halted for the night—a very little town, with the purple and brown moor close upon its one street; a curious little ancient market-cross set up in the midst of it; and the town itself looking much as if it were a collection of great stones piled on end by the Druids long ago, which a few recluse people had since hollowed out for habitations.

"Is there a doctor here?" asked Mr. Goodchild, on his knee, of the motherly landlady of the little Inn: stopping in his examination of Mr. Idle's ankle, with the aid of a candle.

"Ey, my word!" said the landlady, glancing doubtfully at the ankle for herself; "there's Doctor Speddie."

"Is he a good Doctor?"

"Ey!" said the landlady, "I ca' him so. A' cooms efther nae doctor that I ken. Mair nor which, a's just THE doctor heer."

"Do you think he is at home?"

Her reply was, "Gang awa', Jock, and bring him."

Jock, a white-headed boy, who, under pretence of stirring up some bay salt in a basin of water for the laving of this unfortunate ankle, had greatly enjoyed himself for the last ten minutes in splashing the carpet, set off promptly. A very few minutes had elapsed when he showed the Doctor in, by tumbling against the door before him and bursting it open with his head.

"Gently, Jock, gently," said the Doctor as he advanced with a quiet step. "Gentlemen, a good evening. I am sorry that my presence is required here. A slight accident, I hope? A slip and a fall? Yes, yes, yes. Carrock, indeed? Hah! Does that pain you, Sir? No doubt, it does. It is the great connecting ligament here, you see, that has been badly strained. Time and rest, Sir! They are often the recipe in greater cases," with a slight sigh, "and often the recipe in small. I can send a lotion to relieve you, but we must leave the cure to time and rest."

This he said, holding Idle's foot on his knee between his two hands, as he sat over against him. He had touched it tenderly and skilfully in explanation of what he said, and, when his careful examination was completed, softly returned it to its former horizontal position on a chair.

He spoke with a little irresolution whenever he began, but afterwards fluently. He was a tall, thin, large-boned, old gentleman, with an appearance at first sight of being hard-featured; but, at a second glance, the mild expression of his face and some particular touches of sweetness and patience about his mouth, corrected this impression and assigned his long professional rides, by day and night, in the bleak hill-weather, as the true cause of that appearance. He stooped very little, though past seventy and very grey. His dress was more like that of a clergyman than a country doctor, being a plain black suit, and a plain white neck-kerchief tied behind like a band. His black was the worse for wear, and there were darns in his coat, and his linen was a little frayed at the hems and edges. He might have been poor—it was likely enough in that out-of-the-way spot—or he might have been a little self-forgetful and eccentric. Any one could have seen directly, that he had neither wife nor child at home. He had a scholarly air with him, and that kind of considerate humanity towards others which claimed a gentle consideration for himself. Mr. Goodchild made this study of him while he was examining the limb, and as he laid it down. Mr. Goodchild wishes to add that he considers it a very good likeness.

It came out in the course of a little conversation, that Doctor Speddie was acquainted with some friends of Thomas Idle's, and had, when a young man, passed some years in Thomas Idle's birthplace on the other side of England. Certain idle labours, the fruit of Mr. Goodchild's apprenticeship, also happened to be well known to him. The lazy travellers were thus placed on a more intimate footing with the Doctor than the casual circumstances of the meeting would of themselves have established; and when Doctor Speddie rose to go home, remarking that he would send his assistant with the lotion, Francis Goodchild said that was unnecessary, for, by the Doctor's leave, he would accompany him, and bring it back. (Having done nothing to fatigue himself for a full quarter of an hour, Francis began to fear that he was not in a state of idleness.)

Doctor Speddie politely assented to the proposition of Francis Goodchild, "as it would give him the pleasure of enjoying a few more minutes of Mr. Goodchild's society than he could otherwise have hoped for," and they went out together into the village street. The rain had nearly ceased, the clouds had broken before a cool wind from the north-east, and stars were shining from the peaceful heights beyond them.

Doctor Speddie's house was the last house in the place. Beyond it, lay the moor, all dark and lonesome. The wind moaned in a low, dull, shivering manner round the little garden, like a houseless creature that knew the winter was coming. It was exceedingly wild and solitary. "Roses," said the Doctor, when Goodchild touched some wet leaves overhanging the stone porch; "but they get cut to pieces."

The Doctor opened the door with a key he carried, and led the way into a low but pretty ample hall with rooms on either side. The door of one of these stood open, and the Doctor entered it, with a word of welcome to his guest. It, too, was a low room, half surgery and half parlour, with shelves of books and bottles against the walls, which were of a very dark hue. There was a fire in the grate, the night being damp and chill. Leaning against the chimneypiece looking down into it, stood the Doctor's Assistant.

A man of a most remarkable appearance. Much older than Mr. Goodchild had expected, for he was at least two-and-fifty; but, that was nothing. What was startling in him was his remarkable paleness. His large black eyes, his sunken cheeks, his long and heavy iron-grey hair, his wasted hands, and even the attenuation of his figure, were at first forgotten in his extraordinary pallor. There was no vestige of colour in the man. When he turned his face, Francis Goodchild started as if a stone figure had looked round at him.

"Mr. Lorn," said the Doctor. "Mr. Goodchild."

The Assistant, in a distraught way—as if he had forgotten something—as if he had forgotten everything, even to his own name and himself—acknowledged the visitor's presence, and stepped further back into the shadow of the wall behind him. But, he was so pale that his face stood out in relief again the dark wall, and really could not be hidden so.

"Mr. Goodchild's friend has met with accident, Lorn," said Doctor Speddie. "We want the lotion for a bad sprain."

A pause.

"My dear fellow, you are more than usually absent to-night. The lotion for a bad sprain."

"Ah! yes! Directly."

He was evidently relieved to turn away, and to take his white face and his wild eyes to a table in a recess among the bottles. But, though he stood there, compounding the lotion with his back towards them, Goodchild could not, for many moments, withdraw his gaze from the man. When he at length did so, he found the Doctor observing him, with some trouble in his face. "He is absent," explained the Doctor, in a low voice. "Always absent. Very absent."

"Is he ill?"

"No, not ill."

"Unhappy?"

"I have my suspicions that he was," assented the Doctor, "once."

Francis Goodchild could not but observe that the Doctor accompanied these words with a benignant and protecting glance at their subject, in which there was much of the expression with which an attached father might have looked at a heavily afflicted son. Yet, that they were not father and son must have been plain to most eyes. The Assistant, on the other hand, turning presently to ask the Doctor some question, looked at him with a wan smile as if he were his whole reliance and sustainment in life.

It was in vain for the Doctor in his easy-chair, to try to lead the mind of Mr. Goodchild in the opposite easy-chair, away from what was before him. Let Mr. Goodchild do what he would to follow the Doctor, his eyes and thoughts reverted to the Assistant. The Doctor soon perceived it, and, after falling silent, and musing in a little perplexity, said:

"Lorn!"

"My dear Doctor."

"Would you go to the Inn, and apply that lotion? You will show the best way of applying it, far better than Mr. Goodchild can."

"With pleasure."

The Assistant took his hat, and passed like a shadow to the door.

"Lorn!" said the Doctor, calling after him.

He returned.

"Mr. Goodchild will keep me company till you come home. Don't hurry. Excuse my calling you back."

"It is not," said the Assistant, with his former smile, "the first time you have called me back, dear Doctor." With those words he went away.

"Mr. Goodchild," said Doctor Speddie, in a low voice, and with his former troubled expression of face, "I have seen that your attention has been concentrated on my friend."

"He fascinates me. I must apologise to you, but he has quite bewildered and mastered me."

"I find that a lonely existence and a long secret," said the Doctor, drawing his chair a little nearer to Mr. Goodchild's, "become in the course of time very heavy.

I will tell you something. You may make what use you will of it, under fictitious names. I know I may trust you. I am the more inclined to confidence to-night, through having been unexpectedly led back, by the current of our conversation at the Inn, to scenes in my early life. Will you please to draw a little nearer?"

Mr. Goodchild drew a little nearer, and the Doctor went on thus: speaking, for the most part, in so cautious a voice, that the wind, though it was far from high, occasionally got the better of him.

When this present nineteenth century was younger by a good many years than it is now, a certain friend of mine, named Arthur Holliday, happened to arrive in the town of Doncaster, exactly in the middle of a race-week, or, in other words, in the middle of the month of September. He was one of those reckless, rattle-pated, open-hearted, and open-mouthed young gentlemen, who possess the gift of familiarity in its highest perfection, and who scramble carelessly along the journey of life making friends, as the phrase is, wherever they go. His father was a rich manufacturer, and had bought landed property enough in one of the midland counties to make all the born squires in his neighbourhood thoroughly envious of him. Arthur was his only son, possessor in prospect of the great estate and the great business after his father's death; well supplied with money, and not too rigidly looked after, during his father's lifetime. Report, or scandal, whichever you please, said that the old gentleman had been rather wild in his youthful days, and that, unlike most parents, he was not disposed to be violently indignant when he found that his son took after him. This may be true or not. I myself only knew the elder Mr. Holliday when he was getting on in years; and then he was as quiet and as respectable a gentleman as ever I met with.

Well, one September, as I told you, young Arthur comes to Doncaster, having decided all of a sudden, in his harebrained way, that he would go to the races. He did not reach the town till towards the close of the evening, and he went at once to see about his dinner and bed at the principal hotel. Dinner they were ready enough to give him; but as for a bed, they laughed when he mentioned it. In the race-week at Doncaster, it is no uncommon thing for visitors who have not bespoken apartments, to pass the night in their carriages at the inn doors. As for the lower sort of strangers, I myself have often seen them, at that full time, sleeping out on the doorsteps for want of a covered place to creep under. Rich as he was, Arthur's chance of getting a night's lodging (seeing that he had not written beforehand to secure one) was more than doubtful. He tried the second hotel, and the third hotel, and two of the inferior inns after that; and was met everywhere by the same form of answer. No accommodation for the night of any sort was left. All the bright golden sovereigns in his pocket would not buy him a bed at Doncaster in the race-week.

To a young fellow of Arthur's temperament, the novelty of being turned away into the street, like a penniless vagabond, at every house where he asked for a lodging, presented itself in the light of a new and highly amusing piece of experience. He went on, with his carpet-bag in his hand, applying for a bed at every place of entertainment for travellers that he could find in Doncaster, until he wandered into the outskirts of the town. By this time, the last glimmer of twilight had faded out, the moon was rising dimly in a mist, the wind was getting cold, the clouds were gathering heavily, and there was every prospect that it was soon going to rain.

The look of the night had rather a lowering effect on young Holliday's good spirits. He began to contemplate the houseless situation in which he was placed, from the serious rather than the humorous point of view; and he looked about him, for another public-house to inquire at, with something very like downright anxiety in his mind on the subject of a lodging for the night. The suburban part of the town towards which he had now strayed was hardly lighted at all, and he could see nothing of the houses as he passed them, except that they got progressively smaller and dirtier, the farther he went. Down the winding road before him shone the dull gleam of an oil lamp, the one faint, lonely light that struggled ineffectually with the foggy darkness all round him. He resolved to go on as far as this lamp, and then, if it showed him nothing in the shape of an Inn, to return to the central part of the town and to try if he could not at least secure a chair to sit down on, through the night, at one of the principal Hotels.

As he got near the lamp, he heard voices; and, walking close under it, found that it lighted the entrance to a narrow court, on the wall of which was painted a long hand in faded flesh-colour, pointing with a lean forefinger, to this inscription:—

THE TWO ROBINS

Arthur turned into the court without hesitation, to see what The Two Robins could do for him. Four or five men were standing together round the door of the house which was at the bottom of the court, facing the entrance from the street. The men were all listening to one other man, better dressed than the rest, who was telling his audience something, in a low voice, in which they were apparently very much interested.

On entering the passage, Arthur was passed by a stranger with a knapsack in his hand, who was evidently leaving the house.

"No," said the traveller with the knapsack, turning round and addressing himself cheerfully to a fat, sly-looking, bald-headed man, with a dirty white apron on, who had followed him down the passage. "No, Mr. landlord, I am not easily scared by trifles; but, I don't mind confessing that I can't quite stand *that*."

It occurred to young Holliday, the moment he heard these words, that the stranger had been asked an exorbitant price for a bed at The Two Robins; and that he was unable or unwilling to pay it. The moment his back was turned, Arthur, comfortably conscious of his own well-filled pockets, addressed himself in a great hurry, for fear any other benighted traveller should slip in and forestall him, to the sly-looking landlord with the dirty apron and the bald head.

"If you have got a bed to let," he said, "and if that gentleman who has just gone out won't pay your price for it, I will."

The sly landlord looked hard at Arthur.

"Will you, Sir?" he asked, in a meditative, doubtful way.

"Name your price," said young Holliday, thinking that the landlord's hesitation sprang from some boorish distrust of him. "Name your price, and I'll give you the money at once if you like?"

"Are you game for five shillings?" inquired the landlord, rubbing his stubbly double chin, and looking up thoughtfully at the ceiling above him.

Arthur nearly laughed in the man's face; but thinking it prudent to control himself, offered the five shillings as seriously as he could. The sly landlord held out his hand, then suddenly drew it back again.

"You're acting all fair and above-board by me," he said: "and, before I take your money, I'll do the same by you. Look here, this is how it stands. You can have a bed all to yourself for five shillings; but you can't have more than a half-share of the room it stands in. Do you see what I mean, young gentleman?"

"Of course I do," returned Arthur, a little irritably. "You mean that it is a double-bedded room, and that one of the beds is occupied?"

The landlord nodded his head, and rubbed his double chin harder than ever. Arthur hesitated, and mechanically moved back a step or two towards the door. The idea of sleeping in the same room with a total stranger, did not present an attractive prospect to him. He felt more than half inclined to drop his five shillings into his pocket, and to go out into the street once more.

"Is it yes, or no?" asked the landlord. "Settle it as quick as you can, because there's lots of people wanting a bed at Doncaster to-night, besides you."

Arthur looked towards the court, and heard the rain falling heavily in the street outside. He thought he would ask a question or two before he rashly decided on leaving the shelter of The Two Robins.

"What sort of a man is it who has got the other bed?" he inquired. "Is he a gentleman? I mean, is he a quiet, well-behaved person?"

"The quietest man I ever came across," said the landlord, rubbing his fat hands stealthily one over the other. "As sober as a judge, and as regular as clock-work in his habits. It hasn't struck nine, not ten minutes ago, and he's in his bed already. I don't know whether that comes up to your notion of a quiet man: it goes a long way ahead of mine, I can tell you."

"Is he asleep, do you think?" asked Arthur.

"I know he's asleep," returned the landlord. "And what's more, he's gone off so fast, that I'll warrant you don't wake him. This way, Sir," said the landlord, speaking over young Holliday's shoulder, as if he was addressing some new guest who was approaching the house.

"Here you are," said Arthur, determined to be beforehand with the stranger, whoever he might be. "I'll take the bed." And he handed the five shillings to the landlord, who nodded, dropped the money carelessly into his waistcoat-pocket, and lighted the candle.

"Come up and see the room," said the host of The Two Robins, leading the way to the staircase quite briskly, considering how fat he was.

They mounted to the second-floor of the house. The landlord half opened a door, fronting the landing, then stopped, and turned round to Arthur.

"It's a fair bargain, mind, on my side as well as on yours," he said. "You give me five shillings, I give you in return a clean, comfortable bed; and I warrant, beforehand, that you won't be interfered with, or annoyed in any way, by the man who sleeps in the same room as you." Saying those words, he looked hard, for a moment, in young Holliday's face, and then led the way into the room.

It was larger and cleaner than Arthur had expected it would be. The two beds stood parallel with each other—a space of about six feet intervening between them. They were both of the same medium size, and both had the same plain white curtains, made to draw, if necessary, all round them. The occupied bed was the bed nearest the window. The curtains were all drawn round this, except the half curtain at the bottom, on the side of the bed farthest from the window. Arthur saw the feet of the sleeping man raising the scanty clothes into a sharp little eminence, as if he was lying flat on his back. He took the candle, and advanced softly to draw the curtain—stopped half-way, and listened for a moment—then turned to the landlord.

"He's a very quiet sleeper," said Arthur.

"Yes," said the landlord, "very quiet."

Young Holliday advanced with the candle, and looked in at the man cautiously.

"How pale he is!" said Arthur.

"Yes," returned the landlord, "pale enough, isn't he?"

Arthur looked closer at the man. The bedclothes were drawn up to his chin, and they lay perfectly still over the region of his chest. Surprised and vaguely startled, as he noticed this, Arthur stooped down closer over the stranger; looked at his ashy, parted lips; listened breathlessly for an instant; looked again at the strangely still face, and the motionless lips and chest; and turned round suddenly on the landlord, with his own cheeks as pale for the moment as the hollow cheeks of the man on the bed.

"Come here," he whispered, under his breath. "Come here, for God's sake! The man's not asleep—he is dead!"

"You have found that out sooner than I thought you would," said the landlord, composedly. "Yes, he's dead, sure enough. He died at five o'clock to-day."

"How did he die? Who is he?" asked Arthur, staggered, for a moment, by the audacious coolness of the answer.

"As to who is he," rejoined the landlord, "I know no more about him than you do. There are his books and letters and things, all sealed up in that brown-paper parcel, for the Coroner's inquest to open to-morrow or next day. He's been here a week, paying his way fairly enough, and stopping in-doors, for the most part, as if he was ailing. My girl brought him up his tea at five to-day; and as he was pouring of it out, he fell down in a faint, or a fit, or a compound of both, for anything I know. We could not bring him to—and I said he was dead. And the doctor couldn't bring him to—and the doctor said he was dead. And there he is. And the Coroner's inquest's coming as soon as it can. And that's as much as I know about it."

Arthur held the candle close to the man's lips. The flame still burnt straight up, as steadily as before. There was a moment of silence; and the rain pattered drearily through it against the panes of the window.

"If you haven't got nothing more to say to me," continued the landlord, "I suppose I may go. You don't expect your five shillings back, do you? There's the bed I promised you, clean and comfortable. There's the man I warranted not to disturb you, quiet in this world for ever. If you're frightened to stop alone with him, that's not my look out. I've kept my part of the bargain, and I mean to keep the money. I'm not Yorkshire, myself, young gentleman; but I've lived long enough in these parts to have my wits sharpened; and I shouldn't wonder if you found out the way to brighten up yours, next time you come amongst us." With these words, the landlord turned towards the door, and laughed to himself softly, in high satisfaction at his own sharpness.

Startled and shocked as he was, Arthur had by this time sufficiently recovered himself to feel indignant at the trick that had been played on him, and at the insolent manner in which the landlord exulted in it.

"Don't laugh," he said sharply, "till you are quite sure you have got the laugh against me. You shan't have the five shillings for nothing, my man. I'll keep the bed."

"Will you?" said the landlord. "Then I wish you a good night's rest." With that brief farewell, he went out, and shut the door after him.

A good night's rest! The words had hardly been spoken, the door had hardly been closed, before Arthur half-repented the hasty words that had just escaped him. Though not naturally over-sensitive, and not wanting in courage of the moral as well as the physical sort, the presence of the dead man had an instantaneously chilling effect on his mind when he found himself alone in the room—alone, and bound by his own rash words to stay there till the next morning. An older man would have thought nothing of those words, and would have acted, without reference to them, as his calmer sense suggested. But Arthur was too young to treat the ridicule, even of his inferiors, with contempt—too young not to fear the momentary humiliation of falsifying his own foolish boast, more than he feared the trial of watching out the long night in the same chamber with the dead.

"It is but a few hours," he thought to himself, "and I can get away the first thing in the morning."

He was looking towards the occupied bed as that idea passed through his mind, and the sharp, angular eminence made in the clothes by the dead man's upturned feet again caught his eye. He advanced and drew the curtains, purposely abstaining, as he did so, from looking at the face of the corpse, lest he might unnerve himself at the outset by fastening some ghastly impression of it on his mind. He drew the curtain very gently, and sighed involuntarily as he closed it. "Poor fellow," he said, almost as sadly as if he had known the man. "Ah, poor fellow!"

He went next to the window. The night was black, and he could see nothing from it. The rain still pattered heavily against the glass. He inferred, from hearing it, that the window was at the back of the house; remembering that the front was sheltered from the weather by the court and the buildings over it.

While he was still standing at the window—for even the dreary rain was a relief, because of the sound it made; a relief, also, because it moved, and had some faint suggestion, in consequence, of life and companionship in it—while he was standing at the window, and looking vacantly into the black darkness outside, he heard a distant church-clock strike ten. Only ten! How was he to pass the time till the house was astir the next morning?

Under any other circumstances, he would have gone down to the public-house parlour, would have called for his grog, and would have laughed and talked with the company assembled as familiarly as if he had known them all his life. But the very thought of whiling away the time in this manner was distasteful to him. The new situation in which he was placed seemed to have altered him to himself already. Thus far, his life had been the common, trifling, prosaic, surface-life of a prosperous young man, with no troubles to conquer, and no trials to face. He had lost no relation whom he loved, no friend whom he treasured. Till this night, what share he had of the immortal inheritance that is divided amongst us all, had laid dormant within him. Till this night, Death and he had not once met, even in thought.

He took a few turns up and down the room—then stopped. The noise made by his boots on the poorly carpeted floor, jarred on his ear. He hesitated a little, and ended by taking the boots off, and walking backwards and forwards noiselessly. All desire to sleep or to rest had left him. The bare thought of lying down on the unoccupied bed instantly drew the picture on his mind of a dreadful mimicry of the position of the dead man. Who was he? What was the story of his past life? Poor he must have been, or he would not have stopped at such a place as The Two Robins Inn—and weakened, probably, by long illness, or he could hardly have died in the manner in which the landlord had described. Poor, ill, lonely,—dead in a strange place; dead, with nobody but a stranger to pity him. A sad story: truly, on the mere face of it, a very sad story.

While these thoughts were passing through his mind, he had stopped insensibly at the window, close to which stood the foot of the bed with the closed curtains. At first he looked at it absently; then he became conscious that his eyes were fixed on it; and then, a perverse desire took possession of him to do the very thing which he had resolved not to do, up to this time—to look at the dead man.

He stretched out his hand towards the curtains; but checked himself in the very act of undrawing them, turned his back sharply on the bed, and walked towards the chimneypiece, to see what things were placed on it, and to try if he could keep the dead man out of his mind in that way.

There was a pewter inkstand on the chimneypiece, with some mildewed remains of ink in the bottle. There were two coarse china ornaments of the commonest kind; and there was a square of embossed card, dirty and fly-blown, with a collection of wretched riddles printed on it, in all sorts of zig-zag directions, and in variously coloured inks. He took the card, and went away, to read it, to the table on which the candle was placed; sitting down, with his back resolutely turned to the curtained bed.

He read the first riddle, the second, the third, all in one corner of the card—then turned it round impatiently to look at another. Before he could begin reading the riddles printed here, the sound of the church-clock stopped him. Eleven. He had got through an hour of the time, in the room with the dead man.

Once more he looked at the card. It was not easy to make out the letters printed on it, in consequence of the dimness of the light which the landlord had left him—a common tallow candle, furnished with a pair of heavy old-fashioned steel snuffers. Up to this time, his mind had been too much occupied to think of the light. He had left the wick of the candle unsnuffed, till it had risen higher than the flame, and had burnt into an odd pent-house shape at the top, from which morsels of the charred cotton fell off, from time to time, in little flakes. He took up the snuffers now, and trimmed the wick. The light brightened directly, and the room became less dismal.

Again he turned to the riddles; reading them doggedly and resolutely, now in one corner of the card, now in another. All his efforts, however, could not fix his attention on them. He pursued his occupation mechanically, deriving no sort of impression from what he was reading. It was as if a shadow from the curtained bed had got between his mind and the gaily printed letters—a shadow that nothing could dispel. At last, he gave up the struggle, and threw the card from him impatiently, and took to walking softly up and down the room again.

The dead man, the dead man, the *hidden* dead man on the bed! There was the one persistent idea still haunting him. Hidden? Was it only the body being there, or was it the body being there, concealed, that was preying on his mind? He stopped at the window, with that doubt in him; once more listening to the pattering rain, once more looking out into the black darkness.

Still the dead man! The darkness forced his mind back upon itself, and set his memory at work, reviving, with a painfully-vivid distinctness the momentary impression it had received from the first sight of the corpse. Before long the face seemed to be hovering out in the middle of the darkness, confronting him through the window, with the paleness whiter, with the dreadful dull line of light between the imperfectly-closed eyelids broader than he had seen it—with the parted lips slowly dropping farther and farther away from each other—with the features growing larger and moving closer, till they seemed to fill the window and to silence the rain, and to shut out the night.

The sound of a voice, shouting below-stairs, woke him suddenly from the dream of his own distempered fancy. He recognised it as the voice of the landlord. "Shut up at twelve, Ben," he heard it say. "I'm off to bed."

He wiped away the damp that had gathered on his forehead, reasoned with himself for a little while, and resolved to shake his mind free of the ghastly counterfeit which still clung to it, by forcing himself to confront, if it was only for a moment, the solemn reality. Without allowing himself an instant to hesitate, he parted the curtains at the foot of the bed, and looked through.

There was a sad, peaceful, white face, with the awful mystery of stillness on it, laid back upon the pillow. No stir, no change there! He only looked at it for a moment before he closed the curtains again—but that moment steadied him, calmed him, restored him—mind and body—to himself.

He returned to his old occupation of walking up and down the room; persevering in it, this time, till the clock struck again. Twelve.

As the sound of the clock-bell died away, it was succeeded by the confused noise, downstairs, of the drinkers in the tap-room leaving the house. The next sound, after an interval of silence, was caused by the barring of the door, and the closing of the shutters, at the back of the Inn. Then the silence followed again, and was disturbed no more.

He was alone now—absolutely, utterly, alone with the dead man, till the next morning.

The wick of the candle wanted trimming again. He took up the snuffers—but paused suddenly on the very point of using them, and looked attentively at the candle—then back, over his shoulder, at the curtained bed—then again at the candle. It had been lighted, for the first time, to show him the way upstairs, and three parts of it, at least, were already consumed. In another hour it would be burnt out. In another hour—unless he called at once to the man who had shut up the Inn, for a fresh candle—he would be left in the dark.

Strongly as his mind had been affected since he had entered his room, his unreasonable dread of encountering ridicule, and of exposing his courage to suspicion, had not altogether lost its influence over him, even yet. He lingered irresolutely by the table, waiting till he could prevail on himself to open the door, and call, from the landing, to the man who had shut up the Inn. In his present hesitating frame of mind, it was a kind of relief to gain a few moments only by engaging in the trifling occupation of snuffing the candle. His hand trembled a little, and the snuffers were heavy and awkward to use. When he closed them on the wick, he closed them a hair's breadth too low. In an instant the candle was out, and the room was plunged in pitch darkness.

The one impression which the absence of light immediately produced on his mind, was distrust of the curtained bed—distrust which shaped itself into no distinct idea, but which was powerful enough in its very vagueness, to bind him down to his chair, to make his heart beat fast, and to set him listening intently. No sound stirred in the room but the familiar sound of the rain against the window, louder and sharper now than he had heard it yet.

Still the vague distrust, the inexpressible dread possessed him, and kept him to his chair. He had put his carpet-bag on the table, when he first entered the room; and he now took the key from his pocket, reached out his hand softly, opened the bag, and groped in it for his travelling writing-case, in which he knew that there was a small store of matches. When he had got one of the matches, he waited before he struck it on the coarse wooden table, and listened intently again, without knowing why. Still there was no sound in the room but the steady, ceaseless, rattling sound of the rain.

He lighted the candle again, without another moment of delay and, on the instant of its burning up, the first object in the room that his eyes sought for was the curtained bed.

Just before the light had been put out, he had looked in that direction, and had seen no change, no disarrangement of any sort, in the folds of the closely-drawn curtains.

When he looked at the bed, now, he saw, hanging over the side of it, a long white hand.

It lay perfectly motionless, midway on the side of the bed, where the curtain at the head and the curtain at the foot met. Nothing more was visible. The clinging curtains hid everything but the long white hand.

He stood looking at it unable to stir, unable to call out; feeling nothing, knowing nothing, every faculty he possessed gathered up and lost in the one seeing faculty. How long that first panic held him he never could tell afterwards. It might have been only for a moment; it might have been for many minutes together. How he got to the bed—whether he ran to it headlong, or whether he approached it slowly—how he wrought himself up to unclose the curtains and look in, he never has remembered, and never will remember to his dying day. It is enough that he did go to the bed, and that he did look inside the curtains.

The man had moved. One of his arms was outside the clothes; his face was turned a little on the pillow; his eyelids were wide open. Changed as to position, and as to one of the features, the face was, otherwise, fearfully and wonderfully unaltered. The dead paleness and the dead quiet were on it still.

One glance showed Arthur this—one glance, before he flew breathlessly to the door, and alarmed the house.

The man whom the landlord called "Ben," was the first to appear on the stairs. In three words, Arthur told him what had happened, and sent him for the nearest doctor.

I, who tell you this story, was then staying with a medical friend of mine, in practice at Doncaster, taking care of his patients for him, during his absence in London; and I, for the time being, was the nearest doctor. They had sent for me from the Inn, when the stranger was taken ill in the afternoon; but I was not at home, and medical assistance was sought for elsewhere. When the man from The Two Robins rang the night-bell, I was just thinking of going to bed. Naturally enough, I did not believe a word of his story about "a dead man who had come to life again." However, I put on my hat, armed myself with one or two bottles of restorative medicine, and ran to the Inn, expecting to find nothing more remarkable, when I got there, than a patient in a fit.

My surprise at finding that the man had spoken the literal truth was almost, if not quite, equalled by my astonishment at finding myself face to face with Arthur Holliday as soon as I entered the bedroom. It was no time then for giving or seeking explanations. We just shook hands amazedly; and then I ordered everybody but Arthur out of the room, and hurried to the man on the bed.

The kitchen fire had not been long out. There was plenty of hot water in the boiler, and plenty of flannel to be had. With these, with my medicines, and with such help as Arthur could render under my direction, I dragged the man, literally, out of the jaws of death. In less than an hour from the time when I had been called in, he was alive and talking in the bed on which he had been laid out to wait for the Coroner's inquest.

You will naturally ask me, what had been the matter with him; and I might treat you, in reply, to a long theory, plentifully sprinkled with, what the children call, hard words. I prefer telling you that, in this case, cause and effect could not be satisfactorily joined together by any theory whatever. There are mysteries in life, and the condition of it, which human science has not fathomed yet; and I candidly confess to you, that, in bringing that man back to existence, I was, morally speaking, groping haphazard in the dark. I know (from the testimony of the doctor who attended him in the afternoon) that the vital machinery, so far as its action is appreciable by our senses, had, in this case, unquestionably stopped; and I am equally certain (seeing that I recovered him) that the vital principle was not extinct. When I add, that he had suffered from a long and complicated illness, and that his whole nervous system was utterly deranged, I have told you all I really know of the physical condition of my dead-alive patient at The Two Robins Inn.

When he "came to," as the phrase goes, he was a startling object to look at, with his colourless face, his sunken cheeks, his wild black eyes, and his long black hair. The first question he asked me about himself, when he could speak, made me suspect that I had been called in to a man in my own profession. I mentioned to him my surmise; and he told me that I was right.

He said he had come last from Paris, where he had been attached to a hospital. That he had lately returned to England, on his way to Edinburgh, to continue his studies; that he had been taken ill on the journey; and that he had stopped to rest and recover himself at Doncaster. He did not add a word about his name, or who he was: and, of course, I did not question him on the subject. All I inquired, when he ceased speaking, was what branch of the profession he intended to follow.

"Any branch," he said, bitterly, "which will put bread into the mouth of a poor man."

At this, Arthur, who had been hitherto watching him in silent curiosity, burst out impetuously in his usual good-humoured way:—

"My dear fellow!" (everybody was "my dear fellow" with Arthur) "now you have come to life again, don't begin by being downhearted about your prospects. I'll answer for it, I can help you to some capital thing in the medical line—or, if I can't, I know my father can."

The medical student looked at him steadily.

"Thank you," he said, coldly. Then added, "May I ask who your father is?"

"He's well enough known all about this part of the country," replied Arthur. "He is a great manufacturer, and his name is Holliday."

My hand was on the man's wrist during this brief conversation. The instant the name of Holliday was pronounced I felt the pulse under my fingers flutter, stop, go on suddenly with a bound, and beat afterwards, for a minute or two, at the fever rate.

"How did you come here?" asked the stranger, quickly, excitably, passionately almost.

Arthur related briefly what had happened from the time of his first taking the bed at the inn.

"I am indebted to Mr. Holliday's son then for the help that has saved my life," said the medical student, speaking to himself, with a singular sarcasm in his voice. "Come here!"

He held out, as he spoke, his long, white, bony, right hand.

"With all my heart," said Arthur, taking the hand cordially. "I may confess it now," he continued, laughing. "Upon my honour, you almost frightened me out of my wits."

The stranger did not seem to listen. His wild black eyes were fixed with a look of eager interest on Arthur's face, and his long bony fingers kept tight hold of Arthur's hand. Young Holliday, on his side, returned the gaze, amazed and puzzled by the medical student's odd language and manners. The two faces were close together; I looked at them; and, to my amazement, I was suddenly impressed by the sense of a likeness between them—not in features, or complexion, but solely in expression. It must have been a strong likeness, or I should certainly not have found it out, for I am naturally slow at detecting resemblances between faces.

"You have saved my life," said the strange man, still looking hard in Arthur's face, still holding tightly by his hand. "If you had been my own brother, you could not have done more for me than that."

He laid a singularly strong emphasis on those three words "my own brother," and a change passed over his face as he pronounced them,—a change that no language of mine is competent to describe.

"I hope I have not done being of service to you yet," said Arthur. "I'll speak to my father, as soon as I get home."

"You seem to be fond and proud of your father," said the medical student. "I suppose, in return, he is fond and proud of you?"

"Of course, he is!" answered Arthur, laughing. "Is there anything wonderful in that? Isn't *your* father fond—"

The stranger suddenly dropped young Holliday's hand, and turned his face away.

"I beg your pardon," said Arthur. "I hope I have not unintentionally pained you. I hope you have not lost your father."

"I can't well lose what I have never had," retorted the medical student, with a harsh, mocking laugh.

"What you have never had!"

The strange man suddenly caught Arthur's hand again, suddenly looked once more hard in his face.

"Yes," he said, with a repetition of the bitter laugh. "You have brought a poor devil back into the world, who has no business there. Do I astonish you? Well! I have a fancy of my own for telling you what men in my situation generally keep a secret. I have no name and no father. The merciful law of Society tells me I am Nobody's Son! Ask your father if he will be my father too, and help me on in life with the family name."

Arthur looked at me, more puzzled than ever. I signed to him to say nothing, and then laid my fingers again on the man's wrist. No! In spite of the extraordinary speech that he had just made, he was not, as I had been disposed to suspect, beginning to get light-headed. His pulse, by this time, had fallen back to a quiet, slow beat, and his skin was moist and cool. Not a symptom of fever or agitation about him.

Finding that neither of us answered him, he turned to me, and began talking of the extraordinary nature of his case, and asking my advice about the future course of medical treatment to which he ought to subject himself. I said the matter required careful thinking over, and suggested that I should submit certain prescriptions to him the next morning. He told me to write them at once, as he would, most likely, be leaving Doncaster, in the morning, before I was up. It was quite useless to represent to him the folly and danger of such a proceeding as this. He heard me politely and patiently, but held to his resolution, without offering any reasons or any explanations, and repeated to me, that if I wished to give him a chance of seeing my prescription, I must write it at once. Hearing this, Arthur volunteered the loan of a travelling writing-case, which, he said, he had with him; and, bringing it to the bed, shook the note-paper out of the pocket of the case forthwith in his usual careless way. With the paper, there fell out on the counterpane of the bed a small packet of sticking-plaster, and a little water-colour drawing of a landscape.

The medical student took up the drawing and looked at it. His eye fell on some initials neatly written, in cypher, in one corner. He started and trembled; his pale face grew whiter than ever; his wild black eyes turned on Arthur, and looked through and through him.

"A pretty drawing," he said in a remarkably quiet tone of voice.

"Ah! and done by such a pretty girl," said Arthur. "Oh, such a pretty girl! I wish it was not a landscape—I wish it was a portrait of her!"

"You admire her very much?"

Arthur, half in jest, half in earnest, kissed his hand for answer.

"Love at first sight!" he said, putting the drawing away again. "But the course of it doesn't run smooth. It's the old story. She's monopolised as usual. Trammelled by a rash engagement to some poor man who is never likely to get money enough to marry her. It was lucky I heard of it in time, or I should certainly have risked a declaration when she gave me that drawing. Here, doctor! Here is pen, ink, and paper all ready for you."

"When she gave you that drawing? Gave it. Gave it." He repeated the words slowly to himself, and suddenly closed his eyes. A momentary distortion passed across his face, and I saw one of his hands clutch up the bedclothes and squeeze them hard. I thought he was going to be ill again, and begged that there might be no more talking. He opened his eyes when I spoke, fixed them once more searchingly on Arthur, and said, slowly and distinctly, "You like her, and she likes you. The poor man may die out of your way. Who can tell that she may not give you herself as well as her drawing, after all?"

Before young Holliday could answer, he turned to me, and said in a whisper, "Now for the prescription." From that time, though he spoke to Arthur again, he never looked at him more.

When I had written the prescription, he examined it, approved of it, and then astonished us both by abruptly wishing us good night. I offered to sit up with him, and he shook his head. Arthur offered to sit up with him, and he said, shortly, with his face turned away, "No." I insisted on having somebody left to watch him. He gave way when he found I was determined, and said he would accept the services of the waiter at the Inn.

"Thank you, both," he said, as we rose to go. "I have one last favour to ask—not of you, doctor, for I leave you to exercise your professional discretion—but of Mr. Holliday." His eyes, while he spoke, still rested steadily on me, and never once turned towards Arthur. "I beg that Mr. Holliday will not mention to any one—least of all to his father—the events that have occurred, and the words that have passed, in this room. I entreat him to bury me in his memory, as, but for him, I might have been buried in my grave. I cannot give my reasons for making this strange request. I can only implore him to grant it."

His voice faltered for the first time, and he hid his face on the pillow. Arthur, completely bewildered, gave the required pledge. I took young Holliday away with me, immediately afterwards, to the house of my friend; determining to go back to the Inn, and to see the medical student again before he had left in the morning.

I returned to the Inn at eight o'clock, purposely abstaining from waking Arthur, who was sleeping off the past night's excitement on one of my friend's sofas. A suspicion had occurred to me as soon as I was alone in my bedroom, which made me resolve that Holliday and the stranger whose life he had saved should not meet again, if I could prevent it. I have already alluded to certain reports, or scandals, which I knew of, relating to the early life of Arthur's father. While I was thinking, in my bed, of what had passed at the Inn—of the change in the student's pulse when he heard the name of Holliday; of the resemblance of expression that I had discovered between his face and Arthur's; of the emphasis he had laid on those three words, "my own brother"; and of his incomprehensible acknowledgment of his own illegitimacy—while I was thinking of these things, the reports I have mentioned suddenly flew into my mind, and linked themselves fast to the chain of my previous reflections. Something within me whispered, "It is best that those two young men should not meet again." I felt it before I slept; I felt it when I woke; and I went, as I told you, alone to the Inn the next morning.

I had missed my only opportunity of seeing my nameless patient again. He had been gone nearly an hour when I inquired for him.

I have now told you everything that I know for certain, in relation to the man whom I brought back to life in the double-bedded room of the Inn at Doncaster. What I have next to add is matter for inference and surmise, and is not, strictly speaking, matter of fact.

I have to tell you, first, that the medical student turned out to be strangely and unaccountably right in assuming it as more than probable that Arthur Holliday would marry the young lady who had given him the water-colour drawing of the landscape. That marriage took place a little more than a year after the events occurred which I have just been relating. The young couple came to live in the neighbourhood in which I was then established in practice. I was present at the wedding, and was rather surprised to find that Arthur was singularly reserved with me, both before and after his marriage, on the subject of the young lady's prior engagement. He only referred to it once, when we were alone, merely telling me, on that occasion, that his wife had done all that honour and duty required of her in the matter, and that the engagement had been broken off with the full approval of her parents. I never heard more from him than this. For three years he and his wife lived together happily. At the expiration of that time, the symptoms of a serious illness first declared themselves in Mrs. Arthur Holliday. It turned out to be a long, lingering, hopeless malady. I attended her throughout. We had been great friends when she was well, and we became more attached to each other than ever when she was ill. I had many long and interesting conversations with her in the intervals when she suffered least. The result of one of these conversations I may briefly relate, leaving you to draw any inferences from it that you please.

The interview to which I refer, occurred shortly before her death. I called one evening, as usual, and found her alone, with a look in her eyes which told me that she had been crying. She only informed me at first, that she had been depressed in spirits; but, by little and little, she became more communicative, and confessed to me that she had been looking over some old letters, which had been addressed to her, before she had seen Arthur, by a man to whom she had been engaged to be married.

I asked her how the engagement came to be broken off. She replied that it had not been broken off, but that it had died out in a very mysterious way. The person to whom she was engaged—her first love, she called him—was very poor, and there was no immediate prospect of their being married. He followed my profession, and went abroad to study. They had corresponded regularly, until the time when, as she believed, he had returned to England. From that period she heard no more of him. He was of a fretful, sensitive temperament; and she feared that she might have inadvertently done or said something that offended him. However that might be, he had never written to her again; and, after waiting a year, she had married Arthur. I asked when the first estrangement had begun, and found that the time at which she ceased to hear anything of her first lover exactly corresponded with the time at which I had been called in to my mysterious patient at The Two Robins Inn.

A fortnight after that conversation, she died. In course of time, Arthur married again. Of late years, he has lived principally in London, and I have seen little or nothing of him.

I have many years to pass over before I can approach to anything like a conclusion of this fragmentary narrative. And even when that later period is reached, the little that I have to say will not occupy your attention for more than a few minutes. Between six and seven years ago, the gentleman to whom I introduced you in this room, came to me, with good professional recommendations, to fill the position of my assistant. We met, not like strangers, but like friends—the only difference between us being, that I was very much surprised to see him, and that he did not appear to be at all surprised to see me. If he was my son or my brother, I believe he could not be fonder of me than he is; but he has never volunteered any confidences since he has been here, on the subject of his past life. I saw something that was familiar to me in his face when we first met; and yet it was also something that suggested the idea of change. I had a notion once that my patient at the Inn might be a natural son of Mr. Holliday's; I had another idea that he might also have been the man who was engaged to Arthur's first wife; and I have a third idea, still clinging to me, that Mr. Lorn is the only man in England who could really enlighten me, if he chose, on both those doubtful points. His hair is not black, now, and his eyes are dimmer than the piercing eyes that I remember, but, for all that, he is very like the nameless medical student of my young days—very like him. And, sometimes, when I come home late at night, and find him asleep, and wake him, he looks, in coming to, wonderfully like the stranger at Doncaster, as he raised himself in the bed on that memorable night!

The Doctor paused. Mr. Goodchild, who had been following every word that fell from his lips up to this time, leaned forward eagerly to ask a question. Before he could say a word, the latch of the door was raised, without any warning sound of footsteps in the passage outside. A long, white, bony hand appeared through the opening, gently pushing the door, which was prevented from working freely on its hinges by a fold in the carpet under it.

"That hand! Look at that hand, Doctor!" said Mr. Goodchild, touching him.

At the same moment, the Doctor looked at Mr. Goodchild, and whispered to him, significantly:

"Hush! he has come back."

Chapter III

THE CUMBERLAND DOCTOR'S MENTION OF DONCASTER RACES, INSPIRED MR. Francis Goodchild with the idea of going down to Doncaster to see the races. Doncaster being a good way off, and quite out of the way of the Idle Apprentices (if anything could be out of their way, who had no way), it necessarily followed that Francis perceived Doncaster in the race-week to be, of all possible idleness, the particular idleness that would completely satisfy him.

Thomas, with an enforced idleness grafted on the natural and voluntary power of his disposition, was not of this mind; objecting that a man compelled to lie on his back on a floor, a sofa, a table, a line of chairs, or anything he could get to lie upon, was not in racing condition, and that he desired nothing better than to lie where he was, enjoying himself in looking at the flies on the ceiling. But, Francis Goodchild, who had been walking round his companion in a circuit of twelve miles for two days, and had begun to doubt whether it was reserved for him ever to be idle in his life, not only overpowered this objection, but even converted Thomas Idle to a scheme he formed (another idle inspiration), of conveying the said Thomas to the sea-coast, and putting his injured leg under a stream of salt-water.

Plunging into this happy conception headforemost, Mr. Goodchild immediately referred to the county-map, and ardently discovered that the most delicious piece of sea-coast to be found within the limits of England, Ireland, Scotland, Wales, the Isle of Man, and the Channel Islands, all summed up together, was Allonby on the coast of Cumberland. There was the coast of Scotland opposite to Allonby, said Mr. Goodchild with enthusiasm; there was a fine Scottish mountain on that Scottish coast; there were Scottish lights to be seen shining across the glorious Channel, and at Allonby itself there was every idle luxury (no doubt) that a watering-place could offer to the heart of idle man. Moreover, said Mr. Goodchild, with his finger on the map, this exquisite retreat was approached by a coach-road, from a railway-station called Aspatria—a name, in a manner, suggestive of the departed glories of Greece, associated with one of the most engaging and most famous of Greek women. On this point, Mr. Goodchild continued at intervals to breathe a vein of classic fancy and eloquence exceedingly irksome to Mr. Idle, until it appeared that the honest English pronunciation of that Cumberland country shortened Aspatria into "Spatter." After this supplementary discovery, Mr. Goodchild said no more about it.

By way of Spatter, the crippled Idle was carried, hoisted, pushed, poked, and packed, into and out of carriages, into and out of beds, into and out of tavern resting-places, until he was brought at length within sniff of the sea. And now, behold the apprentices gallantly riding into Allonby in a one-horse fly, bent upon staying in that peaceful marine valley until the turbulent Doncaster time shall come round upon the wheel, in its turn among what are in sporting registers called the "Fixtures" for the month.

"Do you see Allonby!" asked Thomas Idle.

"I don't see it yet," said Francis, looking out of window.

"It must be there," said Thomas Idle.

"I don't see it," returned Francis.

"It must be there," repeated Thomas Idle, fretfully.

"Lord bless me!" exclaimed Francis, drawing in his head, "I suppose this is it!"

"A watering-place," retorted Thomas Idle, with the pardonable sharpness of an invalid, "can't be five gentlemen in straw hats, on a form on one side of a door, and four ladies in hats and falls, on a form on another side of a door, and three geese in a dirty little brook before them, and a boy's legs hanging over a bridge (with a boy's body I suppose on the other side of the parapet), and a donkey running away. What are you talking about?"

"Allonby, gentlemen," said the most comfortable of landladies as she opened one door of the carriage; "Allonby, gentlemen," said the most attentive of landlords, as he opened the other.

Thomas Idle yielded his arm to the ready Goodchild, and descended from the vehicle. Thomas, now just able to grope his way along, in a doubled-up condition, with the aid of two thick sticks, was no bad embodiment of Commodore Trunnion, or of one of those many gallant Admirals of the stage, who have all ample fortunes, gout, thick sticks, tempers, wards, and nephews. With this distinguished naval appearance upon him, Thomas made a crab-like progress up a clean little bulk-headed staircase, into a clean little bulk-headed room, where he slowly deposited himself on a sofa, with a stick on either hand of him, looking exceedingly grim.

"Francis," said Thomas Idle, "what do you think of this place?"

"I think," returned Mr. Goodchild, in a glowing way, "it is everything we expected."

"Hah!" said Thomas Idle.

"There is the sea," cried Mr. Goodchild, pointing out of window; "and here," pointing to the lunch on the table, "are shrimps. Let us—" here Mr. Goodchild looked out of window, as if in search of something, and looked in again,—"let us eat 'em."

The shrimps eaten and the dinner ordered, Mr. Goodchild went out to survey the watering-place. As Chorus of the Drama, without whom Thomas could make nothing of the scenery, he by-and-by returned, to have the following report screwed out of him.

In brief, it was the most delightful place ever seen.

"But," Thomas Idle asked, "where is it?"

"It's what you may call generally up and down the beach, here and there," said Mr. Goodchild, with a twist of his hand.

"Proceed," said Thomas Idle.

It was, Mr. Goodchild went on to say, in cross-examination, what you might call a primitive place. Large? No, it was not large. Who ever expected it would be large? Shape? What a question to ask! No shape. What sort of a street? Why, no street. Shops? Yes, of course (quite indignant). How many? Who ever went into a place to count the shops? Ever so many. Six? Perhaps. A library? Why, of course (indignant again). Good collection of books? Most likely—couldn't say—had seen nothing in it but a pair of scales. Any reading-room? Of course, there was a reading-room. Where? Where! why, over there. Where was over there? Why, *there*! Let Mr. Idle carry his eye to that bit of waste ground above high-water mark, where the rank grass and loose stones were most in a litter; and he would see a sort of long, ruinous brick loft, next door to a ruinous brick outhouse, which loft had a ladder outside, to get up by. That was the reading-room, and if Mr. Idle didn't like the idea of a weaver's shuttle throbbing under a reading-room, that was his look out. *He* was not to dictate, Mr. Goodchild supposed (indignant again), to the company.

"By-the-by," Thomas Idle observed; "the company?"

Well! (Mr. Goodchild went on to report) very nice company. Where were they? Why, there they were. Mr. Idle could see the tops of their hats, he supposed. What? Those nine straw hats again, five gentlemen's and four ladies'? Yes, to be sure. Mr. Goodchild hoped the company were not to be expected to wear helmets, to please Mr. Idle.

Beginning to recover his temper at about this point, Mr. Goodchild voluntarily reported that if you wanted to be primitive, you could be primitive here, and that if you wanted to be idle, you could be idle here. In the course of some days, he added, that there were three fishing-boats, but no rigging, and that there were plenty of fishermen who never fished. That they got their living entirely by looking at the ocean. What nourishment they looked out of it to support their strength, he couldn't say; but, he supposed it was some sort of Iodine. The place was full of their children, who were always upside down on the public buildings (two small bridges over the brook), and always hurting themselves or one another, so that their wailings made more continual noise in the air than could have been got in a busy place. The houses people lodged in, were nowhere in particular, and were in capital accordance with the beach; being all more or less cracked and damaged as its shells were, and all empty—as its shells were. Among them, was an edifice of destitute appearance, with a number of wall-eyed windows in it, looking desperately out to Scotland as if for help, which said it was a Bazaar (and it ought to know), and where you might buy anything you wanted—supposing what you wanted, was a little camp-stool or a child's wheelbarrow. The brook crawled or stopped between the houses and the sea, and the donkey was always running away, and when he got into the brook he was pelted out with stones, which never hit him, and which always hit some of the children who were upside down on the public buildings, and made their lamentations louder. This donkey was the public excitement of Allonby, and was probably supported at the public expense.

The foregoing descriptions, delivered in separate items, on separate days of adventurous discovery, Mr. Goodchild severally wound up, by looking out of window, looking in again, and saying, "But there is the sea, and here are the shrimps—let us eat 'em."

There were fine sunsets at Allonby when the low flat beach, with its pools of water and its dry patches, changed into long bars of silver and gold in various states of burnishing, and there were fine views—on fine days—of the Scottish coast. But, when it rained at Allonby, Allonby thrown back upon its ragged self, became a kind of place which the donkey seemed to have found out, and to have his highly sagacious reasons for wishing to bolt from. Thomas Idle observed, too, that Mr. Goodchild, with a noble show of disinterestedness, became every day more ready to walk to Maryport and back, for letters; and suspicions began to harbour in the mind of Thomas, that his friend deceived him, and that Maryport was a preferable place.

Therefore, Thomas said to Francis on a day when they had looked at the sea and eaten the shrimps, "My mind misgives me, Goodchild, that you go to Maryport, like the boy in the story-book, to ask *it* to be idle with you."

"Judge, then," returned Francis, adopting the style of the story-book, "with what success. I go to a region which is a bit of water-side Bristol, with a slice of Wapping, a seasoning of Wolverhampton, and a garnish of Portsmouth, and I say, 'Will *you* come and be idle with me?' And it answers, 'No; for I am a great deal too vaporous, and a great deal too rusty, and a great deal too muddy, and a great deal too dirty altogether; and I have ships to load, and pitch and tar to boil, and iron to hammer, and steam to get up, and smoke to make, and stone to quarry, and fifty other disagreeable things to do, and I can't be idle with you.' Then I go into jagged up-hill and down-hill streets, where I am in the pastrycook's shop at one moment, and next moment in savage fastnesses of moor and morass, beyond the confines of civilisation, and I say to those murky and black-dusty streets, 'Will *you* come and be idle with me?' To which they reply, 'No, we can't, indeed, for we haven't the spirits, and we are startled by the echo of your feet on the sharp pavement, and we have so many goods in our shop-windows which nobody wants, and we have so much to do for a limited public which never comes to us to be done for, that we are altogether out of sorts and can't enjoy ourselves with any one.' So I go to the Post-office, and knock at the shutter, and I say to the Post-master, 'Will *you* come and be idle with me?' To which he rejoins, 'No, I really can't, for I live, as you may see, in such a very little Post-office, and pass my life behind such a very little shutter, that my hand, when I put it out, is as the hand of a giant crammed through the window of a dwarf's house at a fair, and I am a mere Post-office anchorite in a cell much too small for him, and I can't get out, and I can't get in, and I have no space to be idle in, even if I would.' So, the boy," said Mr. Goodchild, concluding the tale, "comes back with the letters after all, and lives happy never afterwards."

But it may, not unreasonably, be asked—while Francis Goodchild was wandering hither and thither, storing his mind with perpetual observation of men and things, and sincerely believing himself to be the laziest creature in existence all the time—how did Thomas Idle, crippled and confined to the house, contrive to get through the hours of the day?

Prone on the sofa, Thomas made no attempt to get through the hours, but passively allowed the hours to get through *him*. Where other men in his situation would have read books and improved their minds, Thomas slept and rested his body. Where other men would have pondered anxiously over their future prospects, Thomas dreamed lazily of his past life. The one solitary thing he did, which most other people would have done in his place, was to resolve on making certain alterations and improvements in his mode of existence, as soon as the effects of the misfortune that had overtaken him had all passed away. Remembering that the current of his life had hitherto oozed along in one smooth stream of laziness, occasionally troubled on the surface by a slight passing ripple of industry, his present ideas on the subject of self-reform, inclined him—not as the reader may be disposed to imagine, to project schemes for a new existence of enterprise and exertion—but, on the contrary, to resolve that he would never, if he could possibly help it, be active or industrious again, throughout the whole of his future career.

It is due to Mr. Idle to relate that his mind sauntered towards this peculiar conclusion on distinct and logically-producible grounds. After reviewing, quite at his ease, and with many needful intervals of repose, the generally-placid spectacle of his past existence, he arrived at the discovery that all the great disasters which had tried his patience and equanimity in early life, had been caused by his having allowed himself to be deluded into imitating some pernicious example of activity and industry that had been set him by others. The trials to which he here alludes were three in number, and may be thus reckoned up: First, the disaster of being an unpopular and a thrashed boy at school; secondly, the disaster of falling seriously ill; thirdly, the disaster of becoming acquainted with a great bore.

The first disaster occurred after Thomas had been an idle and a popular boy at school, for some happy years. One Christmas-time, he was stimulated by the evil example of a companion, whom he had always trusted and liked, to be untrue to himself, and to try for a prize at the ensuing half-yearly examination. He did try, and he got a prize—how, he did not distinctly know at the moment, and cannot remember now. No sooner, however, had the book—Moral Hints to the Young on the Value of Time—been placed in his hands, than the first troubles of his life began. The idle boys deserted him, as a traitor to their cause. The industrious boys avoided him, as a dangerous interloper; one of their number, who had always won the prize on previous occasions, expressing just resentment at the invasion of his privileges by calling Thomas into the playground, and then and there administering to him the first sound and genuine thrashing that he had ever received in his life. Unpopular from that moment, as a beaten boy, who belonged to no side and was rejected by all parties, young Idle soon lost caste with his masters, as he had previously lost caste with his schoolfellows. He had forfeited the comfortable reputation of being the one lazy member of the youthful community whom it was quite hopeless to punish. Never again did he hear the headmaster say reproachfully to an industrious boy who had committed a fault, "I might have expected this in Thomas Idle, but it is inexcusable, Sir, in you, who know better." Never more, after winning that fatal prize, did he escape the retributive imposition, or the avenging birch. From that time, the masters made him work, and the boys would not let him play. From that time his social position steadily declined, and his life at school became a perpetual burden to him.

So, again, with the second disaster. While Thomas was lazy, he was a model of health. His first attempt at active exertion and his first suffering from severe illness are connected together by the intimate relations of cause and effect. Shortly after leaving school, he accompanied a party of friends to a cricket-field, in his natural and appropriate character of spectator only. On the ground it was discovered that the players fell short of the required number, and facile Thomas was persuaded to assist in making up the complement. At a certain appointed time, he was roused from peaceful slumber in a dry ditch, and placed before three wickets with a bat in his hand. Opposite to him, behind three more wickets, stood one of his bosom friends, filling the situation (as he was informed) of bowler. No words can describe Mr. Idle's horror and amazement, when he saw this young man—on ordinary occasions, the meekest and mildest of human beings—suddenly contract his eye-brows, compress his lips, assume the aspect of an infuriated savage, run back a few steps, then run forward, and, without the slightest previous provocation, hurl a detestably hard ball with all his might straight at Thomas's legs. Stimulated to preternatural activity of body and sharpness of eye by the instinct of self-preservation, Mr. Idle contrived, by jumping deftly aside at the right moment, and by using his bat (ridiculously narrow as it was for the purpose) as a shield, to preserve his life and limbs from the dastardly attack that had been made on both, to leave the full force of the deadly missile to strike his wicket instead of his leg; and to end the innings, so far as his side was concerned, by being immediately bowled out. Grateful for his escape, he was about to return to the dry ditch, when he was peremptorily stopped, and told that the other side was "going in," and that he was expected to "field." His conception of the whole art and mystery of "fielding," may be summed up in the three words of serious advice which he privately administered to himself on that trying occasion—avoid the ball. Fortified by this sound and salutary principle, he took his own course, impervious alike to ridicule and abuse. Whenever the ball came near him, he thought of his shins, and got out of the way immediately. "Catch it!" "Stop it!" "Pitch it up!" were cries that passed by him like the idle wind that he regarded not. He ducked under it, he jumped over it, he whisked himself away from it on either side. Never once, through the whole innings did he and the ball come together on anything approaching to intimate terms. The unnatural activity of body which was necessarily called forth for the accomplishment of this result threw Thomas Idle, for the first time in his life, into a perspiration. The perspiration, in consequence of his want of practice in the management of that particular result of bodily activity, was suddenly checked; the inevitable chill succeeded; and that, in its turn, was followed by a fever. For the first time since his birth, Mr. Idle found himself confined to his bed for many weeks together, wasted and worn by a long illness, of which his own disastrous muscular exertion had been the sole first cause.

The third occasion on which Thomas found reason to reproach himself bitterly for the mistake of having attempted to be industrious, was connected with his choice of a calling in life. Having no interest in the Church, he appropriately selected the next best profession for a lazy man in England—the Bar. Although the Benchers of the Inns of Court have lately abandoned their good old principles, and oblige their students to make some show of studying, in Mr. Idle's time no such innovation as this existed. Young men who aspired to the honourable title of barrister were, very properly, not asked to learn anything of the law, but were merely required to eat a certain number of dinners at the table of their Hall, and to pay a certain sum of money; and were called to the Bar as soon as they could prove that they had sufficiently complied with these extremely sensible regulations. Never did Thomas move more harmoniously in concert with his elders and betters than when he was qualifying himself for admission among the barristers of his native country. Never did he feel more deeply what real laziness was in all the serene majesty of its nature, than on the memorable day when he was called to the Bar, after having carefully abstained from opening his law-books during his period of probation, except to fall asleep over them. How he could ever again have become industrious, even for the shortest period, after that great reward conferred upon his idleness, quite passes his comprehension. The kind Benchers did everything they could to show him the folly of exerting himself. They wrote out his probationary exercise for him, and never expected him even to take the trouble of reading it through when it was written. They invited him, with seven other choice spirits as lazy as himself, to come and be called to the Bar, while they were sitting over their wine and fruit after dinner. They put his oaths of allegiance, and his dreadful official denunciations of the Pope and the Pretender, so gently into his mouth, that he hardly knew how the words got there. They wheeled all their chairs softly round from the table, and sat surveying the young barristers with their backs to their bottles, rather than stand up, or adjourn to hear the exercises read. And when Mr. Idle and the seven unlabouring neophytes, ranged in order, as a class, with their backs considerately placed against a screen, had begun, in rotation, to read the exercises which they had not written, even then, each Bencher, true to the great lazy principle of the whole proceeding, stopped each neophyte before he had stammered through his first line, and bowed to him, and told him politely that he was a barrister from that moment. This was all the ceremony. It was followed by a social supper, and by the presentation, in accordance with ancient custom, of a pound of sweetmeats and a bottle of Madeira, offered in the way of needful refreshment, by each grateful neophyte to each beneficent Bencher. It may seem inconceivable that Thomas should ever have forgotten the great do-nothing principle instilled by such a ceremony as this; but it is, nevertheless, true, that certain designing students of industrious habits found him out, took advantage of his easy humour, persuaded him that it was discreditable to be a barrister and to know nothing whatever about the law, and lured him, by the force of their own evil example, into a conveyancer's chambers, to make up for lost time, and to qualify himself for practice at the Bar. After a fortnight of self-delusion, the curtain fell from his eyes; he resumed his natural character, and shut up his books. But the retribution which had hitherto always followed his little casual errors of industry followed them still. He could get away from the conveyancer's chambers, but he could not get away from one of the pupils, who had taken a fancy to him,—a tall, serious, raw-boned, hard-working, disputatious pupil, with ideas of his own about reforming the Law of Real Property, who has been the scourge of Mr.

Idle's existence ever since the fatal day when he fell into the mistake of attempting to study the law. Before that time his friends were all sociable idlers like himself. Since that time the burden of bearing with a hard-working young man has become part of his lot in life. Go where he will now, he can never feel certain that the raw-boned pupil is not affectionately waiting for him round a corner, to tell him a little more about the Law of Real Property. Suffer as he may under the infliction, he can never complain, for he must always remember, with unavailing regret, that he has his own thoughtless industry to thank for first exposing him to the great social calamity of knowing a bore.

These events of his past life, with the significant results that they brought about, pass drowsily through Thomas Idle's memory, while he lies alone on the sofa at Allonby and elsewhere, dreaming away the time which his fellow-apprentice gets through so actively out of doors. Remembering the lesson of laziness which his past disasters teach, and bearing in mind also the fact that he is crippled in one leg because he exerted himself to go up a mountain, when he ought to have known that his proper course of conduct was to stop at the bottom of it, he holds now, and will for the future firmly continue to hold, by his new resolution never to be industrious again, on any pretence whatever, for the rest of his life. The physical results of his accident have been related in a previous chapter. The moral results now stand on record; and, with the enumeration of these, that part of the present narrative which is occupied by the Episode of The Sprained Ankle may now perhaps be considered, in all its aspects, as finished and complete.

"How do you propose that we get through this present afternoon and evening?" demanded Thomas Idle, after two or three hours of the foregoing reflections at Allonby.

Mr. Goodchild faltered, looked out of window, looked in again, and said, as he had so often said before, "There is the sea, and here are the shrimps;—let us eat 'em!"

But, the wise donkey was at that moment in the act of bolting: not with the irresolution of his previous efforts which had been wanting in sustained force of character, but with real vigour of purpose: shaking the dust off his mane and hind-feet at Allonby, and tearing away from it, as if he had nobly made up his mind that he never would be taken alive. At sight of this inspiring spectacle, which was visible from his sofa, Thomas Idle stretched his neck and dwelt upon it rapturously.

"Francis Goodchild," he then said, turning to his companion with a solemn air, "this is a delightful little Inn, excellently kept by the most comfortable of landladies and the most attentive of landlords, but—the donkey's right!"

The words, "There is the sea, and here are the—" again trembled on the lips of Goodchild, unaccompanied however by any sound.

"Let us instantly pack the portmanteaus," said Thomas Idle, "pay the bill, and order a fly out, with instructions to the driver to follow the donkey!"

Mr. Goodchild, who had only wanted encouragement to disclose the real state of his feelings, and who had been pining beneath his weary secret, now burst into tears, and confessed that he thought another day in the place would be the death of him.

So, the two idle apprentices followed the donkey until the night was far advanced. Whether he was recaptured by the town-council, or is bolting at this hour through the United Kingdom, they know not. They hope he may be still bolting; if so, their best wishes are with him.

It entered Mr. Idle's head, on the borders of Cumberland, that there could be no idler place to stay at, except by snatches of a few minutes each, than a railway station. "An intermediate station on a line—a junction—anything of that sort," Thomas suggested. Mr. Goodchild approved of the idea as eccentric, and they journeyed on and on, until they came to such a station where there was an Inn.

"Here," said Thomas, "we may be luxuriously lazy; other people will travel for us, as it were, and we shall laugh at their folly."

It was a Junction-Station, where the wooden razors before mentioned shaved the air very often, and where the sharp electric-telegraph bell was in a very restless condition. All manner of cross-lines of rails came zig-zagging into it, like a Congress of iron vipers; and, a little way out of it, a pointsman in an elevated signal-box was constantly going through the motions of drawing immense quantities of beer at a public-house bar. In one direction, confused perspectives of embankments and arches were to be seen from the platform; in the other, the rails soon disentangled themselves into two tracks and shot away under a bridge, and curved round a corner. Sidings were there, in which empty luggage-vans and cattle-boxes often butted against each other as if they couldn't agree; and warehouses were there, in which great quantities of goods seemed to have taken the veil (of the consistency of tarpaulin), and to have retired from the world without any hope of getting back to it. Refreshment-rooms were there; one, for the hungry and thirsty Iron Locomotives where their coke and water were ready, and of good quality, for they were dangerous to play tricks with; the other, for the hungry and thirsty human Locomotives, who might take what they could get, and whose chief consolation was provided in the form of three terrific urns or vases of white metal, containing nothing, each forming a breastwork for a defiant and apparently much-injured woman.

Established at this Station, Mr. Thomas Idle and Mr. Francis Goodchild resolved to enjoy it. But, its contrasts were very violent, and there was also an infection in it.

First, as to its contrasts. They were only two, but they were Lethargy and Madness. The Station was either totally unconscious, or wildly raving. By day, in its unconscious state, it looked as if no life could come to it,—as if it were all rust, dust, and ashes—as if the last train for ever, had gone without issuing any Return-Tickets—as if the last Engine had uttered its last shriek and burst. One awkward shave of the air from the wooden razor, and everything changed. Tight office-doors flew open, panels yielded, books, newspapers, travelling-caps and wrappers broke out of brick walls, money chinked, conveyances oppressed by nightmares of luggage came careering into the yard, porters started up from secret places, ditto the much-injured women, the shining bell, who lived in a little tray on stilts by himself, flew into a man's hand and clamoured violently. The pointsman aloft in the signal-box made the motions of drawing, with some difficulty, hogsheads of beer. Down Train! More beer! Up Train! More beer. Cross Junction Train! More beer! Cattle Train! More beer. Goods Train! Simmering, whistling, trembling, rumbling, thundering. Trains on the whole confusion of intersecting rails, crossing one another, bumping one another, hissing one another, backing to go forward, tearing into distance to come close. People frantic. Exiles seeking restoration to their native carriages, and banished to remoter climes. More beer and more bell. Then, in a minute, the Station relapsed into stupor as the stoker of the Cattle Train, the last to depart, went gliding out of it, wiping the long nose of his oil-can with a dirty pocket-handkerchief.

By night, in its unconscious state, the Station was not so much as visible. Something in the air, like an enterprising chemist's established in business on one of the boughs of Jack's beanstalk, was all that could be discerned of it under the stars. In a moment it would break out, a constellation of gas. In another moment, twenty rival chemists, on twenty rival beanstalks, came into existence. Then, the Furies would be seen, waving their lurid torches up and down the confused perspectives of embankments and arches—would be heard, too, wailing and shrieking. Then, the Station would be full of palpitating trains, as in the day; with the heightening difference that they were not so clearly seen as in the day, whereas the Station walls, starting forward under the gas, like a hippopotamus's eyes, dazzled the human locomotives with the sauce-bottle, the cheap music, the bedstead, the distorted range of buildings where the patent safes are made, the gentleman in the rain with the registered umbrella, the lady returning from the ball with the registered respirator, and all their other embellishments. And now, the human locomotives, creased as to their countenances and purblind as to their eyes, would swarm forth in a heap, addressing themselves to the mysterious urns and the much-injured women; while the iron locomotives, dripping fire and water, shed their steam about plentifully, making the dull oxen in their cages, with heads depressed, and foam hanging from their mouths as their red looks glanced fearfully at the surrounding terrors, seem as though they had been drinking at half-frozen waters and were hung with icicles. Through the same steam would be caught glimpses of their fellow-travellers, the sheep, getting their white kid faces together, away from the bars, and stuffing the interstices with trembling wool. Also, down among the wheels, of the man with the sledge-hammer, ringing the axles of the fast night-train; against whom the oxen have a misgiving that he is the man with the pole-axe who is to come by-and-by, and so the nearest of them try to get back, and get a purchase for a thrust at him through the bars. Suddenly, the bell would ring, the steam would stop with one hiss and a yell, the chemists on the beanstalks would be busy, the avenging Furies would bestir themselves, the fast night-train would melt from eye and ear, the other trains going their ways more slowly would be heard faintly rattling in the distance like old-fashioned watches running down, the sauce-bottle and cheap music retired from view, even the bedstead went to bed, and there was no such visible thing as the Station to vex the cool wind in its blowing, or perhaps the autumn lightning, as it found out the iron rails.

The infection of the Station was this:—When it was in its raving state, the Apprentices found it impossible to be there, without labouring under the delusion that they were in a hurry. To Mr. Goodchild, whose ideas of idleness were so imperfect, this was no unpleasant hallucination, and accordingly that gentleman went through great exertions in yielding to it, and running up and down the platform, jostling everybody, under the impression that he had a highly important mission somewhere, and had not a moment to lose. But, to Thomas Idle, this contagion was so very unacceptable an incident of the situation, that he struck on the fourth day, and requested to be moved.

"This place fills me with a dreadful sensation," said Thomas, "of having something to do. Remove me, Francis."

"Where would you like to go next?" was the question of the ever-engaging Goodchild.

"I have heard there is a good old Inn at Lancaster, established in a fine old house: an Inn where they give you Bride-cake every day after dinner," said Thomas Idle. "Let us eat Bride-cake without the trouble of being married, or of knowing anybody in that ridiculous dilemma."

Mr. Goodchild, with a lover's sigh, assented. They departed from the Station in a violent hurry (for which, it is unnecessary to observe, there was not the least occasion), and were delivered at the fine old house at Lancaster, on the same night.

It is Mr. Goodchild's opinion, that if a visitor on his arrival at Lancaster could be accommodated with a pole which would push the opposite side of the street some yards farther off, it would be better for all parties. Protesting against being required to live in a trench, and obliged to speculate all day upon what the people can possibly be doing within a mysterious opposite window, which is a shop-window to look at, but not a shop-window in respect of its offering nothing for sale and declining to give any account whatever of itself, Mr. Goodchild concedes Lancaster to be a pleasant place. A place dropped in the midst of a charming landscape, a place with a fine ancient fragment of castle, a place of lovely walks, a place possessing staid old houses richly fitted with old Honduras mahogany, which has grown so dark with time that it seems to have got something of a retrospective mirror-quality into itself, and to show the visitor, in the depth of its grain, through all its polish, the hue of the wretched slaves who groaned long ago under old Lancaster merchants. And Mr. Goodchild adds that the stones of Lancaster do sometimes whisper, even yet, of rich men passed away—upon whose great prosperity some of these old doorways frowned sullen in the brightest weather—that their slave-gain turned to curses, as the Arabian Wizard's money turned to leaves, and that no good ever came of it, even unto the third and fourth generations, until it was wasted and gone.

It was a gallant sight to behold, the Sunday procession of the Lancaster elders to Church—all in black, and looking fearfully like a funeral without the Body—under the escort of Three Beadles.

"Think," said Francis, as he stood at the Inn window, admiring, "of being taken to the sacred edifice by three Beadles! I have, in my early time, been taken out of it by one Beadle; but, to be taken into it by three, O Thomas, is a distinction I shall never enjoy!"

Chapter IV

When Mr. Goodchild had looked out of the Lancaster Inn window for two hours on end, with great perseverance, he begun to entertain a misgiving that he was growing industrious. He therefore set himself next, to explore the country from the tops of all the steep hills in the neighbourhood.

He came back at dinner-time, red and glowing, to tell Thomas Idle what he had seen. Thomas, on his back reading, listened with great composure, and asked him whether he really had gone up those hills, and bothered himself with those views, and walked all those miles?

"Because I want to know," added Thomas, "what you would say of it, if you were obliged to do it?"

"It would be different, then," said Francis. "It would be work, then; now, it's play."

"Play!" replied Thomas Idle, utterly repudiating the reply. "Play! Here is a man goes systematically tearing himself to pieces, and putting himself through an incessant course of training, as if he were always under articles to fight a match for the champion's belt, and he calls it Play! Play!" exclaimed Thomas Idle, scornfully contemplating his one boot in the air. "You *can't* play. You don't know what it is. You make work of everything."

The bright Goodchild amiably smiled.

"So you do," said Thomas. "I mean it. To me you are an absolutely terrible fellow. You do nothing like another man. Where another fellow would fall into a footbath of action or emotion, you fall into a mine. Where any other fellow would be a painted butterfly, you are a fiery dragon. Where another man would stake a sixpence, you stake your existence. If you were to go up in a balloon, you would make for Heaven; and if you were to dive into the depths of the earth, nothing short of the other place would content you. What a fellow you are, Francis!" The cheerful Goodchild laughed.

"It's all very well to laugh, but I wonder you don't feel it to be serious," said Idle. "A man who can do nothing by halves appears to me to be a fearful man."

"Tom, Tom," returned Goodchild, "if I can do nothing by halves, and be nothing by halves, it's pretty clear that you must take me as a whole, and make the best of me."

With this philosophical rejoinder, the airy Goodchild clapped Mr. Idle on the shoulder in a final manner, and they sat down to dinner.

"By-the-by," said Goodchild, "I have been over a lunatic asylum too, since I have been out."

"He has been," exclaimed Thomas Idle, casting up his eyes, "over a lunatic asylum! Not content with being as great an Ass as Captain Barclay in the pedestrian way, he makes a Lunacy Commissioner of himself—for nothing!"

"An immense place," said Goodchild, "admirable offices, very good arrangements, very good attendants; altogether a remarkable place."

"And what did you see there?" asked Mr. Idle, adapting Hamlet's advice to the occasion, and assuming the virtue of interest, though he had it not.

"The usual thing," said Francis Goodchild, with a sigh. "Long groves of blighted men-and-women-trees; interminable avenues of hopeless faces; numbers, without the slightest power of really combining for any earthly purpose; a society of human creatures who have nothing in common but that they have all lost the power of being humanly social with one another."

"Take a glass of wine with me," said Thomas Idle, "and let *us* be social."

"In one gallery, Tom," pursued Francis Goodchild, "which looked to me about the length of the Long Walk at Windsor, more or less—"

"Probably less," observed Thomas Idle.

"In one gallery, which was otherwise clear of patients (for they were all out), there was a poor little dark-chinned, meagre man, with a perplexed brow and a pensive face, stooping low over the matting on the floor, and picking out with his thumb and forefinger the course of its fibres. The afternoon sun was slanting in at the large end-window, and there were cross patches of light and shade all down the vista, made by the unseen windows and the open doors of the little sleeping-cells on either side. In about the centre of the perspective, under an arch, regardless of the pleasant weather, regardless of the solitude, regardless of approaching footsteps, was the poor little dark-chinned, meagre man, poring over the matting. 'What are you doing there?' said my conductor, when we came to him. He looked up, and pointed to the matting. 'I wouldn't do that, I think,' said my conductor, kindly; 'if I were you, I would go and read, or I would lie down if I felt tired; but I wouldn't do that.' The patient considered a moment, and vacantly answered, 'No, Sir, I won't; I'll—I'll go and read,' and so he lamely shuffled away into one of the little rooms. I turned my head before we had gone many paces. He had already come out again, and was again poring over the matting, and tracking out its fibres with his thumb and forefinger. I stopped to look at him, and it came into my mind, that probably the course of those fibres as they plaited in and out, over and under, was the only course of things in the whole wide world that it was left to him to understand—that his darkening intellect had narrowed down to the small cleft of light which showed him, 'This piece was twisted this way, went in here, passed under, came out there, was carried on away here to the right where I now put my finger on it, and in this progress of events, the thing was made and came to be here.' Then, I wondered whether he looked into the matting, next, to see if it could show him anything of the process through which *he* came to be there, so strangely poring over it. Then, I thought how all of us, GOD help us! in our different ways are poring over our bits of matting, blindly enough, and what confusions and mysteries we make in the pattern. I had a sadder fellow-feeling with the little dark-chinned, meagre man, by that time, and I came away."

Mr. Idle diverting the conversation to grouse, custards, and bride-cake, Mr. Goodchild followed in the same direction. The bride-cake was as bilious and indigestible as if a real Bride had cut it, and the dinner it completed was an admirable performance.

The house was a genuine old house of a very quaint description, teeming with old carvings, and beams, and panels, and having an excellent old staircase, with a gallery or upper staircase, cut off from it by a curious fence-work of old oak, or of the old Honduras Mahogany wood. It was, and is, and will be, for many a long year to come, a remarkably picturesque house; and a certain grave mystery lurking in the depth of the old mahogany panels, as if they were so many deep pools of dark water—such, indeed, as they had been much among when they were trees—gave it a very mysterious character after nightfall.

When Mr. Goodchild and Mr. Idle had first alighted at the door, and stepped into the sombre, handsome old hall, they had been received by half-a-dozen noiseless old men in black, all dressed exactly alike, who glided up the stairs with the obliging landlord and waiter—but without appearing to get into their way, or to mind whether they did or no—and who had filed off to the right and left on the old staircase, as the guests entered their sitting-room. It was then broad, bright day. But, Mr. Goodchild had said, when their door was shut, "Who on earth are those old men?"

And afterwards, both on going out and coming in, he had noticed that there were no old men to be seen.

Neither, had the old men, or any one of the old men, reappeared since. The two friends had passed a night in the house, but had seen nothing more of the old men. Mr. Goodchild, in rambling about it, had looked along passages, and glanced in at doorways, but had encountered no old men; neither did it appear that any old men were, by any member of the establishment, missed or expected.

Another odd circumstance impressed itself on their attention. It was, that the door of their sitting-room was never left untouched for a quarter of an hour. It was opened with hesitation, opened with confidence, opened a little way, opened a good way,—always clapped-to again without a word of explanation. They were reading, they were writing, they were eating, they were drinking, they were talking, they were dozing; the door was always opened at an unexpected moment, and they looked towards it, and it was clapped-to again, and nobody was to be seen. When this had happened fifty times or so, Mr. Goodchild had said to his companion, jestingly: "I begin to think, Tom, there was something wrong with those six old men."

Night had come again, and they had been writing for two or three hours: writing, in short, a portion of the lazy notes from which these lazy sheets are taken. They had left off writing, and glasses were on the table between them. The house was closed and quiet. Around the head of Thomas Idle, as he lay upon his sofa, hovered light wreaths of fragrant smoke. The temples of Francis Goodchild, as he leaned back in his chair, with his two hands clasped behind his head, and his legs crossed, were similarly decorated.

They had been discussing several idle subjects of speculation, not omitting the strange old men, and were still so occupied, when Mr. Goodchild abruptly changed his attitude to wind up his watch. They were just becoming drowsy enough to be stopped in their talk by any such slight check. Thomas Idle, who was speaking at the moment, paused and said, "How goes it?"

"One," said Goodchild.

As if he had ordered One old man, and the order were promptly executed (truly, all orders were so, in that excellent hotel), the door opened, and One old man stood there.

He did not come in, but stood with the door in his hand.

"One of the six, Tom, at last!" said Mr. Goodchild, in a surprised whisper.—"Sir, your pleasure?"

"Sir, *your* pleasure?" said the One old man.

"I didn't ring."

"The bell did," said the One old man.

He said BELL, in a deep, strong way, that would have expressed the church Bell.

"I had the pleasure, I believe, of seeing you, yesterday?" said Goodchild.

"I cannot undertake to say for certain," was the grim reply of the One old man.

"I think you saw me? Did you not?"

"Saw *you*?" said the old man. "O yes, I saw you. But, I see many who never see me."

A chilled, slow, earthy, fixed old man. A cadaverous old man of measured speech. An old man who seemed as unable to wink, as if his eyelids had been nailed to his forehead. An old man whose eyes—two spots of fire—had no more motion than if they had been connected with the back of his skull by screws driven through it, and rivetted and bolted outside, among his grey hair.

The night had turned so cold, to Mr. Goodchild's sensations, that he shivered. He remarked lightly, and half apologetically, "I think somebody is walking over my grave."

"No," said the weird old man, "there is no one there."

Mr. Goodchild looked at Idle, but Idle lay with his head enwreathed in smoke.

"No one there?" said Goodchild.

"There is no one at your grave, I assure you," said the old man.

He had come in and shut the door, and he now sat down. He did not bend himself to sit, as other people do, but seemed to sink bolt upright, as if in water, until the chair stopped him.

"My friend, Mr. Idle," said Goodchild, extremely anxious to introduce a third person into the conversation.

"I am," said the old man, without looking at him, "at Mr. Idle's service."

"If you are an old inhabitant of this place," Francis Goodchild resumed.

"Yes."

"Perhaps you can decide a point my friend and I were in doubt upon, this morning. They hang condemned criminals at the Castle, I believe?"

"*I* believe so," said the old man.

"Are their faces turned towards that noble prospect?"

"Your face is turned," replied the old man, "to the Castle wall. When you are tied up, you see its stones expanding and contracting violently, and a similar expansion and contraction seem to take place in your own head and breast. Then, there is a rush of fire and an earthquake, and the Castle springs into the air, and you tumble down a precipice."

His cravat appeared to trouble him. He put his hand to his throat, and moved his neck from side to side. He was an old man of a swollen character of face, and his nose was immoveably hitched up on one side, as if by a little hook inserted in that nostril. Mr. Goodchild felt exceedingly uncomfortable, and began to think the night was hot, and not cold.

"A strong description, Sir," he observed.

"A strong sensation," the old man rejoined.

Again, Mr. Goodchild looked to Mr. Thomas Idle; but Thomas lay on his back with his face attentively turned towards the One old man, and made no sign. At this time Mr. Goodchild believed that he saw threads of fire stretch from the old man's eyes to his own, and there attach themselves. (Mr. Goodchild writes the present account of his experience, and, with the utmost solemnity, protests that he had the strongest sensation upon him of being forced to look at the old man along those two fiery films, from that moment.)

"I must tell it to you," said the old man, with a ghastly and a stony stare.

"What?" asked Francis Goodchild.

"You know where it took place. Yonder!"

Whether he pointed to the room above, or to the room below, or to any room in that old house, or to a room in some other old house in that old town, Mr. Goodchild was not, nor is, nor ever can be, sure. He was confused by the circumstance that the right forefinger of the One old man seemed to dip itself in one of the threads of fire, light itself, and make a fiery start in the air, as it pointed somewhere. Having pointed somewhere, it went out.

"You know she was a Bride," said the old man.

"I know they still send up Bride-cake," Mr. Goodchild faltered. "This is a very oppressive air."

"She was a Bride," said the old man. "She was a fair, flaxen-haired, large-eyed girl, who had no character, no purpose. A weak, credulous, incapable, helpless nothing. Not like her mother. No, no. It was her father whose character she reflected.

"Her mother had taken care to secure everything to herself, for her own life, when the father of this girl (a child at that time) died—of sheer helplessness; no other disorder—and then He renewed the acquaintance that had once subsisted between the mother and Him. He had been put aside for the flaxen-haired, large-eyed man (or nonentity) with Money. He could overlook that for Money. He wanted compensation in Money.

"So, he returned to the side of that woman the mother, made love to her again, danced attendance on her, and submitted himself to her whims. She wreaked upon him every whim she had, or could invent. He bore it. And the more he bore, the more he wanted compensation in Money, and the more he was resolved to have it.

"But, lo! Before he got it, she cheated him. In one of her imperious states, she froze, and never thawed again. She put her hands to her head one night, uttered a cry, stiffened, lay in that attitude certain hours, and died. And he had got no compensation from her in Money, yet. Blight and Murrain on her! Not a penny.

"He had hated her throughout that second pursuit, and had longed for retaliation on her. He now counterfeited her signature to an instrument, leaving all she had to leave, to her daughter—ten years old then—to whom the property passed absolutely, and appointing himself the daughter's Guardian. When He slid it under the pillow of the bed on which she lay, He bent down in the deaf ear of Death, and whispered: "Mistress Pride, I have determined a long time that, dead or alive, you must make me compensation in Money."

"So, now there were only two left. Which two were, He, and the fair flaxen-haired, large-eyed foolish daughter, who afterwards became the Bride.

"He put her to school. In a secret, dark, oppressive, ancient house, he put her to school with a watchful and unscrupulous woman. "My worthy lady," he said, "here is a mind to be formed; will you help me to form it?" She accepted the trust. For which she, too, wanted compensation in Money, and had it.

"The girl was formed in the fear of him, and in the conviction, that there was no escape from him. She was taught, from the first, to regard him as her future husband—the man who must marry her—the destiny that overshadowed her—the appointed certainty that could never be evaded. The poor fool was soft white wax in their hands, and took the impression that they put upon her. It hardened with time. It became a part of herself. Inseparable from herself, and only to be torn away from her, by tearing life away from her.

"Eleven years she had lived in the dark house and its gloomy garden. He was jealous of the very light and air getting to her, and they kept her close. He stopped the wide chimneys, shaded the little windows, left the strong-stemmed ivy to wander where it would over the house-front, the moss to accumulate on the untrimmed fruit-trees in the red-walled garden, the weeds to over-run its green and yellow walks. He surrounded her with images of sorrow and desolation. He caused her to be filled with fears of the place and of the stories that were told of it, and then on pretext of correcting them, to be left in it in solitude, or made to shrink about it in the dark. When her mind was most depressed and fullest of terrors, then, he would come out of one of the hiding-places from which he overlooked her, and present himself as her sole resource.

"Thus, by being from her childhood the one embodiment her life presented to her of power to coerce and power to relieve, power to bind and power to loose, the ascendency over her weakness was secured. She was twenty-one years and twenty-one days old, when he brought her home to the gloomy house, his half-witted, frightened, and submissive Bride of three weeks.

"He had dismissed the governess by that time—what he had left to do, he could best do alone—and they came back, upon a rain night, to the scene of her long preparation. She turned to him upon the threshold, as the rain was dripping from the porch, and said:

"'O sir, it is the Death-watch ticking for me!'

"'Well!' he answered. "And if it were?'

"'O Sir!' she returned to him, 'look kindly on me, and be merciful to me! I beg your pardon. I will do anything you wish, if you will only forgive me!'

"That had become the poor fool's constant song: 'I beg your pardon,' and 'Forgive me!'

"She was not worth hating; he felt nothing but contempt for her. But, she had long been in the way, and he had long been weary, and the work was near its end, and had to be worked out.

"'You fool,' he said. 'Go up the stairs!'

"She obeyed very quickly, murmuring, 'I will do anything you wish!' When he came into the Bride's Chamber, having been a little retarded by the heavy fastenings of the great door (for they were alone in the house, and he had arranged that the people who attended on them should come and go in the day), he found her withdrawn to the furthest corner, and there standing pressed against the paneling as if she would have shrunk through it: her flaxen hair all wild about her face, and her large eyes staring at him in vague terror.

"'What are you afraid of? Come and sit down by me.'

"'I will do anything you wish. I beg your pardon, Sir. Forgive me!' Her monotonous tune as usual.

"'Ellen, here is a writing that you must write out to-morrow, in your own hand. You may as well be seen by others, busily engaged upon it. When you have written it all fairly, and corrected all mistakes, call in any two people there may be about the house, and sign your name to it before them. Then, put it in your bosom to keep it safe, and when I sit here again to-morrow night, give it to me.'

"'I will do it all, with the greatest care. I will do anything you wish.'

"'Don't shake and tremble, then.'

"'I will try my utmost not to do it—if you will only forgive me!'

"Next day, she sat down at her desk, and did as she had been told. He often passed in and out of the room, to observe her, and always saw her slowly and laboriously writing: repeating to herself the words she copied, in appearance quite mechanically, and without caring or endeavouring to comprehend them, so that she did her task. He saw her follow the directions she had received, in all particulars; and at night, when they were alone again in the same Bride's Chamber, and he drew his chair to the hearth, she timidly approached him from her distant seat, took the paper from her bosom, and gave it into his hand.

"It secured all her possessions to him, in the event of her death. He put her before him, face to face, that he might look at her steadily; and he asked her, in so many plain words, neither fewer nor more, did she know that?

"There were spots of ink upon the bosom of her white dress, and they made her face look whiter and her eyes look larger as she nodded her head. There were spots of ink upon the hand with which she stood before him, nervously plaiting and folding her white skirts.

"He took her by the arm, and looked her, yet more closely and steadily, in the face. 'Now, die! I have done with you.'

"She shrunk, and uttered a low, suppressed cry.

"'I am not going to kill you. I will not endanger my life for yours. Die!'

"He sat before her in the gloomy Bride's Chamber, day after day, night after night, looking the word at her when he did not utter it. As often as her large unmeaning eyes were raised from the hands in which she rocked her head, to the stern figure, sitting with crossed arms and knitted forehead, in the chair, they read in it, 'Die!' When she dropped asleep in exhaustion, she was called back to shuddering consciousness, by the whisper, 'Die!' When she fell upon her old entreaty to be pardoned, she was answered 'Die!' When she had out-watched and out-suffered the long night, and the rising sun flamed into the sombre room, she heard it hailed with, 'Another day and not dead?—Die!'

"Shut up in the deserted mansion, aloof from all mankind, and engaged alone in such a struggle without any respite, it came to this—that either he must die, or she. He knew it very well, and concentrated his strength against her feebleness. Hours upon hours he held her by the arm when her arm was black where he held it, and bade her Die!

"It was done, upon a windy morning, before sunrise. He computed the time to be half-past four; but, his forgotten watch had run down, and he could not be sure. She had broken away from him in the night, with loud and sudden cries—the first of that kind to which she had given vent—and he had had to put his hands over her mouth. Since then, she had been quiet in the corner of the paneling where she had sunk down; and he had left her, and had gone back with his folded arms and his knitted forehead to his chair.

"Paler in the pale light, more colourless than ever in the leaden dawn, he saw her coming, trailing herself along the floor towards him—a white wreck of hair, and dress, and wild eyes, pushing itself on by an irresolute and bending hand.

"'O, forgive me! I will do anything. O, Sir, pray tell me I may live!'

"'Die!'

"'Are you so resolved? Is there no hope for me?'

"'Die!'

"Her large eyes strained themselves with wonder and fear; wonder and fear changed to reproach; reproach to blank nothing. It was done. He was not at first so sure it was done, but that the morning sun was hanging jewels in her hair—he saw the diamond, emerald, and ruby, glittering among it in little points, as he stood looking down at her—when he lifted her and laid her on her bed.

"She was soon laid in the ground. And now they were all gone, and he had compensated himself well.

"He had a mind to travel. Not that he meant to waste his Money, for he was a pinching man and liked his Money dearly (liked nothing else, indeed), but, that he had grown tired of the desolate house and wished to turn his back upon it and have done with it. But, the house was worth Money, and Money must not be thrown away. He determined to sell it before he went. That it might look the less wretched and bring a better price, he hired some labourers to work in the overgrown garden; to cut out the dead wood, trim the ivy that drooped in heavy masses over the windows and gables, and clear the walks in which the weeds were growing mid-leg high.

"He worked, himself, along with them. He worked later than they did, and, one evening at dusk, was left working alone, with his bill-hook in his hand. One autumn evening, when the Bride was five weeks dead.

"'It grows too dark to work longer,' he said to himself, 'I must give over for the night.'

"He detested the house, and was loath to enter it. He looked at the dark porch waiting for him like a tomb, and felt that it was an accursed house. Near to the porch, and near to where he stood, was a tree whose branches waved before the old bay-window of the Bride's Chamber, where it had been done. The tree swung suddenly, and made him start. It swung again, although the night was still. Looking up into it, he saw a figure among the branches.

"It was the figure of a young man. The face looked down, as his looked up; the branches cracked and swayed; the figure rapidly descended, and slid upon its feet before him. A slender youth of about her age, with long light brown hair.

"'What thief are you?' he said, seizing the youth by the collar.

"The young man, in shaking himself free, swung him a blow with his arm across the face and throat. They closed, but the young man got from him and stepped back, crying, with great eagerness and horror, 'Don't touch me! I would as lieve be touched by the Devil!'

"He stood still, with his bill-hook in his hand, looking at the young man. For, the young man's look was the counterpart of her last look, and he had not expected ever to see that again.

"'I am no thief. Even if I were, I would not have a coin of your wealth, if it would buy me the Indies. You murderer!'

"'What!'

"'I climbed it,' said the young man, pointing up into the tree, 'for the first time, nigh four years ago. I climbed it, to look at her. I saw her. I spoke to her. I have climbed it, many a time, to watch and listen for her. I was a boy, hidden among its leaves, when from that bay-window she gave me this!'

"He showed a tress of flaxen hair, tied with a mourning ribbon.

"'Her life,' said the young man, 'was a life of mourning. She gave me this, as a token of it, and a sign that she was dead to every one but you. If I had been older, if I had seen her sooner, I might have saved her from you. But, she was fast in the web when I first climbed the tree, and what could I do then to break it!'

"In saying those words, he burst into a fit of sobbing and crying: weakly at first, then passionately.

"'Murderer! I climbed the tree on the night when you brought her back. I heard her, from the tree, speak of the Death-watch at the door. I was three times in the tree while you were shut up with her, slowly killing her. I saw her, from the tree, lie dead upon her bed. I have watched you, from the tree, for proofs and traces of your guilt. The manner of it, is a mystery to me yet, but I will pursue you until you have rendered up your life to the hangman. You shall never, until then, be rid of me. I loved her! I can know no relenting towards you. Murderer, I loved her!'

"The youth was bareheaded, his hat having fluttered away in his descent from the tree. He moved towards the gate. He had to pass—Him—to get to it. There was breadth for two old-fashioned carriages abreast; and the youth's abhorrence, openly expressed in every feature of his face and limb of his body, and very hard to bear, had verge enough to keep itself at a distance in. He (by which I mean the other) had not stirred hand or foot, since he had stood still to look at the boy. He faced round, now, to follow him with his eyes. As the back of the bare light-brown head was turned to him, he saw a red curve stretch from his hand to it. He knew, before he threw the bill-hook, where it had alighted—I say, had alighted, and not, would alight; for, to his clear perception the thing was done before he did it. It cleft the head, and it remained there, and the boy lay on his face.

"He buried the body in the night, at the foot of the tree. As soon as it was light in the morning, he worked at turning up all the ground near the tree, and hacking and hewing at the neighbouring bushes and undergrowth. When the labourers came, there was nothing suspicious, and nothing suspected.

"But, he had, in a moment, defeated all his precautions, and destroyed the triumph of the scheme he had so long concerted, and so successfully worked out. He had got rid of the Bride, and had acquired her fortune without endangering his life;

but now, for a death by which he had gained nothing, he had evermore to live with a rope around his neck.

"Beyond this, he was chained to the house of gloom and horror, which he could not endure. Being afraid to sell it or to quit it, lest discovery should be made, he was forced to live in it. He hired two old people, man and wife, for his servants; and dwelt in it, and dreaded it. His great difficulty, for a long time, was the garden. Whether he should keep it trim, whether he should suffer it to fall into its former state of neglect, what would be the least likely way of attracting attention to it?

"He took the middle course of gardening, himself, in his evening leisure, and of then calling the old serving-man to help him; but, of never letting him work there alone. And he made himself an arbour over against the tree, where he could sit and see that it was safe.

"As the seasons changed, and the tree changed, his mind perceived dangers that were always changing. In the leafy time, he perceived that the upper boughs were growing into the form of the young man—that they made the shape of him exactly, sitting in a forked branch swinging in the wind. In the time of the falling leaves, he perceived that they came down from the tree, forming tell-tale letters on the path, or that they had a tendency to heap themselves into a churchyard mound above the grave. In the winter, when the tree was bare, he perceived that the boughs swung at him the ghost of the blow the young man had given, and that they threatened him openly. In the spring, when the sap was mounting in the trunk, he asked himself, were the dried-up particles of blood mounting with it: to make out more obviously this year than last, the leaf-screened figure of the young man, swinging in the wind?

"However, he turned his Money over and over, and still over. He was in the dark trade, the gold-dust trade, and most secret trades that yielded great returns. In ten years, he had turned his Money over, so many times, that the traders and shippers who had dealings with him, absolutely did not lie—for once—when they declared that he had increased his fortune, Twelve Hundred Per Cent.

"He possessed his riches one hundred years ago, when people could be lost easily. He had heard who the youth was, from hearing of the search that was made after him; but, it died away, and the youth was forgotten.

"The annual round of changes in the tree had been repeated ten times since the night of the burial at its foot, when there was a great thunder-storm over this place. It broke at midnight, and roared until morning. The first intelligence he heard from his old serving-man that morning, was, that the tree had been struck by Lightning.

"It had been riven down the stem, in a very surprising manner, and the stem lay in two blighted shafts: one resting against the house, and one against a portion of the old red garden-wall in which its fall had made a gap. The fissure went down the tree to a little above the earth, and there stopped. There was great curiosity to see the tree, and, with most of his former fears revived, he sat in his arbour—grown quite an old man—watching the people who came to see it.

"They quickly began to come, in such dangerous numbers, that he closed his garden-gate and refused to admit any more. But, there were certain men of science who travelled from a distance to examine the tree, and, in an evil hour, he let them in!—Blight and Murrain on them, let them in!

"They wanted to dig up the ruin by the roots, and closely examine it, and the earth about it. Never, while he lived! They offered money for it. They! Men of science, whom he could have bought by the gross, with a scratch of his pen! He showed them the garden-gate again, and locked and barred it.

"But they were bent on doing what they wanted to do, and they bribed the old serving-man—a thankless wretch who regularly complained when he received his wages, of being underpaid—and they stole into the garden by night with their lanterns, picks, and shovels, and fell to at the tree. He was lying in a turret-room on the other side of the house (the Bride's Chamber had been unoccupied ever since), but he soon dreamed of picks and shovels, and got up.

"He came to an upper window on that side, whence he could see their lanterns, and them, and the loose earth in a heap which he had himself disturbed and put back, when it was last turned to the air. It was found! They had that minute lighted on it. They were all bending over it. One of them said, 'The skull is fractured'; and another, 'See here the bones'; and another, 'See here the clothes'; and then the first struck in again, and said, 'A rusty bill-hook!'

"He became sensible, next day, that he was already put under a strict watch, and that he could go nowhere without being followed. Before a week was out, he was taken and laid in hold. The circumstances were gradually pieced together against him, with a desperate malignity, and an appalling ingenuity. But, see the justice of men, and how it was extended to him! He was further accused of having poisoned that girl in the Bride's Chamber. He, who had carefully and expressly avoided imperilling a hair of his head for her, and who had seen her die of her own incapacity!

"There was doubt for which of the two murders he should be first tried; but, the real one was chosen, and he was found Guilty, and cast for death. Bloodthirsty wretches! They would have made him Guilty of anything, so set they were upon having his life.

"His money could do nothing to save him, and he was hanged. *I* am He, and I was hanged at Lancaster Castle with my face to the wall, a hundred years ago!"

At this terrific announcement, Mr. Goodchild tried to rise and cry out. But, the two fiery lines extending from the old man's eyes to his own, kept him down, and he could not utter a sound. His sense of hearing, however, was acute, and he could hear the clock strike Two. No sooner had he heard the clock strike Two, than he saw before him Two old men!

Two.

The eyes of each, connected with his eyes by two films of fire: each, exactly like the other: each, addressing him at precisely one and the same instant: each, gnashing the same teeth in the same head, with the same twitched nostril above them, and the same suffused expression around it. Two old men. Differing in nothing, equally distinct to the sight, the copy no fainter than the original, the second as real as the first.

"At what time," said the Two old men, "did you arrive at the door below?"

"At Six."

"And there were Six old men upon the stairs!"

Mr. Goodchild having wiped the perspiration from his brow, or tried to do it, the Two old men proceeded in one voice, and in the singular number:

"I had been anatomised, but had not yet had my skeleton put together and re-hung on an iron hook, when it began to be whispered that the Bride's Chamber was haunted. It *was* haunted, and I was there.

"*We* were there. She and I were there. I, in the chair upon the hearth; she, a white wreck again, trailing itself towards me on the floor. But, I was the speaker no more, and the one word that she said to me from midnight until dawn was, "Live!"

"The youth was there, likewise. In the tree outside the window. Coming and going in the moonlight, as the tree bent and gave. He has, ever since, been there, peeping in at me in my torment; revealing to me by snatches, in the pale lights and slatey shadows where he comes and goes, bare-headed—a bill-hook, standing edgewise in his hair.

"In the Bride's Chamber, every night from midnight until dawn—one month in the year excepted, as I am going to tell you—he hides in the tree, and she comes towards me on the floor; always approaching; never coming nearer; always visible as if by moon-light, whether the moon shines or no; always saying, from midnight until dawn, her one word, "Live!"

"But, in the month wherein I was forced out of this life—this present month of thirty days—the Bride's Chamber is empty and quiet. Not so my old dungeon. Not so the rooms where I was restless and afraid, ten years. Both are fitfully haunted then. At One in the morning. I am what you saw me when the clock struck that hour—One old man. At Two in the morning, I am Two old men. At Three, I am Three. By Twelve at noon, I am Twelve old men, One for every hundred per cent. of old gain. Every one of the Twelve, with Twelve times my old power of suffering and agony. From that hour until Twelve at night, I, Twelve old men in anguish and fearful foreboding, wait for the coming of the executioner. At Twelve at night, I, Twelve old men turned off, swing invisible outside Lancaster Castle, with Twelve faces to the wall!

"When the Bride's Chamber was first haunted, it was known to me that this punishment would never cease, until I could make its nature, and my story, known to two living men together. I waited for the coming of two living men together into the Bride's Chamber, years upon years. It was infused into my knowledge (of the means I am ignorant) that if two living men, with their eyes open, could be in the Bride's Chamber at One in the morning, they would see me sitting in my chair.

"At length, the whispers that the room was spiritually troubled, brought two men to try the adventure. I was scarcely struck upon the hearth at midnight (I come there as if the Lightning blasted me into being), when I heard them ascending the stairs. Next, I saw them enter. One of them was a bold, gay, active man, in the prime of life, some five and forty years of age; the other, a dozen years younger. They brought provisions with them in a basket, and bottles. A young woman accompanied them, with wood and coals for the lighting of the fire. When she had lighted it, the bold, gay, active man accompanied her along the gallery outside the room, to see her safely down the staircase, and came back laughing.

"He locked the door, examined the chamber, put out the contents of the basket on the table before the fire—little recking of me, in my appointed station on the hearth, close to him—and filled the glasses, and ate and drank. His companion did the same, and was as cheerful and confident as he: though he was the leader. When they had supped, they laid pistols on the table, turned to the fire, and began to smoke their pipes of foreign make.

"They had travelled together, and had been much together, and had an abundance of subjects in common. In the midst of their talking and laughing, the younger man made a reference to the leader's being always ready for any adventure; that one, or any other. He replied in these words:

"'Not quite so, Dick; if I am afraid of nothing else, I am afraid of myself.'

"His companion seeming to grow a little dull, asked him, in what sense? How?

"'Why, thus," he returned. "Here is a Ghost to be disproved. Well! I cannot answer for what my fancy might do if I were alone here, or what tricks my senses might play with me if they had me to themselves. But, in company with another man, and especially with Dick, I would consent to outface all the Ghosts that were ever of in the universe.'

"'I had not the vanity to suppose that I was of so much importance to-night,' said the other.

"'Of so much,' rejoined the leader, more seriously than he had spoken yet, 'that I would, for the reason I have given, on no account have undertaken to pass the night here alone.'

"It was within a few minutes of One. The head of the younger man had drooped when he made his last remark, and it drooped lower now.

"'Keep awake, Dick!' said the leader, gaily. 'The small hours are the worst.'

"He tried, but his head drooped again.

"'Dick!' urged the leader. 'Keep awake!'

"'I can't,' he indistinctly muttered. 'I don't know what strange influence is stealing over me. I can't.'

"His companion looked at him with a sudden horror, and I, in my different way, felt a new horror also; for, it was on the stroke of One, and I felt that the second watcher was yielding to me, and that the curse was upon me that I must send him to sleep.

"'Get up and walk, Dick!' cried the leader. 'Try!'

"It was in vain to go behind the slumber's chair and shake him. One o'clock sounded, and I was present to the elder man, and he stood transfixed before me.

"To him alone, I was obliged to relate my story, without hope of benefit. To him alone, I was an awful phantom making a quite useless confession. I foresee it will ever be the same. The two living men together will never come to release me. When I appear, the senses of one of the two will be locked in sleep; he will neither see nor hear me; my communication will ever be made to a solitary listener, and will ever be unserviceable. Woe! Woe! Woe!"

As the Two old men, with these words, wrung their hands, it shot into Mr. Goodchild's mind that he was in the terrible situation of being virtually alone with the spectre, and that Mr. Idle's immoveability was explained by his having been charmed asleep at One o'clock. In the terror of this sudden discovery which produced an indescribable dread, he struggled so hard to get free from the four fiery threads, that he snapped them, after he had pulled them out to a great width. Being then out of bonds, he caught up Mr. Idle from the sofa and rushed downstairs with him.

"What are you about, Francis?" demanded Mr. Idle. "My bedroom is not down here. What the deuce are you carrying me at all for? I can walk with a stick now. I don't want to be carried. Put me down."

Mr. Goodchild put him down in the old hall, and looked about him wildly.

"What are you doing? Idiotically plunging at your own sex, and rescuing them or perishing in the attempt?" asked Mr. Idle, in a highly petulant state.

"The One old man!" cried Mr. Goodchild, distractedly,—"and the Two old men!"

Mr. Idle deigned no other reply than "The One old woman, I think you mean," as he began hobbling his way back up the staircase, with the assistance of its broad balustrade.

"I assure you, Tom," began Mr. Goodchild, attending at his side, "that since you fell asleep—"

"Come, I like that!" said Thomas Idle, "I haven't closed an eye!"

With the peculiar sensitiveness on the subject of the disgraceful action of going to sleep out of bed, which is the lot of all mankind, Mr. Idle persisted in this declaration. The same peculiar sensitiveness impelled Mr. Goodchild, on being taxed with the same crime, to repudiate it with honourable resentment. The settlement of the question of The One old man and The Two old men was thus presently complicated, and soon made quite impracticable. Mr. Idle said it was all Bride-cake, and fragments, newly arranged, of things seen and thought about in the day. Mr. Goodchild said how could that be, when he hadn't been asleep, and what right could Mr. Idle have to say so, who had been asleep? Mr. Idle said he had never been asleep, and never did go to sleep, and that Mr. Goodchild, as a general rule, was always asleep. They consequently parted for the rest of the night, at their bedroom doors, a little ruffled. Mr. Goodchild's last words were, that he had had, in that real and tangible old sitting-room of that real and tangible old Inn (he supposed Mr. Idle denied its existence?), every sensation and experience, the present record of which is now within a line or two of completion; and that he would write it out and print it every word. Mr. Idle returned that he might if he liked—and he did like, and has now done it.

Chapter V

TWO OF THE MANY PASSENGERS BY A CERTAIN LATE SUNDAY EVENING TRAIN, Mr. Thomas Idle and Mr. Francis Goodchild, yielded up their tickets at a little rotten platform (converted into artificial touchwood by smoke and ashes), deep in the manufacturing bosom of Yorkshire. A mysterious bosom it appeared, upon a damp, dark, Sunday night, dashed through in the train to the music of the whirling wheels, the panting of the engine, and the part-singing of hundreds of third-class excursionists, whose vocal efforts "bobbed arayound" from sacred to profane, from hymns, to our transatlantic sisters the Yankee Gal and Mairy Anne, in a remarkable way. There seemed to have been some large vocal gathering near to every lonely station on the line. No town was visible, no village was visible, no light was visible; but, a multitude got out singing, and a multitude got in singing, and the second multitude took up the hymns, and adopted our transatlantic sisters, and sang of their own egregious wickedness, and of their bobbing arayound, and of how the ship it was ready and the wind it was fair, and they were bayound for the sea, Mairy Anne, until they in their turn became a getting-out multitude, and were replaced by another getting-in multitude, who did the same. And at every station, the getting-in multitude, with an artistic reference to the completeness of their chorus, incessantly cried, as with one voice while scuffling into the carriages, "We mun aa' gang toogither!"

The singing and the multitudes had trailed off as the lonely places were left and the great towns were neared, and the way had lain as silently as a train's way ever can, over the vague black streets of the great gulfs of towns, and among their branchless woods of vague black chimneys. These towns looked, in the cinderous wet, as though they had one and all been on fire and were just put out—a dreary and quenched panorama, many miles long.

Thus, Thomas and Francis got to Leeds; of which enterprising and important commercial centre it may be observed with delicacy, that you must either like it very much or not at all. Next day, the first of the Race-Week, they took train to Doncaster.

And instantly the character, both of travellers and of luggage, entirely changed, and no other business than race-business any longer existed on the face of the earth. The talk was all of horses and "John Scott." Guards whispered behind their hands to station-masters, of horses and John Scott. Men in cut-away coats and speckled cravats fastened with peculiar pins, and with the large bones of their legs developed under tight trousers, so that they should look as much as possible like horses' legs, paced up and down by twos at junction-stations, speaking low and moodily of horses and John Scott. The young clergyman in the black strait-waistcoat, who occupied the middle seat of the carriage, expounded in his peculiar pulpit-accent to the young and lovely Reverend Mrs. Crinoline, who occupied the opposite middle-seat, a few passages of rumour relative to "Oartheth, my love, and Mithter John Eth-COTT." A bandy vagabond, with a head like a Dutch cheese, in a fustian stable-suit, attending on a horse-box and going about the platforms with a halter hanging round his neck like a Calais burgher of the ancient period much degenerated, was courted by the best society, by reason of what he had to hint, when not engaged in eating straw, concerning "t'harses and Joon Scott." The engine-driver himself, as he applied one eye to his large stationary double-eye-glass on the engine, seemed to keep the other open, sideways, upon horses and John Scott.

Breaks and barriers at Doncaster Station to keep the crowd off; temporary wooden avenues of ingress and egress, to help the crowd on. Forty extra porters sent down for this present blessed Race-Week, and all of them making up their betting-books in the lamp-room or somewhere else, and none of them to come and touch the luggage. Travellers disgorged into an open space, a howling wilderness of idle men. All work but race-work at a stand-still; all men at a stand-still. "Ey my word! Deant ask noon o' us to help wi' t'luggage. Bock your opinion loike a mon. Coom! Dang it, coom, t'harses and Joon Scott!" In the midst of the idle men, all the fly horses and omnibus horses of Doncaster and parts adjacent, rampant, rearing, backing, plunging, shying—apparently the result of their hearing of nothing but their own order and John Scott.

Grand Dramatic Company from London for the Race-Week. Poses Plastiques in the Grand Assembly Room up the Stable-Yard at seven and nine each evening, for the Race-Week. Grand Alliance Circus in the field beyond the bridge, for the

Race-Week. Grand Exhibition of Aztec Lilliputians, important to all who want to be horrified cheap, for the Race-Week. Lodgings, grand and not grand, but all at grand prices, ranging from ten pounds to twenty, for the Grand Race-Week!

Rendered giddy enough by these things, Messieurs Idle and Goodchild repaired to the quarters they had secured beforehand, and Mr. Goodchild looked down from the window into the surging street.

"By Heaven, Tom!" cried he, after contemplating it, "I am in the Lunatic Asylum again, and these are all mad people under the charge of a body of designing keepers!"

All through the Race-Week, Mr. Goodchild never divested himself of this idea. Every day he looked out of window, with something of the dread of Lemuel Gulliver looking down at men after he returned home from the horse-country; and every day he saw the Lunatics, horse-mad, betting-mad, drunken-mad, vice-mad, and the designing Keepers always after them. The idea pervaded, like the second colour in shot-silk, the whole of Mr. Goodchild's impressions. They were much as follows:

Monday, mid-day. Races not to begin until to-morrow, but all the mob-Lunatics out, crowding the pavements of the one main street of pretty and pleasant Doncaster, crowding the road, particularly crowding the outside of the Betting Rooms, whooping and shouting loudly after all passing vehicles. Frightened lunatic horses occasionally running away, with infinite clatter. All degrees of men, from peers to paupers, betting incessantly. Keepers very watchful, and taking all good chances. An awful family likeness among the Keepers, to Mr. Palmer and Mr. Thurtell. With some knowledge of expression and some acquaintance with heads (thus writes Mr. Goodchild), I never have seen anywhere, so many repetitions of one class of countenance and one character of head (both evil) as in this street at this time. Cunning, covetousness, secrecy, cold calculation, hard callousness and dire insensibility, are the uniform Keeper characteristics. Mr. Palmer passes me five times in five minutes, and, so I go down the street, the back of Mr. Thurtell's skull is always going on before me.

Monday evening. Town lighted up; more Lunatics out than ever; a complete choke and stoppage of the thoroughfare outside the Betting Rooms. Keepers, having dined, pervade the Betting Rooms, and sharply snap at the moneyed Lunatics. Some Keepers flushed with drink, and some not, but all close and calculating. A vague echoing roar of "t'harses" and "t'races" always rising in the air, until midnight, at about which period it dies away in occasional drunken songs and straggling yells. But, all night, some unmannerly drinking-house in the neighbourhood opens its mouth at intervals and spits out a man too drunk to be retained: who thereupon makes what uproarious protest may be left in him, and either falls asleep where he tumbles, or is carried off in custody.

Tuesday morning, at daybreak. A sudden rising, as it were out of the earth, of all the obscene creatures, who sell "correct cards of the races." They may have been coiled in corners, or sleeping on door-steps, and, having all passed the night under the same set of circumstances, may all want to circulate their blood at the same time; but, however that may be, they spring into existence all at once and together, as though a new Cadmus had sown a race-horse's teeth. There is nobody up, to buy the cards; but, the cards are madly cried. There is no patronage to quarrel for; but, they madly quarrel and fight. Conspicuous among these hyaenas, as breakfast-time discloses, is a fearful creature in the general semblance of a man: shaken off his next-to-no legs by drink and devilry, bare-headed and bare-footed, with a great shock of hair like a horrible broom, and nothing on him but a ragged pair of trousers and a pink glazed-calico coat—made on him—so very tight that it is as evident that he could never take it off, as that he never does. This hideous apparition, inconceivably drunk, has a terrible power of making a gong-like imitation of the braying of an ass: which feat requires that he should lay his right jaw in his begrimed right paw, double himself up, and shake his bray out of himself, with much staggering on his next-to-no legs, and much twirling of his horrible broom, as if it were a mop. From the present minute, when he comes in sight holding up his cards to the windows, and hoarsely proposing purchase to My Lord, Your Excellency, Colonel, the Noble Captain, and Your Honourable Worship—from the present minute until the Grand Race-Week is finished, at all hours of the morning, evening, day, and night, shall the town reverberate, at capricious intervals, to the brays of this frightful animal the Gong-donkey.

No very great racing to-day, so no very great amount of vehicles: though there is a good sprinkling, too: from farmers' carts and gigs, to carriages with post-horses and to fours-in-hand, mostly coming by the road from York, and passing on straight through the main street to the Course. A walk in the wrong direction may be a better thing for Mr. Goodchild to-day than the Course, so he walks in the wrong direction. Everybody gone to the races. Only children in the street. Grand Alliance Circus deserted; not one Star-Rider left; omnibus which forms the Pay-Place, having on separate panels Pay here for the Boxes, Pay here for the Pit, Pay here for the Gallery, hove down in a corner and locked up; nobody near the tent but the man on his knees on the grass, who is making the paper balloons for the Star young gentlemen to jump through to-night. A pleasant road, pleasantly wooded. No labourers working in the fields; all gone "t'races." The few late wenders of their way "t'races," who are yet left driving on the road, stare in amazement at the recluse who is not going "t'races." Roadside innkeeper has gone "t'races." Turnpike-man has gone "t'races." His thrifty wife, washing clothes at the toll-house door, is going "t'races' to-morrow. Perhaps there may be no one left to take the toll to-morrow; who knows? Though assuredly that would be neither turnpike-like nor Yorkshire-like. The very wind and dust seem to be hurrying "t'races," as they briskly pass the only wayfarer on the road. In the distance, the Railway Engine, waiting at the town-end, shrieks despairingly. Nothing but the difficulty of getting off the Line, restrains that Engine from going "t'races," too, it is very clear.

At night, more Lunatics out than last night—and more Keepers. The latter very active at the Betting Rooms, the street in front of which is now impassable. Mr. Palmer as before. Mr. Thurtell as before. Roar and uproar as before. Gradual subsidence as before. Unmannerly drinking-house expectorates as before. Drunken negro-melodists, Gong-donkey, and correct cards, in the night.

On Wednesday morning, the morning of the great St. Leger, it becomes apparent that there has been a great influx since yesterday, both of Lunatics and Keepers. The families of the tradesmen over the way are no longer within human ken; their places know them no more; ten, fifteen, and twenty guinea-lodgers fill them. At the pastry-cook's second-floor window, a Keeper is brushing Mr. Thurtell's hair—thinking it his own. In the wax-chandler's attic, another Keeper is putting on Mr. Palmer's braces. In the gunsmith's nursery, a Lunatic is shaving himself. In the serious stationer's best sitting-room, three Lunatics are taking a combination-breakfast, praising the (cook's) devil, and drinking neat brandy in an atmosphere of last midnight's cigars. No family sanctuary is free from our Angelic messengers—we put up at the Angel—who in the guise of extra waiters for the grand Race-Week, rattle in and out of the most secret chambers of everybody's house, with dishes and tin covers, decanters, soda-water bottles, and glasses. An hour later. Down the street and up the street, as far as eyes can see and a good deal farther, there is a dense crowd; outside the Betting Rooms it is like a great struggle at a theatre door—in the days of theatres; or at the vestibule of the Spurgeon temple—in the days of Spurgeon. An hour later. Fusing into this crowd, and somehow getting through it, are all kinds of conveyances, and all kinds of foot-passengers; carts, with brick-makers and brick-makeresses jolting up and down on planks; drags, with the needful grooms behind, sitting cross-armed in the needful manner, and slanting themselves backward from the soles of their boots at the needful angle; postboys, in the shining hats and smart jackets of the olden time, when stokers were not; beautiful Yorkshire horses, gallantly driven by their own breeders and masters. Under every pole, and every shaft, and every horse, and every wheel as it would seem, the Gong-donkey—metallically braying, when not struggling for life, or whipped out of the way.

By one o'clock, all this stir has gone out of the streets, and there is no one left in them but Francis Goodchild. Francis Goodchild will not be left in them long; for, he too is on his way, "t'races."

A most beautiful sight, Francis Goodchild finds "t'races" to be, when he has left fair Doncaster behind him, and comes out on the free course, with its agreeable prospect, its quaint Red House oddly changing and turning as Francis turns, its green grass, and fresh heath. A free course and an easy one, where Francis can roll smoothly where he will, and can choose between the start, or the coming-in, or the turn behind the brow of the hill, or any out-of-the-way point where he lists to see the throbbing horses straining every nerve, and making the sympathetic earth throb as they come by. Francis much delights to be, not in the Grand Stand, but where he can see it, rising against the sky with its vast tiers of little white dots of faces, and its last high rows and corners of people, looking like pins stuck into an enormous pincushion—not quite so symmetrically as his orderly eye could wish, when people change or go away. When the race is nearly run out, it is as good as the race to him to see the flutter among the pins, and the change in them from dark to light, as hats are taken off and waved. Not less full of interest, the loud anticipation of the winner's name, the swelling, and the final, roar; then, the quick dropping of all the pins out of their places, the revelation of the shape of the bare pincushion, and the closing-in of the whole host of Lunatics and Keepers, in the rear of the three horses with bright-coloured riders, who have not yet quite subdued their gallop though the contest is over.

Mr. Goodchild would appear to have been by no means free from lunacy himself at "t'races," though not of the prevalent kind. He is suspected by Mr. Idle to have fallen into a dreadful state concerning a pair of little lilac gloves and a little bonnet that he saw there. Mr. Idle asserts, that he did afterwards repeat at the Angel, with an appearance of being lunatically seized, some rhapsody to the following effect: "O little lilac gloves! And O winning little bonnet, making in conjunction with her golden hair quite a Glory in the sunlight round the pretty head, why anything in the world but you and me! Why may not this day's running-of horses, to all the rest: of precious sands of life to me—be prolonged through an everlasting autumn-sunshine, without a sunset! Slave of the Lamp, or Ring, strike me yonder gallant equestrian Clerk of the Course, in the scarlet coat, motionless on the green grass for ages! Friendly Devil on Two Sticks, for ten times ten thousands years, keep Blink-Bonny jibbing at the post, and let us have no start! Arab drums, powerful of old to summon Genii in the desert, sound of yourselves and raise a troop for me in the desert of my heart, which shall so enchant this dusty barouche (with a conspicuous excise-plate, resembling the Collector's door-plate at a turnpike), that I, within it, loving the little lilac gloves, the winning little bonnet, and the dear unknown-wearer with the golden hair, may wait by her side for ever, to see a Great St. Leger that shall never be run!"

Thursday morning. After a tremendous night of crowding, shouting, drinking-house expectoration, Gong-donkey, and correct cards. Symptoms of yesterday's gains in the way of drink, and of yesterday's losses in the way of money, abundant. Money-losses very great. As usual, nobody seems to have won; but, large losses and many losers are unquestionable facts. Both Lunatics and Keepers, in general very low. Several of both kinds look in at the chemist's while Mr. Goodchild is making a purchase there, to be "picked up." One red-eyed Lunatic, flushed, faded, and disordered, enters hurriedly and cries savagely, "Hond us a gloss of sal volatile in wather, or soom dommed thing o' thot sart!" Faces at the Betting Rooms very long, and a tendency to bite nails observable. Keepers likewise given this morning to standing about solitary, with their hands in their pockets, looking down at their boots as they fit them into cracks of the pavement, and then looking up whistling and walking away. Grand Alliance Circus out, in procession; buxom lady-member of Grand Alliance, in crimson riding-habit, fresher to look at, even in her paint under the day sky, than the cheeks of Lunatics or Keepers. Spanish Cavalier appears to have lost yesterday, and jingles his bossed bridle with disgust, as if he were paying. Reaction also apparent at the Guildhall opposite, whence certain pickpockets come out handcuffed together, with that peculiar walk which is never seen under any other circumstances—a walk expressive of going to jail, game, but still of jails being in bad taste and arbitrary, and how would *you* like it if it was you instead of me, as it ought to be! Mid-day. Town filled as yesterday, but not so full; and emptied as yesterday, but not so empty. In the evening, Angel ordinary where every Lunatic and Keeper has his modest daily meal of turtle, venison, and wine, not so crowded as yesterday, and not so noisy. At night, the theatre. More abstracted faces in it than one ever sees at public assemblies; such faces wearing an expression which strongly reminds Mr. Goodchild of the boys at school who were "going up next," with their arithmetic or mathematics. These boys are, no doubt, going up to-morrow with *their* sums and figures. Mr. Palmer and Mr. Thurtell in the boxes O. P. Mr. Thurtell and Mr. Palmer in the boxes P. S. The firm of Thurtell, Palmer, and Thurtell, in the boxes Centre. A most odious tendency observable in these distinguished gentlemen to put vile constructions on sufficiently innocent phrases in the play, and then to applaud them in a Satyr-like manner. Behind Mr. Goodchild, with a party of other Lunatics and one Keeper, the express incarnation of the thing called a "gent." A gentleman born; a gent manufactured. A something with a scarf round its neck, and a slipshod speech issuing from behind the scarf; more depraved, more foolish, more ignorant, more unable to believe in any noble or good thing of any kind, than the stupidest Bosjesman. The thing is but a boy in years, and is addled with drink. To do its company justice, even its company is ashamed of it, as it drawls its slang criticisms on the representation, and inflames Mr. Goodchild with a burning ardour to fling it into the pit. Its remarks are so horrible, that Mr. Goodchild, for the moment, even doubts whether that *is* a wholesome Art, which sets women apart on a high floor before such a thing as this, though as good as its own sisters, or its own mother—whom Heaven forgive for bringing it into the world! But, the consideration that a low nature must make a low world of its own to live in, whatever the real materials, or it could no more exist than any of us could without the sense of touch, brings Mr. Goodchild to reason: the rather, because the thing soon drops its downy chin upon its scarf, and slobbers itself asleep.

Friday Morning. Early fights. Gong-donkey, and correct cards. Again, a great set towards the races, though not so great a set as on Wednesday. Much packing going on too, upstairs at the gun-smith's, the wax-chandler's, and the serious stationer's; for there will be a heavy drift of Lunatics and Keepers to London by the afternoon train. The course as pretty as ever; the great pincushion as like a pincushion, but not nearly so full of pins; whole rows of pins wanting. On the great event of the day, both Lunatics and Keepers become inspired with rage; and there is a violent scuffling, and a rushing at the losing jockey, and an emergence of the said jockey from a swaying and menacing crowd, protected by friends, and looking the worse for wear; which is a rough proceeding, though animating to see from a pleasant distance. After the great event, rills begin to flow from the pincushion towards the railroad; the rills swell into rivers; the rivers soon unite into a lake. The lake floats Mr. Goodchild into Doncaster, past the Itinerant personage in black, by the way-side telling him from the vantage ground of a legibly printed placard on a pole that for all these things the Lord will bring him to judgment. No turtle and venison ordinary this evening; that is all over. No Betting at the rooms; nothing there but the plants in pots, which have, all the week, been stood about the entry to give it an innocent appearance, and which have sorely sickened by this time.

Saturday. Mr. Idle wishes to know at breakfast, what were those dreadful groanings in his bedroom doorway in the night? Mr. Goodchild answers, Nightmare. Mr. Idle repels the calumny, and calls the waiter. The Angel is very sorry—had intended to explain; but you see, gentlemen, there was a gentleman dined downstairs with two more, and he had lost a deal of money, and he would drink a deal of wine, and in the night he "took the horrors," and got up; and as his friends could do nothing with him he laid himself down and groaned at Mr. Idle's door. "And he DID groan there," Mr. Idle says; 'and you will please to imagine me inside, "taking the horrors" too!"

So far, the picture of Doncaster on the occasion of its great sporting anniversary, offers probably a general representation of the social condition of the town, in the past as well as in the present time. The sole local phenomenon of the current year, which may be considered as entirely unprecedented in its way, and which certainly claims, on that account, some slight share of notice, consists in the actual existence of one remarkable individual, who is sojourning in Doncaster, and who, neither directly nor indirectly, has anything at all to do, in any capacity whatever, with the racing amusements of the week. Ranging throughout the entire crowd that fills the town, and including the inhabitants as well as the visitors, nobody is to be found altogether disconnected with the business of the day, excepting this one unparalleled man. He does not bet on the races, like the sporting men. He does not assist the races, like the jockeys, starters, judges, and grooms. He does not look on at the races, like Mr. Goodchild and his fellow-spectators. He does not profit by the races, like the hotel-keepers and the tradespeople. He does not minister to the necessities of the races, like the booth-keepers, the postilions, the waiters, and the hawkers of Lists. He does not assist the attractions of the races, like the actors at the theatre, the riders at the circus, or the posturers at the Poses Plastiques. Absolutely and literally, he is the only individual in Doncaster who stands by the brink of the full-flowing race-stream, and is not swept away by it in common with all the rest of his species. Who is this modern hermit, this recluse of the St. Leger-week, this inscrutably ungregarious being, who lives apart from the amusements and activities of his fellow-creatures? Surely, there is little difficulty in guessing that clearest and easiest of all riddles. Who could he be, but Mr. Thomas Idle?

Thomas had suffered himself to be taken to Doncaster, just as he would have suffered himself to be taken to any other place in the habitable globe which would guarantee him the temporary possession of a comfortable sofa to rest his ankle on. Once established at the hotel, with his leg on one cushion and his back against another, he formally declined taking the slightest interest in any circumstance whatever connected with the races, or with the people who were assembled to see them. Francis Goodchild, anxious that the hours should pass by his crippled travelling-companion as lightly as possible, suggested that his sofa should be moved to the window, and that he should amuse himself by looking out at the moving panorama of humanity, which the view from it of the principal street presented. Thomas, however, steadily declined profiting by the suggestion.

"The farther I am from the window," he said, "the better, Brother Francis, I shall be pleased. I have nothing in common with the one prevalent idea of all those people who are passing in the street. Why should I care to look at them?"

"I hope I have nothing in common with the prevalent idea of a great many of them, either," answered Goodchild, thinking of the sporting gentlemen whom he had met in the course of his wanderings about Doncaster. "But, surely, among all the people who are walking by the house, at this very moment, you may find—"

"Not one living creature," interposed Thomas, "who is not, in one way or another, interested in horses, and who is not, in a greater or less degree, an admirer of them. Now, I hold opinions in reference to these particular members of the quadruped creation, which may lay claim (as I believe) to the disastrous distinction of being unpartaken by any other human being, civilised or savage, over the whole surface of the earth. Taking the horse as an animal in the abstract, Francis, I cordially despise him from every point of view."

"Thomas," said Goodchild, "confinement to the house has begun to affect your biliary secretions. I shall go to the chemist's and get you some physic."

"I object," continued Thomas, quietly possessing himself of his friend's hat, which stood on a table near him,—"I object, first, to the personal appearance of the horse. I protest against the conventional idea of beauty, as attached to that animal. I think his nose too long, his forehead too low, and his legs (except in the case of the cart-horse) ridiculously thin by comparison with the size of his body. Again, considering how big an animal he is, I object to the contemptible delicacy of his constitution. Is he not the sickliest creature in creation? Does any child catch cold as easily as a horse? Does he not sprain his fetlock, for all his appearance of superior strength, as easily as I sprained my ankle! Furthermore, to take him from another point of view, what a helpless wretch he is! No fine lady requires more constant waiting-on than a horse. Other animals can make their own toilette: he must have a groom. You will tell me that this is because we want to make his coat artificially glossy. Glossy! Come home with me, and see my cat,—my clever cat, who can groom herself! Look at your own dog! see how the intelligent creature curry-combs himself with his own honest teeth! Then, again, what a fool the horse is, what a poor, nervous fool! He will start at a piece of white paper in the road as if it was a lion. His one idea, when he hears a noise that he is not accustomed to, is to run away from it. What do you say to those two common instances of the sense and courage of this absurdly overpraised animal? I might multiply them to two hundred, if I chose to exert my mind and waste my breath, which I never do. I prefer coming at once to my last charge against the horse, which is the most serious of all, because it affects his moral character. I accuse him boldly, in his capacity of servant to man, of slyness and treachery. I brand him publicly, no matter how mild he may look about the eyes, or how sleek he may be about the coat, as a systematic betrayer, whenever he can get the chance, of the confidence reposed in him. What do you mean by laughing and shaking your head at me?"

"Oh, Thomas, Thomas!" said Goodchild. "You had better give me my hat; you had better let me get you that physic."

"I will let you get anything you like, including a composing draught for yourself," said Thomas, irritably alluding to his fellow-apprentice's inexhaustible activity, "if you will only sit quiet for five minutes longer, and hear me out. I say again the horse is a betrayer of the confidence reposed in him; and that opinion, let me add, is drawn from my own personal experience, and is not based on any fanciful theory whatever. You shall have two instances, two overwhelming instances. Let me start the first of these by asking, what is the distinguishing quality which the Shetland Pony has arrogated to himself, and is still perpetually trumpeting through the world by means of popular report and books on Natural History? I see the answer in your face: it is the quality of being Sure-Footed. He professes to have other virtues, such as hardiness and strength, which you may discover on trial; but the one thing which he insists on your believing, when you get on his back, is that he may be safely depended on not to tumble down with you. Very good. Some years ago, I was in Shetland with a party of friends. They insisted on taking me with them to the top of a precipice that overhung the sea. It was a great distance off, but they all determined to walk to it except me. I was wiser then than I was with you at Carrock, and I determined to be carried to the precipice. There was no carriage-road in the island, and nobody offered (in consequence, as I suppose, of the imperfectly-civilised state of the country) to bring me a sedan-chair, which is naturally what I should have liked best. A Shetland pony was produced instead. I remembered my Natural History, I recalled popular report, and I got on the little beast's back, as any other man would have done in my position, placing implicit confidence in the sureness of his feet. And how did he repay that confidence? Brother Francis, carry your mind on from morning to noon. Picture to yourself a howling wilderness of grass and bog, bounded by low stony hills. Pick out one particular spot in that imaginary scene, and sketch me in it, with outstretched arms, curved back, and heels in the air, plunging headforemost into a black patch of water and mud. Place just behind me the legs, the body, and the head of a sure-footed Shetland pony, all stretched flat on the ground, and you will have produced an accurate representation of a very lamentable fact. And the moral device, Francis, of this picture will be to testify that when gentlemen put confidence in the legs of Shetland ponies, they will find to their cost that they are leaning on nothing but broken reeds. There is my first instance—and what have you got to say to that?"

"Nothing, but that I want my hat," answered Goodchild, starting up and walking restlessly about the room.

"You shall have it in a minute," rejoined Thomas. "My second instance"—(Goodchild groaned, and sat down again)—"My second instance is more appropriate to the present time and place, for it refers to a race-horse. Two years ago an excellent friend of mine, who was desirous of prevailing on me to take regular exercise, and who was well enough acquainted with the weakness of my legs to expect no very active compliance with his wishes on their part, offered to make me a present of one of his horses. Hearing that the animal in question had started in life on the turf, I declined accepting the gift with many thanks; adding, by way of explanation, that I looked on a race-horse as a kind of embodied hurricane, upon which no sane man of my character and habits could be expected to seat himself. My friend replied that, however appropriate my metaphor might be as applied to race-horses in general, it was singularly unsuitable as applied to the particular horse which he proposed to give me. From a foal upwards this remarkable animal had been the idlest and most sluggish of his race. Whatever capacities for speed he might possess he had kept so strictly to himself, that no amount of training had ever brought them out. He had been found hopelessly slow as a racer, and hopelessly lazy as a hunter, and was fit for nothing but a quiet, easy life of it with an old gentleman or an invalid. When I heard this account of the horse, I don't mind confessing that my heart warmed to him. Visions of Thomas Idle ambling serenely on the back of a steed as lazy as himself, presenting to a restless world the soothing and composite spectacle of a kind of sluggardly Centaur, too peaceable in his habits to alarm anybody, swam attractively before my eyes. I went to look at the horse in the stable. Nice fellow! he was fast asleep with a kitten on his back. I saw him taken out for an airing by the groom. If he had had trousers on his legs I should not have known them from my own, so deliberately were they lifted up, so gently were they put down, so slowly did they get over the ground. From that moment I gratefully accepted my friend's offer. I went home; the horse followed me—by a slow train. Oh, Francis, how devoutly I believed in that horse! how carefully I looked after all his little comforts! I had never gone the length of hiring a man-servant to wait on myself; but I went to the expense of hiring one to wait upon him. If I thought a little of myself when I bought the softest saddle that could be had for money, I thought also of my horse. When the man at the shop afterwards offered me spurs and a whip, I turned from him with horror. When I sallied out for my first ride, I went purposely unarmed with the means of hurrying my steed. He proceeded at his own pace every step of the way; and when he stopped, at last, and blew out both his sides with a heavy sigh, and turned his sleepy head and looked behind him, I took him home again, as I might take home an artless child who said to me, 'If you please, sir, I am tired.' For a week this complete harmony between me and my horse lasted undisturbed. At the end of that time, when he had made quite sure of my friendly confidence in his laziness, when he had thoroughly acquainted himself with all the little weaknesses of my seat (and their name is Legion), the smouldering treachery and ingratitude of the equine nature blazed out in an instant. Without the slightest provocation from me, with nothing passing him at the time but a pony-chaise driven by an old lady, he started in one instant from a state of sluggish depression to a state of frantic high spirits. He kicked, he plunged, he shied, he pranced, he capered fearfully. I sat on him as long as I could, and when I could sit no longer, I fell off. No, Francis! this is not a circumstance to be laughed at, but to be wept over. What would be said of a Man who had requited my kindness in that way? Range over all the rest of the animal creation, and where will you find me an instance of treachery so black as this? The cow that kicks down the milking-pail may have some reason for it; she may think herself taxed too heavily to contribute to the dilution of human tea and the greasing of human bread. The tiger who springs out on me unawares has the excuse of being hungry at the time, to say nothing of the further justification of being a total stranger to me. The very flea who surprises me in my sleep may defend his act of assassination on the ground that I, in my turn, am always ready to murder him when I am awake. I defy the whole body of Natural

Historians to move me, logically, off the ground that I have taken in regard to the horse. Receive back your hat, Brother Francis, and go to the chemist's, if you please; for I have now done. Ask me to take anything you like, except an interest in the Doncaster races. Ask me to look at anything you like, except an assemblage of people all animated by feelings of a friendly and admiring nature towards the horse. You are a remarkably well-informed man, and you have heard of hermits. Look upon me as a member of that ancient fraternity, and you will sensibly add to the many obligations which Thomas Idle is proud to owe to Francis Goodchild."

Here, fatigued by the effort of excessive talking, disputatious Thomas waved one hand languidly, laid his head back on the sofa-pillow, and calmly closed his eyes.

At a later period, Mr. Goodchild assailed his travelling companion boldly from the impregnable fortress of common sense. But Thomas, though tamed in body by drastic discipline, was still as mentally unapproachable as ever on the subject of his favourite delusion.

The view from the window after Saturday's breakfast is altogether changed. The tradesmen's families have all come back again. The serious stationer's young woman of all work is shaking a duster out of the window of the combination breakfast-room; a child is playing with a doll, where Mr. Thurtell's hair was brushed; a sanitary scrubbing is in progress on the spot where Mr. Palmer's braces were put on. No signs of the Races are in the streets, but the tramps and the tumble-down-carts and trucks laden with drinking-forms and tables and remnants of booths, that are making their way out of the town as fast as they can. The Angel, which has been cleared for action all the week, already begins restoring every neat and comfortable article of furniture to its own neat and comfortable place. The Angel's daughters (pleasanter angels Mr. Idle and Mr. Goodchild never saw, nor more quietly expert in their business, nor more superior to the common vice of being above it), have a little time to rest, and to air their cheerful faces among the flowers in the yard. It is market-day. The market looks unusually natural, comfortable, and wholesome; the market-people too. The town seems quite restored, when, hark! a metallic bray—The Gong-donkey!

The wretched animal has not cleared off with the rest, but is here, under the window. How much more inconceivably drunk now, how much more begrimed of paw, how much more tight of calico hide, how much more stained and daubed and dirty and dunghilly, from his horrible broom to his tender toes, who shall say! He cannot even shake the bray out of himself now, without laying his cheek so near to the mud of the street, that he pitches over after delivering it. Now, prone in the mud, and now backing himself up against shop-windows, the owners of which come out in terror to remove him; now, in the drinking-shop, and now in the tobacconist's, where he goes to buy tobacco, and makes his way into the parlour, and where he gets a cigar, which in half-a-minute he forgets to smoke; now dancing, now dozing, now cursing, and now complimenting My Lord, the Colonel, the Noble Captain, and Your Honourable Worship, the Gong-donkey kicks up his heels, occasionally braying, until suddenly, he beholds the dearest friend he has in the world coming down the street.

The dearest friend the Gong-donkey has in the world, is a sort of Jackall, in a dull, mangy, black hide, of such small pieces that it looks as if it were made of blacking bottles turned inside out and cobbled together. The dearest friend in the world (inconceivably drunk too) advances at the Gong-donkey, with a hand on each thigh, in a series of humorous springs and stops, wagging his head as he comes. The Gong-donkey regarding him with attention and with the warmest affection, suddenly perceives that he is the greatest enemy he has in the world, and hits him hard in the countenance. The astonished Jackall closes with the Donkey, and they roll over and over in the mud, pummelling one another. A Police Inspector, supernaturally endowed with patience, who has long been looking on from the Guildhall-steps, says, to a myrmidon, "Lock 'em up! Bring 'em in!"

Appropriate finish to the Grand Race-Week. The Gong-donkey, captive and last trace of it, conveyed into limbo, where they cannot do better than keep him until next Race-Week. The Jackall is wanted too, and is much looked for, over the way and up and down. But, having had the good fortune to be undermost at the time of the capture, he has vanished into air.

On Saturday afternoon, Mr. Goodchild walks out and looks at the Course. It is quite deserted; heaps of broken crockery and bottles are raised to its memory; and correct cards and other fragments of paper are blowing about it, as the regulation little paper-books, carried by the French soldiers in their breasts, were seen, soon after the battle was fought, blowing idly about the plains of Waterloo.

Where will these present idle leaves be blown by the idle winds, and where will the last of them be one day lost and forgotten? An idle question, and an idle thought; and with it Mr. Idle fitly makes his bow, and Mr. Goodchild his, and thus ends the Lazy Tour of Two Idle Apprentices.